I0819846

The Short Stories of Sheridan Le Fanu

By

Sheridan Le Fanu

Cover Photograph: Elliott Brown

ISBN: 978-1-78139-495-3

Contents

THE PURCELL PAPERS VOLUME I

THE PURCELL PAPERS VOLUME II

THE PURCELL PAPERS VOLUME III

IN A GLASS DARKLY VOLUME I

GREEN TEA

THE FAMILIAR.

MR. JUSTICE HARBOTTLE.

IN A GLASS DARKLY VOLUME II

THE ROOM IN THE DRAGON VOLANT.

IN A GLASS DARKLY VOLUME III

THE ROOM IN THE DRAGON VOLANT.

CARMILLA.

THE WATCHER AND OTHER WEIRD STORIES

A STABLE FOR NIGHTMARES

GHOSTLY TALES VOLUME I

GHOSTLY TALES VOLUME II

ULTOR DE LACY: A LEGEND OF CAPPERCULLEN

GHOSTLY TALES VOLUME III

THE HAUNTED BARONET

GHOSTLY TALES VOLUME IV

GHOSTLY TALES VOLUME V

WICKED CAPTAIN WALSHAWE, OF WAULING

GHOSTLY TALES VOLUME V (con't)

THE MURDERED COUSIN

MADAM CROWL'S GHOST

THE DEAD SEXTON

THE PURCELL PAPERS VOLUME I

With a Memoir by ALFRED PERCEVAL GRAVES

MEMOIR OF JOSEPH SHERIDAN LE FANU.

A noble Huguenot family, owning considerable property in Normandy, the Le Fanus of Caen, were, upon the revocation of the Edict of Nantes, deprived of their ancestral estates of Mandeville, Sequeville, and Cresseron; but, owing to their possessing influential relatives at the court of Louis the Fourteenth, were allowed to quit their country for England, unmolested, with their personal property. We meet with John Le Fanu de Sequeville and Charles Le Fanu de Cresseron, as cavalry officers in William the Third's army; Charles being so distinguished a member of the King's staff that he was presented with William's portrait from his master's own hand. He afterwards served as a major of dragoons under Marlborough.

At the beginning of the eighteenth century, William Le Fanu was the sole survivor of his family. He married Henrietta Raboteau de Puggibaut, the last of another great and noble Huguenot family, whose escape from France, as a child, by the aid of a Roman Catholic uncle in high position at the French court, was effected after adventures of the most romantic danger.

Joseph Le Fanu, the eldest of the sons of this marriage who left issue, held the office of Clerk of the Coast in Ireland. He married for the second time Alicia, daughter of Thomas Sheridan and sister of Richard Brinsley Sheridan; his brother, Captain Henry Le Fanu, of Leamington, being united to the only other sister of the great wit and orator.

Dean Thomas Philip Le Fanu, the eldest son of Joseph Le Fanu, became by his wife Emma, daughter of Dr. Dobbin, F.T.C.D., the father of Joseph Sheridan Le Fanu, the subject of this memoir, whose name is so familiar to English and American readers as one of the greatest masters of the weird and the terrible amongst our modern novelists.

Born in Dublin on the 28th of August, 1814, he did not begin to speak until he was more than two years of age; but when he had once started, the boy showed an unusual aptitude in acquiring fresh words, and using them correctly.

The first evidence of literary taste which he gave was in his sixth year, when he made several little sketches with explanatory remarks written beneath them, after the manner of Du Maurier's, or Charles Keene's humorous illustrations in 'Punch.'

One of these, preserved long afterwards by his mother, represented a balloon in mid-air, and two aeronauts, who had occupied it, falling headlong to earth, the disaster being explained by these words: 'See the effects of trying to go to Heaven.'

As a mere child, he was a remarkably good actor, both in tragic and comic pieces, and was hardly twelve years old when he began to write verses of singular spirit for one so young. At fourteen, he produced a long Irish poem, which he never permitted anyone but his mother and brother to read. To that brother, Mr. William Le Fanu, Commissioner of Public Works, Ireland, to whom, as the suggester of Sheridan Le Fanu's 'Phaudrig Croohore' and 'Shamus O'Brien,' Irish ballad literature owes a delightful debt, and whose richly humorous and passionately pathetic powers as a raconteur of these poems have only doubled that obligation in the hearts of those who have been happy enough to be his hearers—to Mr. William Le Fanu we are indebted for the following extracts from the first of his works, which the boy-author seems to have set any store by:

'Muse of Green Erin, break thine icy slumbers!
  Strike once again thy wreathed lyre!
Burst forth once more and wake thy tuneful numbers!
  Kindle again thy long-extinguished fire!

'Why should I bid thee, Muse of Erin, waken?
  Why should I bid thee strike thy harp once more?
Better to leave thee silent and forsaken
  Than wake thee but thy glories to deplore.

'How could I bid thee tell of Tara's Towers,
  Where once thy sceptred Princes sate in state—
Where rose thy music, at the festive hours,
  Through the proud halls where listening thousands
    sate?

'Fallen are thy fair palaces, thy country's glory,
  Thy tuneful bards were banished or were slain,
Some rest in glory on their deathbeds gory,
  And some have lived to feel a foeman's chain.

'Yet for the sake of thy unhappy nation,
  Yet for the sake of Freedom's spirit fled,
Let thy wild harpstrings, thrilled with indignation,
  Peal a deep requiem o'er thy sons that bled.

'O yes! like the last breath of evening sighing,
  Sweep thy cold hand the silent strings along,
Flash like the lamp beside the hero dying,

Then hushed for ever be thy plaintive song.'

To Mr. William Le Fanu we are further indebted for the accompanying specimens of his brother's serious and humorous powers in verse, written when he was quite a lad, as valentines to a Miss G. K.:

'Life were too long for me to bear
If banished from thy view;
Life were too short, a thousand year,
If life were passed with you.

'Wise men have said "Man's lot on earth
Is grief and melancholy,"
But where thou art, there joyous mirth
Proves all their wisdom folly.

'If fate withhold thy love from me,
All else in vain were given;
Heaven were imperfect wanting thee,
And with thee earth were heaven.'

A few days after, he sent the following sequel:

'My dear good Madam, You can't think how very sad I'm. I sent you, or I mistake myself foully, A very excellent imitation of the poet Cowley, Containing three very fair stanzas, Which number Longinus, a very critical man, says, And Aristotle, who was a critic ten times more caustic, To a nicety fits a valentine or an acrostic. And yet for all my pains to this moving epistle, I have got no answer, so I suppose I may go whistle. Perhaps you'd have preferred that like an old monk I had pattered on In the style and after the manner of the unfortunate Chatterton; Or that, unlike my reverend daddy's son, I had attempted the classicalities of the dull, though immortal Addison.

I can't endure this silence another week;
What shall I do in order to make you speak?
Shall I give you a trope
In the manner of Pope,
Or hammer my brains like an old smith
To get out something like Goldsmith?
Or shall I aspire on
To tune my poetic lyre on
The same key touched by Byron,
And laying my hand its wire on,
With its music your soul set fire on
By themes you ne'er could tire on?
Or say,
I pray,

Would a lay
Like Gay
Be more in your way?
I leave it to you,
Which am I to do?
It plain on the surface is
That any metamorphosis,
To affect your study
You may work on my soul or body.
Your frown or your smile makes me Savage or Gay
In action, as well as in song;
And if 'tis decreed I at length become Gray,
Express but the word and I'm Young;
And if in the Church I should ever aspire
With friars and abbots to cope,
By a nod, if you please, you can make me a Prior—
By a word you render me Pope.
If you'd eat, I'm a Crab; if you'd cut, I'm your Steel,
As sharp as you'd get from the cutler;
I'm your Cotton whene'er you're in want of a reel,
And your livery carry, as Butler.
I'll ever rest your debtor
If you'll answer my first letter;
Or must, alas, eternity
Witness your taciturnity?
Speak—and oh! speak quickly
Or else I shall grow sickly,
And pine,
And whine,
And grow yellow and brown
As e'er was mahogany,
And lie me down
And die in agony.

P.S.—You'll allow I have the gift
To write like the immortal Swift.'

But besides the poetical powers with which he was endowed, in common with the great Brinsley, Lady Dufferin, and the Hon. Mrs. Norton, young Sheridan Le Fanu also possessed an irresistible humour and oratorical gift that, as a student of Old Trinity, made him a formidable rival of the best of the young debaters of his time at the 'College Historical,' not a few of whom have since reached the highest eminence at the Irish Bar, after having long enlivened and charmed St. Stephen's by their wit and oratory.

Amongst his compeers he was remarkable for his sudden fiery eloquence of attack, and ready and rapid powers of repartee when on his defence. But Le Fanu, whose understanding was elevated by a deep love of the classics, in which he took university honours, and further heightened by an admirable knowledge of our own great authors, was not to be tempted away by oratory from literature, his first and, as it proved, his last love.

Very soon after leaving college, and just when he was called to the Bar, about the year 1838, he bought the 'Warder,' a Dublin newspaper, of which he was editor, and took what many of his best friends and admirers, looking to his high prospects as a barrister, regarded at the time as a fatal step in his career to fame.

Just before this period, Le Fanu had taken to writing humorous Irish stories, afterwards published in the 'Dublin University Magazine,' such as the 'Quare Gander,' 'Jim Sulivan's Adventure,' 'The Ghost and the Bone-setter,' etc.

These stories his brother William Le Fanu was in the habit of repeating for his friends' amusement, and about the year 1837, when he was about twenty-three years of age, Joseph Le Fanu said to him that he thought an Irish story in verse would tell well, and that if he would choose him a subject suitable for recitation, he would write him one. 'Write me an Irish "Young Lochinvar,"' said his brother; and in a few days he handed him 'Phaudrig Croohore'—Anglice, 'Patrick Crohore.'

Of course this poem has the disadvantage not only of being written after 'Young Lochinvar,' but also that of having been directly inspired by it; and yet, although wanting in the rare and graceful finish of the original, the Irish copy has, we feel, so much fire and feeling that it at least tempts us to regret that Scott's po em was not written in that heart-stirring Northern dialect without which the noblest of our British ballads would lose half their spirit. Indeed, we may safely say that some of Le Fanu's lines are finer than any in 'Young Lochinvar,' simply because they seem to speak straight from a people's heart, not to be the mere echoes of medieval romance.

'Phaudrig Croohore' did not appear in print in the 'Dublin University Magazine' till 1844, twelve years after its composition, when it was included amongst the Purcell Papers.

To return to the year 1837. Mr. William Le Fanu, the suggester of this ballad, who was from home at the time, now received daily instalments of the second and more remarkable of his brother's Irish poems—'Shamus O'Brien' (James O'Brien)—learning them by heart as they reached him, and, fortunately, never forgetting them, for his brother Joseph kept no copy of the ballad, and he had himself to write it out from memory ten years after, when the poem appeared in the 'University Magazine.'

Few will deny that this poem contains passages most faithfully, if fearfully, picturesque, and that it is characterised throughout by a profound pathos, and an abundant though at times a too grotesquely incongruous humour. Can we wonder, then, at the immense popularity with which Samuel Lover recited it in the United States? For to Lover's admiration of the poem, and his addition of it to his entertainment, 'Shamus O'Brien' owes its introduction into America, where it is now so popular. Lover added some lines of his own to the poem, made Shamus emigrate to the States, and set up a public-house. These added lines appeared in most of the published versions of the poem. But they are indifferent as verse, and certainly injure the dramatic effect of the poem.

'Shamus O'Brien' is so generally attributed to Lover (indeed we remember seeing it advertised for recitation on the occasion of a benefit at a leading London theatre as 'by Samuel Lover') that it is a satisfaction to be able to reproduce the following letter upon the subject from Lover to William le Fanu:

'Astor House,
'New York, U.S. America.
'Sept. 30, 1846.

'My dear Le Fanu,

'In reading over your brother's poem while I crossed the Atlantic, I became more and more impressed with its great beauty and dramatic effect—so much so that I determined to test its effect in public, and have done so here, on my first appearance, with the greatest success. Now I have no doubt there will be great praises of the poem, and people will suppose, most likely, that the composition is mine, and as you know (I take for granted) that I would not wish to wear a borrowed feather, I should be glad to give your brother's name as the author, should he not object to have it known; but as his writings are often of so different a tone, I would not speak without permission to do so. It is true that in my programme my name is attached to other pieces, and no name appended to the recitation; so far, you will see, I have done all I could to avoid "appropriating," the spirit of which I might have caught here, with Irish aptitude; but I would like to have the means of telling all whom it may concern the name of the author, to whose head and heart it does so much honour. Pray, my dear Le Fanu, inquire, and answer me here by next packet, or as soon as convenient. My success here has been quite triumphant.

'Yours very truly,

'SAMUEL LOVER.'

We have heard it said (though without having inquired into the truth of the tradition) that 'Shamus O'Brien' was the result of a match at pseudo-national ballad writing made between Le Fanu and several of the most brilliant of his young literary confreres at T. C. D. But however this may be, Le Fanu undoubtedly was no young Irelander; indeed he did the stoutest service as a press writer in the Conservative interest, and was no doubt provoked as well as amused at the unexpected popularity to which his poem attained amongst the Irish Nationalists. And here it should be remembered that the ballad was written some eleven years before the outbreak of '48, and at a time when a '98 subject might fairly have been regarded as legitimate literary property amongst the most loyal.

We left Le Fanu as editor of the 'Warder.' He afterwards purchased the 'Dublin Evening Packet,' and much later the half-proprietorship of the 'Dublin Evening Mail.' Eleven or twelve years ago he also became the owner and editor of the 'Dublin University Magazine,' in which his later as well as earlier Irish Stories appeared. He sold it about a year before his death in 1873, having previously parted with the 'Warder' and his share in the 'Evening Mail.'

He had previously published in the 'Dublin University Magazine' a number of charming lyrics, generally anonymously, and it is to be feared that all clue to the identification of most of these is lost, except that of internal evidence.

The following poem, undoubtedly his, should make general our regret at being unable to fix with certainty upon its fellows:

'One wild and distant bugle sound
Breathed o'er Killarney's magic shore
Will shed sweet floating echoes round
When that which made them is no more.

'So slumber in the human heart
Wild echoes, that will sweetly thrill
The words of kindness when the voice
That uttered them for aye is still.

'Oh! memory, though thy records tell
Full many a tale of grief and sorrow,
Of mad excess, of hope decayed,
Of dark and cheerless melancholy;

'Still, memory, to me thou art
The dearest of the gifts of mind,
For all the joys that touch my heart
Are joys that I have left behind.

Le Fanu's literary life may be divided into three distinct periods. During the first of these, and till his thirtieth year, he was an Irish ballad, song, and story writer, his first published story being the 'Adventures of Sir Robert Ardagh,' which appeared in the 'Dublin University Magazine' of 1838.

In 1844 he was united to Miss Susan Bennett, the beautiful daughter of the late George Bennett, Q.C. From this time until her decease, in 1858, he devoted his energies almost entirely to press work, making, however, his first essays in novel writing during that period. The 'Cock and Anchor,' a chronicle of old Dublin city, his first and, in the opinion of competent critics, one of the best of his novels, seeing the light about the year 1850. This work, it is to be feared, is out of print, though there is now a cheap edition of 'Torlogh O'Brien,' its immediate successor. The comparative want of success of these novels seems to have deterred Le Fanu from using his pen, except as a press writer, until 1863, when the 'House by the

Churchyard' was published, and was soon followed by 'Uncle Silas' and his five other well-known novels.

We have considered Le Fanu as a ballad writer and poet. As a press writer he is still most honourably remembered for his learning and brilliancy, and the power and point of his sarcasm, which long made the 'Dublin Evening Mail' one of the most formidable of Irish press critics; but let us now pass to the consideration of him in the capacity of a novelist, and in particular as the author of 'Uncle Silas.'

There are evidences in 'Shamus O'Brien,' and even in 'Phaudrig Croohore,' of a power over the mysterious, the grotesque, and the horrible, which so singularly distinguish him as a writer of prose fiction.

'Uncle Silas,' the fairest as well as most familiar instance of this enthralling spell over his readers, is too well known a story to tell in detail. But how intensely and painfully distinct is the opening description of the silent, inflexible Austin Ruthyn of Knowl, and his shy, sweet daughter Maude, the one so resolutely confident in his brother's honour, the other so romantically and yet anxiously interested in her uncle—the sudden arrival of Dr. Bryerly, the strange Swedenborgian, followed by the equally unexpected apparition of Madame de la Rougiere, Austin Ruthyn's painful death, and the reading of his strange will consigning poor Maude to the protection of her unknown Uncle Silas—her cousin, good, bright devoted Monica Knollys, and her dreadful distrust of Silas—Bartram Haugh and its uncanny occupants, and foremost amongst them Uncle Silas.

This is his portrait:

'A face like marble, with a fearful monumental look, and for an old man, singularly vivid, strange eyes, the singularity of which rather grew upon me as I looked; for his eyebrows were still black, though his hair descended from his temples in long locks of the purest silver and fine as silk, nearly to his shoulders.

'He rose, tall and slight, a little stooped, all in black, with an ample black velvet tunic, which was rather a gown than a coat....

'I know I can't convey in words an idea of this apparition, drawn, as it seemed, in black and white, venerable, bloodless, fiery-eyed, with its singular look of power, and an expression so bewildering—was it derision, or anguish, or cruelty, or patience?

'The wild eyes of this strange old man were fixed on me as he rose; an habitual contraction, which in certain lights took the character of a scowl, did not relax as he advanced towards me with a thin-lipped smile.'

Old Dicken and his daughter Beauty, old L'Amour and Dudley Ruthyn, now enter upon the scene, each a fresh shadow to deepen its already sombre hue, while the gloom gathers in spite of the glimpse of sunshine shot through it by the visit to Elverston. Dudley's brutal encounter with Captain Oakley, and vile persecution of poor Maude till his love marriage comes to light, lead us on to the ghastly catastrophe, the hideous conspiracy of Silas and his son against the life of the innocent girl.

It is interesting to know that the germ of Uncle Silas first appeared in the 'Dublin University Magazine' of 1837 or 1838, as the short tale, entitled, 'A Passage from the Secret History of an Irish Countess,' which is printed in this collection of Stories. It next was published as 'The Murdered Cousin' in a collection of Christmas stories, and finally developed into the three-volume novel we have just no-noticed.

There are about Le Fanu's narratives touches of nature which reconcile us to their always remarkable and often supernatural incidents. His characters are well conceived and distinctly drawn, and strong soliloquy and easy dialogue spring unaffectedly from their lips. He is a close observer of Nature, and reproduces her wilder effects of storm and gloom with singular vividness; while he is equally at home in his descriptions of still life, some of which remind us of the faithfully minute detail of old Dutch pictures.

Mr. Wilkie Collins, amongst our living novelists, best compares with Le Fanu. Both of these writers are remarkable for the ingenious mystery with which they develop their plots, and for the absorbing, if often over-sensational, nature of their incidents; but whilst Mr. Collins excites and fascinates our attention by an intense power of realism which carries us with unreasoning haste from cover to cover of his works, Le Fanu is an idealist, full of high imagination, and an artist who devotes deep attention to the most delicate detail in his portraiture of men and women, and his descriptions of the outdoor and indoor worlds—a writer, therefore, through whose pages it would be often an indignity to hasten. And this more leisurely, and certainly more classical, conduct of his stories makes us remember them more fully and faithfully than those of the author of the 'Woman in White.' Mr. Collins is generally dramatic, and sometimes stagy, in his effects. Le Fanu, while less careful to arrange his plots, so as to admit of their being readily adapted for the stage, often surprises us by scenes of so much greater tragic intensity that we cannot but lament that he did not, as Mr. Collins has done, attempt the drama, and so furnish another ground of comparison with his fellow-countryman, Maturin (also, if we mistake not, of French origin), whom, in his writings, Le Fanu far more closely resembles than Mr. Collins, as a master of the darker and stronger emotions of human character. But, to institute a broader ground of comparison between Le Fanu and Mr. Collins, whilst the idiosyncrasies of the former's characters, however immaterial those characters may be, seem always to suggest the minutest detail of his story, the latter would appear to consider plot as the prime, character as a subsidiary element in the art of novel writing.

Those who possessed the rare privilege of Le Fanu's friendship, and only they, can form any idea of the true character of the man; for after the death of his wife, to whom he was most deeply devoted, he quite forsook general society, in which his fine features, distinguished bearing, and charm of conversation marked him out as the beau-ideal of an Irish wit and scholar of the old school.

From this society he vanished so entirely that Dublin, always ready with a nickname, dubbed him 'The Invisible Prince;' and indeed he was for long almost invisible, except to his family and most familiar friends, unless at odd hours of the evening, when he might occasionally be seen stealing, like the ghost of his former self, between his newspaper office and his home in Merrion Square; sometimes, too, he was to be encountered in an old out-of-the-way bookshop poring over some rare black letter Astrology or Demonology.

To one of these old bookshops he was at one time a pretty frequent visitor, and the bookseller relates how he used to come in and ask with his peculiarly pleasant voice and smile, 'Any more ghost stories for me, Mr. ——-?' and how, on a fresh one being handed to him, he would seldom leave the shop until he had looked it through. This taste for the supernatural seems to have grown upon him after his wife's death, and influenced him so deeply that, had he not been possessed of a deal of shrewd common sense, there might have been danger of his embracing some of the visionary doctrines in which he was so learned. But no! even Spiritualism, to which not a few of his brother novelists succumbed, whilst affording congenial material for our artist of the superhuman to work upon, did not escape his severest satire.

Shortly after completing his last novel, strange to say, bearing the title 'Willing to Die,' Le Fanu breathed his last at his home No. 18, Merrion Square South, at the age of fifty-nine.

'He was a man,' writes the author of a brief memoir of him in the 'Dublin University Magazine,' 'who thought deeply, especially on religious subjects. To those who knew him he was very dear; they admired him for his learning, his sparkling wit, and pleasant conversation, and loved him for his manly virtues, for his noble and generous qualities, his gentleness, and his loving, affectionate nature.' And all who knew the man must feel how deeply deserved are these simple words of sincere regard for Joseph Sheridan Le Fanu.

Le Fanu's novels are accessible to all; but his Purcell Papers are now for the first time collected and published, by the permission of his eldest son (the late Mr. Philip Le Fanu), and very much owing to the friendly and active assistance of his brother, Mr. William Le Fanu.

THE GHOST AND THE BONE SETTER.

In looking over the papers of my late valued and respected friend, Francis Purcell, who for nearly fifty years discharged the arduous duties of a parish priest in the south of Ireland, I met with the following document. It is one of many such; for he was a curious and industrious collector of old local traditions—a commodity in which the quarter where he resided mightily abounded. The collection and arrangement of such legends was, as long as I can remember him, his hobby; but I had never learned that his love of the marvellous and whimsical had carried him so far as to prompt him to commit the results of his inquiries to writing, until, in the character of residuary legatee, his will put me in possession of all his manuscript papers. To such as may think the composing of such productions as these inconsistent with the character and habits of a country priest, it is necessary to observe, that there did exist a race of priests—those of the old school, a race now nearly extinct—whose education abroad tended to produce in them tastes more literary than have yet been evinced by the alumni of Maynooth.

It is perhaps necessary to add that the superstition illustrated by the following story, namely, that the corpse last buried is obliged, during his juniority of interment, to supply his brother tenants of the churchyard in which he lies, with fresh water to allay the burning thirst of purgatory, is prevalent throughout the south of Ireland.

The writer can vouch for a case in which a respectable and wealthy farmer, on the borders of Tipperary, in tenderness to the corns of his departed helpmate, enclosed in her coffin two pair of brogues, a light and a heavy, the one for dry, the other for sloppy weather; seeking thus to mitigate the fatigues of her inevitable perambulations in procuring water and administering it to the thirsty souls of purgatory. Fierce and desperate conflicts have ensued in the case of two funeral parties approaching the same churchyard together, each endeavouring to secure to his own dead priority of sepulture, and a consequent immunity from the tax levied upon the pedestrian powers of the last-comer. An instance not long since occurred, in which one of two such parties, through fear of losing to their deceased friend this inestimable advantage, made their way to the churchyard by a short cut, and, in violation of one of their strongest prejudices, actually threw the coffin over the wall, lest time should be lost in making their entrance through the gate. Innumerable instances of the same kind might be quoted, all tending to show how strongly among the peasantry of the south this superstition is entertained. However, I shall not detain the reader further by any prefatory remarks, but shall proceed to lay before him the following:

Extract from the MS. Papers of the late Rev. Francis Purcell, of Drumcoolagh.

I tell the following particulars, as nearly as I can recollect them, in the words of the narrator. It may be necessary to observe that he was what is termed a well-spoken man, having for a considerable time instructed the ingenious youth of his native parish in such of the liberal arts and sciences as he found it convenient to profess—a circumstance which may account for the occurrence of several big words in the course of this narrative, more distinguished for euphonious effect than for correctness of application. I proceed then, without further preface, to lay before you the wonderful adventures of Terry Neil.

'Why, thin, 'tis a quare story, an' as thrue as you're sittin' there; and I'd make bould to say there isn't a boy in the seven parishes could tell it better nor crickther than myself, for 'twas my father himself it happened to, an' many's the time I heerd it out iv his own mouth; an' I can say, an' I'm proud av that same, my father's word was as incredible as any squire's oath in the counthry; and so signs an' if a poor man got into any unlucky throuble, he was the boy id go into the court an' prove; but that doesn't signify—he was as honest and as sober a man, barrin' he was a little bit too partial to the glass, as you'd find in a day's walk; an' there wasn't the likes of him in the counthry round for nate labourin' an' baan diggin'; and he was mighty handy entirely for carpenther's work, and men din' ould spudethrees, an' the likes i' that. An' so he tuk up with bone-settin', as was most nathural, for none of them could come up to him in mendin' the leg iv a stool or a table; an' sure, there never was a bone-setter got so much custom-man an' child, young an' ould—there never was such breakin' and mendin' of bones known in the memory of man. Well, Terry Neil—for that was my father's name—began to feel his heart growin' light, and his purse heavy; an' he took a bit iv a farm in Squire Phelim's ground, just undher the ould castle, an' a pleasant little spot it was; an' day an' mornin' poor crathurs not able to put a foot to the ground, with broken arms and broken legs, id be comin' ramblin' in from all quarters to have their bones spliced up. Well, yer honour, all this was as well as well could be; but it was customary when Sir Phelim id go anywhere out iv the country, for some iv the tinants to sit up to watch in the ould castle, just for a kind of compliment to the ould family—an' a mighty unplisant compliment it was for the tinants, for there wasn't a man of them but knew there was something quare about the ould castle. The neighbours had it, that the squire's ould grandfather, as good a gintlenlan—God be with him—as I heer'd, as ever stood in shoe-leather, used to keep walkin' about in the middle iv the night, ever sinst he bursted a blood vessel pullin' out a cork out iv a bottle, as you or I might be doin', and will too, plase God—but that doesn't signify. So, as I was sayin', the ould squire used to come down out of the frame, where his picthur was hung up, and to break the bottles and glasses—God be marciful to us all—an' dthrink all he could come at—an' small blame to him for that same; and then if any of the family id be comin' in, he id be up again in his place, looking as quite an' as innocent as if he didn't know anything about it—the mischievous ould chap.

'Well, your honour, as I was sayin', one time the family up at the castle was stayin' in Dublin for a week or two; and so, as usual, some of the tinants had to sit up in the castle, and the third night it kem to my father's turn. "Oh, tare an' ouns!" says he unto himself, "an' must I sit up all night, and that ould vagabone of a sperit, glory be to God," says he, "serenadin' through the house, an' doin' all sorts iv mischief?" However, there was no gettin' aff, and so he put a bould face on it, an' he went up at nightfall with a bottle of pottieen, and another of holy wather.

'It was rainin' smart enough, an' the evenin' was darksome and gloomy, when my father got in; and what with the rain he got, and the holy wather he sprinkled on himself, it wasn't long till he had to swally a cup iv the pottieen, to keep the cowld out iv his heart. It was the ould steward, Lawrence Connor, that opened the door—and he an' my father wor always very great. So when he seen who it was, an' my father tould him how it was his turn to watch in the castle, he offered to sit up along with him; and you may be sure my father wasn't sorry for that same. So says Larry:

'"We'll have a bit iv fire in the parlour," says he.

'"An' why not in the hall?" says my father, for he knew that the squire's picthur was hung in the parlour.

'"No fire can be lit in the hall," says Lawrence, "for there's an ould jackdaw's nest in the chimney."

'"Oh thin," says my father, "let us stop in the kitchen, for it's very unproper for the likes iv me to be sittin' in the parlour," says he.

'"Oh, Terry, that can't be," says Lawrence; "if we keep up the ould custom at all, we may as well keep it up properly," says he.

'"Divil sweep the ould custom!" says my father—to himself, do ye mind, for he didn't like to let Lawrence see that he was more afeard himself.

'"Oh, very well," says he. "I'm agreeable, Lawrence," says he; and so down they both wint to the kitchen, until the fire id be lit in the parlour—an' that same wasn't long doin'.

'Well, your honour, they soon wint up again, an' sat down mighty comfortable by the parlour fire, and they beginned to talk, an' to smoke, an' to dhrink a small taste iv the pottieen; and, moreover, they had a good rousin' fire o' bogwood and turf, to warm their shins over.

'Well, sir, as I was sayin' they kep' convarsin' and smokin' together most agreeable, until Lawrence beginn'd to get sleepy, as was but nathural for him, for he was an ould sarvint man, and was used to a great dale iv sleep.

'"Sure it's impossible," says my father, "it's gettin' sleepy you are?"

'"Oh, divil a taste," says Larry; "I'm only shuttin' my eyes," says he, "to keep out the parfume o' the tibacky smoke, that's makin' them wather," says he. "So don't you mind other people's business," says he, stiff enough, for he had a mighty high stomach av his own (rest his sowl), "and go on," says he, "with your story, for I'm listenin'," says he, shuttin' down his eyes.

'Well, when my father seen spakin' was no use, he went on with his story. By the same token, it was the story of Jim Soolivan and his ould goat he was tellin'—an' a plisant story it is—an' there was so much divarsion in it, that it was enough to waken a dormouse, let alone to pervint a Christian goin' asleep. But, faix, the way my father tould it, I believe there never was the likes heerd sinst nor before, for he bawled out every word av it, as if the life was fairly lavin' him, thrying to keep ould Larry awake; but, faix, it was no use, for the hoorsness came an him, an' before he kem to the end of his story Larry O'Connor beginned to snore like a bagpipes.

'"Oh, blur an' agres," says my father, "isn't this a hard case," says he, "that ould villain, lettin' on to be my friend, and to go asleep this way, an' us both in the very room with a sperit," says he. "The crass o' Christ about us!" says he; and with that he was goin' to shake Lawrence to waken him, but he just remimbered if he roused him, that he'd surely go off to his bed, an' lave him complately alone, an' that id be by far worse.

'"Oh thin," says my father, "I'll not disturb the poor boy. It id be neither friendly nor good-nathured," says he, "to tormint him while he is asleep," says he; "only I wish I was the same way, myself," says he.

'An' with that he beginned to walk up an' down, an' sayin' his prayers, until he worked himself into a sweat, savin' your presence. But it was all no good; so he dthrunk about a pint of sperits, to compose his mind.

'"Oh," says he, "I wish to the Lord I was as asy in my mind as Larry there. Maybe," says he, "if I thried I could go asleep;" an' with that he pulled a big arm-chair close beside Lawrence, an' settled himself in it as well as he could.

'But there was one quare thing I forgot to tell you. He couldn't help, in spite av himself, lookin' now an' thin at the picthur, an' he immediately obsarved that the eyes av it was follyin' him about, an' starin' at him, an' winkin' at him, wheriver he wint. "Oh," says he, when he seen that, "it's a poor chance I have," says he; "an' bad luck was with me the day I kem into this unforthunate place," says he. "But any way there's no use in bein' freckened now," says he; "for if I am to die, I may as well parspire undaunted," says he.

'Well, your honour, he thried to keep himself quite an' asy, an' he thought two or three times he might have wint asleep, but for the way the storm was groanin' and creakin' through the great heavy branches outside, an' whistlin' through the ould chimleys iv the castle. Well, afther one great roarin' blast iv the wind, you'd think the walls iv the castle was just goin' to fall, quite an' clane, with the shakin' iv it. All av a suddint the storm stopt, as silent an' as quite as if it was a July evenin'. Well, your honour, it wasn't stopped blowin' for three minnites, before he thought he hard a sort iv a noise over the chimley-piece; an' with that my father just opened his eyes the smallest taste in life, an' sure enough he seen the ould squire gettin' out iv the picthur, for all the world as if he was throwin' aff his ridin' coat, until he stept out clane an' complate, out av the chimley-piece, an' thrun himself down an the floor. Well, the slieveen ould chap—an' my father thought it was the dirtiest turn iv all—before he beginned to do anything out iv the way, he stopped for a while to listen wor they both asleep; an' as soon as he thought all was quite, he put out his hand and tuk hould iv the whisky bottle, an dhrank at laste a pint iv it. Well, your honour, when he tuk his turn out iv it, he settled it back mighty cute entirely, in the very same spot it was in before. An' he beginned to walk up an' down the room, lookin' as sober an' as solid as if he never done the likes at all. An' whinever he went apast my father, he thought he felt a great scent of brimstone, an' it was that that freckened him entirely; for he knew it was brimstone that was burned in hell, savin' your presence. At any rate, he often heerd it from Father Murphy, an' he had a right to know what belonged to it—he's dead since, God rest him. Well, your honour, my father was asy enough until the sperit kem past him; so close, God be marciful to us all, that the smell iv the sulphur tuk the breath clane out iv him; an' with that he tuk such a fit iv coughin', that it al-a-most shuk him out iv the chair he was sittin' in.

'"Ho, ho!" says the squire, stoppin' short about two steps aff, and turnin' round facin' my father, "is it you that's in it?—an' how's all with you, Terry Neil?"

'"At your honour's sarvice," says my father (as well as the fright id let him, for he was more dead than alive), "an' it's proud I am to see your honour to-night," says he.

'"Terence," says the squire, "you're a respectable man" (an' it was thrue for him), "an industhrious, sober man, an' an example of inebriety to the whole parish," says he.

'"Thank your honour," says my father, gettin' courage, "you were always a civil spoken gintleman, God rest your honour."

'"REST my honour?" says the sperit (fairly gettin' red in the face with the madness), "Rest my honour?" says he. "Why, you ignorant spalpeen," says he, "you mane, niggarly ignoramush," says he, "where did you lave your manners?" says he. "If I AM dead, it's no fault iv mine," says he; "an' it's not to be thrun in my teeth at every hand's turn, by the likes iv you," says he, stampin' his foot an the flure, that you'd think the boords id smash undther him.

'"Oh," says my father, "I'm only a foolish, ignorant poor man," says he.

'"You're nothing else," says the squire: "but any way," says he, "it's not to be listenin' to your gosther, nor convarsin' with the likes iv you, that I came UP—down I mane," says he—(an' as little as the mistake was, my father tuk notice iv it). "Listen to me now, Terence Neil," says he: "I was always a good masther to Pathrick Neil, your grandfather," says he.

'"'Tis thrue for your honour," says my father.

'"And, moreover, I think I was always a sober, riglar gintleman," says the squire.

'"That's your name, sure enough," says my father (though it was a big lie for him, but he could not help it).

'"Well," says the sperit, "although I was as sober as most men—at laste as most gintlemin," says he; "an' though I was at different pariods a most extempory Christian, and most charitable and inhuman to the poor," says he; "for all that I'm not as asy where I am now," says he, "as I had a right to expect," says he.

'"An' more's the pity," says my father. "Maybe your honour id wish to have a word with Father Murphy?"

'"Hould your tongue, you misherable bliggard," says the squire; "it's not iv my sowl I'm thinkin'—an' I wondther you'd have the impitence to talk to a gintleman consarnin' his sowl; and when I want THAT fixed," says he, slappin' his thigh, "I'll go to them that knows what belongs to the likes," says he. "It's not my sowl," says he, sittin' down opossite my father; "it's not my sowl that's annoyin' me most—I'm unasy on my right leg," says he, "that I bruk at Glenvarloch cover the day I killed black Barney."

'My father found out afther, it was a favourite horse that fell undher him, afther leapin' the big fence that runs along by the glin.

'"I hope," says my father, "your honour's not unasy about the killin' iv him?"

'"Hould your tongue, ye fool," said the squire, "an' I'll tell you why I'm unasy on my leg," says he. "In the place, where I spend most iv my time," says he, "except the little leisure I have for lookin' about me here," says he, "I have to walk a great dale more than I was ever used to," says he, "and by far more than is good for me either," says he; "for I must tell you," says he, "the people where I am is ancommonly fond iv cowld wather, for there is nothin' betther to be had; an', moreover, the weather is hotter than is altogether plisant," says he; "and I'm appinted," says he, "to assist in carryin' the wather, an' gets a mighty poor share iv it myself," says he, "an' a mighty throublesome, wearin' job it is, I can tell you," says he; "for they're all iv them surprisinly dthry, an' dthrinks it as fast as my legs can carry it," says he; "but what kills me intirely," says he, "is the wakeness in my leg," says he, "an' I want you to give it a pull or two to bring it to shape," says he, "and that's the long an' the short iv it," says he.

'"Oh, plase your honour," says my father (for he didn't like to handle the sperit at all), "I wouldn't have the impidence to do the likes to your honour," says he; "it's only to poor crathurs like myself I'd do it to," says he.

'"None iv your blarney," says the squire. "Here's my leg," says he, cockin' it up to him—"pull it for the bare life," says he; an'"if you don't, by the immortial powers I'll not lave a bone in your carcish I'll not powdher," says he.

'When my father heerd that, he seen there was no use in purtendin', so he tuk hould iv the leg, an' he kep' pullin' an' pullin', till the sweat, God bless us, beginned to pour down his face.

'"Pull, you divil!" says the squire.

'"At your sarvice, your honour," says my father.

'"Pull harder," says the squire.

'My father pulled like the divil.

'"I'll take a little sup," says the squire, rachin' over his hand to the bottle, "to keep up my courage," says he, lettin' an to be very wake in himself intirely. But, as cute as he was, he was out here, for he tuk the wrong one. "Here's to your good health, Terence," says he; "an' now pull like the very divil." An' with that he lifted the bottle of holy wather, but it was hardly to his mouth, whin he let a screech out, you'd think the room id fairly split with it, an' made one chuck that sent the leg clane aff his body in my father's hands. Down wint the squire over the table, an' bang wint my father half-way across the room on his back, upon the flure. Whin he kem to himself the cheerful mornin' sun was shinin' through the windy shutthers, an' he was lying flat an his back, with the leg iv one of the great ould chairs pulled clane out iv the socket an' tight in his hand, pintin' up to the ceilin', an' ould Larry fast asleep, an' snorin' as loud as ever. My father wint that mornin' to Father Murphy, an' from that to the day of his death, he never neglected confission nor mass, an' what he tould was betther believed that he spake av it but seldom. An', as for the squire, that is the sperit, whether it was that he did not like his liquor, or by rason iv the loss iv his leg, he was never known to walk agin.'

THE FORTUNES OF SIR ROBERT ARDAGH.

Being a second Extract from the Papers of the late Father Purcell.

'The earth hath bubbles as the water hath—
And these are of them.'

In the south of Ireland, and on the borders of the county of Limerick, there lies a district of two or three miles in length, which is rendered interesting by the fact that it is one of the very few spots throughout this country, in which some vestiges of aboriginal forest still remain. It has little or none of the lordly character of the American forest, for the axe has felled its oldest and its grandest trees; but in the close wood which survives, live all the wild and pleasing peculiarities of nature: its complete irregularity, its vistas, in whose perspective the quiet cattle are peacefully browsing; its refreshing glades, where the grey rocks arise from amid the nodding fern; the silvery shafts of the old birch trees; the knotted trunks of the hoary oak, the grotesque but graceful branches which never shed their honours under the tyrant pruning-hook; the soft green sward; the chequered light and shade; the wild luxuriant weeds; the lichen and the moss—all, all are beautiful alike in the green freshness of spring, or in the sadness and sere of autumn. Their beauty is of that kind which makes the heart full with joy—appealing to the affections with a power which belongs to nature only. This wood runs up, from below the base, to the ridge of a long line of irregular hills, having perhaps, in primitive times, formed but the skirting of some mighty forest which occupied the level below.

But now, alas! whither have we drifted? whither has the tide of civilisation borne us? It has passed over a land unprepared for it—it has left nakedness behind it; we have lost our forests, but our marauders remain; we have destroyed all that is picturesque, while we have retained everything that is revolting in barbarism. Through the midst of this woodland there runs a deep gully or glen, where the stillness of the scene is broken in upon by the brawling of a mountain-stream, which, however, in the winter season, swells into a rapid and formidable torrent.

There is one point at which the glen becomes extremely deep and narrow; the sides descend to the depth of some hundred feet, and are so steep as to be nearly perpendicular. The wild trees which have taken root in the crannies and chasms of the rock have so intersected and entangled, that one can with difficulty catch a glimpse of the stream, which wheels, flashes, and foams below, as if exulting in the surrounding silence and solitude.

This spot was not unwisely chosen, as a point of no ordinary strength, for the erection of a massive square tower or keep, one side of which rises as if in continuation of the precipitous cliff on which it is based. Originally, the only mode of ingress was by a narrow portal in the very wall which overtopped the precipice, opening upon a ledge of rock which afforded a precarious pathway, cautiously intersected, however, by a deep trench cut with great labour in the living rock; so that, in its original state, and before the introduction of artillery into the art of war, this tower might have been pronounced, and that not presumptuously, almost impregnable.

The progress of improvement and the increasing security of the times had, however, tempted its successive proprietors, if not to adorn, at least to enlarge their premises, and at about the middle of the last century, when the castle was last inhabited, the original square tower formed but a small part of the edifice.

The castle, and a wide tract of the surrounding country, had from time immemorial belonged to a family which, for distinctness, we shall call by the name of Ardagh; and owing to the associations which, in Ireland, almost always attach to scenes which have long witnessed alike the exercise of stern feudal authority, and of that savage hospitality which distinguished the good old times, this building has become the subject and the scene of many wild and extraordinary traditions. One of them I have been enabled, by a personal acquaintance with an eye-witness of the events, to trace to its origin, and yet it is hard to say whether the events which I am about to record appear more strange or improbable as seen through the distorting medium of tradition, or in the appalling dimness of uncertainty which surrounds the reality.

Tradition says that, sometime in the last century, Sir Robert Ardagh, a young man, and the last heir of that family, went abroad and served in foreign armies; and that, having acquired considerable honour and emolument, he settled at Castle Ardagh, the building we have just now attempted to describe. He was what the country people call a DARK man; that is, he was considered morose, reserved, and ill-tempered; and, as it was supposed from the utter solitude of his life, was upon no terms of cordiality with the other members of his family.

The only occasion upon which he broke through the solitary monotony of his life was during the continuance of the racing season, and immediately subsequent to it; at which time he was to be seen among the busiest upon the course, betting deeply and unhesitatingly, and invariably with success. Sir Robert was, however, too well known as a man of honour, and of too high a family, to be suspected of any unfair dealing. He was, moreover, a soldier, and a man of an intrepid as well as of a haughty character; and no one cared to hazard a surmise, the consequences of which would be felt most probably by its originator only.

Gossip, however, was not silent; it was remarked that Sir Robert never appeared at the race-ground, which was the only place of public resort which he frequented, except in company with a certain strange-looking person, who was never seen elsewhere, or under other circumstances. It was remarked, too, that this man, whose relation to Sir Robert was never distinctly ascertained, was the only person to whom he seemed to speak unnecessarily; it was observed that while with the country gentry he exchanged no further communication than what was unavoidable in arranging his sporting transactions, with this person he would converse earnestly and frequently. Tradition asserts that, to enhance the curiosity which this unaccountable and exclusive preference excited, the stranger possessed some striking and unpleasant peculiarities of person and of garb—she does not say, however, what these were—but they, in conjunction with Sir Robert's secluded habits and extraordinary run of luck—a success which was supposed to result from the suggestions and immediate advice of the unknown—were sufficient to warrant report in pronouncing that there was something QUEER in the wind, and in surmising that Sir Robert was playing a fearful and a hazardous game, and that, in short, his strange companion was little better than the devil himself.

Years, however, rolled quietly away, and nothing novel occurred in the arrangements of Castle Ardagh, excepting that Sir Robert parted with his odd companion, but as nobody could tell whence he came, so nobody could say whither he had gone. Sir Robert's habits, however, underwent no consequent change; he continued regularly to frequent the race meetings, without mixing at all in the convivialities of the gentry, and immediately afterwards to relapse into the secluded monotony of his ordinary life.

It was said that he had accumulated vast sums of money—and, as his bets were always successful, and always large, such must have been the case. He did not suffer the acquisition of wealth, however, to influence his hospitality or his housekeeping—he neither purchased land, nor extended his establishment; and his mode of enjoying his money must have been altogether that of the miser—consisting merely in the pleasure of touching and telling his gold, and in the consciousness of wealth.

Sir Robert's temper, so far from improving, became more than ever gloomy and morose. He sometimes carried the indulgence of his evil dispositions to such a height that it bordered upon insanity. During these paroxysms he would neither eat, drink, nor sleep. On such occasions he insisted on perfect privacy, even from the intrusion of his most trusted servants; his voice was frequently heard, sometimes in earnest supplication, sometime as if in loud and angry altercation with some unknown visitant; sometimes he would, for hours together, walk to and fro throughout the long oak wainscoted apartment, which he generally occupied, with wild gesticulations and agitated pace, in the manner of one who has been roused to a state of unnatural excitement by some sudden and appalling intimation.

These paroxysms of apparent lunacy were so frightful, that during their continuance even his oldest and most-faithful domestics dared not approach him; consequently, his hours of agony were never intruded upon, and the mysterious causes of his sufferings appeared likely to remain hidden for ever.

On one occasion a fit of this kind continued for an unusual time, the ordinary term of their duration—about two days—had been long past, and the old servant who generally waited upon Sir Robert after these visitations, having in vain listened for the well-known tinkle of his master's hand-bell, began to feel extremely anxious; he feared that his master might have died from sheer exhaustion, or perhaps put an end to his own existence during his miserable depression. These fears at length became so strong, that having in vain urged some of his brother servants to accompany him, he determined to go up alone, and himself see whether any accident had befallen Sir Robert.

He traversed the several passages which conducted from the new to the more ancient parts of the mansion, and having arrived in the old hall of the castle, the utter silence of the hour, for it was very late in the night, the idea of the nature of the enterprise in which he was engaging himself, a sensation of remoteness from anything like human companionship, but, more than all, the vivid but undefined anticipation of something horrible, came upon him with such oppressive weight that he hesitated as to whether he should proceed. Real uneasiness, however, respecting the fate of his master, for whom he felt that kind of attachment which the force of habitual intercourse not unfrequently engenders respecting objects not in themselves amiable, and also a latent unwillingness to expose his weakness to the ridicule of his fellow-servants, combined to overcome his reluctance; and he had just placed his foot upon the first step of the staircase which conducted to his master's chamber, when his attention was arrested by a low but distinct knocking at the hall-door. Not, perhaps, very sorry at finding thus an excuse even for deferring his intended expedition, he placed the candle upon a stone block which lay in the hall, and approached the door, uncertain whether his ears had not deceived him. This doubt was justified by the circumstance that the hall entrance had been for nearly fifty years disused as a mode of ingress to the castle. The situation of this gate also, which we have endeavoured to describe, opening upon a narrow ledge of rock which overhangs a perilous cliff, rendered it at all times, but particularly at night, a dangerous entrance. This shelving platform of rock, which formed the only avenue to the door, was divided, as I have already stated, by a broad chasm, the planks across which had long disappeared by decay or otherwise, so that it seemed at least highly improbable that any man could have found his way across the passage in safety to the door, more particularly on a night like that, of singular darkness. The old man, therefore, listened attentively, to ascertain whether the first application should be followed by another. He had not long to wait; the same low but singularly distinct knocking was repeated; so low that it seemed as if the applicant had employed no harder or heavier instrument than his hand, and yet, despite the immense thickness of the door, with such strength that the sound was distinctly audible.

The knock was repeated a third time, without any increase of loudness; and the old man, obeying an impulse for which to his dying hour he could never account, proceeded to remove, one by one, the three great oaken bars which secured the door. Time and damp had effectually corroded the iron chambers of the lock, so that it afforded little resistance. With some effort, as he believed, assisted from without, the old servant succeeded in opening the door; and a low, square-built figure, apparently that of a man wrapped in a large black cloak, entered the hall. The servant could not see much of this visitant with any distinctness; his dress appeared foreign, the skirt of his ample cloak was thrown over one shoulder; he wore a large felt hat, with a very heavy leaf, from under which escaped what appeared to be a mass of long sooty-black hair; his feet were cased in heavy riding-boots. Such were the few particulars which the servant had time and light to observe. The stranger desired him to let his master know instantly that a friend had come, by appointment, to settle some business with him. The servant hesitated, but a slight motion on the part of his visitor, as if to possess himself of the candle, determined him; so, taking it in his hand, he ascended the castle stairs, leaving his guest in the hall.

On reaching the apartment which opened upon the oak-chamber he was surprised to observe the door of that room partly open, and the room itself lit up. He paused, but there was no sound; he looked in, and saw Sir Robert, his head and the upper part of his body reclining on a table, upon which burned a lamp; his arms were stretched forward on either side, and perfectly motionless; it appeared that, having been sitting at the table, he had thus sunk forward, either dead or in a swoon. There was no sound of breathing; all was silent, except the sharp ticking of a watch, which lay beside the lamp. The servant coughed twice or thrice, but with no effect; his fears now almost amounted to certainty, and he was approaching the table on which his master partly lay, to satisfy himself of his death, when Sir Robert slowly raised his head, and throwing himself back in his chair, fixed his eyes in a ghastly and uncertain gaze upon his attendant. At length he said, slowly and painfully, as if he dreaded the answer:

'In God's name, what are you?'

'Sir,' said the servant, 'a strange gentleman wants to see you below.'

At this intimation Sir Robert, starting on his feet and tossing his arms wildly upwards, uttered a shriek of such appalling and despairing terror that it was almost too fearful for human endurance; and long after the sound had ceased it seemed to the terrified imagination of the old servant to roll through the deserted passages in bursts of unnatural laughter. After a few moments Sir Robert said:

'Can't you send him away? Why does he come so soon? O God! O God! let him leave me for an hour; a little time. I can't see him now; try to get him away. You see I can't go down now; I have not strength. O God! O God! let him come back in an hour; it is not long to wait. He cannot lose anything by it; nothing, nothing, nothing. Tell him that; say anything to him.'

The servant went down. In his own words, he did not feel the stairs under him till he got to the hall. The figure stood exactly as he had left it. He delivered his master's message as coherently as he could. The stranger replied in a careless tone:

'If Sir Robert will not come down to me, I must go up to him.'

The man returned, and to his surprise he found his master much more composed in manner. He listened to the message, and though the cold perspiration rose in drops upon his forehead faster than he could wipe it away, his manner had lost the dreadful agitation which had marked it before. He rose feebly, and casting a last look of agony behind him, passed from the room to the lobby, where he signed to his attendant not to follow him. The man moved as far as the head of the staircase, from whence he had a tolerably distinct view of the hall, which was imperfectly lighted by the candle he had left there.

He saw his master reel, rather than walk down the stairs, clinging all the way to the banisters. He walked on, as if about to sink every moment from weakness. The figure advanced as if to meet him, and in passing struck down the light. The servant could see no more; but there was a sound of struggling, renewed at intervals with silent but fearful energy. It was evident, however, that the parties were approaching the door, for he heard the solid oak sound twice or thrice, as the feet of the combatants, in shuffling hither and thither over the floor, struck upon it. After a slight pause he heard the door thrown open with such violence that the leaf seemed to strike the side-wall of the hall, for it was so dark without that this could only be surmised by the sound. The struggle was renewed with an agony and intenseness of energy that betrayed itself in deep-drawn gasps. One desperate effort, which terminated in the breaking of some part of the door, producing a sound as if the door-post was wrenched from its position, was followed by another wrestle, evidently upon the narrow ledge which ran outside the door, overtopping the precipice. This proved to be the final struggle, for it was followed by a crashing sound as if some heavy body had fallen over, and was rushing down the precipice, through the light boughs that crossed near the top. All then became still as the grave, except when the moan of the night wind sighed up the wooded glen.

The old servant had not nerve to return through the hall, and to him the darkness seemed all but endless; but morning at length came, and with it the disclosure of the events of the night. Near the door, upon the ground, lay Sir Robert's sword-belt, which had given way in the scuffle. A huge splinter from the massive door-post had been wrenched off by an almost superhuman effort—one which nothing but the gripe of a despairing man could have severed—and on the rock outside were left the marks of the slipping and sliding of feet.

At the foot of the precipice, not immediately under the castle, but dragged some way up the glen, were found the remains of Sir Robert, with hardly a vestige of a limb or feature left distinguishable. The right hand, however, was uninjured, and in its fingers were clutched, with the fixedness of death, a long lock of coarse sooty hair—the only direct circumstantial evidence of the presence of a second person. So says tradition.

This story, as I have mentioned, was current among the dealers in such lore; but the original facts are so dissimilar in all but the name of the principal person mentioned and his mode of life, and the fact that his death was accompanied with circumstances of extraordinary mystery, that the two narratives are totally irreconcilable (even allowing the utmost for the exaggerating influence of tradition), except by supposing report to have combined and blended together the fabulous histories of several distinct bearers of the family name. However this may be, I shall lay before the reader a distinct recital of the events from which the foregoing tradition arose. With respect to these there can be no mistake; they are authenticated as fully as anything can be by human testimony; and I state them principally upon the evidence of a lady who herself bore a prominent part in the strange events which she related, and which I now record as being among the few well-attested tales of the marvellous which it has been my fate to hear. I shall, as far as I am able, arrange in one combined narrative the evidence of several distinct persons who were eye-witnesses of what they related, and with the truth of whose testimony I am solemnly and deeply impressed.

Sir Robert Ardagh, as we choose to call him, was the heir and representative of the family whose name he bore; but owing to the prodigality of his father, the estates descended to him in a very impaired condition. Urged by the restless spirit of youth, or more probably by a feeling of pride which could not submit to witness, in the paternal mansion, what he considered a humiliating alteration in the style and hospitality which up to that time had distinguished his family, Sir Robert left Ireland and went abroad. How he occupied himself, or what countries he visited during his absence, was never known, nor did he afterwards make any allusion or encourage any inquiries touching his foreign sojourn. He left Ireland in the year 1742, being then just of age, and was not heard of until the year 1760—about eighteen years afterwards—at which time he returned. His personal appearance was, as might have been expected, very greatly altered, more altered, indeed, than the time of his absence might have warranted one in supposing likely. But to counterbalance the unfavourable change which time had wrought in his form and features, he had acquired all the advantages of polish of manner and refinement of taste which foreign travel is supposed to bestow. But what was truly surprising was that it soon became evident that Sir Robert was very wealthy—wealthy to an extraordinary and unaccountable degree; and this fact was made manifest, not only by his expensive style of living, but by his proceeding to disembarrass his property, and to purchase extensive estates in addition. Moreover, there could be nothing deceptive in these appearances, for he paid ready money for everything, from the most important purchase to the most trifling.

Sir Robert was a remarkably agreeable man, and possessing the combined advantages of birth and property, he was, as a matter of course, gladly received into the highest society which the metropolis then commanded. It was thus that he became acquainted with the two beautiful Miss F——ds, then among the brightest ornaments of the highest circle of Dublin fashion. Their family was in more than one direction allied to nobility; and Lady D——, their elder sister by many years, and sometime married to a once well-known nobleman, was now their protectress. These considerations, beside the fact that the young ladies were what is usually termed heiresses, though not to a very great amount, secured to them a high position in the best society which Ireland then produced. The two young ladies differed strongly, alike in appearance and in character. The elder of the two, Emily, was generally considered the handsomer—for her beauty was of that impressive kind which never failed to strike even at the first glance, possessing as it did all the advantages of a fine person and a commanding carriage. The beauty of her features strikingly assorted in character with that of her figure and deportment. Her hair was raven-black and richly luxuriant, beautifully contrasting with the perfect whiteness of her forehead—her finely pencilled brows were black as the ringlets that clustered near them—and her blue eyes, full, lustrous, and animated, possessed all the power and brilliancy of brown ones, with more than their softness and variety of expression. She was not, however, merely the tragedy queen. When she smiled, and that was not seldom, the dimpling of cheek and chin, the laughing display of the small and beautiful teeth—but, more than all, the roguish archness of her deep, bright eye, showed that nature had not neglected in her the lighter and the softer characteristics of woman.

Her younger sister Mary was, as I believe not unfrequently occurs in the case of sisters, quite in the opposite style of beauty. She was light-haired, had more colour, had nearly equal grace, with much more liveliness of manner. Her eyes were of that dark grey which poets so much admire—full of expression and vivacity. She was altogether a very beautiful and animated girl—though as unlike her sister as the presence of those two qualities would permit her to be. Their dissimilarity did not stop here—it was deeper than mere appearance—the character of their minds differed almost as strikingly as did their complexion. The fair-haired beauty had a large proportion of that softness and pliability of temper which physiognomists assign as the characteristics of such complexions. She was much more the creature of impulse than of feeling, and consequently more the victim of extrinsic circumstances than was her sister. Emily, on the contrary, possessed considerable firmness and decision. She was less excitable, but when excited her feelings were more intense and enduring. She wanted much of the gaiety, but with it the volatility of her younger sister. Her opinions were adopted, and her friendships formed more reflectively, and her affections seemed to move, as it were, more slowly, but more determinedly. This firmness of character did not amount to anything masculine, and did not at all impair the feminine grace of her manners.

Sir Robert Ardagh was for a long time apparently equally attentive to the two sisters, and many were the conjectures and the surmises as to which would be the lady of his choice. At length, however, these doubts were determined; he proposed for and was accepted by the dark beauty, Emily F——d.

The bridals were celebrated in a manner becoming the wealth and connections of the parties; and Sir Robert and Lady Ardagh left Dublin to pass the honeymoon at the family mansion, Castle Ardagh, which had lately been fitted up in a style bordering upon magnificent. Whether in compliance with the wishes of his lady, or owing to some whim of his own, his habits were henceforward strikingly altered; and from having moved among the gayest if not the most profligate of the votaries of fashion, he suddenly settled down into a quiet, domestic, country gentleman, and seldom, if ever, visited the capital, and then his sojourns were as brief as the nature of his business would permit.

Lady Ardagh, however, did not suffer from this change further than in being secluded from general society; for Sir Robert's wealth, and the hospitality which he had established in the family mansion, commanded that of such of his lady's friends and relatives as had leisure or inclination to visit the castle; and as their style of living was very handsome, and its internal resources of amusement considerable, few invitations from Sir Robert or his lady were neglected.

Many years passed quietly away, during which Sir Robert's and Lady Ardagh's hopes of issue were several times disappointed. In the lapse of all this time there occurred but one event worth recording. Sir Robert had brought with him from abroad a valet, who sometimes professed himself to be French, at others Italian, and at others again German. He spoke all these languages with equal fluency, and seemed to take a kind of pleasure in puzzling the sagacity and balking the curiosity of such of the visitors at the castle as at any time happened to enter into conversation with him, or who, struck by his singularities, became inquisitive respecting his country and origin. Sir Robert called him by the French name, JACQUE, and among the lower orders he was familiarly known by the title of 'Jack, the devil,' an appellation which originated in a supposed malignity of disposition and a real reluctance to mix in the society of those who were believed to be his equals. This morose reserve, coupled with the mystery which enveloped all about him, rendered him an object of suspicion and inquiry to his fellow-servants, amongst whom it was whispered that this man in secret governed the actions of Sir Robert with a despotic dictation, and that, as if to indemnify himself for his public and apparent servitude and self-denial, he in private exacted a degree of respectful homage from his so-called master, totally inconsistent with the relation generally supposed to exist between them.

This man's personal appearance was, to say the least of it, extremely odd; he was low in stature; and this defect was enhanced by a distortion of the spine, so considerable as almost to amount to a hunch; his features, too, had all that sharpness and sickliness of hue which generally accompany deformity; he wore his hair, which was black as soot, in heavy neglected ringlets about his shoulders, and always without powder—a peculiarity in those days. There was something unpleasant, too, in the circumstance that he never raised his eyes to meet those of another; this fact was often cited as a proof of his being something not quite right, and said to result not from the timidity which is supposed in most cases to induce this habit, but from a consciousness that his eye possessed a power which, if exhibited, would betray a supernatural origin. Once, and once only, had he violated this sinister observance: it was on the occasion of Sir Robert's hopes having been most bitterly disappointed; his lady, after a severe and dangerous confinement, gave birth to a dead child. Immediately after the intelligence had been made known, a servant, having upon some business passed outside the gate of the castle-yard, was met by Jacque, who, contrary to his wont, accosted him, observing, 'So, after all the pother, the son and heir is still-born.' This remark was accompanied by a chuckling laugh, the only approach to merriment which he was ever known to exhibit. The servant, who was really disappointed, having hoped for holiday times, feasting and debauchery with impunity during the rejoicings which would have accompanied a christening, turned tartly upon the little valet, telling him that he should let Sir Robert know how he had received the tidings which should have filled any faithful servant with sorrow; and having once broken the ice, he was proceeding with increasing fluency, when his harangue was cut short and his temerity punished, by the little man raising his head and treating him to a scowl so fearful, half-demoniac, half-insane, that it haunted his imagination in nightmares and nervous tremors for months after.

To this man Lady Ardagh had, at first sight, conceived an antipathy amounting to horror, a mixture of loathing and dread so very powerful that she had made it a particular and urgent request to Sir Robert, that he would dismiss him, offering herself, from that property which Sir Robert had by the marriage settlements left at her own disposal, to provide handsomely for him, provided only she might be relieved from the continual anxiety and discomfort which the fear of encountering him induced.

Sir Robert, however, would not hear of it; the request seemed at first to agitate and distress him; but when still urged in defiance of his peremptory refusal, he burst into a violent fit of fury; he spoke darkly of great sacrifices which he had made, and threatened that if the request were at any time renewed he would leave both her and the country for ever. This was, however, a solitary instance of violence; his general conduct towards Lady Ardagh, though at no time uxorious, was certainly kind and respectful, and he was more than repaid in the fervent attachment which she bore him in return.

Some short time after this strange interview between Sir Robert and Lady Ardagh; one night after the family had retired to bed, and when everything had been quiet for some time, the bell of Sir Robert's dressing-room rang suddenly and violently; the ringing was repeated again and again at still shorter intervals, and with increasing violence, as if the person who pulled the bell was agitated by the presence of some terrifying and imminent danger. A servant named Donovan was the first to answer it; he threw on his clothes, and hurried to the room.

Sir Robert had selected for his private room an apartment remote from the bedchambers of the castle, most of which lay in the more modern parts of the mansion, and secured at its entrance by a double door. As the servant opened the first of these, Sir Robert's bell again sounded with a longer and louder peal; the inner door resisted his efforts to open it; but after a few violent struggles, not having been perfectly secured, or owing to the inadequacy of the bolt itself, it gave way, and the servant rushed into the apartment, advancing several paces before he could recover himself. As he entered, he heard Sir Robert's voice exclaiming loudly—'Wait without, do not come in yet;' but the prohibition came too late. Near a low truckle-bed, upon which Sir Robert sometimes slept, for he was a whimsical man, in a large armchair, sat, or rather lounged, the form of the valet Jacque, his arms folded, and his heels stretched forward on the floor, so as fully to exhibit his misshapen legs, his head thrown back, and his eyes fixed upon his master with a look of indescribable defiance and derision, while, as if to add to the strange insolence of his attitude and expression, he had placed upon his head the black cloth cap which it was his habit to wear.

Sir Robert was standing before him, at the distance of several yards, in a posture expressive of despair, terror, and what might be called an agony of humility. He waved his hand twice or thrice, as if to dismiss the servant, who, however, remained fixed on the spot where he had first stood; and then, as if forgetting everything but the agony within him, he pressed his clenched hands on his cold damp brow, and dashed away the heavy drops that gathered chill and thickly there.

Jacque broke the silence.

'Donovan,' said he, 'shake up that drone and drunkard, Carlton; tell him that his master directs that the travelling carriage shall be at the door within half-an-hour.'

The servant paused, as if in doubt as to what he should do; but his scruples were resolved by Sir Robert's saying hurriedly, 'Go—go, do whatever he directs; his commands are mine; tell Carlton the same.'

The servant hurried to obey, and in about half-an-hour the carriage was at the door, and Jacque, having directed the coachman to drive to B——n, a small town at about the distance of twelve miles—the nearest point, however, at which post-horses could be obtained—stepped into the vehicle, which accordingly quitted the castle immediately.

Although it was a fine moonlight night, the carriage made its way but very slowly, and after the lapse of two hours the travellers had arrived at a point about eight miles from the castle, at which the road strikes through a desolate and heathy flat, sloping up distantly at either side into bleak undulatory hills, in whose monotonous sweep the imagination beholds the heaving of some dark sluggish sea, arrested in its first commotion by some preternatural power. It is a gloomy and divested spot; there is neither tree nor habitation near it; its monotony is unbroken, except by here and there the grey front of a rock peering above the heath, and the effect is rendered yet more dreary and spectral by the exaggerated and misty shadows which the moon casts along the sloping sides of the hills.

When they had gained about the centre of this tract, Carlton, the coachman, was surprised to see a figure standing at some distance in advance, immediately beside the road, and still more so when, on coming up, he observed that it was no other than Jacque whom he believed to be at that moment quietly seated in the carriage; the coachman drew up, and nodding to him, the little valet exclaimed:

'Carlton, I have got the start of you; the roads are heavy, so I shall even take care of myself the rest of the way. Do you make your way back as best you can, and I shall follow my own nose.'

So saying, he chucked a purse into the lap of the coachman, and turning off at a right angle with the road, he began to move rapidly away in the direction of the dark ridge that lowered in the distance.

The servant watched him until he was lost in the shadowy haze of night; and neither he nor any of the inmates of the castle saw Jacque again. His disappearance, as might have been expected, did not cause any regret among the servants and dependants at the castle; and Lady Ardagh did not attempt to conceal her delight; but with Sir Robert matters were different, for two or three days subsequent to this event he confined himself to his room, and when he did return to his ordinary occupations, it was with a gloomy indifference, which showed that he did so more from habit than from any interest he felt in them. He appeared from that moment unaccountably and strikingly changed, and thenceforward walked through life as a thing from which he could derive neither profit nor pleasure. His temper, however, so far from growing wayward or morose, became, though gloomy, very—almost unnaturally—placid and cold; but his spirits totally failed, and he grew silent and abstracted.

These sombre habits of mind, as might have been anticipated, very materially affected the gay house-keeping of the castle; and the dark and melancholy spirit of its master seemed to have communicated itself to the very domestics, almost to the very walls of the mansion.

Several years rolled on in this way, and the sounds of mirth and wassail had long been strangers to the castle, when Sir Robert requested his lady, to her great astonishment, to invite some twenty or thirty of their friends to spend the Christmas, which was fast approaching, at the castle. Lady Ardagh gladly complied, and her sister Mary, who still continued unmarried, and Lady D—— were of course included in the invitations. Lady Ardagh had requested her sisters to set forward as early as possible, in order that she might enjoy a little of their society before the arrival of the other guests; and in compliance with this request they left Dublin almost immediately upon receiving the invitation, a little more than a week before the arrival of the festival which was to be the period at which the whole party were to muster.

For expedition's sake it was arranged that they should post, while Lady D——'s groom was to follow with her horses, she taking with herself her own maid and one male servant. They left the city when the day was considerably spent, and consequently made but three stages in the first day; upon the second, at about eight in the evening, they had reached the town of K——k, distant about fifteen miles from Castle Ardagh. Here, owing to Miss F——d's great fatigue, she having been for a considerable time in a very delicate state of health, it was determined to put up for the night. They, accordingly, took possession of the best sitting-room which the inn commanded, and Lady D——remained in it to direct and urge the preparations for some refreshment, which the fatigues of the day had rendered necessary, while her younger sister retired to her bed-chamber to rest there for a little time, as the parlour commanded no such luxury as a sofa.

Miss F——d was, as I have already stated, at this time in very delicate health; and upon this occasion the exhaustion of fatigue, and the dreary badness of the weather, combined to depress her spirits. Lady D—— had not been left long to herself, when the door communicating with the passage was abruptly opened, and her sister Mary entered in a state of great agitation; she sat down pale and trembling upon one of the chairs, and it was not until a copious flood of tears had relieved her, that she became sufficiently calm to relate the cause of her excitement and distress. It was simply this. Almost immediately upon lying down upon the bed she sank into a feverish and unrefreshing slumber; images of all grotesque shapes and startling colours flitted before her sleeping fancy with all the rapidity and variety of the changes in a kaleidoscope. At length, as she described it, a mist seemed to interpose itself between her sight and the ever-shifting scenery which sported before her imagination, and out of this cloudy shadow gradually emerged a figure whose back seemed turned towards the sleeper; it was that of a lady, who, in perfect silence, was expressing as far as pantomimic gesture could, by wringing her hands, and throwing her head from side to side, in the manner of one who is exhausted by the over indulgence, by the very sickness and impatience of grief; the extremity of misery. For a long time she sought in vain to catch a glimpse of the face of the apparition, who thus seemed to stir and live before her. But at length the figure seemed to move with an air of authority, as if about to give directions to some inferior, and in doing so, it turned its head so as to display, with a ghastly distinctness, the features of Lady Ardagh, pale as death, with her dark hair all dishevelled, and her eyes dim and sunken with weeping. The revulsion of feeling which Miss F——d experienced at this disclosure—for up to that point she had contemplated the appearance rather with a sense of curiosity and of interest, than of anything deeper—was so horrible, that the shock awoke her perfectly. She sat up in the bed, and looked fearfully around the room, which was imperfectly lighted by a single candle burning dimly, as if she almost expected to see the reality of her dreadful vision lurking in some corner of the chamber. Her fears were, however, verified, though not in the way she expected; yet in a manner sufficiently horrible—for she had hardly time to breathe and to collect her thoughts, when she heard, or thought she heard, the voice of her sister, Lady Ardagh, sometimes sobbing violently, and sometimes almost shrieking as if in terror, and calling upon her and Lady D——, with the most imploring earnestness of despair, for God's sake to lose no time in coming to her. All this was so horribly distinct, that it seemed as if the mourner was standing within a few yards of the spot where Miss F——d lay. She sprang from the bed, and leaving the candle in the room behind her, she made her way in the dark through the passage, the voice still following her, until as she arrived at the door of the sitting-room it seemed to die away in low sobbing.

As soon as Miss F——d was tolerably recovered, she declared her determination to proceed directly, and without further loss of time, to Castle Ardagh. It was not without much difficulty that Lady D—— at length prevailed upon her to consent to remain where they then were, until morning should arrive, when it was to be expected that the young lady would be much refreshed by at least remaining quiet for the night, even though sleep were out of the question. Lady D—— was convinced, from the nervous and feverish symptoms which her sister exhibited, that she had already done too much, and was more than ever satisfied of the necessity of prosecuting the journey no further upon that day. After some time she persuaded her sister to return to her room, where she remained with her until she had gone to bed, and appeared comparatively composed. Lady D—— then returned to the parlour, and not finding herself sleepy, she remained sitting by the fire. Her solitude was a second time broken in upon, by the entrance of her sister, who now appeared, if possible, more agitated than before. She said that Lady D—— had not long left the room, when she was roused by a repetition of the same wailing and lamentations, accompanied by the wildest and most agonized supplications that no time should be lost in coming to Castle Ardagh, and all in her sister's voice, and uttered at the same proximity as before. This time the voice had followed her to the very door of the sitting-room, and until she closed it, seemed to pour forth its cries and sobs at the very threshold.

Miss F——d now most positively declared that nothing should prevent her proceeding instantly to the castle, adding that if Lady D—— would not accompany her, she would go on by herself. Superstitious feelings are at all times more or less contagious, and the last century afforded a soil much more congenial to their growth than the present. Lady D—— was so far affected by her sister's terrors, that she became, at least, uneasy; and seeing that her sister was immovably determined upon setting forward immediately, she consented to accompany her forthwith. After a slight delay, fresh horses were procured, and the two ladies and their attendants renewed their journey, with strong injunctions to the driver to quicken their rate of travelling as much as possible, and promises of reward in case of his doing so.

Roads were then in much worse condition throughout the south, even than they now are; and the fifteen miles which modern posting would have passed in little more than an hour and a half, were not completed even with every possible exertion in twice the time. Miss F——d had been nervously restless during the journey. Her head had been constantly out of the carriage window; and as they approached the entrance to the castle demesne, which lay about a mile from the building, her anxiety began to communicate itself to her sister. The postillion had just dismounted, and was endeavouring to open the gate—at that time a necessary trouble; for in the middle of the last century porter's lodges were not common in the south of Ireland, and locks and keys almost unknown. He had just succeeded in rolling back the heavy oaken gate so as to admit the vehicle, when a mounted servant rode rapidly down the avenue, and drawing up at the carriage, asked of the postillion who the party were; and on hearing, he rode round to the carriage window and handed in a note, which Lady D—— received. By the assistance of one of the coach-lamps they succeeded in deciphering it. It was scrawled in great agitation, and ran thus:

'MY DEAR SISTER—MY DEAR SISTERS BOTH,—In God's name lose no time, I am frightened and miserable; I cannot explain all till you come. I am too much terrified to write coherently; but understand me—hasten—do not waste a minute. I am afraid you will come too late.

'E. A.'

The servant could tell nothing more than that the castle was in great confusion, and that Lady Ardagh had been crying bitterly all the night. Sir Robert was perfectly well. Altogether at a loss as to the cause of Lady Ardagh's great distress, they urged their way up the steep and broken avenue which wound through the crowding trees, whose wild and grotesque branches, now left stripped and naked by the blasts of winter, stretched drearily across the road. As the carriage drew up in the area before the door, the anxiety of the ladies almost amounted to agony; and scarcely waiting for the assistance of their attendant, they sprang to the ground, and in an instant stood at the castle door. From within were distinctly audible the sounds of lamentation and weeping, and the suppressed hum of voices as if of those endeavouring to soothe the mourner. The door was speedily opened, and when the ladies entered, the first object which met their view was their sister, Lady Ardagh, sitting on a form in the hall, weeping and wringing her hands in deep agony. Beside her stood two old, withered crones, who were each endeavouring in their own way to administer consolation, without even knowing or caring what the subject of her grief might be.

Immediately on Lady Ardagh's seeing her sisters, she started up, fell on their necks, and kissed them again and again without speaking, and then taking them each by a hand, still weeping bitterly, she led them into a small room adjoining the hall, in which burned a light, and, having closed the door, she sat down between them. After thanking them for the haste they had made, she proceeded to tell them, in words incoherent from agitation, that Sir Robert had in private, and in the most solemn manner, told her that he should die upon that night, and that he had occupied himself during the evening in giving minute directions respecting the arrangements of his funeral. Lady D—— here suggested the possibility of his labouring under the hallucinations of a fever, but to this Lady Ardagh quickly replied:

'Oh! no, no! Would to God I could think it. Oh! no, no! Wait till you have seen him. There is a frightful calmness about all he says and does; and his directions are all so clear, and his mind so perfectly collected, it is impossible, quite impossible.' And she wept yet more bitterly.

At that moment Sir Robert's voice was heard in issuing some directions, as he came downstairs; and Lady Ardagh exclaimed, hurriedly:

'Go now and see him yourself. He is in the hall.'

Lady D—— accordingly went out into the hall, where Sir Robert met her; and, saluting her with kind politeness, he said, after a pause:

'You are come upon a melancholy mission—the house is in great confusion, and some of its inmates in considerable grief.' He took her hand, and looking fixedly in her face, continued: 'I shall not live to see to-morrow's sun shine.'

'You are ill, sir, I have no doubt,' replied she; 'but I am very certain we shall see you much better to-morrow, and still better the day following.'

'I am NOT ill, sister,' replied he. 'Feel my temples, they are cool; lay your finger to my pulse, its throb is slow and temperate. I never was more perfectly in health, and yet do I know that ere three hours be past, I shall be no more.'

'Sir, sir,' said she, a good deal startled, but wishing to conceal the impression which the calm solemnity of his manner had, in her own despite, made upon her,

'Sir, you should not jest; you should not even speak lightly upon such subjects. You trifle with what is sacred—you are sporting with the best affections of your wife——'

'Stay, my good lady,' said he; 'if when this clock shall strike the hour of three, I shall be anything but a helpless clod, then upbraid me. Pray return now to your sister. Lady Ardagh is, indeed, much to be pitied; but what is past cannot now be helped. I have now a few papers to arrange, and some to destroy. I shall see you and Lady Ardagh before my death; try to compose her—her sufferings distress me much; but what is past cannot now be mended.'

Thus saying, he went upstairs, and Lady D—— returned to the room where her sisters were sitting.

'Well,' exclaimed Lady Ardagh, as she re-entered, 'is it not so?—do you still doubt?—do you think there is any hope?'

Lady D—— was silent.

'Oh! none, none, none,' continued she; 'I see, I see you are convinced.' And she wrung her hands in bitter agony.

'My dear sister,' said Lady D——, 'there is, no doubt, something strange in all that has appeared in this matter; but still I cannot but hope that there may be something deceptive in all the apparent calmness of Sir Robert. I still must believe that some latent fever has affected his mind, or that, owing to the state of nervous depression into which he has been sinking, some trivial occurrence has been converted, in his disordered imagination, into an augury foreboding his immediate dissolution.'

In such suggestions, unsatisfactory even to those who originated them, and doubly so to her whom they were intended to comfort, more than two hours passed; and Lady D—— was beginning to hope that the fated term might elapse without the occurrence of any tragical event, when Sir Robert entered the room. On coming in, he placed his finger with a warning gesture upon his lips, as if to enjoin silence; and then having successively pressed the hands of his two sisters-in-law, he stooped sadly over the fainting form of his lady, and twice pressed her cold, pale forehead, with his lips, and then passed silently out of the room.

Lady D——, starting up, followed to the door, and saw him take a candle in the hall, and walk deliberately up the stairs. Stimulated by a feeling of horrible curiosity, she continued to follow him at a distance. She saw him enter his own private room, and heard him close and lock the door after him. Continuing to follow him as far as she could, she placed herself at the door of the chamber, as noiselessly as possible, where after a little time she was joined by her two sisters, Lady Ardagh and Miss F——d. In breathless silence they listened to what should pass within. They distinctly heard Sir Robert pacing up and down the room for some time; and then, after a pause, a sound as if some one had thrown himself heavily upon the bed. At this moment Lady D——, forgetting that the door had been secured within, turned the handle for the purpose of entering; when some one from the inside, close to the door, said, 'Hush! hush!' The same lady, now much alarmed, knocked violently at the door; there was no answer. She knocked again more violently, with no further success. Lady Ardagh, now uttering a piercing shriek, sank in a swoon upon the floor. Three or four servants, alarmed by the noise, now hurried upstairs, and Lady Ardagh was carried apparently lifeless to her own chamber. They then, after having knocked long and loudly in vain, applied themselves to forcing an entrance into Sir Robert's room. After resisting some violent efforts, the door at length gave way, and all entered the room nearly together. There was a single candle burning upon a table at the far end of the apartment; and stretched upon the bed lay Sir Robert Ardagh. He was a corpse—the eyes were open—no convulsion had passed over the features, or distorted the limbs—it seemed as if the soul had sped from the body without a struggle to remain there. On touching the body it was found to be cold as clay—all lingering of the vital heat had left it. They closed the ghastly eyes of the corpse, and leaving it to the care of those who seem to consider it a privilege of their age and sex to gloat over the revolting spectacle of death in all its stages, they returned to Lady Ardagh, now a widow. The party assembled at the castle, but the atmosphere was tainted with death. Grief there was not much, but awe and panic were expressed in every face. The guests talked in whispers, and the servants walked on tiptoe, as if afraid of the very noise of their own footsteps.

The funeral was conducted almost with splendour. The body, having been conveyed, in compliance with Sir Robert's last directions, to Dublin, was there laid within the ancient walls of St. Audoen's Church—where I have read the epitaph, telling the age and titles of the departed dust. Neither painted escutcheon, nor marble slab, have served to rescue from oblivion the story of the dead, whose very name will ere long moulder from their tracery,

'Et sunt sua fata sepulchris[1].'

The events which I have recorded are not imaginary. They are FACTS; and there lives one whose authority none would venture to question, who could vindicate the accuracy of every statement which I have set down, and that, too, with all the circumstantiality of an eye-witness[2].

---

[1] This prophecy has since been realised; for the aisle in which Sir Robert's remains were laid has been suffered to fall completely to decay; and the tomb which marked his grave, and other monuments more curious, form now one indistinguishable mass of rubbish.

[2] This paper, from a memorandum, I find to have been written in 1803. The lady to whom allusion is made, I believe to be Miss Mary F——d. She never married, and survived both her sisters, living to a very advanced age.

THE LAST HEIR OF CASTLE CONNOR.

Being a third Extract from the legacy of the late Francis Purcell, P. P. of Drumcoolagh.

There is something in the decay of ancient grandeur to interest even the most unconcerned spectator—the evidences of greatness, of power, and of pride that survive the wreck of time, proving, in mournful contrast with present desolation and decay, what WAS in other days, appeal, with a resistless power, to the sympathies of our nature. And when, as we gaze on the scion of some ruined family, the first impulse of nature that bids us regard his fate with interest and respect is justified by the recollection of great exertions and self-devotion and sacrifices in the cause of a lost country and of a despised religion—sacrifices and efforts made with all the motives of faithfulness and of honour, and terminating in ruin—in such a case respect becomes veneration, and the interest we feel amounts almost to a passion.

It is this feeling which has thrown the magic veil of romance over every roofless castle and ruined turret throughout our country; it is this feeling that, so long as a tower remains above the level of the soil, so long as one scion of a prostrate and impoverished family survives, will never suffer Ireland to yield to the stranger more than the 'mouth honour' which fear compels[1]. I who have conversed viva voce et propria persona with those whose recollections could run back so far as the times previous to the confiscations which followed the Revolution of 1688—whose memory could repeople halls long roofless and desolate, and point out the places where greatness once had been, may feel all this more strongly, and with a more vivid interest, than can those whose sympathies are awakened by the feebler influence of what may be called the PICTURESQUE effects of ruin and decay.

---

[1] This passage serves (mirabile dictu) to corroborate a statement of Mr. O'Connell's, which occurs in his evidence given before the House of Commons, wherein he affirms that the principles of the Irish priesthood 'ARE democratic, and were those of Jacobinism.'—See digest of the evidence upon the state of Ireland, given before the House of Commons.

There do, indeed, still exist some fragments of the ancient Catholic families of Ireland; but, alas! what VERY fragments! They linger like the remnants of her aboriginal forests, reft indeed of their strength and greatness, but proud even in decay. Every winter thins their ranks, and strews the ground with the wreck of their loftiest branches; they are at best but tolerated in the land which gave them birth—objects of curiosity, perhaps of pity, to one class, but of veneration to another.

The O'Connors, of Castle Connor, were an ancient Irish family. The name recurs frequently in our history, and is generally to be found in a prominent place whenever periods of tumult or of peril called forth the courage and the enterprise of this country. After the accession of William III., the storm of confiscation which swept over the land made woeful havoc in their broad domains. Some fragments of property, however, did remain to them, and with it the building which had for ages formed the family residence.

About the year 17—, my uncle, a Catholic priest, became acquainted with the inmates of Castle Connor, and after a time introduced me, then a lad of about fifteen, full of spirits, and little dreaming that a profession so grave as his should ever become mine.

The family at that time consisted of but two members, a widow lady and her only son, a young man aged about eighteen. In our early days the progress from acquaintance to intimacy, and from intimacy to friendship is proverbially rapid; and young O'Connor and I became, in less than a month, close and confidential companions—an intercourse which ripened gradually into an attachment ardent, deep, and devoted such as I believe young hearts only are capable of forming.

He had been left early fatherless, and the representative and heir of his family. His mother's affection for him was intense in proportion as there existed no other object to divide it—indeed—such love as that she bore him I have never seen elsewhere. Her love was better bestowed than that of mothers generally is, for young O'Connor, not without some of the faults, had certainly many of the most engaging qualities of youth. He had all the frankness and gaiety which attract, and the generosity of heart which confirms friendship; indeed, I never saw a person so universally popular; his very faults seemed to recommend him; he was wild, extravagant, thoughtless, and fearlessly adventurous—defects of character which, among the peasantry of Ireland, are honoured as virtues. The combination of these qualities, and the position which O'Connor occupied as representative of an ancient Irish Catholic family—a peculiarly interesting one to me, one of the old faith—endeared him to me so much that I have never felt the pangs of parting more keenly than when it became necessary, for the finishing of his education, that he should go abroad.

Three years had passed away before I saw him again. During the interval, however, I had frequently heard from him, so that absence had not abated the warmth of our attachment. Who could tell of the rejoicings that marked the evening of his return? The horses were removed from the chaise at the distance of a mile from the castle, while it and its contents were borne rapidly onward almost by the pressure of the multitude, like a log upon a torrent. Bonfires blared far and near—bagpipes roared and fiddles squeaked; and, amid the thundering shouts of thousands, the carriage drew up before the castle.

In an instant young O'Connor was upon the ground, crying, 'Thank you, boys—thank you, boys;' while a thousand hands were stretched out from all sides to grasp even a finger of his. Still, amid shouts of 'God bless your honour—long may you reign!' and 'Make room there, boys! clear the road for the masther!' he reached the threshold of the castle, where stood his mother weeping for joy.

Oh! who could describe that embrace, or the enthusiasm with which it was witnessed? 'God bless him to you, my lady—glory to ye both!' and 'Oh, but he is a fine young gentleman, God bless him!' resounded on all sides, while hats flew up in volleys that darkened the moon; and when at length, amid the broad delighted grins of the thronging domestics, whose sense of decorum precluded any more boisterous evidence of joy, they reached the parlour, then giving way to the fulness of her joy the widowed mother kissed and blessed him and wept in turn. Well might any parent be proud to claim as son the handsome stripling who now represented the Castle Connor family; but to her his beauty had a peculiar charm, for it bore a striking resemblance to that of her husband, the last O'Connor.

I know not whether partiality blinded me, or that I did no more than justice to my friend in believing that I had never seen so handsome a young man. I am inclined to think the latter. He was rather tall, very slightly and elegantly made; his face was oval, and his features decidedly Spanish in cast and complexion, but with far more vivacity of expression than generally belongs to the beauty of that nation. The extreme delicacy of his features and the varied animation of his countenance made him appear even younger than his years—an illusion which the total absence of everything studied in his manners seemed to confirm. Time had wrought no small change in me, alike in mind and spirits; but in the case of O'Connor it seemed to have lost its power to alter. His gaiety was undamped, his generosity unchilled; and though the space which had intervened between our parting and reunion was but brief, yet at the period of life at which we were, even a shorter interval than that of three years has frequently served to form or DEform a character.

Weeks had passed away since the return of O'Connor, and scarce a day had elapsed without my seeing him, when the neighbourhood was thrown into an unusual state of excitement by the announcement of a race-ball to be celebrated at the assembly-room of the town of T——, distant scarcely two miles from Castle Connor.

Young O'Connor, as I had expected, determined at once to attend it; and having directed in vain all the powers of his rhetoric to persuade his mother to accompany him, he turned the whole battery of his logic upon me, who, at that time, felt a reluctance stronger than that of mere apathy to mixing in any of these scenes of noisy pleasure for which for many reasons I felt myself unfitted. He was so urgent and persevering, however, that I could not refuse; and I found myself reluctantly obliged to make up my mind to attend him upon the important night to the spacious but ill-finished building, which the fashion and beauty of the county were pleased to term an assembly-room.

When we entered the apartment, we found a select few, surrounded by a crowd of spectators, busily performing a minuet, with all the congees and flourishes which belonged to that courtly dance; and my companion, infected by the contagion of example, was soon, as I had anticipated, waving his chapeau bras, and gracefully bowing before one of the prettiest girls in the room. I had neither skill nor spirits to qualify me to follow his example; and as the fulness of the room rendered it easy to do so without its appearing singular, I determined to be merely a spectator of the scene which surrounded me, without taking an active part in its amusements.

The room was indeed very much crowded, so that its various groups, formed as design or accident had thrown the parties together, afforded no small fund of entertainment to the contemplative observer. There were the dancers, all gaiety and good-humour; a little further off were the tables at which sat the card-players, some plying their vocation with deep and silent anxiety—for in those days gaming often ran very high in such places—and others disputing with all the vociferous pertinacity of undisguised ill-temper. There, again, were the sallow, blue-nosed, grey-eyed dealers in whispered scandal; and, in short, there is scarcely a group or combination to be met with in the court of kings which might not have found a humble parallel in the assembly-room of T——.

I was allowed to indulge in undisturbed contemplation, for I suppose I was not known to more than five or six in the room. I thus had leisure not only to observe the different classes into which the company had divided itself, but to amuse myself by speculating as to the rank and character of many of the individual actors in the drama.

Among many who have long since passed from my memory, one person for some time engaged my attention, and that person, for many reasons, I shall not soon forget. He was a tall, square-shouldered man, who stood in a careless attitude, leaning with his back to the wall; he seemed to have secluded himself from the busy multitudes which moved noisily and gaily around him, and nobody seemed to observe or to converse with him. He was fashionably dressed, but perhaps rather extravagantly; his face was full and heavy, expressive of sullenness and stupidity, and marked with the lines of strong vulgarity; his age might be somewhere between forty and fifty. Such as I have endeavoured to describe him, he remained motionless, his arms doggedly folded across his broad chest, and turning his sullen eyes from corner to corner of the room, as if eager to detect some object on which to vent his ill-humour.

It is strange, and yet it is true, that one sometimes finds even in the most commonplace countenance an undefinable something, which fascinates the attention, and forces it to recur again and again, while it is impossible to tell whether the peculiarity which thus attracts us lies in feature or in expression, or in both combined, and why it is that our observation should be engrossed by an object which, when analysed, seems to possess no claim to interest or even to notice. This unaccountable feeling I have often experienced, and I believe I am not singular. but never in so remarkable a degree as upon this occasion. My friend O'Connor, having disposed of his fair partner, was crossing the room for the purpose of joining me, in doing which I was surprised to see him exchange a familiar, almost a cordial, greeting with the object of my curiosity. I say I was surprised, for independent of his very questionable appearance, it struck me as strange that though so constantly associated with O'Connor, and, as I thought, personally acquainted with all his intimates, I had never before even seen this individual. I did not fail immediately to ask him who this gentleman was. I thought he seemed slightly embarrassed, but after a moment's pause he laughingly said that his friend over the way was too mysterious a personage to have his name announced in so giddy a scene as the present; but that on the morrow he would furnish me with all the information which I could desire. There was, I thought, in his affected jocularity a real awkwardness which appeared to me unaccountable, and consequently increased my curiosity; its gratification, however, I was obliged to defer. At length, wearied with witnessing amusements in which I could not sympathise, I left the room, and did not see O'Connor until late in the next day.

I had ridden down towards the castle for the purpose of visiting the O'Connors, and had nearly reached the avenue leading to the mansion, when I met my friend. He was also mounted; and having answered my inquiries respecting his mother, he easily persuaded me to accompany him in his ramble. We had chatted as usual for some time, when, after a pause, O'Connor said:

'By the way, Purcell, you expressed some curiosity respecting the tall, handsome fellow to whom I spoke last night.'

'I certainly did question you about a TALL gentleman, but was not aware of his claims to beauty,' replied I.

'Well, that is as it may be,' said he; 'the ladies think him handsome, and their opinion upon that score is more valuable than yours or mine. Do you know,' he continued, 'I sometimes feel half sorry that I ever made the fellow's acquaintance: he is quite a marked man here, and they tell stories of him that are anything but reputable, though I am sure without foundation. I think I know enough about him to warrant me in saying so.'

'May I ask his name?' inquired I.

'Oh! did not I tell you his name?' rejoined he. 'You should have heard that first; he and his name are equally well known. You will recognise the individual at once when I tell you that his name is—Fitzgerald.'

'Fitzgerald!' I repeated. 'Fitzgerald!—can it be Fitzgerald the duellist?'

'Upon my word you have hit it,' replied he, laughing; 'but you have accompanied the discovery with a look of horror more tragic than appropriate. He is not the monster you take him for—he has a good deal of old Irish pride; his temper is hasty, and he has been unfortunately thrown in the way of men who have not made allowance for these things. I am convinced that in every case in which Fitzgerald has fought, if the truth could be discovered, he would be found to have acted throughout upon the defensive. No man is mad enough to risk his own life, except when the doing so is an alternative to submitting tamely to what he considers an insult. I am certain that no man ever engaged in a duel under the consciousness that he had acted an intentionally aggressive part.'

'When did you make his acquaintance?' said I.

'About two years ago,' he replied. 'I met him in France, and you know when one is abroad it is an ungracious task to reject the advances of one's countryman, otherwise I think I should have avoided his society—less upon my own account than because I am sure the acquaintance would be a source of continual though groundless uneasiness to my mother. I know, therefore, that you will not unnecessarily mention its existence to her.'

I gave him the desired assurance, and added:

'May I ask you. O'Connor, if, indeed, it be a fair question, whether this Fitzgerald at any time attempted to engage you in anything like gaming?'

This question was suggested by my having frequently heard Fitzgerald mentioned as a noted gambler, and sometimes even as a blackleg. O'Connor seemed, I thought, slightly embarrassed. He answered:

'No, no—I cannot say that he ever attempted anything of the kind. I certainly have played with him, but never lost to any serious amount; nor can I recollect that he ever solicited me—indeed he knows that I have a strong objection to deep play. YOU must be aware that my finances could not bear much pruning down. I never lost more to him at a sitting than about five pounds, which you know is nothing. No, you wrong him if you imagine that he attached himself to me merely for the sake of such contemptible winnings as those which a broken-down Irish gentleman could afford him. Come, Purcell, you are too hard upon him—you judge only by report; you must see him, and decide for yourself.—Suppose we call upon him now; he is at the inn, in the High Street, not a mile off.'

I declined the proposal drily.

'Your caution is too easily alarmed,' said he. 'I do not wish you to make this man your bosom friend: I merely desire that you should see and speak to him, and if you form any acquaintance with him, it must be of that slight nature which can be dropped or continued at pleasure.'

From the time that O'Connor had announced the fact that his friend was no other than the notorious Fitzgerald, a foreboding of something calamitous had come upon me, and it now occurred to me that if any unpleasantness were to be feared as likely to result to O'Connor from their connection, I might find my attempts to extricate him much facilitated by my being acquainted, however slightly, with Fitzgerald. I know not whether the idea was reasonable—it was certainly natural; and I told O'Connor that upon second thoughts I would ride down with him to the town, and wait upon Mr. Fitzgerald.

We found him at home; and chatted with him for a considerable time. To my surprise his manners were perfectly those of a gentleman, and his conversation, if not peculiarly engaging, was certainly amusing. The politeness of his demeanour, and the easy fluency with which he told his stories and his anecdotes, many of them curious, and all more or less entertaining, accounted to my mind at once for the facility with which he had improved his acquaintance with O'Connor; and when he pressed upon us an invitation to sup with him that night, I had almost joined O'Connor in accepting it. I determined, however, against doing so, for I had no wish to be on terms of familiarity with Mr. Fitzgerald; and I knew that one evening spent together as he proposed would go further towards establishing an intimacy between us than fifty morning visits could do. When I arose to depart, it was with feelings almost favourable to Fitzgerald; indeed I was more than half ashamed to acknowledge to my companion how complete a revolution in my opinion respecting his friend half an hour's conversation with him had wrought. His appearance certainly WAS against him; but then, under the influence of his manner, one lost sight of much of its ungainliness, and of nearly all its vulgarity; and, on the whole, I felt convinced that report had done him grievous wrong, inasmuch as anybody, by an observance of the common courtesies of society, might easily avoid coming into personal collision with a gentleman so studiously polite as Fitzgerald. At parting, O'Connor requested me to call upon him the next day, as he intended to make trial of the merits of a pair of greyhounds, which he had thoughts of purchasing; adding, that if he could escape in anything like tolerable time from Fitzgerald's supper-party, he would take the field soon after ten on the next morning. At the appointed hour, or perhaps a little later, I dismounted at Castle Connor; and, on entering the hall, I observed a gentleman issuing from O'Connor's private room. I recognised him, as he approached, as a Mr. M'Donough, and, being but slightly acquainted with him, was about to pass him with a bow, when he stopped me. There was something in his manner which struck me as odd; he seemed a good deal flurried if not agitated, and said, in a hurried tone:

'This is a very foolish business, Mr. Purcell. You have some influence with my friend O'Connor; I hope you can induce him to adopt some more moderate line of conduct than that he has decided upon. If you will allow me, I will return for a moment with you, and talk over the matter again with O'Connor.'

As M'Donough uttered these words, I felt that sudden sinking of the heart which accompanies the immediate anticipation of something dreaded and dreadful. I was instantly convinced that O'Connor had quarrelled with Fitzgerald, and I knew that if such were the case, nothing short of a miracle could extricate him from the consequences. I signed to M'Donough to lead the way, and we entered the little study together. O'Connor was standing with his back to the fire; on the table lay the breakfast-things in the disorder in which a hurried meal had left them; and on another smaller table, placed near the hearth, lay pen, ink, and paper. As soon as O'Connor saw me, he came forward and shook me cordially by the hand.

'My dear Purcell,' said he, 'you are the very man I wanted. I have got into an ugly scrape, and I trust to my friends to get me out of it.'

'You have had no dispute with that man—that Fitzgerald, I hope,' said I, giving utterance to the conjecture whose truth I most dreaded.

'Faith, I cannot say exactly what passed between us,' said he, 'inasmuch as I was at the time nearly half seas over; but of this much I am certain, that we exchanged angry words last night. I lost my temper most confoundedly; but, as well as I can recollect, he appeared perfectly cool and collected. What he said was, therefore, deliberately said, and on that account must be resented.'

'My dear O'Connor, are you mad?' I exclaimed. 'Why will you seek to drive to a deadly issue a few hasty words, uttered under the influence of wine, and forgotten almost as soon as uttered? A quarrel with Fitzgerald it is twenty chances to one would terminate fatally to you.'

'It is exactly because Fitzgerald IS such an accomplished shot,' said he, 'that I become liable to the most injurious and intolerable suspicions if I submit to anything from him which could be construed into an affront; and for that reason Fitzgerald is the very last man to whom I would concede an inch in a case of honour.'

'I do not require you to make any, the slightest sacrifice of what you term your honour,' I replied; 'but if you have actually written a challenge to Fitzgerald, as I suspect you have done, I conjure you to reconsider the matter before you despatch it. From all that I have heard you say, Fitzgerald has more to complain of in the altercation which has taken place than you. You owe it to your only surviving parent not to thrust yourself thus wantonly upon—I will say it, the most appalling danger. Nobody, my dear O'Connor, can have a doubt of your courage; and if at any time, which God forbid, you shall be called upon thus to risk your life, you should have it in your power to enter the field under the consciousness that you have acted throughout temperately and like a man, and not, as I fear you now would do, having rashly and most causelessly endangered your own life and that of your friend.'

'I believe, Purcell, your are right,' said he. 'I believe I HAVE viewed the matter in too decided a light; my note, I think, scarcely allows him an honourable alternative, and that is certainly going a step too far—further than I intended. Mr. M'Donough, I'll thank you to hand me the note.'

He broke the seal, and, casting his eye hastily over it, he continued:

'It is, indeed, a monument of folly. I am very glad, Purcell, you happened to come in, otherwise it would have reached its destination by this time.'

He threw it into the fire; and, after a moment's pause, resumed:

'You must not mistake me, however. I am perfectly satisfied as to the propriety, nay, the necessity, of communicating with Fitzgerald. The difficulty is in what tone I should address him. I cannot say that the man directly affronted me—I cannot recollect any one expression which I could lay hold upon as offensive—but his language was ambiguous, and admitted frequently of the most insulting construction, and his manner throughout was insupportably domineering. I know it impressed me with the idea that he presumed upon his reputation as a DEAD SHOT, and that would be utterly unendurable.'

'I would now recommend, as I have already done,' said M'Donough, 'that if you write to Fitzgerald, it should be in such a strain as to leave him at perfect liberty, without a compromise of honour, in a friendly way, to satisfy your doubts as to his conduct.'

I seconded the proposal warmly, and O'Connor, in a few minutes, finished a note, which he desired us to read. It was to this effect:

'O'Connor, of Castle Connor, feeling that some expressions employed by Mr. Fitzgerald upon last night, admitted of a construction offensive to him, and injurious to his character, requests to know whether Mr. Fitzgerald intended to convey such a meaning.

'Castle Connor, Thursday morning.'

This note was consigned to the care of Mr. M'Donough, who forthwith departed to execute his mission. The sound of his horse's hoofs, as he rode rapidly away, struck heavily at my heart; but I found some satisfaction in the reflection that M'Donough appeared as averse from extreme measures as I was myself, for I well knew, with respect to the final result of the affair, that as much depended upon the tone adopted by the SECOND, as upon the nature of the written communication.

I have seldom passed a more anxious hour than that which intervened between the departure and the return of that gentleman. Every instant I imagined I heard the tramp of a horse approaching, and every time that a door opened I fancied it was to give entrance to the eagerly expected courier. At length I did hear the hollow and rapid tread of a horse's hoof upon the avenue. It approached—it stopped—a hurried step traversed the hall—the room door opened, and M'Donough entered.

'You have made great haste,' said O'Connor; 'did you find him at home?'

'I did,' replied M'Donough, 'and made the greater haste as Fitzgerald did not let me know the contents of his reply.'

At the same time he handed a note to O'Connor, who instantly broke the seal. The words were as follow:

'Mr. Fitzgerald regrets that anything which has fallen from him should have appeared to Mr. O'Connor to be intended to convey a reflection upon his honour (none such having been meant), and begs leave to disavow any wish to quarrel unnecessarily with Mr. O'Connor.

'T—— Inn, Thursday morning.'

I cannot describe how much I felt relieved on reading the above communication. I took O'Connor's hand and pressed it warmly, but my emotions were deeper and stronger than I cared to show, for I was convinced that he had escaped a most imminent danger. Nobody whose notions upon the subject are derived from the duelling of modern times, in which matters are conducted without any very sanguinary determination upon either side, and with equal want of skill and coolness by both parties, can form a just estimate of the danger incurred by one who ventured to encounter a duellist of the old school. Perfect coolness in the field, and a steadiness and accuracy (which to the unpractised appeared almost miraculous) in the use of the pistol, formed the characteristics of this class; and in addition to this there generally existed a kind of professional pride, which prompted the duellist, in default of any more malignant feeling, from motives of mere vanity, to seek the life of his antagonist. Fitzgerald's career had been a remarkably successful one, and I knew that out of thirteen duels which he had fought in Ireland, in nine cases he had KILLED his man. In those days one never heard of the parties leaving the field, as not unfrequently now occurs, without blood having been spilt; and the odds were, of course, in all cases tremendously against a young and unpractised man, when matched with an experienced antagonist. My impression respecting the magnitude of the danger which my friend had incurred was therefore by no means unwarranted.

I now questioned O'Connor more accurately respecting the circumstances of his quarrel with Fitzgerald. It arose from some dispute respecting the application of a rule of piquet, at which game they had been playing, each interpreting it favourably to himself, and O'Connor, having lost considerably, was in no mood to conduct an argument with temper—an altercation ensued, and that of rather a pungent nature, and the result was that he left Fitzgerald's room rather abruptly, determined to demand an explanation in the most peremptory tone. For this purpose he had sent for M'Donough, and had commissioned him to deliver the note, which my arrival had fortunately intercepted.

As it was now past noon, O'Connor made me promise to remain with him to dinner; and we sat down a party of three, all in high spirits at the termination of our anxieties. It is necessary to mention, for the purpose of accounting for what follows, that Mrs. O'Connor, or, as she was more euphoniously styled, the lady of Castle Connor, was precluded by ill-health from taking her place at the dinner-table, and, indeed, seldom left her room before four o'clock[1]. We were sitting after dinner sipping our claret, and talking, and laughing, and enjoying ourselves exceedingly, when a servant, stepping into the room, informed his master that a gentleman wanted to speak with him.

'Request him, with my compliments, to walk in,' said O'Connor; and in a few moments a gentleman entered the room.

His appearance was anything but prepossessing. He was a little above the middle size, spare, and raw-boned; his face very red, his features sharp and bluish, and his age might be about sixty. His attire savoured a good deal of the SHABBY-GENTEEL; his clothes, which had much of tarnished and faded pretension about them, did not fit him, and had not improbably fluttered in the stalls of Plunket Street. We had risen on his entrance, and O'Connor had twice requested of him to take a chair at the table, without his hearing, or at least noticing, the invitation; while with a slow pace, and with an air of mingled importance and effrontery, he advanced into the centre of the apartment, and regarding our small party with a supercilious air, he said:

'I take the liberty of introducing myself—I am Captain M'Creagh, formerly of the—infantry. My business here is with a Mr. O'Connor, and the sooner it is despatched the better.'

---

[1] It is scarcely necessary to remind the reader, that at the period spoken of, the important hour of dinner occurred very nearly at noon.

'I am the gentleman you name,' said O'Connor; 'and as you appear impatient, we had better proceed to your commission without delay.'

'Then, Mr. O'Connor, you will please to read that note,' said the captain, placing a sealed paper in his hand.

O'Connor read it through, and then observed:

'This is very extraordinary indeed. This note appears to me perfectly unaccountable.'

'You are very young, Mr. O'Connor,' said the captain, with vulgar familiarity; 'but, without much experience in these matters, I think you might have anticipated something like this. You know the old saying, "Second thoughts are best;" and so they are like to prove, by G—!'

'You will have no objection, Captain M'Creagh, on the part of your friend, to my reading this note to these gentlemen; they are both confidential friends of mine, and one of them has already acted for me in this business.'

'I can have no objection,' replied the captain, 'to your doing what you please with your own. I have nothing more to do with that note once I put it safe into your hand; and when that is once done, it is all one to me, if you read it to half the world—that's YOUR concern, and no affair of mine.'

O'Connor then read the following:

'Mr. Fitzgerald begs leave to state, that upon re-perusing Mr. O'Connor's communication of this morning carefully, with an experienced friend, he is forced to consider himself as challenged. His friend, Captain M'Creagh, has been empowered by him to make all the necessary arrangements.

'T—— Inn, Thursday.'

I can hardly describe the astonishment with which I heard this note. I turned to the captain, and said:

'Surely, sir, there is some mistake in all this?'

'Not the slightest, I'll assure you, sir.' said he, coolly; 'the case is a very clear one, and I think my friend has pretty well made up his mind upon it. May I request your answer?' he continued, turning to O'Connor; 'time is precious, you know.'

O'Connor expressed his willingness to comply with the suggestion, and in a few minutes had folded and directed the following rejoinder:

'Mr. O'Connor having received a satisfactory explanation from Mr. Fitzgerald, of the language used by that gentleman, feels that there no longer exists any grounds for misunderstanding, and wishes further to state, that the note of which Mr. Fitzgerald speaks was not intended as a challenge.'

With this note the captain departed; and as we did not doubt that the message which he had delivered had been suggested by some unintentional misconstruction of O'Connor's first billet, we felt assured that the conclusion of his last note would set the matter at rest. In this belief, however, we were mistaken; before we had left the table, and in an incredibly short time, the captain returned. He entered the room with a countenance evidently tasked to avoid expressing the satisfaction which a consciousness of the nature of his mission had conferred; but in spite of all his efforts to look gravely unconcerned, there was a twinkle in the small grey eye, and an almost imperceptible motion in the corner of the mouth, which sufficiently betrayed his internal glee, as he placed a note in the hand of O'Connor. As the young man cast his eye over it, he coloured deeply, and turning to M'Donough, he said:

'You will have the goodness to make all the necessary arrangements for a meeting. Something has occurred to render one between me and Mr. Fitzgerald inevitable. Understand me literally, when I say that it is now totally impossible that this affair should be amicably arranged. You will have the goodness, M'Donough, to let me know as soon as all the particulars are arranged. Purcell,' he continued, 'will you have the kindness to accompany me?' and having bowed to M'Creagh, we left the room.

As I closed the door after me, I heard the captain laugh, and thought I could distinguish the words—'By —— I knew Fitzgerald would bring him to his way of thinking before he stopped.'

I followed O'Connor into his study, and on entering, the door being closed, he showed me the communication which had determined him upon hostilities. Its language was grossly impertinent, and it concluded by actually threatening to 'POST' him, in case he further attempted 'to be OFF.' I cannot describe the agony of indignation in which O'Connor writhed under this insult. He said repeatedly that 'he was a degraded and dishohoured man,' that 'he was dragged into the field,' that 'there was ignominy in the very thought that such a letter should have been directed to him.' It was in vain that I reasoned against this impression; the conviction that he had been disgraced had taken possession of his mind. He said again and again that nothing but his DEATH could remove the stain which his indecision had cast upon the name of his family. I hurried to the hall, on hearing M'Donough and the captain passing, and reached the door just in time to hear the latter say, as he mounted his horse:

'All the rest can be arranged on the spot; and so farewell, Mr. M'Donough—we'll meet at Philippi, you know;' and with this classical allusion, which was accompanied with a grin and a bow, and probably served many such occasions, the captain took his departure.

M'Donough briefly stated the few particulars which had been arranged. The parties were to meet at the stand-house, in the race-ground, which lay at about an equal distance between Castle Connor and the town of T——. The hour appointed was half-past five on the next morning, at which time the twilight would be sufficiently advanced to afford a distinct view; and the weapons to be employed were PISTOLS—M'Creagh having claimed, on the part of his friend, all the advantages of the CHALLENGED party, and having, consequently, insisted upon the choice of 'TOOLS,' as he expressed himself; and it was further stipulated that the utmost secrecy should be observed, as Fitzgerald would incur great risk from the violence of the peasantry, in case the affair took wind. These conditions were, of course, agreed upon by O'Connor, and M'Donough left the castle, having appointed four o'clock upon the next morning as the hour of his return, by which time it would be his business to provide everything necessary for the meeting. On his departure, O'Connor requested me to remain with him upon that evening, saying that 'he could not bear to be alone with his mother.' It was to me a most painful request, but at the same time one which I could not think of refusing. I felt, however, that the difficulty at least of the task which I had to perform would be in some measure mitigated by the arrival of two relations of O'Connor upon that evening.

'It is very fortunate,' said O'Connor, whose thoughts had been running upon the same subject, 'that the O'Gradys will be with us to-night; their gaiety and good-humour will relieve us from a heavy task. I trust that nothing may occur to prevent their coming.' Fervently concurring in the same wish, I accompanied O'Connor into the parlour, there to await the arrival of his mother.

God grant that I may never spend such another evening! The O'Gradys DID come, but their high and noisy spirits, so far from relieving me, did but give additional gloom to the despondency, I might say the despair, which filled my heart with misery—the terrible forebodings which I could not for an instant silence, turned their laughter into discord, and seemed to mock the smiles and jests of the unconscious party. When I turned my eyes upon the mother, I thought I never had seen her look so proudly and so lovingly upon her son before—it cut me to the heart—oh, how cruelly I was deceiving her! I was a hundred times on the very point of starting up, and, at all hazards, declaring to her how matters were; but other feelings subdued my better emotions. Oh, what monsters are we made of by the fashions of the world! how are our kindlier and nobler feelings warped or destroyed by their baleful influences! I felt that it would not be HONOURABLE, that it would not be ETIQUETTE, to betray O'Connor's secret. I sacrificed a higher and a nobler duty than I have since been called upon to perform, to the dastardly fear of bearing the unmerited censure of a world from which I was about to retire. O Fashion! thou gaudy idol, whose feet are red with the blood of human sacrifice, would I had always felt towards thee as I now do!

O'Connor was not dejected; on the contrary, he joined with loud and lively alacrity in the hilarity of the little party; but I could see in the flush of his cheek, and in the unusual brightness of his eye, all the excitement of fever—he was making an effort almost beyond his strength, but he succeeded—and when his mother rose to leave the room, it was with the impression that her son was the gayest and most light-hearted of the company. Twice or thrice she had risen with the intention of retiring, but O'Connor, with an eagerness which I alone could understand, had persuaded her to remain until the usual hour of her departure had long passed; and when at length she arose, declaring that she could not possibly stay longer, I alone could comprehend the desolate change which passed over his manner; and when I saw them part, it was with the sickening conviction that those two beings, so dear to one another, so loved, so cherished, should meet no more.

O'Connor briefly informed his cousins of the position in which he was placed, requesting them at the same time to accompany him to the field, and this having been settled, we separated, each to his own apartment. I had wished to sit up with O'Connor, who had matters to arrange sufficient to employ him until the hour appointed for M'Donough's visit; but he would not hear of it, and I was forced, though sorely against my will, to leave him without a companion. I went to my room, and, in a state of excitement which I cannot describe, I paced for hours up and down its narrow precincts. I could not—who could?—analyse the strange, contradictory, torturing feelings which, while I recoiled in shrinking horror from the scene which the morning was to bring, yet forced me to wish the intervening time annihilated; each hour that the clock told seemed to vibrate and tinkle through every nerve; my agitation was dreadful; fancy conjured up the forms of those who filled my thoughts with more than the vividness of reality; things seemed to glide through the dusky shadows of the room. I saw the dreaded form of Fitzgerald—I heard the hated laugh of the captain—and again the features of O'Connor would appear before me, with ghastly distinctness, pale and writhed in death, the gouts of gore clotted in the mouth, and the eye-balls glared and staring. Scared with the visions which seemed to throng with unceasing rapidity and vividness, I threw open the window and looked out upon the quiet scene around. I turned my eyes in the direction of the town; a heavy cloud was lowering darkly about it, and I, in impious frenzy, prayed to God that it might burst in avenging fires upon the murderous wretch who lay beneath. At length, sick and giddy with excess of excitement, I threw myself upon the bed without removing my clothes, and endeavoured to compose myself so far as to remain quiet until the hour for our assembling should arrive.

A few minutes before four o'clock I stole noiselessly downstairs, and made my way to the small study already mentioned. A candle was burning within; and, when I opened the door, O'Connor was reading a book, which, on seeing me, he hastily closed, colouring slightly as he did so. We exchanged a cordial but mournful greeting; and after a slight pause he said, laying his hand upon the volume which he had shut a moment before:

'Purcell, I feel perfectly calm, though I cannot say that I have much hope as to the issue of this morning's rencounter. I shall avoid half the danger. If I must fall, I am determined I shall not go down to the grave with his blood upon my hands. I have resolved not to fire at Fitzgerald—that is, to fire in such a direction as to assure myself against hitting him. Do not say a word of this to the O'Gradys. Your doing so would only produce fruitless altercation; they could not understand my motives. I feel convinced that I shall not leave the field alive. If I must die to-day, I shall avoid an awful aggravation of wretchedness. Purcell,' he continued, after a little space, 'I was so weak as to feel almost ashamed of the manner in which I was occupied as you entered the room. Yes, *I—I* who will be, before this evening, a cold and lifeless clod, was ashamed to have spent my last moment of reflection in prayer. God pardon me! God pardon me!' he repeated.

I took his hand and pressed it, but I could not speak. I sought for words of comfort, but they would not come. To have uttered one cheering sentence I must have contradicted every impression of my own mind. I felt too much awed to attempt it. Shortly afterwards, M'Donough arrived. No wretched patient ever underwent a more thrilling revulsion at the first sight of the case of surgical instruments under which he had to suffer, than did I upon beholding a certain oblong flat mahogany box, bound with brass, and of about two feet in length, laid upon the table in the hall. O'Connor, thanking him for his punctuality, requested him to come into his study for a moment, when, with a melancholy collectedness, he proceeded to make arrangements for our witnessing his will. The document was a brief one, and the whole matter was just arranged, when the two O'Gradys crept softly into the room.

'So! last will and testament,' said the elder. 'Why, you have a very BLUE notion of these matters. I tell you, you need not be uneasy. I remember very well, when young Ryan of Ballykealey met M'Neil the duellist, bets ran twenty to one against him. I stole away from school, and had a peep at the fun as well as the best of them. They fired together. Ryan received the ball through the collar of his coat, and M'Neil in the temple; he spun like a top: it was a most unexpected thing, and disappointed his friends damnably. It was admitted, however, to have been very pretty shooting upon both sides. To be sure,' he continued, pointing to the will, 'you are in the right to keep upon the safe side of fortune; but then, there is no occasion to be altogether so devilish down in the mouth as you appear to be.'

'You will allow,' said O'Connor, 'that the chances are heavily against me.'

'Why, let me see,' he replied, 'not so hollow a thin, either. Let me see, we'll say about four to one against you; you may chance to throw doublets like him I told you of, and then what becomes of the odds I'd like to know? But let things go as they will, I'll give and take four to one, in pounds and tens of pounds. There, M'Donough, there's a GET for you; b—t me, if it is not. Poh! the fellow is stolen away,' he continued, observing that the object of his proposal had left the room; 'but d—— it, Purcell, you are fond of a SOFT THING, too, in a quiet way—I'm sure you are—so curse me if I do not make you the same offer-is it a go?'

I was too much disgusted to make any reply, but I believe my looks expressed my feelings sufficiently, for in a moment he said:

'Well, I see there is nothing to be done, so we may as well be stirring. M'Donough, myself, and my brother will saddle the horses in a jiffy, while you and Purcell settle anything which remains to be arranged.'

So saying, he left the room with as much alacrity as if it were to prepare for a foxhunt. Selfish, heartless fool! I have often since heard him spoken of as A CURSED GOOD-NATURED DOG and a D—— GOOD FELLOW; but such eulogies as these are not calculated to mitigate the abhorrence with which his conduct upon that morning inspired me.

The chill mists of night were still hovering on the landscape as our party left the castle. It was a raw, comfortless morning—a kind of drizzling fog hung heavily over the scene, dimming the light of the sun, which had now risen, into a pale and even a grey glimmer. As the appointed hour was fast approaching, it was proposed that we should enter the race-ground at a point close to the stand-house—a measure which would save us a ride of nearly two miles, over a broken road; at which distance there was an open entrance into the race-ground. Here, accordingly, we dismounted, and leaving our horses in the care of a country fellow who happened to be stirring at that early hour, we proceeded up a narrow lane, over a side wall of which we were to climb into the open ground where stood the now deserted building, under which the meeting was to take place. Our progress was intercepted by the unexpected appearance of an old woman, who, in the scarlet cloak which is the picturesque characteristic of the female peasantry of the south, was moving slowly down the avenue to meet us, uttering that peculiarly wild and piteous lamentation well known by the name of 'the Irish cry,' accompanied throughout by all the customary gesticulation of passionate grief. This rencounter was more awkward than we had at first anticipated; for, upon a nearer approach, the person proved to be no other than an old attached dependent of the family, and who had herself nursed O'Connor. She quickened her pace as we advanced almost to a run; and, throwing her arms round O'Connor's neck, she poured forth such a torrent of lamentation, reproach, and endearment, as showed that she was aware of the nature of our purpose, whence and by what means I knew not. It was in vain that he sought to satisfy her by evasion, and gently to extricate himself from her embrace. She knelt upon the ground, and clasped her arms round his legs, uttering all the while such touching supplications, such cutting and passionate expressions of woe, as went to my very heart.

At length, with much difficulty, we passed this most painful interruption; and, crossing the boundary wall, were placed beyond her reach. The O'Gradys damned her for a troublesome hag, and passed on with O'Connor, but I remained behind for a moment. The poor woman looked hopelessly at the high wall which separated her from him she had loved from infancy, and to be with whom at that minute she would have given worlds, she took her seat upon a solitary stone under the opposite wall, and there, in a low, subdued key, she continued to utter her sorrow in words so desolate, yet expressing such a tenderness of devotion as wrung my heart.

'My poor woman,' I said, laying my hand gently upon her shoulder, 'you will make yourself ill; the morning is very cold, and your cloak is but a thin defence against the damp and chill. Pray return home and take this; it may be useful to you.'

So saying, I dropped a purse, with what money I had about me, into her lap, but it lay there unheeded; she did not hear me.

'Oh I my child, my child, my darlin',' she sobbed, 'are you gone from me? are you gone from me? Ah, mavourneen, mavourneen, you'll never come back alive to me again. The crathur that slept on my bosom—the lovin' crathur that I was so proud of—they'll kill him, they'll kill him. Oh, voh! voh!'

The affecting tone, the feeling, the abandonment with which all this was uttered, none can conceive who have not heard the lamentations of the Irish peasantry. It brought tears to my eyes. I saw that no consolation of mine could soothe her grief, so I turned and departed; but as I rapidly traversed the level sward which separated me from my companions, now considerably in advance, I could still hear the wailings of the solitary mourner.

As we approached the stand-house, it was evident that our antagonists had already arrived. Our path lay by the side of a high fence constructed of loose stones, and on turning a sharp angle at its extremity, we found ourselves close to the appointed spot, and within a few yards of a crowd of persons, some mounted and some on foot, evidently awaiting our arrival. The affair had unaccountably taken wind, as the number of the expectants clearly showed; but for this there was now no remedy.

As our little party advanced we were met and saluted by several acquaintances, whom curiosity, if no deeper feeling, had brought to the place. Fitzgerald and the Captain had arrived, and having dismounted, were standing upon the sod. The former, as we approached, bowed slightly and sullenly—while the latter, evidently in high good humour, made his most courteous obeisance. No time was to be lost; and the two seconds immediately withdrew to a slight distance, for the purpose of completing the last minute arrangements. It was a brief but horrible interval—each returned to his principal to communicate the result, which was soon caught up and repeated from mouth to mouth throughout the crowd. I felt a strange and insurmountable reluctance to hear the sickening particulars detailed; and as I stood irresolute at some distance from the principal parties, a top-booted squireen, with a hunting whip in his hand, bustling up to a companion of his, exclaimed:

'Not fire together!—did you ever hear the like? If Fitzgerald gets the first shot all is over. M'Donough sold the pass, by——, and that is the long and the short of it.'

The parties now moved down a little to a small level space, suited to the purpose; and the captain, addressing M'Donough, said:

'Mr. M'Donough, you'll now have the goodness to toss for choice of ground; as the light comes from the east the line must of course run north and south. Will you be so obliging as to toss up a crown-piece, while I call?'

A coin was instantly chucked into the air. The captain cried, 'Harp.' The HEAD was uppermost, and M'Donough immediately made choice of the southern point at which to place his friend—a position which it will be easily seen had the advantage of turning his back upon the light—no trifling superiority of location. The captain turned with a kind of laugh, and said:

'By ——, sir, you are as cunning as a dead pig; but you forgot one thing. My friend is a left-handed gunner, though never a bit the worse for that; so you see there is no odds as far as the choice of light goes.'

He then proceeded to measure nine paces in a direction running north and south, and the principals took their ground.

'I must be troublesome to you once again, Mr. M'Donough. One toss more, and everything is complete. We must settle who is to have the FIRST SLAP.'

A piece of money was again thrown into the air; again the captain lost the toss and M'Donough proceeded to load the pistols. I happened to stand near Fitzgerald, and I overheard the captain, with a chuckle, say something to him in which the word 'cravat' was repeated. It instantly occurred to me that the captain's attention was directed to a bright-coloured muffler which O'Connor wore round his neck, and which would afford his antagonist a distinct and favourable mark. I instantly urged him to remove it, and at length, with difficulty, succeeded. He seemed perfectly careless as to any precaution. Everything was now ready; the pistol was placed in O'Connor's hand, and he only awaited the word from the captain.

M'Creagh then said:

'Mr. M'Donough, is your principal ready?'

M'Donough replied in the affirmative; and, after a slight pause, the captain, as had been arranged, uttered the words:

'Ready—fire.'

O'Connor fired, but so wide of the mark that some one in the crowd exclaimed:

'Fired in the air.'

'Who says he fired in the air?' thundered Fitzgerald. 'By —— he lies, whoever he is.' There was a silence. 'But even if he was fool enough to fire in the air, it is not in HIS power to put an end to the quarrel by THAT. D—— my soul, if I am come here to be played with like a child, and by the Almighty —— you shall hear more of this, each and everyone of you, before I'm satisfied.'

A kind of low murmur, or rather groan, was now raised, and a slight motion was observable in the crowd, as if to intercept Fitzgerald's passage to his horse. M'Creagh, drawing the horse close to the spot where Fitzgerald stood, threatened, with the most awful imprecations, 'to blow the brains out of the first man who should dare to press on them.'

O'Connor now interfered, requesting the crowd to forbear, and some degree of order was restored. He then said, 'that in firing as he did, he had no intention whatever of waiving his right of firing upon Fitzgerald, and of depriving that gentleman of his right of prosecuting the affair to the utmost—that if any person present imagined that he intended to fire in the air, he begged to set him right; since, so far from seeking to exort an unwilling reconciliation, he was determined that no power on earth should induce him to concede one inch of ground to Mr. Fitzgerald.'

This announcement was received with a shout by the crowd, who now resumed their places at either side of the plot of ground which had been measured. The principals took their places once more, and M'Creagh proceeded, with the nicest and most anxious care, to load the pistols; and this task being accomplished, Fitzgerald whispered something in the Captain's ear, who instantly drew his friend's horse so as to place him within a step of his rider, and then tightened the girths. This accomplished, Fitzgerald proceeded deliberately to remove his coat, which he threw across his horse in front of the saddle; and then, with the assistance of M'Creagh, he rolled the shirt sleeve up to the shoulder, so as to leave the whole of his muscular arm perfectly naked. A cry of 'Coward, coward! butcher, butcher!' arose from the crowd. Fitzgerald paused.

'Do you object, Mr. M'Donough? and upon what grounds, if you please?' said he.

'Certainly he does not,' replied O'Connor; and, turning to M'Donough, he added, 'pray let there be no unnecessary delay.'

'There is no objection, then,' said Fitzgerald.

'*I* object,' said the younger of the O'Gradys, 'if nobody else will.'

' And who the devil are you, that DARES to object?' shouted Fitzgerald; 'and what d—d presumption prompts you to DARE to wag your tongue here?'

'I am Mr. O'Grady, of Castle Blake,' replied the young man, now much enraged; 'and by ——, you shall answer for your language to me.'

'Shall I, by ——? Shall I?' cried he, with a laugh of brutal scorn; 'the more the merrier, d—n the doubt of it—so now hold your tongue, for I promise you you shall have business enough of your own to think about, and that before long.'

There was an appalling ferocity in his tone and manner which no words could convey. He seemed transformed; he was actually like a man possessed. Was it possible, I thought, that I beheld the courteous gentleman, the gay, good-humoured retailer of amusing anecdote with whom, scarce two days ago, I had laughed and chatted, in the blasphemous and murderous ruffian who glared and stormed before me!

O'Connor interposed, and requested that time should not be unnecessarily lost.

'You have not got a second coat on?' inquired the Captain. 'I beg pardon, but my duty to my friend requires that I should ascertain the point.'

O'Connor replied in the negative. The Captain expressed himself as satisfied, adding, in what he meant to be a complimentary strain, 'that he knew Mr. O'Connor would scorn to employ padding or any unfair mode of protection.'

There was now a breathless silence. O'Connor stood perfectly motionless; and, excepting the death-like paleness of his features, he exhibited no sign of agitation. His eye was steady—his lip did not tremble—his attitude was calm. The Captain, having re-examined the priming of the pistols, placed one of them in the hand of Fitzgerald.—M'Donough inquired whether the parties were prepared, and having been answered in the affirmative, he proceeded to give the word, 'Ready.' Fitzgerald raised his hand, but almost instantly lowered it again. The crowd had pressed too much forward as it appeared, and his eye had been unsteadied by the flapping of the skirt of a frieze riding-coat worn by one of the spectators.

'In the name of my principal,' said the Captain, 'I must and do insist upon these gentlemen moving back a little. We ask but little; fair play, and no favour.'

The crowd moved as requested. M'Donough repeated his former question, and was answered as before. There was a breathless silence. Fitzgerald fixed his eye upon O'Connor. The appointed signal, 'Ready, fire!' was given. There was a pause while one might slowly reckon three—Fitzgerald fired—and O'Connor fell helplessly upon the ground.

'There is no time to be lost,' said M'Creagrh; 'for, by ——, you have done for him.'

So saying, he threw himself upon his horse, and was instantly followed at a hard gallop by Fitzgerald.

'Cold-blooded murder, if ever murder was committed,' said O'Grady. 'He shall hang for it; d—n me, but he shall.'

A hopeless attempt was made to overtake the fugitives; but they were better mounted than any of their pursuers, and escaped with ease. Curses and actual yells of execration followed their course; and as, in crossing the brow of a neighbouring hill, they turned round in the saddle to observe if they were pursued, every gesture which could express fury and defiance was exhausted by the enraged and defeated multitude.

'Clear the way, boys,' said young O'Grady, who with me was kneeling beside O'Connor, while we supported him in our arms; 'do not press so close, and be d—d; can't you let the fresh air to him; don't you see he's dying?'

On opening his waistcoat we easily detected the wound: it was a little below the chest—a small blue mark, from which oozed a single heavy drop of blood.

'He is bleeding but little—that is a comfort at all events,' said one of the gentlemen who surrounded the wounded man.

Another suggested the expediency of his being removed homeward with as little delay as possible, and recommended, for this purpose, that a door should be removed from its hinges, and the patient, laid upon this, should be conveyed from the field. Upon this rude bier my poor friend was carried from that fatal ground towards Castle Connor. I walked close by his side, and observed every motion of his. He seldom opened his eyes, and was perfectly still, excepting a nervous WORKING of the fingers, and a slight, almost imperceptible twitching of the features, which took place, however, only at intervals. The first word he uttered was spoken as we approached the entrance of the castle itself, when he said; repeatedly, 'The back way, the back way.' He feared lest his mother should meet him abruptly and without preparation; but although this fear was groundless, since she never left her room until late in the day, yet it was thought advisable, and, indeed, necessary, to caution all the servants most strongly against breathing a hint to their mistress of the events which had befallen.

Two or three gentlemen had ridden from the field one after another, promising that they should overtake our party before it reached the castle, bringing with them medical aid from one quarter or another; and we determined that Mrs. O'Connor should not know anything of the occurrence until the opinion of some professional man should have determined the extent of the injury which her son had sustained—a course of conduct which would at least have the effect of relieving her from the horrors of suspense. When O'Connor found himself in his own room, and laid upon his own bed, he appeared much revived—so much so, that I could not help admitting a strong hope that all might yet be well.

'After all, Purcell,' said he, with a melancholy smile, and speaking with evident difficulty, 'I believe I have got off with a trifling wound. I am sure it cannot be fatal I feel so little pain—almost none.'

I cautioned him against fatiguing himself by endeavouring to speak; and he remained quiet for a little time. At length he said:

'Purcell, I trust this lesson shall not have been given in vain. God has been very merciful to me; I feel—I have an internal confidence that I am not wounded mortally. Had I been fatally wounded—had I been killed upon the spot, only think on it'—and he closed his eyes as if the very thought made him dizzy—'struck down into the grave, unprepared as I am, in the very blossom of my sins, without a moment of repentance or of reflection; I must have been lost—lost for ever and ever.'

I prevailed upon him, with some difficulty, to abstain from such agitating reflections, and at length induced him to court such repose as his condition admitted of, by remaining perfectly silent, and as much as possible without motion.

O'Connor and I only were in the room; he had lain for some time in tolerable quiet, when I thought I distinguished the bustle attendant upon the arrival of some one at the castle, and went eagerly to the window, believing, or at least hoping, that the sounds might announce the approach of the medical man, whom we all longed most impatiently to see.

My conjecture was right; I had the satisfaction of seeing him dismount and prepare to enter the castle, when my observations were interrupted, and my attention was attracted by a smothered, gurgling sound proceeding from the bed in which lay the wounded man. I instantly turned round, and in doing so the spectacle which met my eyes was sufficiently shocking.

I had left O'Connor lying in the bed, supported by pillows, perfectly calm, and with his cycs closcd: he was now lying nearly in the same position, his eyes open and almost starting from their sockets, with every feature pale and distorted as death, and vomiting blood in quantities that were frightful. I rushed to the door and called for assistance; the paroxysm, though violent, was brief, and O'Connor sank into a swoon so deep and death-like, that I feared he should waken no more.

The surgeon, a little, fussy man, but I believe with some skill to justify his pretensions, now entered the room, carrying his case of instruments, and followed by servants bearing basins and water and bandages of linen. He relieved our doubts by instantly assuring us that 'the patient' was still living; and at the same time professed his determination to take advantage of the muscular relaxation which the faint had induced to examine the wound—adding that a patient was more easily 'handled' when in a swoon than under other circumstances.

After examining the wound in front where the ball had entered, he passed his hand round beneath the shoulder, and after a little pause he shook his head, observing that he feared very much that one of the vertebrae was fatally injured, but that he could not say decidedly until his patient should revive a little. 'Though his language was very technical, and consequently to me nearly unintelligible, I could perceive plainly by his manner that he considered the case as almost hopeless.

O'Connor gradually gave some signs of returning animation, and at length was so far restored as to be enabled to speak. After some few general questions as to how he felt affected, etc., etc., the surgeon, placing his hand upon his leg and pressing it slightly, asked him if he felt any pressure upon the limb? O'Connor answered in the negative—he pressed harder, and repeated the question; still the answer was the same, till at length, by repeated experiments, he ascertained that all that part of the body which lay behind the wound was paralysed, proving that the spine must have received some fatal injury.

'Well, doctor,' said O'Connor, after the examination of the wound was over; 'well, I shall do, shan't I?'

The physician was silent for a moment, and then, as if with an effort, he replied:

'Indeed, my dear sir, it would not be honest to flatter you with much hope.'

'Eh?' said O'Connor with more alacrity than I had seen him exhibit since the morning; 'surely I did not hear you aright; I spoke of my recovery—surely there is no doubt; there can be none—speak frankly, doctor, for God's sake—am I dying?'

The surgeon was evidently no stoic, and his manner had extinguished in me every hope, even before he had uttered a word in reply.

'You are—you are indeed dying. There is no hope; I should but deceive you if I held out any.'

As the surgeon uttered these terrible words, the hands which O'Connor had stretched towards him while awaiting his reply fell powerless by his side; his head sank forward; it seemed as if horror and despair had unstrung every nerve and sinew; he appeared to collapse and shrink together as a plant might under the influence of a withering spell.

It has often been my fate, since then, to visit the chambers of death and of suffering; I have witnessed fearful agonies of body and of soul; the mysterious shudderings of the departing spirit, and the heart-rending desolation of the survivors; the severing of the tenderest ties, the piteous yearnings of unavailing love—of all these things the sad duties of my profession have made me a witness. But, generally speaking, I have observed in such scenes some thing to mitigate, if not the sorrows, at least the terrors, of death; the dying man seldom seems to feel the reality of his situation; a dull consciousness of approaching dissolution, a dim anticipation of unconsciousness and insensibility, are the feelings which most nearly border upon an appreciation of his state; the film of death seems to have overspread the mind's eye, objects lose their distinctness, and float cloudily before it, and the apathy and apparent indifference with which men recognise the sure advances of immediate death, rob that awful hour of much of its terrors, and the death-bed of its otherwise inevitable agonies.

This is a merciful dispensation; but the rule has its exceptions—its terrible exceptions. When a man is brought in an instant, by some sudden accident, to the very verge of the fathomless pit of death, with all his recollections awake, and his perceptions keenly and vividly alive, without previous illness to subdue the tone of the mind as to dull its apprehensions—then, and then only, the death-bed is truly terrible.

Oh, what a contrast did O'Connor afford as he lay in all the abject helplessness of undisguised terror upon his death-bed, to the proud composure with which he had taken the field that morning. I had always before thought of death as of a quiet sleep stealing gradually upon exhausted nature, made welcome by suffering, or, at least, softened by resignation; I had never before stood by the side of one upon whom the hand of death had been thus suddenly laid; I had never seen the tyrant arrayed in his terror till then. Never before or since have I seen horror so intensely depicted. It seemed actually as if O'Connor's mind had been unsettled by the shock; the few words he uttered were marked with all the incoherence of distraction; but it was not words that marked his despair most strongly, the appalling and heart-sickening groans that came from the terror-stricken and dying man must haunt me while I live; the expression, too, of hopeless, imploring agony with which he turned his eyes from object to object, I can never forget. At length, appearing suddenly to recollect himself, he said, with startling alertness, but in a voice so altered that I scarce could recognise the tones:

'Purcell, Purcell, go and tell my poor mother; she must know all, and then, quick, quick, quick, call your uncle, bring him here; I must have a chance.' He made a violent but fruitless effort to rise, and after a slight pause continued, with deep and urgent solemnity: 'Doctor, how long shall I live? Don't flatter me. Compliments at a death-bed are out of place; doctor, for God's sake, as you would not have my soul perish with my body, do not mock a dying man; have I an hour to live?'

'Certainly,' replied the surgeon; 'if you will but endeavour to keep yourself tranquil; otherwise I cannot answer for a moment.'

'Well, doctor,' said the patient, 'I will obey you; now, Purcell, my first and dearest friend, will you inform my poor mother of—of what you see, and return with your uncle; I know you will.'

I took the dear fellow's hand and kissed it, it was the only answer I could give, and left the room. I asked the first female servant I chanced to meet, if her mistress were yet up, and was answered in the affirmative. Without giving myself time to hesitate, I requested her to lead me to her lady's room, which she accordingly did; she entered first, I supposed to announce my name, and I followed closely; the poor mother said something, and held out her hands to welcome me; I strove for words; I could not speak, but nature found expression; I threw myself at her feet and covered her hands with kisses and tears. My manner was enough; with a quickness almost preternatural she understood it all; she simply said the words: 'O'Connor is killed;' she uttered no more.

How I left the room I know not; I rode madly to my uncle's residence, and brought him back with me—all the rest is a blank. I remember standing by O'Connor's bedside, and kissing the cold pallid forehead again and again; I remember the pale serenity of the beautiful features; I remember that I looked upon the dead face of my friend, and I remember no more.

For many months I lay writhing and raving in the frenzy of brain fever; a hundred times I stood tottering at the brink of death, and long after my restoration to bodily health was assured, it appeared doubtful whether I should ever be restored to reason. But God dealt very mercifully with me; His mighty hand rescued me from death and from madness when one or other appeared inevitable. As soon as I was permitted pen and ink, I wrote to the bereaved mother in a tone bordering upon frenzy. I accused myself of having made her childless; I called myself a murderer; I believed myself accursed; I could not find terms strong enough to express my abhorrence of my own conduct. But, oh! what an answer I received, so mild, so sweet, from the desolate, childless mother! its words spoke all that is beautiful in Christianity—it was forgiveness—it was resignation. I am convinced that to that letter, operating as it did upon a mind already predisposed, is owing my final determination to devote myself to that profession in which, for more than half a century, I have been a humble minister.

Years roll away, and we count them not as they pass, but their influence is not the less certain that it is silent; the deepest wounds are gradually healed, the keenest griefs are mitigated, and we, in character, feelings, tastes, and pursuits, become such altered beings, that but for some few indelible marks which past events must leave behind them, which time may soften, but can never efface; our very identity would be dubious. Who has not felt all this at one time or other? Who has not mournfully felt it? This trite, but natural train of reflection filled my mind as I approached the domain of Castle Connor some ten years after the occurrence of the events above narrated. Everything looked the same as when I had left it; the old trees stood as graceful and as grand as ever; no plough had violated the soft green sward; no utilitarian hand had constrained the wanderings of the clear and sportive stream, or disturbed the lichen-covered rocks through which it gushed, or the wild coppice that over-shadowed its sequestered nooks—but the eye that looked upon these things was altered, and memory was busy with other days, shrouding in sadness every beauty that met my sight.

As I approached the castle my emotions became so acutely painful that I had almost returned the way I came, without accomplishing the purpose for which I had gone thus far; and nothing but the conviction that my having been in the neighbourhood of Castle Connor without visiting its desolate mistress would render me justly liable to the severest censure, could overcome my reluctance to encountering the heavy task which was before me. I recognised the old servant who opened the door, but he did not know me. I was completely changed; suffering of body and mind had altered me in feature and in bearing, as much as in character. I asked the man whether his mistress ever saw visitors. He answered:

'But seldom; perhaps, however, if she knew that an old friend wished to see her for a few minutes, she would gratify him so far.'

At the same time I placed my card in his hand, and requested him to deliver it to his mistress. He returned in a few moments, saying that his lady would be happy to see me in the parlour, and I accordingly followed him to the door, which he opened. I entered the room, and was in a moment at the side of my early friend and benefactress. I was too much agitated to speak; I could only hold the hands which she gave me, while, spite of every effort, the tears flowed fast and bitterly.

'It was kind, very, very kind of you to come to see me,' she said, with far more composure than I could have commanded; 'I see it is very painful to you.'

I endeavoured to compose myself, and for a little time we remained silent; she was the first to speak:

'You will be surprised, Mr. Purcell, when you observe the calmness with which I can speak of him who was dearest to me, who is gone; but my thoughts are always with him, and the recollections of his love'—her voice faltered a little—'and the hope of meeting him hereafter enables me to bear existence.'

I said I know not what; something about resignation, I believe.

'I hope I am resigned; God made me more: so,' she said. 'Oh, Mr. Purcell, I have often thought I loved my lost child TOO well. It was natural—he was my only child—he was——' She could not proceed for a few moments: 'It was very natural that I should love him as I did; but it may have been sinful; I have often thought so. I doated upon him—I idolised him—I thought too little of other holier affections; and God may have taken him from me, only to teach me, by this severe lesson, that I owed to heaven a larger share of my heart than to anything earthly. I cannot think of him now without more solemn feelings than if he were with me. There is something holy in our thoughts of the dead; I feel it so.' After a pause, she continued—'Mr. Purcell, do you remember his features well? they were very beautiful.' I assured her that I did. 'Then you can tell me if you think this a faithful likeness.' She took from a drawer a case in which lay a miniature. I took it reverently from her hands; it was indeed very like—touchingly like. I told her so; and she seemed gratified.

As the evening was wearing fast, and I had far to go, I hastened to terminate my visit, as I had intended, by placing in her hand a letter from her son to me, written during his sojourn upon the Continent. I requested her to keep it; it was one in which he spoke much of her, and in terms of the tenderest affection. As she read its contents the heavy tears gathered in her eyes, and fell, one by one, upon the page; she wiped them away, but they still flowed fast and silently. It was in vain that she tried to read it; her eyes were filled with tears: so she folded the letter, and placed it in her bosom. I rose to depart, and she also rose.

'I will not ask you to delay your departure,' said she; 'your visit here must have been a painful one to you. I cannot find words to thank you for the letter as I would wish, or for all your kindness. It has given me a pleasure greater than I thought could have fallen to the lot of a creature so very desolate as I am; may God bless you for it!' And thus we parted; I never saw Castle Connor or its solitary inmate more.

THE DRUNKARD'S DREAM.

Being a Fourth Extract from the Legacy of the late F. Purcell, P. P. of Drumcoolagh.

> 'All this HE told with some confusion and
> Dismay, the usual consequence of dreams
> Of the unpleasant kind, with none at hand
> To expound their vain and visionary gleams,
> I've known some odd ones which seemed really planned
> Prophetically, as that which one deems
> "A strange coincidence," to use a phrase
> By which such things are settled nowadays.'
>
> BYRON.

Dreams! What age, or what country of the world, has not and acknowledged the mystery of their origin and end? I have thought not a little upon the subject, seeing it is one which has been often forced upon my attention, and sometimes strangely enough; and yet I have never arrived at anything which at all appeared a satisfactory conclusion. It does appear that a mental phenomenon so extraordinary cannot be wholly without its use. We know, indeed, that in the olden times it has been made the organ of communication between the Deity and His creatures; and when, as I have seen, a dream produces upon a mind, to all appearance hopelessly reprobate and depraved, an effect so powerful and so lasting as to break down the inveterate habits, and to reform the life of an abandoned sinner, we see in the result, in the reformation of morals which appeared incorrigible, in the reclamation of a human soul which seemed to be irretrievably lost, something more than could be produced by a mere chimera of the slumbering fancy, something more than could arise from the capricious images of a terrified imagination; but once presented, we behold in all these things, and in their tremendous and mysterious results, the operation of the hand of God. And while Reason rejects as absurd the superstition which will read a prophecy in every dream, she may, without violence to herself, recognise, even in the wildest and most incongruous of the wanderings of a slumbering intellect, the evidences and the fragments of a language which may be spoken, which HAS been spoken, to terrify, to warn, and to command. We have reason to believe too, by the promptness of action which in the age of the prophets followed all intimations of this kind, and by the strength of conviction and strange permanence of the effects resulting from certain dreams in latter times, which effects we ourselves may have witnessed, that when this medium of communication has been employed by the Deity, the evidences of His presence have been unequivocal. My thoughts were directed to this subject, in a manner to leave a lasting impression upon my mind, by the events which I shall now relate, the statement of which, however extraordinary, is nevertheless ACCURATELY CORRECT.

About the year 17—, having been appointed to the living of C—-h, I rented a small house in the town, which bears the same name: one morning in the month of November, I was awakened before my usual time by my servant, who bustled into my bedroom for the purpose of announcing a sick call. As the Catholic Church holds her last rites to be totally indispensable to the safety of the departing sinner, no conscientious clergyman can afford a moment's unnecessary delay, and in little more than five minutes I stood ready cloaked and booted for the road, in the small front parlour, in which the messenger, who was to act as my guide, awaited my coming. I found a poor little girl crying piteously near the door, and after some slight difficulty I ascertained that her father was either dead or just dying.

'And what may be your father's name, my poor child?' said I. She held down her head, as if ashamed. I repeated the question, and the wretched little creature burst into floods of tears still more bitter than she had shed before. At length, almost provoked by conduct which appeared to me so unreasonable, I began to lose patience, spite of the pity which I could not help feeling towards her, and I said rather harshly:

'If you will not tell me the name of the person to whom you would lead me, your silence can arise from no good motive, and I might be justified in refusing to go with you at all.'

'Oh, don't say that—don't say that!' cried she. 'Oh, sir, it was that I was afeard of when I would not tell you—I was afeard, when you heard his name, you would not come with me; but it is no use hidin' it now—it's Pat Connell, the carpenter, your honour.'

She looked in my face with the most earnest anxiety, as if her very existence depended upon what she should read there; but I relieved her at once. The name, indeed, was most unpleasantly familiar to me; but, however fruitless my visits and advice might have been at another time, the present was too fearful an occasion to suffer my doubts of their utility or my reluctance to re-attempting what appeared a hopeless task to weigh even against the lightest chance that a consciousness of his imminent danger might produce in him a more docile and tractable disposition. Accordingly I told the child to lead the way, and followed her in silence. She hurried rapidly through the long narrow street which forms the great thoroughfare of the town. The darkness of the hour, rendered still deeper by the close approach of the old-fashioned houses, which lowered in tall obscurity on either side of the way; the damp, dreary chill which renders the advance of morning peculiarly cheerless, combined with the object of my walk, to visit the death-bed of a presumptuous sinner, to endeavour, almost against my own conviction, to infuse a hope into the heart of a dying reprobate—a drunkard but too probably perishing under the consequences of some mad fit of intoxication; all these circumstances united served to enhance the gloom and solemnity of my feelings, as I silently followed my little guide, who with quick steps traversed the uneven pavement of the main street. After a walk of about five minutes she turned off into a narrow lane, of that obscure and comfortless class which is to be found in almost all small oldfashioned towns, chill, without ventilation, reeking with all manner of offensive effluviae, and lined by dingy, smoky, sickly and pent-up buildings, frequently not only in a wretched but in a dangerous condition.

'Your father has changed his abode since I last visited him, and, I am afraid, much for the worse,' said I.

'Indeed he has, sir; but we must not complain,' replied she. 'We have to thank God that we have lodging and food, though it's poor enough, it is, your honour.'

Poor child! thought I, how many an older head might learn wisdom from thee—how many a luxurious philosopher, who is skilled to preach but not to suffer, might not thy patient words put to the blush! The manner and language of this child were alike above her years and station; and, indeed, in all cases in which the cares and sorrows of life have anticipated their usual date, and have fallen, as they sometimes do, with melancholy prematurity to the lot of childhood, I have observed the result to have proved uniformly the same. A young mind, to which joy and indulgence have been strangers, and to which suffering and self-denial have been familiarised from the first, acquires a solidity and an elevation which no other discipline could have bestowed, and which, in the present case, communicated a striking but mournful peculiarity to the manners, even to the voice, of the child. We paused before a narrow, crazy door, which she opened by means of a latch, and we forthwith began to ascend the steep and broken stairs which led upwards to the sick man's room.

As we mounted flight after flight towards the garret-floor, I heard more and more distinctly the hurried talking of many voices. I could also distinguish the low sobbing of a female. On arriving upon the uppermost lobby these sounds became fully audible.

'This way, your honour,' said my little conductress; at the same time, pushing open a door of patched and half-rotten plank, she admitted me into the squalid chamber of death and misery. But one candle, held in the fingers of a scared and haggard-looking child, was burning in the room, and that so dim that all was twilight or darkness except within its immediate influence. The general obscurity, however, served to throw into prominent and startling relief the death-bed and its occupant. The light was nearly approximated to, and fell with horrible clearness upon, the blue and swollen features of the drunkard. I did not think it possible that a human countenance could look so terrific. The lips were black and drawn apart; the teeth were firmly set; the eyes a little unclosed, and nothing but the whites appearing. Every feature was fixed and livid, and the whole face wore a ghastly and rigid expression of despairing terror such as I never saw equalled. His hands were crossed upon his breast, and firmly clenched; while, as if to add to the corpse-like effect of the whole, some white cloths, dipped in water, were wound about the forehead and temples.

As soon as I could remove my eyes from this horrible spectacle, I observed my friend Dr. D——, one of the most humane of a humane profession, standing by the bedside. He had been attempting, but unsuccessfully, to bleed the patient, and had now applied his finger to the pulse.

'Is there any hope?' I inquired in a whisper.

A shake of the head was the reply. There was a pause while he continued to hold the wrist; but he waited in vain for the throb of life—it was not there: and when he let go the hand, it fell stiffly back into its former position upon the other.

'The man is dead,' said the physician, as he turned from the bed where the terrible figure lay.

Dead! thought I, scarcely venturing to look upon the tremendous and revolting spectacle. Dead! without an hour for repentance, even a moment for reflection; dead I without the rites which even the best should have. Is there a hope for him? The glaring eyeball, the grinning mouth, the distorted brow—that unutterable look in which a painter would have sought to embody the fixed despair of the nethermost hell. These were my answer.

The poor wife sat at a little distance, crying as if her heart would break—the younger children clustered round the bed, looking with wondering curiosity upon the form of death never seen before.

When the first tumult of uncontrollable sorrow had passed away, availing myself of the solemnity and impressiveness of the scene, I desired the heart-stricken family to accompany me in prayer, and all knelt down while I solemnly and fervently repeated some of those prayers which appeared most applicable to the occasion. I employed myself thus in a manner which, I trusted, was not unprofitable, at least to the living, for about ten minutes; and having accomplished my task, I was the first to arise.

I looked upon the poor, sobbing, helpless creatures who knelt so humbly around me, and my heart bled for them. With a natural transition I turned my eyes from them to the bed in which the body lay; and, great God! what was the revulsion, the horror which I experienced on seeing the corpse-like terrific thing seated half upright before me; the white cloths which had been wound about the head had now partly slipped from their position, and were hanging in grotesque festoons about the face and shoulders, while the distorted eyes leered from amid them—

'A sight to dream of, not to tell.'

I stood actually riveted to the spot. The figure nodded its head and lifted its arm, I thought, with a menacing gesture. A thousand confused and horrible thoughts at once rushed upon my mind. I had often read that the body of a presumptuous sinner, who, during life, had been the willing creature of every satanic impulse, after the human tenant had deserted it, had been known to become the horrible sport of demoniac possession.

I was roused from the stupefaction of terror in which I stood, by the piercing scream of the mother, who now, for the first time, perceived the change which had taken place. She rushed towards the bed, but stunned by the shock, and overcome by the conflict of violent emotions, before she reached it she fell prostrate upon the floor.

I am perfectly convinced that had I not been startled from the torpidity of horror in which I was bound by some powerful and arousing stimulant, I should have gazed upon this unearthly apparition until I had fairly lost my senses. As it was, however, the spell was broken—superstition gave way to reason: the man whom all believed to have been actually dead was living!

Dr. D—— was instantly standing by the bedside, and upon examination he found that a sudden and copious flow of blood had taken place from the wound which the lancet had left; and this, no doubt, had effected his sudden and almost preternatural restoration to an existence from which all thought he had been for ever removed. The man was still speechless, but he seemed to understand the physician when he forbid his repeating the painful and fruitless attempts which he made to articulate, and he at once resigned himself quietly into his hands.

I left the patient with leeches upon his temples, and bleeding freely, apparently with little of the drowsiness which accompanies apoplexy; indeed, Dr. D—— told me that he had never before witnessed a seizure which seemed to combine the symptoms of so many kinds, and yet which belonged to none of the recognised classes; it certainly was not apoplexy, catalepsy, nor delirium tremens, and yet it seemed, in some degree, to partake of the properties of all. It was strange, but stranger things are coming.

During two or three days Dr. D—— would not allow his patient to converse in a manner which could excite or exhaust him, with anyone; he suffered him merely as briefly as possible to express his immediate wants. And it was not until the fourth day after my early visit, the particulars of which I have just detailed, that it was thought expedient that I should see him, and then only because it appeared that his extreme importunity and impatience to meet me were likely to retard his recovery more than the mere exhaustion attendant upon a short conversation could possibly do; perhaps, too, my friend entertained some hope that if by holy confession his patient's bosom were eased of the perilous stuff which no doubt oppressed it, his recovery would be more assured and rapid. It was then, as I have said, upon the fourth day after my first professional call, that I found myself once more in the dreary chamber of want and sickness.

The man was in bed, and appeared low and restless. On my entering the room he raised himself in the bed, and muttered, twice or thrice:

'Thank God! thank God!'

I signed to those of his family who stood by to leave the room, and took a chair beside the bed. So soon as we were alone, he said, rather doggedly:

'There's no use in telling me of the sinfulness of bad ways—I know it all. I know where they lead to—I seen everything about it with my own eyesight, as plain as I see you.' He rolled himself in the bed, as if to hide his face in the clothes; and then suddenly raising himself, he exclaimed with startling vehemence: 'Look, sir! there is no use in mincing the matter: I'm blasted with the fires of hell; I have been in hell. What do you think of that? In hell—I'm lost for ever—I have not a chance. I am damned already—damned—damned!'

The end of this sentence he actually shouted. His vehemence was perfectly terrific; he threw himself back, and laughed, and sobbed hysterically. I poured some water into a tea-cup, and gave it to him. After he had swallowed it, I told him if he had anything to communicate, to do so as briefly as he could, and in a manner as little agitating to himself as possible; threatening at the same time, though I had no intention of doing so, to leave him at once, in case he again gave way to such passionate excitement.

'It's only foolishness,' he continued, 'for me to try to thank you for coming to such a villain as myself at all. It's no use for me to wish good to you, or to bless you; for such as me has no blessings to give.'

I told him that I had but done my duty, and urged him to proceed to the matter which weighed upon his mind. He then spoke nearly as follows:

'I came in drunk on Friday night last, and got to my bed here; I don't remember how. Sometime in the night it seemed to me I wakened, and feeling unasy in myself, I got up out of the bed. I wanted the fresh air; but I would not make a noise to open the window, for fear I'd waken the crathurs. It was very dark and throublesome to find the door; but at last I did get it, and I groped my way out, and went down as asy as I could. I felt quite sober, and I counted the steps one after another, as I was going down, that I might not stumble at the bottom.

'When I came to the first landing-place—God be about us always!—the floor of it sunk under me, and I went down—down—down, till the senses almost left me. I do not know how long I was falling, but it seemed to me a great while. When I came rightly to myself at last, I was sitting near the top of a great table; and I could not see the end of it, if it had any, it was so far off. And there was men beyond reckoning, sitting down all along by it, at each side, as far as I could see at all. I did not know at first was it in the open air; but there was a close smothering feel in it that was not natural. And there was a kind of light that my eyesight never saw before, red and unsteady; and I did not see for a long time where it was coming from, until I looked straight up, and then I seen that it came from great balls of blood-coloured fire that were rolling high over head with a sort of rushing, trembling sound, and I perceived that they shone on the ribs of a great roof of rock that was arched overhead instead of the sky. When I seen this, scarce knowing what I did, I got up, and I said, "I have no right to be here; I must go." And the man that was sitting at my left hand only smiled, and said, "Sit down again; you can NEVER leave this place." And his voice was weaker than any child's voice I ever heerd; and when he was done speaking he smiled again.

'Then I spoke out very loud and bold, and I said, "In the name of God, let me out of this bad place." And there was a great man that I did not see before, sitting at the end of the table that I was near; and he was taller than twelve men, and his face was very proud and terrible to look at. And he stood up and stretched out his hand before him; and when he stood up, all that was there, great and small, bowed down with a sighing sound, and a dread came on my heart, and he looked at me, and I could not speak. I felt I was his own, to do what he liked with, for I knew at once who he was; and he said, "If you promise to return, you may depart for a season;" and the voice he spoke with was terrible and mournful, and the echoes of it went rolling and swelling down the endless cave, and mixing with the trembling of the fire overhead; so that when he sat down there was a sound after him, all through the place, like the roaring of a furnace, and I said, with all the strength I had, "I promise to come back—in God's name let me go!"

'And with that I lost the sight and the hearing of all that was there, and when my senses came to me again, I was sitting in the bed with the blood all over me, and you and the rest praying around the room.'

Here he paused and wiped away the chill drops of horror which hung upon his forehead.

I remained silent for some moments. The vision which he had just described struck my imagination not a little, for this was long before Vathek and the 'Hall of Eblis' had delighted the world; and the description which he gave had, as I received it, all the attractions of novelty beside the impressiveness which always belongs to the narration of an EYE-WITNESS, whether in the body or in the spirit, of the scenes which he describes. There was something, too, in the stern horror with which the man related these things, and in the incongruity of his description, with the vulgarly received notions of the great place of punishment, and of its presiding spirit, which struck my mind with awe, almost with fear. At length he said, with an expression of horrible, imploring earnestness, which I shall never forget—'Well, sir, is there any hope; is there any chance at all? or, is my soul pledged and promised away for ever? is it gone out of my power? must I go back to the place?'

In answering him, I had no easy task to perform; for however clear might be my internal conviction of the groundlessness of his tears, and however strong my scepticism respecting the reality of what he had described, I nevertheless felt that his impression to the contrary, and his humility and terror resulting from it, might be made available as no mean engines in the work of his conversion from prodigacy, and of his restoration to decent habits, and to religious feeling.

I therefore told him that he was to regard his dream rather in the light of a warning than in that of a prophecy; that our salvation depended not upon the word or deed of a moment, but upon the habits of a life; that, in fine, if he at once discarded his idle companions and evil habits, and firmly adhered to a sober, industrious, and religious course of life, the powers of darkness might claim his soul in vain, for that there were higher and firmer pledges than human tongue could utter, which promised salvation to him who should repent and lead a new life.

I left him much comforted, and with a promise to return upon the next day. I did so, and found him much more cheerful and without any remains of the dogged sullenness which I suppose had arisen from his despair. His promises of amendment were given in that tone of deliberate earnestness, which belongs to deep and solemn determination; and it was with no small delight that I observed, after repeated visits, that his good resolutions, so far from failing, did but gather strength by time; and when I saw that man shake off the idle and debauched companions, whose society had for years formed alike his amusement and his ruin, and revive his long discarded habits of industry and sobriety, I said within myself, there is something more in all this than the operation of an idle dream.

One day, sometime after his perfect restoration to health, I was surprised on ascending the stairs, for the purpose of visiting this man, to find him busily employed in nailing down some planks upon the landing-place, through which, at the commencement of his mysterious vision, it seemed to him that he had sunk. I perceived at once that he was strengthening the floor with a view to securing himself against such a catastrophe, and could scarcely forbear a smile as I bid 'God bless his work.'

He perceived my thoughts, I suppose, for he immediately said:

'I can never pass over that floor without trembling. I'd leave this house if I could, but I can't find another lodging in the town so cheap, and I'll not take a better till I've paid off all my debts, please God; but I could not be asy in my mind till I made it as safe as I could. You'll hardly believe me, your honour, that while I'm working, maybe a mile away, my heart is in a flutter the whole way back, with the bare thoughts of the two little steps I have to walk upon this bit of a floor. So it's no wonder, sir, I'd thry to make it sound and firm with any idle timber I have.'

I applauded his resolution to pay off his debts, and the steadiness with which he perused his plans of conscientious economy, and passed on.

Many months elapsed, and still there appeared no alteration in his resolutions of amendment. He was a good workman, and with his better habits he recovered his former extensive and profitable employment. Everything seemed to promise comfort and respectability. I have little more to add, and that shall be told quickly. I had one evening met Pat Connell, as he returned from his work, and as usual, after a mutual, and on his side respectful salutation, I spoke a few words of encouragement and approval. I left him industrious, active, healthy—when next I saw him, not three days after, he was a corpse.

The circumstances which marked the event of his death were somewhat strange—I might say fearful. The unfortunate man had accidentally met an early friend just returned, after a long absence, and in a moment of excitement, forgetting everything in the warmth of his joy, he yielded to his urgent invitation to accompany him into a public-house, which lay close by the spot where the encounter had taken place. Connell, however, previously to entering the room, had announced his determination to take nothing more than the strictest temperance would warrant.

But oh! who can describe the inveterate tenacity with which a drunkard's habits cling to him through life? He may repent—he may reform—he may look with actual abhorrence upon his past profligacy; but amid all this reformation and compunction, who can tell the moment in which the base and ruinous propensity may not recur, triumphing over resolution, remorse, shame, everything, and prostrating its victim once more in all that is destructive and revolting in that fatal vice?

The wretched man left the place in a state of utter intoxication. He was brought home nearly insensible, and placed in his bed, where he lay in the deep calm lethargy of drunkenness. The younger part of the family retired to rest much after their usual hour; but the poor wife remained up sitting by the fire, too much grieved and shocked at the occurrence of what she had so little expected, to settle to rest; fatigue, however, at length overcame her, and she sank gradually into an uneasy slumber. She could not tell how long she had remained in this state, when she awakened, and immediately on opening her eyes, she perceived by the faint red light of the smouldering turf embers, two persons, one of whom she recognised as her husband, noiselessly gliding out of the room.

'Pat, darling, where are you going?' said she. There was no answer—the door closed after them; but in a moment she was startled and terrified by a loud and heavy crash, as if some ponderous body had been hurled down the stair. Much alarmed, she started up, and going to the head of the staircase, she called repeatedly upon her husband, but in vain. She returned to the room, and with the assistance of her daughter, whom I had occasion to mention before, she succeeded in finding and lighting a candle, with which she hurried again to the head of the staircase.

At the bottom lay what seemed to be a bundle of clothes, heaped together, motionless, lifeless—it was her husband. In going down the stair, for what purpose can never now be known, he had fallen helplessly and violently to the bottom, and coming head foremost, the spine at the neck had been dislocated by the shock, and instant death must have ensued. The body lay upon that landing-place to which his dream had referred. It is scarcely worth endeavouring to clear up a single point in a narrative where all is mystery; yet I could not help suspecting that the second figure which had been seen in the room by Connell's wife on the night of his death, might have been no other than his own shadow. I suggested this solution of the difficulty; but she told me that the unknown person had been considerably in advance of the other, and on reaching the door, had turned back as if to communicate something to his companion. It was then a mystery.

Was the dream verified?—whither had the disembodied spirit sped?—who can say? We know not. But I left the house of death that day in a state of horror which I could not describe. It seemed to me that I was scarce awake. I heard and saw everything as if under the spell of a night-mare. The coincidence was terrible.

THE PURCELL PAPERS VOLUME II

PASSAGE IN THE SECRET HISTORY OF AN IRISH COUNTESS.

Being a Fifth Extract from the Legacy of the late Francis Purcell, P.P. of Drumcoolagh.

The following paper is written in a female hand, and was no doubt communicated to my much-regretted friend by the lady whose early history it serves to illustrate, the Countess D——. She is no more—she long since died, a childless and a widowed wife, and, as her letter sadly predicts, none survive to whom the publication of this narrative can prove 'injurious, or even painful.' Strange! two powerful and wealthy families, that in which she was born, and that into which she had married, have ceased to be—they are utterly extinct.

To those who know anything of the history of Irish families, as they were less than a century ago, the facts which immediately follow will at once suggest THE NAMES of the principal actors; and to others their publication would be useless—to us, possibly, if not probably, injurious. I have, therefore, altered such of the names as might, if stated, get us into difficulty; others, belonging to minor characters in the strange story, I have left untouched.

My dear friend,—You have asked me to furnish you with a detail of the strange events which marked my early history, and I have, without hesitation, applied myself to the task, knowing that, while I live, a kind consideration for my feelings will prevent your giving publicity to the statement; and conscious that, when I am no more, there will not survive one to whom the narrative can prove injurious, or even painful.

My mother died when I was quite an infant, and of her I have no recollection, even the faintest. By her death, my education and habits were left solely to the guidance of my surviving parent; and, as far as a stern attention to my religious instruction, and an active anxiety evinced by his procuring for me the best masters to perfect me in those accomplishments which my station and wealth might seem to require, could avail, he amply discharged the task.

My father was what is called an oddity, and his treatment of me, though uniformly kind, flowed less from affection and tenderness than from a sense of obligation and duty. Indeed, I seldom even spoke to him except at meal-times, and then his manner was silent and abrupt; his leisure hours, which were many, were passed either in his study or in solitary walks; in short, he seemed to take no further interest in my happiness or improvement than a conscientious regard to the discharge of his own duty would seem to claim.

Shortly before my birth a circumstance had occurred which had contributed much to form and to confirm my father's secluded habits—it was the fact that a suspicion of MURDER had fallen upon his younger brother, though not sufficiently definite to lead to an indictment, yet strong enough to ruin him in public opinion.

This disgraceful and dreadful doubt cast upon the family name, my father felt deeply and bitterly, and not the less so that he himself was thoroughly convinced of his brother's innocence. The sincerity and strength of this impression he shortly afterwards proved in a manner which produced the dark events which follow. Before, however, I enter upon the statement of them, I ought to relate the circumstances which had awakened the suspicion; inasmuch as they are in themselves somewhat curious, and, in their effects, most intimately connected with my after-history.

My uncle, Sir Arthur T——n, was a gay and extravagant man, and, among other vices, was ruinously addicted to gaming; this unfortunate propensity, even after his fortune had suffered so severely as to render inevitable a reduction in his expenses by no means inconsiderable, nevertheless continued to actuate him, nearly to the exclusion of all other pursuits; he was, however, a proud, or rather a vain man, and could not bear to make the diminution of his income a matter of gratulation and triumph to those with whom he had hitherto competed, and the consequence was, that he frequented no longer the expensive haunts of dissipation, and retired from the gay world, leaving his coterie to discover his reasons as best they might.

He did not, however, forego his favourite vice, for, though he could not worship his great divinity in the costly temples where it was formerly his wont to take his stand, yet he found it very possible to bring about him a sufficient number of the votaries of chance to answer all his ends. The consequence was, that Carrickleigh, which was the name of my uncle's residence, was never without one or more of such visitors as I have described.

It happened that upon one occasion he was visited by one Hugh Tisdall, a gentleman of loose habits, but of considerable wealth, and who had, in early youth, travelled with my uncle upon the Continent; the period of his visit was winter, and, consequently, the house was nearly deserted excepting by its regular inmates; it was therefore highly acceptable, particularly as my uncle was aware that his visitor's tastes accorded exactly with his own.

Both parties seemed determined to avail themselves of their suitability during the brief stay which Mr. Tisdall had promised; the consequence was, that they shut themselves up in Sir Arthur's private room for nearly all the day and the greater part of the night, during the space of nearly a week, at the end of which the servant having one morning, as usual, knocked at Mr. Tisdall's bedroom door repeatedly, received no answer, and, upon attempting to enter, found that it was locked; this appeared suspicious, and, the inmates of the house having been alarmed, the door was forced open, and, on proceeding to the bed, they found the body of its occupant perfectly lifeless, and hanging half-way out, the head downwards, and near the floor. One deep wound had been inflicted upon the temple, apparently with some blunt instrument which had penetrated the brain; and another blow, less effective, probably the first aimed, had grazed the head, removing some of the scalp, but leaving the skull untouched. The door had been double-locked upon the INSIDE, in evidence of which the key still lay where it had been placed in the lock.

The window, though not secured on the interior, was closed—a circumstance not a little puzzling, as it afforded the only other mode of escape from the room; it looked out, too, upon a kind of courtyard, round which the old buildings stood, formerly accessible by a narrow doorway and passage lying in the oldest side of the quadrangle, but which had since been built up, so as to preclude all ingress or egress; the room was also upon the second story, and the height of the window considerable. Near the bed were found a pair of razors belonging to the murdered man, one of them upon the ground, and both of them open. The weapon which had inflicted the mortal wound was not to be found in the room, nor were any footsteps or other traces of the murderer discoverable.

At the suggestion of Sir Arthur himself, a coroner was instantly summoned to attend, and an inquest was held; nothing, however, in any degree conclusive was elicited; the walls, ceiling, and floor of the room were carefully examined, in order to ascertain whether they contained a trap-door or other concealed mode of entrance—but no such thing appeared.

Such was the minuteness of investigation employed, that, although the grate had contained a large fire during the night, they proceeded to examine even the very chimney, in order to discover whether escape by it were possible; but this attempt, too, was fruitless, for the chimney, built in the old fashion, rose in a perfectly perpendicular line from the hearth to a height of nearly fourteen feet above the roof, affording in its interior scarcely the possibility of ascent, the flue being smoothly plastered, and sloping towards the top like an inverted funnel, promising, too, even if the summit were attained, owing to its great height, but a precarious descent upon the sharp and steep-ridged roof; the ashes, too, which lay in the grate, and the soot, as far as it could be seen, were undisturbed, a circumstance almost conclusive of the question.

Sir Arthur was of course examined; his evidence was given with clearness and unreserve, which seemed calculated to silence all suspicion. He stated that, up to the day and night immediately preceding the catastrophe, he had lost to a heavy amount, but that, at their last sitting, he had not only won back his original loss, but upwards of four thousand pounds in addition; in evidence of which he produced an acknowledgment of debt to that amount in the handwriting of the deceased, and bearing the date of the fatal night. He had mentioned the circumstance to his lady, and in presence of some of the domestics; which statement was supported by THEIR respective evidence.

One of the jury shrewdly observed, that the circumstance of Mr. Tisdall's having sustained so heavy a loss might have suggested to some ill-minded persons accidentally hearing it, the plan of robbing him, after having murdered him in such a manner as might make it appear that he had committed suicide; a supposition which was strongly supported by the razors having been found thus displaced, and removed from their case. Two persons had probably been engaged in the attempt, one watching by the sleeping man, and ready to strike him in case of his awakening suddenly, while the other was procuring the razors and employed in inflicting the fatal gash, so as to make it appear to have been the act of the murdered man himself. It was said that while the juror was making this suggestion Sir Arthur changed colour.

Nothing, however, like legal evidence appeared against him, and the consequence was that the verdict was found against a person or persons unknown; and for some time the matter was suffered to rest, until, after about five months, my father received a letter from a person signing himself Andrew Collis, and representing himself to be the cousin of the deceased. This letter stated that Sir Arthur was likely to incur not merely suspicion, but personal risk, unless he could account for certain circumstances connected with the recent murder, and contained a copy of a letter written by the deceased, and bearing date, the day of the week, and of the month, upon the night of which the deed of blood had been perpetrated. Tisdall's note ran as follows:

> 'DEAR COLLIS,
>
> 'I have had sharp work with Sir Arthur; he tried some of his stale tricks, but soon found that *I* was Yorkshire too: it would not do—you understand me. We went to the work like good ones, head, heart and soul; and, in fact, since I came here, I have lost no time. I am rather fagged, but I am sure to be well paid for my hardship; I never want sleep so long as I can have the music of a dice-box, and wherewithal to pay the piper. As I told you, he tried some of his queer turns, but I foiled him like a man, and, in return, gave him more than he could relish of the genuine DEAD KNOWLEDGE.
>
> 'In short, I have plucked the old baronet as never baronet was plucked before; I have scarce left him the stump of a quill; I have got promissory notes in his hand to the amount of—if you like round numbers, say, thirty thousand pounds, safely deposited in my portable strong-box, alias double-clasped pocket-book. I leave this ruinous old rat-hole early on to-morrow, for two reasons—first, I do not want to play with Sir Arthur deeper than I think his security, that is, his money, or his money's worth, would warrant; and, secondly, because I am safer a hundred miles from Sir Arthur than in the house with him. Look you, my worthy, I tell you this between ourselves—I may be wrong, but, by G—, I am as sure as that I am now living, that Sir A—— attempted to poison me last night; so much for old friendship on both sides.

'When I won the last stake, a heavy one enough, my friend leant his forehead upon his hands, and you'll laugh when I tell you that his head literally smoked like a hot dumpling. I do not know whether his agitation was produced by the plan which he had against me, or by his having lost so heavily—though it must be allowed that he had reason to be a little funked, whichever way his thoughts went; but he pulled the bell, and ordered two bottles of champagne. While the fellow was bringing them he drew out a promissory note to the full amount, which he signed, and, as the man came in with the bottles and glasses, he desired him to be off; he filled out a glass for me, and, while he thought my eyes were off, for I was putting up his note at the time, he dropped something slyly into it, no doubt to sweeten it; but I saw it all, and, when he handed it to me, I said, with an emphasis which he might or might not understand:

'"There is some sediment in this; I'll not drink it."

'"Is there?" said he, and at the same time snatched it from my hand and threw it into the fire. What do you think of that? have I not a tender chicken to manage? Win or lose, I will not play beyond five thousand to-night, and to-morrow sees me safe out of the reach of Sir Arthur's champagne. So, all things considered, I think you must allow that you are not the last who have found a knowing boy in

'Yours to command,

'HUGH TISDALL.'

Of the authenticity of this document I never heard my father express a doubt; and I am satisfied that, owing to his strong conviction in favour of his brother, he would not have admitted it without sufficient inquiry, inasmuch as it tended to confirm the suspicions which already existed to his prejudice.

Now, the only point in this letter which made strongly against my uncle, was the mention of the 'double-clasped pocket-book' as the receptacle of the papers likely to involve him, for this pocket-book was not forthcoming, nor anywhere to be found, nor had any papers referring to his gaming transactions been found upon the dead man. However, whatever might have been the original intention of this Collis, neither my uncle nor my father ever heard more of him; but he published the letter in Faulkner's newspaper, which was shortly afterwards made the vehicle of a much more mysterious attack. The passage in that periodical to which I allude, occurred about four years afterwards, and while the fatal occurrence was still fresh in public recollection. It commenced by a rambling preface, stating that 'a CERTAIN PERSON whom CERTAIN persons thought to be dead, was not so, but living, and in full possession of his memory, and moreover ready and able to make GREAT delinquents tremble.' It then went on to describe the murder, without, however, mentioning names; and in doing so, it entered into minute and circumstantial particulars of which none but an EYE-WITNESS could have been possessed, and by implications almost too unequivocal to be regarded in the light of insinuation, to involve the 'TITLED GAMBLER' in the guilt of the transaction.

My father at once urged Sir Arthur to proceed against the paper in an action of libel; but he would not hear of it, nor consent to my father's taking any legal steps whatever in the matter. My father, however, wrote in a threatening tone to Faulkner, demanding a surrender of the author of the obnoxious article. The answer to this application is still in my possession, and is penned in an apologetic tone: it states that the manuscript had been handed in, paid for, and inserted as an advertisement, without sufficient inquiry, or any knowledge as to whom it referred.

No step, however, was taken to clear my uncle's character in the judgment of the public; and as he immediately sold a small property, the application of the proceeds of which was known to none, he was said to have disposed of it to enable himself to buy off the threatened information. However the truth might have been, it is certain that no charges respecting the mysterious murder were afterwards publicly made against my uncle, and, as far as external disturbances were concerned, he enjoyed henceforward perfect security and quiet.

A deep and lasting impression, however, had been made upon the public mind, and Sir Arthur T——n was no longer visited or noticed by the gentry and aristocracy of the county, whose attention and courtesies he had hitherto received. He accordingly affected to despise these enjoyments which he could not procure, and shunned even that society which he might have commanded.

This is all that I need recapitulate of my uncle's history, and I now recur to my own. Although my father had never, within my recollection, visited, or been visited by, my uncle, each being of sedentary, procrastinating, and secluded habits, and their respective residences being very far apart—the one lying in the county of Galway, the other in that of Cork—he was strongly attached to his brother, and evinced his affection by an active correspondence, and by deeply and proudly resenting that neglect which had marked Sir Arthur as unfit to mix in society.

When I was about eighteen years of age, my father, whose health had been gradually declining, died, leaving me in heart wretched and desolate, and, owing to his previous seclusion, with few acquaintances, and almost no friends.

The provisions of his will were curious, and when I had sufficiently come to myself to listen to or comprehend them, surprised me not a little: all his vast property was left to me, and to the heirs of my body, for ever; and, in default of such heirs, it was to go after my death to my uncle, Sir Arthur, without any entail.

At the same time, the will appointed him my guardian, desiring that I might be received within his house, and reside with his family, and under his care, during the term of my minority; and in consideration of the increased expense consequent upon such an arrangement, a handsome annuity was allotted to him during the term of my proposed residence.

The object of this last provision I at once understood: my father desired, by making it the direct, apparent interest of Sir Arthur that I should die without issue, while at the same time he placed me wholly in his power, to prove to the world how great and unshaken was his confidence in his brother's innocence and honour, and also to afford him an opportunity of showing that this mark of confidence was not unworthily bestowed.

It was a strange, perhaps an idle scheme; but as I had been always brought up in the habit of considering my uncle as a deeply-injured man, and had been taught, almost as a part of my religion, to regard him as the very soul of honour, I felt no further uneasiness respecting the arrangement than that likely to result to a timid girl, of secluded habits, from the immediate prospect of taking up her abode for the first time in her life among total strangers. Previous to leaving my home, which I felt I should do with a heavy heart, I received a most tender and affectionate letter from my uncle, calculated, if anything could do so, to remove the bitterness of parting from scenes familiar and dear from my earliest childhood, and in some degree to reconcile me to the measure.

It was during a fine autumn that I approached the old domain of Carrickleigh. I shall not soon forget the impression of sadness and of gloom which all that I saw produced upon my mind; the sunbeams were falling with a rich and melancholy tint upon the fine old trees, which stood in lordly groups, casting their long, sweeping shadows over rock and sward. There was an air of neglect and decay about the spot, which amounted almost to desolation; the symptoms of this increased in number as we approached the building itself, near which the ground had been originally more artificially and carefully cultivated than elsewhere, and whose neglect consequently more immediately and strikingly betrayed itself.

As we proceeded, the road wound near the beds of what had been formally two fish-ponds, which were now nothing more than stagnant swamps, overgrown with rank weeds, and here and there encroached upon by the straggling underwood; the avenue itself was much broken, and in many places the stones were almost concealed by grass and nettles, the loose stone walls which had here and there intersected the broad park were, in many places, broken down, so as no longer to answer their original purpose as fences; piers were now and then to be seen, but the gates were gone; and, to add to the general air of dilapidation, some huge trunks were lying scattered through the venerable old trees, either the work of the winter storms, or perhaps the victims of some extensive but desultory scheme of denudation, which the projector had not capital or perseverance to carry into full effect.

After the carriage had travelled a mile of this avenue, we reached the summit of rather an abrupt eminence, one of the many which added to the picturesqueness, if not to the convenience of this rude passage. From the top of this ridge the grey walls of Carrickleigh were visible, rising at a small distance in front, and darkened by the hoary wood which crowded around them. It was a quadrangular building of considerable extent, and the front which lay towards us, and in which the great entrance was placed, bore unequivocal marks of antiquity; the time-worn, solemn aspect of the old building, the ruinous and deserted appearance of the whole place, and the associations which connected it with a dark page in the history of my family, combined to depress spirits already predisposed for the reception of sombre and dejecting impressions.

When the carriage drew up in the grass-grown court yard before the hall-door, two lazy-looking men, whose appearance well accorded with that of the place which they tenanted, alarmed by the obstreperous barking of a great chained dog, ran out from some half-ruinous out-houses, and took charge of the horses; the hall-door stood open, and I entered a gloomy and imperfectly lighted apartment, and found no one within. However, I had not long to wait in this awkward predicament, for before my luggage had been deposited in the house, indeed, before I had well removed my cloak and other wraps, so as to enable me to look around, a young girl ran lightly into the hall, and kissing me heartily, and somewhat boisterously, exclaimed:

'My dear cousin, my dear Margaret—I am so delighted—so out of breath. We did not expect you till ten o'clock; my father is somewhere about the place, he must be close at hand. James—Corney—run out and tell your master—my brother is seldom at home, at least at any reasonable hour—you must be so tired—so fatigued—let me show you to your room—see that Lady Margaret's luggage is all brought up—you must lie down and rest yourself—Deborah, bring some coffee—up these stairs; we are so delighted to see you—you cannot think how lonely I have been—how steep these stairs are, are not they? I am so glad you are come—I could hardly bring myself to believe that you were really coming—how good of you, dear Lady Margaret.'

There was real good-nature and delight in my cousin's greeting, and a kind of constitutional confidence of manner which placed me at once at ease, and made me feel immediately upon terms of intimacy with her. The room into which she ushered me, although partaking in the general air of decay which pervaded the mansion and all about it, had nevertheless been fitted up with evident attention to comfort, and even with some dingy attempt at luxury; but what pleased me most was that it opened, by a second door, upon a lobby which communicated with my fair cousin's apartment; a circumstance which divested the room, in my eyes, of the air of solitude and sadness which would otherwise have characterised it, to a degree almost painful to one so dejected in spirits as I was.

After such arrangements as I found necessary were completed, we both went down to the parlour, a large wainscoted room, hung round with grim old portraits, and, as I was not sorry to see, containing in its ample grate a large and cheerful fire. Here my cousin had leisure to talk more at her ease; and from her I learned something of the manners and the habits of the two remaining members of her family, whom I had not yet seen.

On my arrival I had known nothing of the family among whom I was come to reside, except that it consisted of three individuals, my uncle, and his son and daughter, Lady T——n having been long dead. In addition to this very scanty stock of information, I shortly learned from my communicative companion that my uncle was, as I had suspected, completely retired in his habits, and besides that, having been so far back as she could well recollect, always rather strict, as reformed rakes frequently become, he had latterly been growing more gloomily and sternly religious than heretofore.

Her account of her brother was far less favourable, though she did not say anything directly to his disadvantage. From all that I could gather from her, I was led to suppose that he was a specimen of the idle, coarse-mannered, profligate, low-minded 'squirearchy'—a result which might naturally have flowed from the circumstance of his being, as it were, outlawed from society, and driven for companionship to grades below his own—enjoying, too, the dangerous prerogative of spending much money.

However, you may easily suppose that I found nothing in my cousin's communication fully to bear me out in so very decided a conclusion.

I awaited the arrival of my uncle, which was every moment to be expected, with feelings half of alarm, half of curiosity—a sensation which I have often since experienced, though to a less degree, when upon the point of standing for the first time in the presence of one of whom I have long been in the habit of hearing or thinking with interest.

It was, therefore, with some little perturbation that I heard, first a slight bustle at the outer door, then a slow step traverse the hall, and finally witnessed the door open, and my uncle enter the room. He was a striking-looking man; from peculiarities both of person and of garb, the whole effect of his appearance amounted to extreme singularity. He was tall, and when young his figure must have been strikingly elegant; as it was, however, its effect was marred by a very decided stoop. His dress was of a sober colour, and in fashion anterior to anything which I could remember. It was, however, handsome, and by no means carelessly put on; but what completed the singularity of his appearance was his uncut, white hair, which hung in long, but not at all neglected curls, even so far as his shoulders, and which combined with his regularly classic features, and fine dark eyes, to bestow upon him an air of venerable dignity and pride, which I have never seen equalled elsewhere. I rose as he entered, and met him about the middle of the room; he kissed my cheek and both my hands, saying:

'You are most welcome, dear child, as welcome as the command of this poor place and all that it contains can make you. I am most rejoiced to see you—truly rejoiced. I trust that you are not much fatigued—pray be seated again.' He led me to my chair, and continued: 'I am glad to perceive you have made acquaintance with Emily already; I see, in your being thus brought together, the foundation of a lasting friendship. You are both innocent, and both young. God bless you—God bless you, and make you all that I could wish.'

He raised his eyes, and remained for a few moments silent, as if in secret prayer. I felt that it was impossible that this man, with feelings so quick, so warm, so tender, could be the wretch that public opinion had represented him to be. I was more than ever convinced of his innocence.

His manner was, or appeared to me, most fascinating; there was a mingled kindness and courtesy in it which seemed to speak benevolence itself. It was a manner which I felt cold art could never have taught; it owed most of its charm to its appearing to emanate directly from the heart; it must be a genuine index of the owner's mind. So I thought.

My uncle having given me fully to understand that I was most welcome, and might command whatever was his own, pressed me to take some refreshment; and on my refusing, he observed that previously to bidding me good-night, he had one duty further to perform, one in whose observance he was convinced I would cheerfully acquiesce.

He then proceeded to read a chapter from the Bible; after which he took his leave with the same affectionate kindness with which he had greeted me, having repeated his desire that I should consider everything in his house as altogether at my disposal. It is needless to say that I was much pleased with my uncle—it was impossible to avoid being so; and I could not help saying to myself, if such a man as this is not safe from the assaults of slander, who is? I felt much happier than I had done since my father's death, and enjoyed that night the first refreshing sleep which had visited me since that event.

My curiosity respecting my male cousin did not long remain unsatisfied—he appeared the next day at dinner. His manners, though not so coarse as I had expected, were exceedingly disagreeable; there was an assurance and a forwardness for which I was not prepared; there was less of the vulgarity of manner, and almost more of that of the mind, than I had anticipated. I felt quite uncomfortable in his presence; there was just that confidence in his look and tone which would read encouragement even in mere toleration; and I felt more disgusted and annoyed at the coarse and extravagant compliments which he was pleased from time to time to pay me, than perhaps the extent of the atrocity might fully have warranted. It was, however, one consolation that he did not often appear, being much engrossed by pursuits about which I neither knew nor cared anything; but when he did appear, his attentions, either with a view to his amusement or to some more serious advantage, were so obviously and perseveringly directed to me, that young and inexperienced as I was, even *I* could not be ignorant of his preference. I felt more provoked by this odious persecution than I can express, and discouraged him with so much vigour, that I employed even rudeness to convince him that his assiduities were unwelcome; but all in vain.

This had gone on for nearly a twelve-month, to my infinite annoyance, when one day as I was sitting at some needle-work with my companion Emily, as was my habit, in the parlour, the door opened, and my cousin Edward entered the room. There was something, I thought, odd in his manner—a kind of struggle between shame and impudence—a kind of flurry and ambiguity which made him appear, if possible, more than ordinarily disagreeable.

'Your servant, ladies,' he said, seating himself at the same time; 'sorry to spoil your tete-a-tete, but never mind, I'll only take Emily's place for a minute or two; and then we part for a while, fair cousin. Emily, my father wants you in the corner turret. No shilly-shally; he's in a hurry.' She hesitated. 'Be off—tramp, march!' he exclaimed, in a tone which the poor girl dared not disobey.

She left the room, and Edward followed her to the door. He stood there for a minute or two, as if reflecting what he should say, perhaps satisfying himself that no one was within hearing in the hall.

At length he turned about, having closed the door, as if carelessly, with his foot; and advancing slowly, as if in deep thought, he took his seat at the side of the table opposite to mine.

There was a brief interval of silence, after which he said:

'I imagine that you have a shrewd suspicion of the object of my early visit; but I suppose I must go into particulars. Must I?'

'I have no conception,' I replied, 'what your object may be.'

'Well, well,' said he, becoming more at his ease as he proceeded, 'it may be told in a few words. You know that it is totally impossible—quite out of the question—that an offhand young fellow like me, and a good-looking girl like yourself, could meet continually, as you and I have done, without an attachment—a liking growing up on one side or other; in short, I think I have let you know as plain as if I spoke it, that I have been in love with you almost from the first time I saw you.'

He paused; but I was too much horrified to speak. He interpreted my silence favourably.

'I can tell you,' he continued, 'I'm reckoned rather hard to please, and very hard to HIT. I can't say when I was taken with a girl before; so you see fortune reserved me——'

Here the odious wretch wound his arm round my waist. The action at once restored me to utterance, and with the most indignant vehemence I released myself from his hold, and at the same time said:

'I have not been insensible, sir, of your most disagreeable attentions—they have long been a source of much annoyance to me; and you must be aware that I have marked my disapprobation—my disgust—as unequivocally as I possibly could, without actual indelicacy.'

I paused, almost out of breath from the rapidity with which I had spoken; and without giving him time to renew the conversation, I hastily quitted the room, leaving him in a paroxysm of rage and mortification. As I ascended the stairs, I heard him open the parlour-door with violence, and take two or three rapid strides in the direction in which I was moving. I was now much frightened, and ran the whole way until I reached my room; and having locked the door, I listened breathlessly, but heard no sound. This relieved me for the present; but so much had I been overcome by the agitation and annoyance attendant upon the scene which I had just gone through, that when my cousin Emily knocked at my door, I was weeping in strong hysterics.

You will readily conceive my distress, when you reflect upon my strong dislike to my cousin Edward, combined with my youth and extreme inexperience. Any proposal of such a nature must have agitated me; but that it should have come from the man whom of all others I most loathed and abhorred, and to whom I had, as clearly as manner could do it, expressed the state of my feelings, was almost too overwhelming to be borne. It was a calamity, too, in which I could not claim the sympathy of my cousin Emily, which had always been extended to me in my minor grievances. Still I hoped that it might not be unattended with good; for I thought that one inevitable and most welcome consequence would result from this painful eclaircissment, in the discontinuance of my cousin's odious persecution.

When I arose next morning, it was with the fervent hope that I might never again behold the face, or even hear the name, of my cousin Edward; but such a consummation, though devoutly to be wished, was hardly likely to occur. The painful impressions of yesterday were too vivid to be at once erased; and I could not help feeling some dim foreboding of coming annoyance and evil.

To expect on my cousin's part anything like delicacy or consideration for me, was out of the question. I saw that he had set his heart upon my property, and that he was not likely easily to forego such an acquisition—possessing what might have been considered opportunities and facilities almost to compel my compliance.

I now keenly felt the unreasonableness of my father's conduct in placing me to reside with a family of all whose members, with one exception, he was wholly ignorant, and I bitterly felt the helplessness of my situation. I determined, however, in case of my cousin's persevering in his addresses, to lay all the particulars before my uncle, although he had never in kindness or intimacy gone a step beyond our first interview, and to throw myself upon his hospitality and his sense of honour for protection against a repetition of such scenes.

My cousin's conduct may appear to have been an inadequate cause for such serious uneasiness; but my alarm was caused neither by his acts nor words, but entirely by his manner, which was strange and even intimidating to excess. At the beginning of the yesterday's interview there was a sort of bullying swagger in his air, which towards the end gave place to the brutal vehemence of an undisguised ruffian—a transition which had tempted me into a belief that he might seek even forcibly to extort from me a consent to his wishes, or by means still more horrible, of which I scarcely dared to trust myself to think, to possess himself of my property.

I was early next day summoned to attend my uncle in his private room, which lay in a corner turret of the old building; and thither I accordingly went, wondering all the way what this unusual measure might prelude. When I entered the room, he did not rise in his usual courteous way to greet me, but simply pointed to a chair opposite to his own. This boded nothing agreeable. I sat down, however, silently waiting until he should open the conversation.

'Lady Margaret,' at length he said, in a tone of greater sternness than I thought him capable of using, 'I have hitherto spoken to you as a friend, but I have not forgotten that I am also your guardian, and that my authority as such gives me a right to control your conduct. I shall put a question to you, and I expect and will demand a plain, direct answer. Have I rightly been informed that you have contemptuously rejected the suit and hand of my son Edward?'

I stammered forth with a good deal of trepidation:

'I believe—that is, I have, sir, rejected my cousin's proposals; and my coldness and discouragement might have convinced him that I had determined to do so.'

'Madam,' replied he, with suppressed, but, as it appeared to me, intense anger, 'I have lived long enough to know that COLDNESS and discouragement, and such terms, form the common cant of a worthless coquette. You know to the full, as well as I, that COLDNESS AND DISCOURAGEMENT may be so exhibited as to convince their object that he is neither distasteful or indifferent to the person who wears this manner. You know, too, none better, that an affected neglect, when skilfully managed, is amongst the most formidable of the engines which artful beauty can employ. I tell you, madam, that having, without one word spoken in discouragement, permitted my son's most marked attentions for a twelvemonth or more, you have no right to dismiss him with no further explanation than demurely telling him that you had always looked coldly upon him; and neither your wealth nor your LADYSHIP' (there was an emphasis of scorn on the word, which would have become Sir Giles Overreach himself) 'can warrant you in treating with contempt the affectionate regard of an honest heart.'

I was too much shocked at this undisguised attempt to bully me into an acquiescence in the interested and unprincipled plan for their own aggrandisement, which I now perceived my uncle and his son to have deliberately entered into, at once to find strength or collectedness to frame an answer to what he had said. At length I replied, with some firmness:

'In all that you have just now said, sir, you have grossly misstated my conduct and motives. Your information must have been most incorrect as far as it regards my conduct towards my cousin; my manner towards him could have conveyed nothing but dislike; and if anything could have added to the strong aversion which I have long felt towards him, it would be his attempting thus to trick and frighten me into a marriage which he knows to be revolting to me, and which is sought by him only as a means for securing to himself whatever property is mine.'

As I said this, I fixed my eyes upon those of my uncle, but he was too old in the world's ways to falter beneath the gaze of more searching eyes than mine; he simply said:

'Are you acquainted with the provisions of your father's will?'

I answered in the affirmative; and he continued:

'Then you must be aware that if my son Edward were—which God forbid—the unprincipled, reckless man you pretend to think him'—(here he spoke very slowly, as if he intended that every word which escaped him should be registered in my memory, while at the same time the expression of his countenance underwent a gradual but horrible change, and the eyes which he fixed upon me became so darkly vivid, that I almost lost sight of everything else)—'if he were what you have described him, think you, girl, he could find no briefer means than wedding contracts to gain his ends? 'twas but to gripe your slender neck until the breath had stopped, and lands, and lakes, and all were his.'

I stood staring at him for many minutes after he had ceased to speak, fascinated by the terrible serpent-like gaze, until he continued with a welcome change of countenance:

'I will not speak again to you upon this—topic until one month has passed. You shall have time to consider the relative advantages of the two courses which are open to you. I should be sorry to hurry you to a decision. I am satisfied with having stated my feelings upon the subject, and pointed out to you the path of duty. Remember this day month—not one word sooner.'

He then rose, and I left the room, much agitated and exhausted.

This interview, all thc circumstances attending it, but most particularly the formidable expression of my uncle's countenance while he talked, though hypothetically, of murder, combined to arouse all my worst suspicions of him. I dreaded to look upon the face that had so recently worn the appalling livery of guilt and malignity. I regarded it with the mingled fear and loathing with which one looks upon an object which has tortured them in a nightmare.

In a few days after the interview, the particulars of which I have just related, I found a note upon my toilet-table, and on opening it I read as follows:

> 'MY DEAR LADY MARGARET,
>
> 'You will be perhaps surprised to see a strange face in your room to-day. I have dismissed your Irish maid, and secured a French one to wait upon you—a step rendered necessary by my proposing shortly to visit the Continent, with all my family.
>
> 'Your faithful guardian,
>
> 'ARTHUR T——N.'

On inquiry, I found that my faithful attendant was actually gone, and far on her way to the town of Galway; and in her stead there appeared a tall, raw-boned, ill-looking, elderly Frenchwoman, whose sullen and presuming manners seemed to imply that her vocation had never before been that of a lady's-maid. I could not help regarding her as a creature of my uncle's, and therefore to be dreaded, even had she been in no other way suspicious.

Days and weeks passed away without any, even a momentary doubt upon my part, as to the course to be pursued by me. The allotted period had at length elapsed; the day arrived on which I was to communicate my decision to my uncle. Although my resolution had never for a moment wavered, I could not shake of the dread of the approaching colloquy; and my heart sunk within me as I heard the expected summons.

I had not seen my cousin Edward since the occurrence of the grand eclaircissment; he must have studiously avoided me—I suppose from policy, it could not have been from delicacy. I was prepared for a terrific burst of fury from my uncle, as soon as I should make known my determination; and I not unreasonably feared that some act of violence or of intimidation would next be resorted to.

Filled with these dreary forebodings, I fearfully opened the study door, and the next minute I stood in my uncle's presence. He received me with a politeness which I dreaded, as arguing a favourable anticipation respecting the answer which I was to give; and after some slight delay, he began by saying:

'It will be a relief to both of us, I believe, to bring this conversation as soon as possible to an issue. You will excuse me, then, my dear niece, for speaking with an abruptness which, under other circumstances, would be unpardonable. You have, I am certain, given the subject of our last interview fair and serious consideration; and I trust that you are now prepared with candour to lay your answer before me. A few words will suffice—we perfectly understand one another.'

He paused, and I, though feeling that I stood upon a mine which might in an instant explode, nevertheless answered with perfect composure:

'I must now, sir, make the same reply which I did upon the last occasion, and I reiterate the declaration which I then made, that I never can nor will, while life and reason remain, consent to a union with my cousin Edward.'

This announcement wrought no apparent change in Sir Arthur, except that he became deadly, almost lividly pale. He seemed lost in dark thought for a minute, and then with a slight effort said:

'You have answered me honestly and directly; and you say your resolution is unchangeable. Well, would it had been otherwise—would it had been otherwise—but be it as it is—I am satisfied.'

He gave me his hand—it was cold and damp as death; under an assumed calmness, it was evident that he was fearfully agitated. He continued to hold my hand with an almost painful pressure, while, as if unconsciously, seeming to forget my presence, he muttered:

'Strange, strange, strange, indeed! fatuity, helpless fatuity!' there was here a long pause. 'Madness INDEED to strain a cable that is rotten to the very heart—it must break—and then—all goes.'

There was again a pause of some minutes, after which, suddenly changing his voice and manner to one of wakeful alacrity, he exclaimed:

'Margaret, my son Edward shall plague you no more. He leaves this country on to-morrow for France—he shall speak no more upon this subject—never, never more—whatever events depended upon your answer must now take their own course; but, as for this fruitless proposal, it has been tried enough; it can be repeated no more.'

At these words he coldly suffered my hand to drop, as if to express his total abandonment of all his projected schemes of alliance; and certainly the action, with the accompanying words, produced upon my mind a more solemn and depressing effect than I believed possible to have been caused by the course which I had determined to pursue; it struck upon my heart with an awe and heaviness which WILL accompany the accomplishment of an important and irrevocable act, even though no doubt or scruple remains to make it possible that the agent should wish it undone.

'Well,' said my uncle, after a little time, 'we now cease to speak upon this topic, never to resume it again. Remember you shall have no farther uneasiness from Edward; he leaves Ireland for France on to-morrow; this will be a relief to you. May I depend upon your HONOUR that no word touching the subject of this interview shall ever escape you?'

I gave him the desired assurance; he said:

'It is well—I am satisfied—we have nothing more, I believe, to say upon either side, and my presence must be a restraint upon you, I shall therefore bid you farewell.'

I then left the apartment, scarcely knowing what to think of the strange interview which had just taken place.

On the next day my uncle took occasion to tell me that Edward had actually sailed, if his intention had not been interfered with by adverse circumstances; and two days subsequently he actually produced a letter from his son, written, as it said, ON BOARD, and despatched while the ship was getting under weigh. This was a great satisfaction to me, and as being likely to prove so, it was no doubt communicated to me by Sir Arthur.

During all this trying period, I had found infinite consolation in the society and sympathy of my dear cousin Emily. I never in after-life formed a friendship so close, so fervent, and upon which, in all its progress, I could look back with feelings of such unalloyed pleasure, upon whose termination I must ever dwell with so deep, yet so unembittered regret. In cheerful converse with her I soon recovered my spirits considerably, and passed my time agreeably enough, although still in the strictest seclusion.

Matters went on sufficiently smooth, although I could not help sometimes feeling a momentary, but horrible uncertainty respecting my uncle's character; which was not altogether unwarranted by the circumstances of the two trying interviews whose particulars I have just detailed. The unpleasant impression which these conferences were calculated to leave upon my mind, was fast wearing away, when there occurred a circumstance, slight indeed in itself, but calculated irresistibly to awaken all my worst suspicions, and to overwhelm me again with anxiety and terror.

I had one day left the house with my cousin Emily, in order to take a ramble of considerable length, for the purpose of sketching some favourite views, and we had walked about half a mile when I perceived that we had forgotten our drawing materials, the absence of which would have defeated the object of our walk. Laughing at our own thoughtlessness, we returned to the house, and leaving Emily without, I ran upstairs to procure the drawing-books and pencils, which lay in my bedroom.

As I ran up the stairs I was met by the tall, ill-looking Frenchwoman, evidently a good deal flurried.

'Que veut, madame?' said she, with a more decided effort to be polite than I had ever known her make before.

'No, no—no matter,' said I, hastily running by her in the direction of my room.

'Madame,' cried she, in a high key, 'restez ici, s'il vous plait; votre chambre n'est pas faite—your room is not ready for your reception yet.'

I continued to move on without heeding her. She was some way behind me, and feeling that she could not otherwise prevent my entrance, for I was now upon the very lobby, she made a desperate attempt to seize hold of my person: she succeeded in grasping the end of my shawl, which she drew from my shoulders; but slipping at the same time upon the polished oak floor, she fell at full length upon the boards.

A little frightened as well as angry at the rudeness of this strange woman, I hastily pushed open the door of my room, at which I now stood, in order to escape from her; but great was my amazement on entering to find the apartment preoccupied.

The window was open, and beside it stood two male figures; they appeared to be examining the fastenings of the casement, and their backs were turned towards the door. One of them was my uncle; they both turned on my entrance, as if startled. The stranger was booted and cloaked, and wore a heavy broad-leafed hat over his brows. He turned but for a moment, and averted his face; but I had seen enough to convince me that he was no other than my cousin Edward. My uncle had some iron instrument in his hand, which he hastily concealed behind his back; and coming towards me, said something as if in an explanatory tone; but I was too much shocked and confounded to understand what it might be. He said something about 'REPAIRS—window—frames—cold, and safety.'

I did not wait, however, to ask or to receive explanations, but hastily left the room. As I went down the stairs I thought I heard the voice of the Frenchwoman in all the shrill volubility of excuse, which was met, however, by suppressed but vehement imprecations, or what seemed to me to be such, in which the voice of my cousin Edward distinctly mingled.

I joined my cousin Emily quite out of breath. I need not say that my head was too full of other things to think much of drawing for that day. I imparted to her frankly the cause of my alarms, but at the same time as gently as I could; and with tears she promised vigilance, and devotion, and love. I never had reason for a moment to repent the unreserved confidence which I then reposed in her. She was no less surprised than I at the unexpected appearance of Edward, whose departure for France neither of us had for a moment doubted, but which was now proved by his actual presence to be nothing more than an imposture, practised, I feared, for no good end.

The situation in which I had found my uncle had removed completely all my doubts as to his designs. I magnified suspicions into certainties, and dreaded night after night that I should be murdered in my bed. The nervousness produced by sleepless nights and days of anxious fears increased the horrors of my situation to such a degree, that I at length wrote a letter to a Mr. Jefferies, an old and faithful friend of my father's, and perfectly acquainted with all his affairs, praying him, for God's sake, to relieve me from my present terrible situation, and communicating without reserve the nature and grounds of my suspicions.

This letter I kept sealed and directed for two or three days always about my person, for discovery would have been ruinous, in expectation of an opportunity which might be safely trusted, whereby to have it placed in the post-office. As neither Emily nor I were permitted to pass beyond the precincts of the demesne itself, which was surrounded by high walls formed of dry stone, the difficulty of procuring such an opportunity was greatly enhanced.

At this time Emily had a short conversation with her father, which she reported to me instantly.

After some indifferent matter, he had asked her whether she and I were upon good terms, and whether I was unreserved in my disposition. She answered in the affirmative; and he then inquired whether I had been much surprised to find him in my chamber on the other day. She answered that I had been both surprised and amused.

'And what did she think of George Wilson's appearance?'

'Who?' inquired she.

'Oh, the architect,' he answered, 'who is to contract for the repairs of the house; he is accounted a handsome fellow.'

'She could not see his face,' said Emily, 'and she was in such a hurry to escape that she scarcely noticed him.'

Sir Arthur appeared satisfied, and the conversation ended.

This slight conversation, repeated accurately to me by Emily, had the effect of confirming, if indeed anything was required to do so, all that I had before believed as to Edward's actual presence; and I naturally became, if possible, more anxious than ever to despatch the letter to Mr. Jefferies. An opportunity at length occurred.

As Emily and I were walking one day near the gate of the demesne, a lad from the village happened to be passing down the avenue from the house; the spot was secluded, and as this person was not connected by service with those whose observation I dreaded, I committed the letter to his keeping, with strict injunctions that he should put it without delay into the receiver of the town post-office; at the same time I added a suitable gratuity, and the man having made many protestations of punctuality, was soon out of sight.

He was hardly gone when I began to doubt my discretion in having trusted this person; but I had no better or safer means of despatching the letter, and I was not warranted in suspecting him of such wanton dishonesty as an inclination to tamper with it; but I could not be quite satisfied of its safety until I had received an answer, which could not arrive for a few days. Before I did, however, an event occurred which a little surprised me.

I was sitting in my bedroom early in the day, reading by myself, when I heard a knock at the door.

'Come in,' said I; and my uncle entered the room.

'Will you excuse me?' said he. 'I sought you in the parlour, and thence I have come here. I desired to say a word with you. I trust that you have hitherto found my conduct to you such as that of a guardian towards his ward should be.'

I dared not withhold my consent.

'And,' he continued, 'I trust that you have not found me harsh or unjust, and that you have perceived, my dear niece, that I have sought to make this poor place as agreeable to you as may be.'

I assented again; and he put his hand in his pocket, whence he drew a folded paper, and dashing it upon the table with startling emphasis, he said:

'Did you write that letter?'

The sudden and tearful alteration of his voice, manner, and face, but, more than all, the unexpected production of my letter to Mr. Jefferies, which I at once recognised, so confounded and terrified me, that I felt almost choking.

I could not utter a word.

'Did you write that letter?' he repeated with slow and intense emphasis.' You did, liar and hypocrite! You dared to write this foul and infamous libel; but it shall be your last. Men will universally believe you mad, if I choose to call for an inquiry. I can make you appear so. The suspicions expressed in this letter are the hallucinations and alarms of moping lunacy. I have defeated your first attempt, madam; and by the holy God, if ever you make another, chains, straw, darkness, and the keeper's whip shall be your lasting portion!'

With these astounding words he left the room, leaving me almost fainting.

I was now almost reduced to despair; my last cast had failed; I had no course left but that of eloping secretly from the castle, and placing myself under the protection of the nearest magistrate. I felt if this were not done, and speedily, that I should be MURDERED.

No one, from mere description, can have an idea of the unmitigated horror of my situation—a helpless, weak, inexperienced girl, placed under the power and wholly at the mercy of evil men, and feeling that she had it not in her power to escape for a moment from the malignant influences under which she was probably fated to fall; and with a consciousness that if violence, if murder were designed, her dying shriek would be lost in void space; no human being would be near to aid her, no human interposition could deliver her.

I had seen Edward but once during his visit, and as I did not meet with him again, I began to think that he must have taken his departure—a conviction which was to a certain degree satisfactory, as I regarded his absence as indicating the removal of immediate danger.

Emily also arrived circuitously at the same conclusion, and not without good grounds, for she managed indirectly to learn that Edward's black horse had actually been for a day and part of a night in the castle stables, just at the time of her brother's supposed visit. The horse had gone, and, as she argued, the rider must have departed with it.

This point being so far settled, I felt a little less uncomfortable: when being one day alone in my bedroom, I happened to look out from the window, and, to my unutterable horror, I beheld, peering through an opposite casement, my cousin Edward's face. Had I seen the evil one himself in bodily shape, I could not have experienced a more sickening revulsion.

I was too much appalled to move at once from the window, but I did so soon enough to avoid his eye. He was looking fixedly into the narrow quadrangle upon which the window opened. I shrank back unperceived, to pass the rest of the day in terror and despair. I went to my room early that night, but I was too miserable to sleep.

At about twelve o'clock, feeling very nervous, I determined to call my cousin Emily, who slept, you will remember, in the next room, which communicated with mine by a second door. By this private entrance I found my way into her chamber, and without difficulty persuaded her to return to my room and sleep with me. We accordingly lay down together, she undressed, and I with my clothes on, for I was every moment walking up and down the room, and felt too nervous and miserable to think of rest or comfort.

Emily was soon fast asleep, and I lay awake, fervently longing for the first pale gleam of morning, reckoning every stroke of the old clock with an impatience which made every hour appear like six.

It must have been about one o'clock when I thought I heard a slight noise at the partition-door between Emily's room and mine, as if caused by somebody's turning the key in the lock. I held my breath, and the same sound was repeated at the second door of my room—that which opened upon the lobby—the sound was here distinctly caused by the revolution of the bolt in the lock, and it was followed by a slight pressure upon the door itself, as if to ascertain the security of the lock.

The person, whoever it might be, was probably satisfied, for I heard the old boards of the lobby creak and strain, as if under the weight of somebody moving cautiously over them. My sense of hearing became unnaturally, almost painfully acute. I suppose the imagination added distinctness to sounds vague in themselves. I thought that I could actually hear the breathing of the person who was slowly returning down the lobby. At the head of the staircase there appeared to occur a pause; and I could distinctly hear two or three sentences hastily whispered; the steps then descended the stairs with apparently less caution. I now ventured to walk quickly and lightly to the lobby-door, and attempted to open it; it was indeed fast locked upon the outside, as was also the other.

I now felt that the dreadful hour was come; but one desperate expedient remained—it was to awaken Emily, and by our united strength to attempt to force the partition-door, which was slighter than the other, and through this to pass to the lower part of the house, whence it might be possible to escape to the grounds, and forth to the village.

I returned to the bedside and shook Emily, but in vain. Nothing that I could do availed to produce from her more than a few incoherent words—it was a deathlike sleep. She had certainly drank of some narcotic, as had I probably also, spite of all the caution with which I had examined everything presented to us to eat or drink.

I now attempted, with as little noise as possible, to force first one door, then the other—but all in vain. I believe no strength could have effected my object, for both doors opened inwards. I therefore collected whatever movables I could carry thither, and piled them against the doors, so as to assist me in whatever attempts I should make to resist the entrance of those without. I then returned to the bed and endeavoured again, but fruitlessly, to awaken my cousin. It was not sleep, it was torpor, lethargy, death. I knelt down and prayed with an agony of earnestness; and then seating myself upon the bed, I awaited my fate with a kind of terrible tranquillity.

I heard a faint clanking sound from the narrow court which I have already mentioned, as if caused by the scraping of some iron instrument against stones or rubbish. I at first determined not to disturb the calmness which I now felt, by uselessly watching the proceedings of those who sought my life; but as the sounds continued, the horrible curiosity which I felt overcame every other emotion, and I determined, at all hazards, to gratify it. I therefore crawled upon my knees to the window, so as to let the smallest portion of my head appear above the sill.

The moon was shining with an uncertain radiance upon the antique grey buildings, and obliquely upon the narrow court beneath, one side of which was therefore clearly illuminated, while the other was lost in obscurity, the sharp outlines of the old gables, with their nodding clusters of ivy, being at first alone visible.

Whoever or whatever occasioned the noise which had excited my curiosity, was concealed under the shadow of the dark side of the quadrangle. I placed my hand over my eyes to shade them from the moonlight, which was so bright as to be almost dazzling, and, peering into the darkness, I first dimly, but afterwards gradually, almost with full distinctness, beheld the form of a man engaged in digging what appeared to be a rude hole close under the wall. Some implements, probably a shovel and pickaxe, lay beside him, and to these he every now and then applied himself as the nature of the ground required. He pursued his task rapidly, and with as little noise as possible.

'So,' thought I, as, shovelful after shovelful, the dislodged rubbish mounted into a heap, 'they are digging the grave in which, before two hours pass, I must lie, a cold, mangled corpse. I am THEIRS—I cannot escape.'

I felt as if my reason was leaving me. I started to my feet, and in mere despair I applied myself again to each of the two doors alternately. I strained every nerve and sinew, but I might as well have attempted, with my single strength, to force the building itself from its foundation. I threw myself madly upon the ground, and clasped my hands over my eyes as if to shut out the horrible images which crowded upon me.

The paroxysm passed away. I prayed once more, with the bitter, agonised fervour of one who feels that the hour of death is present and inevitable. When I arose, I went once more to the window and looked out, just in time to see a shadowy figure glide stealthily along the wall. The task was finished. The catastrophe of the tragedy must soon be accomplished.

I determined now to defend my life to the last; and that I might be able to do so with some effect, I searched the room for something which might serve as a weapon; but either through accident, or from an anticipation of such a possibility, everything which might have been made available for such a purpose had been carefully removed. I must then die tamely and without an effort to defend myself.

A thought suddenly struck me—might it not be possible to escape through the door, which the assassin must open in order to enter the room? I resolved to make the attempt. I felt assured that the door through which ingress to the room would be effected, was that which opened upon the lobby. It was the more direct way, besides being, for obvious reasons, less liable to interruption than the other. I resolved, then, to place myself behind a projection of the wall, whose shadow would serve fully to conceal me, and when the door should be opened, and before they should have discovered the identity of the occupant of the bed, to creep noiselessly from the room, and then to trust to Providence for escape.

In order to facilitate this scheme, I removed all the lumber which I had heaped against the door; and I had nearly completed my arrangements, when I perceived the room suddenly darkened by the close approach of some shadowy object to the window. On turning my eyes in that direction, I observed at the top of the casement, as if suspended from above, first the feet, then the legs, then the body, and at length the whole figure of a man present himself. It was Edward T——n.

He appeared to be guiding his descent so as to bring his feet upon the centre of the stone block which occupied the lower part of the window; and, having secured his footing upon this, he kneeled down and began to gaze into the room. As the moon was gleaming into the chamber, and the bed-curtains were drawn, he was able to distinguish the bed itself and its contents. He appeared satisfied with his scrutiny, for he looked up and made a sign with his hand, upon which the rope by which his descent had been effected was slackened from above, and he proceeded to disengage it from his waist; this accomplished, he applied his hands to the window-frame, which must have been ingeniously contrived for the purpose, for, with apparently no resistance, the whole frame, containing casement and all, slipped from its position in the wall, and was by him lowered into the room.

The cold night wind waved the bed-curtains, and he paused for a moment—all was still again—and he stepped in upon the floor of the room. He held in his hand what appeared to be a steel instrument, shaped something like a hammer, but larger and sharper at the extremities. This he held rather behind him, while, with three long, tip-toe strides, he brought himself to the bedside.

I felt that the discovery must now be made, and held my breath in momentary expectation of the execration in which he would vent his surprise and disappointment. I closed my eyes—there was a pause, but it was a short one. I heard two dull blows, given in rapid succession: a quivering sigh, and the long-drawn, heavy breathing of the sleeper was for ever suspended. I unclosed my eyes, and saw the murderer fling the quilt across the head of his victim: he then, with the instrument of death still in his hand, proceeded to the lobby-door, upon which he tapped sharply twice or thrice. A quick step was then heard approaching, and a voice whispered something from without. Edward answered, with a kind of chuckle, 'Her ladyship is past complaining; unlock the door, in the devil's name, unless you're afraid to come in, and help me to lift the body out of the window.'

The key was turned in the lock—the door opened—and my uncle entered the room.

I have told you already that I had placed myself under the shade of a projection of the wall, close to the door. I had instinctively shrunk down, cowering towards the ground on the entrance of Edward through the window. When my uncle entered the room he and his son both stood so very close to me that his hand was every moment upon the point of touching my face. I held my breath, and remained motionless as death.

'You had no interruption from the next room?' said my uncle.

'No,' was the brief reply.

'Secure the jewels, Ned; the French harpy must not lay her claws upon them. You're a steady hand, by G——! not much blood—eh?'

'Not twenty drops,' replied his son, 'and those on the quilt.'

'I'm glad it's over,' whispered my uncle again. 'We must lift the—the THING through the window, and lay the rubbish over it.'

They then turned to the bedside, and, winding the bed-clothes round the body, carried it between them slowly to the window, and, exchanging a few brief words with some one below, they shoved it over the window-sill, and I heard it fall heavily on the ground underneath.

'I'll take the jewels,' said my uncle; 'there are two caskets in the lower drawer.'

He proceeded, with an accuracy which, had I been more at ease, would have furnished me with matter of astonishment, to lay his hand upon the very spot where my jewels lay; and having possessed himself of them, he called to his son:

'Is the rope made fast above?'

'I'm not a fool—to be sure it is,' replied he.

They then lowered themselves from the window. I now rose lightly and cautiously, scarcely daring to breathe, from my place of concealment, and was creeping towards the door, when I heard my cousin's voice, in a sharp whisper, exclaim: 'Scramble up again! G—d d——n you, you've forgot to lock the room-door!' and I perceived, by the straining of the rope which hung from above, that the mandate was instantly obeyed.

Not a second was to be lost. I passed through the door, which was only closed, and moved as rapidly as I could, consistently with stillness, along the lobby. Before I had gone many yards, I heard the door through which I had just passed double-locked on the inside. I glided down the stairs in terror, lest, at every corner, I should meet the murderer or one of his accomplices.

I reached the hall, and listened for a moment to ascertain whether all was silent around; no sound was audible. The parlour windows opened on the park, and through one of them I might, I thought, easily effect my escape. Accordingly, I hastily entered; but, to my consternation, a candle was burning in the room, and by its light I saw a figure seated at the dinner-table, upon which lay glasses, bottles, and the other accompaniments of a drinking-party. Two or three chairs were placed about the table irregularly, as if hastily abandoned by their occupants.

A single glance satisfied me that the figure was that of my French attendant. She was fast asleep, having probably drank deeply. There was something malignant and ghastly in the calmness of this bad woman's features, dimly illuminated as they were by the flickering blaze of the candle. A knife lay upon the table, and the terrible thought struck me—'Should I kill this sleeping accomplice in the guilt of the murderer, and thus secure my retreat?'

Nothing could be easier—it was but to draw the blade across her throat—the work of a second. An instant's pause, however, corrected me. 'No,' thought I, 'the God who has conducted me thus far through the valley of the shadow of death, will not abandon me now. I will fall into their hands, or I will escape hence, but it shall be free from the stain of blood. His will be done.'

I felt a confidence arising from this reflection, an assurance of protection which I cannot describe. There was no other means of escape, so I advanced, with a firm step and collected mind, to the window. I noiselessly withdrew the bars and unclosed the shutters—I pushed open the casement, and, without waiting to look behind me, I ran with my utmost speed, scarcely feeling the ground under me, down the avenue, taking care to keep upon the grass which bordered it.

I did not for a moment slack my speed, and I had now gained the centre point between the park-gate and the mansion-house. Here the avenue made a wider circuit, and in order to avoid delay, I directed my way across the smooth sward round which the pathway wound, intending, at the opposite side of the flat, at a point which I distinguished by a group of old birch-trees, to enter again upon the beaten track, which was from thence tolerably direct to the gate.

I had, with my utmost speed, got about half way across this broad flat, when the rapid treading of a horse's hoofs struck upon my ear. My heart swelled in my bosom as though I would smother. The clattering of galloping hoofs approached—I was pursued—they were now upon the sward on which I was running—there was not a bush or a bramble to shelter me—and, as if to render escape altogether desperate, the moon, which had hitherto been obscured, at this moment shone forth with a broad clear light, which made every object distinctly visible.

The sounds were now close behind me. I felt my knees bending under me, with the sensation which torments one in dreams. I reeled—I stumbled—I fell—and at the same instant the cause of my alarm wheeled past me at full gallop. It was one of the young fillies which pastured loose about the park, whose frolics had thus all but maddened me with terror. I scrambled to my feet, and rushed on with weak but rapid steps, my sportive companion still galloping round and round me with many a frisk and fling, until, at length, more dead than alive, I reached the avenue-gate and crossed the stile, I scarce knew how.

I ran through the village, in which all was silent as the grave, until my progress was arrested by the hoarse voice of a sentinel, who cried: 'Who goes there?' I felt that I was now safe. I turned in the direction of the voice, and fell fainting at the soldier's feet. When I came to myself; I was sitting in a miserable hovel, surrounded by strange faces, all bespeaking curiosity and compassion.

Many soldiers were in it also: indeed, as I afterwards found, it was employed as a guard-room by a detachment of troops quartered for that night in the town. In a few words I informed their officer of the circumstances which had occurred, describing also the appearance of the persons engaged in the murder; and he, without loss of time, proceeded to the mansion-house of Carrickleigh, taking with him a party of his men. But the villains had discovered their mistake, and had effected their escape before the arrival of the military.

The Frenchwoman was, however, arrested in the neighbourhood upon the next day. She was tried and condemned upon the ensuing assizes; and previous to her execution, confessed that 'SHE HAD A HAND IN MAKING HUGH TISDAL'S BED.' She had been a housekeeper in the castle at the time, and a kind of chere amie of my uncle's. She was, in reality, able to speak English like a native, but had exclusively used the French language, I suppose to facilitate her disguise. She died the same hardened wretch which she had lived, confessing her crimes only, as she alleged, that her doing so might involve Sir Arthur T——n, the great author of her guilt and misery, and whom she now regarded with unmitigated detestation.

With the particulars of Sir Arthur's and his son's escape, as far as they are known, you are acquainted. You are also in possession of their after fate—the terrible, the tremendous retribution which, after long delays of many years, finally overtook and crushed them. Wonderful and inscrutable are the dealings of God with His creatures.

Deep and fervent as must always be my gratitude to heaven for my deliverance, effected by a chain of providential occurrences, the failing of a single link of which must have ensured my destruction, I was long before I could look back upon it with other feelings than those of bitterness, almost of agony.

The only being that had ever really loved me, my nearest and dearest friend, ever ready to sympathise, to counsel, and to assist—the gayest, the gentlest, the warmest heart—the only creature on earth that cared for me—HER life had been the price of my deliverance; and I then uttered the wish, which no event of my long and sorrowful life has taught me to recall, that she had been spared, and that, in her stead, *I* were mouldering in the grave, forgotten and at rest.

THE BRIDAL OF CARRIGVARAH.

Being a Sixth Extract from the Legacy of the late Francis Purcell, P. P. of Drumcoolagh.

In a sequestered district of the county of Limerick, there stood my early life, some forty years ago, one of those strong stone buildings, half castle, half farm-house, which are not unfrequent in the South of Ireland, and whose solid masonry and massive construction seem to prove at once the insecurity and the caution of the Cromwellite settlers who erected them. At the time of which I speak, this building was tenanted by an elderly man, whose starch and puritanic mien and manners might have become the morose preaching parliamentarian captain, who had raised the house and ruled the household more than a hundred years before; but this man, though Protestant by descent as by name, was not so in religion; he was a strict, and in outward observances, an exemplary Catholic; his father had returned in early youth to the true faith, and died in the bosom of the church.

Martin Heathcote was, at the time of which I speak, a widower, but his house-keeping was not on that account altogether solitary, for he had a daughter, whose age was now sufficiently advanced to warrant her father in imposing upon her the grave duties of domestic superintendence.

This little establishment was perfectly isolated, and very little intruded upon by acts of neighbourhood; for the rank of its occupants was of that equivocal kind which precludes all familiar association with those of a decidedly inferior rank, while it is not sufficient to entitle its possessors to the society of established gentility, among whom the nearest residents were the O'Maras of Carrigvarah, whose mansion-house, constructed out of the ruins of an old abbey, whose towers and cloisters had been levelled by the shot of Cromwell's artillery, stood not half a mile lower upon the river banks.

Colonel O'Mara, the possessor of the estates, was then in a declining state of health, and absent with his lady from the country, leaving at the castle, his son young O'Mara, and a kind of humble companion, named Edward Dwyer, who, if report belied him not, had done in his early days some PECULIAR SERVICES for the Colonel, who had been a gay man—perhaps worse—but enough of recapitulation.

It was in the autumn of the year 17— that the events which led to the catastrophe which I have to detail occurred. I shall run through the said recital as briefly as clearness will permit, and leave you to moralise, if such be your mood, upon the story of real life, which I even now trace at this distant period not without emotion.

It was upon a beautiful autumn evening, at that glad period of the season when the harvest yields its abundance, that two figures were seen sauntering along the banks of the winding river, which I described as bounding the farm occupied by Heathcote; they had been, as the rods and landing-nets which they listlessly carried went to show, plying the gentle, but in this case not altogether solitary craft of the fisherman. One of those persons was a tall and singularly handsome young man, whose dark hair and complexion might almost have belonged to a Spaniard, as might also the proud but melancholy expression which gave to his countenance a character which contrasts sadly, but not uninterestingly, with extreme youth; his air, as he spoke with his companion, was marked by that careless familiarity which denotes a conscious superiority of one kind or other, or which may be construed into a species of contempt; his comrade afforded to him in every respect a striking contrast. He was rather low in stature—a defect which was enhanced by a broad and square-built figure—his face was sallow, and his features had that prominence and sharpness which frequently accompany personal deformity—a remarkably wide mouth, with teeth white as the fangs of a wolf, and a pair of quick, dark eyes, whose effect was heightened by the shadow of a heavy black brow, gave to his face a power of expression, particularly when sarcastic or malignant emotions were to be exhibited, which features regularly handsome could scarcely have possessed.

'Well, sir,' said the latter personage, 'I have lived in hall and abbey, town and country, here and abroad for forty years and more, and should know a thing or two, and as I am a living man, I swear I think the girl loves you.'

'You are a fool, Ned,' said the younger.

'I may be a fool,' replied the first speaker, 'in matters where my own advantage is staked, but my eye is keen enough to see through the flimsy disguise of a country damsel at a glance; and I tell you, as surely as I hold this rod, the girl loves you.'

'Oh I this is downright headstrong folly,' replied the young fisherman. 'Why, Ned, you try to persuade me against my reason, that the event which is most to be deprecated has actually occurred. She is, no doubt, a pretty girl—a beautiful girl—but I have not lost my heart to her; and why should I wish her to be in love with me? Tush, man, the days of romance are gone, and a young gentleman may talk, and walk, and laugh with a pretty country maiden, and never breathe aspirations, or vows, or sighs about the matter; unequal matches are much oftener read of than made, and the man who could, even in thought, conceive a wish against the honour of an unsuspecting, artless girl, is a villain, for whom hanging is too good.'

This concluding sentence was uttered with an animation and excitement, which the mere announcement of an abstract moral sentiment could hardly account for.

'You are, then, indifferent, honestly and in sober earnest, indifferent to the girl?' inquired Dwyer.

'Altogether so,' was the reply.

'Then I have a request to make,' continued Dwyer, 'and I may as well urge it now as at any other time. I have been for nearly twenty years the faithful, and by no means useless, servant of your family; you know that I have rendered your father critical and important services——' he paused, and added hastily: 'you are not in the mood—I tire you, sir.'

'Nay,' cried O'Mara, 'I listen patiently—proceed.'

'For all these services, and they were not, as I have said, few or valueless, I have received little more reward than liberal promises; you have told me often that this should be mended—I'll make it easily done—I'm not unreasonable—I should be contented to hold Heathcote's ground, along with this small farm on which we stand, as full quittance of all obligations and promises between us.'

'But how the devil can I effect that for you; this farm, it is true, I, or my father, rather, may lease to you, but Heathcote's title we cannot impugn; and even if we could, you would not expect us to ruin an honest man, in order to make way for YOU, Ned.'

'What I am,' replied Dwyer, with the calmness of one who is so accustomed to contemptuous insinuations as to receive them with perfect indifference, 'is to be attributed to my devotedness to your honourable family—but that is neither here nor there. I do not ask you to displace Heathcote, in order to made room for me. I know it is out of your power to do so. Now hearken to me for a moment; Heathcote's property, that which he has set out to tenants, is worth, say in rents, at most, one hundred pounds: half of this yearly amount is assigned to your father, until payment be made of a bond for a thousand pounds, with interest and soforth. Hear me patiently for a moment and I have done. Now go you to Heathcote, and tell him your father will burn the bond, and cancel the debt, upon one condition—that when I am in possession of this farm, which you can lease to me on what terms you think suitable, he will convey over his property to me, reserving what life-interest may appear fair, I engaging at the same time to marry his daughter, and make such settlements upon her as shall be thought fitting—he is not a fool—the man will close with the offer.'

O'Mara turned shortly upon Dwyer, and gazed upon him for a moment with an expression of almost unmixed resentment.

'How,' said he at length, 'YOU contract to marry Ellen Heathcote? the poor, innocent, confiding, light-hearted girl. No, no, Edward Dwyer, I know you too well for that—your services, be they what they will, must not, shall not go unrewarded—your avarice shall be appeased—but not with a human sacrifice! Dwyer, I speak to you without disguise; you know me to be acquainted with your history, and what's more, with your character. Now tell me frankly, were I to do as you desire me, in cool blood, should I not prove myself a more uncompromising and unfeeling villain than humanity even in its most monstrous shapes has ever yet given birth to?'

Dwyer met this impetuous language with the unmoved and impenetrable calmness which always marked him when excitement would have appeared in others; he even smiled as he replied: (and Dwyer's smile, for I have seen it, was characteristically of that unfortunate kind which implies, as regards the emotions of others, not sympathy but derision).

'This eloquence goes to prove Ellen Heathcote something nearer to your heart than your great indifference would have led me to suppose.'

There was something in the tone, perhaps in the truth of the insinuation, which at once kindled the quick pride and the anger of O'Mara, and he instantly replied:

'Be silent, sir, this is insolent folly.'

Whether it was that Dwyer was more keenly interested in the success of his suit, or more deeply disappointed at its failure than he cared to express, or that he was in a less complacent mood than was his wont, it is certain that his countenance expressed more emotion at this direct insult than it had ever exhibited before under similar circumstances; for his eyes gleamed for an instant with savage and undisguised ferocity upon the young man, and a dark glow crossed his brow, and for the moment he looked about to spring at the throat of his insolent patron; but the impulse whatever it might be, was quickly suppressed, and before O'Mara had time to detect the scowl, it had vanished.

'Nay, sir,' said Dwyer, 'I meant no offence, and I will take none, at your hands at least. I will confess I care not, in love and soforth, a single bean for the girl; she was the mere channel through which her father's wealth, if such a pittance deserves the name, was to have flowed into my possession—'twas in respect of your family finances the most economical provision for myself which I could devise—a matter in which you, not I, are interested. As for women, they are all pretty much alike to me. I am too old myself to make nice distinctions, and too ugly to succeed by Cupid's arts; and when a man despairs of success, he soon ceases to care for it. So, if you know me, as you profess to do, rest satisfied "caeteris paribus;" the money part of the transaction being equally advantageous, I should regret the loss of Ellen Heathcote just as little as I should the escape of a minnow from my landing-net.'

They walked on for a few minutes in silence, which was not broken till Dwyer, who had climbed a stile in order to pass a low stone wall which lay in their way, exclaimed:

'By the rood, she's here—how like a philosopher you look.'

The conscious blood mounted to O'Mara's cheek; he crossed the stile, and, separated from him only by a slight fence and a gate, stood the subject of their recent and somewhat angry discussion.

'God save you, Miss Heathcote,' cried Dwyer, approaching the gate.

The salutation was cheerfully returned, and before anything more could pass, O'Mara had joined the party.

My friend, that you may understand the strength and depth of those impetuous passions, that you may account for the fatal infatuation which led to the catastrophe which I have to relate, I must tell you, that though I have seen the beauties of cities and of courts, with all the splendour of studied ornament about them to enhance their graces, possessing charms which had made them known almost throughout the world, and worshipped with the incense of a thousand votaries, yet never, nowhere did I behold a being of such exquisite and touching beauty, as that possessed by the creature of whom I have just spoken. At the moment of which I write, she was standing near the gate, close to which several brown-armed, rosy-cheeked damsels were engaged in milking the peaceful cows, who stood picturesquely grouped together. She had just thrown back the hood which is the graceful characteristic of the Irish girl's attire, so that her small and classic head was quite uncovered, save only by the dark-brown hair, which with graceful simplicity was parted above her forehead. There was nothing to shade the clearness of her beautiful complexion; the delicately-formed features, so exquisite when taken singly, so indescribable when combined, so purely artless, yet so meet for all expression. She was a thing so very beautiful, you could not look on her without feeling your heart touched as by sweet music. Whose lightest action was a grace—whose lightest word a spell—no limner's art, though ne'er so perfect, could shadow forth her beauty; and do I dare with feeble words try to make you see it[1]? Providence is indeed no respecter of persons, its blessings and its inflictions are apportioned with an undistinguishing hand, and until the race is over, and life be done, none can know whether those perfections, which seemed its goodliest gifts, many not prove its most fatal; but enough of this.

Dwyer strolled carelessly onward by the banks of the stream, leaving his young companion leaning over the gate in close and interesting parlance with Ellen Heathcote; as he moved on, he half thought, half uttered words to this effect:

'Insolent young spawn of ingratitude and guilt, how long must I submit to be trod upon thus; and yet why should I murmur—his day is even now declining—and if I live a year, I shall see the darkness cover him and his for ever. Scarce half his broad estates shall save him—but I must wait—I am but a pauper now—a beggar's accusation is always a libel—they must reward me soon—and were I independent once, I'd make them feel my power, and feel it SO, that I should die the richest or the best avenged servant of a great man that has ever been heard of—yes, I must wait—I must make sure of something at least—I must be able to stand by myself—and then—and then—' He clutched his fingers together, as if in the act of strangling the object of his hatred. 'But one thing shall save him—but one thing only—he shall pay me my own price—and if he acts liberally, as no doubt he will do, upon compulsion, why he saves his reputation—perhaps his

[1] Father Purcell seems to have had an admiration for the beauties of nature, particularly as developed in the fair sex; a habit of mind which has been rather improved upon than discontinued by his successors from Maynooth.—ED.

neck—the insolent young whelp yonder would speak in an humbler key if he but knew his father's jeopardy—but all in good time.'

He now stood upon the long, steep, narrow bridge, which crossed the river close to Carrigvarah, the family mansion of the O'Maras; he looked back in the direction in which he had left his companion, and leaning upon the battlement, he ruminated long and moodily. At length he raised himself and said:

'He loves the girl, and WILL love her more—I have an opportunity of winning favour, of doing service, which shall bind him to me; yes, he shall have the girl, if I have art to compass the matter. I must think upon it.'

He entered the avenue and was soon lost in the distance.

Days and weeks passed on, and young O'Mara daily took his rod and net, and rambled up the river; and scarce twelve hours elapsed in which some of those accidents, which invariably bring lovers together, did not secure him a meeting of longer or shorter duration, with the beautiful girl whom he so fatally loved.

One evening, after a long interview with her, in which he had been almost irresistibly prompted to declare his love, and had all but yielded himself up to the passionate impulse, upon his arrival at home he found a letter on the table awaiting his return; it was from his father to the following effect:

To Richard O'Mara.

'September, 17—, L——m, England.

'MY DEAR SON,—

'I have just had a severe attack of my old and almost forgotten enemy, the gout. This I regard as a good sign; the doctors telling me that it is the safest development of peccant humours; and I think my chest is less tormenting and oppressed than I have known it for some years. My chief reason for writing to you now, as I do it not without difficulty, is to let you know my pleasure in certain matters, in which I suspect some shameful, and, indeed, infatuated neglect on your part, "quem perdere vult deus prius dementat:" how comes it that you have neglected to write to Lady Emily or any of that family? the understood relation subsisting between you is one of extreme delicacy, and which calls for marked and courteous, nay, devoted attention upon your side. Lord —— is already offended; beware what you do; for as you will find, if this match be lost by your fault or folly, by —— I will cut you off with a shilling. I am not in the habit of using threats when I do not mean to fulfil them, and that you well know; however I do not think you have much real cause for alarm in this case. Lady Emily, who, by the way, looks if possible more charming than ever, is anything but hard-hearted, at least when YOU solicit; but do as I desire, and lose no time in making what excuse you may, and let me hear from you when you can fix a time to join me and your mother here.

'Your sincere well-wisher and father,

'RICHARD O'MARA.'

In this letter was inclosed a smaller one, directed to Dwyer, and containing a cheque for twelve pounds, with the following words:

'Make use of the enclosed, and let me hear if Richard is upon any wild scheme at present: I am uneasy about him, and not without reason; report to me speedily the result of your vigilance.

'R. O'MARA.'

Dwyer just glanced through this brief, but not unwelcome, epistle; and deposited it and its contents in the secret recesses of his breeches pocket, and then fixed his eyes upon the face of his companion, who sat opposite, utterly absorbed in the perusal of his father's letter, which he read again and again, pausing and muttering between whiles, and apparently lost in no very pleasing reflections. At length he very abruptly exclaimed:

'A delicate epistle, truly—and a politic—would that my tongue had been burned through before I assented to that doubly-cursed contract. Why, I am not pledged yet—I am not; there is neither writing, nor troth, nor word of honour, passed between us. My father has no right to pledge me, even though I told him I liked the girl, and would wish the match. 'Tis not enough that my father offers her my heart and hand; he has no right to do it; a delicate woman would not accept professions made by proxy. Lady Emily! Lady Emily! with all the tawdry frippery, and finery of dress and demeanour—compare HER with—— Pshaw! Ridiculous! How blind, how idiotic I have been.'

He relapsed into moody reflections, which Dwyer did not care to disturb, and some ten minutes might have passed before he spoke again. When he did, it was in the calm tone of one who has irrevocably resolved upon some decided and important act.

'Dwyer,' he said, rising and approaching that person, 'whatever god or demon told you, even before my own heart knew it, that I loved Ellen Heathcote, spoke truth. I love her madly—I never dreamed till now how fervently, how irrevocably, I am hers—how dead to me all other interests are. Dwyer, I know something of your disposition, and you no doubt think it strange that I should tell to you, of all persons, SUCH a secret; but whatever be your faults, I think you are attached to our family. I am satisfied you will not betray me. I know——'

'Pardon me,' said Dwyer, 'if I say that great professions of confidence too frequently mark distrust. I have no possible motive to induce me to betray you; on the contrary, I would gladly assist and direct whatever plans you may have formed. Command me as you please; I have said enough.'

'I will not doubt you, Dwyer,' said O'Mara; 'I have taken my resolution—I have, I think, firmness to act up to it. To marry Ellen Heathcote, situated as I am, were madness; to propose anything else were worse, were villainy not to be named. I will leave the country to-morrow, cost what pain it may, for England. I will at once break off the proposed alliance with Lady Emily, and will wait until I am my own master, to open my heart to Ellen. My father may say and do what he likes; but his passion will not last. He will forgive me; and even were he to disinherit me, as he threatens, there is some property which must descend to me, which his will cannot affect. He cannot ruin my interests; he SHALL NOT ruin my happiness. Dwyer, give me pen and ink; I will write this moment.'

This bold plan of proceeding for many reasons appeared inexpedient to Dwyer, and he determined not to consent to its adoption without a struggle.

'I commend your prudence,' said he, 'in determining to remove yourself from the fascinating influence which has so long bound you here; but beware of offending your father. Colonel O'Mara is not a man to forgive an act of deliberate disobedience, and surely you are not mad enough to ruin yourself with him by offering an outrageous insult to Lady Emily and to her family in her person; therefore you must not break off the understood contract which subsists between you by any formal act—hear me out patiently. You must let Lady Emily perceive, as you easily may, without rudeness or even coldness of manner, that she is perfectly indifferent to you; and when she understands this to be the case, it she possesses either delicacy or spirit, she will herself break off the engagement. Make what delay it is possible to effect; it is very possible that your father, who cannot, in all probability, live many months, may not live as many days if harassed and excited by such scenes as your breaking off your engagement must produce.'

'Dwyer,' said O'Mara, 'I will hear you out—proceed.'

'Besides, sir, remember,' he continued, 'the understanding which we have termed an engagement was entered into without any direct sanction upon your part; your father has committed HIMSELF, not YOU, to Lord ——. Before a real contract can subsist, you must be an assenting party to it. I know of no casuistry subtle enough to involve you in any engagement whatever, without such an ingredient. Tush! you have an easy card to play.'

'Well,' said the young man, 'I will think on what you have said; in the meantime, I will write to my father to announce my immediate departure, in order to join him.'

'Excuse me,' said Dwyer, 'but I would suggest that by hastening your departure you but bring your dangers nearer. While you are in this country a letter now and then keeps everything quiet; but once across the Channel and with the colonel, you must either quarrel with him to your own destruction, or you must dance attendance upon Lady Emily with such assiduity as to commit yourself as completely as if you had been thrice called with her in the parish church. No, no; keep to this side of the Channel as long as you decently can. Besides, your sudden departure must appear suspicious, and will probably excite inquiry. Every good end likely to be accomplished by your absence will be effected as well by your departure for Dublin, where you may remain for three weeks or a month without giving rise to curiosity or doubt of an unpleasant kind; I would therefore advise you strongly to write immediately to the colonel, stating that business has occurred to defer your departure for a month, and you can then leave this place, if you think fit, immediately, that is, within a week or so.'

Young O'Mara was not hard to be persuaded. Perhaps it was that, unacknowledged by himself, any argument which recommended his staying, even for an hour longer than his first decision had announced, in the neighbourhood of Ellen Heathcote, appeared peculiarly cogent and convincing; however this may have been, it is certain that he followed the counsel of his cool-headed follower, who retired that night to bed with the pleasing conviction that he was likely soon to involve his young patron in all the intricacies of disguise and intrigue—a consummation which would leave him totally at the mercy of the favoured confidant who should possess his secret.

Young O'Mara's reflections were more agitating and less satisfactory than those of his companion. He resolved upon leaving the country before two days had passed. He felt that he could not fairly seek to involve Ellen Heathcote in his fate by pledge or promise, until he had extricated himself from those trammels which constrained and embarrassed all his actions. His determination was so far prudent; but, alas! he also resolved that it was but right, but necessary, that he should see her before his departure. His leaving the country without a look or a word of parting kindness interchanged, must to her appear an act of cold and heartless caprice; he could not bear the thought.

'No,' said he, 'I am not child enough to say more than prudence tells me ought to say; this cowardly distrust of my firmness I should and will contemn. Besides, why should I commit myself? It is possible the girl may not care for me. No, no; I need not shrink from this interview. I have no reason to doubt my firmness—none—none. I must cease to be governed by impulse. I am involved in rocks and quicksands; and a collected spirit, a quick eye, and a steady hand, alone can pilot me through. God grant me a safe voyage!'

The next day came, and young O'Mara did not take his fishing rod as usual, but wrote two letters; the one to his father, announcing his intention of departing speedily for England; the other to Lady Emily, containing a cold but courteous apology for his apparent neglect. Both these were despatched to the post-office that evening, and upon the next morning he was to leave the country.

Upon the night of the momentous day of which we have just spoken, Ellen Heathcote glided silently and unperceived from among the busy crowds who were engaged in the gay dissipation furnished by what is in Ireland commonly called a dance (the expenses attendant upon which, music, etc., are defrayed by a subscription of one halfpenny each), and having drawn her mantle closely about her, was proceeding with quick steps to traverse the small field which separated her from her father's abode. She had not walked many yards when she became aware that a solitary figure, muffled in a cloak, stood in the pathway. It approached; a low voice whispered:

'Ellen.'

'Is it you, Master Richard?' she replied.

He threw back the cloak which had concealed his features.

'It is I, Ellen, he said; 'I have been watching for you. I will not delay you long.'

He took her hand, and she did not attempt to withdraw it; for she was too artless to think any evil, too confiding to dread it.

'Ellen,' he continued, even now unconsciously departing from the rigid course which prudence had marked out; 'Ellen, I am going to leave the country; going to-morrow. I have had letters from England. I must go; and the sea will soon be between us.'

He paused, and she was silent.

'There is one request, one entreaty I have to make,' he continued; 'I would, when I am far away, have something to look at which belonged to you. Will you give me—do not refuse it—one little lock of your beautiful hair?'

With artless alacrity, but with trembling hand, she took the scissors, which in simple fashion hung by her side, and detached one of the long and beautiful locks which parted over her forehead. She placed it in his hand.

Again he took her hand, and twice he attempted to speak in vain; at length he said:

'Ellen, when I am gone—when I am away—will you sometimes remember, sometimes think of me?'

Ellen Heathcote had as much, perhaps more, of what is noble in pride than the haughtiest beauty that ever trod a court; but the effort was useless; the honest struggle was in vain; and she burst into floods of tears, bitterer than she had ever shed before.

I cannot tell how passions rise and fall; I cannot describe the impetuous words of the young lover, as pressing again and again to his lips the cold, passive hand, which had been resigned to him, prudence, caution, doubts, resolutions, all vanished from his view, and melted into nothing. 'Tis for me to tell the simple fact, that from that brief interview they both departed promised and pledged to each other for ever.

Through the rest of this story events follow one another rapidly.

A few nights after that which I have just mentioned, Ellen Heathcote disappeared; but her father was not left long in suspense as to her fate, for Dwyer, accompanied by one of those mendicant friars who traversed the country then even more commonly than they now do, called upon Heathcote before he had had time to take any active measures for the recovery of his child, and put him in possession of a document which appeared to contain satisfactory evidence of the marriage of Ellen Heathcote with Richard O'Mara, executed upon the evening previous, as the date went to show; and signed by both parties, as well as by Dwyer and a servant of young O'Mara's, both these having acted as witnesses; and further supported by the signature of Peter Nicholls, a brother of the order of St. Francis, by whom the ceremony had been performed, and whom Heathcote had no difficulty in recognising in the person of his visitant.

This document, and the prompt personal visit of the two men, and above all, the known identity of the Franciscan, satisfied Heathcote as fully as anything short of complete publicity could have done. And his conviction was not a mistaken one.

Dwyer, before he took his leave, impressed upon Heathcote the necessity of keeping the affair so secret as to render it impossible that it should reach Colonel

O'Mara's ears, an event which would have been attended with ruinous consequences to all parties. He refused, also, to permit Heathcote to see his daughter, and even to tell him where she was, until circumstances rendered it safe for him to visit her.

Heathcote was a harsh and sullen man; and though his temper was anything but tractable, there was so much to please, almost to dazzle him, in the event, that he accepted the terms which Dwyer imposed upon him without any further token of disapprobation than a shake of the head, and a gruff wish that 'it might prove all for the best.'

Nearly two months had passed, and young O'Mara had not yet departed for England. His letters had been strangely few and far between; and in short, his conduct was such as to induce Colonel O'Mara to hasten his return to Ireland, and at the same time to press an engagement, which Lord ——, his son Captain N——, and Lady Emily had made to spend some weeks with him at his residence in Dublin.

A letter arrived for young O'Mara, stating the arrangement, and requiring his attendance in Dublin, which was accordingly immediately afforded.

He arrived, with Dwyer, in time to welcome his father and his distinguished guests. He resolved to break off his embarrassing connection with Lady Emily, without, however, stating the real motive, which he felt would exasperate the resentment which his father and Lord —— would no doubt feel at his conduct.

He strongly felt how dishonourably he would act if, in obedience to Dwyer's advice, he seemed tacitly to acquiesce in an engagement which it was impossible for him to fulfil. He knew that Lady Emily was not capable of anything like strong attachment; and that even if she were, he had no reason whatever to suppose that she cared at all for him.

He had not at any time desired the alliance; nor had he any reason to suppose the young lady in any degree less indifferent. He regarded it now, and not without some appearance of justice, as nothing more than a kind of understood stipulation, entered into by their parents, and to be considered rather as a matter of business and calculation than as involving anything of mutual inclination on the part of the parties most nearly interested in the matter.

He anxiously, therefore, watched for an opportunity of making known his feelings to Lord ——, as he could not with propriety do so to Lady Emily; but what at a distance appeared to be a matter of easy accomplishment, now, upon a nearer approach, and when the immediate impulse which had prompted the act had subsided, appeared so full of difficulty and almost inextricable embarrassments, that he involuntarily shrunk from the task day after day.

Though it was a source of indescribable anxiety to him, he did not venture to write to Ellen, for he could not disguise from himself the danger which the secrecy of his connection with her must incur by his communicating with her, even through a public office, where their letters might be permitted to lie longer than the gossiping inquisitiveness of a country town would warrant him in supposing safe.

It was about a fortnight after young O'Mara had arrived in Dublin, where all things, and places, and amusements; and persons seemed thoroughly stale, flat, and unprofitable, when one day, tempted by the unusual fineness of the weather, Lady Emily proposed a walk in the College Park, a favourite promenade at that time. She therefore with young O'Mara, accompanied by Dwyer (who, by-the-by, when he pleased, could act the gentleman sufficiently well), proceeded to the place proposed, where they continued to walk for some time.

'Why, Richard,' said Lady Emily, after a tedious and unbroken pause of some minutes, 'you are becoming worse and worse every day. You are growing absolutely intolerable; perfectly stupid! not one good thing have I heard since I left the house.'

O'Mara smiled, and was seeking for a suitable reply, when his design was interrupted, and his attention suddenly and painfully arrested, by the appearance of two figures, who were slowly passing the broad walk on which he and his party moved; the one was that of Captain N——, the other was the form of—Martin Heathcote!

O'Mara felt confounded, almost stunned; the anticipation of some impending mischief—of an immediate and violent collision with a young man whom he had ever regarded as his friend, were apprehensions which such a juxtaposition could not fail to produce.

'Is Heathcote mad?' thought he. 'What devil can have brought him here?'

Dwyer having exchanged a significant glance with O'Mara, said slightly to Lady Emily:

'Will your ladyship excuse me for a moment? I have a word to say to Captain N——, and will, with your permission, immediately rejoin you.'

He bowed, and walking rapidly on, was in a few moments beside the object of his and his patron's uneasiness.

Whatever Heathcote's object might be, he certainly had not yet declared the secret, whose safety O'Mara had so naturally desired, for Captain N—— appeared in good spirits; and on coming up to his sister and her companion, he joined them for a moment, telling O'Mara, laughingly, that an old quiz had come from the country for the express purpose of telling tales, as it was to be supposed, of him (young O'Mara), in whose neighbourhood he lived.

During this speech it required all the effort which it was possible to exert to prevent O'Mara's betraying the extreme agitation to which his situation gave rise. Captain N——, however, suspected nothing, and passed on without further delay.

Dinner was an early meal in those days, and Lady Emily was obliged to leave the Park in less than half an hour after the unpleasant meeting which we have just mentioned.

Young O'Mara and, at a sign from him, Dwyer having escorted the lady to the door of Colonel O'Mara's house, pretended an engagement, and departed together.

Richard O'Mara instantly questioned his comrade upon the subject of his anxiety; but Dwyer had nothing to communicate of a satisfactory nature. He had only time, while the captain had been engaged with Lady Emily and her companion, to say to Heathcote:

'Be secret, as you value your existence: everything will be right, if you be but secret.'

To this Heathcote had replied: 'Never fear me; I understand what I am about.'

This was said in such an ambiguous manner that it was impossible to conjecture whether he intended or not to act upon Dwyer's exhortation. The conclusion which appeared most natural, was by no means an agreeable one.

It was much to be feared that Heathcote having heard some vague report of O'Mara's engagement with Lady Emily, perhaps exaggerated, by the repetition, into a speedily approaching marriage, had become alarmed for his daughter's interest, and had taken this decisive step in order to prevent, by a disclosure of the circumstances of his clandestine union with Ellen, the possibility of his completing a guilty alliance with Captain N——'s sister. If he entertained the suspicions which they attributed to him, he had certainly taken the most effectual means to prevent their being realised. Whatever his object might be, his presence in Dublin, in company with Captain N——, boded nothing good to O'Mara.

They entered ——'s tavern, in Dame Street, together; and there, over a hasty and by no means a comfortable meal, they talked over their plans and conjectures. Evening closed in, and found them still closeted together, with nothing to interrupt, and a large tankard of claret to sustain their desultory conversation.

Nothing had been determined upon, except that Dwyer and O'Mara should proceed under cover of the darkness to search the town for Heathcote, and by minute inquiries at the most frequented houses of entertainment, to ascertain his place of residence, in order to procuring a full and explanatory interview with him. They had each filled their last glass, and were sipping it slowly, seated with their feet stretched towards a bright cheerful fire; the small table which sustained the flagon of which we have spoken, together with two pair of wax candles, placed between them, so as to afford a convenient resting-place for the long glasses out of which they drank.

'One good result, at all events, will be effected by Heathcote's visit,' said O'Mara. 'Before twenty-four hours I shall do that which I should have done long ago. I shall, without reserve, state everything. I can no longer endure this suspense—this dishonourable secrecy—this apparent dissimulation. Every moment I have passed since my departure from the country has been one of embarrassment, of pain, of humiliation. To-morrow I will brave the storm, whether successfully or not is doubtful; but I had rather walk the high roads a beggar, than submit a day longer to be made the degraded sport of every accident—the miserable dependent upon a successful system of deception. Though PASSIVE deception, it is still unmanly, unworthy, unjustifiable deception. I cannot bear to think of it. I despise myself, but I will cease to be the despicable thing I have become. To-morrow sees me free, and this harassing subject for ever at rest.'

He was interrupted here by the sound of footsteps heavily but rapidly ascending the tavern staircase. The room door opened, and Captain N——, accompanied by a fashionably-attired young man, entered the room.

Young O'Mara had risen from his seat on the entrance of their unexpected visitants; and the moment Captain N—— recognised his person, an evident and ominous change passed over his countenance. He turned hastily to withdraw, but, as it seemed, almost instantly changed his mind, for he turned again abruptly.

'This chamber is engaged, sir,' said the waiter.

'Leave the room, sir,' was his only reply.

'The room is engaged, sir,' repeated the waiter, probably believing that his first suggestion had been unheard.

'Leave the room, or go to hell!' shouted Captain N——; at the same time seizing the astounded waiter by the shoulder, he hurled him headlong into the passage, and flung the door to with a crash that shook the walls. 'Sir,' continued he, addressing himself to O'Mara, 'I did not hope to have met you until to-morrow. Fortune has been kind to me—draw, and defend yourself.'

At the same time he drew his sword, and placed himself in an attitude of attack.

'I will not draw upon YOU,' said O'Mara. 'I have, indeed, wronged you. I have given you just cause for resentment; but against your life I will never lift my hand.'

'You are a coward, sir,' replied Captain N——, with almost frightful vehemence, 'as every trickster and swindler IS. You are a contemptible dastard—a despicable, damned villain! Draw your sword, sir, and defend your life, or every post and pillar in this town shall tell your infamy.'

'Perhaps,' said his friend, with a sneer, 'the gentleman can do better without his honour than without his wife.'

'Yes,' shouted the captain, 'his wife—a trull—a common——'

'Silence, sir!' cried O'Mara, all the fierceness of his nature roused by this last insult—'your object is gained; your blood be upon your own head.' At the same time he sprang across a bench which stood in his way, and pushing aside the table which supported the lights, in an instant their swords crossed, and they were engaged in close and deadly strife.

Captain N—— was far the stronger of the two; but, on the other hand, O'Mara possessed far more skill in the use of the fatal weapon which they employed. But the narrowness of the room rendered this advantage hardly available.

Almost instantly O'Mara received a slight wound upon the forehead, which, though little more than a scratch, bled so fast as to obstruct his sight considerably.

Those who have used the foil can tell how slight a derangement of eye or of hand is sufficient to determine a contest of this kind; and this knowledge will prevent their being surprised when I say, that, spite of O'Mara's superior skill and practice, his adversary's sword passed twice through and through his body, and he fell heavily and helplessly upon the floor of the chamber.

Without saying a word, the successful combatant quitted the room along with his companion, leaving Dwyer to shift as best he might for his fallen comrade.

With the assistance of some of the wondering menials of the place, Dwyer succeeded in conveying the wounded man into an adjoining room, where he was laid upon a bed, in a state bordering upon insensibility—the blood flowing, I might say WELLING, from the wounds so fast as to show that unless the bleeding were speedily and effectually stopped, he could not live for half an hour.

Medical aid was, of course, instantly procured, and Colonel O'Mara, though at the time seriously indisposed, was urgently requested to attend without loss of time. He did so; but human succour and support were all too late. The wound had been truly dealt—the tide of life had ebbed; and his father had not arrived five minutes when young O'Mara was a corpse. His body rests in the vaults of Christ Church, in Dublin, without a stone to mark the spot.

The counsels of the wicked are always dark, and their motives often beyond fathoming; and strange, unaccountable, incredible as it may seem, I do believe, and that upon evidence so clear as to amount almost to demonstration, that Heathcote's visit to Dublin—his betrayal of the secret—and the final and terrible catastrophe which laid O'Mara in the grave, were brought about by no other agent than Dwyer himself.

I have myself seen the letter which induced that visit. The handwriting is exactly what I have seen in other alleged specimens of Dwyer's penmanship. It is written with an affectation of honest alarm at O'Mara's conduct, and expresses a conviction that if some of Lady Emily's family be not informed of O'Mara's real situation, nothing could prevent his concluding with her an advantageous alliance, then upon the tapis, and altogether throwing off his allegiance to Ellen—a step which, as the writer candidly asserted, would finally conduce as inevitably to his own disgrace as it immediately would to her ruin and misery.

The production was formally signed with Dwyer's name, and the postscript contained a strict injunction of secrecy, asserting that if it were ascertained that such an epistle had been despatched from such a quarter, it would be attended with the total ruin of the writer.

It is true that Dwyer, many years after, when this letter came to light, alleged it to be a forgery, an assertion whose truth, even to his dying hour, and long after he had apparently ceased to feel the lash of public scorn, he continued obstinately to maintain. Indeed this matter is full of mystery, for, revenge alone excepted, which I believe, in such minds as Dwyer's, seldom overcomes the sense of interest, the only intelligible motive which could have prompted him to such an act was the hope that since he had, through young O'Mara's interest, procured from the colonel a lease of a small farm upon the terms which he had originally stipulated, he might prosecute his plan touching the property of Martin Heathcote, rendering his daughter's hand free by the removal of young O'Mara. This appears to me too complicated a plan of villany to have entered the mind even of such a man as Dwyer. I must, therefore, suppose his motives to have originated out of circumstances connected with this story which may not have come to my ear, and perhaps never will.

Colonel O'Mara felt the death of his son more deeply than I should have thought possible; but that son had been the last being who had continued to interest his cold heart. Perhaps the pride which he felt in his child had in it more of selfishness than of any generous feeling. But, be this as it may, the melancholy circumstances connected with Ellen Heathcote had reached him, and his conduct towards her proved, more strongly than anything else could have done, that he felt keenly and justly, and, to a certain degree, with a softened heart, the fatal event of which she had been, in some manner, alike the cause and the victim.

He evinced not towards her, as might have been expected, any unreasonable resentment. On the contrary, he exhibited great consideration, even tenderness, for her situation; and having ascertained where his son had placed her, he issued strict orders that she should not be disturbed, and that the fatal tidings, which had not yet reached her, should be withheld until they might be communicated in such a way as to soften as much as possible the inevitable shock.

These last directions were acted upon too scrupulously and too long; and, indeed, I am satisfied that had the event been communicated at once, however terrible and overwhelming the shock might have been, much of the bitterest anguish, of sickening doubts, of harassing suspense, would have been spared her, and the first tempestuous burst of sorrow having passed over, her chastened spirit might have recovered its tone, and her life have been spared. But the mistaken kindness which concealed from her the dreadful truth, instead of relieving her mind of a burden which it could not support, laid upon it a weight of horrible fears and doubts as to the affection of O'Mara, compared with which even the certainty of his death would have been tolerable.

One evening I had just seated myself beside a cheerful turf fire, with that true relish which a long cold ride through a bleak and shelterless country affords, stretching my chilled limbs to meet the genial influence, and imbibing the warmth at every pore, when my comfortable meditations were interrupted by a long and sonorous ringing at the door-bell evidently effected by no timid hand.

A messenger had arrived to request my attendance at the Lodge—such was the name which distinguished a small and somewhat antiquated building, occupying a peculiarly secluded position among the bleak and heathy hills which varied the surface of that not altogether uninteresting district, and which had, I believe, been employed by the keen and hardy ancestors of the O'Mara family as a convenient temporary residence during the sporting season.

Thither my attendance was required, in order to administer to a deeply distressed lady such comforts as an afflicted mind can gather from the sublime hopes and consolations of Christianity.

I had long suspected that the occupant of this sequestered, I might say desolate, dwelling-house was the poor girl whose brief story we are following; and feeling a keen interest in her fate—as who that had ever seen her DID NOT?—I started from my comfortable seat with more eager alacrity than, I will confess it, I might have evinced had my duty called me in another direction.

In a few minutes I was trotting rapidly onward, preceded by my guide, who urged his horse with the remorseless rapidity of one who seeks by the speed of his progress to escape observation. Over roads and through bogs we splashed and clattered, until at length traversing the brow of a wild and rocky hill, whose aspect seemed so barren and forbidding that it might have been a lasting barrier alike to mortal sight and step, the lonely building became visible, lying in a kind of swampy flat, with a broad reedy pond or lake stretching away to its side, and backed by a farther range of monotonous sweeping hills, marked with irregular lines of grey rock, which, in the distance, bore a rude and colossal resemblance to the walls of a fortification.

Riding with undiminished speed along a kind of wild horse-track, we turned the corner of a high and somewhat ruinous wall of loose stones, and making a sudden wheel we found ourselves in a small quadrangle, surmounted on two sides by dilapidated stables and kennels, on another by a broken stone wall, and upon the fourth by the front of the lodge itself.

The whole character of the place was that of dreary desertion and decay, which would of itself have predisposed the mind for melancholy impressions. My guide dismounted, and with respectful attention held my horse's bridle while I got down; and knocking at the door with the handle of his whip, it was speedily opened by a neatly-dressed female domestic, and I was admitted to the interior of the house, and conducted into a small room, where a fire in some degree dispelled the cheerless air, which would otherwise have prevailed to a painful degree throughout the place.

I had been waiting but for a very few minutes when another female servant, somewhat older than the first, entered the room. She made some apology on the part of the person whom I had come to visit, for the slight delay which had already occurred, and requested me further to wait for a few minutes longer, intimating that the lady's grief was so violent, that without great effort she could not bring herself to speak calmly at all. As if to beguile the time, the good dame went on in a highly communicative strain to tell me, amongst much that could not interest me, a little of what I had desired to hear. I discovered that the grief of her whom I had come to visit was excited by the sudden death of a little boy, her only child, who was then lying dead in his mother's chamber.

'And the mother's name?' said I, inquiringly.

The woman looked at me for a moment, smiled, and shook her head with the air of mingled mystery and importance which seems to say, 'I am unfathomable.' I did not care to press the question, though I suspected that much of her apparent reluctance was affected, knowing that my doubts respecting the identity of the person whom I had come to visit must soon be set at rest, and after a little pause the worthy Abigail went on as fluently as ever. She told me that her young mistress had been, for the time she had been with her—that was, for about a year and a half—in declining health and spirits, and that she had loved her little child to a degree beyond expression—so devotedly that she could not, in all probability, survive it long.

While she was running on in this way the bell rang, and signing me to follow, she opened the room door, but stopped in the hall, and taking me a little aside, and speaking in a whisper, she told me, as I valued the life of the poor lady, not to say one word of the death of young O'Mara. I nodded acquiescence, and ascending a narrow and ill-constructed staircase, she stopped at a chamber door and knocked.

'Come in,' said a gentle voice from within, and, preceded by my conductress, I entered a moderately-sized, but rather gloomy chamber.

There was but one living form within it—it was the light and graceful figure of a young woman. She had risen as I entered the room; but owing to the obscurity of the apartment, and to the circumstance that her face, as she looked towards the door, was turned away from the light, which found its way in dimly through the narrow windows, I could not instantly recognise the features.

'You do not remember me, sir?' said the same low, mournful voice. 'I am—I WAS—Ellen Heathcote.'

'I do remember you, my poor child,' said I, taking her hand; 'I do remember you very well. Speak to me frankly—speak to me as a friend. Whatever I can do or say for you, is yours already; only speak.'

'You were always very kind, sir, to those—to those that WANTED kindness.'

The tears were almost overflowing, but she checked them; and as if an accession of fortitude had followed the momentary weakness, she continued, in a subdued but firm tone, to tell me briefly the circumstances of her marriage with O'Mara. When she had concluded the recital, she paused for a moment; and I asked again:

'Can I aid you in any way—by advice or otherwise?'

'I wish, sir, to tell you all I have been thinking about,' she continued. 'I am sure, sir, that Master Richard loved me once—I am sure he did not think to deceive me; but there were bad, hard-hearted people about him, and his family were all rich and high, and I am sure he wishes NOW that he had never, never seen me. Well, sir, it is not in my heart to blame him. What was *I* that I should look at him?—an ignorant, poor, country girl—and he so high and great, and so beautiful. The blame was all mine—it was all my fault; I could not think or hope he would care for me more than a little time. Well, sir, I thought over and over again that since his love was gone from me for ever, I should not stand in his way, and hinder whatever great thing his family wished for him. So I thought often and often to write him a letter to get the marriage broken, and to send me home; but for one reason, I would have done it long ago: there was a little child, his and mine—the dearest, the loveliest.' She could not go on for a minute or two. 'The little child that is lying there, on that bed; but it is dead and gone, and there is no reason NOW why I should delay any more about it.'

She put her hand into her breast, and took out a letter, which she opened. She put it into my hands. It ran thus:

'DEAR MASTER RICHARD,

'My little child is dead, and your happiness is all I care about now. Your marriage with me is displeasing to your family, and I would be a burden to you, and in your way in the fine places, and among the great friends where you must be. You ought, therefore, to break the marriage, and I will sign whatever YOU wish, or your family. I will never try to blame you, Master Richard—do not think it—for I never deserved your love, and must not complain now that I have lost it; but I will always pray for you, and be thinking of you while I live.'

While I read this letter, I was satisfied that so far from adding to the poor girl's grief, a full disclosure of what had happened would, on the contrary, mitigate her sorrow, and deprive it of its sharpest sting.

'Ellen,' said I solemnly, 'Richard O'Mara was never unfaithful to you; he is now where human reproach can reach him no more.'

As I said this, the hectic flush upon her cheek gave place to a paleness so deadly, that I almost thought she would drop lifeless upon the spot.

'Is he—is he dead, then?' said she, wildly.

I took her hand in mine, and told her the sad story as best I could. She listened with a calmness which appeared almost unnatural, until I had finished the mournful narration. She then arose, and going to the bedside, she drew the curtain and gazed silently and fixedly on the quiet face of the child: but the feelings which swelled at her heart could not be suppressed; the tears gushed forth, and sobbing as if her heart would break, she leant over the bed and took the dead child in her arms.

She wept and kissed it, and kissed it and wept again, in grief so passionate, so heartrending, as to draw bitter tears from my eyes. I said what little I could to calm her—to have sought to do more would have been a mockery; and observing that the darkness had closed in, I took my leave and departed, being favoured with the services of my former guide.

I expected to have been soon called upon again to visit the poor girl; but the Lodge lay beyond the boundary of my parish, and I felt a reluctance to trespass upon the precincts of my brother minister, and a certain degree of hesitation in intruding upon one whose situation was so very peculiar, and who would, I had no doubt, feel no scruple in requesting my attendance if she desired it.

A month, however, passed away, and I did not hear anything of Ellen. I called at the Lodge, and to my inquiries they answered that she was very much worse in health, and that since the death of the child she had been sinking fast, and so weak that she had been chiefly confined to her bed. I sent frequently to inquire, and often called myself, and all that I heard convinced me that she was rapidly sinking into the grave.

Late one night I was summoned from my rest, by a visit from the person who had upon the former occasion acted as my guide; he had come to summon me to the death-bed of her whom I had then attended. With all celerity I made my preparations, and, not without considerable difficulty and some danger, we made a rapid night-ride to the Lodge, a distance of five miles at least. We arrived safely, and in a very short time—but too late.

I stood by the bed upon which lay the once beautiful form of Ellen Heathcote. The brief but sorrowful trial was past—the desolate mourner was gone to that land where the pangs of grief, the tumults of passion, regrets and cold neglect, are felt no more. I leant over the lifeless face, and scanned the beautiful features which, living, had wrought such magic on all that looked upon them. They were, indeed, much wasted; but it was impossible for the fingers of death or of decay altogether to obliterate the traces of that exquisite beauty which had so distinguished her. As I gazed on this most sad and striking spectacle, remembrances thronged fast upon my mind, and tear after tear fell upon the cold form that slept tranquilly and for ever.

A few days afterwards I was told that a funeral had left the Lodge at the dead of night, and had been conducted with the most scrupulous secrecy. It was, of course, to me no mystery.

Heathcote lived to a very advanced age, being of that hard mould which is not easily impressionable. The selfish and the hard-hearted survive where nobler, more generous, and, above all, more sympathising natures would have sunk for ever.

Dwyer certainly succeeded in extorting, I cannot say how, considerable and advantageous leases from Colonel O'Mara; but after his death he disposed of his interest in these, and having for a time launched into a sea of profligate extravagance, he became bankrupt, and for a long time I totally lost sight of him.

The rebellion of '98, and the events which immediately followed, called him forth from his lurking-places, in the character of an informer; and I myself have seen the hoary-headed, paralytic perjurer, with a scowl of derision and defiance, brave the hootings and the execrations of the indignant multitude.

STRANGE EVENT IN THE LIFE OF SCHALKEN THE PAINTER.

Being a Seventh Extract from the Legacy of the late Francis Purcell, P. P. of Drumcoolagh.

You will no doubt be surprised, my dear friend, at the subject of the following narrative. What had I to do with Schalken, or Schalken with me? He had returned to his native land, and was probably dead and buried, before I was born; I never visited Holland nor spoke with a native of that country. So much I believe you already know. I must, then, give you my authority, and state to you frankly the ground upon which rests the credibility of the strange story which I am, about to lay before you.

I was acquainted, in my early days, with a Captain Vandael, whose father had served King William in the Low Countries, and also in my own unhappy land during the Irish campaigns. I know not how it happened that I liked this man's society, spite of his politics and religion: but so it was; and it was by means of the free intercourse to which our intimacy gave rise that I became possessed of the curious tale which you are about to hear.

I had often been struck, while visiting Vandael, by a remarkable picture, in which, though no connoisseur myself, I could not fail to discern some very strong peculiarities, particularly in the distribution of light and shade, as also a certain oddity in the design itself, which interested my curiosity. It represented the interior of what might be a chamber in some antique religious building—the foreground was occupied by a female figure, arrayed in a species of white robe, part of which is arranged so as to form a veil. The dress, however, is not strictly that of any religious order. In its hand the figure bears a lamp, by whose light alone the form and face are illuminated; the features are marked by an arch smile, such as pretty women wear when engaged in successfully practising some roguish trick; in the background, and, excepting where the dim red light of an expiring fire serves to define the form, totally in the shade, stands the figure of a man equipped in the old fashion, with doublet and so forth, in an attitude of alarm, his hand being placed upon the hilt of his sword, which he appears to be in the act of drawing.

STRANGE EVENT IN THE LIFE OF SCHALKEN THE PAINTER.

'There are some pictures,' said I to my friend, 'which impress one, I know not how, with a conviction that they represent not the mere ideal shapes and combinations which have floated through the imagination of the artist, but scenes, faces, and situations which have actually existed. When I look upon that picture, something assures me that I behold the representation of a reality.'

Vandael smiled, and, fixing his eyes upon the painting musingly, he said:

'Your fancy has not deceived you, my good friend, for that picture is the record, and I believe a faithful one, of a remarkable and mysterious occurrence. It was painted by Schalken, and contains, in the face of the female figure, which occupies the most prominent place in the design, an accurate portrait of Rose Velderkaust, the niece of Gerard Douw, the first and, I believe, the only love of Godfrey Schalken. My father knew the painter well, and from Schalken himself he learned the story of the mysterious drama, one scene of which the picture has embodied. This painting, which is accounted a fine specimen of Schalken's style, was bequeathed to my father by the artist's will, and, as you have observed, is a very striking and interesting production.'

I had only to request Vandael to tell the story of the painting in order to be gratified; and thus it is that I am enabled to submit to you a faithful recital of what I heard myself, leaving you to reject or to allow the evidence upon which the truth of the tradition depends, with this one assurance, that Schalken was an honest, blunt Dutchman, and, I believe, wholly incapable of committing a flight of imagination; and further, that Vandael, from whom I heard the story, appeared firmly convinced of its truth.

There are few forms upon which the mantle of mystery and romance could seem to hang more ungracefully than upon that of the uncouth and clownish Schalken—the Dutch boor—the rude and dogged, but most cunning worker in oils, whose pieces delight the initiated of the present day almost as much as his manners disgusted the refined of his own; and yet this man, so rude, so dogged, so slovenly, I had almost said so savage, in mien and manner, during his after successes, had been selected by the capricious goddess, in his early life, to figure as the hero of a romance by no means devoid of interest or of mystery.

Who can tell how meet he may have been in his young days to play the part of the lover or of the hero—who can say that in early life he had been the same harsh, unlicked, and rugged boor that, in his maturer age, he proved—or how far the neglected rudeness which afterwards marked his air, and garb, and manners, may not have been the growth of that reckless apathy not unfrequently produced by bitter misfortunes and disappointments in early life?

These questions can never now be answered.

We must content ourselves, then, with a plain statement of facts, or what have been received and transmitted as such, leaving matters of speculation to those who like them.

When Schalken studied under the immortal Gerard Douw, he was a young man; and in spite of the phlegmatic constitution and unexcitable manner which he shared, we believe, with his countrymen, he was not incapable of deep and vivid impressions, for it is an established fact that the young painter looked with considerable interest upon the beautiful niece of his wealthy master.

Rose Velderkaust was very young, having, at the period of which we speak, not yet attained her seventeenth year, and, if tradition speaks truth, possessed all the soft dimpling charms of the fail; light-haired Flemish maidens. Schalken had not studied long in the school of Gerard Douw, when he felt this interest deepening into something of a keener and intenser feeling than was quite consistent with the tranquillity of his honest Dutch heart; and at the same time he perceived, or thought he perceived, flattering symptoms of a reciprocity of liking, and this was quite sufficient to determine whatever indecision he might have heretofore experienced, and to lead him to devote exclusively to her every hope and feeling of his heart. In short, he was as much in love as a Dutchman could be. He was not long in making his passion known to the pretty maiden herself, and his declaration was followed by a corresponding confession upon her part.

Schalken, however, was a poor man, and he possessed no counterbalancing advantages of birth or position to induce the old man to consent to a union which must involve his niece and ward in the strugglings and difficulties of a young and nearly friendless artist. He was, therefore, to wait until time had furnished him with opportunity, and accident with success; and then, if his labours were found sufficiently lucrative, it was to be hoped that his proposals might at least be listened to by her jealous guardian. Months passed away, and, cheered by the smiles of the little Rose, Schalken's labours were redoubled, and with such effect and improvement as reasonably to promise the realisation of his hopes, and no contemptible eminence in his art, before many years should have elapsed.

The even course of this cheering prosperity was, however, destined to experience a sudden and formidable interruption, and that, too, in a manner so strange and mysterious as to baffle all investigation, and throw upon the events themselves a shadow of almost supernatural horror.

Schalken had one evening remained in the master's studio considerably longer than his more volatile companions, who had gladly availed themselves of the excuse which the dusk of evening afforded, to withdraw from their several tasks, in order to finish a day of labour in the jollity and conviviality of the tavern.

But Schalken worked for improvement, or rather for love. Besides, he was now engaged merely in sketching a design, an operation which, unlike that of colouring, might be continued as long as there was light sufficient to distinguish between canvas and charcoal. He had not then, nor, indeed, until long after, discovered the peculiar powers of his pencil, and he was engaged in composing a group of extremely roguish-looking and grotesque imps and demons, who were inflicting various ingenious torments upon a perspiring and pot-bellied St. Anthony, who reclined in the midst of them, apparently in the last stage of drunkenness.

The young artist, however, though incapable of executing, or even of appreciating, anything of true sublimity, had nevertheless discernment enough to prevent his being by any means satisfied with his work; and many were the patient erasures and corrections which the limbs and features of saint and devil underwent, yet all without producing in their new arrangement anything of improvement or increased effect.

The large, old-fashioned room was silent, and, with the exception of himself, quite deserted by its usual inmates. An hour had passed—nearly two—without any improved result. Daylight had already declined, and twilight was fast giving way to the darkness of night. The patience of the young man was exhausted, and he stood before his unfinished production, absorbed in no very pleasing ruminations, one hand buried in the folds of his long dark hair, and the other holding the piece of charcoal which had so ill executed its office, and which he now rubbed, without much regard to the sable streaks which it produced, with irritable pressure upon his ample Flemish inexpressibles.

'Pshaw!' said the young man aloud, 'would that picture, devils, saint, and all, were where they should be—in hell!'

A short, sudden laugh, uttered startlingly close to his ear, instantly responded to the ejaculation.

The artist turned sharply round, and now for the first time became aware that his labours had been overlooked by a stranger.

Within about a yard and a half, and rather behind him, there stood what was, or appeared to be, the figure of an elderly man: he wore a short cloak, and broad-brimmed hat with a conical crown, and in his hand, which was protected with a heavy, gauntlet-shaped glove, he carried a long ebony walking-stick, surmounted with what appeared, as it glittered dimly in the twilight, to be a massive head of gold, and upon his breast, through the folds of the cloak, there shone what appeared to be the links of a rich chain of the same metal.

The room was so obscure that nothing further of the appearance of the figure could be ascertained, and the face was altogether overshadowed by the heavy flap of the beaver which overhung it, so that not a feature could be discerned. A quantity of dark hair escaped from beneath this sombre hat, a circumstance which, connected with the firm, upright carriage of the intruder, proved that his years could not yet exceed threescore or thereabouts.

There was an air of gravity and importance about the garb of this person, and something indescribably odd, I might say awful, in the perfect, stone-like movelessness of the figure, that effectually checked the testy comment which had at once risen to the lips of the irritated artist. He therefore, as soon as he had sufficiently recovered the surprise, asked the stranger, civilly, to be seated, and desired to know if he had any message to leave for his master.

'Tell Gerard Douw,' said the unknown, without altering his attitude in the smallest degree, 'that Mynher Vanderhauseny of Rotterdam, desires to speak with him to-morrow evening at this hour, and, if he please, in this room, upon matters of weight—that is all. Good-night.'

The stranger, having finished this message, turned abruptly, and, with a quick but silent step, quitted the room, before Schalken had time to say a word in reply.

The young man felt a curiosity to see in what direction the burgher of Rotterdam would turn on quitting the studio, and for that purpose he went directly to the window which commanded the door.

A lobby of considerable extent intervened between the inner door of the painter's room and the street entrance, so that Schalken occupied the post of observation before the old man could possibly have reached the street.

He watched in vain, however. There was no other mode of exit.

Had the old man vanished, or was he lurking about the recesses of the lobby for some bad purpose? This last suggestion filled the mind of Schalken with a vague horror, which was so unaccountably intense as to make him alike afraid to remain in the room alone and reluctant to pass through the lobby.

However, with an effort which appeared very disproportioned to the occasion, he summoned resolution to leave the room, and, having double-locked the door and thrust the key in his pocket, without looking to the right or left, he traversed the passage which had so recently, perhaps still, contained the person of his mysterious visitant, scarcely venturing to breathe till he had arrived in the open street.

'Mynher Vanderhausen,' said Gerard Douw within himself, as the appointed hour approached, 'Mynher Vanderhausen of Rotterdam! I never heard of the man till yesterday. What can he want of me? A portrait, perhaps, to be painted; or a younger son or a poor relation to be apprenticed; or a collection to be valued; or—pshaw I there's no one in Rotterdam to leave me a legacy. Well, whatever the business may be, we shall soon know it all.'

It was now the close of day, and every easel, except that of Schalken, was deserted. Gerard Douw was pacing the apartment with the restless step of impatient expectation, every now and then humming a passage from a piece of music which he was himself composing; for, though no great proficient, he admired the art; sometimes pausing to glance over the work of one of his absent pupils, but more frequently placing himself at the window, from whence he might observe the passengers who threaded the obscure by-street in which his studio was placed.

'Said you not, Godfrey,' exclaimed Douw, after a long and fruitless gaze from his post of observation, and turning to Schalken—'said you not the hour of appointment was at about seven by the clock of the Stadhouse?'

'It had just told seven when I first saw him, sir,' answered the student.

'The hour is close at hand, then,' said the master, consulting a horologe as large and as round as a full-grown orange. 'Mynher Vanderhausen, from Rotterdam—is it not so?'

'Such was the name.'

'And an elderly man, richly clad?' continued Douw.

'As well as I might see,' replied his pupil; 'he could not be young, nor yet very old neither, and his dress was rich and grave, as might become a citizen of wealth and consideration.'

At this moment the sonorous boom of the Stadhouse clock told, stroke after stroke, the hour of seven; the eyes of both master and student were directed to the door; and it was not until the last peal of the old bell had ceased to vibrate, that Douw exclaimed:

'So, so; we shall have his worship presently—that is, if he means to keep his hour; if not, thou mayst wait for him, Godfrey, if you court the acquaintance of a capricious burgomaster. As for me, I think our old Leyden contains a sufficiency of such commodities, without an importation from Rotterdam.'

Schalken laughed, as in duty bound; and after a pause of some minutes, Douw suddenly exclaimed:

'What if it should all prove a jest, a piece of mummery got up by Vankarp, or some such worthy! I wish you had run all risks, and cudgelled the old burgomaster, stadholder, or whatever else he may be, soundly. I would wager a dozen of Rhenish, his worship would have pleaded old acquaintance before the third application.'

'Here he comes, sir,' said Schalken, in a low admonitory tone; and instantly, upon turning towards the door, Gerard Douw observed the same figure which had, on the day before, so unexpectedly greeted the vision of his pupil Schalken.

There was something in the air and mien of the figure which at once satisfied the painter that there was no mummery in the case, and that he really stood in the presence of a man of worship; and so, without hesitation, he doffed his cap, and courteously saluting the stranger, requested him to be seated.

The visitor waved his hand slightly, as, if in acknowledgment of the courtesy, but remained standing.

'I have the honour to see Mynher Vanderhausen, of Rotterdam?' said Gerard Douw.

'The same,' was the laconic reply of his visitant.

'I understand your worship desires to speak with me,' continued Douw, 'and I am here by appointment to wait your commands.'

'Is that a man of trust?' said Vanderhausen, turning towards Schalken, who stood at a little distance behind his master.

'Certainly,' replied Gerard.

'Then let him take this box and get the nearest jeweller or goldsmith to value its contents, and let him return hither with a certificate of the valuation.'

At the same time he placed a small case, about nine inches square, in the hands of Gerard Douw, who was as much amazed at its weight as at the strange abruptness with which it was handed to him.

In accordance with the wishes of the stranger, he delivered it into the hands of Schalken, and repeating HIS directions, despatched him upon the mission.

Schalken disposed his precious charge securely beneath the folds of his cloak, and rapidly traversing two or three narrow streets, he stopped at a corner house, the lower part of which was then occupied by the shop of a Jewish goldsmith.

Schalken entered the shop, and calling the little Hebrew into the obscurity of its back recesses, he proceeded to lay before him Vanderhausen's packet.

On being examined by the light of a lamp, it appeared entirely cased with lead, the outer surface of which was much scraped and soiled, and nearly white with age. This was with difficulty partially removed, and disclosed beneath a box of some dark and singularly hard wood; this, too, was forced, and after the removal of two or three folds of linen, its contents proved to be a mass of golden ingots, close packed, and, as the Jew declared, of the most perfect quality.

Every ingot underwent the scrutiny of the little Jew, who seemed to feel an epicurean delight in touching and testing these morsels of the glorious metal; and each one of them was replaced in the box with the exclamation:

'Mein Gott, how very perfect! not one grain of alloy—beautiful, beautiful!'

The task was at length finished, and the Jew certified under his hand the value of the ingots submitted to his examination to amount to many thousand rix-dollars.

With the desired document in his bosom, and the rich box of gold carefully pressed under his arm, and concealed by his cloak, he retraced his way, and entering the studio, found his master and the stranger in close conference.

Schalken had no sooner left the room, in order to execute the commission he had taken in charge, than Vanderhausen addressed Gerard Douw in the following terms:

'I may not tarry with you to-night more than a few minutes, and so I shall briefly tell you the matter upon which I come. You visited the town of Rotterdam some four months ago, and then I saw in the church of St. Lawrence your niece, Rose Velderkaust. I desire to marry her, and if I satisfy you as to the fact that I am very wealthy—more wealthy than any husband you could dream of for her—I expect that you will forward my views to the utmost of your authority. If you approve my proposal, you must close with it at once, for I cannot command time enough to wait for calculations and delays.'

Gerard Douw was, perhaps, as much astonished as anyone could be by the very unexpected nature of Mynher Vanderhausen's communication; but he did not give vent to any unseemly expression of surprise, for besides the motives supplied by prudence and politeness, the painter experienced a kind of chill and oppressive sensation, something like that which is supposed to affect a man who is placed unconsciously in immediate contact with something to which he has a natural antipathy—an undefined horror and dread while standing in the presence of the eccentric stranger, which made him very unwilling to say anything which might reasonably prove offensive.

'I have no doubt,' said Gerard, after two or three prefatory hems, 'that the connection which you propose would prove alike advantageous and honourable to my niece; but you must be aware that she has a will of her own, and may not acquiesce in what WE may design for her advantage.'

'Do not seek to deceive me, Sir Painter,' said Vanderhausen; 'you are her guardian—she is your ward. She is mine if YOU like to make her so.'

The man of Rotterdam moved forward a little as he spoke, and Gerard Douw, he scarce knew why, inwardly prayed for the speedy return of Schalken.

'I desire,' said the mysterious gentleman, 'to place in your hands at once an evidence of my wealth, and a security for my liberal dealing with your niece. The lad will return in a minute or two with a sum in value five times the fortune which she has a right to expect from a husband. This shall lie in your hands, together with her dowry, and you may apply the united sum as suits her interest best; it shall be all exclusively hers while she lives. Is that liberal?'

Douw assented, and inwardly thought that fortune had been extraordinarily kind to his niece. The stranger, he thought, must be both wealthy and generous, and such an offer was not to be despised, though made by a humourist, and one of no very prepossessing presence.

Rose had no very high pretensions, for she was almost without dowry; indeed, altogether so, excepting so far as the deficiency had been supplied by the generosity of her uncle. Neither had she any right to raise any scruples against the match on the score of birth, for her own origin was by no means elevated; and as to other objections, Gerard resolved, and, indeed, by the usages of the time was warranted in resolving, not to listen to them for a moment.

'Sir,' said he, addressing the stranger, 'your offer is most liberal, and whatever hesitation I may feel in closing with it immediately, arises solely from my not having the honour of knowing anything of your family or station. Upon these points you can, of course, satisfy me without difficulty?'

'As to my respectability,' said the stranger, drily, 'you must take that for granted at present; pester me with no inquiries; you can discover nothing more about me than I choose to make known. You shall have sufficient security for my respectability—my word, if you are honourable: if you are sordid, my gold.'

'A testy old gentleman,' thought Douw; 'he must have his own way. But, all things considered, I am justified in giving my niece to him. Were she my own daughter, I would do the like by her. I will not pledge myself unnecessarily, however.'

'You will not pledge yourself unnecessarily,' said Vanderhausen, strangely uttering the very words which had just floated through the mind of his companion; 'but you will do so if it IS necessary, I presume; and I will show you that I consider it indispensable. If the gold I mean to leave in your hands satisfy you, and if you desire that my proposal shall not be at once withdrawn, you must, before I leave this room, write your name to this engagement.'

Having thus spoken, he placed a paper in the hands of Gerard, the contents of which expressed an engagement entered into by Gerard Douw, to give to Wilken Vanderhausen, of Rotterdam, in marriage, Rose Velderkaust, and so forth, within one week of the date hereof.

While the painter was employed in reading this covenant, Schalken, as we have stated, entered the studio, and having delivered the box and the valuation of the Jew into the hands of the stranger, he was about to retire, when Vanderhausen called to him to wait; and, presenting the case and the certificate to Gerard Douw, he waited in silence until he had satisfied himself by an inspection of both as to the value of the pledge left in his hands. At length he said:

'Are you content?'

The painter said he would fain have an other day to consider.

'Not an hour,' said the suitor, coolly.

'Well, then,' said Douw, 'I am content; it is a bargain.'

'Then sign at once,' said Vanderhausen; 'I am weary.'

At the same time he produced a small case of writing materials, and Gerard signed the important document.

'Let this youth witness the covenant,' said the old man; and Godfrey Schalken unconsciously signed the instrument which bestowed upon another that hand which he had so long regarded as the object and reward of all his labours.

The compact being thus completed, the strange visitor folded up the paper, and stowed it safely in an inner pocket.

'I will visit you to-morrow night, at nine of the clock, at your house, Gerard Douw, and will see the subject of our contract. Farewell.' And so saying, Wilken Vanderhausen moved stiffly, but rapidly out of the room.

Schalken, eager to resolve his doubts, had placed himself by the window in order to watch the street entrance; but the experiment served only to support his suspicions, for the old man did not issue from the door. This was very strange, very odd, very fearful. He and his master returned together, and talked but little on the way, for each had his own subjects of reflection, of anxiety, and of hope.

Schalken, however, did not know the ruin which threatened his cherished schemes.

Gerard Douw knew nothing of the attachment which had sprung up between his pupil and his niece; and even if he had, it is doubtful whether he would have regarded its existence as any serious obstruction to the wishes of Mynher Vanderhausen.

Marriages were then and there matters of traffic and calculation; and it would have appeared as absurd in the eyes of the guardian to make a mutual attachment an essential element in a contract of marriage, as it would have been to draw up his bonds and receipts in the language of chivalrous romance.

The painter, however, did not communicate to his niece the important step which he had taken in her behalf, and his resolution arose not from any anticipation of opposition on her part, but solely from a ludicrous consciousness that if his ward were, as she very naturally might do, to ask him to describe the appearance of the bridegroom whom he destined for her, he would be forced to confess that he had not seen his face, and, if called upon, would find it impossible to identify him.

Upon the next day, Gerard Douw having dined, called his niece to him, and having scanned her person with an air of satisfaction, he took her hand, and looking upon her pretty, innocent face with a smile of kindness, he said:

'Rose, my girl, that face of yours will make your fortune.' Rose blushed and smiled. 'Such faces and such tempers seldom go together, and, when they do, the compound is a love-potion which few heads or hearts can resist. Trust me, thou wilt soon be a bride, girl. But this is trifling, and I am pressed for time, so make ready the large room by eight o'clock to-night, and give directions for supper at nine. I expect a friend to-night; and observe me, child, do thou trick thyself out handsomely. I would not have him think us poor or sluttish.'

With these words he left the chamber, and took his way to the room to which we have already had occasion to introduce our readers—that in which his pupils worked.

When the evening closed in, Gerard called Schalken, who was about to take his departure to his obscure and comfortless lodgings, and asked him to come home and sup with Rose and Vanderhausen.

The invitation was of course accepted, and Gerard Douw and his pupil soon found themselves in the handsome and somewhat antique-looking room which had been prepared for the reception of the stranger.

A cheerful wood-fire blazed in the capacious hearth; a little at one side an old-fashioned table, with richly-carved legs, was placed—destined, no doubt, to receive the supper, for which preparations were going forward; and ranged with exact regularity, stood the tall-backed chairs, whose ungracefulness was more than counterbalanced by their comfort.

The little party, consisting of Rose, her uncle, and the artist, awaited the arrival of the expected visitor with considerable impatience.

Nine o'clock at length came, and with it a summons at the street-door, which, being speedily answered, was followed by a slow and emphatic tread upon the staircase; the steps moved heavily across the lobby, the door of the room in which the party which we have described were assembled slowly opened, and there entered a figure which startled, almost appalled, the phlegmatic Dutchmen, and nearly made Rose scream with affright; it was the form, and arrayed in the garb, of Mynher Vanderhausen; the air, the gait, the height was the same, but the features had never been seen by any of the party before.

The stranger stopped at the door of the room, and displayed his form and face completely. He wore a dark-coloured cloth cloak, which was short and full, not falling quite to the knees; his legs were cased in dark purple silk stockings, and his shoes were adorned with roses of the same colour. The opening of the cloak in front showed the under-suit to consist of some very dark, perhaps sable material, and his hands were enclosed in a pair of heavy leather gloves which ran up considerably above the wrist, in the manner of a gauntlet. In one hand he carried his walking-stick and his hat, which he had removed, and the other hung heavily by his side. A quantity of grizzled hair descended in long tresses from his head, and its folds rested upon the plaits of a stiff ruff, which effectually concealed his neck.

So far all was well; but the face!—all the flesh of the face was coloured with the bluish leaden hue which is sometimes produced by the operation of metallic medicines administered in excessive quantities; the eyes were enormous, and the white appeared both above and below the iris, which gave to them an expression of insanity, which was heightened by their glassy fixedness; the nose was well enough, but the mouth was writhed considerably to one side, where it opened in order to give egress to two long, discoloured fangs, which projected from the upper jaw, far below the lower lip; the hue of the lips themselves bore the usual relation to that of the face, and was consequently nearly black. The character of the face was malignant, even satanic, to the last degree; and, indeed, such a combination of horror could hardly be accounted for, except by supposing the corpse of some atrocious malefactor, which had long hung blackening upon the gibbet, to have at length become the habitation of a demon—the frightful sport of Satanic possession.

It was remarkable that the worshipful stranger suffered as little as possible of his flesh to appear, and that during his visit he did not once remove his gloves.

Having stood for some moments at the door, Gerard Douw at length found breath and collectedness to bid him welcome, and, with a mute inclination of the head, the stranger stepped forward into the room.

There was something indescribably odd, even horrible, about all his motions, something undefinable, that was unnatural, unhuman—it was as if the limbs were guided and directed by a spirit unused to the management of bodily machinery.

The stranger said hardly anything during his visit, which did not exceed half an hour; and the host himself could scarcely muster courage enough to utter the few necessary salutations and courtesies: and, indeed, such was the nervous terror which the presence of Vanderhausen inspired, that very little would have made all his entertainers fly bellowing from the room.

They had not so far lost all self-possession, however, as to fail to observe two strange peculiarities of their visitor.

During his stay he did not once suffer his eyelids to close, nor even to move in the slightest degree; and further, there was a death-like stillness in his whole person, owing to the total absence of the heaving motion of the chest, caused by the process of respiration.

These two peculiarities, though when told they may appear trifling, produced a very striking and unpleasant effect when seen and observed. Vanderhausen at length relieved the painter of Leyden of his inauspicious presence; and with no small gratification the little party heard the street-door close after him.

'Dear uncle,' said Rose, 'what a frightful man! I would not see him again for the wealth of the States!'

'Tush, foolish girl!' said Douw, whose sensations were anything but comfortable. 'A man may be as ugly as the devil, and yet if his heart and actions are good, he is worth all the pretty-faced, perfumed puppies that walk the Mall. Rose, my girl, it is very true he has not thy pretty face, but I know him to be wealthy and liberal; and were he ten times more ugly——'

'Which is inconceivable,' observed Rose.

'These two virtues would be sufficient,' continued her uncle, 'to counterbalance all his deformity; and if not of power sufficient actually to alter the shape of the features, at least of efficacy enough to prevent one thinking them amiss.'

'Do you know, uncle,' said Rose, 'when I saw him standing at the door, I could not get it out of my head that I saw the old, painted, wooden figure that used to frighten me so much in the church of St. Laurence of Rotterdam.'

Gerard laughed, though he could not help inwardly acknowledging the justness of the comparison. He was resolved, however, as far as he could, to check his niece's inclination to ridicule the ugliness of her intended bridegroom, although he was not a little pleased to observe that she appeared totally exempt from that mysterious dread of the stranger which, he could not disguise it from himself, considerably affected him, as also his pupil Godfrey Schalken.

Early on the next day there arrived, from various quarters of the town, rich presents of silks, velvets, jewellery, and so forth, for Rose; and also a packet directed to Gerard Douw, which, on being opened, was found to contain a contract of marriage, formally drawn up, between Wilken Vanderhausen of the Boom-quay, in Rotterdam, and Rose Velderkaust of Leyden, niece to Gerard Douw, master in the art of painting, also of the same city; and containing engagements on the part of Vanderhausen to make settlements upon his bride, far more splendid than he had before led her guardian to believe likely, and which were to be secured to her use in the most unexceptionable manner possible—the money being placed in the hands of Gerard Douw himself.

I have no sentimental scenes to describe, no cruelty of guardians, or magnanimity of wards, or agonies of lovers. The record I have to make is one of sordidness, levity, and interest. In less than a week after the first interview which we have just described, the contract of marriage was fulfilled, and Schalken saw the prize which he would have risked anything to secure, carried off triumphantly by his formidable rival.

For two or three days he absented himself from the school; he then returned and worked, if with less cheerfulness, with far more dogged resolution than before; the dream of love had given place to that of ambition.

Months passed away, and, contrary to his expectation, and, indeed, to the direct promise of the parties, Gerard Douw heard nothing of his niece, or her worshipful spouse. The interest of the money, which was to have been demanded in quarterly sums, lay unclaimed in his hands. He began to grow extremely uneasy.

Mynher Vanderhausen's direction in Rotterdam he was fully possessed of. After some irresolution he finally determined to journey thither—a trifling undertaking, and easily accomplished—and thus to satisfy himself of the safety and comfort of his ward, for whom he entertained an honest and strong affection.

His search was in vain, however. No one in Rotterdam had ever heard of Mynher Vanderhausen.

Gerard Douw left not a house in the Boom-quay untried; but all in vain. No one could give him any information whatever touching the object of his inquiry; and he was obliged to return to Leyden, nothing wiser than when he had left it.

On his arrival he hastened to the establishment from which Vanderhausen had hired the lumbering though, considering the times, most luxurious vehicle which the bridal party had employed to convey them to Rotterdam. From the driver of this machine he learned, that having proceeded by slow stages, they had late in the evening approached Rotterdam; but that before they entered the city, and while yet nearly a mile from it, a small party of men, soberly clad, and after the old fashion, with peaked beards and moustaches, standing in the centre of the road, obstructed the further progress of the carriage. The driver reined in his horses, much fearing, from the obscurity of the hour, and the loneliness of the road, that some mischief was intended.

His fears were, however, somewhat allayed by his observing that these strange men carried a large litter, of an antique shape, and which they immediately set down upon the pavement, whereupon the bridegroom, having opened the coach-door from within, descended, and having assisted his bride to do likewise, led her, weeping bitterly and wringing her hands, to the litter, which they both entered. It was then raised by the men who surrounded it, and speedily carried towards the city, and before it had proceeded many yards the darkness concealed it from the view of the Dutch charioteer.

In the inside of the vehicle he found a purse, whose contents more than thrice paid the hire of the carriage and man. He saw and could tell nothing more of Mynher Vanderhausen and his beautiful lady. This mystery was a source of deep anxiety and almost of grief to Gerard Douw.

There was evidently fraud in the dealing of Vanderhausen with him, though for what purpose committed he could not imagine. He greatly doubted how far it was possible for a man possessing in his countenance so strong an evidence of the presence of the most demoniac feelings, to be in reality anything but a villain; and every day that passed without his hearing from or of his niece, instead of inducing him to forget his fears, on the contrary tended more and more to exasperate them.

The loss of his niece's cheerful society tended also to depress his spirits; and in order to dispel this despondency, which often crept upon his mind after his daily employment was over, he was wont frequently to prevail upon Schalken to accompany him home, and by his presence to dispel, in some degree, the gloom of his otherwise solitary supper.

One evening, the painter and his pupil were sitting by the fire, having accomplished a comfortable supper, and had yielded to that silent pensiveness sometimes induced by the process of digestion, when their reflections were disturbed by a loud sound at the street-door, as if occasioned by some person rushing forcibly and repeatedly against it. A domestic had run without delay to ascertain the cause of the disturbance, and they heard him twice or thrice interrogate the applicant for admission, but without producing an answer or any cessation of the sounds.

They heard him then open the hall-door, and immediately there followed a light and rapid tread upon the staircase. Schalken laid his hand on his sword, and advanced towards the door. It opened before he reached it, and Rose rushed into the room. She looked wild and haggard, and pale with exhaustion and terror; but her dress surprised them as much even as her unexpected appearance. It consisted of a kind of white woollen wrapper, made close about the neck, and descending to the very ground. It was much deranged and travel-soiled. The poor creature had hardly entered the chamber when she fell senseless on the floor. With some difficulty they succeeded in reviving her, and on recovering her senses she instantly exclaimed, in a tone of eager, terrified impatience:

'Wine, wine, quickly, or I'm lost!'

Much alarmed at the strange agitation in which the call was made, they at once administered to her wishes, and she drank some wine with a haste and eagerness which surprised them. She had hardly swallowed it, when she exclaimed, with the same urgency:

'Food, food, at once, or I perish!'

A considerable fragment of a roast joint was upon the table, and Schalken immediately proceeded to cut some, but he was anticipated; for no sooner had she become aware of its presence than she darted at it with the rapacity of a vulture, and, seizing it in her hands she tore off the flesh with her teeth and swallowed it.

When the paroxysm of hunger had been a little appeased, she appeared suddenly to become aware how strange her conduct had been, or it may have been that other more agitating thoughts recurred to her mind, for she began to weep bitterly and to wring her hands.

'Oh! send for a minister of God,' said she; 'I am not safe till he comes; send for him speedily.'

Gerard Douw despatched a messenger instantly, and prevailed on his niece to allow him to surrender his bedchamber to her use; he also persuaded her to retire to it at once and to rest; her consent was extorted upon the condition that they would not leave her for a moment.

'Oh that the holy man were here!' she said; 'he can deliver me. The dead and the living can never be one—God has forbidden it.'

With these mysterious words she surrendered herself to their guidance, and they proceeded to the chamber which Gerard Douw had assigned to her use.

'Do not—do not leave me for a moment,' said she. 'I am lost for ever if you do.'

Gerard Douw's chamber was approached through a spacious apartment, which they were now about to enter. Gerard Douw and Schalken each carried a was candle, so that a sufficient degree of light was cast upon all surrounding objects. They were now entering the large chamber, which, as I have said, communicated with Douw's apartment, when Rose suddenly stopped, and, in a whisper which seemed to thrill with horror, she said:

'O God! he is here—he is here! See, see—there he goes!'

She pointed towards the door of the inner room, and Schalken thought he saw a shadowy and ill-defined form gliding into that apartment. He drew his sword, and raising the candle so as to throw its light with increased distinctness upon the objects in the room, he entered the chamber into which the shadow had glided. No figure was there—nothing but the furniture which belonged to the room, and yet he could not be deceived as to the fact that something had moved before them into the chamber.

A sickening dread came upon him, and the cold perspiration broke out in heavy drops upon his forehead; nor was he more composed when he heard the increased urgency, the agony of entreaty, with which Rose implored them not to leave her for a moment.

'I saw him,' said she. 'He's here! I cannot be deceived—I know him. He's by me—he's with me—he's in the room. Then, for God's sake, as you would save, do not stir from beside me!'

They at length prevailed upon her to lie down upon the bed, where she continued to urge them to stay by her. She frequently uttered incoherent sentences, repeating again and again, 'The dead and the living cannot be one—God has forbidden it!' and then again, 'Rest to the wakeful—sleep to the sleep-walkers.'

These and such mysterious and broken sentences she continued to utter until the clergyman arrived.

Gerard Douw began to fear, naturally enough, that the poor girl, owing to terror or ill-treatment, had become deranged; and he half suspected, by the suddenness of her appearance, and the unseasonableness of the hour, and, above all, from the wildness and terror of her manner, that she had made her escape from some place of confinement for lunatics, and was in immediate fear of pursuit. He resolved to summon medical advice as soon as the mind of his niece had been in some measure set at rest by the offices of the clergyman whose attendance she had so earnestly desired; and until this object had been attained, he did not venture to put any questions to her, which might possibly, by reviving painful or horrible recollections, increase her agitation.

The clergyman soon arrived—a man of ascetic countenance and venerable age—one whom Gerard Douw respected much, forasmuch as he was a veteran polemic, though one, perhaps, more dreaded as a combatant than beloved as a Christian—of pure morality, subtle brain, and frozen heart. He entered the chamber which communicated with that in which Rose reclined, and immediately on his arrival she requested him to pray for her, as for one who lay in the hands of Satan, and who could hope for deliverance—only from heaven.

That our readers may distinctly understand all the circumstances of the event which we are about imperfectly to describe, it is necessary to state the relative position of the parties who were engaged in it. The old clergyman and Schalken were in the anteroom of which we have already spoken; Rose lay in the inner chamber, the door of which was open; and by the side of the bed, at her urgent desire, stood her guardian; a candle burned in the bedchamber, and three were lighted in the outer apartment.

The old man now cleared his voice, as if about to commence; but before he had time to begin, a sudden gust of air blew out the candle which served to illuminate the room in which the poor girl lay, and she, with hurried alarm, exclaimed:

'Godfrey, bring in another candle; the darkness is unsafe.'

Gerard Douw, forgetting for the moment her repeated injunctions in the immediate impulse, stepped from the bedchamber into the other, in order to supply what she desired.

'O God I do not go, dear uncle!' shrieked the unhappy girl; and at the same time she sprang from the bed and darted after him, in order, by her grasp, to detain him.

But the warning came too late, for scarcely had he passed the threshold, and hardly had his niece had time to utter the startling exclamation, when the door which divided the two rooms closed violently after him, as if swung to by a strong blast of wind.

Schalken and he both rushed to the door, but their united and desperate efforts could not avail so much as to shake it.

Shriek after shriek burst from the inner chamber, with all the piercing loudness of despairing terror. Schalken and Douw applied every energy and strained every nerve to force open the door; but all in vain.

There was no sound of struggling from within, but the screams seemed to increase in loudness, and at the same time they heard the bolts of the latticed window withdrawn, and the window itself grated upon the sill as if thrown open.

One LAST shriek, so long and piercing and agonised as to be scarcely human, swelled from the room, and suddenly there followed a death-like silence.

A light step was heard crossing the floor, as if from the bed to the window; and almost at the same instant the door gave way, and, yielding to the pressure of the external applicants, they were nearly precipitated into the room. It was empty. The window was open, and Schalken sprang to a chair and gazed out upon the street and canal below. He saw no form, but he beheld, or thought he beheld, the waters of the broad canal beneath settling ring after ring in heavy circular ripples, as if a moment before disturbed by the immersion of some large and heavy mass.

No trace of Rose was ever after discovered, nor was anything certain respecting her mysterious wooer detected or even suspected; no clue whereby to trace the intricacies of the labyrinth and to arrive at a distinct conclusion was to be found. But an incident occurred, which, though it will not be received by our rational readers as at all approaching to evidence upon the matter, nevertheless produced a strong and a lasting impression upon the mind of Schalken.

Many years after the events which we have detailed, Schalken, then remotely situated, received an intimation of his father's death, and of his intended burial upon a fixed day in the church of Rotterdam. It was necessary that a very considerable journey should be performed by the funeral procession, which, as it will readily be believed, was not very numerously attended. Schalken with difficulty arrived in Rotterdam late in the day upon which the funeral was appointed to take place. The procession had not then arrived. Evening closed in, and still it did not appear.

Schalken strolled down to the church—he found it open—notice of the arrival of the funeral had been given, and the vault in which the body was to be laid had been opened. The official who corresponds to our sexton, on seeing a well-dressed gentleman, whose object was to attend the expected funeral, pacing the aisle of the church, hospitably invited him to share with him the comforts of a blazing wood fire, which, as was his custom in winter time upon such occasions, he had kindled on the hearth of a chamber which communicated, by a flight of steps, with the vault below.

In this chamber Schalken and his entertainer seated themselves, and the sexton, after some fruitless attempts to engage his guest in conversation, was obliged to apply himself to his tobacco-pipe and can to solace his solitude.

In spite of his grief and cares, the fatigues of a rapid journey of nearly forty hours gradually overcame the mind and body of Godfrey Schalken, and he sank into a deep sleep, from which he was awakened by some one shaking him gently by the shoulder. He first thought that the old sexton had called him, but HE was no longer in the room.

He roused himself, and as soon as he could clearly see what was around him, he perceived a female form, clothed in a kind of light robe of muslin, part of which was so disposed as to act as a veil, and in her hand she carried a lamp. She was moving rather away from him, and towards the flight of steps which conducted towards the vaults.

Schalken felt a vague alarm at the sight of this figure, and at the same time an irresistible impulse to follow its guidance. He followed it towards the vaults, but when it reached the head of the stairs, he paused; the figure paused also, and, turning gently round, displayed, by the light of the lamp it carried, the face and features of his first love, Rose Velderkaust. There was nothing horrible, or even sad, in the countenance. On the contrary, it wore the same arch smile which used to enchant the artist long before in his happy days.

A feeling of awe and of interest, too intense to be resisted, prompted him to follow the spectre, if spectre it were. She descended the stairs he followed; and, turning to the left, through a narrow passage, she led him, to his infinite surprise, into what appeared to be an oldfashioned Dutch apartment, such as the pictures of Gerard Douw have served to immortalise.

Abundance of costly antique furniture was disposed about the room, and in one corner stood a four-post bed, with heavy black-cloth curtains around it; the figure frequently turned towards him with the same arch smile; and when she came to the side of the bed, she drew the curtains, and by the light of the lamp which she held towards its contents, she disclosed to the horror-stricken painter, sitting bolt upright in the bed, the livid and demoniac form of Vanderhausen. Schalken had hardly seen him when he fell senseless upon the floor, where he lay until discovered, on the next morning, by persons employed in closing the passages into the vaults. He was lying in a cell of considerable size, which had not been disturbed for a long time, and he had fallen beside a large coffin which was supported upon small stone pillars, a security against the attacks of vermin.

To his dying day Schalken was satisfied of the reality of the vision which he had witnessed, and he has left behind him a curious evidence of the impression which it wrought upon his fancy, in a painting executed shortly after the event we have narrated, and which is valuable as exhibiting not only the peculiarities which have made Schalken's pictures sought after, but even more so as presenting a portrait, as close and faithful as one taken from memory can be, of his early love, Rose Velderkaust, whose mysterious fate must ever remain matter of speculation.

The picture represents a chamber of antique masonry, such as might be found in most old cathedrals, and is lighted faintly by a lamp carried in the hand of a female figure, such as we have above attempted to describe; and in the background, and to the left of him who examines the painting, there stands the form of a man apparently aroused from sleep, and by his attitude, his hand being laid upon his sword, exhibiting considerable alarm: this last figure is illuminated only by the expiring glare of a wood or charcoal fire.

The whole production exhibits a beautiful specimen of that artful and singular distribution of light and shade which has rendered the name of Schalken immortal among the artists of his country. This tale is traditionary, and the reader will easily perceive, by our studiously omitting to heighten many points of the narrative, when a little additional colouring might have added effect to the recital, that we have desired to lay before him, not a figment of the brain, but a curious tradition connected with, and belonging to, the biography of a famous artist.

SCRAPS OF HIBERNIAN BALLADS.

Being an Eighth Extract from the Legacy of the late Francis Purcell, P. P. of Drumcoolagh.

I have observed, my dear friend, among other grievous misconceptions current among men otherwise well-informed, and which tend to degrade the pretensions of my native land, an impression that there exists no such thing as indigenous modern Irish composition deserving the name of poetry—a belief which has been thoughtlessly sustained and confirmed by the unconscionable literary perverseness of Irishmen themselves, who have preferred the easy task of concocting humorous extravaganzas, which caricature with merciless exaggeration the pedantry, bombast, and blunders incident to the lowest order of Hibernian ballads, to the more pleasurable and patriotic duty of collecting together the many, many specimens of genuine poetic feeling, which have grown up, like its wild flowers, from the warm though neglected soil of Ireland.

In fact, the productions which have long been regarded as pure samples of Irish poetic composition, such as 'The Groves of Blarney,' and 'The Wedding of Ballyporeen,' 'Ally Croker,' etc., etc., are altogether spurious, and as much like the thing they call themselves 'as I to Hercules.'

There are to be sure in Ireland, as in all countries, poems which deserve to be laughed at. The native productions of which I speak, frequently abound in absurdities—absurdities which are often, too, provokingly mixed up with what is beautiful; but I strongly and absolutely deny that the prevailing or even the usual character of Irish poetry is that of comicality. No country, no time, is devoid of real poetry, or something approaching to it; and surely it were a strange thing if Ireland, abounding as she does from shore to shore with all that is beautiful, and grand, and savage in scenery, and filled with wild recollections, vivid passions, warm affections, and keen sorrow, could find no language to speak withal, but that of mummery and jest. No, her language is imperfect, but there is strength in its rudeness, and beauty in its wildness; and, above all, strong feeling flows through it, like fresh fountains in rugged caverns.

And yet I will not say that the language of genuine indigenous Irish composition is always vulgar and uncouth: on the contrary, I am in possession of some specimens, though by no means of the highest order as to poetic merit, which do not possess throughout a single peculiarity of diction. The lines which I now proceed to lay before you, by way of illustration, are from the pen of an unfortunate young man, of very humble birth, whose early hopes were crossed by the untimely death of her whom he loved. He was a self-educated man, and in after-life rose to high distinctions in the Church to which he devoted himself—an act which proves the sincerity of spirit with which these verses were written.

'When moonlight falls on wave and wimple,
And silvers every circling dimple,
  That onward, onward sails:
When fragrant hawthorns wild and simple
  Lend perfume to the gales,
And the pale moon in heaven abiding,
O'er midnight mists and mountains riding,
Shines on the river, smoothly gliding
  Through quiet dales,

'I wander there in solitude,
Charmed by the chiming music rude
  Of streams that fret and flow.
For by that eddying stream SHE stood,
  On such a night I trow:
For HER the thorn its breath was lending,
On this same tide HER eye was bending,
And with its voice HER voice was blending
  Long, long ago.

Wild stream! I walk by thee once more,
I see thy hawthorns dim and hoar,
  I hear thy waters moan,
And night-winds sigh from shore to shore,
  With hushed and hollow tone;
But breezes on their light way winging,
And all thy waters heedless singing,
No more to me are gladness bringing—
  I am alone.

'Years after years, their swift way keeping,
Like sere leaves down thy current sweeping,
  Are lost for aye, and sped—
And Death the wintry soil is heaping
  As fast as flowers are shed.
And she who wandered by my side,
And breathed enchantment o'er thy tide,
That makes thee still my friend and guide—
  And she is dead.'

These lines I have transcribed in order to prove a point which I have heard denied, namely, that an Irish peasant—for their author was no more—may write at least correctly in the matter of measure, language, and rhyme; and I shall add several extracts in further illustration of the same fact, a fact whose assertion, it must be allowed, may appear somewhat paradoxical even to those who are acquainted, though superficially, with Hibernian composition. The rhymes are, it must be granted, in the generality of such productions, very latitudinarian indeed, and as a veteran votary of the muse once assured me, depend wholly upon the wowls (vowels), as may be seen in the following stanza of the famous 'Shanavan Voicth.'

'"What'll we have for supper?"
Says my Shanavan Voicth;
"We'll have turkeys and roast BEEF,
And we'll eat it very SWEET,
And then we'll take a SLEEP,"
Says my Shanavan Voicth.'

But I am desirous of showing you that, although barbarisms may and do exist in our native ballads, there are still to be found exceptions which furnish examples of strict correctness in rhyme and metre. Whether they be one whit the better for this I have my doubts. In order to establish my position, I subjoin a portion of a ballad by one Michael Finley, of whom more anon. The GENTLEMAN spoken of in the song is Lord Edward Fitzgerald.

'The day that traitors sould him and inimies bought him,
The day that the red gold and red blood was paid—
Then the green turned pale and thrembled like the dead leaves in Autumn,
And the heart an' hope iv Ireland in the could grave was laid.

'The day I saw you first, with the sunshine fallin' round ye,
My heart fairly opened with the grandeur of the view:
For ten thousand Irish boys that day did surround ye,
An' I swore to stand by them till death, an' fight for you.

'Ye wor the bravest gentleman, an' the best that ever stood,
And your eyelid never thrembled for danger nor for dread,
An' nobleness was flowin' in each stream of your blood—
My bleasing on you night au' day, an' Glory be your bed.

'My black an' bitter curse on the head, an' heart, an' hand,
That plotted, wished, an' worked the fall of this Irish hero
bold; God's curse upon the Irishman that sould his native land,
An' hell consume to dust the hand that held the thraitor's gold.'

Such were the politics and poetry of Michael Finley, in his day, perhaps, the most noted song-maker of his country; but as genius is never without its eccentricities, Finley had his peculiarities, and among these, perhaps the most amusing was his rooted aversion to pen, ink, and paper, in perfect independence of which, all his compositions were completed. It is impossible to describe the jealousy with which he regarded the presence of writing materials of any kind, and his ever wakeful fears lest some literary pirate should transfer his oral poetry to paper—fears which were not altogether without warrant, inasmuch as the recitation and singing of these original pieces were to him a source of wealth and importance. I recollect upon one occasion his detecting me in the very act of following his recitation with my pencil and I shall not soon forget his indignant scowl, as stopping abruptly in the midst of a line, he sharply exclaimed:

'Is my pome a pigsty, or what, that you want a surveyor's ground-plan of it?'

Owing to this absurd scruple, I have been obliged, with one exception, that of the ballad of 'Phaudhrig Crohoore,' to rest satisfied with such snatches and fragments of his poetry as my memory could bear away—a fact which must account for the mutilated state in which I have been obliged to present the foregoing specimen of his composition.

It was in vain for me to reason with this man of metres upon the unreasonableness of this despotic and exclusive assertion of copyright. I well remember his answer to me when, among other arguments, I urged the advisability of some care for the permanence of his reputation, as a motive to induce him to consent to have his poems written down, and thus reduced to a palpable and enduring form.

'I often noticed,' said he, 'when a mist id be spreadin', a little brier to look as big, you'd think, as an oak tree; an' same way, in the dimmness iv the nightfall, I often seen a man tremblin' and crassin' himself as if a sperit was before him, at the sight iv a small thorn bush, that he'd leap over with ase if the daylight and sunshine was in it. An' that's the rason why I think it id be better for the likes iv me to be remimbered in tradition than to be written in history.'

Finley has now been dead nearly eleven years, and his fame has not prospered by the tactics which he pursued, for his reputation, so far from being magnified, has been wholly obliterated by the mists of obscurity.

With no small difficulty, and no inconsiderable manoeuvring, I succeeded in procuring, at an expense of trouble and conscience which you will no doubt think but poorly rewarded, an accurate 'report' of one of his most popular recitations. It celebrates one of the many daring exploits of the once famous Phaudhrig Crohoore (in prosaic English, Patrick Connor). I have witnessed powerful effects produced upon large assemblies by Finley's recitation of this poem which he was wont, upon pressing invitation, to deliver at weddings, wakes, and the like; of course the power of the narrative was greatly enhanced by the fact that many of his auditors had seen and well knew the chief actors in the drama.

'PHAUDHRIG CROHOORE.

Oh, Phaudhrig Crohoore was the broth of a boy,
  And he stood six foot eight,
And his arm was as round as another man's thigh,
  'Tis Phaudhrig was great,—

And his hair was as black as the shadows of night,
And hung over the scars left by many a fight;
And his voice, like the thunder, was deep, strong, and loud,
And his eye like the lightnin' from under the cloud.
And all the girls liked him, for he could spake civil,
And sweet when he chose it, for he was the divil.
An' there wasn't a girl from thirty-five undher,
Divil a matter how crass, but he could come round her.
But of all the sweet girls that smiled on him, but one
Was the girl of his heart, an' he loved her alone.
An' warm as the sun, as the rock firm an' sure,
Was the love of the heart of Phaudhrig Crohoore;
An' he'd die for one smile from his Kathleen O'Brien,
For his love, like his hatred, was sthrong as the lion.

'But Michael O'Hanlon loved Kathleen as well
As he hated Crohoore—an' that same was like hell.
But O'Brien liked HIM, for they were the same parties,
The O'Briens, O'Hanlons, an' Murphys, and Cartys—
An' they all went together an' hated Crohoore,
For it's many the batin' he gave them before;
An' O'Hanlon made up to O'Brien, an' says he:
"I'll marry your daughter, if you'll give her to me."
And the match was made up, an' when Shrovetide came on,
The company assimbled three hundred if one:
There was all the O'Hanlons, an' Murphys, an' Cartys,
An' the young boys an' girls av all o' them parties;
An' the O'Briens, av coorse, gathered strong on day,
An' the pipers an' fiddlers were tearin' away;
There was roarin', an' jumpin', an' jiggin', an' flingin',
An' jokin', an' blessin', an' kissin', an' singin',
An' they wor all laughin'—why not, to be sure?—
How O'Hanlon came inside of Phaudhrig Crohoore.
An' they all talked an' laughed the length of the table,
Atin' an' dhrinkin' all while they wor able,
And with pipin' an' fiddlin' an' roarin' like tundher,
Your head you'd think fairly was splittin' asundher;
And the priest called out, "Silence, ye blackguards, agin!"
An' he took up his prayer-book, just goin' to begin,
An' they all held their tongues from their funnin' and bawlin',
So silent you'd notice the smallest pin fallin';

An' the priest was just beg'nin' to read, whin the door
Sprung back to the wall, and in walked Crohoore—

Oh! Phaudhrig Crohoore was the broth of a boy,
Ant he stood six foot eight,
An' his arm was as round as another man's thigh,
'Tis Phaudhrig was great—
An' he walked slowly up, watched by many a bright eye,
As a black cloud moves on through the stars of the sky,
An' none sthrove to stop him, for Phaudhrig was great,
Till he stood all alone, just apposit the sate
Where O'Hanlon and Kathleen, his beautiful bride,
Were sitting so illigant out side by side;
An' he gave her one look that her heart almost broke,
An' he turned to O'Brien, her father, and spoke,
An' his voice, like the thunder, was deep, sthrong, and loud,
An' his eye shone like lightnin' from under the cloud:
"I didn't come here like a tame, crawlin' mouse,
But I stand like a man in my inimy's house;
In the field, on the road, Phaudhrig never knew fear,
Of his foemen, an' God knows he scorns it here;

So lave me at aise, for three minutes or four,
To spake to the girl I'll never see more."
An' to Kathleen he turned, and his voice changed its tone,
For he thought of the days when he called her his own,
An' his eye blazed like lightnin' from under the cloud
On his false-hearted girl, reproachful and proud,
An' says he: "Kathleen bawn, is it thrue what I hear,
That you marry of your free choice, without threat or fear?
If so, spake the word, an' I'll turn and depart,
Chated once, and once only by woman's false heart."
Oh! sorrow and love made the poor girl dumb,
An' she thried hard to spake, but the words wouldn't come,
For the sound of his voice, as he stood there fornint her,
Wint could on her heart as the night wind in winther.
An' the tears in her blue eyes stood tremblin' to flow,
And pale was her cheek as the moonshine on snow;
Then the heart of bould Phaudhrig swelled high in its place,
For he knew, by one look in that beautiful face,

That though sthrangers an' foemen their pledged hands might sever, Her true heart was his, and his only, for ever.
An' he lifted his voice, like the agle's hoarse call,
An' says Phaudhrig, "She's mine still, in spite of yez all!"
Then up jumped O'Hanlon, an' a tall boy was he,
An' he looked on bould Phaudhrig as fierce as could be,

An' says he, "By the hokey! before you go out,
Bould Phaudhrig Crohoore, you must fight for a bout."
Then Phaudhrig made answer: "I'll do my endeavour,"
An' with one blow he stretched bould O'Hanlon for ever.
In his arms he took Kathleen, an' stepped to the door;
And he leaped on his horse, and flung her before;
An' they all were so bother'd, that not a man stirred
Till the galloping hoofs on the pavement were heard.
Then up they all started, like bees in the swarm,
An' they riz a great shout, like the burst of a storm,
An' they roared, and they ran, and they shouted galore;
But Kathleen and Phaudhrig they never saw more.

'But them days are gone by, an' he is no more;
An' the green-grass is growin' o'er Phaudhrig Crohoore,
For he couldn't be aisy or quiet at all;
As he lived a brave boy, he resolved so to fall.
And he took a good pike—for Phaudhrig was great—
And he fought, and he died in the year ninety-eight.
An' the day that Crohoore in the green field was killed,
A sthrong boy was sthretched, and a sthrong heart was stilled.'

It is due to the memory of Finley to say that the foregoing ballad, though bearing throughout a strong resemblance to Sir Walter Scott's 'Lochinvar,' was nevertheless composed long before that spirited production had seen the light.

THE PURCELL PAPERS VOLUME III

JIM SULIVAN'S ADVENTURES IN THE GREAT SNOW.

Being a Ninth Extract from the Legacy of the late Francis Purcell, P.P. of Drumcoolagh.

Jim Sulivan was a dacent, honest boy as you'd find in the seven parishes, an' he was a beautiful singer, an' an illegant dancer intirely, an' a mighty plisant boy in himself; but he had the divil's bad luck, for he married for love, an 'av coorse he niver had an asy minute afther.

Nell Gorman was the girl he fancied, an' a beautiful slip of a girl she was, jist twinty to the minute when he married her. She was as round an' as complate in all her shapes as a firkin, you'd think, an' her two cheeks was as fat an' as red, it id open your heart to look at them.

But beauty is not the thing all through, an' as beautiful as she was she had the divil's tongue, an' the divil's timper, an' the divil's behaviour all out; an' it was impossible for him to be in the house with her for while you'd count tin without havin' an argymint, an' as sure as she riz an argymint with him she'd hit him a wipe iv a skillet or whatever lay next to her hand.

Well, this wasn't at all plasin' to Jim Sulivan you may be sure, an' there was scarce a week that his head wasn't plasthered up, or his back bint double, or his nose swelled as big as a pittaty, with the vilence iv her timper, an' his heart was scalded everlastin'ly with her tongue; so he had no pace or quietness in body or soul at all at all, with the way she was goin' an.

Well, your honour, one cowld snowin' evenin' he kim in afther his day's work regulatin' the men in the farm, an' he sat down very quite by the fire, for he had a scrimmidge with her in the mornin', an' all he wanted was an air iv the fire in pace; so divil a word he said but dhrew a stool an' sat down close to the fire. Well, as soon as the woman saw him,

'Move aff,' says she, 'an' don't be inthrudin' an the fire,' says she.

Well, he kept never mindin', an' didn't let an' to hear a word she was sayin', so she kim over an' she had a spoon in her hand, an' she took jist the smallest taste in life iv the boilin' wather out iv the pot, an' she dhropped it down an his shins, an' with that he let a roar you'd think the roof id fly aff iv the house.

'Hould your tongue, you barbarrian,' says she; 'you'll waken the child,' says she.

'An' if I done right,' says he, for the spoonful of boilin' wather riz him entirely, 'I'd take yourself,' says he, 'an' I'd stuff you into the pot an the fire, an' boil you.' says he, 'into castor oil,' says he.

'That's purty behavour,' says she; 'it's fine usage you're givin' me, isn't it?' says she, gettin' wickeder every minute; 'but before I'm boiled,' says she, 'thry how you like THAT,' says she; an', sure enough, before he had time to put up his guard, she hot him a rale terrible clink iv the iron spoon acrass the jaw.

'Hould me, some iv ye, or I'll murdher her,' says he.

'Will you?' says she, an' with that she hot him another tin times as good as the first.

'By jabers,' says he, slappin' himself behind, 'that's the last salute you'll ever give me,' says he; 'so take my last blessin',' says he, 'you ungovernable baste!' says he—an' with that he pulled an his hat an' walked out iv the door.

Well, she never minded a word he said, for he used to say the same thing all as one every time she dhrew blood; an' she had no expectation at all but he'd come back by the time supper id be ready; but faix the story didn't go quite so simple this time, for while he was walkin', lonesome enough, down the borheen, with his heart almost broke with the pain, for his shins an' his jaw was mighty troublesome, av course, with the thratement he got, who did he see but Mick Hanlon, his uncle's sarvint by, ridin' down, quite an asy, an the ould black horse, with a halter as long as himself.

'Is that Mr. Soolivan?' says the by. says he, as soon as he saw him a good bit aff.

'To be sure it is, ye spalpeen, you,' says Jim, roarin' out; 'what do you want wid me this time a-day?' says he.

'Don't you know me?' says the gossoon, 'it's Mick Hanlon that's in it,' says he.

'Oh, blur an agers, thin, it's welcome you are, Micky asthore,' says Jim; 'how is all wid the man an' the woman beyant?' says he.

'Oh!' says Micky, 'bad enough,' says he; 'the ould man's jist aff, an' if you don't hurry like shot,' says he, 'he'll be in glory before you get there,' says he.

'It's jokin' ye are,' says Jim, sorrowful enough, for he was mighty partial to his uncle intirely.

'Oh, not in the smallest taste,' says Micky; 'the breath was jist out iv him,' says he, 'when I left the farm. "An", says he, "take the ould black horse," says he, "for he's shure-footed for the road," says he, "an' bring, Jim Soolivan here," says he, "for I think I'd die asy af I could see him onst," says he.'

'Well,' says Jim, 'will I have time,' says he, 'to go back to the house, for it would be a consolation,' says he, 'to tell the bad news to the woman?' says he.

'It's too late you are already,' says Micky, 'so come up behind me, for God's sake,' says he, 'an' don't waste time;' an' with that he brought the horse up beside the ditch, an' Jim Soolivan mounted up behind Micky, an' they rode off; an' tin good miles it was iv a road, an' at the other side iv Keeper intirely; an' it was snowin' so fast that the ould baste could hardly go an at all at all, an' the two bys an his back was jist like a snowball all as one, an' almost fruz an' smothered at the same time, your honour; an' they wor both mighty sorrowful intirely, an' their toes almost dhroppin' aff wid the could.

And when Jim got to the farm his uncle was gettin' an illegantly, an' he was sittin' up sthrong an' warm in the bed, an' improvin' every minute, an' no signs av dyin' an him at all at all; so he had all his throuble for nothin'.

But this wasn't all, for the snow kem so thick that it was impassible to get along the roads at all at all; an' faix, instead iv gettin' betther, next mornin' it was only tin times worse; so Jim had jist to take it asy, an' stay wid his uncle antil such times as the snow id melt.

Well, your honour, the evenin' Jim Soolivan wint away, whin the dark was closin' in, Nell Gorman, his wife, beginned to get mighty anasy in herself whin she didn't see him comin' back at all; an' she was gettin' more an' more frightful in herself every minute till the dark kem an', an' divil a taste iv her husband was coming at all at all.

'Oh!' says she, 'there's no use in purtendin', I know he's kilt himself; he has committed infantycide an himself,' says she, 'like a dissipated bliggard as he always was,' says she, 'God rest his soul. Oh, thin, isn't it me an' not you, Jim Soolivan, that's the unforthunate woman,' says she, 'for ain't I cryin' here, an' isn't he in heaven, the bliggard,' says she. 'Oh, voh, voh, it's not at home comfortable with your wife an' family that you are, Jim Soolivan,' says she, 'but in the other world, you aumathaun, in glory wid the saints I hope,' says she. 'It's I that's the unforthunate famale,' says she, 'an' not yourself, Jim Soolivan,' says she.

An' this way she kep' an till mornin', cryin' and lamintin; an' wid the first light she called up all the sarvint bys, an' she tould them to go out an' to sarch every inch iv ground to find the corpse, 'for I'm sure,' says she, 'it's not to go hide himself he would,' says she.

Well, they went as well as they could, rummagin' through the snow, antil, at last, what should they come to, sure enough, but the corpse of a poor thravelling man, that fell over the quarry the night before by rason of the snow and some liquor he had, maybe; but, at any rate, he was as dead as a herrin', an' his face was knocked all to pieces jist like an over-boiled pitaty, glory be to God; an' divil a taste iv a nose or a chin, or a hill or a hollow from one end av his face to the other but was all as flat as a pancake. An' he was about Jim Soolivan's size, an' dhressed out exactly the same, wid a ridin' coat an' new corderhoys; so they carried him home, an' they were all as sure as daylight it was Jim Soolivan himself, an' they were wondhering he'd do sich a dirty turn as to go kill himself for spite.

Well, your honour, they waked him as well as they could, with what neighbours they could git togither, but by rason iv the snow, there wasn't enough gothered to make much divarsion; however it was a plisint wake enough, an' the churchyard an' the priest bein' convanient, as soon as the youngsthers had their bit iv fun and divarsion out iv the corpse, they burried it without a great dale iv throuble; an' about three days afther the berrin, ould Jim Mallowney, from th'other side iv the little hill, her own cousin by the mother's side—he had a snug bit iv a farm an' a house close by, by the same token—kem walkin' in to see how she was in her health, an' he dhrew a chair, an' he sot down an' beginned to convarse her about one thing an' another, antil he got her quite an' asy into middlin' good humour, an' as soon as he seen it was time:

'I'm wondherin', says he, 'Nell Gorman, sich a handsome, likely girl, id be thinkin' iv nothin' but lamintin' an' the likes,' says he, 'an' lingerin' away her days without any consolation, or gettin' a husband,' says he.

'Oh,' says she, 'isn't it only three days since I burried the poor man,' says she, 'an' isn't it rather soon to be talkin iv marryin' agin?'

'Divil a taste,' says he, 'three days is jist the time to a minute for cryin' afther a husband, an' there's no occasion in life to be keepin' it up,' says he; 'an' besides all that,' says he, 'Shrovetide is almost over, an' if you don't be sturrin' yourself an' lookin' about you, you'll be late,' says he, 'for this year at any rate, an' that's twelve months lost; an' who's to look afther the farm all that time,' says he, 'an' to keep the men to their work?' says he.

'It's thrue for you, Jim Mallowney,' says she, 'but I'm afeard the neighbours will be all talkin' about it,' says she.

'Divil's cure to the word,' says he.

'An' who would you advise?' says she.

'Young Andy Curtis is the boy,' says he.

'He's a likely boy in himself,' says she.

'An' as handy a gossoon as is out,' says he.

'Well, thin, Jim Mallowney,' says she, 'here's my hand, an' you may be talkin' to Andy Curtis, an' if he's willin' I'm agreeble—is that enough?' says she.

So with that he made off with himself straight to Andy Curtis; an' before three days more was past, the weddin' kem an', an' Nell Gorman an' Andy Curtis was married as complate as possible; an' if the wake was plisint the weddin' was tin times as agreeble, an' all the neighbours that could make their way to it was there, an' there was three fiddlers an' lots iv pipers, an' ould Connor Shamus[1] the piper himself was in it—by the same token it was the last weddin' he ever played music at, for the next mornin', whin he was goin' home, bein' mighty hearty an' plisint in himself, he was smothered in the snow, undher the ould castle; an' by my sowl he was a sore loss to the bys an' girls twenty miles round, for he was the illigantest piper, barrin' the liquor alone, that ever worked a bellas.

Well, a week passed over smart enough, an' Nell an' her new husband was mighty well continted with one another, for it was too soon for her to begin to regulate him the way she used with poor Jim Soolivan, so they wor comfortable enough; but this was too good to last, for the thaw kem an', an' you may be sure Jim Soolivan didn't lose a minute's time as soon as the heavy dhrift iv snow was

---

[1] Literally, Cornelius James—the last name employed as a patronymic. Connor is commonly used. Corney, pronounced Kurny, is just as much used in the South, as the short name for Cornelius.

melted enough between him and home to let him pass, for he didn't hear a word iv news from home sinst he lift it, by rason that no one, good nor bad, could thravel at all, with the way the snow was dhrifted.

So one night, when Nell Gorman an' her new husband, Andy Curtis, was snug an' warm in bed, an' fast asleep, an' everything quite, who should come to the door, sure enough, but Jim Soolivan himself, an' he beginned flakin' the door wid a big blackthorn stick he had, an' roarin' out like the divil to open the door, for he had a dhrop taken.

'What the divil's the matther?' says Andy Curtis, wakenin' out iv his sleep.

'Who's batin' the door?' says Nell; 'what's all the noise for?' says she.

'Who's in it?' says Andy.

'It's me,' says Jim.

'Who are you?' says Andy; 'what's your name?'

'Jim Soolivan,' says he.

'By jabers, you lie,' says Andy.

'Wait till I get at you,' says Jim, hittin' the door a lick iv the wattle you'd hear half a mile off.

'It's him, sure enough,' says Nell; 'I know his speech; it's his wandherin' sowl that can't get rest, the crass o' Christ betune us an' harm.'

'Let me in,' says Jim, 'or I'll dhrive the door in a top iv yis.'

'Jim Soolivan—Jim Soolivan,' says Nell, sittin' up in the bed, an' gropin' for a quart bottle iv holy wather she used to hang by the back iv the bed, 'don't come in, darlin'—there's holy wather here,' says she; 'but tell me from where you are is there anything that's throublin' your poor sinful sowl?' says she. 'An' tell me how many masses 'ill make you asy, an' by this crass, I'll buy you as many as you want,' says she.

'I don't know what the divil you mane,' says Jim.

'Go back,' says she, 'go back to glory, for God's sake,' says she.

'Divil's cure to the bit iv me 'ill go back to glory, or anywhere else,' says he, 'this blessed night; so open the door at onst' an' let me in,' says he.

'The Lord forbid,' says she.

'By jabers, you'd betther,' says he, 'or it 'ill be the worse for you,' says he; an' wid that he fell to wallopin' the door till he was fairly tired, an' Andy an' his wife crassin' themselves an' sayin' their prayers for the bare life all the time.

'Jim Soolivan,' says she, as soon as he was done, 'go back, for God's sake, an' don't be freakenin' me an' your poor fatherless childhren,' says she.

'Why, you bosthoon, you,' says Jim, 'won't you let your husband in,' says he, 'to his own house?' says he.

'You WOR my husband, sure enough,' says she, 'but it's well you know, Jim Soolivan, you're not my husband NOW,' says she.

'You're as dhrunk as can be consaved, says Jim.

'Go back, in God's name, pacibly to your grave,' says Nell.

'By my sowl, it's to my grave you'll sind me, sure enough,' says he, 'you hard-hearted bain', for I'm jist aff wid the cowld,' says he.

'Jim Sulivan,' says she, 'it's in your dacent coffin you should be, you unforthunate sperit,' says she; 'what is it's annoyin' your sowl, in the wide world, at all?' says she; 'hadn't you everything complate?' says she, 'the oil, an' the wake, an' the berrin'?' says she.

'Och, by the hoky,' says Jim, 'it's too long I'm makin' a fool iv mysilf, gostherin' wid you outside iv my own door,' says he, 'for it's plain to be seen,' says he, 'you don't know what your're sayin', an' no one ELSE knows what you mane, you unforthunate fool,' says he; 'so, onst for all, open the door quietly,' says he, 'or, by my sowkins, I'll not lave a splinther together,' says he.

Well, whin Nell an' Andy seen he was getting vexed, they beginned to bawl out their prayers, with the fright, as if the life was lavin' them; an' the more he bate the door, the louder they prayed, until at last Jim was fairly tired out.

'Bad luck to you,' says he; 'for a rale divil av a woman,' says he. I 'can't get any advantage av you, any way; but wait till I get hould iv you, that's all,' says he. An' he turned aff from the door, an' wint round to the cow-house, an' settled himself as well as he could, in the sthraw; an' he was tired enough wid the thravellin' he had in the day-time, an' a good dale bothered with what liquor he had taken; so he was purty sure of sleepin' wherever he thrun himself.

But, by my sowl, it wasn't the same way with the man an' the woman in the house—for divil a wink iv sleep, good or bad, could they get at all, wid the fright iv the sperit, as they supposed; an' with the first light they sint a little gossoon, as fast as he could wag, straight off, like a shot, to the priest, an' to desire him, for the love o' God, to come to them an the minute, an' to bring, if it was plasin' to his raverence, all the little things he had for sayin' mass, an' savin' sowls, an' banishin' sperits, an' freakenin' the divil, an' the likes iv that. An' it wasn't long till his raverence kem down, sure enough, on the ould grey mare, wid the little mass-boy behind him, an' the prayer-books an' Bibles, an' all the other mystarious articles that was wantin', along wid him; an' as soon as he kem in, 'God save all here,' says he.

'God save ye, kindly, your raverence,' says they.

'An' what's gone wrong wid ye?' says he; 'ye must be very bad,' says he,' entirely, to disturb my devotions,' says he, 'this way, jist at breakfast-time,' says he.

'By my sowkins,' says Nell, 'it's bad enough we are, your raverence,' says she, 'for it's poor Jim's sperit,' says she; 'God rest his sowl, wherever it is,' says she, 'that was wandherin' up an' down, opossite the door all night,' says she, 'in the way it was no use at all, thryin' to get a wink iv sleep,' says she.

'It's to lay it, you want me, I suppose,' says the priest.

'If your raverence 'id do that same, it 'id be plasin' to us,' says Andy.

'It'll be rather expinsive,' says the priest.

'We'll not differ about the price, your raverence,' says Andy.

'Did the sperit stop long?' says the priest.

'Most part iv the night,' says Nell, 'the Lord be merciful to us all!' says she.

'That'll make it more costly than I thought,' says he. 'An' did it make much noise?' says he.

'By my sowl, it's it that did,' says Andy; 'leatherin' the door wid sticks and stones,' says he, 'antil I fairly thought every minute,' says he, 'the ould boords id smash, an' the sperit id be in an top iv us—God bless us,' says he.

'Phiew!' says the priest; 'it'll cost a power iv money.'

'Well, your raverence,' says Andy, 'take whatever you like,' says he; 'only make sure it won't annoy us any more,' says he.

'Oh! by my sowkins,' says the priest, 'it'll be the quarest ghost in the siven parishes,' says he, 'if it has the courage to come back,' says he, 'afther what I'll do this mornin', plase God,' says he; 'so we'll say twelve pounds; an' God knows it's chape enough,' says he, 'considherin' all the sarcumstances,' says he.

Well, there wasn't a second word to the bargain; so they paid him the money down, an' he sot the table doun like an althar, before the door, an' he settled it out vid all the things he had wid him; an' he lit a bit iv a holy candle, an' he scathered his holy wather right an' left; an' he took up a big book, an' he wint an readin' for half an hour, good; an' whin he kem to the end, he tuck hould iv his little bell, and he beginned to ring it for the bare life; an', by my sowl, he rung it so well, that he wakened Jim Sulivan in the cowhouse, where he was sleepin', an' up he jumped, widout a minute's delay, an' med right for the house, where all the family, an' the priest, an' the little mass-boy was assimbled, layin' the ghost; an' as soon as his raverence seen him comin' in at the door, wid the fair fright, he flung the bell at his head, an' hot him sich a lick iv it in the forehead, that he sthretched him on the floor; but fain; he didn't wait to ax any questions, but he cut round the table as if the divil was afther him, an' out at the door, an' didn't stop even as much as to mount an his mare, but leathered away down the borheen as fast as his legs could carry him, though the mud was up to his knees, savin' your presence.

Well, by the time Jim kem to himself, the family persaved the mistake, an' Andy wint home, lavin' Nell to make the explanation. An' as soon as Jim heerd it all, he said he was quite contint to lave her to Andy, entirely; but the priest would not hear iv it; an' he jist med him marry his wife over again, an' a merry weddin' it was, an' a fine collection for his raverence. An' Andy was there along wid the rest, an' the priest put a small pinnance upon him, for bein' in too great a hurry to marry a widdy.

An' bad luck to the word he'd allow anyone to say an the business, ever after, at all, at all; so, av coorse, no one offinded his raverence, by spakin' iv the twelve pounds he got for layin' the sperit.

An' the neighbours wor all mighty well plased, to be sure, for gettin' all the diversion of a wake, an' two weddin's for nothin.'

A CHAPTER IN THE HISTORY OF A TYRONE FAMILY

Being a Tenth Extract from the Legacy of the late Francis Purcell, P.P. of Drumcoolagh.

INTRODUCTION.

In the following narrative, I have endeavoured to give as nearly as possible the ipsissima verba of the valued friend from whom I received it, conscious that any aberration from HER mode of telling the tale of her own life would at once impair its accuracy and its effect.

Would that, with her words, I could also bring before you her animated gesture, her expressive countenance, the solemn and thrilling air and accent with which she related the dark passages in her strange story; and, above all, that I could communicate the impressive consciousness that the narrator had seen with her own eyes, and personally acted in the scenes which she described; these accompaniments, taken with the additional circumstance that she who told the tale was one far too deeply and sadly impressed with religious principle to misrepresent or fabricate what she repeated as fact, gave to the tale a depth of interest which the events recorded could hardly, themselves, have produced.

I became acquainted with the lady from whose lips I heard this narrative nearly twenty years since, and the story struck my fancy so much that I committed it to paper while it was still fresh in my mind; and should its perusal afford you entertainment for a listless half hour, my labour shall not have been bestowed in vain.

I find that I have taken the story down as she told it, in the first person, and perhaps this is as it should be.

She began as follows:

My maiden name was Richardson[1], the designation of a family of some distinction in the county of Tyrone. I was the younger of two daughters, and we were

[1] I have carefully altered the names as they appear in the original MSS., for the reader will see that some of the circumstances recorded are not of a kind to reflect honour upon those involved in them; and as many are still living, in every way honoured and honourable,

the only children. There was a difference in our ages of nearly six years, so that I did not, in my childhood, enjoy that close companionship which sisterhood, in other circumstances, necessarily involves; and while I was still a child, my sister was married.

The person upon whom she bestowed her hand was a Mr. Carew, a gentleman of property and consideration in the north of England.

I remember well the eventful day of the wedding; the thronging carriages, the noisy menials, the loud laughter, the merry faces, and the gay dresses. Such sights were then new to me, and harmonised ill with the sorrowful feelings with which I regarded the event which was to separate me, as it turned out, for ever from a sister whose tenderness alone had hitherto more than supplied all that I wanted in my mother's affection.

The day soon arrived which was to remove the happy couple from Ashtown House. The carriage stood at the hall-door, and my poor sister kissed me again and again, telling me that I should see her soon.

The carriage drove away, and I gazed after it until my eyes filled with tears, and, returning slowly to my chamber, I wept more bitterly and, so to speak, more desolately, than ever I had done before.

My father had never seemed to love or to take an interest in me. He had desired a son, and I think he never thoroughly forgave me my unfortunate sex.

My having come into the world at all as his child he regarded as a kind of fraudulent intrusion, and as his antipathy to me had its origin in an imperfection of mine, too radical for removal, I never even hoped to stand high in his good graces.

My mother was, I dare say, as fond of me as she was of anyone; but she was a woman of a masculine and a worldly cast of mind. She had no tenderness or sympathy for the weaknesses, or even for the affections, of woman's nature and her demeanour towards me was peremptory, and often even harsh.

It is not to be supposed, then, that I found in the society of my parents much to supply the loss of my sister. About a year after her marriage, we received letters from Mr. Carew, containing accounts of my sister's health, which, though not actually alarming, were calculated to make us seriously uneasy. The symptoms most dwelt upon were loss of appetite and cough.

The letters concluded by intimating that he would avail himself of my father and mother's repeated invitation to spend some time at Ashtown, particularly as the physician who had been consulted as to my sister's health had strongly advised a removal to her native air.

There were added repeated assurances that nothing serious was apprehended, as it was supposed that a deranged state of the liver was the only source of the symptoms which at first had seemed to intimate consumption.

---

who stand in close relation to the principal actors in this drama, the reader will see the necessity of the course which we have adopted.

In accordance with this announcement, my sister and Mr. Carew arrived in Dublin, where one of my father's carriages awaited them, in readiness to start upon whatever day or hour they might choose for their departure.

It was arranged that Mr. Carew was, as soon as the day upon which they were to leave Dublin was definitely fixed, to write to my father, who intended that the two last stages should be performed by his own horses, upon whose speed and safety far more reliance might be placed than upon those of the ordinary post-horses, which were at that time, almost without exception, of the very worst order. The journey, one of about ninety miles, was to be divided; the larger portion being reserved for the second day.

On Sunday a letter reached us, stating that the party would leave Dublin on Monday, and, in due course, reach Ashtown upon Tuesday evening.

Tuesday came the evening closed in, and yet no carriage; darkness came on, and still no sign of our expected visitors.

Hour after hour passed away, and it was now past twelve; the night was remarkably calm, scarce a breath stirring, so that any sound, such as that produced by the rapid movement of a vehicle, would have been audible at a considerable distance. For some such sound I was feverishly listening.

It was, however, my father's rule to close the house at nightfall, and the window-shutters being fastened, I was unable to reconnoitre the avenue as I would have wished. It was nearly one o'clock, and we began almost to despair of seeing them upon that night, when I thought I distinguished the sound of wheels, but so remote and faint as to make me at first very uncertain. The noise approached; it became louder and clearer; it stopped for a moment.

I now heard the shrill screaming of the rusty iron, as the avenue-gate revolved on its hinges; again came the sound of wheels in rapid motion.

'It is they,' said I, starting up; 'the carriage is in the avenue.'

We all stood for a few moments breathlessly listening. On thundered the vehicle with the speed of a whirlwind; crack went the whip, and clatter went the wheels, as it rattled over the uneven pavement of the court. A general and furious barking from all the dogs about the house, hailed its arrival.

We hurried to the hall in time to hear the steps let down with the sharp clanging noise peculiar to the operation, and the hum of voices exerted in the bustle of arrival. The hall-door was now thrown open, and we all stepped forth to greet our visitors.

The court was perfectly empty; the moon was shining broadly and brightly upon all around; nothing was to be seen but the tall trees with their long spectral shadows, now wet with the dews of midnight.

We stood gazing from right to left, as if suddenly awakened from a dream; the dogs walked suspiciously, growling and snuffing about the court, and by totally and suddenly ceasing their former loud barking, expressing the predominance of fear.

We stared one upon another in perplexity and dismay, and I think I never beheld more pale faces assembled. By my father's direction, we looked about to find anything which might indicate or account for the noise which we had heard; but no such thing was to be seen—even the mire which lay upon the avenue was undisturbed. We returned to the house, more panic-struck than I can describe.

On the next day, we learned by a messenger, who had ridden hard the greater part of the night, that my sister was dead. On Sunday evening, she had retired to bed rather unwell, and, on Monday, her indisposition declared itself unequivocally to be malignant fever. She became hourly worse and, on Tuesday night, a little after midnight, she expired[1].

I mention this circumstance, because it was one upon which a thousand wild and fantastical reports were founded, though one would have thought that the truth scarcely required to be improved upon; and again, because it produced a strong and lasting effect upon my spirits, and indeed, I am inclined to think, upon my character.

I was, for several years after this occurrence, long after the violence of my grief subsided, so wretchedly low-spirited and nervous, that I could scarcely be said to live; and during this time, habits of indecision, arising out of a listless acquiescence in the will of others, a fear of encountering even the slightest opposition, and a disposition to shrink from what are commonly called amusements, grew upon me so strongly, that I have scarcely even yet altogether overcome them.

---

[1] The residuary legatee of the late Frances Purcell, who has the honour of selecting such of his lamented old friend's manuscripts as may appear fit for publication, in order that the lore which they contain may reach the world before scepticism and utility have robbed our species of the precious gift of credulity, and scornfully kicked before them, or trampled into annihilation those harmless fragments of picturesque superstition which it is our object to preserve, has been subjected to the charge of dealing too largely in the marvellous; and it has been half insinuated that such is his love for diablerie, that he is content to wander a mile out of his way, in order to meet a fiend or a goblin, and thus to sacrifice all regard for truth and accuracy to the idle hope of affrighting the imagination, and thus pandering to the bad taste of his reader. He begs leave, then, to take this opportunity of asserting his perfect innocence of all the crimes laid to his charge, and to assure his reader that he never PANDERED TO HIS BAD TASTE, nor went one inch out of his way to introduce witch, fairy, devil, ghost, or any other of the grim fraternity of the redoubted Raw-head-and-bloody-bones. His province, touching these tales, has been attended with no difficulty and little responsibility; indeed, he is accountable for nothing more than an alteration in the names of persons mentioned therein, when such a step seemed necessary, and for an occasional note, whenever he conceived it possible, innocently, to edge in a word. These tales have been WRITTEN DOWN, as the heading of each announces, by the Rev. Francis Purcell, P.P., of Drumcoolagh; and in all the instances, which are many, in which the present writer has had an opportunity of comparing the manuscript of his departed friend with the actual traditions which are current amongst the families whose fortunes they pretend to illustrate, he has uniformly found that whatever of supernatural occurred in the story, so far from having been exaggerated by him, had been rather softened down, and, wherever it could be attempted, accounted for.

We saw nothing more of Mr. Carew. He returned to England as soon as the melancholy rites attendant upon the event which I have just mentioned were performed; and not being altogether inconsolable, he married again within two years; after which, owing to the remoteness of our relative situations, and other circumstances, we gradually lost sight of him.

I was now an only child; and, as my elder sister had died without issue, it was evident that, in the ordinary course of things, my father's property, which was altogether in his power, would go to me; and the consequence was, that before I was fourteen, Ashtown House was besieged by a host of suitors. However, whether it was that I was too young, or that none of the aspirants to my hand stood sufficiently high in rank or wealth, I was suffered by both parents to do exactly as I pleased; and well was it for me, as I afterwards found, that fortune, or rather Providence, had so ordained it, that I had not suffered my affections to become in any degree engaged, for my mother would never have suffered any SILLY FANCY of mine, as she was in the habit of styling an attachment, to stand in the way of her ambitious views—views which she was determined to carry into effect, in defiance of every obstacle, and in order to accomplish which she would not have hesitated to sacrifice anything so unreasonable and contemptible as a girlish passion.

When I reached the age of sixteen, my mother's plans began to develop themselves; and, at her suggestion, we moved to Dublin to sojourn for the winter, in order that no time might be lost in disposing of me to the best advantage.

I had been too long accustomed to consider myself as of no importance whatever, to believe for a moment that I was in reality the cause of all the bustle and preparation which surrounded me, and being thus relieved from the pain which a consciousness of my real situation would have inflicted, I journeyed towards the capital with a feeling of total indifference.

My father's wealth and connection had established him in the best society, and, consequently, upon our arrival in the metropolis we commanded whatever enjoyment or advantages its gaieties afforded.

The tumult and novelty of the scenes in which I was involved did not fail considerably to amuse me, and my mind gradually recovered its tone, which was naturally cheerful.

It was almost immediately known and reported that I was an heiress, and of course my attractions were pretty generally acknowledged.

Among the many gentlemen whom it was my fortune to please, one, ere long, established himself in my mother's good graces, to the exclusion of all less important aspirants. However, I had not understood or even remarked his attentions, nor in the slightest degree suspected his or my mother's plans respecting me, when I was made aware of them rather abruptly by my mother herself.

We had attended a splendid ball, given by Lord M——, at his residence in Stephen's Green, and I was, with the assistance of my waiting-maid, employed in rapidly divesting myself of the rich ornaments which, in profuseness and value, could scarcely have found their equals in any private family in Ireland.

I had thrown myself into a lounging-chair beside the fire, listless and exhausted, after the fatigues of the evening, when I was aroused from the reverie into which I had fallen by the sound of footsteps approaching my chamber, and my mother entered.

'Fanny, my dear,' said she, in her softest tone, 'I wish to say a word or two with you before I go to rest. You are not fatigued, love, I hope?'

'No, no, madam, I thank you,' said I, rising at the same time from my seat, with the formal respect so little practised now.

'Sit down, my dear,' said she, placing herself upon a chair beside me; 'I must chat with you for a quarter of an hour or so. Saunders' (to the maid) 'you may leave the room; do not close the room-door, but shut that of the lobby.'

This precaution against curious ears having been taken as directed, my mother proceeded.

'You have observed, I should suppose, my dearest Fanny—indeed, you MUST have observed Lord Glenfallen's marked attentions to you?'

'I assure you, madam——' I began.

'Well, well, that is all right,' interrupted my mother; 'of course you must be modest upon the matter; but listen to me for a few moments, my love, and I will prove to your satisfaction that your modesty is quite unnecessary in this case. You have done better than we could have hoped, at least so very soon. Lord Glenfallen is in love with you. I give you joy of your conquest;' and saying this, my mother kissed my forehead.

'In love with me!' I exclaimed, in unfeigned astonishment.

'Yes, in love with you,' repeated my mother, 'devotedly, distractedly in love with you. Why, my dear, what is there wonderful in it? Look in the glass, and look at these,' she continued, pointing with a smile to the jewels which I had just removed from my person, and which now lay a glittering heap upon the table.

'May there not,' said I, hesitating between confusion and real alarm—'is it not possible that some mistake may be at the bottom of all this?'

'Mistake, dearest! none,' said my mother. 'None; none in the world. Judge for yourself; read this, my love.' And she placed in my hand a letter, addressed to herself, the seal of which was broken. I read it through with no small surprise. After some very fine complimentary flourishes upon my beauty and perfections, as also upon the antiquity and high reputation of our family, it went on to make a formal proposal of marriage, to be communicated or not to me at present, as my mother should deem expedient; and the letter wound up by a request that the writer might be permitted, upon our return to Ashtown House, which was soon to take place, as the spring was now tolerably advanced, to visit us for a few days, in case his suit was approved.

'Well, well, my dear,' said my mother, impatiently; 'do you know who Lord Glenfallen is?'

'I do, madam,' said I rather timidly, for I dreaded an altercation with my mother.

'Well, dear, and what frightens you?' continued she. 'Are you afraid of a title? What has he done to alarm you? he is neither old nor ugly.'

I was silent, though I might have said, 'He is neither young nor handsome.'

'My dear Fanny,' continued my mother, 'in sober seriousness you have been most fortunate in engaging the affections of a nobleman such as Lord Glenfallen, young and wealthy, with first-rate—yes, acknowledged FIRST-RATE abilities, and of a family whose influence is not exceeded by that of any in Ireland. Of course you see the offer in the same light that I do—indeed I think you MUST.'

This was uttered in no very dubious tone. I was so much astonished by the suddenness of the whole communication that I literally did not know what to say.

'You are not in love?' said my mother, turning sharply, and fixing her dark eyes upon me with severe scrutiny.

'No, madam,' said I, promptly; horrified, as what young lady would not have been, at such a query.

'I'm glad to hear it,' said my mother, drily. 'Once, nearly twenty years ago, a friend of mine consulted me as to how he should deal with a daughter who had made what they call a love-match—beggared herself, and disgraced her family; and I said, without hesitation, take no care for her, but cast her off. Such punishment I awarded for an offence committed against the reputation of a family not my own; and what I advised respecting the child of another, with full as small compunction I would DO with mine. I cannot conceive anything more unreasonable or intolerable than that the fortune and the character of a family should be marred by the idle caprices of a girl.'

She spoke this with great severity, and paused as if she expected some observation from me.

I, however, said nothing.

'But I need not explain to you, my dear Fanny,' she continued, 'my views upon this subject; you have always known them well, and I have never yet had reason to believe you likely, voluntarily, to offend me, or to abuse or neglect any of those advantages which reason and duty tell you should be improved. Come hither, my dear; kiss me, and do not look so frightened. Well, now, about this letter, you need not answer it yet; of course you must be allowed time to make up your mind. In the meantime I will write to his lordship to give him my permission to visit us at Ashtown. Good-night, my love.'

And thus ended one of the most disagreeable, not to say astounding, conversations I had ever had. It would not be easy to describe exactly what were my feelings towards Lord Glenfallen;—whatever might have been my mother's suspicions, my heart was perfectly disengaged—and hitherto, although I had not been made in the slightest degree acquainted with his real views, I had liked him very much, as an agreeable, well-informed man, whom I was always glad to meet in society. He had served in the navy in early life, and the polish which his manners received in his after intercourse with courts and cities had not served to obliterate that frankness of manner which belongs proverbially to the sailor.

Whether this apparent candour went deeper than the outward bearing, I was yet to learn. However, there was no doubt that, as far as I had seen of Lord Glenfallen, he was, though perhaps not so young as might have been desired in a lover, a singularly pleasing man; and whatever feeling unfavourable to him had found its way into my mind, arose altogether from the dread, not an unreasonable one, that constraint might be practised upon my inclinations. I reflected, however, that Lord Glenfallen was a wealthy man, and one highly thought of; and although I could never expect to love him in the romantic sense of the term, yet I had no doubt but that, all things considered, I might be more happy with him than I could hope to be at home.

When next I met him it was with no small embarrassment, his tact and good breeding, however, soon reassured me, and effectually prevented my awkwardness being remarked upon. And I had the satisfaction of leaving Dublin for the country with the full conviction that nobody, not even those most intimate with me, even suspected the fact of Lord Glenfallen's having made me a formal proposal.

This was to me a very serious subject of self-gratulation, for, besides my instinctive dread of becoming the topic of the speculations of gossip, I felt that if the situation which I occupied in relation to him were made publicly known, I should stand committed in a manner which would scarcely leave me the power of retraction.

The period at which Lord Glenfallen had arranged to visit Ashtown House was now fast approaching, and it became my mother's wish to form me thoroughly to her will, and to obtain my consent to the proposed marriage before his arrival, so that all things might proceed smoothly, without apparent opposition or objection upon my part. Whatever objections, therefore, I had entertained were to be subdued; whatever disposition to resistance I had exhibited or had been supposed to feel, were to be completely eradicated before he made his appearance; and my mother addressed herself to the task with a decision and energy against which even the barriers, which her imagination had created, could hardly have stood.

If she had, however, expected any determined opposition from me, she was agreeably disappointed. My heart was perfectly free, and all my feelings of liking and preference were in favour of Lord Glenfallen; and I well knew that in case I refused to dispose of myself as I was desired, my mother had alike the power and the will to render my existence as utterly miserable as even the most ill-assorted marriage could possibly have done.

You will remember, my good friend, that I was very young and very completely under the control of my parents, both of whom, my mother particularly, were unscrupulously determined in matters of this kind, and willing, when voluntary obedience on the part of those within their power was withheld, to compel a forced acquiescence by an unsparing use of all the engines of the most stern and rigorous domestic discipline.

All these combined, not unnaturally, induced me to resolve upon yielding at once, and without useless opposition, to what appeared almost to be my fate.

The appointed time was come, and my now accepted suitor arrived; he was in high spirits, and, if possible, more entertaining than ever.

I was not, however, quite in the mood to enjoy his sprightliness; but whatever I wanted in gaiety was amply made up in the triumphant and gracious good-humour of my mother, whose smiles of benevolence and exultation were showered around as bountifully as the summer sunshine.

I will not weary you with unnecessary prolixity. Let it suffice to say, that I was married to Lord Glenfallen with all the attendant pomp and circumstance of wealth, rank, and grandeur. According to the usage of the times, now humanely reformed, the ceremony was made, until long past midnight, the season of wild, uproarious, and promiscuous feasting and revelry.

Of all this I have a painfully vivid recollection, and particularly of the little annoyances inflicted upon me by the dull and coarse jokes of the wits and wags who abound in all such places, and upon all such occasions.

I was not sorry when, after a few days, Lord Glenfallen's carriage appeared at the door to convey us both from Ashtown; for any change would have been a relief from the irksomeness of ceremonial and formality which the visits received in honour of my newly-acquired titles hourly entailed upon me.

It was arranged that we were to proceed to Cahergillagh, one of the Glenfallen estates, lying, however, in a southern county, so that, owing to the difficulty of the roads at the time, a tedious journey of three days intervened.

I set forth with my noble companion, followed by the regrets of some, and by the envy of many; though God knows I little deserved the latter. The three days of travel were now almost spent, when, passing the brow of a wild heathy hill, the domain of Cahergillagh opened suddenly upon our view.

It formed a striking and a beautiful scene. A lake of considerable extent stretching away towards the west, and reflecting from its broad, smooth waters, the rich glow of the setting sun, was overhung by steep hills, covered by a rich mantle of velvet sward, broken here and there by the grey front of some old rock, and exhibiting on their shelving sides, their slopes and hollows, every variety of light and shade; a thick wood of dwarf oak, birch, and hazel skirted these hills, and clothed the shores of the lake, running out in rich luxuriance upon every promontory, and spreading upward considerably upon the side of the hills.

'There lies the enchanted castle,' said Lord Glenfallen, pointing towards a considerable level space intervening between two of the picturesque hills, which rose dimly around the lake.

This little plain was chiefly occupied by the same low, wild wood which covered the other parts of the domain; but towards the centre a mass of taller and statelier forest trees stood darkly grouped together, and among them stood an ancient square tower, with many buildings of a humbler character, forming together the manorhouse, or, as it was more usually called, the Court of Cahergillagh.

As we approached the level upon which the mansion stood, the winding road gave us many glimpses of the time-worn castle and its surrounding buildings; and seen as it was through the long vistas of the fine old trees, and with the rich glow of evening upon it, I have seldom beheld an object more picturesquely striking.

I was glad to perceive, too, that here and there the blue curling smoke ascended from stacks of chimneys now hidden by the rich, dark ivy which, in a great measure, covered the building. Other indications of comfort made themselves manifest as we approached; and indeed, though the place was evidently one of considerable antiquity, it had nothing whatever of the gloom of decay about it.

'You must not, my love,' said Lord Glenfallen, 'imagine this place worse than it is. I have no taste for antiquity—at least I should not choose a house to reside in because it is old. Indeed I do not recollect that I was even so romantic as to overcome my aversion to rats and rheumatism, those faithful attendants upon your noble relics of feudalism; and I much prefer a snug, modern, unmysterious bedroom, with well-aired sheets, to the waving tapestry, mildewed cushions, and all the other interesting appliances of romance. However, though I cannot promise you all the discomfort generally belonging to an old castle, you will find legends and ghostly lore enough to claim your respect; and if old Martha be still to the fore, as I trust she is, you will soon have a supernatural and appropriate anecdote for every closet and corner of the mansion; but here we are—so, without more ado, welcome to Cahergillagh!'

We now entered the hall of the castle, and while the domestics were employed in conveying our trunks and other luggage which we had brought with us for immediate use to the apartments which Lord Glenfallen had selected for himself and me, I went with him into a spacious sitting-room, wainscoted with finely polished black oak, and hung round with the portraits of various worthies of the Glenfallen family.

This room looked out upon an extensive level covered with the softest green sward, and irregularly bounded by the wild wood I have before mentioned, through the leafy arcade formed by whose boughs and trunks the level beams of the setting sun were pouring. In the distance a group of dairymaids were plying their task, which they accompanied throughout with snatches of Irish songs which, mellowed by the distance, floated not unpleasingly to the ear; and beside them sat or lay, with all the grave importance of conscious protection, six or seven large dogs of various kinds. Farther in the distance, and through the cloisters of the arching wood, two or three ragged urchins were employed in driving such stray kine as had wandered farther than the rest to join their fellows.

As I looked upon this scene which I have described, a feeling of tranquillity and happiness came upon me, which I have never experienced in so strong a degree; and so strange to me was the sensation that my eyes filled with tears.

Lord Glenfallen mistook the cause of my emotion, and taking me kindly and tenderly by the hand, he said:

'Do not suppose, my love, that it is my intention to SETTLE here. Whenever you desire to leave this, you have only to let me know your wish, and it shall be complied with; so I must entreat of you not to suffer any circumstances which I can control to give you one moment's uneasiness. But here is old Martha; you must be introduced to her, one of the heirlooms of our family.'

A hale, good-humoured, erect old woman was Martha, and an agreeable contrast to the grim, decrepid hag which my fancy had conjured up, as the depository of all the horrible tales in which I doubted not this old place was most fruitful.

She welcomed me and her master with a profusion of gratulations, alternately kissing our hands and apologising for the liberty, until at length Lord Glenfallen put an end to this somewhat fatiguing ceremonial by requesting her to conduct me to my chamber if it were prepared for my reception.

I followed Martha up an old-fashioned oak staircase into a long, dim passage, at the end of which lay the door which communicated with the apartments which had been selected for our use; here the old woman stopped, and respectfully requested me to proceed.

I accordingly opened the door, and was about to enter, when something like a mass of black tapestry, as it appeared, disturbed by my sudden approach, fell from above the door, so as completely to screen the aperture; the startling unexpectedness of the occurrence, and the rustling noise which the drapery made in its descent, caused me involuntarily to step two or three paces backwards. I turned, smiling and half-ashamed, to the old servant, and said:

'You see what a coward I am.'

The woman looked puzzled, and, without saying any more, I was about to draw aside the curtain and enter the room, when, upon turning to do so, I was surprised to find that nothing whatever interposed to obstruct the passage.

I went into the room, followed by the servant-woman, and was amazed to find that it, like the one below, was wainscoted, and that nothing like drapery was to be found near the door.

'Where is it?' said I; 'what has become of it?'

'What does your ladyship wish to know?' said the old woman.

'Where is the black curtain that fell across the door, when I attempted first to come to my chamber?' answered I.

'The cross of Christ about us!' said the old woman, turning suddenly pale.

'What is the matter, my good friend?' said I; 'you seem frightened.'

'Oh no, no, your ladyship,' said the old woman, endeavouring to conceal her agitation; but in vain, for tottering towards a chair, she sank into it, looking so deadly pale and horror-struck that I thought every moment she would faint.

'Merciful God, keep us from harm and danger!' muttered she at length.

'What can have terrified you so?' said I, beginning to fear that she had seen something more than had met my eye. 'You appear ill, my poor woman!'

'Nothing, nothing, my lady,' said she, rising. 'I beg your ladyship's pardon for making so bold. May the great God defend us from misfortune!'

'Martha,' said I, 'something HAS frightened you very much, and I insist on knowing what it is; your keeping me in the dark upon the subject will make me much more uneasy than anything you could tell me. I desire you, therefore, to let me know what agitates you; I command you to tell me.'

'Your ladyship said you saw a black curtain falling across the door when you were coming into the room,' said the old woman.

'I did,' said I; 'but though the whole thing appears somewhat strange, I cannot see anything in the matter to agitate you so excessively.'

'It's for no good you saw that, my lady,' said the crone; 'something terrible is coming. It's a sign, my lady—a sign that never fails.'

'Explain, explain what you mean, my good woman,' said I, in spite of myself, catching more than I could account for, of her superstitious terror.

'Whenever something—something BAD is going to happen to the Glenfallen family, some one that belongs to them sees a black handkerchief or curtain just waved or falling before their faces. I saw it myself,' continued she, lowering her voice, 'when I was only a little girl, and I'll never forget it. I often heard of it before, though I never saw it till then, nor since, praised be God. But I was going into Lady Jane's room to waken her in the morning; and sure enough when I got first to the bed and began to draw the curtain, something dark was waved across the division, but only for a moment; and when I saw rightly into the bed, there was she lying cold and dead, God be merciful to me! So, my lady, there is small blame to me to be daunted when any one of the family sees it; for it's many's the story I heard of it, though I saw it but once.'

I was not of a superstitious turn of mind, yet I could not resist a feeling of awe very nearly allied to the fear which my companion had so unreservedly expressed; and when you consider my situation, the loneliness, antiquity, and gloom of the place, you will allow that the weakness was not without excuse.

In spite of old Martha's boding predictions, however, time flowed on in an unruffled course. One little incident however, though trifling in itself, I must relate, as it serves to make what follows more intelligible.

Upon the day after my arrival, Lord Glenfallen of course desired to make me acquainted with the house and domain; and accordingly we set forth upon our ramble. When returning, he became for some time silent and moody, a state so unusual with him as considerably to excite my surprise.

I endeavoured by observations and questions to arouse him—but in vain. At length, as we approached the house, he said, as if speaking to himself:

''Twere madness—madness—madness,' repeating the words bitterly—'sure and speedy ruin.'

There was here a long pause; and at length, turning sharply towards me, in a tone very unlike that in which he had hitherto addressed me, he said:

'Do you think it possible that a woman can keep a secret?'

'I am sure,' said I, 'that women are very much belied upon the score of talkativeness, and that I may answer your question with the same directness with which you put it—I reply that I DO think a woman can keep a secret.'

'But I do not,' said he, drily.

We walked on in silence for a time. I was much astonished at his unwonted abruptness—I had almost said rudeness.

After a considerable pause he seemed to recollect himself, and with an effort resuming his sprightly manner, he said:

'Well, well, the next thing to keeping a secret well is, not to desire to possess one—talkativeness and curiosity generally go together. Now I shall make test of you, in the first place, respecting the latter of these qualities. I shall be your BLUEBEARD—tush, why do I trifle thus? Listen to me, my dear Fanny; I speak now in solemn earnest. What I desire is intimately, inseparably, connected with your happiness and honour as well as my own; and your compliance with my request will not be difficult. It will impose upon you a very trifling restraint during your sojourn here, which certain events which have occurred since our arrival have determined me shall not be a long one. You must promise me, upon your sacred honour, that you will visit ONLY that part of the castle which can be reached from the front entrance, leaving the back entrance and the part of the building commanded immediately by it to the menials, as also the small garden whose high wall you see yonder; and never at any time seek to pry or peep into them, nor to open the door which communicates from the front part of the house through the corridor with the back. I do not urge this in jest or in caprice, but from a solemn conviction that danger and misery will be the certain consequences of your not observing what I prescribe. I cannot explain myself further at present. Promise me, then, these things, as you hope for peace here, and for mercy hereafter.'

I did make the promise as desired, and he appeared relieved; his manner recovered all its gaiety and elasticity: but the recollection of the strange scene which I have just described dwelt painfully upon my mind.

More than a month passed away without any occurrence worth recording; but I was not destined to leave Cahergillagh without further adventure. One day, intending to enjoy the pleasant sunshine in a ramble through the woods, I ran up to my room to procure my bonnet and shawl. Upon entering the chamber, I was surprised and somewhat startled to find it occupied. Beside the fireplace, and nearly opposite the door, seated in a large, old-fashioned elbow-chair, was placed the figure of a lady. She appeared to be nearer fifty than forty, and was dressed suitably to her age, in a handsome suit of flowered silk; she had a profusion of trinkets and jewellery about her person, and many rings upon her fingers. But although very rich, her dress was not gaudy or in ill taste. But what was remarkable in the lady was, that although her features were handsome, and upon the whole pleasing, the pupil of each eye was dimmed with the whiteness of cataract, and she was evidently stone-blind. I was for some seconds so surprised at this unaccountable apparition, that I could not find words to address her.

'Madam,' said I, 'there must be some mistake here—this is my bed-chamber.'

'Marry come up,' said the lady, sharply; 'YOUR chamber! Where is Lord Glenfallen?'

'He is below, madam,' replied I; 'and I am convinced he will be not a little surprised to find you here.'

'I do not think he will,' said she; 'with your good leave, talk of what you know something about. Tell him I want him. Why does the minx dilly-dally so?'

In spite of the awe which this grim lady inspired, there was something in her air of confident superiority which, when I considered our relative situations, was not a little irritating.

'Do you know, madam, to whom you speak?' said I.

'I neither know nor care,' said she; 'but I presume that you are some one about the house, so again I desire you, if you wish to continue here, to bring your master hither forthwith.'

'I must tell you, madam,' said I, 'that I am Lady Glenfallen.'

'What's that?' said the stranger, rapidly.

'I say, madam,' I repeated, approaching her that I might be more distinctly heard, 'that I am Lady Glenfallen.'

'It's a lie, you trull!' cried she, in an accent which made me start, and at the same time, springing forward, she seized me in her grasp, and shook me violently, repeating, 'It's a lie—it's a lie!' with a rapidity and vehemence which swelled every vein of her face. The violence of her action, and the fury which convulsed her face, effectually terrified me, and disengaging myself from her grasp, I screamed as loud as I could for help. The blind woman continued to pour out a torrent of abuse upon me, foaming at the mouth with rage, and impotently shaking her clenched fists towards me.

I heard Lord Glenfallen's step upon the stairs, and I instantly ran out; as I passed him I perceived that he was deadly pale, and just caught the words: 'I hope that demon has not hurt you?'

I made some answer, I forget what, and he entered the chamber, the door of which he locked upon the inside. What passed within I know not; but I heard the voices of the two speakers raised in loud and angry altercation.

I thought I heard the shrill accents of the woman repeat the words, 'Let her look to herself;' but I could not be quite sure. This short sentence, however, was, to my alarmed imagination, pregnant with fearful meaning.

The storm at length subsided, though not until after a conference of more than two long hours. Lord Glenfallen then returned, pale and agitated.

'That unfortunate woman,' said he, 'is out of her mind. I daresay she treated you to some of her ravings; but you need not dread any further interruption from her: I have brought her so far to reason. She did not hurt you, I trust.'

'No, no,' said I; 'but she terrified me beyond measure.'

'Well,' said he, 'she is likely to behave better for the future; and I dare swear that neither you nor she would desire, after what has passed, to meet again.'

This occurrence, so startling and unpleasant, so involved in mystery, and giving rise to so many painful surmises, afforded me no very agreeable food for rumination.

All attempts on my part to arrive at the truth were baffled; Lord Glenfallen evaded all my inquiries, and at length peremptorily forbid any further allusion to the matter. I was thus obliged to rest satisfied with what I had actually seen, and to trust to time to resolve the perplexities in which the whole transaction had involved me.

Lord Glenfallen's temper and spirits gradually underwent a complete and most painful change; he became silent and abstracted, his manner to me was abrupt and often harsh, some grievous anxiety seemed ever present to his mind; and under its influence his spirits sunk and his temper became soured.

I soon perceived that his gaiety was rather that which the stir and excitement of society produce, than the result of a healthy habit of mind; every day confirmed me in the opinion, that the considerate good-nature which I had so much admired in him was little more than a mere manner; and to my infinite grief and surprise, the gay, kind, open-hearted nobleman who had for months followed and flattered me, was rapidly assuming the form of a gloomy, morose, and singularly selfish man. This was a bitter discovery, and I strove to conceal it from myself as long as I could; but the truth was not to be denied, and I was forced to believe that Lord Glenfallen no longer loved me, and that he was at little pains to conceal the alteration in his sentiments.

One morning after breakfast, Lord Glenfallen had been for some time walking silently up and down the room, buried in his moody reflections, when pausing suddenly, and turning towards me, he exclaimed:

'I have it—I have it! We must go abroad, and stay there too; and if that does not answer, why—why, we must try some more effectual expedient. Lady Glenfallen, I have become involved in heavy embarrassments. A wife, you know, must share the fortunes of her husband, for better for worse; but I will waive my right if you prefer remaining here here at Cahergillagh. For I would not have you seen elsewhere without the state to which your rank entitles you; besides, it would break your poor mother's heart,' he added, with sneering gravity. 'So make up your mind—Cahergillagh or France. I will start if possible in a week, so determine between this and then.'

He left the room, and in a few moments I saw him ride past the window, followed by a mounted servant. He had directed a domestic to inform me that he should not be back until the next day.

I was in very great doubt as to what course of conduct I should pursue, as to accompanying him in the continental tour so suddenly determined upon. I felt that it would be a hazard too great to encounter; for at Cahergillagh I had always the consciousness to sustain me, that if his temper at any time led him into violent or unwarrantable treatment of me, I had a remedy within reach, in the protection and support of my own family, from all useful and effective communication with whom, if once in France, I should be entirely debarred.

As to remaining at Cahergillagh in solitude, and, for aught I knew, exposed to hidden dangers, it appeared to me scarcely less objectionable than the former proposition; and yet I feared that with one or other I must comply, unless I was prepared to come to an actual breach with Lord Glenfallen. Full of these unpleasing doubts and perplexities, I retired to rest.

I was wakened, after having slept uneasily for some hours, by some person shaking me rudely by the shoulder; a small lamp burned in my room, and by its light, to my horror and amazement, I discovered that my visitant was the self-same blind old lady who had so terrified me a few weeks before.

I started up in the bed, with a view to ring the bell, and alarm the domestics; but she instantly anticipated me by saying:

'Do not be frightened, silly girl! If I had wished to harm you I could have done it while you were sleeping; I need not have wakened you. Listen to me, now, attentively and fearlessly, for what I have to say interests you to the full as much as it does me. Tell me here, in the presence of God, did Lord Glenfallen marry you—ACTUALLY MARRY you? Speak the truth, woman.'

'As surely as I live and speak,' I replied, 'did Lord Glenfallen marry me, in presence of more than a hundred witnesses.'

'Well,' continued she, 'he should have told you THEN, before you married him, that he had a wife living, which wife I am. I feel you tremble—tush! do not be frightened. I do not mean to harm you. Mark me now—you are NOT his wife. When I make my story known you will be so neither in the eye of God nor of man. You must leave this house upon to-morrow. Let the world know that your husband has another wife living; go you into retirement, and leave him to justice, which will surely overtake him. If you remain in this house after to-morrow you will reap the bitter fruits of your sin.'

So saying, she quitted the room, leaving me very little disposed to sleep.

Here was food for my very worst and most terrible suspicions; still there was not enough to remove all doubt. I had no proof of the truth of this woman's statement.

Taken by itself, there was nothing to induce me to attach weight to it; but when I viewed it in connection with the extraordinary mystery of some of Lord Glenfallen's proceedings, his strange anxiety to exclude me from certain portions of the mansion, doubtless lest I should encounter this person—the strong influence, nay, command which she possessed over him, a circumstance clearly established by the very fact of her residing in the very place where, of all others, he should least have desired to find her—her thus acting, and continuing to act in direct contradiction to his wishes; when, I say, I viewed her disclosure in connection with all these circumstances, I could not help feeling that there was at least a fearful verisimilitude in the allegations which she had made.

Still I was not satisfied, nor nearly so. Young minds have a reluctance almost insurmountable to believing, upon anything short of unquestionable proof, the existence of premeditated guilt in anyone whom they have ever trusted; and in support of this feeling I was assured that if the assertion of Lord Glenfallen, which nothing in this woman's manner had led me to disbelieve, were true, namely that her mind was unsound, the whole fabric of my doubts and fears must fall to the ground.

I determined to state to Lord Glenfallen freely and accurately the substance of the communication which I had just heard, and in his words and looks to seek for its proof or refutation. Full of these thoughts, I remained wakeful and excited all night, every moment fancying that I heard the step or saw the figure of my recent visitor, towards whom I felt a species of horror and dread which I can hardly describe.

There was something in her face, though her features had evidently been handsome, and were not, at first sight, unpleasing, which, upon a nearer inspection, seemed to indicate the habitual prevalence and indulgence of evil passions, and a power of expressing mere animal anger, with an intenseness that I have seldom seen equalled, and to which an almost unearthly effect was given by the convulsive quivering of the sightless eyes.

You may easily suppose that it was no very pleasing reflection to me to consider that, whenever caprice might induce her to return, I was within the reach of this violent and, for aught I knew, insane woman, who had, upon that very night, spoken to me in a tone of menace, of which her mere words, divested of the manner and look with which she uttered them, can convey but a faint idea.

Will you believe me when I tell you that I was actually afraid to leave my bed in order to secure the door, lest I should again encounter the dreadful object lurking in some corner or peeping from behind the window-curtains, so very a child was I in my fears.

The morning came, and with it Lord Glenfallen. I knew not, and indeed I cared not, where he might have been; my thoughts were wholly engrossed by the terrible fears and suspicions which my last night's conference had suggested to me. He was, as usual, gloomy and abstracted, and I feared in no very fitting mood to hear what I had to say with patience, whether the charges were true or false.

I was, however, determined not to suffer the opportunity to pass, or Lord Glenfallen to leave the room, until, at all hazards, I had unburdened my mind.

'My lord,' said I, after a long silence, summoning up all my firmness—'my lord, I wish to say a few words to you upon a matter of very great importance, of very deep concernment to you and to me.'

I fixed my eyes upon him to discern, if possible, whether the announcement caused him any uneasiness; but no symptom of any such feeling was perceptible.

'Well, my dear,' said he, 'this is no doubt a very grave preface, and portends, I have no doubt, something extraordinary. Pray let us have it without more ado.'

He took a chair, and seated himself nearly opposite to me.

'My lord,' said I, 'I have seen the person who alarmed me so much a short time since, the blind lady, again, upon last night.' His face, upon which my eyes were fixed, turned pale; he hesitated for a moment, and then said:

'And did you, pray, madam, so totally forget or spurn my express command, as to enter that portion of the house from which your promise, I might say your oath, excluded you?—answer me that!' he added fiercely.

'My lord,' said I, 'I have neither forgotten your COMMANDS, since such they were, nor disobeyed them. I was, last night, wakened from my sleep, as I lay in my own chamber, and accosted by the person whom I have mentioned. How she found access to the room I cannot pretend to say.'

'Ha! this must be looked to,' said he, half reflectively; 'and pray,' added he, quickly, while in turn he fixed his eyes upon me, 'what did this person say? since some comment upon her communication forms, no doubt, the sequel to your preface.'

'Your lordship is not mistaken,' said I; 'her statement was so extraordinary that I could not think of withholding it from you. She told me, my lord, that you had a wife living at the time you married me, and that she was that wife.'

Lord Glenfallen became ashy pale, almost livid; he made two or three efforts to clear his voice to speak, but in vain, and turning suddenly from me, he walked to the window. The horror and dismay which, in the olden time, overwhelmed the woman of Endor when her spells unexpectedly conjured the dead into her presence, were but types of what I felt when thus presented with what appeared to be almost unequivocal evidence of the guilt whose existence I had before so strongly doubted.

There was a silence of some moments, during which it were hard to conjecture whether I or my companion suffered most.

Lord Glenfallen soon recovered his self-command; he returned to the table, again sat down and said:

'What you have told me has so astonished me, has unfolded such a tissue of motiveless guilt, and in a quarter from which I had so little reason to look for ingratitude or treachery, that your announcement almost deprived me of speech; the person in question, however, has one excuse, her mind is, as I told you before, unsettled. You should have remembered that, and hesitated to receive as unexceptionable evidence against the honour of your husband, the ravings of a lunatic. I now tell you that this is the last time I shall speak to you upon this subject, and, in the presence of the God who is to judge me, and as I hope for mercy in the day of judgment, I swear that the charge thus brought against me is utterly false, unfounded, and ridiculous; I defy the world in any point to taint my honour; and, as I have never taken the opinion of madmen touching your character or morals, I think it but fair to require that you will evince a like tenderness for me; and now, once for all, never again dare to repeat to me your insulting suspicions, or the clumsy and infamous calumnies of fools. I shall instantly let the worthy lady who contrived this somewhat original device, understand fully my opinion upon the matter. Good morning;' and with these words he left me again in doubt, and involved in all horrors of the most agonising suspense.

I had reason to think that Lord Glenfallen wreaked his vengeance upon the author of the strange story which I had heard, with a violence which was not satisfied with mere words, for old Martha, with whom I was a great favourite, while attending me in my room, told me that she feared her master had ill-used the poor blind Dutch woman, for that she had heard her scream as if the very life were leaving her, but added a request that I should not speak of what she had told me to any one, particularly to the master.

'How do you know that she is a Dutch woman?' inquired I, anxious to learn anything whatever that might throw a light upon the history of this person, who seemed to have resolved to mix herself up in my fortunes.

'Why, my lady,' answered Martha, 'the master often calls her the Dutch hag, and other names you would not like to hear, and I am sure she is neither English nor Irish; for, whenever they talk together, they speak some queer foreign lingo, and fast enough, I'll be bound. But I ought not to talk about her at all; it might be as much as my place is worth to mention her—only you saw her first yourself, so there can be no great harm in speaking of her now.'

'How long has this lady been here?' continued I.

'She came early on the morning after your ladyship's arrival,' answered she; 'but do not ask me any more, for the master would think nothing of turning me out of doors for daring to speak of her at all, much less to you, my lady.'

I did not like to press the poor woman further, for her reluctance to speak on this topic was evident and strong.

You will readily believe that upon the very slight grounds which my information afforded, contradicted as it was by the solemn oath of my husband, and derived from what was, at best, a very questionable source, I could not take any very decisive measure whatever; and as to the menace of the strange woman who had thus unaccountably twice intruded herself into my chamber, although, at the moment, it occasioned me some uneasiness, it was not, even in my eyes, sufficiently formidable to induce my departure from Cahergillagh.

A few nights after the scene which I have just mentioned, Lord Glenfallen having, as usual, early retired to his study, I was left alone in the parlour to amuse myself as best I might.

It was not strange that my thoughts should often recur to the agitating scenes in which I had recently taken a part.

The subject of my reflections, the solitude, the silence, and the lateness of the hour, as also the depression of spirits to which I had of late been a constant prey, tended to produce that nervous excitement which places us wholly at the mercy of the imagination.

In order to calm my spirits I was endeavouring to direct my thoughts into some more pleasing channel, when I heard, or thought I heard, uttered, within a few yards of me, in an odd, half-sneering tone, the words,

'There is blood upon your ladyship's throat.'

So vivid was the impression that I started to my feet, and involuntarily placed my hand upon my neck.

I looked around the room for the speaker, but in vain.

I went then to the room-door, which I opened, and peered into the passage, nearly faint with horror lest some leering, shapeless thing should greet me upon the threshold.

When I had gazed long enough to assure myself that no strange object was within sight, 'I have been too much of a rake lately; I am racking out my nerves,' said I, speaking aloud, with a view to reassure myself.

I rang the bell, and, attended by old Martha, I retired to settle for the night.

While the servant was—as was her custom—arranging the lamp which I have already stated always burned during the night in my chamber, I was employed in undressing, and, in doing so, I had recourse to a large looking-glass which occupied a considerable portion of the wall in which it was fixed, rising from the ground to a height of about six feet—this mirror filled the space of a large panel in the wainscoting opposite the foot of the bed.

I had hardly been before it for the lapse of a minute when something like a black pall was slowly waved between me and it.

'Oh, God! there it is,' I exclaimed, wildly. 'I have seen it again, Martha—the black cloth.'

'God be merciful to us, then!' answered she, tremulously crossing herself. 'Some misfortune is over us.'

'No, no, Martha,' said I, almost instantly recovering my collectedness; for, although of a nervous temperament, I had never been superstitious. 'I do not believe in omens. You know I saw, or fancied I saw, this thing before, and nothing followed.'

'The Dutch lady came the next morning,' replied she.

'But surely her coming scarcely deserved such a dreadful warning,' I replied.

'She is a strange woman, my lady,' said Martha; 'and she is not GONE yet—mark my words.'

'Well, well, Martha,' said I, 'I have not wit enough to change your opinions, nor inclination to alter mine; so I will talk no more of the matter. Good-night,' and so I was left to my reflections.

After lying for about an hour awake, I at length fell into a kind of doze; but my imagination was still busy, for I was startled from this unrefreshing sleep by fancying that I heard a voice close to my face exclaim as before:

'There is blood upon your ladyship's throat.'

The words were instantly followed by a loud burst of laughter.

Quaking with horror, I awakened, and heard my husband enter the room. Even this was it relief.

Scared as I was, however, by the tricks which my imagination had played me, I preferred remaining silent, and pretending to sleep, to attempting to engage my husband in conversation, for I well knew that his mood was such, that his words would not, in all probability, convey anything that had not better be unsaid and unheard.

Lord Glenfallen went into his dressing-room, which lay upon the right-hand side of the bed. The door lying open, I could see him by himself, at full length upon a sofa, and, in about half an hour, I became aware, by his deep and regularly drawn respiration, that he was fast asleep.

When slumber refuses to visit one, there is something peculiarly irritating, not to the temper, but to the nerves, in the consciousness that some one is in your immediate presence, actually enjoying the boon which you are seeking in vain; at least, I have always found it so, and never more than upon the present occasion.

A thousand annoying imaginations harassed and excited me; every object which I looked upon, though ever so familiar, seemed to have acquired a strange phantom-like character, the varying shadows thrown by the flickering of the lamplight, seemed shaping themselves into grotesque and unearthly forms, and whenever my eyes wandered to the sleeping figure of my husband, his features appeared to undergo the strangest and most demoniacal contortions.

Hour after hour was told by the old clock, and each succeeding one found me, if possible, less inclined to sleep than its predecessor.

It was now considerably past three; my eyes, in their involuntary wanderings, happened to alight upon the large mirror which was, as I have said, fixed in the wall opposite the foot of the bed. A view of it was commanded from where I lay, through the curtains. As I gazed fixedly upon it, I thought I perceived the broad sheet of glass shifting its position in relation to the bed; I riveted my eyes upon it with intense scrutiny; it was no deception, the mirror, as if acting of its own impulse, moved slowly aside, and disclosed a dark aperture in the wall, nearly as large as an ordinary door; a figure evidently stood in this, but the light was too dim to define it accurately.

It stepped cautiously into the chamber, and with so little noise, that had I not actually seen it, I do not think I should have been aware of its presence. It was arrayed in a kind of woollen night-dress, and a white handkerchief or cloth was bound tightly about the head; I had no difficulty, spite of the strangeness of the attire, in recognising the blind woman whom I so much dreaded.

She stooped down, bringing her head nearly to the ground, and in that attitude she remained motionless for some moments, no doubt in order to ascertain if any suspicious sound were stirring.

She was apparently satisfied by her observations, for she immediately recommenced her silent progress towards a ponderous mahogany dressing-table of my husband's. When she had reached it, she paused again, and appeared to listen attentively for some minutes; she then noiselessly opened one of the drawers, from which, having groped for some time, she took something, which I soon perceived to be a case of razors. She opened it, and tried the edge of each of the two instruments upon the skin of her hand; she quickly selected one, which she fixed firmly in her grasp. She now stooped down as before, and having listened for a time, she, with the hand that was disengaged, groped her way into the dressing-room where Lord Glenfallen lay fast asleep.

I was fixed as if in the tremendous spell of a nightmare. I could not stir even a finger; I could not lift my voice; I could not even breathe; and though I expected every moment to see the sleeping man murdered, I could not even close my eyes to shut out the horrible spectacle, which I had not the power to avert.

I saw the woman approach the sleeping figure, she laid the unoccupied hand lightly along his clothes, and having thus ascertained his identity, she, after a brief interval, turned back and again entered my chamber; here she bent down again to listen.

I had now not a doubt but that the razor was intended for my throat; yet the terrific fascination which had locked all my powers so long, still continued to bind me fast.

I felt that my life depended upon the slightest ordinary exertion, and yet I could not stir one joint from the position in which I lay, nor even make noise enough to waken Lord Glenfallen.

The murderous woman now, with long, silent steps, approached the bed; my very heart seemed turning to ice; her left hand, that which was disengaged, was upon the pillow; she gradually slid it forward towards my head, and in an instant, with the speed of lightning, it was clutched in my hair, while, with the other hand, she dashed the razor at my throat.

A slight inaccuracy saved me from instant death; the blow fell short, the point of the razor grazing my throat. In a moment, I know not how, I found myself at the other side of the bed, uttering shriek after shriek; the wretch was, however, determined if possible to murder me.

Scrambling along by the curtains, she rushed round the bed towards me; I seized the handle of the door to make my escape. It was, however, fastened. At all events, I could not open it. From the mere instinct of recoiling terror, I shrunk back into a corner. She was now within a yard of me. Her hand was upon my face.

I closed my eyes fast, expecting never to open them again, when a blow, inflicted from behind by a strong arm, stretched the monster senseless at my feet. At the same moment the door opened, and several domestics, alarmed by my cries, entered the apartment.

I do not recollect what followed, for I fainted. One swoon succeeded another, so long and death-like, that my life was considered very doubtful.

At about ten o'clock, however, I sunk into a deep and refreshing sleep, from which I was awakened at about two, that I might swear my deposition before a magistrate, who attended for that purpose.

I accordingly did so, as did also Lord Glenfallen, and the woman was fully committed to stand her trial at the ensuing assizes.

I shall never forget the scene which the examination of the blind woman and of the other parties afforded.

She was brought into the room in the custody of two servants. She wore a kind of flannel wrapper which had not been changed since the night before. It was torn and soiled, and here and there smeared with blood, which had flowed in large quantities from a wound in her head. The white handkerchief had fallen off in the scuffle, and her grizzled hair fell in masses about her wild and deadly pale countenance.

She appeared perfectly composed, however, and the only regret she expressed throughout, was at not having succeeded in her attempt, the object of which she did not pretend to conceal.

On being asked her name, she called herself the Countess Glenfallen, and refused to give any other title.

'The woman's name is Flora Van-Kemp,' said Lord Glenfallen.

'It WAS, it WAS, you perjured traitor and cheat!' screamed the woman; and then there followed a volley of words in some foreign language. 'Is there a magistrate here?' she resumed; 'I am Lord Glenfallen's wife—I'll prove it—write down my words. I am willing to be hanged or burned, so HE meets his deserts. I did try to kill that doll of his; but it was he who put it into my head to do it—two wives were too many; I was to murder her, or she was to hang me; listen to all I have to say.'

Here Lord Glenfallen interrupted.

'I think, sir,' said he, addressing the magistrate, 'that we had better proceed to business; this unhappy woman's furious recriminations but waste our time. If she refuses to answer your questions, you had better, I presume, take my depositions.'

'And are you going to swear away my life, you black-perjured murderer?' shrieked the woman. 'Sir, sir, sir, you must hear me,' she continued, addressing the magistrate; 'I can convict him—he bid me murder that girl, and then, when I failed, he came behind me, and struck me down, and now he wants to swear away my life. Take down all I say.'

'If it is your intention,' said the magistrate, 'to confess the crime with which you stand charged, you may, upon producing sufficient evidence, criminate whom you please.'

'Evidence!—I have no evidence but myself,' said the woman. 'I will swear it all—write down my testimony—write it down, I say—we shall hang side by side, my brave lord—all your own handy-work, my gentle husband.'

This was followed by a low, insolent, and sneering laugh, which, from one in her situation, was sufficiently horrible.

'I will not at present hear anything,' replied he, 'but distinct answers to the questions which I shall put to you upon this matter.'

'Then you shall hear nothing,' replied she sullenly, and no inducement or intimidation could bring her to speak again.

Lord Glenfallen's deposition and mine were then given, as also those of the servants who had entered the room at the moment of my rescue.

The magistrate then intimated that she was committed, and must proceed directly to gaol, whither she was brought in a carriage; of Lord Glenfallen's, for his lordship was naturally by no means indifferent to the effect which her vehement accusations against himself might produce, if uttered before every chance hearer whom she might meet with between Cahergillagh and the place of confinement whither she was despatched.

During the time which intervened between the committal and the trial of the prisoner, Lord Glenfallen seemed to suffer agonies of mind which baffle all description; he hardly ever slept, and when he did, his slumbers seemed but the instruments of new tortures, and his waking hours were, if possible, exceeded in intensity of terrors by the dreams which disturbed his sleep.

Lord Glenfallen rested, if to lie in the mere attitude of repose were to do so, in his dressing-room, and thus I had an opportunity of witnessing, far oftener than I wished it, the fearful workings of his mind. His agony often broke out into such fearful paroxysms that delirium and total loss of reason appeared to be impending. He frequently spoke of flying from the country, and bringing with him all the witnesses of the appalling scene upon which the prosecution was founded; then, again, he would fiercely lament that the blow which he had inflicted had not ended all.

The assizes arrived, however, and upon the day appointed Lord Glenfallen and I attended in order to give our evidence.

The cause was called on, and the prisoner appeared at the bar.

Great curiosity and interest were felt respecting the trial, so that the court was crowded to excess.

The prisoner, however, without appearing to take the trouble of listening to the indictment, pleaded guilty, and no representations on the part of the court availed to induce her to retract her plea.

After much time had been wasted in a fruitless attempt to prevail upon her to reconsider her words, the court proceeded, according to the usual form, to pass sentence.

This having been done, the prisoner was about to be removed, when she said, in a low, distinct voice:

'A word—a word, my lord!—Is Lord Glenfallen here in the court?'

On being told that he was, she raised her voice to a tone of loud menace, and continued:

'Hardress, Earl of Glenfallen, I accuse you here in this court of justice of two crimes,—first, that you married a second wife, while the first was living; and again, that you prompted me to the murder, for attempting which I am to die. Secure him—chain him—bring him here.'

There was a laugh through the court at these words, which were naturally treated by the judge as a violent extemporary recrimination, and the woman was desired to be silent.

'You won't take him, then?' she said; 'you won't try him? You'll let him go free?'

It was intimated by the court that he would certainly be allowed 'to go free,' and she was ordered again to be removed.

Before, however, the mandate was executed, she threw her arms wildly into the air, and uttered one piercing shriek so full of preternatural rage and despair, that it might fitly have ushered a soul into those realms where hope can come no more.

The sound still rang in my ears, months after the voice that had uttered it was for ever silent.

The wretched woman was executed in accordance with the sentence which had been pronounced.

For some time after this event, Lord Glenfallen appeared, if possible, to suffer more than he had done before, and altogether his language, which often amounted to half confessions of the guilt imputed to him, and all the circumstances connected with the late occurrences, formed a mass of evidence so convincing that I wrote to my father, detailing the grounds of my fears, and imploring him to come to Cahergillagh without delay, in order to remove me from my husband's control, previously to taking legal steps for a final separation.

Circumstanced as I was, my existence was little short of intolerable, for, besides the fearful suspicions which attached to my husband, I plainly perceived that if Lord Glenfallen were not relieved, and that speedily, insanity must supervene. I therefore expected my father's arrival, or at least a letter to announce it, with indescribable impatience.

About a week after the execution had taken place, Lord Glenfallen one morning met me with an unusually sprightly air.

'Fanny,' said he, 'I have it now for the first time in my power to explain to your satisfaction everything which has hitherto appeared suspicious or mysterious in my conduct. After breakfast come with me to my study, and I shall, I hope, make all things clear.'

This invitation afforded me more real pleasure than I had experienced for months. Something had certainly occurred to tranquillize my husband's mind in no ordinary degree, and I thought it by no means impossible that he would, in the proposed interview, prove himself the most injured and innocent of men.

Full of this hope, I repaired to his study at the appointed hour. He was writing busily when I entered the room, and just raising his eyes, he requested me to be seated.

I took a chair as he desired, and remained silently awaiting his leisure, while he finished, folded, directed, and sealed his letter. Laying it then upon the table with the address downward, he said,

'My dearest Fanny, I know I must have appeared very strange to you and very unkind—often even cruel. Before the end of this week I will show you the necessity of my conduct—how impossible it was that I should have seemed otherwise. I am conscious that many acts of mine must have inevitably given rise to painful suspicions—suspicions which, indeed, upon one occasion, you very properly communicated to me. I have got two letters from a quarter which commands respect, containing information as to the course by which I may be enabled to prove the negative of all the crimes which even the most credulous suspicion could lay to my charge. I expected a third by this morning's post, containing documents which will set the matter for ever at rest, but owing, no doubt, to some neglect, or, perhaps, to some difficulty in collecting the papers, some inevitable delay, it has not come to hand this morning, according to my expectation. I was finishing one to the very same quarter when you came in, and if a sound rousing be worth anything, I think I shall have a special messenger before two days have passed. I have been anxiously considering with myself, as to whether I had better imperfectly clear up your doubts by submitting to your inspection the two letters which I have already received, or wait till I can triumphantly vindicate myself by the production of the documents which I have already mentioned, and I have, I think, not unnaturally decided upon the latter course. However, there is a person in the next room whose testimony is not without its value excuse me for one moment.'

So saying, he arose and went to the door of a closet which opened from the study; this he unlocked, and half opening the door, he said, 'It is only I,' and then slipped into the room and carefully closed and locked the door behind him.

I immediately heard his voice in animated conversation. My curiosity upon the subject of the letter was naturally great, so, smothering any little scruples which I might have felt, I resolved to look at the address of the letter which lay, as my husband had left it, with its face upon the table. I accordingly drew it over to me and turned up the direction.

For two or three moments I could scarce believe my eyes, but there could be no mistake—in large characters were traced the words, 'To the Archangel Gabriel in Heaven.'

I had scarcely returned the letter to its original position, and in some degree recovered the shock which this unequivocal proof of insanity produced, when the closet door was unlocked, and Lord Glenfallen re-entered the study, carefully closing and locking the door again upon the outside.

'Whom have you there?' inquired I, making a strong effort to appear calm.

'Perhaps,' said he, musingly, 'you might have some objection to seeing her, at least for a time.'

'Who is it?' repeated I.

'Why,' said he, 'I see no use in hiding it—the blind Dutchwoman. I have been with her the whole morning. She is very anxious to get out of that closet; but you know she is odd, she is scarcely to be trusted.'

A heavy gust of wind shook the door at this moment with a sound as if something more substantial were pushing against it.

'Ha, ha, ha!—do you hear her?' said he, with an obstreperous burst of laughter.

The wind died away in a long howl, and Lord Glenfallen, suddenly checking his merriment, shrugged his shoulders, and muttered:

'Poor devil, she has been hardly used.'

'We had better not tease her at present with questions,' said I, in as unconcerned a tone as I could assume, although I felt every moment as if I should faint.

'Humph! may be so,' said he. 'Well, come back in an hour or two, or when you please, and you will find us here.'

He again unlocked the door, and entered with the same precautions which he had adopted before, locking the door upon the inside; and as I hurried from the room, I heard his voice again exerted as if in eager parley.

I can hardly describe my emotions; my hopes had been raised to the highest, and now, in an instant, all was gone—the dreadful consummation was accomplished—the fearful retribution had fallen upon the guilty man—the mind was destroyed—the power to repent was gone.

The agony of the hours which followed what I would still call my AWFUL interview with Lord Glenfallen, I cannot describe; my solitude was, however, broken in upon by Martha, who came to inform me of the arrival of a gentleman, who expected me in the parlour.

I accordingly descended, and, to my great joy, found my father seated by the fire.

This expedition upon his part was easily accounted for: my communications had touched the honour of the family. I speedily informed him of the dreadful malady which had fallen upon the wretched man.

My father suggested the necessity of placing some person to watch him, to prevent his injuring himself or others.

I rang the bell, and desired that one Edward Cooke, an attached servant of the family, should be sent to me.

I told him distinctly and briefly the nature of the service required of him, and, attended by him, my father and I proceeded at once to the study. The door of the inner room was still closed, and everything in the outer chamber remained in the same order in which I had left it.

We then advanced to the closet-door, at which we knocked, but without receiving any answer.

We next tried to open the door, but in vain—it was locked upon the inside. We knocked more loudly, but in vain.

Seriously alarmed, I desired the servant to force the door, which was, after several violent efforts, accomplished, and we entered the closet.

Lord Glenfallen was lying on his face upon a sofa.

'Hush!' said I, 'he is asleep.' We paused for a moment.

'He is too still for that,' said my father.

We all of us felt a strong reluctance to approach the figure.

'Edward,' said I, 'try whether your master sleeps.'

The servant approached the sofa where Lord Glenfallen lay. He leant his ear towards the head of the recumbent figure, to ascertain whether the sound of breathing was audible. He turned towards us, and said:

'My lady, you had better not wait here; I am sure he is dead!'

'Let me see the face,' said I, terribly agitated; 'you MAY be mistaken.'

The man then, in obedience to my command, turned the body round, and, gracious God! what a sight met my view. He was, indeed, perfectly dead.

The whole breast of the shirt, with its lace frill, was drenched with gore, as was the couch underneath the spot where he lay.

The head hung back, as it seemed, almost severed from the body by a frightful gash, which yawned across the throat. The instrument which had inflicted it was found under his body.

All, then, was over; I was never to learn the history in whose termination I had been so deeply and so tragically involved.

The severe discipline which my mind had undergone was not bestowed in vain. I directed my thoughts and my hopes to that place where there is no more sin, nor danger, nor sorrow.

Thus ends a brief tale whose prominent incidents many will recognise as having marked the history of a distinguished family; and though it refers to a somewhat distant date, we shall be found not to have taken, upon that account, any liberties with the facts, but in our statement of all the incidents to have rigorously and faithfully adhered to the truth.

AN ADVENTURE OF HARDRESS FITZGERALD, A ROYALIST CAPTAIN.

Being an Eleventh Extract from the Legacy of the late
Francis Purcell, P.P. of Drumcoolagh.

The following brief narrative contains a faithful account of one of the many strange incidents which chequered the life of Hardress Fitzgerald—one of the now-forgotten heroes who flourished during the most stirring and, though the most disastrous, by no means the least glorious period of our eventful history.

He was a captain of horse in the army of James, and shared the fortunes of his master, enduring privations, encountering dangers, and submitting to vicissitudes the most galling and ruinous, with a fortitude and a heroism which would, if coupled with his other virtues have rendered the unhappy monarch whom he served, the most illustrious among unfortunate princes.

I have always preferred, where I could do so with any approach to accuracy, to give such relations as the one which I am about to submit to you, in the first person, and in the words of the original narrator, believing that such a form of recitation not only gives freshness to the tale, but in this particular instance, by bringing before me and steadily fixing in my mind's eye the veteran royalist who himself related the occurrence which I am about to record, furnishes an additional stimulant to my memory, and a proportionate check upon my imagination.

As nearly as I can recollect then, his statement was as follows:

After the fatal battle of the Boyne, I came up in disguise to Dublin, as did many in a like situation, regarding the capital as furnishing at once a good central position of observation, and as secure a lurking-place as I cared to find.

I would not suffer myself to believe that the cause of my royal master was so desperate as it really was; and while I lay in my lodgings, which consisted of the garret of a small dark house, standing in the lane which runs close by Audoen's Arch, I busied myself with continual projects for the raising of the country, and the re-collecting of the fragments of the defeated army—plans, you will allow, sufficiently magnificent for a poor devil who dared scarce show his face abroad in the daylight.

I believe, however, that I had not much reason to fear for my personal safety, for men's minds in the city were greatly occupied with public events, and private amusements and debaucheries, which were, about that time, carried to an excess which our country never knew before, by reason of the raking together from all quarters of the empire, and indeed from most parts of Holland, the most dissolute and desperate adventurers who cared to play at hazard for their lives; and thus there seemed to be but little scrutiny into the characters of those who sought concealment.

I heard much at different times of the intentions of King James and his party, but nothing with certainty.

Some said that the king still lay in Ireland; others, that he had crossed over to Scotland, to encourage the Highlanders, who, with Dundee at their head, had been stirring in his behoof; others, again, said that he had taken ship for France, leaving his followers to shift for themselves, and regarding his kingdom as wholly lost, which last was the true version, as I afterwards learned.

Although I had been very active in the wars in Ireland, and had done many deeds of necessary but dire severity, which have often since troubled me much to think upon, yet I doubted not but that I might easily obtain protection for my person and property from the Prince of Orange, if I sought it by the ordinary submissions; but besides that my conscience and my affections resisted such time-serving concessions, I was resolved in my own mind that the cause of the royalist party was by no means desperate, and I looked to keep myself unimpeded by any pledge or promise given to the usurping Dutchman, that I might freely and honourably take a share in any struggle which might yet remain to be made for the right.

I therefore lay quiet, going forth from my lodgings but little, and that chiefly under cover of the dusk, and conversing hardly at all, except with those whom I well knew.

I had like once to have paid dearly for relaxing this caution; for going into a tavern one evening near the Tholsel, I had the confidence to throw off my hat, and sit there with my face quite exposed, when a fellow coming in with some troopers, they fell a-boozing, and being somewhat warmed, they began to drink 'Confusion to popery,' and the like, and to compel the peaceable persons who happened to sit there, to join them in so doing.

Though I was rather hot-blooded, I was resolved to say nothing to attract notice; but, at the same time, if urged to pledge the toasts which they were compelling others to drink, to resist doing so.

With the intent to withdraw myself quietly from the place, I paid my reckoning, and putting on my hat, was going into the street, when the countryman who had come in with the soldiers called out:

'Stop that popish tom-cat!'

And running across the room, he got to the door before me, and, shutting it, placed his back against it, to prevent my going out.

Though with much difficulty, I kept an appearance of quietness, and turning to the fellow, who, from his accent, I judged to be northern, and whose face I knew—though, to this day, I cannot say where I had seen him before—I observed very calmly:

'Sir, I came in here with no other design than to refresh myself, without offending any man. I have paid my reckoning, and now desire to go forth. If there is anything within reason that I can do to satisfy you, and to prevent trouble and delay to myself, name your terms, and if they be but fair, I will frankly comply with them.'

He quickly replied:

'You are Hardress Fitzgerald, the bloody popish captain, that hanged the twelve men at Derry.'

I felt that I was in some danger, but being a strong man, and used to perils of all kinds, it was not easy to disconcert me.

I looked then steadily at the fellow, and, in a voice of much confidence, I said:

'I am neither a Papist, a Royalist, nor a Fitzgerald, but an honester Protestant, mayhap, than many who make louder professions.'

'Then drink the honest man's toast,' said he. 'Damnation to the pope, and confusion to skulking Jimmy and his runaway crew.'

'Yourself shall hear me,' said I, taking the largest pewter pot that lay within my reach. 'Tapster, fill this with ale; I grieve to say I can afford nothing better.'

I took the vessel of liquor in my hand, and walking up to him, I first made a bow to the troopers who sat laughing at the sprightliness of their facetious friend, and then another to himself, when saying, 'G—— damn yourself and your cause!' I flung the ale straight into his face; and before he had time to recover himself, I struck him with my whole force and weight with the pewter pot upon the head, so strong a blow, that he fell, for aught I know, dead upon the floor, and nothing but the handle of the vessel remained in my hand.

I opened the door, but one of the dragoons drew his sabre, and ran at me to avenge his companion. With my hand I put aside the blade of the sword, narrowly escaping what he had intended for me, the point actually tearing open my vest. Without allowing him time to repeat his thrust, I struck him in the face with my clenched fist so sound a blow that he rolled back into the room with the force of a tennis ball.

It was well for me that the rest were half drunk, and the evening dark; for otherwise my folly would infallibly have cost me my life. As it was, I reached my garret in safety, with a resolution to frequent taverns no more until better times.

My little patience and money were wellnigh exhausted, when, after much doubt and uncertainty, and many conflicting reports, I was assured that the flower of the Royalist army, under the Duke of Berwick and General Boisleau, occupied the city of Limerick, with a determination to hold that fortress against the prince's forces; and that a French fleet of great power, and well freighted with arms, ammunition, and men, was riding in the Shannon, under the walls of the town. But this last report was, like many others then circulated, untrue; there being, indeed, a promise and expectation of such assistance, but no arrival of it till too late.

The army of the Prince of Orange was said to be rapidly approaching the town, in order to commence the siege.

On hearing this, and being made as certain as the vagueness and unsatisfactory nature of my information, which came not from any authentic source, would permit; at least, being sure of the main point, which all allowed—namely, that Limerick was held for the king—and being also naturally fond of enterprise, and impatient of idleness, I took the resolution to travel thither, and, if possible, to throw myself into the city, in order to lend what assistance I might to my former companions in arms, well knowing that any man of strong constitution and of some experience might easily make himself useful to a garrison in their straitened situation.

When I had taken this resolution, I was not long in putting it into execution; and, as the first step in the matter, I turned half of the money which remained with me, in all about seventeen pounds, into small wares and merchandise such as travelling traders used to deal in; and the rest, excepting some shillings which I carried home for my immediate expenses, I sewed carefully in the lining of my breeches waistband, hoping that the sale of my commodities might easily supply me with subsistence upon the road.

I left Dublin upon a Friday morning in the month of September, with a tolerably heavy pack upon my back.

I was a strong man and a good walker, and one day with another travelled easily at the rate of twenty miles in each day, much time being lost in the towns of any note on the way, where, to avoid suspicion, I was obliged to make some stay, as if to sell my wares.

I did not travel directly to Limerick, but turned far into Tipperary, going near to the borders of Cork.

Upon the sixth day after my departure from Dublin I learned, CERTAINLY, from some fellows who were returning from trafficking with the soldiers, that the army of the prince was actually encamped before Limerick, upon the south side of the Shannon.

In order, then, to enter the city without interruption, I must needs cross the river, and I was much in doubt whether to do so by boat from Kerry, which I might have easily done, into the Earl of Clare's land, and thus into the beleaguered city, or to take what seemed the easier way, one, however, about which I had certain misgivings—which, by the way, afterwards turned out to be just enough. This way was to cross the Shannon at O'Brien's Bridge, or at Killaloe, into the county of Clare.

I feared, however, that both these passes were guarded by the prince's forces, and resolved, if such were the case, not to essay to cross, for I was not fitted to sustain a scrutiny, having about me, though pretty safely secured, my commission from King James—which, though a dangerous companion, I would not have parted from but with my life.

I settled, then, in my own mind, that if the bridges were guarded I would walk as far as Portumna, where I might cross, though at a considerable sacrifice of time; and, having determined upon this course, I turned directly towards Killaloe.

I reached the foot of the mountain, or rather high hill, called Keeper—which had been pointed out to me as a landmark—lying directly between me and Killaloe, in the evening, and, having ascended some way, the darkness and fog overtook me.

The evening was very chilly, and myself weary, hungry, and much in need of sleep, so that I preferred seeking to cross the hill, though at some risk, to remaining upon it throughout the night. Stumbling over rocks and sinking into bog-mire, as the nature of the ground varied, I slowly and laboriously plodded on, making very little way in proportion to the toil it cost me.

After half an hour's slow walking, or rather rambling, for, owing to the dark, I very soon lost my direction, I at last heard the sound of running water, and with some little trouble reached the edge of a brook, which ran in the bottom of a deep gully. This I knew would furnish a sure guide to the low grounds, where I might promise myself that I should speedily meet with some house or cabin where I might find shelter for the night.

The stream which I followed flowed at the bottom of a rough and swampy glen, very steep and making many abrupt turns, and so dark, owing more to the fog than to the want of the moon (for, though not high, I believe it had risen at the time), that I continually fell over fragments of rock and stumbled up to my middle into the rivulet, which I sought to follow.

In this way, drenched, weary, and with my patience almost exhausted, I was toiling onward, when, turning a sharp angle in the winding glen, I found myself within some twenty yards of a group of wild-looking men, gathered in various attitudes round a glowing turf fire.

I was so surprised at this rencontre that I stopped short, and for a time was in doubt whether to turn back or to accost them.

A minute's thought satisfied me that I ought to make up to the fellows, and trust to their good faith for whatever assistance they could give me.

I determined, then, to do this, having great faith in the impulses of my mind, which, whenever I have been in jeopardy, as in my life I often have, always prompted me aright.

The strong red light of the fire showed me plainly enough that the group consisted, not of soldiers, but of Irish kernes, or countrymen, most of them wrapped in heavy mantles, and with no other covering for their heads than that afforded by their long, rough hair.

There was nothing about them which I could see to intimate whether their object were peaceful or warlike; but I afterwards found that they had weapons enough, though of their own rude fashion.

There were in all about twenty persons assembled around the fire, some sitting upon such blocks of stone as happened to lie in the way; others stretched at their length upon the ground.

'God save you, boys!' said I, advancing towards the party.

The men who had been talking and laughing together instantly paused, and two of them—tall and powerful fellows—snatched up each a weapon, something like a short halberd with a massive iron head, an instrument which they called among themselves a rapp, and with two or three long strides they came up with me, and laying hold upon my arms, drew me, not, you may easily believe, making much resistance, towards the fire.

When I reached the place where the figures were seated, the two men still held me firmly, and some others threw some handfuls of dry fuel upon the red embers, which, blazing up, cast a strong light upon me.

When they had satisfied themselves as to my appearance, they began to question me very closely as to my purpose in being upon the hill at such an unseasonable hour, asking me what was my occupation, where I had been, and whither I was going.

These questions were put to me in English by an old half-military looking man, who translated into that language the suggestions which his companions for the most part threw out in Irish.

I did not choose to commit myself to these fellows by telling them my real character and purpose, and therefore I represented myself as a poor travelling chapman who had been at Cork, and was seeking his way to Killaloe, in order to cross over into Clare and thence to the city of Galway.

My account did not seem fully to satisfy the men.

I heard one fellow say in Irish, which language I understood, 'Maybe he is a spy.'

They then whispered together for a time, and the little man who was their spokesman came over to me and said:

'Do you know what we do with spies? we knock their brains out, my friend.'

He then turned back to them with whom he had been whispering, and talked in a low tone again with them for a considerable time.

I now felt very uncomfortable, not knowing what these savages—for they appeared nothing better—might design against me.

Twice or thrice I had serious thoughts of breaking from them, but the two guards who were placed upon me held me fast by the arms; and even had I succeeded in shaking them off, I should soon have been overtaken, encumbered as I was with a heavy pack, and wholly ignorant of the lie of the ground; or else, if I were so exceedingly lucky as to escape out of their hands, I still had the chance of falling into those of some other party of the same kind.

I therefore patiently awaited the issue of their deliberations, which I made no doubt affected me nearly.

I turned to the men who held me, and one after the other asked them, in their own language, 'Why they held me?' adding, 'I am but a poor pedlar, as you see. I have neither money nor money's worth, for the sake of which you should do me hurt. You may have my pack and all that it contains, if you desire it—but do not injure me.'

To all this they gave no answer, but savagely desired me to hold my tongue.

I accordingly remained silent, determined, if the worst came, to declare to the whole party, who, I doubted not, were friendly, as were all the Irish peasantry in the south, to the Royal cause, my real character and design; and if this avowal failed me, I was resolved to make a desperate effort to escape, or at least to give my life at the dearest price I could.

I was not kept long in suspense, for the little veteran who had spoken to me at first came over, and desiring the two men to bring me after him, led the way along a broken path, which wound by the side of the steep glen.

I was obliged willy nilly to go with them, and, half-dragging and half-carrying me, they brought me by the path, which now became very steep, for some hundred yards without stopping, when suddenly coming to a stand, I found myself close before the door of some house or hut, I could not see which, through the planks of which a strong light was streaming.

At this door my conductor stopped, and tapping gently at it, it was opened by a stout fellow, with buff-coat and jack-boots, and pistols stuck in his belt, as also a long cavalry sword by his side.

He spoke with my guide, and to my no small satisfaction, in French, which convinced me that he was one of the soldiers whom Louis had sent to support our king, and who were said to have arrived in Limerick, though, as I observed above, not with truth.

I was much assured by this circumstance, and made no doubt but that I had fallen in with one of those marauding parties of native Irish, who, placing themselves under the guidance of men of courage and experience, had done much brave and essential service to the cause of the king.

The soldier entered an inner door in the apartment, which opening disclosed a rude, dreary, and dilapidated room, with a low plank ceiling, much discoloured by the smoke which hung suspended in heavy masses, descending within a few feet of the ground, and completely obscuring the upper regions of the chamber.

A large fire of turf and heath was burning under a kind of rude chimney, shaped like a large funnel, but by no means discharging the functions for which it was intended. Into this inauspicious apartment was I conducted by my strange companions. In the next room I heard voices employed, as it seemed, in brief questioning and answer; and in a minute the soldier reentered the room, and having said, 'Votre prisonnier—le general veut le voir,' he led the way into the inner room, which in point of comfort and cleanliness was not a whit better than the first.

Seated at a clumsy plank table, placed about the middle of the floor, was a powerfully built man, of almost colossal stature—his military accoutrements, cuirass and rich regimental clothes, soiled, deranged, and spattered with recent hard travel; the flowing wig, surmounted by the cocked hat and plume, still rested upon his head. On the table lay his sword-belt with its appendage, and a pair of long holster pistols, some papers, and pen and ink; also a stone jug, and the fragments of a hasty meal. His attitude betokened the languor of fatigue. His left hand was buried beyond the lace ruffle in the breast of his cassock, and the elbow of his right rested upon the table, so as to support his head. From his mouth protruded a tobacco-pipe, which as I entered he slowly withdrew.

A single glance at the honest, good-humoured, comely face of the soldier satisfied me of his identity, and removing my hat from my head I said, 'God save General Sarsfield!'

The general nodded

'I am a prisoner here under strange circumstances,' I continued 'I appear before you in a strange disguise. You do not recognise Captain Hardress Fitzgerald!'

'Eh, how's this?' said he, approaching me with the light.

'I am that Hardress Fitzgerald,' I repeated, 'who served under you at the Boyne, and upon the day of the action had the honour to protect your person at the expense of his own.' At the same time I turned aside the hair which covered the scar which you well know upon my forehead, and which was then much more remarkable than it is now.

The general on seeing this at once recognised me, and embracing me cordially, made me sit down, and while I unstrapped my pack, a tedious job, my fingers being nearly numbed with cold, sent the men forth to procure me some provision.

The general's horse was stabled in a corner of the chamber where we sat, and his war-saddle lay upon the floor. At the far end of the room was a second door, which stood half open; a bogwood fire burned on a hearth somewhat less rude than the one which I had first seen, but still very little better appointed with a chimney, for thick wreaths of smoke were eddying, with every fitful gust, about the room. Close by the fire was strewed a bed of heath, intended, I supposed, for the stalwart limbs of the general.

'Hardress Fitzgerald,' said he, fixing his eyes gravely upon me, while he slowly removed the tobacco-pipe from his mouth, 'I remember you, strong, bold and cunning in your warlike trade; the more desperate an enterprise, the more ready for it, you. I would gladly engage you, for I know you trustworthy, to perform a piece of duty requiring, it may be, no extraordinary quality to fulfil; and yet perhaps, as accidents may happen, demanding every attribute of daring and dexterity which belongs to you.'

Here he paused for some moments.

I own I felt somewhat flattered by the terms in which he spoke of me, knowing him to be but little given to compliments; and not having any plan in my head, farther than the rendering what service I might to the cause of the king, caring very little as to the road in which my duty might lie, I frankly replied:

'Sir, I hope, if opportunity offers, I shall prove to deserve the honourable terms in which you are pleased to speak of me. In a righteous cause I fear not wounds or death; and in discharging my duty to my God and my king, I am ready for any hazard or any fate. Name the service you require, and if it lies within the compass of my wit or power, I will fully and faithfully perform it. Have I said enough?'

'That is well, very well, my friend; you speak well, and manfully,' replied the general. 'I want you to convey to the hands of General Boisleau, now in the city of

Limerick, a small written packet; there is some danger, mark me, of your falling in with some outpost or straggling party of the prince's army. If you are taken unawares by any of the enemy you must dispose of the packet inside your person, rather than let it fall into their hands—that is, you must eat it. And if they go to question you with thumbscrews, or the like, answer nothing; let them knock your brains out first.' In illustration, I suppose, of the latter alternative, he knocked the ashes out of his pipe upon the table as he uttered it.

'The packet,' he continued, 'you shall have to-morrow morning. Meantime comfort yourself with food, and afterwards with sleep; you will want, mayhap, all your strength and wits on the morrow.'

I applied myself forthwith to the homely fare which they had provided, and I confess that I never made a meal so heartily to my satisfaction.

It was a beautiful, clear, autumn morning, and the bright beams of the early sun were slanting over the brown heath which clothed the sides of the mountain, and glittering in the thousand bright drops which the melting hoar-frost had left behind it, and the white mists were lying like broad lakes in the valleys, when, with my pedlar's pack upon my back, and General Sarsfield's precious despatch in my bosom, I set forth, refreshed and courageous.

As I descended the hill, my heart expanded and my spirits rose under the influences which surrounded me. The keen, clear, bracing air of the morning, the bright, slanting sunshine, the merry songs of the small birds, and the distant sounds of awakening labour that floated up from the plains, all conspired to stir my heart within me, and more like a mad-cap boy, broken loose from school, than a man of sober years upon a mission of doubt and danger, I trod lightly on, whistling and singing alternately for very joy.

As I approached the object of my early march, I fell in with a countryman, eager, as are most of his kind, for news.

I gave him what little I had collected, and professing great zeal for the king, which, indeed, I always cherished, I won upon his confidence so far, that he became much more communicative than the peasantry in those quarters are generally wont to be to strangers.

From him I learned that there was a company of dragoons in William's service, quartered at Willaloe; but he could not tell whether the passage of the bridge was stopped by them or not. With a resolution, at all events, to make the attempt to cross, I approached the town. When I came within sight of the river, I quickly perceived that it was so swollen with the recent rains, as, indeed, the countryman had told me, that the fords were wholly impassable.

I stopped then, upon a slight eminence overlooking the village, with a view to reconnoitre and to arrange my plans in case of interruption. While thus engaged, the wind blowing gently from the west, in which quarter Limerick lay, I distinctly heard the explosion of the cannon, which played from and against the city, though at a distance of eleven miles at the least.

I never yet heard the music that had for me half the attractions of that sullen sound, and as I noted again and again the distant thunder that proclaimed the perils, and the valour, and the faithfulness of my brethren, my heart swelled with pride, and the tears rose to my eyes; and lifting up my hands to heaven, I prayed to God that I might be spared to take a part in the righteous quarrel that was there so bravely maintained.

I felt, indeed, at this moment a longing, more intense than I have the power to describe, to be at once with my brave companions in arms, and so inwardly excited and stirred up as if I had been actually within five minutes' march of the field of battle.

It was now almost noon, and I had walked hard since morning across a difficult and broken country, so that I was a little fatigued, and in no small degree hungry. As I approached the hamlet, I was glad to see in the window of a poor hovel several large cakes of meal displayed, as if to induce purchasers to enter.

I was right in regarding this exhibition as an intimation that entertainment might be procured within, for upon entering and inquiring, I was speedily invited by the poor woman, who, it appeared, kept this humble house of refreshment, to lay down my pack and seat myself by a ponderous table, upon which she promised to serve me with a dinner fit for a king; and indeed, to my mind, she amply fulfilled her engagement, supplying me abundantly with eggs, bacon, and wheaten cakes, which I discussed with a zeal which almost surprised myself.

Having disposed of the solid part of my entertainment, I was proceeding to regale myself with a brimming measure of strong waters, when my attention was arrested by the sound of horses' hoofs in brisk motion upon the broken road, and evidently approaching the hovel in which I was at that moment seated.

The ominous clank of sword scabbards and the jingle of brass accoutrements announced, unequivocally, that the horsemen were of the military profession.

'The red-coats will stop here undoubtedly,' said the old woman, observing, I suppose, the anxiety of my countenance; 'they never pass us without coming in for half an hour to drink or smoke. If you desire to avoid them, I can hide you safely; but don't lose a moment. They will be here before you can count a hundred.'

I thanked the good woman for her hospitable zeal; but I felt a repugnance to concealing myself as she suggested, which was enhanced by the consciousness that if by any accident I were detected while lurking in the room, my situation would of itself inevitably lead to suspicions, and probably to discovery.

I therefore declined her offer, and awaited in suspense the entrance of the soldiers.

I had time before they made their appearance to move my seat hurriedly from the table to the hearth, where, under the shade of the large chimney, I might observe the coming visitors with less chance of being myself remarked upon.

As my hostess had anticipated, the horsemen drew up at the door of the hut, and five dragoons entered the dark chamber where I awaited them.

Leaving their horses at the entrance, with much noise and clatter they proceeded to seat themselves and call for liquor.

Three of these fellows were Dutchmen, and, indeed, all belonged, as I afterwards found, to a Dutch regiment, which had been recruited with Irish and English, as also partly officered from the same nations.

Being supplied with pipes and drink they soon became merry; and not suffering their smoking to interfere with their conversation, they talked loud and quickly, for the most part in a sort of barbarous language, neither Dutch nor English, but compounded of both.

They were so occupied with their own jocularity that I had very great hopes of escaping observation altogether, and remained quietly seated in a corner of the chimney, leaning back upon my seat as if asleep.

My taciturnity and quiescence, however, did not avail me, for one of these fellows coming over to the hearth to light his pipe, perceived me, and looking me very hard in the face, he said:

'What countryman are you, brother, that you sit with a covered head in the room with the prince's soldiers?'

At the same time he tossed my hat off my head into the fire. I was not fool enough, though somewhat hot-blooded, to suffer the insolence of this fellow to involve me in a broil so dangerous to my person and ruinous to my schemes as a riot with these soldiers must prove. I therefore, quietly taking up my hat and shaking the ashes out of it, observed:

'Sir, I crave your pardon if I have offended you. I am a stranger in these quarters, and a poor, ignorant, humble man, desiring only to drive my little trade in peace, so far as that may be done in these troublous times.'

'And what may your trade be?' said the same fellow.

'I am a travelling merchant,' I replied; 'and sell my wares as cheap as any trader in the country.'

'Let us see them forthwith,' said he; 'mayhap I or my comrades may want something which you can supply. Where is thy chest, friend? Thou shalt have ready money' (winking at his companions), 'ready money, and good weight, and sound metal; none of your rascally pinchbeck. Eh, my lads? Bring forth the goods, and let us see.'

Thus urged, I should have betrayed myself had I hesitated to do as required; and anxious, upon any terms, to quiet these turbulent men of war, I unbuckled my pack and exhibited its contents upon the table before them.

'A pair of lace ruffles, by the Lord!' said one, unceremoniously seizing upon the articles he named.

'A phial of perfume,' continued another, tumbling over the farrago which I had submitted to them, 'wash-balls, combs, stationery, slippers, small knives, tobacco; by ——, this merchant is a prize! Mark me, honest fellow, the man who wrongs thee shall suffer—'fore Gad he shall; thou shalt be fairly dealt with' (this he said while in the act of pocketing a small silver tobacco-box, the most valuable article in the lot). 'You shall come with me to head-quarters; the captain will deal with you, and never haggle about the price. I promise thee his good will, and thou wilt consider me accordingly. You'll find him a profitable customer—he has money without end, and throws it about like a gentleman. If so be as I tell thee, I shall expect, and my comrades here, a piece or two in the way of a compliment—but of this anon. Come, then, with us; buckle on thy pack quickly, friend.'

There was no use in my declaring my willingness to deal with themselves in preference to their master; it was clear that they had resolved that I should, in the most expeditious and advantageous way, turn my goods into money, that they might excise upon me to the amount of their wishes.

The worthy who had taken a lead in these arrangements, and who by his stripes I perceived to be a corporal, having insisted on my taking a dram with him to cement our newly-formed friendship, for which, however, he requested me to pay, made me mount behind one of his comrades; and the party, of which I thus formed an unwilling member, moved at a slow trot towards the quarters of the troop.

They reined up their horses at the head of the long bridge, which at this village spans the broad waters of the Shannon connecting the opposite counties of Tipperary and Clare.

A small tower, built originally, no doubt, to protect and to defend this pass, occupied the near extremity of the bridge, and in its rear, but connected with it, stood several straggling buildings rather dilapidated.

A dismounted trooper kept guard at the door, and my conductor having, dismounted, as also the corporal, the latter inquired:

'Is the captain in his quarters?'

'He is,' replied the sentinel.

And without more ado my companion shoved me into the entrance of the small dark tower, and opening a door at the extremity of the narrow chamber into which we had passed from the street, we entered a second room in which were seated some half-dozen officers of various ranks and ages, engaged in drinking, and smoking, and play.

I glanced rapidly from man to man, and was nearly satisfied by my inspection, when one of the gentlemen whose back had been turned towards the place where I stood, suddenly changed his position and looked towards me.

As soon as I saw his face my heart sank within me, and I knew that my life or death was balanced, as it were, upon a razor's edge.

The name of this man whose unexpected appearance thus affected me was Hugh Oliver, and good and strong reason had I to dread him, for so bitterly did he hate me, that to this moment I do verily believe he would have compassed my death if it lay in his power to do so, even at the hazard of his own life and soul, for I had been—though God knows with many sore strugglings and at the stern call of public duty—the judge and condemner of his brother; and though the military law, which I was called upon to administer, would permit no other course or sentence than the bloody one which I was compelled to pursue, yet even to this hour the recollection of that deed is heavy at my breast.

As soon as I saw this man I felt that my safety depended upon the accident of his not recognising me through the disguise which I had assumed, an accident against which were many chances, for he well knew my person and appearance.

It was too late now to destroy General Sarsfield's instructions; any attempt to do so would ensure detection. All then depended upon a cast of the die.

When the first moment of dismay and heart-sickening agitation had passed, it seemed to me as if my mind acquired a collectedness and clearness more complete and intense than I had ever experienced before.

I instantly perceived that he did not know me, for turning from me to the soldier with all air of indifference, he said,

'Is this a prisoner or a deserter? What have you brought him here for, sirra?'

'Your wisdom will regard him as you see fit, may it please you,' said the corporal. 'The man is a travelling merchant, and, overtaking him upon the road, close by old Dame MacDonagh's cot, I thought I might as well make a sort of prisoner of him that your honour might use him as it might appear most convenient; he has many commododies which are not unworthy of price in this wilderness, and some which you may condescend to make use of yourself. May he exhibit the goods he has for sale, an't please you?'

'Ay, let us see them,' said he.

'Unbuckle your pack,' exclaimed the corporal, with the same tone of command with which, at the head of his guard, he would have said 'Recover your arms.' 'Unbuckle your pack, fellow, and show your goods to the captain—here, where you are.'

The conclusion of his directions was suggested by my endeavouring to move round in order to get my back towards the windows, hoping, by keeping my face in the shade, to escape detection.

In this manoeuvre, however, I was foiled by the imperiousness of the soldier; and inwardly cursing his ill-timed interference, I proceeded to present my merchandise to the loving contemplation of the officers who thronged around me, with a strong light from an opposite window full upon my face.

As I continued to traffic with these gentlemen, I observed with no small anxiety the eyes of Captain Oliver frequently fixed upon me with a kind of dubious inquiring gaze.

'I think, my honest fellow,' he said at last, 'that I have seen you somewhere before this. Have you often dealt with the military?'

'I have traded, sir,' said I, 'with the soldiery many a time, and always been honourably treated. Will your worship please to buy a pair of lace ruffles?—very cheap, your worship.'

'Why do you wear your hair so much over your face, sir?' said Oliver, without noticing my suggestion. 'I promise you, I think no good of thee; throw back your hair, and let me see thee plainly. Hold up your face, and look straight at me; throw back your hair, sir.'

I felt that all chance of escape was at an end; and stepping forward as near as the table would allow me to him, I raised my head, threw back my hair, and fixed my eyes sternly and boldly upon his face.

I saw that he knew me instantly, for his countenance turned as pale as ashes with surprise and hatred. He started up, placing his hand instinctively upon his sword-hilt, and glaring at me with a look so deadly, that I thought every moment he would strike his sword into my heart. He said in a kind of whisper: 'Hardress Fitzgerald?'

'Yes;' said I, boldly, for the excitement of the scene had effectually stirred my blood, 'Hardress Fitzgerald is before you. I know you well, Captain Oliver. I know how you hate me. I know how you thirst for my blood; but in a good cause, and in the hands of God, I defy you.'

'You are a desperate villain, sir,' said Captain Oliver; 'a rebel and a murderer! Holloa, there! guard, seize him!'

As the soldiers entered, I threw my eyes hastily round the room, and observing a glowing fire upon the hearth, I suddenly drew General Sarsfield's packet from my bosom, and casting it upon the embers, planted my foot upon it.

'Secure the papers!' shouted the captain; and almost instantly I was laid prostrate and senseless upon the floor, by a blow from the butt of a carbine.

I cannot say how long I continued in a state of torpor; but at length, having slowly recovered my senses, I found myself lying firmly handcuffed upon the floor of a small chamber, through a narrow loophole in one of whose walls the evening sun was shining. I was chilled with cold and damp, and drenched in blood, which had flowed in large quantities from the wound on my head. By a strong effort I shook off the sick drowsiness which still hung upon me, and, weak and giddy, I rose with pain and difficulty to my feet.

The chamber, or rather cell, in which I stood was about eight feet square, and of a height very disproportioned to its other dimensions; its altitude from the floor to the ceiling being not less than twelve or fourteen feet. A narrow slit placed high in the wall admitted a scanty light, but sufficient to assure me that my prison contained nothing to render the sojourn of its tenant a whit less comfortless than my worst enemy could have wished.

My first impulse was naturally to examine the security of the door, the loophole which I have mentioned being too high and too narrow to afford a chance of escape. I listened attentively to ascertain if possible whether or not a guard had been placed upon the outside.

Not a sound was to be heard. I now placed my shoulder to the door, and sought with all my combined strength and weight to force it open. It, however, resisted all my efforts, and thus baffled in my appeal to mere animal power, exhausted and disheartened, I threw myself on the ground.

It was not in my nature, however, long to submit to the apathy of despair, and in a few minutes I was on my feet again.

With patient scrutiny I endeavoured to ascertain the nature of the fastenings which secured the door.

The planks, fortunately, having been nailed together fresh, had shrunk considerably, so as to leave wide chinks between each and its neighbour.

By means of these apertures I saw that my dungeon was secured, not by a lock, as I had feared, but by a strong wooden bar, running horizontally across the door, about midway upon the outside.

'Now,' thought I, 'if I can but slip my fingers through the opening of the planks, I can easily remove the bar, and then——'

My attempts, however, were all frustrated by the manner in which my hands were fastened together, each embarrassing the other, and rendering my efforts so hopelessly clumsy, that I was obliged to give them over in despair.

I turned with a sigh from my last hope, and began to pace my narrow prison floor, when my eye suddenly encountered an old rusty nail or holdfast sticking in the wall.

All the gold of Plutus would not have been so welcome as that rusty piece of iron.

I instantly wrung it from the wall, and inserting the point between the planks of the door into the bolt, and working it backwards and forwards, I had at length the unspeakable satisfaction to perceive that the beam was actually yielding to my efforts, and gradually sliding into its berth in the wall.

I have often been engaged in struggles where great bodily strength was required, and every thew and sinew in the system taxed to the uttermost; but, strange as it may appear, I never was so completely exhausted and overcome by any labour as by this comparatively trifling task.

Again and again was I obliged to desist, until my cramped finger-joints recovered their power; but at length my perseverance was rewarded, for, little by little, I succeeded in removing the bolt so far as to allow the door to open sufficiently to permit me to pass.

With some squeezing I succeeded in forcing my way into a small passage, upon which my prison-door opened.

This led into a chamber somewhat more spacious than my cell, but still containing no furniture, and affording no means of escape to one so crippled with bonds as I was.

At the far extremity of this room was a door which stood ajar, and, stealthily passing through it, I found myself in a room containing nothing but a few raw hides, which rendered the atmosphere nearly intolerable.

Here I checked myself, for I heard voices in busy conversation in the next room.

I stole softly to the door which separated the chamber in which I stood from that from which the voices proceeded.

A moment served to convince me that any attempt upon it would be worse than fruitless, for it was secured upon the outside by a strong lock, besides two bars, all which I was enabled to ascertain by means of the same defect in the joining of the planks which I have mentioned as belonging to the inner door.

I had approached this door very softly, so that, my proximity being wholly unsuspected by the speakers within, the conversation continued without interruption.

Planting myself close to the door, I applied my eye to one of the chinks which separated the boards, and thus obtained a full view of the chamber and its occupants.

It was the very apartment into which I had been first conducted. The outer door, which faced the one at which I stood, was closed, and at a small table were seated the only tenants of the room—two officers, one of whom was Captain Oliver. The latter was reading a paper, which I made no doubt was the document with which I had been entrusted.

'The fellow deserves it, no doubt' said the junior officer. 'But, methinks, considering our orders from head-quarters, you deal somewhat too hastily.'

'Nephew, nephew,' said Captain Oliver, 'you mistake the tenor of our orders. We were directed to conciliate the peasantry by fair and gentle treatment, but not to suffer spies and traitors to escape. This packet is of some value, though not, in all its parts, intelligible to me. The bearer has made his way hither under a disguise, which, along with the other circumstances of his appearance here, is sufficient to convict him as a spy.'

There was a pause here, and after a few minutes the younger officer said:

'Spy is a hard term, no doubt, uncle; but it is possible—nay, likely, that this poor devil sought merely to carry the parcel with which he was charged in safety to its destination. Pshaw! he is sufficiently punished if you duck him, for ten minutes or so, between the bridge and the mill-dam.'

'Young man,' said Oliver, somewhat sternly, 'do not obtrude your advice where it is not called for; this man, for whom you plead, murdered your own father!'

I could not see how this announcement affected the person to whom it was addressed, for his back was towards me; but I conjectured, easily, that my last poor chance was gone, for a long silence ensued. Captain Oliver at length resumed:

'I know the villain well. I know him capable of any crime; but, by ——, his last card is played, and the game is up. He shall not see the moon rise to-night.'

There was here another pause.

Oliver rose, and going to the outer door, called:

'Hewson! Hewson!'

A grim-looking corporal entered.

'Hewson, have your guard ready at eight o'clock, with their carbines clean, and a round of ball-cartridge each. Keep them sober; and, further, plant two upright posts at the near end of the bridge, with a cross one at top, in the manner of a gibbet. See to these matters, Hewson: I shall be with you speedily.'

The corporal made his salutations, and retired.

Oliver deliberately folded up the papers with which I had been commissioned, and placing them in the pocket of his vest, he said:

'Cunning, cunning Master Hardress Fitzgerald hath made a false step; the old fox is in the toils. Hardress Fitzgerald, Hardress Fitzgerald, I will blot you out.'

He repeated these words several times, at the same time rubbing his finger strongly upon the table, as if he sought to erase a stain:

'I WILL BLOT YOU OUT!'

There was a kind of glee in his manner and expression which chilled my very heart.

'You shall be first shot like a dog, and then hanged like a dog: shot to-night, and hung to-morrow; hung at the bridgehead—hung, until your bones drop asunder!'

It is impossible to describe the exultation with which he seemed to dwell upon, and to particularise the fate which he intended for me.

I observed, however, that his face was deadly pale, and felt assured that his conscience and inward convictions were struggling against his cruel resolve. Without further comment the two officers left the room, I suppose to oversee the preparations which were being made for the deed of which I was to be the victim.

A chill, sick horror crept over me as they retired, and I felt, for the moment, upon the brink of swooning. This feeling, however, speedily gave place to a sensation still more terrible. A state of excitement so intense and tremendous as to border upon literal madness, supervened; my brain reeled and throbbed as if it would burst; thoughts the wildest and the most hideous flashed through my mind with a spontaneous rapidity that scared my very soul; while, all the time, I felt a strange and frightful impulse to burst into uncontrolled laughter.

Gradually this fearful paroxysm passed away. I kneeled and prayed fervently, and felt comforted and assured; but still I could not view the slow approaches of certain death without an agitation little short of agony.

I have stood in battle many a time when the chances of escape were fearfully small. I have confronted foemen in the deadly breach. I have marched, with a constant heart, against the cannon's mouth. Again and again has the beast which I bestrode been shot under me; again and again have I seen the comrades who walked beside me in an instant laid for ever in the dust; again and again have I been in the thick of battle, and of its mortal dangers, and never felt my heart shake, or a single nerve tremble: but now, helpless, manacled, imprisoned, doomed, forced to watch the approaches of an inevitable fate—to wait, silent and moveless, while death as it were crept towards me, human nature was taxed to the uttermost to bear the horrible situation.

I returned again to the closet in which I had found myself upon recovering from the swoon.

The evening sunshine and twilight was fast melting into darkness, when I heard the outer door, that which communicated with the guard-room in which the officers had been amusing themselves, opened and locked again upon the inside.

A measured step then approached, and the door of the wretched cell in which I lay being rudely pushed open, a soldier entered, who carried something in his hand; but, owing to the obscurity of the place, I could not see what.

'Art thou awake, fellow?' said he, in a gruff voice. 'Stir thyself; get upon thy legs.'

His orders were enforced by no very gentle application of his military boot.

'Friend,' said I, rising with difficulty, 'you need not insult a dying man. You have been sent hither to conduct me to death. Lead on! My trust is in God, that He will forgive me my sins, and receive my soul, redeemed by the blood of His Son.'

There here intervened a pause of some length, at the end of which the soldier said, in the same gruff voice, but in a lower key:

'Look ye, comrade, it will be your own fault if you die this night. On one condition I promise to get you out of this hobble with a whole skin; but if you go to any of your d——d gammon, by G—, before two hours are passed, you will have as many holes in your carcase as a target.'

'Name your conditions,' said I, 'and if they consist with honour, I will never balk at the offer.'

'Here they are: you are to be shot to-night, by Captain Oliver's orders. The carbines are cleaned for the job, and the cartridges served out to the men. By G—, I tell you the truth!'

Of this I needed not much persuasion, and intimated to the man my conviction that he spoke the truth.

'Well, then,' he continued, 'now for the means of avoiding this ugly business. Captain Oliver rides this night to head-quarters, with the papers which you carried. Before he starts he will pay you a visit, to fish what he can out of you with all the fine promises he can make. Humour him a little, and when you find an opportunity, stab him in the throat above the cuirass.'

'A feasible plan, surely,' said I, raising my shackled hands, 'for a man thus completely crippled and without a weapon.'

'I will manage all that presently for you,' said the soldier. 'When you have thus dealt with him, take his cloak and hat, and so forth, and put them on; the papers you will find in the pocket of his vest, in a red leather case. Walk boldly out. I am appointed to ride with Captain Oliver, and you will find me holding his horse and my own by the door. Mount quickly, and I will do the same, and then we will ride for our lives across the bridge. You will find the holster-pistols loaded in case of pursuit; and, with the devil's help, we shall reach Limerick without a hair hurt. My only condition is, that when you strike Oliver, you strike home, and again and again, until he is FINISHED; and I trust to your honour to remember me when we reach the town.'

I cannot say whether I resolved right or wrong, but I thought my situation, and the conduct of Captain Oliver, warranted me in acceding to the conditions propounded by my visitant, and with alacrity I told him so, and desired him to give me the power, as he had promised to do, of executing them.

With speed and promptitude he drew a small key from his pocket, and in an instant the manacles were removed from my hands.

How my heart bounded within me as my wrists were released from the iron gripe of the shackles! The first step toward freedom was made—my self-reliance returned, and I felt assured of success.

'Now for the weapon,' said I.

'I fear me, you will find it rather clumsy,' said he; 'but if well handled, it will do as well as the best Toledo. It is the only thing I could get, but I sharpened it myself; it has an edge like a skean.'

He placed in my hand the steel head of a halberd. Grasping it firmly, I found that it made by no means a bad weapon in point of convenience; for it felt in the hand like a heavy dagger, the portion which formed the blade or point being crossed nearly at the lower extremity by a small bar of metal, at one side shaped into the form of an axe, and at the other into that of a hook. These two transverse appendages being muffled by the folds of my cravat, which I removed for the purpose, formed a perfect guard or hilt, and the lower extremity formed like a tube, in which the pike-handle had been inserted, afforded ample space for the grasp of my hand; the point had been made as sharp as a needle, and the metal he assured me was good.

Thus equipped he left me, having observed, 'The captain sent me to bring you to your senses, and give you some water that he might find you proper for his visit. Here is the pitcher; I think I have revived you sufficiently for the captain's purpose.'

With a low savage laugh he left me to my reflections.

Having examined and adjusted the weapon, I carefully bound the ends of the cravat, with which I had secured the cross part of the spear-head, firmly round my wrist, so that in case of a struggle it might not easily be forced from my hand; and having made these precautionary dispositions, I sat down upon the ground with my back against the wall, and my hands together under my coat, awaiting my visitor.

The time wore slowly on; the dusk became dimmer and dimmer, until it nearly bordered on total darkness.

'How's this?' said I, inwardly; 'Captain Oliver, you said I should not see the moon rise to-night. Methinks you are somewhat tardy in fulfilling your prophecy.'

As I made this reflection, a noise at the outer door announced the entrance of a visitant. I knew that the decisive moment was come, and letting my head sink upon my breast, and assuring myself that my hands were concealed, I waited, in the attitude of deep dejection, the approach of my foe and betrayer.

As I had expected, Captain Oliver entered the room where I lay. He was equipped for instant duty, as far as the imperfect twilight would allow me to see; the long sword clanked upon the floor as he made his way through the lobbies which led to my place of confinement; his ample military cloak hung upon his arm; his cocked hat was upon his head, and in all points he was prepared for the road.

This tallied exactly with what my strange informant had told me.

I felt my heart swell and my breath come thick as the awful moment which was to witness the death-struggle of one or other of us approached.

Captain Oliver stood within a yard or two of the place where I sat, or rather lay; and folding his arms, he remained silent for a minute or two, as if arranging in his mind how he should address me.

'Hardress Fitzgerald,' he began at length, 'are you awake? Stand up, if you desire to hear of matters nearly touching your life or death. Get up, I say.'

I arose doggedly, and affecting the awkward movements of one whose hands were bound,

'Well,' said I, 'what would you of me? Is it not enough that I am thus imprisoned without a cause, and about, as I suspect, to suffer a most unjust and violent sentence, but must I also be disturbed during the few moments left me for reflection and repentance by the presence of my persecutor? What do you want of me?'

'As to your punishment, sir,' said he, 'your own deserts have no doubt suggested the likelihood of it to your mind; but I now am with you to let you know that whatever mitigation of your sentence you may look for, must be earned by your compliance with my orders. You must frankly and fully explain the contents of the packet which you endeavoured this day to destroy; and further, you must tell all that you know of the designs of the popish rebels.'

'And if I do this I am to expect a mitigation of my punishment—is it not so?'

Oliver bowed.

'And what IS this mitigation to be? On the honour of a soldier, what is it to be?' inquired I.

'When you have made the disclosure required,' he replied, 'you shall hear. 'Tis then time to talk of indulgences.'

'Methinks it would then be too late,' answered I. 'But a chance is a chance, and a drowning man will catch at a straw. You are an honourable man, Captain Oliver. I must depend, I suppose, on your good faith. Well, sir, before I make the desired communication I have one question more to put. What is to befall me in case that I, remembering the honour of a soldier and a gentleman, reject your infamous terms, scorn your mitigations, and defy your utmost power?'

'In that case,' replied he, coolly, 'before half an hour you shall be a corpse.'

'Then God have mercy on your soul!' said I; and springing forward, I dashed the weapon which I held at his throat.

I missed my aim, but struck him full in the mouth with such force that most of his front teeth were dislodged, and the point of the spear-head passed out under his jaw, at the ear.

My onset was so sudden and unexpected that he reeled back to the wall, and did not recover his equilibrium in time to prevent my dealing a second blow, which I did with my whole force. The point unfortunately struck the cuirass, near the neck, and glancing aside it inflicted but a flesh wound, tearing the skin and tendons along the throat.

He now grappled with me, strange to say, without uttering any cry of alarm; being a very powerful man, and if anything rather heavier and more strongly built than I, he succeeded in drawing me with him to the ground. We fell together with a heavy crash, tugging and straining in what we were both conscious was a mortal struggle. At length I succeeded in getting over him, and struck him twice more in the face; still he struggled with an energy which nothing but the tremendous stake at issue could have sustained.

I succeeded again in inflicting several more wounds upon him, any one of which might have been mortal. While thus contending he clutched his hands about my throat, so firmly that I felt the blood swelling the veins of my temples and face almost to bursting. Again and again I struck the weapon deep into his face and throat, but life seemed to adhere in him with an almost INSECT tenacity.

My sight now nearly failed, my senses almost forsook me; I felt upon the point of suffocation when, with one desperate effort, I struck him another and a last blow in the face. The weapon which I wielded had lighted upon the eye, and the point penetrated the brain; the body quivered under me, the deadly grasp relaxed, and Oliver lay upon the ground a corpse!

As I arose and shook the weapon and the bloody cloth from my hand, the moon which he had foretold I should never see rise, shone bright and broad into the room, and disclosed, with ghastly distinctness, the mangled features of the dead soldier; the mouth, full of clotting blood and broken teeth, lay open; the eye, close by whose lid the fatal wound had been inflicted, was not, as might have been expected, bathed in blood, but had started forth nearly from the socket, and gave to the face, by its fearful unlikeness to the other glazing orb, a leer more hideous and unearthly than fancy ever saw. The wig, with all its rich curls, had fallen with the hat to the floor, leaving the shorn head exposed, and in many places marked by the recent struggle; the rich lace cravat was drenched in blood, and the gay uniform in many places soiled with the same.

It is hard to say, with what feelings I looked upon the unsightly and revolting mass which had so lately been a living and a comely man. I had not any time, however, to spare for reflection; the deed was done—the responsibility was upon me, and all was registered in the book of that God who judges rightly.

With eager haste I removed from the body such of the military accoutrements as were necessary for the purpose of my disguise. I buckled on the sword, drew off the military boots, and donned them myself, placed the brigadier wig and cocked hat upon my head, threw on the cloak, drew it up about my face, and proceeded, with the papers which I found as the soldier had foretold me, and the key of the outer lobby, to the door of the guard-room; this I opened, and with a firm and rapid tread walked through the officers, who rose as I entered, and passed without question or interruption to the street-door. Here I was met by the grim-looking corporal, Hewson, who, saluting me, said:

'How soon, captain, shall the file be drawn out and the prisoner despatched?'

'In half an hour,' I replied, without raising my voice.

The man again saluted, and in two steps I reached the soldier who held the two horses, as he had intimated.

'Is all right?' said he, eagerly.

'Ay,' said I, 'which horse am I to mount?'

He satisfied me upon this point, and I threw myself into the saddle; the soldier mounted his horse, and dashing the spurs into the flanks of the animal which I bestrode, we thundered along the narrow bridge. At the far extremity a sentinel, as we approached, called out, 'Who goes there? stand, and give the word!' Heedless of the interruption, with my heart bounding with excitement, I dashed on, as did also the soldier who accompanied me.

'Stand, or I fire! give the word!' cried the sentry.

'God save the king, and to hell with the prince!' shouted I, flinging the cocked hat in his face as I galloped by.

The response was the sharp report of a carbine, accompanied by the whiz of a bullet, which passed directly between me and my comrade, now riding beside me.

'Hurrah!' I shouted; 'try it again, my boy.'

And away we went at a gallop, which bid fair to distance anything like pursuit.

Never was spur more needed, however, for soon the clatter of horses' hoofs, in full speed, crossing the bridge, came sharp and clear through the stillness of the night.

Away we went, with our pursuers close behind; one mile was passed, another nearly completed. The moon now shone forth, and, turning in the saddle, I looked back upon the road we had passed.

One trooper had headed the rest, and was within a hundred yards of us.

I saw the fellow throw himself from his horse upon the ground.

I knew his object, and said to my comrade:

'Lower your body—lie flat over the saddle; the fellow is going to fire.'

I had hardly spoken when the report of a carbine startled the echoes, and the ball, striking the hind leg of my companion's horse, the poor animal fell headlong upon the road, throwing his rider head-foremost over the saddle.

My first impulse was to stop and share whatever fate might await my comrade; but my second and wiser one was to spur on, and save myself and my despatch.

I rode on at a gallop, turning to observe my comrade's fate. I saw his pursuer, having remounted, ride rapidly up to him, and, on reaching the spot where the man and horse lay, rein in and dismount.

He was hardly upon the ground, when my companion shot him dead with one of the holster-pistols which he had drawn from the pipe; and, leaping nimbly over a ditch at the side of the road, he was soon lost among the ditches and thornbushes which covered that part of the country.

Another mile being passed, I had the satisfaction to perceive that the pursuit was given over, and in an hour more I crossed Thomond Bridge, and slept that night in the fortress of Limerick, having delivered the packet, the result of whose safe arrival was the destruction of William's great train of artillery, then upon its way to the besiegers.

Years after this adventure, I met in France a young officer, who I found had served in Captain Oliver's regiment; and he explained what I had never before understood—the motives of the man who had wrought my deliverance. Strange to say, he was the foster-brother of Oliver, whom he thus devoted to death, but in revenge for the most grievous wrong which one man can inflict upon another!

'THE QUARE GANDER.'

Being a Twelfth Extract from the Legacy of the late Francis Purcell, P.P. of Drumcoolagh.

As I rode at a slow walk, one soft autumn evening, from the once noted and noticeable town of Emly, now a squalid village, towards the no less remarkable town of Tipperary, I fell into a meditative mood.

My eye wandered over a glorious landscape; a broad sea of corn-fields, that might have gladdened even a golden age, was waving before me; groups of little cabins, with their poplars, osiers, and light mountain ashes, clustered shelteringly around them, were scattered over the plain; the thin blue smoke arose floating through their boughs in the still evening air. And far away with all their broad lights and shades, softened with the haze of approaching twilight, stood the bold wild Galties.

As I gazed on this scene, whose richness was deepened by the melancholy glow of the setting sun, the tears rose to my eyes, and I said:

'Alas, my country! what a mournful beauty is thine. Dressed in loveliness and laughter, there is mortal decay at thy heart: sorrow, sin, and shame have mingled thy cup of misery. Strange rulers have bruised thee, and laughed thee to scorn, and they have made all thy sweetness bitter. Thy shames and sins are the austere fruits of thy miseries, and thy miseries have been poured out upon thee by foreign hands. Alas, my stricken country! clothed with this most pity-moving smile, with this most unutterably mournful loveliness, thou sore-grieved, thou desperately-beloved! Is there for thee, my country, a resurrection?'

I know not how long I might have continued to rhapsodize in this strain, had not my wandering thoughts been suddenly recalled to my own immediate neighbourhood by the monotonous clatter of a horse's hoofs upon the road, evidently moving, at that peculiar pace which is neither a walk nor a trot, and yet partakes of both, so much in vogue among the southern farmers.

In a moment my pursuer was up with me, and checking his steed into a walk he saluted me with much respect. The cavalier was a light-built fellow, with good-humoured sun-burnt features, a shrewd and lively black eye, and a head covered with a crop of close curly black hair, and surmounted with a turf-coloured caubeen, in the packthread band of which was stuck a short pipe, which had evidently seen much service.

My companion was a dealer in all kinds of local lore, and soon took occasion to let me see that he was so.

After two or three short stories, in which the scandalous and supernatural were happily blended, we happened to arrive at a narrow road or bohreen leading to a snug-looking farm-house.

'That's a comfortable bit iv a farm,' observed my comrade, pointing towards the dwelling with his thumb; 'a shnug spot, and belongs to the Mooneys this long time. 'Tis a noted place for what happened wid the famous gandher there in former times.'

'And what was that?' inquired I.

'What was it happened wid the gandher!' ejaculated my companion in a tone of indignant surprise; 'the gandher iv Ballymacrucker, the gandher! Your raverance must be a stranger in these parts. Sure every fool knows all about the gandher, and Terence Mooney, that was, rest his sowl. Begorra, 'tis surprisin' to me how in the world you didn't hear iv the gandher; and may be it's funnin me ye are, your raverance.'

I assured him to the contrary, and conjured him to narrate to me the facts, an unacquaintance with which was sufficient it appeared to stamp me as an ignoramus of the first magnitude.

It did not require much entreaty to induce my communicative friend to relate the circumstance, in nearly the following words:

'Terence Mooney was an honest boy and well to do; an' he rinted the biggest farm on this side iv the Galties; an' bein' mighty cute an' a sevare worker, it was small wonder he turned a good penny every harvest. But unluckily he was blessed with an ilegant large family iv daughters, an' iv coorse his heart was allamost bruck, striving to make up fortunes for the whole of them. An' there wasn't a conthrivance iv any soart or description for makin' money out iv the farm, but he was up to.

'Well, among the other ways he had iv gettin' up in the world, he always kep a power iv turkeys, and all soarts iv poultrey; an' he was out iv all rason partial to geese—an' small blame to him for that same—for twice't a year you can pluck them as bare as my hand—an' get a fine price for the feathers, an' plenty of rale sizable eggs—an' when they are too ould to lay any more, you can kill them, an' sell them to the gintlemen for goslings, d'ye see, let alone that a goose is the most manly bird that is out.

'Well, it happened in the coorse iv time that one ould gandher tuck a wondherful likin' to Terence, an' divil a place he could go serenadin' about the farm, or lookin' afther the men, but the gandher id be at his heels, an' rubbin' himself agin his legs, an' lookin' up in his face jist like any other Christian id do; an' begorra, the likes iv it was never seen—Terence Mooney an' the gandher wor so great.

'An' at last the bird was so engagin' that Terence would not allow it to be plucked any more, an' kep it from that time out for love an' affection—just all as one like one iv his childer.

'But happiness in perfection never lasts long, an' the neighbours begin'd to suspect the nathur an' intentions iv the gandher, an' some iv them said it was the divil, an' more iv them that it was a fairy.

'Well, Terence could not but hear something of what was sayin', an' you may be sure he was not altogether asy in his mind about it, an' from one day to another he was gettin' more ancomfortable in himself, until he detarmined to sind for Jer Garvan, the fairy docthor in Garryowen, an' it's he was the ilegant hand at the business, an' divil a sperit id say a crass word to him, no more nor a priest. An' moreover he was very great wid ould Terence Mooney—this man's father that' was.

'So without more about it he was sint for, an' sure enough the divil a long he was about it, for he kem back that very evenin' along wid the boy that was sint for him, an' as soon as he was there, an' tuck his supper, an' was done talkin' for a while, he begined of coorse to look into the gandher.

'Well, he turned it this away an' that away, to the right an' to the left, an' straight-ways an' upside-down, an' when he was tired handlin' it, says he to Terence Mooney:

'"Terence," says he, "you must remove the bird into the next room," says he, "an' put a petticoat," says he, "or anny other convaynience round his head," says he.

'"An' why so?" says Terence.

'"Becase," says Jer, says he.

'"Becase what?" says Terence.

'"Becase," says Jer, "if it isn't done you'll never be asy again," says he, "or pusilanimous in your mind," says he; "so ax no more questions, but do my biddin'," says he.

'"Well," says Terence, "have your own way," says he.

'An' wid that he tuck the ould gandher, an' giv' it to one iv the gossoons.

'"An' take care," says he, "don't smother the crathur," says he.

'Well, as soon as the bird was gone, says Jer Garvan says he:

'"Do you know what that ould gandher IS, Terence Mooney?"

'"Divil a taste," says Terence.

'"Well then," says Jer, "the gandher is your own father," says he.

'"It's jokin' you are," says Terence, turnin' mighty pale; "how can an ould gandher be my father?" says he.

'"I'm not funnin' you at all," says Jer; "it's thrue what I tell you, it's your father's wandhrin' sowl," says he, "that's naturally tuck pissession iv the ould gandher's body," says he. "I know him many ways, and I wondher," says he, "you do not know the cock iv his eye yourself," says he.

'"Oh blur an' ages!" says Terence, "what the divil will I ever do at all at all," says he; "it's all over wid me, for I plucked him twelve times at the laste," says he.

'"That can't be helped now," says Jer; "it was a sevare act surely," says he, "but it's too late to lamint for it now," says he; "the only way to prevint what's past," says he, "is to put a stop to it before it happens," says he.

'"Thrue for you," says Terence, "but how the divil did you come to the knowledge iv my father's sowl," says he, "bein' in the owld gandher," says he.

'"If I tould you," says Jer, "you would not undherstand me," says he, "without book-larnin' an' gasthronomy," says he; "so ax me no questions," says he, "an' I'll tell you no lies. But blieve me in this much," says he, "it's your father that's in it," says he; "an' if I don't make him spake to-morrow mornin'," says he, "I'll give you lave to call me a fool," says he.

'"Say no more," says Terence, "that settles the business," says he; "an' oh! blur and ages is it not a quare thing," says he, "for a dacent respictable man," says he, "to be walkin' about the counthry in the shape iv an ould gandher," says he; "and oh, murdher, murdher! is not it often I plucked him," says he, "an' tundher and ouns might not I have ate him," says he; and wid that he fell into a could parspiration, savin' your prisince, an was on the pint iv faintin' wid the bare notions iv it.

'Well, whin he was come to himself agin, says Jerry to him quite an' asy:

'"Terence," says he, "don't be aggravatin' yourself," says he; "for I have a plan composed that 'ill make him spake out," says he, "an' tell what it is in the world he's wantin'," says he; "an' mind an' don't be comin' in wid your gosther, an' to say agin anything I tell you," says he, "but jist purtind, as soon as the bird is brought back," says he, "how that we're goin' to sind him to-morrow mornin' to market," says he. "An' if he don't spake to-night," says he, "or gother himself out iv the place," says he, "put him into the hamper airly, and sind him in the cart," says he, "straight to Tipperary, to be sould for ating," says he, "along wid the two gossoons," says he, "an' my name isn't Jer Garvan," says he, "if he doesn't spake out before he's half-way," says he. "An' mind," says he, "as soon as iver he says the first word," says he, "that very minute bring him aff to Father Crotty," says he; "an' if his raverince doesn't make him ratire," says he, "like the rest iv his parishioners, glory be to God," says he, "into the siclusion iv the flames iv purgathory," says he, "there's no vartue in my charums," says he.

'Well, wid that the ould gandher was let into the room agin, an' they all bigined to talk iv sindin' him the nixt mornin' to be sould for roastin' in Tipperary, jist as if it was a thing andoubtingly settled. But divil a notice the gandher tuck, no more nor if they wor spaking iv the Lord-Liftinant; an' Terence desired the boys to get ready the kish for the poulthry, an' to "settle it out wid hay soft an' shnug," says he, "for it's the last jauntin' the poor ould gandher 'ill get in this world," says he.

'Well, as the night was gettin' late, Terence was growin' mighty sorrowful an' down-hearted in himself entirely wid the notions iv what was goin' to happen. An' as soon as the wife an' the crathurs war fairly in bed, he brought out some illigint potteen, an' himself an' Jer Garvan sot down to it; an' begorra, the more anasy Terence got, the more he dhrank, and himself and Jer Garvan finished a quart betune them. It wasn't an imparial though, an' more's the pity, for them wasn't anvinted antil short since; but divil a much matther it signifies any longer if a pint could hould two quarts, let alone what it does, sinst Father Mathew—the Lord purloin his raverence—begin'd to give the pledge, an' wid the blessin' iv timperance to deginerate Ireland.

'An' begorra, I have the medle myself; an' it's proud I am iv that same, for abstamiousness is a fine thing, although it's mighty dhry.

'Well, whin Terence finished his pint, he thought he might as well stop; "for enough is as good as a faste," says he; "an' I pity the vagabond," says he, "that is not able to conthroul his licquor," says he, "an' to keep constantly inside iv a pint measure," said he; an' wid that he wished Jer Garvan a good-night, an' walked out iv the room.

'But he wint out the wrong door, bein' a thrifle hearty in himself, an' not rightly knowin' whether he was standin' on his head or his heels, or both iv them at the same time, an' in place iv gettin' into bed, where did he thrun himself but into the poulthry hamper, that the boys had settled out ready for the gandher in the mornin'. An' sure enough he sunk down soft an' complate through the hay to the bottom; an' wid the turnin' and roulin' about in the night, the divil a bit iv him but was covered up as shnug as a lumper in a pittaty furrow before mornin'.

'So wid the first light, up gets the two boys, that war to take the sperit, as they consaved, to Tipperary; an' they cotched the ould gandher, an' put him in the hamper, and clapped a good wisp iv hay an' the top iv him, and tied it down sthrong wid a bit iv a coard, and med the sign iv the crass over him, in dhread iv any harum, an' put the hamper up an the car, wontherin' all the while what in the world was makin' the ould burd so surprisin' heavy.

'Well, they wint along quite aisy towards Tipperary, wishin' every minute that some iv the neighbours bound the same way id happen to fall in with them, for they didn't half like the notions iv havin' no company but the bewitched gandher, an' small blame to them for that same.

'But although they wor shaking in their skhins in dhread iv the ould bird beginnin' to convarse them every minute, they did not let an' to one another, bud kep singin' an' whistlin' like mad, to keep the dread out iv their hearts.

'Well, afther they war on the road betther nor half an hour, they kem to the bad bit close by Father Crotty's, an' there was one divil of a rut three feet deep at the laste; an' the car got sich a wondherful chuck goin' through it, that it wakened Terence widin in the basket.

'"Bad luck to ye," says he, "my bones is bruck wid yer thricks; what the divil are ye doin' wid me?"

'"Did ye hear anything quare, Thady?" says the boy that was next to the car, turnin' as white as the top iv a musharoon; "did ye hear anything quare soundin' out iv the hamper?" says he.

'"No, nor you," says Thady, turnin' as pale as himself, "it's the ould gandher that's gruntin' wid the shakin' he's gettin'," says he.

'"Where the divil have ye put me into," says Terence inside, "bad luck to your sowls," says he, "let me out, or I'll be smothered this minute," says he.

'"There's no use in purtending," says the boy, "the gandher's spakin', glory be to God," says he.

'"Let me out, you murdherers," says Terence.

'"In the name iv the blessed Vargin," says Thady, "an' iv all the holy saints, hould yer tongue, you unnatheral gandher," says he.

'"Who's that, that dar to call me nicknames?" says Terence inside, roaring wid the fair passion, "let me out, you blasphamious infiddles," says he, "or by this crass I'll stretch ye," says he.

'"In the name iv all the blessed saints in heaven," says Thady, "who the divil are ye?"

'"Who the divil would I be, but Terence Mooney," says he. "It's myself that's in it, you unmerciful bliggards," says he, "let me out, or by the holy, I'll get out in spite iv yes," says he, "an' by jaburs, I'll wallop yes in arnest," says he.

'"It's ould Terence, sure enough," says Thady, "isn't it cute the fairy docthor found him out," says he.

'"I'm an the pint iv snuffication," says Terence, "let me out, I tell you, an' wait till I get at ye," says he, "for begorra, the divil a bone in your body but I'll powdher," says he.

'An' wid that, he biginned kickin' and flingin' inside in the hamper, and dhrivin his legs agin the sides iv it, that it was a wonder he did not knock it to pieces.

'Well, as soon as the boys seen that, they skelped the ould horse into a gallop as hard as he could peg towards the priest's house, through the ruts, an' over the stones; an' you'd see the hamper fairly flyin' three feet up in the air with the joultin'; glory be to God.

'So it was small wondher, by the time they got to his Raverince's door, the breath was fairly knocked out of poor Terence, so that he was lyin' speechless in the bottom iv the hamper.

'Well, whin his Raverince kem down, they up an' they tould him all that happened, an' how they put the gandher into the hamper, an' how he beginned to spake, an' how he confissed that he was ould Terence Mooney; an' they axed his honour to advise them how to get rid iv the spirit for good an' all.

'So says his Raverince, says he:

'"I'll take my booke," says he, "an' I'll read some rale sthrong holy bits out iv it," says he, "an' do you get a rope and put it round the hamper," says he, "an' let it swing over the runnin' wather at the bridge," says he, "an' it's no matther if I don't make the spirit come out iv it," says he.

'Well, wid that, the priest got his horse, and tuck his booke in undher his arum, an' the boys follied his Raverince, ladin' the horse down to the bridge, an' divil a word out iv Terence all the way, for he seen it was no use spakin', an' he was afeard if he med any noise they might thrait him to another gallop an finish him intirely.

'Well, as soon as they war all come to the bridge, the boys tuck the rope they had with them, an' med it fast to the top iv the hamper an' swung it fairly over the bridge, lettin' it hang in the air about twelve feet out iv the wather.

'An' his Raverince rode down to the bank of the river, close by, an' beginned to read mighty loud and bould intirely.

'An' when he was goin' on about five minutes, all at onst the bottom iv the hamper kem out, an' down wint Terence, falling splash dash into the water, an' the ould gandher a-top iv him. Down they both went to the bottom, wid a souse you'd hear half a mile off.

'An' before they had time to rise agin, his Raverince, wid the fair astonishment, giv his horse one dig iv the spurs, an' before he knew where he was, in he went, horse an' all, a-top iv them, an' down to the bottom.

'Up they all kem agin together, gaspin' and puffin', an' off down wid the current wid them, like shot in under the arch iv the bridge till they kem to the shallow wather.

'The ould gandher was the first out, and the priest and Terence kem next, pantin' an' blowin' an' more than half dhrounded, an' his Raverince was so freckened wid the droundin' he got, and wid the sight iv the sperit, as he consaved, that he wasn't the better of it for a month.

'An' as soon as Terence could spake, he swore he'd have the life of the two gossoons; but Father Crotty would not give him his will. An' as soon as he was got quiter, they all endivoured to explain it; but Terence consaved he went raly to bed the night before, and his wife said the same to shilter him from the suspicion for havin' th' dthrop taken. An' his Raverince said it was a mysthery, an' swore if he cotched anyone laughin' at the accident, he'd lay the horsewhip across their shouldhers.

'An' Terence grew fonder an' fonder iv the gandher every day, until at last he died in a wondherful old age, lavin' the gandher afther him an' a large family iv childher.

'An' to this day the farm is rinted by one iv Terence Mooney's lenial and legitimate postariors.'

BILLY MALOWNEY'S TASTE OF LOVE AND GLORY.

Let the reader fancy a soft summer evening, the fresh dews falling on bush and flower. The sun has just gone down, and the thrilling vespers of thrushes and blackbirds ring with a wild joy through the saddened air; the west is piled with fantastic clouds, and clothed in tints of crimson and amber, melting away into a wan green, and so eastward into the deepest blue, through which soon the stars will begin to peep.

Let him fancy himself seated upon the low mossy wall of an ancient churchyard, where hundreds of grey stones rise above the sward, under the fantastic branches of two or three half-withered ash-trees, spreading their arms in everlasting love and sorrow over the dead.

The narrow road upon which I and my companion await the tax-cart that is to carry me and my basket, with its rich fruitage of speckled trout, away, lies at his feet, and far below spreads an undulating plain, rising westward again into soft hills, and traversed (every here and there visibly) by a winding stream which, even through the mists of evening, catches and returns the funereal glories of the skies.

As the eye traces its wayward wanderings, it loses them for a moment in the heaving verdure of white-thorns and ash, from among which floats from some dozen rude chimneys, mostly unseen, the transparent blue film of turf smoke. There we know, although we cannot see it, the steep old bridge of Carrickadrum spans the river; and stretching away far to the right the valley of Lisnamoe: its steeps and hollows, its straggling hedges, its fair-green, its tall scattered trees, and old grey tower, are disappearing fast among the discoloured tints and haze of evening.

Those landmarks, as we sit listlessly expecting the arrival of our modest conveyance, suggest to our companion—a bare-legged Celtic brother of the gentle craft, somewhat at the wrong side of forty, with a turf-coloured caubeen, patched frieze, a clear brown complexion, dark-grey eyes, and a right pleasant dash of roguery in his features—the tale, which, if the reader pleases, he is welcome to hear along with me just as it falls from the lips of our humble comrade.

His words I can give, but your own fancy must supply the advantages of an intelligent, expressive countenance, and, what is perhaps harder still, the harmony of his glorious brogue, that, like the melodies of our own dear country, will leave a burden of mirth or of sorrow with nearly equal propriety, tickling the diaphragm as easily as it plays with the heart-strings, and is in itself a national music that, I trust, may never, never—scouted and despised though it be—never cease, like the lost tones of our harp, to be heard in the fields of my country, in welcome or endearment, in fun or in sorrow, stirring the hearts of Irish men and Irish women.

My friend of the caubeen and naked shanks, then, commenced, and continued his relation, as nearly as possible, in the following words:

Av coorse ye often heerd talk of Billy Malowney, that lived by the bridge of Carrickadrum. 'Leum-a-rinka' was the name they put on him, he was sich a beautiful dancer. An' faix, it's he was the rale sportin' boy, every way—killing the hares, and gaffing the salmons, an' fightin' the men, an' funnin' the women, and coortin' the girls; an' be the same token, there was not a colleen inside iv his jurisdiction but was breakin' her heart wid the fair love iv him.

Well, this was all pleasant enough, to be sure, while it lasted; but inhuman beings is born to misfortune, an' Bill's divarshin was not to last always. A young boy can't be continially coortin' and kissin' the girls (an' more's the pity) without exposin' himself to the most eminent parril; an' so signs all' what should happen Billy Malowney himself, but to fall in love at last wid little Molly Donovan, in Coolnamoe.

I never could ondherstand why in the world it was Bill fell in love wid HER, above all the girls in the country. She was not within four stone weight iv being as fat as Peg Brallaghan; and as for redness in the face, she could not hould a candle to Judy Flaherty. (Poor Judy! she was my sweetheart, the darlin', an' coorted me constant, ever antil she married a boy of the Butlers; an' it's twenty years now since she was buried under the ould white-thorn in Garbally. But that's no matther!)

Well, at any rate, Molly Donovan tuck his fancy, an' that's everything! She had smooth brown hair—as smooth as silk-an' a pair iv soft coaxin' eyes—an' the whitest little teeth you ever seen; an', bedad, she was every taste as much in love wid himself as he was.

Well, now, he was raly stupid wid love: there was not a bit of fun left in him. He was good for nothin' an airth bud sittin' under bushes, smokin' tobacky, and sighin' till you'd wonder how in the world he got wind for it all.

An', bedad, he was an illigant scholar, moreover; an', so signs, it's many's the song he made about her; an' if you'd be walkin' in the evening, a mile away from Carrickadrum, begorra you'd hear him singing out like a bull, all across the country, in her praises.

Well, ye may be sure, ould Tim Donovan and the wife was not a bit too well plased to see Bill Malowney coortin' their daughter Molly; for, do ye mind, she was the only child they had, and her fortune was thirty-five pounds, two cows, and five illigant pigs, three iron pots and a skillet, an' a trifle iv poultry in hand;

and no one knew how much besides, whenever the Lord id be plased to call the ould people out of the way into glory!

So, it was not likely ould Tim Donovan id be fallin' in love wid poor Bill Malowney as aisy as the girls did; for, barrin' his beauty, an' his gun, an' his dhudheen, an' his janius, the divil a taste of property iv any sort or description he had in the wide world!

Well, as bad as that was, Billy would not give in that her father and mother had the smallest taste iv a right to intherfare, good or bad.

'An' you're welcome to rayfuse me,' says he, 'whin I ax your lave,' says he; 'an' I'll ax your lave,' says he, 'whenever I want to coort yourselves,' says he; 'but it's your daughter I'm coortin' at the present,' says he, 'an that's all I'll say,' says he; 'for I'd as soon take a doase of salts as be discoursin' ye,' says he.

So it was a rale blazin' battle betune himself and the ould people; an', begorra, there was no soart iv blaguardin' that did not pass betune them; an' they put a solemn injection on Molly again seein' him or meetin' him for the future.

But it was all iv no use. You might as well be pursuadin' the birds agin flying, or sthrivin' to coax the stars out iv the sky into your hat, as be talking common sinse to them that's fairly bothered and burstin' wid love. There's nothin' like it. The toothache an' cholic together id compose you betther for an argyment than itself. It leaves you fit for nothin' bud nansinse.

It's stronger than whisky, for one good drop iv it will make you drunk for one year, and sick, begorra, for a dozen.

It's stronger than the say, for it'll carry you round the world an' never let you sink, in sunshine or storm; an', begorra, it's stronger than Death himself, for it is not afeard iv him, bedad, but dares him in every shape.

But lovers has quarrels sometimes, and, begorra, when they do, you'd a'most imagine they hated one another like man and wife. An' so, signs an', Billy Malowney and Molly Donovan fell out one evening at ould Tom Dundon's wake; an' whatever came betune them, she made no more about it but just draws her cloak round her, and away wid herself and the sarvant-girl home again, as if there was not a corpse, or a fiddle, or a taste of divarsion in it.

Well, Bill Malowney follied her down the boreen, to try could he deludher her back again; but, if she was bitther before, she gave it to him in airnest when she got him alone to herself, and to that degree that he wished her safe home, short and sulky enough, an' walked back again, as mad as the devil himself, to the wake, to pay a respect to poor Tom Dundon.

Well, my dear, it was aisy seen there was something wrong avid Billy Malowney, for he paid no attintion the rest of the evening to any soart of divarsion but the whisky alone; an' every glass he'd drink it's what he'd be wishing the divil had the women, an' the worst iv bad luck to all soarts iv courting, until, at last, wid the goodness iv the sperits, an' the badness iv his temper, an' the constant flusthration iv cursin', he grew all as one as you might say almost, saving your presince, bastely drunk!

Well, who should he fall in wid, in that childish condition, as he was deploying along the road almost as straight as the letter S, an' cursin' the girls, an' roarin' for more whisky, but the recruiting-sargent iv the Welsh Confusileers.

So, cute enough, the sargent begins to convarse him, an' it was not long until he had him sitting in Murphy's public-house, wid an elegant dandy iv punch before him, an' the king's money safe an' snug in the lowest wrinkle of his breeches-pocket.

So away wid him, and the dhrums and fifes playing, an' a dozen more unforthunate bliggards just listed along with him, an' he shakin' hands wid the sargent, and swearin' agin the women every minute, until, be the time he kem to himself, begorra, he was a good ten miles on the road to Dublin, an' Molly and all behind him.

It id be no good tellin' you iv the letters he wrote to her from the barracks there, nor how she was breaking her heart to go and see him just wanst before he'd go; but the father an' mother would not allow iv it be no manes.

An' so in less time than you'd be thinkin' about it, the colonel had him polished off into it rale elegant soger, wid his gun exercise, and his bagnet exercise, and his small sword, and broad sword, and pistol and dagger, an' all the rest, an' then away wid him on boord a man-a-war to furrin parts, to fight for King George agin Bonyparty, that was great in them times.

Well, it was very soon in everyone's mouth how Billy Malowney was batin' all before him, astonishin' the ginerals, an frightenin' the inimy to that degree, there was not a Frinchman dare say parley voo outside of the rounds iv his camp.

You may be sure Molly was proud iv that same, though she never spoke a word about it; until at last the news kem home that Billy Malowney was surrounded an' murdered by the Frinch army, under Napoleon Bonyparty himself. The news was brought by Jack Brynn Dhas, the peddlar, that said he met the corporal iv the regiment on the quay iv Limerick, an' how he brought him into a public-house and thrated him to a naggin, and got all the news about poor Billy Malowney out iv him while they war dhrinkin' it; an' a sorrowful story it was.

The way it happened, accordin' as the corporal tould him, was jist how the Jook iv Wellington detarmined to fight a rale tarin' battle wid the Frinch, and Bonyparty at the same time was aiqually detarmined to fight the divil's own scrimmidge wid the British foorces.

Well, as soon as the business was pretty near ready at both sides, Bonyparty and the general next undher himself gets up behind a bush, to look at their inimies through spyglasses, and thry would they know any iv them at the distance.

'Bedadad!' says the gineral, afther a divil iv a long spy, 'I'd bet half a pint,' says he, 'that's Bill Malowney himself,' says he, 'down there,' says he.

'Och!' says Bonypart, 'do you tell me so?' says he—'I'm fairly heart-scalded with that same Billy Malowney,' says he; 'an' I think if I was wanst shut iv him I'd bate the rest iv them aisy,' says he.

'I'm thinking so myself,' says the gineral, says he; 'but he's a tough bye,' says he.

'Tough!' says Bonypart, 'he's the divil,' says he.

'Begorra, I'd be better plased.' says the gineral, says he, 'to take himself than the Duke iv Willinton,' says he, 'an' Sir Edward Blakeney into the bargain,' says he.

'The Duke of Wellinton and Gineral Blakeney,' says Bonypart, 'is great for planning, no doubt,' says he; 'but Billy Malowney's the boy for ACTION,' says he—'an' action's everything, just now,' says he.

So wid that Bonypart pushes up his cocked hat, and begins scratching his head, and thinning and considherin' for the bare life, and at last says he to the gineral:

'Gineral Commandher iv all the Foorces,' says he, 'I've hot it,' says he: 'ordher out the forlorn hope,' says he, 'an' give them as much powdher, both glazed and blasting,' says he, 'an' as much bullets do ye mind, an' swan-dhrops an' chain-shot,' says he, 'an' all soorts iv waipons an' combustables as they can carry; an' let them surround Bill Malowney,' says he, 'an' if they can get any soort iv an advantage,' says he, 'let them knock him to smithereens,' says he, 'an' then take him presner,' says he; 'an' tell all the bandmen iv the Frinch army,' says he, 'to play up "Garryowen," to keep up their sperits,' says he, 'all the time they're advancin'. An' you may promise them anything you like in my name,' says he; for, by my sowl, I don't think its many iv them 'ill come back to throuble us,' says he, winkin' at him.

So away with the gineral, an' he ordhers out the forlorn hope, all' tells the band to play, an' everything else, just as Bonypart desired him. An' sure enough, whin Billy Malowney heerd the music where he was standin' taking a blast of the dhudheen to compose his mind for murdherin' the Frinchmen as usual, being mighty partial to that tune intirely, he cocks his ear a one side, an' down he stoops to listen to the music; but, begorra, who should be in his rare all the time but a Frinch grannideer behind a bush, and seeing him stooped in a convanient forum, bedad he let flies at him sthraight, and fired him right forward between the legs an' the small iv the back, glory be to God! with what they call (saving your presence) a bum-shell.

Well, Bill Malowney let one roar out iv him, an' away he rowled over the field iv battle like a slitther (as Bonypart and the Duke iv Wellington, that was watching the manoeuvres from a distance, both consayved) into glory.

An' sure enough the Frinch was overjoyed beyant all bounds, an' small blame to them—an' the Duke of Wellington, I'm toult, was never all out the same man sinst.

At any rate, the news kem home how Billy Malowney was murdhered by the Frinch in furrin parts.

Well, all this time, you may be sure, there was no want iv boys comin' to coort purty Molly Donovan; but one way ar another, she always kept puttin' them off constant. An' though her father and mother was nathurally anxious to get rid of her respickably, they did not like to marry her off in spite iv her teeth.

An' this way, promising one while and puttin' it off another, she conthrived to get on from one Shrove to another, until near seven years was over and gone from the time when Billy Malowney listed for furrin sarvice.

It was nigh hand a year from the time whin the news iv Leum-a-rinka bein' killed by the Frinch came home, an' in place iv forgettin' him, as the saisins wint over, it's what Molly was growin' paler and more lonesome every day, antil the neighbours thought she was fallin' into a decline; and this is the way it was with her whin the fair of Lisnamoe kem round.

It was a beautiful evenin', just at the time iv the reapin' iv the oats, and the sun was shinin' through the red clouds far away over the hills iv Cahirmore.

Her father an' mother, an' the boys an' girls, was all away down in the fair, and Molly Sittin' all alone on the step of the stile, listening to the foolish little birds whistlin' among the leaves—and the sound of the mountain-river flowin' through the stones an' bushes—an' the crows flyin' home high overhead to the woods iv Glinvarlogh—an' down in the glen, far away, she could see the fair-green iv Lisnamoe in the mist, an' sunshine among the grey rocks and threes—an' the cows an' the horses, an' the blue frieze, an' the red cloaks, an' the tents, an' the smoke, an' the ould round tower—all as soft an' as sorrowful as a dhrame iv ould times.

An' while she was looking this way, an' thinking iv Leum-a-rinka—poor Bill iv the dance, that was sleepin' in his lonesome glory in the fields iv Spain—she began to sing the song he used to like so well in the ould times—

'Shule, shule, shale a-roon;'

an' when she ended the verse, what do you think but she heard a manly voice just at the other side iv the hedge, singing the last words over again!

Well she knew it; her heart flutthered up like a little bird that id be wounded, and then dhropped still in her breast. It was himself. In a minute he was through the hedge and standing before her.

'Leum!' says she.

'Mavourneen cuishla machree!' says he; and without another word they were locked in one another's arms.

Well, it id only be nansinse for me thryin' an' tell ye all the foolish things they said, and how they looked in one another's faces, an' laughed, an' cried, an' laughed again; and how, when they came to themselves, and she was able at last to believe it was raly Billy himself that was there, actially holdin' her hand, and lookin' in her eyes the same way as ever, barrin' he was browner and boulder, an' did not, maybe, look quite as merry in himself as he used to do in former times—an' fondher for all, an' more lovin' than ever—how he tould her all about the wars wid the Frinchmen—an' how he was wounded, and left for dead in the field iv battle, bein' shot through the breast, and how he was discharged, an' got a pinsion iv a full shillin' a day—and how he was come back to liv the rest iv his days in the sweet glen iv Lisnamoe, an' (if only SHE'D consint) to marry herself in spite iv them all.

Well, ye may aisily think they had plinty to talk about, afther seven years without once seein' one another; and so signs on, the time flew by as swift an' as pleasant as a bird on the wing, an' the sun wint down, an' the moon shone sweet an' soft instead, an' they two never knew a ha'porth about it, but kept talkin' an' whisperin', an' whisperin' an' talkin'; for it's wondherful how often a tinder-hearted girl will bear to hear a purty boy tellin' her the same story constant over an' over; ontil at last, sure enough, they heerd the ould man himself comin' up the boreen, singin' the 'Colleen Rue'—a thing he never done barrin' whin he had a dhrop in; an' the misthress walkin' in front iv him, an' two illigant Kerry cows he just bought in the fair, an' the sarvint boys dhriving them behind.

'Oh, blessed hour!' says Molly, 'here's my father.'

'I'll spake to him this minute,' says Bill.

'Oh, not for the world,' says she; 'he's singin' the "Colleen Rue,"' says she, 'and no one dar raison with him,' says she.

'An' where 'll I go, thin?' says he, 'for they're into the haggard an top iv us,' says he, 'an' they'll see me iv I lep through the hedge,' says he.

'Thry the pig-sty,' says she, 'mavourneen,' says she, 'in the name iv God,' says she.

'Well, darlint,' says he, 'for your sake,' says he, 'I'll condescend to them animals,' says he.

An' wid that he makes a dart to get in; bud, begorra, it was too late—the pigs was all gone home, and the pig-sty was as full as the Burr coach wid six inside.

'Och! blur-an'-agers,' says he, 'there is not room for a suckin'-pig,' says he, 'let alone a Christian,' says he.

'Well, run into the house, Billy,' says she, 'this minute,' says she, 'an' hide yourself antil they're quiet,' says she, 'an' thin you can steal out,' says she, 'anknownst to them all,' says she.

'I'll do your biddin', says he, 'Molly asthore,' says he.

'Run in thin,' says she, 'an' I'll go an' meet them,' says she.

So wid that away wid her, and in wint Billy, an' where 'id he hide himself bud in a little closet that was off iv the room where the ould man and woman slep'. So he closed the doore, and sot down in an ould chair he found there convanient.

Well, he was not well in it when all the rest iv them comes into the kitchen, an' ould Tim Donovan singin' the 'Colleen Rue' for the bare life, an' the rest iv them sthrivin' to humour him, and doin' exactly everything he bid them, because they seen he was foolish be the manes iv the liquor.

Well, to be sure all this kep' them long enough, you may be sure, from goin' to bed, so that Billy could get no manner iv an advantage to get out iv the house, and so he sted sittin' in the dark closet in state, cursin' the 'Colleen Rue,' and wondherin' to the divil whin they'd get the ould man into his bed. An', as if that was not delay enough, who should come in to stop for the night but Father O'Flaherty, of Cahirmore, that was buyin' a horse at the fair! An' av course, there was a bed to be med down for his raverence, an' some other attintions; an' a long discoorse himself an' ould Mrs. Donovan had about the slaughter iv Billy Malowney, an' how he was buried on the field iv battle; an' his raverence hoped he got a dacent funeral, an' all the other convaniences iv religion. An' so you may suppose it was pretty late in the night before all iv them got to their beds.

Well, Tim Donovan could not settle to sleep at all at all, an' so he kep' discoorsin' the wife about the new cows he bought, an' the stripphers he sould, an' so an for better than an hour, ontil from one thing to another he kem to talk about the pigs, an' the poulthry; and at last, having nothing betther to discoorse about, he begun at his daughter Molly, an' all the heartscald she was to him be raison iv refusin' the men. An' at last says he:

'I onderstand,' says he, 'very well how it is,' says he. 'It's how she was in love,' says he, 'wid that bliggard, Billy Malowney,' says he, 'bad luck to him!' says he; for by this time he was coming to his raison.

'Ah!' says the wife, says she, 'Tim darlint, don't be cursin' them that's dead an' buried,' says she.

'An' why would not I,' says he, 'if they desarve it?' says he.

'Whisht,' says she, 'an' listen to that,' says she. 'In the name of the Blessed Vargin,' says she, 'what IS it?' says she.

An' sure enough what was it but Bill Malowney that was dhroppin' asleep in the closet, an' snorin' like a church organ.

'Is it a pig,' says he, 'or is it a Christian?'

'Arra! listen to the tune iv it,' says she; 'sure a pig never done the like is that,' says she.

'Whatever it is,' says he, 'it's in the room wid us,' says he. 'The Lord be marciful to us!' says he.

'I tould you not to be cursin',' says she; 'bad luck to you,' says she, 'for an ommadhaun!' for she was a very religious woman in herself.

'Sure, he's buried in Spain,' says he; 'an' it is not for one little innocent expression,' says he, 'he'd be comin' all that a way to annoy the house,' says he.

Well, while they war talkin', Bill turns in the way he was sleepin' into an aisier imposture; and as soon as he stopped snorin' ould Tim Donovan's courage riz agin, and says he:

'I'll go to the kitchen,' says he, 'an' light a rish,' says he.

An' with that away wid him, an' the wife kep' workin' the beads all the time, an' before he kem back Bill was snorin' as loud as ever.

'Oh! bloody wars—I mane the blessed saints about us!—that deadly sound,' says he; 'it's going on as lively as ever,' says he.

'I'm as wake as a rag,' says his wife, says she, 'wid the fair anasiness,' says she. 'It's out iv the little closet it's comin,' says she.

'Say your prayers,' says he, 'an' hould your tongue,' says he, 'while I discoorse it,' says he. 'An' who are ye,' says he, 'in the name iv of all the holy saints?' says he, givin' the door a dab iv a crusheen that wakened Bill inside. 'I ax,' says he, 'who are you?' says he.

Well, Bill did not rightly remember where in the world he was, but he pushed open the door, an' says he:

'Billy Malowney's my name,' says he, 'an' I'll thank ye to tell me a betther,' says he.

Well, whin Tim Donovan heard that, an' actially seen that it was Bill himself that was in it, he had not strength enough to let a bawl out iv him, but he dhropt the candle out iv his hand, an' down wid himself on his back in the dark.

Well, the wife let a screech you'd hear at the mill iv Killraghlin, an'—

'Oh,' says she, 'the spirit has him, body an' bones!' says she. 'Oh, holy St. Bridget—oh, Mother iv Marcy—oh, Father O'Flaherty!' says she, screechin' murdher from out iv her bed.

Well, Bill Malowney was not a minute remimberin' himself, an' so out wid him quite an' aisy, an' through the kitchen; bud in place iv the door iv the house, it's what he kem to the door iv Father O'Flaherty's little room, where he was jist wakenin' wid the noise iv the screechin' an' battherin'; an' bedad, Bill makes no more about it, but he jumps, wid one boult, clever an' clane into his raverance's bed.

'What do ye mane, you uncivilised bliggard?' says his raverance. 'Is that a venerable way,' says he, 'to approach your clargy?' says he.

'Hould your tongue,' says Bill, 'an' I'll do ye no harum,' says he.

'Who are you, ye scoundhrel iv the world?' says his raverance.

'Whisht!' says he? 'I'm Billy Malowney,' says he.

'You lie!' says his raverance for he was frightened beyont all bearin'—an' he makes but one jump out iv the bed at the wrong side, where there was only jist a little place in the wall for a press, an' his raverance could not as much as turn in it for the wealth iv kingdoms. 'You lie,' says he; 'but for feared it's the truth you're tellin',' says he, 'here's at ye in the name iv all the blessed saints together!' says he.

An' wid that, my dear, he blazes away at him wid a Latin prayer iv the strongest description, an', as he said himself afterwards, that was iv a nature that id dhrive the divil himself up the chimley like a puff iv tobacky smoke, wid his tail betune his legs

'Arra, what are ye sthrivin' to say,' says Bill; says he, 'if ye don't hould your tongue,' says he, 'wid your parly voo;' says he, 'it's what I'll put my thumb on your windpipe,' says he, 'an' Billy Malowney never wint back iv his word yet,' says he.

'Thundher-an-owns,' says his raverance, says he—seein' the Latin took no infect on him, at all at all an' screechin' that you'd think he'd rise the thatch up iv the house wid the fair fright—'and thundher and blazes, boys, will none iv yes come here wid a candle, but lave your clargy to be choked by a spirit in the dark?' says he.

Well, be this time the sarvint boys and the rest iv them wor up an' half dressed, an' in they all run, one on top iv another, wid pitchforks and spades, thinkin' it was only what his raverence slep' a dhrame iv the like, by means of the punch he was afther takin' just before he rowl'd himself into the bed. But, begorra, whin they seen it was raly Bill Malowney himself that was in it, it was only who'd be foremost out agin, tumblin' backways, one over another, and his raverence roarin' an' cursin' them like mad for not waitin' for him.

Well, my dear, it was betther than half an hour before Billy Malowney could explain to them all how it raly was himself, for begorra they were all iv them persuadin' him that he was a spirit to that degree it's a wondher he did not give in to it, if it was only to put a stop to the argiment.

Well, his raverence tould the ould people then, there was no use in sthrivin' agin the will iv Providence an' the vagaries iv love united; an' whin they kem to undherstand to a sartinty how Billy had a shillin' a day for the rest iv his days, begorra they took rather a likin' to him, and considhered at wanst how he must have riz out of all his nansinse entirely, or his gracious Majesty id never have condescinded to show him his countenance that way every day of his life, on a silver shillin'.

An' so, begorra, they never stopt till it was all settled—an' there was not sich a weddin' as that in the counthry sinst. It's more than forty years ago, an' though I was no more nor a gossoon myself, I remimber it like yestherday. Molly never looked so purty before, an' Billy Malowney was plisant beyont all hearin,' to that degree that half the girls in it was fairly tarin' mad—only they would not let on—they had not him to themselves in place iv her. An' begorra I'd be afeared to tell ye, because you would not believe me, since that blessid man Father Mathew put an end to all soorts of sociality, the Lord reward him, how many gallons iv potti-een whisky was dhrank upon that most solemn and tindher occasion.

Pat Hanlon, the piper, had a faver out iv it; an' Neddy Shawn Heigue, mountin' his horse the wrong way, broke his collarbone, by the manes iv fallin' over his tail while he was feelin' for his head; an' Payther Brian, the horse-docther, I am tould, was never quite right in the head ever afther; an' ould Tim Donovan was singin' the 'Colleen Rue' night and day for a full week; an' begorra the weddin' was only the foundation iv fun, and the beginning iv divarsion, for there was not a year for ten years afther, an' more, but brought round a christenin' as regular as the sasins revarted.

IN A GLASS DARKLY
VOLUME I

TO
BRINSLEY HOMAN, ESQ.
THESE VOLUMES ARE INSCRIBED,
WITH MUCH AFFECTION,
BY HIS OLD FRIEND
THE AUTHOR.

GREEN TEA

PROLOGUE.

MARTIN HESSELIUS, THE GERMAN PHYSICIAN.

Though carefully educated in medicine and surgery, I have never practised either. The study of each continues, nevertheless, to interest me profoundly. Neither idleness nor caprice caused my secession from the honourable calling which I had just entered. The cause was a very trifling scratch inflicted by a dissecting knife. This trifle cost me the loss of two fingers, amputated promptly, and the more painful loss of my health, for I have never been quite well since, and have seldom been twelve months together in the same place.

In my wanderings I became acquainted with Dr. Martin Hesselius, a wanderer like myself, like me a physician, and like me an enthusiast in his profession. Unlike me in this, that his wanderings were voluntary, and he a man, if not of fortune, as we estimate fortune in England, at least in what our forefathers used to term "easy circumstances." He was an old man when I first saw him; nearly five-and-thirty years my senior.

In Dr. Martin Hesselius, I found my master. His knowledge was immense, his grasp of a case was an intuition. He was the very man to inspire a young enthusiast, like me, with awe and delight. My admiration has stood the test of time and survived the separation of death. I am sure it was well-founded.

For nearly twenty years I acted as his medical secretary. His immense collection of papers he has left in my care, to be arranged, indexed and bound. His treatment of some of these cases is curious. He writes in two distinct characters. He describes what he saw and heard as an intelligent layman might, and when in this style of narrative he had seen the patient either through his own hall-door, to the light of day, or through the gates of darkness to the caverns of the dead, he returns upon the narrative, and in the terms of his art, and with all the force and originality of genius, proceeds to the work of analysis, diagnosis and illustration.

Here and there a case strikes me as of a kind to amuse or horrify a lay reader with an interest quite different from the peculiar one which it may possess for an expert. With slight modifications, chiefly of language, and of course a change of names, I copy the following. The narrator is Dr. Martin Hesselius. I find it among the voluminous notes of cases which he made during a tour in England about sixty-four years ago.

It is related in a series of letters to his friend Professor Van Loo of Leyden. The professor was not a physician, but a chemist, and a man who read history and metaphysics and medicine, and had, in his day, written a play.

The narrative is therefore, if somewhat less valuable as a medical record, necessarily written in a manner more likely to interest an unlearned reader.

These letters, from a memorandum attached, appear to have been returned on the death of the professor, in 1819, to Dr. Hesselius. They are written, some in English, some in French, but the greater part in German. I am a faithful, though I am conscious, by no means a graceful translator, and although here and there, I omit some passages, and shorten others and disguise names, I have interpolated nothing.

CHAPTER I.

DR. HESSELIUS RELATES HOW HE MET THE REV. MR. JENNINGS.

The Rev. Mr. Jennings is tall and thin. He is middle-aged, and dresses with a natty, old-fashioned, high-church precision. He is naturally a little stately, but not at all stiff. His features, without being handsome, are well formed, and their expression extremely kind, but also shy.

I met him one evening at Lady Mary Heyduke's. The modesty and benevolence of his countenance are extremely prepossessing. We were but a small party, and he joined agreeably enough in the conversation. He seems to enjoy listening very much more than contributing to the talk, but what he says is always to the purpose and well said. He is a great favourite of Lady Mary's, who it seems, consults him upon many things, and thinks him the most happy and blessed person on earth. Little knows she about him.

The Rev. Mr. Jennings is a bachelor, and has, they say, sixty thousand pounds in the funds. He is a charitable man. He is most anxious to be actively employed in his sacred profession, and yet though always tolerably well elsewhere, when he goes down to his vicarage in Warwickshire, to engage in the actual duties of his sacred calling his health soon fails him, and in a very strange way. So says Lady Mary.

There is no doubt that Mr. Jennings' health does break down in, generally a sudden and mysterious way, sometimes in the very act of officiating in his old and pretty church at Kenlis. It may be his heart, it may be his brain. But so it has happened three or four times, or oftener, that after proceeding a certain way in the service, he has on a sudden stopped short, and after a silence, apparently quite unable to resume, he has fallen into solitary, inaudible prayer, his hands and eyes uplifted, and then pale as death, and in the agitation of a strange shame and horror, descended trembling, and got into the vestry-room, leaving his congregation, without explanation, to themselves. This occurred when his curate was absent. When he goes down to Kenlis, now, he always takes care to provide a clergyman to share his duty, and to supply his place on the instant should he become thus suddenly incapacitated.

When Mr. Jennings breaks down quite, and beats a retreat from the vicarage, and returns to London, where, in a dark street off Piccadilly, he inhabits a very narrow house, Lady Mary says that he is always perfectly well. I have my own opinion about that. There are degrees of course. We shall see.

Mr. Jennings is a perfectly gentleman-like man. People, however, remark something odd. There is an impression a little ambiguous. One thing which certainly contributes to it, people I think don't remember; or, perhaps, distinctly remark. But I did, almost immediately. Mr. Jennings has a way of looking sidelong upon the carpet, as if his eye followed the movements of something there. This, of course, is not always. It occurs only now and then. But often enough to give a certain oddity, as I have said to his manner, and in this glance travelling along the floor there is something both shy and anxious.

A medical philosopher, as you are good enough to call me, elaborating theories by the aid of cases sought out by himself, and by him watched and scrutinised with more time at command, and consequently infinitely more minuteness than the ordinary practitioner can afford, falls insensibly into habits of observation, which accompany him everywhere, and are exercised, as some people would say, impertinently, upon every subject that presents itself with the least likelihood of rewarding inquiry.

There was a promise of this kind in the slight, timid, kindly, but reserved gentleman, whom I met for the first time at this agreeable little evening gathering. I observed, of course, more than I here set down; but I reserve all that borders on the technical for a strictly scientific paper.

I may remark, that when I here speak of medical science, I do so, as I hope some day to see it more generally understood, in a much more comprehensive sense than its generally material treatment would warrant. I believe the entire natural world is but the ultimate expression of that spiritual world from which, and in which alone, it has its life. I believe that the essential man is a spirit, that the spirit is an organised substance, but as different in point of material from what we ordinarily understand by matter, as light or electricity is; that the material body is, in the most literal sense, a vesture, and death consequently no interruption of the living man's existence, but simply his extrication from the natural body—a process which commences at the moment of what we term death, and the completion of which, at furthest a few days later, is the resurrection "in power."

The person who weighs the consequences of these positions will probably see their practical bearing upon medical science. This is, however, by no means the proper place for displaying the proofs and discussing the consequences of this too generally unrecognised state of facts.

In pursuance of my habit, I was covertly observing Mr. Jennings, with all my caution—I think he perceived it—and I saw plainly that he was as cautiously observing me. Lady Mary happening to address me by my name, as Dr. Hesselius, I saw that he glanced at me more sharply, and then became thoughtful for a few minutes.

After this, as I conversed with a gentleman at the other end of the room, I saw him look at me more steadily, and with an interest which I thought I understood. I then saw him take an opportunity of chatting with Lady Mary, and was, as one always is, perfectly aware of being the subject of a distant inquiry and answer.

This tall clergyman approached me by-and-by: and in a little time we had got into conversation. When two people, who like reading, and know books and places, having travelled, wish to converse, it is very strange if they can't find topics. It was not accident that brought him near me, and led him into conversation. He knew German, and had read my Essays on Metaphysical Medicine which suggest more than they actually say.

This courteous man, gentle, shy, plainly a man of thought and reading, who moving and talking among us, was not altogether of us, and whom I already suspected of leading a life whose transactions and alarms were carefully concealed, with an impenetrable reserve from, not only the world, but his best beloved friends—was cautiously weighing in his own mind the idea of taking a certain step with regard to me.

I penetrated his thoughts without his being aware of it, and was careful to say nothing which could betray to his sensitive vigilance my suspicions respecting his position, or my surmises about his plans respecting myself.

We chatted upon indifferent subjects for a time; but at last he said:

"I was very much interested by some papers of yours, Dr. Hesselius, upon what you term Metaphysical Medicine—I read them in German, ten or twelve years ago—have they been translated?"

"No, I'm sure they have not—I should have heard. They would have asked my leave, I think."

"I asked the publishers here, a few months ago, to get the book for me in the original German; but they tell me it is out of print."

"So it is, and has been for some years; but it flatters me as an author to find that you have not forgotten my little book, although," I added, laughing, "ten or twelve years is a considerable time to have managed without it; but I suppose you have been turning the subject over again in your mind, or something has happened lately to revive your interest in it."

At this remark, accompanied by a glance of inquiry, a sudden embarrassment disturbed Mr. Jennings, analogous to that which makes a young lady blush and look foolish. He dropped his eyes, and folded his hands together uneasily, and looked oddly, and you would have said, guiltily for a moment.

I helped him out of his awkwardness in the best way, by appearing not to observe it, and going straight on, I said: "Those revivals of interest in a subject happen to me often; one book suggests another, and often sends me back a wild-goose chase over an interval of twenty years. But if you still care to possess a copy, I shall be only too happy to provide you; I have still got two or three by me—and if you allow me to present one I shall be very much honoured."

"You are very good indeed," he said, quite at his ease again, in a moment: "I almost despaired—I don't know how to thank you."

"Pray don't say a word; the thing is really so little worth that I am only ashamed of having offered it, and if you thank me any more I shall throw it into the fire in a fit of modesty."

Mr. Jennings laughed. He inquired where I was staying in London, and after a little more conversation on a variety of subjects, he took his departure.

CHAPTER II.

THE DOCTOR QUESTIONS LADY MARY, AND SHE ANSWERS.

"I like your vicar so much, Lady Mary," said I, so soon as he was gone. "He has read, travelled, and thought, and having also suffered, he ought to be an accomplished companion."

"So he is, and, better still, he is a really good man," said she. "His advice is invaluable about my schools, and all my little undertakings at Dawlbridge, and he's so painstaking, he takes so much trouble—you have no idea—wherever he thinks he can be of use: he's so good-natured and so sensible."

"It is pleasant to hear so good an account of his neighbourly virtues. I can only testify to his being an agreeable and gentle companion, and in addition to what you have told me, I think I can tell you two or three things about him," said I.

"Really!"

"Yes, to begin with, he's unmarried."

"Yes, that's right,—go on."

"He has been writing, that is he was, but for two or three years perhaps, he has not gone on with his work, and the book was upon some rather abstract subject—perhaps theology."

"Well, he was writing a book, as you say; I'm not quite sure what it was about, but only that it was nothing that I cared for, very likely you are right, and he certainly did stop—yes."

"And although he only drank a little coffee here to-night, he likes tea, at least, did like it, extravagantly."

"Yes, that's *quite* true."

"He drank green tea, a good deal, didn't he?" I pursued.

"Well, that's very odd! Green tea was a subject on which we used almost to quarrel."

"But he has quite given that up," said I.

"So he has."

"And, now, one more fact. His mother or his father, did you know them?"

"Yes, both; his father is only ten years dead, and their place is near Dawlbridge. We knew them very well," she answered.

"Well, either his mother or his father—I should rather think his father, saw a ghost," said I.

"Well, you really are a conjurer, Dr. Hesselius."

"Conjurer or no, haven't I said right?" I answered merrily.

"You certainly have, and it was his father: he was a silent, whimsical man, and he used to bore my father about his dreams, and at last he told him a story about a ghost he had seen and talked with, and a very odd story it was. I remember it particularly, because I was so afraid of him. This story was long before he died—when I was quite a child—and his ways were so silent and moping, and he used to drop in, sometimes, in the dusk, when I was alone in the drawing-room, and I used to fancy there were ghosts about him."

I smiled and nodded.

"And now having established my character as a conjurer I think I must say good-night," said I.

"But how *did* you find it out?"

"By the planets of course, as the gipsies do," I answered, and so, gaily, we said good-night.

Next morning I sent the little book he had been inquiring after, and a note to Mr. Jennings, and on returning late that evening, I found that he had called, at my lodgings, and left his card. He asked whether I was at home, and asked at what hour he would be most likely to find me.

Does he intend opening his case, and consulting me "professionally," as they say? I hope so. I have already conceived a theory about him. It is supported by Lady Mary's answers to my parting questions. I should like much to ascertain from his own lips. But what can I do consistently with good breeding to invite a confession? Nothing. I rather think he meditates one. At all events, my dear Van L., I shan't make myself difficult of access; I mean to return his visit to-morrow. It will be only civil in return for his politeness, to ask to see him. Perhaps something may come of it. Whether much, little, or nothing, my dear Van L., you shall hear.

CHAPTER III.

DR. HESSELIUS PICKS UP SOMETHING IN LATIN BOOKS.

Well, I have called at Blank-street.

On inquiring at the door, the servant told me that Mr. Jennings was engaged very particularly with a gentleman, a clergyman from Kenlis, his parish in the country. Intending to reserve my privilege and to call again, I merely intimated that I should try another time, and had turned to go, when the servant begged my pardon, and asked me, looking at me a little more attentively than well-bred persons of his order usually do, whether I was Dr. Hesselius; and, on learning that I was, he said, "Perhaps then, sir, you would allow me to mention it to Mr. Jennings, for I am sure he wishes to see you."

The servant returned in a moment, with a message from Mr. Jennings, asking me to go into his study, which was in effect his back drawing-room, promising to be with me in a very few minutes.

This was really a study—almost a library. The room was lofty, with two tall slender windows, and rich dark curtains. It was much larger than I had expected, and stored with books on every side, from the floor to the ceiling. The upper carpet—for to my tread it felt that there were two or three—was a Turkey carpet. My steps fell noiselessly. The book-cases standing out, placed the windows, particularly narrow ones, in deep recesses. The effect of the room was, although extremely comfortable, and even luxurious, decidedly gloomy, and aided by the silence, almost oppressive. Perhaps, however, I ought to have allowed something for association. My mind had connected peculiar ideas with Mr. Jennings. I stepped into this perfectly silent room, of a very silent house, with a peculiar foreboding; and its darkness, and solemn clothing of books, for except where two narrow looking-glasses were set in the wall, they were everywhere, helped this sombre feeling.

While awaiting Mr. Jennings' arrival, I amused myself by looking into some of the books with which his shelves were laden. Not among these, but immediately under them, with their backs upward, on the floor, I lighted upon a complete set of Swedenborg's Arcana Cælestia, in the original Latin, a very fine folio set, bound in the natty livery which theology affects, pure vellum, namely, gold letters, and carmine edges. There were paper markers in several of these volumes, I raised and placed them, one after the other, upon the table, and opening where these papers were placed, I read in the solemn Latin phraseology, a series of sentences indicated by a pencilled line at the margin. Of these I copy here a few, translating them into English.

"When man's interior sight is opened, which is that of his spirit, then there appear the things of another life, which cannot possibly be made visible to the bodily sight."...

"By the internal sight it has been granted me to see the things that are in the other life, more clearly than I see those that are in the world. From these considerations, it is evident that external vision exists from interior vision, and this from a vision still more interior, and so on."...

"There are with every man at least two evil spirits."...

"With wicked genii there is also a fluent speech, but harsh and grating. There is also among them a speech which is not fluent, wherein the dissent of the thoughts is perceived as something secretly creeping along within it."...

"The evil spirits associated with man are, indeed, from the hells, but when with man they are not then in hell, but are taken out thence. The place where they then are is in the midst between heaven and hell, and is called the world of spirits—when the evil spirits who are with man, are in that world, they are not in any infernal torment, but in every thought and affection of the man, and so, in all that the man himself enjoys. But when they are remitted into their hell, they return to their former state."...

"If evil spirits could perceive that they were associated with man, and yet that they were spirits separate from him, and if they could flow in into the things of his body, they would attempt by a thousand means to destroy him; for they hate man with a deadly hatred."...

"Knowing, therefore, that I was a man in the body, they were continually striving to destroy me, not as to the body only, but especially as to the soul; for to destroy any man or spirit is the very delight of the life of all who are in hell; but I have been continually protected by the Lord. Hence it appears how dangerous it is for man to be in a living consort with spirits, unless he be in the good of faith."...

"Nothing is more carefully guarded from the knowledge of associate spirits than their being thus conjoint with a man, for if they knew it they would speak to him, with the intention to destroy him."...

"The delight of hell is to do evil to man, and to hasten his eternal ruin."

A long note, written with a very sharp and fine pencil, in Mr. Jennings' neat hand, at the foot of the page, caught my eye. Expecting his criticism upon the text, I read a word or two, and stopped, for it was something quite different, and began with these words, *Deus misereatur mei*—"May God compassionate me." Thus warned of its private nature, I averted my eyes, and shut the book, replacing all the volumes as I had found them, except one which interested me, and in which, as men studious and solitary in their habits will do, I grew so absorbed as to take no cognisance of the outer world, nor to remember where I was.

I was reading some pages which refer to "representatives" and "correspondents," in the technical language of Swedenborg, and had arrived at a passage, the substance of which is, that evil spirits, when seen by other eyes than those of their infernal associates, present themselves, by "correspondence," in the shape of the beast (*fera*) which represents their particular lust and life, in aspect direful and atrocious. This is a long passage, and particularises a number of those bestial forms.

CHAPTER IV.

FOUR EYES WERE READING THE PASSAGE.

I was running the head of my pencil-case along the line as I read it, and something caused me to raise my eyes.

Directly before me was one of the mirrors I have mentioned, in which I saw reflected the tall shape of my friend Mr. Jennings leaning over my shoulder, and reading the page at which I was busy, and with a face so dark and wild that I should hardly have known him.

I turned and rose. He stood erect also, and with an effort laughed a little, saying:

"I came in and asked you how you did, but without succeeding in awaking you from your book; so I could not restrain my curiosity, and very impertinently, I'm afraid, peeped over your shoulder. This is not your first time of looking into those pages. You have looked into Swedenborg, no doubt, long ago?"

"Oh dear, yes! I owe Swedenborg a great deal; you will discover traces of him in the little book on Metaphysical Medicine, which you were so good as to remember."

Although my friend affected a gaiety of manner, there was a slight flush in his face, and I could perceive that he was inwardly much perturbed.

"I'm scarcely yet qualified, I know so little of Swedenborg. I've only had them a fortnight," he answered, "and I think they are rather likely to make a solitary man nervous—that is, judging from the very little I have read—I don't say that they have made me so," he laughed; "and I'm so very much obliged for the book. I hope you got my note?"

I made all proper acknowledgments and modest disclaimers.

"I never read a book that I go with, so entirely, as that of yours," he continued. "I saw at once there is more in it than is quite unfolded. Do you know Dr. Harley?" he asked, rather abruptly.

In passing, the editor remarks that the physician here named was one of the most eminent who had ever practised in England.

I did, having had letters to him, and had experienced from him great courtesy and considerable assistance during my visit to England.

"I think that man one of the very greatest fools I ever met in my life," said Mr. Jennings.

This was the first time I had ever heard him say a sharp thing of anybody, and such a term applied to so high a name a little startled me.

"Really! and in what way?" I asked.

"In his profession," he answered.

I smiled.

"I mean this," he said: "he seems to me, one half, blind—I mean one half of all he looks at is dark—preternaturally bright and vivid all the rest; and the worst of it is, it seems *wilful.* I can't get him—I mean he won't—I've had some experience of him as a physician, but I look on him as, in that sense, no better than a paralytic mind, an intellect half dead, I'll tell you—I know I shall some time—all about it," he said, with a little agitation. "You stay some months longer in England. If I should be out of town during your stay for a little time, would you allow me to trouble you with a letter?"

"I should be only too happy," I assured him.

"Very good of you. I am so utterly dissatisfied with Harley."

"A little leaning to the materialistic school," I said.

"A *mere* materialist," he corrected me; "you can't think how that sort of thing worries one who knows better. You won't tell any one—any of my friends you know—that I am hippish; now, for instance, no one knows—not even Lady Mary—that I have seen Dr. Harley, or any other doctor. So pray don't mention it; and, if I should have any threatening of an attack, you'll kindly let me write, or, should I be in town, have a little talk with you."

I was full of conjecture, and unconsciously I found I had fixed my eyes gravely on him, for he lowered his for a moment, and he said:

"I see you think I might as well tell you now, or else you are forming a conjecture; but you may as well give it up. If you were guessing all the rest of your life, you will never hit on it."

He shook his head smiling, and over that wintry sunshine a black cloud suddenly came down, and he drew his breath in, through his teeth as men do in pain.

"Sorry, of course, to learn that you apprehend occasion to consult any of us; but, command me when and how you like, and I need not assure you that your confidence is sacred."

He then talked of quite other things, and in a comparatively cheerful way and after a little time, I took my leave.

CHAPTER V.

DOCTOR HESSELIUS IS SUMMONED TO RICHMOND.

We parted cheerfully, but he was not cheerful, nor was I. There are certain expressions of that powerful organ of spirit—the human face—which, although I have seen them often, and possess a doctor's nerve, yet disturb me profoundly. One look of Mr. Jennings haunted me. It had seized my imagination with so dismal a power that I changed my plans for the evening, and went to the opera, feeling that I wanted a change of ideas.

I heard nothing of or from him for two or three days, when a note in his hand reached me. It was cheerful, and full of hope. He said that he had been for some little time so much better quite well, in fact that he was going to make a little experiment, and run down for a month or so to his parish, to try whether a little work might not quite set him up. There was in it a fervent religious expression of gratitude for his restoration, as he now almost hoped he might call it.

A day or two later I saw Lady Mary, who repeated what his note had announced, and told me that he was actually in Warwickshire, having resumed his clerical duties at Kenlis; and she added, "I begin to think that he is really perfectly well, and that there never was anything the matter, more than nerves and fancy; we are all nervous, but I fancy there is nothing like a little hard work for that kind of weakness, and he has made up his mind to try it. I should not be surprised if he did not come back for a year."

Notwithstanding all this confidence, only two days later I had this note, dated from his house off Piccadilly:

"Dear Sir.—I have returned disappointed. If I should feel at all able to see you, I shall write to ask you kindly to call. At present I am too low, and, in fact, simply unable to say all I wish to say. Pray don't mention my name to my friends. I can see no one. By-and-by, please God, you shall hear from me. I mean to take a run into Shropshire, where some of my people are. God bless you! May we, on my return, meet more happily than I can now write."

About a week after this I saw Lady Mary at her own house, the last person, she said, left in town, and just on the wing for Brighton, for the London season was quite over. She told me that she had heard from Mr. Jennings' niece, Martha, in

Shropshire. There was nothing to be gathered from her letter, more than that he was low and nervous. In those words, of which healthy people think so lightly, what a world of suffering is sometimes hidden!

Nearly five weeks passed without any further news of Mr. Jennings. At the end of that time I received a note from him. He wrote:

"I have been in the country, and have had change of air, change of scene, change of faces, change of everything and in everything—but *myself*. I have made up my mind, so far as the most irresolute creature on earth can do it, to tell my case fully to you. If your engagements will permit, pray come to me to-day, to-morrow, or the next day; but, pray defer as little as possible. You know not how much I need help. I have a quiet house at Richmond, where I now am. Perhaps you can manage to come to dinner, or to luncheon, or even to tea. You shall have no trouble in finding me out. The servant at Blank street, who takes this note, will have a carriage at your door at any hour you please; and I am always to be found. You will say that I ought not to be alone. I have tried everything. Come and see."

I called up the servant, and decided on going out the same evening, which accordingly I did.

He would have been much better in a lodging-house, or hotel, I thought, as I drove up through a short double row of sombre elms to a very old-fashioned brick house, darkened by the foliage of these trees, which over-topped, and nearly surrounded it. It was a perverse choice, for nothing could be imagined more triste and silent. The house, I found, belonged to him. He had stayed for a day or two in town, and, finding it for some cause insupportable, had come out here, probably because being furnished and his own, he was relieved of the thought and delay of selection, by coming here.

The sun had already set, and the red reflected light of the western sky illuminated the scene with the peculiar effect with which we are all familiar. The hall seemed very dark, but, getting to the back drawing-room, whose windows command the west, I was again in the same dusky light.

I sat down, looking out upon the richly-wooded landscape that glowed in the grand and melancholy light which was every moment fading. The corners of the room were already dark; all was growing dim, and the gloom was insensibly toning my mind, already prepared for what was sinister. I was waiting alone for his arrival, which soon took place. The door communicating with the front room opened, and the tall figure of Mr. Jennings, faintly seen in the ruddy twilight, came, with quiet stealthy steps, into the room.

We shook hands, and, taking a chair to the window, where there was still light enough to enable us to see each other's faces, he sat down beside me, and, placing his hand upon my arm, with scarcely a word of preface began his narrative.

CHAPTER VI.

HOW MR. JENNINGS MET HIS COMPANION.

The faint glow of the west, the pomp of the then lonely woods of Richmond, were before us, behind and about us the darkening room, and on the stony face or the sufferer—for the character of his face, though still gentle and sweet, was changed—rested that dim, odd glow which seems to descend and produce, where it touches, lights, sudden though faint, which are lost, almost without gradation, in darkness. The silence, too, was utter; not a distant wheel, or bark, or whistle from without; and within the depressing stillness of an invalid bachelor's house.

I guessed well the nature, though not even vaguely the particulars of the revelations I was about to receive, from that fixed face of suffering that so oddly flushed stood out, like a portrait of Schalken's, before its background of darkness.

"It began," he said, "on the 15th of October, three years and eleven weeks ago, and two days—I keep very accurate count, for every day is torment. If I leave anywhere a chasm in my narrative tell me.

"About four years ago I began a work, which had cost me very much thought and reading. It was upon the religious metaphysics of the ancients."

"I know," said I; "the actual religion of educated and thinking paganism, quite apart from symbolic worship? A wide and very interesting field."

"Yes; but not good for the mind—the Christian mind, I mean. Paganism is all bound together in essential unity, and, with evil sympathy, their religion involves their art, and both their manners, and the subject is a degrading fascination and the nemesis sure. God forgive me!

"I wrote a great deal; I wrote late at night. I was always thinking on the subject, walking about, wherever I was, everywhere. It thoroughly infected me. You are to remember that all the material ideas connected with it were more or less of the beautiful, the subject itself delightfully interesting, and I, then, without a care."

He sighed heavily.

"I believe that every one who sets about writing in earnest does his work, as a friend of mine phrased it, *on* something—tea, or coffee, or tobacco. I suppose there is a material waste that must be hourly supplied in such occupations, or that we should grow too abstracted, and the mind, as it were, pass out of the body, unless it were reminded often of the connection by actual sensation. At all events, I felt the want, and I supplied it. Tea was my companion—at first the ordinary black tea, made in the usual way, not too strong: but I drank a good deal, and increased its strength as I went on. I never experienced an uncomfortable symptom from it. I began to take a little green tea. I found the effect pleasanter, it cleared and intensified the power of thought so. I had come to take it frequently, but not stronger than one might take it for pleasure. I wrote a great deal out here, it was so quiet, and in this room. I used to sit up very late, and it became a habit with me to sip my tea—green tea—every now and then as my work proceeded. I had a little kettle on my table, that swung over a lamp, and made tea two or three times between eleven o'clock and two or three in the morning, my hours of going to bed. I used to go into town every day. I was not a monk, and, although I spent an hour or two in a library, hunting up authorities and looking out lights upon my theme, I was in no morbid state as far as I can judge. I met my friends pretty much as usual, and enjoyed their society, and, on the whole, existence had never been, I think, so pleasant before.

"I had met with a man who had some odd old books, German editions in mediæval Latin, and I was only too happy to be permitted access to them. This obliging person's books were in the City, a very out-of-the-way part of it. I had rather out-stayed my intended hour, and, on coming out, seeing no cab near, I was tempted to get into the omnibus which used to drive past this house. It was darker than this by the time the 'bus had reached an old house, you may have remarked, with four poplars at each side of the door, and there the last passenger but myself got out. We drove along rather faster. It was twilight now. I leaned back in my corner next the door ruminating pleasantly.

"The interior of the omnibus was nearly dark. I had observed in the corner opposite to me at the other side, and at the end next the horses, two small circular reflections, as it seemed to me of a reddish light. They were about two inches apart, and about the size of those small brass buttons that yachting men used to put upon their jackets. I began to speculate, as listless men will, upon this trifle, as it seemed. From what centre did that faint but deep red light come, and from what—glass beads, buttons, toy decorations—was it reflected? We were lumbering along gently, having nearly a mile still to go. I had not solved the puzzle, and it became in another minute more odd, for these two luminous points, with a sudden jerk, descended nearer the floor, keeping still their relative distance and horizontal position, and then, as suddenly, they rose to the level of the seat on which I was sitting, and I saw them no more.

"My curiosity was now really excited, and, before I had time to think, I saw again these two dull lamps, again together near the floor; again they disappeared, and again in their old corner I saw them.

"So, keeping my eyes upon them, I edged quietly up my own side, towards the end at which I still saw these tiny discs of red.

"There was very little light in the 'bus. It was nearly dark. I leaned forward to aid my endeavour to discover what these little circles really were. They shifted their position a little as I did so. I began now to perceive an outline of something black, and I soon saw with tolerable distinctness the outline of a small black monkey, pushing its face forward in mimicry to meet mine; those were its eyes, and I now dimly saw its teeth grinning at me.

"I drew back, not knowing whcther it might not meditate a spring. I fancied that one of the passengers had forgot this ugly pet, and wishing to ascertain something of its temper, though not caring to trust my fingers to it, I poked my umbrella softly towards it. It remained immovable—up to it—*through* it! For through it, and back and forward, it passed, without the slightest resistance.

"I can't, in the least, convey to you the kind of horror that I felt. When I had ascertained that the thing was an illusion, as I then supposed, there came a misgiving about myself and a terror that fascinated me in impotence to remove my gaze from the eyes of the brute for some moments. As I looked, it made a little skip back, quite into the corner, and I, in a panic, found myself at the door, having put my head out, drawing deep breaths of the outer air, and staring at the lights and trees we were passing, too glad to reassure myself of reality.

"I stopped the 'bus and got out. I perceived the man look oddly at me as I paid him. I daresay there was something unusual in my looks and manner, for I had never felt so strangely before."

CHAPTER VII.

THE JOURNEY: FIRST STAGE.

"When the omnibus drove on, and I was alone upon the road, I looked carefully round to ascertain whether the monkey had followed me. To my indescribable relief I saw it nowhere. I can't describe easily what a shock I had received, and my sense of genuine gratitude on finding myself, as I supposed, quite rid of it.

"I had got out a little before we reached this house, two or three hundred steps. A brick wall runs along the footpath, and inside the wall is a hedge of yew or some dark evergreen of that kind, and within that again the row of fine trees which you may have remarked as you came.

"This brick wall is about as high as my shoulder, and happening to raise my eyes I saw the monkey, with that stooping gait, on all fours, walking or creeping, close beside me on top of the wall. I stopped looking at it with a feeling of loathing and horror. As I stopped so did it. It sat up on the wall with its long hands on its knees looking at me. There was not light enough to see it much more than in outline, nor was it dark enough to bring the peculiar light of its eyes into strong relief. I still saw, however, that red foggy light plainly enough. It did not show its teeth, nor exhibit any sign of irritation, but seemed jaded and sulky, and was observing me steadily.

"I drew back into the middle of the road. It was an unconscious recoil, and there I stood, still looking at it, it did not move.

"With an instinctive determination to try something—anything, I turned about and walked briskly towards town with a skance look, all the time, watching the movements of the beast. It crept swiftly along the wall, at exactly my pace.

"Where the wall ends, near the turn of the road, it came down and with a wiry spring or two brought itself close to my feet, and continued to keep up with me, as I quickened my pace. It was at my left side, so close to my leg that I felt every moment as if I should tread upon it.

"The road was quite deserted and silent, and it was darker every moment. I stopped dismayed and bewildered, turning as I did so, the other way—I mean, towards this house, away from which I had been walking. When I stood still, the monkey drew back to a distance of, I suppose, about five or six yards, and remained stationary, watching me.

"I had been more agitated than I have said. I had read, of course, as every one has, something about 'spectral illusions,' as you physicians term the phenomena of such cases. I considered my situation, and looked my misfortune in the face.

"These affections, I had read, are sometimes transitory and sometimes obstinate. I had read of cases in which the appearance, at first harmless, had, step by step, degenerated into something direful and insupportable, and ended by wearing its victim out. Still as I stood there, but for my bestial companion, quite alone, I tried to comfort myself by repeating again and again the assurance, 'the thing is purely disease, a well-known physical affection, as distinctly as small-pox or neuralgia. Doctors are all agreed on that, philosophy demonstrates it. I must not be a fool. I've been sitting up too late, and I daresay my digestion is quite wrong, and with God's help, I shall be all right, and this is but a symptom of nervous dyspepsia.' Did I believe all this? Not one word of it, no more than any other miserable being ever did who is once seized and riveted in this satanic captivity. Against my convictions, I might say my knowledge, I was simply bullying myself into a false courage.

"I now walked homeward. I had only a few hundred yards to go. I had forced myself into a sort of resignation, but I had not got over the sickening shock and the flurry of the first certainty of my misfortune.

"I made up my mind to pass the night at home. The brute moved close beside me, and I fancied there was the sort of anxious drawing toward the house, which one sees in tired horses or dogs, sometimes as they come toward home.

"I was afraid to go into town, I was afraid of any one's seeing and recognising me. I was conscious of an irrepressible agitation in my manner. Also, I was afraid of any violent change in my habits, such as going to a place of amusement, or walking from home in order to fatigue myself. At the hall door it waited till I mounted the steps, and when the door was opened entered with me.

"I drank no tea that night. I got cigars and some brandy-and-water. My idea was that I should act upon my material system, and by living for a while in sensation apart from thought, send myself forcibly, as it were, into a new groove. I came up here to this drawing-room. I sat just here. The monkey then got upon a small table that then stood *there*. It looked dazed and languid. An irrepressible uneasiness as to its movements kept my eyes always upon it. Its eyes were half closed, but I could see them glow. It was looking steadily at me. In all situations, at all hours, it is awake and looking at me. That never changes.

"I shall not continue in detail my narrative of this particular night. I shall describe, rather, the phenomena of the first year, which never varied, essentially. I shall describe the monkey as it appeared in daylight. In the dark, as you shall presently hear, there are peculiarities. It is a small monkey, perfectly black. It had only one peculiarity—a character of malignity—unfathomable malignity. During the first year it looked sullen and sick. But this character of intense malice and vigilance was always underlying that surly languor. During all that time it acted as if on a plan of giving me as little trouble as was consistent with watching me. Its eyes were never off me, I have never lost sight of it, except in my sleep, light or dark, day or night, since it came here, excepting when it withdraws for some weeks at a time, unaccountably.

"In total dark it is visible as in daylight. I do not mean merely its eyes. It is *all* visible distinctly in a halo that resembles a glow of red embers, and which accompanies it in all its movements.

"When it leaves me for a time, it is always at night, in the dark, and in the same way. It grows at first uneasy, and then furious, and then advances towards me, grinning and shaking its paws clenched, and, at the same time, there comes the appearance of fire in the grate. I never have any fire. I can't sleep in the room where there is any, and it draws nearer and nearer to the chimney, quivering, it seems, with rage, and when its fury rises to the highest pitch, it springs into the grate, and up the chimney, and I see it no more.

"When first this happened I thought I was released. I was a new man. A day passed—a night—and no return, and a blessed week—a week—another week. I was always on my knees, Dr. Hesselius, always, thanking God and praying. A whole month passed of liberty, but on a sudden, it was with me again."

CHAPTER VIII.

THE SECOND STAGE.

"It was with me, and the malice which before was torpid under a sullen exterior, was now active. It was perfectly unchanged in every other respect. This new energy was apparent in its activity and its looks, and soon in other ways.

"For a time, you will understand, the change was shown only in an increased vivacity, and an air of menace, as if it was always brooding over some atrocious plan. Its eyes, as before, were never off me."

"Is it here now?" I asked.

"No," he replied, "it has been absent exactly a fortnight and a day—fifteen days. It has sometimes been away so long as nearly two months, once for three. Its absence always exceeds a fortnight, although it may be but by a single day. Fifteen days having past since I saw it last, it may return now at any moment."

"Is its return," I asked, "accompanied by any peculiar manifestation?"

"Nothing—no," he said. "It is simply with me again. On lifting my eyes from a book, or turning my head, I see it as usual, looking at me, and then it remains, as before, for its appointed time. I have never told so much and so minutely before to any one."

I perceived that he was agitated, and looking like death, and he repeatedly applied his handkerchief to his forehead; I suggested that he might be tired, and told him that I would call, with pleasure, in the morning, but he said:

"No, if you don't mind hearing it all now. I have got so far, and I should prefer making one effort of it. When I spoke to Dr. Harley, I had nothing like so much to tell. You are a philosophic physician. You give spirit its proper rank. If this thing is real—"

He paused, looking at me with agitated inquiry.

"We can discuss it by-and-by, and very fully. I will give you all I think," I answered, after an interval.

"Well—very well. If it is anything real, I say, it is prevailing, little by little, and drawing me more interiorly into hell. Optic nerves, he talked of. Ah! well—there are other nerves of communication. May God Almighty help me! You shall hear.

"Its power of action, I tell you, had increased. Its malice became, in a way aggressive. About two years ago, some questions that were pending between me and the bishop having been settled, I went down to my parish in Warwickshire, anxious to find occupation in my profession. I was not prepared for what happened, although I have since thought I might have apprehended something like it. The reason of my saying so, is this—"

He was beginning to speak with a great deal more effort and reluctance, and sighed often, and seemed at times nearly overcome. But at this time his manner was not agitated. It was more like that of a sinking patient, who has given himself up.

"Yes, but I will first tell you about Kenlis, my parish.

"It was with me when I left this place for Dawlbridge. It was my silent travelling companion, and it remained with me at the vicarage. When I entered on the discharge of my duties, another change took place. The thing exhibited an atrocious determination to thwart me. It was with me in the church—in the reading-desk—in the pulpit—within the communion rails. At last, it reached this extremity, that while I was reading to the congregation, it would spring upon the open book and squat there, so that I was unable to see the page. This happened more than once.

"I left Dawlbridge for a time. I placed myself in Dr. Harley's hands. I did everything he told me. He gave my case a great deal of thought. It interested him, I think. He seemed successful. For nearly three months I was perfectly free from a return. I began to think I was safe. With his full assent I returned to Dawlbridge.

"I travelled in a chaise. I was in good spirits. I was more—I was happy and grateful. I was returning, as I thought delivered from a dreadful hallucination, to the scene of duties which I longed to enter upon. It was a beautiful sunny evening, everything looked serene and cheerful, and I was delighted. I remember looking out of the window to see the spire of my church at Kenlis among the trees, at the point where one has the earliest view of it. It is exactly where the little stream that bounds the parish passes under the road by a culvert, and where it emerges at the road-side, a stone with an old inscription is placed. As we passed this point, I drew my head in and sat down, and in the corner of the chaise was the monkey.

"For a moment I felt faint, and then quite wild with despair and horror. I called to the driver, and got out, and sat down at the road-side, and prayed to God silently for mercy. A despairing resignation supervened. My companion was with me as I re-entered the vicarage. The same persecution followed. After a short struggle I submitted, and soon I left the place.

"I told you," he said, "that the beast has before this become in certain ways aggressive. I will explain a little. It seemed to be actuated by intense and increasing fury, whenever I said my prayers, or even meditated prayer. It amounted at last to a dreadful interruption. You will ask, how could a silent immaterial phantom effect that? It was thus, whenever I meditated praying; it was always before me, and nearer and nearer.

"It used to spring on a table, on the back of a chair, on the chimney-piece, and slowly to swing itself from side to side, looking at me all the time. There is in its motion an indefinable power to dissipate thought, and to contract one's attention to that monotony, till the ideas shrink, as it were, to a point, and at last to nothing—and unless I had started up, and shook off the catalepsy I have felt as if my mind were on the point of losing itself. There are other ways," he sighed heavily; "thus, for instance, while I pray with my eyes closed, it comes closer and closer, and I see it. I know it is not to be accounted for physically, but I do actually see it, though my lids are closed, and so it rocks my mind, as it were, and overpowers me, and I am obliged to rise from my knees. If you had ever yourself known this, you would be acquainted with desperation."

CHAPTER IX.

THE THIRD STAGE.

"I see, Dr. Hesselius, that you don't lose one word of my statement. I need not ask you to listen specially to what I am now going to tell you. They talk of the optic nerves, and of spectral illusions, as if the organ of sight was the only point assailable by the influences that have fastened upon me—I know better. For two years in my direful case that limitation prevailed. But as food is taken in softly at the lips, and then brought under the teeth, as the tip of the little finger caught in a mill crank will draw in the hand, and the arm, and the whole body, so the miserable mortal who has been once caught firmly by the end of the finest fibre of his nerve, is drawn in and in, by the enormous machinery of hell, until he is as I am. Yes, Doctor, as *I* am, for while I talk to you, and implore relief, I feel that my prayer is for the impossible, and my pleading with the inexorable."

I endeavoured to calm his visibly increasing agitation, and told him that he must not despair.

While we talked the night had overtaken us. The filmy moonlight was wide over the scene which the window commanded, and I said:

"Perhaps you would prefer having candles. This light, you know, is odd. I should wish you, as much as possible, under your usual conditions while I make my diagnosis, shall I call it—otherwise I don't care."

"All lights are the same to me," he said: "except when I read or write, I care not if night were perpetual. I am going to tell you what happened about a year ago. The thing began to speak to me."

"Speak! How do you mean—speak as a man does, do you mean?"

"Yes; speak in words and consecutive sentences, with perfect coherence and articulation; but there is a peculiarity. It is not like the tone of a human voice. It is not by my ears it reaches me—it comes like a singing through my head.

"This faculty, the power of speaking to me, will be my undoing. It won't let me pray, it interrupts me with dreadful blasphemies. I dare not go on, I could not. Oh! Doctor, can the skill, and thought, and prayers of man avail me nothing!"

"You must promise me, my dear sir, not to trouble yourself with unnecessarily exciting thoughts; confine yourself strictly to the narrative of *facts*; and recollect, above all, that even if the thing that infests you be as you seem to suppose, a reality with an actual independent life and will, yet it can have no power to hurt you, unless it be given from above: its access to your senses depends mainly upon your physical condition—this is, under God, your comfort and reliance: we are all alike environed. It is only that in your case, the '*paries*,' the veil of the flesh, the screen, is a little out of repair, and sights and sounds are transmitted. We must enter on a new course, sir—be encouraged. I'll give to-night to the careful consideration of the whole case."

"You are very good, sir; you think it worth trying, you don't give me quite up; but, sir, you don't know, it is gaining such an influence over me: it orders me about, it is such a tyrant, and I'm growing so helpless. May God deliver me!"

"It orders you about—of course you mean by speech?"

"Yes, yes; it is always urging me to crimes, to injure others, or myself. You see, Doctor, the situation is urgent, it is indeed. When I was in Shropshire, a few weeks ago" (Mr. Jennings was speaking rapidly and trembling now, holding my arm with one hand, and looking in my face), "I went out one day with a party of friends for a walk: my persecutor, I tell you, was with me at the time. I lagged behind the rest: the country near the Dee, you know, is beautiful. Our path happened to lie near a coal mine, and at the verge of the wood is a perpendicular shaft, they say, a hundred and fifty feet deep. My niece had remained behind with me—she knows, of course, nothing of the nature of my sufferings. She knew, however, that I had been ill, and was low, and she remained to prevent my being quite alone. As we loitered slowly on together the brute that accompanied me was urging me to throw myself down the shaft. I tell you now—oh, sir, think of it!—the one consideration that saved me from that hideous death was the fear lest the shock of witnessing the occurrence should be too much for the poor girl. I asked her to go on and take her walk with her friends, saying that I could go no further. She made excuses, and the more I urged her the firmer she became. She looked doubtful and frightened. I suppose there was something in my looks or manner that alarmed her; but she would not go, and that literally saved me. You had no idea, sir, that a living man could be made so abject a slave of Satan," he said, with a ghastly groan and a shudder.

There was a pause here, and I said, "You were preserved nevertheless. It was the act of God. You are in his hands and in the power of no other being: be therefore confident for the future."

CHAPTER X.

HOME.

I made him have candles lighted, and saw the room looking cheery and inhabited before I left him. I told him that he must regard his illness strictly as one dependent on physical, though *subtle* physical, causes. I told him that he had evidence of God's care and love in the deliverance which he had just described, and that I had perceived with pain that he seemed to regard its peculiar features as indicating that he had been delivered over to spiritual reprobation. Than such a conclusion nothing could be, I insisted, less warranted; and not only so, but more contrary to facts, as disclosed in his mysterious deliverance from that murderous influence during his Shropshire excursion. First, his niece had been retained by his side without his intending to keep her near him; and, secondly, there had been infused into his mind an irresistible repugnance to execute the dreadful suggestion in her presence.

As I reasoned this point with him, Mr. Jennings wept. He seemed comforted. One promise I exacted, which was that should the monkey at any time return, I should be sent for immediately; and, repeating my assurance that I would give neither time nor thought to any other subject until I had thoroughly investigated his case, and that to-morrow he should hear the result, I took my leave.

Before getting into the carriage I told the servant that his master was far from well, and that he should make a point of frequently looking into his room.

My own arrangements I made with a view to being quite secure from interruption.

I merely called at my lodgings, and with a travelling-desk and carpet-bag, set off in a hackney-carriage for an inn about two miles out of town, called The Horns, a very quiet and comfortable house, with good thick walls. And there I resolved, without the possibility of intrusion or distraction, to devote some hours of the night, in my comfortable sitting-room, to Mr. Jennings' case, and so much of the morning as it might require.

(There occurs here a careful note of Dr. Hesselius' opinion upon the case and of the habits, dietary, and medicines which he prescribed. It is curious—some persons would say mystical. But on the whole I doubt whether it would sufficiently interest a reader of the kind I am likely to meet with, to warrant its being here reprinted. The whole letter was plainly written at the inn where he had hid himself for the occasion. The next letter is dated from his town lodgings.)

I left town for the inn where I slept last night at half-past nine, and did not arrive at my room in town until one o'clock this afternoon. I found a letter in Mr. Jennings' hand upon my table. It had not come by post, and, on inquiry, I learned that Mr. Jennings' servant had brought it, and on learning that I was not to return until to-day, and that no one could tell him my address, he seemed very uncomfortable, and said that his orders from his master were that he was not to return without an answer.

I opened the letter, and read:

"Dear Dr. Hesselius. It is here. You had not been an hour gone when it returned. It is speaking. It knows all that has happened. It knows everything—it knows you, and is frantic and atrocious. It reviles. I send you this. It knows every word I have written—I write. This I promised, and I therefore write, but I fear very confused, very incoherently. I am so interrupted, disturbed.

"Ever yours, sincerely yours,

"ROBERT LYNDER JENNINGS."

"When did this come?" I asked.

"About eleven last night: the man was here again, and has been here three times to-day. The last time is about an hour since."

Thus answered, and with the notes I had made upon his case in my pocket, I was in a few minutes driving towards Richmond, to see Mr. Jennings.

I by no means, as you perceive, despaired of Mr. Jennings' case. He had himself remembered and applied, though quite in a mistaken way, the principle which I lay down in my Metaphysical Medicine, and which governs all such cases. I was about to apply it in earnest. I was profoundly interested, and very anxious to see and examine him while the "enemy" was actually present.

I drove up to the sombre house, and ran up the steps, and knocked. The door, in a little time, was opened by a tall woman in black silk. She looked ill, and as if she had been crying. She curtseyed, and heard my question, but she did not answer. She turned her face away, extending her hand towards two men who were coming down-stairs; and thus having, as it were, tacitly made me over to them, she passed through a side-door hastily and shut it.

The man who was nearest the hall, I at once accosted, but being now close to him, I was shocked to see that both his hands were covered with blood.

I drew back a little, and the man passing down-stairs merely said in a low tone, "Here's the servant, sir."

The servant had stopped on the stairs, confounded and dumb at seeing me. He was rubbing his hands in a handkerchief, and it was steeped in blood.

"Jones, what is it, what has happened?" I asked, while a sickening suspicion overpowered me.

The man asked me to come up to the lobby. I was beside him in a moment, and frowning and pallid, with contracted eyes, he told me the horror which I already half guessed.

His master had made away with himself.

I went upstairs with him to the room—what I saw there I won't tell you. He had cut his throat with his razor. It was a frightful gash. The two men had laid him on the bed and composed his limbs. It had happened as the immense pool of blood on the floor declared, at some distance between the bed and the window. There was carpet round his bed, and a carpet under his dressing-table, but none on the rest of the floor, for the man said he did not like a carpet on his bedroom. In this sombre, and now terrible room, one of the great elms that darkened the house was slowly moving the shadow of one of its great boughs upon this dreadful floor.

I beckoned to the servant and we went down-stairs together. I turned off the hall into an old-fashioned pannelled room, and there standing, I heard all the servant had to tell. It was not a great deal.

"I concluded, sir, from your words, and looks, sir, as you left last night, that you thought my master seriously ill. I thought it might be that you were afraid of a fit, or something. So I attended very close to your directions. He sat up late, till past three o'clock. He was not writing or reading. He was talking a great deal to himself, but that was nothing unusual. At about that hour I assisted him to undress, and left him in his slippers and dressing-gown. I went back softly in about half an hour. He was in his bed, quite undressed, and a pair of candles lighted on the table beside his bed. He was leaning on his elbow and looking out at the other side of the bed when I came in. I asked him if he wanted anything, and he said no.

"I don't know whether it was what you said to me, sir, or something a little unusual about him, but I was uneasy, uncommon uneasy about him last night.

"In another half hour, or it might be a little more, I went up again. I did not hear him talking as before. I opened the door a little. The candles were both out, which was not usual. I had a bedroom candle, and I let the light in, a little bit, looking softly round. I saw him sitting in that chair beside the dressing-table with his clothes on again. He turned round and looked at me. I thought it strange he should get up and dress, and put out the candles to sit in the dark, that way. But I only asked him again if I could do anything for him. He said, no, rather sharp, I thought. I asked if I might light the candles, and he said, 'Do as you like, Jones,' So I lighted them, and I lingered about the room, and he said, 'Tell me truth, Jones, why did you come again—you did not hear any one cursing?' 'No, sir,' I said, wondering what he could mean.

"'No,' said he, after me, 'of course, no;' and I said to him, 'Wouldn't it be well, sir, you went to bed? It's just five o'clock;' and he said nothing but, 'Very likely; good-night, Jones.' So I went, sir, but in less than hour I came again. The door was fast, and he heard me, and called as I thought from the bed to know what I wanted, and he desired me not to disturb him again. I lay down and slept for a little. It must have been between six and seven when I went up again. The door was still fast, and he made no answer, so I did not like to disturb him, and thinking he was asleep, I left him till nine. It was his custom to ring when he wished me to come, and I had no particular hour for calling him. I tapped very gently, and getting no answer, I stayed away a good while, supposing he was getting some rest then. It was not till eleven o'clock I grew really uncomfortable about him—for at the latest he was never, that I could remember, later than half-past ten. I got no answer. I knocked and called, and still no answer. So not being able to force the door, I called Thomas from the stables, and together we forced it, and found him in the shocking way you saw."

Jones had no more to tell. Poor Mr. Jennings was very gentle, and very kind. All his people were fond of him. I could see that the servant was very much moved.

So, dejected and agitated, I passed from that terrible house, and its dark canopy of elms, and I hope I shall never see it more. While I write to you I feel like a man who has but half waked from a frightful and monotonous dream. My memory rejects the picture with incredulity and horror. Yet I know it is true. It is the story of the process of a poison, a poison which excites the reciprocal action of spirit and nerve, and paralyses the tissue that separates those cognate functions of the senses, the external and the interior. Thus we find strange bed-fellows, and the mortal and immortal prematurely make acquaintance.

CONCLUSION.

A WORD FOR THOSE WHO SUFFER.

My dear Van L——, you have suffered from an affection similar to that which I have just described. You twice complained of a return of it.

Who, under God, cured you? Your humble servant, Martin Hesselius. Let me rather adopt the more emphasised piety of a certain good old French surgeon of three hundred years ago: "I treated, and God cured you."

Come, my friend, you are not to be hippish. Let me tell you a fact.

I have met with, and treated, as my book shows, fifty-seven cases of this kind of vision, which I term indifferently "sublimated," "precocious," and "interior."

There is another class of affections which are truly termed—though commonly confounded with those which I describe—spectral illusions. These latter I look upon as being no less simply curable than a cold in the head or a trifling dyspepsia.

It is those which rank in the first category that test our promptitude of thought. Fifty-seven such cases have I encountered, neither more nor less. And in how many of these have I failed? In no one single instance.

There is no one affliction of mortality more easily and certainly reducible, with a little patience, and a rational confidence in the physician. With these simple conditions, I look upon the cure as absolutely certain.

You are to remember that I had not even commenced to treat Mr. Jennings' case. I have not any doubt that I should have cured him perfectly in eighteen months, or possibly it might have extended to two years. Some cases are very rapidly curable, others extremely tedious. Every intelligent physician who will give thought and diligence to the task, will effect a cure.

You know my tract on The Cardinal Functions of the Brain. I there, by the evidence of innumerable facts, prove, as I think, the high probability of a circulation arterial and venous in its mechanism, through the nerves. Of this system, thus considered, the brain is the heart. The fluid, which is propagated hence through one class of nerves, returns in an altered state through another, and the nature of that fluid is spiritual, though not immaterial, any more than, as I before remarked, light or electricity are so.

By various abuses, among which the habitual use of such agents as green tea is one, this fluid may be affected as to its quality, but it is more frequently disturbed as to equilibrium. This fluid being that which we have in common with spirits, a congestion found upon the masses of brain or nerve, connected with the interior sense, forms a surface unduly exposed, on which disembodied spirits may operate: communication is thus more or less effectually established. Between this brain circulation and the heart circulation there is an intimate sympathy. The seat, or rather the instrument of exterior vision, is the eye. The seat of interior vision is the nervous tissue and brain, immediately about and above the eyebrow. You remember how effectually I dissipated your pictures by the simple application of iced eau-de-cologne. Few cases, however, can be treated exactly alike with anything like rapid success. Cold acts powerfully as a repellant of the nervous fluid. Long enough continued it will even produce that permanent insensibility which we call numbness, and a little longer, muscular as well as sensational paralysis.

I have not, I repeat, the slightest doubt that I should have first dimmed and ultimately sealed that inner eye which Mr. Jennings had inadvertently opened. The same senses are opened in delirium tremens, and entirely shut up again when the over-action of the cerebral heart, and the prodigious nervous congestions that attend it, are terminated by a decided change in the state of the body. It is by acting steadily upon the body, by a simple process, that this result is produced—and inevitably produced—I have never yet failed.

Poor Mr. Jennings made away with himself. But that catastrophe was the result of a totally different malady, which, as it were, projected itself upon that disease which was established. His case was in the distinctive manner a complication, and the complaint under which he really succumbed, was hereditary suicidal mania. Poor Mr. Jennings I cannot call a patient of mine, for I had not even begun to treat his case, and he had not yet given me, I am convinced, his full and unreserved confidence. If the patient do not array himself on the side of the disease, his cure is certain.

THE FAMILIAR.

PROLOGUE.

Out of about two hundred and thirty cases, more or less nearly akin to that I have entitled "Green Tea," I select the following, which I call "The Familiar."

To this MS. Doctor Hesselius, has, after his wont, attached some sheets of letter-paper, on which are written, in his hand nearly as compact as print, his own remarks upon the case. He says—

"In point of conscience, no more unexceptionable narrator, than the venerable Irish Clergyman who has given me this paper, on Mr. Barton's case, could have been chosen. The statement is, however, medically imperfect. The report of an intelligent physician, who had marked its progress, and attended the patient, from its earlier stages to its close, would have supplied what is wanting to enable me to pronounce with confidence. I should have been acquainted with Mr. Barton's probable hereditary pre-dispositions; I should have known, possibly, by very early indications, something of a remoter origin of the disease than can now be ascertained.

"In a rough way, we may reduce all similar cases to three distinct classes. They are founded on the primary distinction between the subjective and the objective. Of those whose senses are alleged to be subject to supernatural impressions—some are simply visionaries, and propagate the illusions of which they complain, from diseased brain or nerves. Others are, unquestionably, infested by, as we term them, spiritual agencies, exterior to themselves. Others, again, owe their sufferings to a mixed condition. The interior sense, it is true, is opened; but it has been and continues open by the action of disease. This form of disease may, in one sense, be compared to the loss of the scarf-skin, and a consequent exposure of surfaces for whose excessive sensitiveness, nature has provided a muffling. The loss of this covering is attended by an habitual impassability, by influences against which we were intended to be guarded. But in the case of the brain, and the nerves immediately connected with its functions and its sensuous impressions, the cerebral circulation undergoes periodically that vibratory disturbance, which, I believe, I have satisfactorily examined and demonstrated, in my MS. Essay, A. 17. This vibratory disturbance differs, as I there prove, essentially from the congestive disturbance, the phenomena of which are examined in A. 19. It is, when excessive, invariably accompanied by *illusions.*

"Had I seen Mr. Barton, and examined him upon the points, in his case, which need elucidation, I should have without difficulty referred those phenomena to their proper disease. My diagnosis is now, necessarily, conjectural."

Thus writes Doctor Hesselius; and adds a great deal which is of interest only to a scientific physician.

The Narrative of the Rev. Thomas Herbert, which furnishes all that is known of the case, will be found in the chapters that follow.

CHAPTER I.

FOOT-STEPS.

I was a young man at the time, and intimately acquainted with some of the actors in this strange tale; the impression which its incidents made on me, therefore, were deep, and lasting. I shall now endeavour, with precision, to relate them all, combining, of course, in the narrative, whatever I have learned from various sources, tending, however imperfectly, to illuminate the darkness which involves its progress and termination.

Somewhere about the year 1794, the younger brother of a certain baronet, whom I shall call Sir James Barton, returned to Dublin. He had served in the navy with some distinction, having commanded one of His Majesty's frigates during the greater part of the American war. Captain Barton was apparently some two or three-and-forty years of age. He was an intelligent and agreeable companion when he pleased it, though generally reserved, and occasionally even moody.

In society, however, he deported himself as a man of the world, and a gentleman. He had not contracted any of the noisy brusqueness sometimes acquired at sea; on the contrary, his manners were remarkably easy, quiet, and even polished. He was in person about the middle size, and somewhat strongly formed—his countenance was marked with the lines of thought, and on the whole wore an expression of gravity and melancholy; being, however, as I have said, a man of perfect breeding, as well as of good family, and in affluent circumstances, he had, of course, ready access to the best society of Dublin, without the necessity of any other credentials.

In his personal habits Mr. Barton was unexpensive. He occupied lodgings in one of the *then* fashionable streets in the south side of the town—kept but one horse and one servant—and though a reputed free-thinker, yet lived an orderly and moral life—indulging neither in gaming, drinking, nor any other vicious pursuit—living very much to himself, without forming intimacies, or choosing any companions, and appearing to mix in gay society rather for the sake of its bustle and distraction, than for any opportunities it offered of interchanging thought or feeling with its votaries.

Barton was therefore pronounced a saving, prudent, unsocial sort of fellow, who bid fair to maintain his celibacy alike against stratagem and assault, and was likely to live to a good old age, die rich, and leave his money to an hospital.

It was now apparent, however, that the nature of Mr. Barton's plans had been totally misconceived. A young lady, whom I shall call Miss Montague, was at this time introduced into the gay world, by her aunt, the Dowager Lady L——. Miss Montague was decidedly pretty and accomplished, and having some natural cleverness, and a great deal of gaiety, became for a while a reigning toast.

Her popularity, however, gained her, for a time, nothing more than that unsubstantial admiration which, however, pleasant as an incense to vanity, is by no means necessarily antecedent to matrimony—for, unhappily for the young lady in question, it was an understood thing, that beyond her personal attractions, she had no kind of earthly provision. Such being the state of affairs, it will readily be believed that no little surprise was consequent upon the appearance of Captain Barton as the avowed lover of the penniless Miss Montague.

His suit prospered, as might have been expected, and in a short time it was communicated by old Lady L—— to each of her hundred-and-fifty particular friends in succession, that Captain Barton had actually tendered proposals of marriage, with her approbation, to her niece, Miss Montague, who had, moreover, accepted the offer of his hand, conditionally upon the consent of her father, who was then upon his homeward voyage from India, and expected in two or three weeks at the furthest.

About this consent there could be no doubt—the delay, therefore, was one merely of form—they were looked upon as absolutely engaged, and Lady L——, with a rigour of old-fashioned decorum with which her niece would, no doubt, gladly have dispensed, withdrew her thenceforward from all further participation in the gaieties of the town.

Captain Barton was a constant visitor, as well as a frequent guest at the house, and was permitted all the privileges of intimacy which a betrothed suitor is usually accorded. Such was the relation of parties, when the mysterious circumstances which darken this narrative first begun to unfold themselves.

Lady L—— resided in a handsome mansion at the north side of Dublin, and Captain Barton's lodgings, as we have already said, were situated at the south. The distance intervening was considerable, and it was Captain Barton's habit generally to walk home without an attendant, as often as he passed the evening with the old lady and her fair charge.

His shortest way in such nocturnal walks, lay, for a considerable space, through a line of street which had as yet merely been laid out, and little more than the foundations of the houses constructed.

One night, shortly after his engagement with Miss Montague had commenced, he happened to remain unusually late, in company with her and Lady L——. The conversation had turned upon the evidences of revelation, which he had disputed with the callous scepticism of a confirmed infidel. What were called "French principles," had in those days found their way a good deal into fashionable society, especially that portion of it which professed allegiance to Whiggism, and neither the old lady nor her charge were so perfectly free from the taint, as to look upon Mr. Barton's views as any serious objection to the proposed union.

The discussion had degenerated into one upon the supernatural and the marvellous, in which he had pursued precisely the same line of argument and ridicule. In all this, it is but truth to state, Captain Barton, was guilty of no affectation—the doctrines upon which he insisted, were, in reality, but, too truly the basis of his own fixed belief, if so it might be called; and perhaps not the least strange of the many strange circumstances connected with my narrative, was the fact, that the subject of the fearful influences I am about to describe, was himself, from the deliberate conviction of years, an utter disbeliever in what are usually termed preternatural agencies.

It was considerably past midnight when Mr. Barton took his leave, and set out upon his solitary walk homeward. He had now reached the lonely road, with its unfinished dwarf walls tracing the foundations of the projected row of houses on either side—the moon was shining mistily, and its imperfect light made the road he trod but additionally dreary—that utter silence which has in it something indefinably exciting, reigned there, and made the sound of his steps, which alone broke it, unnaturally loud and distinct.

He had proceeded thus some way, when he, on a sudden, heard other footfalls, pattering at a measured pace, and, as it seemed, about two score steps behind him.

The suspicion of being dogged is at all times unpleasant; it is, however, especially so in a spot so lonely; and this suspicion became so strong in the mind of Captain Barton, that he abruptly turned about to confront his pursuer, but, though there was quite sufficient moonlight to disclose any object upon the road he had traversed, no form of any kind was visible there.

The steps he had heard could not have been the reverberation of his own, for he stamped his foot upon the ground, and walked briskly up and down, in the vain attempt to awake an echo; though by no means a fanciful person, therefore he was at last fain to charge the sounds upon his imagination, and treat them as an illusion. Thus satisfying himself, he resumed his walk, and before he had proceeded a dozen paces, the mysterious footfall was again audible from behind, and this time, as if with the special design of showing that the sounds were not the responses of an echo—the steps sometimes slackened nearly to a halt, and sometimes hurried for six or eight strides to a run, and again abated to a walk.

Captain Barton, as before, turned suddenly round, and with the same result—no object was visible above the deserted level of the road. He walked back over the same ground, determined that, whatever might have been the cause of the sounds which had so disconcerted him, it should not escape his search—the endeavour, however, was unrewarded.

In spite of all his scepticism, he felt something like a superstitious fear stealing fast upon him, and with these unwonted and uncomfortable sensations, he once more turned and pursued his way. There was no repetition of these haunting sounds, until he had reached the point where he had last stopped to retrace his steps—here they were resumed—and with sudden starts of running, which threatened to bring the unseen pursuer up to the alarmed pedestrian.

Captain Barton arrested his course as formerly—the unaccountable nature of the occurrence filled him with vague and disagreeable sensations—and yielding to the excitement that was gaining upon him, he shouted sternly, "Who goes there?" The sound of one's own voice, thus exerted, in utter solitude, and followed by total silence, has in it something unpleasantly dismaying, and he felt a degree of nervousness which, perhaps, from no cause had he ever known before.

To the very end of this solitary street the steps pursued him—and it required a strong effort of stubborn pride on his part, to resist the impulse that prompted him every moment to run for safety at the top of his speed. It was not until he had reached his lodging, and sate by his own fire-side, that he felt sufficiently reassured to rearrange and reconsider in his own mind the occurrences which had so discomposed him. So little a matter, after all, is sufficient to upset the pride of scepticism and vindicate the old simple laws of nature within us.

CHAPTER II.

THE WATCHER.

Mr. Barton was next morning sitting at a late breakfast, reflecting upon the incidents of the previous night, with more of inquisitiveness than awe, so speedily do gloomy impressions upon the fancy disappear under the cheerful influence of day, when a letter just delivered by the postman was placed upon the table before him.

There was nothing remarkable in the address of this missive, except that it was written in a hand which he did not know—perhaps it was disguised—for the tall narrow characters were sloped backward; and with the self-inflicted suspense which we often see practised in such cases, he puzzled over the inscription for a full minute before he broke the seal. When he did so, he read the following words, written in the same hand:—

"Mr. Barton, late captain of the 'Dolphin,' is warned of DANGER. He will do wisely to avoid —— street—[here the locality of his last night's adventure was named]—if he walks there as usual he will meet with something unlucky—let him take warning, once for all, for he has reason to dread

"THE WATCHER."

Captain Barton read and re-read this strange effusion; in every light and in every direction he turned it over and over; he examined the paper on which it was written, and scrutinized the hand-writing once more. Defeated here, he turned to the seal; it was nothing but a patch of wax, upon which the accidental impression of a thumb was imperfectly visible.

There was not the slightest mark, or clue of any kind, to lead him to even a guess as to its possible origin. The writer's object seemed a friendly one, and yet he subscribed himself as one whom he had "reason to dread." Altogether the letter, its author, and its real purpose were to him an inexplicable puzzle, and one, moreover, unpleasantly suggestive, in his mind, of other associations connected with his last night's adventure.

In obedience to some feeling—perhaps of pride—Mr. Barton did not communicate, even to his intended bride, the occurrences which I have just detailed. Trifling as they might appear, they had in reality most disagreeably affected his imagination, and he cared not to disclose, even to the young lady in question, what she might possibly look upon as evidences of weakness. The letter might very well be but a hoax, and the mysterious footfall but a delusion or a trick. But although he affected to treat the whole affair as unworthy of a thought, it yet haunted him pertinaciously, tormenting him with perplexing doubts, and depressing him with undefined apprehensions. Certain it is, that for a considerable time afterwards he carefully avoided the street indicated in the letter as the scene of danger.

It was not until about a week after the receipt of the letter which I have transcribed, that anything further occurred to remind Captain Barton of its contents, or to counteract the gradual disappearance from his mind of the disagreeable impressions then received.

He was returning one night, after the interval I have stated, from the theatre, which was then situated in Crow-street, and having there seen Miss Montague and Lady L—— into their carriage, he loitered for some time with two or three acquaintances.

With these, however, he parted close to the college, and pursued his way alone. It was now fully one o'clock, and the streets were quite deserted. During the whole of his walk with the companions from whom he had just parted, he had been at times painfully aware of the sound of steps, as it seemed, dogging them on their way.

Once or twice he had looked back, in the uneasy anticipation that he was again about to experience the same mysterious annoyances which had so disconcerted him a week before, and earnestly hoping that he might see some form to account naturally for the sounds. But the street was deserted—no one was visible.

Proceeding now quite alone upon his homeward way, he grew really nervous and uncomfortable, as he became sensible, with increased distinctness, of the well-known and now absolutely dreaded sounds.

By the side of the dead wall which bounded the college park, the sounds followed, recommencing almost simultaneously with his own steps. The same unequal pace—sometimes slow, sometimes for a score yards or so, quickened almost to a run—was audible from behind him. Again and again he turned; quickly and stealthily he glanced over his shoulder—almost at every half-dozen steps; but no one was visible.

The irritation of this intangible and unseen pursuit became gradually all but intolerable; and when at last he reached his home, his nerves were strung to such a pitch of excitement that he could not rest, and did not attempt even to lie down until after the daylight had broken.

He was awakened by a knock at his chamber-door, and his servant entering, handed him several letters which had just been received by the penny post. One among them instantly arrested his attention—a single glance at the direction aroused him thoroughly. He at once recognized its character, and read as follows:—

"You may as well think, Captain Barton, to escape from your own shadow as from me; do what you may, I will see you as often as I please, and you shall see me, for I do not want to hide myself, as you fancy. Do not let it trouble your rest, Captain Barton; for, with a *good conscience*, what need you fear from the eye of

"THE WATCHER."

It is scarcely necessary to dwell upon the feelings that accompanied a perusal of this strange communication. Captain Barton was observed to be unusually absent and out of spirits for several days afterwards, but no one divined the cause.

Whatever he might think as to the phantom steps which followed him, there could be no possible illusion about the letters he had received; and, to say the least, their immediate sequence upon the mysterious sounds which had haunted him, was an odd coincidence.

The whole circumstance was, in his own mind, vaguely and instinctively connected with certain passages in his past life, which, of all others, he hated to remember.

It happened, however, that in addition to his own approaching nuptials, Captain Barton had just then—fortunately, perhaps, for himself—some business of an engrossing kind connected with the adjustment of a large and long-litigated claim upon certain properties.

The hurry and excitement of business had its natural effect in gradually dispelling the gloom which had for a time occasionally oppressed him, and in a little while his spirits had entirely recovered their accustomed tone.

During all this time, however, he was, now and then, dismayed by indistinct and half-heard repetitions of the same annoyance, and that in lonely places, in the day-time as well as after nightfall. These renewals of the strange impressions from which he had suffered so much, were, however, desultory and faint, insomuch that often he really could not, to his own satisfaction, distinguish between them and the mere suggestions of an excited imagination.

One evening he walked down to the House of Commons with a Member, an acquaintance of his and mine. This was one of the few occasions upon which I have been in company with Captain Barton. As we walked down together, I observed that he became absent and silent, and to a degree that seemed to argue the pressure of some urgent and absorbing anxiety.

I afterwards learned that during the whole of our walk, he had heard the well-known footsteps tracking him as we proceeded.

This, however, was the last time he suffered from this phase of the persecution, of which he was already the anxious victim. A new and a very different one was about to be presented.

CHAPTER III.

AN ADVERTISEMENT.

Of the new series of impressions which were afterwards gradually to work out his destiny, I that evening witnessed the first; and but for its relation to the train of events which followed, the incident would scarcely have been now remembered by me.

As we were walking in at the passage from College-Green, a man, of whom I remember only that he was short in stature, looked like a foreigner, and wore a kind of fur travelling-cap, walked very rapidly, and as if under fierce excitement, directly towards us, muttering to himself, fast and vehemently the while.

This odd-looking person walked straight toward Barton, who was foremost of the three, and halted, regarding him for a moment or two with a look of maniacal menace and fury; and then turning about as abruptly, he walked before us at the same agitated pace, and disappeared at a side passage. I do distinctly remember being a good deal shocked at the countenance and bearing of this man, which indeed irresistibly impressed me with an undefined sense of danger, such as I have never felt before or since from the presence of anything human; but these sensations were, on my part, far from amounting to anything so disconcerting as to flurry or excite me—I had seen only a singularly evil countenance, agitated, as it seemed, with the excitement of madness.

I was absolutely astonished, however, at the effect of this apparition upon Captain Barton. I knew him to be a man of proud courage and coolness in real danger—a circumstance which made his conduct upon this occasion the more conspicuously odd. He recoiled a step or two as the stranger advanced, and clutched my arm in silence, with what seemed to be a spasm of agony or terror! and then, as the figure disappeared, shoving me roughly back, he followed it for a few paces, stopped in great disorder, and sat down upon a form. I never beheld a countenance more ghastly and haggard.

"For God's sake, Barton, what is the matter?" said ——, our companion, really alarmed at his appearance. "You're not hurt, are you?—or unwell? What is it?"

"What did he say?—I did not hear it—what was it?" asked Barton, wholly disregarding the question.

"Nonsense," said ——, greatly surprised; "who cares what the fellow said. You are unwell, Barton—decidedly unwell; let me call a coach."

"Unwell! No—not unwell," he said, evidently making an effort to recover his self-possession; "but, to say the truth, I am fatigued—a little over-worked—and perhaps over anxious. You know I have been in chancery, and the winding up of a suit is always a nervous affair. I have felt uncomfortable all this evening; but I am better now. Come, come—shall we go on?"

"No, no. Take my advice, Barton, and go home; you really do need rest! you are looking quite ill. I really do insist on your allowing me to see you home," replied his friend.

I seconded ——'s advice, the more readily as it was obvious that Barton was not himself disinclined to be persuaded. He left us, declining our offered escort. I was not sufficiently intimate with —— to discuss the scene we had both just witnessed. I was, however, convinced from his manner in the few common-place comments and regrets we exchanged, that he was just as little satisfied as I with the extempore plea of illness with which he had accounted for the strange exhibition, and that we were both agreed in suspecting some lurking mystery in the matter.

I called next day at Barton's lodgings, to enquire for him, and learned from the servant that he had not left his room since his return the night before; but that he was not seriously indisposed, and hoped to be out in a few days. That evening he sent for Dr. R——, then in large and fashionable practice in Dublin, and their interview was, it is said, an odd one.

He entered into a detail of his own symptoms in an abstracted and desultory way which seemed to argue a strange want of interest in his own cure, and, at all events, made it manifest that there was some topic engaging his mind of more engrossing importance than his present ailment. He complained of occasional palpitations and headache.

Doctor R——, asked him among other questions, whether there was any irritating circumstance or anxiety then occupying his thoughts. This he denied quickly and almost peevishly; and the physician thereupon declared his opinion, that there was nothing amiss except some slight derangement of the digestion, for which he accordingly wrote a prescription, and was about to withdraw, when Mr. Barton, with the air of a man who recollects a topic which had nearly escaped him, recalled him.

"I beg your pardon, Doctor, but I really almost forgot; will you permit me to ask you two or three medical questions—rather odd ones, perhaps, but a wager depends upon their solution, you will, I hope, excuse my unreasonableness."

The physician readily undertook to satisfy the inquirer.

Barton seemed to have some difficulty about opening the proposed interrogatories, for he was silent for a minute, then walked to his book-case, and returned as he had gone; at last he sat down and said—

"You'll think them very childish questions, but I can't recover my wager without a decision; so I must put them. I want to know first about lock-jaw. If a man actually has had that complaint, and appears to have died of it—so much so, that a physician of average skill pronounces him actually dead—may he, after all, recover?"

The physician smiled, and shook his head.

"But—but a blunder may be made," resumed Barton. "Suppose an ignorant pretender to medical skill; may *he* be so deceived by any stage of the complaint, as to mistake what is only a part of the progress of the disease, for death itself?"

"No one who had ever seen death," answered he, "could mistake it in a case of lock-jaw."

Barton mused for a few minutes. "I am going to ask you a question, perhaps, still more childish; but first, tell me, are the regulations of foreign hospitals, such as that of, let us say, Naples, very lax and bungling. May not all kinds of blunders and slips occur in their entries of names, and soforth?"

Doctor R—— professed his incompetence to answer that query.

"Well, then, Doctor, here is the last of my questions. You will, probably, laugh at it; but it must out, nevertheless. Is there any disease, in all the range of human maladies, which would have the effect of perceptibly contracting the stature, and the whole frame—causing the man to shrink in all his proportions, and yet to preserve his exact resemblance to himself in every particular—with the one exception, his height and bulk; any disease, mark—no matter how rare—how little believed in, generally—which could possibly result in producing such an effect?"

The physician replied with a smile, and a very decided negative.

"Tell me, then," said Barton, abruptly, "if a man be in reasonable fear of assault from a lunatic who is at large, can he not procure a warrant for his arrest and detention?"

"Really that is more a lawyer's question than one in my way," replied Dr. R——: "but I believe, on applying to a magistrate, such a course would be directed."

The physician then took his leave; but, just as he reached the hall-door, remembered that he had left his cane up stairs, and returned. His reappearance was awkward, for a piece of paper, which he recognised as his own prescription, was slowly burning upon the fire, and Barton sitting close by with an expression of settled gloom and dismay.

Doctor R—— had too much tact to observe what presented itself; but he had seen quite enough to assure him that the mind, and not the body, of Captain Barton was in reality the seat of suffering.

A few days afterwards, the following advertisement appeared in the Dublin newspapers.

"If Sylvester Yelland, formerly a foremast-man on board his Majesty's frigate Dolphin, or his nearest of kin, will apply to Mr. Hubert Smith, attorney, at his office, Dame Street, he or they may hear of something greatly to his or their advantage. Admission may be had at any hour up to twelve o'clock at night, should parties desire to avoid observation; and the strictest secrecy, as to all communications intended to be confidential, shall be honourably observed."

The Dolphin, as I have mentioned, was the vessel which Captain Barton had commanded; and this circumstance, connected with the extraordinary exertions made by the circulation of hand-bills, &c., as well as by repeated advertisements, to secure for this strange notice the utmost possible publicity, suggested to Dr. R—— the idea that Captain Barton's extreme uneasiness was somehow connected with the individual to whom the advertisement was addressed, and he himself the author of it.

This, however, it is needless to add, was no more than a conjecture. No information whatsoever, as to the real purpose of the advertisement was divulged by the agent, nor yet any hint as to who his employer might be.

CHAPTER IV.

HE TALKS WITH A CLERGYMAN.

Mr. Barton, although he had latterly begun to earn for himself the character of an hypochondriac, was yet very far from deserving it. Though by no means lively, he had yet, naturally, what are termed "even spirits," and was not subject to undue depressions.

He soon, therefore, began to return to his former habits; and one of the earliest symptoms of this healthier tone of spirits was, his appearing at a grand dinner of the Freemasons, of which worthy fraternity he was himself a brother. Barton, who had been at first gloomy and abstracted, drank much more freely than was his wont—possibly with the purpose of dispelling his own secret anxieties—and under the influence of good wine, and pleasant company, became gradually (unlike himself) talkative, and even noisy.

It was under this unwonted excitement that he left his company at about half-past ten o'clock; and, as conviviality is a strong incentive to gallantry, it occurred to him to proceed forthwith to Lady L——'s and pass the remainder of the evening with her and his destined bride.

Accordingly, he was soon at —— street, and chatting gaily with the ladies. It is not to be supposed that Captain Barton had exceeded the limits which propriety prescribes to good fellowship—he had merely taken enough wine to raise his spirits, without, however, in the least degree unsteadying his mind, or affecting his manners.

With this undue elevation of spirits had supervened an entire oblivion or contempt of those undefined apprehensions which had for so long weighed upon his mind, and to a certain extent estranged him from society; but as the night wore away, and his artificial gaiety began to flag, these painful feelings gradually intruded themselves again, and he grew abstracted and anxious as heretofore.

He took his leave at length, with an unpleasant foreboding of some coming mischief, and with a mind haunted with a thousand mysterious apprehensions, such as, even while he acutely felt their pressure, he, nevertheless, inwardly strove, or affected to contemn.

It was this proud defiance of what he regarded as his own weakness, which prompted him upon the present occasion to that course which brought about the adventure I am now about to relate.

Mr. Barton might have easily called a coach, but he was conscious that his strong inclination to do so proceeded from no cause other than what he desperately persisted in representing to himself to be his own superstitious tremors.

He might also have returned home by a *route* different from that against which he had been warned by his mysterious correspondent; but for the same reason he dismissed this idea also, and with a dogged and half desperate resolution to force matters to a crisis of some kind, if there were any reality in the causes of his former suffering, and if not, satisfactorily to bring their delusiveness to the proof, he determined to follow precisely the course which he had trodden upon the night so painfully memorable in his own mind as that on which his strange persecution commenced. Though, sooth to say, the pilot who for the first time steers his vessel under the muzzles of a hostile battery, never felt his resolution more severely tasked than did Captain Barton as he breathlessly pursued this solitary path—a path which, spite of every effort of scepticism and reason, he felt to be infested by some (as respected *him*) malignant being.

He pursued his way steadily and rapidly, scarcely breathing from intensity of suspense; he, however, was troubled by no renewal of the dreaded footsteps, and was beginning to feel a return of confidence, as more than three-fourths of the way being accomplished with impunity, he approached the long line of twinkling oil lamps which indicated the frequented streets.

This feeling of self-congratulation was, however, but momentary. The report of a musket at some hundred yards behind him, and the whistle of a bullet close to his head, disagreeably and startlingly dispelled it. His first impulse was to retrace his steps in pursuit of the assassin; but the road on either side was, as we have said, embarrassed by the foundations of a street, beyond which extended waste fields, full of rubbish and neglected lime and brick-kilns, and all now as utterly silent as though no sound had ever disturbed their dark and unsightly solitude. The futility of, single-handed, attempting, under such circumstances, a search for the murderer, was apparent, especially as no sound, either of retreating steps or any other kind, was audible to direct his pursuit.

With the tumultuous sensations of one whose life has just been exposed to a murderous attempt, and whose escape has been the narrowest possible, Captain Barton turned again; and without, however, quickening his pace actually to a run, hurriedly pursued his way.

He had turned, as I have said, after a pause of a few seconds, and had just commenced his rapid retreat, when on a sudden he met the well-remembered little man in the fur cap. The encounter was but momentary. The figure was walking at the same exaggerated pace, and with the same strange air of menace as before; and as it passed him, he thought he heard it say, in a furious whisper, "Still alive—still alive!"

The state of Mr. Barton's spirits began now to work a corresponding alteration in his health and looks, and to such a degree that it was impossible that the change should escape general remark.

For some reasons, known but to himself, he took no step whatsoever to bring the attempt upon his life, which he had so narrowly escaped, under the notice of the authorities; on the contrary, he kept it jealously to himself; and it was not for many weeks after the occurrence that he mentioned it, and then in strict confidence, to a gentleman, whom the torments of his mind at last compelled him to consult.

Spite of his blue devils, however, poor Barton, having no satisfactory reason to render to the public for any undue remissness in the attentions exacted by the relation subsisting between him and Miss Montague was obliged to exert himself, and present to the world a confident and cheerful bearing.

The true source of his sufferings, and every circumstance connected with them, he guarded with a reserve so jealous, that it seemed dictated by at least a suspicion that the origin of his strange persecution was known to himself, and that it was of a nature which, upon his own account, he could not or dared not disclose.

The mind thus turned in upon itself, and constantly occupied with a haunting anxiety which it dared not reveal or confide to any human breast, became daily more excited, and, of course, more vividly impressible, by a system of attack which operated through the nervous system; and in this state he was destined to sustain, with increasing frequency, the stealthy visitations of that apparition which from the first had seemed to possess so terrible a hold upon his imagination.

It was about this time that Captain Barton called upon the then celebrated preacher, Dr. ——, with whom he had a slight acquaintance, and an extraordinary conversation ensued.

The divine was seated in his chambers in college, surrounded with works upon his favourite pursuit, and deep in theology, when Barton was announced.

There was something at once embarrassed and excited in his manner, which, along with his wan and haggard countenance, impressed the student with the unpleasant consciousness that his visitor must have recently suffered terribly indeed, to account for an alteration so striking—almost shocking.

After the usual interchange of polite greeting, and a few common-place remarks, Captain Barton, who obviously perceived the surprise which his visit had excited, and which Doctor —— was unable wholly to conceal, interrupted a brief pause by remarking—

"This is a strange call, Doctor ——, perhaps scarcely warranted by an acquaintance so slight as mine with you. I should not under ordinary circumstances have ventured to disturb you; but my visit is neither an idle nor impertinent intrusion. I am sure you will not so account it, when I tell you how afflicted I am."

Doctor —— interrupted him with assurances such as good breeding suggested, and Barton resumed—

"I am come to task your patience by asking your advice. When I say your patience, I might, indeed, say more; I might have said your humanity—your compassion; for I have been and am a great sufferer."

"My dear sir," replied the churchman, "it will, indeed, afford me infinite gratification if I can give you comfort in any distress of mind; but—you know——"

"I know what you would say," resumed Barton, quickly; "I am an unbeliever, and, therefore, incapable of deriving help from religion; but don't take that for granted. At least you must not assume that, however unsettled my convictions may be, I do not feel a deep—a very deep—interest in the subject. Circumstances have lately forced it upon my attention, in such a way as to compel me to review the whole question in a more candid and teachable spirit, I believe, than I ever studied it in before."

"Your difficulties, I take it for granted, refer to the evidences of revelation," suggested the clergyman.

"Why—no—not altogether; in fact I am ashamed to say I have not considered even my objections sufficiently to state them connectedly; but—but there is one subject on which I feel a peculiar interest."

He paused again, and Doctor —— pressed him to proceed.

"The fact is," said Barton, "whatever may be my uncertainty as to the authenticity of what we are taught to call revelation, of one fact I am deeply and horribly convinced, that there does exist beyond this a spiritual world—a system whose workings are generally in mercy hidden from us—a system which may be, and which is sometimes, partially and terribly revealed. I am sure—I *know*," continued Barton, with increasing excitement, "that there is a God—a dreadful God—and that retribution follows guilt, in ways the most mysterious and stupendous—by agencies the most inexplicable and terrific;—there is a spiritual system—great God, how I have been convinced!—a system malignant, and implacable, and omnipotent, under whose persecutions I am, and have been, suffering the torments of the damned!—yes, sir—yes—the fires and frenzy of hell!"

As Barton spoke, his agitation became so vehement that the Divine was shocked, and even alarmed. The wild and excited rapidity with which he spoke, and, above all, the indefinable horror, that stamped his features, afforded a contrast to his ordinary cool and unimpassioned self-possession striking and painful in the last degree.

CHAPTER V.

MR. BARTON STATES HIS CASE.

"My dear sir," said Doctor ——, after a brief pause, "I fear you have been very unhappy, indeed; but I venture to predict that the depression under which you labour will be found to originate in purely physical causes, and that with a change of air, and the aid of a few tonics, your spirits will return, and the tone of your mind be once more cheerful and tranquil as heretofore. There was, after all, more truth than we are quite willing to admit in the classic theories which assigned the undue predominance of any one affection of the mind, to the undue action or torpidity of one or other of our bodily organs. Believe me, that a little attention to diet, exercise, and the other essentials of health, under competent direction, will make you as much yourself as you can wish."

"Doctor ——" said Barton, with something like a shudder, "I *cannot* delude myself with such a hope. I have no hope to cling to but one, and that is, that by some other spiritual agency more potent than that which tortures me, *it* may be combated, and I delivered. If this may not be, I am lost—now and for ever lost."

"But, Mr. Barton, you must remember," urged his companion, "that others have suffered as you have done, and——"

"No, no, no," interrupted he, with irritability—"no, sir, I am not a credulous—far from a superstitious man. I have been, perhaps, too much the reverse—too sceptical, too slow of belief; but unless I were one whom no amount of evidence could convince, unless I were to contemn the repeated, the *perpetual* evidence of my own senses, I am now—now at last constrained to believe—I have no escape from the conviction—the overwhelming certainty—that I am haunted and dogged, go where I may, by—by a DEMON!"

There was a preternatural energy of horror in Barton's face, as, with its damp and death-like lineaments turned towards his companion, he thus delivered himself.

"God help you, my poor friend," said Dr. ——, much shocked, "God help you; for, indeed, you *are* a sufferer, however your sufferings may have been caused."

"Ay, ay, God help me," echoed Barton, sternly; "but *will* he help me—will he help me?"

"Pray to him—pray in an humble and trusting spirit," said he.

"Pray, pray," echoed he again; "I can't pray—I could as easily move a mountain by an effort of my will. I have not belief enough to pray; there is something within me that will not pray. You prescribe impossibilities—literal impossibilities."

"You will not find it so, if you will but try," said Doctor ——.

"Try! I *have* tried, and the attempt only fills me with confusion; and, sometimes, terror; I have tried in vain, and more than in vain. The awful, unutterable idea of eternity and infinity oppresses and maddens my brain whenever my mind approaches the contemplation of the Creator; I recoil from the effort scared. I tell you, Doctor ——, if I am to be saved, it must be by other means. The idea of an eternal Creator is to me intolerable—my mind cannot support it."

"Say, then, my dear sir," urged he, "say how you would have me serve you—what you would learn of me—what I can do or say to relieve you?"

"Listen to me first," replied Captain Barton, with a subdued air, and an effort to suppress his excitement, "listen to me while I detail the circumstances of the persecution under which my life has become all but intolerable—a persecution which has made me fear *death* and the world beyond the grave as much as I have grown to hate existence."

Barton then proceeded to relate the circumstances which I have already detailed, and then continued:

"This has now become habitual—an accustomed thing. I do not mean the actual seeing him in the flesh—thank God, *that* at least is not permitted daily. Thank God, from the ineffable horrors of that visitation I have been mercifully allowed intervals of repose, though none of security; but from the consciousness that a malignant spirit is following and watching me wherever I go, I have never, for a single instant, a temporary respite. I am pursued with blasphemies, cries of despair and appalling hatred. I hear those dreadful sounds called after me as I turn the corners of the streets; they come in the night-time, while I sit in my chamber alone; they haunt me everywhere, charging me with hideous crimes, and—great God!—threatening me with coming vengeance and eternal misery. Hush! do you hear *that*?" he cried with a horrible smile of triumph; "there, there, will that convince you?"

The clergyman felt a chill of horror steal over him, while, during the wail of a sudden gust of wind, he heard, or fancied he heard, the half articulate sounds of rage and derision mingling in the sough.

"Well, what do you think of *that*?" at length Barton cried, drawing a long breath through his teeth.

"I heard the wind," said Doctor ——.

"What should I think of it—what is there remarkable about it?"

"The prince of the powers of the air," muttered Barton, with a shudder.

"Tut, tut! my dear sir," said the student, with an effort to reassure himself; for though it was broad daylight, there was nevertheless something disagreeably contagious in the nervous excitement under which his visitor so miserably suffered.

"You must not give way to those wild fancies; you must resist these impulses of the imagination."

"Ay, ay; 'resist the devil and he will flee from thee,'" said Barton, in the same tone; "but *how* resist him? ay, there it is—there is the rub. What—*what* am I to do? what *can* I do?"

"My dear sir, this *is* fancy," said the man of folios; "you are your own tormentor."

"No, no, sir—fancy has no part in it," answered Barton, somewhat sternly. "Fancy! was it that made you, as well as me, hear, but this moment, those accents of hell? Fancy, indeed! No, no."

"But you have seen this person frequently," said the ecclesiastic; "why have you not accosted or secured him? Is it not a little precipitate, to say no more, to assume, as you have done, the existence of preternatural agency, when, after all, everything may be easily accountable, if only proper means were taken to sift the matter."

"There are circumstances connected with this—this *appearance*," said Barton, "which it is needless to disclose, but which to *me* are proof of its horrible nature. I know that the being that follows me is not human—I say I know this; I could prove it to your own conviction." He paused for a minute, and then added, "And as to accosting it, I dare not, I could not; when I see it I am powerless; I stand in the gaze of death, in the triumphant presence of infernal power and malignity. My strength, and faculties, and memory, all forsake me. O God, I fear, sir, you know not what you speak of. Mercy, mercy; heaven have pity on me!"

He leaned his elbow on the table, and passed his hand across his eyes, as if to exclude some image of horror, muttering the last words of the sentence he had just concluded, again and again.

"Doctor ——," he said, abruptly raising himself, and looking full upon the clergyman with an imploring eye, "I know you will do for me whatever may be done. You know now fully the circumstances and the nature of my affliction. I tell you I cannot help myself; I cannot hope to escape; I am utterly passive. I conjure you, then, to weigh my case well, and if anything may be done for me by vicarious supplication—by the intercession of the good—or by any aid or influence whatsoever, I implore of you, I adjure you in the name of the Most High, give me the benefit of that influence—deliver me from the body of this death. Strive for me, pity me; I know you will; you cannot refuse this; it is the purpose and object of my visit. Send me away with some hope, however little, some faint hope of ultimate deliverance, and I will nerve myself to endure, from hour to hour, the hideous dream into which my existence has been transformed."

Doctor —— assured him that all he could do was to pray earnestly for him, and that so much he would not fail to do. They parted with a hurried and melancholy valediction. Barton hastened to the carriage that awaited him at the door, drew down the blinds, and drove away, while Doctor —— returned to his chamber, to ruminate at leisure upon the strange interview which had just interrupted his studies.

CHAPTER VI.

SEEN AGAIN.

It was not to be expected that Captain Barton's changed and eccentric habits should long escape remark and discussion. Various were the theories suggested to account for it. Some attributed the alteration to the pressure of secret pecuniary embarrassments; others to a repugnance to fulfil an engagement into which he was presumed to have too precipitately entered; and others, again, to the supposed incipiency of mental disease, which latter, indeed, was the most plausible as well as the most generally, received, of the hypotheses circulated in the gossip of the day.

From the very commencement of this change, at first so gradual in its advances, Miss Montague had of course been aware of it. The intimacy involved in their peculiar relation, as well as the near interest which it inspired afforded, in her case, a like opportunity and motive for the successful exercise of that keen and penetrating observation peculiar to her sex.

His visits became, at length, so interrupted, and his manner, while they lasted, so abstracted, strange, and agitated, that Lady L——, after hinting her anxiety and her suspicions more than once, at length distinctly stated her anxiety, and pressed for an explanation.

The explanation was given, and although its nature at first relieved the worst solicitudes of the old lady and her niece, yet the circumstances which attended it, and the really dreadful consequences which it obviously indicated, as regarded the spirits, and indeed the reason of the now wretched man, who made the strange declaration, were enough, upon little reflection, to fill their minds with perturbation and alarm.

General Montague, the young lady's father, at length arrived. He had himself slightly known Barton, some ten or twelve years previously, and being aware of his fortune and connexions, was disposed to regard him as an unexceptionable and indeed a most desirable match for his daughter. He laughed at the story of Barton's supernatural visitations, and lost no time in calling upon his intended son-in-law.

"My dear Barton," he continued, gaily, after a little conversation, "my sister tells me that you are a victim to blue devils, in quite a new and original shape."

Barton changed countenance, and sighed profoundly.

"Come, come; I protest this will never do," continued the General; "you are more like a man on his way to the gallows than to the altar. These devils have made quite a saint of you."

Barton made an effort to change the conversation.

"No, no, it won't do," said his visitor laughing; "I am resolved to say what I have to say upon this magnificent mock mystery of yours. You must not be angry, but really it is too bad to see you at your time of life, absolutely frightened into good behaviour, like a naughty child by a bugaboo, and as far as I can learn, a very contemptible one. Seriously, I have been a good deal annoyed at what they tell me; but at the same time thoroughly convinced that there is nothing in the matter that may not cleared up, with a little attention and management, within a week at furthest."

"Ah, General, you do not know—" he began.

"Yes, but I do know quite enough to warrant my confidence," interrupted the soldier, "don't I know that all your annoyance proceeds from the occasional appearance of a certain little man in a cap and great-coat, with a red vest and a bad face, who follows you about, and pops upon you at corners of lanes, and throws you into ague fits. Now, my dear fellow, I'll make it my business to catch this mischievous little mountebank, and either beat him to a jelly with my own hands, or have him whipped through the town, at the cart's-tail, before a month passes."

"If *you* knew what *I* know," said Barton, with gloomy agitation, "you would speak very differently. Don't imagine that I am so weak as to assume, without proof the most overwhelming, the conclusion to which I have been forced—the proofs are here, locked up here." As he spoke he tapped upon his breast, and with an anxious sigh continued to walk up and down the room.

"Well, well, Barton," said his visitor, "I'll wager a rump and a dozen I collar the ghost, and convince even you before many days are over."

He was running on in the same strain when he was suddenly arrested, and not a little shocked, by observing Barton, who had approached the window, stagger slowly back, like one who had received a stunning blow; his arm extended toward the street—his face and his very lips white as ashes—while he muttered, "There—by heaven!—there—there!"

General Montague started mechanically to his feet, and from the window of the drawing-room, saw a figure corresponding as well as his hurry would permit him to discern, with the description of the person, whose appearance so persistently disturbed the repose of his friend.

The figure was just turning from the rails of the area upon which it had been leaning, and, without waiting to see more, the old gentleman snatched his cane and hat, and rushed down the stairs and into the street, in the furious hope of securing the person, and punishing the audacity of the mysterious stranger.

He looked round him, but in vain, for any trace of the person he had himself distinctly seen. He ran breathlessly to the nearest corner, expecting to see from thence the retiring figure, but no such form was visible. Back and forward, from crossing to crossing, he ran, at fault, and it was not until the curious gaze and laughing countenances of the passers-by reminded him of the absurdity of his pursuit, that he checked his hurried pace, lowered his walking cane from the menacing altitude which he had mechanically given it, adjusted his hat, and walked composedly back again, inwardly vexed and flurried. He found Barton pale and trembling in every joint; they both remained silent, though under emotions very different. At last Barton whispered, "You saw it?"

"*It!*—him—some one—you mean—to be sure I did," replied Montague, testily. "But where is the good or the harm of seeing him? The fellow runs like a lamp-lighter. I wanted to *catch* him, but he had stole away before I could reach the hall-door. However, it is no great matter; next time, I dare say, I'll do better; and egad, if I once come within reach of him, I'll introduce his shoulders to the weight of my cane."

Notwithstanding General Montague's undertakings and exhortations, however, Barton continued to suffer from the self-same unexplained cause; go how, when, or where he would, he was still constantly dogged or confronted by the being who had established over him so horrible an influence.

Nowhere and at no time was he secure against the odious appearance which haunted him with such diabolic perseverance.

His depression, misery, and excitement became more settled and alarming every day, and the mental agonies that ceaselessly preyed upon him, began at last so sensibly to affect his health, that Lady L—— and General Montague succeeded, without, indeed, much difficulty, in persuading him to try a short tour on the Continent, in the hope that an entire change of scene would, at all events, have the effect of breaking through the influences of local association, which the more sceptical of his friends assumed to be by no means inoperative in suggesting and perpetuating what they conceived to be a mere form of nervous illusion.

General Montague indeed was persuaded that the figure which haunted his intended son-in-law was by no means the creation of his imagination, but, on the contrary, a substantial form of flesh and blood, animated by a resolution, perhaps with some murderous object in perspective, to watch and follow the unfortunate gentleman.

Even this hypothesis was not a very pleasant one; yet it was plain that if Barton could ever be convinced that there was nothing preternatural in the phenomenon which he had hitherto regarded in that light, the affair would lose all its terrors in his eyes, and wholly cease to exercise upon his health and spirits the baleful influence which it had hitherto done. He therefore reasoned, that if the annoyance were actually escaped by mere locomotion and change of scene, it obviously could not have originated in any supernatural agency.

CHAPTER VII.

FLIGHT.

Yielding to their persuasions, Barton left Dublin for England, accompanied by General Montague. They posted rapidly to London, and thence to Dover, whence they took the packet with a fair wind for Calais. The General's confidence in the result of the expedition on Barton's spirits had risen day by day, since their departure from the shores of Ireland; for to the inexpressible relief and delight of the latter, he had not since then, so much as even once fancied a repetition of those impressions which had, when at home, drawn him gradually down to the very depths of despair.

This exemption from what he had begun to regard as the inevitable condition of his existence, and the sense of security which began to pervade his mind, were inexpressibly delightful; and in the exultation of what he considered his deliverance, he indulged in a thousand happy anticipations for a future into which so lately he had hardly dared to look; and in short, both he and his companion secretly congratulated themselves upon the termination of that persecution which had been to its immediate victim a source of such unspeakable agony.

It was a beautiful day, and a crowd of idlers stood upon the jetty to receive the packet, and enjoy the bustle of the new arrivals. Montague walked a few paces in advance of his friend, and as he made his way through the crowd, a little man touched his arm, and said to him, in a broad provincial *patois*—

"Monsieur is walking too fast; he will lose his sick comrade in the throng, for, by my faith, the poor gentleman seems to be fainting."

Montague turned quickly, and observed that Barton did indeed look deadly pale. He hastened to his side.

"My dear fellow, are you ill?" he asked anxiously.

The question was unheeded and twice, repeated, ere Barton stammered—

"I saw him—by——, I saw him!"

"*Him!*—the wretch—who—where now?—where is he?" cried Montague, looking around him.

"I saw him—but he is gone," repeated Barton, faintly.

"But where—where? For God's sake speak," urged Montague, vehemently.

"It is but this moment—*here*," said he.

"But what did he look like—what had he on—what did he wear—quick, quick," urged his excited companion, ready to dart among the crowd and collar the delinquent on the spot.

"He touched your arm—he spoke to you—he pointed to me. God be merciful to me, there is no escape," said Barton, in the low, subdued tones of despair.

Montague had already bustled away in all the flurry of mingled hope and rage; but though the singular *personnel* of the stranger who had accosted him was vividly impressed upon his recollection, he failed to discover among the crowd even the slightest resemblance to him.

After a fruitless search, in which he enlisted the services of several of the bystanders, who aided all the more zealously, as they believed he had been robbed, he at length, out of breath and baffled, gave over the attempt.

"Ah, my friend, it won't do," said Barton, with the faint voice and bewildered, ghastly look of one who had been stunned by some mortal shock; "there is no use in contending; whatever it is, the dreadful association between me and it, is now established—I shall never escape—never!"

"Nonsense, nonsense, my dear Barton; don't talk so," said Montague with something at once of irritation and dismay; "you must not, I say; we'll jockey the scoundrel yet; never mind, I say—never mind."

It was, however, but labour lost to endeavour henceforward to inspire Barton with one ray of hope; he became desponding.

This intangible, and, as it seemed, utterly inadequate influence was fast destroying his energies of intellect, character, and health. His first object was now to return to Ireland, there, as he believed, and now almost hoped, speedily to die.

To Ireland accordingly he came and one of the first faces he saw upon the shore, was again that of his implacable and dreaded attendant. Barton seemed at last to have lost not only all enjoyment and every hope in existence, but all independence of will besides. He now submitted himself passively to the management of the friends most nearly interested in his welfare.

With the apathy of entire despair, he implicitly assented to whatever measures they suggested and advised; and as a last resource, it was determined to remove him to a house of Lady L——'s, in the neighbourhood of Clontarf, where, with the advice of his medical attendant, who persisted in his opinion that the whole train of consequences resulted merely from some nervous derangement, it was resolved that he was to confine himself, strictly to the house, and to make use only of those apartments which commanded a view of an enclosed yard, the gates of which were to be kept jealously locked.

Those precautions would certainly secure him against the casual appearance of any living form, that his excited imagination might possibly confound with the spectre which, as it was contended, his fancy recognised in every figure that bore even a distant or general resemblance to the peculiarities with which his fancy had at first invested it.

A month or six weeks' absolute seclusion under these conditions, it was hoped might, by interrupting the series of these terrible impressions, gradually dispel the predisposing apprehensions, and the associations which had confirmed the supposed disease, and rendered recovery hopeless.

Cheerful society and that of his friends was to be constantly supplied, and on the whole, very sanguine expectations were indulged in, that under the treatment thus detailed, the obstinate hypochondria of the patient might at length give way.

Accompanied, therefore, by Lady L——, General Montague and his daughter—his own affianced bride—poor Barton—himself never daring to cherish a hope of his ultimate emancipation from the horrors under which his life was literally wasting away—took possession of the apartments, whose situation protected him against the intrusions, from which he shrank with such unutterable terror.

After a little time, a steady persistence in this system began to manifest its results, in a very marked though gradual improvement, alike in the health and spirits of the invalid. Not, indeed, that anything at all approaching complete recovery was yet discernible. On the contrary, to those who had not seen him since the commencement of his strange sufferings, such an alteration would have been apparent as might well have shocked them.

The improvement, however, such as it was, was welcomed with gratitude and delight, especially by the young lady, whom her attachment to him, as well as her now singularly painful position, consequent on his protracted illness, rendered an object scarcely one degree less to be commiserated than himself.

A week passed—a fortnight—a month—and yet there had been no recurrence of the hated visitation. The treatment had, so far forth, been followed by complete success. The chain of associations was broken. The constant pressure upon the overtasked spirits had been removed, and, under these comparatively favourable circumstances, the sense of social community with the world about him, and something of human interest, if not of enjoyment, began to reanimate him.

It was about this time that Lady L—— who, like most old ladies of the day, was deep in family receipts, and a great pretender to medical science, dispatched her own maid to the kitchen garden, with a list of herbs, which were there to be carefully culled, and brought back to her housekeeper for the purpose stated. The handmaiden, however, returned with her task scarce half completed, and a good deal flurried and alarmed. Her mode of accounting for her precipitate retreat and evident agitation was odd, and, to the old lady, startling.

CHAPTER VIII.

SOFTENED.

It appeared that she had repaired to the kitchen garden, pursuant to her mistress's directions, and had there begun to make the specified election among the rank and neglected herbs which crowded one corner of the enclosure, and while engaged in this pleasant labour, she carelessly sang a fragment of an old song, as she said, "to keep herself company." She was, however, interrupted by an ill-natured laugh; and, looking up, she saw through the old thorn hedge, which surrounded the garden, a singularly ill-looking little man, whose countenance wore the stamp of menace and malignity, standing close to her, at the other side of the hawthorn screen.

She described herself as utterly unable to move or speak, while he charged her with a message for Captain Barton; the substance of which she distinctly remembered to have been to the effect, that he, Captain Barton, must come abroad as usual, and show himself to his friends, out of doors, or else prepare for a visit in his own chamber.

On concluding this brief message, the stranger had, with a threatening air, got down into the outer ditch, and, seizing the hawthorn stems in his hands, seemed on the point of climbing through the fence—a feat which might have been accomplished without much difficulty.

Without, of course, awaiting this result, the girl—throwing down her treasures of thyme and rosemary—had turned and run, with the swiftness of terror, to the house. Lady L—— commanded her, on pain of instant dismissal, to observe an absolute silence respecting all that passed of the incident which related to Captain Barton; and, at the same time, directed instant search to be made by her men, in the garden and the fields adjacent. This measure, however, was as usual, unsuccessful, and, filled with undefinable misgivings, Lady L—— communicated the incident to her brother. The story, however, until long afterwards, went no further, and, of course, it was jealously guarded from Barton, who continued to amend, though slowly.

Barton now began to walk occasionally in the court-yard which I have mentioned, and which being enclosed by a high wall, commanded no view beyond its own extent. Here he, therefore, considered himself perfectly secure: and, but for a careless violation of orders by one of the grooms, he might have enjoyed, at least for some time longer, his much-prized immunity. Opening upon the public road, this yard was entered by a wooden gate, with a wicket in it, and was further defended by an iron gate upon the outside. Strict orders had been given to keep both carefully locked; but, spite of these, it had happened that one day, as Barton was slowly pacing this narrow enclosure, in his accustomed walk, and reaching the further extremity, was turning to retrace his steps, he saw the boarded wicket ajar, and the face of his tormentor immovably looking at him through the iron bars. For a few seconds he stood rivetted to the earth—breathless and bloodless—in the fascination of that dreaded gaze, and then fell helplessly insensible, upon the pavement.

There he was found a few minutes afterwards, and conveyed to his room—the apartment which he was never afterwards to leave alive. Henceforward a marked and unaccountable change was observable in the tone of his mind. Captain Barton was now no longer the excited and despairing man he had been before; a strange alteration had passed upon him—an unearthly tranquillity reigned in his mind—it was the anticipated stillness of the grave.

"Montague, my friend, this struggle is nearly ended now," he said, tranquilly, but with a look of fixed and fearful awe. "I have, at last, some comfort from that world of spirits, from which my punishment has come. I now know that my sufferings will soon be over."

Montague pressed him to speak on.

"Yes," said he, in a softened voice, "my punishment is nearly ended. From sorrow, perhaps I shall never, in time or eternity, escape; but my *agony* is almost over. Comfort has been revealed to me, and what remains of my allotted struggle I will bear with submission—even with hope."

"I am glad to hear you speak so tranquilly, my dear Barton," said Montague; "peace and cheer of mind are all you need to make you what you were."

"No, no—I never can be that," said he mournfully. "I am no longer fit for life. I am soon to die. I am to see him but once again, and then all is ended."

"He said so, then?" suggested Montague.

"*He?*—No, no: good tidings could scarcely come through him; and these were good and welcome; and they came so solemnly and sweetly—with unutterable love and melancholy, such as I could not—without saying more than is needful, or fitting, of other long-past scenes and persons—fully explain to you." As Barton said this he shed tears.

"Come, come," said Montague, mistaking the source of his emotions, "you must not give way. What is it, after all, but a pack of dreams and nonsense; or, at worst, the practices of a scheming rascal that enjoys his power of playing upon your nerves, and loves to exert it—a sneaking vagabond that owes you a grudge, and pays it off this way, not daring to try a more manly one."

"A grudge, indeed, he owes me—you say rightly," said Barton, with a sudden shudder; "a grudge as you call it. Oh, my God! when the justice of Heaven permits the Evil one to carry out a scheme of vengeance—when its execution is committed to the lost and terrible victim of sin, who owes his own ruin to the man, the very man, whom he is commissioned to pursue—then, indeed, the torments and terrors of hell are anticipated on earth. But heaven has dealt mercifully with me—hope has opened to me at last; and if death could come without the dreadful sight I am doomed to see, I would gladly close my eyes this moment upon the world. But though death is welcome, I shrink with an agony you cannot understand—an actual frenzy of terror—from the last encounter with that—that demon, who has drawn me thus to the verge of the chasm, and who is himself to plunge me down. I am to see him again—once more—but under circumstances unutterably more terrific than ever."

As Barton thus spoke, he trembled so violently that Montague was really alarmed at the extremity of his sudden agitation, and hastened to lead him back to the topic which had before seemed to exert so tranquillizing an effect upon his mind.

"It was not a dream," he said, after a time; "I was in a different state—I felt differently and strangely; and yet it was all as real, as clear, and vivid, as what I now see and hear—it was a reality."

"And what *did* you see and hear?" urged his companion.

"When I wakened from the swoon I fell into on seeing *him*," said Barton, continuing as if he had not heard the question, "it was slowly, very slowly—I was lying by the margin of a broad lake, with misty hills all round, and a soft, melancholy, rose-coloured light illuminated it all. It was unusually sad and lonely, and yet more beautiful than any earthly scene. My head was leaning on the lap of a girl, and she was singing a song, that told, I know not how—whether by words or harmonies—of all my life—all that is past, and all that is still to come; and with the song the old feelings that I thought had perished within me came back, and tears flowed from my eyes—partly for the song and its mysterious beauty, and partly for the unearthly sweetness of her voice; and yet I knew the voice—oh! how well; and I was spell-bound as I listened and looked at the solitary scene, without stirring, almost without breathing—and, alas! alas! without turning my eyes toward the face that I knew was near me, so sweetly powerful was the enchantment that held me. And so, slowly, the song and scene grew fainter, and fainter, to my senses, till all was dark and still again. And then I awoke to this world, as you saw, comforted, for I knew that I was forgiven much." Barton wept again long and bitterly.

From this time, as we have said, the prevailing tone of his mind was one of profound and tranquil melancholy. This, however, was not without its interruptions. He was thoroughly impressed with the conviction that he was to experience another and a final visitation, transcending in horror all he had before experienced. From this anticipated and unknown agony, he often shrank in such paroxysms of abject terror and distraction, as filled the whole household with dismay and superstitious panic. Even those among them who affected to discredit the theory of preternatural agency, were often in their secret souls visited during the silence of night with qualms and apprehensions, which they would not have readily confessed; and none of them attempted to dissuade Barton from the resolution on which he now systematically acted, of shutting himself up in his own apartment. The window-blinds of this room were kept jealously down; and his own man was seldom out of his presence, day or night, his bed being placed in the same chamber.

This man was an attached and respectable servant; and his duties, in addition to those ordinarily imposed upon valets, but which Barton's independent habits generally dispensed with, were to attend carefully to the simple precautions by means of which his master hoped to exclude the dreaded intrusion of the "Watcher." And, in addition to attending to those arrangements, which amounted merely to guarding against the possibility of his master's being, through any unscreened window or open door, exposed to the dreaded influence, the valet was never to suffer him to be alone—total solitude, even for a minute, had become to him now almost as intolerable as the idea of going abroad into the public ways—it was an instinctive anticipation of what was coming.

CHAPTER IX.

REQUIESCAT.

It is needless to say, that under these circumstances, no steps were taken toward the fulfilment of that engagement into which he had entered. There was quite disparity enough in point of years, and indeed of habits, between the young lady and Captain Barton, to have precluded anything like very vehement or romantic attachment on her part. Though grieved and anxious, therefore, she was very far from being heart-broken.

Miss Montague, however, devoted much of her time to the patient but fruitless attempt to cheer the unhappy invalid. She read for him, and conversed with him; but it was apparent that whatever exertions he made, the endeavour to escape from the one ever waking fear that preyed upon him, was utterly and miserably unavailing.

Young ladies are much given to the cultivation of pets; and among those who shared the favour of Miss Montague was a fine old owl, which the gardener, who caught him napping among the ivy of a ruined stable, had dutifully presented to that young lady.

The caprice which regulates such preferences was manifested in the extravagant favour with which this grim and ill-favoured bird was at once distinguished by his mistress; and, trifling as this whimsical circumstance may seem, I am forced to mention it, inasmuch as it is connected, oddly enough, with the concluding scene of the story.

Barton, so far from sharing in this liking for the new favourite, regarded it from the first with an antipathy as violent as it was utterly unaccountable. Its very vicinity was unsupportable to him. He seemed to hate and dread it with a vehemence absolutely laughable, and which to those who have never witnessed the exhibition of antipathies of this kind, would seem all but incredible.

With these few words of preliminary explanation, I shall proceed to state the particulars of the last scene in this strange series of incidents. It was almost two o'clock one winter's night, and Barton was, as usual at that hour, in his bed; the servant we have mentioned occupied a smaller bed in the same room, and a light was burning. The man was on a sudden aroused by his master, who said—

"I can't get it out of my head that that accursed bird has got out somehow, and is lurking in some corner of the room. I have been dreaming about him. Get up, Smith, and look about; search for him. Such hateful dreams!"

The servant rose, and examined the chamber, and while engaged in so doing, he heard the well-known sound, more like a long-drawn gasp than a hiss, with which these birds from their secret haunts affright the quiet of the night.

This ghostly indication of its proximity—for the sound proceeded from the passage upon which Barton's chamber-door opened—determined the search of the servant, who, opening the door, proceeded a step or two forward for the purpose of driving the bird away. He had however, hardly entered the lobby, when the door behind him slowly swung to under the impulse, as it seemed, of some gentle current of air; but as immediately over the door there was a kind of window, intended in the day time to aid in lighting the passage, and through which at present the rays of the candle were issuing, the valet could see quite enough for his purpose.

As he advanced he heard his master—who, lying in a well-curtained bed, had not, as it seemed, perceived his exit from the room—call him by name, and direct him to place the candle on the table by his bed. The servant, who was now some way in the long passage, and not liking to raise his voice for the purpose of replying, lest he should startle the sleeping inmates of the house, began to walk hurriedly and softly back again, when, to his amazement, he heard a voice in the interior of the chamber answering calmly, and actually saw, through the window which over-topped the door, that the light was slowly shifting, as if carried across the room in answer to his master's call. Palsied by a feeling akin to terror, yet not unmingled with curiosity, he stood breathless and listening at the threshold, unable to summon resolution to push open the door and enter. Then came a rustling of the curtains, and a sound like that of one who in a low voice hushes a child to rest, in the midst of which he heard Barton say, in a tone of stifled horror—"Oh, God—oh, my God!" and repeat the same exclamation several times. Then ensued a silence, which again was broken by the same strange soothing sound; and at last there burst forth, in one swelling peal, a yell of agony so appalling and hideous, that, under some impulse of ungovernable horror, the man rushed to the door, and with his whole strength strove to force it open. Whether it was that, in his agitation, he had himself but imperfectly turned the handle, or that the door was really secured upon the inside, he failed to effect an entrance; and as he tugged and pushed, yell after yell rang louder and wilder through the chamber, accompanied all the while by the same hushed sounds. Actually freezing with terror, and scarce knowing what he did, the man turned and ran down the passage, wringing his hands in the extremity of horror and irresolution. At the stair-head he was encountered by General Montague, scared and eager, and just as they met the fearful sounds had ceased.

"What is it? Who—where is your master?" said Montague with the incoherence of extreme agitation. "Has anything—for God's sake is anything wrong?"

"Lord have mercy on us, it's all over," said the man staring wildly towards his master's chamber. "He's dead, sir, I'm sure he's dead."

Without waiting for inquiry or explanation, Montague, closely followed by the servant, hurried to the chamber-door, turned the handle, and pushed it open. As the door yielded to his pressure, the ill-omened bird of which the servant had been in search, uttering its spectral warning, started suddenly from the far side of the bed, and flying through the doorway close over their heads, and extinguishing, in his passage, the candle which Montague carried, crashed through the skylight that overlooked the lobby, and sailed away into the darkness of the outer space.

"There it is, God bless us," whispered the man, after a breathless pause.

"Curse that bird," muttered the General, startled by the suddenness of the apparition, and unable to conceal his discomposure.

"The candle is moved," said the man, after another breathless pause, pointing to the candle that still burned in the room; "see, they put it by the bed."

"Draw the curtains, fellow, and don't stand gaping there," whispered Montague, sternly.

The man hesitated.

"Hold this, then," said Montague, impatiently thrusting the candlestick into the servant's hand, and himself advancing to the bed-side, he drew the curtains apart. The light of the candle, which was still burning at the bedside, fell upon a figure huddled together, and half upright, at the head of the bed. It seemed as though it had slunk back as far as the solid panelling would allow, and the hands were still clutched in the bed-clothes.

"Barton, Barton, *Barton*!" cried the General, with a strange mixture of awe and vehemence. He took the candle, and held it so that it shone full upon the face. The features were fixed, stern, and white; the jaw was fallen; and the sightless eyes, still open, gazed vacantly forward toward the front of the bed. "God Almighty! he's dead," muttered the General, as he looked upon this fearful spectacle. They both continued to gaze upon it in silence for a minute or more. "And cold, too," whispered Montague, withdrawing his hand from that of the dead man.

"And see, see—may I never have life, sir," added the man, after a another pause, with a shudder, "but there was something else on the bed with him. Look there—look there—see that, sir."

As the man thus spoke, he pointed to a deep indenture, as if caused by a heavy pressure, near the foot of the bed.

Montague was silent.

"Come, sir, come away, for God's sake," whispered the man, drawing close up to him, and holding fast by his arm, while he glanced fearfully round; "what good can be done here now—come away, for God's sake!"

At this moment they heard the steps of more than one approaching, and Montague, hastily desiring the servant to arrest their progress, endeavoured to loose the rigid gripe with which the fingers of the dead man were clutched in the bed-clothes, and drew, as well as he was able, the awful figure into a reclining posture; then closing the curtains carefully upon it, he hastened himself to meet those persons that were approaching.

It is needless to follow the personages so slightly connected with this narrative, into the events of their after life; it is enough to say, that no clue to the solution of these mysterious occurrences was ever after discovered; and so long an interval having now passed since the event which I have just described concluded this strange history, it is scarcely to be expected that time can throw any new lights upon its dark and inexplicable outline. Until the secrets of the earth shall be no longer hidden, therefore, these transactions must remain shrouded in their original obscurity.

The only occurrence in Captain Barton's former life to which reference was ever made, as having any possible connexion with the sufferings with which his existence closed, and which he himself seemed to regard as working out a retribution for some grievous sin of his past life, was a circumstance which not for several years after his death was brought to light. The nature of this disclosure was painful to his relatives, and discreditable to his memory.

It appeared that some six years before Captain Barton's final return to Dublin, he had formed, in the town of Plymouth, a guilty attachment, the object of which was the daughter of one of the ship's crew under his command. The father had visited the frailty of his unhappy child with extreme harshness, and even brutality, and it was said that she had died heart-broken. Presuming upon Barton's implication in her guilt, this man had conducted himself toward him with marked insolence, and Barton retaliated this, and what he resented with still more exasperated bitterness his treatment of the unfortunate girl—by a systematic exercise of those terrible and arbitrary severities which the regulations of the navy placed at the command of those who are responsible for its discipline. The man had at length made his escape, while the vessel was in port at Naples, but died, as it was said, in an hospital in that town, of the wounds inflicted in one of his recent and sanguinary punishments.

Whether these circumstances in reality bear, or not, upon the occurrences of Barton's after-life, it is, of course, impossible to say. It seems, however more than probable that they were at least, in his own mind, closely associated with them. But however the truth may be, as to the origin and motives of this mysterious persecution, there can be no doubt that, with respect to the agencies by which it was accomplished, absolute and impenetrable mystery is like to prevail until the day of doom.

POSTSCRIPT BY THE EDITOR.

The preceding narrative is given in the *ipsissima verba* of the good old clergyman, under whose hand it was delivered to Doctor Hesselius. Notwithstanding the occasional stiffness and redundancy of his sentences, I thought it better to reserve to myself the power of assuring the reader, that in handing to the printer, the M.S. of a statement so marvellous, the Editor has not altered one letter of the original text.—[*Ed. Papers of Dr. Hesselius.*]

MR. JUSTICE HARBOTTLE.

PROLOGUE.

On this case, Doctor Hesselius has inscribed nothing more than the words, "Harman's Report," and a simple reference to his own extraordinary Essay on "the Interior Sense, and the Conditions of the opening thereof."

The reference is to Vol. I. Section 317, Note Z[a]. The note to which reference is thus made, simply says: "There are two accounts of the remarkable case of the Honourable Mr. Justice Harbottle, one furnished to me by Mrs. Trimmer of Tunbridge Wells (June, 1805); the other at a much later date, by Anthony Harman, Esq. I much prefer the former; in the first place, because it is minute and detailed, and written, it seems to me, with more caution and knowledge; and in the next, because the letters from Doctor Hedstone, which are embodied in it, furnish matter of the highest value to a right apprehension of the nature of the case. It was one of the best declared cases of an opening of the interior sense, which I have met with. It was affected, too, by the phenomenon, which occurs so frequently as to indicate a law of these eccentric conditions, that is to say, it exhibited, what I may term, the contagious character of this sort of intrusion of the spirit-world upon the proper domain of matter. So soon as the spirit-action has established itself in the case of one patient, its developed energy begins to radiate, more or less effectually, upon others. The interior vision of the child was opened; as was, also, that of its mother, Mrs. Pyneweck; and both the interior vision and hearing of the scullery-maid, were opened on the same occasion. After-appearances are the result of the law explained in Vol. II. Section 17 to 49. The common centre of association, simultaneously recalled, unites, or *re*unites, as the case may be, for a period measured, as we see, in Section 37. The *maximum* will extend to days, the *minimum* is little more than a second. We see the operation of this principle perfectly displayed, in certain cases of lunacy, of epilepsy, of catalepsy, and of mania, of a peculiar and painful character, though unattended by incapacity of business."

The memorandum of the case of Judge Harbottle, which was written by Mrs. Trimmer of Tunbridge Wells, which Doctor Hesselius thought the better of the two, I have been unable to discover among his papers. I found in his escritoire a note to the effect that he had lent the Report of Judge Harbottle's case, written by Mrs. Trimmer to Doctor F. Heyne. To that learned and able gentleman accordingly I wrote, and received from him, in his reply, which was full of alarms and regrets on account of the uncertain safety of that "valuable MS.," a line written long since by Doctor Hesselius, which completely exonerated him, inasmuch as it acknowledged the safe return of the papers. The Narrative of Mr. Harman, is, therefore, the only one available for this collection. The late Dr. Hesselius, in another passage of the note that I have cited, says, "As to the facts (non-medical) of the case, the narrative of Mr. Harman exactly tallies with that furnished by Mrs. Trimmer." The strictly scientific view of the case would scarcely interest the popular reader; and, possibly, for the purposes of this selection, I should, even had I both papers to choose between, have preferred that of Mr. Harman, which is given, in full, in the following pages.

CHAPTER I.

THE JUDGE'S HOUSE.

Thirty years ago, an elderly man, to whom I paid quarterly a small annuity charged on some property of mine, came on the quarter-day to receive it. He was a dry, sad, quiet man, who had known better days, and had always maintained an unexceptionable character. No better authority could be imagined for a ghost story.

He told me one, though with a manifest reluctance; he was drawn into the narration by his choosing to explain what I should not have remarked, that he had called two days earlier than that week after the strict day of payment, which he had usually allowed to elapse. His reason was a sudden determination to change his lodgings, and the consequent necessity of paying his rent a little before it was due.

He lodged in a dark street in Westminster, in a spacious old house, very warm, being wainscoted from top to bottom, and furnished with no undue abundance of windows, and those fitted with thick sashes and small panes.

This house was, as the bills upon the windows testified, offered to be sold or let. But no one seemed to care to look at it.

A thin matron, in rusty black silk, very taciturn, with large, steady, alarmed eyes, that seemed to look in your face, to read what you might have seen in the dark rooms and passages through which you had passed, was in charge of it, with a solitary 'maid-of-all-work' under her command. My poor friend had taken lodgings in this house, on account of their extraordinary cheapness. He had occupied them for nearly a year without the slightest disturbance, and was the only tenant, under rent, in the house. He had two rooms; a sitting-room, and a bedroom with a closet opening from it, in which he kept his books and papers locked up. He had gone to his bed, having also locked the outer door. Unable to sleep, he had lighted a candle, and after having read for a time, had laid the book beside him. He heard the old clock at the stair-head strike one; and very shortly after, to his alarm, he saw the closet-door, which he thought he had locked, open stealthily, and a slight dark man, particularly sinister, and somewhere about fifty, dressed in mourning of a very antique fashion, such a suit as we see in Hogarth, entered the room on tiptoe. He was followed by an elder man, stout, and blotched with scurvy, and whose features, fixed as a corpse's, were stamped with dreadful force with a character of sensuality and villany.

This old man wore a flowered-silk dressing-gown and ruffles, and he remarked a gold ring on his finger, and on his head a cap of velvet, such as, in the days of perukes, gentlemen wore in undress.

This direful old man carried in his ringed and ruffled hand a coil of rope; and these two figures crossed the floor diagonally, passing the foot of his bed, from the closet-door at the farther end of the room, at the left, near the window, to the door opening upon the lobby, close to the bed's head, at his right.

He did not attempt to describe his sensations as these figures passed so near him. He merely said, that so far from sleeping in that room again, no consideration the world could offer would induce him so much as to enter it again alone, even in the daylight. He found both doors, that of the closet, and that of the room opening upon the lobby, in the morning fast locked, as he had left them before going to bed.

In answer to a question of mine, he said that neither appeared the least conscious of his presence. They did not seem to glide, but walked as living men do, but without any sound, and he felt a vibration on the floor as they crossed it. He so obviously suffered from speaking about the apparitions, that I asked him no more questions.

There were in his description, however, certain coincidences so very singular, as to induce me, by that very post, to write to a friend much my senior, then living in a remote part of England, for the information which I knew he could give me. He had himself more than once pointed out that old house to my attention, and told me, though very briefly, the strange story which I now asked him to give me in greater detail.

His answer satisfied me; and the following pages convey its substance.

Your letter (he wrote) tells me you desire some particulars about the closing years of the life of Mr. Justice Harbottle, one of the judges of the Court of Common Pleas. You refer, of course, to the extraordinary occurrences that made that period of his life long after a theme for 'winter tales' and metaphysical speculation. I happen to know perhaps more than any other man living of those mysterious particulars.

The old family mansion, when I revisited London, more than thirty years ago, I examined for the last time. During the years that have passed since then, I hear that improvement, with its preliminary demolitions, has been doing wonders for the quarter of Westminster in which it stood. If I were quite certain that the house had been taken down, I should have no difficulty about naming the street in which it stood. As what I have to tell, however, is not likely to improve its letting value, and as I should not care to get into trouble, I prefer being silent on that particular point.

How old the house was, I can't tell. People said it was built by Roger Harbottle, a Turkey merchant, in the reign of King James I. I am not a good opinion upon such questions; but having been in it, though in its forlorn and deserted state. I can tell you in a general way what it was like. It was built of dark-red brick, and the door and windows were faced with stone that had turned yellow by time. It receded some feet from the line of the other houses in the street; and it had a florid and fanciful rail of iron about the broad steps that invited your ascent to the hall-door, in which were fixed, under a file of lamps, among scrolls and twisted leaves, two immense 'extinguishers,' like the conical caps of fairies, into which, in old times, the footmen used to thrust their flambeaux when their chairs or coaches had set down their great people, in the hall or at the steps, as the case might be. That hall is panelled up to the ceiling, and has a large fire-place. Two or three stately old rooms open from it at each side. The windows of these are tall, with many small panes. Passing through the arch at the back of the hall, you come upon the wide and heavy well-staircase. There is a back staircase also. The mansion is large, and has not as much light, by any means, in proportion to its extent, as modern houses enjoy. When I saw it, it had long been untenanted, and had the gloomy reputation beside of a haunted house. Cobwebs floated from the ceilings or spanned the corners of the cornices, and dust lay thick over everything. The windows were stained with the dust and rain of fifty years, and darkness had thus grown darker.

When I made it my first visit, it was in company with my father, when I was still a boy, in the year 1808. I was about twelve years old, and my imagination impressible, as it always is at that age. I looked about me with great awe. I was here in the very centre and scene of those occurrences which I had heard recounted at the fire-side at home, with so delightful a horror.

My father was an old bachelor of nearly sixty when he married. He had, when a child, seen Judge Harbottle on the bench in his robes and wig a dozen times at least before his death, which took place in 1748, and his appearance made a powerful and unpleasant impression, not only on his imagination, but upon his nerves.

The Judge was at that time a man of some sixty-seven years. He had a great mulberry-coloured face, a big, carbuncled nose, fierce eyes, and a grim and brutal mouth. My father, who was young at the time, thought it the most formidable face he had ever seen; for there were evidences of intellectual power in the formation and lines of the forehead. His voice was loud and harsh, and gave effect to the sarcasm which was his habitual weapon on the bench.

This old gentleman had the reputation of being about the wickedest man in England. Even on the bench he now and then showed his scorn of opinion. He had carried cases his own way, it was said, in spite of counsel, authorities, and even of juries, by a sort of cajolery, violence, and bamboozling, that somehow confused and overpowered resistance. He had never actually committed himself; he was too cunning to do that. He had the character of being, however, a dangerous and unscrupulous judge; but his character did not trouble him. The associates he chose for his hours of relaxation cared as little as he did about it.

CHAPTER II.

MR. PETERS.

One night during the session of 1746 this old Judge went down in his chair to wait in one of the rooms of the House of Lords for the result of a division in which he and his order were interested.

This over, he was about to return to his house close by, in his chair; but the night had become so soft and fine that he changed his mind, sent it home empty, and with two footmen, each with a flambeau, set out on foot in preference. Gout had made him rather a slow pedestrian. It took him some time to get through the two or three streets he had to pass before reaching his house.

In one of those narrow streets of tall houses, perfectly silent at that hour, he overtook, slowly as he was walking, a very singular-looking old gentleman.

He had a bottle-green coat on, with a cape to it, and large stone buttons, a broad-leafed low-crowned hat, from under which a big powdered wig escaped; he stooped very much, and supported his bending knees with the aid of a crutch-handled cane, and so shuffled and tottered along painfully.

"I ask your pardon, sir," said this old man in a very quavering voice, as the burly Judge came up with him, and he extended his hand feebly towards his arm.

Mr. Justice Harbottle saw that the man was by no means poorly dressed, and his manner that of a gentleman.

The Judge stopped short, and said, in his harsh peremptory tones, "Well, sir, how can I serve you?"

"Can you direct me to Judge Harbottle's house? I have some intelligence of the very last importance to communicate to him."

"Can you tell it before witnesses?" asked the Judge.

"By no means; it must reach *his* ear only," quavered the old man earnestly.

"If that be so, sir, you have only to accompany me a few steps farther to reach my house, and obtain a private audience; for I am Judge Harbottle."

With this invitation the infirm gentleman in the white wig complied very readily; and in another minute the stranger stood in what was then termed the front parlour of the Judge's house, *tête-à-tête* with that shrewd and dangerous functionary.

He had to sit down, being very much exhausted, and unable for a little time to speak; and then he had a fit of coughing, and after that a fit of gasping; and thus two or three minutes passed, during which the Judge dropped his roquelaure on an arm-chair, and threw his cocked-hat over that.

The venerable pedestrian in the white wig quickly recovered his voice. With closed doors they remained together for some time.

There were guests waiting in the drawing-rooms, and the sound of men's voices laughing, and then of a female voice singing to a harpsichord, were heard distinctly in the hall over the stairs; for old Judge Harbottle had arranged one of his dubious jollifications, such as might well make the hair of godly men's heads stand upright, for that night.

This old gentleman in the powdered white wig, that rested on his stooped shoulders, must have had something to say that interested the Judge very much; for he would not have parted on easy terms with the ten minutes and upwards which that conference filched from the sort of revelry in which he most delighted, and in which he was the roaring king, and in some sort the tyrant also, of his company.

The footman who showed the aged gentleman out observed that the Judge's mulberry-coloured face, pimples and all, were bleached to a dingy yellow, and there was the abstraction of agitated thought in his manner, as he bid the stranger good-night. The servant saw that the conversation had been of serious import, and that the Judge was frightened.

Instead of stumping upstairs forthwith to his scandalous hilarities, his profane company, and his great china bowl of punch—the identical bowl from which a bygone Bishop of London, good easy man, had baptised this Judge's grandfather, now clinking round the rim with silver ladles, and hung with scrolls of lemon-peel—instead, I say, of stumping and clambering up the great staircase to the cavern of his Circean enchantment, he stood with his big nose flattened against the window-pane, watching the progress of the feeble old man, who clung stiffly to the iron rail as he got down, step by step, to the pavement.

The hall-door had hardly closed, when the old Judge was in the hall bawling hasty orders, with such stimulating expletives as old colonels under excitement sometimes indulge in now-a-days, with a stamp or two of his big foot, and a waving of his clenched fist in the air. He commanded the footman to overtake the old gentleman in the white wig, to offer him his protection on his way home, and in no case to show his face again without having ascertained where he lodged, and who he was, and all about him.

"By ——, sirrah! if you fail me in this, you doff my livery to-night!"

Forth bounced the stalwart footman, with his heavy cane under his arm, and skipped down the steps, and looked up and down the street after the singular figure, so easy to recognise.

What were his adventures I shall not tell you just now.

The old man, in the conference to which he had been admitted in that stately panelled room, had just told the Judge a very strange story. He might be himself a conspirator; he might possibly be crazed; or possibly his whole story was straight and true.

The aged gentleman in the bottle-green coat, on finding himself alone with Mr. Justice Harbottle, had become agitated. He said,

"There is, perhaps you are not aware, my lord, a prisoner in Shrewsbury jail, charged with having forged a bill of exchange for a hundred and twenty pounds, and his name is Lewis Pyneweck, a grocer of that town."

"Is there?" says the Judge, who knew well that there was.

"Yes, my lord," says the old man.

"Then you had better say nothing to affect this case. If you do, by —— I'll commit you; for I'm to try it," says the Judge, with his terrible look and tone.

"I am not going to do anything of the kind, my lord; of him or his case I know nothing, and care nothing. But a fact has come to my knowledge which it behoves you to well consider."

"And what may that fact be?" inquired the Judge; "I'm in haste, sir, and beg you will use dispatch."

"It has come to my knowledge, my lord, that a secret tribunal is in process of formation, the object of which is to take cognisance of the conduct of the judges; and first, of *your* conduct, my lord: it is a wicked conspiracy."

"Who are of it?" demands the Judge.

"I know not a single name as yet. I know but the fact, my lord; it is most certainly true."

"I'll have you before the Privy Council, sir," says the Judge.

"That is what I most desire; but not for a day or two, my lord."

"And why so?"

"I have not as yet a single name, as I told your lordship; but I expect to have a list of the most forward men in it, and some other papers connected with the plot, in two or three days."

"You said one or two just now."

"About that time, my lord."

"Is this a Jacobite plot?"

"In the main I think it is, my lord."

"Why, then, it is political. I have tried no State prisoners, nor am like to try any such. How, then, doth it concern me?"

"From what I can gather, my lord, there are those in it who desire private revenges upon certain judges."

"What do they call their cabal?"

"The High Court of Appeal, my lord."

"Who are you sir? What is your name?"

"Hugh Peters, my lord."

"That should be a Whig name?"

"It is, my lord."

"Where do you lodge, Mr. Peters?"

"In Thames-street, my lord, over against the sign of the Three Kings."

"Three Kings? Take care one be not too many for you, Mr. Peters! How come you, an honest Whig, as you say, to be privy to a Jacobite plot? Answer me that."

"My lord, a person in whom I take an interest has been seduced to take a part in it; and being frightened at the unexpected wickedness of their plans, he is resolved to become an informer for the Crown."

"He resolves like a wise man, sir. What does he say of the persons? Who are in the plot? Doth he know them?"

"Only two, my lord; but he will be introduced to the club in a few days, and he will then have a list, and more exact information of their plans, and above all of their oaths, and their hours and places of meeting, with which he wishes to be acquainted before they can have any suspicions of his intentions. And being so informed, to whom, think you, my lord, had he best go then?"

"To the king's attorney-general straight. But you say this concerns me, sir, in particular? How about this prisoner, Lewis Pyneweck? Is he one of them?"

"I can't tell, my lord; but for some reason, it is thought your lordship will be well advised if you try him not. For if you do, it is feared 'twill shorten your days."

"So far as I can learn, Mr. Peters, this business smells pretty strong of blood and treason. The king's attorney-general will know how to deal with it. When shall I see you again, sir?"

"If you give me leave, my lord, either before your lordship's court sits, or after it rises, to-morrow. I should like to come and tell your lordship what has passed."

"Do so, Mr. Peters, at nine o'clock to-morrow morning. And see you play me no trick, sir, in this matter; if you do, by , sir, I'll lay you by the heels!"

"You need fear no trick from me, my lord; had I not wished to serve you, and acquit my own conscience, I never would have come all this way to talk with your lordship."

"I'm willing to believe you, Mr. Peters; I'm willing to believe you, sir."

And upon this they parted.

"He has either painted his face, or he is consumedly sick," thought the old Judge.

The light had shone more effectually upon his features as he turned to leave the room with a low bow, and they looked, he fancied, unnaturally chalky.

"D— him!" said the judge ungraciously, as he began to scale the stairs: "he has half-spoiled my supper."

But if he had, no one but the Judge himself perceived it, and the evidence was all, as any one might perceive, the other way.

CHAPTER III.

LEWIS PYNEWECK.

In the meantime, the footman dispatched in pursuit of Mr. Peters speedily overtook that feeble gentleman. The old man stopped when he heard the sound of pursuing steps, but any alarms that may have crossed his mind seemed to disappear on his recognising the livery. He very gratefully accepted the proferred assistance, and placed his tremulous arm within the servant's for support. They had not gone far, however, when the old man stopped suddenly, saying,

"Dear me! as I live, I have dropped it. You heard it fall. My eyes, I fear, won't serve me, and I'm unable to stoop low enough; but if you will look, you shall have half the find. It is a guinea; I carried it in my glove."

The street was silent and deserted. The footman had hardly descended to what he termed his "hunkers," and begun to search the pavement about the spot which the old man indicated, when Mr. Peters, who seemed very much exhausted, and breathed with difficulty, struck him a violent blow, from above, over the back of the head with a heavy instrument, and then another; and leaving him bleeding and senseless in the gutter, ran like a lamp-lighter down a lane to the right, and was gone.

When, an hour later, the watchman brought the man in livery home, still stupid and covered with blood, Judge Harbottle cursed his servant roundly, swore he was drunk, threatened him with an indictment for taking bribes to betray his master, and cheered him with a perspective of the broad street leading from the Old Bailey to Tyburn, the cart's tail, and the hangman's lash.

Notwithstanding this demonstration, the Judge was pleased. It was a disguised "affidavit man," or footpad, no doubt, who had been employed to frighten him. The trick had fallen through.

A "court of appeal," such as the false Hugh Peters had indicated, with assassination for its sanction, would be an uncomfortable institution for a "hanging judge" like the Honourable Justice Harbottle. That sarcastic and ferocious administrator of the criminal code of England, at that time a rather pharisaical, bloody, and heinous system of justice, had reasons of his own for choosing to try that very

Lewis Pyneweck, on whose behalf this audacious trick was devised. Try him he would. No man living should take that morsel out of his mouth.

Of Lewis Pyneweck of course, so far as the outer world could see, he knew nothing. He would try him after his fashion, without fear, favour, or affection.

But did he not remember a certain thin man, dressed in mourning, in whose house, in Shrewsbury, the Judge's lodgings used to be, until a scandal of his ill-treating his wife came suddenly to light? A grocer with a demure look, a soft step, and a lean face as dark as mahogany, with a nose sharp and long, standing ever so little awry, and a pair of dark steady brown eyes under thinly-traced black brows—a man whose thin lips wore always a faint unpleasant smile.

Had not that scoundrel an account to settle with the Judge? had he not been troublesome lately? and was not his name Lewis Pyneweck, some time grocer in Shrewsbury, and now prisoner in the jail of that town?

The reader may take it, if he pleases, as a sign that Judge Harbottle was a good Christian, that he suffered nothing ever from remorse. That was undoubtedly true. He had nevertheless done this grocer, forger, what you will, some five or six years before, a grievous wrong; but it was not that, but a possible scandal, and possible complications, that troubled the learned Judge now.

Did he not, as a lawyer, know, that to bring a man from his shop to the dock, the chances must be at least ninety-nine out of a hundred that he is guilty.

A weak man like his learned brother Withershins was not a judge to keep the high-roads safe, and make crime tremble. Old Judge Harbottle was the man to make the evil-disposed quiver, and to refresh the world with showers of wicked blood, and thus save the innocent, to the refrain of the ancient saw he loved to quote:

Foolish pity
Ruins a city.

In hanging that fellow he could not be wrong. The eye of a man accustomed to look upon the dock could not fail to read "villain" written sharp and clear in his plotting face. Of course he would try him, and no one else should.

A saucy-looking woman, still handsome, in a mob-cap gay with blue ribbons, in a saque of flowered silk, with lace and rings on, much too fine for the Judge's housekeeper, which nevertheless she was, peeped into his study next morning, and, seeing the Judge alone, stepped in.

"Here's another letter from him, come by the post this morning. Can't you do nothing for him?" she said wheedlingly, with her arm over his neck, and her delicate finger and thumb fiddling with the lobe of his purple ear.

"I'll try," said Judge Harbottle, not raising his eyes from the paper he was reading.

"I knew you'd do what I asked you," she said.

The Judge clapt his gouty claw over his heart, and made her an ironical bow.

"What," she asked, "will you do?"

"Hang him," said the Judge with a chuckle.

"You don't mean to; no, you don't, my little man," said she, surveying herself in a mirror on the wall.

"I'm d——d but I think you're falling in love with your husband at last!" said Judge Harbottle.

"I'm blest but I think you're growing jealous of him," replied the lady with a laugh. "But no; he was always a bad one to me; I've done with him long ago."

"And he with you, by George! When he took your fortune and your spoons and your ear-rings, he had all he wanted of you. He drove you from his house; and when he discovered you had made yourself comfortable, and found a good situation, he'd have taken your guineas and your silver and your ear-rings over again, and then allowed you half-a-dozen years more to make a new harvest for his mill. You don't wish him good; if you say you do, you lie."

She laughed a wicked saucy laugh, and gave the terrible Rhadamanthus a playful tap on the chops.

"He wants me to send him money to fee a counsellor," she said, while her eyes wandered over the pictures on the wall, and back again to the looking-glass; and certainly she did not look as if his jeopardy troubled her very much.

"Confound his impudence, the *scoundrel*!" thundered the old Judge, throwing himself back in his chair, as he used to do *in furore* on the bench, and the lines of his mouth looked brutal, and his eyes ready to leap from their sockets. "If you answer his letter from my house to please yourself, you'll write your next from somebody else's to please me. You understand, my pretty witch, I'll not be pestered. Come, no pouting; whimpering won't do. You don't care a brass farthing for the villain, body or soul. You came here but to make a row. You are one of Mother Carey's chickens; and where you come, the storm is up. Get you gone, baggage! get you *gone*!" he repeated with a stamp; for a knock at the hall-door made her instantaneous disappearance indispensable.

I need hardly say that the venerable Hugh Peters did not appear again. The Judge never mentioned him. But oddly enough, considering how he laughed to scorn the weak invention which he had blown into dust at the very first puff, his white-wigged visitor and the conference in the dark front parlour was often in his memory.

His shrewd eye told him that allowing for change of tints and such disguises as the playhouse affords every night, the features of this false old man, who had turned out too hard for his tall footman, were identical with those of Lewis Pyneweck.

Judge Harbottle made his registrar call upon the crown solicitor, and tell him that there was a man in town who bore a wonderful resemblance to a prisoner in Shrewsbury jail named Lewis Pyneweck, and to make inquiry through the post forthwith whether any one was personating Pyneweck in prison, and whether he had thus or otherwise made his escape.

The prisoner was safe, however, and no question as to his identity.

CHAPTER IV.

INTERRUPTION IN COURT.

In due time Judge Harbottle went circuit; and in due time the judges were in Shrewsbury. News travelled slowly in those days, and newspapers, like the wagons and stage-coaches, took matters easily. Mrs. Pyneweck, in the Judge's house, with a diminished household—the greater part of the Judge's servants having gone with him, for he had given up riding circuit, and travelled in his coach in state—kept house rather solitarily at home.

In spite of quarrels, in spite of mutual injuries—some of them, inflicted by herself, enormous—in spite of a married life of spited bickerings—a life in which there seemed no love or liking or forbearance, for years now that Pyneweck stood in near danger of death, something like remorse came suddenly upon her. She knew that in Shrewsbury were transacting the scenes which were to determine his fate. She knew she did not love him; but she could not have supposed, even a fortnight before, that the hour of suspense could have affected her so powerfully.

She knew the day on which the trial was expected to take place. She could not get it out of her head for a minute; she felt faint as it drew towards evening.

Two or three days passed; and then she knew that the trial must be over by this time. There were floods between London and Shrewsbury, and news was long delayed. She wished the floods would last for ever. It was dreadful waiting to hear; dreadful to know that the event was over, and that she could not hear till self-willed rivers subsided; dreadful to know that they must subside and the news come at last.

She had some vague trust in the Judge's good-nature, and much in the resources of chance and accident. She had contrived to send the money he wanted. He would not be without legal advice and energetic and skilled support.

At last the news did come—a long arrear all in a gush: a letter from a female friend in Shrewsbury; a return of the sentences, sent up for the Judge; and most important, because most easily got at, being told with great aplomb and brevity, the long-deferred intelligence of the Shrewsbury Assizes in the *Morning Adver-*

tiser. Like an impatient reader of a novel, who reads the last page first, she read with dizzy eyes the list of the executions.

Two were respited, seven were hanged; and in that capital catalogue was this line:

"Lewis Pyneweck—forgery."

She had to read it half-a-dozen times over before she was sure she understood it. Here was the paragraph:

> "*Sentence, Death*—7.
> "Executed accordingly, on Friday the 13th instant, to wit:
> "Thomas Primer, *alias* Duck—highway robbery.
> "Flora Guy—stealing to the value of 11*s. 6d.*
> "Arthur Pounden—burglary.
> "Matilda Mummery—riot.
> "Lewis Pyneweck—forgery, bill of exchange."

And when she reached this, she read it over and over, feeling very cold and sick. This buxom housekeeper was known in the house as Mrs. Carwell—Carwell being her maiden name, which she had resumed.

No one in the house except its master knew her history. Her introduction had been managed craftily. No one suspected that it had been concerted between her and the old reprobate in scarlet and ermine.

Flora Carwell ran up the stairs now, and snatched her little girl, hardly seven years of age, whom she met on the lobby, hurriedly up in her arms, and carried her into her bedroom, without well knowing what she was doing, and sat down, placing the child before her. She was not able to speak. She held the child before her, and looked in the little girl's wondering face, and burst into tears of horror.

She thought, the Judge could have saved him. I daresay he could. For a time she was furious with him; and hugged and kissed her bewildered little girl, who returned her gaze with large round eyes.

That little girl had lost her father, and knew nothing of the matter. She had been always told that her father was dead long ago.

A woman, coarse, uneducated, vain, and violent, does not reason, or even feel, very distinctly; but in these tears of consternation were mingling a self-upbraiding. She felt afraid of that little child.

But Mrs. Carwell was a person who lived not upon sentiment, but upon beef and pudding; she consoled herself with punch; she did not trouble herself long even with resentments; she was a gross and material person, and could not mourn over the irrevocable for more than a limited number of hours, even if she would.

Judge Harbottle was soon in London again. Except the gout, this savage old epicurean never knew a day's sickness. He laughed and coaxed and bullied away the young woman's faint upbraidings, and in a little time Lewis Pyneweck troubled her no more; and the Judge secretly chuckled over the perfectly fair removal of a bore, who might have grown little by little into something very like a tyrant.

It was the lot of the Judge whose adventures I am now recounting to try criminal cases at the Old Bailey shortly after his return. He had commenced his charge to the jury in a case of forgery, and was, after his wont, thundering dead against the prisoner, with many a hard aggravation and cynical gibe, when suddenly all died away in silence, and, instead of looking at the jury, the eloquent Judge was gaping at some person in the body of the court.

Among the persons of small importance who stand and listen at the sides was one tall enough to show with a little prominence; a slight mean figure, dressed in seedy black, lean and dark of visage. He had just handed a letter to the crier, before he caught the Judge's eye.

That Judge descried, to his amazement, the features of Lewis Pyneweck. He has the usual faint thin-lipped smile; and with his blue chin raised in air, and as it seemed quite unconscious of the distinguished notice he has attracted, he was stretching his low cravat with his crooked fingers, while he slowly turned his head from side to side—a process which enabled the Judge to see distinctly a stripe of swollen blue round his neck, which indicated, he thought, the grip of the rope.

This man, with a few others, had got a footing on a step, from which he could better see the court. He now stepped down, and the Judge lost sight of him.

His lordship signed energetically with his hand in the direction in which this man had vanished. He turned to the tipstaff. His first effort to speak ended in a gasp. He cleared his throat, and told the astounded official to arrest that man who had interrupted the court.

"He's but this moment gone down *there*. Bring him in custody before me, within ten minutes' time, or I'll strip your gown from your shoulders and fine the sheriff!" he thundered, while his eyes flashed round the court in search of the functionary.

Attorneys, counsellors, idle spectators, gazed in the direction in which Mr. Justice Harbottle had shaken his gnarled old hand. They compared notes. Not one had seen any one making a disturbance. They asked one another if the Judge was losing his head.

Nothing came of the search. His lordship concluded his charge a great deal more tamely; and when the jury retired, he stared round the court with a wandering mind, and looked as if he would not have given sixpence to see the prisoner hanged.

CHAPTER V.

CALEB SEARCHER.

The Judge had received the letter; had he known from whom it came, he would no doubt have read it instantaneously. As it was he simply read the direction:

To the Honourable
The Lord Justice
Elijah Harbottle,
One of his Majesty's Justices of
the Honourable Court of Common Pleas.

It remained forgotten in his pocket till he reached home.

When he pulled out that and others from the capacious pocket of his coat, it had its turn, as he sat in his library in his thick silk dressing-gown; and then he found its contents to be a closely-written letter, in a clerk's hand, and an enclosure in 'secretary hand,' as I believe the angular scrivinary of law-writings in those days was termed, engrossed on a bit of parchment about the size of this page. The letter said:

"Mr. Justice Harbottle,—My Lord,

"I am ordered by the High Court of Appeal to acquaint your lordship, in order to your better preparing yourself for your trial, that a true bill hath been sent down, and the indictment lieth against your lordship for the murder of one Lewis Pyneweck of Shrewsbury, citizen, wrongfully executed for the forgery of a bill of exchange, on the—the day of —— last, by reason of the wilful perversion of the evidence, and the undue pressure put upon the jury, together with the illegal admission of evidence by your lordship, well knowing the same to be illegal, by all which the promoter of the prosecution of the said indictment, before the High Court of Appeal, hath lost his life.

"And the trial of the said indictment, I am farther ordered to acquaint your lordship is fixed for the 10th day of —— next ensuing, by the right honourable the Lord Chief-Justice Twofold, of the court aforesaid, to wit, the High Court of Appeal, on which day it will most certainly take place. And I am farther to acquaint your lordship, to prevent any surprise or miscarriage, that your case stands first for the said day, and that the said High Court of Appeal sits day and night, and never rises; and herewith, by order of the said court, I furnish your lordship with a copy (extract) of the record in this case, except of the indictment, whereof, notwithstanding, the substance and effect is supplied to your lordship in this Notice. And farther I am to inform you, that in case the jury then to try your lordship should find you guilty, the right honourable the Lord Chief-Justice will, in passing sentence of death upon you, fix the day of execution for the 10th day of ----, being one calendar month from the day of your trial."

It was signed by "CALEB SEARCHER,

"Officer of the Crown Solicitor in the

"Kingdom of Life and Death."

The Judge glanced through the parchment.

"'Sblood! Do they think a man like me is to be bamboozled by their buffoonery?"

The Judge's coarse features were wrung into one of his sneers; but he was pale. Possibly, after all, there was a conspiracy on foot. It was queer. Did they mean to pistol him in his carriage? or did they only aim at frightening him?

Judge Harbottle had more than enough of animal courage. He was not afraid of highwaymen, and he had fought more than his share of duels, being a foul-mouthed advocate while he held briefs at the bar. No one questioned his fighting qualities. But with respect to this particular case of Pyneweck, he lived in a house of glass. Was there not his pretty, dark-eyed, over-dressed housekeeper, Mrs. Flora Carwell? Very easy for people who knew Shrewsbury to identify Mrs. Pyneweck, if once put upon the scent; and had he not stormed and worked hard in that case? Had he not made it hard sailing for the prisoner? Did he not know very well what the bar thought of it? It would be the worst scandal that ever blasted judge.

So much there was intimidating in the matter, but nothing more. The Judge was a little bit gloomy for a day or two after, and more testy with every one than usual.

He locked up the papers; and about a week after he asked his housekeeper, one day, in the library:

"Had your husband never a brother?"

Mrs. Carwell squalled on this sudden introduction of the funereal topic, and cried exemplary "piggins full," as the Judge used pleasantly to say. But he was in no mood for trifling now, and he said sternly:

"Come, madam! this wearies me. Do it another time; and give me an answer to my question." So she did.

Pyneweck had no brother living. He once had one; but he died in Jamaica.

"How do you know he is dead?" asked the Judge.

"Because he told me so."

"Not the dead man?"

"Pyneweck told me so."

"Is that all?" sneered the Judge.

He pondered this matter; and time went on. The Judge was growing a little morose, and less enjoying. The subject struck nearer to his thoughts than he fancied it could have done. But so it is with most undivulged vexations, and there was no one to whom he could tell this one.

It was now the ninth; and Mr. Justice Harbottle was glad. He knew nothing would come of it. Still it bothered him; and to-morrow would see it well over.

[What of the paper, I have cited? No one saw it during his life; no one, after his death. He spoke of it to Dr. Hedstone; and what purported to be "a copy," in the old Judge's hand-writing, was found. The original was nowhere. Was it a copy of an illusion, incident to brain disease? Such is my belief.]

CHAPTER VI.

ARRESTED.

Judge Harbottle went this night to the play at Drury Lane. He was one of those old fellows who care nothing for late hours, and occasional knocking about in pursuit of pleasure. He had appointed with two cronies of Lincoln's Inn to come home in his coach with him to sup after the play.

They were not in his box, but were to meet him near the entrance, and to get into his carriage there; and Mr. Justice Harbottle, who hated waiting, was looking a little impatiently from the window.

The Judge yawned.

He told the footman to watch for Counsellor Thavies and Counsellor Beller, who were coming; and, with another yawn, he laid his cocked-hat on his knees, closed his eyes, leaned back in his corner, wrapped his mantle closer about him, and began to think of pretty Mrs. Abington.

And being a man who could sleep like a sailor, at a moment's notice, he was thinking of taking a nap. Those fellows had no business to keep a judge waiting.

He heard their voices now. Those rake-hell counsellors were laughing, and bantering, and sparring after their wont. The carriage swayed and jerked, as one got in, and then again as the other followed. The door clapped, and the coach was now jogging and rumbling over the pavement. The Judge was a little bit sulky. He did not care to sit up and open his eyes. Let them suppose he was asleep. He heard them laugh with more malice than good-humour, he thought, as they observed it. He would give them a d——d hard knock or two when they got to his door, and till then he would counterfeit his nap.

The clocks were chiming twelve. Beller and Thavies were silent as tomb-stones. They were generally loquacious and merry rascals.

The Judge suddenly felt himself roughly seized and thrust from his corner into the middle of the seat, and opening his eyes, instantly he found himself between his two companions.

Before he could blurt out the oath that was at his lips, he saw that they were two strangers—evil-looking fellows, each with a pistol in his hand, and dressed like Bow Street officers.

The Judge clutched at the check-string. The coach pulled up. He stared about him. They were not among houses; but through the windows, under a broad moonlight, he saw a black moor stretching lifelessly from right to left, with rotting trees, pointing fantastic branches in the air, standing here and there in groups, as if they held up their arms and twigs like fingers, in horrible glee at the Judge's coming.

A footman came to the window. He knew his long face and sunken eyes. He knew it was Dingly Chuff, fifteen years ago a footman in his service, whom he had turned off at a moment's notice, in a burst of jealousy, and indicted for a missing spoon. The man had died in prison of the jail-fever.

The Judge drew back in utter amazement. His armed companions signed mutely; and they were again gliding over this unknown moor.

The bloated and gouty old man, in his horror, considered the question of resistance. But his athletic days were long over. This moor was a desert. There was no help to be had. He was in the hands of strange servants, even if his recognition turned out to be a delusion, and they were under the command of his captors. There was nothing for it but submission, for the present.

Suddenly the coach was brought nearly to a standstill, so that the prisoner saw an ominous sight from the window.

It was a gigantic gallows beside the road; it stood three-sided, and from each of its three broad beams at top depended in chains some eight or ten bodies, from several of which the cere-clothes had dropped away, leaving the skeletons swinging lightly by their chains. A tall ladder reached to the summit of the structure, and on the peat beneath lay bones.

On top of the dark transverse beam facing the road, from which, as from the other two completing the triangle of death, dangled a row of these unfortunates in chains, a hang-man, with a pipe in his mouth, much as we see him in the famous print of the 'Idle Apprentice,' though here his perch was ever so much higher, was reclining at his ease and listlessly shying bones, from a little heap at his elbow, at the skeletons that hung round, bringing down now a rib or two, now a hand, now half a leg. A long-sighted man could have discerned that he was a dark fellow, lean; and from continually looking down on the earth from the elevation over which, in another sense, he always hung, his nose, his lips, his chin were pendulous and loose, and drawn down into a monstrous grotesque.

This fellow took his pipe from his mouth on seeing the coach, stood up, and cut some solemn capers high on his beam, and shook a new rope in the air, crying with a voice high and distant as the caw of a raven hovering over a gibbet, "A rope for Judge Harbottle!"

The coach was now driving on at its old swift pace.

So high a gallows as that, the Judge had never, even in his most hilarious moments, dreamed of. He thought he must be raving. And the dead footman! He shook his ears and strained his eyelids; but if he was dreaming, he was unable to awake himself.

There was no good in threatening these scoundrels. A *brutum fulmen* might bring a real one on his head.

Any submission to get out of their hands; and then heaven and earth he would move to unearth and hunt them down.

Suddenly they drove round a corner of a vast white building, and under a *porte-cochère*.

CHAPTER VII.

CHIEF JUSTICE TWOFOLD.

The Judge found himself in a corridor lighted with dingy oil-lamps, the walls of bare stone; it looked like a passage in a prison. His guards placed him in the hands of other people. Here and there he saw bony and gigantic soldiers passing to and fro, with muskets over their shoulders. They looked straight before them, grinding their teeth, in bleak fury, with no noise but the clank of their shoes. He saw these by glimpses, round corners, and at the ends of passages, but he did not actually pass them by.

And now, passing under a narrow doorway, he found himself in the dock, confronting a judge in his scarlet robes, in a large court-house. There was nothing to elevate this temple of Themis above its vulgar kind elsewhere. Dingy enough it looked, in spite of candles lighted in decent abundance. A case had just closed, and the last juror's back was seen escaping through the door in the wall of the jury-box. There were some dozen barristers, some fiddling with pen and ink, others buried in briefs, some beckoning, with the plumes of their pens, to their attorneys, of whom there were no lack; there were clerks to-ing and fro-ing, and the officers of the court, and the registrar, who was handing up a paper to the judge; and the tipstaff, who was presenting a note at the end of his wand to a king's counsel over the heads of the crowd between. If this was the High Court of Appeal, which never rose day or night, it might account for the pale and jaded aspect of everybody in it. An air of indescribable gloom hung upon the pallid features of all the people here; no one ever smiled; all looked more or less secretly suffering.

"The King against Elijah Harbottle!" shouted the officer.

"Is the appellant Lewis Pyneweck in court?" asked Chief-Justice Twofold, in a voice of thunder, that shook the woodwork of the Court, and boomed down the corridors.

Up stood Pyneweck from his place at the table.

"Arraign the prisoner!" roared the Chief; and Judge Harbottle felt the pannels of the dock round him, and the floor, and the rails quiver in the vibrations of that tremendous voice.

The prisoner, *in limine*, objected to this pretended court, as being a sham, and non-existent in point of law; and then, that, even if it were a court constituted by law, (the Judge was growing dazed), it had not and could not have any jurisdiction to try him for his conduct on the bench.

Whereupon the chief-justice laughed suddenly, and every one in court, turning round upon the prisoner, laughed also, till the laugh grew and roared all round like a deafening acclamation; he saw nothing but glittering eyes and teeth, a universal stare and grin; but though all the voices laughed, not a single face of all those that concentrated their gaze upon him looked like a laughing face. The mirth subsided as suddenly as it began.

The indictment was read. Judge Harbottle actually pleaded! He pleaded "Not guilty." A jury were sworn. The trial proceeded. Judge Harbottle was bewildered.

This could not be real. He must be either mad, or *going* mad, he thought.

One thing could not fail to strike even him. This Chief-Justice Twofold, who was knocking him about at every turn with sneer and gibe, and roaring him down with his tremendous voice, was a dilated effigy of himself; an image of Mr. Justice Harbottle, at least double his size, and with all his fierce colouring, and his ferocity of eye and visage, enhanced awfully.

Nothing the prisoner could argue, cite, or state was permitted to retard for a moment the march of the case towards its catastrophe.

The chief-justice seemed to feel his power over the jury, and to exult and riot in the display of it. He glared at them, he nodded to them; he seemed to have established an understanding with them. The lights were faint in that part of the court. The jurors were mere shadows, sitting in rows; the prisoner could see a dozen pair of white eyes shining, coldly, out of the darkness; and whenever the judge in his charge, which was contemptuously brief, nodded and grinned and gibed, the prisoner could see, in the obscurity, by the dip of all these rows of eyes together, that the jury nodded in acquiescence.

And now the charge was over, the huge chief-justice leaned back panting and gloating on the prisoner. Every one in the court turned about, and gazed with steadfast hatred on the man in the dock. From the jury-box where the twelve sworn brethren were whispering together, a sound in the general stillness like a prolonged "hiss-s-s!" was heard; and then, in answer to the challenge of the officer, "How say you, gentlemen of the jury, guilty or not guilty?" came in a melancholy voice the finding, "Guilty."

The place seemed to the eyes of the prisoner to grow gradually darker and darker, till he could discern nothing distinctly but the lumen of the eyes that were turned upon him from every bench and side and corner and gallery of the building. The prisoner doubtless thought that he had quite enough to say, and conclusive, why sentence of death should not be pronounced upon him; but the lord chief-justice puffed it contemptuously away, like so much smoke, and proceeded to pass sentence of death upon the prisoner, having named the 10th of the ensuing month for his execution.

Before he had recovered the stun of this ominous farce, in obedience to the mandate, 'Remove the prisoner,' he was led from the dock. The lamps seemed all to have gone out, and there were stoves and charcoal-fires here and there, that threw a faint crimson light on the walls of the corridors through which he passed. The stones that composed them looked now enormous, cracked and unhewn.

He came into a vaulted smithy, where two men, naked to the waist, with heads like bulls, round shoulders, and the arms of giants, were welding red-hot chains together with hammers that pelted like thunderbolts.

They looked on the prisoner with fierce red eyes, and rested on their hammers for a minute; and said the elder to his companion, "Take out Elijah Harbottle's gyves;" and with a pincers he plucked the end which lay dazzling in the fire from the furnace.

"One end locks," said he, taking the cool end of the iron in one hand, while with the grip of a vice he seized the leg of the Judge, and locked the ring round his ankle. "The other," he said with a grin, "is welded."

The iron band that was to form the ring for the other leg lay still red-hot upon the stone floor, with brilliant sparks sporting up and down its surface.

His companion in his gigantic hands seized the old Judge's other leg, and pressed his foot immovably to the stone floor; while his senior in a twinkling, with a masterly application of pincers and hammer, sped the glowing bar round his ankle so tight that the skin and sinews smoked and bubbled again, and old Judge Harbottle uttered a yell that seemed to chill the very stones, and make the iron chains quiver on the wall.

Chains, vaults, smiths, and smithy all vanished in a moment; but the pain continued. Mr. Justice Harbottle was suffering torture all round the ankle on which the infernal smiths had just been operating.

His friends Thavies and Beller were startled by the Judge's roar in the midst of their elegant trifling about a marriage à-la-mode case which was going on. The Judge was in panic as well as pain. The street-lamps and the light of his own hall-door restored him.

"I'm very bad," growled he between his set teeth; "my foot's blazing. Who was he that hurt my foot? 'Tis the gout—'tis the gout!" he said, awaking completely. "How many hours have we been coming from the playhouse? 'Sblood, what has happened on the way? I've slept half the night?"

There had been no hitch or delay, and they had driven home at a good pace.

The Judge, however, was in gout; he was feverish too; and the attack, though very short, was sharp; and when, in about a fortnight, it subsided, his ferocious joviality did not return. He could not get this dream, as he chose to call it, out of his head.

CHAPTER VIII.

SOMEBODY HAS GOT INTO THE HOUSE.

People remarked that the Judge was in the vapours. His doctor said he should go for a fortnight to Buxton.

Whenever the Judge fell into a brown study, he was always conning over the terms of the sentence pronounced upon him in his vision—"in one calendar month from the date of this day;" and then the usual form, "and you shall be hanged by the neck till you are dead," &c. "That will be the 10th—I'm not much in the way of being hanged. I know what stuff dreams are, and I laugh at them; but this is continually in my thoughts, as if it forecast misfortune of some sort. I wish the day my dream gave me were passed and over. I wish I were well purged of my gout. I wish I were as I used to be. 'Tis nothing but vapours, nothing but a maggot." The copy of the parchment and letter which had announced his trial with many a snort and sneer he would read over and over again, and the scenery and people of his dream would rise about him in places the most unlikely, and steal him in a moment from all that surrounded him into a world of shadows.

The Judge had lost his iron energy and banter. He was growing taciturn and morose. The Bar remarked the change, as well they might. His friends thought him ill. The doctor said he was troubled with hypochondria, and that his gout was still lurking in his system, and ordered him to that ancient haunt of crutches and chalk-stones, Buxton.

The Judge's spirits were very low; he was frightened about himself; and he described to his housekeeper, having sent for her to his study to drink a dish of tea, his strange dream in his drive home from Drury Lane playhouse. He was sinking into the state of nervous dejection in which men lose their faith in orthodox advice, and in despair consult quacks, astrologers, and nursery story-tellers. Could such a dream mean that he was to have a fit, and so die on the 10th? She did not think so. On the contrary, it was certain some good luck must happen on that day.

The Judge kindled; and for the first time for many days, he looked for a minute or two like himself, and he tapped her on the cheek with the hand that was not in flannel.

"Odsbud! odsheart! you dear rogue! I had forgot. There is young Tom—yellow Tom, my nephew, you know, lies sick at Harrogate; why shouldn't he go that day as well as another, and if he does, I get an estate by it? Why, lookee, I asked Doctor Hedstone yesterday if I was like to take a fit any time, and he laughed, and swore I was the last man in town to go off that way."

The Judge sent most of his servants down to Buxton to make his lodgings and all things comfortable for him. He was to follow in a day or two.

It was now the 9th; and the next day well over, he might laugh at his visions and auguries.

On the evening of the 9th, Doctor Hedstone's footman knocked at the Judge's door. The doctor ran up the dusky stairs to the drawing-room. It was a March evening, near the hour of sunset, with an east wind whistling sharply through the chimney-stacks. A wood fire blazed cheerily on the hearth. And Judge Harbottle, in what was then called a brigadier-wig, with his red roquelaure on, helped the glowing effect of the darkened chamber, which looked red all over like a room on fire.

The Judge had his feet on a stool, and his huge grim purple face confronted the fire and seemed to pant and swell, as the blaze alternately spread upward and collapsed. He had fallen again among his blue devils, and was thinking of retiring from the Bench, and of fifty other gloomy things.

But the doctor, who was an energetic son of Æsculapius, would listen to no croaking, told the Judge he was full of gout, and in his present condition no judge even of his own case, but promised him leave to pronounce on all those melancholy questions, a fortnight later.

In the meantime the Judge must be very careful. He was over-charged with gout, and he must not provoke an attack, till the waters of Buxton should do that office for him, in their own salutary way.

The doctor did not think him perhaps quite so well as he pretended, for he told him he wanted rest, and would be better if he went forthwith to his bed.

Mr. Gerningham, his valet, assisted him, and gave him his drops; and the Judge told him to wait in his bedroom till he should go to sleep.

Three persons that night had specially odd stories to tell.

The housekeeper had got rid of the trouble of amusing her little girl at this anxious time by giving her leave to run about the sitting-rooms and look at the pictures and china, on the usual condition of touching nothing. It was not until the last gleam of sunset had for some time faded, and the twilight had so deepened that she could no longer discern the colours on the china figures on the chimney-piece or in the cabinets, that the child returned to the housekeeper's room to find her mother.

To her she related, after some prattle about the china, and the pictures, and the Judge's two grand wigs in the dressing-room off the library, an adventure of an extraordinary kind.

In the hall was placed, as was customary in those times, the sedan-chair which the master of the house occasionally used, covered with stamped leather, and studded with gilt nails, and with its red silk blinds down. In this case, the doors of this old-fashioned conveyance were locked, the windows up, and, as I said, the blinds down, but not so closely that the curious child could not peep underneath one of them, and see into the interior.

A parting beam from the setting sun, admitted through the window of a back room, shot obliquely through the open door, and lighting on the chair, shone with a dull transparency through the crimson blind.

To her surprise, the child saw in the shadow a thin man dressed in black seated in it; he had sharp dark features; his nose, she fancied, a little awry, and his brown eyes were looking straight before him; his hand was on his thigh, and he stirred no more than the waxen figure she had seen at Southwark fair.

A child is so often lectured for asking questions and on the propriety of silence, and the superior wisdom of its elders, that it accepts most things at last in good faith; and the little girl acquiesced respectfully in the occupation of the chair by this mahogany-faced person as being all right and proper.

It was not until she asked her mother who this man was, and observed her scared face as she questioned her more minutely upon the appearance of the stranger, that she began to understand that she had seen something unaccountable.

Mrs. Carwell took the key of the chair from its nail over the footman's shelf, and led the child by the hand up to the hall, having a lighted candle in her other hand. She stopped at a distance from the chair, and placed the candlestick in the child's hand.

"Peep in, Margery, again, and try if there's anything there," she whispered; "hold the candle near the blind so as to throw its light through the curtain."

The child peeped, this time with a very solemn face, and intimated at once that he was gone.

"Look again, and be sure," urged her mother.

The little girl was quite certain; and Mrs. Carwell, with her mob-cap of lace and cherry-coloured ribbons, and her dark brown hair, not yet powdered, over a very pale face, unlocked the door, looked in, and beheld emptiness.

"All a mistake, child, you see."

"*There*, ma'am! see there! He's gone round the corner," said the child.

"Where?" said Mrs. Carwell, stepping backward a step.

"Into that room."

"Tut, child! 'twas the shadow," cried Mrs. Carwell angrily, because she was frightened. "I moved the candle." But she clutched one of the poles of the chair, which leant against the wall in the corner, and pounded the floor furiously with one end of it, being afraid to pass the open door the child had pointed to.

The cook and two kitchen-maids came running upstairs, not knowing what to make of this unwonted alarm.

They all searched the room; but it was still and empty, and no sign of any one's having been there.

Some people may suppose that the direction given to her thoughts by this odd little incident will account for a very strange illusion which Mrs. Carwell herself experienced about two hours later.

CHAPTER IX.

THE JUDGE LEAVES HIS HOUSE.

Mrs. Flora Carwell was going up the great staircase with a posset for the Judge in a china bowl, on a little silver tray.

Across the top of the well-staircase there runs a massive oak rail; and, raising her eyes accidentally, she saw an extremely odd-looking stranger, slim and long, leaning carelessly over with a pipe between his finger and thumb. Nose, lips, and chin seemed all to droop downward into extraordinary length, as he leant his odd peering face over the banister. In his other hand he held a coil of rope, one end of which escaped from under his elbow and hung over the rail.

Mrs. Carwell, who had no suspicion at the moment, that he was not a real person, and fancied that he was some one employed in cording the Judge's luggage, called to know what he was doing there.

Instead of answering, he turned about, and walked across the lobby, at about the same leisurely pace at which she was ascending, and entered a room, into which she followed him. It was an uncarpeted and unfurnished chamber. An open trunk lay upon the floor empty, and beside it the coil of rope; but except herself there was no one in the room.

Mrs. Carwell was very much frightened, and now concluded that the child must have seen the same ghost that had just appeared to her. Perhaps, when she was able to think it over, it was a relief to believe so; for the face, figure, and dress described by the child were awfully like Pyneweck; and this certainly was not he.

Very much scared and very hysterical, Mrs. Carwell ran down to her room, afraid to look over her shoulder, and got some companions about her, and wept, and talked, and drank more than one cordial, and talked and wept again, and so on, until, in those early days, it was ten o'clock, and time to go to bed.

A scullery-maid remained up finishing some of her scouring and "scalding" for some time after the other servants—who, as I said, were few in number—that night had got to their beds. This was a low-browed, broad-faced, intrepid wench with black hair, who did not "vally a ghost not a button," and treated the house-keeper's hysterics with measureless scorn.

The old house was quiet, now. It was near twelve o'clock, no sounds were audible except the muffled wailing of the wintry winds, piping high among the roofs and chimneys, or rumbling at intervals, in under gusts, through the narrow channels of the street.

The spacious solitudes of the kitchen level were awfully dark, and this sceptical kitchen-wench was the only person now up and about, in the house. She hummed tunes to herself, for a time; and then stopped and listened; and then resumed her work again. At last, she was destined to be more terrified than even was the housekeeper.

There was a back-kitchen in this house, and from this she heard, as if coming from below its foundations, a sound like heavy strokes, that seemed to shake the earth beneath her feet. Sometimes a dozen in sequence, at regular intervals; sometimes fewer. She walked out softly into the passage, and was surprised to see a dusky glow issuing from this room, as if from a charcoal fire.

The room seemed thick with smoke.

Looking in, she very dimly beheld a monstrous figure, over a furnace, beating with a mighty hammer the rings and rivets of a chain.

The strokes, swift and heavy as they looked, sounded hollow and distant. The man stopped, and pointed to something on the floor, that, through the smoky haze, looked, she thought, like a dead body. She remarked no more; but the servants in the room close by, startled from their sleep by a hideous scream, found her in a swoon on the flags, close to the door, where she had just witnessed this ghastly vision.

Startled by the girl's incoherent asseverations that she had seen the Judge's corpse on the floor, two servants having first searched the lower part of the house, went rather frightened upstairs to inquire whether their master was well. They found him, not in his bed, but in his room. He had a table with candles burning at his bedside, and was getting on his clothes again; and he swore and cursed at them roundly in his old style, telling them that he had business, and that he would discharge on the spot any scoundrel who should dare to disturb him again.

So the invalid was left to his quietude.

In the morning it was rumoured here and there in the street that the Judge was dead. A servant was sent from the house three doors away, by Counsellor Traverse, to inquire at Judge Harbottle's hall-door.

The servant who opened it was pale and reserved, and would only say that the Judge was ill. He had had a dangerous accident; Doctor Hedstone had been with him at seven o'clock in the morning.

There were averted looks, short answers, pale and frowning faces, and all the usual signs that there was a secret that sat heavily upon their minds, and the time for disclosing which had not yet come. That time would arrive when the coroner had arrived, and the mortal scandal that had befallen the house could be no longer hidden. For that morning Mr. Justice Harbottle had been found hanging by the neck from the banister at the top of the great staircase, and quite dead.

There was not the smallest sign of any struggle or resistance. There had not been heard a cry or any other noise in the slightest degree indicative of violence. There was medical evidence to show that, in his atrabilious state, it was quite on the cards that he might have made away with himself. The jury found accordingly that it was a case of suicide. But to those who were acquainted with the strange story which Judge Harbottle had related to at least two persons, the fact that the catastrophe occurred on the morning of the 10th March seemed a startling coincidence.

A few days after, the pomp of a great funeral attended him to the grave; and so, in the language of Scripture, "the rich man died, and was buried."

IN A GLASS DARKLY
VOLUME II

THE ROOM IN THE DRAGON VOLANT.

PROLOGUE.

The curious case which I am about to place before you, is referred to, very pointedly, and more than once, in the extraordinary Essay upon the drugs of the Dark and the Middle Ages, from the pen of Doctor Hesselius.

This Essay he entitles "Mortis Imago," and he, therein, discusses the *Vinum letiferum*, the *Beatifica*, the *Somnus Angelorum*, the *Hypnus Sagarum*, the *Aqua Thessalliæ*, and about twenty other infusions and distillations, well known to the sages of eight hundred years ago, and two of which are still, he alleges, known to the fraternity of thieves, and, among them, as police-office inquiries sometimes disclose to this day, in practical use.

The Essay, *Mortis Imago*, will occupy as nearly as I can, at present, calculate, two volumes, the ninth and tenth, of the collected papers of Doctor Martin Hesselius.

This Essay, I may remark, in conclusion, is very curiously enriched by citations, in great abundance, from mediæval verse and prose romance, some of the most valuable of which, strange to say, are Egyptian.

I have selected this particular statement from among many cases equally striking, but hardly, I think, so effective as mere narratives, in this irregular form of publication, it is simply as a story that I present it.

CHAPTER I.

ON THE ROAD.

In the eventful year, 1815, I was exactly three-and-twenty, and had just succeeded to a very large sum in consols, and other securities. The first fall of Napoleon had thrown the continent open to English excursionists, anxious, let us suppose, to improve their minds by foreign travel; and I—the slight check of the 'hundred days' removed, by the genius of Wellington, on the field of Waterloo—was now added to the philosophic throng.

I was posting up to Paris from Bruxelles, following, I presume, the route that the allied army had pursued but a few weeks before—more carriages than you could believe were pursuing the same line. You could not look back or forward, without seeing into far perspective the clouds of dust which marked the line of the long series of vehicles. We were, perpetually, passing relays of return-horses, on their way, jaded and dusty, to the inns from which they had been taken. They were arduous times for those patient public servants. The whole world seemed posting up to Paris.

I ought to have noted it more particularly, but my head was so full of Paris and the future, that I passed the intervening scenery with little patience and less attention; I think, however, that it was about four miles to the frontier side of a rather picturesque little town, the name of which, as of many more important places through which I posted in my hurried journey, I forget, and about two hours before sunset, that we came up with a carriage in distress.

It was not quite an upset. But the two leaders were lying flat. The booted postillions had got down, and two servants who seemed very much at sea in such matters, were by way of assisting them. A pretty little bonnet and head were popped out of the window of the carriage in distress. Its *tournure*, and that of the shoulders that also appeared for a moment, was captivating: I resolved to play the part of a good Samaritan; stopped my chaise, jumped out, and with my servant lent a very willing hand in the emergency. Alas! the lady with the pretty bonnet, wore a very thick, black veil. I could see nothing but the pattern of the Bruxelles lace, as she drew back.

A lean old gentleman, almost at the same time, stuck his head out of the window. An invalid he seemed, for although the day was hot, he wore a black muffler which came up to his ears and nose, quite covering the lower part of his face, an arrangement which he disturbed by pulling it down for a moment, and poured forth a torrent of French thanks, as he uncovered his black wig, and gesticulated with grateful animation.

One of my very few accomplishments besides boxing, which was cultivated by all Englishmen at that time, was French; and I replied, I hope and believe, grammatically. Many bows being exchanged, the old gentleman's head went in again, and the demure, pretty little bonnet once more appeared.

The lady must have heard me speak to my servant, for she framed her little speech in such pretty, broken English, and in a voice so sweet, that I more than ever cursed the black veil that baulked my romantic curiosity.

The arms that were emblazoned on the panel were peculiar; I remember especially, one device, it was the figure of a stork, painted in carmine, upon what the heralds call a 'field or.' The bird was standing upon one leg, and in the other claw held a stone. This is, I believe, the emblem of vigilance. Its oddity struck me, and remained impressed upon my memory. There were supporters besides, but I forget what they were.

The courtly manners of these people, the style of their servants, the elegance of their travelling carriage, and the supporters to their arms, satisfied me that they were noble.

The lady, you may be sure, was not the less interesting on that account. What a fascination a title exercises upon the imagination! I do not mean on that of snobs or moral flunkies. Superiority of rank is a powerful and genuine influence in love. The idea of superior refinement is associated with it. The careless notice of the squire tells more upon the heart of the pretty milkmaid, than years of honest Dobbin's manly devotion, and so on and up. It is an unjust world!

But in this case there was something more. I was conscious of being good-looking. I really believe I was; and there could be no mistake about my being nearly six feet high. Why need this lady have thanked me? Had not her husband, for such I assumed him to be, thanked me quite enough, and for both? I was instinctively aware that the lady was looking on me with no unwilling eyes; and, through her veil, I felt the power of her gaze.

She was now rolling away, with a train of dust behind her wheels, in the golden sunlight, and a wise young gentleman followed her with ardent eyes, and sighed profoundly as the distance increased.

I told the postillions on no account to pass the carriage, but to keep it steadily in view, and to pull up at whatever posting-house it should stop at. We were soon in the little town, and the carriage we followed drew up at the Belle Etoile, a comfortable old inn. They got out of the carriage and entered the house.

At a leisurely pace we followed. I got down, and mounted the steps listlessly, like a man quite apathetic and careless.

Audacious as I was, I did not care to inquire in what room I should find them. I peeped into the apartment to my right, and then into that on my left. *My* people were not there.

I ascended the stairs. A drawing-room door stood open. I entered with the most innocent air in the world. It was a spacious room, and, beside myself, contained but one living figure—a very pretty and lady-like one. There was the very bonnet with which I had fallen in love. The lady stood with her back toward me. I could not tell whether the envious veil was raised; she was reading a letter.

I stood for a minute in fixed attention, gazing upon her, in the vague hope that she might turn about, and give me an opportunity of seeing her features. She did not; but with a step or two she placed herself before a little cabriole-table, which stood against the wall, from which rose a tall mirror, in a tarnished frame.

I might, indeed, have mistaken it for a picture; for it now reflected a half-length portrait of a singularly beautiful woman.

She was looking down upon a letter which she held in her slender fingers, and in which she seemed absorbed.

The face was oval, melancholy, sweet. It had in it, nevertheless, a faint and undefinably sensual quality also. Nothing could exceed the delicacy of its features, or the brilliancy of its tints. The eyes, indeed, were lowered, so that I could not see their colour; nothing but their long lashes, and delicate eyebrows. She continued reading. She must have been deeply interested; I never saw a living form so motionless—I gazed on a tinted statue.

Being at that time blessed with long and keen vision, I saw this beautiful face with perfect distinctness. I saw even the blue veins that traced their wanderings on the whiteness of her full throat.

I ought to have retreated as noiselessly as I came in, before my presence was detected. But I was too much interested to move from the spot, for a few moments longer; and while they were passing, she raised her eyes. Those eyes were large, and of that hue which modern poets term "violet."

These splendid melancholy eyes were turned upon me from the glass, with a haughty stare, and hastily the lady lowered her black veil, and turned about.

I fancied that she hoped I had not seen her. I was watching every look and movement, the minutest, with an attention as intense as if an ordeal involving my life depended on them.

CHAPTER II.

THE INN-YARD OF THE BELLE ETOILE.

The face was, indeed, one to fall in love with at first sight. Those sentiments that take such sudden possession of young men were now dominating my curiosity. My audacity faltered before her; and I felt that my presence in this room was probably an impertinence. This point she quickly settled, for the same very sweet voice I had heard before, now said coldly, and this time in French, "Monsieur cannot be aware that this apartment is not public."

I bowed very low, faltered some apologies, and backed to the door.

I suppose I looked penitent and embarrassed. I certainly felt so; for the lady said, by way it seemed of softening matters, "I am happy, however, to have an opportunity of again thanking Monsieur for the assistance, so prompt and effectual, which he had the goodness to render us to-day."

It was more the altered tone in which it was spoken, than the speech itself that encouraged me. It was also true that she need not have recognized me; and even if she had, she certainly was not obliged to thank me over again.

All this was indescribably flattering, and all the more so that it followed so quickly on her slight reproof.

The tone in which she spoke had become low and timid, and I observed that she turned her head quickly towards a second door of the room, I fancied that the gentleman in the black wig, a jealous husband, perhaps, might reappear through it. Almost at the same moment, a voice at once reedy and nasal, was heard snarling some directions to a servant, and evidently approaching. It was the voice that had thanked me so profusely, from the carriage windows, about an hour before.

"Monsieur will have the goodness to retire," said the lady, in a tone that resembled entreaty, at the same time gently waving her hand toward the door through which I had entered. Bowing again very low, I stepped back, and closed the door.

I ran down the stairs, very much elated. I saw the host of the Belle Etoile which, as I said, was the sign and designation of my inn.

I described the apartment I had just quitted, said I liked it, and asked whether I could have it.

He was extremely troubled, but that apartment and two adjoining rooms were engaged—

"By whom?"

"People of distinction."

"But who are they? They must have names, or titles."

"Undoubtedly, Monsieur, but such a stream is rolling into Paris, that we have ceased to inquire the names or titles of our guests—we designate them simply by the rooms they occupy."

"What stay do they make?"

"Even that, Monsieur, I cannot answer. It does not interest us. Our rooms, while this continues, can never be, for a moment, disengaged."

"I should have liked those rooms so much! Is one of them a sleeping apartment?"

"Yes, sir, and Monsieur will observe that people do not usually engage bedrooms, unless they mean to stay the night."

"Well, I can, I suppose, have some rooms, any, I don't care in what part of the house?"

"Certainly, Monsieur can have two apartments. They are the last at present disengaged."

I took them instantly.

It was plain these people meant to make a stay here; at least they would not go till morning. I began to feel that I was all but engaged in an adventure.

I took possession of my rooms, and looked out of the window, which I found commanded the inn-yard. Many horses were being liberated from the traces, hot and weary, and others fresh from the stables, being put to. A great many vehicles—some private carriages, others, like mine, of that public class, which is equivalent to our old English post-chaise, were standing on the pavement, waiting their turn for relays. Fussy servants were to-ing and fro-ing, and idle ones lounging or laughing, and the scene, on the whole, was animated and amusing.

Among these objects, I thought I recognized the travelling carriage, and one of the servants of the "persons of distinction" about whom I was, just then, so profoundly interested.

I therefore ran down the stairs, made my way to the back door; and so, behold me, in a moment, upon the uneven pavement, among all these sights and sounds which in such a place attend upon a period of extraordinary crush and traffic.

By this time the sun was near its setting, and threw its golden beams on the red brick chimneys of the offices, and made the two barrels, that figured as pigeon-houses, on the tops of poles, look as if they were on fire. Everything in this light becomes picturesque; and things interest us which, in the sober grey of morning, are dull enough.

After a little search, I lighted upon the very carriage, of which I was in quest. A servant was locking one of the doors, for it was made with the security of lock and key. I paused near, looking at the panel of the door.

"A very pretty device that red stork!" I observed, pointing to the shield on the door, "and no doubt indicates a distinguished family?"

The servant looked at me, for a moment, as he placed the little key in his pocket, and said with a slightly sarcastic bow and smile, "Monsieur is at liberty to conjecture."

Nothing daunted, I forthwith administered that laxative which, on occasion, acts so happily upon the tongue—I mean a "tip."

The servant looked at the Napoleon in his hand, and then, in my face, with a sincere expression of surprise.

"Monsieur is very generous!"

"Not worth mentioning—who are the lady and gentleman who came here, in this carriage, and whom, you may remember, I and my servant assisted to-day in an emergency, when their horses had come to the ground?"

"They are the Count, and the young lady we call the Countess—but I know not, she may be his daughter."

"Can you tell me where they live?"

"Upon my honour, Monsieur, I am unable—I know not."

"Not know where your master lives! Surely you know something more about him than his name?"

"Nothing worth relating, Monsieur; in fact, I was hired in Bruxelles, on the very day they started. Monsieur Picard, my fellow-servant, Monsieur the Comte's gentleman, he has been years in his service and knows everything; but he never speaks except to communicate an order. From him I have learned nothing. We are going to Paris, however, and there I shall speedily pick up all about them. At present I am as ignorant of all that as Monsieur himself."

"And where is Monsieur Picard?"

"He has gone to the cutler's to get his razors set. But I do not think he will tell anything."

This was a poor harvest for my golden sowing. The man, I think, spoke truth, and would honestly have betrayed the secrets of the family, if he had possessed any. I took my leave politely; and mounting the stairs, again I found myself once more in my room.

Forthwith I summoned my servant. Though I had brought him with me from England, he was a native of France—a useful fellow, sharp, bustling, and, of course, quite familiar with the ways and tricks of his countrymen.

"St. Clair, shut the door; come here. I can't rest till I have made out something about those people of rank who have got the apartments under mine. Here are fifteen francs; make out the servants we assisted to-day; have them to a *petit souper*, and come back and tell me their entire history. I have, this moment, seen one of them who knows nothing, and has communicated it. The other, whose name I forget, is the unknown nobleman's valet, and knows everything. Him you must pump. It is, of course, the venerable peer, and not the young lady who accompanies him, that interests me—you understand? Begone! fly! and return with all the details I sigh for, and every circumstance that can possibly interest me."

It was a commission which admirably suited the tastes and spirits of my worthy St. Clair, to whom, you will have observed, I had accustomed myself to talk with the peculiar familiarity which the old French comedy establishes between master and valet.

I am sure he laughed at me in secret; but nothing could be more, polite and deferential.

With several wise looks, nods and shrugs, he withdrew; and looking down from my window, I saw him, with incredible quickness, enter the yard, where I soon lost sight of him among the carriages.

CHAPTER III.

DEATH AND LOVE TOGETHER MATED.

When the day drags, when a man is solitary, and in a fever of impatience and suspense; when the minute-hand of his watch travels as slowly as the hour-hand used to do, and the hour-hand has lost all appreciable motion; when he yawns, and beats the devil's tatto, and flattens his handsome nose against the window, and whistles tunes he hates, and, in short, does not know what to do with himself, it is deeply to be regretted that he cannot make a solemn dinner of three courses more than once in a day. The laws of matter, to which we are slaves, deny us that re-source.

But in the times I speak of, supper was still a substantial meal, and its hour was approaching. This was consolatory. Three-quarters of an hour, however, still interposed. How was I to dispose of that interval?

I had two or three idle books, it is true, as travelling-companions; but there are many moods in which one cannot read. My novel lay with my rug and walking-stick on the sofa, and I did not care if the heroine and the hero were both drowned together in the water-barrel that I saw in the inn-yard under my window.

I took a turn or two up and down my room, and sighed, looking at myself in the glass, adjusted my great white "choker," folded and tied after Brummel, the immortal "Beau," put on a buff waistcoat and my blue swallow-tailed coat with gilt buttons; I deluged my pocket handkerchief with Eau-de-Cologne (we had not then the variety of bouquets with which the genius of perfumery has since blessed us); I arranged my hair, on which I piqued myself, and which I loved to groom in those days. That dark-brown *chevelure*, with a natural curl, is now represented by a few dozen perfectly white hairs, and its place—a smooth, bald, pink head—knows it no more. But let us forget these mortifications. It was then rich, thick, and dark-brown. I was making a very careful toilet. I took my unexceptionable hat from its case, and placed it lightly on my wise head, as nearly as memory and practice enabled me to do so, at that very slight inclination which the immortal person I have mentioned was wont to give to his. A pair of light French gloves and a rather club-like knotted walking-stick, such as just then came into vogue, for a year or two again in England, in the phraseology of Sir Walter Scott's romances, "completed my equipment."

All this attention to effect, preparatory to a mere lounge in the yard, or on the steps of the Belle Etoile, was a simple act of devotion to the wonderful eyes which I had that evening beheld for the first time, and never, never could forget! In plain terms, it was all done in the vague, very vague hope that those eyes might behold the unexceptionable get-up of a melancholy slave, and retain the image, not altogether without secret approbation.

As I completed my preparations the light failed me; the last level streak of sunlight disappeared, and a fading twilight only remained. I sighed in unison with the pensive hour, and threw open the window, intending to look out for a moment before going downstairs. I perceived instantly that the window underneath mine was also open, for I heard two voices in conversation, although I could not distinguish what they were saying.

The male voice was peculiar; it was, as I told you, reedy and nasal. I knew it, of course, instantly. The answering voice spoke in those sweet tones which I recognised only too easily. The dialogue was only for a minute; the repulsive male voice laughed, I fancied, with a kind of devilish satire, and retired from the window, so that I almost ceased to hear it.

The other voice remained nearer the window, but not so near as at first.

It was not an altercation; there was evidently nothing the least exciting in the colloquy. What would I not have given that it had been a quarrel—a violent one—and I the redresser of wrongs, and the defender of insulted beauty! Alas! so far as I could pronounce upon the character of the tones I heard, they might be as tranquil a pair as any in existence. In a moment more the lady began to sing an odd little *chanson*. I need not remind you how much farther the voice is heard *singing* than speaking. I could distinguish the words. The voice was of that exquisitely sweet kind which is called, I believe, a semi-contralto; it had something pathetic, and something, I fancied, a little mocking in its tones. I venture a clumsy, but adequate translation of the words:—

"Death and Love, together mated,
  Watch and wait in ambuscade;
 At early morn, or else belated.
  They meet and mark the man or maid.
"Burning sigh, or breath that freezes,
  Numbs or maddens man or maid;
 Death or Love the victim seizes,
  Breathing from their ambuscade."
  Breathing from their ambuscade."

"Enough, Madame!" said the old voice, with sudden severity. "We do not desire, I believe, to amuse the grooms and hostlers in the yard with our music."

The lady's voice laughed gaily.

"You desire to quarrel, Madame!" And the old man, I presume, shut down the window. Down it went, at all events, with a rattle that might easily have broken the glass.

Of all thin partitions, glass is the most effectual excluder of sound. I heard no more, not even the subdued hum of the colloquy.

What a charming voice this Countess had! How it melted, swelled, and trembled! How it moved, and even agitated me! What a pity that a hoarse old jackdaw should have power to crow down such a Philomel! "Alas! what a life it is!" I moralized, wisely. "That beautiful Countess, with the patience of an angel and the beauty of a Venus and the accomplishments of all the Muses, a slave! She knows perfectly who occupies the apartments over hers; she heard me raise my window. One may conjecture pretty well for whom that music was intended—ay, old gentleman, and for whom you suspected it to be intended."

In a very agreeable flutter I left my room, and descending the stairs, passed the Count's door very much at my leisure. There was just a chance that the beautiful songstress might emerge. I dropped my stick on the lobby, near their door, and you may be sure it took me some little time to pick it up! Fortune, nevertheless, did not favour me. I could not stay on the lobby all night picking up my stick, so I went down to the hall.

I consulted the clock, and found that there remained but a quarter of an hour to the moment of supper.

Every one was roughing it now, every inn in confusion; people might do at such a juncture what they never did before. Was it just possible that, for once, the Count and Countess would take their chairs at the table d'hôte?

CHAPTER IV.

MONSIEUR DROQVILLE.

Full of this exciting hope, I sauntered out, upon the steps of the Belle Etoile. It was now night, and a pleasant moonlight over everything. I had entered more into my romance since my arrival, and this poetic light heightened the sentiment. What a drama, if she turned out to be the Count's daughter, and in love with me! What a delightful—*tragedy*, if she turned out to be the Count's wife!

In this luxurious mood, I was accosted by a tall and very elegantly-made gentleman, who appeared to be about fifty. His air was courtly and graceful, and there was in his whole manner and appearance something so distinguished, that it was impossible not to suspect him of being a person of rank.

He had been standing upon the steps, looking out, like me, upon the moonlight effects that transformed, as it were, the objects and buildings in the little street. He accosted me, I say, with the politeness, at once easy and lofty, of a French nobleman of the old school. He asked me if I were not Mr. Beckett? I assented; and he immediately introduced himself as the Marquis d'Harmonville (this information he gave me in a low tone), and asked leave to present me with a letter from Lord R——, who knew my father slightly, and had once done me, also, a trifling kindness.

This English peer, I may mention, stood very high in the political world, and was named as the most probable successor to the distinguished post of English Minister at Paris.

I received it with a low bow, and read:

"MY DEAR BECKETT,

"I beg to introduce my very dear friend, the Marquis d'Harmonville, who will explain to you the nature of the services it may be in your power to render him and us."

He went on to speak of the Marquis as a man whose great wealth, whose intimate relations with the old families, and whose legitimate influence with the court rendered him the fittest possible person for those friendly offices which, at the desire of his own sovereign, and of our government, he has so obligingly undertaken.

It added a great deal to my perplexity, when I read, further—

"By-the-bye, Walton was here yesterday, and told me that your seat was likely to be attacked; something, he says, is unquestionably going on at Domwell. You know there is an awkwardness in my meddling ever so cautiously. But I advise, if it is not very officious, your making Haxton look after it, and report immediately. I fear it is serious. I ought to have mentioned that, for reasons that you will see, when you have talked with him for five minutes, the Marquis—with the concurrence of all our friends—drops his title, for a few weeks, and is at present plain Monsieur Droqville.

"I am this moment going to town, and can say no more.

"Yours faithfully,

"R——."

I was utterly puzzled. I could scarcely boast of Lord ——'s acquaintance. I knew no one named Haxton, and, except my hatter, no one called Walton; and this peer wrote as if we were intimate friends! I looked at the back of the letter, and the mystery was solved. And now, to my consternation—for I was plain Richard Beckett—I read—

"*To George Stanhope Beckett, Esq., M.P.*"

I looked with consternation in the face of the Marquis.

"What apology can I offer to Monsieur the Mar—to Monsieur Droqville? It is true my name is Beckett—it is true I am known, though very slightly to Lord R——; but the letter was not intended for me. My name is Richard Beckett—this is to Mr. Stanhope Beckett, the member for Shillingsworth. What can I say, or do, in this unfortunate situation? I can only give you my honour as a gentleman, that, for me, the letter, which I now return, shall remain as unviolated a secret as before I opened it. I am so shocked and grieved that such a mistake should have occurred!"

I dare say my honest vexation and good faith were pretty legibly written in my countenance; for the look of gloomy embarrassment which had for a moment settled on the face of the Marquis, brightened; he smiled, kindly, and extended his hand.

"I have not the least doubt that Monsieur Beckett will respect my little secret. As a mistake was destined to occur, I have reason to thank my good stars that it should have been with a gentleman of honour. Monsieur Beckett will permit me, I hope, to place his name among those of my friends?"

I thanked the Marquis very much for his kind expressions. He went on to say—

"If, Monsieur, I can persuade you to visit me at Claironville, in Normandy, where I hope to see, on the 15th of August, a great many friends, whose acquaintance it might interest you to make, I shall be too happy."

I thanked him, of course, very gratefully for his hospitality. He continued:

"I cannot, for the present, see my friends, for reasons which you may surmise, at my house in Paris. But Monsieur will be so good as to let me know the hotel he means to stay at in Paris; and he will find that although the Marquis d'Harmonville is not in town, that Monsieur Droqville will not lose sight of him."

With many acknowledgments I gave him the information he desired.

"And in the meantime," he continued, "if you think of any way in which Monsieur Droqville can be of use to you, our communication shall not be interrupted, and I shall so manage matters that you can easily let me know."

I was very much flattered. The Marquis had, as we say, taken a fancy to me. Such likings at first sight often ripen into lasting friendships. To be sure it was just possible that the Marquis might think it prudent to keep the involuntary depository of a political secret, even so vague a one, in good humour.

Very graciously the Marquis took his leave, going up the stairs of the Belle Etoile.

I remained upon the steps, for a minute lost in speculation upon this new theme of interest. But the wonderful eyes, the thrilling voice, the exquisite figure of the beautiful lady who had taken possession of my imagination, quickly reasserted their influence. I was again gazing at the sympathetic moon, and descending the steps, I loitered along the pavements among strange objects, and houses that were antique and picturesque, in a dreamy state, thinking.

In a little while, I turned into the inn-yard again. There had come a lull. Instead of the noisy place it was, an hour or two before, the yard was perfectly still and empty, except for the carriages that stood here and there. Perhaps there was a servants' table-d'hôte just then. I was rather pleased to find solitude; and undisturbed I found out my lady-love's carriage, in the moonlight. I mused, I walked round it; I was as utterly foolish and maudlin as very young men, in my situation, usually are. The blinds were down, the doors, I suppose, locked. The brilliant moonlight revealed everything, and cast sharp, black shadows of wheel, and bar, and spring, on the pavement. I stood before the escutcheon painted on the door, which I had examined in the daylight. I wondered how often her eyes had rested on the same object. I pondered in a charming dream. A harsh, loud voice, over my shoulder, said suddenly,

"A red stork—good! The stork is a bird of prey; it is vigilant, greedy, and catches gudgeons. Red, too!—blood red! Ha! ha! the symbol is appropriate."

I had turned about, and beheld the palest face I ever saw. It was broad, ugly, and malignant. The figure was that of a French officer, in undress, and was six feet high. Across the nose and eyebrow there was a deep scar, which made the repulsive face grimmer.

The officer elevated his chin and his eyebrows, with a scoffing chuckle, and said,—"I have shot a stork, with a rifle bullet, when he thought himself safe in the clouds, for mere sport!" (He shrugged, and laughed malignantly). "See, Monsieur; when a man like me—a man of energy, you understand, a man with all his wits about him, a man who has made the tour of Europe under canvas, and, *parbleu!* often without it—resolves to discover a secret, expose a crime, catch a thief, spit a robber on the point of his sword, it is odd if he does not succeed. Ha! ha! ha! Adieu, Monsieur!"

He turned with an angry whisk on his heel, and swaggered with long strides out of the gate.

CHAPTER V.

SUPPER AT THE BELLE ETOILE.

The French army were in a rather savage temper, just then. The English, especially, had but scant courtesy to expect at their hands. It was plain, however, that the cadaverous gentleman who had just apostrophized the heraldry of the Count's carriage, with such mysterious acrimony, had not intended any of his malevolence for me. He was stung by some old recollection, and had marched off, seething with fury.

I had received one of those unacknowledged shocks which startle us, when fancying ourselves perfectly alone, we discover on a sudden, that our antics have been watched by a spectator, almost at our elbow. In this case, the effect was enhanced by the extreme repulsiveness of the face, and, I may add, its proximity, for, as I think, it almost touched mine. The enigmatical harangue of this person, so full of hatred and implied denunciation, was still in my ears. Here at all events was new matter for the industrious fancy of a lover to work upon.

It was time now to go to the table-d'hôte. Who could tell what lights the gossip of the supper-table might throw upon the subject that interested me so powerfully!

I stepped into the room, my eyes searching the little assembly, about thirty people, for the persons who specially interested me.

It was not easy to induce people, so hurried and overworked as those of the Belle Etoile just now, to send meals up to one's private apartments, in the midst of this unparalleled confusion; and, therefore, many people who did not like it, might find themselves reduced to the alternative of supping at the table-d'hôte, or starving.

The Count was not there, nor his beautiful companion; but the Marquis d'Harmonville, whom I hardly expected to see in so public a place, signed, with a significant smile, to a vacant chair beside himself. I secured it, and he seemed pleased, and almost immediately entered into conversation with me.

"This is, probably, your first visit to France?" he said.

I told him it was, and he said:

"You must not think me very curious and impertinent; but Paris is about the most dangerous capital a high-spirited and generous young gentleman could visit without a Mentor. If you have not an experienced friend as a companion during your visit—" He paused.

I told him I was not so provided, but that I had my wits about me; that I had seen a good deal of life in England, and that, I fancied, human nature was pretty much the same in all parts of the world. The Marquis shook his head, smiling.

"You will find very marked differences, notwithstanding," he said. "Peculiarities of intellect and peculiarities of character, undoubtedly, do pervade different nations; and this results, among the criminal classes, in a style of villainy no less peculiar. In Paris, the class who live by their wits, is three or four times as great as in London; and they live much better; some of them even splendidly. They are more ingenious than the London rogues; they have more animation, and invention, and the dramatic faculty, in which your countrymen are deficient, is everywhere. These invaluable attributes place them upon a totally different level. They can affect the manners and enjoy the luxuries of people of distinction. They live, many of them, by play."

"So do many of our London rogues."

"Yes, but in a totally different way. They are the *habitués* of certain gaming-tables, billiard-rooms, and other places, including your races, where high play goes on; and by superior knowledge of chances, by masking their play, by means of confederates, by means of bribery, and other artifices, varying with the subject of their imposture, they rob the unwary. But here it is more elaborately done, and with a really exquisite *finesse*. There are people whose manners, style, conversation, are unexceptionable, living in handsome houses in the best situations, with everything about them in the most refined taste, and exquisitely luxurious, who impose even upon the Parisian bourgeois, who believe them to be, in good faith, people of rank and fashion, because their habits are expensive and refined, and their houses are frequented by foreigners of distinction, and, to a degree, by foolish young Frenchmen of rank. At all these houses play goes on. The ostensible host and hostess seldom join in it; they provide it simply to plunder their guests, by means of their accomplices, and thus wealthy strangers are inveigled and robbed."

"But I have heard of a young Englishman, a son of Lord Rooksbury, who broke two Parisian gaming-tables only last year."

"I see," he said, laughing, "you are come here to do likewise. I, myself, at about your age, undertook the same spirited enterprise. I raised no less a sum than five hundred thousand francs to begin with; I expected to carry all before me by the simple expedient of going on doubling my stakes. I had heard of it, and I fancied that the sharpers, who kept the table, knew nothing of the matter. I found, however, that they not only knew all about it, but had provided against the possibility of any such experiments; and I was pulled up before I had well begun, by a rule which forbids the doubling of an original stake more than four times, consecutively."

"And is that rule in force still?" I inquired, chap-fallen.

He laughed and shrugged, "Of course it is, my young friend. People who live by an art, always understand it better than an amateur. I see you had formed the same plan, and no doubt came provided."

I confessed I had prepared for conquest upon a still grander scale. I had arrived with a purse of thirty thousand pounds sterling.

"Any acquaintance of my very dear friend, Lord R——, interests me; and, besides my regard for him, I am charmed with you; so you will pardon all my, perhaps, too officious questions and advice."

I thanked him most earnestly for his valuable counsel, and begged that he would have the goodness to give me all the advice in his power.

"Then if you take my advice," said he, "you will leave your money in the bank where it lies. Never risk a Napoleon in a gaming-house. The night I went to break the bank, I lost between seven and eight thousand pounds sterling of your English money; and my next adventure, I had obtained an introduction to one of those elegant gaming-houses which affect to be the private mansions of persons of distinction, and was saved from ruin by a gentleman, whom, ever since, I have regarded with increasing respect and friendship. It oddly happens he is in this house at this moment. I recognized his servant, and made him a visit in his apartments here, and found him the same brave, kind, honourable man I always knew him. But that he is living so entirely out of the world, now, I should have made a point of introducing you. Fifteen years ago he would have been the man of all others to consult. The gentleman I speak of is the Comte de St. Alyre. He represents a very old family. He is the very soul of honour, and the most sensible man in the world, except in one particular."

"And that particular?" I hesitated. I was now deeply interested.

"Is that he has married a charming creature, at least five-and-forty years younger than himself, and is, of course, although I believe absolutely without cause, horribly jealous."

"And the lady?"

"The Countess is, I believe, in every way worthy of so good a man," he answered, a little drily.

"I think I heard her sing this evening."

"Yes, I daresay; she is very accomplished." After a few moments' silence he continued.

"I must not lose sight of you, for I should be sorry, when next you meet my friend Lord R——, that you had to tell him you had been pigeoned in Paris. A rich Englishman as you are, with so large a sum at his Paris bankers, young, gay, generous, a thousand ghouls and harpies will be contending who shall be first to seize and devour you."

At this moment I received something like a jerk from the elbow of the gentleman at my right. It was an accidental jog, as he turned in his seat.

"On the honour of a soldier, there is no man's flesh in this company heals so fast as mine."

The tone in which this was spoken was harsh and stentorian, and almost made me bounce. I looked round and recognised the officer, whose large white face had half scared me in the inn-yard, wiping his mouth furiously, and then with a gulp of Maçon, he went on—

"*No* one! It's not blood; it is ichor! it's miracle! Set aside stature, thew, bone, and muscle—set aside courage, and by all the angels of death, I'd fight a lion naked and dash his teeth down his jaws with my fist, and flog him to death with his own tail! Set aside, I say, all those attributes, which I am allowed to possess, and I am worth six men in any campaign; for that one quality of healing as I do—rip me up; punch me through, tear me to tatters with bomb-shells, and nature has me whole again, while your tailor would fine-draw an old-coat. *Parbleu!* gentlemen, if you saw me naked, you would laugh? Look at my hand, a sabre-cut across the palm, to the bone, to save my head, taken up with three stitches, and five days afterwards I was playing ball with an English general, a prisoner in Madrid, against the wall of the convent of the Santa Maria de la Castita! At Arcola, by the great devil himself! that was an action. Every man there, gentlemen, swallowed as much smoke in five minutes as would smother you all, in this room! I received, at the same moment, two musket balls in the thighs, a grape shot through the calf of my leg, a lance through my left shoulder, a piece of a shrapnel in the left deltoid, a bayonet through the cartilage of my right ribs, a sabre-cut that carried away a pound of flesh from my chest, and the better part of a congreve rocket on my forehead. Pretty well, ha, ha! and all while you'd say *bah!* and in eight days and a half I was making a forced march, without shoes, and only one gaiter, the life and soul of my company, and as sound as a roach!"

"Bravo! Bravissimo! Per Bacco! un gallant uomo!" exclaimed, in a martial ecstacy, a fat little Italian, who manufactured tooth-picks and wicker cradles on the island of Notre Dame; "your exploits shall resound through Europe! and the history of those wars should be written in your blood!"

"Never mind! a trifle!" exclaimed the soldier. "At Ligny, the other day, where we smashed the Prussians into ten hundred thousand milliards of atoms, a bit of a shell cut me across the leg and opened an artery. It was spouting as high as the chimney, and in half a minute I had lost enough to fill a pitcher. I must have expired in another minute, if I had not whipped off my sash like a flash of lightning, tied it round my leg above the wound, whipt a bayonet out of the back of a dead Prussian, and passing it under, made a tournequet of it with a couple of twists, and so stayed the hemorrhage, and saved my life. But, *sacré bleu!* gentlemen, I lost so much blood, I have been as pale as the bottom of a plate ever since. No matter. A trifle. Blood well spent, gentlemen." He applied himself now to his bottle of *vin ordinaire*.

The Marquis had closed his eyes, and looked resigned and disgusted, while all this was going on.

"*Garçon*" said the officer, for the first time, speaking in a low tone over the back of his chair to the waiter; "who came in that travelling carriage, dark yellow and black, that stands in the middle of the yard, with arms and supporters emblazoned on the door, and a red stork, as red as my facings?"

The waiter could not say.

The eye of the eccentric officer, who had suddenly grown grim and serious, and seemed to have abandoned the general conversation to other people, lighted, as it were, accidentally, on me.

"Pardon me, Monsieur," he said. "Did I not see you examining the panel of that carriage at the same time that I did so, this evening? Can you tell me who arrived in it?"

"I rather think the Count and Countess de St. Alyre."

"And are they here, in the Belle Etoile?" he asked.

"They have got apartments upstairs," I answered.

He started up, and half pushed his chair from the table. He quickly sat down again, and I could hear him *sacré*-ing and muttering to himself, and grinning and scowling. I could not tell whether he was alarmed or furious.

I turned to say a word or two to the Marquis, but he was gone. Several other people had dropped out also, and the supper party soon broke up.

Two or three substantial pieces of wood smouldered on the hearth, for the night had turned out chilly. I sat down by the fire in a great arm-chair, of carved oak, with a marvellously high back, that looked as old as the days of Henry IV.

"*Garçon*," said I, "do you happen to know who that officer is?"

"That is Colonel Gaillarde, Monsieur."

"Has he been often here?"

"Once before, Monsieur, for a week; it is a year since."

"He is the palest man I ever saw."

"That is true, Monsieur; he has been often taken for a *revenant*."

"Can you give me a bottle of really good Burgundy?"

"The best in France, Monsieur."

"Place it, and a glass by my side, on this table, if you please. I may sit here for half an hour?"

"Certainly, Monsieur."

I was very comfortable, the wine excellent, and my thoughts glowing and serene. "Beautiful Countess! Beautiful Countess! shall we ever be better acquainted."

CHAPTER VI.

THE NAKED SWORD.

A man who has been posting all day long, and changing the air he breathes every half hour, who is well pleased with himself, and has nothing on earth to trouble him, and who sits alone by a fire in a comfortable chair after having eaten a hearty supper, may be pardoned if he takes an accidental nap.

I had filled my fourth glass when I fell asleep. My head, I daresay, hung uncomfortably; and it is admitted, that a variety of French dishes is not the most favourable precursor to pleasant dreams.

I had a dream as I took mine ease in mine inn on this occasion. I fancied myself in a huge cathedral, without light, except from four tapers that stood at the corners of a raised platform hung with black, on which lay, draped also in black, what seemed to me the dead body of the Countess de St. Alyre. The place seemed empty, it was cold, and I could see only (in the halo of the candles) a little way round.

The little I saw bore the character of Gothic gloom, and helped my fancy to shape and furnish the black void that yawned all round me. I heard a sound like the slow tread of two persons walking up the flagged aisle. A faint echo told of the vastness of the place. An awful sense of expectation was upon me, and I was horribly frightened when the body that lay on the catafalque said (without stirring), in a whisper that froze me, "They come to place me in the grave alive; save me."

I found that I could neither speak nor move. I was horribly frightened.

The two people who approached now emerged from the darkness. One, the Count de St. Alyre glided to the head of the figure and placed his long thin hands under it. The white-faced Colonel, with the scar across his face, and a look of infernal triumph, placed his hands under her feet, and they began to raise her.

With an indescribable effort I broke the spell that bound me, and started to my feet with a gasp.

I was wide awake, but the broad, wicked face of Colonel Gaillarde was staring, white as death, at me, from the other side of the hearth. "Where is she?" I shuddered.

"That depends on who she is, Monsieur," replied the Colonel, curtly.

"Good heavens!" I gasped, looking about me.

The Colonel, who was eyeing me sarcastically, had had his *demi-tasse* of *café noir*, and now drank his *tasse*, diffusing a pleasant perfume of brandy.

"I fell asleep and was dreaming," I said, least any strong language, founded on the *rôle* he played in my dream, should have escaped me. "I did not know for some moments where I was."

"You are the young gentleman who has the apartments over the Count and Countess de St. Alyre?" he said, winking one eye, close in meditation, and glaring at me with the other.

"I believe so—yes," I answered.

"Well, younker, take care you have not worse dreams than that some night," he said, enigmatically, and wagged his head with a chuckle. "Worse dreams," he repeated.

"What does Monsieur the Colonel mean?" I inquired.

"I am trying to find that out myself," said the Colonel; "and I think I shall. When *I* get the first inch of the thread fast between my finger and thumb, it goes hard but I follow it up, bit by bit, little by little, tracing it this way and that, and up and down, and round about, until the whole clue is wound up on my thumb, and the end, and its secret, fast in my fingers. Ingenious! Crafty as five foxes! wide awake as a weazel! *Parbleu!* if I had descended to that occupation I should have made my fortune as a spy. Good wine here?" he glanced interrogatively at my bottle.

"Very good," said I, "Will Monsieur the Colonel try a glass?"

He took the largest he could find, and filled it, raised it with a bow, and drank it slowly. "Ah! ah! Bah! That is not it," he exclaimed, with some disgust, filling it again. "You ought to have told *me* to order your Burgundy, and they would not have brought you that stuff."

I got away from this man as soon as I civilly could, and, putting on my hat, I walked out with no other company than my sturdy walking stick. I visited the inn-yard, and looked up to the windows of the Countess's apartments. They were closed, however, and I had not even the unsubstantial consolation of contemplating the light in which that beautiful lady was at that moment writing, or reading, or sitting and thinking of—any one you please.

I bore this serious privation as well as I could, and took a little saunter through the town. I shan't bore you with moonlight effects, nor with the maunderings of a man who has fallen in love at first sight with a beautiful face. My ramble, it is enough to say, occupied about half-an-hour, and, returning by a slight *détour*, I found myself in a little square, with about two high gabled houses on each side, and a rude stone statue, worn by centuries of rain, on a pedestal in the centre of the pavement. Looking at this statue was a slight and rather tall man, whom I instantly recognized as the Marquis d'Harmonville: he knew me almost as quickly. He walked a step towards me, shrugged and laughed:

"You are surprised to find Monsieur Droqville staring at that old stone figure by moonlight. Anything to pass the time. You, I see, suffer from *ennui*, as I do. These little provincial towns! Heavens! what an effort it is to live in them! If I could regret having formed in early life a friendship that does me honour, I think its condemning me to a sojourn in such a place would make me do so. You go on towards Paris, I suppose, in the morning?"

"I have ordered horses."

"As for me I await a letter, or an arrival, either would emancipate me; but I can't say how soon either event will happen."

"Can I be of any use in this matter?" I began.

"None, Monsieur, I thank you a thousand times. No, this is a piece in which every *rôle* is already cast. I am but an amateur, and induced, solely by friendship, to take a part."

So he talked on, for a time, as we walked slowly toward the Belle Etoile, and then came a silence, which I broke by asking him if he knew anything of Colonel Gaillarde.

"Oh! yes, to be sure. He is a little mad; he has had some bad injuries of the head. He used to plague the people in the War Office to death. He has always some delusion. They contrived some employment for him—not regimental, of course—but in this campaign Napoleon, who could spare nobody, placed him in command of a regiment. He was always a desperate fighter, and such men were more than ever needed."

There is, or was, a second inn, in this town, called l'Ecu de France. At its door the Marquis stopped, bade me a mysterious good night, and disappeared.

As I walked slowly toward my inn, I met, in the shadow of a row of poplars, the *garçon* who had brought me my Burgundy a little time ago. I was thinking of Colonel Gaillarde, and I stopped the little waiter as he passed me.

"You said, I think, that Colonel Gaillarde was at the Belle Etoile for a week at one time."

"Yes, Monsieur."

"Is he perfectly in his right mind?"

The waiter stared. "Perfectly, Monsieur."

"Has he been suspected at any time of being out of his mind?"

"Never, Monsieur; he is a little noisy, but a very shrewd man."

"What is a fellow to think?" I muttered, as I walked on.

I was soon within sight of the lights of the Belle Etoile. A carriage, with four horses, stood in the moonlight at the door, and a furious altercation was going on in the hall, in which the yell of Colonel Gaillarde out-topped all other sounds.

Most young men like, at least, to witness a row. But, intuitively, I felt that this would interest me in a very special manner. I had only fifty yards to run, when I found myself in the hall of the old inn. The principal actor in this strange drama was, indeed, the Colonel, who stood facing the old Count de St. Alyre, who, in his travelling costume, with his black silk scarf covering the lower part of his face, confronted him; he had evidently been intercepted in an endeavour to reach his carriage. A little in the rear of the Count stood the Countess, also in travelling costume, with her thick black veil down, and holding in her delicate fingers a white rose. You can't conceive a more diabolical effigy of hate and fury than the Colonel; the knotted veins stood out on his forehead, his eyes were leaping from their sockets, he was grinding his teeth, and froth was on his lips. His sword was drawn, in his hand, and he accompanied his yelling denunciations with stamps upon the floor and flourishes of his weapon in the air.

The host of the Belle Etoile was talking to the Colonel in soothing terms utterly thrown away. Two waiters, pale with fear, stared uselessly from behind. The Colonel screamed, and thundered, and whirled his sword. "I was not sure of your red birds of prey; I could not believe you would have the audacity to travel on high roads, and to stop at honest inns, and lie under the same roof with honest men. You! *you! both*—vampires, wolves, ghouls. Summon the *gendarmes*, I say. By St. Peter and all the devils, if either of you try to get out of that door I'll take your heads off."

For a moment I had stood aghast. Here was a situation! I walked up to the lady; she laid her hand wildly upon my arm. "Oh! Monsieur," she whispered, in great agitation, "that dreadful madman! What are we to do? He won't let us pass; he will kill my husband."

"Fear nothing, Madame," I answered, with romantic devotion, and stepping between the Count and Gaillarde, as he shrieked his invective, "Hold your tongue, and clear the way, you ruffian, you bully, you coward!" I roared.

A faint cry escaped the lady, which more than repaid the risk I ran, as the sword of the frantic soldier, after a moment's astonished pause, flashed in the air to cut me down.

CHAPTER VII.

THE WHITE ROSE.

I was too quick for Colonel Gaillarde. As he raised his sword, reckless of all consequences but my condign punishment, and quite resolved to cleave me to the teeth, I struck him across the side of his head, with my heavy stick; and while he staggered back, I struck him another blow, nearly in the same place, that felled him to the floor, where he lay as if dead.

I did not care one of his own regimental buttons, whether he was dead or not; I was, at that moment, carried away by such a tumult of delightful and diabolical emotions!

I broke his sword under my foot, and flung the pieces across the street. The old Count de St. Alyre skipped nimbly without looking to the right or left, or thanking anybody, over the floor, out of the door, down the steps, and into his carriage. Instantly I was at the side of the beautiful Countess, thus left to shift for herself; I offered her my arm, which she took, and I led her to her carriage. She entered, and I shut the door. All this without a word.

I was about to ask if there were any commands with which she would honour me—my hand was laid upon the lower edge of the window, which was open.

The lady's hand was laid upon mine timidly and excitedly. Her lips almost touched my cheek as she whispered hurriedly.

"I may never see you more, and, oh! that I could forget you. Go—farewell—for God's sake, go!"

I pressed her hand for a moment. She withdrew it, but tremblingly pressed into mine the rose which she had held in her fingers during the agitating scene she had just passed through.

All this took place while the Count was commanding, entreating, cursing his servants, tipsy, and out of the way during the crisis, my conscience afterwards insinuated, by my clever contrivance. They now mounted to their places with the agility of alarm. The postillions' whips cracked, the horses scrambled into a trot, and away rolled the carriage, with its precious freightage, along the quaint main street, in the moonlight, toward Paris.

I stood on the pavement, till it was quite lost to eye and ear in the distance.

With a deep sigh, I then turned, my white rose folded in my handkerchief—the little parting *gage*—the

"Favour secret, sweet, and precious;"

which no mortal eye but hers and mine had seen conveyed to me.

The care of the host of the Belle Etoile, and his assistants, had raised the wounded hero of a hundred fights partly against the wall, and propped him at each side with portmanteaus and pillows, and poured a glass of brandy, which was duly placed to his account, into his big mouth, where, for the first time, such a God-send remained unswallowed.

A bald-headed little military surgeon of sixty, with spectacles, who had cut off eighty-seven legs and arms to his own share, after the battle of Eylau, having retired with his sword and his saw, his laurels and his sticking-plaster to this, his native town, was called in, and rather thought the gallant Colonel's skull was fractured, at all events there was concussion of the seat of thought, and quite enough work for his remarkable self-healing powers, to occupy him for a fortnight.

I began to grow a little uneasy. A disagreeable surprise, if my excursion, in which I was to break banks and hearts, and, as you see, heads, should end upon the gallows or the guillotine. I was not clear, in those times of political oscillation, which was the established apparatus.

The Colonel was conveyed, snorting apoplectically to his room.

I saw my host in the apartment in which we had supped. Wherever you employ a force of any sort, to carry a point of real importance, reject all nice calculations of economy. Better to be a thousand per cent, over the mark, than the smallest fraction of a unit under it. I instinctively felt this.

I ordered a bottle of my landlord's very best wine; made him partake with me, in the proportion of two glasses to one; and then told him that he must not decline a trifling *souvenir* from a guest who had been so charmed with all he had seen of the renowned Belle Etoile. Thus saying, I placed five-and-thirty Napoleons in his hand. At touch of which his countenance, by no means encouraging before, grew sunny, his manners thawed, and it was plain, as he dropped the coins hastily into his pocket, that benevolent relations had been established between us.

I immediately placed the Colonel's broken head upon the *tapis*. We both agreed that if I had not given him that rather smart tap of my walking-cane, he would have beheaded half the inmates of the Belle Etoile. There was not a waiter in the house who would not verify that statement on oath.

The reader may suppose that I had other motives, beside the desire to escape the tedious inquisition of the law, for desiring to recommence my journey to Paris with the least possible delay. Judge what was my horror then to learn, that for love or money, horses were nowhere to be had that night. The last pair in the town had been obtained from the Ecu de France, by a gentleman who dined and supped at the Belle Etoile, and was obliged to proceed to Paris that night.

Who was the gentleman? Had he actually gone? Could he possibly be induced to wait till morning?

The gentleman was now upstairs getting his things together, and his name was Monsieur Droqville.

I ran upstairs. I found my servant St. Clair in my room. At sight of him, for a moment, my thoughts were turned into a different channel.

"Well, St. Clair, tell me this moment who the lady is?" I demanded.

"The lady is the daughter or wife, it matters not which, of the Count de St. Alyre;—the old gentleman who was so near being sliced like a cucumber to-night, I am informed, by the sword of the general whom Monsieur, by a turn of fortune, has put to bed of an apoplexy."

"Hold your tongue, fool! The man's beastly drunk—he's sulking—he could talk if he liked—who cares? Pack up my things. Which are Monsieur Droqville's apartments?"

He knew, of course; he always knew everything.

Half an hour later Monsieur Droqville and I were travelling towards Paris, in my carriage, and with his horses. I ventured to ask the Marquis d'Harmonville, in a little while, whether the lady, who accompanied the Count, was certainly the Countess. "Has he not a daughter?"

"Yes;—I believe a very beautiful and charming young lady—I cannot say—it may have been she, his daughter by an earlier marriage. I saw only the Count himself to-day."

The Marquis was growing a little sleepy and, in a little while, he actually fell asleep in his corner. I dozed and nodded; but the Marquis slept like a top. He awoke only for a minute or two at the next posting-house, where he had fortunately secured horses by sending on his man, he told me.

"You will excuse my being so dull a companion," he said, "but till to-night I have had but two hours' sleep, for more than sixty hours. I shall have a cup of coffee here; I have had my nap. Permit me to recommend you to do likewise. Their coffee is really excellent." He ordered two cups of *café noir*, and waited, with his head from the window. "We will keep the cups," he said, as he received them from the waiter, "and the tray. Thank you."

There was a little delay as he paid for these things; and then he took in the little tray, and handed me a cup of coffee.

I declined the tray; so he placed it on his own knees, to act as a miniature table.

"I can't endure being waited for and hurried," he said, "I like to sip my coffee at leisure."

I agreed. It really *was* the very perfection of coffee.

"I, like Monsieur le Marquis, have slept very little for the last two or three nights; and find it difficult to keep awake. This coffee will do wonders for me; it refreshes one so."

Before we had half done, the carriage was again in motion.

For a time our coffee made us chatty, and our conversation was animated.

The Marquis was extremely good-natured, as well as clever, and gave me a brilliant and amusing account of Parisian life, schemes, and dangers, all put so as to furnish me with practical warnings of the most valuable kind.

In spite of the amusing and curious stories which the Marquis related, with so much point and colour, I felt myself again becoming gradually drowsy and dreamy.

Perceiving this, no doubt, the Marquis good-naturedly suffered our conversation to subside into silence. The window next him was open. He threw his cup out of it; and did the same kind office for mine, and finally the little tray flew after, and I heard it clank on the road; a valuable waif, no doubt, for some early wayfarer in wooden shoes.

I leaned back in my corner; I had my beloved *souvenir*—my white rose—close to my heart, folded, now, in white paper. It inspired all manner of romantic dreams. I began to grow more and more sleepy. But actual slumber did not come. I was still viewing, with my half-closed eyes, from my corner, diagonally, the interior of the carriage.

I wished for sleep; but the barrier between waking and sleeping seemed absolutely insurmountable; and instead, I entered into a state of novel and indescribable indolence.

The Marquis lifted his despatch-box from the floor, placed it on his knees, unlocked it, and took out what proved to be a lamp, which he hung with two hooks, attached to it, to the window opposite to him. He lighted it with a match, put on his spectacles, and taking out a bundle of letters, began to read them carefully.

We were making way very slowly. My impatience had hitherto employed four horses from stage to stage. We were in this emergency, only too happy to have secured two. But the difference in pace was depressing.

I grew tired of the monotony of seeing the spectacled Marquis reading, folding, and docketing, letter after letter. I wished to shut out the image which wearied me, but something prevented my being able to shut my eyes. I tried again and again; but, positively, I had lost the power of closing them.

I would have rubbed my eyes, but I could not stir my hand, my will no longer acted on my body—I found that I could not move one joint, or muscle, no more than I could, by an effort of my will, have turned the carriage about.

Up to this I had experienced no sense of horror. Whatever it was, simple nightmare was not the cause. I was awfully frightened! Was I in a fit?

It was horrible to see my good-natured companion pursue his occupation so serenely, when he might have dissipated my horrors by a single shake.

I made a stupendous exertion to call out but in vain; I repeated the effort again and again, with no result.

My companion now tied up his letters, and looked out of the window, humming an air from an opera. He drew back his head, and said, turning to me—

"Yes, I see the lights; we shall be there in two or three minutes."

He looked more closely at me, and with a kind smile, and a little shrug, he said, "Poor child! how fatigued he must have been—how profoundly he sleeps! when the carriage stops he will waken."

He then replaced his letters in the despatch-box, locked it, put his spectacles in his pocket, and again looked out of the window.

We had entered a little town. I suppose it was past two o'clock by this time. The carriage drew up, I saw an inn-door open, and a light issuing from it.

"Here we are!" said my companion, turning gaily to me. But I did not awake.

"Yes, how tired he must have been!" he exclaimed, after he had waited for an answer.

My servant was at the carriage door, and opened it.

"Your master sleeps soundly, he is so fatigued! It would be cruel to disturb him. You and I will go in, while they change the horses, and take some refreshment, and choose something that Monsieur Beckett will like to take in the carriage, for when he awakes by-and-by, he will, I am sure, be hungry."

He trimmed his lamp, poured in some oil; and taking care not to disturb me, with another kind smile, and another word or caution to my servant, he got out, and I heard him talking to St. Clair, as they entered the inn-door, and I was left in my corner, in the carriage, in the same state.

CHAPTER VIII.

A THREE MINUTES' VISIT.

I have suffered extreme and protracted bodily pain, at different periods of my life, but anything like that misery, thank God, I never endured before or since. I earnestly hope it may not resemble any type of death, to which we are liable. I was, indeed, a spirit in prison; and unspeakable was my dumb and unmoving agony.

The power of thought remained clear and active. Dull terror filled my mind. How would this end? Was it actual death?

You will understand that my faculty of observing was unimpaired. I could hear and see anything as distinctly as ever I did in my life. It was simply that my will had, as it were, lost its hold of my body.

I told you that the Marquis d'Harmonville had not extinguished his carriage lamp on going into this village inn. I was listening intently, longing for his return, which might result, by some lucky accident, in awaking me from my catalepsy.

Without any sound of steps approaching, to announce an arrival, the carriage-door suddenly opened, and a total stranger got in silently, and shut the door.

The lamp gave about as strong a light as a wax-candle, so I could see the intruder perfectly. He was a young man, with a dark grey, loose surtout, made with a sort of hood, which was pulled over his head. I thought, as he moved, that I saw the gold band of a military undress cap under it; and I certainly saw the lace and buttons of a uniform, on the cuffs of the coat that were visible under the wide sleeves of his outside wrapper.

This young man had thick moustaches, and an imperial, and I observed that he had a red scar running upward from his lip across his cheek.

He entered, shut the door softly, and sat down beside me. It was all done in a moment; leaning toward me, and shading his eyes with his gloved hand, he examined my face closely, for a few seconds.

This man had come as noiselessly as a ghost; and everything he did was accomplished with the rapidity and decision, that indicated a well defined and prearranged plan. His designs were evidently sinister. I thought he was going to rob, and, perhaps, murder me. I lay, nevertheless, like a corpse under his hands.

He inserted his hand in my breast pocket, from which he took my precious white rose and all the letters it contained, among which was a paper of some consequence to me.

My letters he glanced at. They were plainly not what he wanted. My precious rose, too, he laid aside with them. It was evidently about the paper I have mentioned, that he was concerned; for the moment he opened it, he began with a pencil, in a small pocket-book, to make rapid notes of its contents.

This man seemed to glide through his work with a noiseless and cool celerity which argued, I thought, the training of the police-department.

He re-arranged the papers, possibly in the very order in which he had found them, replaced them in my breast-pocket, and was gone.

His visit, I think, did not quite last three minutes. Very soon after his disappearance, I heard the voice of the Marquis once more. He got in, and I saw him look at me, and smile, half envying me, I fancied, my sound repose. If he had but known all!

He resumed his reading and docketing, by the light of the little lamp which had just subserved the purposes of a spy.

We were now out of the town, pursuing our journey at the same moderate pace. We had left the scene of my police visit, as I should have termed it, now two leagues behind us, when I suddenly felt a strange throbbing in one ear, and a sensation as if air passed through it into my throat. It seemed as if a bubble of air, formed deep in my ear, swelled, and burst there. The indescribable tension of my brain seemed all at once to give way; there was an odd humming in my head, and a sort of vibration through every nerve of my body, such as I have experienced in a limb that has been, in popular phraseology, asleep. I uttered a cry and half rose from my seat, and then fell back trembling, and with a sense of mortal faintness.

The Marquis stared at me, took my hand, and earnestly asked if I was ill. I could answer only with a deep groan.

Gradually the process of restoration was completed; and I was able, though very faintly, to tell him how very ill I had been; and then to describe the violation of my letters, during the time of his absence from the carriage.

"Good heaven!" he exclaimed, "the miscreant did not get at my dispatch-box?"

I satisfied him, so far as I had observed, on that point. He placed the box on the seat beside him, and opened and examined its contents very minutely.

"Yes, undisturbed; all safe, thank heaven!" he murmured. "There are half-a-dozen letters here, that I would not have some people read, for a great deal."

He now asked with a very kind anxiety all about the illness I complained of. When he had heard me, he said—

"A friend of mine once had an attack as like yours as possible. It was on board-ship, and followed a state of high excitement. He was a brave man like you; and was called on to exert both his strength and his courage suddenly. An hour or two after, fatigue overpowered him, and he appeared to fall into a sound sleep. He really sank into a state which he afterwards described so, that I think it must have been precisely the same affection as yours."

"I am happy to think that my attack was not unique. Did he ever experience a return of it."

"I knew him for years after, and never heard of any such thing. What strikes me is a parallel in the predisposing causes of each attack. Your unexpected, and gallant hand-to-hand encounter, at such desperate odds, with an experienced swordsman, like that insane colonel of dragoons, your fatigue, and, finally, your composing yourself, as my other friend did, to sleep."

"I wish," he resumed, "one could make out who that *coquin* was, who examined your letters. It is not worth turning back, however, because we should learn nothing. Those people always manage so adroitly. I am satisfied, however, that he must have been an agent of the police. A rogue of any other kind would have robbed you."

I talked very little, being ill and exhausted, but the Marquis talked on agreeably.

"We grow so intimate," said he, at last, "that I must remind you that I am not, for the present, the Marquis d'Harmonville, but only Monsieur Droqville; nevertheless, when we get to Paris, although I cannot see you often, I may be of use. I shall ask you to name to me the hotel at which you mean to put up; because the Marquis being, as you are aware, on his travels, the Hotel d'Harmonville is, for the present, tenanted only by two or three old servants, who must not even see Monsieur Droqville. That gentleman will, nevertheless, contrive to get you access to the box of Monsieur le Marquis, at the Opera; as well, possibly, as to other places more difficult; and so soon as the diplomatic office of the Marquis d'Harmonville is ended, and he at liberty to declare himself, he will not excuse his friend, Monsieur Beckett, from fulfilling his promise to visit him this autumn at the Château d'Harmonville."

You may be sure I thanked the Marquis.

The nearer we got to Paris, the more I valued his protection. The countenance of a great man on the spot, just then, taking so kind an interest in the stranger whom he had, as it were, blundered upon, might make my visit ever so many degrees more delightful than I had anticipated.

Nothing could be more gracious than the manner and looks of the Marquis; and, as I still thanked him, the carriage suddenly stopped in front of the place where a relay of horses awaited us, and where, as it turned out, we were to part.

CHAPTER IX.

GOSSIP AND COUNSEL.

My eventful journey was over, at last. I sat in my hotel window looking out upon brilliant Paris, which had, in a moment, recovered all its gaiety, and more than its accustomed bustle. Every one has read of the kind of excitement that followed the catastrophe of Napoleon, and the second restoration of the Bourbons. I need not, therefore, even if, at this distance, I could, recall and describe my experiences and impressions of the peculiar aspect of Paris, in those strange times. It was, to be sure, my first visit. But, often as I have seen it since, I don't think I ever saw that delightful capital in a state, pleasurably, so excited and exciting.

I had been two days in Paris, and had seen all sorts of sights, and experienced none of that rudeness and insolence of which others complained, from the exasperated officers of the defeated French army.

I must say this, also. My romance had taken complete possession of me; and the chance of seeing the object of my dream, gave a secret and delightful interest to my rambles and drives in the streets and environs, and my visits to the galleries and other sights of the metropolis.

I had neither seen nor heard of Count or Countess, nor had the Marquis d'Harmonville made any sign. I had quite recovered the strange indisposition under which I had suffered during my night journey.

It was now evening, and I was beginning to fear that my patrician acquaintance had quite forgotten me, when the waiter presented me the card of 'Monsieur Droqville;' and, with no small elation and hurry, I desired him to show the gentleman up.

In came the Marquis d'Harmonville, kind and gracious as ever.

"I am a night-bird at present," said he, so soon as we had exchanged the little speeches which are usual. "I keep in the shade, during the daytime, and even now I hardly ventured to come in a close carriage. The friends for whom I have undertaken a rather critical service, have so ordained it. They think all is lost, if I am known to be in Paris. First let me present you with these orders for my box. I am so vexed that I cannot command it oftener during the next fortnight; during my absence, I had directed my secretary to give it for any night to the first of my friends who might apply, and the result is, that I find next to nothing left at my disposal."

I thanked him very much.

"And now, a word, in my office of Mentor. You have not come here, of course, without introductions?"

I produced half-a-dozen letters, the addresses of which he looked at.

"Don't mind these letters," he said. "I will introduce you. I will take you myself from house to house. One friend at your side is worth many letters. Make no intimacies, no acquaintances, until then. You young men like best to exhaust the public amusements of a great city, before embarrassing yourself with the engagements of society. Go to all these. It will occupy you, day and night, for at least three weeks. When this is over, I shall be at liberty, and will myself introduce you to the brilliant but comparatively quiet routine of society. Place yourself in my hands; and in Paris remember, when once in society, you are always there."

I thanked him very much, and promised to follow his counsels implicitly.

He seemed pleased, and said—

"I shall now tell you some of the places you ought to go to. Take your map, and write letters or numbers upon the points I will indicate, and we will make out a little list. All the places that I shall mention to you are worth seeing."

In this methodical way, and with a great deal of amusing and scandalous anecdote, he furnished me with a catalogue and a guide, which, to a seeker of novelty and pleasure, was invaluable.

"In a fortnight, perhaps in a week," he said, "I shall be at leisure to be of real use to you. In the meantime, be on your guard. You must not play; you will be robbed if you do. Remember, you are surrounded, here, by plausible swindlers and villains of all kinds, who subsist by devouring strangers. Trust no one but those you know."

I thanked him again, and promised to profit by his advice. But my heart was too full of the beautiful lady of the Belle Etoile, to allow our interview to close without an effort to learn something about her. I therefore asked for the Count and Countess de St. Alyre, whom I had had the good fortune to extricate from an extremely unpleasant row in the hall of the inn.

Alas! he had not seen them since. He did not know where they were staying. They had a fine old house only a few leagues from Paris; but he thought it probable that they would remain, for a few days at least, in the city, as preparations would, no doubt, be necessary, after so long an absence, for their reception at home.

"How long have they been away?"

"About eight months, I think."

"They are poor, I think you said?"

"What *you* would consider poor. But, Monsieur, the Count has an income which affords them the comforts, and even the elegancies of life, living as they do, in a very quiet and retired way, in this cheap country."

"Then they are very happy?"

"One would say they *ought* to be happy."

"And what prevents?"

"He is jealous."

"But his wife—she gives him no cause?"

"I am afraid she does."

"How, Monsieur?"

"I always thought she was a little too—a *great deal* too—"

"Too *what*, Monsieur?"

"Too handsome. But although she has remarkably fine eyes, exquisite features, and the most delicate complexion in the world, I believe that she is a woman of probity. You have never seen her?"

"There was a lady, muffled up in a cloak, with a very thick veil on, the other night, in the hall of the Belle Etoile, when I broke that fellow's head who was bullying the old Count. But her veil was so thick I could not see a feature through it." My answer was diplomatic, you observe. "She may have been the Count's daughter. Do they quarrel?"

"Who, he and his wife?"

"Yes."

"A little."

"Oh! and what do they quarrel about?" "It is a long story; about the lady's diamonds. They are valuable—they are worth. La Perelleuse says, about a million of francs. The Count wishes them sold and turned into revenue, which he offers to settle as she pleases. The Countess, whose they are, resists, and for a reason which, I rather think, she can't disclose to him."

"And pray what is that?" I asked, my curiosity a good deal piqued.

"She is thinking, I conjecture, how well she will look in them when she marries her second husband."

"Oh?—yes, to be sure. But the Count de St. Alyre is a good man?"

"Admirable, and extremely intelligent."

"I should wish so much to be presented to the Count: you tell me he's so—"

"So agreeably married. But they are living quite out of the world. He takes her now and then to the Opera, or to a public entertainment; but that is all."

"And he must remember so much of the old *régime*, and so many of the scenes of the revolution!"

"Yes, the very man for a philosopher, like you! And he falls asleep after dinner; and his wife don't. But, seriously, he has retired from the gay and the great world, and has grown apathetic; and so has his wife; and nothing seems to interest her now, not even—her husband!"

The Marquis stood up to take his leave.

"Don't risk your money," said he. "You will soon have an opportunity of laying out some of it to great advantage. Several collections of really good pictures, belonging to persons who have mixed themselves up in this Bonapartist restoration, must come within a few weeks to the hammer. You can do wonders when these sales commence. There will be startling bargains! Reserve yourself for them. I shall let you know all about it. By-the-by," he said, stopping short as he approached the door, "I was so near forgetting. There is to be, next week, the very thing you would enjoy so much, because you see so little of it in England—I mean a *bal masqué*, conducted, it is said, with more than usual splendour. It takes place at Versailles—all the world will be there; there is such a rush for cards! But I think I may promise you one. Good-night! Adieu!"

CHAPTER X.

THE BLACK VEIL.

Speaking the language fluently and with unlimited money, there was nothing to prevent my enjoying all that was enjoyable in the French capital. You may easily suppose how two days were passed. At the end of that time, and at about the same hour, Monsieur Droqville called again.

Courtly, good-natured, gay, as usual, he told me that the masquerade ball was fixed for the next Wednesday, and that he had applied for a card for me.

How awfully unlucky. I was so afraid I should not be able to go.

He stared at me for a moment with a suspicious and menacing look which I did not understand, in silence, and then inquired, rather sharply.

"And will Monsieur Beckett be good enough to say, why not?"

I was a little surprised, but answered the simple truth: I had made an engagement for that evening with two or three English friends, and did not see how I could.

"Just so! You English, wherever you are, always look out for your English boors, your beer and '*bifstek*'; and when you come here, instead of trying to learn something of the people you visit, and pretend to study, you are guzzling, and swearing, and smoking with one another, and no wiser or more polished at the end of your travels than if you had been all the time carousing in a booth at Greenwich."

He laughed sarcastically, and looked as if he could have poisoned me.

"There it is," said he, throwing the card on the table. "Take it or leave it, just as you please. I suppose I shall have my trouble for my pains; but it is not usual when a man, such as I, takes trouble, asks a favour, and secures a privilege for an acquaintance, to treat him so."

This was astonishingly impertinent!

I was shocked, offended, penitent. I had possibly committed unwittingly a breach of good-breeding, according to French ideas, which almost justified the brusque severity of the Marquis's undignified rebuke.

In a confusion, therefore, of many feelings, I hastened to make my apologies, and to propitiate the chance friend who had showed me so much disinterested kindness.

I told him that I would, at any cost, break through the engagement in which I had unluckily entangled myself; that I had spoken with too little reflection, and that I certainly had not thanked him at all in proportion to his kindness and to my real estimate of it.

"Pray say not a word more; my vexation was entirely on your account; and I expressed it, I am only too conscious, in terms a great deal too strong, which, I am sure, your goodnature will pardon. Those who know me a little better are aware that I sometimes say a good deal more than I intend; and am always sorry when I do. Monsieur Beckett will forget that his old friend, Monsieur Droqville, has lost his temper in his cause, for a moment, and—we are as good friends as before."

He smiled like the Monsieur Droqville of the Belle Etoile, and extended his hand, which I took very respectfully and cordially.

Our momentary quarrel had left us only better friends.

The Marquis then told me I had better secure a bed in some hotel at Versailles, as a rush would be made to take them; and advised my going down next morning for the purpose.

I ordered horses accordingly for eleven o'clock; and, after a little more conversation, the Marquis d'Harmonville bid me good-night, and ran down the stairs with his handkerchief to his mouth and nose, and, as I saw from my window, jumped into his close carriage again and drove away.

Next day I was at Versailles. As I approached the door of the Hotel de France, it was plain that I was not a moment too soon, if, indeed, I were not already too late.

A crowd of carriages were drawn up about the entrance, so that I had no chance of approaching except by dismounting and pushing my way among the horses. The hall was full of servants and gentlemen screaming to the proprietor, who, in a state of polite distraction, was assuring them, one and all, that there was not a room or a closet disengaged in his entire house.

I slipped out again, leaving the hall to those who were shouting, expostulating, wheedling, in the delusion that the host might, if he pleased, manage something for them. I jumped into my carriage and drove, at my horses' best pace, to the Hotel du Reservoir. The blockade about this door was as complete as the other. The result was the same. It was very provoking, but what was to be done? My postillion had, a little officiously, while I was in the hall talking with the hotel authorities, got his horses, bit by bit, as other carriages moved away, to the very steps of the inn door.

This arrangement was very convenient so far as getting in again was concerned. But, this accomplished, how were we to get on? There were carriages in front, and carriages behind, and no less than four rows of carriages, of all sorts, outside.

I had at this time remarkably long and clear sight, and if I had been impatient before, guess what my feelings were when I saw an open carriage pass along the narrow strip of roadway left open at the other side, a barouche in which I was certain I recognized the veiled Countess and her husband. This carriage had been brought to a walk by a cart which occupied the whole breadth of the narrow way, and was moving with the customary tardiness of such vehicles.

I should have done more wisely if I had jumped down on the *trottoir*, and run round the block of carriages in front of the barouche. But, unfortunately, I was more of a Murat than a Moltke, and preferred a direct charge upon my object to relying on *tactique*. I dashed across the back seat of a carriage which was next mine, I don't know how; tumbled through a sort of gig, in which an old gentleman and a dog were dozing; stepped with an incoherent apology over the side of an open carriage, in which were four gentlemen engaged in a hot dispute; tripped at the far side in getting out, and fell flat across the backs of a pair of horses, who instantly began plunging and threw me head foremost in the dust.

To those who observed my reckless charge without being in the secret of my object I must have appeared demented. Fortunately, the interesting barouche had passed before the catastrophe, and covered as I was with dust, and my hat blocked, you may be sure I did not care to present myself before the object of my Quixotic devotion.

I stood for a while amid a storm of *sacré*-ing, tempered disagreeably with laughter; and in the midst of these, while endeavouring to beat the dust from my clothes with my handkerchief, I heard a voice with which I was acquainted call, "Monsieur Beckett."

I looked and saw the Marquis peeping from a carriage-window. It was a welcome sight. In a moment I was at his carriage side.

"You may as well leave Versailles," he said; "you have learned, no doubt, that there is not a bed to hire in either of the hotels; and I can add that there is not a room to let in the whole town. But I have managed something for you that will answer just as well. Tell your servant to follow us, and get in here and sit beside me."

Fortunately an opening in the closely-packed carriages had just occurred, and mine was approaching.

I directed the servant to follow us; and the Marquis having said a word to his driver, we were immediately in motion.

"I will bring you to a comfortable place, the very existence of which is known to but few Parisians, where, knowing how things were here, I secured a room for you. It is only a mile away, and an old comfortable inn, called Le Dragon Volant. It was fortunate for you that my tiresome business called me to this place so early."

I think we had driven about a mile-and-a-half to the further side of the palace when we found ourselves upon a narrow old road, with the woods of Versailles on one side, and much older trees, of a size seldom seen in France, on the other.

We pulled up before an antique and solid inn, built of Caen stone, in a fashion richer and more florid than was ever usual in such houses, and which indicated that it was originally designed for the private mansion of some person of wealth, and probably, as the wall bore many carved shields and supporters, of distinction also. A kind of porch, less ancient than the rest, projected hospitably with a wide and florid arch, over which, cut in high relief in stone, and painted and gilded, was the sign of the inn. This was the Flying Dragon, with wings of brilliant red and gold, expanded, and its tail, pale green and gold, twisted and knotted into ever so many rings, and ending in a burnished point barbed like the dart of death.

"I shan't go in—but you will find it a comfortable place; at all events better than nothing. I would go in with you, but my incognito forbids. You will, I daresay, be all the better pleased to learn that the inn is haunted—I should have been, in my young days, I know. But don't allude to that awful fact in hearing of your host, for I believe it is a sore subject. Adieu. If you want to enjoy yourself at the ball take my advice, and go in a domino. I think I shall look in; and certainly, if I do, in the same costume. How shall we recognize one another? Let me see, something held in the fingers—a flower won't do, so many people will have flowers. Suppose you get a red cross a couple of inches long—you're an Englishman—stitched or pinned on the breast of your domino, and I a white one? Yes, that will do very well; and whatever room you go into keep near the door till we meet. I shall look for you at all the doors I pass; and you, in the same way, for me; and we *must* find each other soon. So that is understood. I can't enjoy a thing of that kind with any but a young person; a man of my age requires the contagion of young spirits and the companionship of some one who enjoys everything spontaneously. Farewell; we meet to-night."

By this time I was standing *on* the road; I shut the carriage-door; bid him good-bye; and away he drove.

CHAPTER XI.

THE DRAGON VOLANT.

I took one look about me.

The building was picturesque; the trees made it more so. The antique and sequestered character of the scene, contrasted strangely with the glare and bustle of the Parisian life, to which my eye and ear had become accustomed.

Then I examined the gorgeous old sign for a minute or two. Next I surveyed the exterior of the house more carefully. It was large and solid, and squared more with my ideas of an ancient English hostelrie, such as the Canterbury pilgrims might have put up at, than a French house of entertainment. Except, indeed, for a round turret, that rose at the left flank of the house, and terminated in the extinguisher-shaped roof that suggests a French château.

I entered and announced myself as Monsieur Beckett, for whom a room had been taken. I was received with all the consideration due to an English milord, with, of course, an unfathomable purse.

My host conducted me to my apartment. It was a large room, a little sombre, panelled with dark wainscoting, and furnished in a stately and sombre style, long out of date. There was a wide hearth, and a heavy mantelpiece, carved with shields, in which I might, had I been curious enough, have discovered a correspondence with the heraldry on the outer walls. There was something interesting, melancholy, and even depressing in all this. I went to the stone-shafted window, and looked out upon a small park, with a thick wood, forming the background of a château, which presented a cluster of such conical-topped turrets as I have just now mentioned.

The wood and château were melancholy objects. They showed signs of neglect, and almost of decay; and the gloom of fallen grandeur, and a certain air of desertion hung oppressively over the scene.

I asked my host the name of the château.

"That, Monsieur, is the Château de la Carque," he answered.

"It is a pity it is so neglected," I observed. "I should say, perhaps, a pity that its proprietor is not more wealthy?"

"Perhaps so, Monsieur."

"*Perhaps*?"—I repeated, and looked at him. "Then I suppose he is not very popular."

"Neither one thing nor the other, Monsieur," he answered; "I meant only that we could not tell what use he might make of riches."

"And who is he?" I inquired.

"The Count de St. Alyre."

"Oh! The Count! You are quite sure?" I asked, very eagerly.

It was now the innkeeper's turn to look at me.

"*Quite* sure, Monsieur, the Count de St. Alyre."

"Do you see much of him in this part of the world?"

"Not a great deal, Monsieur; he is often absent for a considerable time."

"And is he poor?" I inquired.

"I pay rent to him for this house. It is not much; but I find he cannot wait long for it," he replied, smiling satirically.

"From what I have heard, however, I should think he cannot be very poor?" I continued.

"They say, Monsieur, he plays. I know not. He certainly is not rich. About seven months ago, a relation of his died in a distant place. His body was sent to the Count's house here, and by him buried in Père la Chaise, as the poor gentleman had desired. The Count was in profound affliction; although he got a handsome legacy, they say, by that death. But money never seems to do him good for any time."

"He is old, I believe?"

"Old? we call him the 'Wandering Jew,' except, indeed, that he has not always the five *sous* in his pocket. Yet, Monsieur, his courage does not fail him. He has taken a young and handsome wife."

"And, she?" I urged—

"Is the Countess de St. Alyre."

"Yes; but I fancy we may say something more? She has attributes?"

"Three, Monsieur, three, at least most amiable."

"Ah! And what are they?"

"Youth, beauty, and—diamonds."

I laughed. The sly old gentleman was foiling my curiosity.

"I see, my friend," said I, "you are reluctant—"

"To quarrel with the Count," he concluded. "True. You see, Monsieur, he could vex me in two or three ways; so could I him. But, on the whole, it is better each to mind his business, and to maintain peaceful relations; you understand."

It was, therefore, no use trying, at least for the present. Perhaps he had nothing to relate. Should I think differently, by-and-by, I could try the effect of a few Napoleons. Possibly he meant to extract them.

The host of the Dragon Volant was an elderly man, thin, bronzed, intelligent, and with an air of decision, perfectly military. I learned afterwards that he had served under Napoleon in his early Italian campaigns.

"One question, I think you may answer," I said, "without risking a quarrel. Is the Count at home?"

"He has many homes, I conjecture," said the host evasively. "But—but I think I may say, Monsieur, that he is, I believe, at present staying at the Château de la Carque."

I looked out of the window, more interested than ever, across the undulating grounds to the château, with its gloomy background of foliage.

"I saw him to-day, in his carriage at Versailles," I said.

"Very natural."

"Then his carriage and horses and servants are at the château?"

"The carriage he puts up here, Monsieur, and the servants are hired for the occasion. There is but one who sleeps at the château. Such a life must be terrifying for Madame the Countess," he replied.

"The old screw!" I thought. "By this torture, he hopes to extract her diamonds. What a life! What fiends to contend with—jealousy and extortion!"

The knight having made this speech to himself, cast his eyes once more upon the enchanter's castle, and heaved a gentle sigh—a sigh of longing, of resolution, and of love.

What a fool I was! and yet, in the sight of angels, are we any wiser as we grow older? It seems to me, only, that our illusions change as we go on; but, still, we are madmen all the same.

"Well, St. Clair," said I, as my servant entered, and began to arrange my things. "You have got a bed?"

"In the cock-loft, Monsieur, among the spiders, and, *par ma foi*! the cats and the owls. But we agree very well. *Vive la bagatelle*!"

"I had no idea it was so full."

"Chiefly the servants, Monsieur, of those persons who were fortunate enough to get apartments at Versailles."

"And what do you think of the Dragon Volant?"

"The Dragon Volant! Monsieur; the old fiery dragon! The devil himself, if all is true! On the faith of a Christian, Monsieur, they say that diabolical miracles have taken place in this house."

"What do you mean? *Revenants*?"

"Not at all, sir; I wish it was no worse. *Revenants*? No! People who have *never* returned—who vanished, before the eyes of half-a-dozen men, all looking at them."

"What do you mean, St. Clair? Let us hear the story, or miracle, or whatever it is."

"It is only this, Monsieur, that an ex-master-of-the-horse of the late king, who lost his head—Monsieur will have the goodness to recollect, in the revolution—being permitted by the Emperor to return to France, lived here in this hotel, for a month, and at the end of that time vanished, visibly, as I told you, before the faces of half-a-dozen credible witnesses! The other was a Russian nobleman, six feet high and upwards, who, standing in the centre of the room, downstairs, describing to seven gentlemen of unquestionable veracity, the last moments of Peter the Great, and having a glass of *eau de vie* in his left hand, and his *tasse de café*, nearly finished, in his right, in like manner vanished. His boots were found on the floor where he had been standing; and the gentleman at his right, found, to his astonishment, his cup of coffee in his fingers, and the gentleman at his left, his glass of *eau de vie*—"

"Which he swallowed in his confusion," I suggested.

"Which was preserved for three years among the curious articles of this house, and was broken by the *curé* while conversing with Mademoiselle Fidone in the housekeeper's room; but of the Russian nobleman himself, nothing more was ever seen or heard! *Parbleu!* when *we* go out of the Dragon Volant, I hope it may be by the door. I heard all this, Monsieur, from the postillion who drove us."

"Then it *must* be true!" said I, jocularly: but I was beginning to feel the gloom of the view, and of the chamber in which I stood; there had stolen over me, I know not how, a presentiment of evil; and my joke was with an effort, and my spirit flagged.

CHAPTER XII.

THE MAGICIAN.

No more brilliant spectacle than this masked ball could be imagined. Among other *salons* and galleries, thrown open, was the enormous perspective of the "Grande Galerie des Glaces," lighted up on that occasion with no less than four thousand wax candles, reflected and repeated by all the mirrors, so that the effect was almost dazzling. The grand suite of *salons* was thronged with masques, in every conceivable costume. There was not a single room deserted. Every place was animated with music, voices, brilliant colours, flashing jewels, the hilarity of extemporized comedy, and all the spirited incidents of a cleverly sustained masquerade. I had never seen before anything, in the least, comparable to this magnificent *fête*. I moved along, indolently, in my domino and mask, loitering, now and then, to enjoy a clever dialogue, a farcical song, or an amusing monologue, but, at the same time, keeping my eyes about me, lest my friend in the black domino, with the little white cross on his breast, should pass me by.

I had delayed and looked about me, specially, at every door I passed, as the Marquis and I had agreed; but he had not yet appeared.

While I was thus employed, in the very luxury of lazy amusement, I saw a gilded sedan chair, or, rather, a Chinese palanquin, exhibiting the fantastic exuberance of "Celestial" decoration, borne forward on gilded poles by four richly-dressed Chinese; one with a wand in his hand marched in front, and another behind; and a slight and solemn man, with a long black beard, a tall fez, such as a dervish is represented as wearing, walked close to its side. A strangely-embroidered robe fell over his shoulders, covered with hieroglyphic symbols; the embroidery was in black and gold, upon a variegated ground of brilliant colours. The robe was bound about his waist with a broad belt of gold, with cabalistic devices traced on it, in dark red and black; red stockings, and shoes embroidered with gold, and pointed and curved upward at the toes, in Oriental fashion, appeared below the skirt of the robe. The man's face was dark, fixed, and solemn, and his eyebrows black, and enormously heavy—he carried a singular-looking book under his arm, a wand of polished black wood in his other hand, and walked with his chin sunk on his breast, and his eyes fixed upon the floor. The man in front waved his wand right and left to clear the way for the advancing palanquin, the curtains of which were closed; and there was something so singular, strange, and solemn about the whole thing, that I felt at once interested.

I was very well pleased when I saw the bearers set down their burthen within a few yards of the spot on which I stood.

The bearers and the men with the gilded wands forthwith clapped their hands, and in silence danced round the palanquin a curious and half frantic dance, which was yet, as to figures and postures, perfectly methodical. This was soon accompanied by a clapping of hands and a ha-ha-ing, rhythmically delivered.

While the dance was going on a hand was lightly laid on my arm, and, looking round, a black domino with a white cross stood beside me.

"I am so glad I have found you," said the Marquis; "and at this moment. This is the best group in the rooms. *You* must speak to the wizard. About an hour ago I lighted upon them, in another *salon*, and consulted the oracle, by putting questions. I never was more amazed. Although his answers were a little disguised it was soon perfectly plain that he knew every detail about the business, which no one on earth had heard of but myself, and two or three other men, about the most cautious persons in France. I shall never forget that shock. I saw other people who consulted him, evidently as much surprised, and more frightened than I. I came with the Count St. Alyre and the Countess."

He nodded toward a thin figure, also in a domino. It was the Count.

"Come," he said to me, "I'll introduce you."

I followed, you may suppose, readily enough.

The Marquis presented me, with a very prettily turned allusion to my fortunate intervention in his favour at the Belle Etoile; and the Count overwhelmed me with polite speeches, and ended by saying, what pleased me better still:

"The Countess is near us, in the next *salon* but one, chatting with her old friend the Duchesse d'Argensaque; I shall go for her in a few minutes; and when I bring her here, she shall make your acquaintance; and thank you, also, for your assistance, rendered with so much courage when we were so very disagreeably interrupted."

"You must, positively, speak with the magician," said the Marquis to the Count de St. Alyre, "you will be so much amused. *I* did so; and, I assure you, I could not have anticipated such answers! I don't know what to believe."

"Really! Then, by all means, let us try," he replied.

We three approached, together, the side of the palanquin, at which the black-bearded magician stood.

A young man, in a Spanish dress, who, with a friend at his side, had just conferred with the conjuror, was saying, as he passed us by:

"Ingenious mystification! Who is that in the palanquin. He seems to know everybody."

The Count, in his mask and domino, moved along, stiffly, with us, toward the palanquin. A clear circle was maintained by the Chinese attendants, and the spectators crowded round in a ring.

One of these men—he who with a gilded wand had preceded the procession—advanced, extending his empty hand, palm upward.

"Money?" inquired the Count.

"Gold," replied the usher.

The Count placed a piece of money in his hand; and I and the Marquis were each called on in turn to do likewise as we entered the circle. We paid accordingly.

The conjuror stood beside the palanquin, its silk curtain in his hand; his chin sunk, with its long, jet-black beard, on his chest; the outer hand grasping the black wand, on which he leaned; his eyes were lowered, as before, to the ground; his face looked absolutely lifeless. Indeed, I never saw face or figure so moveless, except in death.

The first question the Count put, was—

"Am I married, or unmarried?"

The conjuror drew back the curtain quickly, and placed his ear toward a richly-dressed Chinese, who sat in the litter; withdrew his head, and closed the curtain again; and then answered—

"Yes."

The same preliminary was observed each time, so that the man with the black wand presented himself, not as a prophet, but as a medium; and answered, as it seemed, in the words of a greater than himself.

Two or three questions followed, the answers to which seemed to amuse the Marquis very much; but the point of which I could not see, for I knew next to nothing of the Count's peculiarities and adventures.

"Does my wife love me?" asked he, playfully.

"As well as you deserve."

"Whom do I love best in the world?"

"Self."

"Oh! That I fancy is pretty much the case with every one. But, putting myself out of the question, do I love anything on earth better than my wife?"

"Her diamonds."

"Oh!" said the Count.

The Marquis, I could see, laughed.

"Is it true," said the Count, changing the conversation peremptorily, "that there has been a battle in Naples?"

"No; in France."

"Indeed," said the Count, satirically, with a glance round. "And may I inquire between what powers, and on what particular quarrel?"

"Between the Count and Countess de St. Alyre, and about a document they subscribed on the 25th July, 1811."

The Marquis afterwards told me that this was the date of their marriage settlement.

The Count stood stock-still for a minute or so; and one could fancy that they saw his face flushing through his mask.

Nobody, but we two, knew that the inquirer was the Count de St. Alyre.

I thought he was puzzled to find a subject for his next question; and, perhaps, repented having entangled himself in such a colloquy. If so, he was relieved; for the Marquis, touching his arm, whispered—

"Look to your right, and see who is coming."

I looked in the direction indicated by the Marquis, and I saw a gaunt figure stalking toward us. It was not a masque. The face was broad, scarred, and white. In a word, it was the ugly face of Colonel Gaillarde, who, in the costume of a corporal of the Imperial Guard, with his left arm so adjusted as to look like a stump, leaving the lower part of the coat-sleeve empty, and pinned up to the breast. There were strips of very real sticking-plaster across his eyebrow and temple, where my stick had left its mark, to score, hereafter, among the more honourable scars of war.

CHAPTER XIII.

THE ORACLE TELLS ME WONDERS.

I forgot for a moment how impervious my mask and domino were to the hard stare of the old campaigner, and was preparing for an animated scuffle. It was only for a moment, of course; but the Count cautiously drew a little back as the gasconading corporal, in blue uniform, white vest, and white gaiters—for my friend Gaillarde was as loud and swaggering in his assumed character as in his real one of a colonel of dragoons—drew near. He had already twice all but got himself turned out of doors for vaunting the exploits of Napoleon le Grand, in terrific mock-heroics, and had very nearly come to hand-grips with a Prussian hussar. In fact, he would have been involved in several sanguinary rows already, had not his discretion reminded him that the object of his coming there at all, namely, to arrange a meeting with an affluent widow, on whom he believed he had made a tender impression, would not have been promoted by his premature removal from the festive scene, of which he was an ornament, in charge of a couple of gendarmes.

"Money! Gold! Bah! What money can a wounded soldier like your humble servant have amassed, with but his sword-hand left, which, being necessarily occupied, places not a finger at his command with which to scrape together the spoils of a routed enemy?"

"No gold from him," said the magician. "His scars frank him."

"Bravo, Monsieur le prophète! Bravissimo! Here I am. Shall I begin, mon *sorcier*, without further loss of time, to question your—"

Without waiting for an answer, he commenced, in Stentorian tones.

After half-a-dozen questions and answers, he asked—

"Whom do I pursue at present?"

"Two persons."

"Ha! Two? Well, who are they?"

"An Englishman, whom, if you catch, he will kill you; and a French widow, whom if you find, she will spit in your face."

"Monsieur le magicien calls a spade a spade, and knows that his cloth protects him. No matter! Why do I pursue them?"

"The widow has inflicted a wound on your heart, and the Englishman a wound on your head. They are each separately too strong for you; take care your pursuit does not unite them."

"Bah! How could that be?"

"The Englishman protects ladies. He has got that fact into your head. The widow, if she sees, will marry him. It takes some time, she will reflect, to become a colonel, and the Englishman is unquestionably young."

"I will cut his cock's-comb for him," he ejaculated with an oath and a grin; and in a softer tone he asked, "Where is she?"

"Near enough to be offended if you fail."

"So she ought, by my faith. You are right, Monsieur le prophète! A hundred thousand thanks! Farewell!" And staring about him, and stretching his lank neck as high as he could, he strode away with his scars, and white waistcoat and gaiters, and his bearskin shako.

I had been trying to see the person who sat in the palanquin. I had only once an opportunity of a tolerably steady peep. What I saw was singular. The oracle was dressed, as I have said, very richly, in the Chinese fashion. He was a figure altogether on a larger scale than the interpreter, who stood outside. The features seemed to me large and heavy, and the head was carried with a downward inclination! the eyes were closed, and the chin rested on the breast of his embroidered pelisse. The face seemed fixed, and the very image of apathy. Its character and *pose* seemed an exaggerated repetition of the immobility of the figure who communicated with the noisy outer world. This face looked blood-red; but that was caused, I concluded, by the light entering through the red silk curtains. All this struck me almost at a glance; I had not many seconds in which to make my observation. The ground was now clear, and the Marquis said, "Go forward, my friend."

I did so. When I reached the magician, as we called the man with the black wand, I glanced over my shoulder to see whether the Count was near.

No, he was some yards behind; and he and the Marquis, whose curiosity seemed to be, by this time, satisfied, were now conversing generally upon some subject of course quite different.

I was relieved, for the sage seemed to blurt out secrets in an unexpected way; and some of mine might not have amused the Count.

I thought for a moment. I wished to test the prophet. A Church-of-England man was a *rara avis* in Paris.

"What is my religion?" I asked.

"A beautiful heresy," answered the oracle instantly.

"A heresy?—and pray how is it named?"

"Love."

"Oh! Then I suppose I am a polytheist, and love a great many?"

"One."

"But, seriously," I asked, intending to turn the course of our colloquy a little out of an embarrassing channel, "have I ever learned any words of devotion by heart?"

"Yes."

"Can you repeat them?"

"Approach."

I did, and lowered my ear.

The man with the black wand closed the curtains, and whispered, slowly and distinctly, these words, which, I need scarcely tell you, I instantly recognized:

I may never see you more; and, oh! that I could forget you! go—farewell—for God's sake, go!

I started as I heard them. They were, you know, the last words whispered to me by the Countess.

Good Heaven! How miraculous! Words heard, most assuredly, by no ear on earth but my own and the lady's who uttered them, till now!

I looked at the impassive face of the spokesman with the wand. There was no trace of meaning, or even of a consciousness that the words he had uttered could possibly interest me.

"What do I most long for?" I asked, scarcely knowing what I said.

"Paradise."

"And what prevents my reaching it?"

"A black veil."

Stronger and stronger! The answers seemed to me to indicate the minutest acquaintance with every detail of my little romance, of which not even the Marquis knew anything! And I, the questioner, masked and robed so that my own brother could not have known me!

"You said I loved some one. Am I loved in return?" I asked.

"Try."

I was speaking lower than before, and stood near the dark man with the beard, to prevent the necessity of his speaking in a loud key.

"Does any one love me?" I repeated.

"Secretly," was the answer.

"Much or little?" I inquired.

"Too well."

"How long will that love last?"

"Till the rose casts its leaves."

"The rose—another allusion!"

"Then—darkness!" I sighed. "But till then I live in light."

"The light of violet eyes."

Love, if not a religion, as the oracle had just pronounced it, is, at least, a superstition. How it exalts the imagination! How it enervates the reason! How credulous it makes us!

All this which, in the case of another, I should have laughed at, most powerfully affected me in my own. It inflamed my ardour, and half crazed my brain, and even influenced my conduct.

The spokesman of this wonderful trick—if trick it were—now waved me backward with his wand, and as I withdrew, my eyes still fixed upon the group, by this time encircled with an aura of mystery in my fancy; backing toward the ring of spectators, I saw him raise his hand suddenly, with a gesture of command, as a signal to the usher who carried the golden wand in front.

The usher struck his wand on the ground, and, in a shrill voice, proclaimed; "The great Confu is silent for an hour."

Instantly the bearers pulled down a sort of blind of bamboo, which descended with a sharp clatter, and secured it at the bottom; and then the man in the tall fez, with the black beard and wand, began a sort of dervish dance. In this the men with the gold wands joined, and finally, in an outer ring, the bearers, the palanquin being the centre of the circles described by these solemn dancers, whose pace, little by little, quickened, whose gestures grew sudden, strange, frantic, as the motion became swifter and swifter, until at length the whirl became so rapid that the dancers seemed to fly by with the speed of a mill-wheel, and amid a general clapping of hands, and universal wonder, these strange performers mingled with the crowd, and the exhibition, for the time at least, ended.

The Marquis d'Harmonville was standing not far away, looking on the ground, as one could judge by his attitude and musing. I approached, and he said:

"The Count has just gone away to look for his wife. It is a pity she was not here to consult the prophet, it would have been amusing, I daresay, to see how the Count bore it. Suppose we follow him. I have asked him to introduce you."

With a beating heart, I accompanied the Marquis d'Harmonville.

CHAPTER XIV.

MADEMOISELLE DE LA VALLIÈRE.

We wandered through the salons, the Marquis and I. It was no easy matter to find a friend in rooms so crowded.

"Stay here," said the Marquis, "I have thought of a way of finding him. Besides, his jealousy may have warned him that there is no particular advantage to be gained by presenting you to his wife, I had better go and reason with him; as you seem to wish an introduction so very much."

This occurred in the room that is now called the "Salon d'Apollon." The paintings remained in my memory, and my adventure of that evening was destined to occur there.

I sat down upon a sofa; and looked about me. Three or four persons beside myself were seated on this roomy piece of gilded furniture. They were chatting all very gaily; all—except the person who sat next me, and she was a lady. Hardly two feet interposed between us. The lady sat apparently in a reverie. Nothing could be more graceful. She wore the costume perpetuated in Collignan's full-length portrait of Mademoiselle de la Vallière. It is, as you know, not only rich, but elegant. Her hair was powdered, but one could perceive that it was naturally a dark brown. One pretty little foot appeared, and could anything be more exquisite than her hand?

It was extremely provoking that this lady wore her mask, and did not, as many did, hold it for a time in her hand.

I was convinced that she was pretty. Availing myself of the privilege of a masquerade, a microcosm in which it is impossible, except by voice and allusion, to distinguish friend from foe, I spoke—

"It is not easy, Mademoiselle, to deceive me," I began.

"So much the better for Monsieur," answered the mask, quietly.

"I mean," I said, determined to tell my fib, "that beauty is a gift more difficult to conceal than Mademoiselle supposes."

"Yet Monsieur has succeeded very well," she said in the same sweet and careless tones.

"I see the costume of this, the beautiful Mademoiselle de la Vallière, upon a form that surpasses her own; I raise my eyes, and I behold a mask, and yet I recognise the lady; beauty is like that precious stone in the 'Arabian Nights,' which emits, no matter how concealed, a light that betrays it."

"I know the story," said the young lady. "The light betrayed it, not in the sun, but in darkness. Is there so little light in these rooms, Monsieur, that a poor glowworm can show so brightly. I thought we were in a luminous atmosphere, wherever a certain countess moved?"

Here was an awkward speech! How was I to answer? This lady might be, as they say some ladies are, a lover of mischief, or an intimate of the Countess de St. Alyre. Cautiously, therefore, I inquired,

"What countess?"

"If you know me, you must know that she is my dearest friend. Is she not beautiful?"

"How can I answer, there are so many countesses."

"Every one who knows me, knows who my best beloved friend is. You don't know me?"

"That is cruel. I can scarcely believe I am mistaken."

"With whom were you walking, just now?" she asked.

"A gentleman, a friend," I answered.

"I saw him, of course, a friend; but I think I know him, and should like to be certain. Is he not a certain marquis?"

Here was another question that was extremely awkward.

"There are so many people here, and one may walk, at one time, with one, and at another with a different one, that—"

"That an unscrupulous person has no difficulty in evading a simple question like mine. Know then, once for all, that nothing disgusts a person of spirit so much as suspicion. You, Monsieur, are a gentleman of discretion. I shall respect you accordingly."

"Mademoiselle would despise me, were I to violate a confidence."

"But you don't deceive me. You imitate your friend's diplomacy. I hate diplomacy. It means fraud and cowardice. Don't you think I know him. The gentleman with the cross of white ribbon on his breast. I know the Marquis d'Harmonville perfectly. You see to what good purpose your ingenuity has been expended."

"To that conjecture I can answer neither yes nor no."

"You need not. But what was your motive in mortifying a lady?"

"It is the last thing on earth I should do."

"You affected to know me, and you don't; through caprice or listlessness or curiosity you wished to converse, not with a lady, but with a costume. You admired, and you pretend to mistake me for another. But who is quite perfect? Is truth any longer to be found on earth?"

"Mademoiselle has formed a mistaken opinion of me."

"And you also of me; you find me less foolish than you supposed. I know perfectly whom you intend amusing with compliments and melancholy declamation, and whom, with that amiable purpose, you have been seeking."

"Tell me whom you mean," I entreated.

"Upon one condition."

"What is that?"

"That you will confess if I name the lady."

"You describe my object unfairly." I objected. "I can't admit that I proposed speaking to any lady in the tone you describe."

"Well, I shan't insist on that; only if I name the lady, you will promise to admit that I am right."

"*Must* I promise?"

"Certainly not, there is no compulsion; but your promise is the only condition on which I will speak to you again."

I hesitated for a moment; but how could she possibly tell? The Countess would scarcely have admitted this little romance to any one; and the mask in the La Vallière costume could not possibly know who the masked domino beside her was.

"I consent," I said, "I promise."

"You must promise on the honour of a gentleman."

"Well, I do; on the honour of a gentleman."

"Then this lady is the Countess de St. Alyre." I was unspeakably surprised; I was disconcerted; but I remembered my promise, and said—

"The Countess de St. Alyre *is*, unquestionably, the lady to whom I hoped for an introduction to-night, but I beg to assure you also on the honour of a gentleman, that she has not the faintest imaginable suspicion that I was seeking such an honour, nor, in all probability, does she remember that such a person as I exists. I had the honour to render her and the Count a trifling service, too trifling, I fear, to have earned more than an hour's recollection."

"The world is not so ungrateful as you suppose; or if it be, there are, nevertheless, a few hearts that redeem it. I can answer for the Countess de St. Alyre, she never forgets a kindness. She does not show all she feels; for she is unhappy, and cannot."

"Unhappy! I feared, indeed, that might be. But for all the rest that you are good enough to suppose, it is but a flattering dream."

"I told you that I am the Countess's friend, and being so I must know something of her character; also, there are confidences between us, and I may know more than you think, of those trifling services of which you suppose the recollection is so transitory."

I was becoming more and more interested. I was as wicked as other young men, and the heinousness of such a pursuit was as nothing, now that self-love and all the passions that mingle in such a romance, were roused. The image of the beautiful Countess had now again quite superseded the pretty counterpart of La Vallière, who was before me. I would have given a great deal to hear, in solemn earnest, that she did remember the champion who, for her sake, had thrown himself before the sabre of an enraged dragoon, with only a cudgel in his hand, and conquered.

"You say the Countess is unhappy," said I. "What causes her unhappiness?"

"Many things. Her husband is old, jealous, and tyrannical. Is not that enough? Even when relieved from his society, she is lonely."

"But you are her friend?" I suggested.

"And you think one friend enough?" she answered; "she has one alone, to whom she can open her heart."

"Is there room for another friend?"

"Try."

"How can I find a way?"

"She will aid you."

"How?"

She answered by a question. "Have you secured rooms in either of the hotels of Versailles?"

"No, I could not. I am lodged in the Dragon Volant, which stands at the verge of the grounds of the Château de la Carque."

"That is better still. I need not ask if you have courage for an adventure. I need not ask if you are a man of honour. A lady may trust herself to you, and fear nothing. There are few men to whom the interview, such as I shall arrange, could be granted with safety. You shall meet her at two o'clock this morning in the Park of the Château de la Carque. What room do you occupy in the Dragon Volant?"

I was amazed at the audacity and decision of this girl. Was she, as we say in England, hoaxing me?

"I can describe that accurately," said I. "As I look from the rear of the house, in which my apartment is, I am at the extreme right, next the angle; and one pair of stairs up, from the hall."

"Very well; you must have observed, if you looked into the park, two or three clumps of chestnut and lime-trees, growing so close together as to form a small grove. You must return to your hotel, change your dress, and, preserving a scrupulous secrecy, as to why or where you go, leave the Dragon Volant, and climb the park-wall, unseen; you will easily recognize the grove I have mentioned; there you will meet the Countess, who will grant you an audience of a few minutes, who will expect the most scrupulous reserve on your part, and who will explain to you, in a few words, a great deal which *I* could not so well tell you here."

I cannot describe the feeling with which I heard these words. I was astounded. Doubt succeeded. I could not believe these agitating words.

"Mademoiselle will believe that if I only dared assure myself that so great a happiness and honour were really intended for me, my gratitude would be as lasting as my life. But how dare I believe that Mademoiselle does not speak, rather from her own sympathy or goodness, than from a certainty that the Countess de St. Alyre would concede so great an honour?"

"Monsieur believes either that I am not, as I pretend to be, in the secret which he hitherto supposed to be shared by no one but the Countess and himself, or else that I am cruelly mystifying him. That I am in her confidence, I swear by all that is dear in a whispered farewell. By the last companion of this flower!" and she took for a moment in her fingers the nodding head of a white rosebud that was nestled in her bouquet. "By my own good star, and hers—or shall I call it our '*belle* étoile?' Have I said enough?"

"Enough?" I repeated, "more than enough—a thousand thanks."

"And being thus in her confidence, I am clearly her friend; and being a friend would it be friendly to use her dear name so; and all for sake of practising a vulgar trick upon you—a stranger?"

"Mademoiselle will forgive me. Remember how very precious is the hope of seeing, and speaking to the Countess. Is it wonderful, then, that I should falter in my belief? You have convinced me, however, and will forgive my hesitation."

"You will be at the place I have described, then, at two o'clock?"

"Assuredly," I answered.

"And Monsieur, I know, will not fail, through fear. No, he need not assure me; his courage is already proved."

"No danger, in such a case, will be unwelcome to me."

"Had you not better go now, Monsieur, and rejoin your friend?"

"I promised to wait here for my friend's return. The Count de St. Alyre said that he intended to introduce me to the Countess."

"And Monsieur is so simple as to believe him?"

"Why should I not?"

"Because he is jealous and cunning. You will see. He will never introduce you to his wife. He will come here and say he cannot find her, and promise another time."

"I think I see him approaching, with my friend. No—there is no lady with him."

"I told you so. You will wait a long time for that happiness, if it is never to reach you except through his hands. In the meantime, you had better not let him see you so near me. He will suspect that we have been talking of his wife; and that will whet his jealousy and his vigilance."

I thanked my unknown friend in the mask, and withdrawing a few steps, came, by a little "circumbendibus," upon the flank of the Count.

I smiled under my mask, as he assured me that the Duchesse de la Roqueme had changed her place, and taken the Countess with her; but he hoped, at some very early time, to have an opportunity of enabling her to make my acquaintance.

I avoided the Marquis d'Harmonville, who was following the Count. I was afraid he might propose accompanying me home, and had no wish to be forced to make an explanation.

I lost myself quickly, therefore, in the crowd, and moved, as rapidly as it would allow me, toward the Galerie des Glaces, which lay in the direction opposite to that in which I saw the Count and my friend the Marquis moving.

CHAPTER XV.

STRANGE STORY OF THE DRAGON VOLANT.

These *fêtes* were earlier in those days, and in France, than our modern balls are in London. I consulted my watch. It was a little past twelve.

It was a still and sultry night; the magnificent suite of rooms, vast as some of them were, could not be kept at a temperature less than oppressive, especially to people with masks on. In some places the crowd was inconvenient, and the profusion of lights added to the heat. I removed my mask, therefore, as I saw some other people do, who were as careless of mystery as I. I had hardly done so, and began to breathe more comfortably, when I heard a friendly English voice call me by my name. It was Tom Whistlewick, of the — th Dragoons. He had unmasked, with a very flushed face, as I did. He was one of those Waterloo heroes, new from the mint of glory, whom, as a body, all the world, except France, revered; and the only thing I knew against him, was a habit of allaying his thirst, which was excessive, at balls, *fêtes*, musical parties, and all gatherings, where it was to be had, with champagne; and, as he introduced me to his friend, Monsieur Carmaignac, I observed that he spoke a little thick. Monsieur Carmaignac was little, lean, and as straight as a ramrod. He was bald, took snuff, and wore spectacles; and, as I soon learned, held an official position.

Tom was facetious, sly, and rather difficult to understand, in his present pleasant mood. He was elevating his eyebrows and screwing his lips oddly, and fanning himself vaguely with his mask.

After some agreeable conversation, I was glad to observe that he preferred silence, and was satisfied with the *rôle* of listener, as I and Monsieur Carmaignac chatted; and he seated himself, with extraordinary caution and indecision, upon a bench, beside us, and seemed very soon to find a difficulty in keeping his eyes open.

"I heard you mention," said the French gentleman, "that you had engaged an apartment in the Dragon Volant, about half a league from this. When I was in a different police department, about four years ago, two very strange cases were connected with that house. One was of a wealthy *émigré*, permitted to return to

France, by the Em—by Napoleon. He vanished. The other—equally strange—was the case of a Russian of rank and wealth. He disappeared just as mysteriously."

"My servant," I said, "gave me a confused account of some occurrences, and, as well as I recollect he described the same persons—I mean a returned French nobleman, and a Russian gentleman. But he made the whole story so marvellous—I mean in the supernatural sense—that, I confess, I did not believe a word of it."

"No, there was nothing supernatural; but a great deal inexplicable," said the French gentleman. "Of course there may be theories; but the thing was never explained, nor, so far as I know, was a ray of light ever thrown upon it."

"Pray let me hear the story," I said. "I think I have a claim, as it affects my quarters. You don't suspect the people of the house?"

"Oh! it has changed hands since then. But there seemed to be a fatality about a particular room."

"Could you describe that room?"

"Certainly. It is a spacious, panelled bed-room, up one pair of stairs, in the back of the house, and at the extreme right, as you look from its windows."

"Ho! Really? Why, then, I have got the very room!" I said, beginning to be more interested—perhaps the least bit in the world, disagreeably. "Did the people die, or were they actually spirited away?"

"No, they did not die—they disappeared very oddly. I'll tell you the particulars—I happen to know them exactly, because I made an official visit, on the first occasion, to the house, to collect evidence; and although I did not go down there, upon the second, the papers came before me, and I dictated the official letter despatched to the relations of the people who had disappeared; they had applied to the government to investigate, the affair. We had letters from the same relations more than two years later, from which we learned that the missing men had never turned up."

He took a pinch of snuff, and looked steadily at me.

"Never! I shall relate all that happened, so far as we could discover. The French noble, who was the Chevalier Chateau Blassemare, unlike most *émigrés*, had taken the matter in time, sold a large portion of his property before the revolution had proceeded so far as to render that next to impossible, and retired with a large sum. He brought with him about half a million of francs, the greater part of which he invested in the French funds; a much larger sum remained in Austrian land and securities. You will observe then that this gentleman was rich, and there was no allegation of his having lost money, or being, in any way, embarrassed. You see?"

I assented.

"This gentleman's habits were not expensive in proportion to his means. He had suitable lodgings in Paris; and for a time, society, the theatres, and other reasonable amusements, engrossed him. He did not play. He was a middle-aged man, affecting youth, with the vanities which are usual in such persons; but, for the rest, he was a gentle and polite person, who disturbed nobody—a person, you see, not likely to provoke an enmity."

"Certainly not," I agreed.

"Early in the summer of 1811, he got an order permitting him to copy a picture in one of these *salons*, and came down here, to Versailles, for the purpose. His work was getting on slowly. After a time he left his hotel, here, and went, by way of change, to the Dragon Volant: there he took, by special choice, the bed-room which has fallen to you by chance. From this time, it appeared, he painted little; and seldom visited his apartments in Paris. One night he saw the host of the Dragon Volant, and told him that he was going into Paris, to remain for a day or two, on very particular business; that his servant would accompany him, but that he would retain his apartments at the Dragon Volant, and return in a few days. He left some clothes there, but packed a portmanteau, took his dressing-case, and the rest, and, with his servant behind his carriage, drove into Paris. You observe all this, Monsieur?"

"Most attentively," I answered.

"Well, Monsieur, as soon as they were approaching his lodgings, he stopped the carriage on a sudden, told his servant that he had changed his mind; that he would sleep elsewhere that night, that he had very particular business in the north of France, not far from Rouen, that he would set out before daylight on his journey, and return in a fortnight. He called a *fiacre*, took in his hand a leather bag which, the servant said, was just large enough to hold a few shirts and a coat, but that it was enormously heavy, as he could testify, for he held it in his hand, while his master took out his purse to count thirty six Napoleons, for which the servant was to account when he should return. He then sent him on, in the carriage; and he, with the bag I have mentioned, got into the *fiacre*. Up to that, you see, the narrative is quite clear."

"Perfectly," I agreed.

"Now comes the mystery," said Monsieur Carmaignac. "After that, the Count Chateau Blassemare was never more seen, so far as we can make out, by acquaintance or friend. We learned that the day before the Count's stockbroker had, by his direction, sold all his stock in the French funds, and handed him the cash it realized. The reason he gave him for this measure tallied with what he said to his servant. He told him that he was going to the north of France to settle some claims, and did not know exactly how much might be required. The bag, which had puzzled the servant by its weight, contained, no doubt, a large sum in gold. Will Monsieur try my snuff?"

He politely tendered his open snuff-box, of which I partook, experimentally.

"A reward was offered," he continued, "when the inquiry was instituted, for any information tending to throw a light upon the mystery, which might be afforded by the driver of the *fiacre* 'employed on the night of' (so-and-so), 'at about the hour of half-past ten, by a gentleman, with a black-leather travelling-bag in his hand, who descended from a private carriage, and gave his servant some money, which he counted twice over.' About a hundred-and-fifty drivers applied, but not one of them was the right man. We did, however, elicit a curious and unexpected piece of evidence in quite another quarter. What a racket that plaguey harlequin makes with his sword!"

"Intolerable!" I chimed in.

The harlequin was soon gone, and he resumed.

"The evidence I speak of, came from a boy, about twelve years old, who knew the appearance of the Count perfectly, having been often employed by him as a messenger. He stated that about half-past twelve o'clock, on the same night—upon which you are to observe, there was a brilliant moon—he was sent, his mother having been suddenly taken ill, for the *sage femme* who lived within a stone's throw of the Dragon Volant. His father's house, from which he started, was a mile away, or more, from that inn, in order to reach which he had to pass round the park of the Château de la Carque, at the site most remote from the point to which he was going. It passes the old churchyard of St. Aubin, which is separated from the road only by a very low fence, and two or three enormous old trees. The boy was a little nervous as he approached this ancient cemetery; and, under the bright moonlight, he saw a man whom he distinctly recognised as the Count, whom they designated by a soubriquet which means 'the man of smiles.' He was looking rueful enough now, and was seated on the side of a tombstone, on which he had laid a pistol, while he was ramming home the charge of another.

"The boy got cautiously by, on tip-toe, with his eyes all the time on the Count Chateau Blassemare, or the man he mistook for him; his dress was not what he usually wore, but the witness swore that he could not be mistaken as to his identity. He said his face looked grave and stern; but though he did not smile, it was the same face he knew so well. Nothing would make him swerve from that. If that were he, it was the last time he was seen. He has never been heard of since. Nothing could be heard of him in the neighbourhood of Rouen. There has been no evidence of his death; and there is no sign that he is living."

"That certainly is a most singular case," I replied; and was about to ask a question or two, when Tom Whistlewick who, without my observing it, had been taking a ramble, returned, a great deal more awake, and a great deal less tipsy.

"I say, Carmaignac, it is getting late, and I must go; I really must, for the reason I told you—and, Beckett, we must soon meet again."

"I regret very much, Monsieur, my not being able at present to relate to you the other case, that of another tenant of the very same room—a case more mysterious and sinister than the last—and which occurred in the autumn of the same year."

"Will you both do a very good-natured thing, and come and dine with me at the Dragon Volant to-morrow?"

So, as we pursued our way along the Galerie des Glaces, I extracted their promise.

"By Jove!" said Whistlewick, when this was done; "look at that pagoda, or sedan chair, or whatever it is, just where those fellows set it down, and not one of them near it! I can't imagine how they tell fortunes so devilish well. Jack Nuffles—I met him here to-night—says they are gipsies—where are they, I wonder? I'll go over and have a peep at the prophet."

I saw him plucking at the blinds, which were constructed something on the principle of Venetian blinds; the red curtains were inside; but they did not yield, and he could only peep under one that did not come quite down.

When he rejoined us, he related: "I could scarcely see the old fellow, it's so dark. He is covered with gold and red, and has an embroidered hat on like a mandarin's; he's fast asleep; and, by Jove, he smells like a pole-cat! It's worth going over only to have it to say. Fiew! pooh! oh! It *is* a perfume. Faugh!"

Not caring to accept this tempting invitation, we got along slowly toward the door. I bid them good-night, reminding them of their promise. And so found my way at last to my carriage; and was soon rolling slowly toward the Dragon Volant, on the loneliest of roads, under old trees, and the soft moonlight.

What a number of things had happened within the last two hours! what a variety of strange and vivid pictures were crowded together in that brief space! What an adventure was before me!

The silent, moonlighted, solitary road, how it contrasted with the many-eddied whirl of pleasure from whose roar and music, lights, diamonds and colours, I had just extricated myself.

The sight of lonely Nature at such an hour, acts like a sudden sedative. The madness and guilt of my pursuit struck me with a momentary compunction and horror. I wished I had never entered the labyrinth which was leading me, I knew not whither. It was too late to think of that now; but the bitter was already stealing into my cup; and vague anticipations lay, for a few minutes, heavy on my heart. It would not have taken much to make me disclose my unmanly state of mind to my lively friend, Alfred Ogle, nor even to the milder ridicule of the agreeable Tom Whistlewick.

CHAPTER XVI.

THE PARC OF THE CHATEAU DE LA CARQUE.

There was no danger of the Dragon Volant's closing its doors on that occasion till three or four in the morning. There were quartered there many servants of great people, whose masters would not leave the ball till the last moment, and who could not return to their corners in the Dragon Volant, till their last services had been rendered.

I knew, therefore, I should have ample time for my mysterious excursion without exciting curiosity by being shut out.

And now we pulled up under the canopy of boughs, before the sign of the Dragon Volant, and the light that shone from its hall door.

I dismissed my carriage, ran up the broad staircase, mask in hand, with my domino fluttering about me, and entered the large bed-room. The black wainscoting and stately furniture, with the dark curtains of the very tall bed, made the night there more sombre.

An oblique patch of moonlight was thrown upon the floor from the window to which I hastened. I looked out upon the landscape slumbering in those silvery beams. There stood the outline of the Château de la Carque, its chimneys, and many turrets with their extinguisher-shaped roofs black against the soft grey sky. There, also, more in the foreground, about midway between the window where I stood, and the château, but a little to the left, I traced the tufted masses of the grove which the lady in the mask had appointed as the trysting-place, where I and the beautiful Countess were to meet that night.

I took "the bearings" of this gloomy bit of wood, whose foliage glimmered softly at top in the light of the moon.

You may guess with what a strange interest and swelling of the heart I gazed on the unknown scene of my coming adventure.

But time was flying, and the hour already near. I threw my robe upon a sofa; I groped out a pair of boots, which I substituted for those thin heelless shoes, in those days called "pumps," without which a gentleman could not attend an evening party. I put on my hat, and lastly, I took a pair of loaded pistols which I had been advised were satisfactory companions in the then unsettled state of French society: swarms of disbanded soldiers, some of them alleged to be desperate characters, being everywhere to be met with. These preparations made, I confess I took a looking-glass to the window to see how I looked in the moonlight; and being satisfied, I replaced it, and ran downstairs.

In the hall I called for my servant.

"St. Clair," said I; "I mean to take a little moonlight ramble, only ten minutes or so. You must not go to bed until I return. If the night is very beautiful, I may possibly extend my ramble a little."

So down the steps I lounged, looking first over my right, and then over my left shoulder, like a man uncertain which direction to take, and I sauntered up the road, gazing now at the moon, and now at the thin white clouds in the opposite direction, whistling, all the time, an air which I had picked up at one of the theatres.

When I had got a couple of hundred yards away from the Dragon Volant, my minstrelsy totally ceased; and I turned about, and glanced sharply down the road that looked as white as hoar-frost under the moon, and saw the gable of the old inn, and a window, partly concealed by the foliage, with a dusky light shining from it.

No sound of footstep was stirring; no sign of human figure in sight. I consulted my watch, which the light was sufficiently strong to enable me to do. It now wanted but eight minutes of the appointed hour. A thick mantle of ivy at this point covered the wall and rose in a clustering head at top.

It afforded me facilities for scaling the wall, and a partial screen for my operations, if any eye should chance to be looking that way. And now it was done. I was in the park of the Château de la Carque, as nefarious a poacher as ever trespassed on the grounds of unsuspicious lord!

Before me rose the appointed grove, which looked as black as a clump of gigantic hearse-plumes. It seemed to tower higher and higher at every step; and cast a broader and blacker shadow toward my feet. On I marched, and was glad when I plunged into the shadow which concealed me. Now I was among the grand old lime and chestnut trees—my heart beat fast with expectation.

This grove opened, a little, near the middle; and in the space thus cleared, there stood with a surrounding flight of steps, a small Greek temple or shrine, with a statue in the centre. It was built of white marble with fluted Corinthian columns, and the crevices were tufted with grass; moss had shown itself on pedestal and cornice, and signs of long neglect and decay were apparent in its discoloured and weather-worn marble. A few feet in front of the steps a fountain, fed from the great ponds at the other side of the château, was making a constant tinkle and plashing in a wide marble basin, and the jet of water glimmered like a shower of diamonds in the broken moonlight. The very neglect and half-ruinous state of all this made it only the prettier, as well as sadder. I was too intently watching for the arrival of the lady, in the direction of the château, to study these things; but the half-noted effect of them was romantic, and suggested somehow the grotto and the fountain, and the apparition of Egeria.

As I watched a voice spoke to me, a little behind my left shoulder. I turned, almost with a start, and the masque, in the costume of Mademoiselle de la Vallière stood there.

"The Countess will be here presently," she said. The lady stood upon the open space, and the moonlight fell unbroken upon her. Nothing could be more becoming; her figure looked more graceful and elegant than ever. "In the meantime I shall tell you some peculiarities of her situation. She is unhappy; miserable in an ill-assorted marriage, with a jealous tyrant who now would constrain her to sell her diamonds, which are—"

"Worth thirty thousand pounds sterling. I heard all that from a friend. Can I aid the Countess in her unequal struggle? Say but how, and the greater the danger or the sacrifice, the happier will it make me. *Can* I aid her?"

"If you despise a danger—which, yet, is not a danger; if you despise, as she does, the tyrannical canons of the world; and, if you are chivalrous enough to devote yourself to a lady's cause, with no reward but her poor gratitude; if you can do these things you can aid her, and earn a foremost place, not in her gratitude only, but in her friendship."

At those words the lady in the mask turned away, and seemed to weep.

I vowed myself the willing slave of the Countess. "But," I added, "you told me she would soon be here."

"That is, if nothing unforeseen should happen; but with the eye of the Count de St. Alyre in the house, and open, it is seldom safe to stir."

"Does she wish to see me?" I asked, with a tender hesitation.

"First, say have you really thought of *her*, more than once, since the adventure of the Belle Etoile."

"She never leaves my thoughts; day and night her beautiful eyes haunt me; her sweet voice is always in my ear."

"Mine is said to resemble hers," said the mask.

"So it does," I answered. "But it is only a resemblance."

"Oh! then mine is better?"

"Pardon me, Mademoiselle, I did not say *that*. Yours is a sweet voice, but I fancy a little higher."

"A little shriller, you would say," answered the De la Vallière, I fancied a good deal vexed.

"No, not shriller: your voice is not shrill, it is beautifully sweet; but not so pathetically sweet as her."

"That is prejudice, Monsieur; it is not true."

I bowed; I could not contradict a lady.

"I see, Monsieur, you laugh at me; you think me vain, because I claim in some points to be equal to the Countess de St. Alyre. I challenge you to say, my hand, at least, is less beautiful than hers." As she thus spoke, she drew her glove off, and extended her hand, back upward, in the moonlight.

The lady seemed really nettled. It was undignified and irritating; for in this uninteresting competition the precious moments were flying, and my interview leading apparently to nothing.

"You will admit, then, that my hand is as beautiful as hers?"

"I cannot admit it, Mademoiselle," said I, with the honesty of irritation. "I will not enter into comparisons, but the Countess de St. Alyre is, in all respects, the most beautiful lady I ever beheld."

The masque laughed coldly, and then, more and more softly, said, with a sigh, "I will prove all I say." And as she spoke she removed the mask: and the Countess de St. Alyre, smiling, confused, bashful, more beautiful than ever, stood before me!

"Good Heavens!" I exclaimed. "How monstrously stupid I have been. And it was to Madame la Comtesse that I spoke for so long in the *salon*!" I gazed on her in silence. And with a low sweet laugh of goodnature she extended her hand. I took it, and carried it to my lips.

"No, you must not do that," she said, quietly, "we are not old enough friends yet. I find, although you were mistaken, that you do remember the Countess of the Belle Etoile, and that you are a champion true and fearless. Had you yielded to the claims just now pressed upon you by the rivalry of Mademoiselle de la Vallière, in her mask, the Countess de St. Alyre should never have trusted or seen you more. I now am sure that you are true, as well as brave. You now know that I have not forgotten you; and, also, that if you would risk your life for me, I, too, would brave some danger, rather than lose my friend for ever. I have but a few moments more. Will you come here again to-morrow night, at a quarter past eleven? I will be here at that moment; you must exercise the most scrupulous care to prevent suspicion that you have come here, Monsieur. *You owe that to me.*"

She spoke these last words with the most solemn entreaty.

I vowed again and again, that I would die rather than permit the least rashness to endanger the secret which made all the interest and value of my life.

She was looking, I thought, more and more beautiful every moment. My enthusiasm expanded in proportion.

"You must come to-morrow night by a different route," she said; "and if you come again, we can change it once more. At the other side of the château there is a little churchyard, with a ruined chapel. The neighbours are afraid to pass it by night. The road is deserted there, and a stile opens a way into these grounds. Cross it and you can find a covert of thickets, to within fifty steps of this spot."

I promised, of course, to observe her instructions implicitly.

"I have lived for more than a year in an agony of irresolution. I have decided at last. I have lived a melancholy life; a lonelier life than is passed in the cloister. I have had no one to confide in; no one to advise me; no one to save me from the horrors of my existence. I have found a brave and prompt friend at last. Shall I ever forget the heroic tableau of the hall of the Belle Etoile? Have you—have you really kept the rose I gave you, as we parted? Yes—you swear it. You need not; I trust you. Richard, how often have I in solitude repeated your name, learned from my servant. Richard, my hero! Oh! Richard! Oh, my king! I love you."

I would have folded her to my heart—thrown myself at her feet. But this beautiful and—shall I say it—inconsistent woman repelled me.

"No, we must not waste our moments in extravagances. Understand my case. There is no such thing as indifference in the married state. Not to love one's husband," she continued, "is to hate him. The Count, ridiculous in all else, is formidable in his jealousy. In mercy, then, to me, observe caution. Affect to all you speak to, the most complete ignorance of all the people in the Château de la Carque; and, if any one in your presence mentions the Count or Countess de St. Alyre, be sure you say you never saw either. I shall have more to say to you to-morrow night. I have reasons that I cannot now explain, for all I do, and all I postpone. Farewell. Go! Leave me."

She waved me back, peremptorily. I echoed her "farewell," and obeyed.

This interview had not lasted, I think, more than ten minutes. I scaled the park-wall again, and reached the Dragon Volant before its doors were closed.

I lay awake in my bed, in a fever of elation. I saw, till the dawn broke, and chased the vision, the beautiful Countess de St. Alyre, always in the dark, before me.

CHAPTER XVII.

THE TENANT OF THE PALANQUIN.

The Marquis called on me next day. My late breakfast was still upon the table.

He had come, he said, to ask a favour. An accident had happened to his carriage in the crowd on leaving the ball, and he begged, if I were going into Paris, a seat in mine—I was going in, and was extremely glad of his company. He came with me to my hotel; we went up to my rooms. I was surprised to see a man seated in an easy chair, with his back towards us, reading a newspaper. He rose. It was the Count de St. Alyre, his gold spectacles on his nose; his black wig, in oily curls, lying close to his narrow head, and showing, like carved ebony over a repulsive visage of boxwood. His black muffler had been pulled down. His right arm was in a sling. I don't know whether there was anything unusual in his countenance that day, or whether it was but the effect of prejudice arising from all I had heard in my mysterious interview in his park, but I thought his countenance was more strikingly forbidding than I had seen it before.

I was not callous enough in the ways of sin to meet this man, injured at least in intent, thus suddenly, without a momentary disturbance.

He smiled.

"I called, Monsieur Beckett, in the hope of finding you here," he croaked, "and I meditated, I fear, taking a great liberty, but my friend the Marquis d'Harmonville, on whom I have perhaps some claim, will perhaps give me the assistance I require so much."

"With great pleasure," said the Marquis, "but not till after six o'clock. I must go this moment to a meeting of three or four people, whom I cannot disappoint, and I know, perfectly, we cannot break up earlier."

"What am I to do?" exclaimed the Count, "an hour would have done it all. Was ever *contre-temps* so unlucky!"

"I'll give you an hour, with pleasure," said I.

"How very good of you, Monsieur, I hardly dare to hope it. The business, for so gay and charming a man as Monsieur Beckett, is a little *funeste*. Pray read this note which reached me this morning."

It certainly was not cheerful. It was a note stating that the body of his, the Count's cousin, Monsieur de St. Amand, who had died at his house, the Château Clery, had been, in accordance with his written directions, sent for burial at Père La Chaise, and, with the permission of the Count de St. Alyre, would reach his house (the Château de la Carque), at about ten o'clock on the night following, to be conveyed thence in a hearse, with any member of the family who might wish to attend the obsequies.

"I did not see the poor gentleman twice in my life," said the Count, "but this office, as he has no other kinsman, disagreeable as it is, I could scarcely decline, and so I want to attend at the office to have the book signed, and the order entered. But here is another misery. By ill luck, I have sprained my thumb, and can't sign my name for a week to come. However, one name answers as well as another. Yours as well as mine. And as you are so good as to come with me, all will go right."

Away, we drove. The Count gave me a memorandum of the christian and surnames of the deceased, his age, the complaint he died of, and the usual particulars; also a note of the exact position in which a grave, the dimensions of which were described, of the ordinary simple kind, was to be dug, between two vaults belonging to the family of St. Amand. The funeral, it was stated, would arrive at half-past one o'clock A.M. (the next night but one); and he handed me the money, with extra fees, for a burial by night. It was a good deal; and I asked him, as he entrusted the whole affair to me, in whose name I should take the receipt.

"Not in mine, my good friend. They wanted me to become an executor, which I, yesterday, wrote to decline; and I am informed that if the receipt were in my name it would constitute me an executor in the eye of the law, and fix me in that position. Take it, pray, if you have no objection, in your own name."

This, accordingly, I did.

"You will see, by-and-by, why I am obliged to mention all these particulars."

The Count, meanwhile, was leaning back in the carriage, with his black silk muffler up to his nose, and his hat shading his eyes, while he dozed in his corner; in which state I found him on my return.

Paris had lost its charm for me. I hurried through the little business I had to do, longed once more for my quiet room in the Dragon Volant, the melancholy woods of the Château de la Carque, and the tumultuous and thrilling influence of proximity to the object of my wild but wicked romance.

I was delayed some time by my stockbroker. I had a very large sum, as I told you, at my banker's, uninvested. I cared very little for a few days' interest—very little for the entire sum, compared with the image that occupied my thoughts, and beckoned me with a white arm, through the dark, toward the spreading lime-trees and chestnuts of the Château de la Carque. But I had fixed this day to meet him, and was relieved when he told me that I had better let it lie in my banker's hands for a few days longer, as the funds would certainly fall immediately. This accident, too, was not without its immediate bearing on my subsequent adventures.

When I reached the Dragon Volant, I found, in my sitting-room, a good deal to my chagrin, my two guests, whom I had quite forgotten. I inwardly cursed my own stupidity for having embarrassed myself with their agreeable society. It could not be helped now, however, and a word to the waiters put all things in train for dinner.

Tom Whistlewick was in great force; and he commenced almost immediately with a very odd story.

He told me that not only Versailles, but all Paris, was in a ferment, in consequence of a revolting, and all but sacrilegious, practical joke, played off on the night before.

The pagoda, as he persisted in calling the palanquin, had been left standing on the spot where we last saw it. Neither conjuror, nor usher, nor bearers had ever returned. When the ball closed, and the company at length retired, the servants who attended to put out the lights, and secure the doors, found it still there.

It was determined, however, to let it stand where it was until next morning, by which time, it was conjectured, its owners would send messengers to remove it.

None arrived. The servants were then ordered to take it away; and its extraordinary weight, for the first time, reminded them of its forgotten human occupant. Its door was forced; and, judge what was their disgust, when they discovered, not a living man, but a corpse! Three or four days must have passed since the death of the burly man in the Chinese tunic and painted cap. Some people thought it was a trick designed to insult the Allies, in whose honour the ball was got up. Others were of opinion that it was nothing worse than a daring and cynical jocularity which, shocking as it was, might yet be forgiven to the high spirits and irrepressible buffoonery of youth. Others, again, fewer in number, and mystically given, insisted that the corpse was *bonâ fide* necessary to the exhibition, and that the disclosures and allusions which had astonished so many people were distinctly due to necromancy.

"The matter, however, is now in the hands of the police," observed Monsieur Carmaignac, "and we are not the body they were two or three months ago, if the offenders against propriety and public feeling are not traced, and convicted, unless, indeed, they have been a great deal more cunning than such fools generally are."

I was thinking within myself how utterly inexplicable was my colloquy with the conjuror, so cavalierly dismissed by Monsieur Carmaignac as a "fool;" and the more I thought the more marvellous it seemed.

"It certainly was an original joke, though not a very clear one," said Whistlewick.

"Not even original," said Carmaignac. "Very nearly the same thing was done, a hundred years ago or more, at a state ball in Paris; and the rascals who played the trick were never found out."

In this Monsieur Carmaignac, as I afterwards discovered, spoke truly; for, among my books of French anecdote and memoirs, the very incident is marked, by my own hand.

While we were thus talking, the waiter told us that dinner was served; and we withdrew accordingly; my guests more than making amends for my comparative taciturnity.

CHAPTER XVIII.

THE CHURCH-YARD.

Our dinner was really good, so were the wines; better, perhaps, at this out-of-the-way inn, than at some of the more pretentious hotels in Paris. The moral effect of a really good dinner is immense—we all felt it. The serenity and goodnature that follow are more solid and comfortable than the tumultuous benevolences of Bacchus.

My friends were happy, therefore, and very chatty; which latter relieved me of the trouble of talking, and prompted them to entertain me and one another incessantly with agreeable stories and conversation, of which, until suddenly a subject emerged, which interested me powerfully, I confess, so much were my thoughts engaged elsewhere, I heard next to nothing.

"Yes," said Carmaignac, continuing a conversation which had escaped me, "there was another case, beside that Russian nobleman, odder still. I remembered it this morning, but cannot recall the name. He was a tenant of the very same room. By-the-by, Monsieur, might it not be as well," he added, turning to me, with a laugh, half joke whole earnest, as they say, "if you were to get into another apartment, now that the house is no longer crowded? that is, if you mean to make any stay here."

"A thousand thanks! no. I'm thinking of changing my hotel; and I can run into town so easily at night; and though I stay here, for this night, at least, I don't expect to vanish like those others. But you say there is another adventure, of the same kind, connected with the same room. Do let us hear it. But take some wine first."

The story he told was curious.

"It happened," said Carmaignac, "as well as I recollect, before either of the other cases. A French gentleman—I wish I could remember his name—the son of a merchant, came to this inn (the Dragon Volant), and was put by the landlord into the same room of which we have been speaking. *Your* apartment, Monsieur. He was by no means young—past forty—and very far from good-looking. The people here said that he was the ugliest man, and the most good-natured, that ever lived. He played on the fiddle, sang, and wrote poetry. His habits were odd and desultory. He would sometimes sit all day in his room writing, singing, and fiddling, and go out at night for a walk. An eccentric man! He was by no means a millionaire, but he had a *modicum bonum* you understand—a trifle more than half a million of francs. He consulted his stockbroker about investing this money in foreign stocks, and drew the entire sum from his banker. You now have the situation of affairs when the catastrophe occurred."

"Pray fill your glass," I said.

"Dutch courage, Monsieur, to face the catastrophe!" said Whistlewick, filling his own.

"Now, that was the last that ever was heard of his money," resumed Carmaignac. "You shall hear about himself. The night after this financial operation, he was seized with a poetic frenzy; he sent for the then landlord of this house, and told him that he long meditated an epic, and meant to commence that night, and that he was on no account to be disturbed until nine o'clock in the morning. He had two pairs of wax candles, a little cold supper on a side-table, his desk open, paper enough upon it to contain the entire Henriade, and a proportionate store of pens and ink.

"Seated at this desk he was seen by the waiter who brought him a cup of coffee at nine o'clock, at which time the intruder said he was writing fast enough to set fire to the paper—that was his phrase; he did not look up, he appeared too much engrossed. But, when the waiter came back, half an hour afterwards, the door was locked; and the poet, from within, answered, that he must not be disturbed.

"Away went the *garçon*; and next morning at nine o'clock knocked at his door, and receiving no answer, looked through the key-hole; the lights were still burning, the window-shutters were closed as he had left them; he renewed his knocking, knocked louder, no answer came. He reported this continued and alarming silence to the inn-keeper, who, finding that his guest had not left his key in the lock, succeeded in finding another that opened it. The candles were just giving up the ghost in their sockets, but there was light enough to ascertain that the tenant of the room was gone! The bed had not been disturbed; the window-shutter was barred. He must have let himself out, and, locking the door on the outside, put the key in his pocket, and so made his way out of the house. Here, however, was another difficulty, the Dragon Volant shut its doors and made all fast at twelve o'clock; after that hour no one could leave the house, except by obtaining the key and letting himself out, and of necessity leaving the door unsecured, or else by collusion and aid of some person in the house.

"Now it happened that, some time after the doors were secured, at half-past twelve, a servant who had not been apprized of his order to be left undisturbed, seeing a light shine through the key-hole, knocked at the door to inquire whether the poet wanted anything. He was very little obliged to his disturber, and dismissed him with a renewed charge that he was not to be interrupted again during the night. This incident established the fact that he was in the house after the doors had been locked and barred. The inn-keeper himself kept the keys, and swore that he found them hung on the wall above his head, in his bed, in their usual place, in the morning; and that nobody could have taken them away without awakening him. That was all we could discover. The Count de St. Alyre, to whom this house belongs, was very active and very much chagrined. But nothing was discovered."

"And nothing heard since of the epic poet?" I asked.

"Nothing—not the slightest clue—he never turned up again. I suppose he is dead; if he is not, he must have got into some devilish bad scrape, of which we have heard nothing, that compelled him to abscond with all the secresy and expedition in his power. All that we know for certain is that, having occupied the room in which you sleep, he vanished, nobody ever knew how, and never was heard of since."

"You have now mentioned three cases," I said, "and all from the same room."

"Three. Yes, all equally unintelligible. When men are murdered, the great and immediate difficulty the assassins encounter is how to conceal the body. It is very hard to believe that three persons should have been consecutively murdered, in the same room, and their bodies so effectually disposed of that no trace of them was ever discovered."

From this we passed to other topics, and the grave Monsieur Carmaignac amused us with a perfectly prodigious collection of scandalous anecdote, which his opportunities in the police department had enabled him to accumulate.

My guests happily had engagements in Paris, and left me about ten.

I went up to my room, and looked out upon the grounds of the Château de la Carque. The moonlight was broken by clouds, and the view of the park in this desultory light, acquired a melancholy and fantastic character.

The strange anecdotes recounted of the room in which I stood, by Monsieur Carmaignac, returned vaguely upon my mind, drowning in sudden shadows the gaiety of the more frivolous stories with which he had followed them. I looked round me on the room that lay in ominous gloom, with an almost disagreeable sensation. I took my pistols now with an undefined apprehension that they might be really needed before my return to-night. This feeling, be it understood, in nowise chilled my ardour. Never had my enthusiasm mounted higher. My adventure absorbed and carried me away; but it added a strange and stern excitement to the expedition.

I loitered for a time in my room. I had ascertained the exact point at which the little churchyard lay. It was about a mile away; I did not wish to reach it earlier than necessary.

I stole quietly out, and sauntered along the road to my left, and thence entered a narrower track, still to my left, which, skirting the park wall, and describing a circuitous route, all the way, under grand old trees, passes the ancient cemetery. That cemetery is embowered in trees, and occupies little more than half an acre of ground, to the left of the road, interposing between it and the park of the Château de la Carque.

Here, at this haunted spot, I paused and listened. The place was utterly silent. A thick cloud had darkened the moon, so that I could distinguish little more than the outlines of near objects, and that vaguely enough; and sometimes, as it were, floating in black fog, the white surface of a tombstone emerged.

Among the forms that met my eye against the iron-grey of the horizon, were some of those shrubs or trees that grow like our junipers, some six feet high, in form like a miniature poplar, with the darker foliage of the yew. I do not know the name of the plant, but I have often seen it in such funereal places.

Knowing that I was a little too early, I sat down upon the edge of a tombstone to wait, as, for aught I knew, the beautiful Countess might have wise reasons for not caring that I should enter the grounds of the château earlier than she had appointed. In the listless state induced by waiting, I sat there, with my eyes on the object straight before me, which chanced to be that faint black outline I have described. It was right before me, about half-a-dozen steps away.

The moon now began to escape from under the skirt of the cloud that had hid her face for so long; and, as the light gradually improved, the tree on which I had been lazily staring began to take a new shape. It was no longer a tree, but a man standing motionless. Brighter and brighter grew the moonlight, clearer and clearer the image became, and at last stood out perfectly distinctly. It was Colonel Gaillarde.

Luckily, he was not looking toward me. I could only see him in profile; but there was no mistaking the white moustache, the *farouche* visage, and the gaunt six-foot stature. There he was, his shoulder toward me, listening and watching, plainly, for some signal or person expected, straight in front of him.

If he were, by chance, to turn his eyes in my direction, I knew that I must reckon upon an instantaneous renewal of the combat only commenced in the hall of the Belle Etoile. In any case, could malignant fortune have posted, at this place and hour, a more dangerous watcher? What ecstasy to him, by a single discovery, to hit me so hard, and blast the Countess de St. Alyre, whom he seemed to hate.

He raised his arm; he whistled softly; I heard an answering whistle as low; and, to my relief, the Colonel advanced in the direction of this sound, widening the distance between us at every step; and immediately I heard talking, but in a low and cautious key.

I recognized, I thought, even so, the peculiar voice of Gaillarde.

I stole softly forward in the direction in which those sounds were audible. In doing so, I had, of course, to use the extremest caution.

I thought I saw a hat above a jagged piece of ruined wall, and then a second—yes, I saw two hats conversing; the voices came from under them. They moved off, not in the direction of the park, but of the road, and I lay along the grass, peeping over a grave, as a skirmisher might, observing the enemy. One after the other, the figures emerged full into view as they mounted the stile at the roadside. The Colonel, who was last, stood on the wall for awhile, looking about him, and then jumped down on the road. I heard their steps and talk as they moved away together, with their backs toward me, in the direction which led them farther and farther from the Dragon Volant.

I waited until these sounds were quite lost in distance before I entered the park. I followed the instructions I had received from the Countess de St. Alyre, and made my way among brushwood and thickets to the point nearest the ruinous temple, and crossed the short intervening space of open ground rapidly.

I was now once more under the gigantic boughs of the old lime and chestnut trees; softly, and with a heart throbbing fast, I approached the little structure.

The moon was now shining steadily, pouring down its radiance on the soft foliage, and here and there mottling the verdure under my feet.

I reached the steps; I was among its worn marble shafts. She was not there, nor in the inner sanctuary, the arched windows of which were screened almost entirely by masses of ivy. The lady had not yet arrived.

CHAPTER XIX.

THE KEY.

I stood now upon the steps, watching and listening. In a minute or two I heard the crackle of withered sticks trod upon, and, looking in the direction, I saw a figure approaching among the trees, wrapped in a mantle.

I advanced eagerly. It was the Countess. She did not speak, but gave me her hand, and I led her to the scene of our last interview. She repressed the ardour of my impassioned greeting with a gentle but peremptory firmness. She removed her hood, shook back her beautiful hair, and, gazing on me with sad and glowing eyes, sighed deeply. Some awful thought seemed to weigh upon her.

"Richard, I must speak plainly. The crisis of my life has come. I am sure you would defend me. I think you pity me; perhaps you even love me."

At these words I became eloquent, as young madmen in my plight do. She silenced me, however, with the same melancholy firmness.

"Listen, dear friend, and then say whether you can aid me. How madly I am trusting you; and yet my heart tells me how wisely! To meet you here as I do—what insanity it seems! How poorly you must think of me! But when you know all, you will judge me fairly. Without your aid I cannot accomplish my purpose. That purpose unaccomplished, I must die. I am chained to a man whom I despise—whom I abhor. I have resolved to fly. I have jewels, principally diamonds, for which I am offered thirty thousand pounds of your English money. They are my separate property by my marriage settlement; I will take them with me. You are a judge, no doubt, of jewels. I was counting mine when the hour came, and brought this in my hand to show you. Look."

"It is magnificent!" I exclaimed, as a collar of diamonds twinkled and flashed in the moonlight, suspended from her pretty fingers. I thought, even at that tragic moment, that she prolonged the show, with a feminine delight in these brilliant toys.

"Yes," she said, "I shall part with them all. I will turn them into money, and break, for ever, the unnatural and wicked bonds that tied me, in the name of a sacrament, to a tyrant. A man young, handsome, generous, brave as you, can hardly be rich. Richard, you say you love me; you shall share all this with me. We will fly together to Switzerland; we will evade pursuit; my powerful friends will intervene and arrange a separation; and I shall, at length, be happy and reward my hero."

You may suppose the style, florid and vehement, in which I poured forth my gratitude, vowed the devotion of my life, and placed myself absolutely at her disposal.

"To-morrow night," she said, "my husband will attend the remains of his cousin, Monsieur de St. Amand, to Père la Chaise. The hearse, he says, will leave this at half-past nine. You must be here, where we stand, at nine o'clock."

I promised punctual obedience.

"I will not meet you here; but you see a red light in the window of the tower at that angle of the château?"

I assented.

"I placed it there, that, to-morrow night, when it comes, you may recognize it. So soon as that rose-coloured light appears at that window, it will be a signal to you that the funeral has left the château, and that you may approach safely. Come, then, to that window; I will open it, and admit you. Five minutes after a travelling-carriage, with four horses, shall stand ready in the *porte-cochère*. I will place my diamonds in your hands; and so soon as we enter the carriage, our flight commences. We shall have at least five hours' start; and with energy, stratagem, and resource, I fear nothing. Are you ready to undertake all this for my sake?"

Again I vowed myself her slave.

"My only difficulty," she said, "is how we shall quickly enough convert my diamonds into money; I dare not remove them while my husband is in the house."

Here was the opportunity I wished for. I now told her that I had in my banker's hands no less a sum than thirty thousand pounds, with which, in the shape of gold and notes, I should come furnished, and thus the risk and loss of disposing of her diamonds in too much haste would be avoided.

"Good heaven!" she exclaimed, with a kind of disappointment. "You are rich, then? and I have lost the felicity of making my generous friend more happy. Be it so! since so it must be. Let us contribute, each, in equal shares, to our common fund. Bring you, your money; I, my jewels. There is a happiness to me even in mingling my resources with yours."

On this there followed a romantic colloquy, all poetry and passion, such as I should, in vain, endeavour to reproduce.

Then came a very special instruction.

"I have come provided, too, with a key, the use of which I must explain."

It was a double key—a long, slender stem, with a key at each end—one about the size which opens an ordinary room door; the other, as small, almost, as the key of a dressing-case.

"You cannot employ too much caution to-morrow night. An interruption would murder all my hopes. I have learned that you occupy the haunted room in the Dragon Volant. It is the very room I would have wished you in. I will tell you why—there is a story of a man who, having shut himself up in that room one night, disappeared before morning. The truth is, he wanted, I believe, to escape from creditors; and the host of the Dragon Volant, at that time, being a rogue, aided him in absconding. My husband investigated the matter, and discovered how his escape was made. It was by means of this key. Here is a memorandum and a plan describing how they are to be applied. I have taken them from the Count's escritoire. And now, once more I must leave to your ingenuity how to mystify the people at the Dragon Volant. Be sure you try the keys first, to see that the locks turn freely. I will have my jewels ready. You, whatever we divide, had better bring your money, because it may be many months before you can revisit Paris, or disclose our place of residence to any one; and our passports—arrange all that; in what names, and whither, you please. And now, dear Richard" (she leaned her arm fondly on my shoulder, and looked with ineffable passion in my eyes, with her other hand clasped in mine), "my very life is in your hands; I have staked all on your fidelity."

As she spoke the last word, she, on a sudden, grew deadly pale, and gasped, "Good God! who is here?"

At the same moment she receded through the door in the marble screen, close to which she stood, and behind which was a small roofless chamber, as small as the shrine, the window of which was darkened by a clustering mass of ivy so dense that hardly a gleam of light came through the leaves.

I stood upon the threshold which she had just crossed, looking in the direction in which she had thrown that one terrified glance. No wonder she was frightened. Quite close upon us, not twenty yards away, and approaching at a quick step, very distinctly lighted by the moon, Colonel Gaillarde and his companion were coming. The shadow of the cornice and a piece of wall were upon me. Unconscious of this, I was expecting the moment when, with one of his frantic yells, he should spring forward to assail me.

I made a step backward, drew one of my pistols from my pocket, and cocked it. It was obvious he had not seen me.

I stood, with my finger on the trigger, determined to shoot him dead if he should attempt to enter the place where the Countess was. It would, no doubt, have been a murder; but, in my mind, I had no question or qualm about it. When once we engage in secret and guilty practices we are nearer other and greater crimes than we at all suspect.

"There's the statue," said the Colonel, in his brief discordant tones. "That's the figure."

"Alluded to in the stanzas?" inquired his companion.

"The very thing. We shall see more next time. Forward, Monsieur; let us march."

And, much to my relief, the gallant Colonel turned on his heel, and marched through the trees, with his back toward the château, striding over the grass, as I quickly saw, to the park wall, which they crossed not far from the gables of the Dragon Volant.

I found the Countess trembling in no affected, but a very real terror. She would not hear of my accompanying her toward the château. But I told her that I would prevent the return of the mad Colonel; and upon that point, at least, that she need fear nothing. She quickly recovered, again bid me a fond and lingering good-night, and left me, gazing after her, with the key in my hand, and such a phantasmagoria floating in my brain as amounted very nearly to madness.

There was I, ready to brave all dangers, all right and reason, plunge into murder itself, on the first summons, and entangle myself in consequences inextricable and horrible (what cared I?) for a woman of whom I knew nothing, but that she was beautiful and reckless!

I have often thanked heaven for its mercy in conducting me through the labyrinths in which I had all but lost myself.

CHAPTER XX.

A HIGH-CAULD CAP.

I was now upon the road, within two or three hundred yards of the Dragon Volant. I had undertaken an adventure with a vengeance! And by way of prelude, there not improbably awaited me, at my inn, another encounter, perhaps, this time, not so lucky, with the grotesque sabreur.

I was glad I had my pistols. I certainly was bound by no law to allow a ruffian to cut me down, unresisting.

Stooping boughs from the old park, gigantic poplars on the other side, and the moonlight over all, made the narrow road to the inn-door picturesque.

I could not think very clearly just now; events were succeeding one another so rapidly, and I, involved in the action of a drama so extravagant and guilty, hardly knew myself or believed my own story, as I slowly paced towards the still open door of the Flying Dragon.

No sign of the Colonel, visible or audible, was there. In the hall I inquired. No gentleman had arrived at the inn for the last half hour. I looked into the public room. It was deserted. The clock struck twelve, and I heard the servant barring the great door. I took my candle. The lights in this rural hostelry were by this time out, and the house had the air of one that had settled to slumber for many hours. The cold moonlight streamed in at the window on the landing, as I ascended the broad staircase; and I paused for a moment to look oyer the wooded grounds to the turreted château, to me, so full of interest. I bethought me, however, that prying eyes might read a meaning in this midnight gazing, and possibly the Count himself might, in his jealous mood, surmise a signal in this unwonted light in the stair-window of the Dragon Volant.

On opening my room door, with a little start, I met an extremely old woman with the longest face I ever saw; she had what used to be termed, a high-cauld-cap, on, the white border of which contrasted with her brown and yellow skin, and made her wrinkled face more ugly. She raised her curved shoulders, and looked up in my face, with eyes unnaturally black and bright.

"I have lighted a little wood, Monsieur, because the night is chill."

I thanked her, but she did not go. She stood with her candle in her tremulous fingers.

"Excuse an old woman. Monsieur," she said; "but what on earth can a young English *milord*, with all Paris at his feet, find to amuse him in the Dragon Volant?"

Had I been at the age of fairy tales, and in daily intercourse with the delightful Countess d'Aulnois, I should have seen in this withered apparition, the *genius loci*, the malignant fairy, at the stamp of whose foot, the ill-fated tenants of this very room had, from time to time, vanished. I was past that, however; but the old woman's dark eyes were fixed on mine, with a steady meaning that plainly told me that my secret was known. I was embarrassed and alarmed; I never thought of asking her what business that was of hers.

"These old eyes saw you in the park of the château to-night."

"*I!*" I began, with all the scornful surprise I could affect.

"It avails nothing, Monsieur; I know why you stay here; and I tell you to begone. Leave this house to-morrow morning, and never come again."

She lifted her disengaged hand, as she looked at me with intense horror in her eyes.

"There is nothing on earth—I don't know what you mean," I answered; "and why should you care about me?"

"I don't care about you, Monsieur—I care about the honour of an ancient family, whom I served in their happier days, when to be noble, was to be honoured. But my words are thrown away, Monsieur; you are insolent. I will keep my secret, and you, yours; that is all. You will soon find it hard enough to divulge it."

The old woman went slowly from the room and shut the door, before I had made up my mind to say anything. I was standing where she had left me, nearly five minutes later. The jealousy of Monsieur the Count, I assumed, appears to this old creature about the most terrible thing in creation. Whatever contempt I might entertain for the dangers which this old lady so darkly intimated, it was by no means pleasant, you may suppose, that a secret so dangerous should be so much as suspected by a stranger, and that stranger a partisan of the Count de St. Alyre.

Ought I not, at all risks, to apprize the Countess, who had trusted me so generously, or, as she said herself, so madly, of the fact that our secret was, at least, suspected by another? But was there not greater danger in attempting to communicate? What did the beldame mean by saying, "Keep your secret, and I'll keep mine?"

I had a thousand distracting questions before me. My progress seemed like a journey through the Spessart, where at every step some new goblin or monster starts from the ground or steps from behind a tree.

Peremptorily I dismissed these harassing and frightful doubts. I secured my door, sat myself down at my table, and with a candle at each side, placed before me the piece of vellum which contained the drawings and notes on which I was to rely for full instructions as to how to use the key.

When I had studied this for awhile, I made my investigation. The angle of the room at the right side of the window was cut off by an oblique turn in the wainscot. I examined this carefully, and, on pressure, a small bit of the frame of the woodwork slid aside, and disclosed a keyhole. On removing my finger, it shot back to its place again, with a spring. So far I had interpreted my instructions successfully. A similar search, next the door, and directly under this, was rewarded by a like discovery. The small end of the key fitted this, as it had the upper keyhole; and now, with two or three hard jerks at the key, a door in the panel opened, showing a strip of the bare wall, and a narrow, arched doorway, piercing the thickness of the wall; and within which I saw a screw-staircase of stone.

Candle in hand I stepped in. I do not know whether the quality of air, long undisturbed, is peculiar; to me it has always seemed so, and the damp smell of the old masonry hung in this atmosphere. My candle faintly lighted the bare stone wall that enclosed the stair, the foot of which I could not see. Down I went, and a few turns brought me to the stone floor. Here was another door, of the simple, old, oak kind, deep sunk in the thickness of the wall. The large end of the key fitted this. The lock was stiff; I set the candle down upon the stair, and applied both hands; it turned with difficulty, and as it revolved, uttered a shriek that alarmed me for my secret.

For some minutes I did not move. In a little time, however, I took courage, and opened the door. The night-air floating in, puffed out the candle. There was a thicket of holly and underwood, as dense as a jungle, close about the door. I should have been in pitch-darkness, were it not that through the topmost leaves, there twinkled, here and there, a glimmer of moonshine.

Softly, lest any one should have opened his window, at the sound of the rusty bolt, I struggled through this, till I gained a view of the open grounds. Here I found that the brushwood spread a good way up the park, uniting with the wood that approached the little temple I have described.

A general could not have chosen a more effectually-covered approach from the Dragon Volant to the trysting-place where hitherto I had conferred with the idol of my lawless adoration.

Looking back upon the old inn, I discovered that the stair I descended, was enclosed in one of those slender turrets that decorate such buildings. It was placed at that angle which corresponded with the part of the paneling of my room indicated in the plan I had been studying.

Thoroughly satisfied with my experiment, I made my way back to the door, with some little difficulty, re-mounted to my room, locked my secret door again; kissed the mysterious key that her hand had pressed that night, and placed it under my pillow, upon which, very soon after, my giddy head was laid, not, for some time, to sleep soundly.

CHAPTER XXI.

I SEE THREE MEN IN A MIRROR.

I awoke very early next morning, and was too excited to sleep again. As soon as I could, without exciting remark, I saw my host. I told him that I was going into town that night, and thence to ——, where I had to see some people on business, and requested him to mention my being there to any friend who might call. That I expected to be back in about a week, and that in the meantime my servant, St. Clair, would keep the key of my room, and look after my things.

Having prepared this mystification for my landlord, I drove into Paris, and there transacted the financial part of the affair. The problem was to reduce my balance, nearly thirty thousand pounds, to a shape in which it would be not only easily portable, but available, wherever I might go, without involving correspondence, or any other incident which would disclose my place of residence, for the time being. All these points were as nearly provided for as they could be. I need not trouble you about my arrangements for passports. It is enough to say that the point I selected for our flight was, in the spirit of romance, one of the most beautiful and sequestered nooks in Switzerland.

Luggage, I should start with none. The first considerable town we reached next morning, would supply an extemporized wardrobe. It was now two o'clock; *only* two! How on earth was I to dispose of the remainder of the day?

I had not yet seen the cathedral of Notre Dame; and thither I drove. I spent an hour or more there; and then to the Conciergerie, the Palais de Justice, and the beautiful Sainte Chapelle. Still there remained some time to get rid of, and I strolled into the narrow streets adjoining the cathedral. I recollect seeing, in one of them, an old house with a mural inscription stating that it had been the residence of Canon Fulbert, the uncle of Abelard's Eloise. I don't know whether these curious old streets, in which I observed fragments of ancient gothic churches fitted up as warehouses, are still extant. I lighted, among other dingy and eccentric shops, upon one that seemed that of a broker of all sorts of old decorations, armour, china, furniture. I entered the shop; it was dark, dusty, and low. The proprietor was busy scouring a piece of inlaid armour, and allowed me to poke about his shop, and examine the curious things accumulated there, just as I pleased. Gradually I made my way to the farther end of it, where there was but one window with many panes, each with a bull's-eye in it, and in the dirtiest possible state. When I reached this window, I turned about, and in a recess, standing at right angles with the side wall of the shop, was a large mirror in an old-fashioned dingy frame. Reflected in this I saw, what in old houses I have heard termed an "alcove," in which, among lumber, and various dusty articles hanging on the wall, there stood a table, at which three persons were seated, as it seemed to me, in earnest conversation. Two of these persons I instantly recognized; one was Colonel Gaillarde, the other was the Marquis d'Harmonville. The third, who was fiddling with a pen, was a lean, pale man, pitted with the small-pox, with lank black hair, and about as mean-looking a person as I had ever seen in my life. The Marquis looked up, and his glance was instantaneously followed by his two companions. For a moment I hesitated what to do. But it was plain that I was not recognized, as indeed I could hardly have been, the light from the window being behind me, and the portion of the shop immediately before me, being very dark indeed.

Perceiving this, I had presence of mind to affect being entirely engrossed by the objects before me, and strolled slowly down the shop again. I paused for a moment to hear whether I was followed, and was relieved when I heard no step. You may be sure I did not waste more time in that shop, where I had just made a discovery so curious and so unexpected.

It was no business of mine to inquire what brought Colonel Gaillarde and the Marquis together, in so shabby, and even dirty a place, or who the mean person, biting the feather end of his pen, might be. Such employments as the Marquis had accepted sometimes make strange bed-fellows.

I was glad to get away, and just as the sun set, I had reached the steps of the Dragon Volant, and dismissed the vehicle in which I arrived, carrying in my hand a strong box, of marvellously small dimensions considering all it contained, strapped in a leather cover, which disguised its real character.

When I got to my room, I summoned St. Clair. I told him nearly the same story, I had already told my host. I gave him fifty pounds, with orders to expend whatever was necessary on himself, and in payment for my rooms till my return. I then eat a slight and hasty dinner. My eyes were often upon the solemn old clock over the chimney-piece, which was my sole accomplice in keeping tryste in this iniquitous venture. The sky favoured my design, and darkened all things with a sea of clouds.

The innkeeper met me in the hall, to ask whether I should want a vehicle to Paris? I was prepared for this question, and instantly answered that I meant to walk to Versailles, and take a carriage there. I called St. Clair.

"Go," said I, "and drink a bottle of wine with your friends. I shall call you if I should want anything; in the meantime, here is the key of my room; I shall be writing some notes, so don't allow any one to disturb me, for at least half an hour. At the end of that time you will probably find that I have left this for Versailles; and should you not find me in the room, you may take that for granted; and you take charge of everything, and lock the door, you understand?"

St. Clair took his leave, wishing me all happiness and no doubt promising himself some little amusement with my money. With my candle in my hand, I hastened upstairs. It wanted now but five minutes to the appointed time. I do not think there is anything of the coward in my nature; but I confess, as the crisis approached, I felt something of the suspense and awe of a soldier going into action. Would I have receded? Not for all this earth could offer.

I bolted my door, put on my great coat, and placed my pistols, one in each pocket. I now applied my key to the secret locks; drew the wainscot-door a little open, took my strong box under my arm, extinguished my candle, unbolted my door, listened at it for a few moments to be sure that no one was approaching, and then crossed the floor of my room swiftly, entered the secret door, and closed the spring lock after me. I was upon the screw-stair in total darkness, the key in my fingers. Thus far the undertaking was successful.

CHAPTER XXII.

RAPTURE.

Down the screw-stair I went in utter darkness; and having reached the stone floor, I discerned the door and groped out the key-hole. With more caution, and less noise than upon the night before, I opened the door, and stepped out into the thick brushwood. It was almost as dark in this jungle.

Having secured the door, I slowly pushed my way through the bushes, which soon became less dense. Then, with more ease, but still under thick cover, I pursued in the track of the wood, keeping near its edge.

At length, in the darkened air, about fifty yards away, the shafts of the marble temple rose like phantoms before me, seen through the trunks of the old trees. Everything favoured my enterprise. I had effectually mystified my servant and the people of the Dragon Volant, and so dark was the night, that even had I alarmed the suspicions of all the tenants of the inn, I might safely defy their united curiosity, though posted at every window of the house.

Through the trunks, over the roots of the old trees, I reached the appointed place of observation. I laid my treasure, in its leathern case, in the embrasure, and leaning my arms upon it, looked steadily in the direction of the château. The outline of the building was scarcely discernible, blending dimly, as it did, with the sky. No light in any window was visible. I was plainly to wait; but for how long?

Leaning on my box of treasure, gazing toward the massive shadow that represented the château, in the midst of my ardent and elated longings, there came upon me an odd thought, which you will think might well have struck me long before. It seemed on a sudden, as it came, that the darkness deepened, and a chill stole into the air around me.

Suppose I were to disappear finally, like those other men whose stories I had listened to! Had I not been at all the pains that mortal could, to obliterate every trace of my real proceedings, and to mislead every one to whom I spoke as to the direction in which I had gone?

This icy, snake-light thought stole through my mind, and was gone.

It was with me the full-blooded season of youth, conscious strength, rashness, passion, pursuit, the adventure! Here were a pair of double-barrelled pistols, four lives in my hands? What could possibly happen? The Count—except for the sake of my dulcinea, what was it to me whether the old coward whom I had seen, in an ague of terror before the brawling Colonel, interposed or not? I was assuming the worst that could happen. But with an ally so clever and courageous as my beautiful Countess, could any such misadventure befall? Bah! I laughed at all such fancies.

As I thus communed with myself, the signal light sprang up. The rose-coloured light, *couleur de rose*, emblem of sanguine hope, and the dawn of a happy day.

Clear, soft, and steady, glowed the light from the window. The stone shafts showed black against it. Murmuring words of passionate love as I gazed upon the signal, I grasped my strong box under my arm, and with rapid strides approached the Château de la Carque. No sign of light or life, no human voice, no tread of foot, no bark of dog, indicated a chance of interruption. A blind was down; and as I came close to the tall window, I found that half-a-dozen steps led up to it, and that a large lattice, answering for a door, lay open.

A shadow from within fell upon the blind; it was drawn aside, and as I ascended the steps, a soft voice murmured—"Richard, dearest Richard, come, oh! come! how I have longed for this moment?"

Never did she look so beautiful. My love rose to passionate enthusiasm. I only wished there were some real danger in the adventure worthy of such a creature. When the first tumultuous greeting was over, she made me sit beside her on a sofa. There we talked for a minute or two. She told me that the Count had gone, and was by that time more than a mile on his way, with the funeral, to Père la Chaise. Here were her diamonds. She exhibited, hastily, an open casket containing a profusion of the largest brilliants.

"What is this?" she asked.

"A box containing money to the amount of thirty thousand pounds," I answered.

"What! all that money?" she exclaimed.

"Every *sou*."

"Was it not unnecessary to bring so much, seeing all these," she said, touching her diamonds. "It would have been kind of you, to allow me to provide for both for a time, at least. It would have made me happier even than I am."

"Dearest, generous angel!" Such was my extravagant declamation. "You forget that it may be necessary, for a long time, to observe silence as to where we are, and impossible to communicate safely with any one."

"You have then here this great sum—are you certain; have you counted it?"

"Yes, certainly; I received it to-day," I answered, perhaps showing a little surprise in my face, "I counted it, of course, on drawing it from my bankers."

"It makes me feel a little nervous, travelling with so much money; but these jewels make as great a danger; *that* can add but little to it. Place them side by side; you shall take off your great coat when we are ready to go, and with it manage to conceal these boxes. I should not like the drivers to suspect that we were conveying such a treasure. I must ask you now to close the curtains of that window, and bar the shutters."

I had hardly done this when a knock was heard at the room-door.

"I know who this is," she said, in a whisper to me.

I saw that she was not alarmed. She went softly to the door, and a whispered conversation for a minute followed.

"My trusty maid, who is coming with us. She says we cannot safely go sooner than ten minutes. She is bringing some coffee to the next room."

She opened the door and looked in.

"I must tell her not to take too much luggage. She is so odd! Don't follow—stay where you are—it is better that she should not see you."

She left the room with a gesture of caution.

A change had come over the manner of this beautiful woman. For the last few minutes a shadow had been stealing over her, an air of abstraction, a look bordering on suspicion. Why was she pale? Why had there come that dark look in her eyes? Why had her very voice become changed? Had anything gone suddenly wrong? Did some danger threaten?

This doubt, however, speedily quieted itself. If there had been anything of the kind, she would, of course, have told me. It was only natural that, as the crisis approached, she should become more and more nervous. She did not return quite so soon as I had expected. To a man in my situation absolute quietude is next to impossible. I moved restlessly about the room. It was a small one. There was a door at the other end. I opened it, rashly enough. I listened, it was perfectly silent. I was in an excited, eager state, and every faculty engrossed about what was coming, and in so far detached from the immediate present. I can't account, in any other way, for my having done so many foolish things that night, for I was, naturally, by no means deficient in cunning. About the most stupid of those was, that instead of immediately closing that door, which I never ought to have opened, I actually took a candle and walked into the room.

There I made, quite unexpectedly, a rather startling discovery.

CHAPTER XXIII.

A CUP OF COFFEE.

The room was carpetless. On the floor were a quantity of shavings, and some score of bricks. Beyond these, on a narrow table, lay an object, which I could hardly believe I saw aright.

I approached and drew from it a sheet which had very slightly disguised its shape. There was no mistake about it. It was a coffin; and on the lid was a plate, with the inscription in French:

PIERRE DE LA ROCHE ST. AMAND.

AGÉE DE XXIII ANS.

I drew back with a double shock. So, then, the funeral after all had not yet left! Here lay the body. I had been deceived. This, no doubt, accounted for the embarrassment so manifest in the Countess's manner. She would have done more wisely had she told me the true state of the case.

I drew back from this melancholy room, and closed the door. Her distrust of me was the worst rashness she could have committed. There is nothing more dangerous than misapplied caution. In entire ignorance of the fact I had entered the room, and there I might have lighted upon some of the very persons it was our special anxiety that I should avoid.

These reflections were interrupted, almost as soon as begun, by the return of the Countess de St. Alyre. I saw at a glance that she detected in my face some evidence of what had happened, for she threw a hasty look towards the door.

"Have you seen anything—anything to disturb you, dear Richard? Have you been out of this room?"

I answered promptly, "Yes," and told her frankly what had happened.

"Well, I did not like to make you more uneasy than necessary. Besides, it is disgusting and horrible. The body *is* there; but the Count had departed a quarter of an hour before I lighted the coloured lamp, and prepared to receive you. The body did not arrive till eight or ten minutes after he had set out. He was afraid lest the people at Père la Chaise should suppose that the funeral was postponed. He knew that the remains of poor Pierre would certainly reach this to-night although an unexpected delay has occurred; and there are reasons why he wishes the funeral completed before to-morrow. The hearse with the body must leave this in ten minutes. So soon as it is gone, we shall be free to set out upon our wild and happy journey. The horses are to the carriage in the *porte-cochère*. As for this *funeste* horror (she shuddered very prettily), let us think of it no more."

She bolted the door of communication, and when she turned, it was with such a pretty penitence in her face and attitude, that I was ready to throw myself at her feet.

"It is the last time," she said, in a sweet sad little pleading, "I shall ever practise a deception on my brave and beautiful Richard—my hero? Am I forgiven."

Here was another scene of passionate effusion, and lovers' raptures and declamations, but only murmured, lest the ears of listeners should be busy.

At length, on a sudden, she raised her hand, as if to prevent my stirring, her eyes fixed on me, and her ear toward the door of the room in which the coffin was placed, and remained breathless in that attitude for a few moments. Then, with a little nod towards me, she moved on tip-toe to the door, and listened, extending her hand backward as if to warn me against advancing; and, after a little time, she returned, still on tip-toe, and whispered to me, "They are removing the coffin—come with me."

I accompanied her into the room from which her maid, as she told me, had spoken to her. Coffee and some old china cups, which appeared to me quite beautiful, stood on a silver tray; and some liqueur glasses, with a flask, which turned out to be noyeau, on a salver beside it.

"I shall attend you. I'm to be your servant here; I am to have my own way; I shall not think myself forgiven by my darling if he refuses to indulge me in anything." She filled a cup with coffee, and handed it to me with her left hand, her right arm she fondly, passed over my shoulder, and with her fingers through my curls caressingly, she whispered, "Take this, I shall take some just now."

It was excellent; and when I had done she handed me the liqueur, which I also drank.

"Come back, dearest, to the next room," she said. "By this time those terrible people must have gone away, and we shall be safer there, for the present, than here."

"You shall direct, and I obey; you shall command me, not only now, but always, and in all things, my beautiful queen!" I murmured.

My heroics were unconsciously, I daresay, founded upon my ideal of the French school of lovemaking. I am, even now, ashamed as I recall the bombast to which I treated the Countess de St. Alyre.

"There, you shall have another miniature glass—a fairy glass—of noyeau," she said, gaily. In this volatile creature, the funereal gloom of the moment before, and the suspense of an adventure on which all her future was staked, disappeared in a moment. She ran and returned with another tiny glass, which, with an eloquent or tender little speech, I placed to my lips and sipped.

I kissed her hand, I kissed her lips, I gazed in her beautiful eyes, and kissed her again unresisting.

"You call me Richard, by what name am I to call my beautiful divinity?" I asked.

"You call me Eugenie, it is my name. Let us be quite real; that is, if you love as entirely as I do."

"Eugenie!" I exclaimed, and broke into a new rapture upon the name.

It ended by my telling her how impatient I was to set out upon our journey; and, as I spoke, suddenly an odd sensation overcame me. It was not in the slightest degree like faintness. I can find no phrase to describe it, but a sudden constraint of the brain; it was as if the membrane in which it lies, if there be such a thing, contracted, and became inflexible.

"Dear Richard! what is the matter?" she exclaimed, with terror in her looks. "Good Heavens! are you ill. I conjure you, sit down; sit in this chair." She almost forced me into one; I was in no condition to offer the least resistance. I recognised but too truly the sensations that supervened. I was lying back in the chair in which I sat without the power, by this time, of uttering a syllable, of closing my eyelids, of moving my eyes, of stirring a muscle. I had in a few seconds glided into precisely the state in which I had passed so many appalling hours when approaching Paris, in my night-drive with the Marquis d'Harmonville.

Great and loud was the lady's agony. She seemed to have lost all sense of fear. She called me by my name, shook me by the shoulder, raised my arm and let it fall, all the time imploring of me, in distracting sentences, to make the slightest sign of life, and vowing that if I did not, she would make away with herself.

These ejaculations, after a minute or two, suddenly subsided. The lady was perfectly silent and cool. In a very business-like way she took a candle and stood before me, pale indeed, very pale, but with an expression only of intense scrutiny with a dash of horror in it. She moved the candle before my eyes slowly, evidently watching the effect. She then set it down, and rang a hand-bell two or three times sharply. She placed the two cases (I mean hers containing the jewels) and my strong box, side by side on the table; and I saw her carefully lock the door that gave access to the room in which I had just now sipped my coffee.

IN A GLASS DARKLY
VOLUME III

THE ROOM IN THE DRAGON VOLANT.

CHAPTER XXIV.

HOPE.

She had scarcely set down my heavy box, which she seemed to have considerable difficulty in raising on the table, when the door of the room in which I had seen the coffin, opened, and a sinister and unexpected apparition entered.

It was the Count de St. Alyre, who had been, as I have told you, reported to me to be, for some considerable time, on his way to Père la Chaise. He stood before me for a moment, with the frame of the doorway and a background of darkness enclosing him, like a portrait. His slight, mean figure was draped in the deepest mourning. He had a pair of black gloves in his hand, and his hat with crape round it.

When he was not speaking his face showed signs of agitation; his mouth was puckering and working. He looked damnably wicked and frightened.

"Well, my dear Eugenie? Well, child—eh? Well, it all goes admirably?"

"Yes," she answered, in a low, hard tone. "But you and Planard should not have left that door open."

This she said sternly. "He went in there and looked about wherever he liked; it was fortunate he did not move aside the lid of the coffin."

"Planard should have seen to that," said the Count, sharply. "Ma foi! I can't be everywhere!" He advanced half-a-dozen short quick steps into the room toward me, and placed his glasses to his eyes.

"Monsieur Beckett," he cried sharply, two or three times, "Hi! don't you know me?"

He approached and peered more closely in my face; raised my hand and shook it, calling me again, then let it drop, and said—"It has set in admirably, my pretty mignonne. When did it commence?"

The Countess came and stood beside him, and looked at me steadily for some seconds.

You can't conceive the effect of the silent gaze of those two pairs of evil eyes.

The lady glanced to where, I recollected, the mantel-piece stood, and upon it a clock, the regular click of which I sharply heard.

"Four—five—six minutes and a half," she said slowly, in a cold hard way.

"Brava! Bravissima! my beautiful queen! my little Venus! my Joan of Arc! my heroine! my paragon of women!"

He was gloating on me with an odious curiosity, smiling, as he groped backward with his thin brown fingers to find the lady's hand; but she, not (I dare say) caring for his caresses, drew back a little.

"Come, ma chère, let us count these things. What is it? Pocket-book? Or—or—what?"

"It is that?" said the lady, pointing with a look of disgust to the box, which lay in its leather case on the table.

"Oh! Let us see—let us count—let us see," he said, as he was unbuckling the straps with his tremulous fingers. "We must count them—we must see to it. I have pencil and pocket-book—but—where's the key? See this cursed lock! My ——! What is it? Where's the key?"

He was standing before the Countess, shuffling his feet, with his hands extended and all his fingers quivering.

"I have not got it; how could I? It is in his pocket, of course," said the lady.

In another instant the fingers of the old miscreant were in my pockets: he plucked out everything they contained, and some keys among the rest.

I lay in precisely the state in which I had been during my drive with the Marquis to Paris. This wretch I knew was about to rob me. The whole drama, and the Countess's rôle in it, I could not yet comprehend. I could not be sure—so much more presence of mind and histrionic resource have women than fall to the lot of our clumsy sex—whether the return of the Count was not, in truth, a surprise to her; and this scrutiny of the contents of my strong box, an extempore undertaking of the Count's. But it was clearing more and more every moment: and I was destined, very soon, to comprehend minutely my appalling situation.

I had not the power of turning my eyes this way or that, the smallest fraction of a hair's breadth. But let any one, placed as I was at the end of a room, ascertain for himself by experiment how wide is the field of sight, without the slightest alteration in the line of vision, he will find that it takes in the entire breadth of a large room, and that up to a very short distance before him; and imperfectly, by a refraction, I believe, in the eye itself, to a point very near indeed. Next to nothing that passed in the room, therefore, was hidden from me.

The old man had, by this time, found the key. The leather case was open. The box cramped round with iron, was next unlocked. He turned out its contents upon the table.

"Rouleaux of a hundred Napoleons each. One, two, three. Yes, quick. Write down a thousand Napoleons. One, two; yes, right. Another thousand, write!" And so, on and on till gold was rapidly counted. Then came the notes.

"Ten thousand francs. Write. Ten thousand francs again: is it written? Another ten thousand francs: is it down? Smaller notes would have been better. They should have been smaller. These are horribly embarrassing. Bolt that door again; Planard would become unreasonable if he knew the amount. Why did you not tell him to get it in smaller notes? No matter now—go on—it can't be helped—

write—another ten thousand francs—another—another." And so on, till my treasure was counted out, before my face, while I saw and heard all that passed with the sharpest distinctness, and my mental perceptions were horribly vivid. But in all other respects I was dead.

He had replaced in the box every note and rouleau as he counted it, and now having ascertained the sum total, he locked it, replaced it, very methodically, in its cover, opened a buffet in the wainscoting, and, having placed the Countess' jewel-case and my strong box in it, he locked it; and immediately on completing these arrangements he began to complain, with fresh acrimony and maledictions of Planard's delay.

He unbolted the door, looked in the dark room beyond, and listened. He closed the door again, and returned. The old man was in a fever of suspense.

"I have kept ten thousand francs for Planard," said the Count, touching his waistcoat pocket.

"Will that satisfy him?" asked the lady.

"Why—curse him!" screamed the Count. "Has he no conscience! I'll swear to him it's half the entire thing."

He and the lady again came and looked at me anxiously for awhile, in silence; and then the old Count began to grumble again about Planard, and to compare his watch with the clock. The lady seemed less impatient; she sat no longer looking at me, but across the room, so that her profile was toward me—and strangely changed, dark and witch-like it looked. My last hope died as I beheld that jaded face from which the mask had dropped. I was certain that they intended to crown their robbery by murder. Why did they not despatch me at once? What object could there be in postponing the catastrophe which would expedite their own safety. I cannot recall, even to myself, adequately the horrors unutterable that I underwent. You must suppose a real night-mare—I mean a nightmare in which the objects and the danger are real, and the spell of corporal death appears to be protractable at the pleasure of the persons who preside at your unearthly torments. I could have no doubt as to the cause of the state in which I was.

In this agony, to which I could not give the slightest expression, I saw the door of the room where the coffin had been, open slowly, and the Marquis d'Harmonville entered the room.

CHAPTER XXV.

DESPAIR.

A moment's hope, hope violent and fluctuating, hope that was nearly torture, and then came a dialogue, and with it the terrors of despair.

"Thank heaven, Planard, you have come at last," said the Count, taking him, with both hands, by the arm and clinging to it, and drawing him toward me. "See, look at him. It has all gone sweetly, sweetly, sweetly up to this. Shall I hold the candle for you?"

My friend d'Harmonville, Planard, whatever he was, came to me, pulling off his gloves, which he popped into his pocket.

"The candle, a little this way," he said, and stooping over me he looked earnestly in my face. He touched my forehead, drew his hand across it, and then looked in my eyes for a time.

"Well, doctor, what do you think?" whispered the Count.

"How much did you give him?" said the Marquis, thus suddenly stunted down to a doctor.

"Seventy drops," said the lady.

"In the hot coffee?"

"Yes; sixty in a hot cup of coffee and ten in the liqueur."

Her voice, low and hard, seemed to me to tremble a little. It takes a long course of guilt to subjugate nature completely, and prevent those exterior signs of agitation that outlive all good.

The doctor, however, was treating me as coolly as he might a subject which he was about to place on the dissecting-table for a lecture.

He looked into my eyes again for awhile, took my wrist, and applied his fingers to the pulse.

"That action suspended," he said to himself.

Then again he placed something that, for the moment I saw it, looked like a piece of gold-beater's leaf, to my lips, holding his head so far that his own breathing could not affect it.

"Yes," he said in soliloquy, very low.

Then he plucked my shirt-breast open and applied the stethoscope, shifted it from point to point, listened with his ear to its end, as if for a very far off sound, raised his head, and said, in like manner, softly to himself, "All appreciable action of the lungs has subsided."

Then turning from the sound, as I conjectured, he said:

"Seventy drops, allowing ten for waste, ought to hold him fast for six hours and a half—that is ample. The experiment I tried in the carriage was only thirty drops, and showed a highly sensitive brain. It would not do to kill him, you know. You are certain you did not exceed seventy?"

"Perfectly," said the lady.

"If he were to die the evaporation would be arrested, and foreign matter, some of it poisonous, would be found in the stomach, don't you see? If you are doubtful, it would be well to use the stomach-pump."

"Dearest Eugenie, be frank, be frank, do be frank," urged the Count.

"I am not doubtful, I am certain," she answered.

"How long ago, exactly? I told you to observe the time."

"I did; the minute-hand was exactly there, under the point of that Cupid's foot."

"It will last, then, probably for seven hours. He will recover then; the evaporation will be complete, and not one particle of the fluid will remain in the stomach."

It was reassuring, at all events, to hear that there was no intention to murder me. No one who has not tried it knows the terror of the approach of death, when the mind is clear, the instincts of life unimpaired, and no excitement to disturb the appreciation of that entirely new horror.

The nature and purpose of this tenderness was very, very peculiar, and as yet I had not a suspicion of it.

"You leave France, I suppose?" said the ex-Marquis.

"Yes, certainly, to-morrow," answered the Count.

"And where do you mean to go?"

"That I have not yet settled," he answered quickly.

"You won't tell a friend, eh?"

"I can't till I know. This has turned out an unprofitable affair."

"We shall settle that by-and-by."

"It is time we should get him lying down, eh?" said the Count, indicating me with one finger.

"Yes, we must proceed rapidly now. Are his night-shirt and night-cap—you understand—here?"

"All ready," said the Count.

"Now, Madame," said the doctor, turning to the lady, and making her, in spite of the emergency, a bow, "it is time you should retire."

The lady passed into the room, in which I had taken my cup of treacherous coffee, and I saw her no more.

The Count took a candle, and passed through the door at the further end of the room, returning with a roll of linen in his hand. He bolted first one door, then the other.

They now, in silence, proceeded to undress me rapidly. They were not many minutes in accomplishing this.

What the doctor had termed my night-shirt, a long garment which reached below my feet, was now on, and a cap, that resembled a female nightcap more than anything I had ever seen upon a male head, was fitted upon mine, and tied under my chin.

And now, I thought, I shall be laid in a bed, to recover how I can, and, in the meantime, the conspirators will have escaped with their booty, and pursuit be in vain.

This was my best hope at the time; but it was soon clear that their plans were very different.

The Count and Planard now went, together, into the room that lay straight before me. I heard them talking low, and a sound of shuffling feet; then a long rumble; it suddenly stopped; it recommenced; it continued; side by side they came in at the door, their backs toward me. They were dragging something along the floor that made a continued boom and rumble, but they interposed between me and it, so that I could not see it until they had dragged it almost beside me; and then, merciful heaven! I saw it plainly enough. It was the coffin I had seen in the next room. It lay now flat on the floor, its edge against the chair in which I sat. Planard removed the lid. The coffin was empty.

CHAPTER XXVI.

CATASTROPHE.

"Those seem to be good horses, and we change on the way," said Planard. "You give the men a Napoleon or two; we must do it within three hours and a quarter. Now, come; I'll lift him, upright, so as to place his feet in their proper berth, and you must keep them together, and draw the white shirt well down over them."

In another moment I was placed, as he described, sustained in Planard's arms, standing at the foot of the coffin, and so lowered backward, gradually, till I lay my length in it. Then the man, whom he called Planard, stretched my arms by my sides, and carefully arranged the frills at my breast, and the folds of the shroud, and after that, taking his stand at the foot of the coffin, made a survey which seemed to satisfy him.

The Count, who was very methodical, took my clothes, which had just been removed, folded them rapidly together and locked them up, as I afterwards heard, in one of the three presses which opened by doors in the panel.

I now understood their frightful plan. This coffin had been prepared for me; the funeral of St. Amand was a sham to mislead inquiry; I had myself given the order at Père la Chaise, signed it, and paid the fees for the interment of the fictitious Pierre de St. Amand, whose place I was to take, to lie in his coffin, with his name on the plate above my breast, and with a ton of clay packed down upon me; to waken from this catalepsy, after I had been for hours in the grave, there to perish by a death the most horrible that imagination can conceive.

If, hereafter, by any caprice of curiosity or suspicion, the coffin should be exhumed, and the body it enclosed examined, no chemistry could detect a trace of poison, nor the most cautious examination the slightest mark of violence.

I had myself been at the utmost pains to mystify inquiry, should my disappearance excite surmises, and had even written to my few correspondents in England to tell them that they were not to look for a letter from me for three weeks at least.

In the moment of my guilty elation death had caught me, and there was no escape. I tried to pray to God in my unearthly panic, but only thoughts of terror, judgment, and eternal anguish, crossed the distraction of my immediate doom.

I must not try to recall what is indeed indescribable—the multiform horrors of my own thoughts. I will relate, simply, what befell, every detail of which remains sharp in my memory as if cut in steel.

"The undertaker's men are in the hall," said the Count.

"They must not come till this is fixed," answered Planard. "Be good enough to take hold of the lower part while I take this end." I was not left long to conjecture what was coming, for in a few seconds more something slid across, a few inches above my face, and entirely excluded the light, and muffled sound, so that nothing that was not very distinct reached my ears henceforward; but very distinctly came the working of a turnscrew, and the crunching home of screws in succession. Than these vulgar sounds, no doom spoken in thunder could have been more tremendous.

The rest I must relate, not as it then reached my ears, which was too imperfectly and interruptedly to supply a connected narrative, but as it was afterwards told me by other people.

The coffin-lid being screwed down, the two gentlemen arranged the room, and adjusted the coffin so that it lay perfectly straight along the boards, the Count being specially anxious that there should be no appearance of hurry or disorder in the room, which might have suggested remark and conjecture.

When this was done, Doctor Planard said he would go to the hall to summon the men who were to carry the coffin out and place it in the hearse. The Count pulled on his black gloves, and held his white handkerchief in his hand, a very impressive chief-mourner. He stood a little behind the head of the coffin, awaiting the arrival of the persons who accompanied Planard, and whose fast steps he soon heard approaching.

Planard came first. He entered the room through the apartment in which the coffin had been originally placed. His manner was changed; there was something of a swagger in it.

"Monsieur le Comte," he said, as he strode through the door, followed by half-a-dozen persons. "I am sorry to have to announce to you a most unseasonable interruption. Here is Monsieur Carmaignac, a gentleman holding an office in the police department, who says that information to the effect that large quantities of smuggled English and other goods have been distributed in this neighbourhood, and that a portion of them is concealed in your house. I have ventured to assure him, of my own knowledge, that nothing can be more false than that information, and that you would be only too happy to throw open for his inspection, at a moment's notice, every room, closet, and cupboard in your house."

"Most assuredly," exclaimed the Count, with a stout voice, but a very white face. "Thank you, my good friend, for having anticipated me. I will place my house and keys at his disposal, for the purpose of his scrutiny, so soon as he is good enough to inform me, of what specific contraband goods he comes in search."

"The Count de St. Alyre will pardon me," answered Carmaignac, a little dryly. "I am forbidden by my instructions to make that disclosure; and that I am instructed to make a general search, this warrant will sufficiently apprise Monsieur le Comte."

"Monsieur Carmaignac, may I hope," interposed Planard, "that you will permit the Count de St. Alyre to attend the funeral of his kinsman, who lies here, as you see—" (he pointed to the plate upon the coffin)—"and to convey whom to Père la Chaise, a hearse waits at this moment at the door."

"That, I regret to say, I cannot permit. My instructions are precise; but the delay, I trust, will be but trifling. Monsieur le Comte will not suppose for a moment that I suspect him; but we have a duty to perform, and I must act as if I did. When I am ordered to search, I search; things are sometimes hid in such bizarre places. I can't say, for instance, what that coffin may contain."

"The body of my kinsman, Monsieur Pierre de St. Amand," answered the Count, loftily.

"Oh! then you've seen him?"

"Seen him? Often, too often?" The Count was evidently a good deal moved.

"I mean the body?"

The Count stole a quick glance at Planard.

"N—no, Monsieur—that is, I mean only for a moment." Another quick glance at Planard.

"But quite long enough, I fancy, to recognize him?" insinuated that gentleman.

"Of course—of course; instantly—perfectly. What! Pierre de St. Amand? Not know him at a glance? No, no, poor fellow, I know him too well for that."

"The things I am in search of," said Monsieur Carmaignac, "would fit in a narrow compass servants are so ingenious sometimes. Let us raise the lid."

"Pardon me, Monsieur," said the Count, peremptorily, advancing to the side of the coffin, and extending his arm across it. "I cannot permit that indignity—that desecration."

"There shall be none, sir,—simply the raising of the lid; you shall remain in the room. If it should prove as we all hope, you shall have the pleasure of one other look, really the last, upon your beloved kinsman."

"But, sir, I can't."

"But, Monsieur, I must."

"But, besides, the thing, the turnscrew, broke when the last screw was turned; and I give you my sacred honour there is nothing but the body in this coffin."

"Of course Monsieur le Comte believes all that; but he does not know so well as I the legerdemain in use among servants, who are accustomed to smuggling. Here, Philippe, you must take off the lid of that coffin."

The Count protested; but Philippe—a man with a bald head, and a smirched face, looking like a working blacksmith—placed on the floor a leather bag of tools, from which, having looked at the coffin, and picked with his nail at the screw-heads, he selected a turnscrew, and, with a few deft twirls at each of the screws, they stood up like little rows of mushrooms, and the lid was raised. I saw the light, of which I thought I had seen my last, once more; but the axis of vision remained fixed. As I was reduced to the cataleptic state in a position nearly perpendicular, I continued looking straight before me, and thus my gaze was now fixed upon the ceiling. I saw the face of Carmaignac leaning over me with a curious frown. It seemed to me that there was no recognition in his eyes. Oh, heaven! that I could have uttered were it but one cry! I saw the dark, mean mask of the little Count staring down at me from the other side; the face of the pseudo-marquis also peering at me, but not so full in the line of vision; there were other faces also.

"I see, I see," said Carmaignac, withdrawing. "Nothing of the kind there."

"You will be good enough to direct your man to re-adjust the lid of the coffin, and to fix the screws," said the Count, taking courage; "and—and—really the funeral must proceed. It is not fair to the people who have but moderate fees for night-work, to keep them hour after hour beyond the time."

"Count de St. Alyre, you shall go in a very few minutes. I will direct, just now, all about the coffin."

The Count looked toward the door, and there saw a gendarme; and two or three more grave and stalwart specimens of the same force were also in the room. The Count was very uncomfortably excited; it was growing insupportable.

"As this gentleman makes a difficulty about my attending the obsequies of my kinsman, I will ask you, Planard, to accompany the funeral in my stead."

"In a few minutes," answered the incorrigible Carmaignac. "I must first trouble you for the key that opens that press."

He pointed direct at the press, in which the clothes had just been locked up.

"I—I have no objection," said the Count—"none, of course; only they have not been used for an age. I'll direct some one to look for the key."

"If you have not got it about you, it is quite unnecessary. Philippe, try your skeleton-keys with that press. I want it opened. Whose clothes are these?" inquired Carmaignac when, the press having been opened, he took out the suit that had been placed there scarcely two minutes since.

"I can't say," answered the Count. "I know nothing of the contents of that press. A roguish servant, named Lablais, whom I dismissed about a year ago, had the key. I have not seen it open for ten years or more. The clothes are probably his.

"Here are visiting cards, see, and here a marked pocket-handkerchief—'R.B.' upon it. He must have stolen them from a person named Beckett—R. Beckett. 'Mr. Beckett, Berkley Square,' the card says; and, my faith! here's a watch and a bunch of seals; one of them with the initials 'R.B.' upon it. That servant, Lablais, must have been a consummate rogue!"

"So he was; you are right, sir."

"It strikes me that he possibly stole these clothes," continued Carmaignac, "from the man in the coffin, who, in that case, would be Monsieur Beckett, and not Monsieur de St. Amand. For, wonderful to relate, Monsieur, the watch is still going! That man in the coffin, I believe, is not dead, but simply drugged. And for having robbed and intended to murder him, I arrest you, Nicolas de la Marque, Count de St. Alyre."

In another moment the old villain was a prisoner. I heard his discordant voice break quaveringly into sudden vehemence and volubility; now croaking—now shrieking, as he oscillated between protests, threats, and impious appeals to the God who will "judge the secrets of men!" And thus lying and raving, he was removed from the room, and placed in the same coach with his beautiful and abandoned accomplice, already arrested; and, with two gendarmes sitting beside them, they were immediately driving at a rapid pace towards the Conciergerie.

There were now added to the general chorus two voices, very different in quality; one was that of the gasconading Colonel Gaillarde, who had with difficulty been kept in the background up to this; the other was that of my jolly friend Whistlewick, who had come to identify me.

I shall tell you, just now, how this project against my property and life, so ingenious and monstrous, was exploded. I must first say a word about myself. I was placed in a hot bath, under the direction of Planard, as consummate a villain as any of the gang, but now thoroughly in the interests of the prosecution. Thence I was laid in a warm bed, the window of the room being open. These simple measures restored me in about three hours; I should otherwise, probably, have continued under the spell for nearly seven.

The practices of these nefarious conspirators had been carried on with consummate skill and secrecy. Their dupes were led, as I was, to be themselves auxiliary to the mystery which made their own destruction both safe and certain.

A search was, of course, instituted. Graves were opened in Père la Chaise. The bodies exhumed had lain there too long, and were too much decomposed to be recognized. One only was identified. The notice for the burial, in this particular case, had been signed, the order given, and the fees paid, by Gabriel Gaillarde, who was known to the official clerk, who had to transact with him this little funereal business. The very trick, that had been arranged for me, had been successfully practised in his case. The person for whom the grave had been ordered, was purely fictitious; and Gabriel Gaillarde himself filled the coffin, on the cover of which that false name was inscribed as well as upon a tomb-stone over the grave. Possibly, the same honour, under my pseudonym, may have been intended for me.

The identification was curious. This Gabriel Gaillarde had had a bad fall from a run-away horse, about five years before his mysterious disappearance. He had lost an eye and some teeth, in this accident, besides sustaining a fracture of the right leg, immediately above the ankle. He had kept the injuries to his face as profound a secret as he could. The result was, that the glass eye which had done duty for the one he had lost, remained in the socket, slightly displaced, of course, but recognizable by the "artist" who had supplied it.

More pointedly recognizable were the teeth, peculiar in workmanship, which one of the ablest dentists in Paris had himself adapted to the chasms, the cast of which, owing to peculiarities in the accident, he happened to have preserved. This cast precisely fitted the gold plate found in the mouth of the skull. The mark, also, above the ankle, in the bone, where it had re-united, corresponded exactly with the place where the fracture had knit in the limb of Gabriel Gaillarde.

The Colonel, his younger brother, had been furious about the disappearance of Gabriel, and still more so about that of his money, which he had long regarded as his proper keepsake, whenever death should remove his brother from the vexations of living. He had suspected for a long time, for certain adroitly discovered reasons, that the Count de St. Alyre and the beautiful lady, his companion, countess, or whatever else she was, had pigeoned him. To this suspicion were added some others of a still darker kind; but in their first shape, rather the exaggerated reflections of his fury, ready to believe anything, than well-defined conjectures.

At length an accident had placed the Colonel very nearly upon the right scent; a chance, possibly lucky for himself, had apprized the scoundrel Planard that the conspirators—himself among the number—were in danger. The result was that he made terms for himself, became an informer, and concerted with the police this visit made to the Château de la Carque, at the critical moment when every measure had been completed that was necessary to construct a perfect case against his guilty accomplices.

I need not describe the minute industry or forethought with which the police agents collected all the details necessary to support the case. They had brought an able physician, who, even had Planard failed, would have supplied the necessary medical evidence.

My trip to Paris, you will believe, had not turned out quite so agreeably as I had anticipated. I was the principal witness for the prosecution in this cause célébre, with all the agrémens that attend that enviable position. Having had an escape, as my friend Whistlewick said, "with a squeak" for my life, I innocently fancied that I should have been an object of considerable interest to Parisian society; but, a good deal to my mortification, I discovered that I was the object of a good-natured but contemptuous merriment. I was a balourd, a benêt, un âne, and figured even in caricatures. I became a sort of public character, a dignity,

"Unto which I was not born,"

and from which I fled as soon as I conveniently could, without even paying my friend the Marquis d'Harmonville a visit at his hospitable château.

The Marquis escaped scot-free. His accomplice, the Count, was executed. The fair Eugenie, under extenuating circumstances—consisting, so far as I could discover of her good looks—got off for six years' imprisonment.

Colonel Gaillarde recovered some of his brother's money, out of the not very affluent estate of the Count and soi-disant Countess. This, and the execution of the Count, put him in high good humour. So far from insisting on a hostile meeting, he shook me very graciously by the hand, told me that he looked upon the wound on his head, inflicted by the knob of my stick, as having been received in an honourable, though irregular duel, in which he had no disadvantage or unfairness to complain of.

I think I have only two additional details to mention. The bricks discovered in the room with the coffin, had been packed in it, in straw, to supply the weight of a dead body, and to prevent the suspicions and contradictions that might have been excited by the arrival of an empty coffin at the château.

Secondly, the Countess's magnificent brilliants were examined by a lapidary, and pronounced to be worth about five pounds to a tragedy-queen, who happened to be in want of a suite of paste.

The Countess had figured some years before as one of the cleverest actresses on the minor stage of Paris, where she had been picked up by the Count and used as his principal accomplice.

She it was who, admirably disguised, had rifled my papers in the carriage on my memorable night-journey to Paris. She also had figured as the interpreting magician of the palanquin at the ball at Versailles. So far as I was affected by that elaborate mystification it was intended to re-animate my interest, which, they feared, might flag in the beautiful Countess. It had its design and action upon other intended victims also; but of them there is, at present, no need to speak. The introduction of a real corpse—procured from a person who supplied the Parisian anatomists—involved no real danger, while it heightened the mystery and kept the prophet alive in the gossip of the town and in the thoughts of the noodles with whom he had conferred.

I divided the remainder of the summer and autumn between Switzerland and Italy.

As the well-worn phrase goes, I was a sadder if not a wiser man. A great deal of the horrible impression left upon my mind was due, of course, to the mere action of nerves and brain. But serious feelings of another and deeper kind remained. My after life was ultimately formed by the shock I had then received. Those impressions led me—but not till after many years—to happier though not less serious thoughts; and I have deep reason to be thankful to the all-merciful Ruler of events, for an early and terrible lesson in the ways of sin.

CARMILLA.

PROLOGUE.

Upon a paper attached to the Narrative which follows, Doctor Hesselius has written a rather elaborate note, which he accompanies with a reference to his Essay on the strange subject which the MS. illuminates.

This mysterious subject, he treats, in that Essay, with his usual learning and acumen, and with remarkable directness and condensation. It will form but one volume of the series of that extraordinary man's collected papers.

As I publish the case, in these volumes, simply to interest the "laity," I shall forestal the intelligent lady, who relates it, in nothing; and, after due consideration, I have determined, therefore, to abstain from presenting any précis of the learned Doctor's reasoning, or extract from his statement on a subject which he describes as "involving, not improbably, some of the profoundest arcana of our dual existence, and its intermediates."

I was anxious, on discovering this paper, to re-open the correspondence commenced by Doctor Hesselius, so many years before, with a person so clever and careful as his informant seems to have been. Much to my regret, however, I found that she had died in the interval.

She, probably, could have added little to the Narrative which she communicates in the following pages, with, so far as I can pronounce, such a conscientious particularity.

CHAPTER I.

AN EARLY FRIGHT.

In Styria, we, though by no means magnificent people, inhabit a castle, or schloss. A small income, in that part of the world, goes a great way. Eight or nine hundred a year does wonders. Scantily enough ours would have answered among wealthy people at home. My father is English, and I bear an English name, although I never saw England. But here, in this lonely and primitive place, where everything is so marvellously cheap, I really don't see how ever so much more money would at all materially add to our comforts, or even luxuries.

My father was in the Austrian service, and retired upon a pension and his patrimony, and purchased this feudal residence, and the small estate on which it stands, a bargain.

Nothing can be more picturesque or solitary. It stands on a slight eminence in a forest. The road, very old and narrow, passes in front of its drawbridge, never raised in my time, and its moat, stocked with perch, and sailed over by many swans, and floating on its surface white fleets of water-lilies.

Over all this the schloss shows its many-windowed front; its towers, and its Gothic chapel.

The forest opens in an irregular and very picturesque glade before its gate, and at the right a steep Gothic bridge carries the road over a stream that winds in deep shadow through the wood.

I have said that this is a very lonely place. Judge whether I say truth. Looking from the hall door towards the road, the forest in which our castle stands extends fifteen miles to the right, and twelve to the left. The nearest inhabited village, is about seven of your English miles to the left. The nearest inhabited schloss of any historic associations, is that of old General Spielsdorf, nearly twenty miles away to the right.

I have said "the nearest inhabited village," because there is, only three miles westward, that is to say in the direction of General Spielsdorf's schloss, a ruined village, with its quaint little church, now roofless, in the aisle of which are the mouldering tombs of the proud family of Karnstein, now extinct, who once owned the equally desolate château which, in the thick of the forest, overlooks the silent ruins of the town.

Respecting the cause of the desertion of this striking and melancholy spot, there is a legend which I shall relate to you another time.

I must tell you now, how very small is the party who constitute the inhabitants of our castle. I don't include servants, or those dependents who occupy rooms in the buildings attached to the schloss. Listen, and wonder! My father, who is the kindest man on earth, but growing old; and I, at the date of my story, only nineteen. Eight years have passed since then. I and my father constituted the family at the schloss. My mother, a Styrian lady, died in my infancy, but I had a good-natured governess, who had been with me from, I might almost say, my infancy. I could not remember the time when her fat, benignant face was not a familiar picture in my memory. This was Madame Perrodon, a native of Berne, whose care and good nature in part supplied to me the loss of my mother, whom I do not even remember, so early I lost her. She made a third at our little dinner party. There was a fourth, Mademoiselle De Lafontaine, a lady such as you term, I believe, a "finishing governess." She spoke French and German, Madame Perrodon French and broken English, to which my father and I added English, which, partly to prevent its becoming a lost language among us, and partly from patriotic motives, we spoke every day. The consequence was a Babel, at which strangers used to laugh, and which I shall make no attempt to reproduce in this narrative. And there were two or three young lady friends besides, pretty nearly of my own age, who were occasional visitors, for longer or shorter terms; and these visits I sometimes returned.

These were our regular social resources; but of course there were chance visits from "neighbours" of only five or six leagues distance. My life was, notwithstanding, rather a solitary one, I can assure you.

My gouvernantes had just so much control over me as you might conjecture such sage persons would have in the case of a rather spoiled girl, whose only parent allowed her pretty nearly her own way in everything.

The first occurrence in my existence, which produced a terrible impression upon my mind, which, in fact, never has been effaced, was one of the very earliest incidents of my life which I can recollect. Some people will think it so trifling that it should not be recorded here. You will see, however, by-and-bye, why I mention it. The nursery, as it was called, though I had it all to myself, was a large room in the upper story of the castle, with a steep oak roof. I can't have been more than six years old, when one night I awoke, and looking round the room from my bed, failed to see the nursery-maid. Neither was my nurse there; and I thought myself alone. I was not frightened, for I was one of those happy children who are studiously kept in ignorance of ghost stories, of fairy tales, and of all such lore as makes us cover up our heads when the door creeks suddenly, or the flicker of an expiring candle makes the shadow of a bed-post dance upon the wall, nearer to our faces. I was vexed and insulted at finding myself, as I conceived, neglected, and I began to whimper, preparatory to a hearty bout of roaring; when to my surprise, I saw a solemn, but very pretty face looking at me from the side of the bed. It was that of a young lady who was kneeling, with her hands under the coverlet. I looked at her with a kind of pleased wonder, and ceased whimpering. She caressed me with her hands, and lay down beside me on the bed, and drew me towards her, smiling; I felt immediately delightfully soothed, and fell asleep again. I was wakened by a sensation as if two needles ran into my breast very deep at the same moment, and I cried loudly. The lady started back, with her eyes fixed on me, and then slipped down upon the floor, and, as I thought, hid herself under the bed.

I was now for the first time frightened, and I yelled with all my might and main. Nurse, nursery-maid, housekeeper, all came running in, and hearing my story, they made light of it, soothing me all they could meanwhile. But, child as I was, I could perceive that their faces were pale with an unwonted look of anxiety, and I saw them look under the bed, and about the room, and peep under tables and pluck open cupboards; and the housekeeper whispered to the nurse: "Lay your hand along that hollow in the bed; some one did lie there, so sure as you did not; the place is still warm."

I remember the nursery-maid petting me, and all three examining my chest, where I told them I felt the puncture, and pronouncing that there was no sign visible that any such thing had happened to me.

The housekeeper and the two other servants who were in charge of the nursery, remained sitting up all night; and from that time a servant always sat up in the nursery until I was about fourteen.

I was very nervous for a long time after this. A doctor was called in, he was pallid and elderly. How well I remember his long saturnine face, slightly pitted with small-pox, and his chesnut wig. For a good while, every second day, he came and gave me medicine, which of course I hated.

The morning after I saw this apparition I was in a state of terror, and could not bear to be left alone, daylight though it was, for a moment.

I remember my father coming up and standing at the bedside, and talking cheerfully, and asking the nurse a number of questions, and laughing very heartily at one of the answers; and patting me on the shoulder, and kissing me, and telling me not to be frightened, that it was nothing but a dream and could not hurt me.

But I was not comforted, for I knew the visit of the strange woman was not a dream; and I was awfully frightened.

I was a little consoled by the nursery-maid's assuring me that it was she who had come and looked at me, and lain down beside me in the bed, and that I must have been half-dreaming not to have known her face. But this, though supported by the nurse, did not quite satisfy me.

I remember, in the course of that day, a venerable old man, in a black cassock, coming into the room with the nurse and housekeeper, and talking a little to them, and very kindly to me; his face was very sweet and gentle, and he told me they were going to pray, and joined my hands together, and desired me to say, softly, while they were praying, "Lord hear all good prayers for us, for Jesus' sake." I think these were the very words, for I often repeated them to myself, and my nurse used for years to make me say them in my prayers.

I remember so well the thoughtful sweet face of that white-haired old man, in his black cossack, as he stood in that rude, lofty, brown room, with the clumsy furniture of a fashion three hundred years old, about him, and the scanty light entering its shadowy atmosphere through the small lattice. He kneeled, and the three women with him, and he prayed aloud with an earnest quavering voice for, what appeared to me, a long time. I forget all my life preceding that event, and for some time after it is all obscure also, but the scenes I have just described stand out vivid as the isolated pictures of the phantasmagoria surrounded by darkness.

CHAPTER II.

A GUEST.

I am now going to tell you something so strange that it will require all your faith in my veracity to believe my story. It is not only true, nevertheless, but truth of which I have been an eye-witness.

It was a sweet summer evening, and my father asked me, as he sometimes did, to take a little ramble with him along that beautiful forest vista which I have mentioned as lying in front of the schloss.

"General Spielsdorf cannot come to us so soon as I had hoped," said my father, as we pursued our walk.

He was to have paid us a visit of some weeks, and we had expected his arrival next day. He was to have brought with him a young lady, his niece and ward, Mademoiselle Rheinfeldt, whom I had never seen, but whom I had heard described as a very charming girl, and in whose society I had promised myself many happy days. I was more disappointed than a young lady living in a town, or a bustling neighbourhood can y possibly imagine. This visit, and the new acquaintance it promised, had furnished my day dream for many weeks.

"And how soon does he come?" I asked.

"Not till autumn. Not for two months, I dare say," he answered. "And I am very glad now, dear, that you never knew Mademoiselle Rheinfeldt."

"And why?" I asked, both mortified and curious.

"Because the poor young lady is dead," he replied. "I quite forgot I had not told you, but you were not in the room when I received the General's letter this evening."

I was very much shocked. General Spielsdorf had mentioned in his first letter, six or seven weeks before, that she was not so well as he would wish her, but there was nothing to suggest the remotest suspicion of danger.

"Here is the General's letter," he said, handing it to me. "I am afraid he is in great affliction; the letter appears to me to have been written very nearly in distraction."

We sat down on a rude bench, under a group of magnificent lime-trees. The sun was setting with all its melancholy splendour behind the sylvan horizon, and the stream that flows beside our home, and passes under the steep old bridge I have mentioned, wound through many a group of noble trees, almost at our feet, reflecting in its current the fading crimson of the sky. General Spielsdorf's letter was so extraordinary, so vehement, and in some places so self-contradictory, that I read it twice over—the second time aloud to my father—and was still unable to account for it, except by supposing that grief had unsettled his mind.

It said "I have lost my darling daughter, for as such I loved her. During the last days of dear Bertha's illness I was not able to write to you. Before then I had no idea of her danger. I have lost her, and now learn all, too late. She died in the peace of innocence, and in the glorious hope of a blessed futurity. The fiend who betrayed our infatuated hospitality has done it all. I thought I was receiving into my house innocence, gaiety, a charming companion for my lost Bertha. Heavens! what a fool have I been! I thank God my child died without a suspicion of the cause of her sufferings. She is gone without so much as conjecturing the nature of her illness, and the accursed passion of the agent of all this misery. I devote my remaining days to tracking and extinguishing a monster. I am told I may hope to accomplish my righteous and merciful purpose. At present there is scarcely a gleam of light to guide me. I curse my conceited incredulity, my despicable affectation of superiority, my blindness, my obstinacy—all—too late. I cannot write or talk collectedly now. I am distracted. So soon as I shall have a little recovered, I mean to devote myself for a time to enquiry, which may possibly lead me as far as Vienna. Some time in the autumn, two months hence, or earlier if I live, I will see you—that is, if you permit me; I will then tell you all that I scarce dare put upon paper now. Farewell. Pray for me, dear friend."

In these terms ended this strange letter. Though I had never seen Bertha Rheinfeldt my eyes filled with tears at the sudden intelligence; I was startled, as well as profoundly disappointed.

The sun had now set, and it was twilight by the time I had returned the General's letter to my father.

It was a soft clear evening, and we loitered, speculating upon the possible meanings of the violent and incoherent sentences which I had just been reading. We had nearly a mile to walk before reaching the road that passes the schloss in front, and by that time the moon was shining brilliantly. At the drawbridge we met Madame Perrodon and Mademoiselle De Lafontaine, who had come out, without their bonnets, to enjoy the exquisite moonlight.

We heard their voices gabbling in animated dialogue as we approached. We joined them at the drawbridge, and turned about to admire with them the beautiful scene.

The glade through which we had just walked lay before us. At our left the narrow road wound away under clumps of lordly trees, and was lost to sight amid the thickening forest. At the right the same road crosses the steep and picturesque bridge, near which stands a ruined tower which once guarded that pass; and beyond the bridge an abrupt eminence rises, covered with trees, and showing in the shadows some grey ivy-clustered rocks.

Over the sward and low grounds a thin film of mist was stealing, like smoke, marking the distances with a transparent veil; and here and there we could see the river faintly flashing in the moonlight.

No softer, sweeter scene could be imagined. The news I had just heard made it melancholy; but nothing could disturb its character of profound serenity, and the enchanted glory and vagueness of the prospect.

My father, who enjoyed the picturesque, and I, stood looking in silence over the expanse beneath us. The two good governesses, standing a little way behind us, discoursed upon the scene, and were eloquent upon the moon.

Madame Perrodon was fat, middle-aged, and romantic, and talked and sighed poetically. Mademoiselle De Lafontaine—in right of her father, who was a German, assumed to be psychological, metaphysical, and something of a mystic—now declared that when the moon shone with a light so intense it was well known that it indicated a special spiritual activity. The effect of the full moon in such a state of brilliancy was manifold. It acted on dreams, it acted on lunacy, it acted on nervous people; it had marvellous physical influences connected with life. Mademoiselle related that her cousin, who was mate of a merchant ship, having taken a nap on deck on such a night, lying on his back, with his face full in the light of the moon, had wakened, after a dream of an old woman clawing him by the cheek, with his features horribly drawn to one side; and his countenance had never quite recovered its equilibrium.

"The moon, this night," she said, "is full of odylic and magnetic influence—and see, when you look behind you at the front of the schloss, how all its windows flash and twinkle with that silvery splendour, as if unseen hands had lighted up the rooms to receive fairy guests."

There are indolent states of the spirits in which, indisposed to talk ourselves, the talk of others is pleasant to our listless ears; and I gazed on, pleased with the tinkle of the ladies' conversation.

"I have got into one of my moping moods to-night," said my father, after a silence, and quoting Shakespeare, whom, by way of keeping up our English, he used to read aloud, he said:

"In truth I know not why I am so sad:
It wearies me; you say it wearies you;
But how I got it—came by it."

"I forget the rest. But I feel as if some great misfortune were hanging over us. I suppose the poor General's afflicted letter has had something to do with it."

At this moment the unwonted sound of carriage wheels and many hoofs upon the road, arrested our attention.

They seemed to be approaching from the high ground overlooking the bridge, and very soon the equipage emerged from that point. Two horsemen first crossed the bridge, then came a carriage drawn by four horses, and two men rode behind.

It seemed to be the travelling carriage of a person of rank; and we were all immediately absorbed in watching that very unusual spectacle. It became, in a few moments, greatly more interesting, for just as the carriage had passed the summit of the steep bridge, one of the leaders, taking fright, communicated his panic to the rest, and after a plunge or two, the whole team broke into a wild gallop together, and dashing between the horsemen who rode in front, came thunder-thundering along the road towards us with the speed of a hurricane.

The excitement of the scene was made more painful by the clear, long-drawn screams of a female voice from the carriage window.

We all advanced in curiosity and horror; my father in silence, the rest with various ejaculations of terror.

Our suspense did not last long. Just before you reach the castle drawbridge, on the route they were coming, there stands by the roadside a magnificent lime-tree, on the other stands an ancient stone cross, at sight of which the horses, now going at a pace that was perfectly frightful, swerved so as to bring the wheel over the projecting roots of the tree.

I knew what was coming. I covered my eyes, unable to see it out, and turned my head away; at the same moment I heard a cry from my lady-friends, who had gone on a little.

Curiosity opened my eyes, and I saw a scene of utter confusion. Two of the horses were on the ground, the carriage lay upon its side with two wheels in the air; the men were busy removing the traces, and a lady, with a commanding air and figure had got out, and stood with clasped hands, raising the handkerchief that was in them every now and then to her eyes. Through the carriage door was now lifted a young lady, who appeared to be lifeless. My dear old father was already beside the elder lady, with his hat in his hand, evidently tendering his aid and the resources of his schloss. The lady did not appear to hear him, or to have eyes for anything but the slender girl who was being placed against the slope of the bank.

I approached; the young lady was apparently stunned, but she was certainly not dead. My father, who piqued himself on being something of a physician, had just had his fingers to her wrist and assured the lady, who declared herself her mother, that her pulse, though faint and irregular, was undoubtedly still distinguishable. The lady clasped her hands and looked upward, as if in a momentary transport of gratitude; but immediately she broke out again in that theatrical way which is, I believe, natural to some people.

She was what is called a fine looking woman for her time of life, and must have been handsome; she was tall, but not thin, and dressed in black velvet, and looked rather pale, but with a proud and commanding countenance, though now agitated strangely.

"Was ever being so born to calamity?" I heard her say, with clasped hands, as I came up. "Here am I, on a journey of life and death, in prosecuting which to lose an hour is possibly to lose all. My child will not have recovered sufficiently to resume her route for who can say how long. I must leave her; I cannot, dare not, delay. How far on, sir, can you tell, is the nearest village? I must leave her there; and shall not see my darling, or even hear of her till my return, three months hence."

I plucked my father by the coat, and whispered earnestly in his ear: "Oh! papa, pray ask her to let her stay with us—it would be so delightful. Do, pray."

"If Madame will entrust her child to the care of my daughter, and of her good gouvernante, Madame Perrodon, and permit her to remain as our guest, under my charge, until her return, it will confer a distinction and an obligation upon us, and we shall treat her with all the care and devotion which so sacred a trust deserves."

"I cannot do that, sir, it would be to task your kindness and chivalry too cruelly," said the lady, distractedly.

"It would, on the contrary, be to confer on us a very great kindness at the moment when we most need it. My daughter has just been disappointed by a cruel misfortune, in a visit from which she had long anticipated a great deal of happiness. If you confide this young lady to our care it will be her best consolation. The nearest village on your route is distant, and affords no such inn as you could think of placing your daughter at; you cannot allow her to continue her journey for any considerable distance without danger. If, as you say, you cannot suspend your journey, you must part with her to-night, and nowhere could you do so with more honest assurances of care and tenderness than here."

There was something in this lady's air and appearance so distinguished, and even imposing, and in her manner so engaging, as to impress one, quite apart from the dignity of her equipage, with a conviction that she was a person of consequence.

By this time the carriage was replaced in its upright position, and the horses, quite tractable, in the traces again.

The lady threw on her daughter a glance which I fancied was not quite so affectionate as one might have anticipated from the beginning of the scene; then she beckoned slightly to my father, and withdrew two or three steps with him out of hearing; and talked to him with a fixed and stern countenance, not at all like that with which she had hitherto spoken.

I was filled with wonder that my father did not seem to perceive the change, and also unspeakably curious to learn what it could be that she was speaking, almost in his ear, with so much earnestness and rapidity.

Two or three minutes at most I think she remained thus employed, then she turned, and a few steps brought her to where her daughter lay, supported by Madame Perrodon. She kneeled beside her for a moment and whispered, as Madame supposed, a little benediction in her ear; then hastily kissing her she stepped into her carriage, the door was closed, the footmen in stately liveries jumped up behind, the outriders spurred on, the postillions cracked their whips, the horses plunged and broke suddenly into a furious canter that threatened soon again to become a gallop, and the carriage whirled away, followed at the same rapid pace by the two horsemen in the rear.

CHAPTER III.

WE COMPARE NOTES.

We followed the cortège with our eyes until it was swiftly lost to sight in the misty wood; and the very sound of the hoofs and the wheels died away in the silent night air.

Nothing remained to assure us that the adventure had not been an illusion of a moment but the young lady, who just at that moment opened her eyes. I could not see, for her face was turned from me, but she raised her head, evidently looking about her, and I heard a very sweet voice ask complainingly, "Where is mamma?"

Our good Madame Perrodon answered tenderly, and added some comfortable assurances.

I then heard her ask:

"Where am I? What is this place?" and after that she said, "I don't see the carriage; and Matska, where is she?"

Madame answered all her questions in so far as she understood them; and gradually the young lady remembered how the misadventure came about, and was glad to hear that no one in, or in attendance on, the carriage was hurt; and on learning that her mamma had left her here, till her return in about three months, she wept.

I was going to add my consolations to those of Madame Perrodon when Mademoiselle De Lafontaine placed her hand upon my arm, saying:

"Don't approach, one at a time is as much as she can at present converse with; a very little excitement would possibly overpower her now."

As soon as she is comfortably in bed, I thought, I will run up to her room and see her.

My father in the meantime had sent a servant on horseback for the physician, who lived about two leagues away; and a bedroom was being prepared for the young lady's reception.

The stranger now rose, and leaning on Madame's arm, walked slowly over the drawbridge and into the castle gate.

In the hall, servants waited to receive her, and she was conducted forthwith to her room.

The room we usually sat in as our drawing-room is long, having four windows, that looked over the moat and drawbridge, upon the forest scene I have just described.

It is furnished in old carved oak, with large carved cabinets, and the chairs are cushioned with crimson Utrecht velvet. The walls are covered with tapestry, and surrounded with great gold frames, the figures being as large as life, in ancient and very curious costume, and the subjects represented are hunting, hawking, and generally festive. It is not too stately to be extremely comfortable; and here we had our tea, for with his usual patriotic leanings he insisted that the national beverage should make its appearance regularly with our coffee and chocolate.

We sat here this night, and with candles lighted, were talking over the adventure of the evening.

Madame Perrodon and Mademoiselle De Lafontaine were both of our party. The young stranger had hardly lain down in her bed when she sank into a deep sleep; and those ladies had left her in the care of a servant.

"How do you like our guest?" I asked, as soon as Madame entered. "Tell me all about her?"

"I like her extremely," answered Madame, "she is, I almost think, the prettiest creature I ever saw; about your age, and so gentle and nice."

"She is absolutely beautiful," threw in Mademoiselle, who had peeped for a moment into the stranger's room.

"And such a sweet voice!" added Madame Perrodon.

"Did you remark a woman in the carriage, after it was set up again, who did not get out," inquired Mademoiselle, "but only looked from the window?"

"No, we had not seen her."

Then she described a hideous black woman, with a sort of coloured turban on her head, who was gazing all the time from the carriage window, nodding and grinning derisively towards the ladies, with gleaming eyes and large white eyeballs, and her teeth set as if in fury.

"Did you remark what an ill-looking pack of men the servants were?" asked Madame.

"Yes," said my father, who had just come in, "ugly, hang-dog looking fellows, as ever I beheld in my life. I hope they mayn't rob the poor lady in the forest. They are clever rogues, however; they got everything to rights in a minute."

"I dare say they are worn out with too long travelling," said Madame. "Besides looking wicked, their faces were so strangely lean, and dark, and sullen. I am very curious, I own; but I dare say the young lady will tell us all about it to-morrow, if she is sufficiently recovered."

"I don't think she will," said my father, with a mysterious smile, and a little nod of his head, as if he knew more about it than he cared to tell us.

This made me all the more inquisitive as to what had passed between him and the lady in the black velvet, in the brief but earnest interview that had immediately preceded her departure.

We were scarcely alone, when I entreated him to tell me. He did not need much pressing.

"There is no particular reason why I should not tell you. She expressed a reluctance to trouble us with the care of her daughter, saying she was in delicate health and nervous, but not subject to any kind of seizure—she volunteered that—nor to any illusion; being, in fact, perfectly sane."

"How very odd to say all that!" I interpolated. "It was so unnecessary."

"At all events it was said," he laughed, "and as you wish to know all that passed, which was indeed very little, I tell you. She then said, "I am making a long journey of vital importance—she emphasized the word—rapid and secret; I shall return for my child in three months; in the meantime, she will be silent as to who we are, whence we come, and whither we are travelling." That is all she said. She spoke very pure French. When she said the word "secret," she paused for a few seconds, looking sternly, her eyes fixed on mine. I fancy she makes a great point of that. You saw how quickly she was gone. I hope I have not done a very foolish thing, in taking charge of the young lady."

For my part, I was delighted. I was longing to see and talk to her; and only waiting till the doctor should give me leave. You, who live in towns, can have no idea how great an event the introduction of a new friend is, in such a solitude as surrounded us.

The doctor did not arrive till nearly one o'clock; but I could no more have gone to my bed and slept, than I could have overtaken, on foot, the carriage in which the princess in black velvet had driven away.

When the physician came down to the drawing room, it was to report very favourably upon his patient. She was now sitting up, her pulse quite regular, apparently perfectly well. She had sustained no injury, and the little shock to her nerves had passed away quite harmlessly. There could be no harm certainly in my seeing her, if we both wished it; and, with this permission, I sent, forthwith, to know whether she would allow me to visit her for a few minutes in her room.

The servant returned immediately to say that she desired nothing more.

You may be sure I was not long in availing myself of this permission.

Our visitor lay in one of the handsomest rooms in the schloss. It was, perhaps, a little stately. There was a sombre piece of tapestry opposite the foot of the bed, representing Cleopatra with the asps to her bosom; and other solemn classic scenes were displayed, a little faded, upon the other walls. But there was gold carving, and rich and varied colour enough in the other decorations of the room, to more than redeem the gloom of the old tapestry.

There were candles at the bed side. She was sitting up; her slender pretty figure enveloped in the soft silk dressing gown, embroidered with flowers, and lined with thick quilted silk, which her mother had thrown over her feet as she lay upon the ground.

What was it that, as I reached the bed-side and had just begun my little greeting, struck me dumb in a moment, and made me recoil a step or two from before her? I will tell you.

I saw the very face which had visited me in my childhood at night, which remained so fixed in my memory, and on which I had for so many years so often ruminated with horror, when no one suspected of what I was thinking.

It was pretty, even beautiful; and when I first beheld it, wore the same melancholy expression.

But this almost instantly lighted into a strange fixed smile of recognition.

There was a silence of fully a minute, and then at length she spoke; I could not.

"How wonderful!" she exclaimed, "Twelve years ago, I saw your face in a dream, and it has haunted me ever since."

"Wonderful indeed!" I repeated, overcoming with an effort the horror that had for a time suspended my utterances. "Twelve years ago, in vision or reality, I certainly saw you. I could not forget your face. It has remained before my eyes ever since."

Her smile had softened. Whatever I had fancied strange in it, was gone, and it and her dimpling cheeks were now delightfully pretty and intelligent.

I felt reassured, and continued more in the vein which hospitality indicated, to bid her welcome, and to tell her how much pleasure her accidental arrival had given us all, and especially what a happiness it was to me.

I took her hand as I spoke. I was a little shy, as lonely people are, but the situation made me eloquent, and even bold. She pressed my hand, she laid hers upon it, and her eyes glowed, as, looking hastily into mine, she smiled again, and blushed.

She answered my welcome very prettily. I sat down beside her, still wondering; and she said:

"I must tell you my vision about you; it is so very strange that you and I should have had, each of the other so vivid a dream, that each should have seen, I you and you me, looking as we do now, when of course we both were mere children. I was a child, about six years old, and I awoke from a confused and troubled dream, and found myself in a room, unlike my nursery, wainscoted clumsily in some dark wood, and with cupboards and bedsteads, and chairs, and benches placed about it. The beds were, I thought, all empty, and the room itself without anyone but myself in it; and I, after looking about me for some time, and admiring especially an iron candlestick, with two branches, which I should certainly know again, crept under one of the beds to reach the window; but as I got from under the bed, I heard some one crying; and looking up, while I was still upon my knees, I saw you—most assuredly you—as I see you now; a beautiful young lady, with golden hair and large blue eyes, and lips—your lips—you, as you are here. Your looks won me; I climbed on the bed and put my arms about you, and I think we both fell asleep. I was aroused by a scream; you were sitting up screaming. I was frightened, and slipped down upon the ground, and, it seemed to me, lost consciousness for a moment; and when I came to myself, I was again in my nursery at home. Your face I have never forgotten since. I could not be misled by mere resemblance. You are the lady whom I then saw."

It was now my turn to relate my corresponding vision, which I did, to the undisguised wonder of my new acquaintance.

"I don't know which should be most afraid of the other," she said, again smiling—"If you were less pretty I think I should be very much afraid of you, but being as you are, and you and I both so young, I feel only that I have made your acquaintance twelve years ago, and have already a right to your intimacy; at all events it does seem as if we were destined, from our earliest childhood, to be friends. I wonder whether you feel as strangely drawn towards me as I do to you; I have never had a friend—shall I find one now?" She sighed, and her fine dark eyes gazed passionately on me.

Now the truth is, I felt rather unaccountably towards the beautiful stranger. I did feel, as she said, "drawn towards her," but there was also something of repulsion. In this ambiguous feeling, however, the sense of attraction immensely prevailed. She interested and won me; she was so beautiful and so indescribably engaging.

I perceived now something of langour and exhaustion stealing over her, and hastened to bid her good night.

"The doctor thinks," I added, "that you ought to have a maid to sit up with you to-night; one of ours is waiting, and you will find her a very useful and quiet creature."

"How kind of you, but I could not sleep, I never could with an attendant in the room. I shan't require any assistance—and, shall I confess my weakness, I am haunted with a terror of robbers. Our house was robbed once, and two servants murdered, so I always lock my door. It has become a habit and you look so kind I know you will forgive me. I see there is a key in the lock."

She held me close in her pretty arms for a moment and whispered in my ear, "Good night, darling, it is very hard to part with you, but good-night; to-morrow, but not early, I shall see you again."

She sank back on the pillow with a sigh, and her fine eyes followed me with a fond and melancholy gaze, and she murmured again "Good night, dear friend."

Young people like, and even love, on impulse. I was flattered by the evident, though as yet undeserved, fondness she showed me. I liked the confidence with which she at once received me. She was determined that we should be very near friends.

Next day came and we met again. I was delighted with my companion; that is to say, in many respects.

Her looks lost nothing in daylight—she was certainly the most beautiful creature I had ever seen, and the unpleasant remembrance of the face presented in my early dream, had lost the effect of the first unexpected recognition.

She confessed that she had experienced a similar shock on seeing me, and precisely the same faint antipathy that had mingled with my admiration of her. We now laughed together over our momentary horrors.

CHAPTER IV.

HER HABITS—A SAUNTER.

I told you that I was charmed with her in most particulars.

There were some that did not please me so well.

She was above the middle height of women. I shall begin by describing her. She was slender, and wonderfully graceful. Except that her movements were languid—very languid—indeed, there was nothing in her appearance to indicate an invalid. Her complexion was rich and brilliant; her features were small and beautifully formed; her eyes large, dark, and lustrous; her hair was quite wonderful, I never saw hair so magnificently thick and long when it was down about her shoulders; I have often placed my hands under it, and laughed with wonder at its weight. It was exquisitely fine and soft, and in colour a rich very dark brown, with something of gold. I loved to let it down, tumbling with its own weight, as, in her room, she lay back in her chair talking, in her sweet low voice, I used to fold and braid it, and spread it out and play with it. Heavens! If I had but known all!

I said there were particulars which did not please me. I have told you that her confidence won me the first night I saw her; but I found that she exercised with respect to herself, her mother, her history, everything in fact connected with her life, plans, and people, an ever wakeful reserve. I dare say I was unreasonable, perhaps I was wrong; I dare say I ought to have respected the solemn injunction laid upon my father by the stately lady in black velvet. But curiosity is a restless and unscrupulous passion, and no one girl can endure, with patience, that her's should be baffled by another. What harm could it do anyone to tell me what I so ardently desired to know? Had she no trust in my good sense or honour? Why would she not believe me when I assured her, so solemnly, that I would not divulge one syllable of what she told me to any mortal breathing.

There was a coldness, it seemed to me, beyond her years, in her smiling melancholy persistent refusal to afford me the least ray of light.

I cannot say we quarrelled upon this point, for she would not quarrel upon any. It was, of course, very unfair of me to press her, very ill-bred, but I really could not help it; and I might just as well have let it alone.

What she did tell me amounted, in my unconscionable estimation—to nothing.

It was all summed up in three very vague disclosures:

First.—Her name was Carmilla.

Second.—Her family was very ancient and noble.

Third.—Her home lay in the direction of the west.

She would not tell me the name of her family, nor their armorial bearings, nor the name of their estate, nor even that of the country they lived in.

You are not to suppose that I worried her incessantly on these subjects. I watched opportunity, and rather insinuated than urged my inquiries. Once or twice, indeed, I did attack her more directly. But no matter what my tactics, utter failure was invariably the result. Reproaches and caresses were all lost upon her. But I must add this, that her evasion was conducted with so pretty a melancholy and deprecation, with so many, and even passionate declarations of her liking for me, and trust in my honour, and with so many promises that I should at last know all, that I could not find it in my heart long to be offended with her.

She used to place her pretty arms about my neck, draw me to her, and laying her cheek to mine, murmur with her lips near my ear, "Dearest, your little heart is wounded; think me not cruel because I obey the irresistible law of my strength and weakness; if your dear heart is wounded, my wild heart bleeds with yours. In the rapture of my enormous humiliation I live in your warm life, and you shall die—die, sweetly die—into mine. I cannot help it; as I draw near to you, you, in your turn, will draw near to others, and learn the rapture of that cruelty, which yet is love; so, for a while, seek to know no more of me and mine, but trust me with all your loving spirit."

And when she had spoken such a rhapsody, she would press me more closely in her trembling embrace, and her lips in soft kisses gently glow upon my cheek.

Her agitations and her language were unintelligible to me.

From these foolish embraces, which were not of very frequent occurrence, I must allow, I used to wish to extricate myself; but my energies seemed to fail me. Her murmured words sounded like a lullaby in my ear, and soothed my resistance into a trance, from which I only seemed to recover myself when she withdrew her arms.

In these mysterious moods I did not like her. I experienced a strange tumultuous excitement that was pleasurable, ever and anon, mingled with a vague sense of fear and disgust. I had no distinct thoughts about her while such scenes lasted, but I was conscious of a love growing into adoration, and also of abhorrence. This I know is paradox, but I can make no other attempt to explain the feeling.

I now write, after an interval of more than ten years, with a trembling hand, with a confused and horrible recollection of certain occurrences and situations, in the ordeal through which I was unconsciously passing; though with a vivid and very sharp remembrance of the main current of my story. But, I suspect, in all lives there are certain emotional scenes, those in which our passions have been most wildly and terribly roused, that are of all others the most vaguely and dimly remembered.

Sometimes after an hour of apathy, my strange and beautiful companion would take my hand and hold it with a fond pressure, renewed again and again; blushing softly, gazing in my face with languid and burning eyes, and breathing so fast that her dress rose and fell with the tumultuous respiration. It was like the ardour of a lover; it embarrassed me; it was hateful and yet over-powering; and with gloating eyes she drew me to her, and her hot lips travelled along my cheek in kisses; and she would whisper, almost in sobs, "You are mine, you shall be mine, you and I are one for ever." Then she has thrown herself back in her chair, with her small hands over her eyes, leaving me trembling.

"Are we related," I used to ask; "what can you mean by all this? I remind you perhaps of some one whom you love; but you must not, I hate it; I don't know you—I don't know myself when you look so and talk so."

She used to sigh at my vehemence, then turn away and drop my hand.

Respecting these very extraordinary manifestations I strove in vain to form any satisfactory theory—I could not refer them to affectation or trick. It was unmistakably the momentary breaking out of suppressed instinct and emotion. Was she, notwithstanding her mother's volunteered denial, subject to brief visitations of insanity; or was there here a disguise and a romance? I had read in old story books of such things. What if a boyish lover had found his way into the house, and sought to prosecute his suit in masquerade, with the assistance of a clever old adventuress. But there were many things against this hypothesis, highly interesting as it was to my vanity.

I could boast of no little attentions such as masculine gallantry delights to offer. Between these passionate moments there were long intervals of common place, of gaiety, of brooding melancholy, during which, except that I detected her eyes so full of melancholy fire, following me, at times I might have been as nothing to her. Except in these brief periods of mysterious excitement her ways were girlish; and there was always a langour about her, quite incompatible with a masculine system in a state of health.

In some respects her habits were odd. Perhaps not so singular in the opinion of a town lady like you, as they appeared to us rustic people. She used to come down very late, generally not till one o'clock, she would then take a cup of chocolate, but eat nothing; we then went out for a walk, which was a mere saunter, and she seemed, almost immediately, exhausted, and either returned to the schloss or sat on one of the benches that were placed, here and there, among the trees. This was a bodily langour in which her mind did not sympathise. She was always an animated talker, and very intelligent.

She sometimes alluded for a moment to her own home, or mentioned an adventure or situation, or an early recollection, which indicated a people of strange manners, and described customs of which we knew nothing. I gathered from these chance hints that her native country was much more remote than I had at first fancied.

As we sat thus one afternoon under the trees a funeral passed us by. It was that of a pretty young girl, whom I had often seen, the daughter of one of the rangers of the forest. The poor man was walking behind the coffin of his darling; she was his only child, and he looked quite heartbroken. Peasants walking two-and-two came behind, they were singing a funeral hymn.

I rose to mark my respect as they passed, and joined in the hymn they were very sweetly singing.

My companion shook me a little roughly, and I turned surprised.

She said brusquely, "Don't you perceive how discordant that is?"

"I think it very sweet, on the contrary," I answered, vexed at the interruption, and very uncomfortable, lest the people who composed the little procession should observe and resent what was passing.

I resumed, therefore, instantly, and was again interrupted. "You pierce my ears," said Carmilla, almost angrily, and stopping her ears with her tiny fingers. "Besides, how can you tell that your religion and mine are the same; your forms wound me, and I hate funerals. What a fuss! Why you must die—everyone must die; and all are happier when they do. Come home."

"My father has gone on with the clergyman to the churchyard. I thought you knew she was to be buried to day."

"She? I don't trouble my head about peasants. I don't know who she is," answered Carmilla, with a flash from her fine eyes.

"She is the poor girl who fancied she saw a ghost a fortnight ago, and has been dying ever since, till yesterday, when she expired."

"Tell me nothing about ghosts. I shan't sleep to-night, if you do."

"I hope there is no plague or fever coming; all this looks very like it," I continued. "The swineherd's young wife died only a week ago, and she thought something seized her by the throat as she lay in her bed, and nearly strangled her. Papa says such horrible fancies do accompany some forms of fever. She was quite well the day before. She sank afterwards, and died before a week."

"Well, her funeral is over, I hope, and her hymn sung; and our ears shan't be tortured with that discord and jargon. It has made me nervous. Sit down here, beside me; sit close; hold my hand; press it hard—hard—harder."

We had moved a little back, and had come to another seat.

She sat down. Her face underwent a change that alarmed and even terrified me for a moment. It darkened, and became horribly livid; her teeth and hands were clenched, and she frowned and compressed her lips, while she stared down upon the ground at her feet, and trembled all over with a continued shudder as irrepressible as ague. All her energies seemed strained to suppress a fit, with which she was then breathlessly tugging; and at length a low convulsive cry of suffering broke from her, and gradually the hysteria subsided. "There! That comes of strangling people with hymns!" she said at last. "Hold me, hold me still. It is passing away."

And so gradually it did; and perhaps to dissipate the sombre impression which the spectacle had left upon me, she became unusually animated and chatty; and so we got home.

This was the first time I had seen her exhibit any definable symptoms of that delicacy of health which her mother had spoken of. It was the first time, also, I had seen her exhibit anything like temper.

Both passed away like a summer cloud; and never but once afterwards did I witness on her part a momentary sign of anger. I will tell you how it happened.

She and I were looking out of one of the long drawing-room windows, when there entered the court-yard, over the drawbridge, a figure of a wanderer whom I knew very well. He used to visit the schloss generally twice a year.

It was the figure of a hunchback, with the sharp lean features that generally accompany deformity. He wore a pointed black beard, and he was smiling from ear to ear, showing his white fangs. He was dressed in buff, black, and scarlet, and crossed with more straps and belts than I could count, from which hung all manner of things. Behind, he carried a magic-lantern, and two boxes, which I well knew, in one of which was a salamander, and in the other a mandrake. These monsters used to make my father laugh. They were compounded of parts of monkeys, parrots, squirrels, fish, and hedge-hogs, dried and stitched together with great neatness and startling effect. He had a fiddle, a box of conjuring apparatus, a pair of foils and masks attached to his belt, several other mysterious cases dangling about him, and a black staff with copper ferrules in his hand. His companion was a rough spare dog, that followed at his heels, but stopped short, suspiciously at the drawbridge, and in a little while began to howl dismally.

In the meantime, the mountebank, standing in the midst of the court-yard, raised his grotesque hat, and made us a very ceremonious bow, paying his compliments very volubly in execrable French, and German not much better. Then, disengaging his fiddle, he began to scrape a lively air, to which he sang with a merry discord, dancing with ludicrous airs and activity, that made me laugh, in spite of the dog's howling.

Then he advanced to the window with many smiles and salutations, and his hat in his left hand, his fiddle under his arm, and with a fluency that never took breath, he gabbled a long advertisement of all his accomplishments, and the resources of the various arts which he placed at our service, and the curiosities and entertainments which it was in his power, at our bidding, to display.

"Will your ladyships be pleased to buy an amulet against the oupire, which is going like the wolf, I hear, through these woods," he said, dropping his hat on the pavement. "They are dying of it right and left, and here is a charm that never fails; only pinned to the pillow, and you may laugh in his face."

These charms consisted of oblong slips of vellum, with cabalistic ciphers and diagrams upon them.

Carmilla instantly purchased one, and so did I.

He was looking up, and we were smiling down upon him, amused; at least, I can answer for myself. His piercing black eye, as he looked up in our faces, seemed to detect something that fixed for a moment his curiosity.

In an instant he unrolled a leather case, full of all manner of odd little steel instruments.

"See here, my lady," he said, displaying it, and addressing me, "I profess, among other things less useful, the art of dentistry. Plague take the dog!" he interpolated. "Silence, beast! He howls so that your ladyships can scarcely hear a word. Your noble friend, the young, lady at your right, has the sharpest tooth,—long, thin, pointed, like an awl, like a needle; ha, ha! With my sharp and long sight, as I look up, I have seen it distinctly; now if it happens to hurt the young lady, and I think it must, here am I, here are my file, my punch, my nippers; I will make it round and blunt, if her ladyship pleases; no longer the tooth of a fish, but of a beautiful young lady as she is. Hey? Is the young lady displeased? Have I been too bold? Have I offended her?"

The young lady, indeed, looked very angry as she drew back from the window.

"How dares that mountebank insult us so? Where is your father? I shall demand redress from him. My father would have had the wretch tied up to the pump, and flogged with a cart-whip, and burnt to the bones with the castle brand!"

She retired from the window a step or two, and sat down, and had hardly lost sight of the offender, when her wrath subsided as suddenly as it had risen, and she gradually recovered her usual tone, and seemed to forget the little hunchback and his follies.

My father was out of spirits that evening. On coming in he told us that there had been another case very similar to the two fatal ones which had lately occurred. The sister of a young peasant on his estate, only a mile away, was very ill, had been, as she described it, attacked very nearly in the same way, and was now slowly but steadily sinking.

"All this," said my father, "is strictly referable to natural causes. These poor people infect one another with their superstitions, and so repeat in imagination the images of terror that have infested their neighbours."

"But that very circumstance frightens one horribly," said Carmilla.

"How so?" inquired my father.

"I am so afraid of fancying I see such things; I think it would be as bad as reality."

"We are in God's hands; nothing can happen without his permission, and all will end well for those who love him. He is our faithful creator; He has made us all, and will take care of us."

"Creator! Nature!" said the young lady in answer to my gentle father. "And this disease that invades the country is natural. Nature. All things proceed from Nature—don't they? All things in the heaven, in the earth, and under the earth, act and live as Nature ordains? I think so."

"The doctor said he would come here to-day," said my father, after a silence. "I want to know what he thinks about it, and what he thinks we had better do."

"Doctors never did me any good," said Carmilla.

"Then you have been ill?" I asked.

"More ill than ever you were," she answered.

"Long ago?"

"Yes, a long time. I suffered from this very illness; but I forget all but my pain and weakness, and they were not so bad as are suffered in other diseases."

"You were very young then?"

"I dare say; let us talk no more of it. You would not wound a friend?" She looked languidly in my eyes, and passed her arm round my waist lovingly, and led me out of the room. My father was busy over some papers near the window.

"Why does your papa like to frighten us?" said the pretty girl, with a sigh and a little shudder.

"He doesn't, dear Carmilla, it is the very furthest thing from his mind."

"Are you afraid, dearest?"

"I should be very much if I fancied there was any real danger of my being attacked as those poor people were."

"You are afraid to die?"

"Yes, every one is."

"But to die as lovers may—to die together, so that they may live together. Girls are caterpillars while they live in the world, to be finally butterflies when the summer comes; but in the meantime there are grubs and larvæ, don't you see—each with their peculiar propensities, necessities and structure. So says Monsieur Buffon, in his big book, in the next room."

Later in the day the doctor came, and was closeted with papa for some time. He was a skilful man, of sixty and upwards, he wore powder, and shaved his pale face as smooth as a pumpkin. He and papa emerged from the room together, and I heard papa laugh, and say as they came out:

"Well, I do wonder at a wise man like you. What do you say to hippogriffs and dragons?"

The doctor was smiling, and made answer, shaking his head—

"Nevertheless life and death are mysterious states, and we know little of the resources of either."

And so they walked on, and I heard no more. I did not then know what the doctor had been broaching, but I think I guess it now.

CHAPTER V.

A WONDERFUL LIKENESS.

This evening there arrived from Gratz the grave, dark-faced son of the picture cleaner, with a horse and cart laden with two large packing cases, having many pictures in each. It was a journey of ten leagues, and whenever a messenger arrived at the schloss from our little capital of Gratz, we used to crowd about him in the hall, to hear the news.

This arrival created in our secluded quarters quite a sensation. The cases remained in the hall, and the messenger was taken charge of by the servants till he had eaten his supper. Then with assistants, and armed with hammer, ripping-chisel, and turnscrew, he met us in the hall, where we had assembled to witness the unpacking of the cases.

Carmilla sat looking listlessly on, while one after the other the old pictures, nearly all portraits, which had undergone the process of renovation, were brought to light. My mother was of an old Hungarian family, and most of these pictures, which were about to be restored to their places, had come to us through her.

My father had a list in his hand, from which he read, as the artist rummaged out the corresponding numbers. I don't know that the pictures were very good, but they were, undoubtedly, very old, and some of them very curious also. They had, for the most part, the merit of being now seen by me, I may say, for the first time; for the smoke and dust of time had all but obliterated them.

"There is a picture that I have not seen yet," said my father. "In one corner, at the top of it, is the name, as well as I could read, 'Marcia Karnstein,' and the date '1698' and I am curious to see how it has turned out."

I remembered it; it was a small picture, about a foot and a half high, and nearly square, without a frame; but it was so blackened by age that I could not make it out.

The artist now produced it, with evident pride. It was quite beautiful; it was startling; it seemed to live. It was the effigy of Carmilla!

"Carmilla, dear, here is an absolute miracle. Here you are, living, smiling, ready to speak, in this picture. Isn't it beautiful, papa? And see, even the little mole on her throat."

My father laughed, and said "Certainly it is a wonderful likeness," but he looked away, and to my surprise seemed but little struck by it, and went on talking to the picture cleaner, who was also something of an artist, and discoursed with intelligence about the portraits or other works, which his art had just brought into light and colour, while I was more and more lost in wonder the more I looked at the picture.

"Will you let me hang this picture in my room, papa?" I asked.

"Certainly, dear," said he, smiling, "I'm very glad you think it so like. It must be prettier even than I thought it, if it is."

The young lady did not acknowledge this pretty speech, did not seem to hear it. She was leaning back in her seat, her fine eyes under their long lashes gazing on me in contemplation, and she smiled in a kind of rapture.

"And now you can read quite plainly the name that is written in the corner. It is not Marcia; it looks as if it was done in gold. The name is Mircalla, Countess Karnstein, and this is a little coronet over it, and underneath A.D. 1698. I am descended from the Karnsteins; that is, mamma was."

"Ah!" said the lady, languidly, "so am I, I think, a very long descent, very ancient. Are there any Karnsteins living now?"

"None who bear the name, I believe. The family were ruined, I believe, in some civil wars, long ago, but the ruins of the castle are only about three miles away."

"How interesting!" she said, languidly. "But see what beautiful moonlight!" She glanced through the hall-door, which stood a little open. "Suppose you take a little ramble round the court, and look down at the road and river."

"It is so like the night you came to us," I said.

She sighed, smiling.

She rose, and each with her arm about the other's waist, we walked out upon the pavement.

In silence, slowly we walked down to the drawbridge, where the beautiful landscape opened before us.

"And so you were thinking of the night I came here?" she almost whispered. "Are you glad I came?"

"Delighted, dear Carmilla," I answered.

"And you asked for the picture you think like me, to hang in your room," she murmured with a sigh, as she drew her arm closer about my waist, and let her pretty head sink upon my shoulder.

"How romantic you are, Carmilla," I said. "Whenever you tell me your story, it will be made up chiefly of some one great romance."

She kissed me silently.

"I am sure, Carmilla, you have been in love; that there is, at this moment, an affair of the heart going on."

"I have been in love with no one, and never shall," she whispered, "unless it should be with you."

How beautiful she looked in the moonlight!

Shy and strange was the look with which she quickly hid her face in my neck and hair, with tumultuous sighs, that seemed almost to sob, and pressed in mine a hand that trembled.

Her soft cheek was glowing against mine. "Darling, darling," she murmured, "I live in you; and you would die for me, I love you so."

I started from her.

She was gazing on me with eyes from which all fire, all meaning had flown, and a face colourless and apathetic.

"Is there a chill in the air, dear?" she said drowsily. "I almost shiver; have I been dreaming? Let us come in. Come; come; come in."

"You look ill, Carmilla; a little faint. You certainly must take some wine," I said.

"Yes, I will. I'm better now. I shall be quite well in a few minutes. Yes, do give me a little wine," answered Carmilla, as we approached the door. "Let us look again for a moment; it is the last time, perhaps, I shall see the moonlight with you."

"How do you feel now, dear Carmilla? Are you really better?" I asked.

I was beginning to take alarm, lest she should have been stricken with the strange epidemic that they said had invaded the country about us.

"Papa would be grieved beyond measure," I added, "if he thought you were ever so little ill, without immediately letting us know. We have a very skilful doctor near this, the physician who was with papa to-day."

"I'm sure he is. I know how kind you all are; but, dear child, I am quite well again. There is nothing ever wrong with me, but a little weakness. People say I am languid; I am incapable of exertion; I can scarcely walk as far as a child of three years old; and every now and then the little strength I have falters, and I become as you have just seen me. But after all I am very easily set up again; in a moment I am perfectly myself. See how I have recovered."

So, indeed, she had; and she and I talked a great deal, and very animated she was; and the remainder of that evening passed without any recurrence of what I called her infatuations. I mean her crazy talk and looks, which embarrassed, and even frightened me.

But there occurred that night an event which gave my thoughts quite a new turn, and seemed to startle even Carmilla's languid nature into momentary energy.

CHAPTER VI.

A VERY STRANGE AGONY.

When we got into the drawing-room, and had sat down to our coffee and chocolate, although Carmilla did not take any, she seemed quite herself again, and Madame, and Mademoiselle De Lafontaine, joined us, and made a little card party, in the course of which papa came in for what he called his "dish of tea."

When the game was over he sat down beside Carmilla on the sofa, and asked her, a little anxiously, whether she had heard from her mother since her arrival.

She answered "No."

He then asked whether she knew where a letter would reach her at present.

"I cannot tell," she answered ambiguously, "but I have been thinking of leaving you; you have been already too hospitable and too kind to me. I have given you an infinity of trouble, and I should wish to take a carriage to-morrow, and post in pursuit of her; I know where I shall ultimately find her, although I dare not yet tell you."

"But you must not dream of any such thing," exclaimed my father, to my great relief. "We can't afford to lose you so, and I won't consent to your leaving us, except under the care of your mother, who was so good as to consent to your remaining with us till she should herself return. I should be quite happy if I knew that you heard from her; but this evening the accounts of the progress of the mysterious disease that has invaded our neighbourhood, grow even more alarming; and my beautiful guest, I do feel the responsibility, unaided by advice from your mother, very much. But I shall do my best; and one thing is certain, that you must not think of leaving us without her distinct direction to that effect. We should suffer too much in parting from you to consent to it easily."

"Thank you, sir, a thousand times for your hospitality," she answered, smiling bashfully. "You have all been too kind to me; I have seldom been so happy in all my life before, as in your beautiful château, under your care, and in the society of your dear daughter."

So he gallantly, in his old-fashioned way, kissed her hand, smiling and pleased at her little speech.

I accompanied Carmilla as usual to her room, and sat and chatted with her while she was preparing for bed.

"Do you think," I said at length, "that you will ever confide fully in me?"

She turned round smiling, but made no answer, only continued to smile on me.

"You won't answer that?" I said. "You can't answer pleasantly; I ought not to have asked you."

"You were quite right to ask me that, or anything. You do not know how dear you are to me, or you could not think any confidence too great to look for. But I am under vows, no nun half so awfully, and I dare not tell my story yet, even to you. The time is very near when you shall know everything. You will think me cruel, very selfish, but love is always selfish; the more ardent the more selfish. How jealous I am you cannot know. You must come with me, loving me,—to death; or else hate me and still come with me, and hating me through death and after. There is no such word as indifference in my apathetic nature."

"Now, Carmilla, you are going to talk your wild nonsense again," I said hastily.

"Not I, silly little fool as I am, and full of whims and fancies; for your sake I'll talk like a sage. Were you ever at a ball?"

"No; how you do run on. What is it like? How charming it must be."

"I almost forget, it is years ago."

I laughed.

"You are not so old. Your first ball can hardly be forgotten yet."

"I remember everything about it—with an effort. I see it all, as divers see what is going on above them, through a medium, dense, rippling, but transparent. There occurred that night what has confused the picture, and made its colours faint. I was all but assassinated in my bed, wounded here," she touched her breast, "and never was the same since."

"Were you near dying?"

"Yes, very—a cruel love—strange love, that would have taken my life. Love will have its sacrifices. No sacrifice without blood. Let us go to sleep now; I feel so lazy. How can I get up just now and lock my door?"

She was lying with her tiny hands buried in her rich wavy hair, under her cheek, her little head upon the pillow, and her glittering eyes followed me wherever I moved, with a kind of shy smile that I could not decipher.

I bid her good-night, and crept from the room with an uncomfortable sensation.

I often wondered whether our pretty guest ever said her prayers. I certainly had never seen her upon her knees. In the morning she never came down until long after our family prayers were over, and at night she never left the drawing-room to attend our brief evening prayers in the hall.

If it had not been that it had casually come out in one of our careless talks that she had been baptised, I should have doubted her being a Christian. Religion was a subject on which I had never heard her speak a word. If I had known the world better, this particular neglect or antipathy would not have so much surprised me.

A VERY STRANGE AGONY.

The precautions of nervous people are infectious, and persons of a like temperament are pretty sure, after a time, to imitate them. I had adopted Carmilla's habit of locking her bedroom door, having taken into my head all her whimsical alarms about midnight invaders and prowling assassins. I had also adopted her precaution of making a brief search through her room, to satisfy herself that no lurking assassin or robber was "ensconced."

These wise measures taken, I got into my bed and fell asleep. A light was burning in my room. This was an old habit, of very early date, and which nothing could have tempted me to dispense with.

Thus fortified I might take my rest in peace. But dreams come through stone walls, light up dark rooms, or darken light ones, and their persons make their exits and their entrances as they please, and laugh at locksmiths.

I had a dream that night that was the beginning of a very strange agony.

I cannot call it a nightmare, for I was quite conscious of being asleep. But I was equally conscious of being in my room, and lying in bed, precisely as I actually was. I saw, or fancied I saw, the room and its furniture just as I had seen it last, except that it was very dark, and I saw something moving round the foot of the bed, which at first I could not accurately distinguish. But I soon saw that it was a sooty-black animal that resembled a monstrous cat. It appeared to me about four or five feet long, for it measured fully the length of the hearth-rug as it passed over it; and it continued to-ing and fro-ing with the lithe sinister restlessness of a beast in a cage. I could not cry out, although as you may suppose, I was terrified. Its pace was growing faster, and the room rapidly darker and darker, and at length so dark that I could no longer see anything of it but its eyes. I felt it spring lightly on the bed. The two broad eyes approached my face, and suddenly I felt a stinging pain as if two large needles darted, an inch or two apart, deep into my breast. I waked with a scream. The room was lighted by the candle that burnt there all through the night, and I saw a female figure standing at the foot of the bed, a little at the right side. It was in a dark loose dress, and its hair was down and covered its shoulders. A block of stone could not have been more still. There was not the slightest stir of respiration. As I stared at it, the figure appeared to have changed its place, and was now nearer the door; then, close to it, the door opened, and it passed out.

I was now relieved, and able to breathe and move. My first thought was that Carmilla had been playing me a trick, and that I had forgotten to secure my door. I hastened to it, and found it locked as usual on the inside. I was afraid to open it—I was horrified. I sprang into my bed and covered my head up in the bedclothes, and lay there more dead than alive till morning.

CHAPTER VII.

DESCENDING.

It would be vain my attempting to tell you the horror with which, even now, I recall the occurrence of that night. It was no such transitory terror as a dream leaves behind it. It seemed to deepen by time, and communicated itself to the room and the very furniture that had encompassed the apparition.

I could not bear next day to be alone for a moment. I should have told papa, but for two opposite reasons. At one time I thought he would laugh at my story, and I could not bear its being treated as a jest; and at another, I thought he might fancy that I had been attacked by the mysterious complaint which had invaded our neighbourhood. I had myself no misgivings of the kind, and as he had been rather an invalid for some time, I was afraid of alarming him.

I was comfortable enough with my good-natured companions, Madame Paradon, and the vivacious Mademoiselle Lafontaine. They both perceived that I was out of spirits and nervous, and at length I told them what lay so heavy at my heart.

Mademoiselle laughed, but I fancied that Madame Paradon looked anxious.

"By-the-by," said Mademoiselle, laughing, "the long lime-tree walk, behind Carmilla's bedroom-window, is haunted!"

"Nonsense!" exclaimed Madame, who probably thought the theme rather inopportune, "and who tells that story, my dear?"

"Martin says that he came up twice, when the old yard-gate was being repaired, before sunrise, and twice saw the same female figure walking down the lime-tree avenue."

"So he well might, as long as there are cows to milk in the river fields," said Madame.

"I daresay; but Martin chooses to be frightened, and never did I see fool more frightened."

"You must not say a word about it to Carmilla, because she can see down that walk from her room window," I interposed, "and she is, if possible, a greater coward than I."

Carmilla came down rather later than usual that day.

"I was so frightened last night," she said, so soon as were together, "and I am sure I should have seen something dreadful if it had not been for that charm I bought from the poor little hunchback whom I called such hard names. I had a dream of something black coming round my bed, and I awoke in a perfect horror, and I really thought, for some seconds, I saw a dark figure near the chimney-piece, but I felt under my pillow for my charm, and the moment my fingers touched it, the figure disappeared, and I felt quite certain, only that I had it by me, that something frightful would have made its appearance, and, perhaps, throttled me, as it did those poor people we heard of."

"Well, listen to me," I began, and recounted my adventure, at the recital of which she appeared horrified.

"And had you the charm near you?" she asked, earnestly.

"No, I had dropped it into a china vase in the drawing-room, but I shall certainly take it with me to-night, as you have so much faith in it."

At this distance of time I cannot tell you, or even understand, how I overcame my horror so effectually as to lie alone in my room that night. I remember distinctly that I pinned the charm to my pillow. I fell asleep almost immediately, and slept even more soundly than usual all night.

Next night I passed as well. My sleep was delightfully deep and dreamless. But I wakened with a sense of lassitude and melancholy, which, however, did not exceed a degree that was almost luxurious.

"Well, I told you so," said Carmilla, when I described my quiet sleep, "I had such delightful sleep myself last night; I pinned the charm to the breast of my night-dress. It was too far away the night before. I am quite sure it was all fancy, except the dreams. I used to think that evil spirits made dreams, but our doctor told me it is no such thing. Only a fever passing by, or some other malady, as they often do, he said, knocks at the door, and not being able to get in, passes on, with that alarm."

"And what do you think the charm is?" said I.

"It has been fumigated or immersed in some drug, and is an antidote against the malaria," she answered.

"Then it acts only on the body?"

"Certainly; you don't suppose that evil spirits are frightened by bits of ribbon, or the perfumes of a druggist's shop? No, these complaints, wandering in the air, begin by trying the nerves, and so infect the brain, but before they can seize upon you, the antidote repels them. That I am sure is what the charm has done for us. It is nothing magical, it is simply natural."

I should have been happier if I could have quite agreed with Carmilla, but I did my best, and the impression was a little losing its force.

For some nights I slept profoundly; but still every morning I felt the same lassitude, and a languor weighed upon me all day. I felt myself a changed girl. A strange melancholy was stealing over me, a melancholy that I would not have interrupted. Dim thoughts of death began to open, and an idea that I was slowly sinking took gentle, and, somehow, not unwelcome, possession of me. If it was sad, the tone of mind which this induced was also sweet. Whatever it might be, my soul acquiesced in it.

I would not admit that I was ill, I would not consent to tell my papa, or to have the doctor sent for.

Carmilla became more devoted to me than ever, and her strange paroxysms of languid adoration more frequent. She used to gloat on me with increasing ardour the more my strength and spirits waned. This always shocked me like a momentary glare of insanity.

Without knowing it, I was now in a pretty advanced stage of the strangest illness under which mortal ever suffered. There was an unaccountable fascination in its earlier symptoms that more than reconciled me to the incapacitating effect of that stage of the malady. This fascination increased for a time, until it reached a certain point, when gradually a sense of the horrible mingled itself with it, deepening, as you shall hear, until it discoloured and perverted the whole state of my life.

The first change I experienced was rather agreeable. It was very near the turning point from which began the descent of Avernus.

Certain vague and strange sensations visited me in my sleep. The prevailing one was of that pleasant, peculiar cold thrill which we feel in bathing, when we move against the current of a river. This was soon accompanied by dreams that seemed interminable, and were so vague that I could never recollect their scenery and persons, or any one connected portion of their action. But they left an awful impression, and a sense of exhaustion, as if I had passed through a long period of great mental exertion and danger. After all these dreams there remained on waking a remembrance of having been in a place very nearly dark, and of having spoken to people whom I could not see; and especially of one clear voice, of a female's, very deep, that spoke as if at a distance, slowly, and producing always the same sensation of indescribable solemnity and fear. Sometimes there came a sensation as if a hand was drawn softly along my cheek and neck. Sometimes it was as if warm lips kissed me, and longer and more lovingly as they reached my throat, but there the caress fixed itself. My heart beat faster, my breathing rose and fell rapidly and full drawn; a sobbing, that rose into a sense of strangulation, supervened, and turned into a dreadful convulsion, in which my senses left me and I became unconscious.

It was now three weeks since the commencement of this unaccountable state. My sufferings had, during the last week, told upon my appearance. I had grown pale, my eyes were dilated and darkened underneath, and the languor which I had long felt began to display itself in my countenance.

My father asked me often whether I was ill; but, with an obstinacy which now seems to me unaccountable, I persisted in assuring him that I was quite well.

In a sense this was true. I had no pain, I could complain of no bodily derangement. My complaint seemed to be one of the imagination, or the nerves, and, horrible as my sufferings were, I kept them, with a morbid reserve, very nearly to myself.

It could not be that terrible complaint which the peasants called the oupire, for I had now been suffering for three weeks, and they were seldom ill for much more than three days, when death put an end to their miseries.

Carmilla complained of dreams and feverish sensations, but by no means of so alarming a kind as mine. I say that mine were extremely alarming. Had I been capable of comprehending my condition, I would have invoked aid and advice on my knees. The narcotic of an unsuspected influence was acting upon me, and my perceptions were benumbed.

I am going to tell you now of a dream that led immediately to an odd discovery.

One night, instead of the voice I was accustomed to hear in the dark, I heard one, sweet and tender, and at the same time terrible, which said, "Your mother warns you to beware of the assassin." At the same time a light unexpectedly sprang up, and I saw Carmilla, standing, near the foot of my bed, in her white night-dress, bathed, from her chin to her feet, in one great stain of blood.

I wakened with a shriek, possessed with the one idea that Carmilla was being murdered. I remember springing from my bed, and my next recollection is that of standing on the lobby, crying for help.

Madame and Mademoiselle came scurrying out of their rooms in alarm; a lamp burned always on the lobby, and seeing me, they soon learned the cause of my terror.

I insisted on our knocking at Carmilla's door. Our knocking was unanswered. It soon became a pounding and an uproar. We shrieked her name, but all was vain.

We all grew frightened, for the door was locked. We hurried back, in panic, to my room. There we rang the bell long and furiously. If my father's room had been at that side of the house, we would have called him up at once to our aid. But, alas! he was quite out of hearing, and to reach him involved an excursion for which we none of us had courage.

Servants, however, soon came running up the stairs; I had got on my dressing-gown and slippers meanwhile, and my companions were already similarly furnished. Recognising the voices of the servants on the lobby, we sallied out together; and having renewed, as fruitlessly, our summons at Carmilla's door, I ordered the men to force the lock. They did so, and we stood, holding our lights aloft, in the doorway, and so stared into the room.

We called her by name; but there was still no reply. We looked round the room. Everything was undisturbed. It was exactly in the state in which I had left it on bidding her good night. But Carmilla was gone.

CHAPTER VIII.

SEARCH.

At sight of the room, perfectly undisturbed except for our violent entrance, we began to cool a little, and soon recovered our senses sufficiently to dismiss the men. It had struck Mademoiselle that possibly Carmilla had been wakened by the uproar at her door, and in her first panic had jumped from her bed, and hid herself in a press, or behind a curtain, from which she could not, of course, emerge until the majordomo and his myrmidons had withdrawn. We now recommenced our search, and began to call her by name again.

It was all to no purpose. Our perplexity and agitation increased. We examined the windows, but they were secured. I implored of Carmilla, if she had concealed herself, to play this cruel trick no longer—to come out, and to end our anxieties. It was all useless. I was by this time convinced that she was not in the room, nor in the dressing room, the door of which was still locked on this side. She could not have passed it. I was utterly puzzled. Had Carmilla discovered one of those secret passages which the old house-keeper said were known to exist in the schloss, although the tradition of their exact situation had been lost. A little time would, no doubt, explain all—utterly perplexed as, for the present, we were.

It was past four o'clock, and I preferred passing the remaining hours of darkness in Madame's room. Daylight brought no solution of the difficulty.

The whole household, with my father at its head, was in a state of agitation next morning. Every part of the château was searched. The grounds were explored. Not a trace of the missing lady could be discovered. The stream was about to be dragged; my father was in distraction; what a tale to have to tell the poor girl's mother on her return. I, too, was almost beside myself, though my grief was quite of a different kind.

The morning was passed in alarm and excitement. It was now one o'clock, and still no tidings. I ran up to Carmilla's room, and found her standing at her dressing-table. I was astounded. I could not believe my eyes. She beckoned me to her with her pretty finger, in silence. Her face expressed extreme fear.

I ran to her in an ecstasy of joy; I kissed and embraced her again and again. I ran to the bell and rang it vehemently, to bring others to the spot, who might at once relieve my father's anxiety.

"Dear Carmilla, what has become of you all this time? We have been in agonies of anxiety about you," I exclaimed. "Where have you been? How did you come back?"

"Last night has been a night of wonders," she said.

"For mercy's sake, explain all you can."

"It was past two last night," she said, "when I went to sleep as usual in my bed, with my doors locked, that of the dressing-room, and that opening upon the gallery. My sleep was uninterrupted, and, so far as I know, dreamless; but I awoke just now on the sofa in the dressing-room there, and I found the door between the rooms open, and the other door forced. How could all this have happened without my being wakened? It must have been accompanied with a great deal of noise, and I am particularly easily wakened; and how could I have been carried out of my bed without my sleep having been interrupted, I whom the slightest stir startles?"

By this time, Madame, Mademoiselle, my father, and a number of the servants were in the room. Carmilla was, of course, overwhelmed with inquiries, congratulations, and welcomes. She had but one story to tell, and seemed the least able of all the party to suggest any way of accounting for what had happened.

My father took a turn up and down the room, thinking. I saw Carmilla's eye follow him for a moment with a sly, dark glance.

When my father had sent the servants away, Mademoiselle having gone in search of a little bottle of valerian and sal-volatile, and there being no one now in the room with Carmilla, except my father, Madame, and myself, he came to her thoughtfully, took her hand very kindly, led her to the sofa, and sat down beside her.

"Will you forgive me, my dear, if I risk a conjecture, and ask a question?"

"Who can have a better right?" she said. "Ask what you please, and I will tell you everything. But my story is simply one of bewilderment and darkness. I know absolutely nothing. Put any question you please. But you know, of course, the limitations mamma has placed me under."

"Perfectly, my dear child. I need not approach the topics on which she desires our silence. Now, the marvel of last night consists in your having been removed from your bed and your room, without being wakened, and this removal having occurred apparently while the windows were still secured, and the two doors locked upon the inside. I will tell you my theory, and first ask you a question."

Carmilla was leaning on her hand dejectedly; Madame and I were listening breathlessly.

"Now, my question is this. Have you ever been suspected of walking in your sleep?"

"Never, since I was very young indeed."

"But you did walk in your sleep when you were young?"

"Yes; I know I did. I have been told so often by my old nurse."

My father smiled and nodded.

"Well, what has happened is this. You got up in your sleep, unlocked the door, not leaving the key, as usual, in the lock, but taking it out and locking it on the outside; you again took the key out, and carried it away with you to some one of the five-and-twenty rooms on this floor, or perhaps up-stairs or down-stairs. There are so many rooms and closets, so much heavy furniture, and such accumulations of lumber, that it would require a week to search this old house thoroughly. Do you see, now, what I mean?"

"I do, but not all," she answered.

"And how, papa, do you account for her finding herself on the sofa in the dressing-room, which we had searched so carefully?"

"She came there after you had searched it, still in her sleep, and at last awoke spontaneously, and was as much surprised to find herself where she was as any one else. I wish all mysteries were as easily and innocently explained as yours, Carmilla," he said, laughing. "And so we may congratulate ourselves on the certainty that the most natural explanation of the occurrence is one that involves no drugging, no tampering with locks, no burglars, or poisoners, or witches—nothing that need alarm Carmilla, or any one else, for our safety."

Carmilla was looking charmingly. Nothing could be more beautiful than her tints. Her beauty was, I think, enhanced by that graceful languor that was peculiar to her. I think my father was silently contrasting her looks with mine, for he said:

"I wish my poor Laura was looking more like herself," and he sighed.

So our alarms were happily ended, and Carmilla restored to her friends

CHAPTER IX.

THE DOCTOR.

As Carmilla would not hear of an attendant sleeping in her room, my father arranged that a servant should sleep outside her door, so that she could not attempt to make another such excursion without being arrested at her own door.

That night passed quietly; and next morning early, the doctor, whom my father had sent for without telling me a word about it, arrived to see me.

Madame accompanied me to the library; and there the grave little doctor, with white hair and spectacles, whom I mentioned before, was waiting to receive me.

I told him my story, and as I proceeded he grew graver and graver.

We were standing, he and I, in the recess of one of the windows, facing one another. When my statement was over, he leaned with his shoulders against the wall, and with his eyes fixed on me earnestly, with an interest in which was a dash of horror.

After a minute's reflection, he asked Madame if he could see my father.

He was sent for accordingly, and as he entered, smiling, he said:

"I dare say, doctor, you are going to tell me that I am an old fool for having brought you here; I hope I am."

But his smile faded into shadow as the doctor, with a very grave face, beckoned him to him.

He and the doctor talked for some time in the same recess where I had just conferred with the physician. It seemed an earnest and argumentative conversation. The room is very large, and I and Madame stood together, burning with curiosity, at the further end. Not a word could we hear, however, for they spoke in a very low tone, and the deep recess of the window quite concealed the doctor from view, and very nearly my father, whose foot, arm, and shoulder only could we see; and the voices were, I suppose, all the less audible for the sort of closet which the thick wall and window formed.

After a time my father's face looked into the room; it was pale, thoughtful, and, I fancied, agitated.

"Laura, dear, come here for a moment. Madame, we shan't trouble you, the doctor says, at present."

Accordingly I approached, for the first time a little alarmed; for, although I felt very weak, I did not feel ill; and strength, one always fancies, is a thing that may be picked up when we please.

My father held out his hand to me, as I drew near, but he was looking at the doctor, and he said:

"It certainly is very odd; I don't understand it quite. Laura, come here, dear; now attend to Doctor Spielsberg, and recollect yourself."

"You mentioned a sensation like that of two needles piercing the skin, somewhere about your neck, on the night when you experienced your first horrible dream. Is there still any soreness?"

"None at all," I answered.

"Can you indicate with your finger about the point at which you think this occurred?"

"Very little below my throat—here," I answered.

I wore a morning dress, which covered the place I pointed to.

"Now you can satisfy yourself," said the doctor. "You won't mind your papa's lowering your dress a very little. It is necessary, to detect a symptom of the complaint under which you have been suffering."

I acquiesced. It was only an inch or two below the edge of my collar.

"God bless me!—so it is," exclaimed my father, growing pale.

"You see it now with your own eyes," said the doctor, with a gloomy triumph.

"What is it?" I exclaimed, beginning to be frightened.

"Nothing, my dear young lady, but a small blue spot, about the size of the tip of your little ringer; and now," he continued, turning to papa, "the question is what is best to be done?"

"Is there any danger?" I urged, in great trepidation.

"I trust not, my dear," answered the doctor. "I don't see why you should not recover. I don't see why you should not begin immediately to get better. That is the point at which the sense of strangulation begins?"

"Yes," I answered.

"And—recollect as well as you can—the same point was a kind of centre of that thrill which you described just now, like the current of a cold stream running against you?"

"It may have been; I think it was."

"Ay, you see?" he added, turning to my father. "Shall I say a word to Madame?"

"Certainly," said my father.

He called Madame to him, and said:

"I find my young friend here far from well. It won't be of any great consequence, I hope; but it will be necessary that some steps be taken, which I will explain by-and-bye; but in the meantime, Madame, you will be so good as not to let Miss Laura be alone for one moment. That is the only direction I need give for the present. It is indispensable."

"We may rely upon your kindness, Madame, I know," added my father.

Madame satisfied him eagerly.

"And you, dear Laura, I know you will observe the doctor's direction."

"I shall have to ask your opinion upon another patient, whose symptoms slightly resemble those of my daughter, that have just been detailed to you—very much milder in degree, but I believe quite of the same sort. She is a young lady—our guest; but as you say you will be passing this way again this evening, you can't do better than take your supper here, and you can then see her. She does not come down till the afternoon."

"I thank you," said the doctor. "I shall be with you, then, at about seven this evening."

And then they repeated their directions to me and to Madame, and with this parting charge my father left us, and walked out with the doctor; and I saw them pacing together up and down between the road and the moat, on the grassy platform in front of the castle, evidently absorbed in earnest conversation.

The doctor did not return. I saw him mount his horse there, take his leave, and ride away eastward through the forest.

Nearly at the same time I saw the man arrive from Dranfeld with the letters, and dismount and hand the bag to my father.

In the meantime, Madame and I were both busy, lost in conjecture as to the reasons of the singular and earnest direction which the doctor and my father had concurred in imposing. Madame, as she afterwards told me, was afraid the doctor apprehended a sudden seizure, and that, without prompt assistance, I might either lose my life in a fit, or at least be seriously hurt.

This interpretation did not strike me; and I fancied, perhaps luckily for my nerves, that the arrangement was prescribed simply to secure a companion, who would prevent my taking too much exercise, or eating unripe fruit, or doing any of the fifty foolish things to which young people are supposed to be prone.

About half-an-hour after my father came in—he had a letter in his hand—and said:

"This letter had been delayed; it is from General Spielsdorf. He might have been here yesterday, he may not come till to-morrow, or he may be here to-day."

He put the open letter into my hand; but he did not look pleased, as he used when a guest, especially one so much loved as the General, was coming. On the contrary, he looked as if he wished him at the bottom of the Red Sea. There was plainly something on his mind which he did not choose to divulge.

"Papa, darling, will you tell me this?" said I, suddenly laying my hand on his arm, and looking, I am sure, imploringly in his face.

"Perhaps," he answered, smoothing my hair caressingly over my eyes.

"Does the doctor think me very ill?"

"No, dear; he thinks, if right steps are taken, you will be quite well again, at least, on the high road to a complete recovery, in a day or two," he answered, a little drily. "I wish our good friend, the General, had chosen any other time; that is, I wish you had been perfectly well to receive him."

"But do tell me, papa," I insisted, "what does he think is the matter with me?"

"Nothing; you must not plague me with questions," he answered, with more irritation than I ever remember him to have displayed before; and seeing that I looked wounded, I suppose, he kissed me, and added, "You shall know all about it in a day or two; that is, all that I know. In the meantime you are not to trouble your head about it."

He turned and left the room, but came back before I had done wondering and puzzling over the oddity of all this; it was merely to say that he was going to Karnstein, and had ordered the carriage to be ready at twelve, and that I and Madame should accompany him; he was going to see the priest who lived near those picturesque grounds, upon business, and as Carmilla had never seen them, she could follow, when she came down, with Mademoiselle, who would bring materials for what you call a pic-nic, which might be laid for us in the ruined castle.

At twelve o'clock, accordingly, I was ready, and not long after, my father, Madame and I set out upon our projected drive.

Passing the drawbridge we turn to the right, and follow the road over the steep gothic bridge, westward, to reach the deserted village and ruined castle of Karnstein.

No sylvan drive can be fancied prettier. The ground breaks into gentle hills and hollows, all clothed with beautiful wood, totally destitute of the comparative formality which artificial planting and early culture and pruning impart.

The irregularities of the ground often lead the road out of its course, and cause it to wind beautifully round the sides of broken hollows and the steeper sides of the hills, among varieties of ground almost inexhaustible.

Turning one of these points, we suddenly encountered our old friend, the General, riding towards us, attended by a mounted servant. His portmanteaus were following in a hired waggon, such as we term a cart.

The General dismounted as we pulled up, and, after the usual greetings, was easily persuaded to accept the vacant seat in the carriage, and send his horse on with his servant to the schloss.

CHAPTER X.

BEREAVED.

It was about ten months since we had last seen him; but that time had sufficed to make an alteration of years in his appearance. He had grown thinner; something of gloom and anxiety had taken the place of that cordial serenity which used to characterise his features. His dark blue eyes, always penetrating, now gleamed with a sterner light from under his shaggy grey eyebrows. It was not such a change as grief alone usually induces, and angrier passions seemed to have had their share in bringing it about.

We had not long resumed our drive, when the General began to talk, with his usual soldierly directness, of the bereavement, as he termed it, which he had sustained in the death of his beloved niece and ward; and he then broke out in a tone of intense bitterness and fury, inveighing against the "hellish arts" to which she had fallen a victim, and expressing, with more exasperation than piety, his wonder that Heaven should tolerate so monstrous an indulgence of the lusts and malignity of hell.

My father, who saw at once that something very extraordinary had befallen, asked him, if not too painful to him, to detail the circumstances which he thought justified the strong terms in which he expressed himself.

"I should tell you all with pleasure," said the General, "but you would not believe me."

"Why should I not?" he asked.

"Because," he answered testily, "you believe in nothing but what consists with your own prejudices and illusions. I remember when I was like you, but I have learned better."

"Try me," said my father; "I am not such a dogmatist as you suppose. Besides which, I very well know that you generally require proof for what you believe, and am, therefore, very strongly pre-disposed to respect your conclusions."

"You are right in supposing that I have not been led lightly into a belief in the marvellous—for what I have experienced is marvellous—and I have been forced by extraordinary evidence to credit that which ran counter, diametrically, to all my theories. I have been made the dupe of a preternatural conspiracy."

Notwithstanding his professions of confidence in the General's penetration, I saw my father, at this point, glance at the General, with, as I thought, a marked suspicion of his sanity.

The General did not see it, luckily. He was looking gloomily and curiously into the glades and vistas of the woods that were opening before us.

"You are going to the Ruins of Karnstein?" he said. "Yes, it is a lucky coincidence; do you know I was going to ask you to bring me there to inspect them. I have a special object in exploring. There is a ruined chapel, ain't there, with a great many tombs of that extinct family?"

"So there are—highly interesting," said my father. "I hope you are thinking of claiming the title and estates?"

My father said this gaily, but the General did not recollect the laugh, or even the smile, which courtesy exacts for a friend's joke; on the contrary, he looked grave and even fierce, ruminating on a matter that stirred his anger and horror.

"Something very different," he said, gruffly. "I mean to unearth some of those fine people. I hope, by God's blessing, to accomplish a pious sacrilege here, which will relieve our earth of certain monsters, and enable honest people to sleep in their beds without being assailed by murderers. I have strange things to tell you, my dear friend, such as I myself would have scouted as incredible a few months since."

My father looked at him again, but this time not with a glance of suspicion—with an eye, rather, of keen intelligence and alarm.

"The house of Karnstein," he said, "has been long extinct: a hundred years at least. My dear wife was maternally descended from the Karnsteins. But the name and title have long ceased to exist. The castle is a ruin; the very village is deserted; it is fifty years since the smoke of a chimney was seen there; not a roof left."

"Quite true. I have heard a great deal about that since I last saw you; a great deal that will astonish you. But I had better relate everything in the order in which it occurred," said the General. "You saw my dear ward—my child, I may call her. No creature could have been more beautiful, and only three months ago none more blooming."

"Yes, poor thing! when I saw her last she certainly was quite lovely," said my father. "I was grieved and shocked more than I can tell you, my dear friend; I knew what a blow it was to you."

He took the General's hand, and they exchanged a kind pressure. Tears gathered in the old soldier's eyes. He did not seek to conceal them. He said:

"We have been very old friends; I knew you would feel for me, childless as I am. She had become an object of very near interest to me, and repaid my care by an affection that cheered my home and made my life happy. That is all gone. The years that remain to me on earth may not be very long; but by God's mercy I hope to accomplish a service to mankind before I die, and to subserve the vengeance of Heaven upon the fiends who have murdered my poor child in the spring of her hopes and beauty!"

"You said, just now, that you intended relating everything as it occurred," said my father. "Pray do; I assure you that it is not mere curiosity that prompts me."

By this time we had reached the point at which the Drunstall road, by which the General had come, diverges from the road which we were travelling to Karnstein.

"How far is it to the ruins?" inquired the General, looking anxiously forward.

"About half a league," answered my father. "Pray let us hear the story you were so good as to promise."

CHAPTER XI.

THE STORY.

"With all my heart," said the General, with an effort; and after a short pause in which to arrange his subject, he commenced one of the strangest narratives I ever heard.

"My dear child was looking forward with great pleasure to the visit you had been so good as to arrange for her to your charming daughter." Here he made me a gallant but melancholy bow. "In the meantime we had an invitation to my old friend the Count Carlsfeld, whose schloss is about six leagues to the other side of Karnstein. It was to attend the series of fêtes which, you remember, were given by him in honour of his illustrious visitor, the Grand Duke Charles."

"Yes; and very splendid, I believe, they were," said my father.

"Princely! But then his hospitalities are quite regal. He has Aladdin's lamp. The night from which my sorrow dates was devoted to a magnificent masquerade. The grounds were thrown open, the trees hung with coloured lamps. There was such a display of fireworks as Paris itself had never witnessed. And such music—music, you know, is my weakness—such ravishing music! The finest instrumental band, perhaps, in the world, and the finest singers who could be collected from all the great operas in Europe. As you wandered through these fantastically illuminated grounds, the moon-lighted château throwing a rosy light from its long rows of windows, you would suddenly hear these ravishing voices stealing from the silence of some grove, or rising from boats upon the lake. I felt myself, as I looked and listened, carried back into the romance and poetry of my early youth.

"When the fireworks were ended, and the ball beginning, we returned to the noble suite of rooms that were thrown open to the dancers. A masked ball, you know, is a beautiful sight; but so brilliant a spectacle of the kind I never saw before.

"It was a very aristocratic assembly. I was myself almost the only 'nobody' present.

"My dear child was looking quite beautiful. She wore no mask. Her excitement and delight added an unspeakable charm to her features, always lovely. I remarked a young lady, dressed magnificently, but wearing a mask, who appeared to me to be observing my ward with extraordinary interest. I had seen her, earlier in the evening, in the great hall, and again, for a few minutes, walking near us, on the terrace under the castle windows, similarly employed. A lady, also masked, richly and gravely dressed, and with a stately air, like a person of rank, accompanied her as a chaperon. Had the young lady not worn a mask, I could, of course, have been much more certain upon the question whether she was really watching my poor darling. I am now well assured that she was.

"We were now in one of the salons. My poor dear child had been dancing, and was resting a little in one of the chairs near the door; I was standing near. The two ladies I have mentioned had approached, and the younger took the chair next my ward; while her companion stood beside me, and for a little time addressed herself, in a low tone, to her charge.

"Availing herself of the privilege of her mask, she turned to me, and in the tone of an old friend, and calling me by my name, opened a conversation with me, which piqued my curiosity a good deal. She referred to many scenes where she had met me—at Court, and at distinguished houses. She alluded to little incidents which I had long ceased to think of, but which, I found, had only lain in abeyance in my memory, for they instantly started into life at her touch.

"I became more and more curious to ascertain who she was, every moment. She parried my attempts to discover very adroitly and pleasantly. The knowledge she showed of many passages in my life seemed to me all but unaccountable; and she appeared to take a not unnatural pleasure in foiling my curiosity, and in seeing me flounder, in my eager perplexity, from one conjecture to another.

"In the meantime the young lady, whom her mother called by the odd name of Millarca, when she once or twice addressed her, had, with the same ease and grace, got into conversation with my ward.

"She introduced herself by saying that her mother was a very old acquaintance of mine. She spoke of the agreeable audacity which a mask rendered practicable; she talked like a friend; she admired her dress, and insinuated very prettily her admiration of her beauty. She amused her with laughing criticisms upon the people who crowded the ball-room, and laughed at my poor child's fun. She was very witty and lively when she pleased, and after a time they had grown very good friends, and the young stranger lowered her mask, displaying a remarkably beautiful face. I had never seen it before, neither had my dear child. But though it was new to us, the features were so engaging, as well as lovely, that it was impossible not to feel the attraction powerfully. My poor girl did so. I never saw anyone more taken with another at first sight, unless, indeed, it was the stranger herself, who seemed quite to have lost her heart to her.

"In the meantime, availing myself of the licence of a masquerade, I put not a few questions to the elder lady.

"'You have puzzled me utterly,' I said, laughing. 'Is that not enough? won't you, now, consent to stand on equal terms, and do me the kindness to remove your mask?'

"'Can any request be more unreasonable?' she replied. 'Ask a lady to yield an advantage! Beside, how do you know you should recognise me? Years make changes.'

"'As you see,' I said, with a bow, and, I suppose, a rather melancholy little laugh.

"'As philosophers tell us,' she said; 'and how do you know that a sight of my face would help you?'

"'I should take chance for that,' I answered. 'It is vain trying to make yourself out an old woman; your figure betrays you.'

"'Years, nevertheless, have passed since I saw you, rather since you saw me, for that is what I am considering. Millarca, there, is my daughter; I cannot then be young, even in the opinion of people whom time has taught to be indulgent, and I may not like to be compared with what you remember me. You have no mask to remove. You can offer me nothing in exchange.'

"'My petition is to your pity, to remove it.'

"'And mine to yours, to let it stay where it is,' she replied.

"'Well, then, at least you will tell me whether you are French or German; you speak both languages so perfectly.'

"'I don't think I shall tell you that, General; you intend a surprise, and are meditating the particular point of attack.'

'At all events, you won't deny this,' I said, 'that being honoured by your permission to converse, I ought to know how to address you. Shall I say Madame la Comtesse?'

"She laughed, and she would, no doubt, have met me with another evasion if, indeed, I can treat any occurrence in an interview every circumstance of which was pre-arranged, as I now believe, with the profoundest cunning, as liable to be modified by accident.

"'As to that,' she began; but she was interrupted, almost as she opened her lips, by a gentleman, dressed in black, who looked particularly elegant and distinguished, with this drawback, that his face was the most deadly pale I ever saw, except in death. He was in no masquerade—in the plain evening dress of a gentleman; and he said, without a smile, but with a courtly and unusually low bow:—

"'Will Madame la Comtesse permit me to say a very few words which may interest her?'

"The lady turned quickly to him, and touched her lip in token of silence; she then said to me, 'Keep my place for me, General; I shall return when I have said a few words.'

"And with this injunction, playfully given, she walked a little aside with the gentleman in black, and talked for some minutes, apparently very earnestly. They then walked away slowly together in the crowd, and I lost them for some minutes.

"I spent the interval in cudgelling my brains for a conjecture as to the identity of the lady who seemed to remember me so kindly, and I was thinking of turning about and joining in the conversation between my pretty ward and the Countess's daughter, and trying whether, by the time she returned, I might not have a surprise in store for her, by having her name, title, château, and estates at my fingers' ends. But at this moment she returned, accompanied by the pale man in black, who said:

"'I shall return and inform Madame la Comtesse when her carriage is at the door.'

"He withdrew with a bow."

CHAPTER XII.

A PETITION.

"'Then we are to lose Madame la Comtesse, but I hope only for a few hours,' I said, with a low bow.

"'It may be that only, or it may be a few weeks. It was very unlucky his speaking to me just now as he did. Do you now know me?'

"I assured her I did not.

"'You shall know me,' she said, 'but not at present. We are older and better friends than, perhaps, you suspect. I cannot yet declare myself. I shall in three weeks pass your beautiful schloss, about which I have been making enquiries. I shall then look in upon you for an hour or two, and renew a friendship which I never think of without a thousand pleasant recollections. This moment a piece of news has reached me like a thunderbolt. I must set out now, and travel by a devious route, nearly a hundred miles, with all the dispatch I can possibly make. My perplexities multiply. I am only deterred by the compulsory reserve I practise as to my name from making a very singular request of you. My poor child has not quite recovered her strength. Her horse fell with her, at a hunt which she had ridden out to witness, her nerves have not yet recovered the shock, and our physician says that she must on no account exert herself for some time to come. We came here, in consequence, by very easy stages—hardly six leagues a day. I must now travel day and night, on a mission of life and death—a mission the critical and momentous nature of which I shall be able to explain to you when we meet, as I hope we shall, in a few weeks, without the necessity of any concealment.'

"She went on to make her petition, and it was in the tone of a person from whom such a request amounted to conferring, rather than seeking a favour. This was only in manner, and, as it seemed, quite unconsciously. Than the terms in which it was expressed, nothing could be more deprecatory. It was simply that I would consent to take charge of her daughter during her absence.

"This was, all things considered, a strange, not to say, an audacious request. She in some sort disarmed me, by stating and admitting everything that could be urged against it, and throwing herself entirely upon my chivalry. At the same moment, by a fatality that seems to have predetermined all that happened, my poor child came to my side, and, in an undertone, besought me to invite her new friend, Millarca, to pay us a visit. She had just been sounding her, and thought, if her mamma would allow her, she would like it extremely.

"At another time I should have told her to wait a little, until, at least, we knew who they were. But I had not a moment to think in. The two ladies assailed me together, and I must confess the refined and beautiful face of the young lady, about which there was something extremely engaging, as well as the elegance and fire of high birth, determined me; and, quite overpowered, I submitted, and undertook, too easily, the care of the young lady, whom her mother called Millarca.

"The Countess beckoned to her daughter, who listened with grave attention while she told her, in general terms, how suddenly and peremptorily she had been summoned, and also of the arrangement she had made for her under my care, adding that I was one of her earliest and most valued friends.

"I made, of course, such speeches as the case seemed to call for, and found myself, on reflection, in a position which I did not half like.

"The gentleman in black returned, and very ceremoniously conducted the lady from the room.

"The demeanour of this gentleman was such as to impress me with the conviction that the Countess was a lady of very much more importance than her modest title alone might have led me to assume.

"Her last charge to me was that no attempt was to be made to learn more about her than I might have already guessed, until her return. Our distinguished host, whose guest she was, knew her reasons.

"'But here,' she said, 'neither I nor my daughter could safely remain for more than a day. I removed my mask imprudently for a moment, about an hour ago, and, too late, I fancied you saw me. So I resolved to seek an opportunity of talking a little to you. Had I found that you had seen me, I should have thrown myself on your high sense of honour to keep my secret for some weeks. As it is, I am satisfied that you did not see me; but if you now suspect, or, on reflection, should suspect, who I am, I commit myself, in like manner, entirely to your honour. My daughter will observe the same secresy, and I well know that you will, from time to time, remind her, lest she should thoughtlessly disclose it.'

"She whispered a few words to her daughter, kissed her hurriedly twice, and went away, accompanied by the pale gentleman in black, and disappeared in the crowd.

"'In the next room,' said Millarca, 'there is a window that looks upon the hall door. I should like to see the last of mamma, and to kiss my hand to her.'

"We assented, of course, and accompanied her to the window. We looked out, and saw a handsome old-fashioned carriage, with a troop of couriers and footmen. We saw the slim figure of the pale gentleman in black, as he held a thick velvet cloak, and placed it about her shoulders and threw the hood over her head. She nodded to him, and just touched his hand with hers. He bowed low repeatedly as the door closed, and the carriage began to move.

"'She is gone,' said Millarca, with a sigh.

"'She is gone,' I repeated to myself, for the first time—in the hurried moments that had elapsed since my consent—reflecting upon the folly of my act.

"'She did not look up,' said the young lady, plaintively.

"'The Countess had taken off her mask, perhaps, and did not care to show her face,' I said; 'and she could not know that you were in the window.'

"She sighed, and looked in my face. She was so beautiful that I relented. I was sorry I had for a moment repented of my hospitality, and I determined to make her amends for the unavowed churlishness of my reception.

"The young lady, replacing her mask, joined my ward in persuading me to return to the grounds, where the concert was soon to be renewed. We did so, and walked up and down the terrace that lies under the castle windows. Millarca became very intimate with us, and amused us with lively descriptions and stories of most of the great people whom we saw upon the terrace. I liked her more and more every minute. Her gossip, without being ill-natured, was extremely diverting to me, who had been so long out of the great world. I thought what life she would give to our sometimes lonely evenings at home.

"This ball was not over until the morning sun had almost reached the horizon. It pleased the Grand Duke to dance till then, so loyal people could not go away, or think of bed.

"We had just got through a crowded saloon, when my ward asked me what had become of Millarca. I thought she had been by her side, and she fancied she was by mine. The fact was, we had lost her.

"All my efforts to find her were vain. I feared that she had mistaken, in the confusion of a momentary separation from us, other people for her new friends, and had, possibly, pursued and lost them in the extensive grounds which were thrown open to us.

"Now, in its full force, I recognised a new folly in my having undertaken the charge of a young lady without so much as knowing her name; and fettered as I was by promises, of the reasons for imposing which I knew nothing, I could not even point my inquiries by saying that the missing young lady was the daughter of the Countess who had taken her departure a few hours before.

"Morning broke. It was clear daylight before I gave up my search. It was not till near two o'clock next day that we heard anything of my missing charge.

"At about that time a servant knocked at my niece's door, to say that he had been earnestly requested by a young lady, who appeared to be in great distress, to make out where she could find the General Baron Spielsdorf and the young lady his daughter, in whose charge she had been left by her mother.

"There could be no doubt, notwithstanding the slight inaccuracy, that our young friend had turned up; and so she had. Would to heaven we had lost her!

"She told my poor child a story to account for her having failed to recover us for so long. Very late, she said, she had got to the housekeeper's bedroom in despair of finding us, and had then fallen into a deep sleep which, long as it was, had hardly sufficed to recruit her strength after the fatigues of the ball.

"That day Millarca came home with us. I was only too happy, after all, to have secured so charming a companion for my dear girl."

CHAPTER XIII.

THE WOOD-MAN.

"There soon, however, appeared some drawbacks. In the first place, Millarca complained of extreme languor—the weakness that remained after her late illness—and she never emerged from her room till the afternoon was pretty far advanced. In the next place, it was accidentally discovered, although she always locked her door on the inside, and never disturbed the key from its place till she admitted the maid to assist at her toilet, that she was undoubtedly sometimes absent from her room in the very early morning, and at various times later in the day, before she wished it to be understood that she was stirring. She was repeatedly seen from the windows of the schloss, in the first faint grey of the morning, walking through the trees, in an easterly direction, and looking like a person in a trance. This convinced me that, she walked in her sleep. But this hypothesis did not solve the puzzle. How did she pass out from her room, leaving the door locked on the inside? How did she escape from the house without unbarring door or window?

"In the midst of my perplexities, an anxiety of a far more urgent kind presented itself.

"My dear child began to lose her looks and health, and that in a manner so mysterious, and even horrible, that I became thoroughly frightened.

"She was at first visited by appalling dreams; then, as she fancied, by a spectre, sometimes resembling Millarca, sometimes in the shape of a beast, indistinctly seen, walking round the foot of her bed, from side to side. Lastly came sensations. One, not unpleasant, but very peculiar, she said, resembled the flow of an icy stream against her breast. At a later time, she felt something like a pair of large needles pierce her, a little below the throat, with a very sharp pain. A few nights after, followed a gradual and convulsive sense of strangulation; then came unconsciousness."

I could hear distinctly every word the kind old General was saying, because by this time we were driving upon the short grass that spreads on either side of the road as you approach the roofless village which had not shown the smoke of a chimney for more than half a century.

You may guess how strangely I felt as I heard my own symptoms so exactly described in those which had been experienced by the poor girl who, but for the catastrophe which followed, would have been at that moment a visitor at my father's château. You may suppose, also, how I felt as I heard him detail habits and mysterious peculiarities which were, in fact, those of our beautiful guest, Carmilla!

A vista opened in the forest; we were on a sudden under the chimneys and gables of the ruined village, and the towers and battlements of the dismantled castle, round which gigantic trees are grouped, overhung us from a slight eminence.

In a frightened dream I got down from the carriage, and in silence, for we had each abundant matter for thinking; we soon mounted the ascent, and were among the spacious chambers, winding stairs, and dark corridors of the castle.

"And this was once the palatial residence of the Karnsteins!" said the old General at length, as from a great window he looked out across the village, and saw the wide, undulating expanse of forest. "It was a bad family, and here its blood-stained annals were written," he continued. "It is hard that they should, after death, continue to plague the human race with their atrocious lusts. That is the chapel of the Karnsteins, down there."

He pointed down to the grey walls of the gothic building, partly visible through the foliage, a little way down the steep. "And I hear the axe of a woodman," he added, "busy among the trees that surround it; he possibly may give us the information of which I am in search, and point out the grave of Mircalla, Countess of Karnstein. These rustics preserve the local traditions of great families, whose stories die out among the rich and titled so soon as the families themselves become extinct."

"We have a portrait, at home, of Mircalla, the Countess Karnstein; should you like to see it?" asked my father.

"Time enough, dear friend," replied the General. "I believe that I have seen the original; and one motive which has led me to you earlier than I at first intended, was to explore the chapel which we are now approaching."

"What! see the Countess Mircalla," exclaimed my father; "why, she has been dead more than a century!"

"Not so dead as you fancy, I am told," answered the General.

"I confess, General, you puzzle me utterly," replied my father, looking at him, I fancied, for a moment with a return of the suspicion I detected before. But although there was anger and detestation, at times, in the old General's manner, there was nothing flighty.

"There remains to me," he said, as we passed under the heavy arch of the gothic church—for its dimensions would have justified its being so styled—"but one object which can interest me during the few years that remain to me on earth, and that is to wreak on her the vengeance which, I thank God, may still be accomplished by a mortal arm."

"What vengeance can you mean?" asked my father, in increasing amazement.

"I mean, to decapitate the monster," he answered, with a fierce flush, and a stamp that echoed mournfully through the hollow ruin, and his clenched hand was at the same moment raised, as if it grasped the handle of an axe, while he shook it ferociously in the air.

"What?" exclaimed my father, more than ever bewildered.

"To strike her head off."

"Cut her head off!"

"Aye, with a hatchet, with a spade, or with anything that can cleave through her murderous throat. You shall hear," he answered, trembling with rage. And hurrying forward he said:

"That beam will answer for a seat; your dear child is fatigued; let her be seated, and I will, in a few sentences, close my dreadful story."

The squared block of wood, which lay on the grass-grown pavement of the chapel, formed a bench on which I was very glad to seat myself, and in the meantime the General called to the woodman, who had been removing some boughs which leaned upon the old walls; and, axe in hand, the hardy old fellow stood before us.

He could not tell us anything of these monuments; but there was an old man, he said, a ranger of this forest, at present sojourning in the house of the priest, about two miles away, who could point out every monument of the old Karnstein family; and, for a trifle, he undertook to bring him back with him, if we would lend him one of our horses, in little more than half-an-hour.

"Have you been long employed about this forest?" asked my father of the old man.

"I have been a woodman here," he answered in his patois, "under the forester, all my days; so has my father before me, and so on, as many generations as I can count up. I could show you the very house in the village here, in which my ancestors lived."

"How came the village to be deserted?" asked the General.

"It was troubled by revenants, sir; several were tracked to their graves, there detected by the usual tests, and extinguished in the usual way, by decapitation, by the stake, and by burning; but not until many of the villagers were killed.

"But after all these proceedings according to law," he continued—"so many graves opened, and so many vampires deprived of their horrible animation—the village was not relieved. But a Moravian nobleman, who happened to be travelling this way, heard how matters were, and being skilled—as many people are in his country—in such affairs, he offered to deliver the village from its tormentor. He did so thus: There being a bright moon that night, he ascended, shortly after sunset, the towers of the chapel here, from whence he could distinctly see the churchyard beneath him; you can see it from that window. From this point he watched until he saw the vampire come out of his grave, and place near it the linen clothes in which he had been folded, and then glide away towards the village to plague its inhabitants.

"The stranger, having seen all this, came down from the steeple, took the linen wrappings of the vampire, and carried them up to the top of the tower, which he again mounted. When the vampire returned from his prowlings and missed his clothes, he cried furiously to the Moravian, whom he saw at the summit of the tower, and who, in reply, beckoned him to ascend and take them. Whereupon the vampire, accepting his invitation, began to climb the steeple, and so soon as he had reached the battlements, the Moravian, with a stroke of his sword, clove his skull in twain, hurling him down to the churchyard, whither, descending by the winding stairs, the stranger followed and cut his head off, and next day delivered it and the body to the villagers, who duly impaled and burnt them.

"This Moravian nobleman had authority from the then head of the family to remove the tomb of Mircalla, Countess Karnstein, which he did effectually, so that in a little while its site was quite forgotten."

"Can you point out where it stood?" asked the General, eagerly.

The forester shook his head and smiled.

"Not a soul living could tell you that now," he said; "besides, they say her body was removed; but no one is sure of that either."

Having thus spoken, as time pressed, he dropped his axe and departed, leaving us to hear the remainder of the General's strange story.

CHAPTER XIV.

THE MEETING.

"My beloved child," he resumed, "was now growing rapidly worse. The physician who attended her had failed to produce the slightest impression upon her disease, for such I then supposed it to be. He saw my alarm, and suggested a consultation. I called in an abler physician, from Gratz. Several days elapsed before he arrived. He was a good and pious, as well as a learned man. Having seen my poor ward together, they withdrew to my library to confer and discuss. I, from the adjoining room, where I awaited their summons, heard these two gentlemen's voices raised in something sharper than a strictly philosophical discussion. I knocked at the door and entered. I found the old physician from Gratz maintaining his theory. His rival was combatting it with undisguised ridicule, accompanied with bursts of laughter. This unseemly manifestation subsided and the altercation ended on my entrance.

"'Sir,' said my first physician, 'my learned brother seems to think that you want a conjuror, and not a doctor.'

"'Pardon me,' said the old physician from Gratz, looking displeased, 'I shall state my own view of the case in my own way another time. I grieve, Monsieur le Général, that by my skill and science I can be of no use. Before I go I shall do myself the honour to suggest something to you.'

"He seemed thoughtful, and sat down at a table and began to write. Profoundly disappointed, I made my bow, and as I turned to go, the other doctor pointed over his shoulder to his companion who was writing, and then, with a shrug, significantly touched his forehead.

"This consultation, then, left me precisely where I was. I walked out into the grounds, all but distracted. The doctor from Gratz, in ten or fifteen minutes, overtook me. He apologised for having followed me, but said that he could not conscientiously take his leave without a few words more. He told me that he could not be mistaken; no natural disease exhibited the same symptoms; and that death was already very near. There remained, however, a day, or possibly two, of life. If the fatal seizure were at once arrested, with great care and skill her strength might possibly return. But all hung now upon the confines of the irrevocable. One more assault might extinguish the last spark of vitality which is, every moment, ready to die.

"'And what is the nature of the seizure you speak of?' I entreated.

"'I have stated all fully in this note, which I place in your hands upon the distinct condition that you send for the nearest clergyman, and open my letter in his presence, and on no account read it till he is with you; you would despise it else, and it is a matter of life and death. Should the priest fail you, then, indeed, you may read it.'

"He asked me, before taking his leave finally, whether I would wish to see a man curiously learned upon the very subject, which, after I had read his letter, would probably interest me above all others, and he urged me earnestly to invite him to visit him there; and so took his leave.

"The ecclesiastic was absent, and I read the letter by myself. At another time, or in another case, it might have excited my ridicule. But into what quackeries will not people rush for a last chance, where all accustomed means have failed, and the life of a beloved object is at stake?

"Nothing, you will say, could be more absurd than the learned man's letter. It was monstrous enough to have consigned him to a madhouse. He said that the patient was suffering from the visits of a vampire! The punctures which she described as having occurred near the throat, were, he insisted, the insertion of those two long, thin, and sharp teeth which, it is well known, are peculiar to vampires; and there could be no doubt, he added, as to the well-defined presence of the small livid mark which all concurred in describing as that induced by the demon's lips, and every symptom described by the sufferer was in exact conformity with those recorded in every case of a similar visitation.

"Being myself wholly sceptical as to the existence of any such portent as the vampire, the supernatural theory of the good doctor furnished, in my opinion, but another instance of learning and intelligence oddly associated with some one hallucination. I was so miserable, however, that, rather than try nothing, I acted upon the instructions of the letter.

"I concealed myself in the dark dressing-room, that opened upon the poor patient's room, in which a candle was burning, and watched there till she was fast asleep. I stood at the door, peeping through the small crevice, my sword laid on the table beside me, as my directions prescribed, until, a little after one, I saw a large black object, very ill-defined, crawl, as it seemed to me, over the foot of the bed, and swiftly spread itself up to the poor girl's throat, where it swelled, in a moment, into a great, palpitating mass.

"For a few moments I had stood petrified. I now sprang forward, with my sword in my hand. The black creature suddenly contracted toward the foot of the bed, glided over it, and, standing on the floor about a yard below the foot of the bed, with a glare of skulking ferocity and horror fixed on me, I saw Millarca. Speculating I know not what, I struck at her instantly with my sword; but I saw her standing near the door, unscathed. Horrified, I pursued, and struck again. She was gone; and my sword flew to shivers against the door.

"I can't describe to you all that passed on that horrible night. The whole house was up and stirring. The spectre Millarca was gone. But her victim was sinking fast, and before the morning dawned, she died."

The old General was agitated. We did not speak to him. My father walked to some little distance, and began reading the inscriptions on the tombstones; and thus occupied, he strolled into the door of a side-chapel to prosecute his researches. The General leaned against the wall, dried his eyes, and sighed heavily. I was relieved on hearing the voices of Carmilla and Madame, who were at that moment approaching. The voices died away.

In this solitude, having just listened to so strange a story, connected, as it was, with the great and titled dead, whose monuments were mouldering among the dust and ivy round us, and every incident of which bore so awfully upon my own mysterious case—in this haunted spot, darkened by the towering foliage that rose on every side, dense and high above its noiseless walls—a horror began to steal over me, and my heart sank as I thought that my friends were, after all, not about to enter and disturb this triste and ominous scene.

The old General's eyes were fixed on the ground, as he leaned with his hand upon the basement of a shattered monument.

Under a narrow, arched doorway, surmounted by one of those demoniacal grotesques in which the cynical and ghastly fancy of old Gothic carving delights, I saw very gladly the beautiful face and figure of Carmilla enter the shadowy chapel.

I was just about to rise and speak, and nodded smiling, in answer to her peculiarly engaging smile; when with a cry, the old man by my side caught up the woodman's hatchet, and started forward. On seeing him a brutalised change came over her features. It was an instantaneous and horrible transformation, as she made a crouching step backwards. Before I could utter a scream, he struck at her with all his force, but she dived under his blow, and unscathed, caught him in her tiny grasp by the wrist. He struggled for a moment to release his arm, but his hand opened, the axe fell to the ground, and the girl was gone.

He staggered against the wall. His grey hair stood upon his head, and a moisture shone over his face, as if he were at the point of death.

The frightful scene had passed in a moment. The first thing I recollect after, is Madame standing before me, and impatiently repeating again and again, the question, "Where is Mademoiselle Carmilla?"

I answered at length, "I don't know—I can't tell—she went there," and I pointed to the door through which Madame had just entered; "only a minute or two since."

"But I have been standing there, in the passage, ever since Mademoiselle Carmilla entered; and she did not return."

She then began to call "Carmilla," through every door and passage and from the windows, but no answer came.

"She called herself Carmilla?" asked the General, still agitated.

"Carmilla, yes," I answered.

"Aye," he said; "that is Millarca. That is the same person who long ago was called Mircalla, Countess Karnstein. Depart from this accursed ground, my poor child, as quickly as you can. Drive to the clergyman's house, and stay there till we come. Begone! May you never behold Carmilla more; you will not find her here."

CHAPTER XV.

ORDEAL AND EXECUTION.

As he spoke one of the strangest looking men I ever beheld, entered the chapel at the door through which Carmilla had made her entrance and her exit. He was tall, narrow-chested, stooping, with high shoulders, and dressed in black. His face was brown and dried in with deep furrows; he wore an oddly-shaped hat with a broad leaf. His hair, long and grizzled, hung on his shoulders. He wore a pair of gold spectacles, and walked slowly, with an odd shambling gait, with his face sometimes turned up to the sky, and sometimes bowed down toward the ground, seemed to wear a perpetual smile; his long thin arms were swinging, and his lank hands, in old black gloves ever so much too wide for them, waving and gesticulating in utter abstraction.

"The very man!" exclaimed the General, advancing with manifest delight. "My dear Baron, how happy I am to see you, I had no hope of meeting you so soon." He signed to my father, who had by this time returned, and leading the fantastic old gentleman, whom he called the Baron to meet him. He introduced him formally, and they at once entered into earnest conversation. The stranger took a roll of paper from his pocket, and spread it on the worn surface of a tomb that stood by. He had a pencil case in his fingers, with which he traced imaginary lines from point to point on the paper, which from their often glancing from it, together, at certain points of the building, I concluded to be a plan of the chapel. He accompanied, what I may term, his lecture, with occasional readings from a dirty little book, whose yellow leaves were closely written over.

They sauntered together down the side aisle, opposite to the spot where I was standing, conversing as they went; then they begun measuring distances by paces, and finally they all stood together, facing a piece of the side-wall, which they began to examine with great minuteness; pulling off the ivy that clung over it, and rapping the plaster with the ends of their sticks, scraping here, and knocking there. At length they ascertained the existence of a broad marble tablet, with letters carved in relief upon it.

With the assistance of the woodman, who soon returned, a monumental inscription, and carved escutcheon, were disclosed. They proved to be those of the long lost monument of Mircalla, Countess Karnstein.

The old General, though not I fear given to the praying mood, raised his hands and eyes to heaven, in mute thanksgiving for some moments.

"To-morrow," I heard him say; "the commissioner will be here, and the Inquisition will be held according to law."

Then turning to the old man with the gold spectacles, whom I have described, he shook him warmly by both hands and said:

"Baron, how can I thank you? How can we all thank you? You will have delivered this region from a plague that has scourged its inhabitants for more than a century. The horrible enemy, thank God, is at last tracked."

My father led the stranger aside, and the General followed. I knew that he had led them out of hearing, that he might relate my case, and I saw them glance often quickly at me, as the discussion proceeded.

My father came to me, kissed me again and again, and leading me from the chapel, said:

"It is time to return, but before we go home, we must add to our party the good priest, who lives but a little way from this; and persuade him to accompany us to the schloss."

In this quest we were successful: and I was glad, being unspeakably fatigued when we reached home. But my satisfaction was changed to dismay, on discovering that there were no tidings of Carmilla. Of the scene that had occurred in the ruined chapel, no explanation was offered to me, and it was clear that it was a secret which my father for the present determined to keep from me.

The sinister absence of Carmilla made the remembrance of the scene more horrible to me. The arrangements for that night were singular. Two servants, and Madame were to sit up in my room that night; and the ecclesiastic with my father kept watch in the adjoining dressing-room.

The priest had performed certain solemn rites that night, the purport of which I did not understand any more than I comprehended the reason of this extraordinary precaution taken for my safety during sleep.

I saw all clearly a few days later.

The disappearance of Carmilla was followed by the discontinuance of my nightly sufferings.

You have heard, no doubt, of the appalling superstition that prevails in Upper and Lower Styria, in Moravia, Silisia, in Turkish Servia, in Poland, even in Russia; the superstition, so we must call it, of the Vampire.

If human testimony, taken with every care and solemnity, judicially, before commissions innumerable, each consisting of many members, all chosen for integrity and intelligence, and constituting reports more voluminous perhaps than exist upon any one other class of cases, is worth anything, it is difficult to deny, or even to doubt the existence of such a phenomenon as the Vampire.

For my part I have heard no theory by which to explain what I myself have witnessed and experienced, other than that supplied by the ancient and well-attested belief of the country.

The next day the formal proceedings took place in the Chapel of Karnstein. The grave of the Countess Mircalla was opened; and the General and my father recognised each his perfidious and beautiful guest, in the face now disclosed to view. The features, though a hundred and fifty years had passed since her funeral, were tinted with the warmth of life. Her eyes were open; no cadaverous smell exhaled from the coffin. The two medical men, one officially present, the other on the part of the promoter of the inquiry, attested the marvellous fact, that there was a faint but appreciable respiration, and a corresponding action of the heart. The limbs were perfectly flexible, the flesh elastic; and the leaden coffin floated with blood, in which to a depth of seven inches, the body lay immersed. Here then, were all the admitted signs and proofs of vampirism. The body, therefore, in accordance with the ancient practice, was raised, and a sharp stake driven through the heart of the vampire, who uttered a piercing shriek at the moment, in all respects such as might escape from a living person in the last agony. Then the head was struck off, and a torrent of blood flowed from the severed neck. The body and head were next placed on a pile of wood, and reduced to ashes, which were thrown upon the river and borne away, and that territory has never since been plagued by the visits of a vampire.

My father has a copy of the report of the Imperial Commission, with the signatures of all who were present at these proceedings, attached in verification of the statement. It is from this official paper that I have summarized my account of this last shocking scene.

CHAPTER XVI.

CONCLUSION.

I write all this you suppose with composure. But far from it; I cannot think of it without agitation. Nothing but your earnest desire so repeatedly expressed, could have induced me to sit down to a task that has unstrung my nerves for months to come, and reinduced a shadow of the unspeakable horror which years after my deliverance continued to make my days and nights dreadful, and solitude insupportably terrific.

Let me add a word or two about that quaint Baron Vordenburg, to whose curious lore we were indebted for the discovery of the Countess Mircalla's grave.

He had taken up his abode in Gratz, where, living upon a mere pittance, which was all that remained to him of the once princely estates of his family, in Upper Styria, he devoted himself to the minute and laborious investigation of the marvellously authenticated tradition of Vampirism. He had at his fingers' ends all the great and little works upon the subject. "Magia Posthuma," "Phlegon de Mirabilibus," "Augustinus de curâ pro Mortuis," "Philosophicæ et Christiæ Cogitationes de Vampiris," by John Christofer Herenberg; and a thousand others, among which I remember only a few of those which he lent to my father. He had a voluminous digest of all the judicial cases, from which he had extracted a system of principles that appear to govern—some always, and others occasionally only—the condition of the vampire. I may mention, in passing, that the deadly pallor attributed to that sort of revenants, is a mere melodramatic fiction. They present, in the grave, and when they show themselves in human society, the appearance of healthy life. When disclosed to light in their coffins, the exhibit all the symptoms that are enumerated as those which proved the vampire-life of the long-dead Countess Karnstein.

How they escape from their graves and return to them for certain hours every day, without displacing the clay or leaving any trace of disturbance in the state of the coffin or the cerements, has always been admitted to be utterly inexplicable. The amphibious existence of the vampire is sustained by daily renewed slumber in the grave. Its horrible lust for living blood supplies the vigour of its waking existence. The vampire is prone to be fascinated with an engrossing vehemence, resembling the passion of love, by particular persons. In pursuit of these it will exercise inexhaustible patience and stratagem, for access to a particular object may be obstructed in a hundred ways. It will never desist until it has satiated its passion, and drained the very life of its coveted victim. But it will, in these cases, husband and protract its murderous enjoyment with the refinement of an epicure, and heighten it by the gradual approaches of an artful courtship. In these cases it seems to yearn for something like sympathy and consent. In ordinary ones it goes direct to its object, overpowers with violence, and strangles and exhausts often at a single feast.

The vampire is, apparently, subject, in certain situations, to special conditions. In the particular instance of which I have given you a relation, Mircalla seemed to be limited to a name which, if not her real one, should at least reproduce, without the omission or addition of a single letter, those, as we say, anagrammatically, which compose it. Carmilla did this; so did Millarca.

My father related to the Baron Vordenburg, who remained with us for two or three weeks after the expulsion of Carmilla, the story about the Moravian nobleman and the vampire at Karnstein churchyard, and then he asked the Baron how he had discovered the exact position of the long-concealed tomb of the Countess Millarca? The Baron's grotesque features puckered up into a mysterious smile; he looked down, still smiling on his worn spectacle-case and fumbled with it. Then looking up, he said:

"I have many journals, and other papers, written by that remarkable man; the most curious among them is one treating of the visit of which you speak, to Karnstein. The tradition, of course, discolours and distorts a little. He might have been termed a Moravian nobleman, for he had changed his abode to that territory, and was, beside, a noble. But he was, in truth, a native of Upper Styria. It is enough to say that in very early youth he had been a passionate and favoured lover of the beautiful Mircalla, Countess Karnstein. Her early death plunged him into inconsolable grief. It is the nature of vampires to increase and multiply, but according to an ascertained and ghostly law.

"Assume, at starting, a territory perfectly free from that pest. How does it begin, and how does it multiply itself? I will tell you. A person, more or less wicked, puts an end to himself. A suicide, under certain circumstances, becomes a vampire. That spectre visits living people in their slumbers; they die, and almost invariably, in the grave, develope into vampires. This happened in the case of the beautiful Mircalla, who was haunted by one of those demons. My ancestor, Vordenburg, whose title I still bear, soon discovered this, and in the course of the studies to which he devoted himself, learned a great deal more.

"Among other things, he concluded that suspicion of vampirism would probably fall, sooner or later, upon the dead Countess, who in life had been his idol. He conceived a horror, be she what she might, of her remains being profaned by the outrage of a posthumous execution. He has left a curious paper to prove that the vampire, on its expulsion from its amphibious existence, is projected into a far more horrible life; and he resolved to save his once beloved Mircalla from this.

"He adopted the stratagem of a journey here, a pretended removal of her remains, and a real obliteration of her monument. When age had stolen upon him, and from the vale of years he looked back on the scenes he was leaving, he considered, in a different spirit, what he had done, and a horror took possession of him. He made the tracings and notes which have guided me to the very spot, and drew up a confession of the deception that he had practised. If he had intended any further action in this matter, death prevented him; and the hand of a remote descendant has, too late for many, directed the pursuit to the lair of the beast."

We talked a little more, and among other things he said was this:

"One sign of the vampire is the power of the hand. The slender hand of Mircalla closed like a vice of steel on the General's wrist when he raised the hatchet to strike. But its power is not confined to its grasp; it leaves a numbness in the limb it seizes, which is slowly, if ever, recovered from."

The following Spring my father took me on a tour through Italy. We remained away for more than a year. It was long before the terror of recent events subsided; and to this hour the image of Carmilla returns to memory with ambiguous alternations—sometimes the playful, languid, beautiful girl; sometimes the writhing fiend I saw in the ruined church; and often from a reverie I have started, fancying I heard the light step of Carmilla at the drawing-room door.

THE WATCHER AND OTHER WEIRD STORIES

PREFACE.

Most of the tales in this volume were written prior to the publication of "Uncle Silas," which is, perhaps, the novel by which my father is best known. All the stories, with the exception of "The Watcher," were included in "The Purcell Papers," edited by Mr. Alfred Perceval Graves after my father's death, and published by Messrs. Bentley.

It may be of interest to point out that the central idea in the story entitled "Passage in the Secret History of an Irish Countess" is embodied in "Uncle Silas."

When "The Purcell Papers" were appearing in The Dublin University Magazine my father supplied the following note, which was reproduced by Mr. Graves in his edition of the book:—

> "The residuary legatee of the late Francis Purcell, who has the honour of selecting such of his lamented old friend's manuscripts as may appear fit for publication, in order that the lore which they contain may reach the world before scepticism and utility have robbed our species of the precious gift of credulity, and scornfully kicked before them, or trampled into annihilation those harmless fragments of picturesque superstition which it is our object to preserve, has been subjected to the charge of dealing too largely in the marvellous; and it has been half insinuated that such is his love for diablerie, that he is content to wander a mile out of his way in order to meet a fiend or a goblin, and thus to sacrifice all regard for truth and accuracy to the idle hope of affrighting the imagination, and thus pandering to the bad taste of his reader. He begs leave, then, to take this opportunity of asserting his perfect innocence of all the crimes laid to his charge, and to assure his reader that he never pandered to his bad taste, nor went one inch out of his way to introduce witch, fairy, devil, ghost, or any other of the grim fraternity of the redoubted Rawhead-and-bloody-bones. His province touching these tales has been attended with no difficulty and little responsibility; indeed, he is accountable for nothing more than an alteration in the names of persons mentioned therein, when such a step seemed necessary, and for an occasional note, whenever he conceived it possible innocently to

edge in a word. These tales have been written down by the Rev. Francis Purcell, P.P., of Drumcoolagh; and in all the instances, which are many, in which the present writer has had an opportunity of comparing the manuscript of his departed friend with the actual traditions current amongst the families whose fortunes they pretend to illustrate, he has uniformly found that whatever of supernatural occurred in the story, so far from being exaggerated by him, had been rather softened down, and, wherever it could be attempted, accounted for."

Brinsley Le Fanu.
London,
November, 1894.

THE WATCHER

It is now more than fifty years since the occurrences which I am about to relate caused a strange sensation in the gay society of Dublin. The fashionable world, however, is no recorder of traditions; the memory of selfishness seldom reaches far; and the events which occasionally disturb the polite monotony of its pleasant and heartless progress, however stamped with the characters of misery and horror, scarcely outlive the gossip of a season, and (except, perhaps, in the remembrance of a few more directly interested in the consequences of the catastrophe) are in a little time lost to the recollection of all. The appetite for scandal, or for horror, has been sated; the incident can yield no more of interest or novelty; curiosity, frustrated by impenetrable mystery, gives over the pursuit in despair; the tale has ceased to be new, grows stale and flat; and so, in a few years, inquiry subsides into indifference.

Somewhere about the year 1794, the younger brother of a certain baronet, whom I shall call Sir James Barton, returned to Dublin. He had served in the navy with some distinction, having commanded one of his Majesty's frigates during the greater part of the American war. Captain Barton was now apparently some two or three-and-forty years of age. He was an intelligent and agreeable companion, when he chose it, though generally reserved, and occasionally even moody. In society, however, he deported himself as a man of the world and a gentleman. He had not contracted any of the noisy brusqueness sometimes acquired at sea; on the contrary, his manners were remarkably easy, quiet, and even polished. He was in person about the middle size, and somewhat strongly formed; his countenance was marked with the lines of thought, and on the whole wore an expression of gravity and even of melancholy. Being, however, as we have said, a man of perfect breeding, as well as of affluent circumstances and good family, he had, of course, ready access to the best society of the metropolis, without the necessity of any other credentials. In his personal habits Captain Barton was economical. He occupied lodgings in one of the then fashionable streets in the south side of the town, kept but one horse and one servant, and though a reputed free-thinker, he lived an orderly and moral life, indulging neither in gaming, drinking, nor any other vicious pursuit, living very much to himself, without forming any intimacies, or choosing any companions, and appearing to mix in gay society rather for the sake of its bustle and distraction, than for any opportunities which it offered of interchanging either thoughts or feelings with its votaries. Barton was therefore pronounced a saving, prudent, unsocial sort of a fellow, who bid fair to maintain his celibacy alike against stratagem and assault, and was likely to live to a good old age, die rich and leave his money to a hospital.

It was soon apparent, however, that the nature of Captain Barton's plans had been totally misconceived. A young lady, whom we shall call Miss Montague, was at this time introduced into the fashionable world of Dublin by her aunt, the Dowager Lady Rochdale. Miss Montague was decidedly pretty and accomplished, and having some natural cleverness, and a great deal of gaiety, became for a while the reigning toast. Her popularity, however, gained her, for a time, nothing more than that unsubstantial admiration which, however pleasant as an incense to vanity, is by no means necessarily antecedent to matrimony, for, unhappily for the young lady in question, it was an understood thing, that, beyond her personal attractions, she had no kind of earthly provision. Such being the state of affairs, it will readily be believed that no little surprise was consequent upon the appearance of Captain Barton as the avowed lover of the penniless Miss Montague.

His suit prospered, as might have been expected, and in a short time it was confidentially communicated by old Lady Rochdale to each of her hundred and fifty particular friends in succession, that Captain Barton had actually tendered proposals of marriage, with her approbation, to her niece, Miss Montague, who had, moreover, accepted the offer of his hand, conditionally upon the consent of her father, who was then upon his homeward voyage from India, and expected in two or three months at furthest. About his consent there could be no doubt. The delay, therefore, was one merely of form; they were looked upon as absolutely engaged, and Lady Rochdale, with a vigour of old-fashioned decorum with which her niece would, no doubt, gladly have dispensed, withdrew her thenceforward from all further participation in the gaieties of the town. Captain Barton was a constant visitor as well as a frequent guest at the house, and was permitted all the privileges and intimacy which a betrothed suitor is usually accorded. Such was the relation of parties, when the mysterious circumstances which darken this narrative with inexplicable melancholy first began to unfold themselves.

Lady Rochdale resided in a handsome mansion at the north side of Dublin, and Captain Barton's lodgings, as we have already said, were situated at the south. The distance intervening was considerable, and it was Captain Barton's habit generally to walk home without an attendant, as often as he passed the evening with the old lady and her fair charge. His shortest way in such nocturnal walks lay, for a considerable space, through a line of streets which had as yet been merely laid out, and little more than the foundations of the houses constructed. One night, shortly after his engagement with Miss Montague had commenced, he happened to remain unusually late, in company only with her and Lady Rochdale. The conversation had turned upon the evidences of revelation, which he had disputed with the callous scepticism of a confirmed infidel. What were called "French principles" had, in those days, found their way a good deal into fashionable society, especially that portion of it which professed allegiance to Whiggism, and neither the old lady nor her charge was so perfectly free from the taint as to look upon Captain Barton's views as any serious objection to the proposed union. The discussion had degenerated into one upon the supernatural and the marvellous, in which he had pursued precisely the same line of argument and ridicule. In all this, it is but true to state, Captain Barton was guilty of no affectation; the doctrines upon which he insisted were, in reality, but too truly the basis of his own fixed belief, if so it might be called; and perhaps not the least strange of the many strange circumstances connected with this narrative, was the fact that the subject of the fearful influences we are about to describe was himself, from the deliberate conviction of years, an utter disbeliever in what are usually termed preternatural agencies.

It was considerably past midnight when Mr. Barton took his leave, and set out upon his solitary walk homeward. He rapidly reached the lonely road, with its unfinished dwarf walls tracing the foundations of the projected rows of houses on either side. The moon was shining mistily, and its imperfect light made the road he trod but additionally dreary; that utter silence, which has in it something indefinably exciting, reigned there, and made the sound of his steps, which alone broke it, unnaturally loud and distinct. He had proceeded thus some way, when on a sudden he heard other footsteps, pattering at a measured pace, and, as it seemed, about two score steps behind him. The suspicion of being dogged is at all times unpleasant; it is, however, especially so in a spot so desolate and lonely: and this suspicion became so strong in the mind of Captain Barton, that he abruptly turned about to confront his pursuers, but, though there was quite sufficient moonlight to disclose any object upon the road he had traversed, no form of any kind was visible.

The steps he had heard could not have been the reverberation of his own, for he stamped his foot upon the ground, and walked briskly up and down, in the vain attempt to wake an echo. Though by no means a fanciful person, he was at last compelled to charge the sounds upon his imagination, and treat them as an illusion. Thus satisfying himself, he resumed his walk, and before he had proceeded a dozen paces, the mysterious footfalls were again audible from behind, and this time, as if with the special design of showing that the sounds were not the responses of an echo, the steps sometimes slackened nearly to a halt, and sometimes hurried for six or eight strides to a run, and again abated to a walk.

Captain Barton, as before, turned suddenly round, and with the same result; no object was visible above the deserted level of the road. He walked back over the same ground, determined that, whatever might have been the cause of the sounds which had so disconcerted him, it should not escape his search; the endeavour, however, was unrewarded. In spite of all his scepticism, he felt something like a superstitious fear stealing fast upon him, and, with these unwonted and uncomfortable sensations, he once more turned and pursued his way. There was no repetition of these haunting sounds, until he had reached the point where he had last stopped to retrace his steps. Here they were resumed, and with sudden starts of running, which threatened to bring the unseen pursuer close up to the alarmed pedestrian. Captain Barton arrested his course as formerly; the unaccountable nature of the occurrence filled him with vague and almost horrible sensations, and, yielding to the excitement he felt gaining upon him, he shouted, sternly, "Who goes there?"

The sound of one's own voice, thus exerted, in utter solitude, and followed by total silence, has in it something unpleasantly exciting, and he felt a degree of nervousness which, perhaps, from no cause had he ever known before. To the very end of this solitary street the steps pursued him, and it required a strong effort of stubborn pride on his part to resist the impulse that prompted him every moment to run for safety at the top of his speed. It was not until he had reached his lodging, and sat by his own fireside, that he felt sufficiently reassured to arrange and reconsider in his own mind the occurrences which had so discomposed him: so little a matter, after all, is sufficient to upset the pride of scepticism, and vindicate the old simple laws of nature within us.

Mr. Barton was next morning sitting at a late breakfast, reflecting upon the incidents of the previous night, with more of inquisitiveness than awe—so speedily do gloomy impressions upon the fancy disappear under the cheerful influences of day—when a letter just delivered by the postman was placed upon the table before him. There was nothing remarkable in the address of this missive, except that it was written in a hand which he did not know—perhaps it was disguised—for the tall narrow characters were sloped backward; and with the self-inflicted suspense which we so often see practised in such cases, he puzzled over the inscription for a full minute before he broke the seal. When he did so, he read the following words, written in the same hand:

> "Mr. Barton, late Captain of the Dolphin, is warned of danger. He will do wisely to avoid —— Street—(here the locality of his last night's adventure was named)—if he walks there as usual, he will meet with something bad. Let him take warning, once for all, for he has good reason to dread
>
> "The Watcher."

Captain Barton read and re-read this strange effusion; in every light and in every direction he turned it over and over. He examined the paper on which it was written, and closely scrutinized the handwriting. Defeated here, he turned to the seal; it was nothing but a patch of wax, upon which the accidental impression of a coarse thumb was imperfectly visible. There was not the slightest mark, no clue or indication of any kind, to lead him to even a guess as to its possible origin. The writer's object seemed a friendly one, and yet he subscribed himself as one whom he had "good reason to dread." Altogether, the letter, its author, and its real purpose, were to him an inexplicable puzzle, and one, moreover, unpleasantly suggestive, in his mind, of associations connected with the last night's adventure.

In obedience to some feeling—perhaps of pride—Mr. Barton did not communicate, even to his intended bride, the occurrences which we have just detailed. Trifling as they might appear, they had in reality most disagreeably affected his imagination, and he cared not to disclose, even to the young lady in question, what she might possibly look upon as evidences of weakness. The letter might very well be but a hoax, and the mysterious footfall but a delusion of his fancy. But although he affected to treat the whole affair as unworthy of a thought, it yet haunted him pertinaciously, tormenting him with perplexing doubts, and depressing him with undefined apprehensions. Certain it is, that for a considerable time afterwards he carefully avoided the street indicated in the letter as the scene of danger.

It was not until about a week after the receipt of the letter which I have transcribed, that anything further occurred to remind Captain Barton of its contents, or to counteract the gradual disappearance from his mind of the disagreeable impressions which he had then received. He was returning one night, after the interval I have stated, from the theatre, which was then situated in Crow Street, and having there handed Miss Montague and Lady Rochdale into their carriage, he loitered for some time with two or three acquaintances. With these, however, he parted close to the College, and pursued his way alone. It was now about one o'clock, and the streets were quite deserted. During the whole of his walk with the companions from whom he had just parted, he had been at times painfully aware of the sound of steps, as it seemed, dogging them on their way. Once or twice he had looked back, in the uneasy anticipation that he was again about to experience the same mysterious annoyances which had so much disconcerted him a week before, and earnestly hoping that he might see some form from whom the sounds might naturally proceed. But the street was deserted; no form was visible. Proceeding now quite alone upon his homeward way, he grew really nervous and uncomfortable, as he became sensible, with increased distinctness, of the well known and now absolutely dreaded sounds.

By the side of the dead wall which bounded the College Park, the sounds followed, recommencing almost simultaneously with his own steps. The same unequal pace, sometimes slow, sometimes, for a score yards or so, quickened to a run, was audible from behind him. Again and again he turned, quickly and stealthily he glanced over his shoulder almost at every half-dozen steps; but no one was visible. The horrors of this intangible and unseen persecution became gradually all but intolerable; and when at last he reached his home his nerves were strung to such a pitch of excitement that he could not rest, and did not attempt even to lie down until after the daylight had broken.

He was awakened by a knock at his chamber-door, and his servant entering, handed him several letters which had just been received by the early post. One among them instantly arrested his attention; a single glance at the direction aroused him thoroughly. He at once recognized its character, and read as follows:—

> "You may as well think, Captain Barton, to escape from your own shadow as from me; do what you may, I will see you as often as I please, and you shall see me, for I do not want to hide myself, as you fancy. Do not let it trouble your rest, Captain Barton; for, with a good conscience, what need you fear from the eye of

"The Watcher?"

It is scarcely necessary to dwell upon the feelings elicited by a perusal of this strange communication. Captain Barton was observed to be unusually absent and out of spirits for several days afterwards; but no one divined the cause. Whatever he might think as to the phantom steps which followed him, there could be no possible illusion about the letters he had received; and, to say the least of it, their immediate sequence upon the mysterious sounds which had haunted him was an odd coincidence. The whole circumstance, in his own mind, was vaguely and instinctively connected with certain passages in his past life, which, of all others, he hated to remember.

It so happened that just about this time, in addition to his approaching nuptials, Captain Barton had fortunately, perhaps, for himself, some business of an engrossing kind connected with the adjustment of a large and long-litigated claim upon certain properties. The hurry and excitement of business had its natural effect in gradually dispelling the marked gloom which had for a time occasionally oppressed him, and in a little while his spirits had entirely resumed their accustomed tone.

During all this period, however, he was occasionally dismayed by indistinct and half-heard repetitions of the same annoyance, and that in lonely places, in the day time as well as after nightfall. These renewals of the strange impressions from which he had suffered so much were, however, desultory and faint, insomuch that often he really could not, to his own satisfaction, distinguish between them and the mere suggestions of an excited imagination. One evening he walked down to the House of Commons with a Mr. Norcott, a Member. As they walked down together he was observed to become absent and silent, and to a degree so marked as scarcely to consist with good breeding; and this, in one who was obviously in all his habits so perfectly a gentleman, seemed to argue the pressure of some urgent and absorbing anxiety. It was afterwards known that, during the whole of that walk, he had heard the well-known footsteps dogging him as he proceeded. This, however, was the last time he suffered from this phase of the persecution of which he was already the anxious victim. A new and a very different one was about to be presented.

Of the new series of impressions which were afterwards gradually to work out his destiny, that evening disclosed the first; and but for its relation to the train of events which followed, the incident would scarcely have been remembered by any one. As they were walking in at the passage, a man (of whom his friend could afterwards remember only that he was short in stature, looked like a foreigner, and wore a kind of travelling-cap) walked very rapidly, and, as if under some fierce excitement, directly towards them, muttering to himself fast and vehemently the while. This odd-looking person proceeded straight toward Barton, who was foremost, and halted, regarding him for a moment or two with a look of menace and fury almost maniacal; and then turning about as abruptly, he walked before them at the same agitated pace, and disappeared by a side passage. Norcott distinctly remembered being a good deal shocked at the countenance and bearing of this man, which indeed irresistibly impressed him with an undefined sense of danger, such as he never felt before or since from the presence of anything human; but these sensations were far from amounting to anything so disconcerting as to flurry or excite him—he had seen only a singularly evil countenance, agitated, as it seemed, with the excitement of madness. He was absolutely astonished, however, at the effect of this apparition upon Captain Barton. He knew him to be a man of proved courage and coolness in real danger, a circumstance which made his conduct upon this occasion the more conspicuously odd. He recoiled a step or two as the stranger advanced, and clutched his companion's arm in silence, with a spasm of agony or terror; and then, as the figure disappeared, shoving him roughly back, he followed it for a few paces, stopped in great disorder, and sat down upon a form. A countenance more ghastly and haggard it was impossible to fancy.

"For God's sake, Barton, what is the matter?" said Norcott, really alarmed at his friend's appearance. "You're not hurt, are you? nor unwell? What is it?"

"What did he say? I did not hear it. What was it?" asked Barton, wholly disregarding the question.

"Tut, tut, nonsense!" said Norcott, greatly surprised; "who cares what the fellow said? You are unwell, Barton, decidedly unwell; let me call a coach."

"Unwell! Yes, no, not exactly unwell," he said, evidently making an effort to recover his self-possession; "but, to say the truth, I am fatigued, a little overworked, and perhaps over anxious. You know I have been in Chancery, and the winding up of a suit is always a nervous affair. I have felt uncomfortable all this evening; but I am better now. Come, come, shall we go on?"

"No, no. Take my advice, Barton, and go home; you really do need rest; you are looking absolutely ill. I really do insist on your allowing me to see you home," replied his companion.

It was obvious that Barton was not himself disinclined to be persuaded. He accordingly took his leave, politely declining his friend's offered escort. Notwithstanding the few commonplace regrets which Norcott had expressed, it was plain that he was just as little deceived as Barton himself by the extempore plea of illness with which he had accounted for the strange exhibition, and that he even then suspected some lurking mystery in the matter.

Norcott called next day at Barton's lodgings, to inquire for him, and learned from the servant that he had not left his room since his return the night before; but that he was not seriously indisposed, and hoped to be out again in a few days. That evening he sent for Doctor Richards, then in large and fashionable practice in Dublin, and their interview was, it is said, an odd one.

He entered into a detail of his own symptoms in an abstracted and desultory kind of way, which seemed to argue a strange want of interest in his own cure, and, at all events, made it manifest that there was some topic engaging his mind of more engrossing importance than his present ailment. He complained of occasional palpitations, and headache. Doctor Richards asked him, among other questions, whether there was any irritating circumstance or anxiety to account for it. This he denied quickly and peevishly; and the physician thereupon declared his opinion, that there was nothing amiss except some slight derangement of the digestion, for which he accordingly wrote a prescription, and was about to withdraw, when Mr. Barton, with the air of a man who suddenly recollects a topic which had nearly escaped him, recalled him.

"I beg your pardon, doctor, but I had really almost forgot; will you permit me to ask you two or three medical questions?—rather odd ones, perhaps, but as a wager depends upon their solution, you will, I hope, excuse my unreasonableness."

The physician readily undertook to satisfy the inquirer.

Barton seemed to have some difficulty about opening the proposed interrogatories, for he was silent for a minute, then walked to his book-case and returned as he had gone; at last he sat down, and said,—

"You'll think them very childish questions, but I can't recover my wager without a decision; so I must put them. I want to know first about lock-jaw. If a man actually has had that complaint, and appears to have died of it—so that in fact a physician of average skill pronounces him actually dead—may he, after all, recover?"

Doctor Richards smiled, and shook his head.

"But—but a blunder may be made," resumed Barton. "Suppose an ignorant pretender to medical skill; may he be so deceived by any stage of the complaint, as to mistake what is only a part of the progress of the disease, for death itself?"

"No one who had ever seen death," answered he, "could mistake it in the case of lock-jaw."

Barton mused for a few minutes. "I am going to ask you a question, perhaps still more childish; but first tell me, are not the regulations of foreign hospitals, such as those of, let us say, Lisbon, very lax and bungling? May not all kinds of blunders and slips occur in their entries of names, and so forth?"

Doctor Richards professed his inability to answer that query.

"Well, then, doctor, here is the last of my questions. You will probably laugh at it; but it must out nevertheless. Is there any disease, in all the range of human maladies, which would have the effect of perceptibly contracting the stature, and the whole frame—causing the man to shrink in all his proportions, and yet to preserve his exact resemblance to himself in every particular—with the one exception, his height and bulk; any disease, mark, no matter how rare, how little believed in, generally, which could possibly result in producing such an effect?"

The physician replied with a smile, and a very decided negative.

"Tell me, then," said Barton, abruptly, "if a man be in reasonable fear of assault from a lunatic who is at large, can he not procure a warrant for his arrest and detention?"

"Really, that is more a lawyer's question than one in my way," replied Doctor Richards; "but I believe, on applying to a magistrate, such a course would be directed."

The physician then took his leave; but, just as he reached the hall-door, remembered that he had left his cane upstairs, and returned. His reappearance was awkward, for a piece of paper, which he recognized as his own prescription, was slowly burning upon the fire, and Barton sitting close by with an expression of settled gloom and dismay. Doctor Richards had too much tact to appear to observe what presented itself; but he had seen quite enough to assure him that the mind, and not the body, of Captain Barton was in reality the seat of his sufferings.

A few days afterwards, the following advertisement appeared in the Dublin newspapers:—

"If Sylvester Yelland, formerly a foremast man on board his Majesty's frigate Dolphin, or his nearest of kin, will apply to Mr. Robery Smith, solicitor, at his office, Dame Street, he or they may hear of something greatly to his or their advantage. Admission may be had at any hour up to twelve o'clock at night for the next fortnight, should parties desire to avoid observation; and the strictest secrecy, as to all communications intended to be confidential, shall be honourably observed."

The Dolphin, as we have mentioned, was the vessel which Captain Barton had commanded; and this circumstance, connected with the extraordinary exertions made by the circulation of hand-bills, etc., as well as by repeated advertisements, to secure for this strange notice the utmost possible publicity, suggested to Doctor Richards the idea that Captain Barton's extreme uneasiness was somehow connected with the individual to whom the advertisement was addressed, and he himself the author of it. This, however, it is needless to add, was no more than a conjecture. No information whatsoever, as to the real purpose of the advertisement itself, was divulged by the agent, nor yet any hint as to who his employer might be.

Mr. Barton, although he had latterly begun to earn for himself the character of a hypochondriac, was yet very far from deserving it. Though by no means lively, he had yet, naturally, what are termed "even spirits," and was not subject to continual depressions. He soon, therefore, began to return to his former habits; and one of the earliest symptoms of this healthier tone of spirits was his appearing at a grand dinner of the Freemasons, of which worthy fraternity he was himself a brother. Barton, who had been at first gloomy and abstracted, drank much more freely than was his wont—possibly with the purpose of dispelling his own secret anxieties—and under the influence of good wine, and pleasant company, became gradually (unlike his usual self) talkative, and even noisy. It was under this unwonted excitement that he left his company at about half-past ten o'clock; and as conviviality is a strong incentive to gallantry, it occurred to him to proceed forthwith to Lady Rochdale's, and pass the remainder of the evening with her and his destined bride.

Accordingly, he was soon at —— Street, and chatting gaily with the ladies. It is not to be supposed that Captain Barton had exceeded the limits which propriety prescribes to good fellowship; he had merely taken enough of wine to raise his spirits, without, however, in the least degree unsteadying his mind, or affecting his manners. With this undue elevation of spirits had supervened an entire oblivion or contempt of those undefined apprehensions which had for so long weighed upon his mind, and to a certain extent estranged him from society; but as the night wore away, and his artificial gaiety began to flag, these painful feelings gradually intruded themselves again, and he grew abstracted and anxious as heretofore. He took his leave at length, with an unpleasant foreboding of some coming mischief, and with a mind haunted with a thousand mysterious apprehensions, such as, even while he acutely felt their pressure, he, nevertheless, inwardly strove, or affected to contemn.

It was his proud defiance of what he considered to be his own weakness which prompted him upon this occasion to the course which brought about the adventure which we are now about to relate. Mr. Barton might have easily called a coach, but he was conscious that his strong inclination to do so proceeded from no cause other than what he desperately persisted in representing to himself to be his own superstitious tremors. He might also have returned home by a route different from that against which he had been warned by his mysterious correspondent; but for the same reason he dismissed this idea also, and with a dogged and half desperate resolution to force matters to a crisis of some kind, to see if there were any reality in the causes of his former suffering, and if not, satisfactorily to bring their delusiveness to the proof, he determined to follow precisely the course which he had trodden upon the night so painfully memorable in his own mind as that on which his strange persecution had commenced. Though, sooth to say, the pilot who for the first time steers his vessel under the muzzles of a hostile battery never felt his resolution more severely tasked than did Captain Barton, as he breathlessly pursued this solitary path; a path which, spite of every effort of scepticism and reason, he felt to be, as respected him, infested by a malignant influence.

He pursued his way steadily and rapidly, scarcely breathing from intensity of suspense; he, however, was troubled by no renewal of the dreaded footsteps, and was beginning to feel a return of confidence, as, more than three-fourths of the way being accomplished with impunity, he approached the long line of twinkling oil lamps which indicated the frequented streets. This feeling of self-congratulation was, however, but momentary. The report of a musket at some two hundred yards behind him, and the whistle of a bullet close to his head, disagreeably and startlingly dispelled it. His first impulse was to retrace his steps in pursuit of the assassin; but the road on either side was, as we have said, embarrassed by the foundations of a street, beyond which extended waste fields, full of rubbish and neglected lime and brick kilns, and all now as utterly silent as though no sound had ever disturbed their dark and unsightly solitude. The futility of attempting, single-handed, under such circumstances, a search for the murderer, was apparent, especially as no further sound whatever was audible to direct his pursuit.

With the tumultuous sensations of one whose life had just been exposed to a murderous attempt, and whose escape has been the narrowest possible, Captain Barton turned, and without, however, quickening his pace actually to a run, hurriedly pursued his way. He had turned, as we have said, after a pause of a few seconds, and had just commenced his rapid retreat, when on a sudden he met the well-remembered little man in the fur cap. The encounter was but momentary. The figure was walking at the same exaggerated pace, and with the same strange air of menace as before; and as it passed him, he thought he heard it say, in a furious whisper, "Still alive, still alive!"

The state of Mr. Barton's spirits began now to work a corresponding alteration in his health and looks, and to such a degree that it was impossible that the change should escape general remark. For some reasons, known but to himself, he took no step whatsoever to bring the attempt upon his life, which he had so narrowly escaped, under the notice of the authorities; on the contrary, he kept it jealously to himself; and it was not for many weeks after the occurrence that he mentioned it, and then in strict confidence to a gentleman, the torments of his mind at last compelled him to consult a friend.

Spite of his blue devils, however, poor Barton, having no satisfactory reason to render to the public for any undue remissness in the attentions which his relation to Miss Montague required, was obliged to exert himself, and present to the world a confident and cheerful bearing. The true source of his sufferings, and every circumstance connected with them, he guarded with a reserve so jealous, that it seemed dictated by at least a suspicion that the origin of his strange persecution was known to himself, and that it was of a nature which, upon his own account, he could not or dare not disclose.

The mind thus turned in upon itself, and constantly occupied with a haunting anxiety which it dared not reveal, or confide to any human breast, became daily more excited; and, of course, more vividly impressible, by a system of attack which operated through the nervous system; and in this state he was destined to sustain, with increasing frequency, the stealthy visitations of that apparition, which from the first had seemed to possess so unearthly and terrible a hold upon his imagination.

……

It was about this time that Captain Barton called upon the then celebrated preacher, Doctor Macklin, with whom he had a slight acquaintance; and an extraordinary conversation ensued. The divine was seated in his chambers in college, surrounded with works upon his favourite pursuit and deep in theology, when Barton was announced. There was something at once embarrassed and excited in his manner, which, along with his wan and haggard countenance, impressed the student with the unpleasant consciousness that his visitor must have recently suffered terribly indeed to account for an alteration so striking, so shocking.

After the usual interchange of polite greeting, and a few commonplace remarks, Captain Barton, who obviously perceived the surprise which his visit had excited, and which Doctor Macklin was unable wholly to conceal, interrupted a brief pause by remarking,—

"This is a strange call, Doctor Macklin, perhaps scarcely warranted by an acquaintance so slight as mine with you. I should not, under ordinary circumstances, have ventured to disturb you, but my visit is neither an idle nor impertinent intrusion. I am sure you will not so account it, when—"

Doctor Macklin interrupted him with assurances, such as good breeding suggested, and Barton resumed,—

"I am come to task your patience by asking your advice. When I say your patience, I might, indeed, say more; I might have said your humanity, your compassion; for I have been, and am a great sufferer."

"My dear sir," replied the churchman, "it will, indeed, afford me infinite gratification if I can give you comfort in any distress of mind, but—but—"

"I know what you would say," resumed Barton, quickly. "I am an unbeliever, and, therefore, incapable of deriving help from religion, but don't take that for granted. At least you must not assume that, however unsettled my convictions may be, I do not feel a deep, a very deep, interest in the subject. Circumstances have lately forced it upon my attention in such a way as to compel me to review the whole question in a more candid and teachable spirit, I believe, than I ever studied it in before."

"Your difficulties, I take it for granted, refer to the evidences of revelation," suggested the clergyman.

"Why—no—yes; in fact I am ashamed to say I have not considered even my objections sufficiently to state them connectedly; but—but there is one subject on which I feel a peculiar interest."

He paused again, and Doctor Macklin pressed him to proceed.

"The fact is," said Barton, "whatever may be my uncertainty as to the authenticity of what we are taught to call revelation, of one fact I am deeply and horribly convinced: that there does exist beyond this a spiritual world—a system whose workings are generally in mercy hidden from us—a system which may be, and which is sometimes, partially and terribly revealed. I am sure, I know," continued Barton, with increasing excitement, "there is a God—a dreadful God—and that retribution follows guilt. In ways, the most mysterious and stupendous; by agencies, the most inexplicable and terrific; there is a spiritual system—great Heavens, how frightfully I have been convinced!—a system malignant, and inexorable, and omnipotent, under whose persecutions I am, and have been, suffering the torments of the damned!—yes, sir—yes—the fires and frenzy of hell!"

As Barton continued, his agitation became so vehement that the divine was shocked and even alarmed. The wild and excited rapidity with which he spoke, and, above all, the indefinable horror which stamped his features, afforded a contrast to his ordinary cool and unimpassioned self-possession, striking and painful in the last degree.

"My dear sir," said Doctor Macklin, after a brief pause, "I fear you have been suffering much, indeed; but I venture to predict that the depression under which you labour will be found to originate in purely physical causes, and that with a change of air and the aid of a few tonics, your spirits will return, and the tone of your mind be once more cheerful and tranquil as heretofore. There was, after all, more truth than we are quite willing to admit in the classic theories which assigned the undue predominance of any one affection of the mind to the undue action or torpidity of one or other of our bodily organs. Believe me, that a little attention to diet, exercise, and the other essentials of health, under competent direction, will make you as much yourself as you can wish."

"Doctor Macklin," said Barton, with something like a shudder, "I cannot delude myself with such a hope. I have no hope to cling to but one, and that is, that by some other spiritual agency more potent than that which tortures me, it may be combated, and I delivered. If this may not be, I am lost—now and for ever lost."

"But, Mr. Barton, you must remember," urged his companion, "that others have suffered as you have done, and—"

"No, no, no," interrupted he with irritability; "no, sir, I am not a credulous—far from a superstitious man. I have been, perhaps, too much the reverse—too sceptical, too slow of belief; but unless I were one whom no amount of evidence could convince, unless I were to contemn the repeated, the perpetual evidence of my own senses, I am now—now at last constrained to believe I have no escape from the conviction, the overwhelming certainty, that I am haunted and dogged, go where I may, by—by a Demon."

There was an almost preternatural energy of horror in Barton's face, as, with its damp and death-like lineaments turned towards his companion, he thus delivered himself.

"God help you, my poor friend!" said Doctor Macklin, much shocked. "God help you; for, indeed, you are a sufferer, however your sufferings may have been caused."

"Ay, ay, God help me," echoed Barton sternly; "but will He help me? will He help me?"

"Pray to Him; pray in an humble and trusting spirit," said he.

"Pray, pray," echoed he again; "I can't pray; I could as easily move a mountain by an effort of my will. I have not belief enough to pray; there is something within me that will not pray. You prescribe impossibilities—literal impossibilities."

"You will not find it so, if you will but try," said Doctor Macklin.

"Try! I have tried, and the attempt only fills me with confusion and terror. I have tried in vain, and more than in vain. The awful, unutterable idea of eternity and infinity oppresses and maddens my brain, whenever my mind approaches the contemplation of the Creator; I recoil from the effort, scared, confounded, terrified. I tell you, Doctor Macklin, if I am to be saved, it must be by other means. The idea of the Creator is to me intolerable; my mind cannot support it."

"Say, then, my dear sir," urged he, "say how you would have me serve you. What you would learn of me. What can I do or say to relieve you?"

"Listen to me first," replied Captain Barton, with a subdued air, and an evident effort to suppress his excitement; "listen to me while I detail the circumstances of the terrible persecution under which my life has become all but intolerable—a persecution which has made me fear death and the world beyond the grave as much as I have grown to hate existence."

Barton then proceeded to relate the circumstances which we have already detailed, and then continued,—

"This has now become habitual—an accustomed thing. I do not mean the actual seeing him in the flesh; thank God, that at least is not permitted daily. Thank God, from the unutterable horrors of that visitation I have been mercifully allowed intervals of repose, though none of security; but from the consciousness that a malignant spirit is following and watching me wherever I go, I have never, for a single instant, a temporary respite: I am pursued with blasphemies, cries of despair, and appalling hatred; I hear those dreadful sounds called after me as I turn the corners of streets; they come in the night-time while I sit in my chamber alone; they haunt me everywhere, charging me with hideous crimes, and—great God!—threatening me with coming vengeance and eternal misery! Hush! do you hear that?" he cried, with a horrible smile of triumph. "There—there, will that convince you?"

The clergyman felt the chillness of horror irresistibly steal over him, while, during the wail of a sudden gust of wind, he heard, or fancied he heard, the half articulate sounds of rage and derision mingling in their sough.

"Well, what do you think of that?" at length Barton cried, drawing a long breath through his teeth.

"I heard the wind," said Doctor Macklin; "what should I think of it? What is there remarkable about it?"

"The prince of the powers of the air," muttered Barton, with a shudder.

"Tut, tut! my dear sir!" said the student, with an effort to reassure himself; for though it was broad daylight, there was nevertheless something disagreeably contagious in the nervous excitement under which his visitor so obviously suffered. "You must not give way to those wild fancies: you must resist those impulses of the imagination."

"Ay, ay; 'resist the devil, and he will flee from thee,'" said Barton, in the same tone; "but how resist him? Ay, there it is: there is the rub. What—what am I to do? What can I do?"

"My dear sir, this is fancy," said the man of folios; "you are your own tormentor."

"No, no, sir; fancy has no part in it," answered Barton, somewhat sternly. "Fancy, forsooth! Was it that made you, as well as me, hear, but this moment, those appalling accents of hell? Fancy, indeed! No, no."

"But you have seen this person frequently," said the ecclesiastic; "why have you not accosted or secured him? Is it not somewhat precipitate, to say no more, to assume, as you have done, the existence of preternatural agency, when, after all, everything may be easily accountable, if only proper means were taken to sift the matter."

"There are circumstances connected with this—this appearance," said Barton, "which it were needless to disclose, but which to me are proofs of its horrible and unearthly nature. I know that the being who haunts me is not man. I say I know this; I could prove it to your own conviction." He paused for a minute, and then added, "And as to accosting it, I dare not—I could not! When I see it I am powerless; I stand in the gaze of death, in the triumphant presence of preterhuman power and malignity; my strength, and faculties, and memory all forsake me. Oh, God! I fear, sir, you know not what you speak of. Mercy, mercy! heaven have pity on me!"

He leaned his elbow on the table, and passed his hand across his eyes, as if to exclude some image of horror, muttering the last words of the sentence he had just concluded, again and again.

"Dr. Macklin," he said, abruptly raising himself, and looking full upon the clergyman with an imploring eye, "I know you will do for me whatever may be done. You know now fully the circumstances and the nature of the mysterious agency of which I am the victim. I tell you I cannot help myself; I cannot hope to escape; I am utterly passive. I conjure you, then, to weigh my case well, and if anything may be done for me by vicarious supplication, by the intercession of the good, or by any aid or influence whatsoever, I implore of you, I adjure you in the name of the Most High, give me the benefit of that influence, deliver me from the body of this death! Strive for me; pity me! I know you will; you cannot refuse this; it is the purpose and object of my visit. Send me away with some hope, however little—some faint hope of ultimate deliverance, and I will nerve myself to endure, from hour to hour, the hideous dream into which my existence is transformed."

Doctor Macklin assured him that all he could do was to pray earnestly for him, and that so much he would not fail to do. They parted with a hurried and melancholy valediction. Barton hastened to the carriage which awaited him at the door, drew the blinds, and drove away, while Dr. Macklin returned to his chamber, to ruminate at leisure upon the strange interview which had just interrupted his studies.

It was not to be expected that Captain Barton's changed and eccentric habits should long escape remark and discussion. Various were the theories suggested to account for it. Some attributed the alteration to the pressure of secret pecuniary embarrassments; others to a repugnance to fulfil an engagement into which he was presumed to have too precipitately entered; and others, again, to the supposed incipiency of mental disease, which latter, indeed, was the most plausible, as well as the most generally received, of the hypotheses circulated in the gossip of the day.

From the very commencement of this change, at first so gradual in its advances, Miss Montague had, of course, been aware of it. The intimacy involved in their peculiar relation, as well as the near interest which it inspired, afforded, in her case, alike opportunity and motive for the successful exercise of that keen and penetrating observation peculiar to the sex. His visits became, at length, so interrupted, and his manner, while they lasted, so abstracted, strange, and agitated, that Lady Rochdale, after hinting her anxiety and her suspicions more than once, at length distinctly stated her anxiety, and pressed for an explanation. The explanation was given, and although its nature at first relieved the worst solicitudes of the old lady and her niece, yet the circumstances which attended it, and the really dreadful consequences which it obviously threatened as regarded the spirits, and, indeed, the reason, of the now wretched man who made the strange declaration, were enough, upon a little reflection, to fill their minds with perturbation and alarm.

General Montague, the young lady's father, at length arrived. He had himself slightly known Barton, some ten or twelve years previously, and being aware of his fortune and connections, was disposed to regard him as an unexceptionable and indeed a most desirable match for his daughter. He laughed at the story of Barton's supernatural visitations, and lost not a moment in calling upon his intended son-in-law.

"My dear Barton," he continued gaily, after a little conversation, "my sister tells me that you are a victim to blue devils in quite a new and original shape."

Barton changed countenance, and sighed profoundly.

"Come, come; I protest this will never do," continued the General; "you are more like a man on his way to the gallows than to the altar. These devils have made quite a saint of you."

Barton made an effort to change the conversation.

"No, no, it won't do," said his visitor, laughing; "I am resolved to say out what I have to say about this magnificent mock mystery of yours. Come, you must not be angry; but, really, it is too bad to see you, at your time of life, absolutely frightened into good behaviour, like a naughty child, by a bugaboo, and, as far as I can learn, a very particularly contemptible one. Seriously, though, my dear Barton, I have been a good deal annoyed at what they tell me; but, at the same time, thoroughly convinced that there is nothing in the matter that may not be cleared up, with just a little attention and management, within a week at furthest."

"Ah, General, you do not know—" he began.

"Yes, but I do know quite enough to warrant my confidence," interrupted the soldier. "I know that all your annoyance proceeds from the occasional appearance of a certain little man in a cap and great-coat, with a red vest and bad countenance, who follows you about, and pops upon you at the corners of lanes, and throws you into ague fits. Now, my dear fellow, I'll make it my business to catch this mischievous little mountebank, and either beat him into a jelly with my own hands, or have him whipped through the town at the cart's tail."

"If you knew what I know," said Barton, with gloomy agitation, "you would speak very differently. Don't imagine that I am so weak and foolish as to assume, without proof the most overwhelming, the conclusion to which I have been forced. The proofs are here, locked up here." As he spoke, he tapped upon his breast, and with an anxious sigh continued to walk up and down the room.

"Well, well, Barton," said his visitor, "I'll wager a rump and a dozen I collar the ghost, and convince yourself before many days are over."

He was running on in the same strain when he was suddenly arrested, and not a little shocked, by observing Barton, who had approached the window, stagger slowly back, like one who had received a stunning blow—his arm feebly extended towards the street, his face and his very lips white as ashes—while he uttered, "There—there—there!"

General Montague started mechanically to his feet, and, from the window of the drawing-room, saw a figure corresponding, as well as his hurry would permit him to discern, with the description of the person whose appearance so constantly and dreadfully disturbed the repose of his friend. The figure was just turning from the rails of the area upon which it had been leaning, and without waiting to see more, the old gentleman snatched his cane and hat, and rushed down the stairs and into the street, in the furious hope of securing the person, and punishing the audacity of the mysterious stranger. He looked around him, but in vain, for any trace of the form he had himself distinctly beheld. He ran breathlessly to the nearest corner, expecting to see from thence the retreating figure, but no such form was visible. Back and forward, from crossing to crossing, he ran at fault, and it was not until the curious gaze and laughing countenances of the passers-by reminded him of the absurdity of his pursuit, that he checked his hurried pace, lowered his walking-cane from the menacing altitude which he had mechanically given it, adjusted his hat, and walked composedly back again, inwardly vexed and flurried. He found Barton pale and trembling in every joint; they both remained silent, though under emotions very different. At last Barton whispered, "You saw it?"

"It!—him—someone—you mean—to be sure I did," replied Montague, testily. "But where is the good or the harm of seeing him? The fellow runs like a lamplighter. I wanted to catch him, but he had stolen away before I could reach the hall door. However, it is no great matter; next time, I dare say, I'll do better; and, egad, if I once come within reach of him, I'll introduce his shoulders to the weight of my cane, in a way to make him cry peccavi."

Notwithstanding General Montague's undertakings and exhortations, however, Barton continued to suffer from the self-same unexplained cause. Go how, when, or where he would, he was still constantly dogged or confronted by the hateful being who had established over him so dreadful and mysterious an influence; nowhere, and at no time, was he secure against the odious appearance which haunted him with such diabolical perseverance. His depression, misery, and excitement became more settled and alarming every day, and the mental agonies that ceaselessly preyed upon him began at last so sensibly to affect his general health, that Lady Rochdale and General Montague succeeded (without, indeed, much difficulty) in persuading him to try a short tour on the Continent, in the hope that an entire change of scene would, at all events, have the effect of breaking through the influences of local association, which the more sceptical of his friends assumed to be by no means inoperative in suggesting and perpetuating what they conceived to be a mere form of nervous illusion. General Montague, moreover, was persuaded that the figure which haunted his intended son-in-law was by no means the creation of his own imagination, but, on the contrary, a substantial form of flesh and blood, animated by a spiteful and obstinate resolution, perhaps with some murderous object in perspective, to watch and follow the unfortunate gentleman. Even this hypothesis was not a very pleasant one; yet it was plain that if Barton could once be convinced that there was nothing preternatural in the phenomenon, which he had hitherto regarded in that light, the affair would lose all its terrors in his eyes, and wholly cease to exercise upon his health and spirits the baneful influence which it had hitherto done. He therefore reasoned, that if the annoyance were actually escaped from by mere change of scene, it obviously could not have originated in any supernatural agency.

Yielding to their persuasions, Barton left Dublin for England, accompanied by General Montague. They posted rapidly to London, and thence to Dover, whence they took the packet with a fair wind for Calais. The General's confidence in the result of the expedition on Barton's spirits had risen day by day since their departure from the shores of Ireland; for, to the inexpressible relief and delight of the latter, he had not, since then, so much as even once fancied a repetition of those impressions which had, when at home, drawn him gradually down to the very abyss of horror and despair. This exemption from what he had begun to regard as the inevitable condition of his existence, and the sense of security which began to pervade his mind, were inexpressibly delightful; and in the exultation of what he considered his deliverance, he indulged in a thousand happy anticipations for a future into which so lately he had hardly dared to look. In short, both he and his companion secretly congratulated themselves upon the termination of that persecution which had been to its immediate victim a source of such unspeakable agony.

It was a beautiful day, and a crowd of idlers stood upon the jetty to receive the packet, and enjoy the bustle of the new arrivals. Montague walked a few paces in advance of his friend, and as he made his way through the crowd, a little man touched his arm, and said to him, in a broad provincial patois,—

"Monsieur is walking too fast; he will lose his sick comrade in the throng, for, by my faith, the poor gentleman seems to be fainting."

Montague turned quickly, and observed that Barton did indeed look deadly pale. He hastened to his side.

"My poor fellow, are you ill?" he asked anxiously.

The question was unheeded, and twice repeated, ere Barton stammered,—

"I saw him—by ——, I saw him!"

"Him!—who?—where?—when did you see him?—where is he?" cried Montague, looking around him.

"I saw him—but he is gone," repeated Barton, faintly.

"But where—where? For God's sake, speak," urged Montague, vehemently.

"It is but this moment—here," said he.

"But what did he look like?—what had he on?—what did he wear?—quick, quick," urged his excited companion, ready to dart among the crowd, and collar the delinquent on the spot.

"He touched your arm—he spoke to you—he pointed to me. God be merciful to me, there is no escape!" said Barton, in the low, subdued tones of intense despair.

Montague had already bustled away in all the flurry of mingled hope and indignation; but though the singular personnel of the stranger who had accosted him was vividly and perfectly impressed upon his recollection, he failed to discover among the crowd even the slightest resemblance to him. After a fruitless search, in which he enlisted the services of several of the bystanders, who aided all the more zealously as they believed he had been robbed, he at length, out of breath and baffled, gave over the attempt.

"Ah, my friend, it won't do," said Barton, with the faint voice and bewildered, ghastly look of one who has been stunned by some mortal shock; "there is no use in contending with it; whatever it is, the dreadful association between me and it is now established; I shall never escape—never, never!"

"Nonsense, nonsense, my dear fellow; don't talk so," said Montague, with something at once of irritation and dismay; "you must not; never mind, I say—never mind, we'll jockey the scoundrel yet."

It was, however, but lost labour to endeavour henceforward to inspire Barton with one ray of hope; he became utterly desponding. This intangible and, as it seemed, utterly inadequate influence was fast destroying his energies of intellect, character, and health. His first object was now to return to Ireland, there, as he believed, and now almost hoped, speedily to die.

To Ireland, accordingly, he came, and one of the first faces he saw upon the shore was again that of his implacable and dreaded persecutor. Barton seemed at last to have lost not only all enjoyment and every hope in existence, but all independence of will besides. He now submitted himself passively to the management of the friends most nearly interested in his welfare. With the apathy of entire despair, he implicitly assented to whatever measures they suggested and advised; and, as a last resource, it was determined to remove him to a house of Lady Rochdale's in the neighbourhood of Clontarf, where, with the advice of his medical attendant (who persisted in his opinion that the whole train of impressions resulted merely from some nervous derangement) it was resolved that he was to confine himself strictly to the house, and to make use only of those apartments which commanded a view of an enclosed yard, the gates of which were to be kept jealously locked. These precautions would at least secure him against the casual appearance of any living form which his excited imagination might possibly confound with the spectre which, as it was contended, his fancy recognized in every figure that bore even a distant or general resemblance to the traits with which he had at first invested it. A month or six weeks' absolute seclusion under these conditions, it was hoped, might, by interrupting the series of these terrible impressions, gradually dispel the predisposing apprehension, and effectually break up the associations which had confirmed the supposed disease, and rendered recovery hopeless. Cheerful society and that of his friends was to be constantly supplied, and on the whole, very sanguine expectations were indulged in, that under this treatment the obstinate hypochondria of the patient might at length give way.

Accompanied, therefore, by Lady Rochdale, General Montague, and his daughter—his own affianced bride—poor Barton, himself never daring to cherish a hope of his ultimate emancipation from the strange horrors under which his life was literally wasting away, took possession of the apartments whose situation protected him against the dreadful intrusions from which he shrank with such unutterable terror.

After a little time, a steady persistence in this system began to manifest its results in a very marked though gradual improvement alike in the health and spirits of the invalid. Not, indeed, that anything at all approaching to complete recovery was yet discernible. On the contrary, to those who had not seen him since the commencement of his strange sufferings, such an alteration would have been apparent as might well have shocked them. The improvement, however, such as it was, was welcomed with gratitude and delight, especially by the poor young lady, whom her attachment to him, as well as her now singularly painful position, consequent on his mysterious and protracted illness, rendered an object of pity scarcely one degree less to be commiserated than himself.

A week passed—a fortnight—a month—and yet no recurrence of the hated visitation had agitated and terrified him as before. The treatment had, so far, been followed by complete success. The chain of association had been broken. The constant pressure upon the overtasked spirits had been removed, and, under these comparatively favourable circumstances, the sense of social community with the world about him, and something of human interest, if not of enjoyment, began to reanimate his mind.

It was about this time that Lady Rochdale, who, like most old ladies of the day, was deep in family receipts, and a great pretender to medical science, being engaged in the concoction of certain unpalatable mixtures of marvellous virtue, despatched her own maid to the kitchen garden with a list of herbs which were there to be carefully culled and brought back to her for the purpose stated. The hand-maiden, however, returned with her task scarce half-completed, and a good deal flurried and alarmed. Her mode of accounting for her precipitate retreat and evident agitation was odd, and to the old lady unpleasantly startling.

It appeared that she had repaired to the kitchen garden, pursuant to her mistress's directions, and had there begun to make the specified selection among the rank and neglected herbs which crowded one corner of the enclosure, and while engaged in this pleasant labour she carelessly sang a fragment of an old song, as she said, "to keep herself company." She was, however, interrupted by a sort of mocking echo of the air she was singing; and looking up, she saw through the old thorn hedge, which surrounded the garden, a singularly ill-looking, little man, whose countenance wore the stamp of menace and malignity, standing close to her at the other side of the hawthorn screen. She described herself as utterly unable to move or speak, while he charged her with a message for Captain Barton, the substance of which she distinctly remembered to have been to the effect that he, Captain Barton, must come abroad as usual, and show himself to his friends out of doors, or else prepare for a visit in his own chamber. On concluding this brief message, the stranger had, with a threatening air, got down into the outer ditch, and seizing the hawthorn stems in his hands, seemed on the point of climbing through the fence, a feat which might have been accomplished without much difficulty. Without, of course, awaiting this result, the girl, throwing down her treasures of thyme and rosemary, had turned and run, with the swiftness of terror, to the house. Lady Rochdale commanded her, on pain of instant dismissal, to observe an absolute silence respecting all that portion of the incident which related to Captain Barton; and, at the same time, directed instant search to be made by her men in the garden and fields adjacent. This measure, however, was attended with the usual unsuccess, and filled with fearful and indefinable misgivings, Lady Rochdale communicated the incident to her brother. The story, however, until long afterwards, went no further, and of course it was jealously guarded from Barton, who continued to mend, though slowly and imperfectly.

Barton now began to walk occasionally in the courtyard which we have mentioned, and which, being surrounded by a high wall, commanded no view beyond its own extent. Here he, therefore, considered himself perfectly secure; and, but for a careless violation of orders by one of the grooms, he might have enjoyed, at least for some time longer, his much-prized immunity. Opening upon the public road, this yard was entered by a wooden gate, with a wicket in it, which was further defended by an iron gate upon the outside. Strict orders had been given to keep them carefully locked; but, in spite of these, it had happened that one day, as Barton was slowly pacing this narrow enclosure, in his accustomed walk, and reaching the further extremity, was turning to retrace his steps, he saw the boarded wicket ajar, and the face of his tormentor immovably looking at him through the iron bars. For a few seconds he stood riveted to the earth, breathless and bloodless, in the fascination of that dreaded gaze, and then fell helplessly upon the pavement.

There was he found a few minutes afterwards, and conveyed to his room, the apartment which he was never afterwards to leave alive. Henceforward, a marked and unaccountable change was observable in the tone of his mind. Captain Barton was now no longer the excited and despairing man he had been before; a strange alteration had passed upon him, an unearthly tranquillity reigned in his mind; it was the anticipated stillness of the grave.

"Montague, my friend, this struggle is nearly ended now," he said, tranquilly, but with a look of fixed and fearful awe. "I have, at last, some comfort from that world of spirits, from which my punishment has come. I know now that my sufferings will be soon over."

Montague pressed him to speak on.

"Yes," said he, in a softened voice, "my punishment is nearly ended. From sorrow perhaps I shall never, in time or eternity, escape; but my agony is almost over. Comfort has been revealed to me, and what remains of my allotted struggle I will bear with submission, even with hope."

"I am glad to hear you speak so tranquilly, my dear fellow," said Montague; "peace and cheerfulness of mind are all you need to make you what you were."

"No, no, I never can be that," said he, mournfully. "I am no longer fit for life. I am soon to die: I do not shrink from death as I did. I am to see him but once again, and then all is ended."

"He said so, then?" suggested Montague.

"He? No, no; good tidings could scarcely come through him; and these were good and welcome; and they came so solemnly and sweetly, with unutterable love and melancholy, such as I could not, without saying more than is needful or fitting, of other long-past scenes and persons, fully explain to you." As Barton said this he shed tears.

"Come, come," said Montague, mistaking the source of his emotions, "you must not give way. What is it, after all, but a pack of dreams and nonsense; or, at worst, the practices of a scheming rascal that enjoys his power of playing upon your nerves, and loves to exert it; a sneaking vagabond that owes you a grudge, and pays it off this way, not daring to try a more manly one."

"A grudge, indeed, he owes me; you say rightly," said Barton, with a sullen shudder; "a grudge as you call it. Oh, God! when the justice of heaven permits the Evil One to carry out a scheme of vengeance, when its execution is committed to the lost and frightful victim of sin, who owes his own ruin to the man, the very man, whom he is commissioned to pursue; then, indeed, the torments and terrors of hell are anticipated on earth. But heaven has dealt mercifully with me: hope has opened to me at last; and if death could come without the dreadful sight I am doomed to see, I would gladly close my eyes this moment upon the world. But though death is welcome, I shrink with an agony you cannot understand; a maddening agony, an actual frenzy of terror, from the last encounter with that—that DEMON, who has drawn me thus to the verge of the chasm, and who is himself to plunge me down. I am to see him again, once more, but under circumstances unutterably more terrific than ever."

As Barton thus spoke, he trembled so violently that Montague was really alarmed at the extremity of his sudden agitation, and hastened to lead him back to the topic which had before seemed to exert so tranquillizing an effect upon his mind.

"It was not a dream," he said, after a time; "I was in a different state, I felt differently and strangely; and yet it was all as real, as clear and vivid, as what I now see and hear; it was a reality."

"And what did you see and hear?" urged his companion.

"When I awakened from the swoon I fell into on seeing him," said Barton, continuing, as if he had not heard the question, "it was slowly, very slowly; I was reclining by the margin of a broad lake, surrounded by misty hills, and a soft, melancholy, rose-coloured light illuminated it all. It was indescribably sad and lonely, and yet more beautiful than any earthly scene. My head was leaning on the lap of a girl, and she was singing a strange and wondrous song, that told, I know not how, whether by words or harmony, of all my life, all that is past, and all that is still to come. And with the song the old feelings that I thought had perished within me came back, and tears flowed from my eyes, partly for the song and its mysterious beauty, and partly for the unearthly sweetness of her voice; yet I know the voice, oh! how well; and I was spell-bound as I listened and looked at the strange and solitary scene, without stirring, almost without breathing, and, alas! alas! without turning my eyes toward the face that I knew was near me, so sweetly powerful was the enchantment that held me. And so, slowly and softly, the song and scene grew fainter, and ever fainter, to my senses, till all was dark and still again. And then I wakened to this world, as you saw, comforted, for I knew that I was forgiven much." Barton wept again long and bitterly.

From this time, as we have said, the prevailing tone of his mind was one of profound and tranquil melancholy. This, however, was not without its interruptions. He was thoroughly impressed with the conviction that he was to experience another and a final visitation, illimitably transcending in horror all he had before experienced. From this anticipated and unknown agony he often shrunk in such paroxysms of abject terror and distraction, as filled the whole household with dismay and superstitious panic. Even those among them who affected to discredit the supposition of preternatural agency in the matter, were often in their secret souls visited during the darkness and solitude of night with qualms and apprehensions which they would not have readily confessed; and none of them attempted to dissuade Barton from the resolution on which he now systematically acted, of shutting himself up in his own apartment. The window-blinds of this room were kept jealously down; and his own man was seldom out of his presence, day or night, his bed being placed in the same chamber.

This man was an attached and respectable servant; and his duties, in addition to those ordinarily imposed upon valets, but which Barton's independent habits generally dispensed with, were to attend carefully to the simple precautions by means of which his master hoped to exclude the dreaded intrusion of the "Watcher," as the strange letter he had at first received had designated his persecutor. And, in addition to attending to these arrangements, which consisted merely in anticipating the possibility of his master's being, through any unscreened window or opened door, exposed to the dreaded influence, the valet was never to suffer him to be for one moment alone: total solitude, even for a minute, had become to him now almost as intolerable as the idea of going abroad into the public ways; it was an instinctive anticipation of what was coming.

It is needless to say, that, under these mysterious and horrible circumstances, no steps were taken toward the fulfilment of that engagement into which he had entered. There was quite disparity enough in point of years, and indeed of habits, between the young lady and Captain Barton, to have precluded anything like very vehement or romantic attachment on her part. Though grieved and anxious, therefore, she was very far from being heart-broken; a circumstance which, for the sentimental purposes of our tale, is much to be deplored. But truth must be told, especially in a narrative whose chief, if not only, pretensions to interest consist in a rigid adherence to facts, or what are so reported to have been.

Miss Montague, nevertheless, devoted much of her time to a patient but fruitless attempt to cheer the unhappy invalid. She read for him, and conversed with him; but it was apparent that whatever exertions he made, the endeavour to escape from the one constant and ever-present fear that preyed upon him was utterly and miserably unavailing.

Young ladies, as all the world knows, are much given to the cultivation of pets; and among those who shared the favour of Miss Montague was a fine old owl, which the gardener, who caught him napping among the ivy of a ruined stable, had dutifully presented to that young lady.

The caprice which regulates such preferences was manifested in the extravagant favour with which this grim and ill-favoured bird was at once distinguished by his mistress; and, trifling as this whimsical circumstance may seem, I am forced to mention it, inasmuch as it is connected, oddly enough, with the concluding scene of the story. Barton, so far from sharing in this liking for the new favourite, regarded it from the first with an antipathy as violent as it was utterly unaccountable. Its very vicinity was insupportable to him. He seemed to hate and dread it with a vehemence absolutely laughable, and to those who have never witnessed the exhibition of antipathies of this kind, his dread would seem all but incredible.

With these few words of preliminary explanation, I shall proceed to state the particulars of the last scene in this strange series of incidents. It was almost two o'clock one winter's night, and Barton was, as usual at that hour, in his bed; the servant we have mentioned occupied a smaller bed in the same room, and a candle was burning. The man was on a sudden aroused by his master, who said,—

"I can't get it out of my head that that accursed bird has escaped somehow, and is lurking in some corner of the room. I have been dreaming of him. Get up, Smith, and look about; search for him. Such hateful dreams!"

The servant rose, and examined the chamber, and while engaged in so doing, he heard the well-known sound, more like a long-drawn gasp than a hiss, with which these birds from their secret haunts affright the quiet of the night. This ghostly indication of its proximity, for the sound proceeded from the passage upon which Barton's chamber-door opened, determined the search of the servant, who, opening the door, proceeded a step or two forward for the purpose of driving the bird away. He had, however, hardly entered the lobby, when the door behind him slowly swung to under the impulse, as it seemed, of some gentle current of air; but as immediately over the door there was a kind of window, intended in the daytime to aid in lighting the passage, and through which the rays of the candle were then issuing, the valet could see quite enough for his purpose. As he advanced he heard his master (who, lying in a well-curtained bed had not, as it seemed, perceived his exit from the room) call him by name, and direct him to place the candle on the table by his bed. The servant, who was now some way in the long passage, did not like to raise his voice for the purpose of replying, lest he should startle the sleeping inmates of the house, began to walk hurriedly and softly back again, when, to his amazement, he heard a voice in the interior of the chamber answering calmly, and the man actually saw, through the window which over-topped the door, that the light was slowly shifting, as if carried across the chamber in answer to his master's call. Palsied by a feeling akin to terror, yet not unmingled with a horrible curiosity, he stood breathless and listening at the threshold, unable to summon resolution to push open the door and enter. Then came a rustling of the curtains, and a sound like that of one who in a low voice hushes a child to rest, in the midst of which he heard Barton say, in a tone of stifled horror—"Oh, God—oh, my God!" and repeat the same exclamation several times. Then ensued a silence, which again was broken by the same strange soothing sound; and at last there burst forth, in one swelling peal, a yell of agony so appalling and hideous, that, under some impulse of ungovernable horror, the man rushed to the door, and with his whole strength strove to force it open. Whether it was that, in his agitation, he had himself but imperfectly turned the handle, or that the door was really secured upon the inside, he failed to effect an entrance; and as he tugged and pushed, yell after yell rang louder and wilder through the chamber, accompanied all the while by the same hushing sounds. Actually freezing with terror, and scarce knowing what he did, the man turned and ran down the passage, wringing his hands in the extremity of horror and irresolution. At the stair-head he was encountered by General Montague, scared and eager, and just as they met the fearful sounds had ceased.

"What is it?—who—where is your master?" said Montague, with the incoherence of extreme agitation. "Has anything—for God's sake, is anything wrong?"

"Lord have mercy on us, it's all over," said the man, staring wildly towards his master's chamber. "He's dead, sir; I'm sure he's dead."

Without waiting for inquiry or explanation, Montague, closely followed by the servant, hurried to the chamber-door, turned the handle, and pushed it open. As the door yielded to his pressure, the ill-omened bird of which the servant had been in search, uttering its spectral warning, started suddenly from the far side of the bed, and flying through the doorway close over their heads, and extinguishing, in its passage, the candle which Montague carried, crashed through the skylight that overlooked the lobby, and sailed away into the darkness of the outer space.

"There it is, God bless us!" whispered the man, after a breathless pause.

"Curse that bird!" muttered the general, startled by the suddenness of the apparition, and unable to conceal his discomposure.

"The candle was moved," said the man, after another breathless pause; "see, they put it by the bed!"

"Draw the curtains, fellow, and don't stand gaping there," whispered Montague, sternly.

The man hesitated.

"Hold this, then," said Montague, impatiently, thrusting the candlestick into the servant's hand; and himself advancing to the bedside, he drew the curtains apart. The light of the candle, which was still burning at the bedside, fell upon a figure huddled together, and half upright, at the head of the bed. It seemed as though it had shrunk back as far as the solid panelling would allow, and the hands were still clutched in the bed-clothes.

"Barton, Barton, Barton!" cried the general, with a strange mixture of awe and vehemence.

He took the candle, and held it so that it shone full upon his face. The features were fixed, stern and white; the jaw was fallen, and the sightless eyes, still open, gazed vacantly forward toward the front of the bed.

"God Almighty, he's dead!" muttered the general, as he looked upon this fearful spectacle. They both continued to gaze upon it in silence for a minute or more. "And cold, too," said Montague, withdrawing his hand from that of the dead man.

"And see, see; may I never have life, sir," added the man, after another pause, with a shudder, "but there was something else on the bed with him! Look there—look there; see that, sir!"

As the man thus spoke, he pointed to a deep indenture, as if caused by a heavy pressure, near the foot of the bed.

Montague was silent.

"Come, sir, come away, for God's sake!" whispered the man, drawing close up to him, and holding fast by his arm, while he glanced fearfully round; "what good can be done here now?—come away, for God's sake!"

At this moment they heard the steps of more than one approaching, and Montague, hastily desiring the servant to arrest their progress, endeavoured to loose the rigid grip with which the fingers of the dead man were clutched in the bedclothes, and drew, as well as he was able, the awful figure into a reclining posture. Then closing the curtains carefully upon it, he hastened himself to meet those who were approaching.

.....

It is needless to follow the personages so slightly connected with this narrative into the events of their after lives; it is enough for us to remark that no clue to the solution of these mysterious occurrences was ever afterwards discovered; and so long an interval having now passed, it is scarcely to be expected that time can throw any new light upon their inexplicable obscurity. Until the secrets of the earth shall be no longer hidden these transactions must remain shrouded in mystery.

The only occurrence in Captain Barton's former life to which reference was ever made, as having any possible connection with the sufferings with which his existence closed, and which he himself seemed to regard as working out a retribution for some grievous sin of his past life, was a circumstance which not for several years after his death was brought to light. The nature of this disclosure was painful to his relatives and discreditable to his memory.

It appeared, then, that some eight years before Captain Barton's final return to Dublin, he had formed, in the town of Plymouth, a guilty attachment, the object of which was the daughter of one of the ship's crew under his command. The father had visited the frailty of his unhappy child with extreme harshness, and even brutality, and it was said that she had died heart-broken. Presuming upon Barton's implication in her guilt, this man had conducted himself towards him with marked insolence, and Barton resented this—and what he resented with still more exasperated bitterness, his treatment of the unfortunate girl—by a systematic exercise of those terrible and arbitrary severities with which the regulations of the navy arm those who are responsible for its discipline. The man had at length made his escape, while the vessel was in port at Lisbon, but died, as it was said, in an hospital in that town, of the wounds inflicted in one of his recent and sanguinary punishments.

Whether these circumstances in reality bear or not upon the occurrences of Barton's after-life, it is of course impossible to say. It seems, however, more than probable that they were, at least in his own mind, closely associated with them. But however the truth may be as to the origin and motives of this mysterious persecution, there can be no doubt that, with respect to the agencies by which it was accomplished, absolute and impenetrable mystery is like to prevail until the day of doom.

PASSAGE IN THE SECRET HISTORY OF AN IRISH COUNTESS

This Story can be found on Page 75 as part of The Purcell Papers.

STRANGE EVENT IN THE LIFE OF SCHALKEN THE PAINTER

This Story can be found on Page 120 as part of The Purcell Papers.

THE FORTUNES OF SIR ROBERT ARDAGH[1]

'The earth hath bubbles as the water hath—
And these are of them.'

In the south of Ireland, and on the borders of the county of Limerick, there lies a district of two or three miles in length, which is rendered interesting by the fact that it is one of the very few spots throughout this country in which some vestiges of aboriginal forests still remain. It has little or none of the lordly character of the American forest, for the axe has felled its oldest and its grandest trees; but in the close wood which survives live all the wild and pleasing peculiarities of nature: its complete irregularity, its vistas, in whose perspective the quiet cattle are browsing; its refreshing glades, where the grey rocks arise from amid the nodding fern; the silvery shafts of the old birch-trees; the knotted trunks of the hoary oak, the grotesque but graceful branches which never shed their honours under the tyrant pruning-hook; the soft green sward; the chequered light and shade; the wild luxuriant weeds; the lichen and the moss—all are beautiful alike in the green freshness of spring or in the sadness and sere of autumn. Their beauty is of that kind which makes the heart full with joy—appealing to the affections with a power which belongs to nature only. This wood runs up, from below the base, to the ridge of a long line of irregular hills, having perhaps, in primitive times, formed but the skirting of some mighty forest which occupied the level below.

But now, alas! whither have we drifted? whither has the tide of civilization borne us? It has passed over a land unprepared for it—it has left nakedness behind it; we have lost our forests, but our marauders remain; we have destroyed all that is picturesque, while we have retained everything that is revolting in barbarism. Through the midst of this woodland there runs a deep gully or glen, where the stillness of the scene is broken in upon by the brawling of a mountain-stream, which, however, in the winter season, swells into a rapid and formidable torrent.

There is one point at which the glen becomes extremely deep and narrow; the sides descend to the depth of some hundred feet, and are so steep as to be nearly perpendicular. The wild trees which have taken root in the crannies and chasms of

[1] A longer version of this Story can be found on Page 20 as part of The Purcell Papers.

the rock are so intersected and entangled, that one can with difficulty catch a glimpse of the stream which wheels, flashes, and foams below, as if exulting in the surrounding silence and solitude.

This spot was not unwisely chosen, as a point of no ordinary strength, for the erection of a massive square tower or keep, one side of which rises as if in continuation of the precipitous cliff on which it is based. Originally, the only mode of ingress was by a narrow portal in the very wall which overtopped the precipice, opening upon a ledge of rock which afforded a precarious pathway, cautiously intersected, however, by a deep trench cut out with great labour in the living rock; so that, in its pristine state, and before the introduction of artillery into the art of war, this tower might have been pronounced, and that not presumptuously, impregnable.

The progress of improvement and the increasing security of the times had, however, tempted its successive proprietors, if not to adorn, at least to enlarge their premises, and about the middle of the last century, when the castle was last inhabited, the original square tower formed but a small part of the edifice.

The castle, and a wide tract of the surrounding country, had from time immemorial belonged to a family which, for distinctness, we shall call by the name of Ardagh; and owing to the associations which, in Ireland, almost always attach to scenes which have long witnessed alike the exercise of stern feudal authority, and of that savage hospitality which distinguished the good old times, this building has become the subject and the scene of many wild and extraordinary traditions. One of them I have been enabled, by a personal acquaintance with an eye-witness of the events, to trace to its origin; and yet it is hard to say whether the events which I am about to record appear more strange and improbable as seen through the distorting medium of tradition, or in the appalling dimness of uncertainty which surrounds the reality.

Tradition says that, sometime in the last century, Sir Robert Ardagh, a young man, and the last heir of that family, went abroad and served in foreign armies; and that, having acquired considerable honour and emolument, he settled at Castle Ardagh, the building we have just now attempted to describe. He was what the country people call a dark man; that is, he was considered morose, reserved, and ill-tempered; and, as it was supposed from the utter solitude of his life, was upon no terms of cordiality with the other members of his family.

The only occasion upon which he broke through the solitary monotony of his life was during the continuance of the racing season, and immediately subsequent to it; at which time he was to be seen among the busiest upon the course, betting deeply and unhesitatingly, and invariably with success. Sir Robert was, however, too well known as a man of honour, and of too high a family, to be suspected of any unfair dealing. He was, moreover, a soldier, and a man of intrepid as well as of a haughty character; and no one cared to hazard a surmise, the consequences of which would be felt most probably by its originator only.

Gossip, however, was not silent; it was remarked that Sir Robert never appeared at the race-ground, which was the only place of public resort which he frequented, except in company with a certain strange-looking person, who was never seen elsewhere, or under other circumstances. It was remarked, too, that this man, whose relation to Sir Robert was never distinctly ascertained, was the only person to whom he seemed to speak unnecessarily; it was observed that while with the country gentry he exchanged no further communication than what was unavoidable in arranging his sporting transactions, with this person he would converse earnestly and frequently. Tradition asserts that, to enhance the curiosity which this unaccountable and exclusive preference excited, the stranger possessed some striking and unpleasant peculiarities of person and of garb—though it is not stated, however, what these were—but they, in conjunction with Sir Robert's secluded habits and extraordinary run of luck—a success which was supposed to result from the suggestions and immediate advice of the unknown—were sufficient to warrant report in pronouncing that there was something queer in the wind, and in surmising that Sir Robert was playing a fearful and a hazardous game, and that, in short, his strange companion was little better than the Devil himself.

Years rolled quietly away, and nothing very novel occurred in the arrangements of Castle Ardagh, excepting that Sir Robert parted with his odd companion, but as nobody could tell whence he came, so nobody could say whither he had gone. Sir Robert's habits, however, underwent no consequent change; he continued regularly to frequent the race meetings, without mixing at all in the convivialities of the gentry, and immediately afterwards to relapse into the secluded monotony of his ordinary life.

It was said that he had accumulated vast sums of money—and, as his bets were always successful and always large, such must have been the case. He did not suffer the acquisition of wealth, however, to influence his hospitality or his housekeeping—he neither purchased land, nor extended his establishment; and his mode of enjoying his money must have been altogether that of the miser—consisting merely in the pleasure of touching and telling his gold, and in the consciousness of wealth.

Sir Robert's temper, so far from improving, became more than ever gloomy and morose. He sometimes carried the indulgence of his evil dispositions to such a height that it bordered upon insanity. During these paroxysms he would neither eat, drink, nor sleep. On such occasions he insisted on perfect privacy, even from the intrusion of his most trusted servants; his voice was frequently heard, sometimes in earnest supplication, sometimes raised, as if in loud and angry altercation with some unknown visitant. Sometimes he would for hours together walk to and fro throughout the long oak-wainscoted apartment which he generally occupied, with wild gesticulations and agitated pace, in the manner of one who has been roused to a state of unnatural excitement by some sudden and appalling intimation.

These paroxysms of apparent lunacy were so frightful, that during their continuance even his oldest and most faithful domestics dared not approach him; consequently his hours of agony were never intruded upon, and the mysterious causes of his sufferings appeared likely to remain hidden for ever.

On one occasion a fit of this kind continued for an unusual time; the ordinary term of their duration—about two days—had been long past, and the old servant who generally waited upon Sir Robert after these visitations, having in vain listened for the well-known tinkle of his master's hand-bell, began to feel extremely anxious; he feared that his master might have died from sheer exhaustion, or perhaps put an end to his own existence during his miserable depression. These fears at length became so strong, that having in vain urged some of his brother servants to accompany him, he determined to go up alone, and himself see whether any accident had befallen Sir Robert.

He traversed the several passages which conducted from the new to the more ancient parts of the mansion, and having arrived in the old hall of the castle, the utter silence of the hour—for it was very late in the night—the idea of the nature of the enterprise in which he was engaging himself, a sensation of remoteness from anything like human companionship, but, more than all, the vivid but undefined anticipation of something horrible, came upon him with such oppressive weight that he hesitated as to whether he should proceed. Real uneasiness, however, respecting the fate of his master, for whom he felt that kind of attachment which the force of habitual intercourse not unfrequently engenders respecting objects not in themselves amiable, and also a latent unwillingness to expose his weakness to the ridicule of his fellow-servants, combined to overcome his reluctance; and he had just placed his foot upon the first step of the staircase which conducted to his master's chamber, when his attention was arrested by a low but distinct knocking at the hall-door. Not, perhaps, very sorry at finding thus an excuse even for deferring his intended expedition, he placed the candle upon a stone block which lay in the hall and approached the door, uncertain whether his ears had not deceived him. This doubt was justified by the circumstance that the hall entrance had been for nearly fifty years disused as a mode of ingress to the castle. The situation of this gate also, which we have endeavoured to describe, opening upon a narrow ledge of rock which overhangs a perilous cliff, rendered it at all times, but particularly at night, a dangerous entrance. This shelving platform of rock, which formed the only avenue to the door, was divided, as I have already stated, by a broad chasm, the planks across which had long disappeared, by decay or otherwise; so that it seemed at least highly improbable that any man could have found his way across the passage in safety to the door, more particularly on a night like this, of singular darkness. The old man, therefore, listened attentively, to ascertain whether the first application should be followed by another. He had not long to wait. The same low but singularly distinct knocking was repeated; so low that it seemed as if the applicant had employed no harder or heavier instrument than his hand, and yet, despite the immense thickness of the door, with such strength that the sound was distinctly audible.

The knock was repeated a third time, without any increase of loudness; and the old man, obeying an impulse for which to his dying hour he could never account, proceeded to remove, one by one, the three great oaken bars which secured the door. Time and damp had effectually corroded the iron chambers of the lock, so that it afforded little resistance. With some effort, as he believed, assisted from without, the old servant succeeded in opening the door; and a low, square-built figure, apparently that of a man wrapped in a large black cloak, entered the hall. The servant could not see much of this visitor with any distinctness; his dress appeared foreign, the skirt of his ample cloak was thrown over one shoulder; he wore a large felt hat, with a very heavy leaf, from under which escaped what appeared to be a mass of long sooty-black hair; his feet were cased in heavy riding-boots. Such were the few particulars which the servant had time and light to observe. The stranger desired him to let his master know instantly that a friend had come, by appointment, to settle some business with him. The servant hesitated, but a slight motion on the part of his visitor, as if to possess himself of the candle, determined him; so, taking it in his hand, he ascended the castle stairs, leaving the guest in the hall.

On reaching the apartment which opened upon the oak-chamber he was surprised to observe the door of that room partly open, and the room itself lit up. He paused, but there was no sound; he looked in, and saw Sir Robert, his head and the upper part of his body reclining on a table, upon which two candles burned; his arms were stretched forward on either side, and perfectly motionless; it appeared that, having been sitting at the table, he had thus sunk forward, either dead or in a swoon. There was no sound of breathing; all was silent, except the sharp ticking of a watch, which lay beside the lamp. The servant coughed twice or thrice, but with no effect; his fears now almost amounted to certainty, and he was approaching the table on which his master partly lay, to satisfy himself of his death, when Sir Robert slowly raised his head, and, throwing himself back in his chair, fixed his eyes in a ghastly and uncertain gaze upon his attendant. At length he said, slowly and painfully, as if he dreaded the answer,—

"In God's name, what are you?"

"Sir," said the servant, "a strange gentleman wants to see you below."

At this intimation Sir Robert, starting to his feet and tossing his arms wildly upwards, uttered a shriek of such appalling and despairing terror that it was almost too fearful for human endurance; and long after the sound had ceased it seemed to the terrified imagination of the old servant to roll through the deserted passages in bursts of unnatural laughter. After a few moments Sir Robert said,—

"Can't you send him away? Why does he come so soon? O Merciful Powers! let him leave me for an hour; a little time. I can't see him now; try to get him away. You see I can't go down now; I have not strength. O God! O God! let him come back in an hour; it is not long to wait. He cannot lose anything by it; nothing, nothing, nothing. Tell him that! Say anything to him."

The servant went down. In his own words, he did not feel the stairs under him till he got to the hall. The figure stood exactly as he had left it. He delivered his master's message as coherently as he could. The stranger replied in a careless tone:

"If Sir Robert will not come down to me; I must go up to him."

The man returned, and to his surprise he found his master much more composed in manner. He listened to the message, and though the cold perspiration rose in drops upon his forehead faster than he could wipe it away, his manner had lost the dreadful agitation which had marked it before. He rose feebly, and casting a last look of agony behind him, passed from the room to the lobby, where he signed to his attendant not to follow him. The man moved as far as the head of the staircase, from whence he had a tolerably distinct view of the hall, which was imperfectly lighted by the candle he had left there.

He saw his master reel, rather than walk, down the stairs, clinging all the way to the banisters. He walked on, as if about to sink every moment from weakness. The figure advanced as if to meet him, and in passing struck down the light. The servant could see no more; but there was a sound of struggling, renewed at intervals with silent but fearful energy. It was evident, however, that the parties were approaching the door, for he heard the solid oak sound twice or thrice, as the feet of the combatants, in shuffling hither and thither over the floor, struck upon it. After a slight pause, he heard the door thrown open with such violence that the leaf seemed to strike the side-wall of the hall, for it was so dark without that this could only be surmised by the sound. The struggle was renewed with an agony and intenseness of energy that betrayed itself in deep-drawn gasps. One desperate effort, which terminated in the breaking of some part of the door, producing a sound as if the door-post was wrenched from its position, was followed by another wrestle, evidently upon the narrow ledge which ran outside the door, overtopping the precipice. This proved to be the final struggle; it was followed by a crashing sound as if some heavy body had fallen over, and was rushing down the precipice through the light boughs that crossed near the top. All then became still as the grave, except when the moan of the night-wind sighed up the wooded glen.

The old servant had not nerve to return through the hall, and to him the darkness seemed all but endless; but morning at length came, and with it the disclosure of the events of the night. Near the door, upon the ground, lay Sir Robert's sword-belt, which had given way in the scuffle. A huge splinter from the massive door-post had been wrenched off by an almost superhuman effort—one which nothing but the gripe of a despairing man could have severed—and on the rocks outside were left the marks of the slipping and sliding of feet.

At the foot of the precipice, not immediately under the castle, but dragged some way up the glen, were found the remains of Sir Robert, with hardly a vestige of a limb or feature left distinguishable. The right hand, however, was uninjured, and in its fingers were clutched, with the fixedness of death, a long lock of coarse sooty hair—the only direct circumstantial evidence of the presence of a second person.

THE DREAM

Dreams! What age, or what country of the world, has not felt and acknowledged the mystery of their origin and end? I have thought not a little upon the subject, seeing it is one which has been often forced upon my attention, and sometimes strangely enough; and yet I have never arrived at anything which at all appeared a satisfactory conclusion. It does appear that a mental phenomenon so extraordinary cannot be wholly without its use. We know, indeed, that in the olden times it has been made the organ of communication between the Deity and His creatures; and when a dream produces upon a mind, to all appearance hopelessly reprobate and depraved, an effect so powerful and so lasting as to break down the inveterate habits, and to reform the life of an abandoned sinner, we see in the result, in the reformation of morals which appeared incorrigible, in the reclamation of a human soul which seemed to be irretrievably lost, something more than could be produced by a mere chimera of the slumbering fancy, something more than could arise from the capricious images of a terrified imagination. And while Reason rejects as absurd the superstition which will read a prophecy in every dream, she may, without violence to herself, recognize, even in the wildest and most incongruous of the wanderings of a slumbering intellect, the evidences and the fragments of a language which may be spoken, which has been spoken, to terrify, to warn and to command. We have reason to believe too, by the promptness of action which in the age of the prophets followed all intimations of this kind, and by the strength of conviction and strange permanence of the effects resulting from certain dreams in latter times—which effects we ourselves may have witnessed—that when this medium of communication has been employed by the Deity, the evidences of His presence have been unequivocal. My thoughts were directed to this subject in a manner to leave a lasting impression upon my mind, by the events which I shall now relate, the statement of which, however extraordinary, is nevertheless accurate.

About the year 17—, having been appointed to the living of C——h, I rented a small house in the town which bears the same name: one morning in the month of November, I was awakened before my usual time by my servant, who bustled into my bedroom for the purpose of announcing a sick call. As the Catholic Church holds her last rites to be totally indispensable to the safety of the departing sinner, no conscientious clergyman can afford a moment's unnecessary delay, and in little more than five minutes I stood ready, cloaked and booted for the road, in the small front parlour in which the messenger, who was to act as my guide, awaited my coming. I found a poor little girl crying piteously near the door, and after some slight difficulty I ascertained that her father was either dead or just dying.

"And what may be your father's name, my poor child?" said I. She held down her head as if ashamed. I repeated the question, and the wretched little creature burst into floods of tears still more bitter than she had shed before. At length, almost angered by conduct which appeared to me so unreasonable, I began to lose patience, and I said rather harshly,—

"If you will not tell me the name of the person to whom you would lead me, your silence can arise from no good motive, and I might be justified in refusing to go with you at all."

"Oh, don't say that—don't say that!" cried she. "Oh, sir, it was that I was afeard of when I would not tell you—I was afeard, when you heard his name, you would not come with me; but it is no use hidin' it now—it's Pat Connell, the carpenter, your honour."

She looked in my face with the most earnest anxiety, as if her very existence depended upon what she should read there. I relieved the child at once. The name, indeed, was most unpleasantly familiar to me; but, however fruitless my visits and advice might have been at another time, the present was too fearful an occasion to suffer my doubts of their utility, or my reluctance to re-attempting what appeared a hopeless task, to weigh even against the lightest chance that a consciousness of his imminent danger might produce in him a more docile and tractable disposition. Accordingly I told the child to lead the way, and followed her in silence. She hurried rapidly through the long narrow street which forms the great thoroughfare of the town. The darkness of the hour, rendered still deeper by the close approach of the old-fashioned houses, which lowered in tall obscurity on either side of the way; the damp, dreary chill which renders the advance of morning peculiarly cheerless, combined with the object of my walk—to visit the death-bed of a presumptuous sinner, to endeavour, almost against my own conviction, to infuse a hope into the heart of a dying reprobate—a drunkard but too probably perishing under the consequences of some mad fit of intoxication; all these circumstances served to enhance the gloom and solemnity of my feelings, as I silently followed my little guide, who with quick steps traversed the uneven pavement of the Main Street. After a walk of about five minutes, she turned off into a narrow lane, of that obscure and comfortless class which is to be found in almost all small old-fashioned towns, chill, without ventilation, reeking with all manner of offensive effluviæ, and lined by dingy, smoky, sickly and pent-up buildings, frequently not only in a wretched but in a dangerous condition.

"Your father has changed his abode since I last visited him, and, I am afraid, much for the worse," said I.

"Indeed he has, sir; but we must not complain," replied she. "We have to thank God that we have lodging and food, though it's poor enough, it is, your honour."

Poor child! thought I. How many an older head might learn wisdom from thee—how many a luxurious philosopher, who is skilled to preach but not to suffer, might not thy patient words put to the blush! The manner and language of my companion were alike above her years and station; and, indeed, in all cases in which the cares and sorrows of life have anticipated their usual date, and have fallen, as they sometimes do, with melancholy prematurity to the lot of childhood, I have observed the result to have proved uniformly the same. A young mind, to which joy and indulgence have been strangers, and to which suffering and self-denial have been familiarized from the first, acquires a solidity and an elevation which no other discipline could have bestowed, and which, in the present case, communicated a striking but mournful peculiarity to the manners, even to the voice, of the child. We paused before a narrow, crazy door, which she opened by means of a latch, and we forthwith began to ascend the steep and broken stairs which led to the sick man's room.

As we mounted flight after flight towards the garret-floor, I heard more and more distinctly the hurried talking of many voices. I could also distinguish the low sobbing of a female. On arriving upon the uppermost lobby, these sounds became fully audible.

"This way, your honour," said my little conductress; at the same time, pushing open a door of patched and half-rotten plank, she admitted me into the squalid chamber of death and misery. But one candle, held in the fingers of a scared and haggard-looking child, was burning in the room, and that so dim that all was twilight or darkness except within its immediate influence. The general obscurity, however, served to throw into prominent and startling relief the death-bed and its occupant. The light fell with horrible clearness upon the blue and swollen features of the drunkard. I did not think it possible that a human countenance could look so terrific. The lips were black and drawn apart; the teeth were firmly set; the eyes a little unclosed, and nothing but the whites appearing. Every feature was fixed and livid, and the whole face wore a ghastly and rigid expression of despairing terror such as I never saw equalled. His hands were crossed upon his breast, and firmly clenched; while, as if to add to the corpse-like effect of the whole, some white cloths, dipped in water, were wound about the forehead and temples.

As soon as I could remove my eyes from this horrible spectacle, I observed my friend Dr. D——, one of the most humane of a humane profession, standing by the bedside. He had been attempting, but unsuccessfully, to bleed the patient, and had now applied his finger to the pulse.

"Is there any hope?" I inquired in a whisper.

A shake of the head was the reply. There was a pause, while he continued to hold the wrist; but he waited in vain for the throb of life—it was not there: and when he let go the hand, it fell stiffly back into its former position upon the other.

"The man is dead," said the physician, as he turned from the bed where the terrible figure lay.

Dead! thought I, scarcely venturing to look upon the tremendous and revolting spectacle. Dead! without an hour for repentance, even a moment for reflection.

Dead! without the rites which even the best should have. Was there a hope for him? The glaring eyeball, the grinning mouth, the distorted brow—that unutterable look in which a painter would have sought to embody the fixed despair of the nethermost hell—These were my answer.

The poor wife sat at a little distance, crying as if her heart would break—the younger children clustered round the bed, looking with wondering curiosity upon the form of death, never seen before.

When the first tumult of uncontrollable sorrow had passed away, availing myself of the solemnity and impressiveness of the scene, I desired the heart-stricken family to accompany me in prayer, and all knelt down while I solemnly and fervently repeated some of those prayers which appeared most applicable to the occasion. I employed myself thus in a manner which I trusted was not unprofitable, at least to the living, for about ten minutes; and having accomplished my task, I was the first to arise.

I looked upon the poor, sobbing, helpless creatures who knelt so humbly around me, and my heart bled for them. With a natural transition I turned my eyes from them to the bed in which the body lay; and, great God! what was the revulsion, the horror which I experienced on seeing the corpse-like, terrific thing seated half upright before me. The white cloths which had been wound about the head had now partly slipped from their position, and were hanging in grotesque festoons about the face and shoulders, while the distorted eyes leered from amid them—

"A sight to dream of, not to tell."

I stood actually riveted to the spot. The figure nodded its head and lifted its arm, I thought, with a menacing gesture. A thousand confused and horrible thoughts at once rushed upon my mind. I had often read that the body of a presumptuous sinner, who, during life, had been the willing creature of every satanic impulse, had been known, after the human tenant had deserted it, to become the horrible sport of demoniac possession.

I was roused by the piercing scream of the mother, who now, for the first time, perceived the change which had taken place. She rushed towards the bed, but, stunned by the shock and overcome by the conflict of violent emotions, before she reached it she fell prostrate upon the floor.

I am perfectly convinced that had I not been startled from the torpidity of horror in which I was bound by some powerful and arousing stimulant, I should have gazed upon this unearthly apparition until I had fairly lost my senses. As it was, however, the spell was broken—superstition gave way to reason: the man whom all believed to have been actually dead was living!

Dr. D—— was instantly standing by the bedside, and upon examination he found that a sudden and copious flow of blood had taken place from the wound which the lancet had left; and this, no doubt, had effected his sudden and almost preternatural restoration to an existence from which all thought he had been for ever removed. The man was still speechless, but he seemed to understand the physician when he forbade his repeating the painful and fruitless attempts which he made to articulate, and he at once resigned himself quietly into his hands.

I left the patient with leeches upon his temples, and bleeding freely, apparently with little of the drowsiness which accompanies apoplexy. Indeed, Dr. D—— told me that he had never before witnessed a seizure which seemed to combine the symptoms of so many kinds, and yet which belonged to none of the recognized classes; it certainly was not apoplexy, catalepsy, nor delirium tremens, and yet it seemed, in some degree, to partake of the properties of all. It was strange, but stranger things are coming.

During two or three days Dr. D—— would not allow his patient to converse in a manner which could excite or exhaust him, with anyone; he suffered him merely as briefly as possible to express his immediate wants. And it was not until the fourth day after my early visit, the particulars of which I have just detailed, that it was thought expedient that I should see him, and then only because it appeared that his extreme importunity and impatience to meet me were likely to retard his recovery more than the mere exhaustion attendant upon a short conversation could possibly do. Perhaps, too, my friend entertained some hope that if by holy confession his patient's bosom were eased of the perilous stuff which no doubt oppressed it, his recovery would be more assured and rapid. It was then, as I have said, upon the fourth day after my first professional call, that I found myself once more in the dreary chamber of want and sickness.

The man was in bed, and appeared low and restless. On my entering the room he raised himself in the bed, and muttered, twice or thrice,—

"Thank God! thank God!"

I signed to those of his family who stood by to leave the room, and took a chair beside the bed. So soon as we were alone, he said, rather doggedly,—

"There's no use in telling me of the sinfulness of bad ways—I know it all. I know where they lead to—I have seen everything about it with my own eyesight, as plain as I see you." He rolled himself in the bed, as if to hide his face in the clothes; and then suddenly raising himself, he exclaimed with startling vehemence, "Look, sir! there is no use in mincing the matter: I'm blasted with the fires of hell; I have been in hell. What do you think of that? In hell—I'm lost for ever—I have not a chance. I am damned already—damned—damned!"

The end of this sentence he actually shouted. His vehemence was perfectly terrific; he threw himself back, and laughed, and sobbed hysterically. I poured some water into a tea-cup, and gave it to him. After he had swallowed it, I told him if he had anything to communicate, to do so as briefly as he could, and in a manner as little agitating to himself as possible; threatening at the same time, though I had no intention of doing so, to leave him at once in case he again gave way to such passionate excitement.

"It's only foolishness," he continued, "for me to try to thank you for coming to such a villain as myself at all. It's no use for me to wish good to you, or to bless you; for such as me has no blessings to give."

I told him that I had but done my duty, and urged him to proceed to the matter which weighed upon his mind. He then spoke nearly as follows:—

"I came in drunk on Friday night last, and got to my bed here; I don't remember how. Sometime in the night it seemed to me I wakened, and feeling unasy in myself, I got up out of the bed. I wanted the fresh air; but I would not make a noise to open the window, for fear I'd waken the crathurs. It was very dark and throublesome to find the door; but at last I did get it, and I groped my way out, and went down as asy as I could. I felt quite sober, and I counted the steps one after another, as I was going down, that I might not stumble at the bottom.

"When I came to the first landing-place—God be about us always!—the floor of it sunk under me, and I went down—down—down, till the senses almost left me. I do not know how long I was falling, but it seemed to me a great while. When I came rightly to myself at last, I was sitting near the top of a great table; and I could not see the end of it, if it had any, it was so far off. And there was men beyond reckoning sitting down all along by it, at each side, as far as I could see at all. I did not know at first was it in the open air; but there was a close smothering feel in it that was not natural. And there was a kind of light that my eyesight never saw before, red and unsteady; and I did not see for a long time where it was coming from, until I looked straight up, and then I seen that it came from great balls of blood-coloured fire that were rolling high overhead with a sort of rushing, trembling sound, and I perceived that they shone on the ribs of a great roof of rock that was arched overhead instead of the sky. When I seen this, scarce knowing what I did, I got up, and I said, 'I have no right to be here; I must go.' And the man that was sitting at my left hand only smiled, and said, 'Sit down again; you can never leave this place.' And his voice was weaker than any child's voice I ever heerd; and when he was done speaking he smiled again.

"Then I spoke out very loud and bold, and I said, 'In the name of God, let me out of this bad place.' And there was a great man that I did not see before, sitting at the end of the table that I was near; and he was taller than twelve men, and his face was very proud and terrible to look at. And he stood up and stretched out his hand before him; and when he stood up, all that was there, great and small, bowed down with a sighing sound; and a dread came on my heart, and he looked at me, and I could not speak. I felt I was his own, to do what he liked with, for I knew at once who he was; and he said, 'If you promise to return, you may depart for a season;' and the voice he spoke with was terrible and mournful, and the echoes of it went rolling and swelling down the endless cave, and mixing with the trembling of the fire overhead; so that when he sat down there was a sound after him, all through the place, like the roaring of a furnace. And I said, with all the strength I had, 'I promise to come back—in God's name let me go!'

"And with that I lost the sight and the hearing of all that was there, and when my senses came to me again, I was sitting in the bed with the blood all over me, and you and the rest praying around the room."

Here he paused, and wiped away the chill drops which hung upon his forehead.

I remained silent for some moments. The vision which he had just described struck my imagination not a little, for this was long before Vathek and the "Hall of Eblis" had delighted the world; and the description which he gave had, as I received it, all the attractions of novelty beside the impressiveness which always belongs to the narration of an eye-witness, whether in the body or in the spirit, of the scenes which he describes. There was something, too, in the stern horror with which the man related these things, and in the incongruity of his description with the vulgarly received notions of the great place of punishment, and of its presiding spirit, which struck my mind with awe, almost with fear. At length he said, with an expression of horrible, imploring earnestness, which I shall never forget,—

"Well, sir, is there any hope; is there any chance at all? or is my soul pledged and promised away for ever? is it gone out of my power? must I go back to the place?"

In answering him, I had no easy task to perform; for however clear might be my internal conviction of the groundlessness of his fears, and however strong my scepticism respecting the reality of what he had described, I nevertheless felt that his impression to the contrary, and his humility and terror resulting from it, might be made available as no mean engines in the work of his conversion from profligacy, and of his restoration to decent habits and to religious feeling.

I therefore told him that he was to regard his dream rather in the light of a warning than in that of a prophecy; that our salvation depended not upon the word or deed of a moment, but upon the habits of a life; that, in fine, if he at once discarded his idle companions and evil habits, and firmly adhered to a sober, industrious, and religious course of life, the powers of darkness might claim his soul in vain, for that there were higher and firmer pledges than human tongue could utter, which promised salvation to him who should repent and lead a new life.

I left him much comforted, and with a promise to return upon the next day. I did so, and found him much more cheerful, and without any remains of the dogged sullenness which I suppose had arisen from his despair. His promises of amendment were given in that tone of deliberate earnestness which belongs to deep and solemn determination; and it was with no small delight that I observed, after repeated visits, that his good resolutions, so far from failing, did but gather strength by time; and when I saw that man shake off the idle and debauched companions whose society had for years formed alike his amusement and his ruin, and revive his long-discarded habits of industry and sobriety, I said within myself, There is something more in all this than the operation of an idle dream.

One day, some time after his perfect restoration to health, I was surprised, on ascending the stairs for the purpose of visiting this man, to find him busily employed in nailing down some planks upon the landing-place, through which, at the commencement of his mysterious vision, it seemed to him that he had sunk. I perceived at once that he was strengthening the floor with a view to securing himself against such a catastrophe, and could scarcely forbear a smile as I bid "God bless his work."

He perceived my thoughts, I suppose, for he immediately said:

"I can never pass over that floor without trembling. I'd leave this house if I could, but I can't find another lodging in the town so cheap, and I'll not take a better till I've paid off all my debts, please God; but I could not be asy in my mind till I made it as safe as I could. You'll hardly believe me, your honour, that while I'm working, maybe a mile away, my heart is in a flutter the whole way back, with the bare thoughts of the two little steps I have to walk upon this bit of a floor. So it's no wonder, sir, I'd thry to make it sound and firm with any idle timber I have."

I applauded his resolution to pay off his debts, and the steadiness with which he perused his plans of conscientious economy, and passed on.

Many months elapsed, and still there appeared no alteration in his resolutions of amendment. He was a good workman, and with his better habits he recovered his former extensive and profitable employment. Everything seemed to promise comfort and respectability. I have little more to add, and that shall be told quickly. I had one evening met Pat Connell, as he returned from his work, and as usual, after a mutual, and on his side respectful salutation, I spoke a few words of encouragement and approval. I left him industrious, active, healthy—when next I saw him, not three days after, he was a corpse.

The circumstances which marked the event of his death were somewhat strange—I might say fearful. The unfortunate man had accidentally met an old friend just returned, after a long absence; and in a moment of excitement, forgetting everything in the warmth of his joy, he yielded to his urgent invitation to accompany him into a public house, which lay close by the spot where the encounter had taken place. Connell, however, previously to entering the room, had announced his determination to take nothing more than the strictest temperance would warrant.

But oh! who can describe the inveterate tenacity with which a drunkard's habits cling to him through life? He may repent, he may reform, he may look with actual abhorrence upon his past profligacy; but amid all this reformation and compunction, who can tell the moment in which the base and ruinous propensity may not recur, triumphing over resolution, remorse, shame, everything, and prostrating its victim once more in all that is destructive and revolting in that fatal vice?

The wretched man left the place in a state of utter intoxication. He was brought home nearly insensible, and placed in his bed. The younger part of the family retired to rest much after their usual hour; but the poor wife remained up sitting by the fire, too much grieved and shocked at the occurrence of what she had so little expected, to settle to rest. Fatigue, however, at length overcame her, and she sank gradually into an uneasy slumber. She could not tell how long she had remained in this state; but when she awakened, and immediately on opening her eyes, she perceived by the faint red light of the smouldering turf embers, two persons, one of whom she recognized as her husband, noiselessly gliding out of the room.

"Pat, darling, where are you going?" said she.

There was no answer—the door closed after them; but in a moment she was startled and terrified by a loud and heavy crash, as if some ponderous body had been hurled down the stair.

Much alarmed, she started up, and going to the head of the staircase, she called repeatedly upon her husband, but in vain.

She returned to the room, and with the assistance of her daughter, whom I had occasion to mention before, she succeeded in finding and lighting a candle, with which she hurried again to the head of the staircase.

At the bottom lay what seemed to be a bundle of clothes, heaped together, motionless, lifeless—it was her husband. In going down the stairs, for what purpose can never now be known, he had fallen helplessly and violently to the bottom, and coming head foremost, the spine of the neck had been dislocated by the shock, and instant death must have ensued.

The body lay upon that landing-place to which his dream had referred.

It is scarcely worth endeavouring to clear up a single point in a narrative where all is mystery; yet I could not help suspecting that the second figure which had been seen in the room by Connell's wife on the night of his death might have been no other than his own shadow.

I suggested this solution of the difficulty; but she told me that the unknown person had been considerably in advance of her husband, and on reaching the door, had turned back as if to communicate something to his companion.

It was, then, a mystery.

Was the dream verified?—whither had the disembodied spirit sped? who can say? We know not. But I left the house of death that day in a state of horror which I could not describe. It seemed to me that I was scarce awake. I heard and saw everything as if under the spell of a nightmare. The coincidence was terrible.

A CHAPTER IN THE HISTORY OF A TYRONE FAMILY

This Story can be found on Page 561 as part of The Purcell Papers.

A STABLE FOR NIGHTMARES

DICKON THE DEVIL.

ABOUT thirty years ago I was selected by two rich old maids to visit a property in that part of Lancashire which lies near the famous forest of Pendle, with which Mr. Ainsworth's "Lancashire Witches" has made us so pleasantly familiar. My business was to make partition of a small property, including a house and demesne to which they had, a long time before, succeeded as coheiresses.

The last forty miles of my journey I was obliged to post, chiefly by cross-roads, little known, and less frequented, and presenting scenery often extremely interesting and pretty. The picturesqueness of the landscape was enhanced by the season, the beginning of September, at which I was travelling.

I had never been in this part of the world before; I am told it is now a great deal less wild, and, consequently, less beautiful.

At the inn where I had stopped for a relay of horses and some dinner—for it was then past five o'clock—I found the host, a hale old fellow of five-and-sixty, as he told me, a man of easy and garrulous benevolence, willing to accommodate his guests with any amount of talk, which the slightest tap sufficed to set flowing, on any subject you pleased.

I was curious to learn something about Barwyke, which was the name of the demesne and house I was going to. As there was no inn within some miles of it, I had written to the steward to put me up there, the best way he could, for a night.

The host of the "Three Nuns," which was the sign under which he entertained wayfarers, had not a great deal to tell. It was twenty years, or more, since old Squire Bowes died, and no one had lived in the Hall ever since, except the gardener and his wife.

"Tom Wyndsour will be as old a man as myself; but he's a bit taller, and not so much in flesh, quite," said the fat innkeeper.

"But there were stories about the house," I repeated, "that, they said, prevented tenants from coming into it?"

"Old wives' tales; many years ago, that will be, sir; I forget 'em; I forget 'em all. Oh yes, there always will be, when a house is left so; foolish folk will always be talkin'; but I han't heard a word about it this twenty year."

It was vain trying to pump him; the old landlord of the "Three Nuns," for some reason, did not choose to tell tales of Barwyke Hall, if he really did, as I suspected, remember them.

I paid my reckoning, and resumed my journey, well pleased with the good cheer of that old-world inn, but a little disappointed.

We had been driving for more than an hour, when we began to cross a wild common; and I knew that, this passed, a quarter of an hour would bring me to the door of Barwyke Hall.

The peat and furze were pretty soon left behind; we were again in the wooded scenery that I enjoyed so much, so entirely natural and pretty, and so little disturbed by traffic of any kind. I was looking from the chaise-window, and soon detected the object of which, for some time, my eye had been in search. Barwyke Hall was a large, quaint house, of that cage-work fashion known as "black-and-white," in which the bars and angles of an oak framework contrast, black as ebony, with the white plaster that overspreads the masonry built into its interstices. This steep-roofed Elizabethan house stood in the midst of park-like grounds of no great extent, but rendered imposing by the noble stature of the old trees that now cast their lengthening shadows eastward over the sward, from the declining sun.

The park-wall was gray with age, and in many places laden with ivy. In deep gray shadow, that contrasted with the dim fires of evening reflected on the foliage above it, in a gentle hollow, stretched a lake that looked cold and black, and seemed, as it were, to skulk from observation with a guilty knowledge.

I had forgot that there was a lake at Barwyke; but the moment this caught my eye, like the cold polish of a snake in the shadow, my instinct seemed to recognize something dangerous, and I knew that the lake was connected, I could not remember how, with the story I had heard of this place in my boyhood.

I drove up a grass-grown avenue, under the boughs of these noble trees, whose foliage, dyed in autumnal red and yellow, returned the beams of the western sun gorgeously.

We drew up at the door. I got out, and had a good look at the front of the house; it was a large and melancholy mansion, with signs of long neglect upon it; great wooden shutters, in the old fashion, were barred, outside, across the windows; grass, and even nettles, were growing thick on the courtyard, and a thin moss streaked the timber beams; the plaster was discolored by time and weather, and bore great russet and yellow stains. The gloom was increased by several grand old trees that crowded close about the house.

I mounted the steps, and looked round; the dark lake lay near me now, a little to the left. It was not large; it may have covered some ten or twelve acres; but it added to the melancholy of the scene. Near the centre of it was a small island, with two old ash-trees, leaning toward each other, their pensive images reflected in the stirless water. The only cheery influence of this scene of antiquity, solitude, and neglect was that the house and landscape were warmed with the ruddy western beams. I knocked, and my summons resounded hollow and ungenial in my ear; and the bell, from far away, returned a deep-mouthed and surly ring, as if it resented being roused from a score years' slumber.

A light-limbed, jolly-looking old fellow, in a barracan jacket and gaiters, with a smirk of welcome, and a very sharp, red nose, that seemed to promise good cheer, opened the door with a promptitude that indicated a hospitable expectation of my arrival.

There was but little light in the hall, and that little lost itself in darkness in the background. It was very spacious and lofty, with a gallery running round it, which, when the door was open, was visible at two or three points. Almost in the dark my new acquaintance led me across this wide hall into the room destined for my reception. It was spacious, and wainscoted up to the ceiling. The furniture of this capacious chamber was old-fashioned and clumsy. There were curtains still to the windows, and a piece of Turkey carpet lay upon the floor; those windows were two in number, looking out, through the trunks of the trees close to the house, upon the lake. It needed all the fire, and all the pleasant associations of my entertainer's red nose, to light up this melancholy chamber. A door at its farther end admitted to the room that was prepared for my sleeping apartment. It was wainscoted, like the other. It had a four-post bed, with heavy tapestry curtains, and in other respects was furnished in the same old-world and ponderous style as the other room. Its window, like those of that apartment, looked out upon the lake.

Sombre and sad as these rooms were, they were yet scrupulously clean. I had nothing to complain of; but the effect was rather dispiriting. Having given some directions about supper—a pleasant incident to look forward to—and made a rapid toilet, I called on my friend with the gaiters and red nose (Tom Wyndsour), whose occupation was that of a "bailiff," or under-steward, of the property, to accompany me, as we had still an hour or so of sun and twilight, in a walk over the grounds.

It was a sweet autumn evening, and my guide, a hardy old fellow, strode at a pace that tasked me to keep up with.

Among clumps of trees at the northern boundary of the demesne we lighted upon the little antique parish church. I was looking down upon it, from an eminence, and the park-wall interposed; but a little way down was a stile affording access to the road, and by this we approached the iron gate of the churchyard. I saw the church door open; the sexton was replacing his pick, shovel, and spade, with which he had just been digging a grave in the churchyard, in their little repository under the stone stair of the tower. He was a polite, shrewd little hunchback, who was very happy to show me over the church. Among the monuments was one that interested me; it was erected to commemorate the very Squire Bowes from whom my two old maids had inherited the house and estate of Barwyke. It spoke of him in terms of grandiloquent eulogy, and informed the Christian reader that he had died, in the bosom of the Church of England, at the age of seventy-one.

I read this inscription by the parting beams of the setting sun, which disappeared behind the horizon just as we passed out from under the porch.

"Twenty years since the Squire died," said I, reflecting, as I loitered still in the churchyard.

"Ay, sir; 'twill be twenty year the ninth o' last month."

"And a very good old gentleman?"

"Good-natured enough, and an easy gentleman he was, sir; I don't think while he lived he ever hurt a fly," acquiesced Tom Wyndsour. "It ain't always easy sayin' what's in 'em, though, and what they may take or turn to afterward; and some o' them sort, I think, goes mad."

"You don't think he was out of his mind?" I asked.

"He? La! no; not he, sir; a bit lazy, mayhap, like other old fellows; but a knew devilish well what he was about."

Tom Wyndsour's account was a little enigmatical; but, like old Squire Bowes, I was "a bit lazy" that evening, and asked no more questions about him.

We got over the stile upon the narrow road that skirts the churchyard. It is overhung by elms more than a hundred years old, and in the twilight, which now prevailed, was growing very dark. As side-by-side we walked along this road, hemmed in by two loose stone-like walls, something running toward us in a zig-zag line passed us at a wild pace, with a sound like a frightened laugh or a shudder, and I saw, as it passed, that it was a human figure. I may confess, now, that I was a little startled. The dress of this figure was, in part, white: I know I mistook it at first for a white horse coming down the road at a gallop. Tom Wyndsour turned about and looked after the retreating figure.

"He'll be on his travels to-night," he said, in a low tone. "Easy served with a bed, *that* lad be; six foot o' dry peat or heath, or a nook in a dry ditch. That lad hasn't slept once in a house this twenty year, and never will while grass grows."

"Is he mad?" I asked.

"Something that way, sir; he's an idiot, an awpy; we call him 'Dickon the devil,' because the devil's almost the only word that's ever in his mouth."

It struck me that this idiot was in some way connected with the story of old Squire Bowes.

"Queer things are told of him, I dare say?" I suggested.

"More or less, sir; more or less. Queer stories, some."

"Twenty years since he slept in a house? That's about the time the Squire died," I continued.

"So it will be, sir; not very long after."

"You must tell me all about that, Tom, to-night, when I can hear it comfortably, after supper."

Tom did not seem to like my invitation; and looking straight before him as we trudged on, he said:

"You see, sir, the house has been quiet, and nout's been troubling folk inside the walls or out, all round the woods of Barwyke, this ten year, or more; and my old woman, down there, is clear against talking about such matters, and thinks it best—and so do I—to let sleepin' dogs be."

He dropped his voice toward the close of the sentence, and nodded significantly.

We soon reached a point where he unlocked a wicket in the park wall, by which we entered the grounds of Barwyke once more.

The twilight deepening over the landscape, the huge and solemn trees, and the distant outline of the haunted house, exercised a sombre influence on me, which, together with the fatigue of a day of travel, and the brisk walk we had had, disinclined me to interrupt the silence in which my companion now indulged.

A certain air of comparative comfort, on our arrival, in great measure dissipated the gloom that was stealing over me. Although it was by no means a cold night, I was very glad to see some wood blazing in the grate; and a pair of candles aiding the light of the fire, made the room look cheerful. A small table, with a very white cloth, and preparations for supper, was also a very agreeable object.

I should have liked very well, under these influences, to have listened to Tom Wyndsour's story; but after supper I grew too sleepy to attempt to lead him to the subject; and after yawning for a time, I found there was no use in contending against my drowsiness, so I betook myself to my bedroom, and by ten o'clock was fast asleep.

What interruption I experienced that night I shall tell you presently. It was not much, but it was very odd.

By next night I had completed my work at Barwyke. From early morning till then I was so incessantly occupied and hard-worked, that I had no time to think over the singular occurrence to which I have just referred. Behold me, however, at length once more seated at my little supper-table, having ended a comfortable meal. It had been a sultry day, and I had thrown one of the large windows up as high as it would go. I was sitting near it, with my brandy and water at my elbow, looking out into the dark. There was no moon, and the trees that are grouped about the house make the darkness round it supernaturally profound on such nights.

"Tom," said I, so soon as the jug of hot punch I had supplied him with began to exercise its genial and communicative influence; "you must tell me who beside your wife and you and myself slept in the house last night."

Tom, sitting near the door, set down his tumbler, and looked at me askance, while you might count seven, without speaking a word.

"Who else slept in the house?" he repeated, very deliberately. "Not a living soul, sir;" and he looked hard at me, still evidently expecting something more.

"That *is* very odd," I said, returning his stare, and feeling really a little odd. "You are sure *you* were not in my room last night?"

"Not till I came to call you, sir, this morning; I can make oath of that."

"Well," said I, "there was some one there, *I* can make oath of that. I was so tired I could not make up my mind to get up; but I was waked by a sound that I thought was some one flinging down the two tin boxes in which my papers were locked up violently on the floor. I heard a slow step on the ground, and there was light in the room, although I remembered having put out my candle. I thought it must have been you, who had come in for my clothes, and upset the boxes by accident. Whoever it was, he went out, and the light with him. I was about to settle again, when, the curtain being a little open at the foot of the bed, I saw a light on the wall opposite; such as a candle from outside would cast if the door were very cautiously opening. I started up in the bed, drew the side curtain, and saw that the door *was* opening, and admitting light from outside. It is close, you know, to the head of the bed. A hand was holding on the edge of the door and pushing it open; not a bit like yours; a very singular hand. Let me look at yours."

He extended it for my inspection.

"Oh no; there's nothing wrong with your hand. This was differently shaped; fatter; and the middle finger was stunted, and shorter than the rest, looking as if it had once been broken, and the nail was crooked like a claw. I called out, "Who's there?" and the light and the hand were withdrawn, and I saw and heard no more of my visitor."

"So sure as you're a living man, that was him!" exclaimed Tom Wyndsour, his very nose growing pale, and his eyes almost starting out of his head.

"Who?" I asked.

"Old Squire Bowes; 'twas *his* hand you saw; the Lord a' mercy on us!" answered Tom. "The broken finger, and the nail bent like a hoop. Well for you, sir, he didn't come back when you called, that time. You came here about them Miss Dymock's business, and he never meant they should have a foot o' ground in Barwyke; and he was making a will to give it away quite different, when death took him short. He never was uncivil to no one; but he couldn't abide them ladies. My mind misgave me when I heard 'twas about their business you were coming; and now you see how it is; he'll be at his old tricks again!"

With some pressure, and a little more punch, I induced Tom Wyndsour to explain his mysterious allusions by recounting the occurrences which followed the old Squire's death.

"Squire Bowes, of Barwyke, died without making a will, as you know," said Tom. "And all the folk round were sorry; that is to say, sir, as sorry as folk will be for an old man that has seen a long tale of years, and has no right to grumble that death has knocked an hour too soon at his door. The Squire was well liked; he was never in a passion, or said a hard word; and he would not hurt a fly; and that made what happened after his decease the more surprising.

"The first thing these ladies did, when they got the property, was to buy stock for the park.

"It was not wise, in any case, to graze the land on their own account. But they little knew all they had to contend with.

"Before long something went wrong with the cattle; first one, and then another, took sick and died, and so on, till the loss began to grow heavy. Then, queer stories, little by little, began to be told. It was said, first by one, then by another, that Squire Bowes was seen, about evening time, walking, just as he used to do when he was alive, among the old trees, leaning on his stick; and, sometimes, when he came up with the cattle, he would stop and lay his hand kindly like on the back of one of them; and that one was sure to fall sick next day, and die soon after.

"No one ever met him in the park, or in the woods, or ever saw him, except a good distance off. But they knew his gait and his figure well, and the clothes he used to wear; and they could tell the beast he laid his hand on by its color—white, dun, or black; and that beast was sure to sicken and die. The neighbors grew shy of taking the path over the park; and no one liked to walk in the woods, or come inside the bounds of Barwyke; and the cattle went on sickening and dying, as before.

"At that time there was one Thomas Pyke; he had been a groom to the old Squire; and he was in care of the place, and was the only one that used to sleep in the house.

"Tom was vexed, hearing these stories; which he did not believe the half on 'em; and more especial as he could not get man or boy to herd the cattle; all being afeared. So he wrote to Matlock, in Derbyshire, for his brother, Richard Pyke, a clever lad, and one that knew nout o' the story of the old Squire walking.

"Dick came; and the cattle was better; folk said they could still see the old Squire, sometimes, walking, as before, in openings of the wood, with his stick in his hand; but he was shy of coming nigh the cattle, whatever his reason might be, since Dickon Pyke came; and he used to stand a long bit off, looking at them, with no more stir in him than a trunk o' one of the old trees, for an hour at a time, till the shape melted away, little by little, like the smoke of a fire that burns out.

"Tom Pyke and his brother Dickon, being the only living souls in the house, lay in the big bed in the servants' room, the house being fast barred and locked, one night in November.

"Tom was lying next the wall, and, he told me, as wide awake as ever he was at noonday. His brother Dickon lay outside, and was sound asleep.

"Well, as Tom lay thinking, with his eyes turned toward the door, it opens slowly, and who should come in but old Squire Bowes, his face lookin' as dead as he was in his coffin.

"Tom's very breath left his body; he could not take his eyes off him; and he felt the hair rising up on his head.

"The Squire came to the side of the bed, and put his arms under Dickon, and lifted the boy—in a dead sleep all the time—and carried him out so, at the door.

"Such was the appearance, to Tom Pyke's eyes, and he was ready to swear to it, anywhere.

"When this happened, the light, wherever it came from, all on a sudden went out, and Tom could not see his own hand before him.

"More dead than alive, he lay till daylight.

"Sure enough his brother Dickon was gone. No sign of him could he discover about the house; and with some trouble he got a couple of the neighbors to help him to search the woods and grounds. Not a sign of him anywhere.

"At last one of them thought of the island in the lake; the little boat was moored to the old post at the water's edge. In they got, though with small hope of finding him there. Find him, nevertheless, they did, sitting under the big ash-tree, quite out of his wits; and to all their questions he answered nothing but one cry—'Bowes, the devil! See him; see him; Bowes, the devil!' An idiot they found him; and so he will be till God sets all things right. No one could ever get him to sleep under roof-tree more. He wanders from house to house while daylight lasts; and no one cares to lock the harmless creature in the workhouse. And folk would rather not meet him after nightfall, for they think where he is there may be worse things near."

A silence followed Tom's story. He and I were alone in that large room; I was sitting near the open window, looking into the dark night air. I fancied I saw something white move across it; and I heard a sound like low talking, that swelled into a discordant shriek—"Hoo-oo-oo! Bowes, the devil! Over your shoulder. Hoo-oo-oo! ha! ha! ha!" I started up, and saw, by the light of the candle with which Tom strode to the window, the wild eyes and blighted face of the idiot, as, with a sudden change of mood, he drew off, whispering and tittering to himself, and holding up his long fingers, and looking at them as if they were lighted at the tips like a "hand of glory."

Tom pulled down the window. The story and its epilogue were over. I confessed I was rather glad when I heard the sound of the horses' hoofs on the courtyard, a few minutes later; and still gladder when, having bidden Tom a kind farewell, I had left the neglected house of Barwyke a mile behind me.

A DEBT OF HONOR.

A GHOST STORY.

HUSH! what was that cry, so low but yet so piercing, so strange but yet so sorrowful? It was not the marmot upon the side of the Righi—it was not the heron down by the lake; no, it was distinctively human. Hush! there it is again—from the churchyard which I have just left!

Not ten minutes have elapsed since I was sitting on the low wall of the churchyard of Weggis, watching the calm glories of the moonlight illuminating with silver splendor the lake of Lucerne; and I am certain there was no one within the inclosure but myself.

I am mistaken, surely. What a silence there is upon the night! Not a breath of air now to break up into a thousand brilliant ripples the long reflection of the August moon, or to stir the foliage of the chestnuts; not a voice in the village; no splash of oar upon the lake. All life seems at perfect rest, and the solemn stillness that reigns about the topmost glaciers of S. Gothard has spread its mantle over the warmer world below.

I must not linger; as it is, I shall have to wake up the porter to let me into the hotel. I hurry on.

Not ten paces, though. Again I hear the cry. This time it sounds to me like the long, sad sob of a wearied and broken heart. Without staying to reason with myself, I quickly retrace my steps.

I stumble about among the iron crosses and the graves, and displace in my confusion wreaths of immortelles and fresher flowers. A huge mausoleum stands between me and the wall upon which I had been sitting not a quarter of an hour ago. The mausoleum casts a deep shadow upon the side nearest to me. Ah! something is stirring there. I strain my eyes—the figure of a man passes slowly out of the shade, and silently occupies my place upon the wall. It must have been his lips that gave out that miserable sound.

What shall I do? Compassion and curiosity are strong. The man whose heart can be rent so sorely ought not to be allowed to linger here with his despair. He is gazing, as I did, upon the lake. I mark his profile—clear-cut and symmetrical; I catch the lustre of large eyes. The face, as I can see it, seems very still and placid. I may be mistaken; he may merely be a wanderer like myself; perhaps he heard the three strange cries, and has also come to seek the cause. I feel impelled to speak to him.

I pass from the path by the church to the east side of the mausoleum, and so come toward him, the moon full upon his features. Great heaven! how pale his face is!

"Good-evening, sir. I thought myself alone here, and wondered that no other travellers had found their way to this lovely spot. Charming, is it not?"

For a moment he says nothing, but his eyes are full upon me. At last he replies:

"It is charming, as you say, Mr. Reginald Westcar."

"You know me?" I exclaim, in astonishment.

"Pardon me, I can scarcely claim a personal acquaintance. But yours is the only English name entered to-day in the Livre des Étrangers."

"You are staying at the Hôtel de la Concorde, then?"

An inclination of the head is all the answer vouchsafed.

"May I ask," I continue, "whether you heard just now a very strange cry repeated three times?"

A pause. The lustrous eyes seem to search me through and through—I can hardly bear their gaze. Then he replies.

"I fancy I heard the echoes of some such sounds as you describe."

The *echoes*! Is this, then, the man who gave utterance to those cries of woe! is it possible? The face seems so passionless; but the pallor of those features bears witness to some terrible agony within.

"I thought some one must be in distress," I rejoin, hastily; "and I hurried back to see if I could be of any service."

"Very good of you," he answers, coldly; "but surely such a place as this is not unaccustomed to the voice of sorrow."

"No doubt. My impulse was a mistaken one."

"But kindly meant. You will not sleep less soundly for acting on that impulse, Reginald Westcar."

He rises as he speaks. He throws his cloak round him, and stands motionless. I take the hint. My mysterious countryman wishes to be alone. Some one that he has loved and lost lies buried here.

"Good-night, sir," I say, as I move in the direction of the little chapel at the gate. "Neither of us will sleep the less soundly for thinking of the perfect repose that reigns around this place."

"What do you mean?" he asks.

"The dead," I reply, as I stretch my hand toward the graves. "Do you not remember the lines in 'King Lear'?

"'After life's fitful fever he sleeps well.'"

"But *you* have never died, Reginald Westcar. You know nothing of the sleep of death."

For the third time he speaks my name almost familiarly, and—I know not why—a shudder passes through me. I have no time, in my turn, to ask him what he means; for he strides silently away into the shadow of the church, and I, with a strange sense of oppression upon me, returned to my hotel.

The events which I have just related passed in vivid recollection through my mind as I travelled northward one cold November day in the year 185—. About six months previously I had taken my degree at Oxford, and had since been enjoying a trip upon the continent; and on my return to London I found a letter awaiting me from my lawyers, informing me somewhat to my astonishment, that I had succeeded to a small estate in Cumberland. I must tell you exactly how this came about. My mother was a Miss Ringwood, and she was the youngest of three children: the eldest was Aldina, the second was Geoffrey, and the third (my mother) Alice. Their mother (who had been a widow since my mother's birth) lived at this little place in Cumberland, and which was known as The Shallows; she died shortly after my mother's marriage with my father, Captain Westcar. My aunt Aldina and my uncle Geoffrey—the one at that time aged twenty-eight, and the other twenty-six—continued to reside at The Shallows. My father and mother had to go to India, where I was born, and where, when quite a child, I was left an orphan. A few months after my mother's marriage my aunt disappeared; a few weeks after that event, and my uncle Geoffrey dropped down dead, as he was playing at cards with Mr. Maryon, the proprietor of a neighboring mansion known as The Mere. A fortnight after my uncle's death, my aunt Aldina returned to The Shallows, and never left it again till she was carried out in her coffin to her grave in the churchyard. Ever since her return from her mysterious disappearance she maintained an impenetrable reserve. As a schoolboy I visited her twice or thrice, but these visits depressed my youthful spirits to such an extent, that as I grew older I excused myself from accepting my aunt's not very pressing invitations; and at the time I am now speaking of I had not seen her for eight or ten years. I was rather surprised, therefore, when she bequeathed me The Shallows, which, as the surviving child, she inherited under her mother's marriage settlement.

But The Shallows had always exercised a grim influence over me, and the knowledge that I was now going to it as my home oppressed me. The road seemed unusually dark, cold, and lonely. At last I passed the lodge, and two hundred yards more brought me to the porch. Very soon the door was opened by an elderly female, whom I well remembered as having been my aunt's housekeeper and cook. I had pleasant recollections of her, and was glad to see her. To tell the truth, I had not anticipated my visit to my newly acquired property with any great degree of enthusiasm; but a very tolerable dinner had an inspiriting effect, and I was pleased to learn that there was a bin of old Madeira in the cellar. Naturally I soon grew cheerful, and consequently talkative; and summoned Mrs. Balk for a little gossip. The substance of what I gathered from her rather diffusive conversation was as follows:

My aunt had resided at The Shallows ever since the death of my uncle Geoffrey, but she had maintained a silent and reserved habit; and Mrs. Balk was of opinion that she had had some great misfortune. She had persistently refused all intercourse with the people at The Mere. Squire Maryon, himself a cold and taciturn man, had once or twice showed a disposition to be friendly, but she had sternly repulsed all such overtures. Mrs. Balk was of opinion that Miss Ringwood was not "quite right," as she expressed it, on some topics; especially did she seem impressed with the idea that The Mere ought to belong to her. It appeared that the Ringwoods and Maryons were distant connections; that The Mere belonged in former times to a certain Sir Henry Benet; that he was a bachelor, and that Squire Maryon's father and old Mr. Ringwood were cousins of his, and that there was some doubt as to which was the real heir; that Sir Henry, who disliked old Maryon, had frequently said he had set any chance of dispute at rest, by bequeathing the Mere property by will to Mr. Ringwood, my mother's father; that, on his death, no such will could be found; and the family lawyers agreed that Mr. Maryon was the legal inheritor, and my uncle Geoffrey and his sisters must be content to take the Shallows, or nothing at all. Mr. Maryon was comparatively rich, and the Ringwoods poor, consequently they were advised not to enter upon a costly lawsuit. My aunt Aldina maintained to the last that Sir Henry had made a will, and that Mr. Maryon knew it, but had destroyed or suppressed the document. I did not gather from Mrs. Balk's narrative that Miss Ringwood had any foundation for her belief, and I dismissed the notion at once as baseless.

"And my uncle Geoffrey died of apoplexy, you say, Mrs. Balk?"

"*I* don't say so, sir, no more did Miss Ringwood; but *they* said so."

"Whom do you mean by *they*?"

"The people at The Mere the young doctor, a friend of Squire Maryon's, who was brought over from York, and the rest; he fell heavily from his chair, and his head struck against the fender."

"Playing at cards with Mr. Maryon, I think you said."

"Yes, sir; he was too fond of cards, I believe, was Mr. Geoffrey."

"Is Mr. Maryon seen much in the county—is he hospitable?"

"Well, sir, he goes up to London a good deal, and has some friends down from town occasionally; but he does not seem to care much about the people in the neighborhood."

"He has some children, Mrs. Balk?"

"Only one daughter, sir; a sweet pretty thing she is. Her mother died when Miss Agnes was born."

"You have no idea, Mrs. Balk, what my aunt Aldina's great misfortune was?"

"Well, sir, I can't help thinking it must have been a love affair. She always hated men so much."

"Then why did she leave The Shallows to me, Mrs. Balk?"

"Ah, you are laughing, sir. No doubt she considered that The Mere ought to belong to you, as the heir of the Ringwoods, and she placed you here, as near as might be to the place."

"In hopes that I might marry Miss Maryon, eh, Mrs. Balk?"

"You are laughing again, sir. I don't imagine she thought so much of that, as of the possibility of your discovering something about the missing will."

I bade the communicative Mrs. Balk good night and retired to my bedroom—a low, wide, sombre, oak-panelled chamber. I must confess that family stories had no great interest for me, living apart from them at school and college as I had done; and as I undressed I thought more of the probabilities of sport the eight hundred acres of wild shooting belonging to The Shallows would afford me, than of the supposed will my poor aunt had evidently worried herself about so much. Thoroughly tired after my long journey, I soon fell fast asleep amid the deep shadows of the huge four-poster I mentally resolved to chop up into firewood at an early date, and substitute for it a more modern iron bedstead.

How long I had been asleep I do not know, but I suddenly started up, the echo of a long, sad cry ringing in my ears.

I listened eagerly—sensitive to the slightest sound—painfully sensitive as one is only in the deep silence of the night.

I heard the old-fashioned clock I had noticed on the stairs strike three. The reverberation seemed to last a long time, then all was silent again. "A dream," I muttered to myself, as I lay down upon the pillow; "Madeira is a heating wine. But what can I have been dreaming of?"

Sleep seemed to have gone altogether, and the busy mind wandered among the continental scenes I had lately visited. By and by I found myself in memory once more within the Weggis churchyard. I was satisfied; I had traced my dream to the cries that I had heard there. I turned round to sleep again. Perhaps I fell into a doze—I cannot say; but again I started up at the repetition, as it seemed outside my window, of that cry of sadness and despair. I hastily drew aside the heavy curtains of my bed—at that moment the room seemed to be illuminated with a dim, unearthly light—and I saw, gradually growing into human shape, the figure of a woman. I recognized in it my aunt, Miss Ringwood. Horror-struck, I gazed at the apparition; it advanced a little—the lips moved—I heard it distinctly say:

"*Reginald Westcar, The Mere belongs to you. Compel John Maryon to pay the debt of honor!*"

I fell back senseless.

When next I returned to consciousness, it was when I was called in the morning; the shutters were opened, and I saw the red light of the dawning winter sun.

There is a strange sympathy between the night and the mind. All one's troubles represent themselves as increased a hundredfold if one wakes in the night, and begins to think about them. A muscular pain becomes the certainty of an incurable internal disease; and a headache suggests incipient softening of the brain. But all these horrors are dissipated with the morning light, and the after-glow of a cold bath turns them into jokes. So it was with me on the morning after my arrival at The Shallows. I accounted most satisfactorily for all that had occurred, or seemed to have occurred, during the night; and resolved that, though the old Madeira was uncommonly good, I must be careful in future not to drink more than a couple of glasses after dinner. I need scarcely say that I said nothing to Mrs. Balk of my bad dreams, and shortly after breakfast I took my gun, and went out in search of such game as I might chance to meet with. At three o'clock I sent the keeper home, as his capacious pockets were pretty well filled, telling him that I thought I knew the country, and should stroll back leisurely. The gray gloom of the November evening was spreading over the sky as I came upon a small plantation which I believed belonged to me. I struck straight across it; emerging from its shadows, I found myself by a small stream and some marshy land; on the other side another small plantation. A snipe got up, I fired, and tailored it. I marked the bird into this other plantation, and followed. Up got a covey of partridges—bang, bang—one down by the side of an oak. I was about to enter this covert, when a lady and gentleman emerged, and, struck with the unpleasant thought that I was possibly trespassing, I at once went forward to apologize.

Before I could say a word, the gentleman addressed me.

"May I ask, sir, if I have given you permission to shoot over my preserves?"

"I beg to express my great regret, sir," I replied, as I lifted my hat in acknowledgment of the lady's presence, "that I should have trespassed upon your land. I can only plead, as my excuse, that I fully believed I was still upon the manor belonging to The Shallows."

"Gentlemen who go out shooting ought to know the limits of their estates," he answered harshly; "the boundaries of The Shallows are well defined, nor is the area they contain so very extensive. You have no right upon this side the stream, sir; oblige me by returning."

I merely bowed, for I was nettled by his tone, and as I turned away I noticed that the young lady whispered to him.

"One moment, sir," he said, "my daughter suggests the possibility of your being the new owner of The Shallows. May I ask if this is so?"

It had not occurred to me before, but I understood in a moment to whom I had been speaking, and I replied:

"Yes, Mr. Maryon—my name is Westcar."

Such was my introduction to Mr. and Miss Maryon. The proprietor of The Mere appeared to be a gentleman, but his manners were cold and reserved, and a careful observer might have remarked a perpetual restlessness in the eyes, as if they were physically incapable of regarding the same object for more than a moment. He was about sixty years of age, apparently; and though he now and again made an effort to carry himself upright, the head and shoulders soon drooped again, as if the weight of years, and, it might be, the memory of the past, were a heavy load to carry. Of Miss Maryon it is sufficient to say that she was nineteen or twenty, and it did not need a second glance to satisfy me that her beauty was of no ordinary kind.

I must hurry over the records of the next few weeks. I became a frequent visitor at The Mere. Mr. Maryon's manner never became cordial, but he did not seem displeased to see me; and as to Agnes,—well, she certainly was not displeased either.

I think it was on Christmas Day that I suddenly discovered that I was desperately in love. Miss Maryon had been for two or three days confined to her room by a bad cold, and I found myself in a great state of anxiety to see her again. I am sorry to say that my thoughts wandered a good deal when I was at church upon that festival, and I could not help thinking what ample room there was for a bridal procession up the spacious aisle. Suddenly my eyes rested upon a mural tablet, inscribed, "To the memory of Aldina Ringwood." Then with a cold thrill there came back upon me what I had almost forgotten, the dream, or whatever it was, that had occurred on that first night at The Shallows; and those strange words—"The Mere belongs to you. Compel John Maryon to pay the debt of honor!" Nothing but the remembrance of Agnes' sweet face availed for the time to banish the vision, the statement, and the bidding.

Miss Maryon was soon down-stairs again. Did I flatter myself too much in thinking that she was as glad to see me as I was to see her? No—I felt sure that I did not. Then I began to reflect seriously upon my position. My fortune was small, quite enough for me, but not enough for two; and as she was heiress of The Mere and a comfortable rent-roll of some six or eight thousand a year, was it not natural that Mr. Maryon expected her to make what is called a "good match"? Still, I could not conceal from myself the fact, that he evinced no objection whatever to my frequent visits at his house, nor to my taking walks with his daughter when he was unable to accompany us.

One bright, frosty day I had been down to the lake with Miss Maryon, and had enjoyed the privilege of teaching her to skate; and on returning to the house, we met Mr. Maryon upon the terrace. He walked with us to the conservatory; we went in to examine the plants, and he remained outside, pacing up and down the terrace. Both Agnes and myself were strangely silent; perhaps my tongue had found an eloquence upon the ice which was well met by a shy thoughtfulness upon her part. But there was a lovely color upon her cheeks, and I experienced a very considerable and unusual fluttering about my heart. It happened as we were standing at the door of the conservatory, both of us silently looking away from the flowers upon the frosty view, that our eyes lighted at the same time upon Mr. Maryon. He, too, was apparently regarding the prospect, when suddenly he paused and staggered back, as if something unexpected met his gaze.

"Oh, poor papa! I hope he is not going to have one of his fits!" exclaimed Agnes.

"Fits! Is he subject to such attacks?" I inquired.

"Not ordinary fits," she answered hurriedly; "I hardly know how to explain them. They come upon him occasionally, and generally at this period of the year."

"Shall we go to him?" I suggested.

"No; you cannot help him; and he cannot bear that they should be noticed."

We both watched him. His arms were stretched up above his head, and again he recoiled a step or two. I sought for an explanation in Agnes' face.

"A stranger!" she exclaimed. "Who can it be?"

I looked toward Mr. Maryon. A tall figure of a man had come from the farther side of the house; he wore a large, loose coat and a kind of military cap upon his head.

"Doubtless you are surprised to see me, John," we heard the new-comer say, in a confident voice, "but I am not the devil, man, that you should greet me with such a peculiar attitude." He held out his hand, and continued, "Come, don't let the warmth of old fellowship be all on one side, this wintry day."

We could see that Mr. Maryon took the proffered right hand with his left for an instant, then seemed to shrink away, but exchanged no word of this greeting.

"I don't understand this," said Agnes, and we both hurried forward. The stranger, seeing Agnes approach, lifted his cap.

"Ah, your daughter, John, no doubt. I see the likeness to her lamented mother. Pray introduce me."

Mr. Maryon's usually pallid features had assumed a still paler hue, and he said in a low voice:

"Colonel Bludyer—my daughter." Agnes barely bowed.

"Charmed to renew your acquaintance, Miss Maryon. When last I saw you, you were quite a baby; but your father and I are very old friends—are we not, John?"

Mr. Maryon vaguely nodded his head.

"Well, John, you have often pressed your hospitality upon me, but till now I have never had an opportunity of availing myself of your kind offers; so I have brought my bag, and intend at last to give you the pleasure of my company for a few days."

I certainly should have thought that a man of Mr. Maryon's disposition would have resented such conduct as this, or, at all events, have given this self-invited guest a chilling welcome. Mr. Maryon, however, in a confused and somewhat stammering tone, said that he was glad Colonel Bludyer had come at last, and bade his daughter go and make the necessary arrangements. Agnes, in silent astonishment, entered the house, and then Mr. Maryon turned to me hastily and bade me good-by. In a by no means comfortable frame of mind I returned to The Shallows.

The sudden advent of this miscellaneous colonel was naturally somewhat irritating to me. Not only did I regard the man as an intolerable bore, but I could not help fancying that he was something more than an old friend of Mr. Maryon's; in fact, I was led to judge, by Mr. Maryon's strange conduct, that this Bludyer had some power over him which might be exercised to the detriment of the Maryon family, and I was convinced there was some mystery it was my business to penetrate.

The following day I went up to The Mere to see if Miss Maryon was desirous of renewing her skating lesson. I found the party in the billiard-room, Agnes marking for her father and the Colonel. Mr. Maryon, whom I knew to be an exceptionally good player, seemed incapable of making a decent stroke; the Colonel, on the other hand, could evidently give a professional fifteen, and beat him easily. We all went down to the lake together. I had no chance of any quiet conversation with Agnes; the Colonel was perpetually beside us.

I returned home disgusted. For two whole days I did not go near The Mere. On the third day I went up, hoping that the horrid Colonel would be gone. It was beginning to snow when I left The Shallows at about two o'clock in the afternoon, and Mrs. Balk foretold a heavy storm, and bade me not be late returning.

The black winter darkness in the sky deepened as I approached The Mere. I was ushered again into the billiard-room. Agnes was marking, as upon the previous occasion, but two days had worked a sad difference in her face. Mr. Maryon hardly noticed my entrance; he was flushed, and playing eagerly; the Colonel was boisterous, declaring that John had never played better twenty years ago. I relieved Agnes of the duty of marking. The snow fell in a thick layer upon the skylight, and the Colonel became seriously anxious about my return home. As I did not think he was the proper person to give me hints, I resolutely remained where I was, encouraged in my behavior by the few words I gained from Agnes, and by the looks of entreaty she gave me. I had always considered Mr. Maryon to be an abstemious man, but he drank a good deal of brandy and soda during the long game of seven hundred up, and when he succeeded in beating the Colonel by forty-three, he was in roaring spirits, and insisted upon my staying to dinner. Need I say that I accepted the invitation?

I made such toilet as I could in a most unattainable chamber that was allotted to me, and hurried back to the drawing-room in the hope that I might get a few private words with Agnes. I was not disappointed. She, too, had hurried down, and in a few words I learned that this abominable Bludyer was paying her his coarse attentions, and with, apparently, the full consent of Mr. Maryon. My indignation was unbounded. Was it possible that Mr. Maryon intended to sacrifice this fair creature to that repulsive man?

Mr. Maryon had appeared in excellent spirits when dinner began, and the first glass or two of champagne made him merrier than I thought it possible for him to be. But by the time the dessert was on the table he had grown silent and thoughtful; nor did he respond to the warm eulogiums the Colonel passed upon the magnum of claret which was set before us.

After dinner we sat in the library. The Colonel left the room to fetch some cigars he had been loudly extolling. Then Agnes had an opportunity of whispering to me.

"Look at papa—see how strangely he sits—his hands clenching the arms of the chair, his eyes fixed upon the blazing coals! How old he seems to be to-night! His terrible fits are coming on—he is always like this toward the end of January!" The Colonel's return put an end to any further confidential talk.

When we separated for the night, I felt that my going to bed would be purposeless. I felt most painfully wide awake. I threw myself down upon my bed, and worried myself by trying to imagine what secret there could be between Maryon and Bludyer—for that a secret of some kind existed, I felt certain. I tossed about till I heard the stroke of one. A dreadful restlessness had come upon me. It seemed as if the solemn night-side of life was busy waking now, but the silence and solitude of my antique chamber became too much for me. I rose from my bed, and paced up and down the room. I raked up the dying embers of the fire, and drew an arm-chair to the hearth. I fell into a doze. By and by I woke up suddenly, and I was conscious of stealthy footsteps in the passage. My sense of hearing became painfully acute. I heard the footsteps retreating down the corridor, until they were lost in the distance. I cautiously opened the door, and, shading the candle with my hand, looked out—there was nothing to be seen; but I felt that I could not remain quietly in my room, and, closing the door behind me, I went out in search of I knew not what.

The sitting-rooms and bedrooms in ordinary use at The Mere were in the modern part of the house; but there was an old Elizabethan wing which I had often longed to explore, and in this strange ramble of mine I soon had reason to be satisfied that I was well within it. At the end of an oak-panelled narrow passage a door stood open, and I entered a low, sombre apartment fitted with furniture in the style of two hundred years ago. There was something awfully ghostly about the look of this room. A great four-post bedstead, with heavy hangings, stood in a deep recess; a round oak table and two high-backed chairs were in the centre of the room. Suddenly, as I gazed on these things, I heard stealthy footsteps in the passage, and saw a dim light advancing. Acting on a sudden impulse, I extinguished my candle and withdrew into the shadow of the recess, watching eagerly. The footsteps came nearer. My heart seemed to stand still with expectation. They paused outside the door, for a moment really—for an age it seemed to me. Then, to my astonishment, I saw Mr. Maryon enter. He carried a small night-lamp in his hand. Another glance satisfied me that he was walking in his sleep. He came straight to the round table, and set down the lamp. He seated himself in one of the high-backed chairs, his vacant eyes staring at the chair opposite; then his lips began to move quickly, as if he were addressing some one. Then he rose, went to the bureau, and seemed to take something from it; then he sat down again. What a strange action of his hands! At first I could not understand it; then it flashed upon me that in this dream of his he must be shuffling cards. Yes, he began to deal; then he was playing with his adversary—his lips moving anxiously at times.

A look of terrible eagerness came over the sleepwalker's countenance. With nimble fingers he dealt the cards, and played. Suddenly with a sweep of his hand he seemed to fling the pack into the fireplace, started from his seat, grappled with his unseen adversary, raised his powerful right hand, and struck a tremendous blow. Hush! more footsteps along the passage! Am I deceived? From my concealment I watch for what is to follow. Colonel Bludyer comes in, half dressed, but wide awake.

"You maniac!" I hear him mutter: "I expected you were given to such tricks as these. Lucky for you no eyes but mine have seen your abject folly. Come back to your room."

Mr. Maryon is still gazing, his arms lifted wildly above his head, upon the imagined foe whom he had felled to the ground. The Colonel touches him on the shoulder, and leads him away, leaving the lamp. My reasoning faculties had fully returned to me. I held a clue to the secret, and for Agnes' sake it must be followed up. I took the lamp away, and placed it on a table where the chamber candlesticks stood, relit my own candle, and found my way back to my bedroom.

The next morning, when I came down to breakfast, I found Colonel Bludyer warming himself satisfactorily at the blazing fire. I learned from him that our host was far from well, and that Miss Maryon was in attendance upon her father; that the Colonel was charged with all kinds of apologies to me, and good wishes for my safe return home across the snow. I thanked him for the delivery of the message, while I felt perfectly convinced that he had never been charged with it. However that might be, I never saw Mr. Maryon that morning; and I started back to The Shallows through the snow.

For the next two or three days the weather was very wild, but I contrived to get up to The Mere, and ask after Mr. Maryon. Better, I was told, but unable to see any one. Miss Maryon, too, was fatigued with nursing her father. So there was nothing to do but to trudge home again.

"*Reginald Westcar, The Mere is yours. Compel John Maryon to pay the debt of honor!*"

Again and again these words forced themselves upon me, as I listlessly gazed out upon the white landscape. The strange scene that I had witnessed on that memorable night I passed beneath Mr. Maryon's roof had brought them back to my memory with redoubled force, and I began to think that the apparition I had seen—or dreamed of—on my first night at The Shallows had more of truth in it than I had been willing to believe.

Three more days passed away, and a carter-boy from The Mere brought me a note. It was Agnes' handwriting. It said:

"DEAR MR. WESTCAR: Pray come up here, if you possibly can. I cannot understand what is the matter with papa; and he wishes me to do a dreadful thing. Do come. I feel that I have no friend but you. I am obliged to send this note privately."

I need scarcely say that five minutes afterward I was plunging through the snow toward The Mere. It was already late on that dark February evening as I gained the shrubbery; and as I was pondering upon the best method of securing admittance, I became aware that the figure of a man was hurrying on some yards in front of me. At first I thought it must be one of the gardeners, but all of a sudden I stood still, and my blood seemed to freeze with horror, as I remarked that the figure in front of me *left no trace of footmarks on the snow*! My brain reeled for a moment, and I thought I should have fallen; but I recovered my nerves, and when I looked before me again, it had disappeared. I pressed on eagerly. I arrived at the front door—it was wide open; and I passed through the hall to the library. I heard Agnes' voice.

"No, no, papa. You must not force me to this! I cannot—will not—marry Colonel Bludyer!"

"You *must*," answered Mr. Maryon, in a hoarse voice; "you *must* marry him, and save your father from something worse than disgrace!"

Not feeling disposed to play the eavesdropper, I entered the room. Mr. Maryon was standing at the fireplace. Agnes was crouching on the ground at his feet. I saw at once that it was no use for me to dissemble the reason of my visit, and, without a word of greeting, I said:

"Miss Maryon, I have come, in obedience to your summons. If I can prevent any misfortune from falling upon you I am ready to help you, with my life. You have guessed that I love you. If my love is returned I am prepared to dispute my claim with any man."

Agnes, with a cry of joy, rose from her knees, and rushed toward me. Ah! how strong I felt as I held her in my arms!

"I have my answer," I continued. "Mr. Maryon, I have reason to believe that your daughter is in fear of the future you have forecast for her. I ask you to regard those fears, and to give her to me, to love and cherish as my wife."

Mr. Maryon covered his face with his hands; and I could hear him murmur, "Too late—too late!"

"No, not too late," I echoed. "What is this Bludyer to you, that you should sacrifice your daughter to a man whose very look proclaims him a villain? Nothing can compel you to such a deed—not even a *debt of honor*!"

What it was impelled me to say these last words I know not, but they had an extraordinary effect upon Mr. Maryon. He started toward me, then checked himself; his face was livid, his eyeballs glaring, and he threw up his arms in the strange manner I had already witnessed.

"What is all this?" exclaimed a harsh voice behind me. "Mr. Westcar insulting Miss Maryon and her father! it is time for me to interfere." And Colonel Bludyer approached me menacingly. All his jovial manner and fulsome courtesy was gone; and in his flushed face and insolent look the savage rascal was revealed.

"You will interfere at your peril," I replied. "I am a younger man than you are, and my strength has not been weakened by drink and dissipation. Take care."

The villain drew himself up to his full height; and, though he must have been at least some sixty years of age, I felt assured that I should meet no ordinary adversary if a personal struggle should ensue. Agnes fainted, and I laid her on a sofa.

"Miss Maryon wants air," said the Colonel, in a calmer voice. "Excuse me, Mr. Maryon, if I open a window." He tore open the shutters, and threw up the sash. "And now, Mr. Westcar, unless you are prepared to be sensible, and make your exit by the door, I shall be under the unpleasant necessity of throwing you out of the window."

The ruffian advanced toward me as he spoke. Suddenly he paused. His jaw dropped; his hair seemed literally to stand on end; his white lips quivered; he shook, as with an ague; his whole form appeared to shrink. I stared in amazement at the awful change. A strange thrill shot through me, as I heard a quiet voice say:

"Richard Bludyer, your grave is waiting for you. Go."

The figure of a man passed between me and him. The wretched man shrank back, and, with a wild cry, leaped from the window he had opened.

All this time Mr. Maryon was standing like a lifeless statue.

In helpless wonder I gazed at the figure before me. I saw clearly the features in profile, and, swift as lightning, my memory was carried back to the unforgotten scene in the churchyard upon the Lake of Lucerne, and I recognized the white face of the young man with whom I there had spoken.

"John Maryon," said the voice, "this is the night upon which, a quarter of a century ago, you killed me. It is your last night on earth. You must go through the tragedy again."

Mr. Maryon, still statue-like, beckoned to the figure, and opened a half-concealed door which led into his study. The strange but opportune visitant seemed to motion to me with a gesture of his hand, which I felt I must obey, and I followed in this weird procession. From the study we mounted by a private staircase to a large, well-furnished bed-chamber. Here we paused. Mr. Maryon looked tremblingly at the stranger, and said, in a low, stammering voice:

"This is my room. In this room, on this night, twenty-five years ago, you told me that you were certain Sir Henry Benet's will was in existence, and that you had made up your mind to dispute my possession to this property. You had discovered letters from Sir Henry to your father which gave you a clue to the spot where that will might be found. You, Geoffrey Ringwood, of generous and extravagant nature, offered to find the will in my presence. It was late at night, as now; all the household slept. I accepted your invitation, and followed you."

Mr. Maryon ceased; he seemed physically unable to continue. The terrible stranger, in his low, echoing voice, replied:

"Go on; confess all."

"You and I, Geoffrey, had been what the world calls friends. We had been much in London together; we were both passionately fond of cards. We had a common acquaintance, Richard Bludyer. He was present on the 2d of February, when I lost a large sum of money to you at *écarté*. He hinted to me that you might possibly use these sums in instituting a lawsuit against me for the recovery of this estate. Your intimation that you knew of the existence of the will alarmed me, as it had become necessary for me to remain owner of The Mere. As I have said, I accepted your invitation, and followed you to Sir Henry Benet's room; and now I follow you again."

As he said these words, Geoffrey Ringwood, or his ghost, passed silently by Mr. Maryon, and led the way into the corridor. At the end of the corridor all three paused outside an oak door which I remembered well. A gesture from the leader made Mr. Maryon continue:

"On this threshold you told me suddenly that Bludyer was a villain, and had betrayed your sister Aldina; that she had fled with him that night; that he could never marry her, as you had reason to know he had a wife alive. You made me swear to help you in your vengeance against him. We entered the room, as we enter it now."

Our leader had opened the door of the room, and we were in the same chamber I had wandered to when I had slept at The Mere. The figure of Geoffrey Ringwood paused at the round table, and looked again at Mr. Maryon, who proceeded:

"You went straight to the fifth panel from the fireplace, and then touched a spring, and the panel opened. You said that the will giving this property to your father and his heirs was to be found there. I was convinced that you spoke the truth, but, suddenly remembering your love of gambling, I suggested that we should play for it. You accepted at once. We searched among the papers, and found the will. We placed the will upon the table, and began to play. We agreed that we would play up to ten thousand pounds. Your luck was marvellous. In two hours the limit was reached. I owed you ten thousand pounds, and had lost The Mere. You laughed, and said, 'Well, John, you have had a fair chance. At ten o'clock this morning I shall expect you to pay me *your debt of honor.*' I rose; the devil of despair strong upon me. With one hand I swept the cards from the table into the fire, and with the other seized you by the throat, and dealt you a blow upon the temple. You fell dead upon the floor."

Need I say that as I heard this fearful narrative, I recognized the actions of the sleep-walker, and understood them all?

"To the end!" said the hollow voice. "Confess to the end!"

"The doctor who examined your body gave his opinion, at the inquest, that you had died of apoplexy, caused by strong cerebral excitement. My evidence was to the effect that I believed you had lost a very large sum of money to Captain Bludyer, and that you had told me you were utterly unable to pay it. The jury found their verdict accordingly, and I was left in undisturbed possession of The Mere. But the memory of my crime haunted me as only such memories can haunt a criminal, and I became a morose and miserable man. One thing bound me to life—my daughter. When Reginald Westcar appeared upon the scene I thought that the debt of honor would be satisfied if he married Agnes. Then Bludyer reappeared, and he told me that he knew that I had killed you. He threatened to revive the story, to exhume your body, and to say that Aldina Ringwood had told him all about the will. I could purchase his silence only by giving him my daughter, the heiress of The Mere. To this I consented."

As he said these last words, Mr. Maryon sunk heavily into the chair.

The figure of Geoffrey Ringwood placed one ghostly hand upon his left temple, and then passed silently out of the room. I started up, and followed the phantom along the corridor—down the staircase—out at the front door, which still stood open—across the snow-covered lawn—into the plantation; and then it disappeared as strangely as I first had seen it; and, hardly knowing whether I was mad or dreaming, I found my way back to The Shallows.

For some weeks I was ill with brain-fever. When I recovered I was told that terrible things had happened at The Mere. Mr. Maryon had been found dead in Sir Henry Benet's room—an effusion of blood upon the brain, the doctors said—and the body of Colonel Bludyer had been discovered in the snow in an old disused gravel-pit not far from the house.

A year afterward I married Agnes Maryon; and, if all that I had seen and heard upon that 3d of February was not merely the invention of a fevered brain, the debt of honor was at last discharged, for I, the nephew of the murdered Geoffrey Ringwood, became the owner of The Mere.

DEVEREUX'S DREAM.

I GIVE you this story only at second-hand; but you have it in substance—and he wasted few words over it—as Paul Devereux told it me.

It was not the only queer story he could have told about himself if he had chosen, by a good many, I should say. Paul's life had been an eminently unconventional one: the man's face certified to that—hard, bronzed, war-worn, seamed and scarred with strange battle-marks—the face of a man who had dared and done most things.

It was not his custom to speak much of what he had done, however. Probably only because he and I were little likely to meet again that he told me this I am free to tell you now.

We had come across one another for the first time for years that afternoon on the Italian Boulevart. Paul had landed a couple of weeks previously at Marseilles from a long yacht-cruise in southern waters, the monotony of which we heard had been agreeably diversified by a little pirate-hunting and slaver-chasing—the evil tongues called it piracy and slave-running; and certainly Devereux was quite equal to either *métier*; and he was about starting on a promising little filibustering expedition across the Atlantic, where the chances were he would be shot, and the certainty was that he would be starved. So perhaps he felt inclined to be a trifle more communicative than usual, as we sat late that night over a blazing pyre of logs and in a cloud of Cavendish. At all events he was, and after this fashion.

I forget now exactly how the subject was led up to. Expression of some philosophic incredulity on my part regarding certain matters, followed by a ten-minutes' silence on his side pregnant with unwonted words to come—that was it, perhaps. At last he said, more to himself, it seemed, than to me:

"'Such stuff as dreams are made of.' Well, who knows? You're a Sadducee, Bertie; you call this sort of thing, politely, indigestion. Perhaps you're right. But yet I had a queer dream once."

"Not unlikely," I assented.

"You're wrong; I never dream, as a rule. But, as I say, I had a queer dream once; and queer because it came literally true three years afterward."

"Queer indeed, Paul."

"Happens to be true. What's queerer still, my dream was the means of my finding a man I owed a long score, and a heavy one, and of my paying him in full."

"Bad for the payee!" I thought.

Paul's face had grown terribly eloquent as he spoke those last words. On a sudden the expression of it changed—another memory was stirring in him. Wonderfully tender the fierce eyes grew; wonderfully tender the faint, sad smile, that was like sunshine on storm-scathed granite. That smile transfigured the man before me.

"Ah, poor child—poor Lucille!" I heard him mutter.

That was it, was it? So I let him be. Presently he lifted his head. If he had let himself get the least thing out of hand for a moment, he had got back his self-mastery the next.

"I'll tell you that queer story, Bertie, if you like," he said.

The proposition was flatteringly unusual, but the voice was quite his own.

"Somehow I'd sooner talk than think about—*her*," he went on after a pause.

I nodded. He might talk about this, you see, but *I* couldn't. He began with a question—an odd one:

"Did you ever hear I'd been married?"

Paul Devereux and a wife had always seemed and been to me a most unheard-of conjunction. So I laconically said:

"No."

"Well, I was once, years ago. She was my wife—that child—for a week. And then——"

I easily filled up the pause; but, as it happened, I filled it up wrongly; for he added:

"And then she was murdered."

I was not unused to our Paul's stony style of talk; but this last sentence was sufficiently startling.

"Eh?"

"Murdered—in her sleep. They never found the man who did it either, though I had Durbec and all the Rue de Jérusalem at work. But I forgave them that, for I found the man myself, and killed him."

He was filling his pipe again as he told me this, and he perhaps rammed the Cavendish in a little tighter, but that was all. The thing was a matter of course; I knew my Paul, well enough to know that. Of course he killed him.

"Mind you," he continued, kindling the black *brûle-gueule* the while—"mind you, I'd never seen this man before, never known of his existence, except in a way that—however, it was this way."

He let his grizzled head drop back on the cushions of his chair, and his eyes seemed to see the queer story he was telling enacted once more before him in the red hollows of the fire.

"As I said, it was years ago. I was waiting here in Paris for some fellows who were to join me in a campaign we'd arranged against the African big game. I never was more fit for anything of that sort than I was then. I only tell you this to show you that the thing can't be accounted for by my nerves having been out of order at all.

"Well: I was dining alone that day, at the Café Anglais. It was late when I sat down to my dinner in the little salon as usual. Only two other men were still lingering over theirs. All the time they stayed they bored me so persistently with some confounded story of a murder they were discussing, that I was once or twice more than half-inclined to tell them so. At last, though, they went away.

"But their talk kept buzzing abominably in my head. When the waiter brought me the evening paper, the first thing that caught my eye was a circumstantial account of the *probable* way the fellow did his murder. I say probable, for they never caught him; and, as you will see directly, they could only suppose how it occurred.

"It seemed that a well-known Paris banker, who was ascertained beyond doubt to have left one station alive and well, and with a couple of hundred thousand francs in a leathern *sac* under his seat, arrived at the next station the train stopped at with his throat cut and *minus* all his money, except a few bank-notes to no great amount, which the assassin had been wise enough to leave behind him. The train was a night express on one of the southern lines; the banker travelled quite alone, in a first-class carriage; and the murder must have taken place between midnight and 1 A.M. next morning. The newspapers supposed—rightly enough, I think—that the murderer must have entered the carriage *from without*, stabbed his victim in his sleep—there were no signs of any struggle—opened the *sac*, taken what he wanted, and retreated, loot and all, by the way he came. I fully indorsed my particular writer's opinion that the murderer was an uncommonly cool and clever individual, especially as I fancy he got clear off and was never afterward laid hands on.

"When I had done that I thought I had done with the affair altogether. Not at all. I was regularly ridden with this confounded murder. You see the banker was rather a swell; everybody knew him: and that, of course, made it so shocking. So everybody kept talking about him: they were talking about him at the Opera, and over the *baccarat* and *bouillotte* at La Topaze's later. To escape him I went to bed and smoked myself to sleep. And then a queer thing came to pass: I had a dream—I who never dream; and this is what I dreamed:

"I saw a wide, rich country that I knew. A starless night hung over it like a pall. I saw a narrow track running through it, straight, both ways, for leagues. Something sped along this track with a hurtling rush and roar. This something that at first had looked like a red-eyed devil, with dark sides full of dim fire, resolved itself, as I watched it, presently, into a more conventional night express-train. It flew along, though, as no express-train ever travelled yet; for all that, I was able to keep it quite easily in view. I could count the carriages as they whirled by. One—two—three—four—five—six; but I could only see distinctly into one. Into that one with perfect distinctness. Into that one I seemed forced to look.

"It was the fourth carriage. Two people were in it. They sat in opposite corners; both were sleeping. The one who sat facing forward was a woman—a girl, rather. I could see that; but I couldn't see her face. The blind was drawn across the lamp in the roof, and the light was very dim; moreover, this girl lay back in the shadow. Yet I seemed to know her, and I knew that her face was very fair. She wore a cloak that shrouded her form completely, yet her form was familiar to me.

"The figure opposite to her was a man's. Strangely familiar to me too this figure was. But, as he slept, his head had sunk upon his breast, and the shadow cast upon his face by the low-drawn travelling-cap he wore hid it from me. Yet if I had seemed to know the girl's face, I was certain I knew the man's. But as I could see, so I could remember, neither. And there was an absolute torture in this which I can't explain to you,—in this inability, and in my inability to wake them from their sleep.

"From the first I had been conscious of a desire to do that. This desire grew stronger every second. I tried to call to them, and my tongue wouldn't move. I tried to spring toward them, to thrust out my arms and touch them, and my limbs were paralyzed. And then I tried to shut my eyes to what I *knew* must happen, and my eyes were held open and dragged to look on in spite of me. And I saw this:

"I saw the door of the carriage where these two sleepers, whose sleep was so horribly sound, were sitting—I saw this door open, and out of the thick darkness another face look in.

"The light, as I have said, was very dim, but I could see his face as plainly as I can see yours. A large yellow face it was, like a wax mask. The lips were full, and lustful and cruel. The eyes were little eyes of an evil gray. Thin yellow streaks marked the absence of the eyebrows; thin yellow hair showed itself under a huge fur travelling-cap. The whole face seemed to grow slowly into absolute distinctness as I looked, by the sort of devilish light that it, as it were, radiated. I had chanced upon a good many damnable visages before then; but there was a cold fiendishness about this one such as I had seen on no man's face, alive or dead, till then.

"The next moment the man this face belonged to was standing in the carriage, that seemed to plunge and sway more furiously, as though to waken them that still slept on. He wore a long fur travelling-robe, girt about the waist with a fur girdle. Abnormally tall and broad as he was, he looked in this dress gigantic. Yet there was a marvellous cat-like lightness and agility about all his movements.

"He bent over the girl lying there helpless in her sleep. I don't make rash bargains as a rule, but I felt I would have given years of my life for five minutes of my lost freedom of limb just then. I tell you the torture was infernal.

"The assassin—I knew he was an assassin—bent awhile, gloatingly, over the girl. His great yellow hands were both bare, and on the forefinger of the right hand I could see some great stone blazing like an evil eye. In that right hand there gleamed something else. I saw him draw it slowly from his sleeve, and, as he drew it, turn round and look at the other sleeper with an infernal triumphant malignity and hate the Devil himself might have envied. But the man he looked at slept heavily on. And then—God! I feel the agony I felt in my dream then now!—then I saw the great yellow hand, with the great evil eye upon it, lifted murderously, and the bright steel it held shimmer as the assassin turned again and bent his yellow face down closer to that other face hidden from me in the shadow—the girl's face, that I knew was so fair.

"How can I tell this?... The blade flashed and fell.... There was the sound of a heavy sigh stifled under a heavy hand....

"Then the huge form of the assassin was reared erect, and the bloated yellow face seemed to laugh silently, while the hand that held the steel pointed at the sleeping man in diabolical menace.

"And so the huge form and the bloated yellow face seemed to fade away while I watched.

"The express rushed and roared through the blinding darkness without; the sleeping man slept on still; till suddenly a strong light fell full upon him, and he woke.

"And then I saw why I had been so certain that I knew him. For as he lifted his head, I saw his face in the strong light.

"*And the face was my own face; and the sleeper was myself!*"

Paul Devereux made a pause in his queer story here. Except when he had spoken of the girl, he had spoken in his usual cool, hard way. The pipe he had been smoking all the time was smoked out. He took time to fill another before he went on. I said never a word, for I guessed who the sleeping girl was.

"Well," Paul remarked presently, "that was a devilish queer dream, wasn't it? You'll account for it by telling me I'd been so pestered with the story of the banker's murder that I naturally had nightmare; perhaps, too, that my digestion was out of order. Call it a nightmare, call it dyspepsia, if you like. I *don't*, because——— But you'll see why I don't directly.

"At the same moment that my dream-self awoke in my dream, my actual self woke in reality, and with the same ghastly horror.

"I say the *same* horror, for neither then nor afterward could I separate my one self from my other self. They seemed identical; so that this queer dream made a more lasting impression upon me than you'd think. However, in the life I led that sort of thing couldn't last very long. Before I came back from Africa I had utterly forgotten all about it. Before I left Paris, though, and while it was quite fresh in my memory, I sketched the big murderer just as I had seen him in my dream. The great yellow face, the great broad frame in the fur travelling-robe, the great hand with the great evil eye upon it—everything, carefully and minutely, as though I had been going to paint a portrait that I wanted to make lifelike. I think at the time I had some such intention. If I had, I never fulfilled it. But I made the sketch, as I say, carefully; and then I forgot all about it.

"Time passed—three years nearly. I was wintering in the south of France that year. There it was that I met her—Lucille. Old D'Avray, her father, and I had met before in Algeria. He was dying now. He left the child on his death-bed to me. The end was I married her.

"Poor little thing! I think I might have made her happy—who knows? She used to tell me often she was happy with me. Poor little thing!

"Well, we were to come straight to London. That was Lucille's notion. She wanted to go to my London first—nowhere else. Now I would rather have gone anywhere else; but, naturally, I let the child have her way. She seemed nervously eager about it, I remembered afterward; seemed to have a nervous objection to every other place I proposed. But I saw or suspected nothing to make me question her very closely, or the reasons for her preference for our grimy old Pandemonium. What could I suspect? Not the truth. If I only had! If I had only guessed what it was that made her, as she said, long to be safe there already. Safe? What had she to fear with me? Ah, what indeed!

"So we started on our journey to England. It was a cold, dark night, early in March. We reached Lyons somewhere about seven. I should have stayed there that night but for Lucille. She entreated me so earnestly and with such strange vehemence to go on by the night-mail to Paris, that at last, to satisfy her, I consented; though it struck me unpleasantly at the time that I had let her travel too long already, and that this feverishness was the consequence of over-fatigue. But she became pacified at once when I told her it should be as she wanted; and declared she should sleep perfectly well in the carriage with me beside her. She should feel quite safe then, she said.

"Safe! Where safer? you might ask. Nowhere, I believe. Alone with me—surely nowhere safer. The Paris express was a short train that night; but I managed to secure a compartment for ourselves. I left Lucille in her corner there while I went across to the *buffet* to fill a flask. I was gone barely five minutes; but when I came back the change in the child's face fairly startled me. I had seen it last with the smile it always wore for me on it, looking so childishly happy in the lamplight. Now it was all gray-pale and distorted; and the great blue eyes told me directly with what.

"Fear—sudden, terrible fear—I thought. But *fear*? Fear of what? I asked her. She clung close to me half-sobbing awhile before she could answer; and then she told me—nothing. There was nothing the matter; only she had felt a pain—a cruel pain—at her heart; and it had frightened her. Yes, that was it; it had frightened her, but it had passed; and she was well, quite well again now.

"All this time her eyes seemed to be telling me another story; but I said nothing; she was obviously too excited already. I did my best to soothe her, and I succeeded. She told me she felt quite well once more before we started. No, she had rather, much rather go on to Paris, as I had promised her she should. She should sleep all the way, if no one came into the carriage to disturb her. No one could come in? Then nothing could be better.

"And so it was that she and I started that night by the Paris mail.

"I made her up a bed of rugs and wraps upon the cushions; but she had rather rest her head upon my shoulder, she said, and feel my arm about her; nothing could hurt her then. Ah, strange how she harped on that.

"She lay there, then, as she loved best—with her head resting on my shoulder, not sleeping much or soundly; uneasily, with sudden waking starts, and with glances round her; till I would speak to her. And then she would look up into my face and smile; and so drop into that uneasy sleep again. And I would think she was over-tired, that was all; and reproach myself with having let her come on. And three or four hours passed like this; and then we had got as far as Dijon.

"But the child was fairly worn out now; and she offered no opposition when I asked her to let me pillow her head on something softer than my shoulder. So I folded, a great thick shawl she was too well cloaked to need, and she made that her pillow.

"We were rushing full swing through the wild, dark night, when she lifted up her face and bade me kiss her and bid her sleep well. And I put my arm round her, and kissed the child's loving lips—for the last time while she lived. Then I flung myself on the seat opposite her; and, watching her till she slept soundly and peacefully, slept at last myself also. I had drawn the blind across the lamp in the roof, and the light in the carriage was very dim.

"How long I slept I don't know; it couldn't have been more than an hour and a half, because the express was slackening speed for its first halt beyond Dijon. I had slept heavily I knew; but I woke with a sudden, sharp sense of danger that made me broad awake, and strung every nerve in a moment. The sort of feeling you have when you wake on a prairie, where you have come across 'Indian sign;' on outpost-duty, when your *feldwebel* plucks gently at your cloak. You know what I mean.

"I was on my feet at once. As I said, the light in the carriage was very dim, and the shadow was deepest where Lucille lay. I looked there instinctively. She must have moved in her sleep, for her face was turned away from me; and the cloak I had put so carefully about her had partly fallen off. But she slept on still. Only soundly, very soundly; she scarcely seemed to breathe. And—*did* she breathe?

"A ghastly fear ran through my blood, and froze it. I understood why I had wakened. In my nostrils was an awful odor that I knew well enough. I bent over her; I touched her. Her face was very cold; her eyes glared glassily at me; my hands were wet with something. My hands were wet with blood—her blood!

"I tore away the blind from the lamp, and then I could see that my wife of a week lay there stabbed straight to the heart—dead—dead beyond doubting; murdered in her sleep."

Devereux's stern, low voice shook ever so little as he spoke those last words; and we both sat very silent after them for a good while. Only when he could trust his utterance again he went on.

"A curious piece of devilry, wasn't it? That child—whom had she ever harmed? Who could hate her like this? I remember I thought that, in a dull, confused sort of way, when I found myself alone in that carriage with her lying dead on the cushions before me. *Alone* with her—you understand? It was confusing.

"I pass over what immediately followed. The express came duly to a halt; and then I called people to me, and—and the Paris express went on without that particular carriage.

"The inquiry began before some local authority next day. Very little came of it. What could come of it, unless they had convicted *me* of the murder of this child I would have given my own life to save?

"They might have done that at home; but they knew better here, and didn't. They couldn't find me the actual assassin, however; though I believe they did their best. All they found was his weapon, which he most purposely have left behind. I asked for this, and got it. It gave their police no clue; and it gave me none. But I had a fancy for it.

"It was a plain, double-edged, admirably-tempered dagger—a very workmanlike article indeed. On the cross hilt of it I swore one day that I would live thenceforth for one thing alone—the discovery of the murderer of old D'Avray's child, whom I had promised him to care for before all. When I had found this man, whoever he was, I also swore that I would kill him. Kill him myself, you understand; without any of the law's delay or uncertainty, without troubling *bourreau* or hangman. Kill him as he had killed her—to do this was what I meant to live for. There was war to the knife between him and me.

"I started, of course, under one heavy disadvantage. He knew me, probably, whereas I didn't know him at all. When he found that his amiable intention of fixing the crime on me had been frustrated, it must, I imagined, have occurred to him that the said crime might eventually be fixed by me on him. And he had proved himself to be a person who didn't stick at trifles. It behooved me, therefore, to go to work cautiously. But I hadn't fought Indians for nothing; and I *was* very cautious. I waited quiet till I got a clue. It was a curious one; and I got it in this way. It struck me one day, suddenly, that I had heard of a murder precisely similar to this already. I could not at first call the thing to mind; but presently I remembered—my dream. And then I asked myself this: *Had not this murder been done before my eyes three years ago?*

"I came to the conclusion that the circumstances of the murder in my dream were absolutely identical with the circumstances of the actual crime. Yes; the girl whose face in that dream I had never been able to see was Lucille. Yes; the assassin whose face I had seen so plainly in that dream was the real assassin. In short, I believe that the murder had been *rehearsed* before me three years previous to its actual committal.

"Now this sounds rather wild. Yet I came to this conviction quite coolly and deliberately. It *was* a conviction. Assuming it to be true, the odds against me grew shorter directly; *for I had the portrait of the man I wanted drawn by myself the day after I had seen him in my dream*. And the original of that portrait was a man not to be easily mistaken, supposing him to exist at all. The day I came across that sketch of him in that old forgotten sketch-book of mine, I was as sure he did exist as that I was alive myself. What I had to do was to find this man, and then I never doubted I should find the man I wanted. You see how the odds had shortened. If he knew me I knew him now, and he had no notion that I did know him. It was a good deal fairer fight between us.

"I fought it out alone. My story was hardly one the Rue de Jérusalem would have acted upon; and, besides, I wanted no interference. So, with the portrait before me, I sat down and began to consider who this man was, and why he had murdered that child. The big, burly frame, the heavy yellow face, the sandy-yellow hair, the physiognomy generally, was Teutonic. My man I put down as a North German. Now there were, and are probably, plenty of men who would have no objection whatever to put a knife into me, if they got the chance; but this man, whom I had never met, could have had no such quarrel as theirs with me. His quarrel with me must have been, then, Lucille. Yes, that was it—Lucille. I began to see clearly: a thwarted, devilish passion—a cool, infernal revenge. The child had feared something of this sort; had perhaps seen him that night. This explained her nervous terror, her nervous anxiety to stop nowhere, to travel on. In that carriage of that express-train, alone with me—where could she be safer? This accounted, too, for her anxiety to reach England. He would not dare follow her there, she had thought, or, at least, could not without my noticing him. And then she would have told me. She had not told me before evidently because she had feared for *me* too, in a quarrel with this man. She must, innocent child as she was, have had some instinctive knowledge of what he was capable.... Ay, a cool, infernal revenge, indeed. To kill her; to fix the murder on me. That dagger he had left behind.... The apparent impossibility of any one's entering the carriage as he must have entered it at all, to say nothing of the almost absolute impossibility of his doing so without disturbing either of us, you see it might have gone hard with me if a British jury had had to decide on the case.

"Well, to cut this as short as may be, I made up my mind that the man I wanted was a North German; that he had conceived a hideous passion for Lucille before I knew her; that she had shrunk from it and him so unmistakably, that he knew he had no chance; that my taking her away as my wife, to which he might have been a witness, drove him to as hideous a revenge; that, hearing we were going to England, and seeing that we were likely to stop nowhere on the way, and so give him a chance of doing what he had made up his mind to do, he had decided to do what he had done as he had done it,—counting on finding us asleep as he had found us, or on his strength if it came to a fight between him and me; but coolly reckless enough to brave everything in any case. And the devil aiding, he had in great part and only too well succeeded. He was now either so far satisfied that, if I made no move against him—and how, he might think, could I?—he, feeling himself all safe, would let me be; or, on the other hand, he did not feel safe, and was not satisfied, and was arranging for my being disposed of by and by. I considered the latter frame of mind as his most probable one; I went to work cautiously, as I say. I ascertained that Lucille had made no mention of any obnoxious *prétendant* at any time; I didn't expect to find she had, her terror of the man was too intense. But this man must have met her somewhere—where?

"When old D'Avray came home to die, his daughter was just leaving her Paris *pensionnat*. All through his last illness he had seen no visitor but me, and Lucille had never quitted him. Besides, I had been there all the time. I presumed, then, that this man and she had met in Paris; and I believe they were only likely to have met at one of the half-dozen houses where the child would now and again be asked. I got a list of all these. One name only struck me; it happened to be a German name—Steinmetz. I wondered if Monsieur Steinmetz was my man. In the mean time, who was he? I had no trouble in finding that out: Monsieur Steinmetz was a German banker of good standing and repute, reasonably well off, and recently left a widower. Personally? *Dame*, personally Monsieur Steinmetz was a great man and a fat, with a big face and blond hair, and the appearance of what he really was—a *bon vivant* and a *bon enfant* yet *n'avait jamais fait de mal à personne—allez!*—All, yes; in effect, Madame had died about a year ago, and Monsieur had been inconsolable for a long time. He had changed his residence now, and inhabited a house in one of the new streets off the Champs Elysées.

"From another source I discovered that in the lifetime of Madame Steinmetz Lucille was frequently at the house. She had ceased to come there about the date of the commencement of Madame's sudden illness. I got this information by degrees, while I lay *perdu* in an old haunt of mine in the Pays Latin yonder; for I had always had an idea that I should find the man I wanted in Paris. When I had got it, I thought I should like to see Monsieur Steinmetz, the agreeable banker. One night I strolled up as far as his new residence in the street off the Champs Elysées. Monsieur Steinmetz lived on the first-floor. There was a brilliant light there: Monsieur Steinmetz was entertaining friends, it seemed.

"It was a fine night; I established myself out of sight under the doorway of an unfinished house opposite, and waited. I don't know why; perhaps I fancied that when his friends were gone, the fineness of the night might induce Monsieur Steinmetz to take a stroll, and that then I should be able to gratify my curiosity. You see, I knew that if he were my man, I should know him directly. I waited a good while: shadows crossed the lighted blinds; once a big, broad shadow appeared there, that made me fancy I mightn't have been waiting for nothing after all, somehow. Presently Monsieur Steinmetz's guests departed, and in a little while after there appeared on the little balcony of Monsieur Steinmetz's apartment *the man I wanted*. There was a moon that night, and the cold white light fell on the great yellow face, with the full lustful lips, and the full cruel chin, just as I had seen the light fall on it in my dream. It was the same face, Bertie; the same face, the same man. I couldn't be mistaken. I had no doubt; I *knew* that the assassin of my wife, of that tender, innocent, helpless child, stood there, twenty yards from me, on that balcony.

"I had got myself pretty well in hand; and it was as well. I never moved. The face I knew turned presently toward the spot where I stood hidden,—the face I had seen in my dream, beyond all doubting. The evil gray eyes glanced carelessly into the shadow, and up and down the quiet street; and then Monsieur Steinmetz, humming an air, got inside the window again, and closed it after him. Once more the great burly shadow that had at first told me I should not wait in that dark doorway in vain crossed the blinds; and then it disappeared. I saw my man no more that night; but I had seen enough. I knew who he was now, and where to find him.

"As I walked along home I thought what I would do. I quite meant to kill Monsieur Steinmetz; but I also meant to have no *démêlés* with an Impérial Procureur and the Cour d'Assizes for doing so. I didn't want to murder him, either. I thought I would wait a little for the chance of a suitable opportunity for settling my business satisfactorily. And I did wait. I turned this delay to account, and got together a case of circumstantial evidence against my man that, though perhaps it might have broken down in a law-court, would have been alone amply sufficient for me.

"The reason why Lucille's visits to the banker's house ceased was, it appeared, because Madame Steinmetz had conceived all at once a jealous dislike to her. How far this was owing to Lucille herself I could well understand; but I could understand Madame's jealousy equally well. Madame's illness, strangely sudden, dated from the cessation of Lucille's visits. Was it hard to find a *cause* for that illness—a cause for the wife's subsequent suspected death? I thought not. Then had followed Lucille's departure from Paris. The child's anxiety for her father hid her *other fear* from his eyes and mine; but that fear must have been on her then. With us she forgot it in time; yet it or another reason had always prevented all mention of what had occasioned it. She became my wife. At that very time I easily ascertained that Steinmetz was absent from Paris; less easily, but indubitably, that he had, at all events, been as far south as Lyons. At Lyons it must have been that Lucille first discovered he was dogging us. Hence her alarm, which I had remembered, and her anxiety to proceed on our journey without stopping for the night, as I had previously arranged. The morning after the murder Steinmetz reappeared in Paris. From the hour at which he was seen at the *gare*, it was certain that he had travelled by the night express train in which Lucille and I had started from Lyons; and he wore that morning a travelling-coat of fur in all respects similar to the one I remembered so well.

"If I had ever had any doubt of my man after actually seeing him, I should probably have convinced myself that he was my man by the general tendency of these facts, which I got at slowly and one by one. But I had no need of such evidence; and of course no case, even with such evidence, for a court of law. However, courts of law I had never intended to trouble in the matter.

"The opportunity I was waiting was some time before it offered. Monsieur Steinmetz was a man of regular habits, I found—from his first-floor in the street off the Champs Elysées, every morning at eleven, to the Bourse; thence to his bureau hard by till four; from his bureau to his café, where he read papers and played dominoes till six; and then home slowly by the Boulevarts. He might consider himself tolerably safe from me while he led this sort of life, even supposing he was aware he was incurring any danger. I don't think he troubled much about that; till one night, when, over the count of the beloved domino-points, his eyes met mine fixed right upon him. I had arranged this little surprise to see how it would affect him.

"Perhaps my gaze may have expressed something more than the mere distraction I intended; but I noticed—though a more indifferent observer might easily have failed to notice—how the great yellow face, expanded in childish interest in the childish game, seemed suddenly to grow gray and harden; how the fat smile became a cruel baring of sharp white teeth; how the fat chin squared itself. The man knew me, and scented danger.

"A moment's reflection convinced Monsieur Steinmetz, though, that it could be by no means so certain that I knew him; five minutes' observation of me more than half satisfied him that I did not. Yet what did I want there? What was I doing in Paris? This might concern him nearly, he must have thought.

"I kept my own face in order, and watched his. It wasn't an easy one to read; but you see I had studied it closely, and in a way he couldn't have dreamed of. Monsieur Steinmetz was outwardly his wonted self, but inwardly not quite comfortable when he rose; and I saw the evil eye gleam on his great yellow finger as he took out his purse to pay the *garçon*, just as I had seen it when that finger pointed at *myself* in my dream. I felt curious sensations, Bertie, as I sat there and looked abstractedly at Monsieur Steinmetz. I wondered how long it would be before——But my time hadn't come yet. He went out without another glance at me. I saw his huge form on the other side of the street when I left the café in my turn. This I had expected. Monsieur Steinmetz was naturally curious. It was hardly possible that I could know him; but it was quite certain that he ought to know all about me. So, when I moved on, he moved on; in short, Monsieur Steinmetz dogged me up one street and down another, till he finally dogged me home to my hiding-place in the Pays Latin. He did it very well, too—much better than you would have expected from so apparently unwieldy a *mouchard*. But I *remembered* how lightly he could move.

"Next day I had, of course, disappeared from my old quarters, and gone no one knew where. I suppose Monsieur Steinmetz didn't like this fact when he heard of it. It might have seemed suspicious. Suppose I *had* recognized him? In that case I had evidently a little game of my own, and was as evidently desirous to keep it dark. He was a cool hand; but I fancy my man began to get a little uneasy. He took some trouble to find me again. After a while I permitted him to do that. Once found, he seemed determined that I should not be lost sight of again for want of watching. I permitted that, too; it helped play my game, and I wanted to bring it to an end. To which intent, Monsieur Steinmetz got to hear from sources best known to himself as much of my plans as should bring him to the state I wanted. That was a murderous state. I wanted to get him to think that I was dangerous enough to be worth putting out of the way. I presume he was aware there were, or would be, weak joints in his armor, impenetrable as it seemed; and he preferred not risking the ordeal of legal battle if he could help it. At all events, he elected at last to rid himself of a person who might be dangerous, and was troublesome, by the shortest and the simplest means.

"I say so because when, believing my man was ripe for this, I left Paris about midday for a certain secluded little spot on the sea-coast, I saw one of Monsieur Steinmetz's employees on the platform; and because, two days after my arrival in my secluded spot, I met Monsieur Steinmetz in person, newly arrived also. Now this was exactly what I had intended and anticipated. Monsieur Steinmetz had come down there to put me out of his way, if he could. He passed me, leisurely strolling in the opposite direction, humming his favorite *aria*, bigger and yellower than ever, the evil eye fiery on his finger. His own eyes shot me as evil fire; but he said nothing.... I saw he was ripe, though.... My time was close at hand.

"It came. Monsieur Steinmetz and I met once more in the very place where I, knowing my ground, had intended we should meet. It was a dip in the cliffs like a hollowed palm, and just there the cliff jutted out a good bit, with a sheer fall on to the rocks below. It was a gray afternoon, at the end of summer. The wind was rising fast; there was a thunder of heavy waves already.

"I think he had been dogging me; but I hadn't chosen to let him get up to me till now. We were quite out of sight when he had reached the level bottom of the dip, where I had halted—quite out of sight, and quite alone. To do him justice, he came on steadily enough. His face was liker the sketch I had made of it, liker the face I had seen in my dream, than it had ever looked before. Evidently he had made up his mind.... At last, then!... Well, I had been waiting long!... He was close beside me.

"'*Ah! bon jour, cher Monsieur Steinmetz.*'

"'So?' he said, his little eyes contracting like a cobra's. 'Ah! Monsieur knows my name?'

"'Among other things about you—yes.'

"'So!' The yellow face was turning grayer and harder every minute—liker and liker to my likeness of it. 'And what other things? Has it never appeared to you that this you do, have been doing—this meddling, may be dangerous, *hein*?'

"He had changed his tone, as he had changed the person in which he addressed me. Yes, he had certainly made up his mind. And his big right hand was hidden inside his waistcoat, so that I could not see the evil eye I knew was on his finger.

"'Dangerous?' he repeated slowly.

"'Possibly.'

"'Ay, surely; I shall crush you!'

"'Try.'

"'In good time; wait. You plot against me. Take care; I am strong; I warn you. There must be an end of this, you understand, or——'

"He nodded his big head significantly.

"'You are right,' I told him; 'there must be an end. It is coming.'

"'So?'

"'Yes; I know you. You know me now.'

"'I know you. What do you want?'

"'To kill you.'

"'So?'

"'Yes; as you killed her.'

"'As I killed her? That is it, then? You know that?'

"'I know that.'

"'Well, it is true. I killed her. Now you can guess what I am going to do to you—to you, curse you!—whom she loved.'

"The very face I had seen in my dream now, Bertie, the very face! There was something besides the evil eye that gleamed in his right hand when he drew it from his breast. Once more he spoke.

"'Yes, I killed her. I meant worse for you. You escaped that; but you will not escape me now. Fool! were you mad to do this? Did not I hate you enough? And I would have let you be. Ah, die, then, if you will have it so!'

"His heavy right arm swung high as he spoke, and I saw the sharp steel gleam as it turned to fall. And I twisted from his grip, and caught the falling arm, and bent it till the dagger dropped to the ground. And then, for a fierce, desperate, devilish minute, I had him in my clutch, dragging him nearer the smooth, slippery edge. He was no match for me at this I knew, and he knew; but he held me with the hold of his despair, and I could not loose myself. Both of us together, he meant; but not I. Yet I only freed myself just as he rolled exhausted, but clutching at the tough, short bushes wildly, toward the brink, and partly over it.... Only the hold of his hands between him and his death. And I knelt above him, with the knife in my hand that was stained with *her* blood.

"The great yellow face, ashen now in its mortal agony, looked silently up at me—for three or four awful seconds; and then—then it disappeared.

"Bah!" Paul concluded, "that was the end of it."

CATHERINE'S QUEST.

IMAGINE to yourself an old, rambling, red-brick house, with odd corners and gables here and there, all bound and clasped together with ivy, and you have Craymoor Grange. It was built long before Queen Elizabeth's time, and that illustrious monarch is said to have slept in it in one of her royal progresses—as where has she not slept?

There still remain some remnants of bygone ages, although it has been much modernized and added to in later days. Among these are the brewhouse and laundry—formerly, it is said, dining-hall and ball-room. The latter of these is chiefly remarkable for an immense arched window, such as you see in churches, with five lights.

When we came to the Grange this window had been partially blocked up, and in front of it, up to one-third of its height, was a wooden daïs, or platform, on which stood a cumbrous mangle, left there, I suppose, by the last tenants of the house.

Of these last tenants we knew very little, for it was so long since it had been inhabited that the oldest authority in the village could not remember it.

There were, however, some half-defaced monuments in the village church of Craymoor, bearing the figures and escutcheons of knights and dames of "the old family," as the villagers said; but the inscriptions were worn and almost illegible, and for some time we none of us took the pains to decipher them.

We first came to Craymoor Grange in the summer of 1849, my husband having discovered the place in one of his rambles, and taken a fancy to it. At first I certainly thought we could never make it our home, it was so dilapidated and tumble-down; but by the time winter came on we had had several repairs done and alterations made, and the rooms really became quite presentable.

As our family was small we confined ourselves chiefly to the newest part of the house, leaving the older rooms to the mice, dust, and darkness. We made use of two of the old rooms, however, one as a servants' bedroom and the other as an extra spare chamber, in case of many visitors. For myself, though I hope I am neither nervous nor superstitious, I confess that I would rather sleep in "our wing," as we called the part of the house we inhabited, than in any of the old rooms.

When Catherine l'Estrange came to us, however, during our first Christmas at Craymoor, I found that she was troubled with no such fancies, but declared that she delighted in queer old rooms, with raftered ceilings and deep window-seats, such as ours, and begged to be allowed to occupy the spare chamber. This I readily acceded to, as we had several visitors, and needed all the available rooms.

As my story has principally to do with Catherine l'Estrange, I suppose I ought to speak more fully about her. She was an old school-friend of my daughter Ella, and at the time of which I am speaking was just one-and-twenty, and the merriest girl I ever knew. She had stayed with us once or twice before we came to the Grange, but we then knew no other particulars concerning her family, than that her father had been an Indian officer, and that he and her mother had both died in India when she was about six years old, leaving her to the care of an aunt living in England.

I now, after a long, and I fear a tedious, preamble, come to my story.

On the eve of the new year of 1850, Catherine had a very bad sore throat, and was obliged, though sorely against her inclination, to stay in bed all day, and forego our small evening gayety.

At about 6 o'clock P.M., Ella took her some tea, and fearing she would be dull, offered to stay with her during the evening. This, however, Catherine would not hear of. "You go and entertain your company," said she laughingly, "and leave me to my own devices; I feel very lazy, and I dare say I shall go to sleep." As she had not slept much on the preceding night, Ella thought it was the best thing she could do; so she went out by the door leading on to the corridor, first placing the night-lamp on a table behind the door opening on to the laundry, so that it might not shine in her face.

She did not again visit Catherine's room until reminded to do so by my son George, at about half-past ten. She then rapped at the door, and receiving no answer, opened it softly, and approached the bed. Catherine lay quite still, and Ella imagined her to be asleep. She therefore returned to the drawing-room without disturbing her.

As it was New Year's eve, we stayed up "to see the old year out and the new year in," and at a few minutes to twelve we all gathered round the open window on the stairs to hear the chimes ring out from the village church.

We were all listening breathlessly as the hall-clock struck twelve, when a piercing cry suddenly echoed through the house, causing us all to start in alarm. I knew that it could only proceed from Catherine's room, for the servants were all assembled at the window beneath us, listening, like ourselves, for the chimes. Thither therefore I flew, followed by Ella, and we found poor Catherine in a truly pitiable state.

She was deadly pale, in an agony of terror, and the perspiration stood in large drops upon her forehead. It was some time before we could succeed at all in composing her, and her first words were to implore us to take her into another room.

She was too weak to stand, so we wrapped her in blankets, and carried her into Ella's bedroom. I noticed that as she was taken through the laundry she shuddered, and put her hands before her eyes. When she was laid on Ella's bed she grew calmer, and apologized for the trouble she had caused, saying that she had had a dreadful dream.

With this explanation we were fain to be content, though I thought it hardly accounted for her excessive terror. I had observed, however, that any allusion to what had passed caused her to tremble and turn pale again, and I thought it best to refrain from exciting her further.

When morning came I found Catherine almost her usual self again; but I persuaded her to remain in bed until the evening, as her cold was not much better. Ella's curiosity to hear the dream which had so much excited her friend could now no longer be restrained; but whenever she asked to hear it, Catherine said, "Not now; another time, perhaps, I may tell you."

When she came down to dinner in the evening, we noticed that she was peculiarly silent, and we endeavored to rally her into her usual spirits, but in vain. She tried to laugh and to appear merry, poor child; but there was evidently something on her mind.

At last, as we all sat round the fire after dinner, she spoke. She addressed herself to my husband, but the tone of her voice caused us all to listen.

"Mr. Fanshawe, I have something to ask of you," said she, and then paused.

"Ask on," said Mr. Fanshawe.

"I know that you will think the request I am going to make a peculiar one; but I have a particular reason for making it," continued she. "It is that you will have the wooden daïs in front of the laundry window removed."

Mr. Fanshawe certainly was taken aback, as were we all. When he had mastered his bewilderment, and assured himself that he had heard aright—

"It is, indeed, a strange request, my dear Catherine," said he; "what can be your reason for asking such a thing?"

"If you will only have it done, and not question me, you will understand my reason," answered Catherine.

Mr. Fanshawe demurred, however, thinking it some foolish whim, and at last Catherine said:

"I must tell you why I wish it done, then: I am sure we shall discover something underneath."

At this we all looked at one another in extreme bewilderment.

"Discover something underneath? No doubt we should—cobwebs, probably, and dust and spiders," answered Mr. Fanshawe, much amused.

But Catherine was not to be laughed down.

"Only do as I wish," said she beseechingly, "and you will see. If you find nothing underneath the daïs but cobwebs and dust, then you may laugh at me as much as you like." And I saw that she was serious, for tears were actually gathering in her eyes. Of course we were all very anxious to know what Catherine expected to find, and how she came to suspect that there was anything to be found; but she would not say, and begged us all not to question her.

And now George took upon himself to interfere.

"Let us do as Catherine wishes, father," said he; "the daïs spoils the laundry, and would be much better away."

"Well, well," said Mr. Fanshawe, "do as you like, only I shall expect my share of the treasure that is found.—And now," added he, "you must have a glass of wine to warm you, Catherine, for you look sadly pale, child."

Here the conversation changed, though we often alluded to the subject again during the evening.

The next morning the first thing in all our thoughts was Catherine's singular request.

I think Mr. Fanshawe had hoped she would have forgotten it, but such was not the case; on the contrary, she enlisted George's services the first thing after breakfast to carry out her design, and they left the room together, accompanied by Ella.

It was a snowy morning, and Mr. Fanshawe was obliged to be away from home all day on business, so I was quite at a loss how to entertain my numerous guests successfully. Happily for me, however, the mystery attendant on the removal of the daïs in the laundry charmed them all; and I have to thank Catherine for contributing to their amusement much better than I could possibly have done.

Not long after the disappearance of Catherine, Ella, and George, a message was sent to us in the drawing-room requesting our presence in the laundry; and on all flocking there with more or less eagerness, we found a fire burning on the old-fashioned hearth and chairs arranged round it.

It appeared that with the help of Sam, our factotum, who was a kind of Jack-of-all-trades, George had succeeded in loosening the planks of the daïs, which, although strongly put together, were rotten and worm-eaten, and that we were now summoned to be witnesses of its removal. We found Catherine trembling with a strange eagerness, and her face quite pale with excitement. This was shared by Ella and George; and, judging by the important expression on their faces, I fancied they were let further into the secret than any one else.

We all sat down in the chairs placed for our accommodation, and the wild whistling of the wind in the huge chimney, together with the sheets of snow which darkened the window-panes, enhanced the mystery of the whole affair, while George and his coadjutor worked lustily on.

At length, after a great deal of panting and puffing, George was heard to exclaim, "Now for the tug of war!" and there followed a minute's pause, and then a crash as the loosened planks were torn asunder, and a cloud of dust enveloped both workmen and spectators.

Involuntarily we all started forward, and a moment of the direst confusion ensued, during which the boys of our party greatly endangered their limbs among the broken boards.

"By George!" exclaimed my son at last—in his eagerness invoking his patron saint—as he stumbled upon something, "there is something here and no mistake;" and, hastily clearing away the rubbish and clinging cobwebs, he disclosed to view what proved on examination to be an immense oaken chest, about four feet in height, heavily carved, and ornamented with brass mouldings corroded with age and damp.

Here was a piece of excitement indeed; never in my most imaginative moments had I thought of anything so mysterious as this. The most sceptical among us grew interested.

"Oh, do open it!" cried Ella, when the first exclamations of surprise were over.

"Easier to say than to do, miss," replied Sam, exerting his Herculean strength in vain. With the aid of a hammer and the kitchen-poker, however, he at last succeeded in forcing it open. We all pressed forward eagerly to peer inside. There was something in it certainly, but we none of us could determine what, until Sam, who was the boldest of us all, thrust in his hand and brought forth—something which caused the bravest to start with horror, while poor Catherine sank down, white and trembling, upon the littered floor. It was a bone, to which adhered fragments of decaying silk.

The consternation and conjectures which followed can be better imagined than described. Seeing the effects of the discovery upon Catherine, and indeed upon all, I bade Sam replace it in the chest, which George closed again, to be left until Mr. Fanshawe came home and could investigate the matter.

The rest of the day I passed in attending to Catherine, who seemed much shocked and overcome by what she had seen, and in trying to divert my guests' thoughts from the subject, and dispel the gloom which had gathered over all. In this I succeeded only partially, and never did I welcome my husband's return more gladly than on that evening.

On his arrival I would not let him be disturbed by the relation of what had happened until he had finished his dinner, and it was not till we were gathered as usual round the fire that George related the whole story to him.

When he ended the two gentlemen left the room together, in order that Mr. Fanshawe might verify by his own eyes what he would hardly believe.

They were some time gone, and on their return I noticed that my husband held in his hand an old piece of soiled parchment, with mouldy seals affixed to it.

"We certainly have discovered much more than I thought for, Catherine," said he, "and possibly more than you thought for either." Here he paused for her to reply, but she did not.

"The bones are most probably those of some animal," added he—I fancied I could detect a certain anxiety in his tone that belied what he said; "but in order to quell the active imaginations which I can see are running away with some of you"—here he looked round with a smile—"I will send for Dr. Driscoll to come and examine them to-morrow. I have also found a piece of parchment in the chest," he added; "but I have not yet looked at its contents."

"Before you do that, Mr. Fanshawe, and before you send for the surgeon," interrupted Catherine suddenly in a clear voice, "I think I can tell you all about the bones found in the chest, and how I guessed them to be there."

"I should certainly be very glad to be told," my husband admitted, much surprised; "though how you can possibly know, I cannot surmise."

"Listen, and I will tell you," answered Catherine; and feeling very glad that our curiosity was at last to be gratified, we all "pricked up our ears," as George would say, to listen.

I here transcribe Catherine's story word for word, as my son George subsequently wrote it down from her dictation.

"You all remember," she began, "my alarming you on New Year's eve at midnight, and that I told you I was disturbed by a dreadful dream.

"I said so because I thought you would make fun of me if I called it a vision; and yet it was much more like a vision, for I seemed to see it waking, and it was more vivid and consecutive than any dream I ever had.

"Before I try to describe it, I want you all to understand that I seemed intuitively to comprehend what I saw, and to recognize all the figures which appeared before me, and their relation to one another, though I am sure I never beheld them before in my life.

"When Ella left me that night, I lay propped up with pillows, staring idly at the strange shadows thrown by the hidden lamp across the laundry ceiling and over the floor. As I looked it seemed to me that a change came over the room—a most unaccountable change.

"Instead of the blocked-up window, the rusty mangle, and the daïs at the farther end, I saw the window clear and distinct from top to bottom, and in front of a deep window-seat at its base stood an oaken chest, exactly corresponding to the one discovered this morning. The room seemed brilliantly lighted, and everything was clearly and distinctly visible; and not only was it changed, but also peopled.

"Many figures passed up and down; brocaded silks swept the floor, and old world forms of men in strange costumes bowed in courtly style to the dames by their side. Among all these figures I noticed only one couple particularly, and I knew them to be bride and bridegroom. The man was tall and broad, with dark hair and eyes, and a sensual and cruel face. He seemed, however, to be quite enslaved by the woman by his side, whom I hardly even now like to think of, there was something to me so repellent in her presence.

"She was tall and of middle age, and would have been handsome were it not for a sinister expression in her dark flashing eyes, which was enhanced by the black eyebrows which met over them.

"She reminded me irresistibly of the effigy on the stone monument in Craymoor church, which Ella and I named "the wicked woman."

"As I gazed on the strange scene before me I presently became aware of three other figures which I had not noticed before. They were standing in a small arched doorway in one corner of the room (where the servants' bedroom now is) furtively watching the gay company. One was a pale, careworn woman, apparently of about five-and-thirty, still beautiful, though haggard and mournful-looking, with blue eyes and a fair complexion.

"Her hands rested on the shoulders of two children, one a boy and the other a girl, of about ten and eleven years of age respectively. They much resembled their mother, and, like her, they were meanly dressed, though no poverty of attire could hide the nobility of their aspect. I noticed that the mother's eyes rested chiefly on the face of the tall stately man before mentioned, who seemed unaware or careless of her presence; and instinctively I knew him to be the father of her children and the blighter of her life.

"As I looked and beheld all this, the lights vanished, the company disappeared, and the room became dark and deserted. No, not quite deserted, for I presently distinguished, seated on the window-seat by the old oaken chest, the fair woman and her children again.

"The moonlight now streamed through the window upon the woman's face, making it appear more ghastly and haggard than before. In her long thin fingers she was holding up to the light a necklace of large pearls, curiously interwoven in a diamond pattern, and on this the children's eyes were fixed.

"She then hung it on the girl's fair neck, who hid it in her bosom. Both children then twined their arms round their mother and kissed her repeatedly, while her head sank lower and lower, and the paleness of death overspread her features.

"This scene faded away as the other had done, and I saw the fair woman no more.

"Then it seemed to me that many figures passed and repassed before the window—the wicked woman (as I shall call her to distinguish her), accompanied by a boy the image of herself, whom I knew to be her son. He was apparently older than the fair-haired children, who also passed to and fro, attired as servants, and generally employed in some menial work.

"At last the wicked woman's son, with haughty gestures, ordered the other boy to pick up something that lay on the ground, and when he refused, he raised his cane as though to strike him. Before he could do so, however, the boy flew at him, and they engaged in a fierce struggle.

"In the midst of this the wicked woman, whom I had learned to dread, came forward and separated them; after which she pointed imperiously to the door, and signed to the younger boy to go out.

"He obeyed her mandate, but first threw his arms round his sister in a last embrace, and she detached the pearl necklace from off her neck and gave it to him. He then went out, waving a last adieu to her, and I saw him no more.

"Confused images seemed to crowd before me after this, and I remember nothing clearly until I beheld an infirm and tottering figure led away through the arched doorway, in whom I recognized the tall and stately man I had first seen in company with the wicked woman, but who was now an old man, apparently being supported to his bed to die. As he passed out he laid one trembling hand upon the head of the fair girl, now a blooming woman, and a softer shade came over his face. This the wicked woman noted, and she marked her disapproval by a vindictive frown.

"She also was older-looking, but age had in no degree softened her features; on the contrary, they appeared to me to wear a harsher expression than before.

"In the next scene which came before me, the wicked woman's son was evidently making love to the girl. Both were standing by the old window-seat, but her face was resolutely turned away from him, and when she at last looked at him it was with an expression of uncontrollable horror and dislike.

"Again this scene changed as those before it had done; the young man was gone, and only the light of a grated lantern illumined the room, or rather made darkness visible. The wicked woman was the only occupant of the laundry; she was kneeling by the oaken chest, trying to raise the heavy lid. In her left hand she held a piece of parchment, with large red seals pendent from it. I knew it to be the old man's will which she was hiding, thus defrauding the just claimants of their rights.

"Her hands trembled, and her whole appearance denoted guilty trepidation. At length, however, the lid was raised, but just as she was about to replace the parchment in the chest, a figure glided silently from a dark corner of the window-seat and confronted her. It was the fair girl, pale, resolute, and extending her hand to claim the will.

"After the first guilty start, which caused her to drop the parchment into the chest, the wicked woman hurriedly tried to close the lid. Her efforts were frustrated, however, by the girl, who leaned with all her force upon it, keeping it back, and still held out her hand as before.

"There followed a pause, which seemed to me very long, but which could in reality have only lasted a minute.

"It was broken by the wicked woman, who, hastily casting a glance behind her into the gloom of the darkened chamber, then seized the girl by the arm and dragged her with all her force into the chest. It was but the work of a moment, for the woman was much the more powerful of the two, and the poor victim was too much taken by surprise to make much resistance. I saw one despairing look in her face as her murderess flashed the lantern before it with a hideous gleam of triumph.

"Then the lid was pressed down upon her, and I saw no more, only I felt an unutterable terror, and tried in vain to scream.

"This was not all the vision, however, for before I had mastered my terror the scene was superseded by another.

"This time it was twilight, and the wicked woman and her son were together. The son seemed to be talking eagerly, and grew more and more excited, while the mother stood still and erect, with a malicious smile upon her lips. Presently she moved toward the chest with a fell purpose in her eyes, unlocked it with a key which hung from her girdle, raised the lid and disclosed the contents.

"I understood it all now: the son was asking for the girl whom he had loved, and whom on his return home he missed, and the wicked woman, enraged at hearing for the first time that he had loved her, was determined to have her revenge.

"He should see her again.

"On beholding the dread contents of the chest, the man staggered back horrified; then, doubtless comprehending the case, he turned suddenly upon the murderess, and threw his arm around her, and there ensued a struggle terrible to witness.

"Her proud triumphant glance of malice was now succeeded by one of abject fear, and, as his strength began to gain the mastery, of despair.

"His iron frame heaved for a moment with the violence of his efforts, the next he had forced her down into the chest upon the mouldering body of her victim. I saw her eyes light up with the terror of death for one second, and then her screams were stifled forever beneath the massive lid.

"The horror of this scene was too much for me; I found voice to scream at last, and I suppose it was my cry which alarmed you all."

When Catherine ceased speaking there was a profound silence for a minute, which Mr. Fanshawe was the first to break as he said with a peculiar intonation in his voice, "It is very strange, very unaccountable," reëchoing all our thoughts.

Now it happened that Mr. Fleet, our family lawyer, was among our guests that Christmas-time, and since the discovery of the chest and bones had taken a great interest in the whole affair. He now questioned and cross-questioned Catherine, and seemed quite satisfied with the result.

"This would have made a fine case," said he, "if only it had been a question of the right of succession, for any lawyer to make out; but unfortunately the events are too long past to have any bearing upon the present." (There Mr. Fleet was wrong, though we none of us knew it at the time.)

We now all launched forth into conjectures and opinions, during which Catherine lay still and weary upon the sofa. I saw this, and thought it quite time to put an end to the day's adventures by suggesting a retirement for the night, and we were soon all dispersed to dream of the mysterious vision and discovery.

I think we were none of us sorry when morning dawned without any further tragedy (by *us*, I mean the female part of the establishment).

When I came down to breakfast I found Mr. Fleet very active on the subject of the night before.

"A surgeon ought to be immediately sent for to pronounce an opinion on the contents of the chest," he said; and Dr. Driscoll presently came, and after examining the bones minutely, decided that they were, as we thought, those of two females, who might have been from one to two hundred years dead.

Mr. Fleet next offered to decipher the will, for such he imagined the parchment to be, and he and Mr. Fanshawe were closeted together for some time.

When they at last appeared again, they looked much interested and excited, and led me away to inform me of the result of their examination.

They told me that the document had proved to be a will, but that there was a circumstance connected with it which greatly added to the mystery of the whole business. This was the mention of the name of L'Estrange. I was, of course, as much surprised as they, and heard the will read with great interest.

I cannot remember the technical terms in which it was expressed. Mr. Fleet read me the translation he had made, for the original was in old English; but it was to this effect:

It purported to be the will of Reginald, Viscount St. Aubyn, in which he bequeathed all his inheritance to his lawful son Francis St. Aubyn—commonly known by the name of Francis l'Estrange—and to his heirs forever. It was signed Reginald, Viscount St. Aubyn, and the witnesses were John Murray and Phœbe Brett, who in the old copy had each affixed their mark.

Mr. Fleet affirmed that it was a perfectly legal document, but this was not all it contained.

There was an appendix which our lawyer translated as follows:

"In order to avoid all disputes and doubts which might otherwise arise, I do hereby declare that my lawful wife was Editha, youngest daughter of Francis l'Estrange, Baronet, and that the register of our marriage may be seen in the church of St. Andrew, Haslet. By this marriage we had two children, a son Francis, and a daughter Catherine, commonly called Francis and Catherine l'Estrange. And I hereby declare that Agatha Thornhaugh was not legally married to me as she imagined, my lawful wife being alive at the time; neither do I leave to her son by her first husband, Ralph Thornhaugh, any part or share in my inheritance."

Both the will and the writing at the foot of it were dated the 14th of May, 1668.

This accumulation of mysteries caused me for a time to feel quite bewildered and unable to think, but Mr. Fleet was in his element.

"Here is a case worth entering into," said he, and he further went on to state that he had no doubt that the L'Estranges mentioned in the will were our Catherine's ancestors, the Christian names being similar rendering it more than probable. She was most likely a direct descendant of Francis l'Estrange, the heir mentioned in the will, who was no doubt also the fair-haired boy Catherine had seen in her vision.

The bones were those of his sister, the murdered Catherine l'Estrange, and of her murderess Agatha Thornhaugh, herself immured by her own son; but the matter ought not to rest on mere surmise, and the first place to go to for corroborating evidence was Craymoor church.

The rapidity with which Mr. Fleet came to his conclusions increased my bewilderment, and I was at a loss to know what evidence he expected to gain from Craymoor church. He reminded me, however, of Catherine's statement that "the wicked woman" of her vision resembled the effigy on the monument there.

Thither, then, the lawyer repaired, accompanied by Mr. Fanshawe and George. It was thought best to keep the sequel of the story from Catherine and the others until it was explained more fully, as Mr. Fleet boldly affirmed it should be. I awaited anxiously the result of their researches, and they exceeded I think even our good investigator's hopes.

Not only had they deciphered the inscription round the old monument, but with leave from the clergyman and the assistance of the sexton they had disinterred the coffin and found it to be filled with stones.

I am aware that this was rather an illegal proceeding, but as Mr. Fleet was only acting *en amateur* and not professionally, he did not stick at trifles.

The inscription was in Latin, and stated that the tomb was erected in memory of Agatha, wife of Reginald, Viscount St. Aubyn, who was buried beneath, and who died on the 31st day of December, 1649—exactly two hundred years before the day on which Catherine had seen the vision.

I could not help thinking it shocking that the villagers had for two centuries been worshipping in the presence of a perpetual lie, but Mr. Fleet thought only of the grand corroboration of his "case." He applied to Mr. Fanshawe to take the next step, namely, to write to Catherine's aunt and only living relative, to tell her the whole story, and beg her to assist in elucidating matters by giving all the information she could respecting the L'Estrange family.

This was done, and we anxiously awaited the answer. Meantime, all my guests were clamorous to hear the contents of the will, and I had to appease them as best I could, by promising that they should know all soon.

In a few days, old Miss l'Estrange's answer came. She said her brother, father, and grandfather had all served in India, and that she believed her great-grandfather, who was a Francis l'Estrange, to have passed most of his life abroad, there having been a cloud over his early youth. What this was, however, she could not say. She affirmed that the L'Estranges had in old times resided in ——shire; and she further stated that her father's family had consisted of herself and her brother, whose only child Catherine was.

This was certainly not much information, but it was enough for our purpose. We no longer remained in doubt as to the truth of Mr. Fleet's version of the story, and when he himself told it to all our family-party one evening, every one agreed that he had certainly succeeded in making out a very clever case.

As for Catherine, on being told that the figures she had beheld in the vision were thought to be those of her ancestors, she was not so much surprised as I expected, but said that she had had a presentiment all along that the tragedies she had witnessed were in some way connected with her own family.

I must not forget to say that on ascertaining that the parish church of Haslet was still standing, we searched the register, and another link of evidence was made clear by the finding of the looked-for entry.

There remains little more to be told. The charge of the old will was committed to Mr. Fleet, and Catherine's story has been carefully laid up among the archives of our family. I say advisedly of *our* family, for the line of the L'Estranges, alias St. Aubyns, has been united to ours by the marriage of Catherine to my son George, which took place in 1850.

I who write this am an old woman now, but I still live with my son and daughter-in-law.

George has bought Craymoor Grange, thus rendering justice after the lapse of two centuries, and restoring the inheritance of her fathers to the rightful owner.

I have but one more incident to relate, and I have done. A short time ago, old Miss l'Estrange died, bequeathing all her worldly possessions to Catherine. Among these were some old family relics. Catherine was looking over them as George unpacked them, and she presently came to a miniature of a young and beautiful girl with fair hair and blue eyes, and a wistful expression, and with it a necklace of pearls strung in a diamond pattern. On seeing these she became suddenly grave, and handing them to me, said: "They are the same; the young girl, and the pearl necklace I told you of." No more was said at the time, for the children were present, and we had always avoided alluding to the horrible family tragedy before them; but if we had still retained any doubt about its truth—which we had not—this would have set it at rest.

If you were to visit Craymoor Grange now, you would find no old laundry. The part of the house containing it has been pulled down, and children play and chickens peckett on the ground where it once stood.

The oaken chest has also long since been destroyed.

HAUNTED.

SOME few years ago one of those great national conventions which draw together all ages and conditions of the sovereign people of America was held in Charleston, South Carolina.

Colonel Demarion, one of the State Representatives, had attended that great national convention; and, after an exciting week, was returning home, having a long and difficult journey before him.

A pair of magnificent horses, attached to a light buggy, flew merrily enough over a rough-country for a while; but toward evening stormy weather reduced the roads to a dangerous condition, and compelled the Colonel to relinquish his purpose of reaching home that night, and to stop at a small wayside tavern, whose interior, illuminated by blazing wood-fires, spread a glowing halo among the dripping trees as he approached it, and gave promise of warmth and shelter at least.

Drawing up to this modest dwelling, Colonel Demarion saw through its uncurtained windows that there was no lack of company within. Beneath the trees, too, an entanglement of rustic vehicles, giving forth red gleams from every dripping angle, told him that beasts as well as men were cared for. At the open door appeared the form of a man, who, at the sound of wheels, but not seeing in the outside darkness whom he addressed, called out, "'Tain't no earthly use a-stoppin' here."

Caring more for his chattels than for himself, the Colonel paid no further regard to this address than to call loudly for the landlord.

At the tone of authority, the man in outline more civilly announced himself to be the host; yet so far from inviting the traveller to alight, insisted that the house was "as full as it could pack;" but that there was a place a little farther down the road where the gentleman would be certain to find excellent accommodation.

"What stables have you here?" demanded the traveller, giving no more heed to this than to the former announcement; but bidding his servant to alight, and preparing to do so himself.

"Stables!" repeated the baffled host, shading his eyes so as to scrutinize the newcomer, "*stables*, Cap'n?"

"Yes, *stables*. I want you to take care of my horses; *I* can take care of myself. Some shelter for cattle you must have by the look of these traps," pointing to the wagons. "I don't want my horses to be kept standing out in this storm, you know."

"No, Major. Why no, cert'n'y; Marion's ain't over a mile, and——"

"Conf—!" muttered the Colonel; "but it's over the *river*, which I don't intend to ford to-night under any consideration."

So saying, the Colonel leaped to the ground, directing his servant to cover the horses and then get out his valise; while the host, thus defeated, assumed the best grace he could to say that he would see what could be done "for the *horses*."

"I am a soldier, my man," added the Colonel in a milder tone, as he stamped his cold feet on the porch and shook off the rain from his travelling-gear; "I am used to rough fare and a hard couch: all we want is shelter. A corner of the floor will suffice for me and my rug; a private room I can dispense with at such times as these."

The landlord seemed no less relieved at this assurance than mollified by the explanation of a traveller whom he now saw was of a very different stamp from those who usually frequented the tavern. "For the matter of *stables*, his were newly put up, and first-rate," he said; and "cert'n'y the Gen'ral was welcome to a seat by the fire while 'twas a-storming so fierce."

Colonel Demarion gave orders to his servant regarding the horses, while the landlord, kicking at what seemed to be a bundle of sacking down behind the door, shouted—"Jo! Ho, Jo! Wake up, you sleepy-headed nigger! Be alive, boy, and show this gentleman's horses to the stables." Upon a repetition of which charges a tall, gaunt, dusky figure lifted itself from out of the dark corner, and grew taller and more gaunt as it stretched itself into waking with a grin which was the most visible part of it, by reason of two long rows of ivory gleaming in the red glare. The hard words had fallen as harmless on Jo's ear-drum as the kicks upon his impassive frame. To do Jo's master justice, the kicks were not vicious kicks, and the rough language was but an intimation that dispatch was needed. Very much of the spaniel's nature had Jo; and as he rolled along the passage to fetch a lantern, his mouth expanded into a still broader grin at the honor of attending so stately a gentleman. Quick, like his master, too, was Jo to discriminate between "real gentlefolks" and the "white trash" whose rough-coated, rope-harnessed mules were the general occupants of his stables.

"Splendid pair, sir," said the now conciliating landlord. "Shove some o' them mules out into the shed, Jo (which your horses 'll feel more to hum in my new stalls, Gen'ral)."

Again cautioning his man Plato not to leave them one moment, Colonel Demarion turned to enter the house.

"You'll find a rough crowd in here, sir," said the host, as he paused on the threshold; "but a good fire, anyhow. 'Tain't many of these loafers as understand this convention business—I *pre*sume, Gen'ral, you've attended the convention—they all on 'em *thinks* they does, tho'. Fact most on 'em thinks they'd orter be on the committee theirselves. Good many on 'em is from Char'ston to-day, but is in the same fix as yerself, Gen'ral—can't get across the river to-night."

"I see, I see," cried the statesman, with a gesture toward the sitting-room. "Now what have you got in your larder, Mr. Landlord? and send some supper out to my servant; he must make a bed of the carriage-mats to-night."

The landlord introduced his guest into a room filled chiefly with that shiftless and noxious element of Southern society known as "mean whites." Pipes and drinks, and excited arguments, engaged these people as they stood or sat in groups. The host addressed those who were gathered round the log-fire, and they opened a way for the new-comer, some few, with republican freedom, inviting him to be seated, the rest giving one furtive glance, and then, in antipathy born of envy, skulking away.

The furniture of this comfortless apartment consisted of sloppy, much-jagged deal tables, dirty whittled benches, and a few uncouth chairs. The walls were dirty with accumulated tobacco stains, and so moist and filthy was the floor, that the sound only of scraping seats and heavy footsteps told that it was of boards and not bare earth.

Seated with his back toward the majority of the crowd, and shielded by his newspaper, Colonel Demarion sat awhile unobserved; but was presently recognized by a man from his own immediate neighborhood, when the information was quickly whispered about that no less a person than their distinguished Congressman was among them.

This piece of news speedily found its way to the ears of the landlord, to whom Colonel Demarion was known by name only, and forthwith he reappeared to overwhelm the representative of his State with apologies for the uncourteous reception which had been given him, and to express his now very sincere regrets that the house offered no suitable accommodation for the gentleman. Satisfied as to the safety of his chattels, the Colonel generously dismissed the idea of having anything either to resent or to forgive; and assured the worthy host that he would accept of no exclusive indulgences.

In spite of which the landlord bustled about to bring in a separate table, on which he spread a clean coarse cloth, and a savory supper of broiled ham, hot corncakes, and coffee; every few minutes stopping to renew his apologies, and even appearing to grow confidentially communicative regarding his domestic economies; until the hungry traveller cut him short with "Don't say another word about it, my friend; you have not a spare sleeping-room, and that is enough. Find me a corner—a clean corner"—looking round upon the most unclean corners of that room—"perhaps up-stairs somewhere, and——"

"Ah! *upsta'rs*, Gen'ral. Now, that's jest what I had in my mind to ax you. Fact is ther' *is* a spar' room upsta'rs, as comfortable a room as the best of folks can wish; but——"

"But it's crammed with sleeping folks, so there's an end of it," cried the senator, thoroughly bored.

"No, sir, ain't no person in it; and ther' ain't no person likely to be in it 'cept 'tis *yerself*, Colonel Demarion. Leastways——"

After a good deal of hesitation and embarrassment, the host, in mysterious whispers, imparted the startling fact that this most desirable sleeping room was *haunted*; that the injury he had sustained in consequence had compelled him to fasten it up altogether; that he had come to be very suspicious of admitting strangers, and had limited his custom of late to what the bar could supply, keeping the matter hushed up in the hope that it might be the sooner forgotten by the neighbors; but that in the case of Colonel Demarion he had now made bold to mention it; "as I can't but think, sir," he urged, "you'd find it prefer'ble to sleepin' on the floor or sittin' up all night along ov these loafers. Fer if 'tis any deceivin' trick got up in the house, maybe they won't try it on, sir, to a gentleman of your reputation."

Colonel Demarion became interested in the landlord's confidences, but could only gather in further explanation that for some time past all travellers who had occupied that room had "made off in the middle of the night, never showin' their faces at the inn again;" that on endeavoring to arrest one or more in their nocturnal flight, they—all more or less terrified—had insisted on escaping without a moment's delay, assigning no other reason than that they had seen a ghost. "Not that folks seem to get much harm by it, Colonel—not by the way they makes off without paying a cent of money!"

Great indeed was the satisfaction evinced by the victim of unpaid bills on the Colonel's declaring that the haunted chamber was the very room for him. "If to be turned out of my bed at midnight is all I have to fear, we will see who comes off master in my case. So, Mr. Landlord, let the chamber be got ready directly, and have a good fire built there at once."

The exultant host hurried away to confide the great news to Jo, and with him to make the necessary preparations. "Come what will, Jo, Colonel Demarion ain't the man to make off without paying down good money for his accommodations."

In reasonable time, Colonel Demarion was beckoned out of the public room, and conducted up-stairs by the landlord, who, after receiving a cheerful "good-night," paused on the landing to hear his guest bolt and bar the door within, and then push a piece of furniture against it. "Ah," murmured the host, as a sort of misgiving came over him, "if a apparishum has a mind to come thar, 'tain't all the bolts and bars in South Carolina as 'll kip'en away."

But the Colonel's precaution of securing his door, as also that of placing his revolvers in readiness, had not the slightest reference to the reputed ghost. Spiritual disturbances of such kind he feared not. Spirits *tangible* were already producing ominous demonstrations in the rooms below, nor was it possible to conjecture what troubles these might evolve. Glad enough to escape from the noisy company, he took a survey of his evil-reputed chamber. The only light was that of the roaring, crackling, blazing wood-fire, and no other was needed. And what storm-benighted traveller, when fierce winds and rains are lashing around his lodging, can withstand the cheering influences of a glorious log-fire? especially if, as in that wooden tenement, that fire be of abundant pine-knots. It rivals the glare of gas and the glow of a furnace; it charms away the mustiness and fustiness of years, and causes all that is dull and dead around to laugh and dance in its bright light.

By the illumination of just such a fire, Colonel Demarion observed that the apartment offered nothing worthier of remark than that the furniture was superior to anything that might be expected in a small wayside tavern. In truth, the landlord had expended a considerable sum in fitting up this, his finest chamber, and had therefore sufficient reason to bemoan its unprofitableness.

Having satisfied himself as to his apparent security, the senator thought no more of spirits palpable or impalpable; but to the far graver issues of the convention his thoughts reverted. It was yet early; he lighted a cigar, and in full appreciation of his retirement, took out his note-book and plunged into the affairs of state. Now and then he was recalled to the circumstances of his situation by the swaggering tread of unsteady feet about the house, or when the boisterous shouts below raged above the outside storm; but even then he only glanced up from his papers to congratulate himself upon his agreeable seclusion.

Thus he sat for above an hour, then he heaped fresh logs upon the hearth, looked again to his revolvers, and retired to rest.

The house-clock was striking twelve as the Colonel awoke. He awoke suddenly from a sound sleep, flashing, as it were, into full consciousness, his mind and memory clear, all his faculties invigorated, his ideas undisturbed, but with a perfect conviction that he was not alone.

He lifted his head. A man was standing a few feet from the bed, and between it and the fire, which was still burning, and burning brightly enough to display every object in the room, and to define the outline of the intruder clearly. His dress also and his features were plainly distinguishable: the dress was a travelling-costume, in fashion somewhat out of date; the features wore a mournful and distressed expression—the eyes were fixed upon the Colonel. The right arm hung down, and the hand, partially concealed, might, for aught the Colonel knew, be grasping one of his own revolvers; the left arm was folded against the waist. The man seemed about to advance still closer to the bed, and returned the occupant's gaze with a fixed stare.

"Stand, or I'll fire!" cried the Colonel, taking in all this at a glance, and starting up in his bed, revolver in hand.

The man remained still.

"What is your business here?" demanded the statesman, thinking he was addressing one of the roughs from below.

The man was silent.

"Leave this room, if you value your life," shouted the indignant soldier, pointing his revolver.

The man was motionless.

"RETIRE! or by heaven I'll send a bullet through you!"

But the man moved not an inch.

The Colonel fired. The bullet lodged in the breast of the stranger, but he started not. The soldier leaped to the floor and fired again. The shot entered the heart, pierced the body, and lodged in the wall beyond; and the Colonel beheld the hole where the bullet had entered, and the firelight glimmering through it. And yet the intruder stirred not. Astounded, the Colonel dropped his revolver, and stood face to face before the unmoved man.

"Colonel Demarion," spake the deep solemn voice of the perforated stranger, "in vain you shoot me—I am dead already."

The soldier, with all his bravery, gasped, spellbound. The firelight gleamed through the hole in the body, and the eyes of the shooter were riveted there.

"Fear nothing," spake the mournful presence; "I seek but to divulge my wrongs. Until my death shall be avenged my unquiet spirit lingers here. Listen."

Speechless, motionless was the statesman; and the mournful apparition thus slowly and distinctly continued:

"Four years ago I travelled with one I trusted. We lodged here. That night my comrade murdered me. He plunged a dagger into my heart while I slept. He covered the wound with a plaster. He feigned to mourn my death. He told the people here I had died of heart complaint; that I had long been ailing. I had gold and treasures. With my treasure secreted beneath his garments he paraded mock grief at my grave. Then he departed. In distant parts he sought to forget his crime; but his stolen gold brought him only the curse of an evil conscience. Rest and peace are not for him. He now prepares to leave his native land forever. Under an assumed name that man is this night in Charleston. In a few hours he will sail for Europe. Colonel Demarion, you must prevent it. Justice and humanity demand that a murderer roam not at large, nor squander more of the wealth that is by right my children's."

The spirit paused. To the extraordinary revelation the Colonel had listened in rapt astonishment. He gazed at the presence, at the firelight glimmering through it—through the very place where a human heart would be—and he felt that he was indeed in the presence of a supernatural being. He thought of the landlord's story; but while earnestly desiring to sift the truth of the mystery, words refused to come to his aid.

"Do you hesitate?" said the mournful spirit. "Will *you* also flee, when my orphan children cry for retribution?" Seeming to anticipate the will of the Colonel, "I await your promise, senator," he said. "There is no time to lose."

With a mighty effort, the South Carolinian said, "I promise. What would you have me do?"

In the same terse, solemn manner, the ghostly visitor gave the real and assumed names of the murderer, described his person and dress at the present time, described a certain curious ring he was then wearing, together with other distinguishing characteristics: all being carefully noted down by Colonel Demarion, who, by degrees, recovered his self-possession, and pledged himself to use every endeavor to bring the murderer to justice.

Then, with a portentous wave of the hand, "It is well," said the apparition. "Not until the spirit of my murderer shall be separated from the mortal clay can *my* spirit rest in peace." And vanished.

Half-past six in the morning was the appointed time for the steamer to leave Charleston; and the Colonel lost not a moment in preparing to depart. As he hurried down the stairs he encountered the landlord, who—his eyes rolling in terror—made an attempt to speak. Unheeding, except to demand his carriage, the Colonel pushed past him, and effected a quick escape toward the back premises, shouting lustily for "Jo" and "Plato," and for his carriage to be got ready immediately. A few minutes more, and the bewildered host was recalled to the terrible truth by the noise of the carriage dashing through the yard and away down the road; and it was some miles nearer Charleston before the unfortunate man ceased to peer after it in the darkness—as if by so doing he could recover damages—and bemoan to Jo the utter ruin of his house and hopes.

Thirty miles of hard driving had to be accomplished in little more than five hours. No great achievement under favorable circumstances; but the horses were only half refreshed from their yesterday's journey, and though the storm was over, the roads were in a worse condition than ever.

Colonel Demarion resolved to be true to his promise; and fired by a curiosity to investigate the extraordinary communication which had been revealed to him, urged on his horses, and reached the wharf at Charleston just as the steamer was being loosed from her moorings.

He hailed her. "Stop her! Business with the captain! STOP HER!"

Her machinery was already in motion; her iron lungs were puffing forth dense clouds of smoke and steam; and as the Colonel shouted—the crowd around, from sheer delight in shouting, echoing his "Stop her! stop her!"—the voices on land were confounded with the voices of the sailors, the rattling of chains, and the haulings of ropes.

Among the passengers standing to wave farewells to their friends on the wharf were some who recognised Colonel Demarion, and drew the captain's attention toward him; and as he continued vehemently to gesticulate, that officer, from his post of observation, demanded the nature of the business which should require the ship's detention. Already the steamer was clear of the wharf. In another minute she might be beyond reach of the voice; therefore, failing by gestures and entreaties to convince the captain of the importance of his errand, Colonel Demarion, in desperation, cried at the top of his voice, "A murderer on board! For God's sake, STOP!" He wished to have made this startling declaration in private, but not a moment was to be lost; and the excitement around him was intense.

In the midst of the confusion another cry of "Man overboard!" might have been heard in a distant part of the ship, had not the attention of the crowd been fastened on the Colonel. Such a cry was, however, uttered, offering a still more urgent motive for stopping; and the steamer being again made fast, Colonel Demarion was received on board.

"Let not a soul leave the vessel!" was his first and prompt suggestion; and the order being issued he drew the captain aside, and concisely explained his grave commission. The captain thereupon conducted him to his private room, and summoned the steward, before whom the details were given, and the description of the murderer was read over. The steward, after considering attentively, seemed inclined to associate the description with that of a passenger whose remarkably dejected appearance had already attracted his observation. In such a grave business it was, however, necessary to proceed with the utmost caution, and the "passenger-book" was produced. Upon reference to its pages, the three gentlemen were totally dismayed by the discovery that the name of this same dejected individual was that under which, according to the apparition, the murderer had engaged his passage.

"I am here to charge that man with murder," said Colonel Demarion. "He must be arrested."

Horrified as the captain was at this astounding declaration, yet, on account of the singular and unusual mode by which the Colonel had become possessed of the facts, and the impossibility of proving the charge, he hesitated in consenting to the arrest of a passenger. The steward proposed that they should repair to the saloons and deck, and while conversing with one or another of the passengers, mention—as it were casually—in the hearing of the suspected party his own proper name, and observe the effect produced on him. To this they agreed, and without loss of time joined the passengers, assigning some feasible cause for a short delay of the ship.

The saloon was nearly empty, and while the steward went below, the other two repaired to the deck, where they observed a crowd gathered seaward, apparently watching something over the ship's side.

During the few minutes which had detained the captain in this necessarily hurried business, a boat had been lowered, and some sailors had put off in her to rescue the person who was supposed to have fallen overboard; and it was only now, on joining the crowd, that the captain learned the particulars of the accident. "Who was it?" "What was he like?" they exclaimed simultaneously. That a man had fallen overboard was all that could be ascertained. Some one had seen him run across the deck, looking wildly about him. A splash in the water had soon afterward attracted attention to the spot, and a body had since been seen struggling on the surface. The waves were rough after the storm, and thick with seaweed, and the sailors had as yet missed the body. The two gentlemen took their post among the watchers, and kept their eyes intently upon the waves, and upon the sailors battling against them. Ere long they see the body rise again to the surface. Floated on a powerful wave, they can for the few moments breathlessly scrutinize it. The color of the dress is observed. A face of agony upturned displays a peculiar contour of forehead; the hair, the beard; and now he struggles—an arm is thrown up, and a remarkable ring catches the Colonel's eye. "Great heavens! The whole description tallies!" The sailors pull hard for the spot, the next stroke and they will rescue——

A monster shark is quicker than they. The sea is tinged with blood. The man is no more!

Shocked and silent, Colonel Demarion and the captain quitted the deck and re-summoned the steward, who had, but without success, visited the berths and various parts of the ship for the individual in question. Every hole and corner was now, by the captain's order carefully searched, but in vain; and as no further information concerning the missing party could be obtained, and the steward persisted in his statement regarding his general appearance, they proceeded to examine his effects. In these he was identified beyond a doubt. Papers and relics proved not only his guilt but his remorse; remorse which, as the apparition had said, permitted him no peace in his wanderings.

Those startling words, "A murderer on board!" had doubtless struck fresh terror to his heart and, unable to face the accusation, he had thus terminated his wretched existence.

Colonel Demarion revisited the little tavern, and on several occasions occupied the haunted chamber; but never again had he the honor of receiving a midnight commission from a ghostly visitor, and never again had the landlord to bemoan the flight of a non-paying customer.

PICHON & SONS, OF THE CROIX ROUSSE.

GIRAUDIER, *pharmacien, première classe*, is the legend, recorded in huge, ill-proportioned letters, which directs the attention of the stranger to the most prosperous-looking shop in the grand *place* of La Croix Rousse, a well-known suburb of the beautiful city of Lyons, which has its share of the shabby gentility and poor pretence common to the suburban commerce of great towns.

Giraudier is not only *pharmacien* but *propriétaire*, though not by inheritance; his possession of one of the prettiest and most prolific of the small vineyards in the beautiful suburb, and a charming inconvenient house, with low ceilings, liliputian bedrooms, and a profusion of *persiennes*, *jalousies*, and *contrevents*, comes by purchase. This enviable little *terre* was sold by the Nation, when that terrible abstraction transacted the public business of France; and it was bought very cheaply by the strong-minded father of the Giraudier of the present, who was not disturbed by the evil reputation which the place had gained, at a time the peasants of France, having been bullied into a renunciation of religion, eagerly cherished superstition. The Giraudier of the present cherishes the particular superstition in question affectionately; it reminds him of an uncommonly good bargain made in his favor, which is always a pleasant association of ideas, especially to a Frenchman, still more especially to a Lyonnais; and it attracts strangers to his *pharmacie*, and leads to transactions in *Grand Chartreuse* and *Créme de Roses*, ensuing naturally on the narration of the history of Pichon & Sons. Giraudier is not of aristocratic principles and sympathies; on the contrary, he has decided republican leanings, and considers *Le Progrès* a masterpiece of journalistic literature; but, as he says simply and strongly, "it is not because a man is a marquis that one is not to keep faith with him; a bad action is not good because it harms a good-for-nothing of a noble; the more when that good-for-nothing is no longer a noble, but *pour rire*." At the easy price of acquiescence in these sentiments, the stranger hears one of the most authentic, best-remembered, most popular of the many traditions of the bad old times "before General Bonaparte," as Giraudier, who has no sympathy with any later designation of *le grand homme*, calls the Emperor, whose statue one can perceive—a speck in the distance—from the threshold of the *pharmacie*.

The Marquis de Sénanges, in the days of the triumph of the great Revolution, was fortunate enough to be out of France, and wise enough to remain away from that country, though he persisted, long after the old *régime* was as dead as the Ptolemies, in believing it merely suspended, and the Revolution a lamentable accident of vulgar complexion, but happily temporary duration. The Marquis de Sénanges, who affected the *style régence*, and was the politest of infidels and the most refined of voluptuaries, got on indifferently in inappreciative foreign parts; but the members of his family—his brother and sisters, two of whom were guillotined, while the third escaped to Savoy and found refuge there in a convent of her order—got on exceedingly ill in France. If the *ci-devant* Marquis had had plenty of money to expend in such feeble imitations of his accustomed pleasures as were to be had out of Paris, he would not have been much affected by the fate of his relatives. But money became exceedingly scarce; the Marquis had actually beheld many of his peers reduced to the necessity of earning the despicable but indispensable article after many ludicrous fashions. And the duration of this absurd upsetting of law, order, privilege, and property began to assume unexpected and very unpleasant proportions.

The Château de Sénanges, with its surrounding lands, was confiscated to the Nation, during the third year of the "emigration" of the Marquis de Sénanges; and the greater part of the estate was purchased by a thrifty, industrious, and rich *avocat*, named Prosper Alix, a widower with an only daughter. Prosper Alix enjoyed the esteem of the entire neighborhood. First, he was rich; secondly, he was of a taciturn disposition, and of a neutral tint in politics. He had done well under the old *régime* and, he was doing well under the new—thank God, or the Supreme Being, or the First Cause, or the goddess Reason herself, for all;—he would have invoked Dagon, Moloch, or Kali, quite as readily as the Saints and the Madonna, who has gone so utterly out of fashion of late. Nobody was afraid to speak out before Prosper Alix; he was not a spy; and though a cold-hearted man, except in the instance of his only daughter, he never harmed anybody.

Very likely it was because he was the last person in the vicinity whom anybody would have suspected of being applied to by the dispossessed family, that the son of the Marquis' brother, a young man of promise, of courage, of intellect, and of morals of decidedly a higher calibre than those actually and traditionally imputed to the family, sought the aid of the new possessor of the Château de Sénanges, which had changed its old title for that of the Maison Alix. The father of M. Paul de Sénanges had perished in the September massacres; his mother had been guillotined at Lyons; and he—who had been saved by the interposition of a young comrade, whose father had, in the wonderful rotations of the wheel of Fate, acquired authority in the place where he had once esteemed the notice of the nephew of the Marquis a crowning honor for his son—had passed through the common vicissitudes of that dreadful time, which would take a volume for their recital in each individual instance.

Paul de Sénanges was a handsome young fellow, frank, high-spirited, and of a brisk and happy temperament; which, however, modified by the many misfortunes he had undergone, was not permanently changed. He had plenty of capacity for enjoyment in him still; and as his position was very isolated, and his mind had become enlightened on social and political matters to an extent in which the men of his family would have discovered utter degradation and the women diabolical possession, he would not have been very unhappy if, under the new condition of things, he could have lived in his native country and gained an honest livelihood. But he could not do that, he was too thoroughly "suspect;" the antecedents of his family were too powerful against him: his only chance would have been to have gone into the popular camp as an extreme, violent partisan, to have out-Heroded the revolutionary Herods; and that Paul de Sénanges was too honest to do. So he was reduced to being thankful that he had escaped with his life, and to watching for an opportunity of leaving France and gaining some country where the reign of liberty, fraternity, and equality was not quite so oppressive.

The long-looked-for opportunity at length offered itself, and Paul de Sénanges was instructed by his uncle the Marquis that he must contrive to reach Marseilles, whence he should be transported to Spain—in which country the illustrious emigrant was then residing—by a certain named date. His uncle's communication arrived safely, and the plan proposed seemed a secure and eligible one. Only in two respects was it calculated to make Paul de Sénanges thoughtful. The first was, that his uncle should take any interest in the matter of his safety; the second, what could be the nature of a certain deposit which the Marquis's letter directed him to procure, if possible, from the Château de Sénanges. The fact of this injunction explained, in some measure, the first of the two difficulties. It was plain that whatever were the contents of this packet which he was to seek for, according to the indications marked on a ground-plan drawn by his uncle and enclosed in the letter, the Marquis wanted them, and could not procure them except by the agency of his nephew. That the Marquis should venture to direct Paul de Sénanges to put himself in communication with Prosper Alix, would have been surprising to any one acquainted only with the external and generally understood features of the character of the new proprietor of the Château de Sénanges. But a few people knew Prosper Alix thoroughly, and the Marquis was one of the number; he was keen enough to know in theory that, in the case of a man with only one weakness, that is likely to be a very weak weakness indeed, and to apply the theory to the *avocat*. The beautiful, pious, and aristocratic mother of Paul de Sénanges—a lady to whose superiority the Marquis had rendered the distinguished testimony of his dislike, not hesitating to avow that she was "much too good for *his* taste"—had been very fond of, and very kind to, the motherless daughter of Prosper Alix, and he held her memory in reverence which he accorded to nothing beside, human or divine, and taught his daughter the matchless worth of the friend she had lost. The Marquis knew this, and though he had little sympathy with the sentiment, he believed he might use it in the present instance to his own profit, with safety. The event proved that he was right. Private negotiations, with the manner of whose transaction we are not concerned, passed between the *avocat* and the *ci-devant* Marquis; and the young man, then leading a life in which skulking had a large share, in the vicinity of Dijon, was instructed to present himself at the Maison Alix, under the designation of Henri Glaire, and in the character of an artist in house-decoration. The circumstances of his life in childhood and boyhood had led to his being almost safe from recognition as a man at Lyons; and, indeed, all the people on the *ci-devant* visiting-list of the château had been pretty nearly killed off, in the noble and patriotic ardor of the revolutionary times.

The ancient Château de Sénanges was proudly placed near the summit of the "Holy Hill," and had suffered terrible depredations when the church at Fourvières was sacked, and the shrine desecrated with that ingenious impiety which is characteristic of the French; but it still retained somewhat of its former heavy grandeur. The château was much too large for the needs, tastes, or ambition of its present owner, who was too wise, if even he had been of an ostentatious disposition, not to have sedulously resisted its promptings. The jealousy of the nation of brothers was easily excited, and departure from simplicity and frugality was apt to be commented upon by domiciliary visits, and the eager imposition of fanciful fines. That portion of the vast building occupied by Prosper Alix and the *citoyenne* Berthe, his daughter, presented an appearance of well-to-do comfort and modest ease, which contrasted with the grandiose proportions and the elaborate decorations of the wide corridors, huge flat staircases, and lofty panelled apartments. The *avocat* and his daughter lived quietly in the old place, hoping, after a general fashion, for better times, but not finding the present very bad; the father becoming day by day more pleasant with his bargain, the daughter growing fonder of the great house, and the noble *bocages*, of the scrappy little vineyards, struggling for existence on the sunny hill-side, and the place where the famous shrine had been. They had done it much damage; they had parted its riches among them; the once ever open doors were shut, and the worn flags were untrodden; but nothing could degrade it, nothing could destroy what had been, in the mind of Berthe Alix, who was as devout as her father was unconcernedly unbelieving. Berthe was wonderfully well educated for a Frenchwoman of that period, and surprisingly handsome for a Frenchwoman of any. Not too tall to offend the taste of her compatriots, and not too short to be dignified and graceful, she had a symmetrical figure, and a small, well-poised head, whose profuse, shining, silken dark-brown hair she wore as nature intended, in a shower of curls, never touched by the hand of the coiffeur,—curls which clustered over her brow, and fell far down on her shapely neck. Her features were fine; the eyes very dark, and the mouth very red; the complexion clear and rather pale, and the style of the face and its expression lofty. When Berthe Alix was a child, people were accustomed to say she was pretty and refined enough to belong to the aristocracy; nobody would have dared to say so now, prettiness and refinement, together with all the other virtues admitted to a place on the patriotic roll, having become national property.

Berthe loved her father dearly. She was deeply impressed with the sense of her supreme importance to him, and fully comprehended that he would be influenced by and through her when all other persuasion or argument would be unavailing. When Prosper Alix wished and intended to do anything rather mean or selfish, he did it without letting Berthe know; and when he wished to leave undone something which he knew his daughter would decide ought to be done, he carefully concealed from her the existence of the dilemma. Nevertheless, this system did not prevent the father and daughter being very good and even confidential friends. Prosper Alix loved his daughter immeasurably, and respected her more than he respected any one in the world. With regard to her persevering religiousness, when such things were not only out of fashion and date, but illegal as well, he was very tolerant. Of course it was weak, and an absurdity; but every woman, even his beautiful, incomparable Berthe, was weak and absurd on some point or other; and, after all, he had come to the conclusion that the safest weakness with which a woman can be afflicted is that romantic and ridiculous *faiblesse* called piety. So these two lived a happy life together, Berthe's share of it being very secluded, and were wonderfully little troubled by the turbulence with which society was making its tumultuous way to the virtuous serenity of republican perfection.

The communication announcing the project of the *ci-devant* Marquis for the secure exportation of his nephew, and containing the skilful appeal before mentioned, grievously disturbed the tranquillity of Prosper, and was precisely one of those incidents which he would especially have liked to conceal from his daughter. But he could not do so; the appeal was too cleverly made; and utter indifference to it, utter neglect of the letter, which naturally suggested itself as the easiest means of getting rid of a difficulty, would have involved an act of direct and uncompromising dishonesty to which Prosper, though of sufficiently elastic conscience within the limit of professional gains, could not contemplate. The Château de Sénanges was indeed his own lawful property; his without prejudice to the former owners, dispossessed by no act of his. But the *ci-devant* Marquis—confiding in him to an extent which was quite astonishing, except on the *pis-aller* theory, which is so unflattering as to be seldom accepted—announced to him the existence of a certain packet, hidden in the château, acknowledging its value, and urging the need of its safe transmission. This was not his property. He heartily wished he had never learned its existence, but wishing that was clearly of no use; then he wished the nephew of the *ci-devant* might come soon, and take himself and the hidden wealth away with all possible speed. This latter was a more realizable desire, and Prosper settled his mind with it, communicated the interesting but decidedly dangerous secret to Berthe, received her warm sanction, and transmitted to the Marquis, by the appointed means, an assurance that his wishes should be punctually carried out. The absence of an interdiction of his visit before a certain date was to be the signal to M. Paul de Sénanges that he was to proceed to act upon his uncle's instructions; he waited the proper time, the reassuring silence was maintained unbroken, and he ultimately set forth on his journey, and accomplished it in safety.

Preparations had been made at the Maison Alix for the reception of M. Glaire, and his supposed occupation had been announced. The apartments were decorated in a heavy, gloomy style, and those of the *citoyenne* in particular (they had been occupied by a lady who had once been designated as *feue Madame la Marquise*, but who was referred to now as *la mère du ci-devant*) were much in need of renovation. The alcove, for instance, was all that was least gay and most far from simple. The *citoyenne* would have all that changed. On the morning of the day of the expected arrival, Berthe said to her father:

"It would seem as if the Marquis did not know the exact spot in which the packet is deposited. M. Paul's assumed character implies the necessity for a search."

M. Henri Glaire arrived at the Maison Alix, was fraternally received, and made acquainted with the sphere of his operations. The young man had a good deal of both ability and taste in the line he had assumed, and the part was not difficult to play. Some days were judiciously allowed to pass before the real object of the masquerade was pursued, and during that time cordial relations established themselves between the *avocat* and his guest. The young man was handsome, elegant, engaging, with all the external advantages, and devoid of the vices, errors, and hopeless infatuated unscrupulousness, of his class; he had naturally quick intelligence, and some real knowledge and comprehension of life had been knocked into him by the hard-hitting blows of Fate. His face was like his mother's, Prosper Alix thought, and his mind and tastes were of the very pattern which, in theory, Berthe approved. Berthe, a very unconventional French girl—who thought the new era of purity, love, virtue, and disinterestedness ought to do away with marriage by barter as one of its most notable reforms, and had been disenchanted by discovering that the abolition of marriage altogether suited the taste of the incorruptible Republic better—might like, might even love, this young man. She saw so few men, and had no fancy for patriots; she would certainly be obstinate about it if she did chance to love him. This would be a nice state of affairs. This would be a pleasant consequence of the confiding request of the *ci-devant*. Prosper wished with all his heart for the arrival of the concerted signal, which should tell Henri Glaire that he might fulfil the purpose of his sojourn at the Maison Alix, and set forth for Marseilles.

But the signal did not come, and the days—long, beautiful, sunny, soothing summer-days—went on. The painting of the panels of the *citoyenne's* apartment, which she vacated for that purpose, progressed slowly; and M. Paul de Sénanges, guided by the ground-plan, and aided by Berthe, had discovered the spot in which the jewels of price, almost the last remnants of the princely wealth of the Sénanges, had been hidden by the *femme-de-chambre* who had perished with her mistress, having confided a general statement of the fact to a priest, for transmission to the Marquis. This spot had been ingeniously chosen. The sleeping-apartment of the late Marquis was extensive, lofty, and provided with an alcove of sufficiently large dimensions to have formed in itself a handsome room. This space, containing a splendid but gloomy bed, on an estrade, and hung with rich faded brocade, was divided from the general extent of the apartment by a low railing of black oak, elaborately carved, opening in the centre, and with a flat wide bar along the top, covered with crimson velvet. The curtains were contrived to hang from the ceiling, and, when let down inside the screen of railing, they matched the draperies which closed before the great stone balcony at the opposite end of the room. Since the *avocat's* daughter had occupied this palatial chamber, the curtains of the alcove had never been drawn, and she had substituted for them a high folding screen of black-and-gold Japanese pattern, also a relic of the grand old times, which stood about six feet on the outside of the rails that shut in her bed. The floor was of shining oak, testifying to the conscientious and successful labors of successive generations of *frotteurs*; and on the spot where the railing of the alcove opened by a pretty quaint device sundering the intertwined arms of a pair of very chubby cherubs, a square space in the floor was also richly carved.

The seekers soon reached the end of their search. A little effort removed the square of carved oak, and underneath they found a casket, evidently of old workmanship, richly wrought in silver, much tarnished but quite intact. It was agreed that this precious deposit should be replaced, and the carved square laid down over it, until the signal for his departure should reach Paul. The little baggage which under any circumstances he could have ventured to allow himself in the dangerous journey he was to undertake, must be reduced, so as to admit of his carrying the casket without exciting suspicion.

The finding of the hidden treasure was not the first joint discovery made by the daughter of the *avocat* and the son of the *ci-devant*. The cogitations of Prosper Alix were very wise, very reasonable; but they were a little tardy. Before he had admitted the possibility of mischief, the mischief was done. Each had found out that the love of the other was indispensable to the happiness of life; and they had exchanged confidences, assurances, protestations, and promises, as freely, as fervently, and as hopefully, as if no such thing as a Republic, one and indivisible, with a keen scent and an unappeasable thirst for the blood of aristocrats, existed. They forgot all about "Liberty, Fraternity, and Equality"—these egotistical, narrow-minded young people;—they also forgot the characteristic alternative to those unparalleled blessings—"Death." But Prosper Alix did not forget any of these things; and his consternation, his provision of suffering for his beloved daughter, were terrible, when she told him, with a simple noble frankness which the *grandes dames* of the dead-and-gone time of great ladies had rarely had a chance of exhibiting, that she loved M. Paul de Sénanges, and intended to marry him when the better times should come. Perhaps she meant when that alternative of *death* should be struck off the sacred formula;—of course she meant to marry him with the sanction of her father, which she made no doubt she should receive.

Prosper Alix was in pitiable perplexity. He could not bear to terrify his daughter by a full explanation of the danger she was incurring; he could not bear to delude her with false hope. If this young man could be got away at once safely, there was not much likelihood that he would ever be able to return to France. Would Berthe pine for him, or would she forget him, and make a rational, sensible, rich, republican marriage, which would not imperil either her reputation for pure patriotism or her father's? The latter would be the very best thing that could possibly happen, and therefore it was decidedly unwise to calculate upon it; but, after all, it was possible; and Prosper had not the courage, in such a strait, to resist the hopeful promptings of a possibility. How ardently he regretted that he had complied with the prayer of the *ci-devant*! When would the signal for Mr. Paul's departure come?

Prosper Alix had made many sacrifices, had exercised much self-control for his daughter's sake; but he had never sustained a more severe trial than this, never suffered more than he did now, under the strong necessity for hiding from her his absolute conviction of the impossibility of a happy result for this attachment, in that future to which the lovers looked so fearlessly. He could not even make his anxiety and apprehension known to Paul de Sénanges; for he did not believe the young man had sufficient strength of will to conceal anything so important from the keen and determined observation of Berthe.

The expected signal was not given, and the lovers were incautious. The seclusion of the Maison Alix had all the danger, as well as all the delight, of solitude, and Paul dropped his disguise too much and too often. The servants, few in number, were of the truest patriotic principles, and to some of them the denunciation of the *citoyen*, whom they condescended to serve because the sacred Revolution had not yet made them as rich as he, would have been a delightful duty, a sweet-smelling sacrifice to be laid on the altar of the country. They heard certain names and places mentioned; they perceived many things which led them to believe that Henri Glaire was not an industrial artist and pure patriot, worthy of respect, but a wretched *ci-devant*, resorting to the dignity of labor to make up for the righteous destruction of every other kind of dignity. One day a gardener, of less stoical virtue than his fellows, gave Prosper Alix a warning that the presence of a *ci-devant* upon his premises was suspected, and that he might be certain a domiciliary visit, attended with dangerous results to himself, would soon take place. Of course the *avocat* did not commit himself by any avowal to this lukewarm patriot; but he casually mentioned that Henri Glaire was about to take his leave. What was to be done? He must not leave the neighborhood without receiving the instructions he was awaiting; but he must leave the house, and be supposed to have gone quite away. Without any delay or hesitation, Prosper explained the facts to Berthe and her lover, and insisted on the necessity for an instant parting. Then the courage and the readiness of the girl told. There was no crying, and very little trembling; she was strong and helpful.

"He must go to Pichon's, father," she said, "and remain there until the signal is given.—Pichon is a master-mason, Paul," she continued, turning to her lover, "and his wife was my nurse. They are avaricious people; but they are fond of me in their way, and they will shelter you faithfully enough, when they know that my father will pay them handsomely. You must go at once, unseen by the servants; they are at supper. Fetch your valise, and bring it to my room. We will put the casket in it, and such of your things as you must take out to make room for it, we can hide under the plank. My father will go with you to Pichon's, and we will communicate with you there as soon as it is safe."

Paul followed her to the large gloomy room where the treasure lay, and they took the casket from its hiding-place. It was heavy, though not large, and an awkward thing to pack away among linen in a small valise. They managed it, however, and, the brief preparation completed, the moment of parting arrived. Firmly and eloquently, though in haste, Berthe assured Paul of her changeless love and faith, and promised him to wait for him for any length of time in France, if better days should be slow of coming, or to join him in some foreign land, if they were never to come. Her father was present, full of compassion and misgiving. At length he said:

"Come, Paul, you must leave her; every moment is of importance."

The young man and his betrothed were standing on the spot whence they had taken the casket; the carved rail with the heavy curtains might have been the outer sanctuary of an altar, and they bride and bridegroom before it, with earnest, loving faces, and clasped hands.

"Farewell, Paul," said Berthe; "promise me once more, in this the moment of our parting, that you will come to me again, if you are alive, when the danger is past."

"Whether I am living or dead, Berthe," said Paul de Sénanges, strongly moved by some sudden inexplicable instinct, "I will come to you again."

In a few more minutes, Prosper Alix and his guest, who carried, not without difficulty, the small but heavy leather valise, had disappeared in the distance, and Berthe was on her knees before the *prie-dieu* of the *ci-devant* Marquise, her face turned toward the "Holy Hill" of Fourvières.

Pichon, *mâitre*, and his sons, *garçons-maçons*, were well-to-do people, rather morose, exceedingly avaricious, and of taciturn dispositions; but they were not ill spoken of by their neighbors. They had amassed a good deal of money in their time, and were just then engaged on a very lucrative job. This was the construction of several of the steep descents, by means of stairs, straight and winding, cut in the face of the *côteaux*, by which pedestrians are enabled to descend into the town. Pichon *père* was a *propriétaire* as well; his property was that which is now in the possession of Giraudier, *pharmacien, première classe*, and which was destined to attain a sinister celebrity during his proprietorship. One of the straightest and steepest of the stairways had been cut close to the *terre* which the mason owned, and a massive wall, destined to bound the high-road at the foot of the declivity, was in course of construction.

When Prosper Alix and Paul de Sénanges reached the abode of Pichon, the master-mason, with his sons and workmen, had just completed their day's work, and were preparing to eat the supper served by the wife and mother, a tall, gaunt woman, who looked as if a more liberal scale of housekeeping would have done her good, but on whose features the stamp of that devouring and degrading avarice which is the commonest vice of the French peasantry, was set as plainly as on the hard faces of her husband and her sons. The *avocat* explained his business and introduced his companion briefly, and awaited the reply of Pichon *père* without any appearance of inquietude.

"You don't run any risk," he said; "at least, you don't run any risk which I cannot make it worth your while to incur. It is not the first time you have received a temporary guest on my recommendation. You know nothing about the citizen

Glaire, except that he is recommended to you by me. I am responsible; you can, on occasion, make me so. The citizen may remain with you a short time; can hardly remain long. Say, citizen, is it agreed? I have no time to spare."

It was agreed, and Prosper Alix departed, leaving M. Paul de Sénanges, convinced that the right, indeed the only, thing had been done, and yet much troubled and depressed.

Pichon *père* was a short, squat, powerfully built man, verging on sixty, whose thick, dark grizzled hair, sturdy limbs, and hard hands, on which the muscles showed like cords, spoke of endurance and strength; he was, indeed, noted in the neighborhood for those qualities. His sons resembled him slightly, and each other closely, as was natural, for they were twins. They were heavy, lumpish fellows, and they made but an ungracious return to the attempted civilities of the stranger, to whom the offer of their mother to show him his room was a decided relief. As he rose to follow the woman, Paul de Sénanges lifted his small valise with difficulty from the floor, on which he had placed it on entering the house, and carried it out of the room in both his arms. The brothers followed these movements with curiosity, and, when the door closed behind their mother and the stranger, their eyes met.

Twenty-four hours had passed away, and nothing new had occurred at the Maison Alix. The servants had not expressed any curiosity respecting the departure of the citizen Glaire, no domiciliary visit had taken place, and Berthe and her father were discussing the propriety of Prosper's venturing, on the pretext of an excursion in another direction, a visit to the isolated and quiet dwelling of the master-mason. No signal had yet arrived. It was agreed that after the lapse of another day, if their tranquillity remained undisturbed, Prosper Alix should visit Paul de Sénanges. Berthe, who was silent and preoccupied, retired to her own room early, and her father, who was uneasy and apprehensive, desperately anxious for the promised communication from the Marquis, was relieved by her absence.

The moon was high in the dark sky, and her beams were flung across the polished oak floor of Berthe's bedroom, through the great window with the stone balcony, when the girl, who had gone to sleep with her lover's name upon her lips in prayer, awoke with a sudden start, and sat up in her bed. An unbearable dread was upon her; and yet she was unable to utter a cry, she was unable to make another movement. Had she heard a voice? No, no one had spoken, nor did she fancy that she heard any sound. But within her, somewhere inside her heaving bosom, something said, "Berthe!"

And she listened, and knew what it was. And it spoke, and said:

"I promised you that, living or dead, I would come to you again. And I have come to you; but not living."

She was quite awake. Even in the agony of her fear she looked around, and tried to move her hands, to feel her dress and the bedclothes, and to fix her eyes on some familiar object, that she might satisfy herself, before this racing and beating, this whirling and yet icy chilliness of her blood should kill her outright, that she was really awake.

"I have come to you; but not living."

What an awful thing that voice speaking within her was! She tried to raise her head and to look toward the place where the moonbeams marked bright lines upon the polished floor, which lost themselves at the foot of the Japanese screen. She forced herself to this effort, and lifted her eyes, wild and haggard with fear, and there, the moonbeams at his feet, the tall black screen behind him, she saw Paul de Sénanges. She saw him; she looked at him quite steadily; she rose, slowly, with a mechanical movement, and stood upright beside her bed, clasping her forehead with her hands, and gazing at him. He stood motionless, in the dress he had worn when he took leave of her, the light-colored riding-coat of the period, with a short cape, and a large white cravat tucked into the double breast. The white muslin was flecked, and the front of the riding-coat was deeply stained, with blood. He looked at her, and she took a step forward—another—then, with a desperate effort, she dashed open the railing and flung herself on her knees before him, with her arms stretched out as if to clasp him. But he was no longer there; the moonbeams fell clear and cold upon the polished floor, and lost themselves where Berthe lay, at the foot of the screen, her head upon the ground, and every sign of life gone from her.

"Where is the citizen Glaire?" asked Prosper Alix of the *citoyenne* Pichon, entering the house of the master-mason abruptly, and with a stern and threatening countenance. "I have a message for him; I must see him."

"I know nothing about him," replied the *citoyenne*, without turning in his direction, or relaxing her culinary labors. "He went away from here the next morning, and I did not trouble myself to ask where; that is his affair."

"He went away? Without letting me know! Be careful, *citoyenne*; this is a serious matter."

"So they tell me," said the woman with a grin, which was not altogether free from pain and fear; "for you! A serious thing to have a *suspect* in your house, and palm him off on honest people. However, he went away peaceably enough when he knew we had found him out, and that we had no desire to go to prison, or worse, on his account, or yours."

She was strangely insolent, this woman, and the listener felt his helplessness; he had brought the young man there with such secrecy, he had so carefully provided for the success of concealment.

"Who carried his valise?" Prosper Alix asked her suddenly.

"How should I know?" she replied; but her hands lost their steadiness, and she upset a stew-pan; "he carried it here, didn't he? and I suppose he carried it away again."

Prosper Alix looked at her steadily—she shunned his gaze, but she showed no other sign of confusion; then horror and disgust of the woman came over him.

"I must see Pichon," he said; "where is he?"

"Where should he be but at the wall? he and the boys are working there, as always. The citizen can see them; but he will remember not to detain them; in a little quarter of an hour the soup will be ready."

The citizen did see the master-mason and his sons, and after an interview of some duration he left the place in a state of violent agitation and complete discomfiture. The master-mason had addressed to him these words at parting:

"I assert that the man went away at his own free will; but if you do not keep very quiet, I shall deny that he came here at all—you cannot prove he did—and I will denounce you for harboring a *suspect* and *ci-devant* under a false name. I know a De Sénanges when I see him as well as you, citizen Alix; and, wishing M. Paul a good journey, I hope you will consider about this matter, for truly, my friend, I think you will sneeze in the sack before I shall."

"We must bear it, Berthe, my child," said Prosper Alix to his daughter many weeks later, when the fever had left her, and she was able to talk with her father of the mysterious and frightful events which had occurred. "We are utterly helpless. There is no proof, only the word of these wretches against mine, and certain destruction to me if I speak. We will go to Spain, and tell the Marquis all the truth, and never return, if you would rather not. But, for the rest, we must bear it."

"Yes, my father," said Berthe submissively, "I know we must; but God need not, and I don't believe He will."

The father and the daughter left France unmolested, and Berthe "bore it" as well as she could. When better times come they returned, Prosper Alix an old man, and Berthe a stern, silent, handsome woman, with whom no one associated any notions of love or marriage. But long before their return the traditions of the Croix Rousse were enriched by circumstances which led to that before-mentioned capital bargain made by the father of the Giraudier of the present. These circumstances were the violent death of Pichon and his two sons, who were killed by the fall of a portion of the great boundary-wall on the very day of its completion, and the discovery, close to its foundation, at the extremity of Pichon's *terre*, of the corpse of a young man attired in a light-colored riding-coat, who had been stabbed through the heart.

Berthe Alix lived alone in the Château de Sénanges, under its restored name, until she was a very old woman. She lived long enough to see the golden figure on the summit of the "Holy Hill," long enough to forget the bad old times, but not long enough to forget or cease to mourn the lover who had kept his promise, and come back to her; the lover who rested in the earth which once covered the bones of the martyrs, and who kept a place for her by his side. She has filled that place for many years. You may see it, when you look down from the second gallery of the bell-tower at Fourvières, following the bend of the outstretched golden arm of Notre Dame.

The château was pulled down some years ago, and there is no trace of its former existence among the vines.

Good times, and bad times, and again good times have come for the Croix Rousse, for Lyons, and for France, since then; but the remembrance of the treachery of Pichon & Sons, and of the retribution which at once exposed and punished their crime, outlives all changes. And once, every year, on a certain summer night, three ghostly figures are seen, by any who have courage and patience to watch for them, gliding along by the foot of the boundary-wall, two of them carrying a dangling corpse, and the other, implements for mason's work and a small leather valise. Giraudier, *pharmacien*, has never seen these ghostly figures, but he describes them with much minuteness; and only the *esprits forts* of the Croix Rousse deny that the ghosts of Pichon & Sons are not yet laid.

THE PHANTOM FOURTH.

THEY were three.

It was in the cheap night-service train from Paris to Calais that I first met them.

Railways, as a rule, are among the many things which they do *not* order better in France, and the French Northern line is one of the worst managed in the world, barring none, not even the Italian *vie ferrate*. I make it a rule, therefore, to punish the directors of, and the shareholders in, that undertaking to the utmost within my limited ability, by spending as little money on their line as I can help.

It was, then, in a third-class compartment of the train that I met the three.

Three as hearty, jolly-looking Saxon faces, with stalwart frames to match, as one would be likely to meet in an hour's walk from the Regent's Park to the Mansion House.

One of the three was dark, the other two were fair. The dark one was the senior of the party. He wore an incipient full beard, evidently in process of training, with a considerable amount of grizzle in it.

The face of one of his companions was graced with a magnificent flowing beard. The third of the party, a fair-haired youth of some twenty-three or four summers, showed a scrupulously smooth-shaven face.

They looked all three much flushed and slightly excited, and, I must say, they turned out the most boisterous set of fellows I ever met.

They were clearly gentlemen, however, and men of education, with considerable linguistic acquirements; for they chatted and sang, and declaimed and "did orations" all the way from Paris to Calais, in a slightly bewildering variety of tongues.

Their jollity had, perhaps, just a little over-tinge of the slap-bang jolly-dog style in it; but there was so much heartiness and good-nature in all they said and in all they did, that it was quite impossible for any of the other occupants of the carriage to vote them a nuisance; and even the sourest of the officials, whom they chaffed most unmercifully and unremittingly at every station on the line, took their punishment with a shrug and a grin. The only person, indeed, who rose against them in indignant protestation was the head-waiter at the Calais station refreshment-room, to whom they would persist in propounding puzzling problems, such as, for instance, "If you charge two shillings for one-and-a-half-ounce slice of breast of veal, how many fools will it take to buy the joint off you?"—and what *he* got by the attempt to stop their chaff was a caution to any other sinner who might have felt similarly inclined.

As for me, I could only give half my sense of hearing to their utterings, the other half being put under strict sequester at the time by my friend O'Kweene, the great Irish philosopher, who was delivering to me, for my own special behoof and benefit, a brilliant, albeit somewhat abstruse, dissertation on the "visible and palpable outward manifestations of the inner consciousness of the soul in a trance;" which occupied all the time from Paris to Calais, full eight hours, and which, to judge from my feelings at the time, would certainly afford matter for three heavy volumes of reading in bed, in cases of inveterate sleeplessness—a hint to enterprising publishers.

My friend O'Kweene, who intended to stay a few days at Calais, took leave of me on the pier, and I went on board the steamer that was to carry us and the mail over to Dover.

Here I found our trio of the railway-car, snugly ensconced under an extemporized awning, artfully constructed with railway-rugs and greatcoats, supported partly against the luggage, and partly upon several oars, purloined from the boats, and turned into tent-poles for the nonce—which made the skipper swear wofully when he found it out some time after.

The three were even more cheery and boisterous on board than they had been on shore. From what I could make out in the dark, they were discussing the contents of divers bottles of liquor; I counted four dead men dropped quietly overboard by them in the course of the hour and a half we had to wait for the arrival of the mail-train, which was late, as usual on this line.

At last we were off, about half-past two o'clock in the morning. It was a beautiful, clear, moonlit night, so clear, indeed, that we could see the Dover lights almost from Calais harbor. But we had considerably more than a capful of wind, and there was a turgent ground-swell on, which made our boat—double-engined, and as trim and tidy a craft as ever sped across the span from shore to shore—behave rather lively, with sportive indulgence in a brisk game of pitch-and-toss that proved anything but comfortable to most of the passengers.

When we were steaming out of Calais harbor, our three friends, emerging from beneath their tent, struck up in chorus Campbell's noble song, "Ye Mariners of England," finishing up with a stave from "Rule, Britannia!"

But, alas for them! however loudly their throats were shouting forth the sway proverbially held by Albion and her sons over the waves, on this occasion at least the said waves seemed determined upon ruling these particular three Britons with a rod of antimony; for barely a few seconds after the last vibrating echoes of the "Britons never, never, never shall be slaves!" had died away upon the wind, I beheld the three leaning lovingly together, in fast friendship linked, over the rail, conversing in deep ventriguttural accents with the denizens of Neptune's watery realm.

We had one of the quickest passages on record—ninety-three minutes' steaming carried us across from shore to shore. When we were just on the point of landing, I heard the dark senior of the party mutter to his companions, in a hollow whisper and mysterious manner, "He is gone again;" to which the others, the bearded and the smooth-shaven, responded in the same way, with deep sighs of evident relief, "Ay, marry! so he is at last."

This mysterious communication roused my curiosity. Who was the party that was said to be gone at last? Where had he come from? where had he been hiding, that *I* had not seen him? and where was he gone to now? I determined to know; if but the opportunity would offer, to screw, by cunning questioning, the secret out of either of the three.

Fate favored my design.

For some inscrutable reason, known only to the company's officials, we cheap-trainers were not permitted to proceed on our journey to London along with the mail, but were left to kick our heels for some two hours at the Dover station.

I went into the refreshment-room to look for my party; I had a notion I should find them where the Briton's unswerving and unerring instinct would be most likely to lead them. It turned out that I was right in my conjecture. There they were, seated round a table with huge bowls of steaming tea and monster piles of buttered toast and muffins spread on the festive board before them. Ay, indeed, there they were; but *quantum mutati ab illis*! how strangely changed from the noisy, rollicking set I had known them in the railway-car and on board the steamer, ere yet the demon of sea-sickness had claimed them for his own! How ghastly sober they looked now, to be sure! And how sternly and silently bent upon devoting themselves to the swilling of the Chinese shrub infusion and to the gorging of indigestible muffins. It was quite clear to me that it would have been worse than folly to venture upon addressing them while thus absorbed in absorbing. So I resolved to await a more favorable opening, and went out meanwhile to walk on the platform.

A short time I was left in solitary possession of the promenade; then I became suddenly aware that another traveller was treading the same ground with me—it was the dark elderly leader of the three. I glanced at him as he passed me under one of the lamps. He looked pale and sad. The furrowed lines on his brow bespoke deliberation deep and pondering profound. All the infinite mirth of the preceding few hours had departed from him, leaving him but a wretched wreck of his former reckless self.

"A fine night, sir," I said to break the ice—"for the season of the year," I added by way of a saving clause, to tone down the absoluteness of the assertion.

He looked at me abstractedly, merely reëchoing my own words, "A fine night, sir, for the season of the year."

"Why look ye so sad now, who were erst so jolly?" I bluntly asked, determined to force him into conversation.

"Ay, indeed, why so sad now?" he replied, looking me full in the face; then, suddenly clasping my arm with a spasmodic grip, he continued hurriedly, "I think

I had best confide our secret to you. You seem a man of thought. I witnessed and admired the patient attention with which you listened to your friend's abstruse talk in the railway-car. Maybe you can find the solution of a mystery which defies the ponderings of our poor brains—mine and my two friends."

Then he proceeded to pour into my attentive ear this gruesome tale of mystery:

"We three—that is, myself, yon tall bearded Briton," pointing to the glass door of the refreshment-room, "whose name is Jack Hobson, and young Emmanuel Topp, junior partner in a great beer firm, whom you may behold now at his fifth bowl of tea and his seventh muffin—are teetotallers——"

"Teetotallers!" I could not help exclaiming. "Lord bless me! that is certainly about the last thing I should have taken you for, either of you."

"Well," he replied with some slight confusion, "at least, we *were total* teetotallers, though I admit we can now only claim the character of partial abstainers. The fact is, when, about a fortnight ago, we were discussing the plan of our projected visit to the great Paris Exhibition, Topp suggested that while in France we should do as the French do, to which Jack Hobson assented, remarking that the French knew nothing about tea, and that a Frenchman's tea would be sure to prove an Englishman's poison. So we resolved to suspend the pledge during our visit to France.

"It was on the second day after our arrival in Paris. We were dining in a private cabinet at Désiré Beaurain's, one of the leading restaurants on the fashionable side of the Montmartre—Italiens Boulevard. Our dinner was what an Irishman might call a most 'illigant' affair. We had sipped several bottles of Sauterne, and tasted a few of Tavel, and we were just topping the entertainment with a solitary bottle of champagne, when I became suddenly aware of the presence of another party in the room—a *fourth man*—who sat him down at our table, and helped himself liberally to our liquor. From what I ascertained afterward from Jack Hobson and Emmanuel Topp, the intruder's presence became revealed to them also, either about the same time or a little later. What was he like? I cannot tell. His figure and face remained indistinct throughout—phantom-like. His features seemed endowed with a stronge weird mobility that would defyingly elude the fixing grasp of our eager eyes. Now, and to my two companions, he would look marvellously like me; then, to me, he would stalk and rave about in the likeness of Jack Hobson; again, he would seem the counterfeit of Emmanuel Topp; then he would look like all the three of us put together; then like neither of us, nor like anybody else. Oh, sir, it was a woful thing to be haunted by this phantom apparition. Yet the strangest part of the affair was that neither of us seemed to feel a whit surprised at the dread presence; that we quietly and uncomplainingly let him drink our wine, and actually give orders for more; that we never objected, in fact, to any of his sayings and doings. What seemed also strange was that the waiter, while yet receiving and executing his orders, was evidently pretending to ignore his presence. But then, as I dare say you know as well as I do, French waiters are *such* actors!

"Well, to resume, there he was, this fourth man, seated at our table and feasting at our expense. And the pranks that he would play us—they were truly stupendous. He began his little game by ordering in half-a-dozen of champagne. And when the waiter seemed slightly doubtful and hesitating about executing the order, Topp, forsooth, must put in his oar, and indorse the command, actually pretending that *I*, who am now speaking to you, and who am the very last man in the world likely to dream of such a preposterous thing, had given the order, and that I was a jolly old brick, and the best of boon companions. Surprise at this barefaced assertion kept me mute, and so, of course, the champagne was brought in, and I thought the best thing to do under the circumstances was to have my share of it at least; and so I had—my fair share; but, bless you, it was nothing to what that fourth man drank of it. In fact, the amount of liquor *he* would swill on this and on the many subsequent occasions he intruded his presence upon us, was a caution.

"We paid our little bill without grumbling, though the presence of the fourth man at our table had added rather heavily to the *addition*, as they call bills at French restaurants.

"We sallied forth into the street to get a whiff of fresh air. *He*, the demon, pertinaciously stuck to us; he familiarly linked his arm through mine, and, suggesting coffee as rather a good thing to take after dinner, took us over to the Café du Cardinal, where he, however, took none of the Arabian beverage himself (there being only three cups placed for us, as I distinctly saw), but drank an interminable succession of *chasse-café*, utterly regardless of the divisional lines of the cognac *carafon*. Part of these he would take neat, another portion he would burn over sugar, gloating glaringly over the bluish flame, while gleams of demoniac delight would flit across his ever-changing features. Jack Hobson and Topp, I am sorry to say, joined him with a will in this double-distilled debauch; and when I attempted to remonstrate with them, they brazenly asserted that *I*, who am now speaking to you, who have always, publicly and privately, declared brandy to be the worst of evil spirits, had taken more of it, to my own cheek, as they slangily expressed it, than the two of them together; and the waiter, who had evidently been bribed by them, boldly maintained that *le vieux monsieur*, as he had the impudence to call me, had swallowed *plus de trois carafons de fine*; whereupon the fourth man, stepping up to him, punched his head, which served him right. Now you will hardly believe me when I tell you that at that very instant Topp forced me back into my chair, while Jack Hobson pinioned my arms from behind, and the waiter had the unblushing effrontery to stamp and rave at me like a maniac, demanding satisfaction or compensation at my hands for the unprovoked assault committed upon him by *me, coram populo*!—by *me*, who, I beg to assure you, am the most peaceable man living, and am actually famed for the mildness of my disposition and the sweetness and suavity of my temper. And, would you believe it? everybody present, waiters and guests, and my own two bosom-friends, joined in the conspiracy against me, and I actually had to give the wretch of a waiter ten francs as a plaster for his broken pate, and a salve for his wounded honor! Where was the real culprit all this time, you ask me—the fourth man? Why, he quietly stood by grinning, and they all and every one of them pretended not to see him, though Topp and Jack Hobson next morning confessed to me that they certainly had an indistinct consciousness of the presence throughout of this miserable intruder.

"How we finished that night I remember not; nor could Jack Hobson or Emmanuel Topp. All we could conscientiously stand by, if we were questioned, is that we awoke next morning—the three of us—with some slight swimming in our heads, and a hazy recollection of a gorgeous dream of brilliant lights and sounds of music and revelry, and bright visions of groves and grottoes, and dancing houris (or hussies, as moral Jack Hobson calls the poor things), and a hot supper at a certain place in the Passage des Princes, of which I think the name is Peter's.

"I will not tire your courteous patience by a detailed narrative of our experiences day after day, during our fortnight's stay in Paris. Suffice it to tell you that from that time forward to yesterday, when we left, the *fourth man*, as we, by mutual consent, agreed to call the phantom apparition, came in regularly to our dinner; with the dessert or a little after; that he would constantly suggest a fresh supply of Côte St. Jacques, Moulin-à-Vent, Beaune, Chambertin, Roederer Carte Blanche, and a variety of other, generally rather more than less expensive, wines—and that he somehow would manage to make us have them, too.

"Then he would sally forth with us to the café, where he would indulge in irritating chaff of the waiters, and in slighting comments upon the great French nation in general, and the Parisians in particular, and upon their institutions and manners and customs.

"He would insist upon singing the Marseillaise; he would speak disparagingly of the Emperor, whom he would irreverently call Lambert; he would pass cutting and unsavory remarks upon the glorious system of the night-carts; he would call down the judgment of Heaven upon the devoted head of poor Mr. Haussmann; he would go up to some unhappy sergent-de-ville, who might, however unwittingly, excite his ire, and tell him a bit of his mind in English, with sarcastic allusions to his cocket-hat and his toasting-fork, and polite inquiries after the health of *ce cher* Monsieur Lambert, or the whereabouts of *cet excellent* Monsieur Godinot. The worst of the matter was that I suppose for the reason that man is an imitative animal, a sort of *πιθηκος μυωρος*, or Monboddian monkey minus the tail—my two companions were, somehow, always sure to join the wretch in his evil behavior, and to go on just as bad as he did. No wonder, then, that we got into no end of rows, and it is a marvel to me now, how ever we have managed to get off with a whole skin to our bodies.

"He would insist upon taking us to Mabille, the Closerie des Lilas, and the Châteaurouge, where he would indulge in the maddest pranks and antics, and somehow lead us to join in the wildest dances, and make us lift our legs as high as the highest lifter among the *habitués*, male or female.

"One night, at about half-past two in the morning (*Hibernicè*), he had the cool assurance to drag us along with him to the then closed entrance to the Passage des Princes, where he frantically shook the gate, and insisted to the frightened concierge, who came running up in his night-shirt, that Peter's must and ought to be open still, as *we* had not had our supper yet; and Topp and Jack Hobson, forsooth, must join in the row. I have no distinct recollection of whether it was our phantom guest or either of my companions that madly strove to detain the hastily retreating form of the concierge by a desperate clutch at the tail of his shirt; I only remember that the garment gave way in the struggle, and that the unhappy functionary was reduced nearly altogether to the primitive buff costume of the father of man in Paradise ere he had put his teeth into that unlucky apple of which, the pips keep so inconveniently sticking in poor humanity's gizzard to the present day. And what I remember also to my cost is, that the sergent-de-ville, whom the bereaved man's shouts of distress brought to the scene, fastened upon *me*, the most inoffensive of mortals, for a compensation fine of twenty francs, as if *I* had been the culprit. And deuced glad we were, I assure you, to get off without more serious damage to our pocket and reputation than this, and a copious volley of *sacrés ivrognes Anglais*, fired at us by the wretched concierge and his friend of the police, who, I am quite sure, went halves with him in the compensation. Ah! they are a lawless set, these French.

"On another occasion we three went to the Exhibition, where we visited one of our colonial departments, in company with several English friends, and some French gentlemen appointed on the wine jury. We went to taste a few samples of colonial wines. *He* was not with us *then*. Barely, however, had we uncorked a poor dozen bottles, which turned out rather good for colonial, though a little raw and slightly uneducated, when *who* should stalk in but our fourth man, as jaunty and unconcerned as ever. Well, *he* fell to tasting, and he soon grew eloquent in praise of the colonial juice, which he declared would, in another twenty years' time, be fit to compete successfully with the best French vintages. Of course, the French gentlemen with us could not stand *this*; they spoke slightingly of the British colonial, and one of them even went so far as to call it rotgut. I cannot say whether it was the spirit of the uncompromising opinion thus pronounced, or the coarsely indelicate way in which the judgment of our French friend was expressed, that riled our phantom guest—enough, it brought him down in full force upon the offender and his countrymen, with most fluent French vituperation and an unconscionable amount of bad jokes and worse puns, finishing up with a general address to them as members of the *disgusting* jury, instead of jury of *dégustation*. Now, this I should not have minded so much; for, I must confess, I felt rather nettled at the national conceit and prejudice of these French. But the wretch, in the impetuous utterance of his invective, must somehow—though I was not aware of it at the time—have mimicked my gestures and imitated the very tones and accent of my voice so closely as to deceive even some of my English companions: or how else to account for the fact of their calling me a noisy brawler and a pestilent nuisance? *me*, the gentlest and mildest-spoken of mortals!

"Before our departure from London we had calculated our probable expenses on a most liberal scale, and we had made comfortable provision accordingly for a few weeks' stay in Paris. But with the additional heavy burden of the franking of so copious an imbiber as our fourth man thus unexpectedly thrown on our shoulders, it was no great wonder that we should find our resources go much faster than we had anticipated; so we had already been forcedly led to bethink ourselves of shortening our intended stay in the French capital when a fresh exploit of the phantom fourth, climaxing all his past misdeeds, brought matters to a crisis.

"It was the day before yesterday, the 4th of September. We had been dining at Marigny, and dancing at Mabille. Our eccentric guest had come in, as usual, with the champagne, and had of course, after dinner, taken us over to the enchanted gardens. We were all very jolly. *He* suggested supper at the Cascades, in the Bois de Boulogne. We chartered a *fiacre* to take us there and back. We supped rather copiously. *He* somehow made our coachman drunk, and took upon himself to drive us home. Need I tell you that he upset us in the Avenue de l'Impératrice, and that we had to walk it, and pretty fast too? It was a mercy there were no bones broken.

"Well, as we were walking along, just barely recovering from the shock of the accident, he suddenly took some new whim into his confounded noddle. Nothing would do for him but he must drag us along with him to the great entrance of the Elysée Napoléon (which erst was, and maybe is soon likely to be once more, the Elysée Bourbon), where he had the brazen impudence to claim admittance, as the Emperor, he pretended, had been graciously pleased to offer us the splendid hospitality of that renowned mansion. What further happened here, neither I nor either of my friends can tell. Our recollections from this period till next morning are doubtful and indistinct. All we can state for certain is, that yesterday morning we awoke, the three of us, in a most wretched state, in a strange, nasty place. We learn soon after from a gentleman in a cocked hat, who came to visit us on business, that the imperial hospitality which we had claimed last night had indeed been extended to us—only in the *violon*, instead of the Elysée. Our phantom guest was gone: he would alway, somehow sneak away in the morning, when there was nothing left for him to drink—the guzzling villain!

"The gentleman in the cocked-hat pressingly invited us to pay a visit to the Commissaire du Quartier. That formidable functionary received us with the customary French-polished veneer of urbanity which, as a rule, constitutes the *suaviter in modo* of the higher class of Gallic officials. He read us a severe lecture, however, upon the alleged impropriety of our conduct; and when I ventured to protest that it was not to us the blame ought to be imputed, but to the *quatrième*, he mistook my meaning, and, ere I could explain myself, he cut me short with a polite remark that the French used the cardinal instead of the ordinal numbers in stating the days of the month, with the exception of the first, and that he had had too much trouble with our countrymen (he took us for Yankees!) on the 4th of July, to be disposed to look with an over-lenient eye upon the vagaries we had chosen to commit on the 4th of September, which he supposed was another great national day with us. He would, however, let us off this time with a simple reprimand, upon payment of one hundred francs, compensation for damage done to the coach—drunken cabby having turned up, of course, to testify against us. Well, we paid the money, and handed the worthy magistrate twenty francs besides, for the benefit of the poor, by way of acknowledgment for the imperial hospitality we had enjoyed. We were then allowed to depart in peace.

"Now, you'll hardly believe it, I dare say, but it is the truth notwithstanding, that we three, who have been fast friends for years, actually began to quarrel among ourselves now, mutually imputing to one another the blame of all our misadventures and misfortunes since our arrival in Paris, while yet we clearly knew and felt, each and every of us, that it was all the doings of that phantom fourth.

"One thing, however, we all agreed to do—to leave Paris by the first train.

"To fortify ourselves for the coming journey, we went to indulge in the luxury of a farewell breakfast at Désiré Beaurain's. Of course we emptied a few bottles to our reconciliation. I do not exactly remember how many, but this I *do* remember, that our irrepressible incubus walked in again, and took his place in the midst of us rather sooner even than he had been wont to do; and he never left us from that time to the moment of our landing at Dover harbor, when he took his, I hope and trust final, departure with a ghastly grin.

"I dare say you must have thought us a most noisy and obstreperous lot: well, with my hand on my heart, I can assure you, on my conscience, that a quieter and milder set of fellows than us three you are not likely to find on this or the other side the Channel. But for that mysterious phantom fourth——"

Here the whistle sounded, and the guard came up to us with a hurried, "Now then, gents, take your seats, please; train is off in half a minnit!"

"What can have become of Topp and Jack Hobson?" muttered my new friend, looking around him with eager scrutiny. "I should not wonder if they were still refreshing." And he started off in the direction of the refreshment-room.

I took my seat. Immediately after the train whirled off. I cannot say whether the three were left behind; all I know is that I did not see them get out at London Bridge.

Remembering, however, that the appalling secret of the supernatural visitation which had thus harassed my three fellow-travellers had been confided to me under the impression that I might be likely to find a solution of the mystery, I have ever since deeply pondered thereon.

Shallow thinkers, and sneerers uncharitably given, may, from a consideration of the times, places, and circumstances at and under which the abnormal phenomena here recited were stated to have been observed, be led to attribute them simply to the promptings and imaginings of brains overheated by excessive indulgence in spirituous liquors. But I, striving to be mindful always of the great scriptural injunction to judge not, lest we be judged, and opportunely remembering my friend O'Kweene's learned dissertation above alluded to, feel disposed to pronounce the apparition of the phantom of the fourth man, and all the sayings, doings, and demeanings of the same, to have been simply so many visible and palpable outward manifestations of the inner consciousness of the souls of the three, and more notably of that of the elderly senior of the party, in a succession of vino-alcoholic trances.

My friend O'Kweene is, of course, welcome to such credit as may attach to this attempted solution of mine.

THE SPIRIT'S WHISPER.

YES, I have been haunted!—haunted so fearfully that for some little time I thought myself insane. I was no raving maniac; I mixed in society as heretofore, although perhaps a trifle more grave and taciturn than usual; I pursued my daily avocations; I employed myself even on literary work. To all appearance I was one of the sanest of the sane; and yet all the while I considered myself the victim of such strange delusions that, in my own mind, I fancied my senses—and one sense in particular—so far erratic and beyond my own control that I was, in real truth, a madman. How far I was then insane it must be for others, who hear my story, to decide. My hallucinations have long since left me, and, at all events, I am now as sane as I suppose most men are.

My first attack came on one afternoon when, being in a listless and an idle mood, I had risen from my work and was amusing myself with speculating at my window on the different personages who were passing before me. At that time I occupied apartments in the Brompton Road. Perhaps, there is no thoroughfare in London where the ordinary passengers are of so varied a description or high life and low life mingle in so perpetual a medley. South-Kensington carriages there jostle costermongers' carts; the clerk in the public office, returning to his suburban dwelling, brushes the laborer coming from his work on the never-ending modern constructions in the new district; and the ladies of some of the surrounding squares flaunt the most gigantic of *chignons*, and the most exuberant of motley dresses, before the envying eyes of the ragged girls with their vegetable-baskets.

There was, as usual, plenty of material for observation and conjecture in the passengers, and their characters or destinations, from my window on that day. Yet I was not in the right cue for the thorough enjoyment of my favorite amusement. I was in a rather melancholy mood. Somehow or other, I don't know why, my memory had reverted to a pretty woman whom I had not seen for many years. She had been my first love, and I had loved her with a boyish passion as genuine as it was intense. I thought my heart would have broken, and I certainly talked seriously of dying, when she formed an attachment to an ill-conditioned, handsome young adventurer, and, on her family objecting to such an alliance, eloped with him. I had never seen the fellow, against whom, however, I cherished a hatred almost as intense as my passion for the infatuated girl who had flown from her home for his sake. We had heard of her being on the Continent with her husband, and learned that the man's shifty life had eventually taken him to the East. For some years nothing more had been heard of the poor girl. It was a melancholy history, and its memory ill-disposed me for amusement.

A sigh was probably just escaping my lips with the half-articulated words, "Poor Julia!" when my eyes fell on a man passing before my window. There was nothing particularly striking about him. He was tall, with fine features, and a long, fair beard, contrasting somewhat with his bronzed complexion. I had seen many of our officers on their return from the Crimea look much the same. Still, the man's aspect gave me a shuddering feeling, I didn't know why. At the same moment, a whispering, low voice uttered aloud in my ear the words, "It is he!" I turned, startled; there was no one near me, no one in the room. There was no fancy in the sound; I had heard the words with painful distinctness. I ran to the door, opened it—not a sound on the staircase, not a sound in the whole house—nothing but the hum from the street. I came back and sat down. It was no use reasoning with myself; I had the ineffaceable conviction that I had heard the voice. Then first the idea crossed my mind that I might be the victim of hallucinations. Yes, it must have been so, for now I recalled to mind that the voice had been that of my poor lost Julia; and at the moment I heard it I had been dreaming of her. I questioned my own state of health. I was well; at least I had been so, I felt fully assured, up to that moment. Now a feeling of chilliness and numbness and faintness had crept over me, a cold sweat was on my forehead. I tried to shake off this feeling by bringing back my thoughts to some other subject. But, involuntarily as it were, I again uttered the words, "Poor Julia!" aloud. At the same time a deep and heavy sigh, almost a groan, was distinctly audible close by me. I sprang up; I was alone—quite alone. It was, once more, an hallucination.

By degrees the first painful impression wore away. Some days had passed, and I had begun to forget my singular delusion. When my thoughts aid revert to it, the recollection was dismissed as that of a ridiculous fancy. One afternoon I was in the Strand, coming from Charing Cross, when I was once more overcome by that peculiar feeling of cold and numbness which I had before experienced. The day was warm and bright and genial, and yet I positively shivered. I had scarce time to interrogate my own strange sensations when a man went by me rapidly. How was it that I recognized him at once as the individual who had only passed my window so casually on that morning of the hallucination? I don't know, and yet I was aware that this man was the tall, fair passer-by of the Brompton Road. At the same moment the voice I had previously heard whispered distinctly in my ear the words, "Follow him!" I stood stupefied. The usual throngs of indifferent persons were hurrying past me in that crowded thoroughfare, but I felt convinced that not one of these had spoken to me. I remained transfixed for a moment. I was bent on a matter of business in the contrary direction to the individual I had remarked, and so, although with unsteady step, I endeavored to proceed on my way. Again that voice said, still more emphatically, in my ear, "Follow him!" I stopped involuntarily. And a third time, "Follow him!" I told myself that the sound was a delusion, a cheat of my senses, and yet I could not resist the spell. I turned to follow. Quickening my pace, I soon came up with the tall, fair man, and, unremarked by him, I followed him. Whither was this foolish pursuit to lead me? It was useless to ask myself the question—I was impelled to follow.

I was not destined to go very far, however. Before long the object of my absurd chase entered a well-known insurance-office. I stopped at the door of the establishment. I had no business within, why should I continue to follow? Had I not already been making a sad fool of myself by my ridiculous conduct? These were my thoughts as I stood heated by my quick walk. Yes, heated; and yet, once more, came the sudden chill. Once more that same low but now awful voice spoke in my ear: "Go in!" it said. I endeavored to resist the spell, and yet I felt that resistance was in vain. Fortunately, as it seemed to me, the thought crossed my mind that an old acquaintance was a clerk in that same insurance-office. I had not seen the fellow for a great length of time, and I never had been very intimate with him. But here was a pretext; and so I went in and inquired for Clement Stanley. My acquaintance came forward. He was very busy, he said. I invented, on the spur of the moment, some excuse of the most frivolous and absurd nature, as far as I can recollect, for my intrusion.

"By the way," I said, as I turned to take my leave, although my question was "by the way" of nothing at all, "who was that tall, fair man who just now entered the office?"

"Oh, that fellow?" was the indifferent reply; "a Captain Campbell, or Canton, or some such name; I forget what. He is gone in before the board—insured his wife's life and she is dead; comes for a settlement, I suppose."

There was nothing more to be gained, and so I left the office. As soon as I came without into the scorching sunlight, again the same feeling of cold, again the same voice—"Wait!" Was I going mad? More and more the conviction forced itself upon me that I was decidedly a monomaniac already. I felt my pulse. It was agitated and yet not feverish. I was determined not to give way to this absurd hallucination; and yet, so far was I out of my senses, that my will was no longer my own. Resolved as I was to go, I listened to the dictates of that voice and waited. What was it to me that this Campbell or Canton had insured his wife's life, that she was dead, and that he wanted a settlement of his claim? Obviously nothing; and I yet waited.

So strong was the spell on me that I had no longer any count of time. I had no consciousness whether the period was long or short that I stood there near the door, heedless of all the throng that passed, gazing on vacancy. The fiercest of policemen might have told me to "move on," and I should not have stirred, spite of all the terrors of the "station." The individual came forth. He paid no heed to me. Why should he? What was I to him? This time I needed no warning voice to bid me follow. I was a madman, and I could not resist the impulses of my madness. It was thus, at least I reasoned with myself. I followed into Regent Street. The object of my insensate observation lingered, and looked around as if in expectation. Presently a fine-looking woman, somewhat extravagantly dressed, and obviously not a lady, advanced toward him on the pavement. At the sight of her he quickened his step, and joined her rapidly. I shuddered again, but this time a sort of dread was mingled with that strange shivering. I knew what was coming, and it came. Again that voice in my ear. "Look and remember!" it said. I passed the man and woman as they stopped at their first meeting!

"Is all right, George?" said the female.

"All right, my girl," was the reply.

I looked. An evil smile, as if of wicked triumph, was on the man's face, I thought. And on the woman's? I looked at her, and I remembered. I could not be mistaken. Spite of her change in manner, dress, and appearance, it was Mary Simms. This woman some years before, when she was still very young, had been a sort of humble companion to my mother. A simple-minded, honest girl, we thought her. Sometimes I had fancied that she had paid me, in a sly way, a marked attention. I had been foolish enough to be flattered by her stealthy glances and her sighs. But I had treated these little demonstrations of partiality as due only to a silly girlish fancy. Mary Simms, however, had come to grief in our household. She had been detected in the abstraction of sundry jewels and petty ornaments. The morning after discovery she had left the house, and we had heard of her no more. As these recollections passed rapidly through my mind I looked behind me. The couple had turned back. I turned to follow again; and spite of carriages and cabs, and shouts and oaths of drivers, I took the middle of the street in order to pass the man and woman at a little distance unobserved. No; I was not mistaken. The woman was Mary Simms, though without any trace of all her former simple-minded airs; Mary Simms, no longer in her humble attire, but flaunting in all the finery of overdone fashion. She wore an air of reckless joyousness in her face; and yet, spite of that, I pitied her. It was clear she had fallen on the evil ways of bettered fortune—bettered, alas! for the worse.

I had an excuse now, in my own mind, for my continued pursuit, without deeming myself an utter madman—the excuse of curiosity to know the destiny of one with whom I had been formerly familiar, and in whom I had taken an interest. Presently the game I was hunting down stopped at the door of the Grand Café. After a little discussion they entered. It was a public place of entertainment; there was no reason why I should not enter also. I found my way to the first floor. They were already seated at a table, Mary holding the *carte* in her hand. They were about to dine. Why should not I dine there too? There was but one little objection,—I had an engagement to dinner. But the strange impulse which overpowered me, and seemed leading me on step by step, spite of myself, quickly overruled all the dictates of propriety toward my intended hosts. Could I not send a prettily devised apology? I glided past the couple, with my head averted, seeking a table, and I was unobserved by my old acquaintance. I was too agitated to eat, but I made a semblance, and little heeded the air of surprise and almost disgust on the bewildered face of the waiter as he bore away the barely touched dishes. I was in a very fever of impatience and doubt what next to do. They still sat on, in evident enjoyment of their meal and their constant draughts of sparkling wine. My impatience was becoming almost unbearable when the man at last rose. The woman seemed to have uttered some expostulation, for he turned at the door and said somewhat harshly aloud, "Nonsense; only one game and I shall be back. The waiter will give you a paper—a magazine—something to while away the time." And he left the room for the billiard-table, as I surmised.

Now was my opportunity. After a little hesitation, I rose, and planted myself abruptly on the vacant seat before the woman.

"Mary," I said.

She started, with a little exclamation of alarm, and dropped the paper she had held. She knew me at once.

"Master John!" she exclaimed, using the familiar term still given me when I was long past boyhood; and then, after a lengthened gaze, she turned away her head. I was embarrassed at first how to address her.

"Mary," I said at last, "I am grieved to see you thus."

"Why should you be grieved for me?" she retorted, looking at me sharply, and speaking in a tone of impatient anger. "I am happy as I am."

"I don't believe you," I replied.

She again turned away her head.

"Mary," I pursued, "can you doubt, that, spite of all, I have still a strong interest in the companion of my youth?"

She looked at me almost mournfully, but did not speak. At that moment I probably grew pale; for suddenly that chilly fit seized me again, and my forehead became clammy. That voice sounded again in my ear: "Speak of him!" were the words it uttered. Mary gazed on me with surprise, and yet I was assured that *she* had not heard that voice, so plain to me. She evidently mistook the nature of my visible emotion.

"O Master John!" she stammered, with tears gathering in her eyes, reverting again to that name of bygone times, "if you had loved me then—if you had consoled my true affection with one word of hope, one look of loving-kindness—if you had not spurned and crushed me, I should not have been what I am now."

I was about to make some answer to this burst of unforgotten passion, when the voice came again: "Speak of him!"

"You have loved others since," I remarked, with a coldness which seemed cruel to myself. "You love *him* now." And I nodded my head toward the door by which the man had disappeared.

"Do I?" she said, with a bitter smile. "Perhaps; who knows?"

"And yet no good can come to you from a connection with that man," I pursued.

"Why not? He adores me, and he is free," was her answer, given with a little triumphant air.

"Yes," I said, "I know he is free: he has lately lost his wife. He has made good his claim to the sum for which he insured her life."

Mary grew deadly pale. "How did you learn this? what do you know of him?" she stammered.

I had no reply to give. She scanned my face anxiously for some time; then in a low voice she added, "What do you suspect?"

I was still silent, and only looked at her fixedly.

"You do not speak," she pursued nervously. "Why do you not speak? Ah, you know more than you would say! Master John, Master John, you might set my tortured mind at rest, and clear or confirm those doubts which *will* come into my poor head, spite of myself. Speak out—O, do speak out!"

"Not here; it is impossible," I replied, looking around. The room as the hour advanced, was becoming more thronged with guests, and the full tables gave a pretext for my reticence, when in truth I had nothing to say.

"Will you come and see me—will you?" she asked with earnest entreaty.

I nodded my head.

"Have you a pocketbook? I will write you my address; and you will come—yes, I am sure you will come!" she said in an agitated way.

I handed her my pocketbook and pencil; she wrote rapidly.

"Between the hours of three and five," she whispered, looking uneasily at the door; "*he* is sure not to be at home."

I rose; Mary held out her hand to me, then withdrew it hastily with an air of shame, and the tears sprang into her eyes again. I left the room hurriedly, and met her companion on the stairs.

That same evening, in the solitude of my own room, I pondered over the little event of the day. I had calmed down from my state of excitement. The living apparition of Mary Simms occupied my mind almost to the exclusion of the terrors of the ghostly voice which had haunted me, and my own fears of coming insanity In truth, what was that man to me? Nothing. What did his doings matter to such a perfect stranger as myself? Nothing. His connection with Mary Simms was our only link; and in what should that affect me? Nothing again. I debated with myself whether it were not foolish of me to comply with my youthful companion's request to visit her; whether it were not imprudent in me to take any further interest in the lost woman; whether there were not even danger in seeking to penetrate mysteries which were no concern of mine. The resolution to which I came pleased me, and I said aloud, "No, I will not go!"

At the same moment came again the voice like an awful echo to my words—"Go!" It came so suddenly and so imperatively, almost without any previous warning of the usual shudder, that the shock was more than I could bear. I believe I fainted; I know I found myself, when I came to consciousness, in my arm-chair, cold and numb, and my candles had almost burned down into their sockets.

The next morning I was really ill. A sort of low fever seemed to have prostrated me, and I would have willingly seized so valid a reason for disobeying, at least for that day—for some days, perhaps—the injunction of that ghostly voice. But all that morning it never left me. My fearful chilly fit was of constant recurrence, and the words "Go! go! go!" were murmured so perpetually in my ears—the sound was one of such urgent entreaty—that all force of will gave way completely. Had I remained in that lone room, I should have gone wholly mad. As yet, to my own feelings, I was but partially out of my senses.

I dressed hastily; and, I scarce know how—by no effort of my own will, it seemed to me—I was in the open air. The address of Mary Simms was in a street not far from my own suburb. Without any power of reasoning, I found myself before the door of the house. I knocked, and asked a slipshod girl who opened the door to me for "Miss Simms." She knew no such person, held a brief shrill colloquy with some female in the back-parlor, and, on coming back, was about to shut the door in my face, when a voice from above—the voice of her I sought—called down the stairs, "Let the gentleman come up!"

I was allowed to pass. In the front drawing-room I found Mary Simms.

"They do not know me under that name," she said with a mournful smile, and again extended, then withdrew, her hand.

"Sit down," she went on to say, after a nervous pause. "I am alone now; told I adjure you, if you have still one latent feeling of old kindness for me, explain your words of yesterday to me."

I muttered something to the effect that I had no explanation to give. No words could be truer; I had not the slightest conception what to say.

"Yes, I am sure you have; you must, you will," pursued Mary excitedly; "you have some knowledge of that matter."

"What matter?" I asked.

"Why, the insurance," she replied impatiently. "You know well what I mean. My mind has been distracted about it. Spite of myself, terrible suspicions have forced themselves on me. No; I don't mean that," she cried, suddenly checking herself and changing her tone; "don't heed what I said; it was madness in me to say what I did. But do, do, do tell me all you know."

The request was a difficult one to comply with, for I knew nothing. It is impossible to say what might have been the end of this strange interview, in which I began to feel myself an unwilling impostor; but suddenly Mary started.

"The noise of the latchkey in the lock!" she cried, alarmed; "He has returned; he must not see you; you must come another time. Here, here, be quick! I'll manage him."

And before I could utter another word she had pushed me into the back drawing-room and closed the door. A man's step on the stairs; then voices. The man was begging Mary to come out with him, as the day was so fine. She excused herself; he would hear no refusal. At last she appeared to consent, on condition that the man would assist at her toilet. There was a little laughter, almost hysterical on the part of Mary, whose voice evidently quivered with trepidation.

Presently both mounted the upper stairs. Then the thought stuck me that I had left my hat in the front room—a sufficient cause for the woman's alarm. I opened the door cautiously, seized my hat, and was about to steal down the stairs, when I was again spellbound by that numb cold.

"Stay!" said the voice. I staggered back to the other room with my hat, and closed the door.

Presently the couple came down. Mary was probably relieved by discovering that my hat was no longer there, and surmised that I had departed; for I heard her laughing as they went down the lower flight. Then I heard them leave the house.

I was alone in that back drawing-room. Why? what did I want there? I was soon to learn. I felt the chill invisible presence near me; and the voice said, "Search!"

The room belonged to the common representative class of back drawing-rooms in "apartments" of the better kind. The only one unfamiliar piece of furniture was an old Indian cabinet; and my eye naturally fell on that. As I stood and looked at it with a strange unaccountable feeling of fascination, again came the voice—"Search!"

I shuddered and obeyed. The cabinet was firmly locked; there was no power of opening it except by burglarious infraction; but still the voice said, "Search!"

A thought suddenly struck me, and I turned the cabinet from its position against the wall. Behind, the woodwork had rotted, and in many portions fallen away, so that the inner drawers were visible. What could my ghostly monitor mean—that I should open those drawers? I would not do such a deed of petty treachery. I turned defiantly, and addressing myself to the invisible as if it were a living creature by my side, I cried, "I must not, will not, do such an act of baseness."

The voice replied, "Search!"

I might have known that, in my state of what I deemed insanity, resistance was in vain. I grasped the most accessible drawer from behind, and pulled it toward me. Uppermost within it lay letters: they were addressed to "Captain Cameron,"—"Captain George Cameron." That name!—the name of Julia's husband, the man with whom she had eloped; for it was he who was the object of my pursuit.

My shuddering fit became so strong that I could scarce hold the papers; and "Search!" was repeated in my ear.

Below the letters lay a small book in a limp black cover. I opened this book with trembling hand; it was filled with manuscript—Julia's well-known handwriting.

"Read!" muttered the voice. I read. There were long entries by poor Julia of her daily life; complaints of her husband's unkindness, neglect, then cruelty. I turned to the last pages: her hand had grown very feeble now, and she was very ill. "George seems kinder now," she wrote; "he brings me all my medicines with his own hand." Later on: "I am dying; I know I am dying: he has poisoned me. I saw him last night through the curtains pour something in my cup; I saw it in his evil eye. I would not drink; I will drink no more; but I feel that I must die."

These were the last words. Below were written, in a man's bold hand, the words "Poor fool!"

This sudden revelation of poor Julia's death and dying thoughts unnerved me quite. I grew colder in my whole frame than ever.

"Take it!" said her voice. I took the book, pushed back the cabinet into its place against the wall, and, leaving that fearful room, stole down the stairs with trembling limbs, and left the house with all the feelings of a guilty thief.

For some days I perused my poor lost Julia's diary again and again. The whole revelation of her sad life and sudden death led but to one conclusion,—she had died of poison by the hands of her unworthy husband. He had insured her life, and then——

It seemed evident to me that Mary Simms had vaguely shared suspicions of the same foul deed. On my own mind came conviction. But what could I do next? how bring this evil man to justice? what proof would be deemed to exist in those writings? I was bewildered, weak, irresolute. Like Hamlet, I shrank back and temporized. But I was not feigning madness; my madness seemed but all too real for me. During all this period the wailing of that wretched voice in my ear was almost incessant. O, I must have been mad!

I wandered about restlessly, like the haunted thing I had become. One day I had come unconsciously and without purpose into Oxford Street. My troubled thoughts were suddenly broken in upon by the solicitations of a beggar. With a heart hardened against begging impostors, and under the influence of the shock rudely given to my absorbing dreams, I answered more hardly than was my wont. The man heaved a heavy sigh, and sobbed forth, "Then Heaven help me!" I caught sight of him before he turned away. He was a ghastly object, with fever in his hollow eyes and sunken cheeks, and fever on his dry, chapped lips. But I knew, or fancied I knew, the tricks of the trade, and I was obdurate. Why, I asked myself, should the cold shudder come over me at such a moment? But it was so strong on me as to make me shake all over. It came—that maddening voice. "Succor!" it said now. I had become so accustomed already to address the ghostly voice that I cried aloud, "Why, Julia, why?" I saw people laughing in my face at this strange cry, and I turned in the direction in which the beggar had gone. I just caught sight of him as he was tottering down a street toward Soho. I determined to have pity for this once, and followed the poor man. He led me on through I know not what streets. His steps was hurried now. In one street I lost sight of him; but I felt convinced he must have turned into a dingy court. I made inquiries, but for a time received only rude jeering answers from the rough men and women whom I questioned. At last a little girl informed me that I must mean the strange man who lodged in the garret of a house she pointed out to me. It was an old dilapidated building, and I had much repugnance on entering it. But again I was no master of my will. I mounted some creaking stairs to the top of the house, until I could go no further. A shattered door was open; I entered a wretched garret; the object of my search lay now on a bundle of rags on the bare floor. He opened his wild eyes as I approached.

"I have come to succor," I said, using unconsciously the word of the voice; "what ails you?"

"Ails me?" gasped the man; "hunger, starvation, fever."

I was horrified. Hurrying to the top of the stairs, I shouted till I had roused the attention of an old woman. I gave her money to bring me food and brandy, promising her a recompense for her trouble.

"Have you no friends?" I asked the wretched man as I returned.

"None," he said feebly. Then as the fever rose in his eyes and even flushed his pallid face, he said excitedly, "I had a master once—one I perilled my soul for. He knows I am dying; but, spite of all my letters, he will not come. He wants me dead, he wants me dead—and his wish is coming to pass now."

"Cannot I find him—bring him here?" I asked.

The man stared at me, shook his head, and at last, as if collecting his faculties with much exertion, muttered, "Yes; it is a last hope; perhaps you may, and I can be revenged on him at least. Yes revenged. I have threatened him already." And the fellow laughed a wild laugh.

"Control yourself," I urged, kneeling by his side; "give me his name—his address."

"Captain George Cameron," he gasped, and then fell back.

"Captain George Cameron!" I cried. "Speak! what of him?"

But the man's senses seemed gone; he only muttered incoherently. The old woman returned with the food and spirits. I had found one honest creature in that foul region. I gave her money—provide her more if she would bring a doctor. She departed on her new errand. I raised the man's head, moistened his lips with the brandy, and then poured some of the spirit down his throat. He gulped at it eagerly, and opened his eyes; but he still raved incoherently, "I did not do it, it was he. He made me buy the poison; he dared not risk the danger himself, the coward! I knew what he meant to do with it, and yet I did not speak; I was her murderer too. Poor Mrs. Cameron! poor Mrs. Cameron! do you forgive?—can you forgive?" And the man screamed aloud and stretched out his arms as if to fright away a phantom.

I had drunk in every word, and knew the meaning of those broken accents well. Could I have found at last the means of bringing justice on the murderer's head? But the man was raving in a delirium, and I was obliged to hold him with all my strength. A step on the stairs. Could it be the medical man I had sent for? That would be indeed a blessing. A man entered—it was Cameron!

He came in jauntily, with the words, "How now, Saunders, you rascal! What more do you want to get out of me?"

He started at the sight of a stranger.

I rose from my kneeling posture like an accusing spirit. I struggled for calm; but passion beyond my control mastered me, and was I not a madman? I seized him by the throat, with the words, "Murderer! poisoner! where is Julia?" He shook me off violently.

"And who the devil are you, sir?" he cried.

"That murdered woman's cousin!" I rushed at him again.

"Lying hound!" he shouted, and grappled me. His strength was far beyond mine. He had his hand on my throat; a crimson darkness was in my eyes; I could not see, I could not hear; there was a torrent of sound pouring in my ears. Suddenly his grasp relaxed. When I recovered my sight, I saw the murderer struggling with the fever-stricken man, who had risen from the floor, and seized him from behind. This unexpected diversion saved my life; but the ex-groom was soon thrown back on the ground.

"Captain George Cameron," I cried, "kill me, but you will only heap another murder on your head!"

He advanced on me with something glittering in his hand. Without a word he came and stabbed at me; but at the same moment I darted at him a heavy blow. What followed was too confused for clear remembrance. I saw—no, I will say I fancied that I saw—the dim form of Julia Staunton standing between me and her vile husband. Did he see the vision too? I cannot say. He reeled back, and fell heavily to the floor. Maybe it was only my blow that felled him. Then came confusion—a dream of a crowd of people—policemen—muttered accusations. I had fainted from the wound in my arm.

Captain George Cameron was arrested. Saunders recovered, and lived long enough to be the principal witness on his trial. The murderer was found guilty. Poor Julia's diary, too, which I had abstracted, told fearfully against him. But he contrived to escape the gallows; he had managed to conceal poison on his person, and he was found dead in his cell. Mary Simms I never saw again. I once received a little scrawl, "I am at peace now, Master John. God bless you!"

I have had no more hallucinations since that time; the voice has never come again. I found out poor Julia's grave, and, as I stood and wept by its side, the cold shudder came over me for the last time. Who shall tell me whether I was once really mad, or whether I was not?

DOCTOR FEVERSHAM'S STORY.

I HAVE made a point all my life," said the doctor, "of believing nothing of the kind."

Much ghost-talk by firelight had been going on in the library at Fordwick Chase, when Doctor Feversham made this remark.

"As much as to say," observed Amy Fordwick, "that you are afraid to tackle the subject, because you pique yourself on being strong-minded, and are afraid of being convinced against your will."

"Not precisely, young lady. A man convinced against his will is in a different state of mind from mine in matters like these. But it is true that cases in which the supernatural element appears at first sight to enter are so numerous in my profession, that I prefer accepting only the solutions of science, so far as they go, to entering on any wild speculations which it would require more time than I should care to devote to them to trace to their origin."

"But without entering fully into the why and wherefore, how can you be sure that the proper treatment is observed in the numerous cases of mental hallucination which must come under your notice?" inquired Latimer Fordwick, who was studying for the Bar.

"I content myself, my young friend, with following the rules laid down for such cases, and I generally find them successful," answered the old Doctor.

"Then you admit that cases have occurred within your knowledge of which the easiest apparent solution could be one which involved a belief in supernatural agencies?" persisted Latimer, who was rather prolix and pedantic in his talk.

"I did not say so," said the Doctor.

"But of course he meant us to infer it," said Amy. "Now, my dear old Doctor, do lay aside professional dignity, and give us one good ghost-story out of your personal experience. I believe you have been dying to tell one for the last hour, if you would only confess it."

"I would rather not help to fill that pretty little head with idle fancies, dear child," answered the old man, looking fondly at Amy, who was his especial pet and darling.

"Nonsense! You know I am even painfully unimaginative and matter-of-fact; and as for idle fancies, is it an idle fancy to think you like to please me?" said Amy coaxingly.

"Well, after all, you have been frightening each other with so many thrilling tales for the last hour or two, that I don't suppose I should do much harm by telling you a circumstance which happened to me when I was a young man, and has always rather puzzled me."

A murmur of approval ran round the party. All disposed themselves to listen; and Doctor Feversham, after a prefatory pinch of snuff, began.

"In my youth I resided for some time with a family in the north of England, in the double capacity of secretary and physician. While I was going through the hospitals of Paris I became acquainted with my employer, whom I will call Sir James Collingham, under rather peculiar circumstances, which have nothing to do with my story. He had an only daughter, who was about sixteen when I first entered the family, and it was on her account that Sir James wished to have some person with a competent knowledge of medicine and physiology as one of his household. Miss Collingham was subject to fits of a very peculiar kind, which threw her into a sort of trance, lasting from half an hour to three or even four days, according to the severity of the visitation. During these attacks she occasionally displayed that extraordinary phenomenon which goes by the name of clairvoyance. She saw scenes and persons who were far distant, and described them with wonderful accuracy. Though quite unconscious of all outward things, and apparently in a state of the deepest insensibility, she would address remarks to those present which bore reference to the thoughts then occupying their minds, though they had given them no outward expression; and her remarks showed an insight into matters which had perhaps been carefully kept secret, which might truly be termed preternatural. Under these circumstances, Sir James was very unwilling to bring her into contact with strangers when it could possibly be avoided; and the events which first brought us together, having also led to my treating Miss Collingham rather successfully in a severe attack of her malady, induced her father to offer me a position in his household which, as a young, friendless man, I was very willing to accept.

"Collingham-Westmore was a very ancient house of great extent, and but indifferently kept in repair. The country surrounding it is of great natural beauty, thinly inhabited, and, especially at the time I speak of, before railways had penetrated so far north, somewhat lonely and inaccessible. A group of small houses clustered round the village church of Westmorton, distant about three miles from the mansion of the Collingham family; and a solitary posting-house, on what was then the great north road, could be reached by a horseman in about an hour, though the only practicable road for carriages was at least fifteen miles from the highway to Collingham-Westmore. Wild and lovely in the eyes of an admirer of nature were the hills and 'cloughs' among which I pursued my botanical studies for many a long, silent summer day. My occupations at the mansion—everybody called it the mansion, and I must do so from force of habit, though it sounds rather like a house-agent's advertisement—were few and light; the society was not particularly to my taste, and the fine old library only attracted me on rainy days, of which, truth to say, we had our full share.

"The Collingham family circle comprised a maiden aunt of Sir James, Miss Patricia, a stern and awful specimen of the female sex in its fossil state; her ward, Miss Henderson, who, having long passed her pupilage, remained at Collingham-Westmore in the capacity of gouvernante and companion to the young heiress; the heiress aforesaid, and myself. A priest—did I say that the Collinghams still professed the old religion?—came on Sundays and holydays to celebrate mass in the gloomy old chapel; but neighbors there were none, and only about half-a-dozen times during the four years I was an inmate of the mansion were strangers introduced into the family party."

"How dreadfully dull it must have been!" exclaimed Amy sympathetically.

"It *was* dull," answered the Doctor. "Even with my naturally cheerful disposition, and the course of study with which I methodically filled up all my leisure hours except those devoted to out-of-door exercise, the gloom of the old mansion weighed upon me till I sometimes felt that I must give up my situation at all risks, and return to the world, though it were to struggle with poverty and friendlessness.

"There was no lack of dismal legends and superstitions connected with the mansion, and every trifling circumstance that occurred was twisted into an omen or presage, whether of good or evil, by the highly wrought fancy of Miss Patricia. These absurdities, together with the past grandeur of their house, and the former glories of their religion, formed the staple subjects of conversation when the family was assembled; and as I became more intimately acquainted with the state of my patient, I felt convinced that the atmosphere of gloomy superstition in which she had been reared had fostered, even if it had not altogether been the cause of, her morbid mental and bodily condition.

"Among the many legends connected with the mansion, one seemed to have a peculiar fascination for Miss Collingham, perhaps because it was the most ghastly and repulsive. One wing of the house was held to be haunted by the spirit of an ancestress of the family, who appeared in the shape of a tall woman, with one hand folded in her white robe and the other pointing upward. It was said, that in a room at the end of the haunted wing this lady had been foully murdered by her jealous husband. The window of the apartment overhung the wild wooded side of one of the 'cloughs' common in the country; and tradition averred that the victim was thrown from this window by her murderer. As she caught hold of the sill in a last frantic struggle for life, he severed her hand at the wrist, and the mutilated body fell, with one fearful shriek, into the depth below. Since then, a white shadowy form has forever been sitting at the fatal window, or wandering along the deserted passages of the haunted wing with the bleeding stump folded in her robe; and in moments of danger or approaching death to any member of the Collingham family, the same long, wild shriek rises slowly from the wooded cliff and peals through the mansion; while to different individuals of the house, a pale hand has now and then been visible, laid on themselves or some other of the family, a never-failing omen of danger or death.

"I need not tell you how false and foolish all this dreary superstition appeared to me; and I exerted all my powers of persuasion to induce Miss Patricia to dwell less on these and similar themes in the presence of Miss Collingham. But there seemed to be something in the very air of the gloomy old mansion which fostered such delusions; for when I spoke to Father O'Connor the priest, and urged on him the pernicious effect which was thus produced on my patient's mind, I found him as fully imbued with the spirit of credulity as the most hysterical housemaid of them all. He solemnly declared to me that he had himself repeatedly seen the pale lady sitting at the fatal window, when on his way to and from his home beyond the hills; and moreover, that on the death of Lady Collingham, which occurred at her daughter's birth, he had heard the long, shrill death-scream echo through the mansion while engaged in the last offices of the Church by the bedside of the dying lady.

"So I found it impossible to fight single-handed against these adverse influences, and could only endeavor to divert the mind of my patient into more healthy channels of thought. In this I succeeded perfectly. She became an enthusiastic botanist, and our rambles in search of the rare and lovely specimens which were to be found among the woods and moors surrounding her dwelling did more for her health, both of body and mind, than all the medical skill I could bring to bear on her melancholy case.

"Four years had elapsed since I first took up my abode at Collingham-Westmore. Miss Collingham had grown from a sickly child into a singularly graceful young woman, full of bright intelligence, eager for information, and with scarcely an outward trace remaining of her former fragile health. Still those mysterious swoons occasionally visited her, forming an insurmountable obstacle to her mingling in general society, which she was in all other respects so well fitted to adorn. They occurred without any warning or apparent cause; one moment she would be engaged in animated conversation, and the next, white and rigid as a statue, she would fall back in her chair insensible to all outward objects, but rapt and carried away into a world of her own, whose visions she would sometimes describe in glowing language, although she retained no recollection whatever of them when she returned, as suddenly and at as uncertain a period, to her normal condition. On one of these occasions we were sitting, after dinner, in a large apartment called the summer dining-room. Fruit and wine were on the table, and the last red beams of the setting sun lighted up the distant woods, which were in the first flush of their autumn glory. I turned to remark on the beautiful effect of light to Miss Collingham, and at the very moment I did so she fell back in one of her strange swoons. But instead of the death-like air which her features usually assumed, a lovely smile lighted them up, and an expression of ecstasy made her beauty appear for the moment almost superhuman. Slowly she raised her right hand, and pointed in the direction of the setting sun. 'He is coming,' she said in soft, clear tones; 'life and light are coming with him,—life and light and liberty!'

"Her hand fell gently by her side; the rapt expression faded from her countenance, and the usual death-like blank overspread it. This trance passed away like others, and by midnight the house was profoundly still. Soon after that hour a vociferous peal at the great hall-bell roused most of the inmates from sleep. My rooms were in a distant quarter of the house, and a door opposite to that of my bedroom led to the haunted wing, but was always kept locked. I started up on hearing a second ring, and looked out, in hopes of seeing a servant pass, and ascertaining the cause of this unusual disturbance. I saw no one, and after listening for a while to the opening of the hall-door, and the sound of distant voices, I made up my mind that I should be sent for if wanted, and re-entered my room. As I was closing the door, I was rather startled to see a tall object, of grayish-white color and indistinct form, issue from the gallery whose door, as I said before, had always been locked in my recollection. For a moment I felt as though rooted to the spot, and a strange sensation crept over me. The next, all trace of the appearance had vanished, and I persuaded myself that what I had seen must have been some effect of light from the open door of my room.

"The cause of the nightly disturbance appeared at breakfast on the following morning in the shape of a remarkably handsome young man, who was introduced by Sir James as his nephew, Don Luis de Cabral, the son of an only sister long dead, who had married a Spaniard of high rank. Don Luis showed but little trace of his southern parentage. If I may so express it, all the depth and warmth of coloring in that portion of his blood which he inherited from his Spanish ancestors came out in the raven-black hair and large lustrous dark eyes, which impressed you at once with their uncommon beauty. For the rest, he was a fine well-grown young man, no darker in complexion than an Englishman might well be, and with a careless, happy boyishness of manner, which won immediately on the regard of strangers, and rendered his presence in the house like that of a perpetual sunbeam. We all wondered, after a little while, what we had done before Luis came among us. He was as a son to Sir James; Miss Patricia softened to this new and pleasing interest in her colorless existence as I could not have believed it was in her fossilized nature to do; Miss Henderson became animated, almost young, under the reviving influence of the youth and joyousness of our new inmate; and I own that I speedily attached myself with a warm and affectionate regard to the happy, unselfish nature that seemed to brighten all who came near it.

"But the most remarkable effect of the presence of Don Luis de Cabral among us was visible in Miss Collingham. 'Love at first sight,' often considered as a mere phrase, was, in the case of these two young creatures, an unmistakable reality. From the moment of their first meeting, the cousins were mutually drawn toward each other; and seeing the bright and wonderful change wrought by the presence of Don Luis in Blanche Collingham, I could not but remember, with the interest that attaches to a curious psychological phenomenon, the words she uttered in her trance on the eve of his arrival. 'Life, light, and liberty,' indeed, appeared given to all that was best and brightest in her nature. Her health improved visibly, and her beauty, always touching, became radiant in its full development. My duties toward her were now merely nominal; and when, about two months later, Sir James announced to me her approaching marriage, and confessed that it was with this object he had invited Don Luis to come and make the acquaintance of his English relations, the strong opinions I entertained against the marriage of first cousins, and also on the especial inadvisability of any project of marriage in the case of Miss Collingham, could not prevent my hearty rejoicing in the fair prospect of happiness in which two persons who deeply interested me were indulging.

"Winter set in early and severely that year among our northern hills, and with a view to Blanche's removal from its withering influence, which I always considered prejudicial to her, the preparations for the marriage were hurried on, and the ceremony was fixed to take place about the middle of December. The travelling-carriage which was to convey the young couple on their way southward was to arrive at the nearest railway-station—then more than thirty miles distant—a week before the marriage; and as some important portions of the trousseau, together with a valuable package of jewels intended by Don Luis as presents for his bride, were expected at the same time, the young man announced his intention of riding across the hills to ——, in order to superintend the conveyance of the carriage and its contents along the rough mountain roads that it must traverse.

"We were all sitting around the great fireplace in the winter parlor on the evening before his departure. Miss Collingham had been languid and depressed throughout the day, and often adverted to the long wintry ride he was to undertake in a strain of apprehension at which Don Luis laughed gayly. To divert her mind, he recounted various adventures which had befallen him in foreign lands, with a vigorous simplicity of description which enchained her attention and interested us all.

"Suddenly, so sitting, Miss Collingham leaned forward, and in a changed, eager voice exclaimed, 'Luis, take away your hand from your throat!'

"We looked. Luis' hands were lying one over the other on his knee in a careless attitude that was habitual to him.

"'Take it away, I say! Oh, take it away!'

"Miss Collingham started to her feet as she uttered these words almost in a shriek, and then fell back rigid and senseless, her outstretched hand still pointing to her betrothed.

"The fit was a severe one, but by morning it had yielded to remedies, and Luis set off early on his ride, to make the most of the short daylight, and intending to return with the carriage on the morrow. All that day Miss Collingham remained in a half-conscious state. It was a dreary day of gloom, with a piercing north wind, and toward evening the snow began to fall in those close, compact flakes which forebode a heavy storm. We were glad to think that Luis must have reached his destination before it began; but when the next morning dawned on a wide expanse of snow, and the air was still thick with fast-falling flakes, it was feared that the state of the roads would preclude all hope of the arrival of the carriage on that day.

"My patient took no heed of the untoward state of the weather. She was still in a drowsy condition, very unlike that which usually succeeded her attacks, and

Miss Henderson, who had watched by her through the night, told me she spoke more than once in a strange, excited manner, as though carrying on a conversation with some one whom she appeared to see by her bedside. As the good lady, however, could give but a very imperfect and incoherent account of what had passed, I was left in some doubt as to whether Miss Collingham had seen more or Miss Henderson less than there really was to be seen, as I had before had reason to believe that she was not a very vigilant nurse.

"So the hours went on, and night closed in. Sir James began to feel some uneasiness at the non-appearance, not only of Don Luis, but also of the priest, who was to have arrived at Collingham-Westmore on that day.

"On questioning some of the servants who had been out of the house, the absence of Father O'Connor at least was satisfactorily accounted for: they all declared that it would be quite impossible for those best acquainted with the hills to find their way across them in the blinding drifts which had never ceased throughout the day. We concluded that Father O'Connor and Don Luis were alike storm-stayed, and had no remedy but patience.

"Late in the evening—it must have been near midnight—I was in Miss Collingham's dressing-room with Miss Patricia, who intended to watch by her through the night. We were talking by the fire, of the snow-storm which still continued, and of the hindrance it might prove to the marriage—the day fixed for which was now less than a week distant—when we heard a voice in the adjoining room, where we imagined the object of our care to be sleeping. We went in. Miss Collingham was sitting up in bed, her eyes wide open, in one of her rigid fits. She was speaking rapidly in a low tone, unlike her usual voice.

"'You cannot get through all that snow,' she said. 'Get help; there are men not far off with spades. Oh, be careful! You are off the road! Stop, stop! that is the way to Armstrong's Clough. Does not the postboy know the road? He is bewildered. I tell you it is madness to go on. See, one of the horses has fallen; he kicks—he will hit you! Oh, how dark it is! And the snow covers your lantern, and you cannot see the edge. Now the horse is up again, but he cannot go on. Do not beat him, Luis; it is not his fault, poor beast; the snow is too thick, and you are on rough ground. Now he rears—he backs—the other one backs also—the wheel of the carriage is over the edge—ah!'

"The scream with which these wild, hurried words ended seemed to be taken up and echoed from a distance. Miss Patricia stared at me with a ghastly white face of horror, and I felt my blood curdle as that long, shrill, unearthly shriek pealed through the silent passages. It grew louder and nearer, and seemed to sweep through the room, dying away in the opposite direction. Miss Patricia fell forward without a word in a dead faint.

"I looked at Miss Collingham; she had not moved, or shown any sign of hearing or heeding that awful sound. In a few seconds the room was filled with terrified women, roused from their sleep by the weird cry which rang through the house. Miss Patricia was conveyed by some of them to her own room, where, after much difficulty, we restored her to consciousness. Her first act was to grasp me by the arm.

"'Mr. Feversham, for the love of the Holy Virgin do not leave me! I have seen that which I cannot look upon and live.'

"I soothed her as best I might, and at last persuaded her to allow me to leave her with her own maid in order to visit my other patient, promising to return shortly.

"I found no change whatever in Miss Collingham. Sir James was in the room trying to establish some degree of calmness and order among the terrified women. We succeeded in persuading most of them to take a restorative and return to bed, and leaving two of the most self-possessed to watch beside Miss Collingham, who was still completely insensible, we went together to Miss Patricia's room.

"'Brother, I have seen her!' she exclaimed on Sir James' entrance.

"'Seen who, my dear Patricia?'

"'The pale lady—the spectre of our house,' she replied, shuddering from head to foot. 'She passed through the room, her hand upraised, and the blood-spots on her garment. Oh, James! my time is come, and Father O'Connor is not here.'

"Sir James did not attempt to combat his sister's superstitious terrors, but appeared, on the contrary, almost as deeply impressed as herself, and questioned her closely about the apparition. Her answers led to some mention of the strange vision which Miss Collingham was describing in her trance just before the scream was heard. At Sir James' request I put down in writing, as nearly as I could remember, all she had said, and so great was the impression it made on my mind that I believe I recalled her very words. Knowing all we did of her abnormal condition while in a state of trance, it was impossible not to fear that she might have been describing a scene that was actually occurring at the time; and Sir James determined to send out a party, as soon as daylight came, on the road by which Don Luis must arrive.

"The morning dawned brightly, with a keen frost, and several men were sent off along the road to —— with the first rays of light.

"Some hours afterward Father O'Connor arrived, having made his way with considerable difficulty across the hill. Miss Patricia claimed his first attention, for my unhappy charge remained senseless and motionless as ever.

"After a long conference, he came to me with grave looks.

"'She is at the window this day,' he said, shaking his head sorrowfully, when I had told him my share of the last night's singular experiences. 'The pale lady is there; I saw her as I came by the bridge as plainly as now I see you. We shall have evil tidings of that poor lad before nightfall, or I am strangely mistaken.'

"Evil tidings indeed they were that reached us on the return of some of the exploring-party. They were first attracted from following as nearly as they could the line of road, blocked as it was with drifts of snow by hearing the howling of a dog at some little distance, in the direction of the precipitous ravine which went by the name of 'Armstrong's Clough.' Following the sound, they came upon traces of wheels in the hill-side, where no carriage could have gone had it not been for the deep snow which concealed and smoothed away the inequalities of the ground. These marks were traced here and there till they led to the verge of the precipice, where a struggle had evidently taken place, and masses of snow had been dislodged and fallen into the ravine.

"Looking below, the only thing they could see in the waste of snow was a little dog, who was known to be in the habit of running with the post-horses from ——, which was scraping wildly in the snow and filling the air with its dismal howlings. A considerable circuit had to be made before the bottom of the clough could be reached, and then the whole tragedy was revealed. There lay the broken carriage, the dead horses, and two stiffened corpses under the snow, that had drifted over and around them.

"I need not pursue the melancholy story; I was an old fool for telling it to you," said the Doctor.

"But Miss Collingham—what became of her?" asked an eager listener.

"Well, she did not recover," answered the Doctor with a slight trembling in his voice. "It was a sad matter altogether; and within a short time she lay beside her betrothed in the family vault below the chapel. Sir James broke up his establishment and went abroad, and I never saw any of the family again."

"And what did you do, Doctor?"

"I went to London, to seek my fortune as best I might; and I hope you may all prosper as well, my young friends."

"And is it all really true?" asked Amy, who had listened with breathless attention.

"That is the worst of it; it really is," said the Doctor.

THE SECRET OF THE TWO PLASTER CASTS.

YEARS before the accession of her Majesty Queen Victoria, and yet at not so remote a date as to be utterly beyond the period to which the reminiscences of our middle-aged readers extend, it happened that two English gentlemen sat at table on a summer's evening, after dinner, quietly sipping their wine and engaged in desultory conversation. They were both men known to fame. One of them was a sculptor whose statues adorned the palaces of princes, and whose chiselled busts were the pride of half the nobility of his nation; the other was no less renowned as an anatomist and surgeon. The age of the anatomist might have been guessed at fifty, but the guess would have erred on the side of youth by at least ten years. That of the sculptor could scarcely be more than five-and-thirty. A bust of the anatomist, so admirably executed as to present, although in stone, the perfect similitude of life and flesh, stood upon a pedestal opposite to the table at which sat the pair, and at once explained at least one connecting-link of companionship between them. The anatomist was exhibiting for the criticism of his friend a rare gem which he had just drawn from his cabinet: it was a crucifix magnificently carved in ivory, and incased in a setting of pure gold.

"The carving, my dear sir," observed Mr. Fiddyes, the sculptor, "is indeed, as you say, exquisite. The muscles are admirably made out, the flesh well modelled, wonderfully so for the size and material; and yet—by the bye, on this point you must know more than I—the more I think upon the matter, the more I regard the artistic conception as utterly false and wrong."

"You speak in a riddle," replied Dr. Carnell; "but pray go on, and explain."

"It is a fancy I first had in my student-days," replied Fiddyes. "Conventionality, not to say a most proper and becoming reverence, prevents people by no means ignorant from considering the point. But once think upon it, and you at least, of all men, must at once perceive how utterly impossible it would be for a victim nailed upon a cross by hands and feet to preserve the position invariably displayed in figures of the Crucifixion. Those who so portray it fail in what should be their most awful and agonizing effect. Think for one moment, and imagine, if you can, what would be the attitude of a man, living or dead, under this frightful torture."

"You startle me," returned the great surgeon, "not only by the truth of your remarks, but by their obviousness. It is strange indeed that such a matter should have so long been overlooked. The more I think upon it the more the bare idea of actual crucifixion seems to horrify me, though heaven knows I am accustomed enough to scenes of suffering. How would you represent such a terrible agony?"

"Indeed I cannot tell," replied the sculptor; "to guess would be almost vain. The fearful strain upon the muscles, their utter helplessness and inactivity, the frightful swellings, the effect of weight upon the racked and tortured sinews, appal me too much even for speculation."

"But this," replied the surgeon, "one might think a matter of importance, not only to art, but, higher still, to religion itself."

"Maybe so," returned the sculptor. "But perhaps the appeal to the senses through a true representation might be too horrible for either the one or the other."

"Still," persisted the surgeon, "I should like—say for curiosity—though I am weak enough to believe even in my own motive as a higher one—to ascertain the effect from actual observation."

"So should I, could it be done, and of course without pain to the object, which, as a condition, seems to present at the outset an impossibility."

"Perhaps not," mused the anatomist; "I think I have a notion. Stay—we may contrive this matter. I will tell you my plan, and it will be strange indeed if we two cannot manage to carry it out."

The discourse here, owing to the rapt attention of both speakers, assumed a low and earnest tone, but had perhaps better be narrated by a relation of the events to which it gave rise. Suffice it to say that the Sovereign was more than once mentioned during its progress, and in a manner which plainly told that the two speakers each possessed sufficient influence to obtain the assistance of royalty, and that such assistance would be required in their scheme.

The shades of evening deepened while the two were still conversing. And leaving this scene, let us cast one hurried glimpse at another taking place contemporaneously.

Between Pimlico and Chelsea, and across a canal of which the bed has since been used for the railway terminating at Victoria Station, there was at the time of which we speak a rude timber footway, long since replaced by a more substantial and convenient erection, but then known as the Wooden Bridge. It was named shortly afterward Cutthroat Bridge, and for this reason.

While Mr. Fiddyes and Dr. Carnell were discoursing over their wine, as we have already seen, one Peter Starke, a drunken Chelsea pensioner, was murdering his wife upon the spot we have last indicated. The coincidence was curious.

In those days the punishment of criminals followed closely upon their conviction. The Chelsea pensioner whom we have mentioned was found guilty one Friday and sentenced to die on the following Monday. He was a sad scoundrel, impenitent to the last, glorying in the deeds of slaughter which he had witnessed and acted during the series of campaigns which had ended just previously at Waterloo. He was a tall, well-built fellow enough, of middle age, for his class was not then, as now, composed chiefly of veterans, but comprised many young men, just sufficiently disabled to be unfit for service. Peter Starke, although but slightly wounded, had nearly completed his term of service, and had obtained his pension and presentment to Chelsea Hospital. With his life we have but little to do, save as regards its close, which we shall shortly endeavor to describe far more veraciously, and at some greater length than set forth in the brief account which satisfied the public of his own day, and which, as embodied in the columns of the few journals then appearing, ran thus:

> "On Monday last Peter Starke was executed at Newgate for the murder at the Wooden Bridge, Chelsea, with four others for various offences. After he had been hanging only for a few minutes a respite arrived, but although he was promptly cut down, life was pronounced to be extinct. His body was buried within the prison walls."

Thus far history. But the conciseness of history far more frequently embodies falsehood than truth. Perhaps the following narration may approach more nearly to the facts.

A room within the prison had been, upon that special occasion and by high authority, allotted to the use of Dr. Carnell and Mr. Fiddyes, the famous sculptor, for the purpose of certain investigations connected with art and science. In that room Mr. Fiddyes, while wretched Peter Starke was yet swinging between heaven and earth, was busily engaged in arranging a variety of implements and materials, consisting of a large quantity of plaster-of-Paris, two large pails of water, some tubs, and other necessaries of the moulder's art. The room contained a large deal table, and a wooden cross, not neatly planed and squared at the angles, but of thick, narrow, rudely-sawn oaken plank, fixed by strong, heavy nails. And while Mr. Fiddyes was thus occupied, the executioner entered, bearing upon his shoulders the body of the wretched Peter, which he flung heavily upon the table.

"You are sure he is dead?" asked Mr. Fiddyes.

"Dead as a herring," replied the other. "And yet just as warm and limp as if he had only fainted."

"Then go to work at once," replied the sculptor, as turning his back upon the hangman, he resumed his occupation.

The "work" was soon done. Peter was stripped and nailed upon the timber, which was instantly propped against the wall.

"As fine a one as ever I see," exclaimed the executioner, as he regarded the defunct murderer with an expression of admiration, as if at his own handiwork, in having abruptly demolished such a magnificent animal. "Drops a good bit for'ard, though. Shall I tie him up round the waist, sir?"

"Certainly not," returned the sculptor. "Just rub him well over with this oil, especially his head, and then you can go. Dr. Carnell will settle with you."

"All right, sir."

The fellow did as ordered, and retired without another word; leaving this strange couple, the living and the dead, in that dismal chamber.

Mr. Fiddyes was a man of strong nerve in such matters. He had been too much accustomed to taking posthumous casts to trouble himself with any sentiment of repugnance at his approaching task of taking what is called a "piece-mould" from a body. He emptied a number of bags of the white powdery plaster-of-Paris into one of the larger vessels, poured into it a pail of water, and was carefully stirring up the mass, when a sound of dropping arrested his ear.

Drip, drip.

"There's something leaking," he muttered, as he took a second pail, and emptying it, again stirred the composition.

Drip, drip, drip.

"It's strange," he soliloquized, half aloud. "There is no more water, and yet——"

The sound was heard again.

He gazed at the ceiling; there was no sign of damp. He turned his eyes to the body, and something suddenly caused him a violent start. The murderer was bleeding.

The sculptor, spite of his command over himself, turned pale. At that moment the head of Starke moved—clearly moved. It raised itself convulsively for a single moment; its eyes rolled, and it gave vent to a subdued moan of intense agony. Mr. Fiddyes fell fainting on the floor as Dr. Carnell entered. It needed but a glance to tell the doctor what had happened, even had not Peter just then given vent to another low cry. The surgeon's measures were soon taken. Locking the door, he bore a chair to the wall which supported the body of the malefactor. He drew from his pocket a case of glittering instruments, and with one of these, so small and delicate that it scarcely seemed larger than a needle, he rapidly, but dexterously and firmly, touched Peter just at the back of the neck. There was no wound larger than the head of a small pin, and yet the head fell instantly as though the heart had been pierced. The doctor had divided the spinal cord, and Peter Starke was dead indeed.

A few minutes sufficed to recall the sculptor to his senses. He at first gazed wildly upon the still suspended body, so painfully recalled to life by the rough venesection of the hangman and the subsequent friction of anointing his body to prevent the adhesion of the plaster.

"You need not fear now," said Dr. Carnell; "I assure you he is dead."

"But he *was* alive, surely!"

"Only for a moment, and even that scarcely to be called life—mere muscular contraction, my dear sir, mere muscular contraction."

The sculptor resumed his labor. The body was girt at various circumferences with fine twine, to be afterward withdrawn through a thick coating of plaster, so as to separate the various pieces of the mould, which was at last completed; and after this Dr. Carnell skilfully flayed the body, to enable a second mould to be taken of the entire figure, showing every muscle of the outer layer.

The two moulds were thus taken. It is difficult to conceive more ghastly appearances than they presented. For sculptor's work they were utterly useless; for no artist except the most daring of realists would have ventured to indicate the horrors which they presented. Fiddyes refused to receive them. Dr. Carnell, hard and cruel as he was, for kindness' sake, in his profession, was a gentle, genial father of a family of daughters. He received the casts, and at once consigned them to a garret, to which he forbade access. His youngest daughter, one unfortunate day, during her father's absence, was impelled by feminine curiosity—perhaps a little increased by the prohibition—to enter the mysterious chamber.

Whether she imagined in the pallid figure upon the cross a celestial rebuke for her disobedience, or whether she was overcome by the mere mortal horror of one or both of those dreadful casts, can now never be known. But this is true: she became a maniac.

The writer of this has more than once seen (as, no doubt, have many others) the plaster effigies of Peter Starke, after their removal from Dr. Carnell's to a famous studio near the Regent's Park. It was there that he heard whispered the strange story of their origin. Sculptor and surgeon are now both long since dead, and it is no longer necessary to keep *the secret of the two plaster casts*.

WHAT WAS IT?

IT is, I confess, with considerable diffidence that I approached the strange narrative which I am about to relate. The events which I purpose detailing are of so extraordinary a character that I am quite prepared to meet with an unusual amount of incredulity and scorn. I accept all such beforehand. I have, I trust, the literary courage to face unbelief. I have, after mature consideration, resolved to narrate, in as simple and straightforward a manner as I can compass, some facts that passed under my observation, in the month of July last, and which, in the annals of the mysteries of physical science, are wholly unparalleled.

I live at No. — Twenty-sixth Street, in New York. The house is in some respects a curious one. It has enjoyed for the last two years the reputation of being haunted. The house is very spacious. A hall of noble size leads to a large spiral staircase winding through its centre, while the various apartments are of imposing dimensions. It was built some fifteen or twenty years since by Mr. A——, the well-known New York merchant, who five years ago threw the commercial world into convulsions by a stupendous bank fraud. Mr. A——, as every one knows, escaped to Europe, and died not long after, of a broken heart. Almost immediately after the news of his decease reached this country and was verified, the report spread in Twenty-sixth Street that No. — was haunted. Legal measures had dispossessed the widow of its former owner, and it was inhabited merely by a care-taker and his wife, placed there by the house-agent into whose hands it had passed for purposes of renting or sale. These people declared that they were troubled with unnatural noises. Doors were opened without any visible agency. The remnants of furniture scattered through the various rooms were, during the night, piled one upon the other by unknown hands. Invisible feet passed up and down the stairs in broad daylight, accompanied by the rustle of unseen silk dresses, and the gliding of viewless hands along the massive balusters. The care-taker and his wife declared they would live there no longer. The house-agent laughed, dismissed them, and put others in their place. The noises and supernatural manifestations continued. The neighborhood caught up the story, and the house remained untenanted for three years. Several persons negotiated for it; but, somehow, always before the bargain was closed they heard the unpleasant rumors and declined to treat any further.

It was in this state of things that my landlady, who at that time kept a boarding-house in Bleecker Street, and who wished to move farther up town, conceived the bold idea of renting No. — Twenty-sixth Street. Happening to have in her house rather a plucky and philosophical set of boarders, she laid her scheme before us, stating candidly everything she had heard respecting the ghostly qualities of the establishment to which she wished to remove us. With the exception of two timid persons—a sea-captain and a returned Californian, who immediately gave notice that they would leave—all of Mrs. Moffat's guests declared that they would accompany her in her incursion into the abode of spirits.

Our removal was effected in the month of May, and we were charmed with our new residence.

Of course we had no sooner established ourselves at No. — than we began to expect the ghosts. We absolutely awaited their advent with eagerness. Our dinner conversation was supernatural. I found myself a person of immense importance, it having leaked out that I was tolerably well versed in the history of supernaturalism, and had once written a story the foundation of which was a ghost. If a table or wainscot panel happened to warp when we were assembled in the large drawing-room, there was an instant silence, and every one was prepared for an immediate clanking of chains and a spectral form.

After a month of psychological excitement, it was with the utmost dissatisfaction that we were forced to acknowledge that nothing in the remotest degree approaching the supernatural had manifested itself.

Things were in this state when an incident took place so awful and inexplicable in its character that my reason fairly reels at the bare memory of the occurrence. It was the tenth of July. After dinner was over I repaired, with my friend Dr. Hammond, to the garden to smoke my evening pipe. Independent of certain mental sympathies which existed between the doctor and myself, we were linked together by a vice. We both smoked opium. We knew each other's secret and respected it. We enjoyed together that wonderful expansion of thought, that marvellous intensifying of the perceptive faculties, that boundless feeling of existence when we seem to have points of contact with the whole universe—in short, that unimaginable spiritual bliss, which I would not surrender for a throne, and which I hope you, reader, will never—never taste.

On the evening in question, the tenth of July, the doctor and myself drifted into an unusually metaphysical mood. We lit our large meerschaums, filled with fine Turkish tobacco, in the core of which burned a little black nut of opium, that, like the nut in the fairy tale, held within its narrow limits wonders beyond the reach of kings; we paced to and fro, conversing. A strange perversity dominated the currents of our thoughts. They would not flow through the sun-lit channels into which we strove to divert them. For some unaccountable reason, they constantly diverged into dark and lonesome beds, where a continual gloom brooded. It was in vain that, after our old fashion, we flung ourselves on the shores of the East, and talked of its gay bazaars, of the splendors of the time of Haroun, of harems and golden palaces. Black afreets continually arose from the depths of our talk, and expanded, like the one the fisherman released from the copper vessel, until they blotted everything bright from our vision. Insensibly, we yielded to the occult force that swayed us, and indulged in gloomy speculation. We had talked some time upon the proneness of the human mind to mysticism, and the almost universal love of the terrible, when Hammond suddenly said to me, "What do you consider to be the greatest element of terror?"

The question puzzled me. That many things were terrible, I knew. But it now struck me, for the first time, that there must be one great and ruling embodiment of fear—a King of Terrors, to which all others must succumb. What might it be? To what train of circumstances would it owe its existence?

"I confess, Hammond," I replied to my friend, "I never considered the subject before. That there must be one Something more terrible than any other thing, I feel. I cannot attempt, however, even the most vague definition."

"I am somewhat like you, Harry," he answered. "I feel my capacity to experience a terror greater than anything yet conceived by the human mind—something combining in fearful and unnatural amalgamation hitherto supposed incompatible elements. The calling of the voices in Brockden Brown's novel of 'Wieland' is awful; so is the picture of the Dweller on the Threshold, in Bulwer's 'Zanoni;' but," he added, shaking his head gloomily, "there is something more horrible still than these."

"Look here, Hammond," I rejoined, "let us drop this kind of talk, for Heaven's sake! We shall suffer for it, depend on it."

"I don't know what's the matter with me to-night," he replied, "but my brain is running upon all sorts of weird and awful thoughts. I feel as if I could write a sto ry like Hoffman, to-night, if I were only master of a literary style."

"Well, if we are going to be Hoffmanesque in our talk, I'm off to bed. Opium and nightmares should never be brought together. How sultry it is! Good-night, Hammond."

"Good-night, Harry. Pleasant dreams to you."

"To you, gloomy wretch, afreets, ghouls, and enchanters."

We parted, and each sought his respective chamber. I undressed quickly and got into bed, taking with me, according to my usual custom, a book over which I generally read myself to sleep. I opened the volume as soon as I had laid my head upon the pillow, and instantly flung it to the other side of the room. It was Goudon's "History of Monsters,"—a curious French work, which I had lately imported from Paris, but which, in the state of mind I had then reached, was anything but an agreeable companion. I resolved to go to sleep at once; so, turning down my gas until nothing but a little blue point of light glimmered on the top of the tube, I composed myself to rest.

The room was in total darkness. The atom of gas that still remained alight did not illuminate a distance of three inches round the burner. I desperately drew my arm across my eyes, as if to shut out even the darkness and tried to think of nothing. It was in vain. The confounded themes touched on by Hammond in the garden kept obtruding themselves on my brain. I battled against them. I erected ramparts of would-be blankness of intellect to keep them out. They still crowded upon me. While I was lying still as a corpse, hoping that by a perfect physical inaction I should hasten mental repose, an awful incident occurred. A Something dropped, as it seemed, from the ceiling, plumb upon my chest, and the next instant I felt two bony hands encircling my throat, endeavoring to choke me.

I am no coward, and am possessed of considerable physical strength. The suddenness of the attack, instead of stunning me, strung every nerve to its highest tension. My body acted from instinct, before my brain had time to realize the terrors of my position. In an instant I wound two muscular arms around the creature, and squeezed it, with all the strength of despair, against my chest. In a few seconds the bony hands that had fastened on my throat loosened their hold, and I was free to breathe once more. Then commenced a struggle of awful intensity. Immersed in the most profound darkness, totally ignorant of the nature of the Thing by which I was so suddenly attacked, finding my grasp slipping every moment, by reason, it seemed to me, of the entire nakedness of my assailant, bitten with sharp teeth in the shoulder, neck, and chest, having every moment to protect my throat against a pair of sinewy, agile hands, which my utmost efforts could not confine—these were a combination of circumstances to combat which required all the strength, skill, and courage that I possessed.

At last, after a silent, deadly, exhausting struggle, I got my assailant under by a series of incredible efforts of strength. Once pinned, with my knee on what I made out to be its chest, I knew that I was victor. I rested for a moment to breathe. I heard the creature beneath me panting in the darkness, and felt the violent throbbing of a heart. It was apparently as exhausted as I was; that was one comfort. At this moment I remembered that I usually placed under my pillow, before going to bed, a large yellow silk pocket-handkerchief. I felt for it instantly; it was there. In a few seconds more I had, after a fashion, pinioned the creature's arms.

I now felt tolerably secure. There was nothing more to be done but to turn on the gas, and, having first seen what my midnight assailant was like, arouse the household. I will confess to being actuated by a certain pride in not giving the alarm before; I wished to make the capture alone and unaided.

Never losing my hold for an instant, I slipped from the bed to the floor, dragging my captive with me. I had but a few steps to make to reach the gas-burner; these I made with the greatest caution, holding the creature in a grip like a vice. At last I got within arm's length of the tiny speck of blue light which told me where the gas-burner lay. Quick as lightning I released my grasp with one hand and let on the full flood of light. Then I turned to look at my captive.

I cannot even attempt to give any definition of my sensations the instant after I turned on the gas. I suppose I must have shrieked with terror, for in less than a minute afterward my room was crowded with the inmates of the house. I shudder now as I think of that awful moment. *I saw nothing!* Yes; I had one arm firmly clasped round a breathing, panting, corporeal shape, my other hand gripped with all its strength a throat as warm, and apparently fleshly, as my own; and yet, with this living substance in my grasp, with its body pressed against my own, and all in the bright glare of a large jet of gas, I absolutely beheld nothing! Not even an outline—a vapor!

I do not, even at this hour, realize the situation in which I found myself. I cannot recall the astounding incident thoroughly. Imagination in vain tries to compass the awful paradox.

It breathed. I felt its warm breath upon my cheek. It struggled fiercely. It had hands. They clutched me. Its skin was smooth, like my own. There it lay, pressed close up against me, solid as stone—and yet utterly invisible!

I wonder that I did not faint or go mad on the instant. Some wonderful instinct must have sustained me; for absolutely, in place of loosening my hold on the terrible Enigma, I seemed to gain an additional strength in my moment of horror, and tightened my grasp with such wonderful force that I felt the creature shivering with agony.

Just then Hammond entered my room at the head of the household. As soon as he beheld my face—which, I suppose, must have been an awful sight to look at—he hastened forward, crying, "Great Heaven, what has happened?"

"Hammond! Hammond!" I cried, "come here. Oh, this is awful! I have been attacked in bed by something or other, which I have hold of; but I can't see it—I can't see it!"

Hammond, doubtless struck by the unfeigned horror expressed in my countenance, made one or two steps forward with an anxious yet puzzled expression. A very audible titter burst from the remainder of my visitors. This suppressed laughter made me furious. To laugh at a human being in my position! It was the worst species of cruelty. *Now*, I can understand why the appearance of a man struggling violently, as it would seem, with an airy nothing, and calling for assistance against a vision, should have appeared ludicrous. *Then*, so great was my rage against the mocking crowd that had I the power I would have stricken them dead where they stood.

"Hammond! Hammond!" I cried again, despairingly, "for God's sake come to me. I can hold the—the thing but a short while longer. It is overpowering me. Help me! Help me!"

"Harry," whispered Hammond, approaching me, "you have been smoking too much opium."

"I swear to you, Hammond, that this is no vision," I answered, in the same low tone. "Don't you see how it shakes my whole frame with its struggles? If you don't believe me convince yourself. Feel it—touch it."

Hammond advanced and laid his hand in the spot I indicated. A wild cry of horror burst from him. He had felt it!

In a moment he had discovered somewhere in my room a long piece of cord, and was the next instant winding it and knotting it about the body of the unseen being that I clasped in my arms.

"Harry," he said, in a hoarse, agitated voice, for, though he preserved his presence of mind, he was deeply moved, "Harry, it's all safe now. You may let go, old fellow, if you're tired. The Thing can't move."

I was utterly exhausted, and I gladly loosed my hold.

Hammond stood holding the ends of the cord, that bound the Invisible, twisted round his hand, while before him, self-supporting as it were, he beheld a rope laced and interlaced, and stretching tightly around a vacant space. I never saw a man look so thoroughly stricken with awe. Nevertheless his face expressed all the courage and determination which I knew him to possess. His lips, although white, were set firmly, and one could perceive at a glance that, although stricken with fear, he was not daunted.

The confusion that ensued among the guests of the house who were witnesses of this extraordinary scene between Hammond and myself—who beheld the pantomime of binding this struggling Something—who beheld me almost sinking from physical exhaustion when my task of jailer was over—the confusion and terror that took possession of the bystanders, when they saw all this, was beyond description. The weaker ones fled from the apartment. The few who remained clustered near the door and could not be induced to approach Hammond and his Charge. Still incredulity broke out through their terror. They had not the courage to satisfy themselves, and yet they doubted. It was in vain that I begged of some of the men to come near and convince themselves by touch of the existence in that room of a living being which was invisible. They were incredulous, but did not dare to undeceive themselves. How could a solid, living, breathing body be invisible, they asked. My reply was this. I gave a sign to Hammond, and both of us—conquering our fearful repugnance to touch the invisible creature—lifted it from the ground, manacled as it was, and took it to my bed. Its weight was about that of a boy of fourteen.

"Now, my friends," I said, as Hammond and myself held the creature suspended over the bed, "I can give you self-evident proof that here is a solid, ponderable body, which, nevertheless, you cannot see. Be good enough to watch the surface of the bed attentively."

I was astonished at my own courage in treating this strange event so calmly; but I had recovered from my first terror, and felt a sort of scientific pride in the affair, which dominated every other feeling.

The eyes of the bystanders were immediately fixed on my bed. At a given signal Hammond and I let the creature fall. There was the dull sound of a heavy body alighting on a soft mass. The timbers of the bed creaked. A deep impression marked itself distinctly on the pillow, and on the bed itself. The crowd who witnessed this gave a low cry, and rushed from the room. Hammond and I were left alone with our Mystery.

We remained silent for some time, listening to the low irregular breathing of the creature on the bed and watching the rustle of the bed-clothes as it impotently struggled to free itself from confinement. Then Hammond spoke.

"Harry, this is awful."

"Ay, awful."

"But not unaccountable."

"Not unaccountable! What do you mean? Such a thing has never occurred since the birth of the world. I know not what to think, Hammond. God grant that I am not mad and that this is not an insane fantasy!"

"Let us reason a little, Harry. Here is a solid body which we touch but which we cannot see. The fact is so unusual that it strikes us with terror. Is there no parallel, though, for such a phenomenon? Take a piece of pure glass. It is tangible and transparent. A certain chemical coarseness is all that prevents its being so entirely transparent as to be totally invisible. It is not *theoretically impossible*, mind you, to make a glass which shall not reflect a single ray of light—a glass so pure and homogeneous in its atoms that the rays from the sun will pass through it as they do through the air, refracted but not reflected. We do not see the air, and yet we feel it."

"That's all very well, Hammond, but these are inanimate substances. Glass does not breathe, air does not breathe. This thing has a heart that palpitates—a will that moves it—lungs that play, and inspire and respire."

"You forget the phenomena of which we have so often heard of late," answered the doctor gravely. "At the meetings called 'spirit circles,' invisible hands have been thrust into the hands of those persons round the table—warm, fleshly hands that seemed to pulsate with mortal life."

"What? Do you think, then, that this thing is——"

"I don't know what it is," was the solemn reply; "but please the gods I will, with your assistance, thoroughly investigate it."

We watched together, smoking many pipes, all night long, by the bedside of the unearthly being that tossed and panted until it was apparently wearied out. Then we learned by the low, regular breathing that it slept.

The next morning the house was all astir. The boarders congregated on the landing outside my room, and Hammond and myself were lions. We had to answer a thousand questions as to the state of our extraordinary prisoner, for as yet not one person in the house except ourselves could be induced to set foot in the apartment.

The creature was awake. This was evidenced by the convulsive manner in which the bed-clothes were moved in its efforts to escape. There was something truly terrible in beholding, as it were, those second-hand indications of the terrible writhings and agonized struggles for liberty which themselves were invisible.

Hammond and myself had racked our brains during the long night to discover some means by which we might realize the shape and general appearance of the Enigma. As well as we could make out by passing our hands over the creature's form, its outlines and lineaments were human. There was a mouth; a round, smooth head without hair; a nose, which, however, was little elevated above the cheeks; and its hands and feet felt like those of a boy. At first we thought of placing the being on a smooth surface and tracing its outlines with chalk, as shoemakers trace the outline of the foot. This plan was given up as being of no value. Such an outline would give not the slightest idea of its conformation.

A happy thought struck me. We would take a cast of it in plaster-of-Paris. This would give us the solid figure, and satisfy all our wishes. But how to do it. The movements of the creature would disturb the setting of the plastic covering, and distort the mould. Another thought. Why not give it chloroform? It had respiratory organs—that was evident by its breathing. Once reduced to a state of insensibility, we could do with it what we would. Doctor X—— was sent for; and after the worthy physician had recovered from the first shock of amazement, he proceeded to administer the chloroform. In three minutes afterward we were enabled to remove the fetters from the creature's body, and a modeller was busily engaged in covering the invisible form with the moist clay. In five minutes more we had a mould, and before evening a rough fac-simile of the Mystery. It was shaped like a man—distorted, uncouth, and horrible, but still a man. It was small, not over four feet and some inches in height, and its limbs revealed a muscular development that was unparalleled. Its face surpassed in hideousness anything I had ever seen. Gustave Doré, or Callot, or Tony Johannot, never conceived anything so horrible. There is a face in one of the latter's illustrations to *Un Voyage où il vous plaira*, which somewhat approaches the countenance of this creature, but does not equal it. It was the physiognomy of what I should fancy a ghoul might be. It looked as if it was capable of feeding on human flesh.

Having satisfied our curiosity, and bound every one in the house to secrecy, it became a question what was to be done with our Enigma? It was impossible that we should keep such a horror in our house; it was equally impossible that such an awful being should be let loose upon the world. I confess that I would have gladly voted for the creature's destruction. But who would shoulder the responsibility? Who would undertake the execution of this horrible semblance to a human being? Day after day this question was deliberated gravely. The boarders all left the house. Mrs. Moffat was in despair, and threatened Hammond and myself with all sorts of legal penalties if we did not remove the Horror. Our answer was, "We will go if you like, but we decline taking this creature with us. Remove it yourself if you please. It appeared in your house. On you the responsibility rests." To this there was, of course, no answer. Mrs. Moffat could not obtain for love or money a person who would even approach the Mystery.

At last it died. Hammond and I found it cold and stiff one morning in the bed. The heart had ceased to beat, the lungs to inspire. We hastened to bury it in the garden. It was a strange funeral, the dropping of that viewless corpse into the damp hole. The cast of its form I gave to Doctor X——, who keeps it in his museum in Tenth Street.

As I am on the eve of a long journey from which I may not return, I have drawn up this narrative of an event the most singular that has ever come to my knowledge.

GHOSTLY TALES VOLUME I

SCHALKEN THE PAINTER

"For he is not a man as I am that we should come together; neither is there any that might lay his hand upon us both. Let him, therefore, take his rod away from me, and let not his fear terrify me."

There exists, at this moment, in good preservation a remarkable work of Schalken's. The curious management of its lights constitutes, as usual in his pieces, the chief apparent merit of the picture. I say *apparent*, for in its subject, and not in its handling, however exquisite, consists its real value. The picture represents the interior of what might be a chamber in some antique religious building; and its foreground is occupied by a female figure, in a species of white robe, part of which is arranged so as to form a veil. The dress, however, is not that of any religious order. In her hand the figure bears a lamp, by which alone her figure and face are illuminated; and her features wear such an arch smile, as well becomes a pretty woman when practising some prankish roguery; in the background, and, excepting where the dim red light of an expiring fire serves to define the form, in total shadow, stands the figure of a man dressed in the old Flemish fashion, in an attitude of alarm, his hand being placed upon the hilt of his sword, which he appears to be in the act of drawing.

There are some pictures, which impress one, I know not how, with a conviction that they represent not the mere ideal shapes and combinations which have floated through the imagination of the artist, but scenes, faces, and situations which have actually existed. There is in that strange picture, something that stamps it as the representation of a reality.

And such in truth it is, for it faithfully records a remarkable and mysterious occurrence, and perpetuates, in the face of the female figure, which occupies the most prominent place in the design, an accurate portrait of Rose Velderkaust, the niece of Gerard Douw, the first, and, I believe, the only love of Godfrey Schalken. My great grandfather knew the painter well; and from Schalken himself he learned the fearful story of the painting, and from him too he ultimately received the picture itself as a bequest. The story and the picture have become heir-looms in my family, and having described the latter, I shall, if you please, attempt to relate the tradition which has descended with the canvas.

There are few forms on which the mantle of romance hangs more ungracefully than upon that of the uncouth Schalken—the boorish but most cunning worker in oils, whose pieces delight the critics of our day almost as much as his manners disgusted the refined of his own; and yet this man, so rude, so dogged, so slovenly, in the midst of his celebrity, had in his obscure, but happier days, played the hero in a wild romance of mystery and passion.

When Schalken studied under the immortal Gerard Douw, he was a very young man; and in spite of his phlegmatic temperament, he at once fell over head and ears in love with the beautiful niece of his wealthy master. Rose Velderkaust was still younger than he, having not yet attained her seventeenth year, and, if tradition speaks truth, possessed all the soft and dimpling charms of the fair, light-haired Flemish maidens. The young painter loved honestly and fervently. His frank adoration was rewarded. He declared his love, and extracted a faltering confession in return. He was the happiest and proudest painter in all Christendom. But there was somewhat to dash his elation; he was poor and undistinguished. He dared not ask old Gerard for the hand of his sweet ward. He must first win a reputation and a competence.

There were, therefore, many dread uncertainties and cold days before him; he had to fight his way against sore odds. But he had won the heart of dear Rose Velderkaust, and that was half the battle. It is needless to say his exertions were redoubled, and his lasting celebrity proves that his industry was not unrewarded by success.

These ardent labours, and worse still, the hopes that elevated and beguiled them, were however, destined to experience a sudden interruption of a character so strange and mysterious as to baffle all inquiry and to throw over the events themselves a shadow of preternatural horror.

Schalken had one evening outstayed all his fellow-pupils, and still pursued his work in the deserted room. As the daylight was fast falling, he laid aside his colours, and applied himself to the completion of a sketch on which he had expressed extraordinary pains. It was a religious composition, and represented the temptations of a pot-bellied Saint Anthony. The young artist, however destitute of elevation, had, nevertheless, discernment enough to be dissatisfied with his own work, and many were the patient erasures and improvements which saint and devil underwent, yet all in vain. The large, old-fashioned room was silent, and, with the exception of himself, quite emptied of its usual inmates. An hour had thus passed away, nearly two, without any improved result. Daylight had already declined, and twilight was deepening into the darkness of night. The patience of the young painter was exhausted, and he stood before his unfinished production, angry and mortified, one hand buried in the folds of his long hair, and the other holding the piece of charcoal which had so ill-performed its office, and which he now rubbed, without much regard to the sable streaks it produced, with irritable pressure upon his ample Flemish inexpressibles. "Curse the subject!" said the young man aloud; "curse the picture, the devils, the saint—"

At this moment a short, sudden sniff uttered close beside him made the artist turn sharply round, and he now, for the first time, became aware that his labours had been overlooked by a stranger. Within about a yard and half, and rather behind him, there stood the figure of an elderly man in a cloak and broad-brimmed, conical hat; in his hand, which was protected with a heavy gauntlet-shaped glove, he carried a long ebony walking-stick, surmounted with what appeared, as it glittered dimly in the twilight, to be a massive head of gold, and upon his breast, through the folds of the cloak, there shone the links of a rich chain of the same metal. The room was so obscure that nothing further of the appearance of the figure could be ascertained, and his hat threw his features into profound shadow. It would not have been easy to conjecture the age of the intruder; but a quantity of dark hair escaping from beneath this sombre hat, as well as his firm and upright carriage served to indicate that his years could not yet exceed threescore, or thereabouts. There was an air of gravity and importance about the garb of the person, and something indescribably odd, I might say awful, in the perfect, stone-like stillness of the figure, that effectually checked the testy comment which had at once risen to the lips of the irritated artist. He, therefore, as soon as he had sufficiently recovered his surprise, asked the stranger, civilly, to be seated, and desired to know if he had any message to leave for his master.

"Tell Gerard Douw," said the unknown, without altering his attitude in the smallest degree, "that Minheer Vanderhausen, of Rotterdam, desires to speak with him on tomorrow evening at this hour, and if he please, in this room, upon matters of weight; that is all."

The stranger, having finished this message, turned abruptly, and, with a quick, but silent step quitted the room, before Schalken had time to say a word in reply. The young man felt a curiosity to see in what direction the burgher of Rotterdam would turn, on quitting the studio, and for that purpose he went directly to the window which commanded the door. A lobby of considerable extent intervened between the inner door of the painter's room and the street entrance, so that Schalken occupied the post of observation before the old man could possibly have reached the street. He watched in vain, however. There was no other mode of exit. Had the queer old man vanished, or was he lurking about the recesses of the lobby for some sinister purpose? This last suggestion filled the mind of Schalken with a vague uneasiness, which was so unaccountably intense as to make him alike afraid to remain in the room alone, and reluctant to pass through the lobby. However, with an effort which appeared very disproportioned to the occasion, he summoned resolution to leave the room, and, having locked the door and thrust the key in his pocket, without looking to the right or left, he traversed the passage which had so recently, perhaps still, contained the person of his mysterious visitant, scarcely venturing to breathe till he had arrived in the open street.

"Minheer Vanderhausen!" said Gerard Douw within himself, as the appointed hour approached, "Minheer Vanderhausen, of Rotterdam! I never heard of the man till yesterday. What can he want of me? A portrait, perhaps, to be painted; or a poor relation to be apprenticed; or a collection to be valued; or—pshaw! there's no one in Rotterdam to leave me a legacy. Well, whatever the business may be, we shall soon know it all."

It was now the close of day, and again every easel, except that of Schalken, was deserted. Gerard Douw was pacing the apartment with the restless step of impatient expectation, sometimes pausing to glance over the work of one of his absent pupils, but more frequently placing himself at the window, from whence he might observe the passengers who threaded the obscure by-street in which his studio was placed.

"Said you not, Godfrey," exclaimed Douw, after a long and fruitful gaze from his post of observation, and turning to Schalken, "that the hour he appointed was about seven by the clock of the Stadhouse?"

"It had just told seven when I first saw him, sir," answered the student.

"The hour is close at hand, then," said the master, consulting a horologe as large and as round as an orange. "Minheer Vanderhausen from Rotterdam—is it not so?"

"Such was the name."

"And an elderly man, richly clad?" pursued Douw, musingly.

"As well as I might see," replied his pupil; "he could not be young, nor yet very old, neither; and his dress was rich and grave, as might become a citizen of wealth and consideration."

At this moment the sonorous boom of the Stadhouse clock told, stroke after stroke, the hour of seven; the eyes of both master and student were directed to the door; and it was not until the last peal of the bell had ceased to vibrate, that Douw exclaimed

"So, so; we shall have his worship presently, that is, if he means to keep his hour; if not, you may wait for him, Godfrey, if you court his acquaintance. But what, after all, if it should prove but a mummery got up by Vankarp, or some such wag? I wish you had run all risks, and cudgelled the old burgomaster soundly. I'd wager a dozen of Rhenish, his worship would have unmasked, and pleaded old acquaintance in a trice."

"Here he comes, sir," said Schalken, in a low monitory tone; and instantly, upon turning towards the door, Gerard Douw observed the same figure which had, on the day before, so unexpectedly greeted his pupil Schalken.

There was something in the air of the figure which at once satisfied the painter that there was no masquerading in the case, and that he really stood in the presence of a man of worship; and so, without hesitation, he doffed his cap, and courteously saluting the stranger, requested him to be seated. The visitor waved his hand slightly, as if in acknowledgment of the courtesy, but remained standing.

"I have the honour to see Minheer Vanderhausen of Rotterdam?" said Gerard Douw.

"The same," was the laconic reply of his visitor.

"I understand your worship desires to speak with me," continued Douw, "and I am here by appointment to wait your commands."

"Is that a man of trust?" said Vanderhausen, turning towards Schalken, who stood at a little distance behind his master.

"Certainly," replied Gerard.

"Then let him take this box, and get the nearest jeweller or goldsmith to value its contents, and let him return hither with a certificate of the valuation."

At the same time, he placed a small case about nine inches square in the hands of Gerard Douw, who was as much amazed at its weight as at the strange abruptness with which it was handed to him. In accordance with the wishes of the stranger, he delivered it into the hands of Schalken, and repeating his direction, despatched him upon the mission.

Schalken disposed his precious charge securely beneath the folds of his cloak, and rapidly traversing two or three narrow streets, he stopped at a corner house, the lower part of which was then occupied by the shop of a Jewish goldsmith. He entered the shop, and calling the little Hebrew into the obscurity of its back recesses, he proceeded to lay before him Vanderhausen's casket. On being examined by the light of a lamp, it appeared entirely cased with lead, the outer surface of which was much scraped and soiled, and nearly white with age. This having been partially removed, there appeared beneath a box of some hard wood; which also they forced open and after the removal of two or three folds of linen, they discovered its contents to be a mass of golden ingots, closely packed, and, as the Jew declared, of the most perfect quality. Every ingot underwent the scrutiny of the little Jew, who seemed to feel an epicurean delight in touching and testing these morsels of the glorious metal; and each one of them was replaced in its berth with the exclamation: "*Mein Gott*, how very perfect! not one grain of alloy—beautiful, beautiful!" The task was at length finished, and the Jew certified under his hand the value of the ingots submitted to his examination, to amount to many thousand rix-dollars. With the desired document in his pocket, and the rich box of gold carefully pressed under his arm, and concealed by his cloak, he retraced his way, and entering the studio, found his master and the stranger in close conference. Schalken had no sooner left the room, in order to execute the commission he had taken in charge, than Vanderhausen addressed Gerard Douw in the following terms:----

"I cannot tarry with you to-night more than a few minutes, and so I shall shortly tell you the matter upon which I come. You visited the town of Rotterdam some four months ago, and then I saw in the church of St. Lawrence your niece, Rose Velderkaust. I desire to marry her; and if I satisfy you that I am wealthier than any husband you can dream of for her, I expect that you will forward my suit with your authority. If you approve my proposal, you must close with it here and now, for I cannot wait for calculations and delays."

Gerard Douw was hugely astonished by the nature of Minheer Vanderhausen's communication, but he did not venture to express surprise; for besides the motives supplied by prudence and politeness, the painter experienced a kind of chill and oppression like that which is said to intervene when one is placed in unconscious proximity with the object of a natural antipathy—an undefined but overpowering sensation, while standing in the presence of the eccentric stranger, which made him very unwilling to say anything which might reasonably offend him.

"I have no doubt," said Gerard, after two or three prefatory hems, "that the alliance which you propose would prove alike advantageous and honourable to my niece; but you must be aware that she has a will of her own, and may not acquiesce in what *we* may design for her advantage."

"Do not seek to deceive me, sir painter," said Vanderhausen; "you are her guardian—she is your ward—she is mine if *you* like to make her so."

The man of Rotterdam moved forward a little as he spoke, and Gerard Douw, he scarce knew why, inwardly prayed for the speedy return of Schalken.

"I desire," said the mysterious gentleman, "to place in your hands at once an evidence of my wealth, and a security for my liberal dealing with your niece. The lad will return in a minute or two with a sum in value five times the fortune which she has a right to expect from her husband. This shall lie in your hands, together with her dowry, and you may apply the united sum as suits her interest best; it shall be all exclusively hers while she lives: is that liberal?"

Douw assented, and inwardly acknowledged that fortune had been extraordinarily kind to his niece; the stranger, he thought, must be both wealthy and generous, and such an offer was not to be despised, though made by a humourist, and one of no very prepossessing presence. Rose had no very high pretensions for she had but a modest dowry, which she owed entirely to the generosity of her uncle; neither had she any right to raise exceptions on the score of birth, for her own origin was far from splendid, and as the other objections, Gerald resolved, and indeed, by the usages of the time, was warranted in resolving, not to listen to them for a moment.

"Sir" said he, addressing the stranger, "your offer is liberal, and whatever hesitation I may feel in closing with it immediately, arises solely from my not having the honour of knowing anything of your family or station. Upon these points you can, of course, satisfy me without difficulty?'

"As to my respectability," said the stranger, drily, "you must take that for granted at present; pester me with no inquiries; you can discover nothing more about me than I choose to make known. You shall have sufficient security for my respectability—my word, if you are honourable: if you are sordid, my gold."

"A testy old gentleman," thought Douw, "he must have his own way; but, all things considered, I am not justified to declining his offer. I will not pledge myself unnecessarily, however."

"You will not pledge yourself unnecessarily," said Vanderhausen, strangely uttering the very words which had just floated through the mind of his companion; "but you will do so if it is necessary, I presume; and I will show you that I consider it indispensable. If the gold I mean to leave in your hands satisfy you, and if you don't wish my proposal to be at once withdrawn, you must, before I leave this room, write your name to this engagement."

Having thus spoken, he placed a paper in the hands of the master, the contents of which expressed an engagement entered into by Gerard Douw, to give to

Wilken Vanderhausen of Rotterdam, in marriage, Rose Velderkaust, and so forth, within one week of the date thereof. While the painter was employed in reading this covenant, by the light of a twinkling oil lamp in the far wall of the room, Schalken, as we have stated, entered the studio, and having delivered the box and the valuation of the Jew, into the hands of the stranger, he was about to retire, when Vanderhausen called to him to wait; and, presenting the case and the certificate to Gerard Douw, he paused in silence until he had satisfied himself, by an inspection of both, respecting the value of the pledge left in his hands. At length he said----

"Are you content?"

The painter said he would fain have another day to consider.

"Not an hour," said the suitor, apathetically.

"Well then," said Douw, with a sore effort, "I am content, it is a bargain."

"Then sign at once," said Vanderhausen, "for I am weary."

At the same time he produced a small case of writing materials, and Gerard signed the important document.

"Let this youth witness the covenant," said the old man; and Godfrey Schalken unconsciously attested the instrument which for ever bereft him of his dear Rose Velderkaust.

The compact being thus completed, the strange visitor folded up the paper, and stowed it safely in an inner pocket.

"I will visit you to-morrow night at nine o'clock, at your own house, Gerard Douw, and will see the object of our contract;" and so saying Wilken Vanderhausen moved stiffly, but rapidly, out of the room.

Schalken, eager to resolve his doubts, had placed himself by the window, in order to watch the street entrance; but the experiment served only to support his suspicions, for the old man did not issue from the door. This was *very* strange, odd, nay fearful. He and his master returned together, and talked but little on the way, for each had his own subjects of reflection, of anxiety, and of hope. Schalken, however, did not know the ruin which menaced his dearest projects.

Gerard Douw knew nothing of the attachment which had sprung up between his pupil and his niece; and even if he had, it is doubtful whether he would have regarded its existence as any serious obstruction to the wishes of Minheer Vanderhausen. Marriages were then and there matters of traffic and calculation; and it would have appeared as absurd in the eyes of the guardian to make a mutual attachment an essential element in a contract of the sort, as it would have been to draw up his bonds and receipts in the language of romance.

The painter, however, did not communicate to his niece the important step which he had taken in her behalf, a forebearance caused not by any anticipated opposition on her part, but solely by a ludicrous consciousness that if she were to ask him for a description of her destined bridegroom, he would be forced to confess that he had not once seen his face, and if called upon, would find it absolutely impossible to identify him. Upon the next day, Gerard Douw, after dinner, called his niece to him and having scanned her person with an air of satisfaction, he took her hand, and looking upon her pretty innocent face with a smile of kindness, he said:----

"Rose, my girl, that face of yours will make your fortune." Rose blushed and smiled. "Such faces and such tempers seldom go together, and when they do, the compound is a love charm, few heads or hearts can resist; trust me, you will soon be a bride, girl. But this is trifling, and I am pressed for time, so make ready the large room by eight o'clock to-night, and give directions for supper at nine. I expect a friend; and observe me, child, do you trick yourself out handsomely. I will not have him think us poor or sluttish."

With these words he left her, and took his way to the room in which his pupils worked.

When the evening closed in, Gerard called Schalken, who was about to take his departure to his own obscure and comfortless lodgings, and asked him to come home and sup with Rose and Vanderhausen. The invitation was, of course, accepted and Gerard Douw and his pupil soon found themselves in the handsome and, even then, antique chamber, which had been prepared for the reception of the stranger. A cheerful wood fire blazed in the hearth, a little at one side of which an old-fashioned table, which shone in the fire-light like burnished gold, was awaiting the supper, for which preparations were going forward; and ranged with exact regularity, stood the tall-backed chairs, whose ungracefulness was more than compensated by their comfort. The little party, consisting of Rose, her uncle, and the artist, awaited the arrival of the expected visitor with considerable impatience. Nine o'clock at length came, and with it a summons at the street door, which being speedily answered, was followed by a slow and emphatic tread upon the staircase; the steps moved heavily across the lobby, the door of the room in which the party we have described were assembled slowly opened, and there entered a figure which startled, almost appalled, the phlegmatic Dutchmen, and nearly made Rose scream with terror. It was the form, and arrayed in the garb of Minheer Vanderhausen; the air, the gait, the height were the same, but the features had never been seen by any of the party before. The stranger stopped at the door of the room, and displayed his form and face completely. He wore a dark-coloured cloth cloak, which was short and full, not falling quite to his knees; his legs were cased in dark purple silk stockings, and his shoes were adorned with roses of the same colour. The opening of the cloak in front showed the under-suit to consist of some very dark, perhaps sable material, and his hands were enclosed in a pair of heavy leather gloves, which ran up considerably above the wrist, in the manner of a gauntlet. In one hand he carried his walking-stick and his hat, which he had removed, and the other hung heavily by his side. A quantity of grizzled hair descended in long tresses from his head, and rested upon the plaits of a stiff ruff, which effectually concealed his neck. So far all was well; but the face!--all the flesh of the face was coloured with the bluish leaden hue, which is sometimes produced by metallic medicines, administered in excessive quantities; the eyes showed an undue proportion of muddy white, and had a certain indefinable character of insanity; the hue of the lips bearing the usual relation to that of the face, was, consequently, nearly black; and the entire character of the face was sensual, malignant, and even satanic. It was remarkable that the worshipful stranger suffered as little as possible of his flesh to appear, and that during his visit he did not once remove his gloves. Having stood for some moments at the door, Gerard Douw at length found breath and collectedness to bid him welcome, and with a mute inclination of the head, the stranger stepped forward into the room. There was something indescribably odd, even horrible, about all his motions, something undefinable, that was unnatural, unhuman; it was as if the limbs were guided and directed by a spirit unused to the management of bodily machinery. The stranger spoke hardly at all during his visit, which did not exceed half an hour; and the host himself could scarcely muster courage enough to utter the few necessary salutations and courtesies; and, indeed, such was the nervous terror which the presence of Vanderhausen inspired, that very little would have made all his entertainers fly in downright panic from the room. They had not so far lost all self-possession, however, as to fail to observe two strange peculiarities of their visitor. During his stay his eyelids did not once close, or, indeed, move in the slightest degree; and farther, there was a deathlike stillness in his whole person, owing to the absence of the heaving motion of the chest, caused by the process of respiration. These two peculiarities, though when told they may appear trifling, produced a very striking and unpleasant effect when seen and observed. Vanderhausen at length relieved the painter of Leyden of his inauspicious presence; and with no trifling sense of relief the little party heard the street door close after him.

"Dear uncle," said Rose, "what a frightful man! I would not see him again for the wealth of the States."

"Tush, foolish girl," said Douw, whose sensations were anything but comfortable. "A man may be as ugly as the devil, and yet, if his heart and actions are good, he is worth all the pretty-faced perfumed puppies that walk the Mall. Rose, my girl, it is very true he has not thy pretty face, but I know him to be wealthy and liberal; and were he ten times more ugly, these two virtues would be enough to counter balance all his deformity, and if not sufficient actually to alter the shape and hue of his features, at least enough to prevent one thinking them so much amiss."

"Do you know, uncle," said Rose, "when I saw him standing at the door, I could not get it out of my head that I saw the old painted wooden figure that used to frighten me so much in the Church of St. Laurence at Rotterdam."

Gerard laughed, though he could not help inwardly acknowledging the justness of the comparison. He was resolved, however, as far as he could, to check his niece's disposition to dilate upon the ugliness of her intended bridegroom, although he was not a little pleased, as well as puzzled, to observe that she appeared totally exempt from that mysterious dread of the stranger which, he could not disguise it from himself, considerably affected him, as also his pupil Godfrey Schalken.

Early on the next day there arrived, from various quarters of the town, rich presents of silks, velvets, jewellery, and so forth, for Rose; and also a packet directed to Gerard Douw, which on being opened, was found to contain a contract of marriage, formally drawn up, between Wilken Vanderhausen of the *Boom-quay*, in Rotterdam, and Rose Velderkaust of Leyden, niece to Gerard Douw, master in the art of painting, also of the same city; and containing engagements on the part of Vanderhausen to make settlements upon his bride, far more splendid than he had before led her guardian to believe likely, and which were to be secured to her use in the most unexceptionable manner possible—the money being placed in the hand of Gerard Douw himself.

I have no sentimental scenes to describe, no cruelty of guardians, no magnanimity of wards, no agonies, or transport of lovers. The record I have to make is one of sordidness, levity, and heartlessness. In less than a week after the first interview which we have just described, the contract of marriage was fulfilled, and Schalken saw the prize which he would have risked existence to secure, carried off in solemn pomp by his repulsive rival. For two or three days he absented himself from the school; he then returned and worked, if with less cheerfulness, with far more dogged resolution than before; the stimulus of love had given place to that of ambition. Months passed away, and, contrary to his expectation, and, indeed, to the direct promise of the parties, Gerard Douw heard nothing of his niece or her worshipful spouse. The interest of the money, which was to have been demanded in quarterly sums, lay unclaimed in his hands.

He began to grow extremely uneasy. Minheer Vanderhausen's direction in Rotterdam he was fully possessed of; after some irresolution he finally determined to journey thither—a trifling undertaking, and easily accomplished—and thus to satisfy himself of the safety and comfort of his ward, for whom he entertained an honest and strong affection. His search was in vain, however; no one in Rotterdam had ever heard of Minheer Vanderhausen. Gerard Douw left not a house in the *Boom-quay* untried, but all in vain. No one could give him any information whatever touching the object of his inquiry, and he was obliged to return to Leyden nothing wiser and far more anxious, than when he had left it.

On his arrival he hastened to the establishment from which Vanderhausen had hired the lumbering, though, considering the times, most luxurious vehicle, which the bridal party had employed to convey them to Rotterdam. From the driver of this machine he learned, that having proceeded by slow stages, they had late in the evening approached Rotterdam; but that before they entered the city, and while yet nearly a mile from it, a small party of men, soberly clad, and after the old fashion, with peaked beards and moustaches, standing in the centre of the road, obstructed the further progress of the carriage. The driver reined in his horses, much fearing, from the obscurity of the hour, and the loneliness, of the road, that some mischief was intended. His fears were, however, somewhat allayed by his observing that these strange men carried a large litter, of an antique shape, and which they immediately set down upon the pavement, whereupon the bridegroom, having opened the coach-door from within, descended, and having assisted his bride to do likewise, led her, weeping bitterly, and wringing her hands, to the litter, which they both entered. It was then raised by the men who surrounded it, and speedily carried towards the city, and before it had proceeded very far, the darkness concealed it from the view of the Dutch coachman. In the inside of the vehicle he found a purse, whose contents more than thrice paid the hire of the carriage and man. He saw and could tell nothing more of Minheer Vanderhausen and his beautiful lady.

This mystery was a source of profound anxiety and even grief to Gerard Douw. There was evidently fraud in the dealing of Vanderhausen with him, though for what purpose committed he could not imagine. He greatly doubted how far it was possible for a man possessing such a countenance to be anything but a villain, and every day that passed without his hearing from or of his niece, instead of inducing him to forget his fears, on the contrary tended more and more to aggravate them. The loss of her cheerful society tended also to depress his spirits; and in order to dispel the gloom, which often crept upon his mind after his daily occupations were over, he was wont frequently to ask Schalken to accompany him home, and share his otherwise solitary supper.

One evening, the painter and his pupil were sitting by the fire, having accomplished a comfortable meal, and had yielded to the silent and delicious melancholy of digestion, when their ruminations were disturbed by a loud sound at the street door, as if occasioned by some person rushing and scrambling vehemently against it. A domestic had run without delay to ascertain the cause of the disturbance, and they heard him twice or thrice interrogate the applicant for admission, but without eliciting any other answer but a sustained reiteration of the sounds. They heard him then open the hall-door, and immediately there followed a light and rapid tread on the staircase. Schalken advanced towards the door. It opened before he reached it, and Rose rushed into the room. She looked wild, fierce and haggard with terror and exhaustion, but her dress surprised them as much as even her unexpected appearance. It consisted of a kind of white woollen wrapper, made close about the neck, and descending to the very ground. It was much deranged and travel-soiled. The poor creature had hardly entered the chamber when she fell senseless on the floor. With some difficulty they succeeded in reviving her, and on recovering her senses, she instantly exclaimed, in a tone of terror rather than mere impatience:----

"Wine! wine! quickly, or I'm lost!"

Astonished and almost scared at the strange agitation in which the call was made, they at once administered to her wishes, and she drank some wine with a haste and eagerness which surprised them. She had hardly swallowed it, when she exclaimed, with the same urgency:

"Food, for God's sake, food, at once, or I perish."

A considerable fragment of a roast joint was upon the table, and Schalken immediately began to cut some, but he was anticipated, for no sooner did she see it than she caught it, a more than mortal image of famine, and with her hands, and even with her teeth, she tore off the flesh, and swallowed it. When the paroxysm of hunger had been a little appeased, she appeared on a sudden overcome with shame, or it may have been that other more agitating thoughts overpowered and scared her, for she began to weep bitterly and to wring her hands.

"Oh, send for a minister of God," said she; "I am not safe till he comes; send for him speedily."

Gerard Douw despatched a messenger instantly, and prevailed on his niece to allow him to surrender his bed chamber to her use. He also persuaded her to retire to it at once to rest; her consent was extorted upon the condition that they would not leave her for a moment.

"Oh that the holy man were here," she said; "he can deliver me: the dead and the living can never be one: God has forbidden it."

With these mysterious words she surrendered herself to their guidance, and they proceeded to the chamber which Gerard Douw had assigned to her use.

"Do not, do not leave me for a moment," said she; "I am lost for ever if you do."

Gerard Douw's chamber was approached through a spacious apartment, which they were now about to enter. He and Schalken each carried a candle, so that a sufficiency of light was cast upon all surrounding objects. They were now entering the large chamber, which as I have said, communicated with Douw's apartment, when Rose suddenly stopped, and, in a whisper which thrilled them both with horror, she said:----

"Oh, God! he is here! he is here! See, see! there he goes!"

She pointed towards the door of the inner room, and Schalken thought he saw a shadowy and ill-defined form gliding into that apartment. He drew his sword, and, raising the candle so as to throw its light with increased distinctness upon the objects in the room, he entered the chamber into which the shadow had glided. No figure was there—nothing but the furniture which belonged to the room, and yet he could not be deceived as to the fact that something had moved before them into the chamber. A sickening dread came upon him, and the cold perspiration broke out in heavy drops upon his forehead; nor was he more composed, when he heard the increased urgency and agony of entreaty, with which Rose implored them not to leave her for a moment.

"I saw him," said she; "he's here. I cannot be deceived; I know him; he's by me; he is with me; he's in the room. Then, for God's sake, as you would save me, do not stir from beside me."

They at length prevailed upon her to lie down upon the bed, where she continued to urge them to stay by her. She frequently uttered incoherent sentences, repeating, again and again, "the dead and the living cannot be one: God has forbidden it." And then again, "Rest to the wakeful—sleep to the sleep-walkers." These and such mysterious and broken sentences, she continued to utter until the clergyman arrived. Gerard Douw began to fear, naturally enough, that terror or ill-treatment, had unsettled the poor girl's intellect, and he half suspected, by the suddenness of her appearance, the unseasonableness of the hour, and above all, from the wildness and terror of her manner, that she had made her escape from some place of confinement for lunatics, and was in imminent fear of pursuit. He resolved to summon medical advice as soon as the mind of his niece had been in some measure set at rest by the offices of the clergyman whose attendance she had so earnestly desired; and until this object had been attained, he did not venture to put any questions to her, which might possibly, by reviving painful or horrible recollections, increase her agitation. The clergyman soon arrived—a man of ascetic countenance and venerable age—one whom Gerard Douw respected very much, forasmuch as he was a veteran polemic, though one perhaps more dreaded as a combatant than beloved as a Christian—of pure morality, subtle brain, and frozen heart. He entered the chamber which communicated with that in which Rose reclined and immediately on his arrival, she requested him to pray for her, as for one who lay in the hands of Satan, and who could hope for deliverance only from heaven.

That you may distinctly understand all the circumstances of the event which I am going to describe, it is necessary to state the relative position of the parties who were engaged in it. The old clergyman and Schalken were in the anteroom of which I have already spoken; Rose lay in the inner chamber, the door of which was open; and by the side of the bed, at her urgent desire, stood her guardian; a candle burned in the bedchamber, and three were lighted in the outer apartment. The old man now cleared his voice as if about to commence, but before he had time to begin, a sudden gust of air blew out the candle which served to illuminate the room in which the poor girl lay, and she, with hurried alarm, exclaimed:----

"Godfrey, bring in another candle; the darkness is unsafe."

Gerard Douw forgetting for the moment her repeated injunctions, in the immediate impulse, stepped from the bedchamber into the other, in order to supply what she desired.

"Oh God! do not go, dear uncle," shrieked the unhappy girl—and at the same time she sprung from the bed, and darted after him, in order, by her grasp, to detain him. But the warning came too late, for scarcely had he passed the threshold, and hardly had his niece had time to utter the startling exclamation, when the door which divided the two rooms closed violently after him, as if swung by a strong blast of wind. Schalken and he both rushed to the door, but their united and desperate efforts could not avail so much as to shake it. Shriek after shriek burst from the inner chamber, with all the piercing loudness of despairing terror. Schalken and Douw applied every nerve to force open the door; but all in vain. There was no sound of struggling from within, but the screams seemed to increase in loudness, and at the same time they heard the bolts of the latticed window withdrawn, and the window itself grated upon the sill as if thrown open. One *last* shriek, so long and piercing and agonized as to be scarcely human, swelled from the room, and suddenly there followed a death-like silence. A light step was heard crossing the floor, as if from the bed to the window; and almost at the same instant the door gave way, and, yielding to the pressure of the external applicants, nearly precipitated them into the room. It was empty. The window was open, and Schalken sprung to a chair and gazed out upon the street and canal below. He saw no form, but he saw, or thought he saw, the waters of the broad canal beneath settling ring after ring in heavy circles, as if a moment before disturbed by the submission of some ponderous body.

No trace of Rose was ever after found, nor was anything certain respecting her mysterious wooer discovered or even suspected—no clue whereby to trace the intricacies of the labyrinth and to arrive at its solution, presented itself. But an incident occurred, which, though it will not be received by our rational readers in lieu of evidence, produced nevertheless a strong and a lasting impression upon the mind of Schalken. Many years after the events which we have detailed, Schalken, then residing far away received an intimation of his father's death, and of his intended burial upon a fixed day in the church of Rotterdam. It was necessary that a very considerable journey should be performed by the funeral procession, which as it will be readily believed, was not very numerously attended. Schalken with difficulty arrived in Rotterdam late in the day upon which the funeral was appointed to take place. It had not then arrived. Evening closed in, and still it did not appear.

Schalken strolled down to the church; he found it open; notice of the arrival of the funeral had been given, and the vault in which the body was to be laid had been opened. The sexton, on seeing a well-dressed gentleman, whose object was to attend the expected obsequies, pacing the aisle of the church, hospitably invited him to share with him the comforts of a blazing fire, which, as was his custom in winter time upon such occasions, he had kindled in the hearth of a chamber in which he was accustomed to await the arrival of such grisly guests and which communicated, by a flight of steps, with the vault below. In this chamber, Schalken and his entertainer seated themselves; and the sexton, after some fruitless attempts to engage his guest in conversation, was obliged to apply himself to his tobacco-pipe and can, to solace his solitude. In spite of his grief and cares, the fatigues of a rapid journey of nearly forty hours gradually overcame the mind and body of Godfrey Schalken, and he sank into a deep sleep, from which he awakened by someone's shaking him gently by the shoulder. He first thought that the old sexton had called him, but *he* was no longer in the room. He roused himself, and as soon as he could clearly see what was around him, he perceived a female form, clothed in a kind of light robe of white, part of which was so disposed as to form a veil, and in her hand she carried a lamp. She was moving rather away from him, in the direction of the flight of steps which conducted towards the vaults. Schalken felt a vague alarm at the sight of this figure and at the same time an irresistible impulse to follow its guidance. He followed it towards the vaults, but when it reached the head of the stairs, he paused; the figure paused also, and, turning gently round, displayed, by the light of the lamp it carried, the face and features of his first love, Rose Velderkaust. There was nothing horrible, or even sad, in the countenance. On the contrary, it wore the same arch smile which used to enchant the artist long before in his happy days. A feeling of awe and interest, too intense to be resisted, prompted him to follow the spectre, if spectre it were. She descended the stairs—he followed—and turning to the left, through a narrow passage, she led him, to his infinite surprise, into what appeared to be an old-fashioned Dutch apartment, such as the pictures of Gerard Douw have served to immortalize. Abundance of costly antique furniture was disposed about the room, and in one corner stood a four-post bed, with heavy black cloth curtains around it; the figure frequently turned towards him with the same arch smile; and when she came to the side of the bed, she drew the curtains, and, by the light of the lamp, which she held towards its contents, she disclosed to the horror-stricken painter, sitting bolt upright in the bed, the livid and demoniac form of Vanderhausen. Schalken had hardly seen him, when he fell senseless upon the floor, where he lay until discovered, on the next morning, by persons employed in closing the passages into the vaults. He was lying in a cell of considerable size, which had not been disturbed for a long time, and he had fallen beside a large coffin, which was supported upon small pillars, a security against the attacks of vermin.

To his dying day Schalken was satisfied of the reality of the vision which he had witnessed, and he has left behind him a curious evidence of the impression which it wrought upon his fancy, in a painting executed shortly after the event I have narrated, and which is valuable as exhibiting not only the peculiarities which have made Schalken's pictures sought after, but even more so as presenting a portrait of his early love, Rose Velderkaust, whose mysterious fate must always remain matter of speculation.

AN ACCOUNT OF SOME STRANGE DISTURBANCES IN AUNGIER STREET

It is not worth telling, this story of mine—at least, not worth writing. Told, indeed, as I have sometimes been called upon to tell it, to a circle of intelligent and eager faces, lighted up by a good after-dinner fire on a winter's evening, with a cold wind rising and wailing outside, and all snug and cosy within, it has gone off—though I say it, who should not—indifferent well. But it is a venture to do as you would have me. Pen, ink, and paper are cold vehicles for the marvellous, and a "reader" decidedly a more critical animal than a "listener." If, however, you can induce your friends to read it after nightfall, and when the fireside talk has run for a while on thrilling tales of shapeless terror; in short, if you will secure me the *mollia tempora fandi*, I will go to my work, and say my say, with better heart. Well, then, these conditions presupposed, I shall waste no more words, but tell you simply how it all happened.

My cousin (Tom Ludlow) and I studied medicine together. I think he would have succeeded, had he stuck to the profession; but he preferred the Church, poor fellow, and died early, a sacrifice to contagion, contracted in the noble discharge of his duties. For my present purpose, I say enough of his character when I mention that he was of a sedate but frank and cheerful nature; very exact in his observance of truth, and not by any means like myself—of an excitable or nervous temperament.

My Uncle Ludlow—Tom's father—while we were attending lectures, purchased three or four old houses in Aungier Street, one of which was unoccupied. *He* resided in the country, and Tom proposed that we should take up our abode in the untenanted house, so long as it should continue unlet; a move which would accomplish the double end of settling us nearer alike to our lecture-rooms and to our amusements, and of relieving us from the weekly charge of rent for our lodgings.

Our furniture was very scant—our whole equipage remarkably modest and primitive; and, in short, our arrangements pretty nearly as simple as those of a bivouac. Our new plan was, therefore, executed almost as soon as conceived. The front drawing-room was our sitting-room. I had the bedroom over it, and Tom the back bedroom on the same floor, which nothing could have induced me to occupy.

The house, to begin with, was a very old one. It had been, I believe, newly fronted about fifty years before; but with this exception, it had nothing modern about it. The agent who bought it and looked into the titles for my uncle, told me that it was sold, along with much other forfeited property, at Chichester House, I think, in 1702; and had belonged to Sir Thomas Hacket, who was Lord Mayor of Dublin in James II.'s time. How old it was *then*, I can't say; but, at all events, it had seen years and changes enough to have contracted all that mysterious and saddened air, at once exciting and depressing, which belongs to most old mansions.

There had been very little done in the way of modernising details; and, perhaps, it was better so; for there was something queer and by-gone in the very walls and ceilings—in the shape of doors and windows—in the odd diagonal site of the chimney-pieces—in the beams and ponderous cornices—not to mention the singular solidity of all the woodwork, from the banisters to the window-frames, which hopelessly defied disguise, and would have emphatically proclaimed their antiquity through any conceivable amount of modern finery and varnish.

An effort had, indeed, been made, to the extent of papering the drawing-rooms; but somehow, the paper looked raw and out of keeping; and the old woman, who kept a little dirt-pie of a shop in the lane, and whose daughter—a girl of two and fifty—was our solitary handmaid, coming in at sunrise, and chastely receding again as soon as she had made all ready for tea in our state apartment;—this woman, I say, remembered it, when old Judge Horrocks (who, having earned the reputation of a particularly "hanging judge," ended by hanging himself, as the coroner's jury found, under an impulse of "temporary insanity," with a child's skipping-rope, over the massive old bannisters) resided there, entertaining good company, with fine venison and rare old port. In those halcyon days, the drawing-rooms were hung with gilded leather, and, I dare say, cut a good figure, for they were really spacious rooms.

The bedrooms were wainscoted, but the front one was not gloomy; and in it the cosiness of antiquity quite overcame its sombre associations. But the back bedroom, with its two queerly-placed melancholy windows, staring vacantly at the foot of the bed, and with the shadowy recess to be found in most old houses in Dublin, like a large ghostly closet, which, from congeniality of temperament, had amalgamated with the bedchamber, and dissolved the partition. At night-time, this "alcove"—as our "maid" was wont to call it—had, in my eyes, a specially sinister and suggestive character. Tom's distant and solitary candle glimmered vainly into its darkness. *There* it was always overlooking him—always itself impenetrable. But this was only part of the effect. The whole room was, I can't tell how, repulsive to me. There was, I suppose, in its proportions and features, a latent discord—a certain mysterious and indescribable relation, which jarred indistinctly upon some secret sense of the fitting and the safe, and raised indefinable suspicions and apprehensions of the imagination. On the whole, as I began by saying, nothing could have induced me to pass a night alone in it.

I had never pretended to conceal from poor Tom my superstitious weakness; and he, on the other hand, most unaffectedly ridiculed my tremors. The sceptic was, however, destined to receive a lesson, as you shall hear.

We had not been very long in occupation of our respective dormitories, when I began to complain of uneasy nights and disturbed sleep. I was, I suppose, the more impatient under this annoyance, as I was usually a sound sleeper, and by no means prone to nightmares. It was now, however, my destiny, instead of enjoying my customary repose, every night to "sup full of horrors." After a preliminary course of disagreeable and frightful dreams, my troubles took a definite form, and the same vision, without an appreciable variation in a single detail, visited me at least (on an average) every second night in the week.

Now, this dream, nightmare, or infernal illusion—which you please—of which I was the miserable sport, was on this wise:----

I saw, or thought I saw, with the most abominable distinctness, although at the time in profound darkness, every article of furniture and accidental arrangement of the chamber in which I lay. This, as you know, is incidental to ordinary nightmare. Well, while in this clairvoyant condition, which seemed but the lighting up of the theatre in which was to be exhibited the monotonous tableau of horror, which made my nights insupportable, my attention invariably became, I know not why, fixed upon the windows opposite the foot of my bed; and, uniformly with the same effect, a sense of dreadful anticipation always took slow but sure possession of me. I became somehow conscious of a sort of horrid but undefined preparation going forward in some unknown quarter, and by some unknown agency, for my torment; and, after an interval, which always seemed to me of the same length, a picture suddenly flew up to the window, where it remained fixed, as if by an electrical attraction, and my discipline of horror then commenced, to last perhaps for hours. The picture thus mysteriously glued to the window-panes, was the portrait of an old man, in a crimson flowered silk dressing-gown, the folds of which I could now describe, with a countenance embodying a strange mixture of intellect, sensuality, and power, but withal sinister and full of malignant omen. His nose was hooked, like the beak of a vulture; his eyes large, grey, and prominent, and lighted up with a more than mortal cruelty and coldness. These features were surmounted by a crimson velvet cap, the hair that peeped from under which was white with age, while the eyebrows retained their original blackness. Well I remember every line, hue, and shadow of that stony countenance, and well I may! The gaze of this hellish visage was fixed upon me, and mine returned it with the inexplicable fascination of nightmare, for what appeared to me to be hours of agony. At last----

The cock he crew, away then flew

the fiend who had enslaved me through the awful watches of the night; and, harassed and nervous, I rose to the duties of the day.

I had—I can't say exactly why, but it may have been from the exquisite anguish and profound impressions of unearthly horror, with which this strange phantasmagoria was associated—an insurmountable antipathy to describing the exact nature of my nightly troubles to my friend and comrade. Generally, however, I told him that I was haunted by abominable dreams; and, true to the imputed materialism of medicine, we put our heads together to dispel my horrors, not by exorcism, but by a tonic.

I will do this tonic justice, and frankly admit that the accursed portrait began to intermit its visits under its influence. What of that? Was this singular apparition—as full of character as of terror—therefore the creature of my fancy, or the invention of my poor stomach? Was it, in short, *subjective* (to borrow the technical slang of the day) and not the palpable aggression and intrusion of an external agent? That, good friend, as we will both admit, by no means follows. The evil spirit, who enthralled my senses in the shape of that portrait, may have been just as near me, just as energetic, just as malignant, though I saw him not. What means the whole moral code of revealed religion regarding the due keeping of our own bodies, soberness, temperance, etc.? here is an obvious connexion between the material and the invisible; the healthy tone of the system, and its unimpaired energy, may, for aught we can tell, guard us against influences which would otherwise render life itself terrific. The mesmerist and the electro-biologist will fail upon an average with nine patients out of ten—so may the evil spirit. Special conditions of the corporeal system are indispensable to the production of certain spiritual phenomena. The operation succeeds sometimes—sometimes fails—that is all.

I found afterwards that my would-be sceptical companion had his troubles too. But of these I knew nothing yet. One night, for a wonder, I was sleeping soundly, when I was roused by a step on the lobby outside my room, followed by the loud clang of what turned out to be a large brass candlestick, flung with all his force by poor Tom Ludlow over the banisters, and rattling with a rebound down the second flight of stairs; and almost concurrently with this, Tom burst open my door, and bounced into my room backwards, in a state of extraordinary agitation.

I had jumped out of bed and clutched him by the arm before I had any distinct idea of my own whereabouts. There we were—in our shirts—standing before the open door—staring through the great old banister opposite, at the lobby window, through which the sickly light of a clouded moon was gleaming.

"What's the matter, Tom? What's the matter with you? What the devil's the matter with you, Tom?" I demanded shaking him with nervous impatience.

He took a long breath before he answered me, and then it was not very coherently.

"It's nothing, nothing at all—did I speak?—what did I say?—where's the candle, Richard? It's dark; I—I had a candle!"

"Yes, dark enough," I said; "but what's the matter?—what *is* it?—why don't you speak, Tom?—have you lost your wits?—what is the matter?"

"The matter?—oh, it is all over. It must have been a dream—nothing at all but a dream—don't you think so? It could not be anything more than a dream."

"Of *course*" said I, feeling uncommonly nervous, "it *was* a dream."

"I thought," he said, "there was a man in my room, and—and I jumped out of bed; and—and—where's the candle?"

"In your room, most likely," I said, "shall I go and bring it?"

"No; stay here—don't go; it's no matter—don't, I tell you; it was all a dream. Bolt the door, Dick; I'll stay here with you—I feel nervous. So, Dick, like a good fellow, light your candle and open the window—I am in a *shocking state*."

I did as he asked me, and robing himself like Granuaile in one of my blankets, he seated himself close beside my bed.

Every body knows how contagious is fear of all sorts, but more especially that particular kind of fear under which poor Tom was at that moment labouring. I would not have heard, nor I believe would he have recapitulated, just at that moment, for half the world, the details of the hideous vision which had so unmanned him.

"Don't mind telling me anything about your nonsensical dream, Tom," said I, affecting contempt, really in a panic; "let us talk about something else; but it is quite plain that this dirty old house disagrees with us both, and hang me if I stay here any longer, to be pestered with indigestion and—and—bad nights, so we may as well look out for lodgings—don't you think so?—at once."

Tom agreed, and, after an interval, said----

"I have been thinking, Richard, that it is a long time since I saw my father, and I have made up my mind to go down to-morrow and return in a day or two, and you can take rooms for us in the meantime."

I fancied that this resolution, obviously the result of the vision which had so profoundly scared him, would probably vanish next morning with the damps and shadows of night. But I was mistaken. Off went Tom at peep of day to the country, having agreed that so soon as I had secured suitable lodgings, I was to recall him by letter from his visit to my Uncle Ludlow.

Now, anxious as I was to change my quarters, it so happened, owing to a series of petty procrastinations and accidents, that nearly a week elapsed before my bargain was made and my letter of recall on the wing to Tom; and, in the meantime, a trifling adventure or two had occurred to your humble servant, which, absurd as they now appear, diminished by distance, did certainly at the time serve to whet my appetite for change considerably.

A night or two after the departure of my comrade, I was sitting by my bedroom fire, the door locked, and the ingredients of a tumbler of hot whisky-punch upon the crazy spider-table; for, as the best mode of keeping the

Black spirits and white,
Blue spirits and grey,

with which I was environed, at bay, I had adopted the practice recommended by the wisdom of my ancestors, and "kept my spirits up by pouring spirits down." I had thrown aside my volume of Anatomy, and was treating myself by way of a tonic, preparatory to my punch and bed, to half-a-dozen pages of the *Spectator*, when I heard a step on the flight of stairs descending from the attics. It was two o'clock, and the streets were as silent as a churchyard—the sounds were, therefore, perfectly distinct. There was a slow, heavy tread, characterised by the emphasis and deliberation of age, descending by the narrow staircase from above; and, what made the sound more singular, it was plain that the feet which produced it were perfectly bare, measuring the descent with something between a pound and a flop, very ugly to hear.

I knew quite well that my attendant had gone away many hours before, and that nobody but myself had any business in the house. It was quite plain also that the person who was coming down stairs had no intention whatever of concealing his movements; but, on the contrary, appeared disposed to make even more noise, and proceed more deliberately, than was at all necessary. When the step reached the foot of the stairs outside my room, it seemed to stop; and I expected every moment to see my door open spontaneously, and give admission to the original of my detested portrait. I was, however, relieved in a few seconds by hearing the descent renewed, just in the same manner, upon the staircase leading down to the drawing-rooms, and thence, after another pause, down the next flight, and so on to the hall, whence I heard no more.

Now, by the time the sound had ceased, I was wound up, as they say, to a very unpleasant pitch of excitement. I listened, but there was not a stir. I screwed up my courage to a decisive experiment—opened my door, and in a stentorian voice bawled over the banisters, "Who's there?" There was no answer but the ringing of my own voice through the empty old house, no renewal of the movement; nothing, in short, to give my unpleasant sensations a definite direction. There is, I think, something most disagreeably disenchanting in the sound of one's own voice under such circumstances, exerted in solitude, and in vain. It redoubled my sense of isolation, and my misgivings increased on perceiving that the door, which I certainly thought I had left open, was closed behind me; in a vague alarm, lest my retreat should be cut off, I got again into my room as quickly as I could, where I remained in a state of imaginary blockade, and very uncomfortable indeed, till morning.

Next night brought no return of my barefooted fellow-lodger; but the night following, being in my bed, and in the dark—somewhere, I suppose, about the same hour as before, I distinctly heard the old fellow again descending from the garrets.

This time I had had my punch, and the *morale* of the garrison was consequently excellent. I jumped out of bed, clutched the poker as I passed the expiring fire, and in a moment was upon the lobby. The sound had ceased by this time—the dark and chill were discouraging; and, guess my horror, when I saw, or thought I saw, a black monster, whether in the shape of a man or a bear I could not say, standing, with its back to the wall, on the lobby, facing me, with a pair of great greenish eyes shining dimly out. Now, I must be frank, and confess that the cupboard which displayed our plates and cups stood just there, though at the moment I did not recollect it. At the same time I must honestly say, that making every allowance for an excited imagination, I never could satisfy myself that I was made the dupe of my own fancy in this matter; for this apparition, after one or two shiftings of shape, as if in the act of incipient transformation, began, as it seemed on second thoughts, to advance upon me in its original form. From an instinct of terror rather than of courage, I hurled the poker, with all my force, at its head; and to the music of a horrid crash made my way into my room, and double-locked the door. Then, in a minute more, I heard the horrid bare feet walk down the stairs, till the sound ceased in the hall, as on the former occasion.

If the apparition of the night before was an ocular delusion of my fancy sporting with the dark outlines of our cupboard, and if its horrid eyes were nothing but a pair of inverted teacups, I had, at all events, the satisfaction of having launched the poker with admirable effect, and in true "fancy" phrase, "knocked its two daylights into one," as the commingled fragments of my tea-service testified. I did my best to gather comfort and courage from these evidences; but it would not do. And then what could I say of those horrid bare feet, and the regular tramp, tramp, tramp, which measured the distance of the entire staircase through the solitude of my haunted dwelling, and at an hour when no good influence was stirring? Confound it!--the whole affair was abominable. I was out of spirits, and dreaded the approach of night.

It came, ushered ominously in with a thunder-storm and dull torrents of depressing rain. Earlier than usual the streets grew silent; and by twelve o'clock nothing but the comfortless pattering of the rain was to be heard.

I made myself as snug as I could. I lighted *two* candles instead of one. I forswore bed, and held myself in readiness for a sally, candle in hand; for, *coûte qui coûte*, I was resolved to *see* the being, if visible at all, who troubled the nightly stillness of my mansion. I was fidgetty and nervous and tried in vain to interest myself with my books. I walked up and down my room, whistling in turn martial and hilarious music, and listening ever and anon for the dreaded noise. I sate down and stared at the square label on the solemn and reserved-looking black bottle, until "FLANAGAN & CO'S BEST OLD MALT WHISKY" grew into a sort of subdued accompaniment to all the fantastic and horrible speculations which chased one another through my brain.

Silence, meanwhile, grew more silent, and darkness darker. I listened in vain for the rumble of a vehicle, or the dull clamour of a distant row. There was nothing but the sound of a rising wind, which had succeeded the thunder-storm that had travelled over the Dublin mountains quite out of hearing. In the middle of this great city I began to feel myself alone with nature, and Heaven knows what beside. My courage was ebbing. Punch, however, which makes beasts of so many, made a man of me again—just in time to hear with tolerable nerve and firmness the lumpy, flabby, naked feet deliberately descending the stairs again.

I took a candle, not without a tremour. As I crossed the floor I tried to extemporise a prayer, but stopped short to listen, and never finished it. The steps continued. I confess I hesitated for some seconds at the door before I took heart of grace and opened it. When I peeped out the lobby was perfectly empty—there was no monster standing on the staircase; and as the detested sound ceased, I was reassured enough to venture forward nearly to the banisters. Horror of horrors! within a stair or two beneath the spot where I stood the unearthly tread smote the floor. My eye caught something in motion; it was about the size of Goliah's foot—it was grey, heavy, and flapped with a dead weight from one step to another. As I am alive, it was the most monstrous grey rat I ever beheld or imagined.

Shakespeare says—"Some men there are cannot abide a gaping pig, and some that are mad if they behold a cat." I went well-nigh out of my wits when I beheld this *rat*; for, laugh at me as you may, it fixed upon me, I thought, a perfectly human expression of malice; and, as it shuffled about and looked up into my face almost from between my feet, I saw, I could swear it—I felt it then, and know it now, the infernal gaze and the accursed countenance of my old friend in the portrait, transfused into the visage of the bloated vermin before me.

I bounced into my room again with a feeling of loathing and horror I cannot describe, and locked and bolted my door as if a lion had been at the other side. D—n him or *it*; curse the portrait and its original! I felt in my soul that the rat—yes, the *rat*, the RAT I had just seen, was that evil being in masquerade, and rambling through the house upon some infernal night lark.

Next morning I was early trudging through the miry streets; and, among other transactions, posted a peremptory note recalling Tom. On my return, however, I found a note from my absent "chum," announcing his intended return next day. I was doubly rejoiced at this, because I had succeeded in getting rooms; and because the change of scene and return of my comrade were rendered specially pleasant by the last night's half ridiculous half horrible adventure.

I slept extemporaneously in my new quarters in Digges' Street that night, and next morning returned for breakfast to the haunted mansion, where I was certain Tom would call immediately on his arrival.

I was quite right—he came; and almost his first question referred to the primary object of our change of residence.

"Thank God," he said with genuine fervour, on hearing that all was arranged. "On *your* account I am delighted. As to myself, I assure you that no earthly consideration could have induced me ever again to pass a night in this disastrous old house."

"Confound the house!" I ejaculated, with a genuine mixture of fear and detestation, "we have not had a pleasant hour since we came to live here"; and so I went on, and related incidentally my adventure with the plethoric old rat.

"Well, if that were *all*," said my cousin, affecting to make light of the matter, "I don't think I should have minded it very much."

"Ay, but its eye—its countenance, my dear Tom," urged I; "if you had seen *that*, you would have felt it might be *anything* but what it seemed."

"I inclined to think the best conjurer in such a case would be an able-bodied cat," he said, with a provoking chuckle.

"But let us hear your own adventure," I said tartly.

At this challenge he looked uneasily round him. I had poked up a very unpleasant recollection.

"You shall hear it, Dick; I'll tell it to you," he said. "Begad, sir, I should feel quite queer, though, telling it *here*, though we are too strong a body for ghosts to meddle with just now."

Though he spoke this like a joke, I think it was serious calculation. Our Hebe was in a corner of the room, packing our cracked delft tea and dinner-services in a basket. She soon suspended operations, and with mouth and eyes wide open became an absorbed listener. Tom's experiences were told nearly in these words:----

"I saw it three times, Dick—three distinct times; and I am perfectly certain it meant me some infernal harm. I was, I say, in danger—in *extreme* danger; for, if nothing else had happened, my reason would most certainly have failed me, unless I had escaped so soon. Thank God. I *did* escape.

"The first night of this hateful disturbance, I was lying in the attitude of sleep, in that lumbering old bed. I hate to think of it. I was really wide awake, though I had put out my candle, and was lying as quietly as if I had been asleep; and although accidentally restless, my thoughts were running in a cheerful and agreeable channel.

"I think it must have been two o'clock at least when I thought I heard a sound in that—that odious dark recess at the far end of the bedroom. It was as if someone was drawing a piece of cord slowly along the floor, lifting it up, and dropping it softly down again in coils. I sate up once or twice in my bed, but could see nothing, so I concluded it must be mice in the wainscot. I felt no emotion graver than curiosity, and after a few minutes ceased to observe it.

"While lying in this state, strange to say; without at first a suspicion of anything supernatural, on a sudden I saw an old man, rather stout and square, in a sort of roan-red dressing-gown, and with a black cap on his head, moving stiffly and slowly in a diagonal direction, from the recess, across the floor of the bedroom, passing my bed at the foot, and entering the lumber-closet at the left. He had something under his arm; his head hung a little at one side; and, merciful God! when I saw his face."

Tom stopped for a while, and then said----

"That awful countenance, which living or dying I never can forget, disclosed what he was. Without turning to the right or left, he passed beside me, and entered the closet by the bed's head.

"While this fearful and indescribable type of death and guilt was passing, I felt that I had no more power to speak or stir than if I had been myself a corpse. For hours after it had disappeared, I was too terrified and weak to move. As soon as daylight came, I took courage, and examined the room, and especially the course which the frightful intruder had seemed to take, but there was not a vestige to indicate anybody's having passed there; no sign of any disturbing agency visible among the lumber that strewed the floor of the closet.

"I now began to recover a little. I was fagged and exhausted, and at last, overpowered by a feverish sleep. I came down late; and finding you out of spirits, on account of your dreams about the portrait, whose *original* I am now certain disclosed himself to me, I did not care to talk about the infernal vision. In fact, I was trying to persuade myself that the whole thing was an illusion, and I did not like to revive in their intensity the hated impressions of the past night—or to risk the constancy of my scepticism, by recounting the tale of my sufferings.

"It required some nerve, I can tell you, to go to my haunted chamber next night, and lie down quietly in the same bed," continued Tom. "I did so with a degree of trepidation, which, I am not ashamed to say, a very little matter would have sufficed to stimulate to downright panic. This night, however, passed off quietly enough, as also the next; and so too did two or three more. I grew more confident, and began to fancy that I believed in the theories of spectral illusions, with which I had at first vainly tried to impose upon my convictions.

"The apparition had been, indeed, altogether anomalous. It had crossed the room without any recognition of my presence: I had not disturbed *it*, and *it* had no mission to *me*. What, then, was the imaginable use of its crossing the room in a visible shape at all? Of course it might have *been* in the closet instead of *going* there, as easily as it introduced itself into the recess without entering the chamber in a shape discernible by the senses. Besides, how the deuce *had* I seen it? It was a dark night; I had no candle; there was no fire; and yet I saw it as distinctly, in colouring and outline, as ever I beheld human form! A cataleptic dream would explain it all; and I was determined that a dream it should be.

"One of the most remarkable phenomena connected with the practice of mendacity is the vast number of deliberate lies we tell ourselves, whom, of all persons, we can least expect to deceive. In all this, I need hardly tell you, Dick, I was simply lying to myself, and did not believe one word of the wretched humbug. Yet I went on, as men will do, like persevering charlatans and impostors, who tire people into credulity by the mere force of reiteration; so I hoped to win myself over at last to a comfortable scepticism about the ghost.

"He had not appeared a second time—that certainly was a comfort; and what, after all, did I care for him, and his queer old toggery and strange looks? Not a fig! I was nothing the worse for having seen him, and a good story the better. So I tumbled into bed, put out my candle, and, cheered by a loud drunken quarrel in the back lane, went fast asleep.

"From this deep slumber I awoke with a start. I knew I had had a horrible dream; but what it was I could not remember. My heart was thumping furiously; I felt bewildered and feverish; I sate up in the bed and looked about the room. A broad flood of moonlight came in through the curtainless window; everything was as I had last seen it; and though the domestic squabble in the back lane was, unhappily for me, allayed, I yet could hear a pleasant fellow singing, on his way home, the then popular comic ditty called, 'Murphy Delany.' Taking advantage of this diversion I lay down again, with my face towards the fireplace, and closing my eyes, did my best to think of nothing else but the song, which was every moment growing fainter in the distance:----

"'Twas Murphy Delany, so funny and frisky,

Stept into a shebeen shop to get his skin full;
He reeled out again pretty well lined with whiskey,
As fresh as a shamrock, as blind as a bull.

"The singer, whose condition I dare say resembled that of his hero, was soon too far off to regale my ears any more; and as his music died away, I myself sank into a doze, neither sound nor refreshing. Somehow the song had got into my head, and I went meandering on through the adventures of my respectable fellow-countryman, who, on emerging from the 'shebeen shop,' fell into a river, from which he was fished up to be 'sat upon' by a coroner's jury, who having learned from a 'horse-doctor' that he was 'dead as a door-nail, so there was an end,' returned their verdict accordingly, just as he returned to his senses, when an angry altercation and a pitched battle between the body and the coroner winds up the lay with due spirit and pleasantry.

"Through this ballad I continued with a weary monotony to plod, down to the very last line, and then *da capo*, and so on, in my uncomfortable half-sleep, for how long, I can't conjecture. I found myself at last, however, muttering, '*dead* as a door-nail, so there was an end'; and something like another voice within me, seemed to say, very faintly, but sharply, 'dead! dead! *dead*! and may the Lord have mercy on your soul!' and instantaneously I was wide awake, and staring right before me from the pillow.

"Now—will you believe it, Dick?—I saw the same accursed figure standing full front, and gazing at me with its stony and fiendish countenance, not two yards from the bedside."

Tom stopped here, and wiped the perspiration from his face. I felt very queer. The girl was as pale as Tom; and, assembled as we were in the very scene of these adventures, we were all, I dare say, equally grateful for the clear daylight and the resuming bustle out of doors.

"For about three seconds only I saw it plainly; then it grew indistinct; but, for a long time, there was something like a column of dark vapour where it had been standing, between me and the wall; and I felt sure that he was still there. After a good while, this appearance went too. I took my clothes downstairs to the hall, and dressed there, with the door half open; then went out into the street, and walked about the town till morning, when I came back, in a miserable state of nervousness and exhaustion. I was such a fool, Dick, as to be ashamed to tell you how I came to be so upset. I thought you would laugh at me; especially as I had always talked philosophy, and treated *your* ghosts with contempt. I concluded you would give me no quarter; and so kept my tale of horror to myself.

"Now, Dick, you will hardly believe me, when I assure you, that for many nights after this last experience, I did not go to my room at all. I used to sit up for a while in the drawing-room after you had gone up to your bed; and then steal down softly to the hall-door, let myself out, and sit in the 'Robin Hood' tavern until the last guest went off; and then I got through the night like a sentry, pacing the streets till morning.

"For more than a week I never slept in bed. I sometimes had a snooze on a form in the 'Robin Hood,' and sometimes a nap in a chair during the day; but regular sleep I had absolutely none.

"I was quite resolved that we should get into another house; but I could not bring myself to tell you the reason, and I somehow put it off from day to day, although my life was, during every hour of this procrastination, rendered as miserable as that of a felon with the constables on his track. I was growing absolutely ill from this wretched mode of life.

"One afternoon I determined to enjoy an hour's sleep upon your bed. I hated mine; so that I had never, except in a stealthy visit every day to unmake it, lest Martha should discover the secret of my nightly absence, entered the ill-omened chamber.

"As ill-luck would have it, you had locked your bedroom, and taken away the key. I went into my own to unsettle the bedclothes, as usual, and give the bed the appearance of having been slept in. Now, a variety of circumstances concurred to bring about the dreadful scene through which I was that night to pass. In the first place, I was literally overpowered with fatigue, and longing for sleep; in the next place, the effect of this extreme exhaustion upon my nerves resembled that of a narcotic, and rendered me less susceptible than, perhaps, I should in any other condition have been, of the exciting fears which had become habitual to me. Then again, a little bit of the window was open, a pleasant freshness pervaded the room, and, to crown all, the cheerful sun of day was making the room quite pleasant. What was to prevent my enjoying an hour's nap *here*? The whole air was resonant with the cheerful hum of life, and the broad matter-of-fact light of day filled every corner of the room.

"I yielded—stifling my qualms—to the almost overpowering temptation; and merely throwing off my coat, and loosening my cravat, I lay down, limiting myself to *half*-an-hour's doze in the unwonted enjoyment of a feather bed, a coverlet, and a bolster.

"It was horribly insidious; and the demon, no doubt, marked my infatuated preparations. Dolt that I was, I fancied, with mind and body worn out for want of sleep, and an arrear of a full week's rest to my credit, that such measure as *half*-an-hour's sleep, in such a situation, was possible. My sleep was death-like, long, and dreamless.

"Without a start or fearful sensation of any kind, I waked gently, but completely. It was, as you have good reason to remember, long past midnight—I believe, about two o'clock. When sleep has been deep and long enough to satisfy nature thoroughly, one often wakens in this way, suddenly, tranquilly, and completely.

"There was a figure seated in that lumbering, old sofa-chair, near the fireplace. Its back was rather towards me, but I could not be mistaken; it turned slowly round, and, merciful heavens! there was the stony face, with its infernal lineaments of malignity and despair, gloating on me. There was now no doubt as to its consciousness of my presence, and the hellish malice with which it was animated, for it arose, and drew close to the bedside. There was a rope about its neck, and the other end, coiled up, it held stiffly in its hand.

"My good angel nerved me for this horrible crisis. I remained for some seconds transfixed by the gaze of this tremendous phantom. He came close to the bed, and appeared on the point of mounting upon it. The next instant I was upon the floor at the far side, and in a moment more was, I don't know how, upon the lobby.

"But the spell was not yet broken; the valley of the shadow of death was not yet traversed. The abhorred phantom was before me there; it was standing near the banisters, stooping a little, and with one end of the rope round its own neck, was poising a noose at the other, as if to throw over mine; and while engaged in this baleful pantomime, it wore a smile so sensual, so unspeakably dreadful, that my senses were nearly overpowered. I saw and remember nothing more, until I found myself in your room.

"I had a wonderful escape, Dick—there is no disputing *that*—an escape for which, while I live, I shall bless the mercy of heaven. No one can conceive or imagine what it is for flesh and blood to stand in the presence of such a thing, but one who has had the terrific experience. Dick, Dick, a shadow has passed over me—a chill has crossed my blood and marrow, and I will never be the same again—never, Dick—never!"

Our handmaid, a mature girl of two-and-fifty, as I have said, stayed her hand, as Tom's story proceeded, and by little and little drew near to us, with open mouth, and her brows contracted over her little, beady black eyes, till stealing a glance over her shoulder now and then, she established herself close behind us. During the relation, she had made various earnest comments, in an undertone; but these and her ejaculations, for the sake of brevity and simplicity, I have omitted in my narration.

"It's often I heard tell of it," she now said, "but I never believed it rightly till now—though, indeed, why should not I? Does not my mother, down there in the lane, know quare stories, God bless us, beyant telling about it? But you ought not to have slept in the back bedroom. She was loath to let me be going in and out of that room even in the day time, let alone for any Christian to spend the night in it; for sure she says it was his own bedroom."

"*Whose* own bedroom?" we asked, in a breath.

"Why, *his*—the ould Judge's—Judge Horrock's, to be sure, God rest his sowl"; and she looked fearfully round.

"Amen!" I muttered. "But did he die there?"

"Die there! No, not quite *there*," she said. "Shure, was not it over the banisters he hung himself, the ould sinner, God be merciful to us all? and was not it in the alcove they found the handles of the skipping-rope cut off, and the knife where he was settling the cord, God bless us, to hang himself with? It was his housekeeper's daughter owned the rope, my mother often told me, and the child never throve after, and used to be starting up out of her sleep, and screeching in the night time, wid dhrames and frights that cum an her; and they said how it was the speerit of the ould Judge that was tormentin' her; and she used to be roaring and yelling out to hould back the big ould fellow with the crooked neck; and then she'd screech 'Oh, the master! the master! he's stampin' at me, and beckoning to me! Mother, darling, don't let me go!' And so the poor crathure died at last, and the docthers said it was wather on the brain, for it was all they could say."

"How long ago was all this?" I asked.

"Oh, then, how would I know?" she answered. "But it must be a wondherful long time ago, for the housekeeper was an ould woman, with a pipe in her mouth, and not a tooth left, and better nor eighty years ould when my mother was first married; and they said she was a rale buxom, fine-dressed woman when the ould Judge come to his end; an', indeed, my mother's not far from eighty years ould herself this day; and what made it worse for the unnatural ould villain, God rest his soul, to frighten the little girl out of the world the way he did, was what was mostly thought and believed by every one. My mother says how the poor little crathure was his own child; for he was by all accounts an ould villain every way, an' the hangin'est judge that ever was known in Ireland's ground."

"From what you said about the danger of sleeping in that bedroom," said I, "I suppose there were stories about the ghost having appeared there to others."

"Well, there was things said—quare things, surely," she answered, as it seemed, with some reluctance. "And why would not there? Sure was it not up in that same room he slept for more than twenty years? and was it not in the *alcove* he got the rope ready that done his own business at last, the way he done many a betther man's in his lifetime?—and was not the body lying in the same bed after death, and put in the coffin there, too, and carried out to his grave from it in Pether's churchyard, after the coroner was done? But there was quare stories—my mother has them all—about how one Nicholas Spaight got into trouble on the head of it."

"And what did they say of this Nicholas Spaight?" I asked.

"Oh, for that matther, it's soon told," she answered.

And she certainly did relate a very strange story, which so piqued my curiosity, that I took occasion to visit the ancient lady, her mother, from whom I learned many very curious particulars. Indeed, I am tempted to tell the tale, but my fingers are weary, and I must defer it. But if you wish to hear it another time, I shall do my best.

When we had heard the strange tale I have *not* told you, we put one or two further questions to her about the alleged spectral visitations, to which the house had, ever since the death of the wicked old Judge, been subjected.

"No one ever had luck in it," she told us. "There was always cross accidents, sudden deaths, and short times in it. The first that tuck, it was a family—I forget their name—but at any rate there was two young ladies and their papa. He was about sixty, and a stout healthy gentleman as you'd wish to see at that age. Well, he slept in that unlucky back bedroom; and, God between us an' harm! sure enough he was found dead one morning, half out of the bed, with his head as black as a sloe, and swelled like a puddin', hanging down near the floor. It was a fit, they said. He was as dead as a mackerel, and so *he* could not say what it was; but the ould people was all sure that it was nothing at all but the ould Judge, God bless us! that frightened him out of his senses and his life together.

"Some time after there was a rich old maiden lady took the house. I don't know which room *she* slept in, but she lived alone; and at any rate, one morning, the servants going down early to their work, found her sitting on the passage-stairs, shivering and talkin' to herself, quite mad; and never a word more could any of *them* or her friends get from her ever afterwards but, 'Don't ask me to go, for I promised to wait for him.' They never made out from her who it was she meant by *him*, but of course those that knew all about the ould house were at no loss for the meaning of all that happened to her.

"Then afterwards, when the house was let out in lodgings, there was Micky Byrne that took the same room, with his wife and three little children; and sure I heard Mrs. Byrne myself telling how the children used to be lifted up in the bed at night, she could not see by what mains; and how they were starting and screeching every hour, just all as one as the housekeeper's little girl that died, till at last one night poor Micky had a dhrop in him, the way he used now and again; and what do you think in the middle of the night he thought he heard a noise on the stairs, and being in liquor, nothing less id do him but out he must go himself to see what was wrong. Well, after that, all she ever heard of him was himself sayin', 'Oh, God!' and a tumble that shook the very house; and there, sure enough, he was lying on the lower stairs, under the lobby, with his neck smashed double undher him, where he was flung over the banisters."

Then the handmaiden added

"I'll go down to the lane, and send up Joe Gavvey to pack up the rest of the taythings, and bring all the things across to your new lodgings."

And so we all sallied out together, each of us breathing more freely, I have no doubt, as we crossed that ill-omened threshold for the last time.

Now, I may add thus much, in compliance with the immemorial usage of the realm of fiction, which sees the hero not only through his adventures, but fairly out of the world. You must have perceived that what the flesh, blood, and bone hero of romance proper is to the regular compounder of fiction, this old house of brick, wood, and mortar is to the humble recorder of this true tale. I, therefore, relate, as in duty bound, the catastrophe which ultimately befell it, which was simply this—that about two years subsequently to my story it was taken by a quack doctor, who called himself Baron Duhlstoerf, and filled the parlour windows with bottles of indescribable horrors preserved in brandy, and the newspapers with the usual grandiloquent and mendacious advertisements. This gentleman among his virtues did not reckon sobriety, and one night, being overcome with much wine, he set fire to his bed curtains, partially burned himself, and totally consumed the house. It was afterwards rebuilt, and for a time an undertaker established himself in the premises.

I have now told you my own and Tom's adventures, together with some valuable collateral particulars; and having acquitted myself of my engagement, I wish you a very good night, and pleasant dreams.

GHOSTLY TALES VOLUME II

AN AUTHENTIC NARRATIVE OF A HAUNTED HOUSE

[The Editor of the UNIVERSITY MAGAZINE submits the following very remarkable statement, with every detail of which he has been for some years acquainted, upon the ground that it affords the most authentic and ample relation of a series of marvellous phenoma, in nowise connected with what is technically termed "spiritualism," which he has anywhere met with. All the persons—and there are many of them living—upon whose separate evidence some parts, and upon whose united testimony others, of this most singular recital depend, are, in their several walks of life, respectable, and such as would in any matter of judicial investigation be deemed wholly unexceptionable witnesses. There is not an incident here recorded which would not have been distinctly deposed to on oath had any necessity existed, by the persons who severally, and some of them in great fear, related their own distinct experiences. The Editor begs most pointedly to meet *in limine* the suspicion, that he is elaborating a trick, or vouching for another ghost of Mrs. Veal. As a mere story the narrative is valueless: its sole claim to attention is its absolute truth. For the good faith of its relator he pledges his own and the character of this Magazine. With the Editor's concurrence, the name of the watering-place, and some special circumstances in no essential way bearing upon the peculiar character of the story, but which might have indicated the locality, and possibly annoyed persons interested in house property there, have been suppressed by the narrator. Not the slightest liberty has been taken with the narrative, which is presented precisely in the terms in which the writer of it, who employs throughout the first person, would, if need were, fix it in the form of an affidavit.]

Within the last eight years—the precise date I purposely omit—I was ordered by my physician, my health being in an unsatisfactory state, to change my residence to one upon the sea-coast; and accordingly, I took a house for a year in a fashionable watering-place, at a moderate distance from the city in which I had previously resided, and connected with it by a railway.

Winter was setting in when my removal thither was decided upon; but there was nothing whatever dismal or depressing in the change. The house I had taken was to all appearance, and in point of convenience, too, quite a modern one. It formed one in a cheerful row, with small gardens in front, facing the sea, and commanding sea air and sea views in perfection. In the rear it had coach-house and stable, and between them and the house a considerable grass-plot, with some flower-beds, interposed.

Our family consisted of my wife and myself, with three children, the eldest about nine years old, she and the next in age being girls; and the youngest, between six and seven, a boy. To these were added six servants, whom, although for certain reasons I decline giving their real names, I shall indicate, for the sake of clearness, by arbitrary ones. There was a nurse, Mrs. Southerland; a nursery-maid, Ellen Page; the cook, Mrs. Greenwood; and the housemaid, Ellen Faith; a butler, whom I shall call Smith, and his son, James, about two-and-twenty.

We came out to take possession at about seven o'clock in the evening; every thing was comfortable and cheery; good fires lighted, the rooms neat and airy, and a general air of preparation and comfort, highly conducive to good spirits and pleasant anticipations.

The sitting-rooms were large and cheerful, and they and the bed-rooms more than ordinarily lofty, the kitchen and servants' rooms, on the same level, were well and comfortably furnished, and had, like the rest of the house, an air of recent painting and fitting up, and a completely modern character, which imparted a very cheerful air of cleanliness and convenience.

There had been just enough of the fuss of settling agreeably to occupy us, and to give a pleasant turn to our thoughts after we had retired to our rooms. Being an invalid, I had a small bed to myself—resigning the four-poster to my wife. The candle was extinguished, but a night-light was burning. I was coming up stairs, and she, already in bed, had just dismissed her maid, when we were both startled by a wild scream from her room; I found her in a state of the extremest agitation and terror. She insisted that she had seen an unnaturally tall figure come beside her bed and stand there. The light was too faint to enable her to define any thing respecting this apparition, beyond the fact of her having most distinctly seen such a shape, colourless from the insufficiency of the light to disclose more than its dark outline.

We both endeavoured to re-assure her. The room once more looked so cheerful in the candlelight, that we were quite uninfluenced by the contagion of her terrors. The movements and voices of the servants down stairs still getting things into their places and completing our comfortable arrangements, had also their effect in steeling us against any such influence, and we set the whole thing down as a dream, or an imperfectly-seen outline of the bed-curtains. When, however, we were alone, my wife reiterated, still in great agitation, her clear assertion that she had most positively seen, being at the time as completely awake as ever she was, precisely what she had described to us. And in this conviction she continued perfectly firm.

A day or two after this, it came out that our servants were under an apprehension that, somehow or other, thieves had established a secret mode of access to the lower part of the house. The butler, Smith, had seen an ill-looking woman in his room on the first night of our arrival; and he and other servants constantly saw, for many days subsequently, glimpses of a retreating figure, which corresponded with that so seen by him, passing through a passage which led to a back area in which were some coal-vaults.

This figure was seen always in the act of retreating, its back turned, generally getting round the corner of the passage into the area, in a stealthy and hurried way, and, when closely followed, imperfectly seen again entering one of the coal-vaults, and when pursued into it, nowhere to be found.

The idea of any thing supernatural in the matter had, strange to say, not yet entered the mind of any one of the servants. They had heard some stories of smugglers having secret passages into houses, and using their means of access for purposes of pillage, or with a view to frighten superstitious people out of houses which they needed for their own objects, and a suspicion of similar practices here, caused them extreme uneasiness. The apparent anxiety also manifested by this retreating figure to escape observation, and her always appearing to make her egress at the same point, favoured this romantic hypothesis. The men, however, made a most careful examination of the back area, and of the coal-vaults, with a view to discover some mode of egress, but entirely without success. On the contrary, the result was, so far as it went, subversive of the theory; solid masonry met them on every hand.

I called the man, Smith, up, to hear from his own lips the particulars of what he had seen; and certainly his report was very curious. I give it as literally as my memory enables me:----

His son slept in the same room, and was sound asleep; but he lay awake, as men sometimes will on a change of bed, and having many things on his mind. He was lying with his face towards the wall, but observing a light and some little stir in the room, he turned round in his bed, and saw the figure of a woman, squalid, and ragged in dress; her figure rather low and broad; as well as I recollect, she had something—either a cloak or shawl—on, and wore a bonnet. Her back was turned, and she appeared to be searching or rummaging for something on the floor, and, without appearing to observe him, she turned in doing so towards him. The light, which was more like the intense glow of a coal, as he described it, being of a deep red colour, proceeded from the hollow of her hand, which she held beside her head, and he saw her perfectly distinctly. She appeared middle-aged, was deeply pitted with the smallpox, and blind of one eye. His phrase in describing her general appearance was, that she was "a miserable, poor-looking creature."

He was under the impression that she must be the woman who had been left by the proprietor in charge of the house, and who had that evening, after having given up the keys, remained for some little time with the female servants. He coughed, therefore, to apprize her of his presence, and turned again towards the wall. When he again looked round she and the light were gone; and odd as was her method of lighting herself in her search, the circumstances excited neither uneasiness nor curiosity in his mind, until he discovered next morning that the woman in question had left the house long before he had gone to his bed.

I examined the man very closely as to the appearance of the person who had visited him, and the result was what I have described. It struck me as an odd thing, that even then, considering how prone to superstition persons in his rank of life usually are, he did not seem to suspect any thing supernatural in the occurrence; and, on the contrary, was thoroughly persuaded that his visitant was a living person, who had got into the house by some hidden entrance.

On Sunday, on his return from his place of worship, he told me that, when the service was ended, and the congregation making their way slowly out, he saw the very woman in the crowd, and kept his eye upon her for several minutes, but such was the crush, that all his efforts to reach her were unavailing, and when he got into the open street she was gone. He was quite positive as to his having distinctly seen her, however, for several minutes, and scouted the possibility of any mistake as to identity; and fully impressed with the substantial and living reality of his visitant, he was very much provoked at her having escaped him. He made inquiries also in the neighbourhood, but could procure no information, nor hear of any other persons having seen any woman corresponding with his visitant.

The cook and the housemaid occupied a bed-room on the kitchen floor. It had whitewashed walls, and they were actually terrified by the appearance of the shadow of a woman passing and repassing across the side wall opposite to their beds. They suspected that this had been going on much longer than they were aware, for its presence was discovered by a sort of accident, its movements happening to take a direction in distinct contrariety to theirs.

This shadow always moved upon one particular wall, returning after short intervals, and causing them extreme terror. They placed the candle, as the most obvious specific, so close to the infested wall, that the flame all but touched it; and believed for some time that they had effectually got rid of this annoyance; but one night, notwithstanding this arrangement of the light, the shadow returned, passing and repassing, as heretofore, upon the same wall, although their only candle was burning within an inch of it, and it was obvious that no substance capable of casting such a shadow could have interposed; and, indeed, as they described it, the shadow seemed to have no sort of relation to the position of the light, and appeared, as I have said, in manifest defiance of the laws of optics.

I ought to mention that the housemaid was a particularly fearless sort of person, as well as a very honest one; and her companion, the cook, a scrupulously religious woman, and both agreed in every particular in their relation of what occurred.

Meanwhile, the nursery was not without its annoyances, though as yet of a comparatively trivial kind. Sometimes, at night, the handle of the door was turned hurriedly as if by a person trying to come in, and at others a knocking was made at it. These sounds occurred after the children had settled to sleep, and while the nurse still remained awake. Whenever she called to know "who is there," the sounds ceased; but several times, and particularly at first, she was under the impression that they were caused by her mistress, who had come to see the children, and thus impressed she had got up and opened the door, expecting to see her, but discovering only darkness, and receiving no answer to her inquiries.

With respect to this nurse, I must mention that I believe no more perfectly trustworthy servant was ever employed in her capacity; and, in addition to her integrity, she was remarkably gifted with sound common sense.

One morning, I think about three or four weeks after our arrival, I was sitting at the parlour window which looked to the front, when I saw the little iron door which admitted into the small garden that lay between the window where I was sitting and the public road, pushed open by a woman who so exactly answered the description given by Smith of the woman who had visited his room on the night of his arrival as instantaneously to impress me with the conviction that she must be the identical person. She was a square, short woman, dressed in soiled and tattered clothes, scarred and pitted with small-pox, and blind of an eye. She stepped hurriedly into the little enclosure, and peered from a distance of a few yards into the room where I was sitting. I felt that now was the moment to clear the matter up; but there was something stealthy in the manner and look of the woman which convinced me that I must not appear to notice her until her retreat was fairly cut off. Unfortunately, I was suffering from a lame foot, and could not reach the bell as quickly as I wished. I made all the haste I could, and rang violently to bring up the servant Smith. In the short interval that intervened, I observed the woman from the window, who having in a leisurely way, and with a kind of scrutiny, looked along the front windows of the house, passed quickly out again, closing the gate after her, and followed a lady who was walking along the footpath at a quick pace, as if with the intention of begging from her. The moment the man entered I told him—"the blind woman you described to me has this instant followed a lady in that direction, try to overtake her." He was, if possible, more eager than I in the chase, but returned in a short time after a vain pursuit, very hot, and utterly disappointed. And, thereafter, we saw her face no more.

All this time, and up to the period of our leaving the house, which was not for two or three months later, there occurred at intervals the only phenomenon in the entire series having any resemblance to what we hear described of "Spiritualism." This was a knocking, like a soft hammering with a wooden mallet, as it seemed in the timbers between the bedroom ceilings and the roof. It had this special peculiarity, that it was always rythmical, and, I think, invariably, the emphasis upon the last stroke. It would sound rapidly "one, two, three, *four*—one, two, three, *four*;" or "one, two, *three*—one, two, *three*," and sometimes "one, *two*—one, *two*," &c., and this, with intervals and resumptions, monotonously for hours at a time.

At first this caused my wife, who was a good deal confined to her bed, much annoyance; and we sent to our neighbours to inquire if any hammering or carpentering was going on in their houses but were informed that nothing of the sort was taking place. I have myself heard it frequently, always in the same inaccessible part of the house, and with the same monotonous emphasis. One odd thing about it was, that on my wife's calling out, as she used to do when it became more than usually troublesome, "stop that noise," it was invariably arrested for a longer or shorter time.

Of course none of these occurrences were ever mentioned in hearing of the children. They would have been, no doubt, like most children, greatly terrified had they heard any thing of the matter, and known that their elders were unable to account for what was passing; and their fears would have made them wretched and troublesome.

They used to play for some hours every day in the back garden—the house forming one end of this oblong inclosure, the stable and coach-house the other, and two parallel walls of considerable height the sides. Here, as it afforded a perfectly safe playground, they were frequently left quite to themselves; and in talking over their days' adventures, as children will, they happened to mention a woman, or rather the woman, for they had long grown familiar with her appearance, whom they used to see in the garden while they were at play. They assumed that she came in and went out at the stable door, but they never actually saw her enter or depart. They merely saw a figure—that of a very poor woman, soiled and ragged—near the stable wall, stooping over the ground, and apparently grubbing in the loose clay in search of something. She did not disturb, or appear to observe them; and they left her in undisturbed possession of her nook of ground. When seen it was always in the same spot, and similarly occupied; and the description they gave of her general appearance—for they never saw her face—corresponded with that of the one-eyed woman whom Smith, and subsequently as it seemed, I had seen.

The other man, James, who looked after a mare which I had purchased for the purpose of riding exercise, had, like every one else in the house, his little trouble to report, though it was not much. The stall in which, as the most comfortable, it was decided to place her, she peremptorily declined to enter. Though a very docile and gentle little animal, there was no getting her into it. She would snort and rear, and, in fact, do or suffer any thing rather than set her hoof in it. He was fain, therefore, to place her in another. And on several occasions he found her there, exhibiting all the equine symptoms of extreme fear. Like the rest of us, however, this man was not troubled in the particular case with any superstitious qualms. The mare had evidently been frightened; and he was puzzled to find out how, or by whom, for the stable was well-secured, and had, I am nearly certain, a lock-up yard outside.

One morning I was greeted with the intelligence that robbers had certainly got into the house in the night; and that one of them had actually been seen in the nursery. The witness, I found, was my eldest child, then, as I have said, about nine years of age. Having awoke in the night, and lain awake for some time in her bed, she heard the handle of the door turn, and a person whom she distinctly saw—for it was a light night, and the window-shutters unclosed—but whom she had never seen before, stepped in on tiptoe, and with an appearance of great caution. He was a rather small man, with a very red face; he wore an oddly cut frock coat, the collar of which stood up, and trousers, rough and wide, like those of a sailor, turned up at the ankles, and either short boots or clumsy shoes, covered with mud. This man listened beside the nurse's bed, which stood next the door, as if to satisfy himself that she was sleeping soundly; and having done so for some seconds, he began to move cautiously in a diagonal line, across the room to the chimney-piece, where he stood for a while, and so resumed his tiptoe walk, skirting the wall, until he reached a chest of drawers, some of which were open, and into which he looked, and began to rummage in a hurried way, as the child supposed, making search for something worth taking away. He then passed on to the window, where was a dressing-table, at which he also stopped, turning over the things upon it, and standing for some time at the window as if looking out, and then resuming his walk by the side wall opposite to that by which he had moved up to the window, he returned in the same way toward the nurse's bed, so as to reach it at the foot. With its side to the end wall, in which was the door, was placed the little bed in which lay my eldest child, who watched his proceedings with the extremest terror. As he drew near she instinctively moved herself in the bed, with her head and shoulders to the wall, drawing up her feet; but he passed by without appearing to observe, or, at least, to care for her presence. Immediately after the nurse turned in her bed as if about to waken; and when the child, who had drawn the clothes about her head, again ventured to peep out, the man was gone.

The child had no idea of her having seen any thing more formidable than a thief. With the prowling, cautious, and noiseless manner of proceeding common to such marauders, the air and movements of the man whom she had seen entirely corresponded. And on hearing her perfectly distinct and consistent account, I could myself arrive at no other conclusion than that a stranger had actually got into the house. I had, therefore, in the first instance, a most careful examination made to discover any traces of an entrance having been made by any window into the house. The doors had been found barred and locked as usual; but no sign of any thing of the sort was discernible. I then had the various articles—plate, wearing apparel, books, &c., counted; and after having conned over and reckoned up every thing, it became quite clear that nothing whatever had been removed from the house, nor was there the slightest indication of any thing having been so much as disturbed there. I must here state that this child was remarkably clear, intelligent, and observant; and that her description of the man, and of all that had occurred, was most exact, and as detailed as the want of perfect light rendered possible.

I felt assured that an entrance had actually been effected into the house, though for what purpose was not easily to be conjectured. The man, Smith, was equally confident upon this point; and his theory was that the object was simply to frighten us out of the house by making us believe it haunted; and he was more than ever anxious and on the alert to discover the conspirators. It often since appeared to me odd. Every year, indeed, more odd, as this cumulative case of the marvellous becomes to my mind more and more inexplicable—that underlying my sense of mystery and puzzle, was all along the quiet assumption that all these occurrences were one way or another referable to natural causes. I could not account for them, indeed, myself; but during the whole period I inhabited that house, I never once felt, though much alone, and often up very late at night, any of those tremors and thrills which every one has at times experienced when situation and the hour are favourable. Except the cook and housemaid, who were plagued with the shadow I mentioned crossing and recrossing upon the bedroom wall, we all, without exception, experienced the same strange sense of security, and regarded these phenomena rather with a perplexed sort of interest and curiosity, than with any more unpleasant sensations.

The knockings which I have mentioned at the nursery door, preceded generally by the sound of a step on the lobby, meanwhile continued. At that time (for my wife, like myself, was an invalid) two eminent physicians, who came out occasionally by rail, were attending us. These gentlemen were at first only amused, but ultimately interested, and very much puzzled by the occurrences which we described. One of them, at last, recommended that a candle should be kept burning upon the lobby. It was in fact a recurrence to an old woman's recipe against ghosts—of course it might be serviceable, too, against impostors; at all events, seeming, as I have said, very much interested and puzzled, he advised it, and it was tried. We fancied that it was successful; for there was an interval of quiet for, I think, three or four nights. But after that, the noises—the footsteps on the lobby—the knocking at the door, and the turning of the handle recommenced in full force, notwithstanding the light upon the table outside; and these particular phenomena became only more perplexing than ever.

The alarm of robbers and smugglers gradually subsided after a week or two; but we were again to hear news from the nursery. Our second little girl, then between seven and eight years of age, saw in the night time—she alone being awake—a young woman, with black, or very dark hair, which hung loose, and with a black cloak on, standing near the middle of the floor, opposite the hearthstone, and fronting the foot of her bed. She appeared quite unobservant of the children and nurse sleeping in the room. She was very pale, and looked, the child said, both "sorry and frightened," and with something very peculiar and terrible about her eyes, which made the child conclude that she was dead. She was looking, not at, but in the direction of the child's bed, and there was a dark streak across her throat, like a scar with blood upon it. This figure was not motionless; but once or twice turned slowly, and without appearing to be conscious of the presence of the child, or the other occupants of the room, like a person in vacancy or abstraction. There was on this occasion a night-light burning in the chamber; and the child saw, or thought she saw, all these particulars with the most perfect distinctness. She got her head under the bed-clothes; and although a good many years have passed since then, she cannot recall the spectacle without feelings of peculiar horror.

One day, when the children were playing in the back garden, I asked them to point out to me the spot where they were accustomed to see the woman who occasionally showed herself as I have described, near the stable wall. There was no division of opinion as to this precise point, which they indicated in the most distinct and confident way. I suggested that, perhaps, something might be hidden there in the ground; and advised them digging a hole there with their little spades, to try for it. Accordingly, to work they went, and by my return in the evening they had grubbed up a piece of a jawbone, with several teeth in it. The bone was very much decayed, and ready to crumble to pieces, but the teeth were quite sound. I could not tell whether they were human grinders; but I showed the fossil to one of the physicians I have mentioned, who came out the next evening, and he pronounced them human teeth. The same conclusion was come to a day or two later by the other medical man. It appears to me now, on reviewing the whole matter, almost unaccountable that, with such evidence before me, I should not have got in a labourer, and had the spot effectually dug and searched. I can only say, that so it was. I was quite satisfied of the moral truth of every word that had been related to me, and which I have here set down with scrupulous accuracy. But I experienced an apathy, for which neither then nor afterwards did I quite know how to account. I had a vague, but immovable impression that the whole affair was referable to natural agencies. It was not until some time after we had left the house, which, by-the-by, we afterwards found had had the reputation of being haunted before we had come to live in it, that on reconsideration I discovered the serious difficulty of accounting satisfactorily for all that had occurred upon ordinary principles. A great deal we might arbitrarily set down to imagination. But even in so doing there was, *in limine*, the oddity, not to say improbability, of so many different persons having nearly simultaneously suffered from different spectral and other illusions during the short period for which we had occupied that house, who never before, nor so far as we learned, afterwards were troubled by any fears or fancies of the sort. There were other things, too, not to be so accounted for. The odd knockings in the roof I frequently heard myself.

There were also, which I before forgot to mention, in the daytime, rappings at the doors of the sitting-rooms, which constantly deceived us; and it was not till our "come in" was unanswered, and the hall or passage outside the door was discovered to be empty, that we learned that whatever else caused them, human hands did not. All the persons who reported having seen the different persons or appearances here described by me, were just as confident of having literally and distinctly seen them, as I was of having seen the hard-featured woman with the blind eye, so remarkably corresponding with Smith's description.

About a week after the discovery of the teeth, which were found, I think, about two feet under the ground, a friend, much advanced in years, and who remembered the town in which we had now taken up our abode, for a very long time, happened to pay us a visit. He good-humouredly pooh-poohed the whole thing; but at the same time was evidently curious about it. "We might construct a sort of story," said I (I am giving, of course, the substance and purport, not the exact words, of our dialogue), "and assign to each of the three figures who appeared their respective parts in some dreadful tragedy enacted in this house. The male figure represents the murderer; the ill-looking, one-eyed woman his accomplice, who, we will suppose, buried the body where she is now so often seen grubbing in the earth, and where the human teeth and jawbone have so lately been disinterred; and the young woman with dishevelled tresses, and black cloak, and the bloody scar across her throat, their victim. A difficulty, however, which I cannot get over, exists in the cheerfulness, the great publicity, and the evident very recent date of the house." "Why, as to that," said he, "the house is *not* modern; it and those beside it formed an old government store, altered and fitted up recently as you see. I remember it well in my young days, fifty years ago, before the town had grown out in this direction, and a more entirely lonely spot, or one more fitted for the commission of a secret crime, could not have been imagined."

I have nothing to add, for very soon after this my physician pronounced a longer stay unnecessary for my health, and we took our departure for another place of abode. I may add, that although I have resided for considerable periods in many other houses, I never experienced any annoyances of a similar kind elsewhere; neither have I made (stupid dog! you will say), any inquiries respecting either the antecedents or subsequent history of the house in which we made so disturbed a sojourn. I was content with what I knew, and have here related as clearly as I could, and I think it a very pretty puzzle as it stands.

[Thus ends the statement, which we abandon to the ingenuity of our readers, having ourselves no satisfactory explanation to suggest; and simply repeating the assurance with which we prefaced it, namely, that we can vouch for the perfect good faith and the accuracy of the narrator.—E.D.U.M.]

ULTOR DE LACY: A LEGEND OF CAPPERCULLEN

CHAPTER I

The Jacobite's Legacy In my youth I heard a great many Irish family traditions, more or less of a supernatural character, some of them very peculiar, and all, to a child at least, highly interesting. One of these I will now relate, though the translation to cold type from oral narrative, with all the aids of animated human voice and countenance, and the appropriate *mise-en-scène* of the old-fashioned parlour fireside and its listening circle of excited faces, and, outside, the wintry blast and the moan of leafless boughs, with the occasional rattle of the clumsy old window-frame behind shutter and curtain, as the blast swept by, is at best a trying one.

About midway up the romantic glen of Cappercullen, near the point where the counties of Limerick, Clare, and Tipperary converge, upon the then sequestered and forest-bound range of the Slieve-Felim hills, there stood, in the reigns of the two earliest Georges, the picturesque and massive remains of one of the finest of the Anglo-Irish castles of Munster—perhaps of Ireland.

It crowned the precipitous edge of the wooded glen, itself half-buried among the wild forest that covered that long and solitary range. There was no human habitation within a circle of many miles, except the half-dozen hovels and the small thatched chapel composing the little village of Murroa, which lay at the foot of the glen among the straggling skirts of the noble forest.

Its remoteness and difficulty of access saved it from demolition. It was worth nobody's while to pull down and remove the ponderous and clumsy oak, much less the masonry or flagged roofing of the pile. Whatever would pay the cost of removal had been long since carried away. The rest was abandoned to time—the destroyer.

The hereditary owners of this noble building and of a wide territory in the contiguous counties I have named, were English—the De Lacys—long naturalized in Ireland. They had acquired at least this portion of their estate in the reign of Henry VIII, and held it, with some vicissitudes, down to the establishment of the revolution in Ireland, when they suffered attainder, and, like other great families of that period, underwent a final eclipse.

The De Lacy of that day retired to France, and held a brief command in the Irish Brigade, interrupted by sickness. He retired, became a poor hanger-on of the Court of St. Germains, and died early in the eighteenth century—as well as I remember, 1705—leaving an only son, hardly twelve years old, called by the strange but significant name of Ultor.

At this point commences the marvellous ingredient of my tale.

When his father was dying, he had him to his bedside, with no one by except his confessor; and having told him, first, that on reaching the age of twenty-one, he was to lay claim to a certain small estate in the county of Clare, in Ireland, in right of his mother—the title-deeds of which he gave him—and next, having enjoined him not to marry before the age of thirty, on the ground that earlier marriages destroyed the spirit and the power of enterprise, and would incapacitate him from the accomplishment of his destiny—the restoration of his family—he then went on to open to the child a matter which so terrified him that he cried lamentably, trembling all over, clinging to the priest's gown with one hand and to his father's cold wrist with the other, and imploring him, with screams of horror, to desist from his communication.

But the priest, impressed, no doubt, himself, with its necessity, compelled him to listen. And then his father showed him a small picture, from which also the child turned with shrieks, until similarly constrained to look. They did not let him go until he had carefully conned the features, and was able to tell them, from memory, the colour of the eyes and hair, and the fashion and hues of the dress. Then his father gave him a black box containing this portrait, which was a full-length miniature, about nine inches long, painted very finely in oils, as smooth as enamel, and folded above it a sheet of paper, written over in a careful and very legible hand.

The deeds and this black box constituted the most important legacy bequeathed to his only child by the ruined Jacobite, and he deposited them in the hands of the priest, in trust, till his boy, Ultor, should have attained to an age to understand their value, and to keep them securely.

When this scene was ended, the dying exile's mind, I suppose, was relieved, for he spoke cheerily, and said he believed he would recover; and they soothed the crying child, and his father kissed him, and gave him a little silver coin to buy fruit with; and so they sent him off with another boy for a walk, and when he came back his father was dead.

He remained in France under the care of this ecclesiastic until he had attained the age of twenty-one, when he repaired to Ireland, and his title being unaffected by his father's attainder, he easily made good his claim to the small estate in the county of Clare.

There he settled, making a dismal and solitary tour now and then of the vast territories which had once been his father's, and nursing those gloomy and impatient thoughts which befitted the enterprises to which he was devoted.

Occasionally he visited Paris, that common centre of English, Irish, and Scottish disaffection; and there, when a little past thirty, he married the daughter of another ruined Irish house. His bride returned with him to the melancholy seclusion of their Munster residence, where she bore him in succession two daughters—Alice, the elder, dark-eyed and dark-haired, grave and sensible—Una, four years younger, with large blue eyes and long and beautiful golden hair.

Their poor mother was, I believe, naturally a lighthearted, sociable, high-spirited little creature; and her gay and childish nature pined in the isolation and gloom of her lot. At all events she died young, and the children were left to the sole care of their melancholy and embittered father. In process of time the girls grew up, tradition says, beautiful. The elder was designed for a convent, the younger her father hoped to mate as nobly as her high blood and splendid beauty seemed to promise, if only the great game on which he had resolved to stake all succeeded.

CHAPTER II

The Fairies in the Castle The Rebellion of '45 came, and Ultor de Lacy was one of the few Irishmen implicated treasonably in that daring and romantic insurrection. Of course there were warrants out against him, but he was not to be found. The young ladies, indeed, remained as heretofore in their father's lonely house in Clare; but whether he had crossed the water or was still in Ireland was for some time unknown, even to them. In due course he was attainted, and his little estate forfeited. It was a miserable catastrophe—a tremendous and beggarly waking up from a life-long dream of returning principality.

In due course the officers of the crown came down to take possession, and it behoved the young ladies to flit. Happily for them the ecclesiastic I have mentioned was not quite so confident as their father, of his winning back the magnificent patrimony of his ancestors; and by his advice the daughters had been secured twenty pounds a year each, under the marriage settlement of their parents, which was all that stood between this proud house and literal destitution.

Late one evening, as some little boys from the village were returning from a ramble through the dark and devious glen of Cappercullen, with their pockets laden with nuts and "frahans," to their amazement and even terror they saw a light streaming redly from the narrow window of one of the towers overhanging the precipice among the ivy and the lofty branches, across the glen, already dim in the shadows of the deepening night.

"Look—look—look—'tis the Phooka's tower!" was the general cry, in the vernacular Irish, and a universal scamper commenced.

The bed of the glen, strewn with great fragments of rock, among which rose the tall stems of ancient trees, and overgrown with a tangled copse, was at the best no favourable ground for a run. Now it was dark; and, terrible work breaking through brambles and hazels and tumbling over rocks. Little Shaeen Mull Ryan, the last of the panic rout, screaming to his mates to wait for him—saw a whitish figure emerge from the thicket at the base of the stone flight of steps that descended the side of the glen, close by the castle-wall, intercepting his flight, and a discordant male voice shrieked----

"I have you!"

At the same time the boy, with a cry of terror, tripped and tumbled; and felt himself roughly caught by the arm, and hauled to his feet with a shake.

A wild yell from the child, and a volley of terror and entreaty followed.

"Who is it, Larry; what's the matter?" cried a voice, high in air, from the turret window, The words floated down through the trees, clear and sweet as the low notes of a flute.

"Only a child, my lady; a boy."

"Is he hurt?"

"Are you hurted?" demanded the whitish man, who held him fast, and repeated the question in Irish; but the child only kept blubbering and crying for mercy, with his hands clasped, and trying to drop on his knees.

Larry's strong old hand held him up. He *was* hurt, and bleeding from over his eye.

"Just a trifle hurted, my lady!"

"Bring him up here."

Shaeen Mull Ryan gave himself over. He was among "the good people," who he knew would keep him prisoner for ever and a day. There was no good in resisting. He grew bewildered, and yielded himself passively to his fate, and emerged from the glen on the platform above; his captor's knotted old hand still on his arm, and looked round on the tall mysterious trees, and the gray front of the castle, revealed in the imperfect moonlight, as upon the scenery of a dream.

The old man who, with thin wiry legs, walked by his side, in a dingy white coat, and blue facings, and great pewter buttons, with his silver gray hair escaping from under his battered three-cocked hat; and his shrewd puckered resolute face, in which the boy could read no promise of sympathy, showing so white and phantom-like in the moonlight, was, as he thought, the incarnate ideal of a fairy.

This figure led him in silence under the great arched gateway, and across the grass-grown court, to the door in the far angle of the building; and so, in the dark, round and round, up a stone screw stair, and with a short turn into a large room, with a fire of turf and wood, burning on its long unused hearth, over which hung a pot, and about it an old woman with a great wooden spoon was busy. An iron candlestick supported their solitary candle; and about the floor of the room, as well as on the table and chairs, lay a litter of all sorts of things; piles of old faded hangings, boxes, trunks, clothes, pewter-plates, and cups; and I know not what more.

CHAPTER II

But what instantly engaged the fearful gaze of the boy were the figures of two ladies; red drugget cloaks they had on, like the peasant girls of Munster and Connaught, and the rest of their dress was pretty much in keeping. But they had the grand air, the refined expression and beauty, and above all, the serene air of command that belong to people of a higher rank.

The elder, with black hair and full brown eyes, sat writing at the deal table on which the candle stood, and raised her dark gaze to the boy as he came in. The other, with her hood thrown back, beautiful and *riant*, with a flood of wavy golden hair, and great blue eyes, and with something kind, and arch, and strange in her countenance, struck him as the most wonderful beauty he could have imagined.

They questioned the man in a language strange to the child. It was not English, for he had a smattering of that, and the man's story seemed to amuse them. The two young ladies exchanged a glance, and smiled mysteriously. He was more convinced than ever that he was among the good people. The younger stepped gaily forward and said----

"Do you know who *I* am, my little man? Well, I'm the fairy Una, and this is my palace; and that fairy you see there (pointing to the dark lady, who was looking out something in a box), is my sister and family physician, the Lady Graveairs; and these (glancing at the old man and woman), are some of my courtiers; and I'm considering now what I shall do with *you*, whether I shall send you to-night to Lough Guir, riding on a rush, to make my compliments to the Earl of Desmond in his enchanted castle; or, straight to your bed, two thousand miles under ground, among the gnomes; or to prison in that little corner of the moon you see through the window—with the man-in-the-moon for your gaoler, for thrice three hundred years and a day! There, don't cry. You only see how serious a thing it is for you, little boys, to come so near my castle. Now, for this once, I'll let you go. But, henceforward, any boys I, or my people, may find within half a mile round my castle, shall belong to me for life, and never behold their home or their people more."

And she sang a little air and chased mystically half a dozen steps before him, holding out her cloak with her pretty fingers, and courtesying very low, to his indescribable alarm.

Then, with a little laugh, she said----

"My little man, we must mend your head."

And so they washed his scratch, and the elder one applied a plaister to it. And she of the great blue eyes took out of her pocket a little French box of bon-bons and emptied it into his hand, and she said----

"You need not be afraid to eat these—they are very good—and I'll send my fairy, Blanc-et-bleu, to set you free. Take him (she addressed Larry), and let him go, with a solemn charge."

The elder, with a grave and affectionate smile, said, looking on the fairy----

"Brave, dear, wild Una! nothing can ever quell your gaiety of heart."

And Una kissed her merrily on the cheek.

So the oak door of the room again opened, and Shaeen, with his conductor, descended the stair. He walked with the scared boy in grim silence near half way down the wild hill-side toward Murroa, and then he stopped, and said in Irish----

"You never saw the fairies before, my fine fellow, and 'tisn't often those who once set eyes on us return to tell it. Whoever comes nearer, night or day, than this stone," and he tapped it with the end of his cane, "will never see his home again, for we'll keep him till the day of judgment; goodnight, little gossoon—and away with you."

So these young ladies, Alice and Una, with two old servants, by their father's direction, had taken up their abode in a portion of that side of the old castle which overhung the glen; and with the furniture and hangings they had removed from their late residence, and with the aid of glass in the casements and some other indispensable repairs, and a thorough airing, they made the rooms they had selected just habitable, as a rude and temporary shelter.

CHAPTER III

The Priest's Adventures in the Glen At first, of course, they saw or heard little of their father. In general, however, they knew that his plan was to procure some employment in France, and to remove them there. Their present strange abode was only an adventure and an episode, and they believed that any day they might receive instructions to commence their journey.

After a little while the pursuit relaxed. The government, I believe, did not care, provided he did not obtrude himself, what became of him, or where he concealed himself. At all events, the local authorities showed no disposition to hunt him down. The young ladies' charges on the little forfeited property were paid without any dispute, and no vexatious inquiries were raised as to what had become of the furniture and other personal property which had been carried away from the forfeited house.

The haunted reputation of the castle—for in those days, in matters of the marvellous, the oldest were children—secured the little family in the seclusion they coveted. Once, or sometimes twice a week, old Laurence, with a shaggy little pony, made a secret expedition to the city of Limerick, starting before dawn, and returning under the cover of the night, with his purchases. There was beside an occasional sly moonlit visit from the old parish priest, and a midnight mass in the old castle for the little outlawed congregation.

As the alarm and inquiry subsided, their father made them, now and then, a brief and stealthy visit. At first these were but of a night's duration, and with great precaution; but gradually they were extended and less guarded. Still he was, as the phrase is in Munster, "on his keeping." He had firearms always by his bed, and had arranged places of concealment in the castle in the event of a surprise. But no attempt nor any disposition to molest him appearing, he grew more at ease, if not more cheerful.

CHAPTER III

It came, at last, that he would sometimes stay so long as two whole months at a time, and then depart as suddenly and mysteriously as he came. I suppose he had always some promising plot on hand, and his head full of ingenious treason, and lived on the sickly and exciting dietary of hope deferred.

Was there a poetical justice in this, that the little *ménage* thus secretly established, in the solitary and timeworn pile, should have themselves experienced, but from causes not so easily explicable, those very supernatural perturbations which they had themselves essayed to inspire?

The interruption of the old priest's secret visits was the earliest consequence of the mysterious interference which now began to display itself. One night, having left his cob in care of his old sacristan in the little village, he trudged on foot along the winding pathway, among the gray rocks and ferns that threaded the glen, intending a ghostly visit to the fair recluses of the castle, and he lost his way in this strange fashion.

There was moonlight, indeed, but it was little more than quarter-moon, and a long train of funereal clouds were sailing slowly across the sky—so that, faint and wan as it was, the light seldom shone full out, and was often hidden for a minute or two altogether. When he reached the point in the glen where the castle-stairs were wont to be, he could see nothing of them, and above, no trace of the castle-towers. So, puzzled somewhat, he pursued his way up the ravine, wondering how his walk had become so unusually protracted and fatiguing.

At last, sure enough, he saw the castle as plain as could be, and a lonely streak of candle-light issuing from the tower, just as usual, when his visit was expected. But he could not find the stair; and had to clamber among the rocks and copse wood the best way he could. But when he emerged at top, there was nothing but the bare heath. Then the clouds stole over the moon again, and he moved along with hesitation and difficulty, and once more he saw the outline of the castle against the sky, quite sharp and clear. But this time it proved to be a great battlemented mass of cloud on the horizon. In a few minutes more he was quite close, all of a sudden, to the great front, rising gray and dim in the feeble light, and not till he could have struck it with his good oak "wattle" did he discover it to be only one of those wild, gray frontages of living rock that rise here and there in picturesque tiers along the slopes of those solitary mountains. And so, till dawn, pursuing this mirage of the castle, through pools and among ravines, he wore out a night of miserable misadventure and fatigue.

Another night, riding up the glen, so far as the level way at bottom would allow, and intending to make his nag fast at his customary tree, he heard on a sudden a horrid shriek at top of the steep rocks above his head, and something—a gigantic human form, it seemed—came tumbling and bounding headlong down through the rocks, and fell with a fearful impetus just before his horse's hoofs and there lay like a huge palpitating carcass. The horse was scared, as, indeed, was his rider, too, and more so when this apparently lifeless thing sprang up to his legs, and throwing his arms apart to bar their further progress, advanced his white and gigantic face towards them. Then the horse started about, with a snort of terror, nearly unseating the priest, and broke away into a furious and uncontrollable gallop.

I need not recount all the strange and various misadventures which the honest priest sustained in his endeavours to visit the castle, and its isolated tenants. They were enough to wear out his resolution, and frighten him into submission. And so at last these spiritual visits quite ceased; and fearing to awaken inquiry and suspicion, he thought it only prudent to abstain from attempting them in the daytime.

So the young ladies of the castle were more alone than ever. Their father, whose visits were frequently of long duration, had of late ceased altogether to speak of their contemplated departure for France, grew angry at any allusion to it, and they feared, had abandoned the plan altogether.

CHAPTER IV

The Light in the Bell Tower Shortly after the discontinuance of the priest's visits, old Laurence, one night, to his surprise, saw light issuing from a window in the Bell Tower. It was at first only a tremulous red ray, visible only for a few minutes, which seemed to pass from the room, through whose window it escaped upon the courtyard of the castle, and so to lose itself. This tower and casement were in the angle of the building, exactly confronting that in which the little outlawed family had taken up their quarters.

The whole family were troubled at the appearance of this dull red ray from the chamber in the Bell Tower. Nobody knew what to make of it. But Laurence, who had campaigned in Italy with his old master, the young ladies' grandfather—"the heavens be his bed this night!"—was resolved to see it out, and took his great horse-pistols with him, and ascended to the corridor leading to the tower. But his search was vain.

This light left a sense of great uneasiness among the inmates, and most certainly it was not pleasant to suspect the establishment of an independent and possibly dangerous lodger or even colony, within the walls of the same old building.

The light very soon appeared again, steadier and somewhat brighter, in the same chamber. Again old Laurence buckled on his armour, swearing ominously to himself, and this time bent in earnest upon conflict. The young ladies watched in thrilling suspense from the great window in *their* stronghold, looking diagonally across the court. But as Laurence, who had entered the massive range of buildings opposite, might be supposed to be approaching the chamber from which this ill-omened glare proceeded, it steadily waned, finally disappearing altogether, just a few seconds before his voice was heard shouting from the arched window to know which way the light had gone.

This lighting up of the great chamber of the Bell Tower grew at last to be of frequent and almost continual recurrence. It was, there, long ago, in times of trouble and danger, that the De Lacys of those evil days used to sit in feudal judgment upon captive adversaries, and, as tradition alleged, often gave them no more time for shrift and prayer, than it needed to mount to the battlement of the turret overhead, from which they were forthwith hung by the necks, for a caveat and admonition to all evil disposed persons viewing the same from the country beneath.

Old Laurence observed these mysterious glimmerings with an evil and an anxious eye, and many and various were the stratagems he tried, but in vain, to surprise the audacious intruders. It is, however, I believe, a fact that no phenomenon, no matter how startling at first, if prosecuted with tolerable regularity, and unattended with any new circumstances of terror, will very long continue to excite alarm or even wonder.

So the family came to acquiesce in this mysterious light. No harm accompanied it. Old Laurence, as he smoked his lonely pipe in the grass-grown courtyard, would cast a disturbed glance at it, as it softly glowed out through the darking aperture, and mutter a prayer or an oath. But he had given over the chase as a hopeless business. And Peggy Sullivan, the old dame of all work, when, by chance, for she never willingly looked toward the haunted quarter, she caught the faint reflection of its dull effulgence with the corner of her eye, would sign herself with the cross or fumble at her beads, and deeper furrows would gather in her forehead, and her face grow ashen and perturbed. And this was not mended by the levity with which the young ladies, with whom the spectre had lost his influence, familiarity, as usual, breeding contempt, had come to talk, and even to jest, about it.

CHAPTER V

The Man with the Claret Mark But as the former excitement flagged, old Peggy Sullivan produced a new one; for she solemnly avowed that she had seen a thin-faced man, with an ugly red mark all over the side of his cheek, looking out of the same window, just at sunset, before the young ladies returned from their evening walk.

This sounded in their ears like an old woman's dream, but still it was an excitement, jocular in the morning, and just, perhaps, a little fearful as night overspread the vast and desolate building, but still, not wholly unpleasant. This little flicker of credulity suddenly, however, blazed up into the full light of conviction.

Old Laurence, who was not given to dreaming, and had a cool, hard head, and an eye like a hawk, saw the same figure, just about the same hour, when the last level gleam of sunset was tinting the summits of the towers and the tops of the tall trees that surrounded them.

He had just entered the court from the great gate, when he heard all at once the hard peculiar twitter of alarm which sparrows make when a cat or a hawk invades their safety, rising all round from the thick ivy that overclimbed the wall on his left, and raising his eyes listlessly, he saw, with a sort of shock, a thin, ungainly man, standing with his legs crossed, in the recess of the window from which the light was wont to issue, leaning with his elbows on the stone mullion, and looking down with a sort of sickly sneer, his hollow yellow cheeks being deeply stained on one side with what is called a "claret-mark."

"I have you at last, you villain!" cried Larry, in a strange rage and panic: "drop down out of that on the grass here, and give yourself up, or I'll shoot you."

The threat was backed with an oath, and he drew from his coat pocket the long holster pistol he was wont to carry, and covered his man cleverly.

"I give you while I count ten—one-two-three-four. If you draw back, I'll fire, mind; five-six—you'd better be lively—seven-eight-nine—one chance more; will you come down? Then take it—ten!"

Bang went the pistol. The sinister stranger was hardly fifteen feet removed from him, and Larry was a dead shot. But this time he made a scandalous miss, for the shot knocked a little white dust from the stone wall a full yard at one side; and the fellow never shifted his negligent posture or qualified his sardonic smile during the procedure.

Larry was mortified and angry.

"You'll not get off this time, my tulip!" he said with a grin, exchanging the smoking weapon for the loaded pistol in reserve.

"What are you pistolling, Larry?" said a familiar voice close by his elbow, and he saw his master, accompanied by a handsome young man in a cloak.

"That villain, your honour, in the window, there."

"Why there's nobody there, Larry," said De Lacy, with a laugh, though that was no common indulgence with him.

As Larry gazed, the figure somehow dissolved and broke up without receding. A hanging tuft of yellow and red ivy nodded queerly in place of the face, some broken and discoloured masonry in perspective took up the outline and colouring of the arms and figure, and two imperfect red and yellow lichen streaks carried on the curved tracing of the long spindle shanks. Larry blessed himself, and drew his hand across his damp forehead, over his bewildered eyes, and could not speak for a minute. It was all some devilish trick; he could take his oath he saw every feature in the fellow's face, the lace and buttons of his cloak and doublet, and even his long finger nails and thin yellow fingers that overhung the cross-shaft of the window, where there was now nothing but a rusty stain left.

The young gentleman who had arrived with De Lacy, stayed that night and shared with great apparent relish the homely fare of the family. He was a gay and gallant Frenchman, and the beauty of the younger lady, and her pleasantry and spirit, seemed to make his hours pass but too swiftly, and the moment of parting sad.

When he had departed early in the morning, Ultor De Lacy had a long talk with his elder daughter, while the younger was busy with her early dairy task, for among their retainers this *proles generosa* reckoned a "kind" little Kerry cow.

He told her that he had visited France since he had been last at Cappercullen, and how good and gracious their sovereign had been, and how he had arranged a noble alliance for her sister Una. The young gentleman was of high blood, and though not rich, had, nevertheless, his acres and his *nom de terre*, besides a captain's rank in the army. He was, in short, the very gentleman with whom they had parted only that morning. On what special business he was now in Ireland there was no necessity that he should speak; but being here he had brought him hither to present him to his daughter, and found that the impression she had made was quite what was desirable.

"You, you know, dear Alice, are promised to a conventual life. Had it been otherwise—"

He hesitated for a moment.

"You are right, dear father," she said, kissing his hand, "I *am* so promised, and no earthly tie or allurement has power to draw me from that holy engagement."

"Well," he said, returning her caress, "I do not mean to urge you upon that point. It must not, however, be until Una's marriage has taken place. That cannot be, for many good reasons, sooner than this time twelve months; we shall then exchange this strange and barbarous abode for Paris, where are many eligible convents, in which are entertained as sisters some of the noblest ladies of France; and there, too, in Una's marriage will be continued, though not the name, at all events the blood, the lineage, and the title which, so sure as justice ultimately governs the course of human events, will be again established, powerful and honoured in this country, the scene of their ancient glory and transitory misfortunes. Meanwhile, we must not mention this engagement to Una. Here she runs no risk of being sought or won; but the mere knowledge that her hand was absolutely pledged, might excite a capricious opposition and repining such as neither I nor you would like to see; therefore be secret."

The same evening he took Alice with him for a ramble round the castle wall, while they talked of grave matters, and he as usual allowed her a dim and doubtful view of some of those cloud-built castles in which he habitually dwelt, and among which his jaded hopes revived.

They were walking upon a pleasant short sward of darkest green, on one side overhung by the gray castle walls, and on the other by the forest trees that here and there closely approached it, when precisely as they turned the angle of the Bell Tower, they were encountered by a person walking directly towards them. The sight of a stranger, with the exception of the one visitor introduced by her father, was in this place so absolutely unprecedented, that Alice was amazed and affrighted to such a degree that for a moment she stood stock-still.

But there was more in this apparition to excite unpleasant emotions, than the mere circumstance of its unexpectedness. The figure was very strange, being that of a tall, lean, ungainly man, dressed in a dingy suit, somewhat of a Spanish fashion, with a brown laced cloak, and faded red stockings. He had long lank legs, long arms, hands, and fingers, and a very long sickly face, with a drooping nose, and a sly, sarcastic leer, and a great purplish stain over-spreading more than half of one cheek.

As he strode past, he touched his cap with his thin, discoloured fingers, and an ugly side glance, and disappeared round the corner. The eyes of father and daughter followed him in silence.

Ultor De Lacy seemed first absolutely terror-stricken, and then suddenly inflamed with ungovernable fury. He dropped his cane on the ground, drew his rapier, and, without wasting a thought on his daughter, pursued.

He just had a glimpse of the retreating figure as it disappeared round the far angle. The plume, and the lank hair, the point of the rapier-scabbard, the flutter of the skirt of the cloak, and one red stocking and heel; and this was the last he saw of him.

When Alice reached his side, his drawn sword still in his hand, he was in a state of abject agitation.

"Thank Heaven, he's gone!" she exclaimed.

"He's gone," echoed Ultor, with a strange glare.

"And you are safe," she added, clasping his hand.

He sighed a great sigh.

"And you don't think he's coming back?"

"He!--who?"

"The stranger who passed us but now. Do you know him, father?"

"Yes—and—no, child—I know him not—and yet I know him too well. Would to heaven we could leave this accursed haunt to-night. Cursed be the stupid malice that first provoked this horrible feud, which no sacrifice and misery can appease, and no exorcism can quell or even suspend. The wretch has come from afar with a sure instinct to devour my last hope—to dog us into our last retreat—and to blast with his triumph the very dust and ruins of our house. What ails that stupid priest that he has given over his visits? Are *my* children to be left without mass or confession the sacraments which *guard* as well as save because he once loses his way in a mist, or mistakes a streak of foam in the brook for a dead man's face? D—n him!"

"See, Alice, if he won't come," he resumed, "you must only *write* your confession to him in full—you and Una. Laurence is trusty, and will carry it—and we'll get the bishop's—or, if need be, the Pope's leave for him to give you absolution. I'll move heaven and earth, but you *shall* have the sacraments, poor children!--and see him. I've been a wild fellow in my youth, and never pretended to sanctity; but I know there's but one safe way—and—and—keep you each a bit of this—(he opened a small silver box)—about you while you stay here—fold and sew it up reverently in a bit of the old psaltery parchment and wear it next your hearts—'tis a fragment of the consecrated wafer—and will help, with the saints' protection, to guard you from harm—and be strict in fasts, and constant in prayer—*I* can do nothing—nor devise any help. The curse has fallen, indeed, on me and mine."

And Alice, saw, in silence, the tears of despair roll down his pale and agitated face.

This adventure was also a secret, and Una was to hear nothing of it.

CHAPTER VI

Voices Now Una, nobody knew why, began to lose spirit, and to grow pale. Her fun and frolic were quite gone! Even her songs ceased. She was silent with her sister, and loved solitude better. She said she was well, and quite happy, and could in no wise be got to account for the lamentable change that had stolen over her. She had grown odd too, and obstinate in trifles; and strangely reserved and cold.

Alice was very unhappy in consequence. What was the cause of this estrangement—had she offended her, and how? But Una had never before borne resentment for an hour. What could have altered her entire nature so? Could it be the shadow and chill of coming insanity?

Once or twice, when her sister urged her with tears and entreaties to disclose the secret of her changed spirits and demeanour, she seemed to listen with a sort of silent wonder and suspicion, and then she looked for a moment full upon her, and seemed on the very point of revealing all. But the earnest dilated gaze stole downward to the floor, and subsided into an odd wily smile, and she began to whisper to herself, and the smile and the whisper were both a mystery to Alice.

She and Alice slept in the same bedroom—a chamber in a projecting tower—which on their arrival, when poor Una was so merry, they had hung round with old tapestry, and decorated fantastically according to their skill and frolic. One night, as they went to bed, Una said, as if speaking to herself----

"'Tis my last night in this room—I shall sleep no more with Alice."

"And what has poor Alice done, Una, to deserve your strange unkindness?"

Una looked on her curiously, and half frightened, and then the odd smile stole over her face like a gleam of moonlight.

"My poor Alice, what have you to do with it?" she whispered.

"And why do you talk of sleeping no more with me?" said Alice.

"Why? Alice dear—no why—no reason—only a knowledge that it must be so, or Una will die."

"Die, Una darling!--what can you mean?"

"Yes, sweet Alice, die, indeed. We must all die some time, you know, or—or undergo a change; and my time is near—*very* near—unless I sleep apart from you."

"Indeed, Una, sweetheart, I think you *are* ill, but not near death."

"Una knows what you think, wise Alice—but she's not mad—on the contrary, she's wiser than other folks."

"She's sadder and stranger too," said Alice, tenderly.

"Knowledge is sorrow," answered Una, and she looked across the room through her golden hair which she was combing—and through the window, beyond which lay the tops of the great trees, and the still foliage of the glen in the misty moonlight.

"'Tis enough, Alice dear; it must be so. The bed must move hence, or Una's bed will be low enough ere long. See, it shan't be far though, only into that small room."

She pointed to an inner room or closet opening from that in which they lay. The walls of the building were hugely thick, and there were double doors of oak between the chambers, and Alice thought, with a sigh, how completely separated they were going to be.

However she offered no opposition. The change was made, and the girls for the first time since childhood lay in separate chambers. A few nights afterwards Alice awoke late in the night from a dreadful dream, in which the sinister figure which she and her father had encountered in their ramble round the castle walls, bore a principal part.

When she awoke there were still in her ears the sounds which had mingled in her dream. They were the notes of a deep, ringing, bass voice rising from the glen beneath the castle walls—something between humming and singing—listlessly unequal and intermittent, like the melody of a man whiling away the hours over his work. While she was wondering at this unwonted minstrelsy, there came a silence, and—could she believe her ears?—it certainly was Una's clear low contralto—softly singing a bar or two from the window. Then once more silence—and then again the strange manly voice, faintly chaunting from the leafy abyss.

With a strange wild feeling of suspicion and terror, Alice glided to the window. The moon who sees so many things, and keeps all secrets, with her cold impenetrable smile, was high in the sky. But Alice saw the red flicker of a candle from Una's window, and, she thought, the shadow of her head against the deep side wall of its recess. Then this was gone, and there were no more sights or sounds that night.

As they sate at breakfast, the small birds were singing merrily from among the sun-tipped foliage.

"I love this music," said Alice, unusually pale and sad; "it comes with the pleasant light of morning. I remember, Una, when you used to sing, like those gay birds, in the fresh beams of the morning; that was in the old time, when Una kept no secret from poor Alice."

"And Una knows what her sage Alice means; but there are other birds, silent all day long, and, they say, the sweetest too, that love to sing by *night* alone."

So things went on—the elder girl pained and melancholy—the younger silent, changed, and unaccountable.

A little while after this, very late one night, on awaking, Alice heard a conversation being carried on in her sister's room. There seemed to be no disguise about it. She could not distinguish the words, indeed, the walls being some six feet thick, and two great oak doors intercepting. But Una's clear voice, and the deep bell-like tones of the unknown, made up the dialogue.

Alice sprung from her bed, threw her clothes about her, and tried to enter her sister's room; but the inner door was bolted. The voices ceased to speak as she knocked, and Una opened it, and stood before her in her nightdress, candle in hand.

"Una—Una, darling, as you hope for peace, tell me who is here?" cried frightened Alice, with her trembling arms about her neck.

Una drew back, with her large innocent blue eyes fixed full upon her.

"Come in, Alice," she said, coldly.

And in came Alice, with a fearful glance around. There was no hiding place there; a chair, a table, a little bedstead, and two or three pegs in the wall to hang clothes on; a narrow window, with two iron bars across; no hearth or chimney—nothing but bare walls.

Alice looked round in amazement, and her eyes glanced with painful inquiry into those of her sister. Una smiled one of her peculiar sidelong smiles, and said----

"Strange dreams! I've been dreaming—so has Alice. She hears and sees Una's dreams, and wonders—and well she may."

And she kissed her sister's cheek with a cold kiss, and lay down in her little bed, her slender hand under her head, and spoke no more.

Alice, not knowing what to think, went back to hers.

About this time Ultor De Lacy returned. He heard his elder daughter's strange narrative with marked uneasiness, and his agitation seemed to grow rather than subside. He enjoined her, however, not to mention it to the old servant, nor in presence of anybody she might chance to see, but only to him and to the priest, if he could be persuaded to resume his duty and return. The trial, however, such as it was, could not endure very long; matters had turned out favourably. The union of his younger daughter might be accomplished within a few months, and in eight or nine weeks they should be on their way to Paris.

A night or two after her father's arrival, Alice, in the dead of the night, heard the well-known strange deep voice speaking softly, as it seemed, close to her own window on the outside; and Una's voice, clear and tender, spoke in answer. She hurried to her own casement, and pushed it open, kneeling in the deep embrasure, and looking with a stealthy and affrighted gaze towards her sister's window. As she crossed the floor the voices subsided, and she saw a light withdrawn from within. The moonbeams slanted bright and clear on the whole side of the castle overlooking the glen, and she plainly beheld the shadow of a man projected on the wall as on a screen.

This black shadow recalled with a horrid thrill the outline and fashion of the figure in the Spanish dress. There were the cap and mantle, the rapier, the long thin limbs and sinister angularity. It was so thrown obliquely that the hands reached to the window-sill, and the feet stretched and stretched, longer and longer as she looked, toward the ground, and disappeared in the general darkness; and the rest, with a sudden flicker, shot downwards, as shadows will on the sudden movement of a light, and was lost in one gigantic leap down the castle wall.

"I do not know whether I dream or wake when I hear and see these sights; but I will ask my father to sit up with me, and we *two* surely cannot be mistaken. May the holy saints keep and guard us!" And in her terror she buried her head under the bed-clothes, and whispered her prayers for an hour.

CHAPTER VII

Una's Love "I have been with Father Denis," said De Lacy, next day, "and he will come to-morrow; and, thank Heaven! you may both make your confession and hear mass, and my mind will be at rest; and you'll find poor Una happier and more like herself."

But 'tween cup and lip there's many a slip. The priest was not destined to hear poor Una's shrift. When she bid her sister goodnight she looked on her with her large, cold, wild eyes, till something of her old human affections seemed to gather there, and they slowly filled with tears, which dropped one after the other on her homely dress as she gazed in her sister's face.

Alice, delighted, sprang up, and clasped her arms about her neck. "My own darling treasure,'tis all over; you love your poor Alice again, and will be happier than ever."

But while she held her in her embrace Una's eyes were turned towards the window, and her lips apart, and Alice felt instinctively that her thoughts were already far away.

"Hark!--listen!--hush!" and Una, with her delighted gaze fixed, as if she saw far away beyond the castle wall, the trees, the glen, and the night's dark curtain, held her hand raised near her ear, and waved her head slightly in time, as it seemed, to music that reached not Alice's ear, and smiled her strange pleased smile, and then the smile slowly faded away, leaving that sly suspicious light behind it which somehow scared her sister with an uncertain sense of danger; and she sang in tones so sweet and low that it seemed but a reverie of a song, recalling, as Alice fancied, the strain to which she had just listened in that strange ecstasy, the plaintive and beautiful Irish ballad, "Shule, shule, shule, aroon," the midnight summons of the outlawed Irish soldier to his darling to follow him.

Alice had slept little the night before. She was now overpowered with fatigue; and leaving her candle burning by her bedside, she fell into a deep sleep. From this she awoke suddenly, and completely, as will sometimes happen without any apparent cause, and she saw Una come into the room. She had a little purse of embroidery—her own work—in her hand; and she stole lightly to the bedside, with her peculiar oblique smile, and evidently thinking that her sister was asleep.

Alice was thrilled with a strange terror, and did not speak or move; and her sister slipped her hand softly under her bolster, and withdrew it. Then Una stood for while by the hearth, and stretched her hand up to the mantelpiece, from which she took a little bit of chalk, and Alice thought she saw her place it in the fingers of a long yellow hand that was stealthily introduced from her own chamber-door to receive it; and Una paused in the dark recess of the door, and smiled over her shoulder toward her sister, and then glided into her room, closing the doors.

CHAPTER VII

Almost freezing with terror, Alice rose and glided after her, and stood in her chamber, screaming----

"Una, Una, in heaven's name what troubles you?"

But Una seemed to have been sound asleep in her bed, and raised herself with a start, and looking upon her with a peevish surprise, said----

"What does Alice seek here?"

"You were in my room, Una, dear; you seem disturbed and troubled."

"Dreams, Alice. My dreams crossing your brain; only dreams—dreams. Get you to bed, and sleep."

And to bed she went, but *not* to sleep. She lay awake more than an hour; and then Una emerged once more from her room. This time she was fully dressed, and had her cloak and thick shoes on, as their rattle on the floor plainly discovered. She had a little bundle tied up in a handkerchief in her hand, and her hood was drawn about her head; and thus equipped, as it seemed, for a journey, she came and stood at the foot of Alice's bed, and stared on her with a look so soulless and terrible that her senses almost forsook her. Then she turned and went back into her own chamber.

She may have returned; but Alice thought not—at least she did not see her. But she lay in great excitement and perturbation; and was terrified, about an hour later, by a knock at her chamber door—not that opening into Una's room, but upon the little passage from the stone screw staircase. She sprang from her bed; but the door was secured on the inside, and she felt relieved. The knock was repeated, and she heard some one laughing softly on the outside.

The morning came at last, that dreadful night was over. But Una! Where was Una?

Alice never saw her more. On the head of her empty bed were traced in chalk the words—Ultor De Lacy, Ultor O'Donnell. And Alice found beneath her own pillow the little purse of embroidery she had seen in Una's hand. It was her little parting token, and bore the simple legend—"Una's love!"

De Lacy's rage and horror were boundless. He charged the priest, in frantic language, with having exposed his child, by his cowardice and neglect, to the machinations of the Fiend, and raved and blasphemed like a man demented.

It is said that he procured a solemn exorcism to be performed, in the hope of disenthralling and recovering his daughter. Several times, it is alleged, she was seen by the old servants. Once on a sweet summer morning, in the window of the tower, she was perceived combing her beautiful golden tresses, and holding a little mirror in her hand; and first, when she saw herself discovered, she looked affrighted, and then smiled, her slanting, cunning smile. Sometimes, too, in the glen, by moonlight, it was said belated villagers had met her, always startled first, and then smiling, generally singing snatches of old Irish ballads, that seemed to bear a sort of dim resemblance to her melancholy fate. The apparition has long ceased. But it is said that now and again, perhaps once in two or three years, late on a summer night, you may hear—but faint and far away in the recesses of the glen—the sweet, sad notes of Una's voice, singing those plaintive melodies. This, too, of course, in time will cease, and all be forgotten.

CHAPTER VIII

Sister Agnes and the Portrait When Ultor De Lacy died, his daughter Alice found among his effects a small box, containing a portrait such as I have described. When she looked on it, she recoiled in horror. There, in the plenitude of its sinister peculiarities, was faithfully portrayed the phantom which lived with a vivid and horrible accuracy in her remembrance. Folded in the same box was a brief narrative, stating that, "A.D. 1601, in the month of December, Walter De Lacy, of Cappercullen, made many prisoners at the ford of Ownhey, or Abington, of Irish and Spanish soldiers, flying from the great overthrow of the rebel powers at Kinsale, and among the number one Roderic O'Donnell, an arch traitor, and near kinsman to that other O'Donnell who led the rebels; who, claiming kindred through his mother to De Lacy, sued for his life with instant and miserable entreaty, and offered great ransom, but was by De Lacy, through great zeal for the queen, as some thought, cruelly put to death. When he went to the tower-top, where was the gallows, finding himself in extremity, and no hope of mercy, he swore that though he could work them no evil before his death, yet that he would devote himself thereafter to blast the greatness of the De Lacys, and never leave them till his work was done. He hath been seen often since, and always for that family perniciously, insomuch that it hath been the custom to show to young children of that lineage the picture of the said O'Donnell, in little, taken among his few valuables, to prevent their being misled by him unawares, so that he should not have his will, who by devilish wiles and hell-born cunning, hath steadfastly sought the ruin of that ancient house, and especially to leave that *stemma generosum* destitute of issue for the transmission of their pure blood and worshipful name."

Old Miss Croker, of Ross House, who was near seventy in the year 1821, when she related this story to me, had seen and conversed with Alice De Lacy, a professed nun, under the name of Sister Agnes, in a religious house in King-street, in Dublin, founded by the famous Duchess of Tyrconnell, and had the narrative from her own lips. I thought the tale worth preserving, and have no more to say.

GHOSTLY TALES VOLUME III

THE HAUNTED BARONET

CHAPTER I

The George and Dragon The pretty little town of Golden Friars—standing by the margin of the lake, hemmed round by an amphitheatre of purple mountain, rich in tint and furrowed by ravines, high in air, when the tall gables and narrow windows of its ancient graystone houses, and the tower of the old church, from which every evening the curfew still rings, show like silver in the moonbeams, and the black elms that stand round throw moveless shadows upon the short level grass—is one of the most singular and beautiful sights I have ever seen.

There it rises, 'as from the stroke of the enchanter's wand,' looking so light and filmy, that you could scarcely believe it more than a picture reflected on the thin mist of night.

On such a still summer night the moon shone splendidly upon the front of the George and Dragon, the comfortable graystone inn of Golden Friars, with the grandest specimen of the old inn-sign, perhaps, left in England. It looks right across the lake; the road that skirts its margin running by the steps of the hall-door, opposite to which, at the other side of the road, between two great posts, and framed in a fanciful wrought-iron border splendid with gilding, swings the famous sign of St. George and the Dragon, gorgeous with colour and gold.

In the great room of the George and Dragon, three or four of the old *habitués* of that cozy lounge were refreshing a little after the fatigues of the day.

This is a comfortable chamber, with an oak wainscot; and whenever in summer months the air is sharp enough, as on the present occasion, a fire helped to light it up; which fire, being chiefly wood, made a pleasant broad flicker on panel and ceiling, and yet did not make the room too hot.

On one side sat Doctor Torvey, the doctor of Golden Friars, who knew the weak point of every man in the town, and what medicine agreed with each inhabitant—a fat gentleman, with a jolly laugh and an appetite for all sorts of news, big and little, and who liked a pipe, and made a tumbler of punch at about this hour, with a bit of lemon-peel in it. Beside him sat William Peers, a thin old gentleman, who had lived for more than thirty years in India, and was quiet and benevolent, and the last man in Golden Friars who wore a pigtail. Old Jack Amerald, an ex-captain of the navy, with his short stout leg on a chair, and its wooden companion beside it, sipped his grog, and bawled in the old-fashioned navy way, and called his friends his 'hearties.' In the middle, opposite the hearth, sat deaf Tom Hollar, always placid, and smoked his pipe, looking serenely at the fire. And the landlord of the George and Dragon every now and then strutted in, and sat down in the high-backed wooden arm-chair, according to the old-fashioned republican ways of the place, and took his share in the talk gravely, and was heartily welcome.

"And so Sir Bale is coming home at last," said the Doctor. "Tell us any more you heard since."

"Nothing," answered Richard Turnbull, the host of the George. "Nothing to speak of; only 'tis certain sure, and so best; the old house won't look so dowly now."

"Twyne says the estate owes a good capful o' money by this time, hey?" said the Doctor, lowering his voice and winking.

"Weel, they do say he's been nout at dow. I don't mind saying so to *you*, mind, sir, where all's friends together; but he'll get that right in time."

"More like to save here than where he is," said the Doctor with another grave nod.

"He does very wisely," said Mr. Peers, having blown out a thin stream of smoke, "and creditably, to pull-up in time. He's coming here to save a little, and perhaps he'll marry; and it is the more creditable, if, as they say, he dislikes the place, and would prefer staying where he is."

And having spoken thus gently, Mr. Peers resumed his pipe cheerfully.

"No, he don't like the place; that is, I'm told he *didn't*," said the innkeeper.

"He *hates* it," said the Doctor with another dark nod.

"And no wonder, if all's true I've heard," cried old Jack Amerald. "Didn't he drown a woman and her child in the lake?"

"Hollo! my dear boy, don't let them hear you say that; you're all in the clouds."

"By Jen!" exclaimed the landlord after an alarmed silence, with his mouth and eyes open, and his pipe in his hand, "why, sir, I pay rent for the house up there. I'm thankful—dear knows, I *am* thankful—we're all to ourselves!"

Jack Amerald put his foot on the floor, leaving his wooden leg in its horizontal position, and looked round a little curiously.

"Well, if it wasn't him, it was some one else. I'm sure it happened up at Mardykes. I took the bearings on the water myself from Glads Scaur to Mardykes Jetty, and from the George and Dragon sign down here—down to the white house under Forrick Fells. I could fix a buoy over the very spot. Some one here told me the bearings, I'd take my oath, where the body was seen; and yet no boat could ever come up with it; and that was queer, you know, so I clapt it down in my log."

"Ay, sir, there *was* some flummery like that, Captain," said Turnbull; "for folk will be gabbin'. But 'twas his grandsire was talked o', not him; and 'twould play the hangment wi' me doun here, if 'twas thought there was stories like that passin' in the George and Dragon.'

"Well, his grandfather; 'twas all one to him, I take it."

"There never was no proof, Captain, no more than smoke; and the family up at Mardykes wouldn't allow the king to talk o' them like that, sir; for though they be lang deod that had most right to be angered in the matter, there's none o' the name but would be half daft to think 'twas still believed, and he full out as mich as any. Not that I need care more than another, though they do say he's a bit frowsy and short-waisted; for he can't shouther me out o' the George while I pay my rent, till nine hundred and ninety-nine year be rin oot; and a man, be he ne'er sa het, has time to cool before then. But there's no good quarrellin' wi' teathy folk; and it may lie in his way to do the George mony an ill turn, and mony a gude one; an' it's only fair to say it happened a long way before he was born, and there's no good in vexin' him; and I lay ye a pound, Captain, the Doctor hods wi' me."

The Doctor, whose business was also sensitive, nodded; and then he said, "But for all that, the story's old, Dick Turnbull—older than you or I, my jolly good friend."

"And best forgotten," interposed the host of the George.

"Ay, best forgotten; but that it's not like to be," said the Doctor, plucking up courage. "Here's our friend the Captain has heard it; and the mistake he has made shows there's one thing worse than its being quite remembered, and that is, its being *half* remembered. We can't stop people talking; and a story like that will see us all off the hooks, and be in folks' mouths, still, as strong as ever."

"Ay, and now I think on it, 'twas Dick Harman that has the boat down there—an old tar like myself—that told me that yarn. I was trying for pike, and he pulled me over the place, and that's how I came to hear it. I say, Tom, my hearty, serve us out another glass of brandy, will you?" shouted the Captain's voice as the waiter crossed the room; and that florid and grizzled naval hero clapped his leg again on the chair by its wooden companion, which he was wont to call his jury-mast.

"Well, I do believe it will be spoke of longer than we are like to hear," said the host, "and I don't much matter the story, if it baint told o' the wrong man." Here he touched his tumbler with the spoon, indicating by that little ring that Tom, who had returned with the Captain's grog, was to replenish it with punch. "And Sir Bale is like to be a friend to this house. I don't see no reason why he shouldn't. The George and Dragon has bin in our family ever since the reign of King Charles the Second. It was William Turnbull in that time, which they called it the Restoration, he taking the lease from Sir Tony Mardykes that was then. They was but knights then. They was made baronets first in the reign of King George the Second; you may see it in the list of baronets and the nobility. The lease was made to William Turnbull, which came from London; and he built the stables, which they was out o' repair, as you may read to this day in the lease; and the house has never had but one sign since—the George and Dragon, it is pretty well known in England—and one name to its master. It has been owned by a Turnbull from that day to this, and they have not been counted bad men." A murmur of applause testified the assent of his guests. "They has been steady churchgoin' folk, and brewed good drink, and maintained the best o' characters, hereaways and farther off too, though 'tis I, Richard Turnbull, that says it; and while they pay their rent, no man has power to put them out; for their title's as good to the George and Dragon, and the two fields, and the croft, and the grazing o' their kye on the green, as Sir Bale Mardykes to the Hall up there and estate. So 'tis nout to me, except in the way o' friendliness, what the family may think o' me; only the George and they has always been kind and friendly, and I don't want to break the old custom."

"Well said, Dick!" exclaimed Doctor Torvey; "I own to your conclusion; but there ain't a soul here but ourselves—and we're all friends, and you are your own master—and, hang it, you'll tell us that story about the drowned woman, as you heard it from your father long ago."

"Ay, do, and keep us to our liquor, my hearty!" cried the Captain.

Mr. Peers looked his entreaty; and deaf Mr. Hollar, having no interest in the petition, was at least a safe witness, and, with his pipe in his lips, a cozy piece of furniture.

Richard Turnbull had his punch beside him; he looked over his shoulder. The door was closed, the fire was cheery, and the punch was fragrant, and all friendly faces about him. So said he:

"Gentlemen, as you're pleased to wish it, I don't see no great harm in it; and at any rate, 'twill prevent mistakes. It is more than ninety years since. My father was but a boy then; and many a time I have heard him tell it in this very room."

And looking into his glass he mused, and stirred his punch slowly.

CHAPTER II

The Drowned Woman "It ain't much of a homminy," said the host of the George. "I'll not keep you long over it, gentlemen. There was a handsome young lady, Miss Mary Feltram o' Cloostedd by name. She was the last o' that family; and had gone very poor. There's but the walls o' the house left now; grass growing in the hall, and ivy over the gables; there's no one livin' has ever hard tell o' smoke out o' they chimblies. It stands on t'other side o' the lake, on the level wi' a deal o' a'ad trees behint and aside it at the gap o' the clough, under the pike o' Maiden Fells. Ye may see it wi' a spyin'-glass from the boatbield at Mardykes Hall."

"I've been there fifty times," said the Doctor.

"Well there was dealin's betwixt the two families; and there's good and bad in every family; but the Mardykes, in them days, was a wild lot. And when old Feltram o' Cloostedd died, and the young lady his daughter was left a ward o' Sir Jasper Mardykes—an ill day for her, poor lass!--twenty year older than her he was, an' more; and nothin' about him, they say, to make anyone like or love him, ill-faur'd and little and dow."

"Dow—that's gloomy," Doctor Torvey instructed the Captain aside.

"But they do say, they has an old blud-stean ring in the family that has a charm in't; and happen how it might, the poor lass fell in love wi' him. Some said they was married. Some said it hang'd i' the bell-ropes, and never had the priest's blessing; but anyhow, married or no, there was talk enough amang the folk, and out o' doors she would na budge. And there was two wee barns; and she prayed him hard to confess the marriage, poor thing! But t'was a bootlese bene, and he would not allow they should bear his name, but their mother's; he was a hard man, and hed the bit in his teeth, and went his ain gait. And having tired of her, he took in his head to marry a lady of the Barnets, and it behoved him to be shut o' her and her children; and so she nor them was seen no more at Mardykes Hall. And the eldest, a boy, was left in care of my grandfather's father here in the George."

"That queer Philip Feltram that's travelling with Sir Bale so long is a descendant of his?" said the Doctor.

"Grandson," observed Mr. Peers, removing his pipe for a moment; "and is the last of that stock."

"Well, no one could tell where she had gone to. Some said to distant parts, some said to the madhouse, some one thing, some another; but neither she nor the barn was ever seen or spoke to by the folk at Mardykes in life again. There was one Mr. Wigram that lived in them times down at Moultry, and had sarved, like the Captain here, in the king's navy in his day; and early of a morning down he comes to the town for a boat, sayin' he was looking towards Snakes Island through his spyin'-glass, and he seen a woman about a hundred and fifty yards outside of it; the Captain here has heard the bearings right enough. From her hips upwards she was stark and straight out o' the water, and a baby in her arms. Well, no one else could see it, nor he neither, when they went down to the boat. But next morning he saw the same thing, and the boatman saw it too; and they rowed for it, both pulling might and main; but after a mile or so they could see it no more, and gave over. The next that saw it was the vicar, I forget his name now—but he was up the lake to a funeral at Mortlock Church; and coming back with a bit of a sail up, just passin' Snakes Island, what should they hear on a sudden but a wowl like a death-cry, shrill and bleak, as made the very blood hoot in their veins; and looking along the water not a hundred yards away, saw the same grizzled sight in the moonlight; so they turned the tiller, and came near enough to see her face—blea it was, and drenched wi' water—and she was above the lake to her middle, stiff as a post, holdin' the weeny barn out to them, and flyrin' [smiling scornfully] on them as they drew nigh her. They were half-frighted, not knowing what to make of it; but passing as close as the boatman could bring her side, the vicar stretched over the gunwale to catch her, and she bent forward, pushing the dead bab forward; and as she did, on a sudden she gave a yelloch that scared them, and they saw her no more. 'Twas no livin' woman, for she couldn't rise that height above the water, as they well knew when they came to think; and knew it was a dobby they saw; and ye may be sure they didn't spare prayer and blessin', and went on their course straight before the wind; for neither would a-took the worth o' all the Mardykes to look sich a freetin' i' the face again. 'Twas seen another time by market-folk crossin' fra Gyllenstan in the self-same place; and Snakes Island got a bad neam, and none cared to go nar it after nightfall."

"Do you know anything of that Feltram that has been with him abroad?" asked the Doctor.

"They say he's no good at anything—a harmless mafflin; he was a long gaumless gawky when he went awa," said Richard Turnbull. "The Feltrams and the Mardykes was sib, ye know; and that made what passed in the misfortune o' that young lady spoken of all the harder; and this young man ye speak of is a grandson o' the lad that was put here in care o' my grandfather."

"*Great*-grandson. His father was grandson," said Mr. Peers; "he held a commission in the army and died in the West Indies. This Philip Feltram is the last o' that line—illegitimate, you know, it is held—and the little that remained of the Feltram property went nearly fourscore years ago to the Mardykes, and this Philip is maintained by Sir Bale; it is pleasant, notwithstanding all the stories one hears, gentlemen, that the only thing we know of him for certain should be so creditable to his kindness."

"To be sure," acquiesced Mr. Turnbull.

While they talked the horn sounded, and the mail-coach drew up at the door of the George and Dragon to set down a passenger and his luggage.

Dick Turnbull rose and went out to the hall with careful bustle, and Doctor Torvey followed as far as the door, which commanded a view of it, and saw several trunks cased in canvas pitched into the hall, and by careful Tom and a boy lifted one on top of the other, behind the corner of the banister. It would have been below the dignity of his cloth to go out and read the labels on these, or the Doctor would have done otherwise, so great was his curiosity.

CHAPTER III

Philip Feltram The new guest was now in the hall of the George, and Doctor Torvey could hear him talking with Mr. Turnbull. Being himself one of the dignitaries of Golden Friars, the Doctor, having regard to first impressions, did not care to be seen in his post of observation; and closing the door gently, returned to his chair by the fire, and in an under-tone informed his cronies that there was a new arrival in the George, and he could not hear, but would not wonder if he were taking a private room; and he seemed to have trunks enough to build a church with.

"Don't be too sure we haven't Sir Bale on board," said Amerald, who would have followed his crony the Doctor to the door—for never was retired naval hero of a village more curious than he—were it not that his wooden leg made a distinct pounding on the floor that was inimical, as experience had taught him, to mystery.

"That can't be," answered the Doctor; "Charley Twyne knows everything about it, and has a letter every second day; and there's no chance of Sir Bale before the tenth; this is a tourist, you'll find. I don't know what the d---l keeps Turnbull; he knows well enough we are all naturally willing to hear who it is."

"Well, he won't trouble us here, I bet ye;" and catching deaf Mr. Hollar's eye, the Captain nodded, and pointed to the little table beside him, and made a gesture imitative of the rattling of a dice-box; at which that quiet old gentleman also nodded sunnily; and up got the Captain and conveyed the backgammon-box to the table, near Hollar's elbow, and the two worthies were soon sinc-ducing and catre-acing, with the pleasant clatter that accompanies that ancient game. Hollar had thrown sizes and made his double point, and the honest Captain, who could stand many things better than Hollar's throwing such throws so early in the evening, cursed his opponent's luck and sneered at his play, and called the company to witness, with a distinctness which a stranger to smiling Hollar's deafness would have thought hardly civil; and just at this moment the door opened, and Richard Turnbull showed his new guest into the room, and ushered him to a vacant seat near the other corner of the table before the fire.

The stranger advanced slowly and shyly, with something a little deprecatory in his air, to which a lathy figure, a slight stoop, and a very gentle and even heart-broken look in his pale long face, gave a more marked character of shrinking and timidity.

He thanked the landlord aside, as it were, and took his seat with a furtive glance round, as if he had no right to come in and intrude upon the happiness of these honest gentlemen.

He saw the Captain scanning him from under his shaggy grey eyebrows while he was pretending to look only at his game; and the Doctor was able to recount to Mrs. Torvey when he went home every article of the stranger's dress.

It was odd and melancholy as his peaked face.

He had come into the room with a short black cloak on, and a rather tall foreign felt hat, and a pair of shiny leather gaiters or leggings on his thin legs; and altogether presented a general resemblance to the conventional figure of Guy Fawkes.

Not one of the company assembled knew the appearance of the Baronet. The Doctor and old Mr. Peers remembered something of his looks; and certainly they had no likeness, but the reverse, to those presented by the new-comer. The Baronet, as now described by people who had chanced to see him, was a dark man, not above the middle size, and with a certain decision in his air and talk; whereas this person was tall, pale, and in air and manner feeble. So this broken trader in the world's commerce, with whom all seemed to have gone wrong, could not possibly be he.

Presently, in one of his stealthy glances, the Doctor's eye encountered that of the stranger, who was by this time drinking his tea—a thin and feminine liquor little used in that room.

The stranger did not seem put out; and the Doctor, interpreting his look as a permission to converse, cleared his voice, and said urbanely,

"We have had a little frost by night, down here, sir, and a little fire is no great harm—it is rather pleasant, don't you think?"

The stranger bowed acquiescence with a transient wintry smile, and looked gratefully on the fire.

"This place is a good deal admired, sir, and people come a good way to see it; you have been here perhaps before?"

"Many years ago."

Here was another pause.

"Places change imperceptibly—in detail, at least—a good deal," said the Doctor, making an effort to keep up a conversation that plainly would not go on of itself; "and people too; population shifts—there's an old fellow, sir, they call *Death.*"

"And an old fellow they call the *Doctor*, that helps him," threw in the Captain humorously, allowing his attention to get entangled in the conversation, and treating them to one of his tempestuous ha-ha-ha's.

"We are expecting the return of a gentleman who would be a very leading member of our little society down here," said the Doctor, not noticing the Captain's joke. "I mean Sir Bale Mardykes. Mardykes Hall is a pretty object from the water, sir, and a very fine old place."

The melancholy stranger bowed slightly, but rather in courtesy to the relator, it seemed, than that the Doctor's lore interested him much.

"And on the opposite side of the lake," continued Doctor Torvey, "there is a building that contrasts very well with it—the old house of the Feltrams—quite a ruin now, at the mouth of the glen—Cloostedd House, a very picturesque object."

"Exactly opposite," said the stranger dreamily, but whether in the tone of acquiescence or interrogatory, the Doctor could not be quite sure.

"That was one of our great families down here that has disappeared. It has dwindled down to nothing."

"Duce ace," remarked Mr. Hollar, who was attending to his game.

"While others have mounted more suddenly and amazingly still," observed gentle Mr. Peers, who was great upon county genealogies.

"Sizes!" thundered the Captain, thumping the table with an oath of disgust.

"And Snakes Island is a very pretty object; they say there used to be snakes there," said the Doctor, enlightening the visitor.

"Ah! that's a mistake," said the dejected guest, making his first original observation. "It should be spelt *Snaiks*. In the old papers it is called Sen-aiks Island from the seven oaks that grew in a clump there."

"Hey? that's very curious, egad! I daresay," said the Doctor, set right thus by the stranger, and eyeing him curiously.

"Very true, sir," observed Mr. Peers; "three of those oaks, though, two of them little better than stumps, are there still; and Clewson of Heckleston has an old document——"

Here, unhappily, the landlord entered the room in a fuss, and walking up to the stranger, said, "The chaise is at the door, Mr. Feltram, and the trunks up, sir."

Mr. Feltram rose quietly and took out his purse, and said,

"I suppose I had better pay at the bar?"

"As you like best, sir," said Richard Turnbull.

Mr. Feltram bowed all round to the gentlemen, who smiled, ducked or waved their hands; and the Doctor fussily followed him to the hall-door, and welcomed him back to Golden Friars—there was real kindness in this welcome—and proffered his broad brown hand, which Mr. Feltram took; and then he plunged into his chaise, and the door being shut, away he glided, chaise, horses, and driver, like shadows, by the margin of the moonlighted lake, towards Mardykes Hall.

And after a few minutes' stand upon the steps, looking along the shadowy track of the chaise, they returned to the glow of the room, in which a pleasant perfume of punch still prevailed; and beside Mr. Philip Feltram's deserted tea-things, the host of the George enlightened his guests by communicating freely the little he had picked up. The principal fact he had to tell was, that Sir Bale adhered strictly to his original plan, and was to arrive on the tenth. A few days would bring them to that, and the nine-days wonder run its course and lose its interest. But in the meantime, all Golden Friars was anxious to see what Sir Bale Mardykes was like.

CHAPTER IV

The Baronet Appears As the candles burn blue and the air smells of brimstone at the approach of the Evil One, so, in the quiet and healthy air of Golden Friars, a depressing and agitating influence announced the coming of the long-absent Baronet.

From abroad, no good whatever had been at any time heard of him, and a great deal that was, in the ears of simple folk living in that unsophisticated part of the world, vaguely awful.

Stories that travel so far, however, lose something of their authority, as well as definiteness, on the way; there was always room for charity to suggest a mistake or exaggeration; and if good men turned up their hands and eyes after a new story, and ladies of experience, who knew mankind, held their heads high and looked grim and mysterious at mention of his name, nevertheless an interval of silence softened matters a little, and the sulphureous perfume dissipated itself in time.

Now that Sir Bale Mardykes had arrived at the Hall, there were hurried consultations held in many households. And though he was tried and sentenced by drum-head over some austere hearths, as a rule the law of gravitation prevailed, and the greater house drew the lesser about it, and county people within the visiting radius paid their respects at the Hall.

The Reverend Martin Bedel, the then vicar of Golden Friars, a stout short man, with a mulberry-coloured face and small gray eyes, and taciturn habits, called and entered the drawing-room at Mardykes Hall, with his fat and garrulous wife on his arm.

The drawing-room has a great projecting Tudor window looking out on the lake, with its magnificent background of furrowed and purple mountains.

Sir Bale was not there, and Mrs. Bedel examined the pictures, and ornaments, and the books, making such remarks as she saw fit; and then she looked out of the window, and admired the prospect. She wished to stand well with the Baronet, and was in a mood to praise everything.

You may suppose she was curious to see him, having heard for years such strange tales of his doings.

She expected the hero of a brilliant and wicked romance; and listened for the step of the truant Lovelace who was to fulfil her idea of manly beauty and fascination.

She sustained a slight shock when he did appear.

Sir Bale Mardykes was, as she might easily have remembered, a middle-aged man—and he looked it. He was not even an imposing-looking man for his time of life: he was of about the middle height, slightly made, and dark featured. She had expected something of the gaiety and animation of Versailles, and an evident cultivation of the art of pleasing. What she did see was a remarkable gravity, not to say gloom, of countenance—the only feature of which that struck her being a pair of large dark-gray eyes, that were cold and earnest. His manners had the ease of perfect confidence; and his talk and air were those of a person who might have known how to please, if it were worth the trouble, but who did not care twopence whether he pleased or not.

He made them each a bow, courtly enough, but there was no smile—not even an affectation of cordiality. Sir Bale, however, was chatty, and did not seem to care much what he said, or what people thought of him; and there was a suspicion of sarcasm in what he said that the rustic literality of good Mrs. Bedel did not always detect.

"I believe I have not a clergyman but *you*, sir, within any reasonable distance?"

"Golden Friars *is* the nearest," said Mrs. Bedel, answering, as was her pleasure on all practicable occasions, for her husband. "And southwards, the nearest is Wyllarden—and by a bird's flight that is thirteen miles and a half, and by the road more than nineteen—twenty, I may say, by the road. Ha, ha, ha! it is a long way to look for a clergyman."

"Twenty miles of road to carry you thirteen miles across, hey? The road-makers lead you a pretty dance here; those gentlemen know how to make money, and like to show people the scenery from a variety of points. No one likes a straight road but the man who pays for it, or who, when he travels, is brute enough to wish to get to his journey's end."

"That is so true, Sir Bale; one never cares if one is not in a hurry. That's what Martin thinks—don't we, Martin?—And then, you know, coming home is the time you *are* in a hurry—when you are thinking of your cup of tea and the children; and *then*, you know, you have the fall of the ground all in your favour."

"It's well to have anything in your favour in this place. And so there are children?"

"A good many," said Mrs. Bedel, with a proud and mysterious smile, and a nod; "you wouldn't guess how many."

"Not I; I only wonder you did not bring them all."

"That's very good-natured of you, Sir Bale, but all could not come at *one* bout; there are—tell him, Martin—ha, ha, ha! there are eleven."

"It must be very cheerful down at the vicarage," said Sir Bale graciously; and turning to the vicar he added, "But how unequally blessings are divided! You have eleven, and I not one—that I'm aware of."

"And then, in that direction straight before you, you have the lake, and then the fells; and five miles from the foot of the mountain at the other side, before you reach Fottrell—and that is twenty-five miles by the road——"

"Dear me! how far apart they are set! My gardener told me this morning that asparagus grows very thinly in this part of the world. How thinly clergymen grow also down here—in one sense," he added politely, for the vicar was stout.

"We were looking out of the window—we amused ourselves that way before you came—and your view is certainly the very best anywhere round this side; your view of the lake and the fells—what mountains they are, Sir Bale!"

"'Pon my soul, they are! I wish I could blow them asunder with a charge of duck-shot, and I shouldn't be stifled by them long. But I suppose, as we can't get rid of them, the next best thing is to admire them. We are pretty well married to them, and there is no use in quarrelling."

"I know you don't think so, Sir Bale, ha, ha, ha! You wouldn't take a good deal and spoil Mardykes Hall."

"You can't get a mouthful or air, or see the sun of a morning, for those frightful mountains," he said with a peevish frown at them.

"Well, the lake at all events—that you *must* admire, Sir Bale?"

"No ma'am, I don't admire the lake. I'd drain the lake if I could—I hate the lake. There's nothing so gloomy as a lake pent up among barren mountains. I can't conceive what possessed my people to build our house down here, at the edge of a lake; unless it was the fish, and precious fish it is—pike! I don't know how people digest it—*I* can't. I'd as soon think of eating a watchman's pike."

"I thought that having travelled so much abroad, you would have acquired a great liking for that kind of scenery, Sir Bale; there is a great deal of it on the Continent, ain't there?" said Mrs. Bedel. "And the boating."

"Boating, my dear Mrs. Bedel, is the dullest of all things; don't you think so? Because a boat looks very pretty from the shore, we fancy the shore must look very pretty from a boat; and when we try it, we find we have only got down into a pit and can see nothing rightly. For my part I hate boating, and I hate the water; and I'd rather have my house, like Haworth, at the edge of a moss, with good wholesome peat to look at, and an open horizon—savage and stupid and bleak as all that is—than be suffocated among impassable mountains, or upset in a black lake and drowned like a kitten. O, there's luncheon in the next room; won't you take some?"

CHAPTER V

Mrs. Julaper's Room Sir Bale Mardykes being now established in his ancestral house, people had time to form conclusions respecting him. It must be allowed he was not popular. There was, perhaps, in his conduct something of the caprice of contempt. At all events his temper and conduct were uncertain, and his moods sometimes violent and insulting.

With respect to but one person was his conduct uniform, and that was Philip Feltram. He was a sort of aide-de-camp near Sir Bale's person, and chargeable with all the commissions and offices which could not be suitably intrusted to a mere servant. But in many respects he was treated worse than any servant of the Baronet's. Sir Bale swore at him, and cursed him; laid the blame of everything that went wrong in house, stable, or field upon his shoulders; railed at him, and used him, as people said, worse than a dog.

Why did Feltram endure this contumelious life? What could he do but endure it? was the answer. What was the power that induced strong soldiers to put off their jackets and shirts, and present their hands to be tied up, and tortured for hours, it might be, under the scourge, with an air of ready volition? The moral coercion of despair; the result of an unconscious calculation of chances which satisfies them that it is ultimately better to do all that, bad as it is, than try the alternative. These unconscious calculations are going on every day with each of us, and the results embody themselves in our lives; and no one knows that there has been a process and a balance struck, and that what they see, and very likely blame, is by the fiat of an invisible but quite irresistible power.

A man of spirit would rather break stones on the highway than eat that bitter bread, was the burden of every man's song on Feltram's bondage. But he was not so sure that even the stone-breaker's employment was open to him, or that he could break stones well enough to retain it on a fair trial. And he had other ideas of providing for himself, and a different alternative in his mind.

Good-natured Mrs. Julaper, the old housekeeper at Mardykes Hall, was kind to Feltram, as to all others who lay in her way and were in affliction.

She was one of those good women whom Nature provides to receive the burden of other people's secrets, as the reeds did long ago, only that no chance wind could steal them away, and send them singing into strange ears.

You may still see her snuggery in Mardykes Hall, though the housekeeper's room is now in a different part of the house.

Mrs. Julaper's room was in the oldest quarter of that old house. It was wainscoted, in black panels, up to the ceiling, which was stuccoed over in the fanciful diagrams of James the First's time. Several dingy portraits, banished from time to time from other statelier rooms, found a temporary abode in this quiet spot, where they had come finally to settle and drop out of remembrance. There is a lady in white satin and a ruff; a gentleman whose legs have faded out of view, with a peaked beard, and a hawk on his wrist. There is another in a black periwig lost in the dark background, and with a steel cuirass, the gleam of which out of the darkness strikes the eye, and a scarf is dimly discoverable across it. This is that foolish Sir Guy Mardykes, who crossed the Border and joined Dundee, and was shot through the temple at Killiecrankie and whom more prudent and whiggish scions of the Mardykes family removed forthwith from his place in the Hall, and found a retirement here, from which he has not since emerged.

CHAPTER V

At the far end of this snug room is a second door, on opening which you find yourself looking down upon the great kitchen, with a little balcony before you, from which the housekeeper used to issue her commands to the cook, and exercise a sovereign supervision.

There is a shelf on which Mrs Julaper had her Bible, her *Whole Duty of Man*, and her *Pilgrim's Progress*; and, in a file beside them, her books of housewifery, and among them volumes of MS. recipes, cookery-books, and some too on surgery and medicine, as practised by the Ladies Bountiful of the Elizabethan age, for which an antiquarian would nowadays give an eye or a hand.

Gentle half-foolish Philip Feltram would tell the story of his wrongs, and weep and wish he was dead; and kind Mrs. Julaper, who remembered him a child, would comfort him with cold pie and cherry-brandy, or a cup of coffee, or some little dainty.

"O, ma'am, I'm tired of my life. What's the good of living, if a poor devil is never let alone, and called worse names than a dog? Would not it be better, Mrs. Julaper, to be dead? Wouldn't it be better, ma'am? I think so; I think it night and day. I'm always thinking the same thing. I don't care, I'll just tell him what I think, and have it off my mind. I'll tell him I can't live and bear it longer."

"There now, don't you be frettin'; but just sip this, and remember you're not to judge a friend by a wry word. He does not mean it, not he. They all had a rough side to their tongue now and again; but no one minded that. I don't, nor you needn't, no more than other folk; for the tongue, be it never so bitin', it can't draw blood, mind ye, and hard words break no bones; and I'll make a cup o' tea—ye like a cup o' tea—and we'll take a cup together, and ye'll chirp up a bit, and see how pleasant and ruddy the sun shines on the lake this evening."

She was patting him gently on the shoulder, as she stood slim and stiff in her dark silk by his chair, and her rosy little face smiled down on him. She was, for an old woman, wonderfully pretty still. What a delicate skin she must have had! The wrinkles were etched upon it with so fine a needle, you scarcely could see them a little way off; and as she smiled her cheeks looked fresh and smooth as two ruddy little apples.

"Look out, I say," and she nodded towards the window, deep set in the thick wall. "See how bright and soft everything looks in that pleasant light; *that's* better, child, than the finest picture man's hand ever painted yet, and God gives it us for nothing; and how pretty Snakes Island glows up in that light!"

The dejected man, hardly raising his head, followed with his eyes the glance of the old woman, and looked mournfully through the window.

"That island troubles me, Mrs. Julaper."

"Everything troubles you, my poor goose-cap. I'll pull your lug for ye, child, if ye be so dowly;" and with a mimic pluck the good-natured old housekeeper pinched his ear and laughed.

"I'll go to the still-room now, where the water's boiling, and I'll make a cup of tea; and if I find ye so dow when I come back, I'll throw it all out o' the window, mind."

It was indeed a beautiful picture that Feltram saw in its deep frame of old masonry. The near part of the lake was flushed all over with the low western light; the more distant waters lay dark in the shadow of the mountains; and against this shadow of purple the rocks on Snakes Island, illuminated by the setting sun, started into sharp clear yellow.

But this beautiful view had no charm—at least, none powerful enough to master the latent horror associated with its prettiest feature—for the weak and dismal man who was looking at it; and being now alone, he rose and leant on the window, and looked out, and then with a kind of shudder clutching his hands together, and walking distractedly about the room.

Without his perceiving, while his back was turned, the housekeeper came back; and seeing him walking in this distracted way, she thought to herself, as he leant again upon the window:

"Well, it *is* a burning shame to worrit any poor soul into that state. Sir Bale was always down on someone or something, man or beast; there always was something he hated, and could never let alone. It was not pretty; it was his nature. Happen, poor fellow, he could not help it; but so it was."

A maid came in and set the tea-things down; and Mrs. Julaper drew her sad guest over by the arm, and made him sit down, and she said: "What has a man to do, frettin' in that way? By Jen, I'm ashamed o' ye, Master Philip! Ye like three lumps o' sugar, I think, and—look cheerful, ye must!--a good deal o' cream?"

"You're so kind, Mrs. Julaper, you're so cheery. I feel quite comfortable after awhile when I'm with you; I feel quite happy," and he began to cry.

She understood him very well by this time and took no notice, but went on chatting gaily, and made his tea as he liked it; and he dried his tears hastily, thinking she had not observed.

So the clouds began to clear. This innocent fellow liked nothing better than a cup of tea and a chat with gentle and cheery old Mrs. Julaper, and a talk in which the shadowy old times which he remembered as a child emerged into sunlight and lived again.

When he began to feel better, drawn into the kindly old times by the tinkle of that harmless old woman's tongue, he said:

"I sometimes think I would not so much mind—I should not care so much—if my spirits were not so depressed, and I so agitated. I suppose I am not quite well."

"Well, tell me what's wrong, child, and it's odd but I have a recipe on the shelf there that will do you good."

"It is not a matter of that sort I mean; though I'd rather have you than any doctor, if I needed medicine, to prescribe for me."

Mrs. Julaper smiled in spite of herself, well pleased; for her skill in pharmacy was a point on which the good lady prided herself, and was open to flattery, which, without intending it, the simple fellow administered.

"No, I'm well enough; I can't say I ever was better. It is only, ma'am, that I have such dreams—you have no idea."

"There are dreams and dreams, my dear: there's some signifies no more than the babble of the lake down there on the pebbles, and there's others that has a meaning; there's dreams that is but vanity, and there's dreams that is good, and dreams that is bad. Lady Mardykes—heavens be her bed this day! that's his grandmother I mean—was very sharp for reading dreams. Take another cup of tea. Dear me! what a noise the crows keep aboon our heads, going home! and how high they wing it!--that's a sure sign of fine weather. An' what do you dream about? Tell me your dream, and I may show you it's a good one, after all. For many a dream is ugly to see and ugly to tell, and a good dream, with a happy meaning, for all that."

CHAPTER VI

The Intruder "Well, Mrs. Julaper, dreams I've dreamed like other people, old and young; but this, ma'am, has taken a fast hold of me," said Mr. Feltram dejectedly, leaning back in his chair and looking down with his hands in his pockets. "I think, Mrs. Julaper, it is getting into me. I think it's like possession."

"Possession, child! what do you mean?"

"I think there is something trying to influence me. Perhaps it is the way fellows go mad; but it won't let me alone. I've seen it three times, think of that!"

"Well, dear, and what *have* ye seen?" she asked, with an uneasy cheerfulness, smiling, with eyes fixed steadily upon him; for the idea of a madman—even gentle Philip in that state—was not quieting.

"Do you remember the picture, full-length, that had no frame the lady in the white-satin saque—she was beautiful, *funeste*," he added, talking more to himself; and then more distinctly to Mrs. Julaper again——"in the white-satin saque; and with the little mob cap and blue ribbons to it, and a bouquet in her fingers; that was—that—you know who she was?"

"That was your great-grandmother, my dear," said Mrs. Julaper, lowering her eyes. "It was a dreadful pity it was spoiled. The boys in the pantry had it for a year there on the table for a tray, to wash the glasses on and the like. It was a shame; that was the prettiest picture in the house, with the gentlest, rosiest face."

"It ain't so gentle or rosy now, I can tell you," said Philip. "As fixed as marble; with thin lips, and a curve at the nostril. Do you remember the woman that was found dead in the clough, when I was a boy, that the gipsies murdered, it was thought,—a cruel-looking woman?"

"Agoy! Master Philip, dear! ye would not name that terrible-looking creature with the pretty, fresh, kindly face!"

"Faces change, you see; no matter what she's like; it's her talk that frightens me. She wants to make use of me; and, you see, it is like getting a share in my mind, and a voice in my thoughts, and a command over me gradually; and it is just one idea, as straight as a line of light across the lake—see what she's come to. O Lord, help me!"

"Well, now, don't you be talkin' like that. It is just a little bit dowly and troubled, because the master says a wry word now and then; and so ye let your spirits go down, don't ye see, and all sorts o' fancies comes into your head."

"There's no fancy in my head," he said with a quick look of suspicion; "only you asked me what I dreamed. I don't care if all the world knew. I dreamed I went down a flight of steps under the lake, and got a message. There are no steps near Snakes Island, we all know that," and he laughed chillily. "I'm out of spirits, as you say; and—and—O dear! I wish—Mrs. Julaper—I wish I was in my coffin, and quiet."

"Now that's very wrong of you, Master Philip; you should think of all the blessings you have, and not be makin' mountains o' molehills; and those little bits o' temper Sir Bale shows, why, no one minds 'em—that is, to take 'em to heart like you do, don't ye see?"

"I daresay; I suppose, Mrs. Julaper, you are right. I'm unreasonable often, I know," said gentle Philip Feltram. "I daresay I make too much of it; I'll try. I'm his secretary, and I know I'm not so bright as he is, and it is natural he should sometimes be a little impatient; I ought to be more reasonable, I'm sure. It is all that thing that has been disturbing me—I mean fretting, and, I think, I'm not quite well; and—and letting myself think too much of vexations. It's my own fault, I'm sure, Mrs. Julaper; and I know I'm to blame."

"That's quite right, that's spoken like a wise lad; only I don't say you're to blame, nor no one; for folk can't help frettin' sometimes, no more than they can help a headache—none but a mafflin would say that—and I'll not deny but he has dowly ways when the fit's on him, and he frumps us all round, if such be his humour. But who is there hasn't his faults? We must bear and forbear, and take what we get and be cheerful. So chirp up, my lad; Philip, didn't I often ring the a'd rhyme in your ear long ago?

"Be always as merry as ever you can,
For no one delights in a sorrowful man.

"So don't ye be gettin' up off your chair like that, and tramping about the room wi' your hands in your pockets, looking out o' this window, and staring out o' that, and sighing and crying, and looking so black-ox-trodden, 'twould break a body's heart to see you. Ye must be cheery; and happen you're hungry, and don't know it. I'll tell the cook to grill a hot bit for ye."

"But I'm not hungry, Mrs. Julaper. How kind you are! dear me, Mrs. Julaper, I'm not worthy of it; I don't deserve half your kindness. I'd have been heartbroken long ago, but for you."

"And I'll make a sup of something hot for you; you'll take a rummer-glass of punch—you must."

"But I like the tea better; I do, indeed, Mrs. Julaper."

"Tea is no drink for a man when his heart's down. It should be something with a leg in it, lad; something hot that will warm your courage for ye, and set your blood a-dancing, and make ye talk brave and merry; and will you have a bit of a broil first? No? Well then, you'll have a drop o' punch?—ye sha'n't say no."

CHAPTER VI

And so, all resistance overpowered, the consolation of Philip Feltram proceeded.

A gentler spirit than poor Feltram, a more good-natured soul than the old housekeeper, were nowhere among the children of earth.

Philip Feltram, who was reserved enough elsewhere, used to come into her room and cry, and take her by both hands piteously, standing before her and looking down in her face, while tears ran deviously down his cheeks.

"Did you ever know such a case? was there ever a fellow like *me*? did you ever *know* such a thing? You know what I am, Mrs. Julaper, and who I am. They call me Feltram; but Sir Bale knows as well as I that my true name is not that. I'm Philip Mardykes; and another fellow would make a row about it, and claim his name and his rights, as she is always croaking in my ear I ought. But you know that is not reasonable. My grandmother was married; she was the true Lady Mardykes; *think* what it was to see a woman like that turned out of doors, and her children robbed of their name. O, ma'am, you *can't* think it; unless you were me, you couldn't—you couldn't—you couldn't!"

"Come, come, Master Philip, don't you be taking on so; and ye mustn't be talking like that, d'ye mind? You know he wouldn't stand that; and it's an old story now, and there's naught can be proved concerning it; and what I think is this—I wouldn't wonder the poor lady was beguiled. But anyhow she surely thought she was his lawful wife; and though the law may hev found a flaw somewhere—and I take it 'twas so—yet sure I am she was an honourable lady. But where's the use of stirring that old sorrow? or how can ye prove aught? and the dead hold their peace, you know; dead mice, they say, feels no cold; and dead folks are past fooling. So don't you talk like that; for stone walls have ears, and ye might say that ye couldn't *un*say; and death's day is doom's day. So leave all in the keeping of God; and, above all, never lift hand when ye can't strike."

"Lift my hand! O, Mrs. Julaper, you couldn't think that; you little know me; I did not mean that; I never dreamed of hurting Sir Bale. Good heavens! Mrs. Julaper, you couldn't think that! It all comes of my poor impatient temper, and complaining as I do, and my misery; but O, Mrs. Julaper, you could not think I ever meant to trouble him by law, or any other annoyance! I'd like to see a stain removed from my family, and my name restored; but to touch his property, O, no!--O, no! that never entered my mind, by heaven! that never entered my mind, Mrs. Julaper. I'm not cruel; I'm not rapacious; I don't care for money; don't you know that, Mrs. Julaper? O, surely you won't think me capable of attacking the man whose bread I have eaten so long! I never dreamed of it; I should hate myself. Tell me you don't believe it; O, Mrs. Julaper, say you don't!"

And the gentle feeble creature burst into tears and good Mrs. Julaper comforted him with kind words; and he said,

"Thank you, ma'am; thank you. God knows I would not hurt Bale, nor give him one uneasy hour. It is only this: that I'm—I'm so miserable; and I'm only casting in my mind where to turn to, and what to do. So little a thing would be enough, and then I shall leave Mardykes. I'll go; not in any anger, Mrs. Julaper—don't think that; but I can't stay, I must be gone."

"Well, now, there's nothing yet, Master Philip, to fret you like that. You should not be talking so wild-like. Master Bale has his sharp word and his short temper now and again; but I'm sure he likes you. If he didn't, he'd a-said so to me long ago. I'm sure he likes you well."

"Hollo! I say, who's there? Where the devil's Mr. Feltram?" called the voice of the baronet, at a fierce pitch, along the passage.

"La! Mr. Feltram, it's him! Ye'd better run to him," whispered Mrs. Julaper.

"D—n me! does nobody hear? Mrs. Julaper! Hollo! ho! house, there! ho! D—n me, will nobody answer?"

And Sir Bale began to slap the wainscot fast and furiously with his walking-cane with a clatter like a harlequin's lath in a pantomime.

Mrs. Julaper, a little paler than usual, opened her door, and stood with the handle in her hand, making a little curtsey, enframed in the door-case; and Sir Bale, being in a fume, when he saw her, ceased whacking the panels of the corridor, and stamped on the floor, crying,

"Upon my soul, ma'am, I'm glad to see you! Perhaps you can tell me where Feltram is?"

"He is in my room, Sir Bale. Shall I tell him you want him, please?"

"Never mind; thanks," said the Baronet. "I've a tongue in my head;" marching down the passage to the housekeeper's room, with his cane clutched hard, glaring savagely, and with his teeth fast set, like a fellow advancing to beat a vicious horse that has chafed his temper.

CHAPTER VII

The Bank Note Sir Bale brushed by the housekeeper as he strode into her sanctuary, and there found Philip Feltram awaiting him dejectedly, but with no signs of agitation.

If one were to judge by the appearance the master of Mardykes presented, very grave surmises as to impending violence would have suggested themselves; but though he clutched his cane so hard that it quivered in his grasp, he had no notion of committing the outrage of a blow. The Baronet was unusually angry notwithstanding, and stopping short about three steps away, addressed Feltram with a pale face and gleaming eyes. It was quite plain that there was something very exciting upon his mind.

"I've been looking for you, Mr. Feltram; I want a word or two, if you have done your—your—whatever it is." He whisked the point of his stick towards the modest tea-tray. "I should like five minutes in the library."

The Baronet was all this time eyeing Feltram with a hard suspicious gaze, as if he expected to read in his face the shrinkings and trepidations of guilt; and then turning suddenly on his heel he led the way to his library—a good long march, with a good many turnings. He walked very fast, and was not long in getting there. And as Sir Bale reached the hearth, on which was smouldering a great log of wood, and turned about suddenly, facing the door, Philip Feltram entered.

The Baronet looked oddly and stern—so oddly, it seemed to Feltram, that he could not take his eyes off him, and returned his grim and somewhat embarrassed gaze with a stare of alarm and speculation.

And so doing, his step was shortened, and grew slow and slower, and came quite to a stop before he had got far from the door—a wide stretch of that wide floor still intervening between him and Sir Bale, who stood upon the hearthrug, with his heels together and his back to the fire, cane in hand, like a drill-sergeant, facing him.

"Shut that door, please; that will do; come nearer now. I don't want to bawl what I have to say. Now listen."

The Baronet cleared his voice and paused, with his eyes upon Feltram.

"It is only two or three days ago," said he, "that you said you wished you had a hundred pounds. Am I right?"

"Yes; I think so."

"*Think*? you know it, sir, devilish well. You said that you wished to get away. I have nothing particular to say against that, more especially now. Do you understand what I say?"

"Understand, Sir Bale? I do, sir—quite."

"I daresay quite" he repeated with an angry sneer. "Here, sir, is an odd coincidence: you want a hundred pounds, and you can't earn it, and you can't borrow it—there's another way, it seems—but I have got it—a Bank-of-England note of £100—locked up in that desk;" and he poked the end of his cane against the brass lock of it viciously. "There it is, and there are the papers you work at; and there are two keys—I've got one and you have the other—and devil another key in or out of the house has any one living. Well, do you begin to see? Don't mind. I don't want any d----d lying about it."

Feltram was indeed beginning to see that he was suspected of something very bad, but exactly what, he was not yet sure; and being a man of that unhappy temperament which shrinks from suspicion, as others do from detection, he looked very much put out indeed.

"Ha, ha! I think we do begin to see," said Sir Bale savagely. "It's a bore, I know, troubling a fellow with a story that he knows before; but I'll make mine short. When I take my key, intending to send the note to pay the crown and quit-rents that you know—you—you—no matter—you know well enough must be paid, I open it so—and so—and look *there*, where I left it, for my note; and the note's gone—you understand, the note's *gone*!"

Here was a pause, during which, under the Baronet's hard insulting eye, poor Feltram winced, and cleared his voice, and essayed to speak, but said nothing.

"It's gone, and we know where. Now, Mr. Feltram, *I* did not steal that note, and no one but you and I have access to this desk. You wish to go away, and I have no objection to that—but d—n me if you take away that note with you; and you may as well produce it now and here, as hereafter in a worse place."

"O, my good heaven!" exclaimed poor Feltram at last. "I'm very ill."

"So you are, of course. It takes a stiff emetic to get all that money off a fellow's stomach; and it's like parting with a tooth to give up a bank-note. Of course you're ill, but that's no sign of innocence, and I'm no fool. You had better give the thing up quietly."

"May my Maker strike me——"

"So He will, you d----d rascal, if there's justice in heaven, unless you produce the money. I don't want to hang you. I'm willing to let you off if you'll let me, but I'm cursed if I let my note off along with you; and unless you give it up forthwith, I'll get a warrant and have you searched, pockets, bag, and baggage."

"Lord! am I awake?" exclaimed Philip Feltram.

"Wide awake, and so am I," replied Sir Bale. "You don't happen to have got it about you?"

"God forbid, sir! O, Sir—O, Sir Bale—why, Bale, *Bale*, it's impossible! You *can't* believe it. When did I ever wrong you? You know me since I was not higher than the table, and—and——"

He burst into tears.

"Stop your snivelling, sir, and give up the note. You know devilish well I can't spare it; and I won't spare you if you put me to it. I've said my say."

Sir Bale signed towards the door; and like a somnambulist, with dilated gaze and pale as death, Philip Feltram, at his wit's end, went out of the room. It was not till he had again reached the housekeeper's door that he recollected in what direction he was going. His shut hand was pressed with all his force to his heart, and the first breath he was conscious of was a deep wild sob or two that quivered from his heart as he looked from the lobby-window upon a landscape which he did not see.

All he had ever suffered before was mild in comparison with this dire paroxysm. Now, for the first time, was he made acquainted with his real capacity for pain, and how near he might be to madness and yet retain intellect enough to weigh every scruple, and calculate every chance and consequence, in his torture.

Sir Bale, in the meantime, had walked out a little more excited than he would have allowed. He was still convinced that Feltram had stolen the note, but not quite so certain as he had been. There were things in his manner that confirmed, and others that perplexed, Sir Bale.

The Baronet stood upon the margin of the lake, almost under the evening shadow of the house, looking towards Snakes Island. There were two things about Mardykes he specially disliked.

One was Philip Feltram, who, right or wrong, he fancied knew more than was pleasant of his past life.

The other was the lake. It was a beautiful piece of water, his eye, educated at least in the excellences of landscape-painting, acknowledged. But although he could pull a good oar, and liked other lakes, to this particular sheet of water there lurked within him an insurmountable antipathy. It was engendered by a variety of associations.

There is a faculty in man that will acknowledge the unseen. He may scout and scare religion from him; but if he does, superstition perches near. His boding was made-up of omens, dreams, and such stuff as he most affected to despise, and there fluttered at his heart a presentiment and disgust.

His foot was on the gunwale of the boat, that was chained to its ring at the margin; but he would not have crossed that water in it for any reason that man could urge.

What was the mischief that sooner or later was to befall him from that lake, he could not define; but that some fatal danger lurked there, was the one idea concerning it that had possession of his fancy.

He was now looking along its still waters, towards the copse and rocks of Snakes Island, thinking of Philip Feltram; and the yellow level sunbeams touched his dark features, that bore a saturnine resemblance to those of Charles II, and marked sharply their firm grim lines, and left his deep-set eyes in shadow.

Who has the happy gift to seize the present, as a child does, and live in it? Who is not often looking far off for his happiness, as Sidney Smith says, like a man looking for his hat when it is upon his head? Sir Bale was brooding over his double hatred, of Feltram and of the lake. It would have been better had he struck down the raven that croaked upon his shoulder, and listened to the harmless birds that were whistling all round among the branches in the golden sunset.

CHAPTER VIII

Feltram's Plan This horror of the beautiful lake, which other people thought so lovely, was, in that mind which affected to scoff at the unseen, a distinct creation of downright superstition.

The nursery tales which had scared him in his childhood were founded on the tragedy of Snakes Island, and haunted him with an unavowed persistence still. Strange dreams untold had visited him, and a German conjuror, who had made some strangely successful vaticinations, had told him that his worst enemy would come up to him from a lake. He had heard very nearly the same thing from a fortune-teller in France; and once at Lucerne, when he was waiting alone in his room for the hour at which he had appointed to go upon the lake, all being quiet, there came to the window, which was open, a sunburnt, lean, wicked face. Its ragged owner leaned his arm on the window-frame, and with his head in the room, said in his patois, "Ho! waiting are you? You'll have enough of the lake one day. Don't you mind watching; they'll send when you're wanted;" and twisting his yellow face into a malicious distortion, he went on.

This thing had occurred so suddenly, and chimed-in so oddly with his thoughts, which were at that moment at distant Mardykes and the haunted lake, that it disconcerted him. He laughed, he looked out of the window. He would have given that fellow money to tell him why he said that. But there was no good in looking for the scamp; he was gone.

A memory not preoccupied with that lake and its omens, and a presentiment about himself, would not have noted such things. But *his* mind they touched indelibly; and he was ashamed of his childish slavery, but could not help it.

The foundation of all this had been laid in the nursery, in the winter's tales told by its fireside, and which seized upon his fancy and his fears with a strange congeniality.

There is a large bedroom at Mardykes Hall, which tradition assigns to the lady who had perished tragically in the lake. Mrs. Julaper was sure of it; for her aunt, who died a very old woman twenty years before, remembered the time of the lady's death, and when she grew to woman's estate had opportunity in abundance; for the old people who surrounded her could remember forty years farther back, and tell everything connected with the old house in beautiful Miss Feltram's time.

This large old-fashioned room, commanding a view of Snakes Island, the fells, and the lake—somewhat vast and gloomy, and furnished in a stately old fashion—was said to be haunted, especially when the wind blew from the direction of Golden Friars, the point from which it blew on the night of her death in the lake; or when the sky was overcast, and thunder rolled among the lofty fells, and lightning gleamed on the wide sheet of water.

It was on a night like this that a lady visitor, who long after that event occupied, in entire ignorance of its supernatural character, that large room; and being herself a lady of a picturesque turn, and loving the grander melodrama of Nature, bid her maid leave the shutters open, and watched the splendid effects from her bed, until, the storm being still distant, she fell asleep.

It was travelling slowly across the lake, and it was the deep mouthed clangour of its near approach that startled her, at dead of night, from her slumber, to witness the same phenomena in the tremendous loudness and brilliancy of their near approach.

At this magnificent spectacle she was looking with the awful ecstasy of an observer in whom the sense of danger is subordinated to that of the sublime, when she saw suddenly at the window a woman, whose long hair and dress seemed drenched with water. She was gazing in with a look of terror, and was shaking the sash of the window with vehemence. Having stood there for a few seconds, and before the lady, who beheld all this from her bed, could make up her mind what to do, the storm-beaten figure, wringing her hands, seemed to throw herself backward, and was gone.

Possessed with the idea that she had seen some poor woman overtaken in the storm, who, failing to procure admission there, had gone round to some of the many doors of the mansion, and obtained an entry there, she again fell asleep.

It was not till the morning, when she went to her window to look out upon the now tranquil scene, that she discovered what, being a stranger to the house, she had quite forgotten, that this room was at a great height—some thirty feet—from the ground.

Another story was that of good old Mr. Randal Rymer, who was often a visitor at the house in the late Lady Mardykes' day. In his youth he had been a campaigner; and now that he was a preacher he maintained his hardy habits, and always slept, summer and winter, with a bit of his window up. Being in that room in his bed, and after a short sleep lying awake, the moon shining softly through the window, there passed by that aperture into the room a figure dressed, it seemed to him, in gray that was nearly white. It passed straight to the hearth, where was an expiring wood fire; and cowering over it with outstretched hands, it appeared to be gathering what little heat was to be had. Mr. Rymer, amazed and awestruck, made a movement in his bed; and the figure looked round, with large eyes that in the moonlight looked like melting snow, and stretching its long arms up the chimney, they and the figure itself seemed to blend with the smoke, and so pass up and away.

Sir Bale, I have said, did not like Feltram. His father, Sir William, had left a letter creating a trust, it was said, in favour of Philip Feltram. The document had been found with the will, addressed to Sir Bale in the form of a letter.

"That is mine," said the Baronet, when it dropped out of the will; and he slipped it into his pocket, and no one ever saw it after.

But Mr. Charles Twyne, the attorney of Golden Friars, whenever he got drunk, which was pretty often, used to tell his friends with a grave wink that he knew a thing or two about that letter. It gave Philip Feltram two hundred a-year, charged on Harfax. It was only a direction. It made Sir Bale a trustee, however; and having made away with the "letter," the Baronet had been robbing Philip Feltram ever since.

Old Twyne was cautious, even in his cups, in his choice of an audience, and was a little enigmatical in his revelations. For he was afraid of Sir Bale, though he hated him for employing a lawyer who lived seven miles away, and was a rival. So people were not quite sure whether Mr. Twyne was telling lies or truth, and the principal fact that corroborated his story was Sir Bale's manifest hatred of his secretary. In fact, Sir Bale's retaining him in his house, detesting him as he seemed to do, was not easily to be accounted for, except on the principle of a tacit compromise—a miserable compensation for having robbed him of his rights.

The battle about the bank-note proceeded. Sir Bale certainly had doubts, and vacillated; for moral evidence made powerfully in favour of poor Feltram, though the evidence of circumstance made as powerfully against him. But Sir Bale admitted suspicion easily, and in weighing probabilities would count a virtue very lightly against temptation and opportunity; and whatever his doubts might sometimes be, he resisted and quenched them, and never let that ungrateful scoundrel Philip Feltram so much as suspect their existence.

For two days Sir Bale had not spoken to Feltram. He passed by on stair and passage, carrying his head high, and with a thundrous countenance, rolling conclusions and revenges in his soul.

Poor Feltram all this time existed in one long agony. He would have left Mardykes, were it not that he looked vaguely to some just power—to chance itself—against this hideous imputation. To go with this indictment ringing in his ears, would amount to a confession and flight.

Mrs. Julaper consoled him with might and main. She was a sympathetic and trusting spirit, and knew poor Philip Feltram, in her simplicity, better than the shrewdest profligate on earth could have known him. She cried with him in his misery. She was fired with indignation by these suspicions, and still more at what followed.

Sir Bale showed no signs of relenting. It might have been that he was rather glad of so unexceptionable an opportunity of getting rid of Feltram, who, people thought, knew something which it galled the Baronet's pride that he should know.

The Baronet had another shorter and sterner interview with Feltram in his study. The result was, that unless he restored the missing note before ten o'clock next morning, he should leave Mardykes.

To leave Mardykes was no more than Philip Feltram, feeble as he was of will, had already resolved. But what was to become of him? He did not very much care, if he could find any calling, however humble, that would just give him bread.

There was an old fellow and his wife (an ancient dame,) who lived at the other side of the lake, on the old territories of the Feltrams, and who, from some tradition of loyalty, perhaps, were fond of poor Philip Feltram. They lived somewhat high up on the fells—about as high as trees would grow—and those which were clumped about their rude dwelling were nearly the last you passed in your ascent of the mountain. These people had a multitude of sheep and goats, and lived in their airy solitude a pastoral and simple life, and were childless. Philip Feltram was hardy and active, having passed his early days among that arduous scenery. Cold and rain did not trouble him; and these people being wealthy in their way, and loving him, would be glad to find him employment of that desultory pastoral kind which would best suit him.

This vague idea was the only thing resembling a plan in his mind.

When Philip Feltram came to Mrs. Julaper's room, and told her that he had made up his mind to leave the house forthwith—to cross the lake to the Cloostedd side in Tom Marlin's boat, and then to make his way up the hill alone to Trebeck's lonely farmstead, Mrs. Julaper was overwhelmed.

"Ye'll do no such thing to-night, anyhow. You're not to go like that. Ye'll come into the small room here, where he can't follow; and we'll sit down and talk it over a bit, and ye'll find 'twill all come straight; and this will be no night, anyhow, for such a march. Why, man,'twould take an hour and more to cross the lake, and then a long uphill walk before ye could reach Trebeck's place; and if the night should fall while you were still on the mountain, ye might lose your life among the rocks. It can't be 'tis come to that yet; and the call was in the air, I'm told, all yesterday, and distant thunder to-day, travelling this way over Blarwyn Fells; and 'twill be a night no one will be out, much less on the mountain side."

CHAPTER IX

The Crazy Parson Mrs. Julaper had grown weather-wise, living for so long among this noble and solitary scenery, where people must observe Nature or else nothing—where signs of coming storm or change are almost local, and record themselves on particular cliffs and mountain-peaks, or in the mists, or in mirrored tints of the familiar lake, and are easily learned or remembered. At all events, her presage proved too true.

The sun had set an hour and more. It was dark; and an awful thunder-storm, whose march, like the distant reverberations of an invading army, had been faintly heard beyond the barriers of Blarwyn Fells throughout the afternoon, was near them now, and had burst in deep-mouthed battle among the ravines at the other side, and over the broad lake, that glared like a sheet of burnished steel under its flashes of dazzling blue. Wild and fitful blasts sweeping down the hollows and cloughs of the fells of Golden Friars agitated the lake, and bent the trees low, and whirled away their sere leaves in melancholy drift in their tremendous gusts. And from the window, looking on a scene enveloped in more than the darkness of the night, you saw in the pulsations of the lightning, before "the speedy gleams the darkness swallowed," the tossing trees and the flying foam and eddies on the lake.

In the midst of the hurlyburly, a loud and long knocking came at the hall-door of Mardykes. How long it had lasted before a chance lull made it audible I do not know.

There was nothing picturesquely poor, any more than there were evidences of wealth, anywhere in Sir Bale Mardykes' household. He had no lack of servants, but they were of an inexpensive and homely sort; and the hall-door being opened by the son of an old tenant on the estate—the tempest beating on the other side of the house, and comparative shelter under the gables at the front—he saw standing before him, in the agitated air, a thin old man, who muttering, it might be, a benediction, stepped into the hall, and displayed long silver tresses, just as the storm had blown them, ascetic and eager features, and a pair of large light eyes that wandered wildly. He was dressed in threadbare black; a pair of long leather gaiters, buckled high above his knee, protecting his thin shanks through moss and pool; and the singularity of his appearance was heightened by a wide-leafed felt hat, over which he had tied his handkerchief, so as to bring the leaf of it over his ears, and to secure it from being whirled from his head by the storm.

This odd and storm-beaten figure—tall, and a little stooping, as well as thin—was not unknown to the servant, who saluted him with something of fear as well as of respect as he bid him reverently welcome, and asked him to come in and sit by the fire.

"Get you to your master, and tell him I have a message to him from one he has not seen for two-and-forty years."

As the old man, with his harsh old voice, thus spoke, he unknotted his handkerchief and bet the rain-drops from his hat upon his knee.

The servant knocked at the library-door, where he found Sir Bale.

"Well, what's the matter?" cried Sir Bale sharply, from his chair before the fire, with angry eyes looking over his shoulder.

"Here's 't sir cumman, Sir Bale," he answered.

"Sir," or "the Sir," is still used as the clergyman's title in the Northumbrian counties.

"What sir?"

"Sir Hugh Creswell, if you please, Sir Bale."

"Ho!--mad Creswell?—O, the crazy parson. Well, tell Mrs. Julaper to let him have some supper—and—and to let him have a bed in some suitable place. That's what he wants. These mad fellows know what they are about."

"No, Sir Bale Mardykes, that is not what he wants," said the loud wild voice of the daft sir over the servant's shoulder. "Often has Mardykes Hall given me share of its cheer and its shelter and the warmth of its fire; and I bless the house that has been an inn to the wayfarer of the Lord. But to-night I go up the lake to Pindar's Bield, three miles on; and there I rest and refresh—not here."

"And why not *here*, Mr. Creswell?" asked the Baronet; for about this crazy old man, who preached in the fields, and appeared and disappeared so suddenly in the orbit of his wide and unknown perambulations of those northern and border counties, there was that sort of superstitious feeling which attaches to the mysterious and the good—an idea that it was lucky to harbour and dangerous to offend him. No one knew whence he came or whither he went. Once in a year, perhaps, he might appear at a lonely farmstead door among the fells, salute the house, enter, and be gone in the morning. His life was austere; his piety enthusiastic, severe, and tinged with the craze which inspired among the rustic population a sort of awe.

"I'll not sleep at Mardykes to-night; neither will I eat, nor drink, nor sit me down—no, nor so much as stretch my hands to the fire. As the man of God came out of Judah to king Jeroboam, so come I to you, sent by a vision, to bear a warning; and as he said, 'If thou wilt give me half thy house, I will not go in with thee, neither will I eat bread nor drink water in this place,' so also say I."

"Do as you please," said Sir Bale, a little sulkily. "Say your say; and you are welcome to stay or go, if go you will on so mad a night as this."

"Leave us," said Creswell, beckoning the servant back with his thin hands; "what I have to say is to your master."

The servant went, in obedience to a gesture from Sir Bale, and shut the door.

The old man drew nearer to the Baronet, and lowering his loud stern voice a little, and interrupting his discourse from time to time, to allow the near thunder-peals to subside, he said,

"Answer me, Sir Bale—what is this that has chanced between you and Philip Feltram?"

The Baronet, under the influence of that blunt and peremptory demand, told him shortly and sternly enough.

"And of all these facts you are sure, else ye would not blast your early companion and kinsman with the name of thief?"

"I *am* sure," said Sir Bale grimly.

"Unlock that cabinet," said the old man with the long white locks.

"I've no objection," said Sir Bale; and he did unlock an old oak cabinet that stood, carved in high relief with strange figures and gothic grotesques, against the wall, opposite the fireplace. On opening it there were displayed a system of little drawers and pigeon-holes such as we see in more modern escritoires.

"Open that drawer with the red mark of a seal upon it," continued Hugh Creswell, pointing to it with his lank finger.

Sir Bale did so; and to his momentary amazement, and even consternation, there lay the missing note, which now, with one of those sudden caprices of memory which depend on the laws of suggestion and association, he remembered having placed there with his own hand.

"That is it," said old Creswell with a pallid smile, and fixing his wild eyes on the Baronet. The smile subsided into a frown, and said he: "Last night I slept near Haworth Moss; and your father came to me in a dream, and said: 'My son Bale accuses Philip of having stolen a bank-note from his desk. He forgets that he himself placed it in his cabinet. Come with me.' I was, in the spirit, in this room; and he led me to this cabinet, which he opened; and in that drawer he showed me that note. 'Go,' said he, 'and tell him to ask Philip Feltram's pardon, else he will but go in weakness to return in power;' and he said that which it is not lawful to repeat. My message is told. Now a word from myself," he added sternly. "The dead, through my lips, has spoken, and under God's thunder and lightning his words have found ye. Why so uppish wi' Philip Feltram? See how ye threaped, and yet were wrong. He's no tazzle—he's no taggelt. Ask his pardon. Ye must change, or he will no taggelt. Go, in weakness, come in power: mark ye the words. 'Twill make a peal that will be heard in toon and desert, in the swirls o' the mountain, through pikes and valleys, and mak' a waaly man o' thee."

The old man with these words, uttered in the broad northern dialect of his common speech, strode from the room and shut the door. In another minute he was forth into the storm, pursuing what remained of his long march to Pindar's Bield.

"Upon my soul!" said Sir Bale, recovering from his sort of stun which the sudden and strange visit had left, "that's a cool old fellow! Come to rate me and teach me my own business in my own house!" and he rapped out a fierce oath. "Change his mind or no, here he sha'n't stay to-night—not an hour."

Sir Bale was in the lobby in a moment, and thundered to his servants:

"I say, put that fool out of the door—put him out by the shoulder, and never let him put his foot inside it more!"

But the old man's yea was yea, and his nay nay. He had quite meant what he said; and, as I related, was beyond the reach of the indignity of extrusion.

Sir Bale on his return shut his door as violently as if it were in the face of the old prophet.

"Ask Feltram's pardon, by Jove! For what? Why, any jury on earth would have hanged him on half the evidence; and I, like a fool, was going to let him off with his liberty and my hundred pound-note! Ask his pardon indeed!"

Still there were misgivings in his mind; a consciousness that he did owe explanation and apology to Feltram, and an insurmountable reluctance to undertake either. The old dislike—a contempt mingled with fear—not any fear of his malevolence, a fear only of his carelessness and folly; for, as I have said, Feltram knew many things, it was believed, of the Baronet's Continental and Asiatic life, and had even gently remonstrated with him upon the dangers into which he was running. A simple fellow like Philip Feltram is a dangerous depository of a secret. This Baronet was proud, too; and the mere possession of his secrets by Feltram was an involuntary insult, which Sir Bale could not forgive. He wished him far away; and except for the recovery of his bank-note, which he could ill spare, he was sorry that this suspicion was cleared up.

The thunder and storm were unabated; it seemed indeed that they were growing wilder and more awful.

He opened the window-shutter and looked out upon that sublimest of scenes; and so intense and magnificent were its phenomena, that Sir Bale, for a while, was absorbed in this contemplation.

When he turned about, the sight of his £100 note, still between his finger and thumb, made him smile grimly.

The more he thought of it, the clearer it was that he could not leave matters exactly as they were. Well, what should he do? He would send for Mrs. Julaper, and tell her vaguely that he had changed his mind about Feltram, and that he might continue to stay at Mardykes Hall as usual. That would suffice. She could speak to Feltram.

He sent for her; and soon, in the lulls of the great uproar without, he could hear the jingle of Mrs. Julaper's keys and her light tread upon the lobby.

"Mrs. Julaper," said the Baronet, in his dry careless way, "Feltram may remain; your eloquence has prevailed. What have you been crying about?" he asked, observing that his housekeeper's usually cheerful face was, in her own phrase, 'all cried.'

"It is too late, sir; he's gone."

"And when did he go?" asked Sir Bale, a little put out. "He chose an odd evening, didn't he? So like him!"

"He went about half an hour ago; and I'm very sorry, sir; it's a sore sight to see the poor lad going from the place he was reared in, and a hard thing, sir; and on such a night, above all."

"No one asked him to go to-night. Where is he gone to?"

"I don't know, I'm sure; he left my room, sir, when I was upstairs; and Janet saw him pass the window not ten minutes after Mr. Creswell left the house."

"Well, then, there's no good, Mrs. Julaper, in thinking more about it; he has settled the matter his own way; and as he so ordains it—amen, say I. Goodnight."

CHAPTER X

Adventure in Tom Marlin's Boat Philip Feltram was liked very well—a gentle, kindly, and very timid creature, and, before he became so heart-broken, a fellow who liked a joke or a pleasant story, and could laugh heartily. Where will Sir Bale find so unresisting and respectful a butt and retainer? and whom will he bully now?

Something like remorse was worrying Sir Bale's heart a little; and the more he thought on the strange visit of Hugh Creswell that night, with its unexplained menace, the more uneasy he became.

The storm continued; and even to him there seemed something exaggerated and inhuman in the severity of his expulsion on such a night. It was his own doing, it was true; but would people believe that? and would he have thought of leaving Mardykes at all if it had not been for his kinsman's severity? Nay, was it not certain that if Sir Bale had done as Hugh Creswell had urged him, and sent for Feltram forthwith, and told him how all had been cleared up, and been a little friendly with him, he would have found him still in the house?—for he had not yet gone for ten minutes after Creswell's departure, and thus, all that was to follow might have been averted. But it was too late now, and Sir Bale would let the affair take its own course.

Below him, outside the window at which he stood ruminating, he heard voices mingling with the storm. He could with tolerable certainty perceive, looking into the obscurity, that there were three men passing close under it, carrying some very heavy burden among them.

He did not know what these three black figures in the obscurity were about. He saw them pass round the corner of the building toward the front, and in the lulls of the storm could hear their gruff voices talking.

We have all experienced what a presentiment is, and we all know with what an intuition the faculty of observation is sometimes heightened. It was such an apprehension as sometimes gives its peculiar horror to a dream—a sort of knowledge that what those people were about was in a dreadful way connected with his own fate.

He watched for a time, thinking that they might return; but they did not. He was in a state of uncomfortable suspense.

"If they want me, they won't have much trouble in finding me, nor any scruple, egad, in plaguing me; they never have."

Sir Bale returned to his letters, a score of which he was that night getting off his conscience—an arrear which would not have troubled him had he not ceased, for two or three days, altogether to employ Philip Feltram, who had been accustomed to take all that sort of drudgery off his hands.

All the time he was writing now he had a feeling that the shadows he had seen pass under his window were machinating some trouble for him, and an uneasy suspense made him lift his eyes now and then to the door, fancying sounds and footsteps; and after a resultless wait he would say to himself, "If any one is coming, why the devil don't he come?" and then he would apply himself again to his letters.

But on a sudden he heard good Mrs. Julaper's step trotting along the lobby, and the tiny ringing of her keys.

Here was news coming; and the Baronet stood up looking at the door, on which presently came a hurried rapping; and before he had answered, in the midst of a long thunder-clap that suddenly broke, rattling over the house, the good woman opened the door in great agitation, and cried with a tremulous uplifting of her hands.

"O, Sir Bale! O, la, sir! here's poor dear Philip Feltram come home dead!"

Sir Bale stared at her sternly for some seconds.

"Gome, now, do be distinct," said Sir Bale; "what has happened?"

"He's lying on the sofer in the old still-room. You never saw—my God!--O, sir—what is life?"

"D—n it, can't you cry by-and-by, and tell me what's the matter now?"

"A bit o' fire there, as luck would have it; but what is hot or cold now? La, sir, they're all doin' what they can; he's drowned, sir, and Tom Warren is on the gallop down to Golden Friars for Doctor Torvey."

"*Is* he drowned, or is it only a ducking? Come, bring me to the place. Dead men don't usually want a fire, or consult doctors. I'll see for myself."

So Sir Bale Mardykes, pale and grim, accompanied by the light-footed Mrs. Julaper, strode along the passages, and was led by her into the old still-room, which had ceased to be used for its original purpose. All the servants in the house were now collected there, and three men also who lived by the margin of the lake; one of them thoroughly drenched, with rivulets of water still trickling from his sleeves, water along the wrinkles and pockets of his waistcoat and from the feet of his trousers, and pumping and oozing from his shoes, and streaming from his hair down the channels of his cheeks like a continuous rain of tears.

The people drew back a little as Sir Bale entered with a quick step and a sharp pallid frown on his face. There was a silence as he stooped over Philip Feltram, who lay on a low bed next the wall, dimly lighted by two or three candles here and there about the room.

He laid his hand, for a moment, on his cold wet breast.

Sir Bale knew what should be done in order to give a man in such a case his last chance for life. Everybody was speedily put in motion. Philip's drenched clothes were removed, hot blankets enveloped him, warming-pans and hot bricks lent their aid; he was placed at the prescribed angle, so that the water flowed freely from his mouth. The old expedient for inducing artificial breathing was employed, and a lusty pair of bellows did duty for his lungs.

But these helps to life, and suggestions to nature, availed not. Forlorn and peaceful lay the features of poor Philip Feltram; cold and dull to the touch; no breath through the blue lips; no sight in the fish-like eyes; pulseless and cold in the midst of all the hot bricks and warming-pans about him.

CHAPTER X

At length, everything having been tried, Sir Bale, who had been directing, placed his hand within the clothes, and laid it silently on Philip's shoulder and over his heart; and after a little wait, he shook his head, and looking down on his sunken face, he said,

"I am afraid he's gone. Yes, he's gone, poor fellow! And bear you this in mind, all of you; Mrs. Julaper there can tell you more about it. She knows that it was certainly in no compliance with my wish that he left the house to-night: it was his own obstinate perversity, and perhaps—I forgive him for it—a wish in his unreasonable resentment to throw some blame upon this house, as having refused him shelter on such a night; than which imputation nothing can be more utterly false. Mrs. Julaper there knows how welcome he was to stay the night; but he would not; he had made up his mind, it seems, without telling any person. Had he told you, Mrs. Julaper?"

"No, sir," sobbed Mrs. Julaper from the centre of a pocket-handkerchief in which her face was buried.

"Not a human being: an angry whim of his own. Poor Feltram! and here's the result," said the Baronet. "We have done our best—done everything. I don't think the doctor, when he comes, will say that anything has been omitted; but all won't do. Does any one here know how it happened?"

Two men knew very well—the man who had been ducked, and his companion, a younger man, who was also in the still-room, and had lent a hand in carrying Feltram up to the house.

Tom Marlin had a queer old stone tenement by the edge of the lake just under Mardykes Hall. Some people said it was the stump of an old tower that had once belonged to Mardykes Castle, of which in the modern building scarcely a relic was discoverable.

This Tom Marlin had an ancient right of fishing in the lake, where he caught pike enough for all Golden Friars; and keeping a couple of boats, he made money beside by ferrying passengers over now and then. This fellow, with a furrowed face and shaggy eyebrows, bald at top, but with long grizzled locks falling upon his shoulders, said,

"He wer wi' me this mornin', sayin' he'd want t' boat to cross the lake in, but he didn't say what hour; and when it came on to thunder and blow like this, ye guess I did not look to see him to-night. Well, my wife was just lightin' a pig-tail—tho' light enough and to spare there was in the lift already—when who should come clatterin' at the latch-pin in the blow o' thunder and wind but Philip, poor lad, himself; and an ill hour for him it was. He's been some time in ill fettle, though he was never frowsy, not he, but always kind and dooce, and canty once, like anither; and he asked me to tak the boat across the lake at once to the Clough o' Cloostedd at t'other side. The woman took the pet and wodn't hear o't; and, 'Dall me, if I go to-night,' quoth I. But he would not be put off so, not he; and dingdrive he went to it, cryin' and putrein' ye'd a-said, poor fellow, he was wrang i' his garrets a'most. So at long last I bethought me, there's nout o' a sea to the north o' Snakes Island, so I'll pull him by that side—for the storm is blowin' right up by

Golden Friars, ye mind—and when we get near the point, thinks I, he'll see wi' his een how the lake is, and gie it up. For I liked him, poor lad; and seein' he'd set his heart on't, I wouldn't vex nor frump him wi' a no. So down we three—myself, and Bill there, and Philip Feltram—come to the boat; and we pulled out, keeping Snakes Island atwixt us and the wind. 'Twas smooth water wi' us, for 'twas a scug there, but white enough was all beyont the point; and passing the finger-stone, not forty fathom from thc shorc o' thc island, Bill and me pullin' and he sittin' in the stern, poor lad, up he rises, a bit rabblin' to himself, wi' his hands lifted so.

"'Look a-head!' says I, thinkin' something wos comin' atort us.

"But 'twasn't that. The boat was quiet, for while we looked, oo'er our shouthers, oo'er her bows, we didn't pull, so she lay still; and lookin' back again on Philip, he was rabblin' on all the same.

"'It's nobbut a prass wi' himsel", poor lad,' thinks I.

"But that wasn't it neither; for I sid something white come out o' t' water, by the gunwale, like a hand. By Jen! and he leans oo'er and tuk it; and he sagged like, and so it drew him in, under the mere, before I cud du nout. There was nout to thraa tu him, and no time; down he went, and I followed; and thrice I dived before I found him, and brought him up by the hair at last; and there he is, poor lad! and all one if he lay at the bottom o' t' mere."

As Tom Marlin ended his narrative—often interrupted by the noise of the tempest without, and the peals of thunder that echoed awfully above, like the chorus of a melancholy ballad—the sudden clang of the hall-door bell, and a more faintly-heard knocking, announced a new arrival.

CHAPTER XI

Sir Bale's Dream It was Doctor Torvey who entered the old still-room now, buttoned-up to the chin in his greatcoat, and with a muffler of many colours wrapped partly over that feature.

"Well!--hey? So poor Feltram's had an accident?"

The Doctor was addressing Sir Bale, and getting to the bedside as he pulled off his gloves.

"I see you've been keeping him warm—that's right; and a considerable flow of water from his mouth; turn him a little that way. Hey? O, ho!" said the Doctor, as he placed his hand upon Philip, and gently stirred his limbs. "It's more than an hour since this happened. I'm afraid there's very little to be done now;" and in a lower tone, with his hand on poor Philip Feltram's arm, and so down to his fingers, he said in Sir Bale Mardykes' ear, with a shake of his head,

"Here, you see, poor fellow, here's the cadaveric stiffness; it's very melancholy, but it's all over, he's gone; there's no good trying any more. Come here, Mrs. Julaper. Did you ever see any one dead? Look at his eyes, look at his mouth. You ought to have known that, with half an eye. And you know," he added again confidentially in Sir Bale's ear, "trying any more *now* is all my eye."

CHAPTER XI

Then after a few more words with the Baronet, and having heard his narrative, he said from time to time, "Quite right; nothing could be better; capital practice, sir," and so forth. And at the close of all this, amid the sobs of kind Mrs. Julaper and the general whimpering of the humbler handmaids, the Doctor standing by the bed, with his knuckles on the coverlet, and a glance now and then on the dead face beside him, said—by way of 'quieting men's minds,' as the old tract-writers used to say—a few words to the following effect:

"Everything has been done here that the most experienced physician could have wished. Everything has been done in the best way. I don't know anything that has not been done, in fact. If I had been here myself, I don't know—hot bricks—salt isn't a bad thing. I don't know, I say, that anything of any consequence has been omitted." And looking at the body, "You see," and he drew the fingers a little this way and that, letting them return, as they stiffly did, to their former attitude, "you may be sure that the poor gentleman was quite dead by the time he arrived here. So, since he was laid there, nothing has been lost by delay. And, Sir Bale, if you have any directions to send to Golden Friars, sir, I shall be most happy to undertake your message."

"Nothing, thanks; it is a melancholy ending, poor fellow! You must come to the study with me, Doctor Torvey, and talk a little bit more; and—very sad, doctor—and you must have a glass of sherry, or some port—the port used not to be bad here; I don't take it—but very melancholy it is—bring some port and sherry; and, Mrs. Julaper, you'll be good enough to see that everything that should be done here is looked to; and let Marlin and the men have supper and something to drink. You have been too long in your wet clothes, Marlin."

So, with gracious words all round, he led the Doctor to the library where he had been sitting, and was affable and hospitable, and told him his own version of all that had passed between him and Philip Feltram, and presented himself in an amiable point of view, and pleased the Doctor with his port and flatteries—for he could not afford to lose anyone's good word just now; and the Doctor was a bit of a gossip, and in most houses in that region, in one character or another, every three months in the year.

So in due time the Doctor drove back to Golden Friars, with a high opinion of Sir Bale, and higher still of his port, and highest of all of himself: in the best possible humour with the world, not minding the storm that blew in his face, and which he defied in good-humoured mock-heroics spoken in somewhat thick accents, and regarding the thunder and lightning as a lively gala of fireworks; and if there had been a chance of finding his cronies still in the George and Dragon, he would have been among them forthwith, to relate the tragedy of the night, and tell what a good fellow, after all, Sir Bale was; and what a fool, at best, poor Philip Feltram.

But the George was quiet for that night. The thunder rolled over voiceless chambers; and the lights had been put out within the windows, on whose multitudinous small panes the lightning glared. So the Doctor went home to Mrs. Torvey, whom he charmed into good-humoured curiosity by the tale of wonder he had to relate.

Sir Bale's qualms were symptomatic of something a little less sublime and more selfish than conscience. He was not sorry that Philip Feltram was out of the way. His lips might begin to babble inconveniently at any time, and why should not his mouth be stopped? and what stopper so effectual as that plug of clay which fate had introduced? But he did not want to be charged with the odium of the catastrophe. Every man cares something for the opinion of his fellows. And seeing that Feltram had been well liked, and that his death had excited a vehement commiseration, Sir Bale did not wish it to be said that he had made the house too hot to hold him, and had so driven him to extremity.

Sir Bale's first agitation had subsided. It was now late, he had written many letters, and he was tired. It was not wonderful, then, that having turned his lounging-chair to the fire, he should have fallen asleep in it, as at last he did.

The storm was passing gradually away by this time. The thunder was now echoing among the distant glens and gorges of Daulness Fells, and the angry roar and gusts of the tempest were subsiding into the melancholy soughing and piping that soothe like a lullaby.

Sir Bale therefore had his unpremeditated sleep very comfortably, except that his head was hanging a little uneasily; which, perhaps, helped him to this dream.

It was one of those dreams in which the continuity of the waking state that immediately preceded it seems unbroken; for he thought that he was sitting in the chair which he occupied, and in the room where he actually was. It seemed to him that he got up, took a candle in his hand, and went through the passages to the old still-room where Philip Feltram lay. The house seemed perfectly still. He could hear the chirp of the crickets faintly from the distant kitchen, and the tick of the clock sounded loud and hollow along the passage. In the old still-room, as he opened the door, was no light, except what was admitted from the candle he carried. He found the body of poor Philip Feltram just as he had left it—his gentle face, saddened by the touch of death, was turned upwards, with white lips: with traces of suffering fixed in its outlines, such as caused Sir Bale, standing by the bed, to draw the coverlet over the dead man's features, which seemed silently to upbraid him. "Gone in weakness!" said Sir Bale, repeating the words of the "daft sir," Hugh Creswell; as he did so, a voice whispered near him, with a great sigh, "Come in power!" He looked round, in his dream, but there was no one; the light seemed to fail, and a horror slowly overcame him, especially as he thought he saw the figure under the coverlet stealthily beginning to move. Backing towards the door, for he could not take his eyes off it, he saw something like a huge black ape creep out at the foot of the bed; and springing at him, it griped him by the throat, so that he could not breathe; and a thousand voices were instantly round him, holloaing, cursing, laughing in his ears; and in this direful plight he waked.

Was it the ring of those voices still in his ears, or a real shriek, and another, and a long peal, shriek after shriek, swelling madly through the distant passages, that held him still, freezing in the horror of his dream?

I will tell you what this noise was.

CHAPTER XII

Marcella Bligh and Judith Wale Keep Watch After his bottle of port with Sir Bale, the Doctor had gone down again to the room where poor Philip Feltram lay.

Mrs. Julaper had dried her eyes, and was busy by this time; and two old women were making all their arrangements for a night-watch by the body, which they had washed, and, as their phrase goes, 'laid out' in the humble bed where it had lain while there was still a hope that a spark sufficient to rekindle the fire of life might remain. These old women had points of resemblance: they were lean, sallow, and wonderfully wrinkled, and looked each malign and ugly enough for a witch.

Marcella Bligh's thin hooked nose was now like the beak of a bird of prey over the face of the drowned man, upon whose eyelids she was placing penny-pieces, to keep them from opening; and her one eye was fixed on her work, its sightless companion showing white in its socket, with an ugly leer.

Judith Wale was lifting the pail of hot water with which they had just washed the body. She had long lean arms, a hunched back, a great sharp chin sunk on her hollow breast, and small eyes restless as a ferret's; and she clattered about in great bowls of shoes, old and clouted, that were made for a foot as big as two of hers.

The Doctor knew these two old women, who were often employed in such dismal offices.

"How does Mrs. Bligh? See me with half an eye? Hey—that's rhyme, isn't it?—And, Judy lass—why, I thought you lived nearer the town—here making poor Mr. Feltram's last toilet. You have helped to dress many a poor fellow for his last journey. Not a bad notion of drill either—they stand at attention stiff and straight enough in the sentry-box. Your recruits do you credit, Mrs. Wale."

The Doctor stood at the foot of the bed to inspect, breathing forth a vapour of very fine old port, his hands in his pockets, speaking with a lazy thickness, and looking so comfortable and facetious, that Mrs. Julaper would have liked to turn him out of the room.

But the Doctor was not unkind, only extremely comfortable. He was a good-natured fellow, and had thought and care for the living, but not a great deal of sentiment for the dead, whom he had looked in the face too often to be much disturbed by the spectacle.

"You'll have to keep that bandage on. You should be sharp; you should know all about it, girl, by this time, and not let those muscles stiffen. I need not tell you the mouth shuts as easily as this snuff-box, if you only take it in time.—I suppose, Mrs. Julaper, you'll send to Jos Fringer for the poor fellow's outfit. Fringer is a very proper man—there ain't a properer und-aker in England. I always re-mmend Fringer—in Church-street in Golden Friars. You know Fringer, I daresay."

"I can't say, sir, I'm sure. That will be as Sir Bale may please to direct," answered Mrs. Julaper.

"You've got him very straight—straighter than I thought you could; but the large joints were not so stiff. A very little longer wait, and you'd hardly have got him into his coffin. He'll want a vr-r-ry long one, poor lad. Short cake is life, ma'am. Sad thing this. They'll open their eyes, I promise you, down in the town. 'Twill be cool enough, I'd shay, affre all th-thunr-thunnle, you know. I think I'll take a nip, Mrs. Jool-fr, if you wouldn't mine makin' me out a thimmle-ful bran-band-bran-rand-andy, eh, Mishs Joolfr?"

And the Doctor took a chair by the fire; and Mrs. Julaper, with a dubious conscience and dry hospitality, procured the brandy-flask and wine-glass, and helped the physician in a thin hesitating stream, which left him ample opportunity to cry "Hold—enough!" had he been so minded. But that able physician had no confidence, it would seem, in any dose under a bumper, which he sipped with commendation, and then fell asleep with the firelight on his face—to tender-hearted Mrs. Julaper's disgust—and snored with a sensual disregard of the solemnity of his situation; until with a profound nod, or rather dive, toward the fire, he awoke, got up and shook his ears with a kind of start, and standing with his back to the fire, asked for his muffler and horse; and so took his leave also of the weird sisters, who were still pottering about the body, with croak and whisper, and nod and ogle. He took his leave also of good Mrs. Julaper, who was completing arrangements with teapot and kettle, spiced elderberry wine, and other comforts, to support them through their proposed vigil. And finally, in a sort of way, he took his leave of the body, with a long business-like stare, from the foot of the bed, with his short hands stuffed into his pockets. And so, to Mrs. Julaper's relief, this unseemly doctor, speaking thickly, departed.

And now, the Doctor being gone, and all things prepared for the 'wake' to be observed by withered Mrs. Bligh of the one eye, and yellow Mrs. Wale of the crooked back, the house grew gradually still. The thunder had by this time died into the solid boom of distant battle, and the fury of the gale had subsided to the long sobbing wail that is charged with so eerie a melancholy. Within all was stirless, and the two old women, each a 'Mrs.' by courtesy, who had not much to thank Nature or the world for, sad and cynical, and in a sort outcasts told off by fortune to these sad and grizzly services, sat themselves down by the fire, each perhaps feeling unusually at home in the other's society; and in this soured and forlorn comfort, trimming their fire, quickening the song of the kettle to a boil, and waxing polite and chatty; each treating the other with that deprecatory and formal courtesy which invites a return in kind, and both growing strangely happy in this little world of their own, in the unusual and momentary sense of an importance and consideration which were delightful.

The old still-room of Mardykes Hall is an oblong room wainscoted. From the door you look its full length to the wide stone-shafted Tudor window at the other end. At your left is the ponderous mantelpiece, supported by two spiral stone pillars; and close to the door at the right was the bed in which the two crones had just stretched poor Philip Feltram, who lay as still as an uncoloured wax-work, with a heavy penny-piece on each eye, and a bandage under his jaw, making his mouth look stern. And the two old ladies over their tea by the fire conversed agreeably, compared their rheumatisms and other ailments wordily, and talked of old times, and early recollections, and of sick-beds they had attended, and corpses that "you would not know, so pined and windered" were they; and others so fresh and canny, you'd say the dead had never looked so bonny in life.

Then they began to talk of people who grew tall in their coffins, of others who had been buried alive, and of others who walked after death. Stories as true as holy writ.

"Were you ever down by Hawarth, Mrs. Bligh—hard by Dalworth Moss?" asked crook-backed Mrs. Wale, holding her spoon suspended over her cup.

"Neea whaar sooa far south, Mrs. Wale, ma'am; but ma father was off times down thar cuttin' peat."

"Ah, then ye'll not a kenned farmer Dykes that lived by the Lin-tree Scaur. 'Tweer I that laid him out, poor aad fellow, and a dow man he was when aught went cross wi' him; and he cursed and sweared, twad gar ye dodder to hear him. They said he was a hard man wi' some folk; but he kep a good house, and liked to see plenty, and many a time when I was swaimous about my food, he'd clap t' meat on ma plate, and mak' me eat ma fill. Na, na—there was good as well as bad in farmer Dykes. It was a year after he deed, and Tom Ettles was walking home, down by the Birken Stoop one night, and not a soul nigh, when he sees a big ball, as high as his knee, whirlin' and spangin' away before him on the road. What it wer he could not think; but he never consayted there was a freet or a bo therea-way; so he kep near it, watching every spang and turn it took, till it ran into the gripe by the roadside. There was a gravel pit just there, and Tom Ettles wished to take another gliff at it before he went on. But when he keeked into the pit, what should he see but a man attoppa a horse that could not get up or on: and says he, 'I think ye be at a dead-lift there, gaffer.' And wi' the word, up looks the man, and who sud it be but farmer Dykes himsel; and Tom Ettles saw him plain eneugh, and kenned the horse too for Black Captain, the farmer's aad beast, that broke his leg and was shot two years and more before the farmer died. 'Ay,' says farmer Dykes, lookin' very bad; 'forsett-and-backsett, ye'll tak me oot, Tom Ettles, and clap ye doun behint me quick, or I'll claw ho'd o' thee.' Tom felt his hair risin' stiff on his heed, and his tongue so fast to the roof o' his mouth he could scarce get oot a word; but says he, 'If Black Jack can't do it o' noo, he'll ne'er do't and carry double.' 'I ken my ain business best,' says Dykes. 'If ye gar me gie ye a look, 'twill gie ye the creepin's while ye live; so git ye doun, Tom;' and with that the dobby lifts its neaf, and Tom saw there was a red light round horse and man, like the glow of a peat fire. And says Tom, 'In the name o' God, ye'll let me pass;' and with the word the gooast draws itsel' doun, all a-creaked, like a man wi' a sudden pain; and Tom Ettles took to his heels more deed than alive."

They had approached their heads, and the story had sunk to that mysterious murmur that thrills the listener, when in the brief silence that followed they heard a low odd laugh near the door.

In that direction each lady looked aghast, and saw Feltram sitting straight up in the bed, with the white bandage in his hand, and as it seemed, for one foot was below the coverlet, near the floor, about to glide forth.

Mrs. Bligh, uttering a hideous shriek, clutched Mrs. Wale, and Mrs. Wale, with a scream as dreadful, gripped Mrs. Bligh; and quite forgetting their somewhat formal politeness, they reeled and tugged, wrestling towards the window, each struggling to place her companion between her and the 'dobby,' and both uniting in a direful peal of yells.

This was the uproar which had startled Sir Bale from his dream, and was now startling the servants from theirs.

CHAPTER XIII

The Mist on the Mountain Doctor Torvey was sent for early next morning, and came full of wonder, learning and scepticism. Seeing is believing, however; and there was Philip Feltram living, and soon to be, in all bodily functions, just as usual.

"Upon my soul, Sir Bale, I couldn't have believed it, if I had not seen it with my eyes," said the Doctor impressively, while sipping a glass of sherry in the 'breakfast parlour,' as the great panelled and pictured room next the dining-room was called. "I don't think there is any similar case on record—no pulse, no more than the poker; no respiration, by Jove, no more than the chimney-piece; as cold as a lead image in the garden there. Well, you'll say all that might possibly be fallacious; but what will you say to the cadaveric stiffness? Old Judy Wale can tell you; and my friend Marcella—Monocula would be nearer the mark—Mrs. Bligh, she knows all those common, and I may say up to this, infallible, signs of death, as well as I do. There is no mystery about them; they'll depose to the literality of the symptoms. You heard how they gave tongue. Upon my honour, I'll send the whole case up to my old chief, Sir Hervey Hansard, to London. You'll hear what a noise it will make among the profession. There never was—and it ain't too much to say there never *will* be—another case like it."

During this lecture, and a great deal more, Sir Bale leaned back in his chair, with his legs extended, his heels on the ground, and his arms folded, looking sourly up in the face of a tall lady in white satin, in a ruff, and with a bird on her hand, who smiled down superciliously from her frame on the Baronet. Sir Bale seemed a little bit high and dry with the Doctor.

"You physicians are unquestionably," he said, "a very learned profession."

The Doctor bowed.

"But there's just one thing you know nothing about——"

"Eh? What's that?" inquired Doctor Torvey.

"Medicine," answered Sir Bale. "I was aware you never knew what was the matter with a sick man; but I didn't know, till now, that you couldn't tell when he was dead."

"Ha, ha!--well—ha, ha!--*yes*—well, you see, you—ha, ha!--you certainly have me there. But it's a case without a parallel—it is, upon my honour. You'll find it will not only be talked about, but written about; and, whatever papers appear upon it, will come to me; and I'll take care, Sir Bale, you shall have an opportunity of reading them."

"Of which I shan't avail myself," answered Sir Bale. "Take another glass of sherry, Doctor."

The Doctor made his acknowledgments and filled his glass, and looked through the wine between him and the window.

"Ha, ha!--see there, your port, Sir Bale, gives a fellow such habits—looking for the beeswing, by Jove. It isn't easy, in one sense at least, to get your port out of a fellow's head when once he has tasted it."

But if the honest Doctor meant a hint for a glass of that admirable bin, it fell pointless; and Sir Bale had no notion of making another libation of that precious fluid in honour of Doctor Torvey.

"And I take it for granted," said Sir Bale, "that Feltram will do very well; and, should anything go wrong, I can send for you—unless he should die again; and in that case I think I shall take my own opinion."

So he and the Doctor parted.

Sir Bale, although he did not consult the Doctor on his own case, was not particularly well. "That lonely place, those frightful mountains, and that damp black lake"—which features in the landscape he cursed all round—"are enough to give any man blue devils; and when a fellow's spirits go, he's all gone. That's why I'm dyspeptic—that and those d----d debts—and the post, with its flight of croaking and screeching letters from London. I wish there was no post here. I wish it was like Sir Amyrald's time, when they shot the York mercer that came to dun him, and no one ever took anyone to task about it; and now they can pelt you at any distance they please through the post; and fellows lose their spirits and their appetite and any sort of miserable comfort that is possible in this odious abyss."

Was there gout in Sir Bale's case, or 'vapours'? I know not what the faculty would have called it; but Sir Bale's mode of treatment was simply to work off the attack by long and laborious walking.

This evening his walk was upon the Fells of Golden Friars—long after the landscape below was in the eclipse of twilight, the broad bare sides and angles of these gigantic uplands were still lighted by the misty western sun.

There is no such sense of solitude as that which we experience upon the silent and vast elevations of great mountains. Lifted high above the level of human sounds and habitations, among the wild expanses and colossal features of Nature, we are thrilled in our loneliness with a strange fear and elation—an ascent above the reach of life's vexations or companionship, and the tremblings of a wild and undefined misgiving. The filmy disc of the moon had risen in the east, and was already faintly silvering the shadowy scenery below, while yet Sir Bale stood in the mellow light of the western sun, which still touched also the summits of the opposite peaks of Morvyn Fells.

Sir Bale Mardykes did not, as a stranger might, in prudence, hasten his descent from the heights at which he stood while yet a gleam of daylight remained to him. For he was, from his boyhood, familiar with those solitary regions; and, beside this, the thin circle of the moon, hung in the eastern sky, would brighten as the sunlight sank, and hang like a lamp above his steps.

There was in the bronzed and resolute face of the Baronet, lighted now in the parting beams of sunset, a resemblance to that of Charles the Second—not our "merry" ideal, but the more energetic and saturnine face which the portraits have preserved to us.

He stood with folded arms on the side of the slope, admiring, in spite of his prejudice, the unusual effects of a view so strangely lighted—the sunset tints on the opposite peaks, lost in the misty twilight, now deepening lower down into a darker shade, through which the outlines of the stone gables and tower of Golden Friars and the light of fire or candle in their windows were dimly visible.

As he stood and looked, his more distant sunset went down, and sudden twilight was upon him, and he began to remember the beautiful Homeric picture of a landscape coming out, rock and headland, in the moonlight.

There had hung upon the higher summits, at his right, a heavy fold of white cloud, which on a sudden broke, and, like the smoke of artillery, came rolling down the slopes toward him. Its principal volume, however, unfolded itself in a mighty flood down the side of the mountain towards the lake; and that which spread towards and soon enveloped the ground on which he stood was by no means so dense a fog. A thick mist enough it was; but still, to a distance of twenty or thirty yards, he could discern the outline of a rock or scaur, but not beyond it.

There are few sensations more intimidating than that of being thus enveloped on a lonely mountain-side, which, like this one, here and there breaks into precipice.

There is another sensation, too, which affects the imagination. Overtaken thus on the solitary expanse, there comes a new chill and tremour as this treacherous medium surrounds us, through which unperceived those shapes which fancy conjures up might approach so near and bar our path.

From the risk of being reduced to an actual standstill he knew he was exempt. The point from which the wind blew, light as it was, assured him of that. Still the mist was thick enough seriously to embarrass him. It had overtaken him as he was looking down upon the lake; and he now looked to his left, to try whether in that direction it was too thick to permit a view of the nearest landmarks. Through this white film he saw a figure standing only about five-and-twenty steps away, looking down, as it seemed, in precisely the same direction as he, quite motionless, and standing like a shadow projected upon the smoky vapour. It was the figure of a slight tall man, with his arm extended, as if pointing to a remote object, which no mortal eye certainly could discern through the mist. Sir Bale gazed at this figure, doubtful whether he were in a waking dream, unable to conjecture whence it had come; and as he looked, it moved, and was almost instantly out of sight.

He descended the mountain cautiously. The mist was now thinner, and through the haze he was beginning to see objects more distinctly, and, without danger, to proceed at a quicker pace. He had still a long walk by the uplands towards Mardykes Hall before he descended to the level of the lake.

The mist was still quite thick enough to circumscribe his view and to hide the general features of the landscape; and well was it, perhaps, for Sir Bale that his boyhood had familiarised him with the landmarks on the mountain-side.

He had made nearly four miles on his solitary homeward way, when, passing under a ledge of rock which bears the name of the Cat's Skaitch, he saw the same figure in the short cloak standing within some thirty or forty yards of him—the thin curtain of mist, through which the moonlight touched it, giving to it an airy and unsubstantial character.

Sir Bale came to a standstill. The man in the short cloak nodded and drew back, and was concealed by the angle of the rock.

Sir Bale was now irritated, as men are after a start, and shouting to the stranger to halt, he 'slapped' after him, as the northern phrase goes, at his best pace. But again he was gone, and nowhere could he see him, the mist favouring his evasion.

Looking down the fells that overhang Mardykes Hall, the mountain-side dips gradually into a glen, which, as it descends, becomes precipitous and wooded. A footpath through this ravine conducts the wayfarer to the level ground that borders the lake; and by this dark pass Sir Bale Mardykes strode, in comparatively clear air, along the rocky path dappled with moonlight.

As he emerged upon the lower ground he again encountered the same figure. It approached. It was Philip Feltram.

CHAPTER XIV

A New Philip Feltram The Baronet had not seen Feltram since his strange escape from death. His last interview with him had been stern and threatening; Sir Bale dealing with appearances in the spirit of an incensed judge, Philip Feltram lamenting in the submission of a helpless despair.

Feltram was full in the moonlight now, standing erect, and smiling cynically on the Baronet.

There was that in the bearing and countenance of Feltram that disconcerted him more than the surprise of the sudden meeting.

He had determined to meet Feltram in a friendly way, whenever that not very comfortable interview became inevitable. But he was confused by the suddenness of Feltram's appearance; and the tone, cold and stern, in which he had last spoken to him came first, and he spoke in it after a brief silence.

"I fancied, Mr. Feltram, you were in your bed; I little expected to find you here. I think the Doctor gave very particular directions, and said that you were to remain perfectly quiet."

"But I know more than the Doctor," replied Feltram, still smiling unpleasantly.

"I think, sir, you would have been better in your bed," said Sir Bale loftily.

"Come, come, come, come!" exclaimed Philip Feltram contemptuously.

"It seems to me," said Sir Bale, a good deal astonished, "you rather forget yourself."

"Easier to forget oneself, Sir Bale, than to forgive others, at times," replied Philip Feltram in his unparalleled mood.

"That's the way fools knock themselves up," continued Sir Bale. "You've been walking ever so far—away to the Fells of Golden Friars. It was you whom I saw there. What d----d folly! What brought you there?"

"To observe you," he replied.

"And have you walked the whole way there and back again? How did you get there?"

"Pooh! how did I come—how did you come—how did the fog come? From the lake, I suppose. We all come up, and then down." So spoke Philip Feltram, with serene insolence.

"You are pleased to talk nonsense," said Sir Bale.

"Because I like it—with a *meaning*."

Sir Bale looked at him, not knowing whether to believe his eyes and ears. He did not know what to make of him.

"I had intended speaking to you in a conciliatory way; you seem to wish to make that impossible"—Philip Feltram's face wore its repulsive smile;—"and in fact I don't know what to make of you, unless you are ill; and ill you well may be. You can't have walked much less than twelve miles."

"Wonderful effort for me!" said Feltram with the same sneer.

"Rather surprising for a man so nearly drowned," answered Sir Bale Mardykes.

"A dip: you don't like the lake, sir; but I do. And so it is: as Antaeus touched the earth, so I the water, and rise refreshed."

"I think you'd better get in and refresh there. I meant to tell you that all the unpleasantness about that bank-note is over."

"Is it?"

"Yes. It has been recovered by Mr. Creswell, who came here last night. I've got it, and you're not to blame," said Sir Bale.

"But some one *is* to blame," observed Mr. Feltram, smiling still.

"Well, *you* are not, and that ends it," said the Baronet peremptorily.

"Ends it? Really, how good! how very good!"

Sir Bale looked at him, for there was something ambiguous and even derisive in the tone of Feltram's voice.

But before he could quite make up his mind, Feltram spoke again.

"Everything is settled about you and me?"

"There is nothing to prevent your staying at Mardykes now," said Sir Bale graciously.

"I shall be with you for two years, and then I go on my travels," answered Feltram, with a saturnine and somewhat wild look around him.

"Is he going mad?" thought the Baronet.

"But before I go, I'm to put you in a way of paying off your mortgages. That is my business here."

Sir Bale looked at him sharply. But now there was not the unpleasant smile, but the darkened look of a man in secret pain.

"You shall know it all by and by."

And without more ceremony, and with a darkening face, Philip Feltram made his way under the boughs of the thick oaks that grew there, leaving on Sir Bale's mind an impression that he had been watching some one at a distance, and had gone in consequence of a signal.

In a few seconds he followed in the same direction, halloaing after Feltram; for he did not like the idea of his wandering about the country by moonlight, or possibly losing his life among the precipices, and bringing a new discredit upon his house. But no answer came; nor could he in that thick copse gain sight of him again.

When Sir Bale reached Mardykes Hall he summoned Mrs. Julaper, and had a long talk with her. But she could not say that there appeared anything amiss with Philip Feltram; only he seemed more reserved, and as if he was brooding over something he did not intend to tell.

"But, you know, Sir Bale, what happened might well make a thoughtful man of him. If he's ever to think of Death, it should be after looking him so hard in the face; and I'm not ashamed to say, I'm glad to see he has grace to take the lesson, and I hope his experiences may be sanctified to him, poor fellow! Amen."

"Very good song, and very well sung," said Sir Bale; "but it doesn't seem to me that he has been improved, Mrs. Julaper. He seems, on the contrary, in a queer temper and anything but a heavenly frame of mind; and I thought I'd ask you, because if he is ill—I mean feverish—it might account for his eccentricities, as well as make it necessary to send after him, and bring him home, and put him to bed. But I suppose it is as you say,—his adventure has upset him a little, and he'll sober in a day or two, and return to his old ways."

But this did not happen. A change, more comprehensive than at first appeared, had taken place, and a singular alteration was gradually established.

He grew thin, his eyes hollow, his face gradually forbidding.

His ways and temper were changed: he was a new man with Sir Bale; and the Baronet after a time, people said, began to grow afraid of him. And certainly Feltram had acquired an extraordinary influence over the Baronet, who a little while ago had regarded and treated him with so much contempt.

CHAPTER XV

The Purse of Gold The Baronet was very slightly known in his county. He had led a reserved and inhospitable life. He was pressed upon by heavy debts; and being a proud man, held aloof from society and its doings. He wished people to understand that he was nursing his estate; but somehow the estate did not thrive at nurse. In the country other people's business is admirably well known; and the lord of Mardykes was conscious, perhaps, that his neighbours knew as well he did, that the utmost he could do was to pay the interest charged upon it, and to live in a frugal way enough.

The lake measures some four or five miles across, from the little jetty under the walls of Mardykes Hall to Cloostedd.

Philip Feltram, changed and morose, loved a solitary row upon the lake; and sometimes, with no one to aid him in its management, would take the little sail-boat and pass the whole day upon those lonely waters.

Frequently he crossed to Cloostedd; and mooring the boat under the solemn trees that stand reflected in that dark mirror, he would disembark and wander among the lonely woodlands, as people thought, cherishing in those ancestral scenes the memory of ineffaceable injuries, and the wrath and revenge that seemed of late to darken his countenance, and to hold him always in a moody silence.

One autumnal evening Sir Bale Mardykes was sourly ruminating after his solitary meal. A very red sun was pouring its last low beams through the valley at the western extremity of the lake, across its elsewhere sombre waters, and touching with a sudden and blood-red tint the sail of the skiff in which Feltram was returning from his lonely cruise.

"Here comes my domestic water-fiend," sneered Sir Bale, as he lay back in his cumbrous arm-chair. "Cheerful place, pleasant people, delicious fate! The place alone has been enough to set that fool out of his little senses, d—n him!"

Sir Bale averted his eyes, and another subject not pleasanter entered his mind. He was thinking of the races that were coming off next week at Heckleston Downs, and what sums of money might be made there, and how hard it was that he should be excluded by fortune from that brilliant lottery.

"Ah, Mrs. Julaper, is that you?"

Mrs. Julaper, who was still at the door, curtsied, and said, "I came, Sir Bale, to see whether you'd please to like a jug of mulled claret, sir."

"Not I, my dear. I'll take a mug of beer and my pipe; that homely solace better befits a ruined gentleman."

"H'm, sir; you're not that, Sir Bale; you're no worse than half the lords and great men that are going. I would not hear another say that of you, sir."

"That's very kind of you, Mrs. Julaper; but you won't call *me* out for backbiting myself, especially as it is true, d----d true, Mrs. Julaper! Look ye; there never was a Mardykes here before but he could lay his hundred or his thousand pounds on the winner of the Heckleston Cup; and what could I bet? Little more than that mug of beer I spoke of. It was my great-grandfather who opened the course on the Downs of Heckleston, and now *I* can't show there! Well, what must I do? Grin and bear it, that's all. If you please, Mrs. Julaper, I will have that jug of claret you offered. I want spice and hot wine to keep me alive; but I'll smoke my pipe first, and in an hour's time it will do."

When Mrs. Julaper was gone, he lighted his pipe, and drew near the window, through which he looked upon the now fading sky and the twilight landscape.

CHAPTER XV

He smoked his pipe out, and by that time it had grown nearly dark. He was still looking out upon the faint outlines of the view, and thinking angrily what a little bit of luck at the races would do for many a man who probably did not want it half so much as he. Vague and sombre as his thoughts were, they had, like the darkening landscape outside, shape enough to define their general character. Bitter and impious they were—as those of egotistic men naturally are in suffering. And after brooding, and muttering by fits and starts, he said:

"How many tens and hundreds of thousands of pounds will change hands at Heckleston next week; and not a shilling in all the change and shuffle will stick to me! How many a fellow would sell himself, like Dr. Faustus, just for the knowledge of the name of the winner! But he's no fool, and does not buy his own."

Something caught his eye; something moving on the wall. The fire was lighted, and cast a flickering and gigantic shadow upward; the figure of a man standing behind Sir Bale Mardykes, on whose shoulder he placed a lean hand. Sir Bale turned suddenly about, and saw Philip Feltram. He was looking dark and stern, and did not remove his hand from his shoulder as he peered into the Baronet's face with his deep-set mad eyes.

"Ha, Philip, upon my soul!" exclaimed Sir Bale, surprised. "How time flies! It seems only this minute since I saw the boat a mile and a half away from the shore. Well—yes; there has been time; it is dark now. Ha, ha! I assure you, you startled me. Won't you take something? Do. Shall I touch the bell?"

"You have been troubled about those mortgages. I told you I should pay them off, I thought."

Here there was a pause, and Sir Bale looked hard in Feltram's face. If he had been in his ordinary spirits, or perhaps in some of his haunts less solitary than Mardykes, he would have laughed; but here he had grown unlike himself, gloomy and credulous, and was, in fact, a nervous man.

Sir Bale smiled, and shook his head dismally.

"It is very kind of you, Feltram; the idea shows a kindly disposition. I know you would do me a kindness if you could."

As Sir Bale, each looking in the other's eyes, repeated in this sentence the words "kind," "kindly," "kindness," a smile lighted Feltram's face with at each word an intenser light; and Sir Bale grew sombre in its glare; and when he had done speaking, Feltram's face also on a sudden darkened.

"I have found a fortune-teller in Cloostedd Wood. Look here."

And he drew from his pocket a leathern purse, which he placed on the table in his hand; and Sir Bale heard the pleasant clink of coin in it.

"A fortune-teller! You don't mean to say she gave you that?" said Sir Bale.

Feltram smiled again, and nodded.

"It *was* the custom to give the fortuneteller a trifle. It is a great improvement making *her* fee you," observed Sir Bale, with an approach to his old manner.

"He put that in my hand with a message," said Feltram.

"He? O, then it was a male fortune-teller!"

"Gipsies go in gangs, men and women. *He* might lend, though *she* told fortunes," said Feltram.

"It's the first time I ever heard of gipsies lending money;" and he eyed the purse with a whimsical smile.

With his lean fingers still holding it, Feltram sat down at the table. His face contracted as if in cunning thought, and his chin sank upon his breast as he leaned back.

"I think," continued Sir Bale, "ever since they were spoiled, the Egyptians have been a little shy of lending, and leave that branch of business to the Hebrews."

"What would you give to know, now, the winner at Heckleston races?" said Feltram suddenly, raising his eyes.

"Yes; that would be worth something," answered Sir Bale, looking at him with more interest than the incredulity he affected would quite warrant.

"And this money I have power to lend you, to make your game."

"Do you mean that really?" said Sir Bale, with a new energy in tone, manner, and features.

"That's heavy; there are some guineas there," said Feltram with a dark smile, raising the purse in his hand a little, and letting it drop upon the table with a clang.

"There is *something* there, at all events," said Sir Bale.

Feltram took the purse by the bottom, and poured out on the table a handsome pile of guineas.

"And do you mean to say you got all that from a gipsy in Cloostedd Wood?"

"A friend, who is *myself*," answered Philip Feltram.

"Yourself! Then it is yours—*you* lend it?" said the Baronet, amazed; for there was no getting over the heap of guineas, and the wonder was pretty equal whence they had come.

"Myself, and not myself," said Feltram oracularly; "as like as voice and echo, man and shadow."

Had Feltram in some of his solitary wanderings and potterings lighted upon hidden treasure? There was a story of two Feltrams of Cloostedd, brothers, who had joined the king's army and fought at Marston Moor, having buried in Cloostedd Wood a great deal of gold and plate and jewels. They had, it was said, intrusted one tried servant with the secret; and that servant remained at home. But by a perverse fatality the three witnesses had perished within a month: the two brothers at Marston Moor; and the confidant, of fever, at Cloostedd. From that day forth treasure-seekers had from time to time explored the woods of Cloostedd; and many a tree of mark was dug beside, and the earth beneath many a stone and scar and other landmark in that solitary forest was opened by night, until hope gradually died out, and the tradition had long ceased to prompt to action, and had become a story and nothing more.

The image of the nursery-tale had now recurred to Sir Bale after so long a reach of years; and the only imaginable way, in his mind, of accounting for penniless Philip Feltram having all that gold in his possession was that, in some of his lonely wanderings, chance had led him to the undiscovered hoard of the two Feltrams who had died in the great civil wars.

"Perhaps those gipsies you speak of found the money where you found them; and in that case, as Cloostedd Forest, and all that is in it is my property, their sending it to me is more like my servant's handing me my hat and stick when I'm going out, than making me a present."

"You will not be wise to rely upon the law, Sir Bale, and to refuse the help that comes unasked. But if you like your mortgages as they are, keep them; and if you like my terms as they are, take them; and when you have made up your mind, let me know."

Philip Feltram dropped the heavy purse into his capacious coat-pocket, and walked, muttering, out of the room.

CHAPTER XVI

The Message from Cloostedd "Come back, Feltram; come back, Philip!" cried Sir Bale hastily. "Let us talk, can't we? Come and talk this odd business over a little; you must have mistaken what I meant; I should like to hear all about it."

"All is not much, sir," said Philip Feltram, entering the room again, the door of which he had half closed after him. "In the forest of Cloostedd I met to-day some people, one of whom can foretell events, and told me the names of the winners of the first three races at Heckleston, and gave me this purse, with leave to lend you so much money as you care to stake upon the races. I take no security; you shan't be troubled; and you'll never see the lender, unless you seek him out."

"Well, those are not bad terms," said Sir Bale, smiling wistfully at the purse, which Feltram had again placed upon the table.

"No, not bad," repeated Feltram, in the harsh low tone in which he now habitually spoke.

"You'll tell me what the prophet said about the winners; I should like to hear their names."

"The names I shall tell you if you walk out with me," said Feltram.

"Why not here?" asked Sir Bale.

"My memory does not serve me here so well. Some people, in some places, though they be silent, obstruct thought. Come, let us speak," said Philip Feltram, leading the way.

Sir Bale, with a shrug, followed him.

By this time it was dark. Feltram was walking slowly towards the margin of the lake; and Sir Bale, more curious as the delay increased, followed him, and smiled faintly as he looked after his tall, gaunt figure, as if, even in the dark, expressing a ridicule which he did not honestly feel, and the expression of which, even if there had been light, there was no one near enough to see.

When he reached the edge of the lake, Feltram stooped, and Sir Bale thought that his attitude was that of one who whispers to and caresses a reclining person. What he fancied was a dark figure lying horizontally in the shallow water, near the edge, turned out to be, as he drew near, no more than a shadow on the elsewhere lighter water; and with his change of position it had shifted and was gone, and Philip Feltram was but dabbling his hand this way and that in the water, and muttering faintly to himself. He rose as the Baronet drew near, and standing upright, said,

"I like to listen to the ripple of the water among the grass and pebbles; the tongue and lips of the lake are lapping and whispering all along. It is the merest poetry; but you are so romantic, you excuse me."

There was an angry curve in Feltram's eyebrows, and a cynical smile, and something in the tone which to the satirical Baronet was almost insulting. But even had he been less curious, I don't think he would have betrayed his mortification; for an odd and unavowed influence which he hated was gradually establishing in Feltram an ascendency which sometimes vexed and sometimes cowed him.

"You are not to tell," said Feltram, drawing near him in the dusk. "The secret is yours when you promise."

"Of course I promise," said Sir Bale. "If I believed it, you don't think I could be such an ass as to tell it; and if I didn't believe it, I'd hardly take the trouble."

Feltram stooped, and dipping the hollow of his hand in the water, he raised it full, and said he, "Hold out your hand—the hollow of your hand—like this. I divide the water for a sign—share to me and share to you." And he turned his hand, so as to pour half the water into the hollow palm of Sir Bale, who was smiling, with some uneasiness mixed in his mockery.

"Now, you promise to keep all secrets respecting the teller and the finder, be that who it may?"

"Yes, I promise," said Sir Bale.

"Now do as I do," said Feltram. And he shed the water on the ground, and with his wet fingers touched his forehead and his breast; and then he joined his hand with Sir Bale's, and said, "Now you are my safe man."

Sir Bale laughed. "That's the game they call 'grand mufti,'" said he.

"Exactly; and means nothing," said Feltram, "except that some day it will serve you to remember by. And now the names. Don't speak; listen—you may break the thought else. The winner of the first is *Beeswing*; of the second, *Falcon*; and of the third, *Lightning*."

He had stood for some seconds in silence before he spoke; his eyes were closed; he seemed to bring up thought and speech with difficulty, and spoke faintly and drowsily, both his hands a little raised, and the fingers extended, with the groping air of a man who moves in the dark. In this odd way, slowly, faintly, with many a sigh and scarcely audible groan, he gradually delivered his message and was silent. He stood, it seemed, scarcely half awake, muttering indistinctly and sighing to himself. You would have said that he was exhausted and suffering, like a man at his last hour resigning himself to death.

At length he opened his eyes, looked round a little wildly and languidly, and with another great sigh sat down on a large rock that lies by the margin of the lake, and sighed heavily again and again. You might have fancied that he was a second time recovering from drowning.

Then he got up, and looked drowsily round again, and sighed like a man worn out with fatigue, and was silent.

Sir Bale did not care to speak until he seemed a little more likely to obtain an answer. When that time came, he said, "I wish, for the sake of my believing, that your list was a little less incredible. Not one of the horses you name is the least likely; not one of them has a chance."

"So much the better for you; you'll get what odds you please. You had better seize your luck; on Tuesday Beeswing runs," said Feltram. "When you want money for the purpose, I'm your banker—here is your bank."

He touched his breast, where he had placed the purse, and then he turned and walked swiftly away.

Sir Bale looked after him till he disappeared in the dark. He fluctuated among many surmises about Feltram. Was he insane, or was he practising an imposture? or was he fool enough to believe the predictions of some real gipsies? and had he borrowed this money, which in Sir Bale's eyes seemed the greatest miracle in the matter, from those thriving shepherd mountaineers, the old Trebecks, who, he believed, were attached to him? Feltram had, he thought, borrowed it as if for himself; and having, as Sir Bale in his egotism supposed, "a sneaking regard" for him, had meant the loan for his patron, and conceived the idea of his using his revelations for the purpose of making his fortune. So, seeing no risk, and the temptation being strong, Sir Bale resolved to avail himself of the purse, and use his own judgment as to what horse to back.

About eleven o'clock Feltram, unannounced, walked, with his hat still on, into Sir Bale's library, and sat down at the opposite side of his table, looking gloomily into the Baronet's face for a time.

"Shall you want the purse?" he asked at last.

"Certainly; I always want a purse," said Sir Bale energetically.

"The condition is, that you shall back each of the three horses I have named. But you may back them for much or little, as you like, only the sum must not be less than five pounds in each hundred which this purse contains. That is the condition, and if you violate it, you will make some powerful people very angry, and you will feel it. Do you agree?"

"Of course; five pounds in the hundred—certainly; and how many hundreds are there?"

"Three."

"Well, a fellow with luck may win something with three hundred pounds, but it ain't very much."

"Quite enough, if you use it aright."

"Three hundred pounds," repeated the Baronet, as he emptied the purse, which Feltram had just placed in his hand, upon the table; and contemplating them with grave interest, he began telling them off in little heaps of five-and-twenty each.

He might have thanked Feltram, but he was thinking more of the guineas than of the grizzly donor.

"Ay," said he, after a second counting, "I think there *are* exactly three hundred. Well, so you say I must apply three times five—fifteen of these. It is an awful pity backing those queer horses you have named; but if I must make the sacrifice, I must, I suppose?" he added, with a hesitating inquiry in the tone.

"If you don't, you'll rue it," said Feltram coldly, and walked away.

"Penny in pocket's a merry companion," says the old English proverb, and Sir Bale felt in better spirits and temper than he had for many a day as he replaced the guineas in the purse.

It was long since he had visited either the race-course or any other place of amusement. Now he might face his kind without fear that his pride should be mortified, and dabble in the fascinating agitations of the turf once more.

"Who knows how this little venture may turn out?" he thought. "It is time the luck should turn. My last summer in Germany, my last winter in Paris—d—n me, I'm owed something. It's time I should win a bit."

Sir Bale had suffered the indolence of a solitary and discontented life imperceptibly to steal upon him. It would not do to appear for the first time on Heckleston Lea with any of those signs of negligence which, in his case, might easily be taken for poverty. All his appointments, therefore, were carefully looked after; and on the Monday following, he, followed by his groom, rode away for the Saracen's Head at Heckleston, where he was to put up, for the races that were to begin on the day following, and presented as handsome an appearance as a peer in those days need have cared to show.

CHAPTER XVII

On the Course—Beeswing, Falcon, and Lightning As he rode towards Golden Friars, through which his route lay, in the early morning light, in which the mists of night were clearing, he looked back towards Mardykes with a hope of speedy deliverance from that hated imprisonment, and of a return to the continental life in which he took delight. He saw the summits and angles of the old building touched with the cheerful beams, and the grand old trees, and at the opposite side the fells dark, with their backs towards the east; and down the side of the wooded and precipitous clough of Feltram, the light, with a pleasant contrast against the beetling purple of the fells, was breaking in the faint distance. On the lake he saw the white speck that indicated the sail of Philip Feltram's boat, now midway between Mardykes and the wooded shores of Cloostedd.

"Going on the same errand," thought Sir Bale, "I should not wonder. I wish him the same luck. Yes, he's going to Cloostedd Forest. I hope he may meet his gipsies there—the Trebecks, or whoever they are."

And as a momentary sense of degradation in being thus beholden to such people smote him, "Well," thought he, "who knows? Many a fellow will make a handsome sum of a poorer purse than this at Heckleston. It will be a light matter paying them then."

Through Golden Friars he rode. Some of the spectators who did not like him, wondered audibly at the gallant show, hoped it was paid for, and conjectured that he had ridden out in search of a wife. On the whole, however, the appearance of their Baronet in a smarter style than usual was popular, and accepted as a change to the advantage of the town.

Next morning he was on the race-course of Heckleston, renewing old acquaintance and making himself as agreeable as he could—an object, among some people, of curiosity and even interest. Leaving the carriage-sides, the hoods and bonnets, Sir Bale was soon among the betting men, deep in more serious business.

How did he make his book? He did not break his word. He backed Beeswing, Falcon, and Lightning. But it must be owned not for a shilling more than the five guineas each, to which he stood pledged. The odds were forty-five to one against Beeswing, sixty to one against Lightning, and fifty to one against Falcon.

"A pretty lot to choose!" exclaimed Sir Bale, with vexation. "As if I had money so often, that I should throw it away!"

The Baronet was testy thinking over all this, and looked on Feltram's message as an impertinence and the money as his own.

Let us now see how Sir Bale Mardykes' pocket fared.

Sulkily enough at the close of the week he turned his back on Heckleston racecourse, and took the road to Golden Friars.

He was in a rage with his luck, and by no means satisfied with himself; and yet he had won something. The result of the racing had been curious. In the three principal races the favourites had been beaten: one by an accident, another on a technical point, and the third by fair running. And what horses had won? The names were precisely those which the "fortune-teller" had predicted.

Well, then, how was Sir Bale in pocket as he rode up to his ancestral house of Mardykes, where a few thousand pounds would have been very welcome? He had won exactly 775 guineas; and had he staked a hundred instead of five on each of the names communicated by Feltram, he would have won 15,500 guineas.

He dismounted before his hall-door, therefore, with the discontent of a man who had lost nearly 15,000 pounds. Feltram was upon the steps, and laughed dryly.

"What do you laugh at?" asked Sir Bale tartly.

"You've won, haven't you?"

"Yes, I've won; I've won a trifle."

"On the horses I named?"

"Well, yes; it so turned out, by the merest accident."

Feltram laughed again dryly, and turned away.

Sir Bale entered Mardykes Hall, and was surly. He was in a much worse mood than before he had ridden to Heckleston. But after a week or so ruminating upon the occurrence, he wondered that Feltram spoke no more of it. It was undoubtedly wonderful. There had been no hint of repayment yet, and he had made some hundreds by the loan; and, contrary to all likelihood, the three horses named by the unknown soothsayer had won. Who was this gipsy? It would be worth bringing the soothsayer to Mardykes, and giving his people a camp on the warren, and all the poultry they could catch, and a pig or a sheep every now and then. Why, that seer was worth the philosopher's stone, and could make Sir Bale's fortune in a season. Some one else would be sure to pick him up if he did not.

So, tired of waiting for Feltram to begin, he opened the subject one day himself. He had not seen him for two or three days; and in the wood of Mardykes he saw his lank figure standing among the thick trees, upon a little knoll, leaning on a staff which he sometimes carried with him in his excursions up the mountains.

"Feltram!" shouted Sir Bale.

Feltram turned and beckoned. Sir Bale muttered, but obeyed the signal.

"I brought you here, because you can from this point with unusual clearness today see the opening of the Clough of Feltram at the other side, and the clump of trees, where you will find the way to reach the person about whom you are always thinking."

"Who said I am always thinking about him?" said the Baronet angrily; for he felt like a man detected in a weakness, and resented it.

"*I* say it, because I *know* it; and *you* know it also. See that clump of trees standing solitary in the hollow? Among them, to the left, grows an ancient oak. Cut in its bark are two enormous letters H—F; so large and bold, that the rugged furrows of the oak bark fail to obscure them, although they are ancient and spread by time. Standing against the trunk of this great tree, with your back to these letters, you are looking up the Glen or Clough of Feltram, that opens northward, where stands Cloostedd Forest spreading far and thick. Now, how do you find our fortune-teller?"

"That is exactly what I wish to know," answered Sir Bale; "because, although I can't, of course, believe that he's a witch, yet he has either made the most marvellous fluke I've heard of, or else he has got extraordinary sources of information; or perhaps he acts partly on chance, partly on facts. Be it which you please, I say he's a marvellous fellow; and I should like to see him, and have a talk with him; and perhaps he could arrange with me. I should be very glad to make an arrangement with him to give me the benefit of his advice about any matter of the same kind again."

"I think he's willing to see you; but he's a fellow with a queer fancy and a pig-head. He'll not come here; you must go to him; and approach him his own way too, or you may fail to find him. On these terms he invites you."

Sir Bale laughed.

"He knows his value, and means to make his own terms."

"Well, there's nothing unfair in that; and I don't see that I should dispute it. How is one to find him?"

"Stand, as I told you, with your back to those letters cut in the oak. Right before you lies an old Druidic altar-stone. Cast your eye over its surface, and on some part of it you are sure to see a black stain about the size of a man's head.

Standing, as I suppose you, against the oak, that stain, which changes its place from day to day, will give you the line you must follow through the forest in order to light upon him. Take carefully from it such trees or objects as will guide you; and when the forest thickens, do the best you can to keep to the same line. You are sure to find him."

"You'll come, Feltram. I should lose myself in that wilderness, and probably fail to discover him," said Sir Bale; "and I really wish to see him."

"When two people wish to meet, it is hard if they don't. I can go with you a bit of the way; I can walk a little through the forest by your side, until I see the small flower that grows peeping here and there, that always springs where those people walk; and when I begin to see that sign, I must leave you. And, first, I'll take you across the lake."

"By Jove, you'll do no such thing!" said Sir Bale hastily.

"But that is the way he chooses to be approached," said Philip Feltram.

"I have a sort of feeling about that lake; it's the one childish spot that is left in my imagination. The nursery is to blame for it—old stories and warnings; and I can't think of that. I should feel I had invoked an evil omen if I did. I know it is all nonsense; but we are queer creatures, Feltram. I must only ride there."

"Why, it is five-and-twenty miles round the lake to that; and after all were done, he would not see you. He knows what he's worth, and he'll have his own way," answered Feltram. "The sun will soon set. See that withered branch, near Snakes Island, that looks like fingers rising from the water? When its points grow tipped with red, the sun has but three minutes to live."

"That is a wonder which I can't see; it is too far away."

"Yes, the lake has many signs; but it needs sight to see them," said Feltram.

"So it does," said the Baronet; "more than most men have got. I'll ride round, I say; and I make my visit, for this time, my own way."

"You'll not find him, then; and he wants his money. It would be a pity to vex him."

"It was to you he lent the money," said Sir Bale.

"Yes."

"Well, you are the proper person to find him out and pay him," urged Sir Bale.

"Perhaps so; but he invites you; and if you don't go, he may be offended, and you may hear no more from him."

"We'll try. When can you go? There are races to come off next week, for once and away, at Langton. I should not mind trying my luck there. What do you say?

"You can go there and pay him, and ask the same question—what horses, I mean, are to win. All the county are to be there; and plenty of money will change hands."

"I'll try," said Feltram.

"When will you go?"

"To-morrow," he answered.

"I have an odd idea, Feltram, that you are really going to pay off those cursed mortgages."

He laid his hand with at least a gesture of kindness on the thin arm of Feltram, who coldly answered,

"So have I;" and walked down the side of the little knoll and away, without another word or look.

CHAPTER XVIII

On the Lake, at Last Next day Philip Feltram crossed the lake; and Sir Bale, seeing the boat on the water, guessed its destination, and watched its progress with no little interest, until he saw it moored and its sail drop at the rude pier that affords a landing at the Clough of Feltram. He was now satisfied that Philip had actually gone to seek out the 'cunning man,' and gather hints for the next race.

When that evening Feltram returned, and, later still, entered Sir Bale's library, the master of Mardykes was gladder to see his face and more interested about his news than he would have cared to confess.

Philip Feltram did not affect unconsciousness of that anxiety, but, with great directness, proceeded to satisfy it.

"I was in Cloostedd Forest to-day, nearly all day—and found the old gentleman in a wax. He did not ask me to drink, nor show me any kindness. He was huffed because you would not take the trouble to cross the lake to speak to him yourself. He took the money you sent him and counted it over, and dropped it into his pocket; and he called you hard names enough and to spare; but I brought him round, and at last he did talk."

"And what did he say?"

"He said that the estate of Mardykes would belong to a Feltram."

"He might have said something more likely," said Sir Bale sourly. "Did he say anything more?"

"Yes. He said the winner at Langton Lea would be Silver Bell."

"Any other name?"

"No."

"Silver Bell? Well, that's not so odd as the last. Silver Bell stands high in the list. He has a good many backers—long odds in his favour against most of the field. I should not mind backing Silver Bell."

The fact is, that he had no idea of backing any other horse from the moment he heard the soothsayer's prediction. He made up his mind to no half measures this time. He would go in to win something handsome.

He was in great force and full of confidence on the race-course. He had no fears for the result. He bet heavily. There was a good margin still untouched of the Mardykes estate; and Sir Bale was a good old name in the county. He found a ready market for his offers, and had soon staked—such is the growing frenzy of that excitement—about twenty thousand pounds on his favourite, and stood to win seven.

He did not win, however. He lost his twenty thousand pounds.

CHAPTER XVIII

And now the Mardykes estate was in imminent danger. Sir Bale returned, having distributed I O Us and promissory notes in all directions about him—quite at his wit's end.

Feltram was standing—as on the occasion of his former happier return—on the steps of Mardykes Hall, in the evening sun, throwing eastward a long shadow that was lost in the lake. He received him, as before, with a laugh.

Sir Bale was too much broken to resent this laugh as furiously as he might, had he been a degree less desperate.

He looked at Feltram savagely, and dismounted.

"Last time you would not trust him, and this time he would not trust you. He's huffed, and played you false."

"It was not he. I should have backed that d----d horse in any case," said Sir Bale, grinding his teeth. "What a witch you have discovered! One thing is true, perhaps. If there was a Feltram rich enough, he might have the estate now; but there ain't. They are all beggars. So much for your conjurer."

"He may make amends to you, if you make amends to him."

"He! Why, what can that wretched impostor do? D—n me, I'm past helping now."

"Don't you talk so," said Feltram. "Be civil. You must please the old gentleman. He'll make it up. He's placable when it suits him. Why not go to him his own way? I hear you are nearly ruined. You must go and make it up."

"Make it up! With whom? With a fellow who can't make even a guess at what's coming? Why should I trouble my head about him more?"

"No man, young or old, likes to be frumped. Why did you cross his fancy? He won't see you unless you go to him as he chooses."

"If he waits for that, he may wait till doomsday. I don't choose to go on that water—and cross it I won't," said Sir Bale.

But when his distracting reminders began to pour in upon him, and the idea of dismembering what remained of his property came home to him, his resolution faltered.

"I say, Feltram, what difference can it possibly make to him if I choose to ride round to Cloostedd Forest instead of crossing the lake in a boat?"

Feltram smiled darkly, and answered.

"I can't tell. Can you?"

"Of course I can't—I say I can't; besides, what audacity of a fellow like that presuming to prescribe to me! Utterly ludicrous! And he can't predict—do you really think or believe, Feltram, that he can?"

"I know he can. I know he misled you on purpose. He likes to punish those who don't respect his will; and there is a reason in it, often quite clear—not ill-natured. Now you see he compels you to seek him out, and when you do, I think he'll help you through your trouble. He said he would."

"Then you have seen him since?"

"Yesterday. He has put a pressure on you; but he means to help you."

"If he means to help me, let him remember I want a banker more than a seer. Let him give me a lift, as he did before. He must lend me money."

"He'll not stick at that. When he takes up a man, he carries him through."

"The races of Byermere—I might retrieve at them. But they don't come off for a month nearly; and what is a man like me to do in the meantime?"

"Every man should know his own business best. I'm not like you," said Feltram grimly.

Now Sir Bale's trouble increased, for some people were pressing. Something like panic supervened; for it happened that land was bringing just then a bad price, and more must be sold in consequence.

"All I can tell them is, I am selling land. It can't be done in an hour. I'm selling enough to pay them all twice over. Gentlemen used to be able to wait till a man sold his acres for payment. D—n them! do they want my body, that they can't let me alone for five minutes?"

The end of it was, that before a week Sir Bale told Feltram that he would go by boat, since that fellow insisted on it; and he did not very much care if he were drowned.

It was a beautiful autumnal day. Everything was bright in that mellowed sun, and the deep blue of the lake was tremulous with golden ripples; and crag and peak and scattered wood, faint in the distance, came out with a filmy distinctness on the fells in that pleasant light.

Sir Bale had been ill, and sent down the night before for Doctor Torvey. He was away with a patient. Now, in the morning, he had arrived inopportunely. He met Sir Bale as he issued from the house, and had a word with him in the court, for he would not turn back.

"Well," said the Doctor, after his brief inspection, "you ought to be in your bed; that's all I can say. You are perfectly mad to think of knocking about like this. Your pulse is at a hundred and ten; and, if you go across the lake and walk about Cloostedd, you'll be raving before you come back."

Sir Bale told him, apologetically, as if his life were more to his doctor than to himself, that he would take care not to fatigue himself, and that the air would do him good, and that in any case he could not avoid going; and so they parted.

Sir Bale took his seat beside Feltram in the boat, the sail was spread, and, bending to the light breeze that blew from Golden Friars, she glided from the jetty under Mardykes Hall, and the eventful voyage had begun.

CHAPTER XIX

Mystagogus The sail was loosed, the boat touched the stone step, and Feltram sprang out and made her fast to the old iron ring. The Baronet followed. So! he had ventured upon that water without being drowned. He looked round him as if in a dream. He had not been there since his childhood. There were no regrets, no sentiment, no remorse; only an odd return of the associations and fresh feelings of boyhood, and a long reach of time suddenly annihilated.

CHAPTER XIX

The little hollow in which he stood; the three hawthorn trees at his right; every crease and undulation of the sward, every angle and crack in the lichen-covered rock at his feet, recurred with a sharp and instantaneous recognition to his memory.

"Many a time your brother and I fished for hours together from that bank there, just where the bramble grows. That bramble has not grown an inch ever since, not a leaf altered; we used to pick blackberries off it, with our rods stuck in the bank—it was later in the year than now—till we stript it quite bare after a day or two. The steward used to come over—they were marking timber for cutting and we used to stay here while they rambled through the wood, with an axe marking the trees that were to come down. I wonder whether the big old boat is still anywhere. I suppose she was broken up, or left to rot; I have not seen her since we came home. It was in the wood that lies at the right—the other wood is called the forest; they say in old times it was eight miles long, northward up the shore of the lake, and full of deer; with a forester, and a reeve, and a verderer, and all that. Your brother was older than you; he went to India, or the Colonies; is he living still?"

"I care not."

"That's good-natured, at all events; but do you know?"

"Not I; and what matter? If he's living, I warrant he has his share of the curse, the sweat of his brow and his bitter crust; and if he is dead, he's dust or worse, he's rotten, and smells accordingly."

Sir Bale looked at him; for this was the brother over whom, only a year or two ago, Philip used to cry tears of pathetic longing. Feltram looked darkly in his face, and sneered with a cold laugh.

"I suppose you mean to jest?" said Sir Bale.

"Not I; it is the truth. It is what you'd say, if you were honest. If he's alive, let him keep where he is; and if he's dead, I'll have none of him, body or soul. Do you hear that sound?"

"Like the wind moaning in the forest?"

"Yes."

"But I feel no wind. There's hardly a leaf stirring."

"I think so," said Feltram. "Come along."

And he began striding up the gentle slope of the glen, with many a rock peeping through its sward, and tufted ferns and furze, giving a wild and neglected character to the scene; the background of which, where the glen loses itself in a distant turn, is formed by its craggy and wooded side.

Up they marched, side by side, in silence, towards that irregular clump of trees, to which Feltram had pointed from the Mardykes side.

As they approached, it showed more scattered, and two or three of the trees were of grander dimensions than in the distance they had appeared; and as they walked, the broad valley of Cloostedd Forest opened grandly on their left, studding the sides of the valley with solitary trees or groups, which thickened as it descended to the broad level, in parts nearly three miles wide, on which stands the noble forest of Cloostedd, now majestically reposing in the stirless air, gilded and flushed with the melancholy tints of autumn.

I am now going to relate wonderful things; but they rest on the report, strangely consistent, it is true, of Sir Bale Mardykes. That all his senses, however, were sick and feverish, and his brain not quite to be relied on at that moment, is a fact of which sceptics have a right to make all they please and can.

Startled at their approach, a bird like a huge mackaw bounced from the boughs of the trees, and sped away, every now and then upon the ground, toward the shelter of the forest, fluttering and hopping close by the side of the little brook which, emerging from the forest, winds into the glen, and beside the course of which Sir Bale and Philip Feltram had ascended from the margin of the lake.

It fluttered on, as if one of its wings were hurt, and kept hopping and bobbing and flying along the grass at its swiftest, screaming all the time discordantly.

"That must be old Mrs. Amerald's bird, that got away a week ago," said Sir Bale, stopping and looking after it. "Was not it a mackaw?"

"No," said Feltram; "that was a gray parrot; but there are stranger birds in Cloostedd Forest, for my ancestors collected all that would live in our climate, and were at pains to find them the food and shelter they were accustomed to until they grew hardy—that is how it happens."

"By Jove, that's a secret worth knowing," said Sir Bale. "That would make quite a feature. What a fat brute that bird was! and green and dusky-crimson and yellow; but its head is white—age, I suspect; and what a broken beak—hideous bird! splendid plumage; something between a mackaw and a vulture."

Sir Bale spoke jocularly, but with the interest of a bird-fancier; a taste which, when young, he had indulged; and for the moment forgot his cares and the object of his unwonted excursion.

A moment after, a lank slim bird, perfectly white, started from the same boughs, and winged its way to the forest.

"A kite, I think; but its body is a little too long, isn't it?" said Sir Bale again, stopping and looking after its flight also.

"A foreign kite, I daresay?" said Feltram.

All this time there was hopping near them a jay, with the tameness of a bird accustomed to these solitudes. It peered over its slender wing curiously at the visitors; pecking here and nodding there; and thus hopping, it made a circle round them more than once. Then it fluttered up, and perched on a bough of the old oak, from the deep labyrinth of whose branches the other birds had emerged; and from thence it flew down and lighted on the broad druidic stone, that stood like a cyclopean table on its sunken stone props, before the snakelike roots of the oak.

Across this it hopped conceitedly, as over a stage on which it figured becomingly; and after a momentary hesitation, with a little spring, it rose and winged its way in the same direction which the other birds had taken, and was quickly lost in thick forest to the left.

"Here," said Feltram, "this is the tree."

CHAPTER XIX

"I remember it well! A gigantic trunk; and, yes, those marks; but I never before read them as letters. Yes, H.F., so they are—very odd I should not have remarked them. They are so large, and so strangely drawn-out in some places, and filled-in in others, and distorted, and the moss has grown about them; I don't wonder I took them for natural cracks and chasms in the bark," said Sir Bale.

"Very like," said Feltram.

Sir Bale had remarked, ever since they had begun their walk from the shore, that Feltram seemed to undergo a gloomy change. Sharper, grimmer, wilder grew his features, and shadow after shadow darkened his face wickedly.

The solitude and grandeur of the forest, and the repulsive gloom of his companion's countenance and demeanour, communicated a tone of anxiety to Sir Bale; and they stood still, side by side, in total silence for a time, looking toward the forest glades; between themselves and which, on the level sward of the valley, stood many a noble tree and fantastic group of forked birch and thorn, in the irregular formations into which Nature had thrown them.

"Now you stand between the letters. Cast your eyes on the stone," said Feltram suddenly, and his low stern tones almost startled the Baronet.

Looking round, he perceived that he had so placed himself that his point of vision was exactly from between the two great letters, now half-obliterated, which he had been scrutinizing just as he turned about to look toward the forest of Cloostedd.

"Yes, so I am," said Sir Bale.

There was within him an excitement and misgiving, akin to the sensation of a man going into battle, and which corresponded with the pale and sombre frown which Feltram wore, and the manifest change which had come over him.

"Look on the stone steadily for a time, and tell me if you see a black mark, about the size of your hand, anywhere upon its surface," said Feltram.

Sir Bale affected no airs of scepticism now; his imagination was stirred, and a sense of some unknown reality at the bottom of that which he had affected to treat before as illusion, inspired a strange interest in the experiment.

"Do you see it?" asked Feltram.

Sir Bale was watching patiently, but he had observed nothing of the kind.

Sharper, darker, more eager grew the face of Philip Feltram, as his eyes traversed the surface of that huge horizontal block.

"Now?" asked Feltram again.

No, he had seen nothing.

Feltram was growing manifestly uneasy, angry almost; he walked away a little, and back again, and then two or three times round the tree, with his hands shut, and treading the ground like a man trying to warm his feet, and so impatiently he returned, and looked again on the stone.

Sir Bale was still looking, and very soon said, drawing his brows together and looking hard,

"Ha!--yes—hush. There it is, by Jove!--wait—yes—there; it is growing quite plain."

It seemed not as if a shadow fell upon the stone, but rather as if the stone became semi-transparent, and just under its surface was something dark—a hand, he thought it—and darker and darker it grew, as if coming up toward the surface, and after some little wavering, it fixed itself movelessly, pointing, as he thought, toward the forest.

"It looks like a hand," said he. "By Jove, it is a hand—pointing towards the forest with a finger."

"Don't mind the finger; look only on that black blurred mark, and from the point where you stand, taking that point for your direction, look to the forest. Take some tree or other landmark for an object, enter the forest there, and pursue the same line, as well as you can, until you find little flowers with leaves like wood-sorrel, and with tall stems and a red blossom, not larger than a drop, such as you have not seen before, growing among the trees, and follow wherever they seem to grow thickest, and there you will find him."

All the time that Feltram was making this little address, Sir Bale was endeavouring to fix his route by such indications as Feltram described; and when he had succeeded in quite establishing the form of a peculiar tree—a melancholy ash, one huge limb of which had been blasted by lightning, and its partly stricken arm stood high and barkless, stretching its white fingers, as it were, in invitation into the forest, and signing the way for him——

"I have it now," said he. "Come Feltram, you'll come a bit of the way with me."

Feltram made no answer, but slowly shook his head, and turned and walked away, leaving Sir Bale to undertake his adventure alone.

The strange sound they had heard from the midst of the forest, like the rumble of a storm or the far-off trembling of a furnace, had quite ceased. Not a bird was hopping on the grass, or visible on bough or in the sky. Not a living creature was in sight—never was stillness more complete, or silence more oppressive.

It would have been ridiculous to give way to the old reluctance which struggled within him. Feltram had strode down the slope, and was concealed by a screen of bushes from his view. So alone, and full of an interest quite new to him, he set out in quest of his adventures.

CHAPTER XX

The Haunted Forest Sir Bale Mardykes walked in a straight line, by bush and scaur, over the undulating ground, to the blighted ash-tree; and as he approached it, its withered bough stretched more gigantically into the air, and the forest seemed to open where it pointed.

He passed it by, and in a few minutes had lost sight of it again, and was striding onward under the shadow of the forest, which already enclosed him. He was directing his march with all the care he could, in exactly that line which, according to Feltram's rule, had been laid down for him. Now and then, having, as soldiers say, taken an object, and fixed it well in his memory, he would pause and look about him.

As a boy he had never entered the wood so far; for he was under a prohibition, lest he should lose himself in its intricacies, and be benighted there. He had often heard that it was haunted ground, and that too would, when a boy, have deterred him. It was on this account that the scene was so new to him, and that he cared so often to stop and look about him. Here and there a vista opened, exhibiting the same utter desertion, and opening farther perspectives through the tall stems of the trees faintly visible in the solemn shadow. No flowers could he see, but once or twice a wood anemone, and now and then a tiny grove of wood-sorrel.

Huge oak-trees now began to mingle and show themselves more and more frequently among the other timber; and gradually the forest became a great oak wood unintruded upon by any less noble tree. Vast trunks curving outwards to the roots, and expanding again at the branches, stood like enormous columns, striking out their groining boughs, with the dark vaulting of a crypt.

As he walked under the shadow of these noble trees, suddenly his eye was struck by a strange little flower, nodding quite alone by the knotted root of one of those huge oaks.

He stooped and picked it up, and as he plucked it, with a harsh scream just over his head, a large bird with heavy beating wings broke away from the midst of the branches. He could not see it, but he fancied the scream was like that of the huge mackaw whose ill-poised flight he had watched. This conjecture was but founded on the odd cry he had heard.

The flower was a curious one—a stem fine as a hair supported a little bell, that looked like a drop of blood, and never ceased trembling. He walked on, holding this in his fingers; and soon he saw another of the same odd type, then another at a shorter distance, then one a little to the right and another to the left, and farther on a little group, and at last the dark slope was all over trembling with these little bells, thicker and thicker as he descended a gentle declivity to the bank of the little brook, which flowing through the forest loses itself in the lake. The low murmur of this forest stream was almost the first sound, except the shriek of the bird that startled him a little time ago, which had disturbed the profound silence of the wood since he entered it. Mingling with the faint sound of the brook, he now heard a harsh human voice calling words at intervals, the purport of which he could not yet catch; and walking on, he saw seated upon the grass, a strange figure, corpulent, with a great hanging nose, the whole face glowing like copper. He was dressed in a bottle-green cut-velvet coat, of the style of Queen Anne's reign, with a dusky crimson waistcoat, both overlaid with broad and tarnished gold lace, and his silk stockings on thick swollen legs, with great buckled shoes, straddling on the grass, were rolled up over his knees to his short breeches. This ill-favoured old fellow, with a powdered wig that came down to his shoulders, had a dice-box in each hand, and was apparently playing his left against his right, and calling the throws with a hoarse cawing voice.

Raising his black piggish eyes, he roared to Sir Bale, by name, to come and sit down, raising one of his dice-boxes, and then indicating a place on the grass opposite to him.

Now Sir Bale instantly guessed that this was the man, gipsy, warlock, call him what he might, of whom he had come in search. With a strange feeling of curiosity, disgust, and awe, he drew near. He was resolved to do whatever this old man required of him, and to keep him, this time, in good humour.

Sir Bale did as he bid him, and sat down; and taking the box he presented, they began throwing turn about, with three dice, the copper-faced old man teaching him the value of the throws, as he proceeded, with many a curse and oath; and when he did not like a throw, grinning with a look of such real fury, that the master of Mardykes almost expected him to whip out his sword and prick him through as he sat before him.

After some time spent at this play, in which guineas passed now this way, now that, chucked across the intervening patch of grass, or rather moss, that served them for a green cloth, the old man roared over his shoulder,

"Drink;" and picking up a longstemmed conical glass which Sir Bale had not observed before, he handed it over to the Baronet; and taking another in his fingers, he held it up, while a very tall slim old man, dressed in a white livery, with powdered hair and cadaverous face, which seemed to run out nearly all into a long thin hooked nose, advanced with a flask in each hand. Looking at the unwieldly old man, with his heavy nose, powdered head, and all the bottle-green, crimson, and gold about him, and the long slim serving man, with sharp beak, and white from head to heel, standing by him, Sir Bale was forcibly reminded of the great old macaw and the long and slender kite, whose colours they, after their fashion, reproduced, with something, also indescribable, of the air and character of the birds. Not standing on ceremony, the old fellow held up his own glass first, which the white lackey filled from the flask, and then he filled Sir Bale's glass.

It was a large glass, and might have held about half a pint; and the liquor with which the servant filled it was something of the colour of an opal, and circles of purple and gold seemed to be spreading continually outward from the centre, and running inward from the rim, and crossing one another, so as to form a beautiful rippling net-work.

"I drink to your better luck next time," said the old man, lifting his glass high, and winking with one eye, and leering knowingly with the other; "and you know what I mean."

Sir Bale put the liquor to his lips. Wine? Whatever it was, never had he tasted so delicious a flavour. He drained it to the bottom, and placing it on the grass beside him, and looking again at the old dicer, who was also setting down his glass, he saw, for the first time, the graceful figure of a young woman seated on the grass. She was dressed in deep mourning, had a black hood carelessly over her head, and, strangely, wore a black mask, such as are used at masquerades. So much of her throat and chin as he could see were beautifully white; and there was a prettiness in her air and figure which made him think what a beautiful creature she in all likelihood was. She was reclining slightly against the burly man in bottle-green and gold, and her arm was round his neck, and her slender white hand showed itself over his shoulder.

"Ho! my little Geaiette," cried the old fellow hoarsely; "it will be time that you and I should get home.—So, Bale Mardykes, I have nothing to object to you this time; you've crossed the lake, and you've played with me and won and lost, and drank your glass like a jolly companion, and now we know one another; and an acquaintance is made that will last. I'll let you go, and you'll come when I call for you. And now you'll want to know what horse will win next month at Rindermere races.—Whisper me, lass, and I'll tell him."

So her lips, under the black curtain, crept close to his ear, and she whispered.

"Ay, so it will;" roared the old man, gnashing his teeth; "it will be Rainbow, and now make your best speed out of the forest, or I'll set my black dogs after you, ho, ho, ho! and they may chance to pull you down. Away!"

He cried this last order with a glare so black, and so savage a shake of his huge fist, that Sir Bale, merely making his general bow to the group, clapped his hat on his head, and hastily began his retreat; but the same discordant voice yelled after him:

"You'll want that, you fool; pick it up." And there came hurtling after and beside him a great leather bag, stained, and stuffed with a heavy burden, and bounding by him it stopped with a little wheel that brought it exactly before his feet.

He picked it up, and found it heavy.

Turning about to make his acknowledgments, he saw the two persons in full retreat; the profane old scoundrel in the bottle-green limping and stumbling, yet bowling along at a wonderful rate, with many a jerk and reel, and the slender lady in black gliding away by his side into the inner depths of the forest.

So Sir Bale, with a strange chill, and again in utter solitude, pursued his retreat, with his burden, at a swifter pace, and after an hour or so, had recovered the point where he had entered the forest, and passing by the druidic stone and the mighty oak, saw down the glen at his right, standing by the edge of the lake, Philip Feltram, close to the bow of the boat.

CHAPTER XXI

Rindermere Feltram looked grim and agitated when Sir Bale came up to him, as he stood on the flat-stone by which the boat was moored.

"You found him?" said he.

"Yes."

"The lady in black was there?"

"She was."

"And you played with him?"

"Yes."

"And what is that in your hand?"

"A bag of something, I fancy money; it is heavy; he threw it after me. We shall see just now; let us get away."

"He gave you some of his wine to drink?" said Feltram, looking darkly in his face; but there was a laugh in his eyes.

"Yes; of course I drank it; my object was to please him."

"To be sure."

The faint wind that carried them across the lake had quite subsided by the time they had reached the side where they now were.

There was now not wind enough to fill the sail, and it was already evening.

"Give me an oar; we can pull her over in little more than an hour," said Sir Bale; "only let us get away."

He got into the boat, sat down, and placed the leather bag with its heavy freightage at his feet, and took an oar. Feltram loosed the rope and shoved the boat off; and taking his seat also, they began to pull together, without another word, until, in about ten minutes, they had got a considerable way off the Cloostedd shore.

The leather bag was too clumsy a burden to conceal; besides, Feltram knew all about the transaction, and Sir Bale had no need to make a secret. The bag was old and soiled, and tied about the "neck" with a long leather thong, and it seemed to have been sealed with red wax, fragments of which were still sticking to it.

He got it open, and found it full of guineas.

"Halt!" cried Sir Bale, delighted, for he had half apprehended a trick upon his hopes; "gold it is, and a lot of it, by Jove!"

Feltram did not seem to take the slightest interest in the matter. Sulkily and drowsily he was leaning with his elbow on his knee, and it seemed thinking of something far away. Sir Bale could not wait to count them any longer. He reckoned them on the bench, and found two thousand.

It took some time; and when he had got them back into the leather bag, and tied them up again, Feltram, with a sudden start, said sharply,

"Come, take your oar—unless you like the lake by night; and see, a wind will soon be up from Golden Friars!"

He cast a wild look towards Mardykes Hall and Snakes Island, and applying himself to his oar, told Sir Bale to take his also; and nothing loath, the Baronet did so.

It was slow work, for the boat was not built for speed; and by the time they had got about midway, the sun went down, and twilight and the melancholy flush of the sunset tints were upon the lake and fells.

"Ho! here comes the breeze—up from Golden Friars," said Feltram; "we shall have enough to fill the sails now. If you don't fear spirits and Snakes Island, it is all the better for us it should blow from that point. If it blew from Mardykes now, it would be a stiff pull for you and me to get this tub home."

Talking as if to himself, and laughing low, he adjusted the sail and took the tiller, and so, yielding to the rising breeze, the boat glided slowly toward still distant Mardykes Hall.

CHAPTER XXI

The moon came out, and the shore grew misty, and the towering fells rose like sheeted giants; and leaning on the gunwale of the boat, Sir Bale, with the rush and gurgle of the water on the boat's side sounding faintly in his ear, thought of his day's adventure, which seemed to him like a dream—incredible but for the heavy bag that lay between his feet.

As they passed Snakes Island, a little mist, like a fragment of a fog, seemed to drift with them, and Sir Bale fancied that whenever it came near the boat's side she made a dip, as if strained toward the water; and Feltram always put out his hand, as if waving it from him, and the mist seemed to obey the gesture; but returned again and again, and the same thing always happened.

It was three weeks after, that Sir Bale, sitting up in his bed, very pale and wan, with his silk night-cap nodding on one side, and his thin hand extended on the coverlet, where the doctor had been feeling his pulse, in his darkened room, related all the wonders of this day to Doctor Torvey. The doctor had attended him through a fever which followed immediately upon his visit to Cloostedd.

"And, my dear sir, by Jupiter, can you really believe all that delirium to be sober fact?" said the doctor, sitting by the bedside, and actually laughing.

"I can't help believing it, because I can't distinguish in any way between all that and everything else that actually happened, and which I must believe. And, except that this is more wonderful, I can find no reason to reject it, that does not as well apply to all the rest."

"Come, come, my dear sir, this will never do—nothing is more common. These illusions accompanying fever frequently antedate the attack, and the man is actually raving before he knows he is ill."

"But what do you make of that bag of gold?"

"Some one has lent it. You had better ask all about it of Feltram when you can see him; for in speaking to me he seemed to know all about it, and certainly did not seem to think the matter at all out of the commonplace. It is just like that fisherman's story, about the hand that drew Feltram into the water on the night that he was nearly drowned. Every one can see what that was. Why of course it was simply the reflection of his own hand in the water, in that vivid lightning. When you have been out a little and have gained strength you will shake off these dreams."

"I should not wonder," said Sir Bale.

It is not to be supposed that Sir Bale reported all that was in his memory respecting his strange vision, if such it was, at Cloostedd. He made a selection of the incidents, and threw over the whole adventure an entirely accidental character, and described the money which the old man had thrown to him as amounting to a purse of five guineas, and mentioned nothing of the passages which bore on the coming race.

Good Doctor Torvey, therefore, reported only that Sir Bale's delirium had left two or three illusions sticking in his memory.

But if they were illusions, they survived the event of his recovery, and remained impressed on his memory with the sharpness of very recent and accurately observed fact.

He was resolved on going to the races of Rindermere, where, having in his possession so weighty a guarantee as the leather purse, he was determined to stake it all boldly on Rainbow—against which horse he was glad to hear there were very heavy odds.

The race came off. One horse was scratched, another bolted, the rider of a third turned out to have lost a buckle and three half-pence and so was an ounce and a half under weight, a fourth knocked down the post near Rinderness churchyard, and was held to have done it with his left instead of his right knee, and so had run at the wrong side. The result was that Rainbow came in first, and I should be afraid to say how much Sir Bale won. It was a sum that paid off a heavy debt, and left his affairs in a much more manageable state.

From this time Sir Bale prospered. He visited Cloostedd no more; but Feltram often crossed to that lonely shore as heretofore, and it is believed conveyed to him messages which guided his betting. One thing is certain, his luck never deserted him. His debts disappeared; and his love of continental life seemed to have departed. He became content with Mardykes Hall, laid out money on it, and although he never again cared to cross the lake, he seemed to like the scenery.

In some respects, however, he lived exactly the same odd and unpopular life. He saw no one at Mardykes Hall. He practised a very strict reserve. The neighbours laughed at and disliked him, and he was voted, whenever any accidental contact arose, a very disagreeable man; and he had a shrewd and ready sarcasm that made them afraid of him, and himself more disliked.

Odd rumours prevailed about his household. It was said that his old relations with Philip Feltram had become reversed; and that he was as meek as a mouse, and Feltram the bully now. It was also said that Mrs. Julaper had one Sunday evening when she drank tea at the Vicar's, told his good lady very mysteriously, and with many charges of secrecy, that Sir Bale was none the better of his late-found wealth; that he had a load upon his spirits, that he was afraid of Feltram, and so was every one else, more or less, in the house; that he was either mad or worse; and that it was an eerie dwelling, and strange company, and she should be glad herself of a change.

Good Mrs. Bedel told her friend Mrs. Torvey; and all Golden Friars heard all this, and a good deal more, in an incredibly short time.

All kinds of rumours now prevailed in Golden Friars, connecting Sir Bale's successes on the turf with some mysterious doings in Cloostedd Forest. Philip Feltram laughed when he heard these stories—especially when he heard the story that a supernatural personage had lent the Baronet a purse full of money.

"You should not talk to Doctor Torvey so, sir," said he grimly; "he's the greatest tattler in the town. It was old Farmer Trebeck, who could buy and sell us all down here, who lent that money. Partly from good-will, but not without acknowledgment. He has my hand for the first, not worth much, and yours to a bond for the two thousand guineas you brought home with you. It seems strange you should not remember that venerable and kind old farmer whom you talked with so long that day. His grandson, who expects to stand well in his will, being a trainer in Lord Varney's stables, has sometimes a tip to give, and he is the source of your information."

"By Jove, I must be a bit mad, then, that's all," said Sir Bale, with a smile and a shrug.

Philip Feltram moped about the house, and did precisely what he pleased. The change which had taken place in him became more and more pronounced. Dark and stern he always looked, and often malignant. He was like a man possessed of one evil thought which never left him.

There was, besides, the good old Gothic superstition of a bargain or sale of the Baronet's soul to the arch-fiend. This was, of course, very cautiously whispered in a place where he had influence. It was only a coarser and directer version of a suspicion, that in a more credulous generation penetrated a level of society quite exempt from such follies in our day.

One evening at dusk, Sir Bale, sitting after his dinner in his window, saw the tall figure of Feltram, like a dark streak, standing movelessly by the lake. An unpleasant feeling moved him, and then an impatience. He got up, and having primed himself with two glasses of brandy, walked down to the edge of the lake, and placed himself beside Feltram.

"Looking down from the window," said he, nerved with his Dutch courage, "and seeing you standing like a post, do you know what I began to think of?"

Feltram looked at him, but answered nothing.

"I began to think of taking a wife—*marrying*."

Feltram nodded. The announcement had not produced the least effect.

"Why the devil will you make me so uncomfortable! Can't you be like yourself—what you *were*, I mean? I won't go on living here alone with you. I'll take a wife, I tell you. I'll choose a good church-going woman, that will have every man, woman, and child in the house on their marrow-bones twice a day, morning and evening, and three times on Sundays. How will you like that?"

"Yes, you will be married," said Feltram, with a quiet decision which chilled Sir Bale, for he had by no means made up his mind to that desperate step.

Feltram slowly walked away, and that conversation ended.

Now an odd thing happened about this time. There was a family of Feltram—county genealogists could show how related to the vanished family of Cloostedd—living at that time on their estate not far from Carlisle. Three co-heiresses now represented it. They were great beauties—the belles of their county in their day.

One was married to Sir Oliver Haworth of Haworth, a great family in those times. He was a knight of the shire, and had refused a baronetage, and, it was said, had his eye on a peerage. The other sister was married to Sir William Walsingham, a wealthy baronet; and the third and youngest, Miss Janet, was still unmarried, and at home at Cloudesly Hall, where her aunt, Lady Harbottle, lived with her, and made a dignified chaperon.

Now it so fell out that Sir Bale, having business at Carlisle, and knowing old Lady Harbottle, paid his respects at Cloudesly Hall; and being no less than five-and-forty years of age, was for the first time in his life, seriously in love.

Miss Janet was extremely pretty—a fair beauty with brilliant red lips and large blue eyes, and ever so many pretty dimples when she talked and smiled. It was odd, but not perhaps against the course of nature, that a man, though so old as he, and quite *blasé*, should fall at last under that fascination.

But what are we to say of the strange infatuation of the young lady? No one could tell why she liked him. It was a craze. Her family were against it, her intimates, her old nurse—all would not do; and the oddest thing was, that he seemed to take no pains to please her. The end of this strange courtship was that he married her; and she came home to Mardykes Hall, determined to please everybody, and to be the happiest woman in England.

With her came a female cousin, a good deal her senior, past thirty—Gertrude Mainyard, pale and sad, but very gentle, and with all the prettiness that can belong to her years.

This young lady has a romance. Her hero is far away in India; and she, content to await his uncertain return with means to accomplish the hope of their lives, in that frail chance has long embarked all the purpose and love of her life.

When Lady Mardykes came home, a new leaf was, as the phrase is, turned over. The neighbours and all the country people were willing to give the Hall a new trial. There was visiting and returning of visits; and young Lady Mardykes was liked and admired. It could not indeed have been otherwise. But here the improvement in the relations of Mardykes Hall with other homes ceased. On one excuse or another Sir Bale postponed or evaded the hospitalities which establish intimacies. Some people said he was jealous of his young and beautiful wife. But for the most part his reserve was set down to the old inhospitable cause, some ungenial defect in his character; and in a little time the tramp of horses and roll of carriage-wheels were seldom heard up or down the broad avenue of Mardykes Hall.

Sir Bale liked this seclusion; and his wife, "so infatuated with her idolatry of that graceless old man," as surrounding young ladies said, that she was well content to forego the society of the county people for a less interrupted enjoyment of that of her husband. "What she could see in him" to interest or amuse her so, that for his sake she was willing to be "buried alive in that lonely place," the same critics were perpetually wondering.

A year and more passed thus; for the young wife, happily—*very* happily indeed, had it not been for one topic on which she and her husband could not agree. This was Philip Feltram; and an odd quarrel it was.

CHAPTER XXII

Sir Bale is Frightened To Feltram she had conceived, at first sight, a horror. It was not a mere antipathy; fear mingled largely in it. Although she did not see him often, this restless dread grew upon her so, that she urged his dismissal upon Sir Bale, offering to provide, herself, for him a handsome annuity, charged on that part of her property which, by her marriage settlement, had remained in her power. There was a time when Sir Bale was only too anxious to get rid of him. But that was changed now. Nothing could now induce the Baronet to part with him. He at first evaded and resisted quietly. But, urged with a perseverance to which he was unused, he at last broke into fury that appalled her, and swore that if he was worried more upon the subject, he would leave her and the country, and see neither again. This exhibition of violence affrighted her all the more by reason of the contrast; for up to this he had been an uxorious husband. Lady Mardykes was in hysterics, and thoroughly frightened, and remained in her room for two or three days. Sir Bale went up to London about business, and was not home for more than a week. This was the first little squall that disturbed the serenity of their sky.

This point, therefore, was settled; but soon there came other things to sadden Lady Mardykes. There occurred a little incident, soon after Sir Bale's return from London, which recalled the topic on which they had so nearly quarrelled.

Sir Bale had a dressing-room, remote from the bedrooms, in which he sat and read and sometimes smoked. One night, after the house was all quiet, the Baronet being still up, the bell of this dressing-room rang long and furiously. It was such a peal as a person in extreme terror might ring. Lady Mardykes, with her maid in her room, heard it; and in great alarm she ran in her dressing-gown down the gallery to Sir Bale's room. Mallard the butler had already arrived, and was striving to force the door, which was secured. It gave way just as she reached it, and she rushed through.

Sir Bale was standing with the bell-rope in his hand, in the extremest agitation, looking like a ghost; and Philip Feltram was sitting in his chair, with a dark smile fixed upon him. For a minute she thought he had attempted to assassinate his master. She could not otherwise account for the scene.

There had been nothing of the kind, however; as her husband assured her again and again, as she lay sobbing on his breast, with her arms about his neck.

"To her dying hour," she afterwards said to her cousin, "she never could forget the dreadful look in Feltram's face."

No explanation of that scene did she ever obtain from Sir Bale, nor any clue to the cause of the agony that was so powerfully expressed in his countenance. Thus much only she learned from him, that Feltram had sought that interview for the purpose of announcing his departure, which was to take place within the year.

"You are not sorry to hear that. But if you knew all, you might. Let the curse fly where it may, it will come back to roost. So, darling, let us discuss him no more. Your wish is granted, *dis iratis*."

Some crisis, during this interview, seemed to have occurred in the relations between Sir Bale and Feltram. Henceforward they seldom exchanged a word; and when they did speak, it was coldly and shortly, like men who were nearly strangers.

One day in the courtyard, Sir Bale seeing Feltram leaning upon the parapet that overlooks the lake, approached him, and said in a low tone,

"I've been thinking if we—that is, I—do owe that money to old Trebeck, it is high time I should pay it. I was ill, and had lost my head at the time; but it turned out luckily, and it ought to be paid. I don't like the idea of a bond turning up, and a lot of interest."

"The old fellow meant it for a present. He is richer than you are; he wished to give the family a lift. He has destroyed the bond, I believe, and in no case will he take payment."

"No fellow has a right to force his money on another," answered Sir Bale. "I never asked him. Besides, as you know, I was not really myself, and the whole thing seems to me quite different from what you say it was; and, so far as my brain is concerned, it was all a phantasmagoria; but, you say, it was he."

"Every man is accountable for what he intends and for what he *thinks* he does," said Feltram cynically.

"Well, I'm accountable for dealing with that wicked old dicer I *thought* I saw—isn't that it? But I must pay old Trebeck all the same, since the money was his. Can you manage a meeting?"

"Look down here. Old Trebeck has just landed; he will sleep to-night at the George and Dragon, to meet his cattle in the morning at Golden Friars fair. You can speak to him yourself."

So saying Feltram glided away, leaving Sir Bale the task of opening the matter to the wealthy farmer of Cloostedd Fells.

A broad night of steps leads down from the courtyard to the level of the jetty at the lake: and Sir Bale descended, and accosted the venerable farmer, who was bluff, honest, and as frank as a man can be who speaks a *patois* which hardly a living man but himself can understand.

Sir Bale asked him to come to the Hall and take luncheon; but Trebeck was in haste. Cattle had arrived which he wanted to look at, and a pony awaited him on the road, hard by, to Golden Friars; and the old fellow must mount and away.

Then Sir Bale, laying his hand upon his arm in a manner that was at once lofty and affectionate, told in his ears the subject on which he wished to be understood.

The old farmer looked hard at him, and shook his head and laughed in a way that would have been insupportable in a house, and told him, "I hev narra bond o' thoine, mon."

"I know how that is; so does Philip Feltram."

"Well?"

"Well, I must replace the money."

The old man laughed again, and in his outlandish dialect told him to wait till he asked him. Sir Bale pressed it, but the old fellow put it off with outlandish banter; and as the Baronet grew testy, the farmer only waxed more and more hilarious, and at last, mounting his shaggy pony, rode off, still laughing, at a canter to Golden Friars; and when he reached Golden Friars, and got into the hall of the George and Dragon, he asked Richard Turnbull with a chuckle if he ever knew a man refuse an offer of money, or a man want to pay who did not owe; and inquired whether the Squire down at Mardykes Hall mightn't be a bit "wrang in t' garrets." All this, however, other people said, was intended merely to conceal the fact that he really had, through sheer loyalty, lent the money, or rather bestowed it, thinking the old family in jeopardy, and meaning a gift, was determined to hear no more about it. I can't say; I only know people held, some by one interpretation, some by another.

As the caterpillar sickens and changes its hue when it is about to undergo its transformation, so an odd change took place in Feltram. He grew even more silent and morose; he seemed always in an agitation and a secret rage. He used to walk through the woodlands on the slopes of the fells above Mardykes, muttering to himself, picking up the rotten sticks with which the ground was strewn, breaking them in his hands, and hurling them from him, and stamping on the earth as he paced up and down.

One night a thunder-storm came on, the wind blowing gently up from Golden Friars. It was a night black as pitch, illuminated only by the intermittent glare of the lightning. At the foot of the stairs Sir Bale met Feltram, whom he had not seen for some days. He had his cloak and hat on.

"I am going to Cloostedd to-night," he said, "and if all is as I expect, I sha'n't return. We remember all, you and I." And he nodded and walked down the passage.

Sir Bale knew that a crisis had happened in his own life. He felt faint and ill, and returned to the room where he had been sitting. Throughout that melancholy night he did not go to his bed.

In the morning he learned that Marlin, who had been out late, saw Feltram get the boat off, and sail towards the other side. The night was so dark that he could only see him start; but the wind was light and coming up the lake, so that without a tack he could easily make the other side. Feltram did not return. The boat was found fast to the ring at Cloostedd landing-place.

Lady Mardykes was relieved, and for a time was happier than ever. It was different with Sir Bale; and afterwards her sky grew dark also.

CHAPTER XXIII

A Lady in Black Shortly after this, there arrived at the George and Dragon a stranger. He was a man somewhat past forty, embrowned by distant travel, and, his years considered, wonderfully good-looking. He had good eyes; his dark-brown hair had no sprinkling of gray in it; and his kindly smile showed very white and even teeth. He made inquiries about neighbours, especially respecting Mardykes Hall; and the answers seemed to interest him profoundly. He inquired after Philip Feltram, and shed tears when he heard that he was no longer at Mardykes Hall, and that Trebeck or other friends could give him no tidings of him.

And then he asked Richard Turnbull to show him to a quiet room; and so, taking the honest fellow by the hand, he said,

"Mr. Turnbull, don't you know me?"

"No, sir," said the host of the George and Dragon, after a puzzled stare, "I can't say I do, sir."

The stranger smiled a little sadly, and shook his head: and with a gentle laugh, still holding his hand in a very friendly way, he said, "I should have known you anywhere, Mr. Turnbull—anywhere on earth or water. Had you turned up on the Himalayas, or in a junk on the Canton river, or as a dervish in the mosque of St. Sophia, I should have recognised my old friend, and asked what news from Golden Friars. But of course I'm changed. You were a little my senior; and one advantage among many you have over your juniors is that you don't change as we do. I have played many a game of hand-ball in the inn-yard of the George, Mr. Turnbull. You often wagered a pot of ale on my play; you used to say I'd make the best player of fives, and the best singer of a song, within ten miles round the meer. You used to have me behind the bar when I was a boy, with more of an appetite than I have now. I was then at Mardykes Hall, and used to go back in old Marlin's boat. Is old Marlin still alive?"

"Ay, that—he—is," said Turnbull slowly, as he eyed the stranger again carefully. "I don't know who you can be, sir, unless you are—the boy—William Feltram. La! he was seven or eight years younger than Philip. But, lawk!--Well—By Jen, and *be* you Willie Feltram? But no, you can't!"

"Ay, Mr. Turnbull, that very boy—Willie Feltram—even he, and no other; and now you'll shake hands with me, not so formally, but like an old friend."

"Ay, that I will," said honest Richard Turnbull, with a great smile, and a hearty grasp of his guest's hand; and they both laughed together, and the younger man's eyes, for he was an affectionate fool, filled up with tears.

"And I want you to tell me this," said William, after they had talked a little quietly, "now that there is no one to interrupt us, what has become of my brother Philip? I heard from a friend an account of his health that has caused me unspeakable anxiety."

"His health was not bad; no, he was a hardy lad, and liked a walk over the fells, or a pull on the lake; but he was a bit daft, every one said, and a changed man; and, in troth, they say the air o' Mardykes don't agree with every one, no more than him. But that's a tale that's neither here nor there."

"Yes," said William, "that was what they told me—his mind affected. God help and guard us! I have been unhappy ever since; and if I only knew it was well with poor Philip, I think I should be too happy. And where is Philip now?"

"He crossed the lake one night, having took leave of Sir Bale. They thought he was going to old Trebeck's up the Fells. He likes the Feltrams, and likes the folk at Mardykes Hall—though those two families was not always o'er kind to one another. But Trebeck seed nowt o' him, nor no one else; and what has gone wi' him no one can tell."

"*I* heard that also," said William with a deep sigh. "But *I* hoped it had been cleared up by now, and something happier been known of the poor fellow by this time. I'd give a great deal to know—I don't know what I *would* not give to know—I'm so unhappy about him. And now, my good old friend, tell your people to get me a chaise, for I must go to Mardykes Hall; and, first, let me have a room to dress in."

At Mardykes Hall a pale and pretty lady was looking out, alone, from the stone-shafted drawing-room window across the courtyard and the balustrade, on which stood many a great stone cup with flowers, whose leaves were half shed and gone with the winds—emblem of her hopes. The solemn melancholy of the towering fells, the ripple of the lonely lake, deepened her sadness.

The unwonted sound of carriage-wheels awoke her from her reverie.

Before the chaise reached the steps, a hand from its window had seized the handle, the door was thrown open, and William Feltram jumped out.

She was in the hall, she knew not how; and, with a wild scream and a sob, she threw herself into his arms.

Here at last was an end of the long waiting, the dejection which had reached almost the point of despair. And like two rescued from shipwreck, they clung together in an agony of happiness.

William had come back with no very splendid fortune. It was enough, and only enough, to enable them to marry. Prudent people would have thought it, very likely, too little. But he was now home in England, with health unimpaired by his long sojourn in the East, and with intelligence and energies improved by the discipline of his arduous struggle with fortune. He reckoned, therefore, upon one way or other adding something to their income; and he knew that a few hundreds a year would make them happier than hundreds of thousand could other people.

It was five years since they had parted in France, where a journey of importance to the Indian firm, whose right hand he was, had brought him.

The refined tastes that are supposed to accompany gentle blood, his love of art, his talent for music and drawing, had accidentally attracted the attention of the little travelling-party which old Lady Harbottle chaperoned. Miss Janet, now Lady Mardykes, learning that his name was Feltram, made inquiry through a common friend, and learned what interested her still more about him. It ended in an acquaintance, which his manly and gentle nature and his entertaining qualities soon improved into an intimacy.

Feltram had chosen to work his own way, being proud, and also prosperous enough to prevent his pride, in this respect, from being placed under too severe a pressure of temptation. He heard not from but of his brother, through a friend in London, and more lately from Gertrude, whose account of him was sad and even alarming.

When Lady Mardykes came in, her delight knew no bounds. She had already formed a plan for their future, and was not to be put off—William Feltram was to take the great grazing farm that belonged to the Mardykes estate; or, if he preferred it, to farm it for her, sharing the profits. She wanted something to interest her, and this was just the thing. It was hardly half-a-mile away, up the lake, and there was such a comfortable house and garden, and she and Gertrude could be as much together as ever almost; and, in fact, Gertrude and her husband could be nearly always at Mardykes Hall.

So eager and entreating was she, that there was no escape. The plan was adopted immediately on their marriage, and no happier neighbours for a time were ever known.

But was Lady Mardykes content? was she even exempt from the heartache which each mortal thinks he has all to himself? The longing of her life was for children; and again and again had her hopes been disappointed.

One tiny pretty little baby indeed was born, and lived for two years, and then died; and none had come to supply its place and break the childless silence in the great old nursery. That was her sorrow; a greater one than men can understand.

Another source of grief was this: that Sir Bale Mardykes conceived a dislike to William Feltram that was unaccountable. At first suppressed, it betrayed itself negatively only; but with time it increased; and in the end the Baronet made little secret of his wish to get rid of him. Many and ingenious were the annoyances he contrived; and at last he told his wife plainly that he wished William Feltram to find some other abode for himself.

Lady Mardykes pleaded earnestly, and even with tears; for if Gertrude were to leave the neighbourhood, she well knew how utterly solitary her own life would become.

Sir Bale at last vouchsafed some little light as to his motives. There was an old story, he told her, that his estate would go to a Feltram. He had an instinctive distrust of that family. It was a feeling not given him for nothing; it might be the means of defeating their plotting and strategy. Old Trebeck, he fancied, had a finger in it. Philip Feltram had told him that Mardykes was to pass away to a Feltram. Well, they might conspire; but he would take what care he could that the estate should not be stolen from his family. He did not want his wife stript of her jointure, or his children, if he had any, left without bread.

All this sounded very like madness; but the idea was propounded by Philip Feltram. His own jealousy was at bottom founded on superstition which he would not avow and could hardly define. He bitterly blamed himself for having permitted William Feltram to place himself where he was.

In the midst of these annoyances William Feltram was seriously thinking of throwing up the farm, and seeking similar occupation somewhere else.

One day, walking alone in the thick wood that skirts the lake near his farm, he was discussing this problem with himself; and every now and then he repeated his question, "Shall I throw it up, and give him the lease back if he likes?" On a sudden he heard a voice near him say:

"Hold it, you fool!--hold hard, you fool!--hold it, you fool!"

The situation being lonely, he was utterly puzzled to account for the interruption, until on a sudden a huge parrot, green, crimson, and yellow, plunged from among the boughs over his head to the ground, and partly flying, and partly hopping and tumbling along, got lamely, but swiftly, out of sight among the thick underwood; and he could neither start it nor hear it any more. The interruption reminded him of that which befel Robinson Crusoe. It was more singular, however; for he owned no such bird; and its strangeness impressed the omen all the more.

He related it when he got home to his wife; and as people when living a solitary life, and also suffering, are prone to superstition, she did not laugh at the adventure, as in a healthier state of spirits, I suppose, she would.

They continued, however, to discuss the question together; and all the more industriously as a farm of the same kind, only some fifteen miles away, was now offered to all bidders, under another landlord. Gertrude, who felt Sir Bale's unkindness all the more that she was a distant cousin of his, as it had proved on comparing notes, was very strong in favour of the change, and had been urging it with true feminine ingenuity and persistence upon her husband. A very singular dream rather damped her ardour, however, and it appeared thus:

She had gone to her bed full of this subject; and she thought, although she could not remember having done so, had fallen asleep. She was still thinking, as she had been all the day, about leaving the farm. It seemed to her that she was quite awake, and a candle burning all the time in the room, awaiting the return of her husband, who was away at the fair near Haworth; she saw the interior of the room distinctly. It was a sultry night, and a little bit of the window was raised. A very slight sound in that direction attracted her attention; and to her surprise she saw a jay hop upon the window-sill, and into the room.

Up sat Gertrude, surprised and a little startled at the visit of so large a bird, without presence of mind for the moment even to frighten it away, and staring at it, as they say, with all her eyes. A sofa stood at the foot of the bed; and under this the bird swiftly hopped. She extended her hand now to take the bell-rope at the left side of the bed, and in doing so displaced the curtains, which were open only at the foot. She was amazed there to see a lady dressed entirely in black, and with the old-fashioned hood over her head. She was young and pretty, and looked kindly at her, but with now and then a slight contraction of lips and eyebrows that indicates pain. This little twitching was momentary, and recurred, it seemed, about once or twice in a minute.

How it was that she was not frightened on seeing this lady, standing like an old friend at her bedside, she could not afterwards understand. Some influence besides the kindness of her look prevented any sensation of terror at the time. With a very white hand the young lady in black held a white handkerchief pressed to her bosom at the top of her bodice.

"Who are you?" asked Gertrude.

"I am a kinswoman, although you don't know me; and I have come to tell you that you must not leave Faxwell" (the name of the place) "or Janet. If you go, I will go with you; and I can make you fear me."

Her voice was very distinct, but also very faint, with something undulatory in it, that seemed to enter Gertrude's head rather than her ear.

Saying this she smiled horribly, and, lifting her handkerchief, disclosed for a moment a great wound in her breast, deep in which Gertrude saw darkly the head of a snake writhing.

Hereupon she uttered a wild scream of terror, and, diving under the bed-clothes, remained more dead than alive there, until her maid, alarmed by her cry, came in, and having searched the room, and shut the window at her desire, did all in her power to comfort her.

If this was a nightmare and embodied only by a form of expression which in some states belongs to the imagination, a leading idea in the controversy in which her mind had long been employed, it had at least the effect of deciding her against leaving Faxwell. And so that point was settled; and unpleasant relations continued between the tenants of the farm and the master of Mardykes Hall.

To Lady Mardykes all this was very painful, although Sir Bale did not insist upon making a separation between his wife and her cousin. But to Mardykes Hall that cousin came no more. Even Lady Mardykes thought it better to see her at Faxwell than to risk a meeting in the temper in which Sir Bale then was. And thus several years passed.

No tidings of Philip Feltram were heard; and, in fact, none ever reached that part of the world; and if it had not been highly improbable that he could have drowned himself in the lake without his body sooner or later having risen to the surface, it would have been concluded that he had either accidentally or by design made away with himself in its waters.

Over Mardykes Hall there was a gloom—no sound of children's voices was heard there, and even the hope of that merry advent had died out.

This disappointment had no doubt helped to fix in Sir Bale's mind the idea of the insecurity of his property, and the morbid fancy that William Feltram and old Trebeck were conspiring to seize it; than which, I need hardly say, no imagination more insane could have fixed itself in his mind.

In other things, however, Sir Bale was shrewd and sharp, a clear and rapid man of business, and although this was a strange whim, it was not so unnatural in a man who was by nature so prone to suspicion as Sir Bale Mardykes.

During the years, now seven, that had elapsed since the marriage of Sir Bale and Miss Janet Feltram, there had happened but one event, except the death of their only child, to place them in mourning. That was the decease of Sir William Walsingham, the husband of Lady Mardykes' sister. She now lived in a handsome old dower-house at Islington, and being wealthy, made now and then an excursion to Mardykes Hall, in which she was sometimes accompanied by her sister Lady Haworth. Sir Oliver being a Parliament-man was much in London and deep in politics and intrigue, and subject, as convivial rogues are, to occasional hard hits from gout.

But change and separation had made no alteration in these ladies' mutual affections, and no three sisters were ever more attached.

Was Lady Mardykes happy with her lord? A woman so gentle and loving as she, is a happy wife with any husband who is not an absolute brute. There must have been, I suppose, some good about Sir Bale. His wife was certainly deeply attached to him. She admired his wisdom, and feared his inflexible will, and altogether made of him a domestic idol. To acquire this enviable position, I suspect there must be something not essentially disagreeable about a man. At all events, what her neighbours good-naturedly termed her infatuation continued, and indeed rather improved by time.

CHAPTER XXIV

An Old Portrait Sir Bale—whom some remembered a gay and convivial man, not to say a profligate one—had grown to be a very gloomy man indeed. There was something weighing upon his mind; and I daresay some of the good gossips of Golden Friars, had there been any materials for such a case, would have believed that Sir Bale had murdered Philip Feltram, and was now the victim of the worm and fire of remorse.

The gloom of the master of the house made his very servants gloomy, and the house itself looked sombre, as if it had been startled with strange and dismal sights.

Lady Mardykes was something of an artist. She had lighted lately, in an out-of-the-way room, upon a dozen or more old portraits. Several of these were full-lengths; and she was—with the help of her maid, both in long aprons, amid sponges and basins, soft handkerchiefs and varnish-pots and brushes—busy in removing the dust and smoke-stains, and in laying-on the varnish, which brought out the colouring, and made the transparent shadows yield up their long-buried treasures of finished detail.

Against the wall stood a full-length portrait as Sir Bale entered the room; having for a wonder, a word to say to his wife.

"O," said the pretty lady, turning to him in her apron, and with her brush in her hand, "we are in such in pickle, Munnings and I have been cleaning these old pictures. Mrs. Julaper says they are the pictures that came from Cloostedd Hall long ago. They were buried in dust in the dark room in the clock-tower. Here is such a characteristic one. It has a long powdered wig—George the First or Second, I don't know which—and such a combination of colours, and such a face. It seems starting out of the canvas, and all but speaks. Do look; that is, I mean, Bale, if you can spare time."

Sir Bale abstractedly drew near, and looked over his wife's shoulder on the full-length portrait that stood before him; and as he did so a strange expression for a moment passed over his face.

The picture represented a man of swarthy countenance, with signs of the bottle glowing through the dark skin; small fierce pig eyes, a rather flat pendulous nose, and a grim forbidding mouth, with a large wart a little above it. On the head hung one of those full-bottomed powdered wigs that look like a cloud of cotton-wadding; a lace cravat was about his neck; he wore short black-velvet breeches with stockings rolled over them, a bottle-green coat of cut velvet and a crimson waistcoat with long flaps; coat and waistcoat both heavily laced with gold. He wore a sword, and leaned upon a crutch-handled cane, and his figure and aspect indicated a swollen and gouty state. He could not be far from sixty. There was uncommon force in this fierce and forbidding-looking portrait. Lady Mardykes said, "What wonderful dresses they wore! How like a fine magic-lantern figure he looks! What gorgeous colouring! it looks like the plumage of a mackaw; and what a claw his hand is! and that huge broken beak of a nose! Isn't he like a wicked old mackaw?"

"Where did you find that?" asked Sir Bale.

Surprised at his tone, she looked round, and was still more surprised at his looks.

"I told you, dear Bale, I found them in the clock-tower. I hope I did right; it was not wrong bringing them here? I ought to have asked. Are you vexed, Bale?"

"Vexed! not I. I only wish it was in the fire. I must have seen that picture when I was a child. I hate to look at it. I raved about it once, when I was ill. I don't know who it is; I don't remember when I saw it. I wish you'd tell them to burn it."

"It is one of the Feltrams," she answered. "'Sir Hugh Feltram' is on the frame at the foot; and old Mrs. Julaper says he was the father of the unhappy lady who was said to have been drowned near Snakes Island."

"Well, suppose he is; there's nothing interesting in that. It is a disgusting picture. I connect it with my illness; and I think it is the kind of thing that would make any one half mad, if they only looked at it often enough. Tell them to burn it; and come away, come to the next room; I can't say what I want here."

Sir Bale seemed to grow more and more agitated the longer he remained in the room. He seemed to her both frightened and furious; and taking her a little roughly by the wrist, he led her through the door.

When they were in another apartment alone, he again asked the affrighted lady who had told her that picture was there, and who told her to clean it.

She had only the truth to plead. It was, from beginning to end, the merest accident.

"If I thought, Janet, that you were taking counsel of others, talking me over, and trying clever experiments—" he stopped short with his eyes fixed on hers with black suspicion.

His wife's answer was one pleading look, and to burst into tears.

Sir Bale let-go her wrist, which he had held up to this; and placing his hand gently on her shoulder, he said,

"You must not cry, Janet; I have given you no excuse for tears. I only wished an answer to a very harmless question; and I am sure you would tell me, if by any chance you have lately seen Philip Feltram; he is capable of arranging all that. No one knows him as I do. There, you must not cry any more; but tell me truly, has he turned up? is he at Faxwell?"

She denied all this with perfect truth; and after a hesitation of some time, the matter ended. And as soon as she and he were more themselves, he had something quite different to tell her.

"Sit down, Janet; sit down, and forget that vile picture and all I have been saying. What I came to tell you, I think you will like; I am sure it will please you."

And with this little preface he placed his arm about her neck, and kissed her tenderly. She certainly was pleased; and when his little speech was over, she, smiling, with her tears still wet upon her cheeks, put her arms round her husband's neck, and in turn kissed him with the ardour of gratitude, kissed him affectionately; again and again thanking him all the time.

It was no great matter, but from Sir Bale Mardykes it was something quite unusual.

Was it a sudden whim? What was it? Something had prompted Sir Bale, early in that dark shrewd month of December, to tell his wife that he wished to call together some of his county acquaintances, and to fill his house for a week or so, as near Christmas as she could get them to come. He wished her sisters—Lady Haworth (with her husband) and the Dowager Lady Walsingham—to be invited for an early day, before the coming of the other guests, so that she might enjoy their society for a little time quietly to herself before the less intimate guests should assemble.

Glad was Lady Mardykes to hear the resolve of her husband, and prompt to obey. She wrote to her sisters to beg them to arrange to come, together, by the tenth or twelfth of the month, which they accordingly arranged to do. Sir Oliver, it was true, could not be of the party. A minister of state was drinking the waters at Bath; and Sir Oliver thought it would do him no harm to sip a little also, and his fashionable doctor politely agreed, and "ordered" to those therapeutic springs the knight of the shire, who was "consumedly vexed" to lose the Christmas with that jolly dog, Bale, down at Mardykes Hall. But a fellow must have a stomach for his Christmas pudding, and politics takes it out of a poor gentleman deucedly; and health's the first thing, egad!

So Sir Oliver went down to Bath, and I don't know that he tippled much of the waters, but he did drink the burgundy of that haunt of the ailing; and he had the honour of making a fourth not unfrequently in the secretary of state's whist-parties.

It was about the 8th of December when, in Lady Walsingham's carriage, intending to post all the way, that lady, still young, and Lady Haworth, with all the servants that were usual in such expeditions in those days, started from the great Dower House at Islington in high spirits.

Lady Haworth had not been very well—low and nervous; but the clear frosty sun, and the pleasant nature of the excursion, raised her spirits to the point of enjoyment; and expecting nothing but happiness and gaiety—for, after all, Sir Bale was but one of a large party, and even he could make an effort and be agreeable as well as hospitable on occasion—they set out on their northward expedition. The journey, which is a long one, they had resolved to break into a four days' progress; and the inns had been written to, bespeaking a comfortable reception.

CHAPTER XXV

Through the Wall On the third night they put-up at the comfortable old inn called the Three Nuns. With an effort they might easily have pushed on to Mardykes Hall that night, for the distance is not more than five-and-thirty miles. But, considering her sister's health, Lady Walsingham in planning their route had resolved against anything like a forced march.

Here the ladies took possession of the best sitting-room; and, notwithstanding the fatigue of the journey, Lady Haworth sat up with her sister till near ten o'clock, chatting gaily about a thousand things.

Of the three sisters, Lady Walsingham was the eldest. She had been in the habit of taking the command at home; and now, for advice and decision, her younger sisters, less prompt and courageous than she, were wont, whenever in her neighbourhood, to throw upon her all the cares and agitations of determining what was best to be done in small things and great. It is only fair to say, in addition, that this submission was not by any means exacted; it was the deference of early habit and feebler will, for she was neither officious nor imperious.

It was now time that Lady Haworth, a good deal more fatigued than her sister, should take leave of her for the night.

Accordingly they kissed and bid each other good-night; and Lady Walsingham, not yet disposed to sleep, sat for some time longer in the comfortable room where they had taken tea, amusing the time with the book that had, when conversation flagged, beguiled the weariness of the journey. Her sister had been in her room nearly an hour, when she became herself a little sleepy. She had lighted her candle, and was going to ring for her maid, when, to her surprise, the door opened, and her sister Lady Haworth entered in a dressing-gown, looking frightened.

"My darling Mary!" exclaimed Lady Walsingham, "what is the matter? Are you well?"

"Yes, darling," she answered, "quite well; that is, I don't know what is the matter—I'm frightened." She paused, listening, with her eyes turned towards the wall. "O, darling Maud, I am so frightened! I don't know what it can be."

"You must not be agitated, darling; there's nothing. You have been asleep, and I suppose you have had a dream. Were you asleep?"

Lady Haworth had caught her sister fast by the arm with both hands, and was looking wildly in her face.

"Have *you* heard nothing?" she asked, again looking towards the wall of the room, as if she expected to hear a voice through it.

"Nonsense, darling; you are dreaming still. Nothing; there has been nothing to hear. I have been awake ever since; if there had been anything to hear, I could not have missed it. Come, sit down. Sip a little of this water; you are nervous, and over-tired; and tell me plainly, like a good little soul, what is the matter; for nothing has happened here; and you ought to know that the Three Nuns is the quietest house in England; and I'm no witch, and if you won't tell me what's the matter, I can't divine it."

"Yes, of course," said Mary, sitting down, and glancing round her wildly. "I don't hear it now; *you* don't?"

"Do, my dear Mary, tell me what you mean," said Lady Walsingham kindly but firmly.

Lady Haworth was holding the still untasted glass of water in her hand.

"Yes, I'll tell you; I have been so frightened! You are right; I had a dream, but I can scarcely remember anything of it, except the very end, when I wakened. But it was not the dream; only it was connected with what terrified me so. I was so tired when I went to bed, I thought I should have slept soundly; and indeed I fell asleep immediately; and I must have slept quietly for a good while. How long is it since I left you?"

"More than an hour."

"Yes, I must have slept a good while; for I don't think I have been ten minutes awake. How my dream began I don't know. I remember only that gradually it came to this: I was standing in a recess in a panelled gallery; it was lofty, and, I thought, belonged to a handsome but old-fashioned house. I was looking straight towards the head of a wide staircase, with a great oak banister. At the top of the stairs, as near to me, about, as that window there, was a thick short column of oak, on top of which was a candlestick. There was no other light but from that one candle; and there was a lady standing beside it, looking down the stairs, with her back turned towards me; and from her gestures I should have thought speaking to people on a lower lobby, but whom from my place I could not see. I soon perceived that this lady was in great agony of mind; for she beat her breast and wrung her hands every now and then, and wagged her head slightly from side to side, like a person in great distraction. But one word she said I could not hear. Nor when she struck her hand on the banister, or stamped, as she seemed to do in her pain, upon the floor, could I hear any sound. I found myself somehow waiting upon this lady, and was watching her with awe and sympathy. But who she was I knew not, until turning towards me I plainly saw Janet's face, pale and covered with tears, and with such a look of agony as—O God!--I can never forget."

"Pshaw! Mary darling, what is it but a dream! I have had a thousand more startling; it is only that you are so nervous just now."

"But that is not all—nothing; what followed is so dreadful; for either there is something very horrible going on at Mardykes, or else I am losing my reason," said Lady Haworth in increasing agitation. "I wakened instantly in great alarm, but I suppose no more than I have felt a hundred times on awakening from a frightful dream. I sat up in my bed; I was thinking of ringing for Winnefred, my heart was beating so, but feeling better soon I changed my mind. All this time I heard a faint sound of a voice, as if coming through a thick wall. It came from the wall at the left side of my bed, and I fancied was that of some woman lamenting in a room separated from me by that thick partition. I could only perceive that it was a sound of crying mingled with ejaculations of misery, or fear, or entreaty. I listened with a painful curiosity, wondering who it could be, and what could have happened in the neighbouring rooms of the house; and as I looked and listened, I could distinguish my own name, but at first nothing more. That, of course, might have been an accident; and I knew there were many Marys in the world besides myself. But it made me more curious; and a strange thing struck me, for I was now looking at that very wall through which the sounds were coming. I saw that there was a window in it. Thinking that the rest of the wall might nevertheless be covered by another room, I drew the curtain of it and looked out. But there is no such thing. It is the outer wall the entire way along. And it is equally impossible of the other wall, for it is to the front of the house, and has two windows in it; and the wall that the head of my bed stands against has the gallery outside it all the way; for I remarked that as I came to you."

"Tut, tut, Mary darling, nothing on earth is so deceptive as sound; this and fancy account for everything."

"But hear me out; I have not told you all. I began to hear the voice more clearly, and at last quite distinctly. It was Janet's, and she was conjuring you by name, as well as me, to come to her to Mardykes, without delay, in her extremity; yes, *you*, just as vehemently as me. It was Janet's voice. It still seemed separated by the wall, but I heard every syllable now; and I never heard voice or words of such anguish. She was imploring of us to come on, without a moment's delay, to Mardykes; and crying that, if we were not with her, she should go mad."

"Well, darling," said Lady Walsingham, "you see I'm included in this invitation as well as you, and should hate to disappoint Janet just as much; and I do assure you, in the morning you will laugh over this fancy with me; or rather, she will laugh over it with us, when we get to Mardykes. What you do want is rest, and a little sal-volatile."

So saying she rang the bell for Lady Haworth's maid. Having comforted her sister, and made her take the nervous specific she recommended, she went with her to her room; and taking possession of the arm-chair by the fire, she told her that she would keep her company until she was asleep, and remain long enough to be sure that the sleep was not likely to be interrupted. Lady Haworth had not been ten minutes in her bed, when she raised herself with a start to her elbow, listening with parted lips and wild eyes, her trembling fingers behind her ears. With an exclamation of horror, she cried,

"There it is again, upbraiding us! I can't stay longer."

She sprang from the bed, and rang the bell violently.

"Maud," she cried in an ecstasy of horror, "nothing shall keep me here, whether you go or not. I will set out the moment the horses are put to. If you refuse to come, Maud, mind the responsibility is yours—listen!" and with white face and starting eyes she pointed to the wall. "Have you ears; don't you hear?"

The sight of a person in extremity of terror so mysterious, might have unnerved a ruder system than Lady Walsingham's. She was pale as she replied; for under certain circumstances those terrors which deal with the supernatural are more contagious than any others. Lady Walsingham still, in terms, held to her opinion; but although she tried to smile, her face showed that the panic had touched her.

"Well, dear Mary," she said, "as you will have it so, I see no good in resisting you longer. Here, it is plain, your nerves will not suffer you to rest. Let us go then, in heaven's name; and when you get to Mardykes Hall you will be relieved."

All this time Lady Haworth was getting on her things, with the careless hurry of a person about to fly for her life; and Lady Walsingham issued her orders for horses, and the general preparations for resuming the journey.

It was now between ten and eleven; but the servant who rode armed with them, according to the not unnecessary usage of the times, thought that with a little judicious bribing of postboys they might easily reach Mardykes Hall before three o'clock in the morning.

When the party set forward again, Lady Haworth was comparatively tranquil. She no longer heard the unearthly mimickry of her sister's voice; there remained only the fear and suspense which that illusion or visitation had produced.

Her sister, Lady Walsingham, after a brief effort to induce something like conversation, became silent. A thin sheet of snow had covered the darkened landscape, and some light flakes were still dropping. Lady Walsingham struck her repeater often in the dark, and inquired the distances frequently. She was anxious to get over the ground, though by no means fatigued. Something of the anxiety that lay heavy at her sister's heart had touched her own.

CHAPTER XXVI

Perplexed The roads even then were good, and very good horses the posting-houses turned out; so that by dint of extra pay the rapid rate of travelling undertaken by the servant was fully accomplished in the first two or three stages.

While Lady Walsingham was continually striking her repeater in her ear, and as they neared their destination, growing in spite of herself more anxious, her sister's uneasiness showed itself in a less reserved way; for, cold as it was, with snowflakes actually dropping, Lady Haworth's head was perpetually out at the window, and when she drew it up, sitting again in her place, she would audibly express her alarms, and apply to her sister for consolation and confidence in her suspense.

Under its thin carpet of snow, the pretty village of Golden Friars looked strangely to their eyes. It had long been fast asleep, and both ladies were excited as they drew up at the steps of the George and Dragon, and with bell and knocker roused the slumbering household.

What tidings awaited them here? In a very few minutes the door was opened, and the porter staggered down, after a word with the driver, to the carriage-window, not half awake.

"Is Lady Mardykes well?" demanded Lady Walsingham.

"Is Sir Bale well?"

"Are all the people at Mardykes Hall quite well?"

With clasped hands Lady Haworth listened to the successive answers to these questions which her sister hastily put. The answers were all satisfactory. With a great sigh and a little laugh, Lady Walsingham placed her hand affectionately on that of her sister; who, saying, "God be thanked!" began to weep.

"When had you last news from Mardykes?" asked Lady Walsingham.

"A servant was down here about four o'clock."

"O! no one since?" said she in a disappointed tone.

No one had been from the great house since, but all were well then.

"They are early people, you know, dear; and it is dark at four, and that is as late as they could well have heard, and nothing could have happened since—very unlikely. We have come very fast; it is only a few minutes past two, darling."

But each felt the chill and load of their returning anxiety.

While the people at the George were rapidly getting a team of horses to, Lady Walsingham contrived a moment for an order from the other window to her servant, who knew Golden Friars perfectly, to knock-up the people at Doctor Torvey's, and to inquire whether all were well at Mardykes Hall.

There he learned that a messenger had come for Doctor Torvey at ten o'clock, and that the Doctor had not returned since. There was no news, however, of any one's being ill; and the Doctor himself did not know what he was wanted about. While Lady Haworth was talking to her maid from the window next the steps, Lady Walsingham was, unobserved, receiving this information at the other.

It made her very uncomfortable.

In a few minutes more, however, with a team of fresh horses, they were again rapidly passing the distance between them and Mardykes Hall.

About two miles on, their drivers pulled-up, and they heard a voice talking with them from the roadside. A servant from the Hall had been sent with a note for Lady Walsingham, and had been ordered, if necessary, to ride the whole way to the Three Nuns to deliver it. The note was already in Lady Walsingham's hand; her sister sat beside her, and with the corner of the open note in her fingers, she read it breathlessly at the same time by the light of a carriage-lamp which the man held to the window. It said:

My dearest love—my darling sister—dear sisters both!--in God's name, lose not a moment. I am so overpowered and *terrified.* I cannot explain; I can only implore of you to come with all the haste you can make. Waste no time, darlings. I hardly understand what I write. Only this, dear sisters; I feel that my reason will desert me, unless you come soon. You will not fail me now. Your poor distracted

JANET

The sisters exchanged a pale glance, and Lady Haworth grasped her sister's hand.

"Where is the messenger?" asked Lady Walsingham.

A mounted servant came to the window.

"Is any one ill at home?" she asked.

"No, all were well—my lady, and Sir Bale—no one sick."

"But the Doctor was sent for; what was that for?"

"I can't say, my lady."

"You are quite certain that no one—think—*no* one is ill?"

"There is no one ill at the Hall, my lady, that I have heard of."

"Is Lady Mardykes, my sister, still up?"

"Yes, my lady; and her maid is with her."

"And Sir Bale, are you certain he is quite well?"

"Sir Bale is quite well, my lady; he has been busy settling papers to-night, and was as well as usual."

"That will do, thanks," said the perplexed lady; and to her own servant she added, "On to Mardykes Hall with all the speed they can make. I'll pay them well, tell them."

And in another minute they were gliding along the road at a pace which the muffled beating of the horses' hoofs on the thin sheet of snow that covered the road showed to have broken out of the conventional trot, and to resemble something more like a gallop.

And now they were under the huge trees, that looked black as hearse-plumes in contrast with the snow. The cold gleam of the lake in the moon which had begun to shine out now met their gaze; and the familiar outline of Snakes Island, its solemn timber bleak and leafless, standing in a group, seemed to watch Mardykes Hall with a dismal observation across the water. Through the gate and between the huge files of trees the carriage seemed to fly; and at last the steaming horses stood panting, nodding and snorting, before the steps in the courtyard.

There was a light in an upper window, and a faint light in the hall, the door of which was opened; and an old servant came down and ushered the ladies into the house.

CHAPTER XXVII

The Hour Lightly they stepped over the snow that lay upon the broad steps, and entering the door saw the dim figure of their sister, already in the large and faintly-lighted hall. One candle in the hand of her scared maid, and one burning on the table, leaving the distant parts of that great apartment in total darkness, touched the figures with the odd sharp lights in which Schalken delights; and a streak of chilly moonlight, through the open door, fell upon the floor, and was stretched like a white sheet at her feet. Lady Mardykes, with an exclamation of agitated relief, threw her arms, in turn, round the necks of her sisters, and hugging them, kissed them again and again, murmuring her thanks, calling them her "blessed sisters," and praising God for his mercy in having sent them to her in time, and altogether in a rapture of agitation and gratitude.

Taking them each by a hand, she led them into a large room, on whose panels they could see the faint twinkle of the tall gilded frames, and the darker indication of the old portraits, in which that interesting house abounds. The moonbeams, entering obliquely through the Tudor stone-shafts of the window and thrown upon the floor, reflected an imperfect light; and the candle which the maid who followed her mistress held in her hand shone dimly from the sideboard, where she placed it. Lady Mardykes told her that she need not wait.

"They don't know; they know only that we are in some great confusion; but—God have mercy on me!--nothing of the reality. Sit down, darlings; you are tired."

She sat down between them on a sofa, holding a hand of each. They sat opposite the window, through which appeared the magnificent view commanded from the front of the house: in the foreground the solemn trees of Snakes Island, one great branch stretching upward, bare and moveless, from the side, like an arm raised to heaven in wonder or in menace towards the house; the lake, in part swept by the icy splendour of the moon, trembling with a dazzling glimmer, and farther off lost in blackness; the Fells rising from a base of gloom, into ribs and peaks white with snow, and looking against the pale sky, thin and transparent as a haze. Right across to the storied woods of Cloostedd, and the old domains of the Feltrams, this view extended.

Thus alone, their mufflers still on, their hands clasped in hers, they breathlessly listened to her strange tale.

Connectedly told it amounted to this: Sir Bale seemed to have been relieved of some great anxiety about the time when, ten days before, he had told her to invite her friends to Mardykes Hall. This morning he had gone out for a walk with Trevor, his under-steward, to talk over some plans about thinning the woods at this side; and also to discuss practically a proposal, lately made by a wealthy merchant, to take a very long lease, on advantageous terms to Sir Bale as he thought, of the old park and chase of Cloostedd, with the intention of building there, and making it once more a handsome residence.

In the improved state of his spirits, Sir Bale had taken a shrewd interest in this negotiation; and was actually persuaded to cross the lake that morning with his adviser, and to walk over the grounds with him.

Sir Bale had seemed unusually well, and talked with great animation. He was more like a young man who had just attained his majority, and for the first time grasped his estates, than the grim elderly Baronet who had been moping about Mardykes, and as much afraid as a cat of the water, for so many years.

As they were returning toward the boat, at the roots of that same scathed elm whose barkless bough had seemed, in his former visit to this old wood, to beckon him from a distance, like a skeleton arm, to enter the forest, he and his companion on a sudden missed an old map of the grounds which they had been consulting.

"We must have left it in the corner tower of Cloostedd House, which commands that view of the grounds, you remember; it would not do to lose it. It is the most accurate thing we have. I'll sit down here and rest a little till you come back."

The man was absent little more than twenty minutes. When he returned, he found that Sir Bale had changed his position, and was now walking to and fro, around and about, in what, at a distance, he fancied was mere impatience, on the open space a couple of hundred paces nearer to the turn in the valley towards the boat. It was not impatience. He was agitated. He looked pale, and he took his companion's arm—a thing he had never thought of doing before—and said, "Let us away quickly. I've something to tell at home,—and I forgot it."

Not another word did Sir Bale exchange with his companion. He sat in the stern of the boat, gloomy as a man about to glide under traitor's-gate. He entered his house in the same sombre and agitated state. He entered his library, and sat for a long time as if stunned.

At last he seemed to have made-up his mind to something; and applied himself quietly and diligently to arranging papers, and docketing some and burning others. Dinner-time arrived. He sent to tell Lady Mardykes that he should not join her at dinner, but would see her afterwards.

"It was between eight and nine," she continued, "I forget the exact time, when he came to the tower drawing-room where I was. I did not hear his approach. There is a stone stair, with a thick carpet on it. He told me he wished to speak to me there. It is an out-of-the-way place—a small old room with very thick walls, and there is a double door, the inner one of oak—I suppose he wished to guard against being overheard.

"There was a look in his face that frightened me, I saw he had something dreadful to tell. He looked like a man on whom a lot had fallen to put some one to death," said Lady Mardykes. "O, my poor Bale! my husband, my husband! he knew what it would be to me."

Here she broke into the wildest weeping, and it was some time before she resumed.

"He seemed very kind and very calm," she said at last; "he said but little; and, I think, these were his words: 'I find, Janet, I have made a great miscalculation—I thought my hour of danger had passed. We have been many years together, but a parting must sooner or later be, and my time has come.'

"I don't know what I said. I would not have so much minded—for I could not have believed, if I had not seen him—but there was that in his look and tone which no one could doubt.

"'I shall die before to-morrow morning,' he said. 'You must command yourself, Janet; it can't be altered now.'

"'O, Bale,' I cried nearly distracted, 'you would not kill yourself!'

"'Kill myself! poor child! no, indeed,' he said; 'it is simply that I shall die. No violent death—nothing but the common subsidence of life—I have made up my mind; what happens to everybody can't be so very bad; and millions of worse men than I die every year. You must not follow me to my room, darling; I shall see you by and by.'

"His language was collected and even cold; but his face looked as if it was cut in stone; you never saw, in a dream, a face like it."

Lady Walsingham here said, "I am certain he is ill; he's in a fever. You must not distract and torture yourself about his predictions. You sent for Doctor Torvey; what did he say?"

"I could not tell him all."

"O, no; I don't mean that; they'd only say he was mad, and we little better for minding what he says. But did the Doctor see him? and what did he say of his health?"

"Yes; he says there is nothing wrong—no fever—nothing whatever. Poor Bale has been so kind; he saw him to please me," she sobbed again wildly. "I wrote to implore of him. It was my last hope, strange as it seems; and O, would to God I could think it! But there is nothing of that kind. Wait till you have seen him. There is a frightful calmness about all he says and does; and his directions are all so clear, and his mind so perfectly collected, it is quite impossible."

And poor Lady Mardykes again burst into a frantic agony of tears.

CHAPTER XXVIII

Sir Bale in the Gallery "Now, Janet darling, you are yourself low and nervous, and you treat this fancy of Bale's as seriously as he does himself. The truth is, he is a hypochondriac, as the doctors say; and you will find that I am right; he will be quite well in the morning, and I daresay a little ashamed of himself for having frightened his poor little wife as he has. I will sit up with you. But our poor Mary is not, you know, very strong; and she ought to lie down and rest a little. Suppose you give me a cup of tea in the drawing-room. I will run up to my room and get these things off, and meet you in the drawing-room; or, if you like it better, you can sit with me in my own room; and for goodness' sake let us have candles enough and a bright fire; and I promise you, if you will only exert your own good sense, you shall be a great deal more cheerful in a very little time."

Lady Walsingham's address was kind and cheery, and her air confident. For a moment a ray of hope returned, and her sister Janet acknowledged at least the possibility of her theory. But if confidence is contagious, so also is panic; and Lady Walsingham experienced a sinking of the heart which she dared not confess to her sister, and vainly strove to combat.

Lady Walsingham went up with her sister Mary, and having seen her in her room, and spoken again to her in the same cheery tone in which she had lectured her sister Lady Mardykes, she went on; and having taken possession of her own room, and put off her cloaks and shawls, she was going downstairs again, when she heard Sir Bale's voice, as he approached along the gallery, issuing orders to a servant, as it seemed, exactly in his usual tone.

She turned, with a strange throb at her heart, and met him.

A little sterner, a little paler than usual he looked; she could perceive no other change. He took her hand kindly and held it, as with dilated eyes he looked with a dark inquiry for a moment in her face. He signed to the servant to go on, and said, "I'm glad you have come, Maud. You have heard what is to happen; and I don't know how Janet could have borne it without your support. You did right to come; and you'll stay with her for a day or two, and take her away from this place as soon as you can."

She looked at him with the embarrassment of fear. He was speaking to her with the calmness of a leave-taking in the pressroom—the serenity that overlies the greatest awe and agony of which human nature is capable.

"I am glad to see you, Bale," she began, hardly knowing what she said, and she stopped short.

"You are come, it turns out, on a sad mission," he resumed; "you find all about to change. Poor Janet! it is a blow to her. I shall not live to see to-morrow's sun."

"Come," she said, startled, "you must not talk so. No, Bale, you have no right to speak so; you can have no reason to justify it. It is cruel and wicked to trifle with your wife's feelings. If you are under a delusion, you must make an effort and shake it off, or, at least, cease to talk of it. You are not well; I know by your looks you are ill; but I am very certain we shall see you much better by tomorrow, and still better the day following."

"No, I'm not ill, sister. Feel that pulse, if you doubt me; there is no fever in it. I never was more perfectly in health; and yet I know that before the clock, that has just struck three, shall have struck five, I, who am talking to you, shall be dead."

Lady Walsingham was frightened, and her fear irritated her.

"I have told you what I think and believe," she said vehemently. "I think it wrong and cowardly of you to torture my poor sister with your whimsical predictions. Look into your own mind, and you will see you have absolutely no reason to support what you say. How *can* you inflict all this agony upon a poor creature foolish enough to love you as she does, and weak enough to believe in your idle dreams?"

"Stay, sister; it is not a matter to be debated so. If to-morrow I can hear you, it will be time enough to upbraid me. Pray return now to your sister; she needs all you can do for her. She is much to be pitied; her sufferings afflict me. I shall see you and her again before my death. It would have been more cruel to leave her unprepared. Do all in your power to nerve and tranquillise her. What is past cannot now be helped."

He paused, looking hard at her, as if he had half made up his mind to say something more. But if there was a question of the kind, it was determined in favour of silence.

He dropped her hand, turned quickly, and left her.

CHAPTER XXIX

Dr. Torvey's Opinion When Lady Walsingham reached the head of the stairs, she met her maid, and from her learned that her sister, Lady Mardykes, was downstairs in the same room. On approaching, she heard her sister Mary's voice talking with her, and found them together. Mary, finding that she could not sleep, had put on her clothes again, and come down to keep her sister company. The room looked more comfortable now. There were candles lighted, and a good fire burnt in the grate; tea-things stood on a little table near the fire, and the two sisters were talking, Lady Mardykes appearing more collected, and only they two in the room.

"Have you seen him, Maud?" cried Lady Mardykes, rising and hastily approaching her the moment she entered.

"Yes, dear; and talked with him, and——"

"Well?"

"And I think very much as I did before. I think he is nervous, he says he is not ill; but he is nervous and whimsical, and as men always are when they happen to be out of sorts, very positive; and of course the only thing that can quite undeceive him is the lapse of the time he has fixed for his prediction, as it is sure to pass without any tragic result of any sort. We shall then all see alike the nature of his delusion."

"O, Maud, if I were only sure you thought so! if I were sure you really had hopes! Tell me, Maud, for God's sake, what you really think."

Lady Walsingham was a little disconcerted by the unexpected directness of her appeal.

"Come, darling, you must not be foolish," she said; "we can only talk of impressions, and we are imposed upon by the solemnity of his manner, and the fact that he evidently believes in his own delusion; every one does believe in his own delusion—there is nothing strange in that."

"O, Maud, I see you are not convinced; you are only trying to comfort me. You have no hope—none, none, none!" and she covered her face with her hands, and wept again convulsively.

Lady Walsingham was silent for a moment, and then with an effort said, as she placed her hand on her sister's arm, "You see, dear Janet, there is no use in my saying the same thing over and over again; an hour or two will show who is right. Sit down again, and be like yourself. My maid told me that you had sent to the parlour for Doctor Torvey; he must not find you so. What would he think? Unless you mean to tell him of Bale's strange fancy; and a pretty story that would be to set afloat in Golden Friars. I think I hear him coming."

So, in effect, he was. Doctor Torvey—with the florid gravity of a man who, having just swallowed a bottle of port, besides some glasses of sherry, is admitted to the presence of ladies whom he respects—entered the room, made what he called his "leg and his compliments," and awaited the ladies' commands.

"Sit down, Doctor Torvey," said Lady Walsingham, who in the incapacity of her sister undertook the doing of the honours. "My sister, Lady Mardykes, has got it into her head somehow that Sir Bale is ill. I have been speaking to him; he certainly does not look very well, but he says he is quite well. Do you think him well?—that is, we know you don't think there is anything of importance amiss—but she wishes to know whether you think him *perfectly* well."

The Doctor cleared his voice and delivered his lecture, a little thickly at some words, upon Sir Bale's case; the result of which was that it was no case at all; and that if he would only live something more of a country gentleman's life, he would be as well as any man could desire—as well as any man, gentle or simple, in the country.

"The utmost I should think of doing for him would be, perhaps, a little quinine, nothing mo'—shurely—he is really and toory a very shoun' shtay of health."

Lady Walsingham looked encouragingly at her sister and nodded.

"I've been shen' for, La'y Walsh—Walse—Walsing—*ham*; old Jack Amerald—he likshe his glass o' port," he said roguishly, "and shuvversh accord'n'ly," he continued, with a compassionating paddle of his right hand; "one of thoshe aw—odd feels in his stomach; and as I have pretty well done all I can man-n'ge down here, I must be off, ye shee. Wind up from Golden Friars, and a little flutter ovv zhnow, thazh all;" and with some remarks about the extreme cold of the weather, and the severity of their night journey, and many respectful and polite parting speeches, the Doctor took his leave; and they soon heard the wheels of his gig and the tread of his horse, faint and muffled from the snow in the court-yard, and the Doctor, who had connected that melancholy and agitated household with the outer circle of humanity, was gone.

There was very little snow falling, half-a-dozen flakes now and again, and their flight across the window showed, as the Doctor had in a manner boasted, that the wind was in his face as he returned to Golden Friars. Even these desultory snow-flakes ceased, at times, altogether; and returning, as they say, "by fits and starts," left for long intervals the landscape, under the brilliant light of the moon, in its wide white shroud. The curtain of the great window had not been drawn. It seemed to Lady Walsingham that the moonbeams had grown more dazzling, that Snakes Island was nearer and more distinct, and the outstretched arm of the old tree looked bigger and angrier, like the uplifted arm of an assassin, who draws silently nearer as the catastrophe approaches.

Cold, dazzling, almost repulsive in this intense moonlight and white sheeting, the familiar landscape looked in the eyes of Lady Walsingham. The sisters gradually grew more and more silent, an unearthly suspense overhung them all, and Lady Mardykes rose every now and then and listened at the open door for step or voice in vain. They all were overpowered by the intenser horror that seemed gathering around them. And thus an hour or more passed.

CHAPTER XXX

Hush! Pale and silent those three beautiful sisters sat. The horrible quietude of a suspense that had grown all but insupportable oppressed the guests of Lady Mardykes, and something like the numbness of despair had reduced her to silence, the dreadful counterfeit of peace.

Sir Bale Mardykes on a sudden softly entered the room. Reflected from the floor near the window, the white moonlight somehow gave to his fixed features the character of a smile. With a warning gesture, as he came in, he placed his finger to his lips, as if to enjoin silence; and then, having successively pressed the hands of his two sisters-in-law, he stooped over his almost fainting wife, and twice pressed her cold forehead with his lips; and so, without a word, he went softly from the room.

Some seconds elapsed before Lady Walsingham, recovering her presence of mind, with one of the candlesticks from the table in her hand, opened the door and followed.

She saw Sir Bale mount the last stair of the broad flight visible from the hall, and candle in hand turn the corner of the massive banister, and as the light thrown from his candle showed, he continued, without hurry, to ascend the second flight.

With the irrepressible curiosity of horror she continued to follow him at a distance.

She saw him enter his own private room, and close the door.

Continuing to follow she placed herself noiselessly at the door of the apartment, and in breathless silence, with a throbbing heart, listened for what should pass.

She distinctly heard Sir Bale pace the floor up and down for some time, and then, after a pause, a sound as if some one had thrown himself heavily on the bed. A silence followed, during which her sisters, who had followed more timidly, joined her. She warned them with a look and gesture to be silent.

Lady Haworth stood a little behind, her white lips moving, and her hands clasped in a silent agony of prayer. Lady Mardykes leaned against the massive oak door-case.

With her hand raised to her ear, and her lips parted, Lady Walsingham listened for some seconds—for a minute, two minutes, three. At last, losing heart, she seized the handle in her panic, and turned it sharply. The door was locked on the inside, but some one close to it said from within, "Hush, hush!"

Much alarmed now, the same lady knocked violently at the door. No answer was returned.

She knocked again more violently, and shook the door with all her fragile force. It was something of horror in her countenance as she did so, that, no doubt, terrified Lady Mardykes, who with a loud and long scream sank in a swoon upon the floor.

The servants, alarmed by these sounds, were speedily in the gallery. Lady Mardykes was carried to her room, and laid upon her bed; her sister, Lady Haworth, accompanying her. In the meantime the door was forced. Sir Bale Mardykes was found stretched upon his bed.

Those who have once seen it, will not mistake the aspect of death. Here, in Sir Bale Mardykes' room, in his bed, in his clothes, is a stranger, grim and awful; in a few days to be insupportable, and to pass alone into the prison-house, and to be seen no more.

CHAPTER XXX

Where is Sir Bale Mardykes now, whose roof-tree and whose place at board and bed will know him no more? Here lies a chap-fallen, fish-eyed image, chilling already into clay, and stiffening in every joint.

There is a marble monument in the pretty church of Golden Friars. It stands at the left side of what antiquarians call "the high altar." Two pillars at each end support an arch with several armorial bearings on as many shields sculptured above. Beneath, on a marble flooring raised some four feet, with a cornice round, lies Sir Bale Mardykes, of Mardykes Hall, ninth Baronet of that ancient family, chiseled in marble with knee-breeches and buckled-shoes, and *ailes de pigeon*, and single-breasted coat and long waist-coat, ruffles and sword, such as gentlemen wore about the year 1770, and bearing a strong resemblance to the features of the second Charles. On the broad marble which forms the background is inscribed an epitaph, which has perpetuated to our times the estimate formed by his "inconsolable widow," the Dowager Lady Mardykes, of the virtues and accomplishments of her deceased lord.

Lady Walsingham would have qualified two or three of the more highly-coloured hyperboles, at which the Golden Friars of those days sniffed and tittered. They don't signify now; there is no contemporary left to laugh or whisper. And if there be not much that is true in the letter of that inscription, it at least perpetuates something that *is* true—that wonderful glorificaion of partisanship, the affection of an idolising wife.

Lady Mardykes, a few days after the funeral, left Mardykes Hall for ever. She lived a great deal with her sister, Lady Walsingham; and died, as a line cut at the foot of Sir Bale Mardykes' epitaph records, in the year 1790; her remains being laid beside those of her beloved husband in Golden Friars.

The estates had come to Sir Bale Mardykes free of entail. He had been pottering over a will, but it was never completed, nor even quite planned; and after much doubt and scrutiny, it was at last ascertained that, in default of a will and of issue, a clause in the marriage-settlement gave the entire estates to the Dowager Lady Mardykes.

By her will she bequeathed the estates to "her cousin, also a kinsman of the late Sir Bale Mardykes her husband," William Feltram, on condition of his assuming the name and arms of Mardykes, the arms of Feltram being quartered in the shield.

Thus was oddly fulfilled the prediction which Philip Feltram had repeated, that the estates of Mardykes were to pass into the hands of a Feltram.

About the year 1795 the baronetage was revived, and William Feltram enjoyed the title for fifteen years, as Sir William Mardykes.

GHOSTLY TALES
VOLUME IV

GHOST STORIES OF CHAPELIZOD

Take my word for it, there is no such thing as an ancient village, especially if it has seen better days, unillustrated by its legends of terror. You might as well expect to find a decayed cheese without mites, or an old house without rats, as an antique and dilapidated town without an authentic population of goblins. Now, although this class of inhabitants are in nowise amenable to the police authorities, yet, as their demeanor directly affects the comforts of her Majesty's subjects, I cannot but regard it as a grave omission that the public have hitherto been left without any statistical returns of their numbers, activity, etc., etc. And I am persuaded that a Commission to inquire into and report upon the numerical strength, habits, haunts, etc., etc., of supernatural agents resident in Ireland, would be a great deal more innocent and entertaining than half the Commissions for which the country pays, and at least as instructive. This I say, more from a sense of duty, and to deliver my mind of a grave truth, than with any hope of seeing the suggestion adopted. But, I am sure, my readers will deplore with me that the comprehensive powers of belief, and apparently illimitable leisure, possessed by parliamentary commissions of inquiry, should never have been applied to the subject I have named, and that the collection of that species of information should be confided to the gratuitous and desultory labours of individuals, who, like myself, have other occupations to attend to. This, however, by the way.

Among the village outposts of Dublin, Chapelizod once held a considerable, if not a foremost rank. Without mentioning its connexion with the history of the great Kilmainham Preceptory of the Knights of St. John, it will be enough to remind the reader of its ancient and celebrated Castle, not one vestige of which now remains, and of the fact that it was for, we believe, some centuries, the summer residence of the Viceroys of Ireland. The circumstance of its being up, we believe, to the period at which that corps was disbanded, the headquarters of the Royal Irish Artillery, gave it also a consequence of an humbler, but not less substantial kind. With these advantages in its favour, it is not wonderful that the town exhibited at one time an air of substantial and semi-aristocratic prosperity unknown to Irish villages in modern times.

A broad street, with a well-paved footpath, and houses as lofty as were at that time to be found in the fashionable streets of Dublin; a goodly stone-fronted barrack; an ancient church, vaulted beneath, and with a tower clothed from its summit to its base with the richest ivy; an humble Roman Catholic chapel; a steep bridge spanning the Liffey, and a great old mill at the near end of it, were the principal features of the town. These, or at least most of them, remain still, but the greater part in a very changed and forlorn condition. Some of them indeed are superseded, though not obliterated by modern erections, such as the bridge, the chapel, and the church in part; the rest forsaken by the order who originally raised them, and delivered up to poverty, and in some cases to absolute decay.

The village lies in the lap of the rich and wooded valley of the Liffey, and is overlooked by the high grounds of the beautiful Phoenix Park on the one side, and by the ridge of the Palmerstown hills on the other. Its situation, therefore, is eminently picturesque; and factory-fronts and chimneys notwithstanding, it has, I think, even in its decay, a sort of melancholy picturesqueness of its own. Be that as it may, I mean to relate two or three stories of that sort which may be read with very good effect by a blazing fire on a shrewd winter's night, and are all directly connected with the altered and somewhat melancholy little town I have named.

The first I shall relate concerns

THE VILLAGE BULLY

About thirty years ago there lived in the town of Chapelizod an ill-conditioned fellow of herculean strength, well known throughout the neighbourhood by the title of Bully Larkin. In addition to his remarkable physical superiority, this fellow had acquired a degree of skill as a pugilist which alone would have made him formidable. As it was, he was the autocrat of the village, and carried not the sceptre in vain. Conscious of his superiority, and perfectly secure of impunity, he lorded it over his fellows in a spirit of cowardly and brutal insolence, which made him hated even more profoundly than he was feared.

Upon more than one occasion he had deliberately forced quarrels upon men whom he had singled out for the exhibition of his savage prowess; and in every encounter his over-matched antagonist had received an amount of "punishment" which edified and appalled the spectators, and in some instances left ineffaceable scars and lasting injuries after it.

Bully Larkin's pluck had never been fairly tried. For, owing to his prodigious superiority in weight, strength, and skill, his victories had always been certain and easy; and in proportion to the facility with which he uniformly smashed an antagonist, his pugnacity and insolence were inflamed. He thus became an odious nuisance in the neighbourhood, and the terror of every mother who had a son, and of every wife who had a husband who possessed a spirit to resent insult, or the smallest confidence in his own pugilistic capabilities.

Now it happened that there was a young fellow named Ned Moran—better known by the soubriquet of "Long Ned," from his slender, lathy proportions—at that time living in the town. He was, in truth, a mere lad, nineteen years of age, and fully twelve years younger than the stalwart bully. This, however, as the reader will see, secured for him no exemption from the dastardly provocations of the ill-conditioned pugilist. Long Ned, in an evil hour, had thrown eyes of affection upon a certain buxom damsel, who, notwithstanding Bully Larkin's amorous rivalry, inclined to reciprocate them.

I need not say how easily the spark of jealousy, once kindled, is blown into a flame, and how naturally, in a coarse and ungoverned nature, it explodes in acts of violence and outrage.

"The bully" watched his opportunity, and contrived to provoke Ned Moran, while drinking in a public-house with a party of friends, into an altercation, in the course of which he failed not to put such insults upon his rival as manhood could not tolerate. Long Ned, though a simple, good-natured sort of fellow, was by no means deficient in spirit, and retorted in a tone of defiance which edified the more timid, and gave his opponent the opportunity he secretly coveted.

Bully Larkin challenged the heroic youth, whose pretty face he had privately consigned to the mangling and bloody discipline he was himself so capable of administering. The quarrel, which he had himself contrived to get up, to a certain degree covered the ill blood and malignant premeditation which inspired his proceedings, and Long Ned, being full of generous ire and whiskey punch, accepted the gauge of battle on the instant. The whole party, accompanied by a mob of idle men and boys, and in short by all who could snatch a moment from the calls of business, proceeded in slow procession through the old gate into the Phoenix Park, and mounting the hill overlooking the town, selected near its summit a level spot on which to decide the quarrel.

The combatants stripped, and a child might have seen in the contrast presented by the slight, lank form and limbs of the lad, and the muscular and massive build of his veteran antagonist, how desperate was the chance of poor Ned Moran.

"Seconds" and "bottle-holders"—selected of course for their love of the game—were appointed, and "the fight" commenced.

I will not shock my readers with a description of the cool-blooded butchery that followed. The result of the combat was what anybody might have predicted. At the eleventh round, poor Ned refused to "give in", the brawny pugilist, unhurt, in good wind, and pale with concentrated and as yet unslaked revenge, had the gratification of seeing his opponent seated upon his second's knee, unable to hold up his head, his left arm disabled; his face a bloody, swollen, and shapeless mass; his breast scarred and bloody, and his whole body panting and quivering with rage and exhaustion.

"Give in, Ned, my boy," cried more than one of the bystanders.

"Never, never," shrieked he, with a voice hoarse and choking.

Time being "up," his second placed him on his feet again. Blinded with his own blood, panting and staggering, he presented but a helpless mark for the blows of his stalwart opponent. It was plain that a touch would have been sufficient to throw him to the earth. But Larkin had no notion of letting him off so easily. He closed with him without striking a blow (the effect of which, prematurely dealt, would have been to bring him at once to the ground, and so put an end to the combat), and getting his battered and almost senseless head under his arm, fast in that peculiar "fix" known to the fancy pleasantly by the name of "chancery," he held him firmly, while with monotonous and brutal strokes he beat his fist, as it seemed, almost into his face. A cry of "shame" broke from the crowd, for it was plain that the beaten man was now insensible, and supported only by the herculean arm of the bully. The round and the fight ended by his hurling him upon the ground, falling upon him at the same time with his knee upon his chest.

The bully rose, wiping the perspiration from his white face with his blood-stained hands, but Ned lay stretched and motionless upon the grass. It was impossible to get him upon his legs for another round. So he was carried down, just as he was, to the pond which then lay close to the old Park gate, and his head and body were washed beside it. Contrary to the belief of all he was not dead. He was carried home, and after some months to a certain extent recovered. But he never held up his head again, and before the year was over he had died of consumption. Nobody could doubt how the disease had been induced, but there was no actual proof to connect the cause and effect, and the ruffian Larkin escaped the vengeance of the law. A strange retribution, however, awaited him.

After the death of Long Ned, he became less quarrelsome than before, but more sullen and reserved. Some said "he took it to heart," and others, that his conscience was not at ease about it. Be this as it may, however, his health did not suffer by reason of his presumed agitations, nor was his worldly prosperity marred by the blasting curses with which poor Moran's enraged mother pursued him; on the contrary he had rather risen in the world, and obtained regular and well-remunerated employment from the Chief Secretary's gardener, at the other side of the Park. He still lived in Chapelizod, whither, on the close of his day's work, he used to return across the Fifteen Acres.

It was about three years after the catastrophe we have mentioned, and late in the autumn, when, one night, contrary to his habit, he did not appear at the house where he lodged, neither had he been seen anywhere, during the evening, in the village. His hours of return had been so very regular, that his absence excited considerable surprise, though, of course, no actual alarm; and, at the usual hour, the house was closed for the night, and the absent lodger consigned to the mercy of the elements, and the care of his presiding star. Early in the morning, however, he was found lying in a state of utter helplessness upon the slope immediately overlooking the Chapelizod gate. He had been smitten with a paralytic stroke: his right side was dead; and it was many weeks before he had recovered his speech sufficiently to make himself at all understood.

He then made the following relation:—He had been detained, it appeared, later than usual, and darkness had closed before he commenced his homeward walk across the Park. It was a moonlit night, but masses of ragged clouds were slowly drifting across the heavens. He had not encountered a human figure, and no sounds but the softened rush of the wind sweeping through bushes and hollows met his ear. These wild and monotonous sounds, and the utter solitude which surrounded him, did not, however, excite any of those uneasy sensations which are ascribed to superstition, although he said he did feel depressed, or, in his own phraseology, "lonesome." Just as he crossed the brow of the hill which shelters the town of Chapelizod, the moon shone out for some moments with unclouded lustre, and his eye, which happened to wander by the shadowy enclosures which lay at the foot of the slope, was arrested by the sight of a human figure climbing, with all the haste of one pursued, over the churchyard wall, and running up the steep ascent directly towards him. Stories of "resurrectionists" crossed his recollection, as he observed this suspicious-looking figure. But he began, momentarily, to be aware with a sort of fearful instinct which he could not explain, that the running figure was directing his steps, with a sinister purpose, towards himself.

The form was that of a man with a loose coat about him, which, as he ran, he disengaged, and as well as Larkin could see, for the moon was again wading in clouds, threw from him. The figure thus advanced until within some two score yards of him, it arrested its speed, and approached with a loose, swaggering gait. The moon again shone out bright and clear, and, gracious God! what was the spectacle before him? He saw as distinctly as if he had been presented there in the flesh, Ned Moran, himself, stripped naked from the waist upward, as if for pugilistic combat, and drawing towards him in silence. Larkin would have shouted, prayed, cursed, fled across the Park, but he was absolutely powerless; the apparition stopped within a few steps, and leered on him with a ghastly mimicry of the defiant stare with which pugilists strive to cow one another before combat. For a time, which he could not so much as conjecture, he was held in the fascination of that unearthly gaze, and at last the thing, whatever it was, on a sudden swaggered close up to him with extended palms. With an impulse of horror, Larkin put out his hand to keep the figure off, and their palms touched—at least, so he believed—for a thrill of unspeakable agony, running through his arm, pervaded his entire frame, and he fell senseless to the earth.

Though Larkin lived for many years after, his punishment was terrible. He was incurably maimed; and being unable to work, he was forced, for existence, to beg alms of those who had once feared and flattered him. He suffered, too, increasingly, under his own horrible interpretation of the preternatural encounter which was the beginning of all his miseries. It was vain to endeavour to shake his faith in the reality of the apparition, and equally vain, as some compassionately did, to try to persuade him that the greeting with which his vision closed was intended, while inflicting a temporary trial, to signify a compensating reconciliation.

"No, no," he used to say, "all won't do. I know the meaning of it well enough; it is a challenge to meet him in the other world—in Hell, where I am going—that's what it means, and nothing else."

And so, miserable and refusing comfort, he lived on for some years, and then died, and was buried in the same narrow churchyard which contains the remains of his victim.

I need hardly say, how absolute was the faith of the honest inhabitants, at the time when I heard the story, in the reality of the preternatural summons which, through the portals of terror, sickness, and misery, had summoned Bully Larkin to his long, last home, and that, too, upon the very ground on which he had signalised the guiltiest triumph of his violent and vindictive career.

I recollect another story of the preternatural sort, which made no small sensation, some five-and-thirty years ago, among the good gossips of the town; and, with your leave, courteous reader, I shall relate it.

THE SEXTON'S ADVENTURE

Those who remember Chapelizod a quarter of a century ago, or more, may possibly recollect the parish sexton. Bob Martin was held much in awe by truant boys who sauntered into the churchyard on Sundays, to read the tombstones, or play leap frog over them, or climb the ivy in search of bats or sparrows' nests, or peep into the mysterious aperture under the eastern window, which opened a dim perspective of descending steps losing themselves among profounder darkness, where lidless coffins gaped horribly among tattered velvet, bones, and dust, which time and mortality had strewn there. Of such horribly curious, and otherwise enterprising juveniles, Bob was, of course, the special scourge and terror. But terrible as was the official aspect of the sexton, and repugnant as his lank form, clothed in rusty, sable vesture, his small, frosty visage, suspicious grey eyes, and rusty, brown scratch-wig, might appear to all notions of genial frailty; it was yet true, that Bob Martin's severe morality sometimes nodded, and that Bacchus did not always solicit him in vain.

Bob had a curious mind, a memory well stored with "merry tales," and tales of terror. His profession familiarized him with graves and goblins, and his tastes with weddings, wassail, and sly frolics of all sorts. And as his personal recollections ran back nearly three score years into the perspective of the village history, his fund of local anecdote was copious, accurate, and edifying.

As his ecclesiastical revenues were by no means considerable, he was not unfrequently obliged, for the indulgence of his tastes, to arts which were, at the best, undignified.

He frequently invited himself when his entertainers had forgotten to do so; he dropped in accidentally upon small drinking parties of his acquaintance in public houses, and entertained them with stories, queer or terrible, from his inexhaustible reservoir, never scrupling to accept an acknowledgment in the shape of hot whiskey-punch, or whatever else was going.

There was at that time a certain atrabilious publican, called Philip Slaney, established in a shop nearly opposite the old turnpike. This man was not, when left to himself, immoderately given to drinking; but being naturally of a saturnine complexion, and his spirits constantly requiring a fillip, he acquired a prodigious liking for Bob Martin's company. The sexton's society, in fact, gradually became the solace of his existence, and he seemed to lose his constitutional melancholy in the fascination of his sly jokes and marvellous stories.

This intimacy did not redound to the prosperity or reputation of the convivial allies. Bob Martin drank a good deal more punch than was good for his health, or consistent with the character of an ecclesiastical functionary. Philip Slaney, too, was drawn into similar indulgences, for it was hard to resist the genial seductions of his gifted companion; and as he was obliged to pay for both, his purse was believed to have suffered even more than his head and liver.

Be this as it may, Bob Martin had the credit of having made a drunkard of "black Phil Slaney"—for by this cognomen was he distinguished; and Phil Slaney had also the reputation of having made the sexton, if possible, a "bigger bliggard" than ever. Under these circumstances, the accounts of the concern opposite the turnpike became somewhat entangled; and it came to pass one drowsy summer morning, the weather being at once sultry and cloudy, that Phil Slaney went into a small back parlour, where he kept his books, and which commanded, through its dirty window-panes, a full view of a dead wall, and having bolted the door, he took a loaded pistol, and clapping the muzzle in his mouth, blew the upper part of his skull through the ceiling.

This horrid catastrophe shocked Bob Martin extremely; and partly on this account, and partly because having been, on several late occasions, found at night in a state of abstraction, bordering on insensibility, upon the high road, he had been threatened with dismissal; and, as some said, partly also because of the difficulty of finding anybody to "treat" him as poor Phil Slaney used to do, he for a time forswore alcohol in all its combinations, and became an eminent example of temperance and sobriety.

Bob observed his good resolutions, greatly to the comfort of his wife, and the edification of the neighbourhood, with tolerable punctuality. He was seldom tipsy, and never drunk, and was greeted by the better part of society with all the honours of the prodigal son.

Now it happened, about a year after the grisly event we have mentioned, that the curate having received, by the post, due notice of a funeral to be consummated in the churchyard of Chapelizod, with certain instructions respecting the site of the grave, despatched a summons for Bob Martin, with a view to communicate to that functionary these official details.

It was a lowering autumn night: piles of lurid thunder-clouds, slowly rising from the earth, had loaded the sky with a solemn and boding canopy of storm. The growl of the distant thunder was heard afar off upon the dull, still air, and all nature seemed, as it were, hushed and cowering under the oppressive influence of the approaching tempest.

It was past nine o'clock when Bob, putting on his official coat of seedy black, prepared to attend his professional superior.

"Bobby, darlin'," said his wife, before she delivered the hat she held in her hand to his keeping, "sure you won't, Bobby, darlin'—you won't—you know what."

"I *don't* know what," he retorted, smartly, grasping at his hat.

"You won't be throwing up the little finger, Bobby, acushla?" she said, evading his grasp.

"Arrah, why would I, woman? there, give me my hat, will you?"

"But won't you promise me, Bobby darlin'—won't you, alanna?"

"Ay, ay, to be sure I will—why not?—there, give me my hat, and let me go."

"Ay, but you're not promisin', Bobby, mavourneen; you're not promisin' all the time."

"Well, divil carry me if I drink a drop till I come back again," said the sexton, angrily; "will that do you? And *now* will you give me my hat?"

"Here it is, darlin'," she said, "and God send you safe back."

And with this parting blessing she closed the door upon his retreating figure, for it was now quite dark, and resumed her knitting till his return, very much relieved; for she thought he had of late been oftener tipsy than was consistent with his thorough reformation, and feared the allurements of the half dozen "publics" which he had at that time to pass on his way to the other end of the town.

They were still open, and exhaled a delicious reek of whiskey, as Bob glided wistfully by them; but he stuck his hands in his pockets and looked the other way, whistling resolutely, and filling his mind with the image of the curate and anticipations of his coming fee. Thus he steered his morality safely through these rocks of offence, and reached the curate's lodging in safety.

He had, however, an unexpected sick call to attend, and was not at home, so that Bob Martin had to sit in the hall and amuse himself with the devil's tattoo until his return. This, unfortunately, was very long delayed, and it must have been fully twelve o'clock when Bob Martin set out upon his homeward way. By this time the storm had gathered to a pitchy darkness, the bellowing thunder was heard among the rocks and hollows of the Dublin mountains, and the pale, blue lightning shone upon the staring fronts of the houses.

By this time, too, every door was closed; but as Bob trudged homeward, his eye mechanically sought the public-house which had once belonged to Phil Slaney. A faint light was making its way through the shutters and the glass panes over the doorway, which made a sort of dull, foggy halo about the front of the house.

As Bob's eyes had become accustomed to the obscurity by this time, the light in question was quite sufficient to enable him to see a man in a sort of loose riding-coat seated upon a bench which, at that time, was fixed under the window of the house. He wore his hat very much over his eyes, and was smoking a long pipe. The outline of a glass and a quart bottle were also dimly traceable beside him; and a large horse saddled, but faintly discernible, was patiently awaiting his master's leisure.

There was something odd, no doubt, in the appearance of a traveller refreshing himself at such an hour in the open street; but the sexton accounted for it easily by supposing that, on the closing of the house for the night, he had taken what remained of his refection to the place where he was now discussing it al fresco.

At another time Bob might have saluted the stranger as he passed with a friendly "good night"; but, somehow, he was out of humour and in no genial mood, and was about passing without any courtesy of the sort, when the stranger, without taking the pipe from his mouth, raised the bottle, and with it beckoned him familiarly, while, with a sort of lurch of the head and shoulders, and at the same time shifting his seat to the end of the bench, he pantomimically invited him to share his seat and his cheer. There was a divine fragrance of whiskey about the spot, and Bob half relented; but he remembered his promise just as he began to waver, and said:

"No, I thank you, sir, I can't stop to-night."

The stranger beckoned with vehement welcome, and pointed to the vacant space on the seat beside him.

"I thank you for your polite offer," said Bob, "but it's what I'm too late as it is, and haven't time to spare, so I wish you a good night."

The traveller jingled the glass against the neck of the bottle, as if to intimate that he might at least swallow a dram without losing time. Bob was mentally quite of the same opinion; but, though his mouth watered, he remembered his promise, and shaking his head with incorruptible resolution, walked on.

The stranger, pipe in mouth, rose from his bench, the bottle in one hand, and the glass in the other, and followed at the sexton's heels, his dusky horse keeping close in his wake.

There was something suspicious and unaccountable in this importunity.

Bob quickened his pace, but the stranger followed close. The sexton began to feel queer, and turned about. His pursuer was behind, and still inviting him with impatient gestures to taste his liquor.

"I told you before," said Bob, who was both angry and frightened, "that I would not taste it, and that's enough. I don't want to have anything to say to you or your bottle; and in God's name," he added, more vehemently, observing that he was approaching still closer, "fall back and don't be tormenting me this way."

These words, as it seemed, incensed the stranger, for he shook the bottle with violent menace at Bob Martin; but, notwithstanding this gesture of defiance, he suffered the distance between them to increase. Bob, however, beheld him dogging him still in the distance, for his pipe shed a wonderful red glow, which duskily illuminated his entire figure like the lurid atmosphere of a meteor.

"I wish the devil had his own, my boy," muttered the excited sexton, "and I know well enough where you'd be."

The next time he looked over his shoulder, to his dismay he observed the importunate stranger as close as ever upon his track.

"Confound you," cried the man of skulls and shovels, almost beside himself with rage and horror, "what is it you want of me?"

The stranger appeared more confident, and kept wagging his head and extending both glass and bottle toward him as he drew near, and Bob Martin heard the horse snorting as it followed in the dark.

"Keep it to yourself, whatever it is, for there is neither grace nor luck about you," cried Bob Martin, freezing with terror; "leave me alone, will you."

And he fumbled in vain among the seething confusion of his ideas for a prayer or an exorcism. He quickened his pace almost to a run; he was now close to his own door, under the impending bank by the river side.

"Let me in, let me in, for God's sake; Molly, open the door," he cried, as he ran to the threshold, and leant his back against the plank. His pursuer confronted him upon the road; the pipe was no longer in his mouth, but the dusky red glow still lingered round him. He uttered some inarticulate cavernous sounds, which were wolfish and indescribable, while he seemed employed in pouring out a glass from the bottle.

The sexton kicked with all his force against the door, and cried at the same time with a despairing voice.

"In the name of God Almighty, once for all, leave me alone."

His pursuer furiously flung the contents of the bottle at Bob Martin; but instead of fluid it issued out in a stream of flame, which expanded and whirled round them, and for a moment they were both enveloped in a faint blaze; at the same instant a sudden gust whisked off the stranger's hat, and the sexton beheld that his skull was roofless. For an instant he beheld the gaping aperture, black and shattered, and then he fell senseless into his own doorway, which his affrighted wife had just unbarred.

I need hardly give my reader the key to this most intelligible and authentic narrative. The traveller was acknowledged by all to have been the spectre of the suicide, called up by the Evil One to tempt the convivial sexton into a violation of his promise, sealed, as it was, by an imprecation. Had he succeeded, no doubt the dusky steed, which Bob had seen saddled in attendance, was destined to have carried back a double burden to the place from whence he came.

As an attestation of the reality of this visitation, the old thorn tree which overhung the doorway was found in the morning to have been blasted with the infernal fires which had issued from the bottle, just as if a thunder-bolt had scorched it.

The moral of the above tale is upon the surface, apparent, and, so to speak, *self-acting*—a circumstance which happily obviates the necessity of our discussing it together. Taking our leave, therefore, of honest Bob Martin, who now sleeps soundly in the same solemn dormitory where, in his day, he made so many beds for others, I come to a legend of the Royal Irish Artillery, whose headquarters were for so long a time in the town of Chapelizod. I don't mean to say that I cannot tell a great many more stories, equally authentic and marvellous, touching this old town; but as I may possibly have to perform a like office for other localities, and as Anthony Poplar is known, like Atropos, to carry a shears, wherewith to snip across all "yarns" which exceed reasonable bounds, I consider it, on the whole, safer to despatch the traditions of Chapelizod with one tale more.

Let me, however, first give it a name; for an author can no more despatch a tale without a title, than an apothecary can deliver his physic without a label. We shall, therefore, call it—

THE SPECTRE LOVERS

There lived some fifteen years since in a small and ruinous house, little better than a hovel, an old woman who was reported to have considerably exceeded her eightieth year, and who rejoiced in the name of Alice, or popularly, Ally Moran. Her society was not much courted, for she was neither rich, nor, as the reader may suppose, beautiful. In addition to a lean cur and a cat she had one human companion, her grandson, Peter Brien, whom, with laudable good nature, she had supported from the period of his orphanage down to that of my story, which finds him in his twentieth year. Peter was a good-natured slob of a fellow, much more addicted to wrestling, dancing, and love-making, than to hard work, and fonder of whiskey-punch than good advice. His grandmother had a high opinion of his accomplishments, which indeed was but natural, and also of his genius, for Peter had of late years begun to apply his mind to politics; and as it was plain that he had a mortal hatred of honest labour, his grandmother predicted, like a true fortuneteller, that he was born to marry an heiress, and Peter himself (who had no mind to forego his freedom even on such terms) that he was destined to find a pot of gold. Upon one point both agreed, that being unfitted by the peculiar bias of his genius for work, he was to acquire the immense fortune to which his merits entitled him by means of a pure run of good luck. This solution of Peter's future had the double effect of reconciling both himself and his grandmother to his idle courses, and also of maintaining that even flow of hilarious spirits which made him everywhere welcome, and which was in truth the natural result of his consciousness of approaching affluence.

It happened one night that Peter had enjoyed himself to a very late hour with two or three choice spirits near Palmerstown. They had talked politics and love, sung songs, and told stories, and, above all, had swallowed, in the chastened disguise of punch, at least a pint of good whiskey, every man.

It was considerably past one o'clock when Peter bid his companions goodbye, with a sigh and a hiccough, and lighting his pipe set forth on his solitary homeward way.

The bridge of Chapelizod was pretty nearly the midway point of his night march, and from one cause or another his progress was rather slow, and it was past two o'clock by the time he found himself leaning over its old battlements, and looking up the river, over whose winding current and wooded banks the soft moonlight was falling.

The cold breeze that blew lightly down the stream was grateful to him. It cooled his throbbing head, and he drank it in at his hot lips. The scene, too, had, without his being well sensible of it, a secret fascination. The village was sunk in the profoundest slumber, not a mortal stirring, not a sound afloat, a soft haze covered it all, and the fairy moonlight hovered over the entire landscape.

In a state between rumination and rapture, Peter continued to lean over the battlements of the old bridge, and as he did so he saw, or fancied he saw, emerging one after another along the river bank in the little gardens and enclosures in the rear of the street of Chapelizod, the queerest little white-washed huts and cabins he had ever seen there before. They had not been there that evening when he passed the bridge on the way to his merry tryst. But the most remarkable thing about it was the odd way in which these quaint little cabins showed themselves. First he saw one or two of them just with the corner of his eye, and when he looked full at them, strange to say, they faded away and disappeared. Then another and another came in view, but all in the same coy way, just appearing and gone again before he could well fix his gaze upon them; in a little while, however, they began to bear a fuller gaze, and he found, as it seemed to himself, that he was able by an effort of attention to fix the vision for a longer and a longer time, and when they waxed faint and nearly vanished, he had the power of recalling them into light and substance, until at last their vacillating indistinctness became less and less, and they assumed a permanent place in the moonlit landscape.

"Be the hokey," said Peter, lost in amazement, and dropping his pipe into the river unconsciously, "them is the quarist bits iv mud cabins I ever seen, growing up like musharoons in the dew of an evening, and poppin' up here and down again there, and up again in another place, like so many white rabbits in a warren; and there they stand at last as firm and fast as if they were there from the Deluge; bedad it's enough to make a man a'most believe in the fairies."

This latter was a large concession from Peter, who was a bit of a free-thinker, and spoke contemptuously in his ordinary conversation of that class of agencies.

Having treated himself to a long last stare at these mysterious fabrics, Peter prepared to pursue his homeward way; having crossed the bridge and passed the mill, he arrived at the corner of the main-street of the little town, and casting a careless look up the Dublin road, his eye was arrested by a most unexpected spectacle.

This was no other than a column of foot soldiers, marching with perfect regularity towards the village, and headed by an officer on horseback. They were at the far side of the turnpike, which was closed; but much to his perplexity he perceived that they marched on through it without appearing to sustain the least check from that barrier.

On they came at a slow march; and what was most singular in the matter was, that they were drawing several cannons along with them; some held ropes, others spoked the wheels, and others again marched in front of the guns and behind them, with muskets shouldered, giving a stately character of parade and regularity to this, as it seemed to Peter, most unmilitary procedure.

It was owing either to some temporary defect in Peter's vision, or to some illusion attendant upon mist and moonlight, or perhaps to some other cause, that the whole procession had a certain waving and vapoury character which perplexed and tasked his eyes not a little. It was like the pictured pageant of a phantasmagoria reflected upon smoke. It was as if every breath disturbed it; sometimes it was blurred, sometimes obliterated; now here, now there. Sometimes, while the upper part was quite distinct, the legs of the column would nearly fade away or vanish outright, and then again they would come out into clear relief, marching on with measured tread, while the cocked hats and shoulders grew, as it were, transparent, and all but disappeared.

Notwithstanding these strange optical fluctuations, however, the column continued steadily to advance. Peter crossed the street from the corner near the old bridge, running on tip-toe, and with his body stooped to avoid observation, and took up a position upon the raised footpath in the shadow of the houses, where, as the soldiers kept the middle of the road, he calculated that he might, himself undetected, see them distinctly enough as they passed.

"What the div—, what on airth," he muttered, checking the irreligious ejaculation with which he was about to start, for certain queer misgivings were hovering about his heart, notwithstanding the factitious courage of the whiskey bottle. "What on airth is the manin' of all this? is it the French that's landed at last to give us a hand and help us in airnest to this blessed repale? If it is not them, I simply ask who the div—, I mane who on airth are they, for such sogers as them I never seen before in my born days?"

By this time the foremost of them were quite near, and truth to say they were the queerest soldiers he had ever seen in the course of his life. They wore long gaiters and leather breeches, three-cornered hats, bound with silver lace, long blue coats, with scarlet facings and linings, which latter were shewn by a fastening which held together the two opposite corners of the skirt behind; and in front the breasts were in like manner connected at a single point, where and below which they sloped back, disclosing a long-flapped waistcoat of snowy whiteness; they had very large, long cross-belts, and wore enormous pouches of white leather hung extraordinarily low, and on each of which a little silver star was glittering. But what struck him as most grotesque and outlandish in their costume was their extraordinary display of shirt-frill in front, and of ruffle about their wrists, and the strange manner in which their hair was frizzled out and powdered under their hats, and clubbed up into great rolls behind. But one of the party was mounted. He rode a tall white horse, with high action and arching neck; he had a snow-white feather in his three-cornered hat, and his coat was shimmering all over with a profusion of silver lace. From these circumstances Peter concluded that he must be the commander of the detachment, and examined him as he passed attentively. He was a slight, tall man, whose legs did not half fill his leather breeches, and he appeared to be at the wrong side of sixty. He had a shrunken, weather-beaten, mulberry-coloured face, carried a large black patch over one eye, and turned neither to the right nor to the left, but rode on at the head of his men, with a grim, military inflexibility.

The countenances of these soldiers, officers as well as men, seemed all full of trouble, and, so to speak, scared and wild. He watched in vain for a single contented or comely face. They had, one and all, a melancholy and hang-dog look; and as they passed by, Peter fancied that the air grew cold and thrilling.

He had seated himself upon a stone bench, from which, staring with all his might, he gazed upon the grotesque and noiseless procession as it filed by him. Noiseless it was; he could neither hear the jingle of accoutrements, the tread of feet, nor the rumble of the wheels; and when the old colonel turned his horse a little, and made as though he were giving the word of command, and a trumpeter, with a swollen blue nose and white feather fringe round his hat, who was walking beside him, turned about and put his bugle to his lips, still Peter heard nothing, although it was plain the sound had reached the soldiers, for they instantly changed their front to three abreast.

"Botheration!" muttered Peter, "is it deaf I'm growing?"

But that could not be, for he heard the sighing of the breeze and the rush of the neighbouring Liffey plain enough.

"Well," said he, in the same cautious key, "by the piper, this bangs Banagher fairly! It's either the Frinch army that's in it, come to take the town iv Chapelizod by surprise, an' makin' no noise for feard iv wakenin' the inhabitants; or else it's—it's—what it's—somethin' else. But, tundher-an-ouns, what's gone wid Fitzpatrick's shop across the way?"

The brown, dingy stone building at the opposite side of the street looked newer and cleaner than he had been used to see it; the front door of it stood open, and a sentry, in the same grotesque uniform, with shouldered musket, was pacing noiselessly to and fro before it. At the angle of this building, in like manner, a wide gate (of which Peter had no recollection whatever) stood open, before which, also, a similar sentry was gliding, and into this gateway the whole column gradually passed, and Peter finally lost sight of it.

"I'm not asleep; I'm not dhramin'," said he, rubbing his eyes, and stamping slightly on the pavement, to assure himself that he was wide awake. "It is a quare business, whatever it is; an' it's not alone that, but everything about town looks strange to me. There's Tresham's house new painted, bedad, an' them flowers in the windies! An' Delany's house, too, that had not a whole pane of glass in it this morning, and scarce a slate on the roof of it! It is not possible it's what it's dhrunk I am. Sure there's the big tree, and not a leaf of it changed since I passed, and the stars overhead, all right. I don't think it is in my eyes it is."

And so looking about him, and every moment finding or fancying new food for wonder, he walked along the pavement, intending, without further delay, to make his way home.

But his adventures for the night were not concluded. He had nearly reached the angle of the short land that leads up to the church, when for the first time he perceived that an officer, in the uniform he had just seen, was walking before, only a few yards in advance of him.

The officer was walking along at an easy, swinging gait, and carried his sword under his arm, and was looking down on the pavement with an air of reverie.

In the very fact that he seemed unconscious of Peter's presence, and disposed to keep his reflections to himself, there was something reassuring. Besides, the reader must please to remember that our hero had a quantum sufficit of good punch before his adventure commenced, and was thus fortified against those qualms and terrors under which, in a more reasonable state of mind, he might not impossibly have sunk.

The idea of the French invasion revived in full power in Peter's fuddled imagination, as he pursued the nonchalant swagger of the officer.

"Be the powers iv Moll Kelly, I'll ax him what it is," said Peter, with a sudden accession of rashness. "He may tell me or not, as he plases, but he can't be offinded, anyhow."

With this reflection having inspired himself, Peter cleared his voice and began—

"Captain!" said he, "I ax your pardon, captain, an' maybe you'd be so condescindin' to my ignorance as to tell me, if it's plasin' to yer honour, whether your honour is not a Frinchman, if it's plasin' to you."

This he asked, not thinking that, had it been as he suspected, not one word of his question in all probability would have been intelligible to the person he addressed. He was, however, understood, for the officer answered him in English, at the same time slackening his pace and moving a little to the side of the pathway, as if to invite his interrogator to take his place beside him.

"No; I am an Irishman," he answered.

"I humbly thank your honour," said Peter, drawing nearer—for the affability and the nativity of the officer encouraged him—"but maybe your honour is in the *sarvice* of the King of France?"

"I serve the same King as you do," he answered, with a sorrowful significance which Peter did not comprehend at the time; and, interrogating in turn, he asked, "But what calls you forth at this hour of the day?"

"The *day,* your honour!—the night, you mane."

"It was always our way to turn night into day, and we keep to it still," remarked the soldier. "But, no matter, come up here to my house; I have a job for you, if you wish to earn some money easily. I live here."

As he said this, he beckoned authoritatively to Peter, who followed almost mechanically at his heels, and they turned up a little lane near the old Roman

Catholic chapel, at the end of which stood, in Peter's time, the ruins of a tall, stone-built house.

Like everything else in the town, it had suffered a metamorphosis. The stained and ragged walls were now erect, perfect, and covered with pebble-dash; window-panes glittered coldly in every window; the green hall-door had a bright brass knocker on it. Peter did not know whether to believe his previous or his present impressions; seeing is believing, and Peter could not dispute the reality of the scene. All the records of his memory seemed but the images of a tipsy dream. In a trance of astonishment and perplexity, therefore, he submitted himself to the chances of his adventure.

The door opened, the officer beckoned with a melancholy air of authority to Peter, and entered. Our hero followed him into a sort of hall, which was very dark, but he was guided by the steps of the soldier, and, in silence, they ascended the stairs. The moonlight, which shone in at the lobbies, showed an old, dark wainscoting, and a heavy, oak banister. They passed by closed doors at different landing-places, but all was dark and silent as, indeed, became that late hour of the night.

Now they ascended to the topmost floor. The captain paused for a minute at the nearest door, and, with a heavy groan, pushing it open, entered the room. Peter remained at the threshold. A slight female form in a sort of loose, white robe, and with a great deal of dark hair hanging loosely about her, was standing in the middle of the floor, with her back towards them.

The soldier stopped short before he reached her, and said, in a voice of great anguish, "Still the same, sweet bird—sweet bird! still the same." Whereupon, she turned suddenly, and threw her arms about the neck of the officer, with a gesture of fondness and despair, and her frame was agitated as if by a burst of sobs. He held her close to his breast in silence; and honest Peter felt a strange terror creep over him, as he witnessed these mysterious sorrows and endearments.

"To-night, to-night—and then ten years more—ten long years—another ten years."

The officer and the lady seemed to speak these words together; her voice mingled with his in a musical and fearful wail, like a distant summer wind, in the dead hour of night, wandering through ruins. Then he heard the officer say, alone, in a voice of anguish—

"Upon me be it all, for ever, sweet birdie, upon me."

And again they seemed to mourn together in the same soft and desolate wail, like sounds of grief heard from a great distance.

Peter was thrilled with horror, but he was also under a strange fascination; and an intense and dreadful curiosity held him fast.

The moon was shining obliquely into the room, and through the window Peter saw the familiar slopes of the Park, sleeping mistily under its shimmer. He could also see the furniture of the room with tolerable distinctness—the old balloon-backed chairs, a four-post bed in a sort of recess, and a rack against the wall, from which hung some military clothes and accoutrements; and the sight of all these homely objects reassured him somewhat, and he could not help feeling unspeakably curious to see the face of the girl whose long hair was streaming over the officer's epaulet.

Peter, accordingly, coughed, at first slightly, and afterward more loudly, to recall her from her reverie of grief; and, apparently, he succeeded; for she turned round, as did her companion, and both, standing hand in hand, gazed upon him fixedly. He thought he had never seen such large, strange eyes in all his life; and their gaze seemed to chill the very air around him, and arrest the pulses of his heart. An eternity of misery and remorse was in the shadowy faces that looked upon him.

If Peter had taken less whisky by a single thimbleful, it is probable that he would have lost heart altogether before these figures, which seemed every moment to assume a more marked and fearful, though hardly definable, contrast to ordinary human shapes.

"What is it you want with me?" he stammered.

"To bring my lost treasure to the churchyard," replied the lady, in a silvery voice of more than mortal desolation.

The word "treasure" revived the resolution of Peter, although a cold sweat was covering him, and his hair was bristling with horror; he believed, however, that he was on the brink of fortune, if he could but command nerve to brave the interview to its close.

"And where," he gasped, "is it hid—where will I find it?"

They both pointed to the sill of the window, through which the moon was shining at the far end of the room, and the soldier said

"Under that stone."

Peter drew a long breath, and wiped the cold dew from his face, preparatory to passing to the window, where he expected to secure the reward of his protracted terrors. But looking steadfastly at the window, he saw the faint image of a newborn child sitting upon the sill in the moonlight, with its little arms stretched toward him, and a smile so heavenly as he never beheld before.

At sight of this, strange to say, his heart entirely failed him, he looked on the figures that stood near, and beheld them gazing on the infantine form with a smile so guilty and distorted, that he felt as if he were entering alive among the scenery of hell, and shuddering, he cried in an irrepressible agony of horror—

"I'll have nothing to say with you, and nothing to do with you; I don't know what yez are or what yez want iv me, but let me go this minute, every one of yez, in the name of God."

With these words there came a strange rumbling and sighing about Peter's ears; he lost sight of everything, and felt that peculiar and not unpleasant sensation of falling softly, that sometimes supervenes in sleep, ending in a dull shock. After that he had neither dream nor consciousness till he wakened, chill and stiff, stretched between two piles of old rubbish, among the black and roofless walls of the ruined house.

We need hardly mention that the village had put on its wonted air of neglect and decay, or that Peter looked around him in vain for traces of those novelties which had so puzzled and distracted him upon the previous night.

"Ay, ay," said his grandmother, removing her pipe, as he ended his description of the view from the bridge, "sure enough I remember myself, when I was a slip of a girl, these little white cabins among the gardens by the river side. The artillery sogers that was married, or had not room in the barracks, used to be in them, but they're all gone long ago.

"The Lord be merciful to us!" she resumed, when he had described the military procession, "It's often I seen the regiment marchin' into the town, jist as you saw it last night, acushla. Oh, voch, but it makes my heart sore to think iv them days; they were pleasant times, sure enough; but is not it terrible, avick, to think it's what it was the ghost of the rigiment you seen? The Lord betune us an' harm, for it was nothing else, as sure as I'm sittin' here."

When he mentioned the peculiar physiognomy and figure of the old officer who rode at the head of the regiment—

"That," said the old crone, dogmatically, "was ould Colonel Grimshaw, the Lord presarve us! he's buried in the churchyard iv Chapelizod, and well I remember him, when I was a young thing, an' a cross ould floggin' fellow he was wid the men, an' a devil's boy among the girls—rest his soul!"

"Amen!" said Peter; "it's often I read his tombstone myself; but he's a long time dead."

"Sure, I tell you he died when I was no more nor a slip iv a girl—the

Lord betune us and harm!"

"I'm afeard it is what I'm not long for this world myself, afther seeing such a sight as that," said Peter, fearfully.

"Nonsinse, avourneen," retorted his grandmother, indignantly, though she had herself misgivings on the subject; "sure there was Phil Doolan, the ferryman, that seen black Ann Scanlan in his own boat, and what harm ever kem of it?"

Peter proceeded with his narrative, but when he came to the description of the house, in which his adventure had had so sinister a conclusion, the old woman was at fault.

"I know the house and the ould walls well, an' I can remember the time there was a roof on it, and the doors an' windows in it, but it had a bad name about being haunted, but by who, or for what, I forget intirely."

"Did you ever hear was there goold or silver there?" he inquired.

"No, no, avick, don't be thinking about the likes; take a fool's advice, and never go next to near them ugly black walls again the longest day you have to live; an' I'd take my davy, it's what it's the same word the priest himself id be afther sayin' to you if you wor to ax his raverence consarnin' it, for it's plain to be seen it was nothing good you seen there, and there's neither luck nor grace about it."

Peter's adventure made no little noise in the neighbourhood, as the reader may well suppose; and a few evenings after it, being on an errand to old Major Vandeleur, who lived in a snug old-fashioned house, close by the river, under a perfect bower of ancient trees, he was called on to relate the story in the parlour.

The Major was, as I have said, an old man; he was small, lean, and upright, with a mahogany complexion, and a wooden inflexibility of face; he was a man, besides, of few words, and if *he* was old, it follows plainly that his mother was older still. Nobody could guess or tell *how* old, but it was admitted that her own generation had long passed away, and that she had not a competitor left. She had French blood in her veins, and although she did not retain her charms quite so well as Ninon de l'Enclos, she was in full possession of all her mental activity, and talked quite enough for herself and the Major.

"So, Peter," she said, "you have seen the dear, old Royal Irish again in the streets of Chapelizod. Make him a tumbler of punch, Frank; and Peter, sit down, and while you take it let us have the story."

Peter accordingly, seated, near the door, with a tumbler of the nectarian stimulant steaming beside him, proceeded with marvellous courage, considering they had no light but the uncertain glare of the fire, to relate with minute particularity his awful adventure. The old lady listened at first with a smile of good-natured incredulity; her cross-examination touching the drinking-bout at Palmerstown had been teazing, but as the narrative proceeded she became attentive, and at length absorbed, and once or twice she uttered ejaculations of pity or awe. When it was over, the old lady looked with a somewhat sad and stern abstraction on the table, patting her cat assiduously meanwhile, and then suddenly looking upon her son, the Major, she said—

"Frank, as sure as I live he has seen the wicked Captain Devereux."

The Major uttered an inarticulate expression of wonder.

"The house was precisely that he has described. I have told you the story often, as I heard it from your dear grandmother, about the poor young lady he ruined, and the dreadful suspicion about the little baby. *She*, poor thing, died in that house heart-broken, and you know he was shot shortly after in a duel."

This was the only light that Peter ever received respecting his adventure. It was supposed, however, that he still clung to the hope that treasure of some sort was hidden about the old house, for he was often seen lurking about its walls, and at last his fate overtook him, poor fellow, in the pursuit; for climbing near the summit one day, his holding gave way, and he fell upon the hard uneven ground, fracturing a leg and a rib, and after a short interval died, and he, like the other heroes of these true tales, lies buried in the little churchyard of Chapelizod.

* * * * *

THE DRUNKARD'S DREAM

This Story can be found on Page 62 as part of The Purcell Papers.

THE GHOST AND THE BONE-SETTER

This Story can be found on Page 13 as part of The Purcell Papers.

THE MYSTERIOUS LODGER

PART I

About the year 1822 I resided in a comfortable and roomy old house, the exact locality of which I need not particularise, further than to say that it was not very far from Old Brompton, in the immediate neighbourhood, or rather continuity (as even my Connemara readers perfectly well know), of the renowned city of London.

Though this house was roomy and comfortable, as I have said, it was not, by any means, a handsome one. It was composed of dark red brick, with small windows, and thick white sashes; a porch, too—none of your flimsy trellis-work, but a solid projection of the same vermillion masonry—surmounted by a leaded balcony, with heavy, half-rotten balustrades, darkened the hall-door with a perennial gloom. The mansion itself stood in a walled enclosure, which had, perhaps, from the date of the erection itself, been devoted to shrubs and flowers. Some of the former had grown there almost to the dignity of trees; and two dark little yews stood at each side of the porch, like swart and inauspicious dwarfs, guarding the entrance of an enchanted castle. Not that my domicile in any respect deserved the comparison: it had no reputation as a haunted house; if it ever had any ghosts, nobody remembered them. Its history was not known to me: it may have witnessed plots, cabals, and forgeries, bloody suicides and cruel murders. It was certainly old enough to have become acquainted with iniquity; a small stone slab, under the balustrade, and over the arch of the porch I mentioned, had the date 1672, and a half-effaced coat of arms, which I might have deciphered any day, had I taken the trouble to get a ladder, but always put it off. All I can say for the house is, that it was well stricken in years, with a certain air of sombre comfort about it; contained a vast number of rooms and closets; and, what was of far greater importance, was got by me a dead bargain.

Its individuality attracted me. I grew fond of it for itself, and for its associations, until other associations of a hateful kind first disturbed, and then destroyed, their charm. I forgave its dull red brick, and pinched white windows, for the sake of the beloved and cheerful faces within: its ugliness was softened by its age; and its sombre evergreens, and moss-grown stone flower-pots, were relieved by the brilliant hues of a thousand gay and graceful flowers that peeped among them, or nodded over the grass.

Within that old house lay my life's treasure! I had a darling little girl of nine, and another little darling—a boy—just four years of age; and dearer, unspeakably, than either—a wife—the prettiest, gayest, best little wife in all London. When I tell you that our income was scarcely £380 a-year, you will perceive that our establishment cannot have been a magnificent one; yet, I do assure you, we were more comfortable than a great many lords, and happier, I dare say, than the whole peerage put together.

This happiness was not, however, what it ought to have been. The reader will understand at once, and save me a world of moralising circumlocution, when he learns, bluntly and nakedly, that, among all my comforts and blessings, I was an infidel.

I had not been without religious training; on the contrary, more than average pains had been bestowed upon my religious instruction from my earliest childhood. My father, a good, plain, country clergyman, had worked hard to make me as good as himself; and had succeeded, at least, in training me in godly habits. He died, however, when I was but twelve years of age; and fate had long before deprived me of the gentle care of a mother. A boarding-school, followed by a college life, where nobody having any very direct interest in realising in my behalf the ancient blessing, that in fulness of time I should "die a good old man," I was left very much to my own devices, which, in truth, were none of the best.

Among these were the study of Voltaire, Tom Paine, Hume, Shelley, and the whole school of infidels, poetical as well as prose. This pursuit, and the all but blasphemous vehemence with which I gave myself up to it, was, perhaps, partly reactionary. A somewhat injudicious austerity and precision had indissolubly associated in my childish days the ideas of restraint and gloom with religion. I bore it a grudge; and so, when I became thus early my own master, I set about paying off, after my own fashion, the old score I owed it. I was besides, like every other young infidel whom it has been my fate to meet, a conceited coxcomb. A smattering of literature, without any real knowledge, and a great assortment of all the cut-and-dry flippancies of the school I had embraced, constituted my intellectual stock in trade. I was, like most of my school of philosophy, very proud of being an unbeliever; and fancied myself, in the complacency of my wretched ignorance, at an immeasurable elevation above the church-going, Bible-reading herd, whom I treated with a good-humoured superciliousness which I thought vastly indulgent.

My wife was an excellent little creature and truly pious. She had married me in the full confidence that my levity was merely put on, and would at once give way before the influence she hoped to exert upon my mind. Poor little thing! she deceived herself. I allowed her, indeed, to do entirely as she pleased; but for myself, I carried my infidelity to the length of an absolute superstition. I made an ostentation of it. I would rather have been in a "hell" than in a church on Sunday; and though I did not prevent my wife's instilling her own principles into the minds of our children, I, in turn, took especial care to deliver mine upon all occasions in their hearing, by which means I trusted to sow the seeds of that unprejudiced scepticism in which I prided myself, at least as early as my good little partner dropped those of her own gentle "superstition" into their infant minds. Had I had my own absurd and impious will in this matter, my children should have had absolutely no religious education whatsoever, and been left wholly unshackled to choose for themselves among all existing systems, infidelity included, precisely as chance, fancy, or interest might hereafter determine.

It is not to be supposed that such a state of things did not afford her great uneasiness. Nevertheless, we were so very fond of one another, and in our humble way enjoyed so many blessings, that we were as entirely happy as any pair can be without the holy influence of religious sympathy.

But the even flow of prosperity which had for so long gladdened my little household was not destined to last for ever. It was ordained that I should experience the bitter truth of more than one of the wise man's proverbs, and first, especially, of that which declares that "he that hateth suretyship is sure." I found myself involved (as how many have been before) by a "d—d good-natured friend," for more than two hundred pounds. This agreeable intelligence was conveyed to me in an attorney's letter, which, to obviate unpleasant measures, considerately advised my paying the entire amount within just one week of the date of his pleasant epistle. Had I been called upon within that time to produce the Pitt diamond, or to make title to the Buckingham estates, the demand would have been just as easily complied with.

I have no wish to bore my reader further with this little worry—a very serious one to me, however—and it will be enough to mention, that the kindness of a friend extricated me from the clutches of the law by a timely advance, which, however, I was bound to replace within two years. To enable me to fulfill this engagement, my wife and I, after repeated consultations, resolved upon the course which resulted in the odd and unpleasant consequences which form the subject of this narrative.

We resolved to advertise for a lodger, with or without board, &c.; and by resolutely submitting, for a single year, to the economy we had prescribed for ourselves, as well as to the annoyance of a stranger's intrusion, we calculated that at the end of that term we should have liquidated our debt.

Accordingly, without losing time, we composed an advertisement in the most tempting phraseology we could devise, consistently with that economic laconism which the cost per line in the columns of the *Times* newspaper imposes upon the rhetoric of the advertising public.

Somehow we were unlucky; for although we repeated our public notification three times in the course of a fortnight, we had but two applications. The one was from a clergyman in ill health—a man of great ability and zealous piety, whom we both knew by reputation, and who has since been called to his rest. My good little wife was very anxious that we should close with his offer, which was very considerably under what we had fixed upon; and I have no doubt that she was influenced by the hope that his talents and zeal might exert a happy influence upon my stubborn and unbelieving heart. For my part, his religious character displeased me. I did not wish my children's heads to be filled with mythic dogmas—for so I judged the doctrines of our holy faith—and instinctively wished him away. I therefore declined his offer; and I have often since thought not quite so graciously as I ought to have done. The other offer—if so it can be called—was so very inadequate that we could not entertain it.

I was now beginning to grow seriously uneasy—our little project, so far from bringing in the gains on which we had calculated, had put me considerably out of pocket; for, independently of the cost of the advertisement I have mentioned, there were sundry little expenses involved in preparing for the meet reception of our expected inmate, which, under ordinary circumstances, we should not have dreamed of. Matters were in this posture, when an occurrence took place which immediately revived my flagging hopes.

As we had no superfluity of servants, our children were early obliged to acquire habits of independence; and my little girl, then just nine years of age, was frequently consigned with no other care than that of her own good sense, to the companionship of a little band of playmates, pretty similarly circumstanced, with whom it was her wont to play. Having one fine summer afternoon gone out as usual with these little companions, she did not return quite so soon as we had expected her; when she did so, she was out of breath, and excited.

"Oh, papa," she said, "I have seen such a nice old, kind gentleman, and he told me to tell you that he has a particular friend who wants a lodging in a quiet place, and that he thinks your house would suit him exactly, and ever so much more; and, look here, he gave me this."

She opened her hand, and shewed me a sovereign.

"Well, this does look promisingly," I said, my wife and I having first exchanged a smiling glance.

"And what kind of gentleman was he, dear?" inquired she. "Was he well dressed—whom was he like?"

"He was not like any one that I know," she answered; "but he had very nice new clothes on, and he was one of the fattest men I ever saw; and I am sure he is sick, for he looks very pale, and he had a crutch beside him."

"Dear me, how strange!" exclaimed my wife; though, in truth there was nothing very wonderful in the matter. "Go on, child," I said; "let us hear it all out."

"Well, papa, he had such an immense yellow waistcoat!—I never did see such a waistcoat," she resumed; "and he was sitting or leaning, I can't say which, against the bank of the green lane; I suppose to rest himself, for he seems very weak, poor gentleman!"

"And how did you happen to speak to him?" asked my wife.

"When we were passing by, none of us saw him at all but I suppose he heard them talking to me, and saying my name; for he said, 'Fanny—little Fanny—so, that's your name—come here child, I have a question to ask you.'"

"And so you went to him?" I said.

"Yes," she continued, "he beckoned to me, and I did go over to him, but not very near, for I was greatly afraid of him at first."

"Afraid! dear, and why afraid?" asked I.

"I was afraid, because he looked very old, very frightful, and as if he would hurt me."

"What was there so old and frightful about him?" I asked.

She paused and reflected a little, and then said—

"His face was very large and pale, and it was looking upwards: it seemed very angry, I thought, but maybe it was angry from pain; and sometimes one side of it used to twitch and tremble for a minute, and then to grow quite still again; and all the time he was speaking to me, he never looked at me once, but always kept his face and eyes turned upwards; but his voice was very soft, and he called me little Fanny, and gave me this pound to buy toys with; so I was not so frightened in a little time, and then he sent a long message to you, papa, and told me if I forgot it he would beat me; but I knew he was only joking, so that did not frighten me either."

"And what was the message, my girl?" I asked, patting her pretty head with my hand.

"Now, let me remember it all," she said, reflectively; "for he told it to me twice. He asked me if there was a good bedroom at the top of the house, standing by itself—and you know there is, so I told him so; it was exactly the kind of room that he described. And then he said that his friend would pay two hundred pounds a-year for that bedroom, his board and attendance; and he told me to ask you, and have your answer when he should next meet me."

"Two hundred pounds!" ejaculated my poor little wife; "why that is nearly twice as much as we expected."

"But did he say that his friend was sick, or very old; or that he had any servant to be supported also?" I asked.

"Oh! no; he told me that he was quite able to take care of himself, and that he had, I think he called it, an asthma, but nothing else the matter; and that he would give no trouble at all, and that any friend who came to see him, he would see, not in the house, but only in the garden."

"In the garden!" I echoed, laughing in spite of myself.

"Yes, indeed he said so; and he told me to say that he would pay one hundred pounds when he came here, and the next hundred in six months, and so on," continued she.

"Oh, ho! half-yearly in advance—better and better," said I.

"And he bid me say, too, if you should ask about his character, that he is just as good as the master of the house himself," she added; "and when he said that, he laughed a little."

"Why, if he gives us a hundred pounds in advance," I answered, turning to my wife, "we are safe enough; for he will not find half that value in plate and jewels in the entire household, if he is disposed to rob us. So I see no reason against closing with the offer, should it be seriously meant—do you, dear?"

"Quite the contrary, love," said she. "I think it most desirable—indeed, most *providential*."

"Providential! my dear little bigot!" I repeated, with a smile. "Well, be it so. I call it *lucky* merely; but, perhaps, you are happier in your faith, than I in my philosophy. Yes, you are *grateful* for the chance that I only rejoice at. You receive it as a proof of a divine and tender love—I as an accident. Delusions are often more elevating than truth."

And so saying, I kissed away the saddened cloud that for a moment overcast her face.

"Papa, he bid me be sure to have an answer for him when we meet again," resumed the child. "What shall I say to him when he asks me?"

"Say that we agree to his proposal, my dear—or stay," I said, addressing my wife, "may it not be prudent to reduce what the child says to writing, and accept the offer so? This will prevent misunderstanding, as she may possibly have made some mistake."

My wife agreed, and I wrote a brief note, stating that I was willing to receive an inmate upon the terms recounted by little Fanny, and which I distinctly specified, so that no mistake could possibly arise owing to the vagueness of what lawyers term a parole agreement. This important memorandum I placed in the hands of my little girl, who was to deliver it whenever the old gentleman in the yellow waistcoat should chance to meet her. And all these arrangements completed, I awaited the issue of the affair with as much patience as I could affect. Meanwhile, my wife and I talked it over incessantly; and she, good little soul, almost wore herself to death in settling and unsettling the furniture and decorations of our expected inmate's apartments. Days passed away—days of hopes deferred, tedious and anxious. We were beginning to despond again, when one morning our little girl ran into the breakfast-parlour, more excited even than she had been before, and fresh from a new interview with the gentleman in the yellow waistcoat. She had encountered him suddenly, pretty nearly where she had met him before, and the result was, that he had read the little note I have mentioned, and desired the child to inform me that his friend, *Mr. Smith*, would take possession of the apartments I proposed setting, on the terms agreed between us, that very evening.

"This evening!" exclaimed my wife and I simultaneously—*I* full of the idea of making a first instalment on the day following; *she*, of the hundred-and-one preparations which still remained to be completed.

"And so Smith is his name! Well, that does not tell us much," said I; "but where did you meet your friend on this occasion, and how long is it since?"

"Near the corner of the wall-flower lane (so we indicated one which abounded in these fragrant plants); he was leaning with his back against the old tree you cut my name on, and his crutch was under his arm."

"But how long ago?" I urged.

"Only this moment; I ran home as fast as I could," she replied.

"Why, you little blockhead, you should have told me that at first," I cried, snatching up my hat, and darting away in pursuit of the yellow waistcoat, whose acquaintance I not unnaturally coveted, inasmuch as a man who, for the first time, admits a stranger into his house, on the footing of permanent residence, desires generally to know a little more about him than that his name is Smith.

The place indicated was only, as we say, a step away; and as yellow waistcoat was fat, and used a crutch, I calculated on easily overtaking him. I was, however, disappointed; crutch, waistcoat, and all had disappeared. I climbed to the top of the wall, and from this commanding point of view made a sweeping observation—but in vain. I returned home, cursing my ill-luck, the child's dulness, and the fat old fellow's activity.

I need hardly say that Mr. Smith, in all his aspects, moral, social, physical, and monetary, formed a fruitful and interesting topic of speculation during dinner. How many phantom Smiths, short and long, stout and lean, ill-tempered and well-tempered—rich, respectable, or highly dangerous merchants, spies, forgers, nabobs, swindlers, danced before us, in the endless mazes of fanciful conjecture, during that anxious *tête-à-tête*, which was probably to be interrupted by the arrival of the gentleman himself.

My wife and I puzzled over the problem as people would over the possible *dénouement* of a French novel; and at last, by mutual consent, we came to the conclusion that Smith could, and would turn out to be no other than the good-natured valetudinarian in the yellow waistcoat himself, a humorist, as was evident enough, and a millionaire, as we unhesitatingly pronounced, who had no immediate relatives, and as I hoped, and my wife "was certain," taken a decided fancy to our little Fanny; I patted the child's head with something akin to pride, as I thought of the magnificent, though remote possibilities, in store for her.

Meanwhile, hour after hour stole away. It was a beautiful autumn evening, and the amber lustre of the declining sun fell softly upon the yews and flowers, and gave an air, half melancholy, half cheerful, to the dark-red brick piers surmounted with their cracked and grass-grown stone urns, and furnished with the light foliage of untended creeping plants. Down the short broad walk leading to this sombre entrance, my eye constantly wandered; but no impatient rattle on the latch, no battering at the gate, indicated the presence of a visited, and the lazy bell hung dumbly among the honey-suckles.

"When will he come? Yellow waistcoat promised *this evening*! It has been evening a good hour and a half, and yet he is not here. When will he come? It will soon be dark—the evening will have passed—will he come at all?"

Such were the uneasy speculations which began to trouble us. Redder and duskier grew the light of the setting sun, till it saddened into the mists of night. Twilight came, and then darkness, and still no arrival, no summons at the gate. I would not admit even to my wife the excess of my own impatience. I could, however, stand it no longer; so I took my hat and walked to the gate, where I stood by the side of the public road, watching every vehicle and person that approached, in a fever of expectation. Even these, however, began to fail me, and the road grew comparatively quiet and deserted. Having kept guard like a sentinel for more than half an hour, I returned in no very good humour, with the punctuality of an expected inmate—ordered the servant to draw the curtains and secure the hall-door; and so my wife and I sate down to our disconsolate cup of tea. It must have been about ten o'clock, and we were both sitting silently—she working, I looking moodily into a paper—and neither of us any longer entertaining a hope that anything but disappointment would come of the matter, when a sudden tapping, very loud and sustained, upon the window pane, startled us both in an instant from our reveries.

I am not sure whether I mentioned before that the sitting-room we occupied was upon the ground-floor, and the sward came close under the window. I drew the curtains, and opened the shutters with a revived hope; and looking out, saw a very tall thin figure, a good deal wrapped up, standing about a yard before me, and motioning with head and hand impatiently towards the hall-door. Though the night was clear, there was no moon, and therefore I could see no more than the black outline, like that of an *ombre chinoise* figure, signing to me with mop and moe. In a moment I was at the hall-door, candle in hand; the stranger stept in—his long fingers clutched in the handle of a valise, and a bag which trailed upon the ground behind him.

The light fell full upon him. He wore a long, ill-made, black surtout, buttoned across, and which wrinkled and bagged about his lank figure; his hat was none of the best, and rather broad in the brim; a sort of white woollen muffler enveloped the lower part of his face; a pair of prominent green goggles, fenced round with leather, completely concealed his eyes; and nothing of the genuine man, but a little bit of yellow forehead, and a small transverse segment of equally yellow cheek and nose, encountered the curious gaze of your humble servant.

"You are—I suppose"—I began; for I really was a little doubtful about my man.

"Mr. Smith—the same; be good enough to show me to my bedchamber," interrupted the stranger, brusquely, and in a tone which, spite of the muffler that enveloped his mouth, was sharp and grating enough.

"Ha!—Mr. Smith—so I supposed. I hope you may find everything as comfortable as we desire to make it—"

I was about making a speech, but was cut short by a slight bow, and a decisive gesture of the hand in the direction of the staircase. It was plain that the stranger hated ceremony.

Together, accordingly, we mounted the staircase; he still pulling his luggage after him, and striding lightly up without articulating a word; and on reaching his bedroom, he immediately removed his hat, showing a sinister, black scratch-wig underneath, and then began unrolling the mighty woolen wrapping of his mouth and chin.

"Come," thought I, "we *shall* see something of your face after all."

This something, however, proved to be very little; for under his muffler was a loose cravat, which stood up in front of his chin and upon his mouth, he wore a respirator—an instrument which I had never seen before, and of the use of which I was wholly ignorant.

There was something so excessively odd in the effect of this piece of unknown mechanism upon his mouth, surmounted by the huge goggles which encased his eyes, that I believe I should have laughed outright, were it not for a certain unpleasant and peculiar impressiveness in the *tout ensemble* of the narrow-chested, long-limbed, and cadaverous figure in black. As it was, we stood looking at one another in silence for several seconds.

"Thank you, sir," at last he said, abruptly. "I shan't want anything whatever to-night; if you can only spare me this candle."

I assented; and, becoming more communicative, he added—

"I am, though an invalid, an independent sort of fellow enough. I am a bit of a philosopher; I am my own servant, and, I hope, my own master, too. I rely upon myself in matters of the body and of the mind. I place valets and priests in the same category—fellows who live by our laziness, intellectual or corporeal. I am a Voltaire, without his luxuries—a Robinson Crusoe, without his Bible—an anchorite, without a superstition—in short, my indulgence is asceticism, and my faith infidelity. Therefore, I shan't disturb your servants much with my bell, nor yourselves with my psalmody. You have got a rational lodger, who knows how to attend upon himself."

During this singular address he was drawing off his ill-fitting black gloves, and when he had done so, a bank-note, which had been slipped underneath for safety, remained in his hand.

"Punctuality, sir, is one of my poor pleasures," he said; "will you allow me to enjoy it now? To-morrow you may acknowledge this; I should not rest were you to decline it."

He extended his bony and discoloured fingers, and placed the note in my hand. Oh, Fortune and Plutus! It was a £100 bank-note.

"Pray, not one word, my dear sir," he continued, unbending still further; "it is simply done pursuant to agreement. We shall know one another better, I hope, in a little time; you will find me always equally punctual. At present pray give yourself no further trouble; I require nothing more. Good night."

I returned the valediction, closed his door, and groped my way down the stairs. It was not until I had nearly reached the hall, that I recollected that I had omitted to ask our new inmate at what hour he would desire to be called in the morning, and so I groped my way back again. As I reached the lobby on which his chamber opened, I perceived a long line of light issuing from the partially-opened door, within which stood Mr. Smith, the same odd figure I had just left; while along the boards was creeping towards him across the lobby, a great, big-headed, buff-coloured cat. I had never seen this ugly animal before; and it had reached the threshold of his door, arching its back, and rubbing itself on the post, before either appeared conscious of my approach, when, with an angry growl, it sprang into the stranger's room.

"What do you want?" he demanded, sharply, standing in the doorway.

I explained my errand.

"I shall call myself," was his sole reply; and he shut the door with a crash that indicated no very pleasurable emotions.

I cared very little about my lodger's temper. The stealthy rustle of his bank-note in my waistcoat pocket was music enough to sweeten the harshest tones of his voice, and to keep alive a cheerful good humour in my heart; and although there was, indisputably, something queer about him, I was, on the whole, very well pleased with my bargain.

The next day our new inmate did not ring his bell until noon. As soon as he had had some breakfast, of which he very sparingly partook, he told the servant that, for the future, he desired that a certain quantity of milk and bread might be left outside his door; and this being done, he would dispense with regular meals. He desired, too, that, on my return, I should be acquainted that he wished to see me in his own room at about nine o'clock; and, meanwhile, he directed that he should be left undisturbed. I found my little wife full of astonishment at Mr. Smith's strange frugality and seclusion, and very curious to learn the object of the interview he had desired with me. At nine o'clock I repaired to his room.

I found him in precisely the costume in which I had left him—the same green goggles—the same muffling of the mouth, except that being now no more than a broadly-folded black silk handkerchief, very loose, and covering even the lower part of the nose, it was obviously intended for the sole purpose of concealment. It was plain I was not to see more of his features than he had chosen to disclose at our first interview. The effect was as if the lower part of his face had some hideous wound or sore. He closed the door with his own hand on my entrance, nodded slightly, and took his seat. I expected him to begin, but he was so long silent that I was at last constrained to address him.

I said, for want of something more to the purpose, that I hoped he had not been tormented by the strange cat the night before.

"What cat?" he asked, abruptly; "what the plague do you mean?"

"Why, I certainly did see a cat go into your room last night," I resumed.

"Hey, and what if you did—though I fancy you dreamed it—I'm not afraid of a cat; are you?" he interrupted, tartly.

At this moment there came a low growling mew from the closet which opened from the room in which we sat.

"Talk of the devil," said I, pointing towards the closet. My companion, without any exact change of expression, looked, I thought, somehow still more sinister and lowering; and I felt for a moment a sort of superstitious misgiving, which made the rest of the sentence die away on my lips.

Perhaps Mr. Smith perceived this, for he said, in a tone calculated to reassure me—

"Well, sir, I think I am bound to tell you that I like my apartments very well; they suit me, and I shall probably be your tenant for much longer than at first you anticipated."

I expressed my gratification.

He then began to talk, something in the strain in which he had spoken of his own peculiarities of habit and thinking upon the previous evening. He disposed of all classes and denominations of superstition with an easy sarcastic slang, which for me was so captivating, that I soon lost all reserve, and found myself listening and suggesting by turns—acquiescent and pleased—sometimes hazarding dissent; but whenever I did, foiled and floored by a few pointed satirical sentences, whose sophistry, for such I must now believe it, confounded me with a rapidity which, were it not for the admiration with which he had insensibly inspired me, would have piqued and irritated my vanity not a little.

While this was going on, from time to time the mewing and growling of a cat within the closet became more and more audible. At last these sounds became so loud, accompanied by scratching at the door, that I paused in the midst of a sentence, and observed—

"There certainly is a cat shut up in the closet?"

"Is there?" he ejaculated, in a surprised tone; "nay, I do not hear it."

He rose abruptly and approached the door; his back was towards me, but I observed he raised the goggles which usually covered his eyes, and looked steadfastly at the closet door. The angry sounds all died away into a low, protracted growl, which again subsided into silence. He continued in the same attitude for some moments, and then returned.

"I do not hear it," he said, as he resumed his place, and taking a book from his capacious pocket, asked me if I had seen it before? I never had, and this surprised me, for I had flattered myself that I knew, at least by name, every work published in England during the last fifty years in favour of that philosophy in which we both delighted. The book, moreover, was an odd one, as both its title and table of contents demonstrated.

While we were discoursing upon these subjects, I became more and more distinctly conscious of a new class of sounds proceeding from the same closet. I plainly heard a measured and heavy tread, accompanied by the tapping of some hard and heavy substance like the end of a staff, pass up and down the floor—first, as it seemed, stealthily, and then more and more unconcealedly. I began to feel very uncomfortable and suspicious. As the noise proceeded, and became more and more unequivocal, Mr. Smith abruptly rose, opened the closet door, just enough to admit his own lath-like person, and steal within the threshold for some seconds. What he did I could not see—I felt conscious he had an associate concealed there; and though my eyes remained fixed on the book, I could not avoid listening for some audible words, or signal of caution. I heard, however, nothing of the kind. Mr. Smith turned back—walked a step or two towards me, and said—

"I fancied I heard a sound from that closet, but there is nothing—nothing—nothing whatever; bring the candle, let us both look."

I obeyed with some little trepidation, for I fully anticipated that I should detect the intruder, of whose presence my own ears had given me, for nearly half an hour, the most unequivocal proofs. We entered the closet together; it contained but a few chairs and a small spider table. At the far end of the room there was a sort of grey woollen cloth upon the floor, and a bundle of something underneath it. I looked jealously at it, and half thought I could trace the outline of a human figure; but, if so, it was perfectly motionless.

"Some of my poor wardrobe," he muttered, as he pointed his lean finger in the direction. "It did not sound like a cat, did it—hey—did it?" he muttered; and without attending to my answer, he went about the apartment, clapping his hands, and crying, "Hish—hish—hish!"

The game, however, whatever it was, did not start. As I entered I had seen, however, a large crutch reposing against the wall in the corner opposite to the door. This was the only article in the room, except that I have mentioned, with which I was not familiar. With the exception of our two selves, there was not a living creature to be seen there; no shadow but ours upon the bare walls; no feet but our own upon the comfortless floor.

I had never before felt so strange and unpleasant a sensation.

"There is nothing unusual in the room but that crutch," I said.

"What crutch, you dolt? I see no crutch," he ejaculated, in a tone of sudden but suppressed fury.

"Why, *that* crutch," I answered (for somehow I neither felt nor resented his rudeness), turning and pointing to the spot where I had seen it. It was gone!—it was neither there nor anywhere else. It must have been an illusion—rather an odd one, to be sure. And yet I could at this moment, with a safe conscience, *swear* that I never saw an object more distinctly than I had seen it but a second before.

My companion was muttering fast to himself as we withdrew; his presence rather scared than reassured me; and I felt something almost amounting to horror, as, holding the candle above his cadaverous and sable figure, he stood at his threshold, while I descended the stairs, and said, in a sort of whisper—

"Why, but that I am, like yourself, a philosopher, I should say that your house is—is—a—ha! ha! ha!—HAUNTED!"

"You look very pale, my love," said my wife, as I entered the drawing-room, where she had been long awaiting my return. "Nothing unpleasant has happened?"

"Nothing, nothing, I assure you. Pale!—*do* I look pale?" I answered. "We are excellent friends, I assure you. So far from having had the smallest disagreement, there is every prospect of our agreeing but too well, as you will say; for I find that he holds all my opinions upon speculative subjects. We have had a great deal of conversation this evening, I assure you; and I never met, I think, so scholarlike and able a man."

"I am sorry for it, dearest," she said, sadly. "The greater his talents, if such be his opinions, the more dangerous a companion is he."

We turned, however, to more cheerful topics, and it was late before we retired to rest. I believe it was pride—perhaps only vanity—but, at all events, some obstructive and stubborn instinct of my nature, which I could not overcome—that prevented my telling my wife the odd occurrences which had disturbed my visit to our guest. I was unable or ashamed to confess that so slight a matter had disturbed me; and, above all, that any accident could possibly have clouded, even for a moment, the frosty clearness of my pure and lofty scepticism with the shadows of superstition.

Almost every day seemed to develop some new eccentricity of our strange guest. His dietary consisted, without any variety or relief, of the monotonous bread and milk with which he started; his bed had not been made for nearly a week; nobody had been admitted into his room since my visit, just described; and he never ventured down stairs, or out of doors, until after nightfall, when he used sometimes to glide swiftly round our little enclosed shrubbery, and at others stand quite motionless, composed, as if in an attitude of deep attention. After employing about an hour in this way, he would return, and steal up stairs to his room, when he would shut himself up, and not be seen again until the next night—or, it might be, the night after that—when, perhaps, he would repeat his odd excursion.

Strange as his habits were, their eccentricity was all upon the side least troublesome to us. He required literally no attendance; and as to his occasional night ramble, even *it* caused not the slightest disturbance of our routine hour for securing the house and locking up the hall-door for the night, inasmuch as he had invariably retired before that hour arrived.

All this stimulated curiosity, and, in no small degree, that of my wife, who, notwithstanding her vigilance and her anxiety to see our strange inmate, had been hitherto foiled by a series of cross accidents. We were sitting together somewhere about ten o'clock at night, when there came a tap at the room-door. We had just been discussing the unaccountable Smith; and I felt a sheepish consciousness that he might be himself at the door, and have possibly even overheard our speculation—some of them anything but complimentary, respecting himself.

"Come in," cried, I, with an effort; and the tall form of our lodger glided into the room. My wife was positively frightened, and stood looking at him, as he advanced, with a stare of manifest apprehension, and even recoiled mechanically, and caught my hand.

Sensitiveness, however, was not his fault: he made a kind of stiff nod as I mumbled an introduction; and seating himself unasked, began at once to chat in that odd, off-hand, and sneering style, in which he excelled, and which had, as he wielded it, a sort of fascination of which I can pretend to convey no idea.

My wife's alarm subsided, and although she still manifestly felt some sort of misgiving about our visitor, she yet listened to his conversation, and, spite of herself, soon began to enjoy it. He stayed for nearly half an hour. But although he glanced at a great variety of topics, he did not approach the subject of religion. As soon as he was gone, my wife delivered judgment upon him in form. She admitted he was agreeable; but then he was such an unnatural, awful-looking object: there was, besides, something indescribably frightful, she thought, in his manner—the very tone of his voice was strange and hateful; and, on the whole, she felt unutterably relieved at his departure.

A few days after, on my return, I found my poor little wife agitated and dispirited. Mr. Smith had paid her a visit, and brought with him a book, which he stated he had been reading, and which contained some references to the Bible which he begged of her to explain in that profounder and less obvious sense in which they had been cited. This she had endeavoured to do; and affecting to be much gratified by her satisfactory exposition, he had requested her to reconcile some discrepancies which he said had often troubled him when reading the Scriptures. Some of them were quite new to my good little wife; they startled and even horrified her. He pursued this theme, still pretending only to seek for information to quiet his own doubts, while in reality he was sowing in her mind the seeds of the first perturbations that had ever troubled the sources of her peace. He had been with her, she thought, no more than a quarter of an hour; but he had contrived to leave her abundant topics on which to ruminate for days. I found her shocked and horrified at the doubts which this potent Magus had summoned from the pit—doubts which she knew not how to combat, and from the torment of which she could not escape.

"He has made me very miserable with his deceitful questions. I never thought of them before; and, merciful Heaven! I cannot answer them! What am I to do? My serenity is gone; I shall never be happy again."

In truth, she was so very miserable, and, as it seemed to me, so disproportionately excited, that, inconsistent in me as the task would have been, I would gladly have explained away her difficulties, and restored to her mind its wonted confidence and serenity, had I possessed sufficient knowledge for the purpose. I really pitied her, and heartily wished Mr. Smith, for the nonce, at the devil.

I observed after this that my wife's spirits appeared permanently affected. There was a constantly-recurring anxiety, and I thought something was lying still more heavily at her heart than the uncertainties inspired by our lodger.

One evening, as we two were sitting together, after a long silence, she suddenly laid her hand upon my arm, and said—

"Oh, Richard, my darling! would to God you could pray for me!"

There was something so agitated, and even terrified, in her manner, that I was absolutely startled. I urged her to disclose whatever preyed upon her mind.

"You can't sympathise with me—you can't help me—you can scarcely compassionate me in my misery! Oh, dearest Richard! Some evil influence has been gaining upon my heart, dulling and destroying my convictions, killing all my holy affections, and—and absolutely transforming me. I look inward upon myself with amazement, with terror—with—oh, God!—with actual despair!"

Saying this, she threw herself on her knees, and wept an agonised flood of tears, with her head reposing in my lap.

Poor little thing, my heart bled for her! But what could I do or say?

All I could suggest was what I really thought, that she was unwell—hysterical—and needed to take better care of her precious self; that her change of feeling was fancied, not real; and that a few days would restore her to her old health and former spirits and serenity.

"And sometimes," she resumed, after I had ended a consolatory discussion, which it was but too manifest had fallen unprofitably upon her ear, "such dreadful, impious thoughts come into my mind, whether I choose it or not; they come, and stay, and return, strive as I may; and I can't pray against them. They are forced upon me with the strength of an independent will; and oh!—horrible—frightful—they blaspheme the character of God himself. They upbraid the Almighty upon his throne, and I can't pray against them; there is something in me now that resists prayer."

There was such a real and fearful anguish in the agitation of my gentle companion, that it shook my very soul within me, even while I was affecting to make light of her confessions. I had never before witnessed a struggle at all like this, and I was awe-struck at the spectacle.

At length she became comparatively calm. I did gradually succeed, though very imperfectly, in reassuring her. She strove hard against her depression, and recovered a little of her wonted cheerfulness.

After a while, however, the cloud returned. She grew sad and earnest, though no longer excited; and entreated, or rather implored, of me to grant her one special favour, and this was, to avoid the society of our lodger.

"I never," she said, "could understand till now the instinctive dread with which poor Margaret, in *Faust*, shrinks from the hateful presence of Mephistopheles. I now feel it in myself. The dislike and suspicion I first felt for that man—Smith, or whatever else he may call himself—has grown into literal detestation and terror. I hate him—I am afraid of him—I never knew what anguish of mind was until he entered our doors; and would to God—would to God he were gone."

I reasoned with her—kissed her—laughed at her; but could not dissipate, in the least degree, the intense and preternatural horror with which she had grown to regard the poor philosophic invalid, who was probably, at that moment, poring over some metaphysical book in his solitary bedchamber.

The circumstance I am about to mention will give you some notion of the extreme to which these excited feelings had worked upon her nerves. I was that night suddenly awakened by a piercing scream—I started upright in the bed, and saw my wife standing at the bedside, white as ashes with terror. It was some seconds, so startled was I, before I could find words to ask her the cause of her affright. She caught my wrist in her icy grasp, and climbed, trembling violently, into bed. Notwithstanding my repeated entreaties, she continued for a long time stupified and dumb. At length, however, she told me, that having lain awake for a long time, she felt, on a sudden, that she could pray, and lighting the candle, she had stolen from beside me, and kneeled down for the purpose. She had, however, scarcely assumed the attitude of prayer, when somebody, she said, clutched her arm violently near the wrist, and she heard, at the same instant, some blasphemous menace, the import of which escaped her the moment it was spoken, muttered close in her ear. This terrifying interruption was the cause of the scream which had awakened me; and the condition in which she continued during the remainder of the night confirmed me more than ever in the conviction, that she was suffering under some morbid action of the nervous system.

After this event, which *I* had no hesitation in attributing to fancy, she became literally afraid to pray, and her misery and despondency increased proportionately.

It was shortly after this that an unusual pressure of business called me into town one evening after office hours. I had left my dear little wife tolerably well, and little Fanny was to be her companion until I returned. She and her little companion occupied the same room in which we sat on the memorable evening which witnessed the arrival of our eccentric guest. Though usually a lively child, it most provokingly happened upon this night that Fanny was heavy and drowsy to excess. Her mamma would have sent her to bed, but that she now literally feared to be left alone; although, however, she could not so far overcome her horror of solitude as to do this, she yet would not persist in combating the poor child's sleepiness.

Accordingly, little Fanny was soon locked in a sound sleep, while her mamma quietly pursued her work beside her. They had been perhaps some ten minutes thus circumstanced, when my wife heard the window softly raised from without—a bony hand parted the curtains, and Mr. Smith leaned into the room.

She was so utterly overpowered at sight of this apparition, that even had it, as she expected, climbed into the room, she told me she could not have uttered a sound, or stirred from the spot where she sate transfixed and petrified.

"Ha, ha!" he said gently, "I hope you'll excuse this, I must admit, very odd intrusion; but I knew I should find you here, and could not resist the opportunity of raising the window just for a moment, to look in upon a little family picture, and say a word to yourself. I understand that you are troubled, because for some cause you cannot say your prayers—because what you call your 'faith' is, so to speak, dead and gone, and also because what *you* consider bad thoughts are constantly recurring to your mind. Now, all that is very silly. If it is really impossible for you to believe and to pray, what are you to infer from that? It is perfectly plain your Christian system can't be a true one—faith and *prayer* it everywhere represents as the conditions of grace, acceptance, and salvation; and yet your Creator will not *permit* you either to believe or pray. The Christian system is, forsooth, a *free* gift, and yet he who formed *you* and *it*, makes it absolutely impossible for you to accept it. *Is* it, I ask you, from your own experience—is it a free gift? And if your own experience, in which you can't be mistaken, gives its pretensions the lie, why, in the name of common sense, will you persist in believing it? I say it is downright blasphemy to think it has emanated from the Good Spirit—assuming that there is one. It tells you that you must be tormented hereafter in a way only to be made intelligible by the image of eternal fires—pretty strong, we must all allow—unless you comply with certain conditions, which it pretends are so easy that it is a positive pleasure to embrace and perform them; and yet, for the life of you, you can't—physically *can't*—do either. Is this truth and mercy?—or is it swindling and cruelty? Is it the part of the Redeemer, or that of the tyrant, deceiver, and tormentor?"

Up to that moment, my wife had sate breathless and motionless, listening, in the catalepsy of nightmare, to a sort of echo of the vile and impious reasoning which had haunted her for so long. At the last words of the sentence his voice became harsh and thrilling; and his whole manner bespoke a sort of crouching and terrific hatred, the like of which she could not have conceived.

Whatever may have been the cause, she was on a sudden disenchanted. She started to her feet; and, freezing with horror though she was, in a shrill cry of agony commanded him, in the name of God, to depart from her. His whole frame seemed to darken; he drew back silently; the curtains dropped into their places, the window was let down again as stealthily as it had just been raised; and my wife found herself alone in the chamber with our little child, who had been startled from her sleep by her mother's cry of anguish, and with the fearful words, "tempter," "destroyer," "devil," still ringing in her ears, was weeping bitterly, and holding her terrified mother's hand.

There is nothing, I believe, more infectious than that species of nervousness which shows itself in superstitious fears. I began—although I could not bring myself to admit anything the least like it—to partake insensibly, but strongly of the peculiar feelings with which my wife, and indeed my whole household, already regarded the lodger up stairs. The fact was, beside, that the state of my poor wife's mind began to make me seriously uneasy; and, although I was fully sensible of the pecuniary and other advantages attendant upon his stay, they were yet far from outweighing the constant gloom and frequent misery in which the protracted sojourn was involving my once cheerful house. I resolved, therefore, at whatever monetary sacrifice, to put an end to these commotions; and, after several debates with my wife, in which the subject was, as usual, turned in all its possible and impossible bearings, we agreed that, deducting a fair proportion for his five weeks' sojourn, I should return the remainder of his £100, and request immediate possession of his apartments. Like a man suddenly relieved of an insufferable load, and breathing freely once more, I instantly prepared to carry into effect the result of our deliberations.

In pursuance of this resolution, I waited upon Mr. Smith. This time my call was made in the morning, somewhere about nine o'clock. He received me at his door, standing as usual in the stealthy opening which barely admitted his lank person. There he stood, fully equipped with goggles and respirator, and swathed, rather than dressed, in his puckered black garments.

As he did not seem disposed to invite me into his apartment, although I had announced my visit as one of business, I was obliged to open my errand where I stood; and after a great deal of fumbling and muttering, I contrived to place before him distinctly the resolution to which I had come.

"But I can't think of taking back any portion of the sum I have paid you," said he, with a cool, dry emphasis.

"Your reluctance to do so, Mr. Smith, is most handsome, and I assure you, appreciated," I replied. "It is very generous; but, at the same time, it is quite impossible for me to accept what I have no right to take, and I must beg of you not to mention that part of the subject again."

"And why should *I* take it?" demanded Mr. Smith.

"Because you have paid this hundred pounds for six months, and you are leaving me with nearly five months of the term still unexpired," I replied. "I expect to receive fair play myself, and always give it."

"But who on earth said that I was going away so soon?" pursued Mr. Smith, in the same dry, sarcastic key. "*I* have not said so—because I really don't intend it; I mean to stay here to the last day of the six months for which I have paid you. I have no notion of vacating my hired lodgings, simply because you say, *go*. I shan't quarrel with you—I never quarrel with anybody. I'm as much your friend as ever; but, without the least wish to disoblige, I can't do this, positively I cannot. Is there anything else?"

I had not anticipated in the least the difficulty which thus encountered and upset our plans. I had so set my heart upon effecting the immediate retirement of our inauspicious inmate, that the disappointment literally stunned me for a moment. I, however, returned to the charge: I urged, and prayed, and almost besought him to give up his apartments, and to leave us. I offered to repay every farthing of the sum he had paid me—reserving nothing on account of the time he had already been with us. I suggested all the disadvantages of the house. I shifted my ground, and told him that my wife wanted the rooms; I pressed his gallantry—his good nature—his economy; in short, I assailed him upon every point—but in vain, he did not even take the trouble of repeating what he had said before—he neither relented, nor showed the least irritation, but simply said—

"I can't do this; here I am, and here I stay until the half-year has expired. You wanted a lodger, and you have got one—the quietest, least troublesome, least expensive person you could have; and though your house, servants, and furniture are none of the best, I don't care for that. I pursue my own poor business and enjoyments here entirely to my satisfaction."

Having thus spoken, he gave me a sort of nod, and closed the door.

So, instead of getting rid of him the next day, as we had hoped, we had nearly five months more of his company in expectancy; I hated, and my wife dreaded the prospect. She was literally miserable and panic-struck at her disappointment—and grew so nervous and wretched that I made up my mind to look out for lodgings for her and the children (subversive of all our schemes of retrenchment as such a step would be), and surrendering the house absolutely to Mr. Smith and the servants during the remainder of his term.

Circumstances, however, occurred to prevent our putting this plan in execution. My wife, meanwhile, was, if possible, more depressed and nervous every day. The servants seemed to sympathise in the dread and gloom which involved ourselves; the very children grew timid and spiritless, without knowing why—and the entire house was pervaded with an atmosphere of uncertainty and fear. A poorhouse or a dungeon would have been cheerful, compared with a dwelling haunted unceasingly with unearthly suspicions and alarms. I would have made any sacrifice short of ruin, to emancipate our household from the odious mental and moral thraldom which was invisibly established over us—overcasting us with strange anxieties and an undefined terror.

About this time my wife had a dream which troubled her much, although she could not explain its supposed significance satisfactorily by any of the ordinary rules of interpretation in such matters. The vision was as follows.

She dreamed that we were busily employed in carrying out our scheme of removal, and that I came into the parlour where she was making some arrangements, and, with rather an agitated manner, told her that the carriage had come for the children. She thought she went out to the hall, in consequence, holding little Fanny by one hand, and the boy—or, as we still called him, "baby,"—by the other, and feeling, as she did so, an unaccountable gloom, almost amounting to terror, steal over her. The children, too, seemed, she thought, frightened, and disposed to cry.

So close to the hall-door as to exclude the light, stood some kind of vehicle, of which she could see nothing but that its door was wide open, and the interior involved in total darkness. The children, she thought, shrunk back in great trepidation, and she addressed herself to induce them, by persuasion, to enter, telling them that they were only "going to their new home." So, in a while, little Fanny approached it; but, at the same instant, some person came swiftly up from behind, and, raising the little boy in his hands, said fiercely, "No, the baby first"; and placed him in the carriage. This person was our lodger, Mr. Smith, and was gone as soon as seen. My wife, even in her dream, could not act or speak; but as the child was lifted into the carriage-door, a man, whose face was full of beautiful tenderness and compassion, leaned forward from the carriage and received the little child, which, stretching his arms to the stranger, looked back with a strange smile upon his mother.

"He is safe with me, and I will deliver him to you when you come."

These words the man spoke, looking upon her, as he received him, and immediately the carriage-door shut, and the noise of its closing wakened my wife from her nightmare.

This dream troubled her very much, and even haunted my mind unpleasantly too. We agreed, however, not to speak of it to anybody, not to divulge any of our misgivings respecting the stranger. We were anxious that neither the children nor the servants should catch the contagion of those fears which had seized upon my poor little wife, and, if truth were spoken, upon myself in some degree also. But this precaution was, I believe, needless, for, as I said before, everybody under the same roof with Mr. Smith was, to a certain extent, affected with the same nervous gloom and apprehension.

And now commences a melancholy chapter in my life. My poor little Fanny was attacked with a cough which soon grew very violent, and after a time degenerated into a sharp attack of inflammation. We were seriously alarmed for her life, and nothing that care and medicine could effect was spared to save it. Her mother was indefatigable, and scarcely left her night or day; and, indeed, for some time, we all but despaired of her recovery.

One night, when she was at the worst, her poor mother, who had sat for many a melancholy hour listening, by her bedside, to those plaintive incoherences of delirium and moanings of fever, which have harrowed so many a fond heart, gained gradually from her very despair the courage which she had so long wanted, and knelt down at the side of her sick darling's bed to pray for her deliverance.

With clasped hands, in an agony of supplication, she prayed that God would, in his mercy, spare her little child—that, justly as she herself deserved the sorest chastisement his hand could inflict, he would yet deal patiently and tenderly with her in this one thing. She poured out her sorrows before the mercy-seat—she opened her heart, and declared her only hope to be in his pity; without which, she felt that her darling would only leave the bed where she was lying for her grave.

Exactly as she came to this part of her supplication, the child, who had grown, as it seemed, more and more restless, and moaned and muttered with increasing pain and irritation, on a sudden started upright in her bed, and, in a thrilling voice, cried—

"No! no!—the baby first."

The mysterious sentence which had secretly tormented her for so long, thus piercingly uttered by this delirious, and, perhaps, dying child, with what seemed a preternatural earnestness and strength, arrested her devotions, and froze her with a feeling akin to terror.

"Hush, hush, my darling!" said the poor mother, almost wildly, as she clasped the attenuated frame of the sick child in her arms; "hush, my darling; don't cry out so loudly—there—there—my own love."

The child did not appear to see or hear her, but sate up still with feverish cheeks, and bright unsteady eyes, while her dry lips were muttering inaudible words.

"Lie down, my sweet child—lie down, for your own mother," she said; "if you tire yourself, you can't grow well, and your poor mother will lose you."

At these words, the child suddenly cried out again, in precisely the same loud, strong voice—"No! no! the baby first, the baby first"—and immediately afterwards lay down, and fell, for the first time since her illness into a tranquil sleep.

My good little wife sate, crying bitterly by her bedside. The child was better—*that* was, indeed, delightful. But then there was an omen in the words, thus echoed from her dream, which she dared not trust herself to interpret, and which yet had seized, with a grasp of iron, upon every fibre of her brain.

"Oh, Richard," she cried, as she threw her arms about my neck, "I am terrified at this horrible menace from the unseen world. Oh! poor, darling little baby, I shall lose you—I am sure I shall lose you. Comfort me, darling, and say he is not to die."

And so I did; and tasked all my powers of argument and persuasion to convince her how unsubstantial was the ground of her anxiety. The little boy was perfectly well, and, even were he to die before his sister that event might not occur for seventy years to come. I could not, however, conceal from myself that there was something odd and unpleasant in the coincidence; and my poor wife had grown so nervous and excitable, that a much less ominous conjecture would have sufficed to alarm her.

Meanwhile, the unaccountable terror which our lodger's presence inspired continued to increase. One of our maids gave us warning, solely from her dread of our queer inmate, and the strange accessories which haunted him. She said—and this was corroborated by her fellow-servant—that Mr. Smith seemed to have constantly a companion in his room; that although they never heard them speak, they continually and distinctly heard the tread of two persons walking up and down the room together, and described accurately the peculiar sound of a stick or crutch tapping upon the floor, which my own ears had heard. They also had seen the large, ill-conditioned cat I have mentioned, frequently steal in and out of the stranger's room; and observed that when our little girl was in greatest danger, the hateful animal was constantly writhing, fawning, and crawling about the door of the sick room after nightfall. They were thoroughly persuaded that this ill-omened beast was the foul fiend himself, and I confess I could not—sceptic as I was—bring myself absolutely to the belief that he was nothing more than a "harmless, necessary cat." These and similar reports—implicitly believed as they palpably were by those who made them—were certainly little calculated to allay the perturbation and alarm with which our household was filled.

The evenings had by this time shortened very much, and darkness often overtook us before we sate down to our early tea. It happened just at this period of which I have been speaking, after my little girl had begun decidedly to mend, that I was sitting in our dining-parlour, with my little boy fast asleep upon my knees, and thinking of I know not what, my wife having gone up stairs, as usual, to sit in the room with little Fanny. As I thus sate in what was to me, in effect, total solitude, darkness unperceived stole on us.

On a sudden, as I sate, with my elbow leaning upon the table, and my other arm round the sleeping child, I felt, as I thought, a cold current of air faintly blowing upon my forehead. I raised my head, and saw, as nearly as I could calculate, at the far end of the table on which my arm rested, two large green eyes confronting me. I could see no more, but instantly concluded they were those of the abominable cat. Yielding to an impulse of horror and abhorrence, I caught a water-croft that was close to my hand, and threw it full at it with all my force. I must have missed my object, for the shining eyes continued fixed for a second, and then glided still nearer to me, and then a little nearer still. The noise of the glass smashed with so much force upon the table called in the servant, who happened to be passing. She had a candle in her hand, and, perhaps, the light alarmed the odious beast, for as she came in it was gone.

I had had an undefined idea that its approach was somehow connected with a designed injury of some sort to the sleeping child. I could not be mistaken as to the fact that I had plainly seen the two broad, glaring, green eyes. Where the cursed animal had gone I had not observed: it might, indeed, easily have run out at the door as the servant opened it, but neither of us had seen it do so; and we were every one of us in such a state of nervous excitement, that even this incident was something in the catalogue of our ambiguous experiences.

It was a great happiness to see our darling little Fanny every day mending, and now quite out of danger: this was cheering and delightful. It was also something to know that more than two months of our lodger's term of occupation had already expired; and to realise, as we now could do, by anticipation, the unspeakable relief of his departure.

My wife strove hard to turn our dear child's recovery to good account for me; but the impressions of fear soon depart, and those of religious gratitude must be preceded by religious faith. All as yet was but as seed strewn upon the rock.

Little Fanny, though recovering rapidly, was still very weak, and her mother usually passed a considerable part of every evening in her bedroom—for the child was sometimes uneasy and restless at night. It happened at this period that, sitting as usual at Fanny's bedside, she witnessed an occurrence which agitated her not a little.

The child had been, as it seems, growing sleepy, and was lying listlessly, with eyes half open, apparently taking no note of what was passing. Suddenly, however, with an expression of the wildest terror, she drew up her limbs, and cowered in the bed's head, gazing at some object; which, judging from the motion of her eyes, must have been slowly advancing from the end of the room next the door.

The child made a low shuddering cry, as she grasped her mother's hand, and, with features white and tense with terror, slowly following with her eyes the noiseless course of some unseen spectre, shrinking more and more fearfully backward every moment.

"What is it? Where? What is it that frightens you, my darling?" asked the poor mother, who, thrilled with horror, looked in vain for the apparition which seemed to have all but bereft the child of reason.

"Stay with me—save me—keep it away—look, look at it—making signs to me—don't let it hurt me—it is angry—Oh! mamma, save me, save me!"

The child said this, all the time clinging to her with both her hands, in an ecstasy of panic.

"There—there, my darling," said my poor wife, "don't be afraid; there's nothing but me—your own mamma—and little baby in the room; nothing, my darling; nothing indeed."

"Mamma, mamma, don't move; don't go near him"; the child continued wildly. "It's only his back now; don't make him turn again; he's untying his handkerchief. Oh! baby, baby; he'll *kill* baby! and he's lifting up those green things from his eyes; don't you see him doing it? Mamma, mamma, why does he come here? Oh, mamma, poor baby—poor little baby!"

She was looking with a terrified gaze at the little boy's bed, which lay directly opposite to her own, and in which he was sleeping calmly.

"Hush, hush, my darling child," said my wife, with difficulty restraining an hysterical burst of tears; "for God's sake don't speak so wildly, my own precious love—there, there—don't be frightened—there, darling, there."

"Oh! poor baby—poor little darling baby," the child continued as before; "will no one save him—tell that wicked man to go away—oh—there—why, mamma—don't—oh, sure you won't let him—don't—don't—he'll take the child's life—will you let him lie down that way on the bed—save poor little baby—oh, baby, baby, waken—his head is on your face."

As she said this she raised her voice to a cry of despairing terror which made the whole room ring again.

This cry, or rather yell, reached my ears as I sate reading in the parlour by myself, and fearing I knew not what, I rushed to the apartment; before I reached it, the sound had subsided into low but violent sobbing; and, just as I arrived at the threshold I heard, close at my feet, a fierce protracted growl, and something rubbing along the surbase. I was in the dark, but, with a feeling of mingled terror and fury, I stamped and struck at the abhorred brute with my feet, but in vain. The next moment I was in the room, and heard little Fanny, through her sobs, cry—

"Oh, poor baby is killed—that wicked man has killed him—he uncovered his face, and put it on him, and lay upon the bed and killed poor baby. I knew he came to kill him. Ah, papa, papa, why did you not come up before he went?—he is gone, he went away as soon as he killed our poor little darling baby."

I could not conceal my agitation, quite, and I said to my wife—

"Has he, Smith, been here?"

"No."

"What is it, then?"

"The child has seen *some* one."

"Seen whom? Who? Who has been here?"

"I did not see it; but—but I am sure the child saw—that is, *thought* she saw *him*;—the person you have named. Oh, God, in mercy deliver us! What shall I do—what shall I do!"

Thus saying, the dear little woman burst into tears, and crying, as if her heart would break, sobbed out an entreaty that I would look at baby; adding, that she herself had not courage to see whether her darling was sleeping or dead.

"Dead!" I exclaimed. "Tut, tut, my darling; you must not give way to such morbid fancies—he is very well, I see him breathing;" and so saying, I went over to the bed where our little boy was lying. He was slumbering; though it seemed to me very heavily, and his cheeks were flushed.

"Sleeping tranquilly, my darling—tranquilly, and deeply; and with a warm colour in his cheeks," I said, rearranging the coverlet, and retiring to my wife, who sate almost breathless whilst I was looking at our little boy.

"Thank God—thank God," she said quietly; and she wept again; and rising, came to his bedside.

"Yes, yes—alive; thank God; but it seems to me he is breathing very short, and with difficulty, and he looks—*does* he not look hot and feverish? Yes, he *is* very hot; feel his little hand—feel his neck; merciful heaven! he is burning."

It was, indeed, very true, that his skin was unnaturally dry and hot; his little pulse, too, was going at a fearful rate.

"I do think," said I—resolved to conceal the extent of my own apprehensions—"I do think that he is just a *little* feverish; but he has often been much more so; and will, I dare say, in the morning, be perfectly well again. I dare say, but for little Fanny's *dream*, we should not have observed it at all."

"Oh, my darling, my darling, my darling!" sobbed the poor little woman, leaning over the bed, with her hands locked together, and looking the very picture of despair. "Oh, my darling, what has happened to you? I put you into your bed, looking so well and beautiful, this evening, and here you are, stricken with sickness, my own little love. Oh, you will not—you cannot, leave your poor mother!"

It was quite plain that she despaired of the child from the moment we had ascertained that it was unwell. As it happened, her presentiment was but too truly prophetic. The apothecary said the child's ailment was "suppressed small-pox"; the physician pronounced it "typhus." The only certainty about it was the issue—the child died.

To me few things appear so beautiful as a very young child in its shroud. The little innocent face looks so sublimely simple and confiding amongst the cold terrors of death—crimeless, and fearless, that little mortal has passed alone under the shadow, and explored the mystery of dissolution. There is death in its sublimest and purest image—no hatred, no hypocrisy, no suspicion, no care for the morrow ever darkened that little face; death has come lovingly upon it; there is nothing cruel, or harsh, in his victory. The yearnings of love, indeed, cannot be stifled; for the prattle, and smiles, and all the little world of thoughts that were so delightful, are gone for ever. Awe, too, will overcast us in its presence—for we are looking on death; but we do not fear for the little, lonely voyager—for the child has gone, simple and trusting, into the presence of its all-wise Father; and of such, we know, is the kingdom of heaven.

And so we parted from poor little baby. I and his poor old nurse drove in a mourning carriage, in which lay the little coffin, early in the morning, to the churchyard of ——. Sore, indeed, was my heart, as I followed that little coffin to the grave! Another burial had just concluded as we entered the churchyard, and the mourners stood in clusters round the grave, into which the sexton was now shovelling the mould.

As I stood, with head uncovered, listening to the sublime and touching service which our ritual prescribes, I found that a gentleman had drawn near also, and was standing at my elbow. I did not turn to look at him until the earth had closed over my darling boy; I then walked a little way apart, that I might be alone, and drying my eyes, sat down upon a tombstone, to let the confusion of my mind subside.

While I was thus lost in a sorrowful reverie, the gentleman who had stood near me at the grave was once more at my side. The face of the stranger, though I could not call it handsome, was very remarkable; its expression was the purest and noblest I could conceive, and it was made very beautiful by a look of such compassion as I never saw before.

"Why do you sorrow as one without hope?" he said, gently.

"I *have* no hope," I answered.

"Nay, I think you have," he answered again; "and I am sure you will soon have more. That little child for which you grieve, has escaped the dangers and miseries of life; its body has perished; but he will receive in the end the crown of life. God has given him an early victory."

I know not what it was in him that rebuked my sullen pride, and humbled and saddened me, as I listened to this man. He was dressed in deep mourning, and looked more serene, noble, and sweet than any I had ever seen. He was young, too, as I have said, and his voice very clear and harmonious. He talked to me for a long time, and I listened to him with involuntary reverence. At last, however, he left me, saying he had often seen me walking into town, about the same hour that he used to go that way, and that if he saw me again he would walk with me, and so we might reason of these things together.

It was late when I returned to my home, now a house of mourning.

PART II

Our home was one of sorrow and of fear. The child's death had stricken us with terror no less than grief. Referring it, as we both tacitly did, to the mysterious and fiendish agency of the abhorred being whom, in an evil hour, we had admitted into our house, we both viewed him with a degree and species of fear for which I can find no name.

I felt that some further calamity was impending. I could not hope that we were to be delivered from the presence of the malignant agent who haunted, rather than inhabited our home, without some additional proofs alike of his malice and his power.

My poor wife's presentiments were still more terrible and overpowering, though not more defined, than my own. She was never tranquil while our little girl was out of her sight; always dreading and expecting some new revelation of the evil influence which, as we were indeed both persuaded, had bereft our darling little boy of life. Against an hostility so unearthly and intangible there was no guarding, and the sense of helplessness intensified the misery of our situation. Tormented with doubts of the very basis of her religion, and recoiling from the ordeal of prayer with the strange horror with which the victim of hydrophobia repels the pure water, she no longer found the consolation which, had sorrow reached her in any other shape, she would have drawn from the healing influence of religion. We were both of us unhappy, dismayed, DEMON-STRICKEN.

Meanwhile, our lodger's habits continued precisely the same. If, indeed, the sounds which came from his apartments were to be trusted, he and his agents were more on the alert than ever. I can convey to you, good reader, no notion, even the faintest, of the dreadful sensation always more or less present to my mind, and sometimes with a reality which thrilled me almost to frenzy—the apprehension that I had admitted into my house the incarnate spirit of the dead or damned, to torment me and my family.

It was some nights after the burial of our dear little baby; we had not gone to bed until late, and I had slept, I suppose, some hours, when I was awakened by my wife, who clung to me with the energy of terror. She said nothing, but grasped and shook me with more than her natural strength. She had crept close to me, and was cowering with her head under the bedclothes.

The room was perfectly dark, as usual, for we burned no night-light; but from the side of the bed next her proceeded a voice as of one sitting there with his head within a foot of the curtains—and, merciful heavens! it was the voice of our lodger.

He was discoursing of the death of our baby, and inveighing, in the old mocking tone of hate and suppressed fury, against the justice, mercy, and goodness of God. He did this with a terrible plausibility of sophistry, and with a resolute emphasis and precision, which seemed to imply, "I have got something to tell you, and, whether you like it or like it not, I *will* say out my say."

To pretend that I felt anger at his intrusion, or emotion of any sort, save the one sense of palsied terror, would be to depart from the truth. I lay, cold and breathless, as if frozen to death—unable to move, unable to utter a cry—with the voice of that demon pouring, in the dark, his undisguised blasphemies and temptations close into my ears. At last the dreadful voice ceased whether the speaker went or stayed I could not tell—the silence, which he might be improving for the purpose of some hellish strategem, was to me more tremendous even than his speech.

We both lay awake, not daring to move or speak, scarcely even breathing, but clasping one another fast, until at length the welcome light of day streamed into the room through the opening door, as the servant came in to call us. I need not say that our nocturnal visitant had left us.

The magnanimous reader will, perhaps, pronounce that I ought to have pulled on my boots and inexpressibles with all available despatch, run to my lodger's bedroom, and kicked him forthwith downstairs, and the entire way moreover out to the public road, as some compensation for the scandalous affront put upon me and my wife by his impertinent visit. Now, at that time, I had no scruples against what are termed the laws of honour, was by no means deficient in "pluck," and gifted, moreover, with a somewhat excitable temper. Yet, I will honestly avow that, so far from courting a collision with the dreaded stranger, I would have recoiled at his very sight, and given my eyes to avoid him, such was the ascendancy which he had acquired over me, as well as everybody else in my household, in his own quiet, irresistible, hellish way.

The shuddering antipathy which our guest inspired did not rob his infernal homily of its effect. It was not a new or strange thing which he presented to our minds. There was an awful subtlety in the train of his suggestions. All that he had said had floated through my own mind before, without order, indeed, or shew of logic. From my own rebellious heart the same evil thoughts had risen, like pale apparitions hovering and lost in the fumes of a necromancer's cauldron. His was like the summing up of all this—a reflection of my own feelings and fancies—but reduced to an awful order and definiteness, and clothed with a sophistical form of argument. The effect of it was powerful. It revived and exaggerated these bad emotions—it methodised and justified them—and gave to impulses and impressions, vague and desultory before, something of the compactness of a system.

My misfortune, therefore, did not soften, it exasperated me. I regarded the Great Disposer of events as a persecutor of the human race, who took delight in their miseries. I asked why my innocent child had been smitten down into the grave?—and why my darling wife, whose first object, I knew, had ever been to serve and glorify her Maker, should have been thus tortured and desolated by the cruelest calamity which the malignity of a demon could have devised? I railed and blasphemed, and even in my agony defied God with the impotent rage and desperation of a devil, in his everlasting torment.

In my bitterness, I could not forbear speaking these impenitent repetitions of the language of our nightly visitant, even in the presence of my wife. She heard me with agony, almost with terror. I pitied and loved her too much not to respect even her weaknesses—for so I characterised her humble submission to the chastisements of heaven. But even while I spared her reverential sensitiveness, the spectacle of her patience but enhanced my own gloomy and impenitent rage.

I was walking into town in this evil mood, when I was overtaken by the gentleman whom I had spoken with in the churchyard on the morning when my little boy was buried. I call him *gentleman*, but I could not say *what* was his rank—I never thought about it; there was a grace, a purity, a compassion, and a grandeur of intellect in his countenance, in his language, in his mien, that was beautiful and kinglike. I felt, in his company, a delightful awe, and an humbleness more gratifying than any elation of earthly pride.

He divined my state of feeling, but he said nothing harsh. He did not rebuke, but he reasoned with me—and oh! how mighty was that reasoning—without formality—without effort—as the flower grows and blossoms. Its process was in harmony with the successions of nature—gentle, spontaneous, irresistible.

At last he left me. I was grieved at his departure—I was wonder-stricken. His discourse had made me cry tears at once sweet and bitter; it had sounded depths I knew not of, and my heart was disquieted within me. Yet my trouble was happier than the resentful and defiant calm that had reigned within me before.

When I came home, I told my wife of my having met the same good, wise man I had first seen by the grave of my child. I recounted to her his discourse, and, as I brought it again to mind, my tears flowed afresh, and I was happy while I wept.

I now see that the calamity which bore at first such evil fruit, was good for me. It fixed my mind, however rebelliously, upon God, and it stirred up all the passions of my heart. Levity, inattention, and self-complacency are obstacles harder to be overcome than the violence of evil passions—the transition from hate is easier than from indifference, to love. A mighty change was making on my mind.

I need not particularise the occasions upon which I again met my friend, for so I knew him to be, nor detail the train of reasoning and feeling which in such interviews he followed out; it is enough to say, that he assiduously cultivated the good seed he had sown, and that his benignant teachings took deep root, and flourished in my soul, heretofore so barren.

One evening, having enjoyed on the morning of the same day another of those delightful and convincing conversations, I was returning on foot homeward; and as darkness had nearly closed, and the night threatened cold and fog, the footpaths were nearly deserted.

As I walked on, deeply absorbed in the discourse I had heard on the same morning, a person overtook me, and continued to walk, without much increasing the interval between us, a little in advance of me. There came upon me, at the same moment, an indefinable sinking of the heart, a strange and unaccountable fear. The pleasing topics of my meditations melted away, and gave place to a sense of danger, all the more unpleasant that it was vague and objectless. I looked up. What was that which moved before me? I stared—I faltered; my heart fluttered as if it would choke me, and then stood still. It was the peculiar and unmistakeable form of our lodger.

Exactly as I looked at him, he turned his head, and looked at me over his shoulder. His face was muffled as usual. I cannot have seen its features with any completeness, yet I felt that his look was one of fury. The next instant he was at my side; and my heart quailed within me—my limbs all but refused their office; yet the very emotions of terror, which might have overcome me, acted as a stimulus, and I quickened my pace.

"Hey! what a pious person! So I suppose you have learned at last that 'evil communications corrupt good manners'; and you are absolutely afraid of the old infidel, the old blasphemer, hey?"

I made him no answer; I was indeed too much agitated to speak.

"You'll make a good Christian, no doubt," he continued; "the independent man, who thinks for himself, reasons his way to his principles, and sticks fast to them, is sure to be true to whatever system he embraces. You have been so consistent a philosopher, that I am sure you will make a steady Christian. You're not the man to be led by the nose by a sophistical mumbler. *You* could never be made the prey of a grasping proselytism; *you* are not the sport of every whiff of doctrine, nor the facile slave of whatever superstition is last buzzed in your ear. No, no: you've got a masculine intellect, and think for yourself, hey?"

I was incapable of answering him. I quickened my pace to escape from his detested persecution; but he was close beside me still.

We walked on together thus for a time, during which I heard him muttering fast to himself, like a man under fierce and malignant excitement. We reached, at length, the gateway of my dwelling; and I turned the latch-key in the wicket, and entered the enclosure. As we stood together within, he turned full upon me, and confronting me with an aspect whose character I felt rather than saw, he said—

"And so you mean to be a Christian, after all! Now just reflect how very absurdly you are choosing. Leave the Bible to that class of fanatics who may hope to be saved under its system, and, in the name of common sense, study the Koran, or some less ascetic tome. Don't be gulled by a plausible slave, who wants nothing more than to multiply *professors* of his theory. Why don't you *read* the Bible, you miserable, puling poltroon, before you hug it as a treasure? Why don't you read it, and learn out of the mouth of the founder of Christianity, that there is one sin for which there is *no* forgiveness—blasphemy against the Holy Ghost, hey?—and that sin I myself have heard you commit by the hour—in my presence—in my room. I have heard you commit it in our free discussions a dozen times. The Bible seals against you the lips of mercy. If *it* be true, you are this moment as irrevocably damned as if you had died with those blasphemies on your lips."

Having thus spoken, he glided into the house. I followed slowly.

His words rang in my ears—I was stunned. What he had said I feared might be true. Giant despair felled me to the earth. He had recalled, and lighted up with a glare from the pit, remembrances with which I knew not how to cope. It was true I had spoken with daring impiety of subjects whose sacredness I now began to appreciate. With trembling hands I opened the Bible. I read and re-read the mysterious doom recorded by the Redeemer himself against blasphemers of the Holy Ghost—monsters set apart from the human race, and damned and dead, even while they live and walk upon the earth. I groaned—I wept. Henceforward the Bible, I thought, must be to me a dreadful record of despair. I dared not read it.

I will not weary you with all my mental agonies. My dear little wife did something toward relieving my mind, but it was reserved for the friend, to whose heavenly society I owed so much, to tranquillise it once more. He talked this time to me longer, and even more earnestly than before. I soon encountered him again. He expounded to me the ways of Providence, and showed me how needful sorrow was for every servant of God. How mercy was disguised in tribulation, and our best happiness came to us, like our children, in tears and wailing. He showed me that trials were sent to call us up, with a voice of preternatural power, from the mortal apathy of sin and the world. And then, again, in our new and better state, to prove our patience and our faith—

"The more trouble befalls you, the nearer is God to you. He visits you in sorrow—and sorrow, as well as joy, is a sign of his presence. If, then, other griefs overtake you, remember this—be patient, be faithful; and bless the name of God."

I returned home comforted and happy, although I felt assured that some further and sadder trial was before me.

Still our household was overcast by the same insurmountable dread of our tenant. The same strange habits characterised him, and the same unaccountable sounds disquieted us—an atmosphere of death and malice hovered about his door, and we all hated and feared to pass it.

Let me now tell, as well and briefly as I may, the dreadful circumstances of my last great trial. One morning, my wife being about her household affairs, and I on the point of starting for town, I went into the parlour for some letters which I was to take with me. I cannot easily describe my consternation when, on entering the room, I saw our lodger seated near the window, with our darling little girl upon his knee.

His back was toward the door, but I could plainly perceive that the respirator had been removed from his mouth, and that the odious green goggles were raised. He was sitting, as it seemed, absolutely without motion, and his face was advanced close to that of the child.

I stood looking at this group in a state of stupor for some seconds. He was, I suppose, conscious of my presence, for although he did not turn his head, or otherwise take any note of my arrival, he readjusted the muffler which usually covered his mouth, and lowered the clumsy spectacles to their proper place.

The child was sitting upon his knee as motionless as he himself, with a countenance white and rigid as that of a corpse, and from which every trace of meaning, except some vague character of terror, had fled, and staring with a fixed and dilated gaze into his face.

As it seemed, she did not perceive my presence. Her eyes were transfixed and fascinated. She did not even seem to me to breathe. Horror and anguish at last overcame my stupefaction.

"What—what is it?" I cried; "what ails my child, my darling child?"

"I'd be glad to know, myself," he replied, coolly; "it is certainly something very queer."

"What is it, darling?" I repeated, frantically, addressing the child.

"What is it?" he reiterated. "Why it's pretty plain, I should suppose, that the child is ill."

"Oh merciful God!" I cried, half furious, half terrified—"You have injured her—you have terrified her. Give me my child—give her to me."

These words I absolutely shouted, and stamped upon the floor in my horrid excitement.

"Pooh, pooh!" he said, with a sort of ugly sneer; "the child is nervous—you'll make her more so—be quiet and she'll probably find her tongue presently. I have had her on my knee some minutes, but the sweet bird could not tell what ails her."

"Let the child go," I shouted in a voice of thunder; "let her go, I say—let her go."

He took the passive, death-like child, and placed her standing by the window, and rising, he simply said—

"As soon as you grow cool, you are welcome to ask me what questions you like. The child is plainly ill. I should not wonder if she had seen something that frightened her."

Having thus spoken, he passed from the room. I felt as if I spoke, saw, and walked in a horrid dream. I seized the darling child in my arms, and bore her away to her mother.

"What is it—for mercy's sake what is the matter?" she cried, growing in an instant as pale as the poor child herself.

"I found that—that *demon*—in the parlour with the child on his lap, staring in her face. She is manifestly terrified."

"Oh! gracious God! she is lost—she is killed," cried the poor mother, frantically looking into the white, apathetic, meaningless face of the child.

"Fanny, darling Fanny, tell us if you are ill," I cried, pressing the little girl in terror to my heart.

"Tell your own mother, my darling," echoed my poor little wife. "Oh! darling, darling child, speak to your poor mother."

It was all in vain. Still the same dilated, imploring gaze—the same pale face—wild and dumb. We brought her to the open window—we gave her cold water to drink—we sprinkled it in her face. We sent for the apothecary, who lived hard by, and he arrived in a few moments, with a parcel of tranquillising medicines. These, however, were equally unavailing.

Hour after hour passed away. The darling child looked upon us as if she would have given the world to speak to us, or to weep, but she uttered no sound. Now and then she drew a long breath as though preparing to say something, but still she was mute. She often put her hand to her throat, as if there was some pain or obstruction there.

I never can, while I live, lose one line of that mournful and terrible portrait—the face of my stricken child. As hour after hour passed away, without bringing the smallest change or amendment, we grew both alarmed, and at length absolutely terrified for her safety.

We called in a physician toward night, and told him that we had reason to suspect that the child had somehow been frightened, and that in no other way could we at all account for the extraordinary condition in which he found her.

This was a man, I may as well observe, though I do not name him, of the highest eminence in his profession, and one in whose skill, from past personal experience, I had the best possible reasons for implicitly confiding.

He asked a multiplicity of questions, the answers to which seemed to baffle his attempts to arrive at a satisfactory diagnosis. There was something undoubtedly anomalous in the case, and I saw plainly that there were features in it which puzzled and perplexed him not a little.

At length, however, he wrote his prescription, and promised to return at nine o'clock. I remember there was something to be rubbed along her spine, and some medicines beside.

But these remedies were as entirely unavailing as the others. In a state of dismay and distraction we watched by the bed in which, in accordance with the physician's direction, we had placed her. The absolute changelessness of her condition filled us with despair. The day which had elapsed had not witnessed even a transitory variation in the dreadful character of her seizure. Any change, even a change for the worse, would have been better than this sluggish, hopeless monotony of suffering.

At the appointed hour the physician returned. He appeared disappointed, almost shocked, at the failure of his prescriptions. On feeling her pulse he declared that she must have a little wine. There had been a wonderful prostration of all the vital powers since he had seen her before. He evidently thought the case a strange and precarious one.

She was made to swallow the wine, and her pulse rallied for a time, but soon subsided again. I and the physician were standing by the fire, talking in whispers of the darling child's symptoms, and likelihood of recovery, when we were arrested in our conversation by a cry of anguish from the poor mother, who had never left the bedside of her little child, and this cry broke into bitter and convulsive weeping.

The poor little child had, on a sudden, stretched down her little hands and feet, and died. There is no mistaking the features of death: the filmy eye and dropt jaw once seen, are recognised whenever we meet them again. Yet, spite of our belief, we cling to hope; and the distracted mother called on the physician, in accents which might have moved a statue, to say that her darling was not dead, not quite dead—that something might still be done—that it could not be all over. Silently he satisfied himself that no throb of life still fluttered in that little frame.

"It is, indeed, all over," he said, in tones scarce above a whisper; and pressing my hand kindly, he said, "comfort your poor wife"; and so, after a momentary pause, he left the room.

This blow had smitten me with stunning suddenness. I looked at the dead child, and from her to her poor mother. Grief and pity were both swallowed up in transports of fury and detestation with which the presence in my house of the wretch who had wrought all this destruction and misery filled my soul. My heart swelled with ungovernable rage; for a moment my habitual fear of him was neutralised by the vehemence of these passions. I seized a candle in silence, and mounted the stairs. The sight of the accursed cat, flitting across the lobby, and the loneliness of the hour, made me hesitate for an instant. I had, however, gone so far, that shame sustained me. Overcoming a momentary thrill of dismay, and determined to repel and defy the influence that had so long awed me, I knocked sharply at the door, and, almost at the same instant, pushed it open, and entered our lodger's chamber.

He had had no candle in the room, and it was lighted only by the "darkness visible" that entered through the window. The candle which I held very imperfectly illuminated the large apartment; but I saw his spectral form floating, rather than walking, back and forward in front of the windows.

At sight of him, though I hated him more than ever, my instinctive fear returned. He confronted me, and drew nearer and nearer, without speaking. There was something indefinably fearful in the silent attraction which seemed to be drawing him to me. I could not help recoiling, little by little, as he came toward me, and with an effort I said—

"You know why I have come: the child—she's dead!"

"Dead—ha!—*dead*—is she?" he said, in his odious, mocking tone.

"Yes—dead!" I cried, with an excitement which chilled my very marrow with horror; "and *you* have killed her, as you killed my other."

"How?—I killed her!—eh?—ha, ha!" he said, still edging nearer and nearer.

"Yes; I say you!" I shouted, trembling in every joint, but possessed by that unaccountable infatuation which has made men invoke, spite of themselves, their own destruction, and which I was powerless to resist—"deny it as you may, it is you who killed her—wretch!—FIEND!—no wonder she could not stand the breath and glare of HELL!"

"And you are one of those who believe that not a sparrow falls to the ground without your Creator's consent," he said, with icy sarcasm; "and this is a specimen of Christian resignation—hey? You charge his act upon a poor fellow like me, simply that you may cheat the devil, and rave and rebel against the decrees of heaven, under pretence of abusing me. The breath and flare of hell!—eh? You mean that I removed this and these (touching the covering of his mouth and eyes successively) as I *shall* do now again, and show you there's no great harm in that."

There was a tone of menace in his concluding words not to be mistaken.

"Murderer and liar from the beginning, as you are, I defy you!" I shouted, in a frenzy of hate and horror, stamping furiously on the floor.

As I said this, it seemed to me that he darkened and dilated before my eyes. My senses, thoughts, consciousness, grew horribly confused, as if some powerful, extraneous will, were seizing upon the functions of my brain. Whether I were to be mastered by death, or madness, or possession, I knew not; but hideous destruction of some sort was impending: all hung upon the moment, and I cried aloud, in my agony, an adjuration in the name of the three persons of the Trinity, that he should not torment me.

Stunned, bewildered, like a man recovered from a drunken fall, I stood, freezing and breathless, in the same spot, looking into the room, which wore, in my eyes, a strange, unearthly character. Mr. Smith was cowering darkly in the window, and, after a silence, spoke to me in a croaking, sulky tone, which was, however, unusually submissive.

"Don't it strike you as an odd procedure to break into a gentleman's apartment at such an hour, for the purpose of railing at him in the coarsest language? If you have any charge to make against me, do so; I invite inquiry and defy your worst. If you think you can bring home to me the smallest share of blame in this unlucky matter, call the coroner, and let his inquest examine and cross-examine me, and sift the matter—if, indeed, there is anything to *be* sifted—to the bottom. Meanwhile, go you about your business, and leave me to mine. But I see how the wind sits; you want to get rid of me, and so you make the place odious to me. But it won't do; and if you take to making criminal charges against me, you had better look to yourself; for two can play at that game."

There was a suppressed whine in all this, which strangely contrasted with the cool and threatening tone of his previous conversation.

Without answering a word I hurried from the room, and scarcely felt secure, even when once more in the melancholy chamber, where my poor wife was weeping.

Miserable, horrible was the night that followed. The loss of our child was a calamity which we had not dared to think of. It had come, and with a suddenness enough to bereave me of reason. It seemed all unreal, all fantastic. It needed an effort to convince me, minute after minute, that the dreadful truth was so; and the old accustomed feeling that she was still alive, still running from room to room, and the expectation that I should hear her step and her voice, and see her entering at the door, would return. But still the sense of dismay, of having received some stunning, irreparable blow, remained behind; and then came the horrible effort, like that with which one rouses himself from a haunted sleep, the question, "What disaster is this that has befallen?"—answered, alas! but too easily, too terribly! Amidst all this was perpetually rising before my fancy the obscure, dilated figure of our lodger, as he had confronted me in his malign power that night. I dismissed the image with a shudder as often as it recurred; and even now, at this distance of time, I have felt more than I could well describe in the mere effort to fix my recollection upon its hated traits, while writing the passages I have just concluded.

This hateful scene I did not recount to my poor wife. Its horrors were too fresh upon me. I had not courage to trust myself with the agitating narrative; and so I sate beside her, with her hand locked in mine: I had no comfort to offer but the dear love I bore her.

At last, like a child, she cried herself to sleep—the dull, heavy slumber of worn-out grief. As for me, the agitation of my soul was too fearful and profound for repose. My eye accidentally rested on the holy volume, which lay upon the table open, as I had left it in the morning; and the first words which met my eye were these—"For our light affliction, which is but for a moment, worketh for us a far more exceeding and eternal weight of glory." This blessed sentence riveted my attention, and shed a stream of solemn joy upon my heart; and so the greater part of that mournful night, I continued to draw comfort and heavenly wisdom from the same inspired source.

Next day brought the odious incident, the visit of the undertaker—the carpentery, upholstery, and millinery of death. Why has not civilisation abolished these repulsive and shocking formalities? What has the poor corpse to do with frills, and pillows, and napkins, and all the equipage in which it rides on its last journey? There is no intrusion so jarring to the decent grief of surviving affection, no conceivable mummery more derisive of mortality.

In the room which we had been so long used to call "the nursery," now desolate and mute, the unclosed coffin lay, with our darling shrouded in it. Before we went to our rest at night we visited it. In the morning the lid was to close over that sweet face, and I was to see the child laid by her little brother. We looked upon the well-known and loved features, purified in the sublime serenity of death, for a long time, whispering to one another, among our sobs, how sweet and beautiful we thought she looked; and at length, weeping bitterly, we tore ourselves away.

We talked and wept for many hours, and at last, in sheer exhaustion, dropt asleep. My little wife awaked me, and said—

"I think they have come—the—the undertakers."

It was still dark, so I could not consult my watch; but they were to have arrived early, and as it was winter, and the nights long, the hour of their visit might well have arrived.

"What, darling, is your reason for thinking so?" I asked.

"I am sure I have heard them for some time in the nursery," she answered.

"Oh! dear, dear little Fanny! Don't allow them to close the coffin until

I have seen my darling once more."

I got up, and threw some clothes hastily about me. I opened the door and listened. A sound like a muffled knocking reached me from the nursery.

"Yes, my darling!" I said, "I think they have come. I will go and desire them to wait until you have seen her again."

And, so saying, I hastened from the room.

Our bedchamber lay at the end of a short corridor, opening from the lobby, at the head of the stairs, and the nursery was situated nearly at the end of a corresponding passage, which opened from the same lobby at the opposite side As I hurried along I distinctly heard the same sounds. The light of dawn had not yet appeared, but there was a strong moonlight shining through the windows. I thought the morning could hardly be so far advanced as we had at first supposed; but still, strangely as it now seems to me, suspecting nothing amiss, I walked on in noiseless, slippered feet, to the nursery-door. It stood half open; some one had unquestionably visited it since we had been there. I stepped forward, and entered. At the threshold horror arrested my advance.

The coffin was placed upon tressles at the further extremity of the chamber, with the foot of it nearly towards the door, and a large window at the side of it admitted the cold lustre of the moon full upon the apparatus of mortality, and the objects immediately about it.

At the foot of the coffin stood the ungainly form of our lodger. He seemed to be intently watching the face of the corpse, and was stooped a little, while with his hands he tapped sharply, from time to time at the sides of the coffin, like one who designs to awaken a slumberer. Perched upon the body of the child, and nuzzling among the grave-clothes, with a strange kind of ecstasy, was the detested brute, the cat I have so often mentioned.

The group thus revealed, I looked upon but for one instant; in the next I shouted, in absolute terror—

"In God's name! what are you doing?"

Our lodger shuffled away abruptly, as if disconcerted; but the ill-favoured cat, whisking round, stood like a demon sentinel upon the corpse, growling and hissing, with arched back and glaring eyes.

The lodger, turning abruptly toward me, motioned me to one side.

Mechanically I obeyed his gesture, and he hurried hastily from the room.

Sick and dizzy, I returned to my own chamber. I confess I had not nerve to combat the infernal brute, which still held possession of the room, and so I left it undisturbed.

This incident I did not tell to my wife until some time afterwards; and I mention it here because it was, and is, in my mind associated with a painful circumstance which very soon afterwards came to light.

That morning I witnessed the burial of my darling child. Sore and desolate was my heart; but with infinite gratitude to the great controller of all events, I recognised in it a change which nothing but the spirit of all good can effect. The love and fear of God had grown strong within me—in humbleness I bowed to his awful will—with a sincere trust I relied upon the goodness, the wisdom, and the mercy of him who had sent this great affliction. But a further incident connected with this very calamity was to test this trust and patience to the uttermost.

It was still early when I returned, having completed the last sad office. My wife, as I afterwards learned, still lay weeping upon her bed. But somebody awaited my return in the hall, and opened the door, anticipating my knock. This person was our lodger.

I was too much appalled by the sudden presentation of this abhorred spectre even to retreat, as my instinct would have directed, through the open door.

"I have been expecting your return," he said, "with the design of saying something which it might have profited you to learn, but now I apprehend it is too late. What a pity you are so violent and impatient; you would not have heard me, in all probability, this morning. You cannot think how cross-grained and intemperate you have grown since you became a saint—but that is your affair, not mine. You have buried your little daughter this morning. It requires a good deal of that new attribute of yours, *faith*, which judges all things by a rule of contraries, and can never see anything but kindness in the worst afflictions which malignity could devise, to discover benignity and mercy in the torturing calamity which has just punished you and your wife for *nothing*! But I fancy that it will be harder still when I tell you what I more than suspect—ha, ha. It would be really ridiculous, if it were not heart-rending; that your little girl has been actually buried *alive*; do you comprehend me?—alive. For, upon my life, I fancy she was not dead as she lay in her coffin."

I knew the wretch was exulting in the fresh anguish he had just inflicted. I know not how it was, but any announcement of *disaster* from his lips, seemed to me to be necessarily true. Half-stifled with the dreadful emotions he had raised, palpitating between hope and terror, I rushed frantically back again, the way I had just come, running as fast as my speed could carry me, toward the, alas! distant burial-ground where my darling lay.

I stopped a cab slowly returning to town, at the corner of the lane, sprang into it, directed the man to drive to the church of ——, and promised him anything and everything for despatch. The man seemed amazed; doubtful, perhaps, whether he carried a maniac or a malefactor. Still he took his chance for the promised reward, and galloped his horse, while I, tortured with suspense, yelled my frantic incentives to further speed.

At last, in a space immeasurably short, but which to me was protracted almost beyond endurance, we reached the spot. I halloed to the sexton, who was now employed upon another grave, to follow me. I myself seized a mattock, and in obedience to my incoherent and agonised commands, he worked as he had never worked before. The crumbling mould flew swiftly to the upper soil—deeper and deeper, every moment, grew the narrow grave—at last I sobbed, "Thank God—thank God," as I saw the face of the coffin emerge; a few seconds more and it lay upon the sward beside me, and we both, with the edges of our spades, ripped up the lid.

There was the corpse—but not the tranquil statue I had seen it last. Its knees were both raised, and one of its little hands drawn up and clenched near its throat, as if in a feeble but agonised struggle to force up the superincumbent mass. The eyes, that I had last seen closed, were now open, and the face no longer serenely pale, but livid and distorted.

I had time to see all in an instant; the whole scene reeled and darkened before me, and I swooned away.

When I came to myself, I found that I had been removed to the vestry-room. The open coffin was in the aisle of the church, surrounded by a curious crowd. A medical gentleman had examined the body carefully, and had pronounced life totally extinct. The trepidation and horror I experienced were indescribable. I felt like the murderer of my own child. Desperate as I was of any chance of its life, I dispatched messengers for no less than three of the most eminent physicians then practising in London. All concurred—the child was now as dead as any other, the oldest tenant of the churchyard.

Notwithstanding which, I would not permit the body to be reinterred for several days, until the symptoms of decay became unequivocal, and the most fantastic imagination could no longer cherish a doubt. This, however, I mention only parenthetically, as I hasten to the conclusion of my narrative. The circumstance which I have last described found its way to the public, and caused no small sensation at the time.

I drove part of the way home, and then discharged the cab, and walked the remainder. On my way, with an emotion of ecstasy I cannot describe, I met the good being to whom I owed so much. I ran to meet him, and felt as if I could throw myself at his feet, and kiss the very ground before him. I knew by his heavenly countenance he was come to speak comfort and healing to my heart.

With humbleness and gratitude, I drank in his sage and holy discourse. I need not follow the gracious and delightful exposition of God's revealed will and character with which he cheered and confirmed my faltering spirit. A solemn joy, a peace and trust, streamed on my heart. The wreck and desolation there, lost their bleak and ghastly character, like ruins illuminated by the mellow beams of a solemn summer sunset.

In this conversation, I told him what I had never revealed to any one before—the absolute terror, in all its stupendous and maddening amplitude, with which I regarded our ill-omened lodger, and my agonised anxiety to rid my house of him. My companion answered me—

"I know the person of whom you speak—he designs no good for you or any other. He, too, knows me, and I have intimated to him that he must now leave you, and visit you no more. Be firm and bold, trusting in God, through his Son, like a good soldier, and you will win the victory from a greater and even worse than he—the *unseen* enemy of mankind. You need not see or speak with your evil tenant any more. Call to him from your hall, in the name of the Most Holy, to leave you bodily, with all that appertains to him, this evening. He knows that he must go, and will obey you. But leave the house as soon as may be yourself; you will scarce have peace in it. Your own remembrances will trouble you and *other minds have established associations within its walls and chambers too.*"

These words sounded mysteriously in my ears.

Let me say here, before I bring my reminiscences to a close, a word or two about the house in which these detested scenes occurred, and which I did not long continue to inhabit. What I afterwards learned of it, seemed to supply in part a dim explanation of these words.

In a country village there is no difficulty in accounting for the tenacity with which the sinister character of a haunted tenement cleaves to it. Thin neighbourhoods are favourable to scandal; and in such localities the reputation of a house, like that of a woman, once blown upon, never quite recovers. In huge London, however, it is quite another matter; and, therefore, it was with some surprise that, five years after I had vacated the house in which the occurrences I have described took place, I learned that a respectable family who had taken it were obliged to give it up, on account of annoyances, for which they could not account, and all proceeding from the apartments formerly occupied by our "lodger." Among the sounds described were footsteps restlessly traversing the floor of that room, accompanied by the peculiar tapping of the crutch.

I was so anxious about this occurrence, that I contrived to have strict inquiries made into the matter. The result, however, added little to what I had at first learned—except, indeed, that our old friend, the cat, bore a part in the transaction as I suspected; for the servant, who had been placed to sleep in the room, complained that something bounded on and off, and ran to-and-fro along the foot of the bed, in the dark. The same servant, while in the room, in the broad daylight, had heard the sound of walking, and even the rustling of clothes near him, as of people passing and repassing; and, although he had never seen anything, he yet became so terrified that he would not remain in the house, and ultimately, in a short time, left his situation.

These sounds, attention having been called to them, were now incessantly observed—the measured walking up and down the room, the opening and closing of the door, and the teazing tap of the crutch—all these sounds were continually repeated, until at last, worn out, frightened, and worried, its occupants resolved on abandoning the house.

About four years since, having had occasion to visit the capital, I resolved on a ramble by Old Brompton, just to see if the house were still inhabited. I searched for it, however, in vain, and at length, with difficulty, ascertained its site, upon which now stood two small, staring, bran-new brick houses, with each a gay enclosure of flowers. Every trace of our old mansion, and, let us hope, of our "mysterious lodger," had entirely vanished.

Let me, however, return to my narrative where I left it.

Discoursing upon heavenly matters, my good and gracious friend accompanied me even within the outer gate of my own house. I asked him to come in and rest himself, but he would not; and before he turned to depart, he lifted up his hand, and blessed me and my household.

Having done this, he went away. My eyes followed him till he disappeared, and I turned to the house. My darling wife was standing at the window of the parlour. There was a seraphic smile on her face—pale, pure, and beautiful as death. She was gazing with an humble, heavenly earnestness on us. The parting blessing of the stranger shed a sweet and hallowed influence on my heart. I went into the parlour, to my darling: childless she was now; I had now need to be a tender companion to her.

She raised her arms in a sort of transport, with the same smile of gratitude and purity, and, throwing them round my neck, she said—

"I have seen him—it is he—the man that came with you to the door, and blessed us as he went away—is the same I saw in my dream—the same who took little baby in his arms, and said he would take care of him, and give him safely to me again."

More than a quarter of a century has glided away since then; other children have been given us by the good God—children who have been, from infancy to maturity, a pride and blessing to us. Sorrows and reverses, too, have occasionally visited us; yet, on the whole, we have been greatly blessed; prosperity has long since ended all the cares of the *res angusta domi*, and expanded our power of doing good to our fellow-creatures. God has given it; and God, we trust, directs its dispensation. In our children, and—would you think it?—our *grand*-children, too, the same beneficent God has given us objects that elicit and return all the delightful affections, and exchange the sweet converse that makes home and family dearer than aught else, save that blessed home where the Christian family shall meet at last.

The dear companion of my early love and sorrows still lives, blessed be Heaven! The evening tints of life have fallen upon her; but the dear remembrance of a first love, that never grew cold, makes her beauty changeless for me. As for your humble servant, he is considerably her senior, and looks it: time has stolen away his raven locks, and given him a *chevelure* of snow instead. But, as I said before, I and my wife love, and, I believe, *admire* one another more than ever; and I have often seen our elder children smile archly at one another, when they thought we did not observe them, thinking, no doubt, how like a pair of lovers we two were.

GHOSTLY TALES
VOLUME V

LAURA SILVER BELL

In the five Northumbrian counties you will scarcely find so bleak, ugly, and yet, in a savage way, so picturesque a moor as Dardale Moss. The moor itself spreads north, south, east, and west, a great undulating sea of black peat and heath.

What we may term its shores are wooded wildly with birch, hazel, and dwarf-oak. No towering mountains surround it, but here and there you have a rocky knoll rising among the trees, and many a wooded promontory of the same pretty, because utterly wild, forest, running out into its dark level.

Habitations are thinly scattered in this barren territory, and a full mile away from the meanest was the stone cottage of Mother Carke.

Let not my southern reader who associates ideas of comfort with the term "cot tage" mistake. This thing is built of shingle, with low walls. Its thatch is hollow; the peat-smoke curls stingily from its stunted chimney. It is worthy of its savage surroundings.

The primitive neighbours remark that no rowan-tree grows near, nor holly, nor bracken, and no horseshoe is nailed on the door.

Not far from the birches and hazels that straggle about the rude wall of the little enclosure, on the contrary, they say, you may discover the broom and the ragwort, in which witches mysteriously delight. But this is perhaps a scandal.

Mall Carke was for many a year the *sage femme* of this wild domain. She has renounced practice, however, for some years; and now, under the rose, she dabbles, it is thought, in the black art, in which she has always been secretly skilled, tells fortunes, practises charms, and in popular esteem is little better than a witch.

Mother Carke has been away to the town of Willarden, to sell knit stockings, and is returning to her rude dwelling by Dardale Moss. To her right, as far away as the eye can reach, the moor stretches. The narrow track she has followed here tops a gentle upland, and at her left a sort of jungle of dwarf-oak and brushwood approaches its edge. The sun is sinking blood-red in the west. His disk has touched the broad black level of the moor, and his parting beams glare athwart the gaunt figure of the old beldame, as she strides homeward stick in hand, and bring into relief the folds of her mantle, which gleam like the draperies of a bronze image in the light of a fire. For a few moments this light floods the air—tree, gorse, rock, and bracken glare; and then it is out, and gray twilight over everything.

All is still and sombre. At this hour the simple traffic of the thinly-peopled country is over, and nothing can be more solitary.

From this jungle, nevertheless, through which the mists of evening are already creeping, she sees a gigantic man approaching her.

In that poor and primitive country robbery is a crime unknown. She, therefore, has no fears for her pound of tea, and pint of gin, and sixteen shillings in silver which she is bringing home in her pocket. But there is something that would have frighted another woman about this man.

He is gaunt, sombre, bony, dirty, and dressed in a black suit which a beggar would hardly care to pick out of the dust.

This ill-looking man nodded to her as he stepped on the road.

"I don't know you," she said.

He nodded again.

"I never sid ye neyawheere," she exclaimed sternly.

"Fine evening, Mother Carke," he says, and holds his snuff-box toward her.

She widened the distance between them by a step or so, and said again sternly and pale,

"I hev nowt to say to thee, whoe'er thou beest."

"You know Laura Silver Bell?"

"That's a byneyam; the lass's neyam is Laura Lew," she answered, looking straight before her.

"One name's as good as another for one that was never christened, mother."

"How know ye that?" she asked grimly; for it is a received opinion in that part of the world that the fairies have power over those who have never been baptised.

The stranger turned on her a malignant smile.

"There is a young lord in love with her," the stranger says, "and I'm that lord. Have her at your house to-morrow night at eight o'clock, and you must stick cross pins through the candle, as you have done for many a one before, to bring her lover thither by ten, and her fortune's made. And take this for your trouble."

He extended his long finger and thumb toward her, with a guinea temptingly displayed.

"I have nowt to do wi' thee. I nivver sid thee afoore. Git thee awa'! I earned nea goold o' thee, and I'll tak' nane. Awa' wi' thee, or I'll find ane that will mak' thee!"

The old woman had stopped, and was quivering in every limb as she thus spoke.

He looked very angry. Sulkily he turned away at her words, and strode slowly toward the wood from which he had come; and as he approached it, he seemed to her to grow taller and taller, and stalked into it as high as a tree.

"I conceited there would come something o't", she said to herself. "Farmer Lew must git it done nesht Sunda'. The a'ad awpy!"

Old Farmer Lew was one of that sect who insist that baptism shall be but once administered, and not until the Christian candidate had attained to adult years.

The girl had indeed for some time been of an age not only, according to this theory, to be baptised, but if need be to be married.

Her story was a sad little romance. A lady some seventeen years before had come down and paid Farmer Lew for two rooms in his house. She told him that her husband would follow her in a fortnight, and that he was in the mean time delayed by business in Liverpool.

In ten days after her arrival her baby was born, Mall Carke acting as *sage femme* on the occasion; and on the evening of that day the poor young mother died. No husband came; no wedding-ring, they said, was on her finger. About fifty pounds was found in her desk, which Farmer Lew, who was a kind old fellow and had lost his two children, put in bank for the little girl, and resolved to keep her until a rightful owner should step forward to claim her.

They found half-a-dozen love-letters signed "Francis," and calling the dead woman "Laura."

So Farmer Lew called the little girl Laura; and her *sobriquet* of "Silver Bell" was derived from a tiny silver bell, once gilt, which was found among her poor mother's little treasures after her death, and which the child wore on a ribbon round her neck.

Thus, being very pretty and merry, she grew up as a North-country farmer's daughter; and the old man, as she needed more looking after, grew older and less able to take care of her; so she was, in fact, very nearly her own mistress, and did pretty much in all things as she liked.

Old Mall Carke, by some caprice for which no one could account, cherished an affection for the girl, who saw her often, and paid her many a small fee in exchange for the secret indications of the future.

It was too late when Mother Carke reached her home to look for a visit from Laura Silver Bell that day.

About three o'clock next afternoon, Mother Carke was sitting knitting, with her glasses on, outside her door on the stone bench, when she saw the pretty girl mount lightly to the top of the stile at her left under the birch, against the silver stem of which she leaned her slender hand, and called,

"Mall, Mall! Mother Carke, are ye alane all by yersel'?"

"Ay, Laura lass, we can be clooas enoo, if ye want a word wi' me," says the old woman, rising, with a mysterious nod, and beckoning her stiffly with her long fingers.

The girl was, assuredly, pretty enough for a "lord" to fall in love with. Only look at her. A profusion of brown rippling hair, parted low in the middle of her forehead, almost touched her eyebrows, and made the pretty oval of her face, by the breadth of that rich line, more marked. What a pretty little nose! what scarlet lips, and large, dark, long-fringed eyes!

Her face is transparently tinged with those clear Murillo tints which appear in deeper dyes on her wrists and the backs of her hands. These are the beautiful gipsy-tints with which the sun dyes young skins so richly.

The old woman eyes all this, and her pretty figure, so round and slender, and her shapely little feet, cased in the thick shoes that can't hide their comely proportions, as she stands on the top of the stile. But it is with a dark and saturnine aspect.

"Come, lass, what stand ye for atoppa t' wall, whar folk may chance to see thee? I hev a thing to tell thee, lass."

She beckoned her again.

"An' I hev a thing to tell *thee*, Mall."

"Come hidder," said the old woman peremptorily.

"But ye munna gie me the creepin's" (make me tremble). "I winna look again into the glass o' water, mind ye."

The old woman smiled grimly, and changed her tone.

"Now, hunny, git tha down, and let ma see thy canny feyace," and she beckoned her again.

Laura Silver Bell did get down, and stepped lightly toward the door of the old woman's dwelling.

"Tak this," said the girl, unfolding a piece of bacon from her apron, "and I hev a silver sixpence to gie thee, when I'm gaen away heyam."

They entered the dark kitchen of the cottage, and the old woman stood by the door, lest their conference should be lighted on by surprise.

"Afoore ye begin," said Mother Carke (I soften her patois), "I mun tell ye there's ill folk watchin' ye. What's auld Farmer Lew about, he doesna get t' sir" (the clergyman) "to baptise thee? If he lets Sunda' next pass, I'm afeared ye'll never be sprinkled nor signed wi' cross, while there's a sky aboon us."

"Agoy!" exclaims the girl, "who's lookin' after me?"

"A big black fella, as high as the kipples, came out o' the wood near Deadman's Grike, just after the sun gaed down yester e'en; I knew weel what he was, for his feet ne'er touched the road while he made as if he walked beside me. And he wanted to gie me snuff first, and I wouldna hev that; and then he offered me a gowden guinea, but I was no sic awpy, and to bring you here to-night, and cross the candle wi' pins, to call your lover in. And he said he's a great lord, and in luve wi' thee."

"And you refused him?"

"Well for thee I did, lass," says Mother Carke.

"Why, it's every word true!" cries the girl vehemently, starting to her feet, for she had seated herself on the great oak chest.

"True, lass? Come, say what ye mean," demanded Mall Carke, with a dark and searching gaze.

"Last night I was coming heyam from the wake, wi' auld farmer Dykes and his wife and his daughter Nell, and when we came to the stile, I bid them good-night, and we parted."

"And ye came by the path alone in the night-time, did ye?" exclaimed old Mall Carke sternly.

"I wasna afeared, I don't know why; the path heyam leads down by the wa'as o' auld Hawarth Castle."

"I knaa it weel, and a dowly path it is; ye'll keep indoors o' nights for a while, or ye'll rue it. What saw ye?"

"No freetin, mother; nowt I was feared on."

"Ye heard a voice callin' yer neyame?"

"I heard nowt that was dow, but the hullyhoo in the auld castle wa's," answered the pretty girl. "I heard nor sid nowt that's dow, but mickle that's conny and gladsome. I heard singin' and laughin' a long way off, I consaited; and I stopped a bit to listen. Then I walked on a step or two, and there, sure enough in the Pie-Mag field, under the castle wa's, not twenty steps away, I sid a grand company; silks and satins, and men wi' velvet coats, wi' gowd-lace striped over them, and ladies wi' necklaces that would dazzle ye, and fans as big as griddles; and powdered footmen, like what the shirra hed behind his coach, only these was ten times as grand."

"It was full moon last night," said the old woman.

"Sa bright 'twould blind ye to look at it," said the girl.

"Never an ill sight but the deaul finds a light," quoth the old woman. "There's a rinnin brook thar—you were at this side, and they at that; did they try to mak ye cross over?"

"Agoy! didn't they? Nowt but civility and kindness, though. But ye mun let me tell it my own way. They was talkin' and laughin', and eatin', and drinkin' out o' long glasses and goud cups, seated on the grass, and music was playin'; and I keekin' behind a bush at all the grand doin's; and up they gits to dance; and says a tall fella I didna see afoore, 'Ye mun step across, and dance wi' a young lord that's faan in luv wi' thee, and that's mysel',' and sure enow I keeked at him under my lashes and a conny lad he is, to my teyaste, though he be dressed in black, wi' sword and sash, velvet twice as fine as they sells in the shop at Gouden Friars; and keekin' at me again fra the corners o' his een. And the same fella telt me he was mad in luv wi' me, and his fadder was there, and his sister, and they came all the way from Catstean Castle to see me that night; and that's t' other side o' Gouden Friars."

"Come, lass, yer no mafflin; tell me true. What was he like? Was his feyace grimed wi' sut? a tall fella wi' wide shouthers, and lukt like an ill-thing, wi' black clothes amaist in rags?"

"His feyace was long, but weel-faured, and darker nor a gipsy; and his clothes were black and grand, and made o' velvet, and he said he was the young lord himsel'; and he lukt like it."

"That will be the same fella I sid at Deadman's Grike," said Mall Carke, with an anxious frown.

"Hoot, mudder! how cud that be?" cried the lass, with a toss of her pretty head and a smile of scorn. But the fortune-teller made no answer, and the girl went on with her story.

"When they began to dance," continued Laura Silver Bell, "he urged me again, but I wudna step o'er; 'twas partly pride, coz I wasna dressed fine enough, and partly contrairiness, or something, but gaa I wudna, not a fut. No but I more nor half wished it a' the time."

"Weel for thee thou dudstna cross the brook."

"Hoity-toity, why not?"

"Keep at heyame after nightfall, and don't ye be walking by yersel' by daylight or any light lang lonesome ways, till after ye're baptised," said Mall Carke.

"I'm like to be married first."

"Tak care *that* marriage won't hang i' the bell-ropes," said Mother Carke.

"Leave me alane for that. The young lord said he was maist daft wi' luv o' me. He wanted to gie me a conny ring wi' a beautiful stone in it. But, drat it, I was sic an awpy I wudna tak it, and he a young lord!"

"Lord, indeed! are ye daft or dreamin'? Those fine folk, what were they? I'll tell ye. Dobies and fairies; and if ye don't du as yer bid, they'll tak ye, and ye'll never git out o' their hands again while grass grows," said the old woman grimly.

"Od wite it!" replies the girl impatiently, "who's daft or dreamin' noo? I'd a bin dead wi' fear, if 'twas any such thing. It cudna be; all was sa luvesome, and bonny, and shaply."

"Weel, and what do ye want o' me, lass?" asked the old woman sharply.

"I want to know—here's t' sixpence—what I sud du," said the young lass. "'Twud be a pity to lose such a marrow, hey?"

"Say yer prayers, lass; *I* can't help ye," says the old woman darkly. "If ye gaa wi' *the* people, ye'll never come back. Ye munna talk wi' them, nor eat wi' them, nor drink wi' them, nor tak a pin's-worth by way o' gift fra them—mark weel what I say—or ye're *lost!*"

The girl looked down, plainly much vexed.

The old woman stared at her with a mysterious frown steadily, for a few seconds.

"Tell me, lass, and tell me true, are ye in luve wi' that lad?"

"What for sud I?" said the girl with a careless toss of her head, and blushing up to her very temples.

"I see how it is," said the old woman, with a groan, and repeated the words, sadly thinking; and walked out of the door a step or two, and looked jealously round. "The lass is witched, the lass is witched!"

"Did ye see him since?" asked Mother Carke, returning.

The girl was still embarrassed; and now she spoke in a lower tone, and seemed subdued.

"I thought I sid him as I came here, walkin' beside me among the trees; but I consait it was only the trees themsels that lukt like rinnin' one behind another, as I walked on."

"I can tell thee nowt, lass, but what I telt ye afoore," answered the old woman peremptorily. "Get ye heyame, and don't delay on the way; and say yer prayers as ye gaa; and let none but good thoughts come nigh ye; and put nayer foot autside the door-steyan again till ye gaa to be christened; and get that done a Sunda' next."

And with this charge, given with grizzly earnestness, she saw her over the stile, and stood upon it watching her retreat, until the trees quite hid her and her path from view.

The sky grew cloudy and thunderous, and the air darkened rapidly, as the girl, a little frightened by Mall Carke's view of the case, walked homeward by the lonely path among the trees.

A black cat, which had walked close by her—for these creatures sometimes take a ramble in search of their prey among the woods and thickets—crept from under the hollow of an oak, and was again with her. It seemed to her to grow bigger and bigger as the darkness deepened, and its green eyes glared as large as halfpennies in her affrighted vision as the thunder came booming along the heights from the Willarden-road.

She tried to drive it away; but it growled and hissed awfully, and set up its back as if it would spring at her, and finally it skipped up into a tree, where they grew thickest at each side of her path, and accompanied her, high over head, hopping from bough to bough as if meditating a pounce upon her shoulders. Her fancy being full of strange thoughts, she was frightened, and she fancied that it was haunting her steps, and destined to undergo some hideous transformation, the moment she ceased to guard her path with prayers.

She was frightened for a while after she got home. The dark looks of Mother Carke were always before her eyes, and a secret dread prevented her passing the threshold of her home again that night.

Next day it was different. She had got rid of the awe with which Mother Carke had inspired her. She could not get the tall dark-featured lord, in the black velvet dress, out of her head. He had "taken her fancy"; she was growing to love him. She could think of nothing else.

Bessie Hennock, a neighbour's daughter, came to see her that day, and proposed a walk toward the ruins of Hawarth Castle, to gather "blaebirries." So off the two girls went together.

In the thicket, along the slopes near the ivied walls of Hawarth Castle, the companions began to fill their baskets. Hours passed. The sun was sinking near the west, and Laura Silver Bell had not come home.

Over the hatch of the farm-house door the maids leant ever and anon with outstretched necks, watching for a sign of the girl's return, and wondering, as the shadows lengthened, what had become of her.

At last, just as the rosy sunset gilding began to overspread the landscape, Bessie Hennock, weeping into her apron, made her appearance without her companion.

Her account of their adventures was curious.

I will relate the substance of it more connectedly than her agitation would allow her to give it, and without the disguise of the rude Northumbrian dialect.

The girl said, that, as they got along together among the brambles that grow beside the brook that bounds the Pie-Mag field, she on a sudden saw a very tall big-boned man, with an ill-favoured smirched face, and dressed in worn and rusty black, standing at the other side of a little stream. She was frightened; and while looking at this dirty, wicked, starved figure, Laura Silver Bell touched her, gazing at the same tall scarecrow, but with a countenance full of confusion and even rapture. She was peeping through the bush behind which she stood, and with a sigh she said:

"Is na that a conny lad? Agoy! See his bonny velvet clothes, his sword and sash; that's a lord, I can tell ye; and weel I know who he follows, who he luves, and who he'll wed."

Bessie Hennock thought her companion daft.

"See how luvesome he luks!" whispered Laura.

Bessie looked again, and saw him gazing at her companion with a malignant smile, and at the same time he beckoned her to approach.

"Darrat ta! gaa not near him! he'll wring thy neck!" gasped Bessie in great fear, as she saw Laura step forward with a look of beautiful bashfulness and joy.

She took the hand he stretched across the stream, more for love of the hand than any need of help, and in a moment was across and by his side, and his long arm about her waist.

"Fares te weel, Bessie, I'm gain my ways," she called, leaning her head to his shoulder; "and tell gud Fadder Lew I'm gain my ways to be happy, and may be, at lang last, I'll see him again."

And with a farewell wave of her hand, she went away with her dismal partner; and Laura Silver Bell was never more seen at home, or among the "coppies" and "wickwoods," the bonny fields and bosky hollows, by Dardale Moss.

Bessie Hennock followed them for a time.

She crossed the brook, and though they seemed to move slowly enough, she was obliged to run to keep them in view; and she all the time cried to her continually, "Come back, come back, bonnie Laurie!" until, getting over a bank, she was met by a white-faced old man, and so frightened was she, that she thought she fainted outright. At all events, she did not come to herself until the birds were singing their vespers in the amber light of sunset, and the day was over.

No trace of the direction of the girl's flight was ever discovered. Weeks and months passed, and more than a year.

At the end of that time, one of Mall Carke's goats died, as she suspected, by the envious practices of a rival witch who lived at the far end of Dardale Moss.

All alone in her stone cabin the old woman had prepared her charm to ascertain the author of her misfortune.

The heart of the dead animal, stuck all over with pins, was burnt in the fire; the windows, doors, and every other aperture of the house being first carefully stopped. After the heart, thus prepared with suitable incantations, is consumed in the fire, the first person who comes to the door or passes by it is the offending magician.

Mother Carke completed these lonely rites at dead of night. It was a dark night, with the glimmer of the stars only, and a melancholy night-wind was soughing through the scattered woods that spread around.

After a long and dead silence, there came a heavy thump at the door, and a deep voice called her by name.

She was startled, for she expected no man's voice; and peeping from the window, she saw, in the dim light, a coach and four horses, with gold-laced footmen, and coachman in wig and cocked hat, turned out as if for a state occasion.

She unbarred the door; and a tall gentleman, dressed in black, waiting at the threshold, entreated her, as the only *sage femme* within reach, to come in the coach and attend Lady Lairdale, who was about to give birth to a baby, promising her handsome payment.

Lady Lairdale! She had never heard of her.

"How far away is it?"

"Twelve miles on the old road to Golden Friars."

Her avarice is roused, and she steps into the coach. The footman claps-to the door; the glass jingles with the sound of a laugh. The tall dark-faced gentleman in black is seated opposite; they are driving at a furious pace; they have turned out of the road into a narrower one, dark with thicker and loftier forest than she was accustomed to. She grows anxious; for she knows every road and by-path in the country round, and she has never seen this one.

He encourages her. The moon has risen above the edge of the horizon, and she sees a noble old castle. Its summit of tower, watchtower and battlement, glimmers faintly in the moonlight. This is their destination.

She feels on a sudden all but overpowered by sleep; but although she nods, she is quite conscious of the continued motion, which has become even rougher.

She makes an effort, and rouses herself. What has become of the coach, the castle, the servants? Nothing but the strange forest remains the same.

She is jolting along on a rude hurdle, seated on rushes, and a tall, big-boned man, in rags, sits in front, kicking with his heel the ill-favoured beast that pulls them along, every bone of which sticks out, and holding the halter which serves for reins. They stop at the door of a miserable building of loose stone, with a thatch so sunk and rotten, that the roof-tree and couples protrude in crooked corners, like the bones of the wretched horse, with enormous head and ears, that dragged them to the door.

The long gaunt man gets down, his sinister face grimed like his hands.

It was the same grimy giant who had accosted her on the lonely road near Deadman's Grike. But she feels that she "must go through with it" now, and she follows him into the house.

Two rushlights were burning in the large and miserable room, and on a coarse ragged bed lay a woman groaning piteously.

"That's Lady Lairdale," says the gaunt dark man, who then began to stride up and down the room rolling his head, stamping furiously, and thumping one hand on the palm of the other, and talking and laughing in the corners, where there was no one visible to hear or to answer.

Old Mall Carke recognized in the faded half-starved creature who lay on the bed, as dark now and grimy as the man, and looking as if she had never in her life washed hands or face, the once blithe and pretty Laura Lew.

The hideous being who was her mate continued in the same odd fluctuations of fury, grief, and merriment; and whenever she uttered a groan, he parodied it with another, as Mother Carke thought, in saturnine derision.

At length he strode into another room, and banged the door after him.

In due time the poor woman's pains were over, and a daughter was born.

Such an imp! with long pointed ears, flat nose, and enormous restless eyes and mouth. It instantly began to yell and talk in some unknown language, at the noise of which the father looked into the room, and told the *sage femme* that she should not go unrewarded.

The sick woman seized the moment of his absence to say in the ear of Mall Carke:

"If ye had not been at ill work tonight, he could not hev fetched ye. Tak no more now than your rightful fee, or he'll keep ye here."

At this moment he returned with a bag of gold and silver coins, which he emptied on the table, and told her to help herself.

She took four shillings, which was her primitive fee, neither more nor less; and all his urgency could not prevail with her to take a farthing more. He looked so terrible at her refusal, that she rushed out of the house.

He ran after her.

"You'll take your money with you," he roared, snatching up the bag, still half full, and flung it after her.

It lighted on her shoulder; and partly from the blow, partly from terror, she fell to the ground; and when she came to herself, it was morning, and she was lying across her own door-stone.

It is said that she never more told fortune or practised spell. And though all that happened sixty years ago and more, Laura Silver Bell, wise folk think, is still living, and will so continue till the day of doom among the fairies.

WICKED CAPTAIN WALSHAWE, OF WAULING

CHAPTER I.

PEG O'NEILL PAYS THE CAPTAIN'S DEBTS

A very odd thing happened to my uncle, Mr. Watson, of Haddlestone; and to enable you to understand it, I must begin at the beginning.

In the year 1822, Mr. James Walshawe, more commonly known as Captain Walshawe, died at the age of eighty-one years. The Captain in his early days, and so long as health and strength permitted, was a scamp of the active, intriguing sort; and spent his days and nights in sowing his wild oats, of which he seemed to have an inexhaustible stock. The harvest of this tillage was plentifully interspersed with thorns, nettles, and thistles, which stung the husbandman unpleasantly, and did not enrich him.

Captain Walshawe was very well known in the neighborhood of Wauling, and very generally avoided there. A "captain" by courtesy, for he had never reached that rank in the army list. He had quitted the service in 1766, at the age of twenty-five; immediately previous to which period his debts had grown so troublesome, that he was induced to extricate himself by running away with and marrying an heiress.

Though not so wealthy quite as he had imagined, she proved a very comfortable investment for what remained of his shattered affections; and he lived and enjoyed himself very much in his old way, upon her income, getting into no end of scrapes and scandals, and a good deal of debt and money trouble.

When he married his wife, he was quartered in Ireland, at Clonmel, where was a nunnery, in which, as pensioner, resided Miss O'Neill, or as she was called in the country, Peg O'Neill—the heiress of whom I have spoken.

Her situation was the only ingredient of romance in the affair, for the young lady was decidedly plain, though good-humoured looking, with that style of features which is termed *potato*; and in figure she was a little too plump, and rather short. But she was impressible; and the handsome young English Lieutenant was too much for her monastic tendencies, and she eloped.

In England there are traditions of Irish fortune-hunters, and in Ireland of English. The fact is, it was the vagrant class of each country that chiefly visited the other in old times; and a handsome vagabond, whether at home or abroad, I suppose, made the most of his face, which was also his fortune.

At all events, he carried off the fair one from the sanctuary; and for some sufficient reason, I suppose, they took up their abode at Wauling, in Lancashire.

Here the gallant captain amused himself after his fashion, sometimes running up, of course on business, to London. I believe few wives have ever cried more in a given time than did that poor, dumpy, potato-faced heiress, who got over the nunnery garden wall, and jumped into the handsome Captain's arms, for love.

He spent her income, frightened her out of her wits with oaths and threats, and broke her heart.

Latterly she shut herself up pretty nearly altogether in her room. She had an old, rather grim, Irish servant-woman in attendance upon her. This domestic was tall, lean, and religious, and the Captain knew instinctively she hated him; and he hated her in return, often threatened to put her out of the house, and sometimes even to kick her out of the window. And whenever a wet day confined him to the house, or the stable, and he grew tired of smoking, he would begin to swear and curse at her for a *diddled* old mischief-maker, that could never be easy, and was always troubling the house with her cursed stories, and so forth.

But years passed away, and old Molly Doyle remained still in her original position. Perhaps he thought that there must be somebody there, and that he was not, after all, very likely to change for the better.

CHAPTER II

THE BLESSED CANDLE

He tolerated another intrusion, too, and thought himself a paragon of patience and easy good nature for so doing. A Roman Catholic clergyman, in a long black frock, with a low standing collar, and a little white muslin fillet round his neck—tall, sallow, with blue chin, and dark steady eyes—used to glide up and down the stairs, and through the passages; and the Captain sometimes met him in one place and sometimes in another. But by a caprice incident to such tempers he treated this cleric exceptionally, and even with a surly sort of courtesy, though he grumbled about his visits behind his back.

I do not know that he had a great deal of moral courage, and the ecclesiastic looked severe and self-possessed; and somehow he thought he had no good opinion of him, and if a natural occasion were offered, might say extremely unpleasant things, and hard to be answered.

Well the time came at last, when poor Peg O'Neill—in an evil hour Mrs. James Walshawe—must cry, and quake, and pray her last. The doctor came from Penlynden, and was just as vague as usual, but more gloomy, and for about a week came and went oftener. The cleric in the long black frock was also daily there. And at last came that last sacrament in the gates of death, when the sinner is traversing those dread steps that never can be retraced; when the face is turned for ever from life, and we see a receding shape, and hear a voice already irrevocably in the land of spirits.

So the poor lady died; and some people said the Captain "felt it very much." I don't think he did. But he was not very well just then, and looked the part of mourner and penitent to admiration—being seedy and sick. He drank a great deal of brandy and water that night, and called in Farmer Dobbs, for want of better company, to drink with him; and told him all his grievances, and how happy he and "the poor lady up-stairs" might have been, had it not been for liars, and pick-thanks, and tale-bearers, and the like, who came between them—meaning Molly Doyle—whom, as he waxed eloquent over his liquor, he came at last to curse and rail at by name, with more than his accustomed freedom. And he described his own natural character and amiability in such moving terms, that he wept maudlin tears of sensibility over his theme; and when Dobbs was gone, drank some more grog, and took to railing and cursing again by himself; and then mounted the stairs unsteadily, to see "what the devil Doyle and the other —— old witches were about in poor Peg's room."

When he pushed open the door, he found some half-dozen crones, chiefly Irish, from the neighbouring town of Hackleton, sitting over tea and snuff, etc., with candles lighted round the corpse, which was arrayed in a strangely cut robe of brown serge. She had secretly belonged to some order—I think the Carmelite, but I am not certain—and wore the habit in her coffin.

"What the d—— are you doing with my wife?" cried the Captain, rather thickly. "How dare you dress her up in this —— trumpery, you—you cheating old witch; and what's that candle doing in her hand?"

I think he was a little startled, for the spectacle was grisly enough. The dead lady was arrayed in this strange brown robe, and in her rigid fingers, as in a socket, with the large wooden beads and cross wound round it, burned a wax candle, shedding its white light over the sharp features of the corpse. Moll Doyle was not to be put down by the Captain, whom she hated, and accordingly, in her phrase, "he got as good as he gave." And the Captain's wrath waxed fiercer, and he chucked the wax taper from the dead hand, and was on the point of flinging it at the old serving-woman's head.

"The holy candle, you sinner!" cried she.

"I've a mind to make you eat it, you beast," cried the Captain.

But I think he had not known before what it was, for he subsided a little sulkily, and he stuffed his hand with the candle (quite extinct by this time) into his pocket, and said he—

"You know devilish well you had no business going on with y-y-your d—— *witch*-craft about my poor wife, without my leave—you do—and you'll please take off that d—— brown pinafore, and get her decently into her coffin, and I'll pitch your devil's waxlight into the sink."

And the Captain stalked out of the room.

"An' now her poor sowl's in prison, you wretch, be the mains o' ye; an' may yer own be shut into the wick o' that same candle, till it's burned out, ye savage."

"I'd have you ducked for a witch, for two-pence," roared the Captain up the staircase, with his hand on the banisters, standing on the lobby. But the door of the chamber of death clapped angrily, and he went down to the parlour, where he examined the holy candle for a while, with a tipsy gravity, and then with something of that reverential feeling for the symbolic, which is not uncommon in rakes and scamps, he thoughtfully locked it up in a press, where were accumulated all sorts of obsolete rubbish—soiled packs of cards, disused tobacco pipes, broken powder flasks, his military sword, and a dusky bundle of the "Flash Songster," and other questionable literature.

He did not trouble the dead lady's room any more. Being a volatile man it is probable that more cheerful plans and occupations began to entertain his fancy.

CHAPTER III

MY UNCLE WATSON VISITS WAULING

So the poor lady was buried decently, and Captain Walshawe reigned alone for many years at Wauling. He was too shrewd and too experienced by this time to run violently down the steep hill that leads to ruin. So there was a method in his madness; and after a widowed career of more than forty years, he, too, died at last with some guineas in his purse.

Forty years and upwards is a great *edax rerum*, and a wonderful chemical power. It acted forcibly upon the gay Captain Walshawe. Gout supervened, and was no more conducive to temper than to enjoyment, and made his elegant hands lumpy at all the small joints, and turned them slowly into crippled claws. He grew stout when his exercise was interfered with, and ultimately almost corpulent. He suffered from what Mr. Holloway calls "bad legs," and was wheeled about in a great leathern-backed chair, and his infirmities went on accumulating with his years.

I am sorry to say, I never heard that he repented, or turned his thoughts seriously to the future. On the contrary, his talk grew fouler, and his fun ran upon his favourite sins, and his temper waxed more truculent. But he did not sink into dotage. Considering his bodily infirmities, his energies and his malignities, which were many and active, were marvellously little abated by time. So he went on to the close. When his temper was stirred, he cursed and swore in a way that made decent people tremble. It was a word and a blow with him; the latter, luckily, not very sure now. But he would seize his crutch and make a swoop or a pound at the offender, or shy his medicine-bottle, or his tumbler, at his head.

It was a peculiarity of Captain Walshawe, that he, by this time, hated nearly everybody. My uncle, Mr. Watson, of Haddlestone, was cousin to the Captain, and his heir-at-law. But my uncle had lent him money on mortgage of his estates, and there had been a treaty to sell, and terms and a price were agreed upon, in "articles" which the lawyers said were still in force.

I think the ill-conditioned Captain bore him a grudge for being richer than he, and would have liked to do him an ill turn. But it did not lie in his way; at least while he was living.

My uncle Watson was a Methodist, and what they call a "classleader"; and, on the whole, a very good man. He was now near fifty—grave, as beseemed his profession—somewhat dry—and a little severe, perhaps—but a just man.

A letter from the Penlynden doctor reached him at Haddlestone, announcing the death of the wicked old Captain; and suggesting his attendance at the funeral, and the expediency of his being on the spot to look after things at Wauling. The reasonableness of this striking my good uncle, he made his journey to the old house in Lancashire incontinently, and reached it in time for the funeral.

My uncle, whose traditions of the Captain were derived from his mother, who remembered him in his slim, handsome youth—in shorts, cocked-hat and lace, was amazed at the bulk of the coffin which contained his mortal remains; but the lid being already screwed down, he did not see the face of the bloated old sinner.

CHAPTER IV

IN THE PARLOUR

What I relate, I had from the lips of my uncle, who was a truthful man, and not prone to fancies.

The day turning out awfully rainy and tempestuous, he persuaded the doctor and the attorney to remain for the night at Wauling.

There was no will—the attorney was sure of that; for the Captain's enmities were perpetually shifting, and he could never quite make up his mind, as to how best to give effect to a malignity whose direction was constantly being modified. He had had instructions for drawing a will a dozen times over. But the process had always been arrested by the intending testator.

Search being made, no will was found. The papers, indeed, were all right, with one important exception: the leases were nowhere to be seen. There were special circumstances connected with several of the principal tenancies on the estate—unnecessary here to detail—which rendered the loss of these documents one of very serious moment, and even of very obvious danger.

My uncle, therefore, searched strenuously. The attorney was at his elbow, and the doctor helped with a suggestion now and then. The old serving-man seemed an honest deaf creature, and really knew nothing.

My uncle Watson was very much perturbed. He fancied—but this possibly was only fancy—that he had detected for a moment a queer look in the attorney's face; and from that instant it became fixed in his mind that he knew all about the leases. Mr. Watson expounded that evening in the parlour to the doctor, the attorney, and the deaf servant. Ananias and Sapphira figured in the foreground; and the awful nature of fraud and theft, of tampering in anywise with the plain rule of honesty in matters pertaining to estates, etc., were pointedly dwelt upon; and then came a long and strenuous prayer, in which he entreated with fervour and aplomb that the hard heart of the sinner who had abstracted the leases might be softened or broken in such a way as to lead to their restitution; or that, if he continued reserved and contumacious, it might at least be the will of Heaven to bring him to public justice and the documents to light. The fact is, that he was praying all this time at the attorney.

When these religious exercises were over, the visitors retired to their rooms, and my Uncle Watson wrote two or three pressing letters by the fire. When his task was done, it had grown late; the candles were flaring in their sockets, and all in bed, and, I suppose, asleep, but he.

The fire was nearly out, he chilly, and the flame of the candles throbbing strangely in their sockets, shed alternate glare and shadow round the old wainscoted room and its quaint furniture. Outside were all the wild thunder and piping of the storm; and the rattling of distant windows sounded through the passages, and down the stairs, like angry people astir in the house.

My Uncle Watson belonged to a sect who by no means rejected the supernatural, and whose founder, on the contrary, has sanctioned ghosts in the most emphatic way. He was glad therefore to remember, that in prosecuting his search that day, he had seen some six inches of wax candle in the press in the parlour; for he had no fancy to be overtaken by darkness in his present situation. He had no time to lose; and taking the bunch of keys—of which he was now master—he soon fitted the lock, and secured the candle—a treasure in his circumstances; and lighting it, he stuffed it into the socket of one of the expiring candles, and extinguishing the other, he looked round the room in the steady light reassured. At the same moment, an unusual violent gust of the storm blew a handful of gravel against the parlour window, with a sharp rattle that startled him in the midst of the roar and hubbub; and the flame of the candle itself was agitated by the air.

CHAPTER V

THE BED-CHAMBER

My uncle walked up to bed, guarding his candle with his hand, for the lobby windows were rattling furiously, and he disliked the idea of being left in the dark more than ever.

His bedroom was comfortable, though old-fashioned. He shut and bolted the door. There was a tall looking-glass opposite the foot of his four-poster, on the dressing-table between the windows. He tried to make the curtains meet, but they would not draw; and like many a gentleman in a like perplexity, he did not possess a pin, nor was there one in the huge pincushion beneath the glass.

He turned the face of the mirror away therefore, so that its back was presented to the bed, pulled the curtains together, and placed a chair against them, to prevent their falling open again. There was a good fire, and a reinforcement of round coal and wood inside the fender. So he piled it up to ensure a cheerful blaze through the night, and placing a little black mahogany table, with the legs of a satyr, beside the bed, and his candle upon it, he got between the sheets, and laid his red nightcapped head upon his pillow, and disposed himself to sleep.

The first thing that made him uncomfortable was a sound at the foot of his bed, quite distinct in a momentary lull of the storm. It was only the gentle rustle and rush of the curtains, which fell open again; and as his eyes opened, he saw them resuming their perpendicular dependence, and sat up in his bed almost expecting to see something uncanny in the aperture.

There was nothing, however, but the dressing-table, and other dark furniture, and the window-curtains faintly undulating in the violence of the storm. He did not care to get up, therefore—the fire being bright and cheery—to replace the curtains by a chair, in the position in which he had left them, anticipating possibly a new recurrence of the relapse which had startled him from his incipient doze.

So he got to sleep in a little while again, but he was disturbed by a sound, as he fancied, at the table on which stood the candle. He could not say what it was, only that he wakened with a start, and lying so in some amaze, he did distinctly hear a sound which startled him a good deal, though there was nothing necessarily supernatural in it. He described it as resembling what would occur if you fancied a thinnish table-leaf, with a convex warp in it, depressed the reverse way, and suddenly with a spring recovering its natural convexity. It was a loud, sudden thump, which made the heavy candlestick jump, and there was an end, except that my uncle did not get again into a doze for ten minutes at least.

The next time he awoke, it was in that odd, serene way that sometimes occurs. We open our eyes, we know not why, quite placidly, and are on the instant wide awake. He had had a nap of some duration this time, for his candle-flame was fluttering and flaring, *in articulo*, in the silver socket. But the fire was still bright and cheery; so he popped the extinguisher on the socket, and almost at the same time there came a tap at his door, and a sort of crescendo "hush-sh-sh!" Once more my uncle was sitting up, scared and perturbed, in his bed. He recollected, however, that he had bolted his door; and such inveterate materialists are we in the midst of our spiritualism, that this reassured him, and he breathed a deep sigh, and began to grow tranquil. But after a rest of a minute or two, there came a louder and sharper knock at his door; so that instinctively he called out, "Who's there?" in a loud, stern key. There was no sort of response, however. The nervous effect of the start subsided; and I think my uncle must have remembered how constantly, especially on a stormy night, these creaks or cracks which simulate all manner of goblin noises, make themselves naturally audible.

CHAPTER VI

THE EXTINGUISHER IS LIFTED

After a while, then, he lay down with his back turned toward that side of the bed at which was the door, and his face toward the table on which stood the massive old candlestick, capped with its extinguisher, and in that position he closed his eyes. But sleep would not revisit them. All kinds of queer fancies began to trouble him—some of them I remember.

He felt the point of a finger, he averred, pressed most distinctly on the tip of his great toe, as if a living hand were between his sheets, and making a sort of signal of attention or silence. Then again he felt something as large as a rat make a sudden bounce in the middle of his bolster, just under his head. Then a voice said "Oh!" very gently, close at the back of his head. All these things he felt certain of, and yet investigation led to nothing. He felt odd little cramps stealing now and then about him; and then, on a sudden, the middle finger of his right hand was plucked backwards, with a light playful jerk that frightened him awfully.

Meanwhile the storm kept singing, and howling, and ha-ha-hooing hoarsely among the limbs of the old trees and the chimney-pots; and my Uncle Watson, although he prayed and meditated as was his wont when he lay awake, felt his heart throb excitedly, and sometimes thought he was beset with evil spirits, and at others that he was in the early stage of a fever.

He resolutely kept his eyes closed, however, and, like St. Paul's shipwrecked companions, wished for the day. At last another little doze seems to have stolen upon his senses, for he awoke quietly and completely as before—opening his eyes all at once, and seeing everything as if he had not slept for a moment.

The fire was still blazing redly—nothing uncertain in the light—the massive silver candlestick, topped with its tall extinguisher, stood on the centre of the black mahogany table as before; and, looking by what seemed a sort of accident to the apex of this, he beheld something which made him quite misdoubt the evidence of his eyes.

He saw the extinguisher lifted by a tiny hand, from beneath, and a small human face, no bigger than a thumb-nail, with nicely proportioned features, peep from beneath it. In this Lilliputian countenance was such a ghastly consternation as horrified my uncle unspeakably. Out came a little foot then and there, and a pair of wee legs, in short silk stockings and buckled shoes, then the rest of the figure; and, with the arms holding about the socket, the little legs stretched and stretched, hanging about the stem of the candlestick till the feet reached the base, and so down the satyr-like leg of the table, till they reached the floor, extending elastically, and strangely enlarging in all proportions as they approached the ground, where the feet and buckles were those of a well-shaped, full grown man, and the figure tapering upward until it dwindled to its original fairy dimensions at the top, like an object seen in some strangely curved mirror.

Standing upon the floor he expanded, my amazed uncle could not tell how, into his proper proportions; and stood pretty nearly in profile at the bedside, a handsome and elegantly shaped young man, in a bygone military costume, with a small laced, three-cocked hat and plume on his head, but looking like a man going to be hanged—in unspeakable despair.

He stepped lightly to the hearth, and turned for a few seconds very dejectedly with his back toward the bed and the mantel-piece, and he saw the hilt of his rapier glittering in the firelight; and then walking across the room he placed himself at the dressing-table, visible through the divided curtains at the foot of the bed. The fire was blazing still so brightly that my uncle saw him as distinctly as if half a dozen candles were burning.

CHAPTER VII

THE VISITATION CULMINATES

The looking-glass was an old-fashioned piece of furniture, and had a drawer beneath it. My uncle had searched it carefully for the papers in the daytime; but the silent figure pulled the drawer quite out, pressed a spring at the side, disclosing a false receptable behind it, and from this he drew a parcel of papers tied together with pink tape.

All this time my uncle was staring at him in a horrified state, neither winking nor breathing, and the apparition had not once given the smallest intimation of consciousness that a living person was in the same room. But now, for the first time, it turned its livid stare full upon my uncle with a hateful smile of significance, lifting up the little parcel of papers between his slender finger and thumb. Then he made a long, cunning wink at him, and seemed to blow out one of his cheeks in a burlesque grimace, which, but for the horrific circumstances, would have been ludicrous. My uncle could not tell whether this was really an intentional distortion or only one of those horrid ripples and deflections which were constantly disturbing the proportions of the figure, as if it were seen through some unequal and perverting medium.

The figure now approached the bed, seeming to grow exhausted and malignant as it did so. My uncle's terror nearly culminated at this point, for he believed it was drawing near him with an evil purpose. But it was not so; for the soldier, over whom twenty years seemed to have passed in his brief transit to the dressing-table and back again, threw himself into a great high-backed arm-chair of stuffed leather at the far side of the fire, and placed his heels on the fender. His feet and legs seemed indistinctly to swell, and swathings showed themselves round them, and they grew into something enormous, and the upper figure swayed and shaped itself into corresponding proportions, a great mass of corpulence, with a cadaverous and malignant face, and the furrows of a great old age, and colourless glassy eyes; and with these changes, which came indefinitely but rapidly as those of a sunset cloud, the fine regimentals faded away, and a loose, gray, woollen drapery, somehow, was there in its stead; and all seemed to be stained and rotten, for swarms of worms seemed creeping in and out, while the figure grew paler and paler, till my uncle, who liked his pipe, and employed the simile naturally, said the whole effigy grew to the colour of tobacco ashes, and the clusters of worms into little wriggling knots of sparks such as we see running over the residuum of a burnt sheet of paper. And so with the strong draught caused by the fire, and the current of air from the window, which was rattling in the storm, the feet seemed to be drawn into the fire-place, and the whole figure, light as ashes, floated away with them, and disappeared with a whisk up the capacious old chimney.

It seemed to my uncle that the fire suddenly darkened and the air grew icy cold, and there came an awful roar and riot of tempest, which shook the old house from top to base, and sounded like the yelling of a blood-thirsty mob on receiving a new and long-expected victim.

Good Uncle Watson used to say, "I have been in many situations of fear and danger in the course of my life, but never did I pray with so much agony before or since; for then, as now, it was clear beyond a cavil that I had actually beheld the phantom of an evil spirit."

CONCLUSION

Now there are two curious circumstances to be observed in this relation of my uncle's, who was, as I have said, a perfectly veracious man.

First—The wax candle which he took from the press in the parlour and burnt at his bedside on that horrible night was unquestionably, according to the testimony of the old deaf servant, who had been fifty years at Wauling, that identical piece of "holy candle" which had stood in the fingers of the poor lady's corpse, and concerning which the old Irish crone, long since dead, had delivered the curious curse I have mentioned against the Captain.

Secondly—Behind the drawer under the looking-glass, he did actually discover a second but secret drawer, in which were concealed the identical papers which he had suspected the attorney of having made away with. There were circumstances, too, afterwards disclosed which convinced my uncle that the old man had deposited them there preparatory to burning them, which he had nearly made up his mind to do.

Now, a very remarkable ingredient in this tale of my Uncle Watson was this, that so far as my father, who had never seen Captain Walshawe in the course of his life, could gather, the phantom had exhibited a horrible and grotesque, but unmistakeable resemblance to that defunct scamp in the various stages of his long life.

Wauling was sold in the year 1837, and the old house shortly after pulled down, and a new one built nearer to the river. I often wonder whether it was rumoured to be haunted, and, if so, what stories were current about it. It was a commodious and stanch old house, and withal rather handsome; and its demolition was certainly suspicious.

GHOSTLY TALES
VOLUME V (con’t)

THE CHILD THAT WENT WITH THE FAIRIES

Eastward of the old city of Limerick, about ten Irish miles under the range of mountains known as the Slieveelim hills, famous as having afforded Sarsfield a shelter among their rocks and hollows, when he crossed them in his gallant descent upon the cannon and ammunition of King William, on its way to the beleaguering army, there runs a very old and narrow road. It connects the Limerick road to Tipperary with the old road from Limerick to Dublin, and runs by bog and pasture, hill and hollow, straw-thatched village, and roofless castle, not far from twenty miles.

Skirting the healthy mountains of which I have spoken, at one part it becomes singularly lonely. For more than three Irish miles it traverses a deserted country. A wide, black bog, level as a lake, skirted with copse, spreads at the left, as you journey northward, and the long and irregular line of mountain rises at the right, clothed in heath, broken with lines of grey rock that resemble the bold and irregular outlines of fortifications, and riven with many a gully, expanding here and there into rocky and wooded glens, which open as they approach the road.

A scanty pasturage, on which browsed a few scattered sheep or kine, skirts this solitary road for some miles, and under shelter of a hillock, and of two or three great ash-trees, stood, not many years ago, the little thatched cabin of a widow named Mary Ryan.

Poor was this widow in a land of poverty. The thatch had acquired the grey tint and sunken outlines, that show how the alternations of rain and sun have told upon that perishable shelter.

But whatever other dangers threatened, there was one well provided against by the care of other times. Round the cabin stood half a dozen mountain ashes, as the rowans, inimical to witches, are there called. On the worn planks of the door were nailed two horse-shoes, and over the lintel and spreading along the thatch, grew, luxuriant, patches of that ancient cure for many maladies, and prophylactic against the machinations of the evil one, the house-leek. Descending into the doorway, in the *chiaroscuro* of the interior, when your eye grew sufficiently accustomed to that dim light, you might discover, hanging at the head of the widow's wooden-roofed bed, her beads and a phial of holy water.

Here certainly were defences and bulwarks against the intrusion of that unearthly and evil power, of whose vicinity this solitary family were constantly reminded by the outline of Lisnavoura, that lonely hillhaunt of the "Good people," as the fairies are called euphemistically, whose strangely dome-like summit rose not half a mile away, looking like an outwork of the long line of mountain that sweeps by it.

It was at the fall of the leaf, and an autumnal sunset threw the lengthening shadow of haunted Lisnavoura, close in front of the solitary little cabin, over the undulating slopes and sides of Slieveelim. The birds were singing among the branches in the thinning leaves of the melancholy ash-trees that grew at the road-side in front of the door. The widow's three younger children were playing on the road, and their voices mingled with the evening song of the birds. Their elder sister, Nell, was "within in the house," as their phrase is, seeing after the boiling of the potatoes for supper.

Their mother had gone down to the bog, to carry up a hamper of turf on her back. It is, or was at least, a charitable custom—and if not disused, long may it continue—for the wealthier people when cutting their turf and stacking it in the bog, to make a smaller stack for the behoof of the poor, who were welcome to take from it so long as it lasted, and thus the potato pot was kept boiling, and hearth warm that would have been cold enough but for that good-natured bounty, through wintry months.

Moll Ryan trudged up the steep "bohereen" whose banks were overgrown with thorn and brambles, and stooping under her burden, re-entered her door, where her dark-haired daughter Nell met her with a welcome, and relieved her of her hamper.

Moll Ryan looked round with a sigh of relief, and drying her forehead, uttered the Munster ejaculation:

"Eiah, wisha! It's tired I am with it, God bless it. And where's the craythurs, Nell?"

"Playin' out on the road, mother; didn't ye see them and you comin' up?"

"No; there was no one before me on the road," she said, uneasily; "not a soul, Nell; and why didn't ye keep an eye on them?"

"Well, they're in the haggard, playin' there, or round by the back o' the house. Will I call them in?"

"Do so, good girl, in the name o' God. The hens is comin' home, see, and the sun was just down over Knockdoulah, an' I comin' up."

So out ran tall, dark-haired Nell, and standing on the road, looked up and down it; but not a sign of her two little brothers, Con and Bill, or her little sister, Peg, could she see. She called them; but no answer came from the little haggard, fenced with straggling bushes. She listened, but the sound of their voices was missing. Over the stile, and behind the house she ran—but there all was silent and deserted.

She looked down toward the bog, as far as she could see; but they did not appear. Again she listened—but in vain. At first she had felt angry, but now a different feeling overcame her, and she grew pale. With an undefined boding she looked toward the heathy boss of Lisnavoura, now darkening into the deepest purple against the flaming sky of sunset.

Again she listened with a sinking heart, and heard nothing but the farewell twitter and whistle of the birds in the bushes around. How many stories had she listened to by the winter hearth, of children stolen by the fairies, at nightfall, in lonely places! With this fear she knew her mother was haunted.

No one in the country round gathered her little flock about her so early as this frightened widow, and no door "in the seven parishes" was barred so early.

Sufficiently fearful, as all young people in that part of the world are of such dreaded and subtle agents, Nell was even more than usually afraid of them, for her terrors were infected and redoubled by her mother's. She was looking towards Lisnavoura in a trance of fear, and crossed herself again and again, and whispered prayer after prayer. She was interrupted by her mother's voice on the road calling her loudly. She answered, and ran round to the front of the cabin, where she found her standing.

"And where in the world's the craythurs—did ye see sight o' them anywhere?" cried Mrs. Ryan, as the girl came over the stile.

"Arrah! mother, 'tis only what they're run down the road a bit. We'll see them this minute coming back. It's like goats they are, climbin' here and runnin' there; an' if I had them here, in my hand, maybe I wouldn't give them a hiding all round."

"May the Lord forgive you, Nell! the childhers gone. They're took, and not a soul near us, and Father Tom three miles away! And what'll I do, or who's to help us this night? Oh, wirristhru, wirristhru! The craythurs is gone!"

"Whisht, mother, be aisy: don't ye see them comin' up?"

And then she shouted in menacing accents, waving her arm, and beckoning the children, who were seen approaching on the road, which some little way off made a slight dip, which had concealed them. They were approaching from the westward, and from the direction of the dreaded hill of Lisnavoura.

But there were only two of the children, and one of them, the little girl, was crying. Their mother and sister hurried forward to meet them, more alarmed than ever.

"Where is Billy—where is he?" cried the mother, nearly breathless, so soon as she was within hearing.

"He's gone—they took him away; but they said he'll come back again," answered little Con, with the dark brown hair.

"He's gone away with the grand ladies," blubbered the little girl.

"What ladies—where? Oh, Leum, asthora! My darlin', are you gone away at last? Where is he? Who took him? What ladies are you talkin' about? What way did he go?" she cried in distraction.

"I couldn't see where he went, mother; 'twas like as if he was going to Lisnavoura."

With a wild exclamation the distracted woman ran on towards the hill alone, clapping her hands, and crying aloud the name of her lost child.

Scared and horrified, Nell, not daring to follow, gazed after her, and burst into tears; and the other children raised high their lamentations in shrill rivalry.

Twilight was deepening. It was long past the time when they were usually barred securely within their habitation. Nell led the younger children into the cabin, and made them sit down by the turf fire, while she stood in the open door, watching in great fear for the return of her mother.

After a long while they did see their mother return. She came in and sat down by the fire, and cried as if her heart would break.

"Will I bar the doore, mother?" asked Nell.

"Ay, do—didn't I lose enough, this night, without lavin' the doore open, for more o' yez to go; but first take an' sprinkle a dust o' the holy waters over ye, acuishla, and bring it here till I throw a taste iv it over myself and the craythurs; an' I wondher, Nell, you'd forget to do the like yourself, lettin' the craythurs out so near nightfall. Come here and sit on my knees, asthora, come to me, mavourneen, and hould me fast, in the name o' God, and I'll hould you fast that none can take yez from me, and tell me all about it, and what it was—the Lord between us and harm—an' how it happened, and who was in it."

And the door being barred, the two children, sometimes speaking together, often interrupting one another, often interrupted by their mother, managed to tell this strange story, which I had better relate connectedly and in my own language.

The Widow Ryan's three children were playing, as I have said, upon the narrow old road in front of her door. Little Bill or Leum, about five years old, with golden hair and large blue eyes, was a very pretty boy, with all the clear tints of healthy childhood, and that gaze of earnest simplicity which belongs not to town children of the same age. His little sister Peg, about a year older, and his brother Con, a little more than a year elder than she, made up the little group.

Under the great old ash-trees, whose last leaves were falling at their feet, in the light of an October sunset, they were playing with the hilarity and eagerness of rustic children, clamouring together, and their faces were turned toward the west and storied hill of Lisnavoura.

Suddenly a startling voice with a screech called to them from behind, ordering them to get out of the way, and turning, they saw a sight, such as they never beheld before. It was a carriage drawn by four horses that were pawing and snorting, in impatience, as it just pulled up. The children were almost under their feet, and scrambled to the side of the road next their own door.

This carriage and all its appointments were old-fashioned and gorgeous, and presented to the children, who had never seen anything finer than a turf car, and once, an old chaise that passed that way from Killaloe, a spectacle perfectly dazzling.

Here was antique splendour. The harness and trappings were scarlet, and blazing with gold. The horses were huge, and snow white, with great manes, that as they tossed and shook them in the air, seemed to stream and float sometimes longer and sometimes shorter, like so much smoke—their tails were long, and tied up in bows of broad scarlet and gold ribbon. The coach itself was glowing with colours, gilded and emblazoned. There were footmen in gay liveries, and three-cocked hats, like the coachman's; but he had a great wig, like a judge's, and their hair was frizzed out and powdered, and a long thick "pigtail," with a bow to it, hung down the back of each.

All these servants were diminutive, and ludicrously out of proportion with the enormous horses of the equipage, and had sharp, sallow features, and small, restless fiery eyes, and faces of cunning and malice that chilled the children. The little coachman was scowling and showing his white fangs under his cocked hat, and his little blazing beads of eyes were quivering with fury in their sockets as he whirled his whip round and round over their heads, till the lash of it looked like a streak of fire in the evening sun, and sounded like the cry of a legion of "fillapoueeks" in the air.

"Stop the princess on the highway!" cried the coachman, in a piercing treble.

"Stop the princess on the highway!" piped each footman in turn, scowling over his shoulder down on the children, and grinding his keen teeth.

The children were so frightened they could only gape and turn white in their panic. But a very sweet voice from the open window of the carriage reassured them, and arrested the attack of the lackeys.

A beautiful and "very grand-looking" lady was smiling from it on them, and they all felt pleased in the strange light of that smile.

"The boy with the golden hair, I think," said the lady, bending her large and wonderfully clear eyes on little Leum.

The upper sides of the carriage were chiefly of glass, so that the children could see another woman inside, whom they did not like so well.

This was a black woman, with a wonderfully long neck, hung round with many strings of large variously-coloured beads, and on her head was a sort of turban of silk striped with all the colours of the rainbow, and fixed in it was a golden star.

This black woman had a face as thin almost as a death's-head, with high cheekbones, and great goggle eyes, the whites of which, as well as her wide range of teeth, showed in brilliant contrast with her skin, as she looked over the beautiful lady's shoulder, and whispered something in her ear.

"Yes; the boy with the golden hair, I think," repeated the lady.

And her voice sounded sweet as a silver bell in the children's ears, and her smile beguiled them like the light of an enchanted lamp, as she leaned from the window with a look of ineffable fondness on the golden-haired boy, with the large blue eyes; insomuch that little Billy, looking up, smiled in return with a wondering fondness, and when she stooped down, and stretched her jewelled arms towards him, he stretched his little hands up, and how they touched the other children did not know; but, saying, "Come and give me a kiss, my darling," she raised him, and he seemed to ascend in her small fingers as lightly as a feather, and she held him in her lap and covered him with kisses.

Nothing daunted, the other children would have been only too happy to change places with their favoured little brother. There was only one thing that was unpleasant, and a little frightened them, and that was the black woman, who stood and stretched forward, in the carriage as before. She gathered a rich silk and gold handkerchief that was in her fingers up to her lips, and seemed to thrust ever so much of it, fold after fold, into her capacious mouth, as they thought to smother her laughter, with which she seemed convulsed, for she was shaking and quivering, as it seemed, with suppressed merriment; but her eyes, which remained uncovered, looked angrier than they had ever seen eyes look before.

But the lady was so beautiful they looked on her instead, and she continued to caress and kiss the little boy on her knee; and smiling at the other children she held up a large russet apple in her fingers, and the carriage began to move slowly on, and with a nod inviting them to take the fruit, she dropped it on the road from the window; it rolled some way beside the wheels, they following, and then she dropped another, and then another, and so on. And the same thing happened to all; for just as either of the children who ran beside had caught the rolling apple, somehow it slipt into a hole or ran into a ditch, and looking up they saw the lady drop another from the window, and so the chase was taken up and continued till they got, hardly knowing how far they had gone, to the old cross-road that leads to Owney. It seemed that there the horses' hoofs and carriage wheels rolled up a wonderful dust, which being caught in one of those eddies that whirl the dust up into a column, on the calmest day, enveloped the children for a moment, and passed whirling on towards Lisnavoura, the carriage, as they fancied, driving in the centre of it; but suddenly it subsided, the straws and leaves floated to the ground, the dust dissipated itself, but the white horses and the lackeys, the gilded carriage, the lady and their little golden haired brother were gone.

At the same moment suddenly the upper rim of the clear setting sun disappeared behind the hill of Knockdoula, and it was twilight. Each child felt the transition like a shock—and the sight of the rounded summit of Lisnavoura, now closely overhanging them, struck them with a new fear.

They screamed their brother's name after him, but their cries were lost in the vacant air. At the same time they thought they heard a hollow voice say, close to them, "Go home."

Looking round and seeing no one, they were scared, and hand in hand—the little girl crying wildly, and the boy white as ashes, from fear, they trotted homeward, at their best speed, to tell, as we have seen, their strange story.

Molly Ryan never more saw her darling. But something of the lost little boy was seen by his former playmates.

Sometimes when their mother was away earning a trifle at haymaking, and Nelly washing the potatoes for their dinner, or "beatling" clothes in the little stream that flows in the hollow close by, they saw the pretty face of little Billy peeping in archly at the door, and smiling silently at them, and as they ran to embrace him, with cries of delight, he drew back, still smiling archly, and when they got out into the open day, he was gone, and they could see no trace of him anywhere.

This happened often, with slight variations in the circumstances of the visit. Sometimes he would peep for a longer time, sometimes for a shorter time, sometimes his little hand would come in, and, with bended finger, beckon them to follow; but always he was smiling with the same arch look and wary silence—and always he was gone when they reached the door. Gradually these visits grew less and less frequent, and in about eight months they ceased altogether, and little Billy, irretrievably lost, took rank in their memories with the dead.

One wintry morning, nearly a year and a half after his disappearance, their mother having set out for Limerick soon after cockcrow, to sell some fowls at the market, the little girl, lying by the side of her elder sister, who was fast asleep, just at the grey of the morning heard the latch lifted softly, and saw little Billy enter and close the door gently after him. There was light enough to see that he was barefoot and ragged, and looked pale and famished. He went straight to the fire, and cowered over the turf embers, and rubbed his hands slowly, and seemed to shiver as he gathered the smouldering turf together.

The little girl clutched her sister in terror and whispered, "Waken, Nelly, waken; here's Billy come back!"

Nelly slept soundly on, but the little boy, whose hands were extended close over the coals, turned and looked toward the bed, it seemed to her, in fear, and she saw the glare of the embers reflected on his thin cheek as he turned toward her. He rose and went, on tiptoe, quickly to the door, in silence, and let himself out as softly as he had come in.

After that, the little boy was never seen any more by any one of his kindred.

"Fairy doctors," as the dealers in the preternatural, who in such cases were called in, are termed, did all that in them lay—but in vain. Father Tom came down, and tried what holier rites could do, but equally without result. So little Billy was dead to mother, brother, and sisters; but no grave received him. Others whom affection cherished, lay in holy ground, in the old churchyard of Abington, with headstone to mark the spot over which the survivor might kneel and say a kind prayer for the peace of the departed soul. But there was no landmark to show where little Billy was hidden from their loving eyes, unless it was in the old hill of Lisnavoura, that cast its long shadow at sunset before the cabin-door; or that, white and filmy in the moonlight, in later years, would occupy his brother's gaze as he returned from fair or market, and draw from him a sigh and a prayer for the little brother he had lost so long ago, and was never to see again.

STORIES OF LOUGH GUIR

When the present writer was a boy of twelve or thirteen, he first made the acquaintance of Miss Anne Baily, of Lough Guir, in the county of Limerick. She and her sister were the last representatives at that place, of an extremely good old name in the county. They were both what is termed "old maids," and at that time past sixty. But never were old ladies more hospitable, lively, and kind, especially to young people. They were both remarkably agreeable and clever. Like all old county ladies of their time, they were great genealogists, and could recount the origin, generations, and intermarriages, of every county family of note.

These ladies were visited at their house at Lough Guir by Mr. Crofton Croker; and are, I think, mentioned, by name, in the second series of his fairy legends; the series in which (probably communicated by Miss Anne Baily), he recounts some of the picturesque traditions of those beautiful lakes—lakes, I should no longer say, for the smaller and prettier has since been drained, and gave up from its depths some long lost and very interesting relics.

In their drawing-room stood a curious relic of another sort: old enough, too, though belonging to a much more modern period. It was the ancient stirrup cup of the hospitable house of Lough Guir. Crofton Croker has preserved a sketch of this curious glass. I have often had it in my hand. It had a short stem; and the cup part, having the bottom rounded, rose cylindrically, and, being of a capacity to contain a whole bottle of claret, and almost as narrow as an old-fashioned ale glass, was tall to a degree that filled me with wonder. As it obliged the rider to extend his arm as he raised the glass, it must have tried a tipsy man, sitting in the saddle, pretty severely. The wonder was that the marvellous tall glass had come down to our times without a crack.

There was another glass worthy of remark in the same drawing-room. It was gigantic, and shaped conically, like one of those old-fashioned jelly glasses which used to be seen upon the shelves of confectioners. It was engraved round the rim with the words, "The glorious, pious, and immortal memory"; and on grand occasions, was filled to the brim, and after the manner of a loving cup, made the circuit of the Whig guests, who owed all to the hero whose memory its legend invoked.

It was now but the transparent phantom of those solemn convivialities of a generation, who lived, as it were, within hearing of the cannon and shoutings of those stirring times. When I saw it, this glass had long retired from politics and carousals, and stood peacefully on a little table in the drawing-room, where ladies' hands replenished it with fair water, and crowned it daily with flowers from the garden.

Miss Anne Baily's conversation ran oftener than her sister's upon the legendary and supernatural; she told her stories with the sympathy, the colour, and the mysterious air which contribute so powerfully to effect, and never wearied of answering questions about the old castle, and amusing her young audience with fascinating little glimpses of old adventure and bygone days. My memory retains the picture of my early friend very distinctly. A slim straight figure, above the middle height; a general likeness to the full-length portrait of that delightful Countess d'Aulnois, to whom we all owe our earliest and most brilliant glimpses of fairy-land; something of her gravely-pleasant countenance, plain, but refined and ladylike, with that kindly mystery in her side-long glance and uplifted finger, which indicated the approaching climax of a tale of wonder.

Lough Guir is a kind of centre of the operations of the Munster fairies. When a child is stolen by the "good people," Lough Guir is conjectured to be the place of its unearthly transmutation from the human to the fairy state. And beneath its waters lie enchanted, the grand old castle of the Desmonds, the great earl himself, his beautiful young countess, and all the retinue that surrounded him in the years of his splendour, and at the moment of his catastrophe.

Here, too, are historic associations. The huge square tower that rises at one side of the stable-yard close to the old house, to a height that amazed my young eyes, though robbed of its battlements and one story, was a stronghold of the last rebellious Earl of Desmond, and is specially mentioned in that delightful old folio, the *Hibernia Pacata*, as having, with its Irish garrison on the battlements, defied the army of the lord deputy, then marching by upon the summits of the overhanging hills. The house, built under shelter of this stronghold of the once proud and turbulent Desmonds, is old, but snug, with a multitude of small low rooms, such as I have seen in houses of the same age in Shropshire and the neighbouring English counties.

The hills that overhang the lakes appeared to me, in my young days (and I have not seen them since), to be clothed with a short soft verdure, of a hue so dark and vivid as I had never seen before.

In one of the lakes is a small island, rocky and wooded, which is believed by the peasantry to represent the top of the highest tower of the castle which sank, under a spell, to the bottom. In certain states of the atmosphere, I have heard educated people say, when in a boat you have reached a certain distance, the island appears to rise some feet from the water, its rocks assume the appearance of masonry, and the whole circuit presents very much the effect of the battlements of a castle rising above the surface of the lake.

This was Miss Anne Baily's story of the submersion of this lost castle:

THE MAGICIAN EARL

It is well known that the great Earl of Desmond, though history pretends to dispose of him differently, lives to this hour enchanted in his castle, with all his household, at the bottom of the lake.

There was not, in his day, in all the world, so accomplished a magician as he. His fairest castle stood upon an island in the lake, and to this he brought his young and beautiful bride, whom he loved but too well; for she prevailed upon his folly to risk all to gratify her imperious caprice.

They had not been long in this beautiful castle, when she one day presented herself in the chamber in which her husband studied his forbidden art, and there implored him to exhibit before her some of the wonders of his evil science. He resisted long; but her entreaties, tears, and wheedlings were at length too much for him and he consented.

But before beginning those astonishing transformations with which he was about to amaze her, he explained to her the awful conditions and dangers of the experiment.

Alone in this vast apartment, the walls of which were lapped, far below, by the lake whose dark waters lay waiting to swallow them, she must witness a certain series of frightful phenomena, which once commenced, he could neither abridge nor mitigate; and if throughout their ghastly succession she spoke one word, or uttered one exclamation, the castle and all that it contained would in one instant subside to the bottom of the lake, there to remain, under the servitude of a strong spell, for ages.

The dauntless curiosity of the lady having prevailed, and the oaken door of the study being locked and barred, the fatal experiments commenced.

Muttering a spell, as he stood before her, feathers sprouted thickly over him, his face became contracted and hooked, a cadaverous smell filled the air, and, with heavy winnowing wings, a gigantic vulture rose in his stead, and swept round and round the room, as if on the point of pouncing upon her.

The lady commanded herself through this trial, and instantly another began.

The bird alighted near the door, and in less than a minute changed, she saw not how, into a horribly deformed and dwarfish hag: who, with yellow skin hanging about her face and enormous eyes, swung herself on crutches toward the lady, her mouth foaming with fury, and her grimaces and contortions becoming more and more hideous every moment, till she rolled with a yell on the floor, in a horrible convulsion, at the lady's feet, and then changed into a huge serpent, with crest erect, and quivering tongue. Suddenly, as it seemed on the point of darting at her, she saw her husband in its stead, standing pale before her, and, with his finger on his lip, enforcing the continued necessity of silence. He then placed himself at his length on the floor, and began to stretch himself out and out, longer and longer, until his head nearly reached to one end of the vast room, and his feet to the other.

This horror overcame her. The ill-starred lady uttered a wild scream, whereupon the castle and all that was within it, sank in a moment to the bottom of the lake.

But, once in every seven years, by night, the Earl of Desmond and his retinue emerge, and cross the lake, in shadowy cavalcade. His white horse is shod with silver. On that one night, the earl may ride till daybreak, and it behoves him to make good use of his time; for, until the silver shoes of his steed be worn through, the spell that holds him and his beneath the lake, will retain its power.

When I (Miss Anne Baily) was a child, there was still living a man named Teigue O'Neill, who had a strange story to tell.

He was a smith, and his forge stood on the brow of the hill, overlooking the lake, on a lonely part of the road to Cahir Conlish. One bright moonlight night, he was working very late, and quite alone. The clink of his hammer, and the wavering glow reflected through the open door on the bushes at the other side of the narrow road, were the only tokens that told of life and vigil for miles around.

In one of the pauses of his work, he heard the ring of many hoofs ascending the steep road that passed his forge, and, standing in this doorway, he was just in time to see a gentleman, on a white horse, who was dressed in a fashion the like of which the smith had never seen before. This man was accompanied and followed by a mounted retinue, as strangely dressed as he.

They seemed, by the clang and clatter that announced their approach, to be riding up the hill at a hard hurry-scurry gallop; but the pace abated as they drew near, and the rider of the white horse who, from his grave and lordly air, he assumed to be a man of rank, and accustomed to command, drew bridle and came to a halt before the smith's door.

He did not speak, and all his train were silent, but he beckoned to the smith, and pointed down to one of his horse's hoofs.

Teigue stooped and raised it, and held it just long enough to see that it was shod with a silver shoe; which, in one place, he said, was worn as thin as a shilling. Instantaneously, his situation was made apparent to him by this sign, and he recoiled with a terrified prayer. The lordly rider, with a look of pain and fury, struck at him suddenly, with something that whistled in the air like a whip; and an icy streak seemed to traverse his body as if he had been cut through with a leaf of steel. But he was without scathe or scar, as he afterwards found. At the same moment he saw the whole cavalcade break into a gallop and disappear down the hill, with a momentary hurtling in the air, like the flight of a volley of cannon shot.

Here had been the earl himself. He had tried one of his accustomed stratagems to lead the smith to speak to him. For it is well known that either for the purpose of abridging or of mitigating his period of enchantment, he seeks to lead people to accost him. But what, in the event of his succeeding, would befall the person whom he had thus ensnared, no one knows.

MOLL RIAL'S ADVENTURE

When Miss Anne Baily was a child, Moll Rial was an old woman. She had lived all her days with the Bailys of Lough Guir; in and about whose house, as was the Irish custom of those days, were a troop of bare-footed country girls, scullery maids, or laundresses, or employed about the poultry yard, or running of errands.

Among these was Moll Rial, then a stout good-humoured lass, with little to think of, and nothing to fret about. She was once washing clothes by the process known universally in Munster as beetling. The washer stands up to her ankles in water, in which she has immersed the clothes, which she lays in that state on a great flat stone, and smacks with lusty strokes of an instrument which bears a rude resemblance to a cricket bat, only shorter, broader, and light enough to be wielded freely with one hand. Thus, they smack the dripping clothes, turning them over and over, sousing them in the water, and replacing them on the same stone, to undergo a repetition of the process, until they are thoroughly washed.

Moll Rial was plying her "beetle" at the margin of the lake, close under the old house and castle. It was between eight and nine o'clock on a fine summer morning, everything looked bright and beautiful. Though quite alone, and though she could not see even the windows of the house (hidden from her view by the irregular ascent and some interposing bushes), her loneliness was not depressing.

Standing up from her work, she saw a gentleman walking slowly down the slope toward her. He was a "grand-looking" gentleman, arrayed in a flowered silk dressing-gown, with a cap of velvet on his head, and as he stepped toward her, in his slippered feet, he showed a very handsome leg. He was smiling graciously as he approached, and drawing a ring from his finger with an air of gracious meaning, which seemed to imply that he wished to make her a present, he raised it in his fingers with a pleased look, and placed it on the flat stones beside the clothes she had been beetling so industriously.

He drew back a little, and continued to look at her with an encouraging smile, which seemed to say: "You have earned your reward; you must not be afraid to take it."

The girl fancied that this was some gentleman who had arrived, as often happened in those hospitable and haphazard times, late and unexpectedly the night before, and who was now taking a little indolent ramble before breakfast.

Moll Rial was a little shy, and more so at having been discovered by so grand a gentleman with her petticoats gathered a little high about her bare shins. She looked down, therefore, upon the water at her feet, and then she saw a ripple of blood, and then another, ring after ring, coming and going to and from her feet. She cried out the sacred name in horror, and, lifting her eyes, the courtly gentleman was gone, but the blood-rings about her feet spread with the speed of light over the surface of the lake, which for a moment glowed like one vast estuary of blood.

Here was the earl once again, and Moll Rial declared that if it had not been for that frightful transformation of the water she would have spoken to him next minute, and would thus have passed under a spell, perhaps as direful as his own.

THE BANSHEE

So old a Munster family as the Bailys, of Lough Guir, could not fail to have their attendant banshee. Everyone attached to the family knew this well, and could cite evidences of that unearthly distinction. I heard Miss Baily relate the only experience she had personally had of that wild spiritual sympathy.

She said that, being then young, she and Miss Susan undertook a long attendance upon the sick bed of their sister, Miss Kitty, whom I have heard remembered among her contemporaries as the merriest and most entertaining of human beings. This light-hearted young lady was dying of consumption. The sad duties of such attendance being divided among many sisters, as there then were, the night watches devolved upon the two ladies I have named: I think, as being the eldest.

It is not improbable that these long and melancholy vigils, lowering the spirits and exciting the nervous system, prepared them for illusions. At all events, one night at dead of night, Miss Baily and her sister, sitting in the dying lady's room, heard such sweet and melancholy music as they had never heard before. It seemed to them like distant cathedral music. The room of the dying girl had its windows toward the yard, and the old castle stood near, and full in sight. The music was not in the house, but seemed to come from the yard, or beyond it. Miss Anne Baily took a candle, and went down the back stairs. She opened the back door, and, standing there, heard the same faint but solemn harmony, and could not tell whether it most resembled the distant music of instruments, or a choir of voices. It seemed to come through the windows of the old castle, high in the air. But when she approached the tower, the music, she thought, came from above the house, at the other side of the yard; and thus perplexed, and at last frightened, she returned.

This aerial music both she and her sister, Miss Susan Baily, avowed that they distinctly heard, and for a long time. Of the fact she was clear, and she spoke of it with great awe.

THE GOVERNESS'S DREAM

This lady, one morning, with a grave countenance that indicated something weighty upon her mind, told her pupils that she had, on the night before, had a very remarkable dream.

The first room you enter in the old castle, having reached the foot of the spiral stone stair, is a large hall, dim and lofty, having only a small window or two, set high in deep recesses in the wall. When I saw the castle many years ago, a portion of this capacious chamber was used as a store for the turf laid in to last the year.

Her dream placed her, alone, in this room, and there entered a grave-looking man, having something very remarkable in his countenance: which impressed her, as a fine portrait sometimes will, with a haunting sense of character and individuality.

In his hand this man carried a wand, about the length of an ordinary walking cane. He told her to observe and remember its length, and to mark well the measurements he was about to make, the result of which she was to communicate to Mr. Baily of Lough Guir.

From a certain point in the wall, with this wand, he measured along the floor, at right angles with the wall, a certain number of its lengths, which he counted aloud; and then, in the same way, from the adjoining wall he measured a certain number of its lengths, which he also counted distinctly. He then told her that at the point where these two lines met, at a depth of a certain number of feet which he also told her, treasure lay buried. And so the dream broke up, and her remarkable visitant vanished.

She took the girls with her to the old castle, where, having cut a switch to the length represented to her in her dream, she measured the distances, and ascertained, as she supposed, the point on the floor beneath which the treasure lay. The same day she related her dream to Mr. Baily. But he treated it laughingly, and took no step in consequence.

Some time after this, she again saw, in a dream, the same remarkable-looking man, who repeated his message, and appeared displeased. But the dream was treated by Mr. Baily as before.

The same dream occurred again, and the children became so clamorous to have the castle floor explored, with pick and shovel, at the point indicated by the thrice seen messenger, that at length Mr. Baily consented, and the floor was opened, and a trench was sunk at the spot which the governess had pointed out.

Miss Anne Baily, and nearly all the members of the family, her father included, were present at this operation. As the workmen approached the depth described in the vision, the interest and suspense of all increased; and when the iron implements met the solid resistance of a broad flagstone, which returned a cavernous sound to the stroke, the excitement of all present rose to its acme.

With some difficulty the flag was raised, and a chamber of stone work, large enough to receive a moderately-sized crock or pit, was disclosed. Alas! it was empty. But in the earth at the bottom of it, Miss Baily said, she herself saw, as every other bystander plainly did, the circular impression of a vessel: which had stood there, as the mark seemed to indicate, for a very long time.

Both the Miss Bailys were strong in their belief hereafterwards, that the treasure which they were convinced had actually been deposited there, had been removed by some more trusting and active listener than their father had proved.

This same governess remained with them to the time of her death, which occurred some years later, under the following circumstances as extraordinary as her dream.

THE EARL'S HALL

The good governess had a particular liking for the old castle, and when lessons were over, would take her book or her work into a large room in the ancient building, called the Earl's Hall. Here she caused a table and chair to be placed for her use, and in the chiaroscuro would so sit at her favourite occupations, with just a little ray of subdued light, admitted through one of the glassless windows above her, and falling upon her table.

The Earl's Hall is entered by a narrow-arched door, opening close to the winding stair. It is a very large and gloomy room, pretty nearly square, with a lofty vaulted ceiling, and a stone floor. Being situated high in the castle, the walls of which are immensely thick, and the windows very small and few, the silence that reigns here is like that of a subterranean cavern. You hear nothing in this solitude, except perhaps twice in a day, the twitter of a swallow in one of the small windows high in the wall.

This good lady having one day retired to her accustomed solitude, was missed from the house at her wonted hour of return. This in a country house, such as Irish houses were in those days, excited little surprise, and no harm. But when the dinner hour came, which was then, in country houses, five o'clock, and the governess had not appeared, some of her young friends, it being not yet winter, and sufficient light remaining to guide them through the gloom of the dim ascent and passages, mounted the old stone stair to the level of the Earl's Hall, gaily calling to her as they approached.

There was no answer. On the stone floor, outside the door of the Earl's Hall, to their horror, they found her lying insensible. By the usual means she was restored to consciousness; but she continued very ill, and was conveyed to the house, where she took to her bed.

It was there and then that she related what had occurred to her. She had placed herself, as usual, at her little work table, and had been either working or reading—I forget which—for some time, and felt in her usual health and serene spirits. Raising her eyes, and looking towards the door, she saw a horrible-looking little man enter. He was dressed in red, was very short, had a singularly dark face, and a most atrocious countenance. Having walked some steps into the room, with his eyes fixed on her, he stopped, and beckoning to her to follow, moved back toward the door. About half way, again he stopped once more and turned. She was so terrified that she sat staring at the apparition without moving or speaking. Seeing that she had not obeyed him, his face became more frightful and menacing, and as it underwent this change, he raised his hand and stamped on the floor. Gesture, look, and all, expressed diabolical fury. Through sheer extremity of terror she did rise, and, as he turned again, followed him a step or two in the direction of the door. He again stopped, and with the same mute menace, compelled her again to follow him.

She reached the narrow stone doorway of the Earl's Hall, through which he had passed; from the threshold she saw him standing a little way off, with his eyes still fixed on her. Again he signed to her, and began to move along the short passage that leads to the winding stair. But instead of following him further, she fell on the floor in a fit.

The poor lady was thoroughly persuaded that she was not long to survive this vision, and her foreboding proved true. From her bed she never rose. Fever and delirium supervened in a few days and she died. Of course it is possible that fever, already approaching, had touched her brain when she was visited by the phantom, and that it had no external existence.

THE VISION OF TOM CHUFF

At the edge of melancholy Catstean Moor, in the north of England, with half-a-dozen ancient poplar-trees with rugged and hoary stems around, one smashed across the middle by a flash of lightning thirty summers before, and all by their great height dwarfing the abode near which they stand, there squats a rude stone house, with a thick chimney, a kitchen and bedroom on the ground-floor, and a loft, accessible by a ladder, under the shingle roof, divided into two rooms.

Its owner was a man of ill repute. Tom Chuff was his name. A shock-headed, broad-shouldered, powerful man, though somewhat short, with lowering brows and a sullen eye. He was a poacher, and hardly made an ostensible pretence of earning his bread by any honest industry. He was a drunkard. He beat his wife, and led his children a life of terror and lamentation, when he was at home. It was a blessing to his frightened little family when he absented himself, as he sometimes did, for a week or more together.

On the night I speak of he knocked at the door with his cudgel at about eight o'clock. It was winter, and the night was very dark. Had the summons been that of a bogie from the moor, the inmates of this small house could hardly have heard it with greater terror.

His wife unbarred the door in fear and haste. Her hunchbacked sister stood by the hearth, staring toward the threshold. The children cowered behind.

Tom Chuff entered with his cudgel in his hand, without speaking, and threw himself into a chair opposite the fire. He had been away two or three days. He looked haggard, and his eyes were bloodshot. They knew he had been drinking.

Tom raked and knocked the peat fire with his stick, and thrust his feet close to it. He signed towards the little dresser, and nodded to his wife, and she knew he wanted a cup, which in silence she gave him. He pulled a bottle of gin from his coat-pocket, and nearly filling the teacup, drank off the dram at a few gulps.

He usually refreshed himself with two or three drams of this kind before beating the inmates of his house. His three little children, cowering in a corner, eyed him from under a table, as Jack did the ogre in the nursery tale. His wife, Nell, standing behind a chair, which she was ready to snatch up to meet the blow of the cudgel, which might be levelled at her at any moment, never took her eyes off him; and hunchbacked Mary showed the whites of a large pair of eyes, similarly employed, as she stood against the oaken press, her dark face hardly distinguishable in the distance from the brown panel behind it.

Tom Chuff was at his third dram, and had not yet spoken a word since his entrance, and the suspense was growing dreadful, when, on a sudden, he leaned back in his rude seat, the cudgel slipped from his hand, a change and a death-like pallor came over his face.

For a while they all stared on; such was their fear of him, they dared not speak or move, lest it should prove to have been but a doze, and Tom should wake up and proceed forthwith to gratify his temper and exercise his cudgel.

In a very little time, however, things began to look so odd, that they ventured, his wife and Mary, to exchange glances full of doubt and wonder. He hung so much over the side of the chair, that if it had not been one of cyclopean clumsiness and weight, he would have borne it to the floor. A leaden tint was darkening the pallor of his face. They were becoming alarmed, and finally braving everything his wife timidly said, "Tom!" and then more sharply repeated it, and finally cried the appellative loudly, and again and again, with the terrified accompaniment, "He's dying—he's dying!" her voice rising to a scream, as she found that neither it nor her plucks and shakings of him by the shoulder had the slightest effect in recalling him from his torpor.

And now from sheer terror of a new kind the children added their shrilly piping to the talk and cries of their seniors; and if anything could have called Tom up from his lethargy, it might have been the piercing chorus that made the rude chamber of the poacher's habitation ring again. But Tom continued unmoved, deaf, and stirless.

His wife sent Mary down to the village, hardly a quarter of a mile away, to implore of the doctor, for whose family she did duty as laundress, to come down and look at her husband, who seemed to be dying.

The doctor, who was a good-natured fellow, arrived. With his hat still on, he looked at Tom, examined him, and when he found that the emetic he had brought with him, on conjecture from Mary's description, did not act, and that his lancet brought no blood, and that he felt a pulseless wrist, he shook his head, and inwardly thought:

"What the plague is the woman crying for? Could she have desired a greater blessing for her children and herself than the very thing that has happened?"

Tom, in fact, seemed quite gone. At his lips no breath was perceptible. The doctor could discover no pulse. His hands and feet were cold, and the chill was stealing up into his body.

The doctor, after a stay of twenty minutes, had buttoned up his great-coat again and pulled down his hat, and told Mrs. Chuff that there was no use in his remaining any longer, when, all of a sudden, a little rill of blood began to trickle from the lancet-cut in Tom Chuffs temple.

"That's very odd," said the doctor. "Let us wait a little."

I must describe now the sensations which Tom Chuff had experienced.

With his elbows on his knees, and his chin upon his hands, he was staring into the embers, with his gin beside him, when suddenly a swimming came in his head, he lost sight of the fire, and a sound like one stroke of a loud church bell smote his brain.

Then he heard a confused humming, and the leaden weight of his head held him backward as he sank in his chair, and consciousness quite forsook him.

When he came to himself he felt chilled, and was leaning against a huge leafless tree. The night was moonless, and when he looked up he thought he had never seen stars so large and bright, or sky so black. The stars, too, seemed to blink down with longer intervals of darkness, and fiercer and more dazzling emergence, and something, he vaguely thought, of the character of silent menace and fury.

He had a confused recollection of having come there, or rather of having been carried along, as if on men's shoulders, with a sort of rushing motion. But it was utterly indistinct; the imperfect recollection simply of a sensation. He had seen or heard nothing on his way.

He looked round. There was not a sign of a living creature near. And he began with a sense of awe to recognise the place.

The tree against which he had been leaning was one of the noble old beeches that surround at irregular intervals the churchyard of Shackleton, which spreads its green and wavy lap on the edge of the Moor of Catstean, at the opposite side of which stands the rude cottage in which he had just lost consciousness. It was six miles or more across the moor to his habitation, and the black expanse lay before him, disappearing dismally in the darkness. So that, looking straight before him, sky and land blended together in an undistinguishable and awful blank.

There was a silence quite unnatural over the place. The distant murmur of the brook, which he knew so well, was dead; not a whisper in the leaves about him; the air, earth, everything about and above was indescribably still; and he experienced that quaking of the heart that seems to portend the approach of something awful. He would have set out upon his return across the moor, had he not an undefined presentiment that he was waylaid by something he dared not pass.

The old grey church and tower of Shackleton stood like a shadow in the rear. His eye had grown accustomed to the obscurity, and he could just trace its outline. There were no comforting associations in his mind connected with it; nothing but menace and misgiving. His early training in his lawless calling was connected with this very spot. Here his father used to meet two other poachers, and bring his son, then but a boy, with him.

Under the church porch, towards morning, they used to divide the game they had taken, and take account of the sales they had made on the previous day, and make partition of the money, and drink their gin. It was here he had taken his early lessons in drinking, cursing, and lawlessness. His father's grave was hardly eight steps from the spot where he stood. In his present state of awful dejection, no scene on earth could have so helped to heighten his fear.

There was one object close by which added to his gloom. About a yard away, in rear of the tree, behind himself, and extending to his left, was an open grave, the mould and rubbish piled on the other side. At the head of this grave stood the beech-tree; its columnar stem rose like a huge monumental pillar. He knew every line and crease on its smooth surface. The initial letters of his own name, cut in its bark long ago, had spread out and wrinkled like the grotesque capitals of a fanciful engraver, and now with a sinister significance overlooked the open grave, as if answering his mental question, "Who for is t' grave cut?"

He felt still a little stunned, and there was a faint tremor in his joints that disinclined him to exert himself; and, further, he had a vague apprehension that take what direction he might, there was danger around him worse than that of staying where he was.

On a sudden the stars began to blink more fiercely, a faint wild light overspread for a minute the bleak landscape, and he saw approaching from the moor a figure at a kind of swinging trot, with now and then a zig-zag hop or two, such as men accustomed to cross such places make, to avoid the patches of slob or quag that meet them here and there. This figure resembled his father's, and like him, whistled through his finger by way of signal as he approached; but the whistle sounded not now shrilly and sharp, as in old times, but immensely far away, and seemed to sing strangely through Tom's head. From habit or from fear, in answer to the signal, Tom whistled as he used to do five-and-twenty years ago and more, although he was already chilled with an unearthly fear.

Like his father, too, the figure held up the bag that was in his left hand as he drew near, when it was his custom to call out to him what was in it. It did not reassure the watcher, you may be certain, when a shout unnaturally faint reached him, as the phantom dangled the bag in the air, and he heard with a faint distinctness the words, "Tom Chuff's soul!"

Scarcely fifty yards away from the low churchyard fence at which Tom was standing, there was a wider chasm in the peat, which there threw up a growth of reeds and bulrushes, among which, as the old poacher used to do on a sudden alarm, the approaching figure suddenly cast itself down.

From the same patch of tall reeds and rushes emerged instantaneously what he at first mistook for the same figure creeping on all-fours, but what he soon perceived to be an enormous black dog with a rough coat like a bear's, which at first sniffed about, and then started towards him in what seemed to be a sportive amble, bouncing this way and that, but as it drew near it displayed a pair of fearful eyes that glowed like live coals, and emitted from the monstrous expanse of its jaws a terrifying growl.

This beast seemed on the point of seizing him, and Tom recoiled in panic and fell into the open grave behind him. The edge which he caught as he tumbled gave way, and down he went, expecting almost at the same instant to reach the bottom. But never was such a fall! Bottomless seemed the abyss! Down, down, down, with immeasurable and still increasing speed, through utter darkness, with hair streaming straight upward, breathless, he shot with a rush of air against him, the force of which whirled up his very arms, second after second, minute after minute, through the chasm downward he flew, the icy perspiration of horror covering his body, and suddenly, as he expected to be dashed into annihilation, his descent was in an instant arrested with a tremendous shock, which, however, did not deprive him of consciousness even for a moment.

He looked about him. The place resembled a smoke-stained cavern or catacomb, the roof of which, except for a ribbed arch here and there faintly visible, was lost in darkness. From several rude passages, like the galleries of a gigantic mine, which opened from this centre chamber, was very dimly emitted a dull glow as of charcoal, which was the only light by which he could imperfectly discern the objects immediately about him.

What seemed like a projecting piece of the rock, at the corner of one of these murky entrances, moved on a sudden, and proved to be a human figure, that beckoned to him. He approached, and saw his father. He could barely recognise him, he was so monstrously altered.

"I've been looking for you, Tom. Welcome home, lad; come along to your place."

Tom's heart sank as he heard these words, which were spoken in a hollow and, he thought, derisive voice that made him tremble. But he could not help accompanying the wicked spirit, who led him into a place, in passing which he heard, as it were from within the rock, deadful cries and appeals for mercy.

"What is this?" said he.

"Never mind."

"Who are they?"

"New-comers, like yourself, lad," answered his father apathetically. "They give over that work in time, finding it is no use."

"What shall I do?" said Tom, in an agony.

"It's all one."

"But what shall I do?" reiterated Tom, quivering in every joint and nerve.

"Grin and bear it, I suppose."

"For God's sake, if ever you cared for me, as I am your own child, let me out of this!"

"There's no way out."

"If there's a way in there's a way out, and for Heaven's sake let me out of this."

But the dreadful figure made no further answer, and glided backwards by his shoulder to the rear; and others appeared in view, each with a faint red halo round it, staring on him with frightful eyes, images, all in hideous variety, of eternal fury or derision. He was growing mad, it seemed, under the stare of so many eyes, increasing in number and drawing closer every moment, and at the same time myriads and myriads of voices were calling him by his name, some far away, some near, some from one point, some from another, some from behind, close to his ears. These cries were increased in rapidity and multitude, and mingled with laughter, with flitting blasphemies, with broken insults and mockeries, succeeded and obliterated by others, before he could half catch their meaning.

All this time, in proportion to the rapidity and urgency of these dreadful sights and sounds, the epilepsy of terror was creeping up to his brain, and with a long and dreadful scream he lost consciousness.

When he recovered his senses, he found himself in a small stone chamber, vaulted above, and with a ponderous door. A single point of light in the wall, with a strange brilliancy illuminated this cell.

Seated opposite to him was a venerable man with a snowy beard of immense length; an image of awful purity and severity. He was dressed in a coarse robe, with three large keys suspensed from his girdle. He might have filled one's idea of an ancient porter of a city gate; such spiritual cities, I should say, as John Bunyan loved to describe.

This old man's eyes were brilliant and awful, and fixed on him as they were, Tom Chuff felt himself helplessly in his power. At length he spoke:

"The command is given to let you forth for one trial more. But if you are found again drinking with the drunken, and beating your fellow-servants, you shall return through the door by which you came, and go out no more."

With these words the old man took him by the wrist and led him through the first door, and then unlocking one that stood in the cavern outside, he struck Tom Chuff sharply on the shoulder, and the door shut behind him with a sound that boomed peal after peal of thunder near and far away, and all round and above, till it rolled off gradually into silence. It was totally dark, but there was a fanning of fresh cool air that overpowered him. He felt that he was in the upper world again.

In a few minutes he began to hear voices which he knew, and first a faint point of light appeared before his eyes, and gradually he saw the flame of the candle, and, after that, the familiar faces of his wife and children, and he heard them faintly when they spoke to him, although he was as yet unable to answer.

He also saw the doctor, like an isolated figure in the dark, and heard him say:

"There, now, you have him back. He'll do, I think."

His first words, when he could speak and saw clearly all about him, and felt the blood on his neck and shirt, were:

"Wife, forgie me. I'm a changed man. Send for't sir."

Which last phrase means, "Send for the clergyman."

When the vicar came and entered the little bedroom where the scared poacher, whose soul had died within him, was lying, still sick and weak, in his bed, and with a spirit that was prostrate with terror, Tom Chuff feebly beckoned the rest from the room, and, the door being closed, the good parson heard the strange confession, and with equal amazement the man's earnest and agitated vows of amendment, and his helpless appeals to him for support and counsel.

These, of course, were kindly met; and the visits of the rector, for some time, were frequent.

One day, when he took Tom Chuff's hand on bidding him good-bye, the sick man held it still, and said:

"Ye'r vicar o' Shackleton, sir, and if I sud dee, ye'll promise me a'e thing, as I a promised ye a many. I a said I'll never gie wife, nor barn, nor folk o' no sort, skelp nor sizzup more, and ye'll know o' me no more among the sipers. Nor never will Tom draw trigger, nor set a snare again, but in an honest way, and after that ye'll no make it a bootless bene for me, but bein', as I say, vicar o' Shackleton, and able to do as ye list, ye'll no let them bury me within twenty good yerd-wands measure o' the a'd beech trees that's round the churchyard of Shackleton."

"I see; you would have your grave, when your time really comes, a good way from the place where lay the grave you dreamed of."

"That's jest it. I'd lie at the bottom o' a marl-pit liefer! And I'd be laid in anither churchyard just to be shut o' my fear o' that, but that a' my kinsfolk is buried beyond in Shackleton, and ye'll gie me yer promise, and no break yer word."

"I do promise, certainly. I'm not likely to outlive you; but, if I should, and still be vicar of Shackleton, you shall be buried somewhere as near the middle of the churchyard as we can find space."

"That'll do."

And so content they parted.

The effect of the vision upon Tom Chuff was powerful, and promised to be lasting. With a sore effort he exchanged his life of desultory adventure and comparative idleness for one of regular industry. He gave up drinking; he was as kind as an originally surly nature would allow to his wife and family; he went to church; in fine weather they crossed the moor to Shackleton Church; the vicar said he came there to look at the scenery of his vision, and to fortify his good resolutions by the reminder.

Impressions upon the imagination, however, are but transitory, and a bad man acting under fear is not a free agent; his real character does not appear. But as the images of the imagination fade, and the action of fear abates, the essential qualities of the man reassert themselves.

So, after a time, Tom Chuff began to grow weary of his new life; he grew lazy, and people began to say that he was catching hares, and pursuing his old contraband way of life, under the rose.

He came home one hard night, with signs of the bottle in his thick speech and violent temper. Next day he was sorry, or frightened, at all events repentant, and for a week or more something of the old horror returned, and he was once more on his good behaviour. But in a little time came a relapse, and another repentance, and then a relapse again, and gradually the return of old habits and the flooding in of all his old way of life, with more violence and gloom, in proportion as the man was alarmed and exasperated by the remembrance of his despised, but terrible, warning.

With the old life returned the misery of the cottage. The smiles, which had begun to appear with the unwonted sunshine, were seen no more. Instead, returned to his poor wife's face the old pale and heartbroken look. The cottage lost its neat and cheerful air, and the melancholy of neglect was visible. Sometimes at night were overheard, by a chance passer-by, cries and sobs from that ill-omened dwelling. Tom Chuff was now often drunk, and not very often at home, except when he came in to sweep away his poor wife's earnings.

Tom had long lost sight of the honest old parson. There was shame mixed with his degradation. He had grace enough left when he saw the thin figure of "t' sir" walking along the road to turn out of his way and avoid meeting him. The clergyman shook his head, and sometimes groaned, when his name was mentioned. His horror and regret were more for the poor wife than for the relapsed sinner, for her case was pitiable indeed.

Her brother, Jack Everton, coming over from Hexley, having heard stories of all this, determined to beat Tom, for his ill-treatment of his sister, within an inch of his life. Luckily, perhaps, for all concerned, Tom happened to be away upon one of his long excursions, and poor Nell besought her brother, in extremity of terror, not to interpose between them. So he took his leave and went home muttering and sulky.

Now it happened a few months later that Nelly Chuff fell sick. She had been ailing, as heartbroken people do, for a good while. But now the end had come.

There was a coroner's inquest when she died, for the doctor had doubts as to whether a blow had not, at least, hastened her death. Nothing certain, however, came of the inquiry. Tom Chuff had left his home more than two days before his wife's death. He was absent upon his lawless business still when the coroner had held his quest.

Jack Everton came over from Hexley to attend the dismal obsequies of his sister. He was more incensed than ever with the wicked husband, who, one way or other, had hastened Nelly's death. The inquest had closed early in the day. The husband had not appeared.

An occasional companion—perhaps I ought to say accomplice—of Chuff's happened to turn up. He had left him on the borders of Westmoreland, and said he would probably be home next day. But Everton affected not to believe it. Perhaps it was to Tom Chuff, he suggested, a secret satisfaction to crown the history of his bad married life with the scandal of his absence from the funeral of his neglected and abused wife.

Everton had taken on himself the direction of the melancholy preparations. He had ordered a grave to be opened for his sister beside her mother's, in Shackleton churchyard, at the other side of the moor. For the purpose, as I have said, of marking the callous neglect of her husband, he determined that the funeral should take place that night. His brother Dick had accompanied him, and they and his sister, with Mary and the children, and a couple of the neighbours, formed the humble cortège.

Jack Everton said he would wait behind, on the chance of Tom Chuff coming in time, that he might tell him what had happened, and make him cross the moor with him to meet the funeral. His real object, I think, was to inflict upon the villain the drubbing he had so long wished to give him. Anyhow, he was resolved, by crossing the moor, to reach the churchyard in time to anticipate the arrival of the funeral, and to have a few words with the vicar, clerk, and sexton, all old friends of his, for the parish of Shackleton was the place of his birth and early recollections.

But Tom Chuff did not appear at his house that night. In surly mood, and without a shilling in his pocket, he was making his way homeward. His bottle of gin, his last investment, half emptied, with its neck protruding, as usual on such returns, was in his coat-pocket.

His way home lay across the moor of Catstean, and the point at which he best knew the passage was from the churchyard of Shackleton. He vaulted the low wall that forms its boundary, and strode across the graves, and over many a flat, half-buried tombstone, toward the side of the churchyard next Catstean Moor.

The old church of Shackleton and its tower rose, close at his right, like a black shadow against the sky. It was a moonless night, but clear. By this time he had reached the low boundary wall, at the other side, that overlooks the wide expanse of Catstean Moor. He stood by one of the huge old beech-trees, and leaned his back to its smooth trunk. Had he ever seen the sky look so black, and the stars shine out and blink so vividly? There was a deathlike silence over the scene, like the hush that precedes thunder in sultry weather. The expanse before him was lost in utter blackness. A strange quaking unnerved his heart. It was the sky and scenery of his vision! The same horror and misgiving. The same invincible fear of venturing from the spot where he stood. He would have prayed if he dared. His sinking heart demanded a restorative of some sort, and he grasped the bottle in his coat-pocket. Turning to his left, as he did so, he saw the piled-up mould of an open grave that gaped with its head close to the base of the great tree against which he was leaning.

He stood aghast. His dream was returning and slowly enveloping him. Everything he saw was weaving itself into the texture of his vision. The chill of horror stole over him.

A faint whistle came shrill and clear over the moor, and he saw a figure approaching at a swinging trot, with a zig-zag course, hopping now here and now there, as men do over a surface where one has need to choose their steps. Through the jungle of reeds and bulrushes in the foreground this figure advanced; and with the same unaccountable impulse that had coerced him in his dream, he answered the whistle of the advancing figure.

On that signal it directed its course straight toward him. It mounted the low wall, and, standing there, looked into the graveyard.

"Who med answer?" challenged the new-comer from his post of observation.

"Me," answered Tom.

"Who are you?" repeated the man upon the wall.

"Tom Chuff; and who's this grave cut for?" He answered in a savage tone, to cover the secret shudder of his panic.

"I'll tell you that, ye villain!" answered the stranger, descending from the wall, "I a' looked for you far and near, and waited long, and now you're found at last."

Not knowing what to make of the figure that advanced upon him, Tom Chuff recoiled, stumbled, and fell backward into the open grave. He caught at the sides as he fell, but without retarding his fall.

An hour later, when lights came with the coffin, the corpse of Tom Chuff was found at the bottom of the grave. He had fallen direct upon his head, and his neck was broken. His death must have been simultaneous with his fall. Thus far his dream was accomplished.

It was his brother-in-law who had crossed the moor and approached the churchyard of Shackleton, exactly in the line which the image of his father had seemed to take in his strange vision. Fortunately for Jack Everton, the sexton and clerk of Shackleton church were, unseen by him, crossing the churchyard toward the grave of Nelly Chuff, just as Tom the poacher stumbled and fell. Suspicion of direct violence would otherwise have inevitably attached to the exasperated brother. As it was, the catastrophe was followed by no legal consequences.

The good vicar kept his word, and the grave of Tom Chuff is still pointed out by the old inhabitants of Shackleton pretty nearly in the centre of the churchyard. This conscientious compliance with the entreaty of the panic-stricken man as to the place of his sepulture gave a horrible and mocking emphasis to the strange combination by which fate had defeated his precaution, and fixed the place of his death.

The story was for many a year, and we believe still is, told round many a cottage hearth, and though it appeals to what many would term superstition, it yet sounded, in the ears of a rude and simple audience, a thrilling, and let us hope, not altogether fruitless homily.

DICKON THE DEVIL

This Story can be found on Page 565 as part of A Stable for Nightmares.

THE MURDERED COUSIN

THE MURDERED COUSIN

"And they lay wait for their own blood: they lurk privily for
their own lives.
"So are the ways of every one that is greedy of gain; which taketh
away the life of the owner thereof."

This story of the Irish peerage is written, as nearly as possible, in the very words in which it was related by its "heroine," the late Countess D——, and is therefore told in the first person.

My mother died when I was an infant, and of her I have no recollection, even the faintest. By her death my education was left solely to the direction of my surviving parent. He entered upon his task with a stern appreciation of the responsibility thus cast upon him. My religious instruction was prosecuted with an almost exaggerated anxiety; and I had, of course, the best masters to perfect me in all those accomplishments which my station and wealth might seem to require. My father was what is called an oddity, and his treatment of me, though uniformly kind, was governed less by affection and tenderness, than by a high and unbending sense of duty. Indeed I seldom saw or spoke to him except at meal-times, and then, though gentle, he was usually reserved and gloomy. His leisure hours, which were many, were passed either in his study or in solitary walks; in short, he seemed to take no further interest in my happiness or improvement, than a conscientious regard to the discharge of his own duty would seem to impose.

Shortly before my birth an event occurred which had contributed much to induce and to confirm my father's unsocial habits; it was the fact that a suspicion of *murder* had fallen upon his younger brother, though not sufficiently definite to lead to any public proceedings, yet strong enough to ruin him in public opinion. This disgraceful and dreadful doubt cast upon the family name, my father felt deeply and bitterly, and not the less so that he himself was thoroughly convinced of his brother's innocence. The sincerity and strength of this conviction he shortly afterwards proved in a manner which produced the catastrophe of my story.

Before, however, I enter upon my immediate adventures, I ought to relate the circumstances which had awakened that suspicion to which I have referred, inasmuch as they are in themselves somewhat curious, and in their effects most intimately connected with my own after-history.

My uncle, Sir Arthur Tyrrell, was a gay and extravagant man, and, among other vices, was ruinously addicted to gaming. This unfortunate propensity, even after his fortune had suffered so severely as to render retrenchment imperative, nevertheless continued to engross him, nearly to the exclusion of every other pursuit. He was, however, a proud, or rather a vain man, and could not bear to make the diminution of his income a matter of triumph to those with whom he had hitherto competed; and the consequence was, that he frequented no longer the expensive haunts of his dissipation, and retired from the gay world, leaving his coterie to discover his reasons as best they might. He did not, however, forego his favourite vice, for though he could not worship his great divinity in those costly temples where he was formerly wont to take his place, yet he found it very possible to bring about him a sufficient number of the votaries of chance to answer all his ends. The consequence was, that Carrickleigh, which was the name of my uncle's residence, was never without one or more of such visiters as I have described. It happened that upon one occasion he was visited by one Hugh Tisdall, a gentleman of loose, and, indeed, low habits, but of considerable wealth, and who had, in early youth, travelled with my uncle upon the Continent. The period of this visit was winter, and, consequently, the house was nearly deserted excepting by its ordinary inmates; it was, therefore, highly acceptable, particularly as my uncle was aware that his visiter's tastes accorded exactly with his own.

Both parties seemed determined to avail themselves of their mutual suitability during the brief stay which Mr. Tisdall had promised; the consequence was, that they shut themselves up in Sir Arthur's private room for nearly all the day and the greater part of the night, during the space of almost a week, at the end of which the servant having one morning, as usual, knocked at Mr. Tisdall's bed-room door repeatedly, received no answer, and, upon attempting to enter, found that it was locked. This appeared suspicious, and the inmates of the house having been alarmed, the door was forced open, and, on proceeding to the bed, they found the body of its occupant perfectly lifeless, and hanging halfway out, the head downwards, and near the floor. One deep wound had been inflicted upon the temple, apparently with some blunt instrument, which had penetrated the brain, and another blow, less effective—probably the first aimed—had grazed his head, removing some of the scalp. The door had been double locked upon the *inside*, in evidence of which the key still lay where it had been placed in the lock. The window, though not secured on the interior, was closed; a circumstance not a little puzzling, as it afforded the only other mode of escape from the room. It looked out, too, upon a kind of court-yard, round which the old buildings stood, formerly accessible by a narrow doorway and passage lying in the oldest side of the quadrangle, but which had since been built up, so as to preclude all ingress or egress; the room was also upon the second story, and the height of the window considerable; in addition to all which the stone window-sill was much too narrow to allow of any one's standing upon it when the window was closed. Near the bed were found a pair of razors belonging to the murdered man, one of them upon the ground, and both of them open. The weapon which inflicted the mortal wound was not to be found in the room, nor were any footsteps or other traces of the murderer discoverable. At the suggestion of Sir Arthur himself, the coroner was instantly summoned to attend, and an inquest was held. Nothing, however, in any degree conclusive was elicited. The walls, ceiling, and floor of the room were carefully examined, in order to ascertain whether they contained a trap-door or other concealed mode of entrance, but no such thing appeared. Such was the minuteness of investigation employed, that, although the grate had contained a large fire during the night, they proceeded to examine even the very chimney, in order to discover whether escape by it were possible. But this attempt, too, was fruitless, for the chimney, built in the old fashion, rose in a perfectly perpendicular line from the hearth, to a height of nearly fourteen feet above the roof, affording in its interior scarcely the possibility of ascent, the flue being smoothly plastered, and sloping towards the top like an inverted funnel; promising, too, even if the summit were attained, owing to its great height, but a precarious descent upon the sharp and steep-ridged roof; the ashes, too, which lay in the grate, and the soot, as far as it could be seen, were undisturbed, a circumstance almost conclusive upon the point.

Sir Arthur was of course examined. His evidence was given with clearness and unreserve, which seemed calculated to silence all suspicion. He stated that, up to the day and night immediately preceding the catastrophe, he had lost to a heavy amount, but that, at their last sitting, he had not only won back his original loss, but upwards of £4,000 in addition; in evidence of which he produced an acknowledgment of debt to that amount in the handwriting of the deceased, bearing date the night of the catastrophe. He had mentioned the circumstance to Lady Tyrrell, and in presence of some of his domestics; which statement was supported by *their* respective evidence. One of the jury shrewdly observed, that the circumstance of Mr. Tisdall's having sustained so heavy a loss might have suggested to some ill-minded persons, accidentally hearing it, the plan of robbing him, after having murdered him in such a manner as might make it appear that he had committed suicide; a supposition which was strongly supported by the razors having been found thus displaced and removed from their case. Two persons had probably been engaged in the attempt, one watching by the sleeping man, and ready to strike him in case of his awakening suddenly, while the other was procuring the razors and employed in inflicting the fatal gash, so as to make it appear to have been the act of the murdered man himself. It was said that while the juror was making this suggestion Sir Arthur changed colour. There was nothing, however, like legal evidence to implicate him, and the consequence was that the verdict was found against a person or persons unknown, and for some time the matter was suffered to rest, until, after about five months, my father received a letter from a person signing himself Andrew Collis, and representing himself to be the cousin of the deceased. This letter stated that his brother, Sir Arthur, was likely to incur not merely suspicion but personal risk, unless he could account for certain circumstances connected with the recent murder, and contained a copy of a letter written by the deceased, and dated the very day upon the night of which the murder had been perpetrated. Tisdall's letter contained, among a great deal of other matter, the passages which follow:—

"I have had sharp work with Sir Arthur: he tried some of his stale tricks, but soon found that *I* was Yorkshire, too; it would not do—you understand me. We went to the work like good ones, head, heart, and soul; and in fact, since I came here, I have lost no time. I am rather fagged, but I am sure to be well paid for my hardship; I never want sleep so long as I can have the music of a dice-box, and wherewithal to pay the piper. As I told you, he tried some of his queer turns, but I foiled him like a man, and, in return, gave him more than he could relish of the genuine *dead knowledge.* In short, I have plucked the old baronet as never baronet was plucked before; I have scarce left him the stump of a quill. I have got promissory notes in his hand to the amount of ——; if you like round numbers, say five-and-twenty thousand pounds, safely deposited in my portable strong box, alias, double-clasped pocket-book. I leave this ruinous old rat-hole early on to-morrow, for two reasons: first, I do not want to play with Sir Arthur deeper than I think his security would warrant; and, secondly, because I am safer a hundred miles away from Sir Arthur than in the house with him. Look you, my worthy, I tell you this between ourselves—I may be wrong—but, by ——, I am sure as that I am now living, that Sir A—— attempted to poison me last night. So much for old friendship on both sides. When I won the last stake, a heavy one enough, my friend leant his forehead upon his hands, and you'll laugh when I tell you that his head literally smoked like a hot dumpling. I do not know whether his agitation was produced by the plan which he had against me, or by his having lost so heavily; though it must be allowed that he had reason to be a little funked, whichever way his thoughts went; but he pulled the bell, and ordered two bottles of Champagne. While the fellow was bringing them, he wrote a promissory note to the full amount, which he signed, and, as the man came in with the bottles and glasses, he desired him to be off. He filled a glass for me, and, while he thought my eyes were off, for I was putting up his note at the time, he dropped something slyly into it, no doubt to sweeten it; but I saw it all, and, when he handed it to me, I said, with an emphasis which he might easily understand, 'There is some sediment in it, I'll not drink it.' 'Is there?' said he, and at the same time snatched it from my hand and threw it into the fire. What do you think of that? Have I not a tender bird in hand? Win or lose, I will not play beyond five thousand to-night, and to-morrow sees me safe out of the reach of Sir Arthur's Champagne."

Of the authenticity of this document, I never heard my father express a doubt; and I am satisfied that, owing to his strong conviction in favour of his brother, he would not have admitted it without sufficient inquiry, inasmuch as it tended to confirm the suspicions which already existed to his prejudice. Now, the only point in this letter which made strongly against my uncle, was the mention of the "double-clasped pocket-book," as the receptacle of the papers likely to involve him, for this pocket-book was not forthcoming, nor anywhere to be found, nor had any papers referring to his gaming transactions been discovered upon the dead man.

But whatever might have been the original intention of this man, Collis, neither my uncle nor my father ever heard more of him; he published the letter, however, in Faulkner's newspaper, which was shortly afterwards made the vehicle of a much more mysterious attack. The passage in that journal to which I allude, appeared about four years afterwards, and while the fatal occurrence was still fresh in public recollection. It commenced by a rambling preface, stating that "a *certain person* whom *certain* persons thought to be dead, was not so, but living, and in full possession of his memory, and moreover, ready and able to make *great* delinquents tremble": it then went on to describe the murder, without, however, mentioning names; and in doing so, it entered into minute and circumstantial particulars of which none but an *eye-witness* could have been possessed, and by implications almost too unequivocal to be regarded in the light of insinuation, to involve the "*titled gambler*" in the guilt of the transaction.

My father at once urged Sir Arthur to proceed against the paper in an action of libel, but he would not hear of it, nor consent to my father's taking any legal steps whatever in the matter. My father, however, wrote in a threatening tone to Faulkner, demanding a surrender of the author of the obnoxious article; the answer to this application is still in my possession, and is penned in an apologetic tone: it states that the manuscript had been handed in, paid for, and inserted as an advertisement, without sufficient inquiry, or any knowledge as to whom it referred. No step, however, was taken to clear my uncle's character in the judgment of the public; and, as he immediately sold a small property, the application of the proceeds of which were known to none, he was said to have disposed of it to enable himself to buy off the threatened information; however the truth might have been, it is certain that no charges respecting the mysterious murder were afterwards publicly made against my uncle, and, as far as external disturbances were concerned, he enjoyed henceforward perfect security and quiet

A deep and lasting impression, however, had been made upon the public mind, and Sir Arthur Tyrrell was no longer visited or noticed by the gentry of the county, whose attentions he had hitherto received. He accordingly affected to despise those courtesies which he no longer enjoyed, and shunned even that society which he might have commanded. This is all that I need recapitulate of my uncle's history, and I now recur to my own.

Although my father had never, within my recollection, visited, or been visited by my uncle, each being of unsocial, procrastinating, and indolent habits, and their respective residences being very far apart—the one lying in the county of Galway, the other in that of Cork—he was strongly attached to his brother, and evinced his affection by an active correspondence, and by deeply and proudly resenting that neglect which had branded Sir Arthur as unfit to mix in society.

When I was about eighteen years of age, my father, whose health had been gradually declining, died, leaving me in heart wretched and desolate, and, owing to his habitual seclusion, with few acquaintances, and almost no friends. The provisions of his will were curious, and when I was sufficiently come to myself to listen to, or comprehend them, surprised me not a little: all his vast property was left to me, and to the heirs of my body, for ever; and, in default of such heirs, it was to go after my death to my uncle, Sir Arthur, without any entail. At the same time, the will appointed him my guardian, desiring that I might be received within his house, and reside with his family, and under his care, during the term of my minority; and in consideration of the increased expense consequent upon such an arrangement, a handsome allowance was allotted to him during the term of my proposed residence. The object of this last provision I at once understood; my father desired, by making it the direct apparent interest of Sir Arthur that I should die without issue, while at the same time he placed my person wholly in his power, to prove to the world how great and unshaken was his confidence in his brother's innocence and honour. It was a strange, perhaps an idle scheme, but as I had been always brought up in the habit of considering my uncle as a deeply injured man, and had been taught, almost as a part of my religion, to regard him as the very soul of honour, I felt no further uneasiness respecting the arrangement than that likely to affect a shy and timid girl at the immediate prospect of taking up her abode for the first time in her life among strangers. Previous to leaving my home, which I felt I should do with a heavy heart, I received a most tender and affectionate letter from my uncle, calculated, if anything could do so, to remove the bitterness of parting from scenes familiar and dear from my earliest childhood, and in some degree to reconcile me to the measure. It was upon a fine autumn day that I approached the old domain of Carrickleigh. I shall not soon forget the impression of sadness and of gloom which all that I saw produced upon my mind; the sunbeams were falling with a rich and melancholy lustre upon the fine old trees, which stood in lordly groups, casting their long sweeping shadows over rock and sward; there was an air of neglect and decay about the spot, which amounted almost to desolation, and mournfully increased as we approached the building itself, near which the ground had been originally more artificially and carefully cultivated than elsewhere, and where consequently neglect more immediately and strikingly betrayed itself.

As we proceeded, the road wound near the beds of what had been formerly two fish-ponds, which were now nothing more than stagnant swamps, overgrown with rank weeds, and here and there encroached upon by the straggling underwood; the avenue itself was much broken; and in many places the stones were almost concealed by grass and nettles; the loose stone walls which had here and there intersected the broad park, were, in many places, broken down, so as no longer to answer their original purpose as fences; piers were now and then to be seen, but the gates were gone; and to add to the general air of dilapidation, some huge trunks were lying scattered through the venerable old trees, either the work of the winter storms, or perhaps the victims of some extensive but desultory scheme of denudation, which the projector had not capital or perseverance to carry into full effect.

After the carriage had travelled a full mile of this avenue, we reached the summit of a rather abrupt eminence, one of the many which added to the picturesqueness, if not to the convenience of this rude approach; from the top of this ridge the grey walls of Carrickleigh were visible, rising at a small distance in front, and darkened by the hoary wood which crowded around them; it was a quadrangular building of considerable extent, and the front, where the great entrance was placed, lay towards us, and bore unequivocal marks of antiquity; the time-worn, solemn aspect of the old building, the ruinous and deserted appearance of the whole place, and the associations which connected it with a dark page in the history of my family, combined to depress spirits already predisposed for the reception of sombre and dejecting impressions. When the carriage drew up in the grass-grown court-yard before the hall-door, two lazy-looking men, whose appearance well accorded with that of the place which they tenanted, alarmed by the obstreperous barking of a great chained dog, ran out from some half-ruinous out-houses, and took charge of the horses; the hall-door stood open, and I entered a gloomy and imperfectly-lighted apartment, and found no one within it. However, I had not long to wait in this awkward predicament, for before my luggage had been deposited in the house, indeed before I had well removed my cloak and other muffles, so as to enable me to look around, a young girl ran lightly into the hall, and kissing me heartily and somewhat boisterously exclaimed, "My dear cousin, my dear Margaret—I am so delighted—so out of breath, we did not expect you till ten o'clock; my father is somewhere about the place, he must be close at hand. James—Corney—run out and tell your master; my brother is seldom at home, at least at any reasonable hour; you must be so tired—so fatigued—let me show you to your room; see that Lady Margaret's luggage is all brought up; you must lie down and rest yourself. Deborah, bring some coffee—up these stairs; we are so delighted to see you—you cannot think how lonely I have been; how steep these stairs are, are not they? I am so glad you are come—I could hardly bring myself to believe that you were really coming; how good of you, dear Lady Margaret." There was real good nature and delight in my cousin's greeting, and a kind of constitutional confidence of manner which placed me at once at ease, and made me feel immediately upon terms of intimacy with her. The room into which she ushered me, although partaking in the general air of decay which pervaded the mansion and all about it, had, nevertheless, been fitted up with evident attention to comfort, and even with some dingy attempt at luxury; but what pleased me most was that it opened, by a second door, upon a lobby which communicated with my fair cousin's apartment; a circumstance which divested the room, in my eyes, of the air of solitude and sadness which would otherwise have characterised it, to a degree almost painful to one so depressed and agitated as I was.

After such arrangements as I found necessary were completed, we both went down to the parlour, a large wainscotted room, hung round with grim old portraits, and, as I was not sorry to see, containing, in its ample grate, a large and cheerful fire. Here my cousin had leisure to talk more at her ease; and from her I learned something of the manners and the habits of the two remaining members of her family, whom I had not yet seen. On my arrival I had known nothing of the family among whom I was come to reside, except that it consisted of three individuals, my uncle, and his son and daughter, Lady Tyrrell having been long dead; in addition to this very scanty stock of information, I shortly learned from my communicative companion, that my uncle was, as I had suspected, completely retired in his habits, and besides that, having been, so far back as she could well recollect, always rather strict, as reformed rakes frequently become, he had latterly been growing more gloomily and sternly religious than heretofore. Her account of her brother was far less favourable, though she did not say anything directly to his disadvantage. From all that I could gather from her, I was led to suppose that he was a specimen of the idle, coarse-mannered, profligate "*squirearchy*"—a result which might naturally have followed from the circumstance of his being, as it were, outlawed from society, and driven for companionship to grades below his own—enjoying, too, the dangerous prerogative of spending a good deal of money. However, you may easily suppose that I found nothing in my cousin's communication fully to bear me out in so very decided a conclusion.

I awaited the arrival of my uncle, which was every moment to be expected, with feelings half of alarm, half of curiosity—a sensation which I have often since experienced, though to a less degree, when upon the point of standing for the first time in the presence of one of whom I have long been in the habit of hearing or thinking with interest. It was, therefore, with some little perturbation that I heard, first a slight bustle at the outer door, then a slow step traverse the hall, and finally witnessed the door open, and my uncle enter the room. He was a striking looking man; from peculiarities both of person and of dress, the whole effect of his appearance amounted to extreme singularity. He was tall, and when young his figure must have been strikingly elegant; as it was, however, its effect was marred by a very decided stoop; his dress was of a sober colour, and in fashion anterior to any thing which I could remember. It was, however, handsome, and by no means carelessly put on; but what completed the singularity of his appearance was his uncut, white hair, which hung in long, but not at all neglected curls, even so far as his shoulders, and which combined with his regularly classic features, and fine dark eyes, to bestow upon him an air of venerable dignity and pride, which I have seldom seen equalled elsewhere. I rose as he entered, and met him about the middle of the room; he kissed my cheek and both my hands, saying—

"You are most welcome, dear child, as welcome as the command of this poor place and all that it contains can make you. I am rejoiced to see you—truly rejoiced. I trust that you are not much fatigued; pray be seated again." He led me to my chair, and continued, "I am glad to perceive you have made acquaintance with Emily already; I see, in your being thus brought together, the foundation of a lasting friendship. You are both innocent, and both young. God bless you—God bless you, and make you all that I could wish."

He raised his eyes, and remained for a few moments silent, as if in secret prayer. I felt that it was impossible that this man, with feelings manifestly so tender, could be the wretch that public opinion had represented him to be. I was more than ever convinced of his innocence. His manners were, or appeared to me, most fascinating. I know not how the lights of experience might have altered this estimate. But I was then very young, and I beheld in him a perfect mingling of the courtesy of polished life with the gentlest and most genial virtues of the heart. A feeling of affection and respect towards him began to spring up within me, the more earnest that I remembered how sorely he had suffered in fortune and how cruelly in fame. My uncle having given me fully to understand that I was most welcome, and might command whatever was his own, pressed me to take some supper; and on my refusing, he observed that, before bidding me good night, he had one duty further to perform, one in which he was convinced I would cheerfully acquiesce. He then proceeded to read a chapter from the Bible; after which he took his leave with the same affectionate kindness with which he had greeted me, having repeated his desire that I should consider every thing in his house as altogether at my disposal. It is needless to say how much I was pleased with my uncle—it was impossible to avoid being so; and I could not help saying to myself, if such a man as this is not safe from the assaults of slander, who is? I felt much happier than I had done since my father's death, and enjoyed that night the first refreshing sleep which had visited me since that calamity. My curiosity respecting my male cousin did not long remain unsatisfied; he appeared upon the next day at dinner. His manners, though not so coarse as I had expected, were exceedingly disagreeable; there was an assurance and a forwardness for which I was not prepared; there was less of the vulgarity of manner, and almost more of that of the mind, than I had anticipated. I felt quite uncomfortable in his presence; there was just that confidence in his look and tone, which would read encouragement even in mere toleration; and I felt more disgusted and annoyed at the coarse and extravagant compliments which he was pleased from time to time to pay me, than perhaps the extent of the atrocity might fully have warranted. It was, however, one consolation that he did not often appear, being much engrossed by pursuits about which I neither knew nor cared anything; but when he did, his attentions, either with a view to his amusement, or to some more serious object, were so obviously and perseveringly directed to me, that young and inexperienced as I was, even *I* could not be ignorant of their significance. I felt more provoked by this odious persecution than I can express, and discouraged him with so much vigour, that I did not stop even at rudeness to convince him that his assiduities were unwelcome; but all in vain.

This had gone on for nearly a twelvemonth, to my infinite annoyance, when one day, as I was sitting at some needlework with my companion, Emily, as was my habit, in the parlour, the door opened, and my cousin Edward entered the room. There was something, I thought, odd in his manner, a kind of struggle between shame and impudence, a kind of flurry and ambiguity, which made him appear, if possible, more than ordinarily disagreeable.

"Your servant, ladies," he said, seating himself at the same time; "sorry to spoil your *tête-à-tête*; but never mind, I'll only take Emily's place for a minute or two, and then we part for a while, fair cousin. Emily, my father wants you in the corner turret; no shilly, shally, he's in a hurry." She hesitated. "Be off—tramp, march, I say," he exclaimed, in a tone which the poor girl dared not disobey.

She left the room, and Edward followed her to the door. He stood there for a minute or two, as if reflecting what he should say, perhaps satisfying himself that no one was within hearing in the hall. At length he turned about, having closed the door, as if carelessly, with his foot, and advancing slowly, in deep thought, he took his seat at the side of the table opposite to mine. There was a brief interval of silence, after which he said:—

"I imagine that you have a shrewd suspicion of the object of my early visit; but I suppose I must go into particulars. Must I?"

"I have no conception," I replied, "what your object may be."

"Well, well," said he becoming more at his ease as he proceeded, "it may be told in a few words. You know that it is totally impossible, quite out of the question, that an off-hand young fellow like me, and a good-looking girl like yourself, could meet continually as you and I have done, without an attachment—a liking growing up on one side or other; in short, I think I have let you know as plainly as if I spoke it, that I have been in love with you, almost from the first time I saw you." He paused, but I was too much horrified to speak. He interpreted my silence favourably. "I can tell you," he continued, "I'm reckoned rather hard to please, and very hard to *hit*. I can't say when I was taken with a girl before, so you see fortune reserved me—."

Here the odious wretch actually put his arm round my waist: the action at once restored me to utterance, and with the most indignant vehemence I released myself from his hold, and at the same time said:—

"I *have*, sir, of course, perceived your most disagreeable attentions; they have long been a source of great annoyance to me; and you must be aware that I have marked my disapprobation, my disgust, as unequivocally as I possibly could, without actual indelicacy."

I paused, almost out of breath from the rapidity with which I had spoken; and without giving him time to renew the conversation, I hastily quitted the room, leaving him in a paroxysm of rage and mortification. As I ascended the stairs, I heard him open the parlour-door with violence, and take two or three rapid strides in the direction in which I was moving. I was now much frightened, and ran the whole way until I reached my room, and having locked the door, I listened breathlessly, but heard no sound. This relieved me for the present; but so much had I been overcome by the agitation and annoyance attendant upon the scene which I had just passed through, that when my cousin Emily knocked at the door, I was weeping in great agitation. You will readily conceive my distress, when you reflect upon my strong dislike to my cousin Edward, combined with my youth and extreme inexperience. Any proposal of such a nature must have agitated me; but that it should come from the man whom, of all others, I instinctively most loathed and abhorred, and to whom I had, as clearly as manner could do it, expressed the state of my feelings, was almost too annoying to be borne; it was a calamity, too, in which I could not claim the sympathy of my cousin Emily, which had always been extended to me in my minor grievances. Still I hoped that it might not be unattended with good; for I thought that one inevitable and most welcome consequence would result from this painful *éclaircissement*, in the discontinuance of my cousin's odious persecution.

When I arose next morning, it was with the fervent hope that I might never again behold his face, or even hear his name; but such a consummation, though devoutedly to be wished, was hardly likely to occur. The painful impressions of yesterday were too vivid to be at once erased; and I could not help feeling some dim foreboding of coming annoyance and evil. To expect on my cousin's part anything like delicacy or consideration for me, was out of the question. I saw that he had set his heart upon my property, and that he was not likely easily to forego such a prize, possessing what might have been considered opportunities and facilities almost to compel my compliance. I now keenly felt the unreasonableness of my father's conduct in placing me to reside with a family, with all the members of which, with one exception, he was wholly unacquainted, and I bitterly felt the helplessness of my situation. I determined, however, in the event of my cousin's persevering in his addresses, to lay all the particulars before my uncle, although he had never, in kindness or intimacy, gone a step beyond our first interview, and to throw myself upon his hospitality and his sense of honour for protection against a repetition of such annoyances.

My cousin's conduct may appear to have been an inadequate cause for such serious uneasiness; but my alarm was awakened neither by his acts nor by words, but entirely by his manner, which was strange and even intimidating. At the beginning of our yesterday's interview, there was a sort of bullying swagger in his air, which, towards the end, gave place to something bordering upon the brutal vehemence of an undisguised ruffian, a transition which had tempted me into a belief that he might seek, even forcibly, to extort from me a consent to his wishes, or by means still more horrible, of which I scarcely dared to trust myself to think, to possess himself of my property.

I was early next day summoned to attend my uncle in his private room, which lay in a corner turret of the old building; and thither I accordingly went, wondering all the way what this unusual measure might prelude. When I entered the room, he did not rise in his usual courteous way to greet me, but simply pointed to a chair opposite to his own; this boded nothing agreeable. I sat down, however, silently waiting until he should open the conversation.

"Lady Margaret," at length he said, in a tone of greater sternness than I thought him capable of using, "I have hitherto spoken to you as a friend, but I have not forgotten that I am also your guardian, and that my authority as such gives me a right to controul your conduct. I shall put a question to you, and I expect and will demand a plain, direct answer. Have I rightly been informed that you have contemptuously rejected the suit and hand of my son Edward?"

I stammered forth with a good deal of trepidation:—

"I believe, that is, I have, sir, rejected my cousin's proposals; and my coldness and discouragement might have convinced him that I had determined to do so."

"Madame," replied he, with suppressed, but, as it appeared to me, intense anger, "I have lived long enough to know that *coldness and discouragement*, and such terms, form the common cant of a worthless coquette. You know to the full, as well as I, that *coldness and discouragement* may be so exhibited as to convince their object that he is neither distasteful nor indifferent to the person who wears that manner. You know, too, none better, that an affected neglect, when skillfully managed, is amongst the most formidable of the allurements which artful beauty can employ. I tell you, madame, that having, without one word spoken in discouragement, permitted my son's most marked attentions for a twelvemonth or more, you have no *right* to dismiss him with no further explanation than demurely telling him that you had always looked coldly upon him, and neither your wealth nor *your ladyship* (there was an emphasis of scorn on the word which would have become Sir Giles Overreach himself) can warrant you in treating with contempt the affectionate regard of an honest heart."

I was too much shocked at this undisguised attempt to bully me into an acquiescence in the interested and unprincipled plan for their own aggrandisement, which I now perceived my uncle and his son had deliberately formed, at once to find strength or collectedness to frame an answer to what he had said. At length I replied, with a firmness that surprised myself:—

"In all that you have just now said, sir, you have grossly misstated my conduct and motives. Your information must have been most incorrect, as far as it regards my conduct towards my cousin; my manner towards him could have conveyed nothing but dislike; and if anything could have added to the strong aversion which I have long felt towards him, it would be his attempting thus to frighten me into a marriage which he knows to be revolting to me, and which is sought by him only as a means for securing to himself whatever property is mine."

As I said this, I fixed my eyes upon those of my uncle, but he was too old in the world's ways to falter beneath the gaze of more searching eyes than mine; he simply said—

"Are you acquainted with the provisions of your father's will?"

I answered in the affirmative; and he continued:—"Then you must be aware that if my son Edward were, which God forbid, the unprincipled, reckless man, the ruffian you pretend to think him"—(here he spoke very slowly, as if he intended that every word which escaped him should be registered in my memory, while at the same time the expression of his countenance underwent a gradual but horrible change, and the eyes which he fixed upon me became so darkly vivid, that I almost lost sight of everything else)—"if he were what you have described him, do you think, child, he would have found no shorter way than marriage to gain his ends? A single blow, an outrage not a degree worse than you insinuate, would transfer your property to us!!"

I stood staring at him for many minutes after he had ceased to speak, fascinated by the terrible, serpent-like gaze, until he continued with a welcome change of countenance:—

"I will not speak again to you, upon this topic, until one month has passed. You shall have time to consider the relative advantages of the two courses which are open to you. I should be sorry to hurry you to a decision. I am satisfied with having stated my feelings upon the subject, and pointed out to you the path of duty. Remember this day month; not one word sooner."

He then rose, and I left the room, much agitated and exhausted.

This interview, all the circumstances attending it, but most particularly the formidable expression of my uncle's countenance while he talked, though hypothetically, of *murder*, combined to arouse all my worst suspicions of him. I dreaded to look upon the face that had so recently worn the appalling livery of guilt and malignity. I regarded it with the mingled fear and loathing with which one looks upon an object which has tortured them in a night-mare.

In a few days after the interview, the particulars of which I have just detailed, I found a note upon my toilet-table, and on opening it I read as follows:—

"*My Dear Lady Margaret,*

You will be, perhaps, surprised to see a strange face in your room today. I have dismissed your Irish maid, and secured a French one to wait upon you; a step rendered necessary by my proposing shortly to visit the Continent with all my family.

Your faithful guardian, "*ARTHUR TYRELL.*"

On inquiry, I found that my faithful attendant was actually gone, and far on her way to the town of Galway; and in her stead there appeared a tall, raw-boned, ill-looking, elderly Frenchwoman, whose sullen and presuming manners seemed to imply that her vocation had never before been that of a lady's-maid. I could not help regarding her as a creature of my uncle's, and therefore to be dreaded, even had she been in no other way suspicious.

Days and weeks passed away without any, even a momentary doubt upon my part, as to the course to be pursued by me. The allotted period had at length elapsed; the day arrived upon which I was to communicate my decision to my uncle. Although my resolution had never for a moment wavered, I could not shake off the dread of the approaching colloquy; and my heart sank within me as I heard the expected summons. I had not seen my cousin Edward since the occurrence of the grand *éclaircissement*; he must have studiously avoided me; I suppose from policy, it could not have been from delicacy. I was prepared for a terrific burst of fury from my uncle, as soon as I should make known my determination; and I not unreasonably feared that some act of violence or of intimidation would next be resorted to. Filled with these dreary forebodings, I fearfully opened the study door, and the next minute I stood in my uncle's presence. He received me with a courtesy which I dreaded, as arguing a favourable anticipation respecting the answer which I was to give; and after some slight delay he began by saying—

"It will be a relief to both of us, I believe, to bring this conversation as soon as possible to an issue. You will excuse me, then, my dear niece, for speaking with a bluntness which, under other circumstances, would be unpardonable. You have, I am certain, given the subject of our last interview fair and serious consideration; and I trust that you are now prepared with candour to lay your answer before me. A few words will suffice; we perfectly understand one another."

He paused; and I, though feeling that I stood upon a mine which might in an instant explode, nevertheless answered with perfect composure: "I must now, sir, make the same reply which I did upon the last occasion, and I reiterate the declaration which I then made, that I never can nor will, while life and reason remain, consent to a union with my cousin Edward."

This announcement wrought no apparent change in Sir Arthur, except that he became deadly, almost lividly pale. He seemed lost in dark thought for a minute, and then, with a slight effort, said, "You have answered me honestly and directly; and you say your resolution is unchangeable; well, would it had been otherwise—would it had been otherwise—but be it as it is; I am satisfied."

He gave me his hand—it was cold and damp as death; under an assumed calmness, it was evident that he was fearfully agitated. He continued to hold my hand with an almost painful pressure, while, as if unconsciously, seeming to forget my presence, he muttered, "Strange, strange, strange, indeed! fatuity, helpless fatuity!" there was here a long pause. "Madness *indeed* to strain a cable that is rotten to the very heart; it must break—and then—all goes." There was again a pause of some minutes, after which, suddenly changing his voice and manner to one of wakeful alacrity, he exclaimed,

"Margaret, my son Edward shall plague you no more. He leaves this country to-morrow for France; he shall speak no more upon this subject—never, never more; whatever events depended upon your answer must now take their own course; but as for this fruitless proposal, it has been tried enough; it can be repeated no more."

At these words he coldly suffered my hand to drop, as if to express his total abandonment of all his projected schemes of alliance; and certainly the action, with the accompanying words, produced upon my mind a more solemn and depressing effect than I believed possible to have been caused by the course which I had determined to pursue; it struck upon my heart with an awe and heaviness which *will* accompany the accomplishment of an important and irrevocable act, even though no doubt or scruple remains to make it possible that the agent should wish it undone.

"Well," said my uncle, after a little time, "we now cease to speak upon this topic, never to resume it again. Remember you shall have no farther uneasiness from Edward; he leaves Ireland for France to-morrow; this will be a relief to you; may I depend upon your *honour* that no word touching the subject of this interview shall ever escape you?" I gave him the desired assurance; he said, "It is well; I am satisfied; we have nothing more, I believe, to say upon either side, and my presence must be a restraint upon you, I shall therefore bid you farewell." I then left the apartment, scarcely knowing what to think of the strange interview which had just taken place.

On the next day my uncle took occasion to tell me that Edward had actually sailed, if his intention had not been prevented by adverse winds or weather; and two days after he actually produced a letter from his son, written, as it said, *on board*, and despatched while the ship was getting under weigh. This was a great satisfaction to me, and as being likely to prove so, it was no doubt communicated to me by Sir Arthur.

During all this trying period I had found infinite consolation in the society and sympathy of my dear cousin Emily. I never, in after-life, formed a friendship so close, so fervent, and upon which, in all its progress, I could look back with feelings of such unalloyed pleasure, upon whose termination I must ever dwell with so deep, so yet unembittered a sorrow. In cheerful converse with her I soon recovered my spirits considerably, and passed my time agreeably enough, although still in the utmost seclusion. Matters went on smoothly enough, although I could not help sometimes feeling a momentary, but horrible uncertainty respecting my uncle's character; which was not altogether unwarranted by the circumstances of the two trying interviews, the particulars of which I have just detailed. The unpleasant impression which these conferences were calculated to leave upon my mind was fast wearing away, when there occurred a circumstance, slight indeed in itself, but calculated irrepressibly to awaken all my worst suspicions, and to overwhelm me again with anxiety and terror.

I had one day left the house with my cousin Emily, in order to take a ramble of considerable length, for the purpose of sketching some favourite views, and we had walked about half a mile when I perceived that we had forgotten our drawing materials, the absence of which would have defeated the object of our walk. Laughing at our own thoughtlessness, we returned to the house, and leaving Emily outside, I ran upstairs to procure the drawing-books and pencils which lay in my bed-room. As I ran up the stairs, I was met by the tall, ill-looking Frenchwoman, evidently a good deal flurried; "Que veut Madame?" said she, with a more decided effort to be polite, than I had ever known her make before. "No, no—no matter," said I, hastily running by her in the direction of my room. "Madame," cried she, in a high key, "restez ici s'il vous plaît, votre chambre n'est pas faite." I continued to move on without heeding her. She was some way behind me, and feeling that she could not otherwise prevent my entrance, for I was now upon the very lobby, she made a desperate attempt to seize hold of my person; she succeeded in grasping the end of my shawl, which she drew from my shoulders, but slipping at the same time upon the polished oak floor, she fell at full length upon the boards. A little frightened as well as angry at the rudeness of this strange woman, I hastily pushed open the door of my room, at which I now stood, in order to escape from her; but great was my amazement on entering to find the apartment preoccupied. The window was open, and beside it stood two male figures; they appeared to be examining the fastenings of the casement, and their backs were turned towards the door. One of them was my uncle; they both had turned on my entrance, as if startled; the stranger was booted and cloaked, and wore a heavy, broad-leafed hat over his brows; he turned but for a moment, and averted his face; but I had seen enough to convince me that he was no other than my cousin Edward. My uncle had some iron instrument in his hand, which he hastily concealed behind his back; and coming towards me, said something as if in an explanatory tone; but I was too much shocked and confounded to understand what it might be. He said something about "*repairs*—window-frames—cold, and safety." I did not wait, however, to ask or to receive explanations, but hastily left the room. As I went down stairs I thought I heard the voice of the Frenchwoman in all the shrill volubility of excuse, and others uttering suppressed but vehement imprecations, or what seemed to me to be such.

I joined my cousin Emily quite out of breath. I need not say that my head was too full of other things to think much of drawing for that day. I imparted to her frankly the cause of my alarms, but, at the same time, as gently as I could; and with tears she promised vigilance, devotion, and love. I never had reason for a moment to repent the unreserved confidence which I then reposed in her. She was no less surprised than I at the unexpected appearance of Edward, whose departure for France neither of us had for a moment doubted, but which was now proved by his actual presence to be nothing more than an imposture practised, I feared, for no good end. The situation in which I had found my uncle had very nearly removed all my doubts as to his designs; I magnified suspicions into certainties, and dreaded night after night that I should be murdered in my bed. The nervousness produced by sleepless nights and days of anxious fears increased the horrors of my situation to such a degree, that I at length wrote a letter to a Mr. Jefferies, an old and faithful friend of my father's, and perfectly acquainted with all his affairs, praying him, for God's sake, to relieve me from my present terrible situation, and communicating without reserve the nature and grounds of my suspicions. This letter I kept sealed and directed for two or three days always about my person, for discovery would have been ruinous, in expectation of an opportunity, which might be safely trusted, of having it placed in the post-office; as neither Emily nor I were permitted to pass beyond the precincts of the demesne itself, which was surrounded by high walls formed of dry stone, the difficulty of procuring such an opportunity was greatly enhanced.

At this time Emily had a short conversation with her father, which she reported to me instantly. After some indifferent matter, he had asked her whether she and I were upon good terms, and whether I was unreserved in my disposition. She answered in the affirmative; and he then inquired whether I had been much surprised to find him in my chamber on the other day. She answered that I had been both surprised and amused. "And what did she think of George Wilson's appearance?" "Who?" inquired she. "Oh! the architect," he answered, "who is to contract for the repairs of the house; he is accounted a handsome fellow." "She could not see his face," said Emily, "and she was in such a hurry to escape that she scarcely observed him." Sir Arthur appeared satisfied, and the conversation ended.

This slight conversation, repeated accurately to me by Emily, had the effect of confirming, if indeed any thing was required to do so, all that I had before believed as to Edward's actual presence; and I naturally became, if possible, more anxious than ever to despatch the letter to Mr. Jefferies. An opportunity at length occurred. As Emily and I were walking one day near the gate of the demesne, a lad from the village happened to be passing down the avenue from the house; the spot was secluded, and as this person was not connected by service with those whose observation I dreaded, I committed the letter to his keeping, with strict injunctions that he should put it, without delay, into the receiver of the town post-office; at the same time I added a suitable gratuity, and the man having made many protestations of punctuality, was soon out of sight. He was hardly gone when I began to doubt my discretion in having trusted him; but I had no better or safer means of despatching the letter, and I was not warranted in suspecting him of such wanton dishonesty as a disposition to tamper with it; but I could not be quite satisfied of its safety until I had received an answer, which could not arrive for a few days. Before I did, however, an event occurred which a little surprised me. I was sitting in my bed-room early in the day, reading by myself, when I heard a knock at the door. "Come in," said I, and my uncle entered the room. "Will you excuse me," said he, "I sought you in the parlour, and thence I have come here. I desired to say a word to you. I trust that you have hitherto found my conduct to you such as that of a guardian towards his ward should be." I dared not withhold my assent. "And," he continued, "I trust that you have not found me harsh or unjust, and that you have perceived, my dear niece, that I have sought to make this poor place as agreeable to you as may be?" I assented again; and he put his hand in his pocket, whence he drew a folded paper, and dashing it upon the table with startling emphasis he said, "Did you write that letter?" The sudden and fearful alteration of his voice, manner, and face, but more than all, the unexpected production of my letter to Mr. Jefferies, which I at once recognised, so confounded and terrified me, that I felt almost choking. I could not utter a word. "Did you write that letter?" he repeated, with slow and intense emphasis. "You did, liar and hypocrite. You dared to write that foul and infamous libel; but it shall be your last. Men will universally believe you mad, if I choose to call for an inquiry. I can make you appear so. The suspicions expressed in this letter are the hallucinations and alarms of a moping lunatic. I have defeated your first attempt, madam; and by the holy God, if ever you make another, chains, darkness, and the keeper's whip shall be your portion." With these astounding words he left the room, leaving me almost fainting.

I was now almost reduced to despair; my last cast had failed; I had no course left but that of escaping secretly from the castle, and placing myself under the protection of the nearest magistrate. I felt if this were not done, and speedily, that I should be *murdered*. No one, from mere description, can have an idea of the unmitigated horror of my situation; a helpless, weak, inexperienced girl, placed under the power, and wholly at the mercy of evil men, and feeling that I had it not in my power to escape for one moment from the malignant influences under which I was probably doomed to fall; with a consciousness, too, that if violence, if murder were designed, no human being would be near to aid me; my dying shriek would be lost in void space.

I had seen Edward but once during his visit, and as I did not meet him again, I began to think that he must have taken his departure; a conviction which was to a certain degree satisfactory, as I regarded his absence as indicating the removal of immediate danger. Emily also arrived circuitously at the same conclusion, and not without good grounds, for she managed indirectly to learn that Edward's black horse had actually been for a day and part of a night in the castle stables, just at the time of her brother's supposed visit. The horse had gone, and as she argued, the rider must have departed with it.

This point being so far settled, I felt a little less uncomfortable; when being one day alone in my bed-room, I happened to look out from the window, and to my unutterable horror, I beheld peering through an opposite casement, my cousin Edward's face. Had I seen the evil one himself in bodily shape, I could not have experienced a more sickening revulsion. I was too much appalled to move at once from the window, but I did so soon enough to avoid his eye. He was looking fixedly down into the narrow quadrangle upon which the window opened. I shrunk back unperceived, to pass the rest of the day in terror and despair. I went to my room early that night, but I was too miserable to sleep.

At about twelve o'clock, feeling very nervous, I determined to call my cousin Emily, who slept, you will remember, in the next room, which communicated with mine by a second door. By this private entrance I found my way into her chamber, and without difficulty persuaded her to return to my room and sleep with me. We accordingly lay down together, she undressed, and I with my clothes on, for I was every moment walking up and down the room, and felt too nervous and miserable to think of rest or comfort. Emily was soon fast asleep, and I lay awake, fervently longing for the first pale gleam of morning, and reckoning every stroke of the old clock with an impatience which made every hour appear like six.

It must have been about one o'clock when I thought I heard a slight noise at the partition door between Emily's room and mine, as if caused by somebody's turning the key in the lock. I held my breath, and the same sound was repeated at the second door of my room, that which opened upon the lobby; the sound was here distinctly caused by the revolution of the bolt in the lock, and it was followed by a slight pressure upon the door itself, as if to ascertain the security of the lock. The person, whoever it might be, was probably satisfied, for I heard the old boards of the lobby creak and strain, as if under the weight of somebody moving cautiously over them. My sense of hearing became unnaturally, almost painfully acute. I suppose the imagination added distinctness to sounds vague in themselves. I thought that I could actually hear the breathing of the person who was slowly returning along the lobby.

At the head of the stair-case there appeared to occur a pause; and I could distinctly hear two or three sentences hastily whispered; the steps then descended the stairs with apparently less caution. I ventured to walk quickly and lightly to the lobby door, and attempted to open it; it was indeed fast locked upon the outside, as was also the other. I now felt that the dreadful hour was come; but one desperate expedient remained—it was to awaken Emily, and by our united strength, to attempt to force the partition door, which was slighter than the other, and through this to pass to the lower part of the house, whence it might be possible to escape to the grounds, and so to the village. I returned to the bedside, and shook Emily, but in vain; nothing that I could do availed to produce from her more than a few incoherent words; it was a death-like sleep. She had certainly drunk of some narcotic, as, probably, had I also, in spite of all the caution with which I had examined every thing presented to us to eat or drink. I now attempted, with as little noise as possible, to force first one door, then the other; but all in vain. I believe no strength could have affected my object, for both doors opened inwards. I therefore collected whatever moveables I could carry thither, and piled them against the doors, so as to assist me in whatever attempts I should make to resist the entrance of those without. I then returned to the bed and endeavoured again, but fruitlessly, to awaken my cousin. It was not sleep, it was torpor, lethargy, death. I knelt down and prayed with an agony of earnestness; and then seating myself upon the bed, I awaited my fate with a kind of terrible tranquillity.

I heard a faint clanking sound from the narrow court which I have already mentioned, as if caused by the scraping of some iron instrument against stones or rubbish. I at first determined not to disturb the calmness which I now experienced, by uselessly watching the proceedings of those who sought my life; but as the sounds continued, the horrible curiosity which I felt overcame every other emotion, and I determined, at all hazards, to gratify it. I, therefore, crawled upon my knees to the window, so as to let the smallest possible portion of my head appear above the sill.

The moon was shining with an uncertain radiance upon the antique grey buildings, and obliquely upon the narrow court beneath; one side of it was therefore clearly illuminated, while the other was lost in obscurity, the sharp outlines of the old gables, with their nodding clusters of ivy, being at first alone visible. Whoever or whatever occasioned the noise which had excited my curiosity, was concealed under the shadow of the dark side of the quadrangle. I placed my hand over my eyes to shade them from the moonlight, which was so bright as to be almost dazzling, and, peering into the darkness, I first dimly, but afterwards gradually, almost with full distinctness, beheld the form of a man engaged in digging what appeared to be a rude hole close under the wall. Some implements, probably a shovel and pickaxe, lay beside him, and to these he every now and then applied himself as the nature of the ground required. He pursued his task rapidly, and with as little noise as possible. "So," thought I, as shovelful after shovelful, the dislodged rubbish mounted into a heap, "they are digging the grave in which, before two hours pass, I must lie, a cold, mangled corpse. I am *theirs*—I cannot escape." I felt as if my reason was leaving me. I started to my feet, and in mere despair I applied myself again to each of the two doors alternately. I strained every nerve and sinew, but I might as well have attempted, with my single strength, to force the building itself from its foundations. I threw myself madly upon the ground, and clasped my hands over my eyes as if to shut out the horrible images which crowded upon me.

The paroxysm passed away. I prayed once more with the bitter, agonised fervour of one who feels that the hour of death is present and inevitable. When I arose, I went once more to the window and looked out, just in time to see a shadowy figure glide stealthily along the wall. The task was finished. The catastrophe of the tragedy must soon be accomplished. I determined now to defend my life to the last; and that I might be able to do so with some effect, I searched the room for something which might serve as a weapon; but either through accident, or else in anticipation of such a possibility, every thing which might have been made available for such a purpose had been removed.

I must then die tamely and without an effort to defend myself. A thought suddenly struck me; might it not be possible to escape through the door, which the assassin must open in order to enter the room? I resolved to make the attempt. I felt assured that the door through which ingress to the room would be effected was that which opened upon the lobby. It was the more direct way, besides being, for obvious reasons, less liable to interruption than the other. I resolved, then, to place myself behind a projection of the wall, the shadow would serve fully to conceal me, and when the door should be opened, and before they should have discovered the identity of the occupant of the bed, to creep noiselessly from the room, and then to trust to Providence for escape. In order to facilitate this scheme, I removed all the lumber which I had heaped against the door; and I had nearly completed my arrangements, when I perceived the room suddenly darkened, by the close approach of some shadowy object to the window. On turning my eyes in that direction, I observed at the top of the casement, as if suspended from above, first the feet, then the legs, then the body, and at length the whole figure of a man present itself. It was Edward Tyrrell. He appeared to be guiding his descent so as to bring his feet upon the centre of the stone block which occupied the lower part of the window; and having secured his footing upon this, he kneeled down and began to gaze into the room. As the moon was gleaming into the chamber, and the bed-curtains were drawn, he was able to distinguish the bed itself and its contents. He appeared satisfied with his scrutiny, for he looked up and made a sign with his hand. He then applied his hands to the window-frame, which must have been ingeniously contrived for the purpose, for with apparently no resistance the whole frame, containing casement and all, slipped from its position in the wall, and was by him lowered into the room. The cold night wind waved the bed-curtains, and he paused for a moment; all was still again, and he stepped in upon the floor of the room. He held in his hand what appeared to be a steel instrument, shaped something like a long hammer. This he held rather behind him, while, with three long, *tip-toe* strides, he brought himself to the bedside. I felt that the discovery must now be made, and held my breath in momentary expectation of the execration in which he would vent his surprise and disappointment. I closed my eyes; there was a pause, but it was a short one. I heard two dull blows, given in rapid succession; a quivering sigh, and the long-drawn, heavy breathing of the sleeper was for ever suspended. I unclosed my eyes, and saw the murderer fling the quilt across the head of his victim; he then, with the instrument of death still in his hand, proceeded to the lobby-door, upon which he tapped sharply twice or thrice. A quick step was then heard approaching, and a voice whispered something from without. Edward answered, with a kind of shuddering chuckle, "Her ladyship is past complaining; unlock the door, in the devil's name, unless you're afraid to come in, and help me to lift her out of the window." The key was turned in the lock, the door opened, and my uncle entered the room. I have told you already that I had placed myself under the shade of a projection of the wall, close to the door. I had instinctively shrunk down cowering towards the ground on the entrance of Edward through the window. When my uncle entered the room, he and his son both stood so very close to me that his hand was every moment upon the point of touching my face. I held my breath, and remained motionless as death.

"You had no interruption from the next room?" said my uncle.

"No," was the brief reply.

"Secure the jewels, Ned; the French harpy must not lay her claws upon them. You're a steady hand, by G—d; not much blood—eh?"

"Not twenty drops," replied his son, "and those on the quilt."

"I'm glad it's over," whispered my uncle again; "we must lift the—the *thing* through the window, and lay the rubbish over it."

They then turned to the bedside, and, winding the bed-clothes round the body, carried it between them slowly to the window, and exchanging a few brief words with some one below, they shoved it over the window-sill, and I heard it fall heavily on the ground underneath.

"I'll take the jewels," said my uncle; "there are two caskets in the lower drawer."

He proceeded, with an accuracy which, had I been more at ease, would have furnished me with matter of astonishment, to lay his hand upon the very spot where my jewels lay; and having possessed himself of them, he called to his son:—

"Is the rope made fast above?"

"I'm no fool; to be sure it is," replied he.

They then lowered themselves from the window; and I rose lightly and cautiously, scarcely daring to breathe, from my place of concealment, and was creeping towards the door, when I heard my uncle's voice, in a sharp whisper, exclaim, "Get up again; G—d d—n you, you've forgot to lock the room door"; and I perceived, by the straining of the rope which hung from above, that the mandate was instantly obeyed. Not a second was to be lost. I passed through the door, which was only closed, and moved as rapidly as I could, consistently with stillness, along the lobby. Before I had gone many yards, I heard the door through which I had just passed roughly locked on the inside. I glided down the stairs in terror, lest, at every corner, I should meet the murderer or one of his accomplices. I reached the hall, and listened, for a moment, to ascertain whether all was silent around. No sound was audible; the parlour windows opened on the park, and through one of them I might, I thought, easily effect my escape. Accordingly, I hastily entered; but, to my consternation, a candle was burning in the room, and by its light I saw a figure seated at the dinner-table, upon which lay glasses, bottles, and the other accompaniments of a drinking party. Two or three chairs were placed about the table, irregularly, as if hastily abandoned by their occupants. A single glance satisfied me that the figure was that of my French attendant. She was fast asleep, having, probably, drank deeply. There was something malignant and ghastly in the calmness of this bad woman's features, dimly illuminated as they were by the flickering blaze of the candle. A knife lay upon the table, and the terrible thought struck me—"Should I kill this sleeping accomplice in the guilt of the murderer, and thus secure my retreat?" Nothing could be easier; it was but to draw the blade across her throat, the work of a second.

An instant's pause, however, corrected me. "No," thought I, "the God who has conducted me thus far through the valley of the shadow of death, will not abandon me now. I will fall into their hands, or I will escape hence, but it shall be free from the stain of blood; His will be done." I felt a confidence arising from this reflection, an assurance of protection which I cannot describe. There were no other means of escape, so I advanced, with a firm step and collected mind, to the window. I noiselessly withdrew the bars, and unclosed the shutters; I pushed open the casement, and without waiting to look behind me, I ran with my utmost speed, scarcely feeling the ground beneath me, down the avenue, taking care to keep upon the grass which bordered it. I did not for a moment slacken my speed, and I had now gained the central point between the park-gate and the mansion-house. Here the avenue made a wider circuit, and in order to avoid delay, I directed my way across the smooth sward round which the carriageway wound, intending, at the opposite side of the level, at a point which I distinguished by a group of old birch trees, to enter again upon the beaten track, which was from thence tolerably direct to the gate. I had, with my utmost speed, got about half way across this broad flat, when the rapid tramp of a horse's hoofs struck upon my ear. My heart swelled in my bosom, as though I would smother. The clattering of galloping hoofs approached; I was pursued, they were now upon the sward on which I was running; there was not a bush or a bramble to shelter me; and, as if to render escape altogether desperate, the moon, which had hitherto been obscured, at this moment shone forth with a broad, clear light, which made every object distinctly visible. The sounds were now close behind me. I felt my knees bending under me, with the sensation which unnerves one in a dream. I reeled, I stumbled, I fell; and at the same instant the cause of my alarm wheeled past me at full gallop. It was one of the young fillies which pastured loose about the park, whose frolics had thus all but maddened me with terror. I scrambled to my feet, and rushed on with weak but rapid steps, my sportive companion still galloping round and round me with many a frisk and fling, until, at length, more dead than alive, I reached the avenue-gate, and crossed the stile, I scarce knew how. I ran through the village, in which all was silent as the grave, until my progress was arrested by the hoarse voice of a sentinel, who cried "Who goes there?" I felt that I was now safe. I turned in the direction of the voice, and fell fainting at the soldier's feet. When I came to myself, I was sitting in a miserable hovel, surrounded by strange faces, all bespeaking curiosity and compassion. Many soldiers were in it also; indeed, as I afterwards found, it was employed as a guard-room by a detachment of troops quartered for that night in the town. In a few words I informed their officer of the circumstances which had occurred, describing also the appearance of the persons engaged in the murder; and he, without further loss of time than was necessary to procure the attendance of a magistrate, proceeded to the mansion-house of Carrickleigh, taking with him a party of his men. But the villains had discovered their mistake, and had effected their escape before the arrival of the military.

The Frenchwoman was, however, arrested in the neighbourhood upon the next day. She was tried and condemned at the ensuing assizes; and previous to her execution confessed that "*she had a hand in making Hugh Tisdall's bed.*" She had been a housekeeper in the castle at the time, and a *chère amie* of my uncle's. She was, in reality, able to speak English like a native, but had exclusively used the French language, I suppose to facilitate her designs. She died the same hardened wretch she had lived, confessing her crimes only, as she alleged, that her doing so might involve Sir Arthur Tyrrell, the great author of her guilt and misery, and whom she now regarded with unmitigated detestation.

With the particulars of Sir Arthur's and his son's escape, as far as they are known, you are acquainted. You are also in possession of their after fate; the terrible, the tremendous retribution which, after long delays of many years, finally overtook and crushed them. Wonderful and inscrutable are the dealings of God with his creatures!

Deep and fervent as must always be my gratitude to heaven for my deliverance, effected by a chain of providential occurrences, the failing of a single link of which must have ensured my destruction, it was long before I could look back upon it with other feelings than those of bitterness, almost of agony. The only being that had ever really loved me, my nearest and dearest friend, ever ready to sympathise, to counsel, and to assist; the gayest, the gentlest, the warmest heart; the only creature on earth that cared for me; *her* life had been the price of my deliverance; and I then uttered the wish, which no event of my long and sorrowful life has taught me to recall, that she had been spared, and that, in her stead, *I* were mouldering in the grave, forgotten, and at rest.

MADAM CROWL'S GHOST

MADAM CROWL'S GHOST

Twenty years have passed since you last saw Mrs. Jolliffe's tall slim figure. She is now past seventy, and can't have many mile-stones more to count on the journey that will bring her to her long home. The hair has grown white as snow, that is parted under her cap, over her shrewd, but kindly face. But her figure is still straight, and her step light and active.

She has taken of late years to the care of adult invalids, having surrendered to younger hands the little people who inhabit cradles, and crawl on all-fours. Those who remember that good-natured face among the earliest that emerge from the darkness of non-entity, and who owe to their first lessons in the accomplishment of walking, and a delighted appreciation of their first babblings and earliest teeth, have "spired up" into tall lads and lasses, now. Some of them shew streaks of white by this time, in brown locks, "the bonny gouden" hair, that she was so proud to brush and shew to admiring mothers, who are seen no more on the green of Golden Friars, and whose names are traced now on the flat grey stones in the church-yard.

So the time is ripening some, and searing others; and the saddening and tender sunset hour has come; and it is evening with the kind old north-country dame, who nursed pretty Laura Mildmay, who now stepping into the room, smiles so gladly, and throws her arms round the old woman's neck, and kisses her twice.

"Now, this is so lucky!" said Mrs. Jenner, "you have just come in time to hear a story."

"Really! That's delightful."

"Na, na, od wite it! no story, ouer true for that, I sid it a wi my aan eyen. But the barn here, would not like, at these hours, just goin' to her bed, to hear tell of freets and boggarts."

"Ghosts? The very thing of all others I should most likely to hear of."

"Well, dear," said Mrs. Jenner, "if you are not afraid, sit ye down here, with us."

"She was just going to tell me all about her first engagement to attend a dying old woman," says Mrs. Jenner, "and of the ghost she saw there. Now, Mrs. Jolliffe, make your tea first, and then begin."

The good woman obeyed, and having prepared a cup of that companionable nectar, she sipped a little, drew her brows slightly together to collect her thoughts, and then looked up with a wondrous solemn face to begin.

Good Mrs. Jenner, and the pretty girl, each gazed with eyes of solemn expectation in the face of the old woman, who seemed to gather awe from the recollections she was summoning.

The old room was a good scene for such a narrative, with the oak-wainscoting, quaint, and clumsy furniture, the heavy beams that crossed its ceiling, and the tall four-post bed, with dark curtains, within which you might imagine what shadows you please.

Mrs. Jolliffe cleared her voice, rolled her eyes slowly round, and began her tale in these words:—

MADAM CROWL'S GHOST

"I'm an ald woman now, and I was but thirteen, my last birthday, the night I came to Applewale House. My aunt was the housekeeper there, and a sort o' one-horse carriage was down at Lexhoe waitin' to take me and my box up to Applewale.

"I was a bit frightened by the time I got to Lexhoe, and when I saw the carriage and horse, I wished myself back again with my mother at Hazelden. I was crying when I got into the 'shay'—that's what we used to call it—and old John Mulbery that drove it, and was a good-natured fellow, bought me a handful of apples at the Golden Lion to cheer me up a bit; and he told me that there was a currant-cake, and tea, and pork-chops, waiting for me, all hot, in my aunt's room at the great house. It was a fine moonlight night, and I eat the apples, lookin' out o' the shay winda.

"It's a shame for gentlemen to frighten a poor foolish child like I was. I sometimes think it might be tricks. There was two on 'em on the tap o' the coach beside me. And they began to question me after nightfall, when the moon rose, where I was going to. Well, I told them it was to wait on Dame Arabella Crowl, of Applewale House, near by Lexhoe.

"'Ho, then,' says one of them, 'you'll not be long there!'

"And I looked at him as much as to say 'Why not?' for I had spoken out when I told them where I was goin', as if 'twas something clever I hed to say.

"'Because,' says he, 'and don't you for your life tell no one, only watch her and see—she's possessed by the devil, and more an half a ghost. Have you got a Bible?'

"'Yes, sir,' says I. For my mother put my little Bible in my box, and I knew it was there: and by the same token, though the print's too small for my ald eyes, I have it in my press to this hour.

"As I looked up at him saying 'Yes, sir,' I thought I saw him winkin' at his friend; but I could not be sure.

"'Well,' says he, 'be sure you put it under your bolster every night, it will keep the ald girl's claws aff ye.'

"And I got such a fright when he said that, you wouldn't fancy! And I'd a liked to ask him a lot about the ald lady, but I was too shy, and he and his friend began talkin' together about their own consarns, and dowly enough I got down, as I told ye, at Lexhoe. My heart sank as I drove into the dark avenue. The trees stand very thick and big, as ald as the ald house almost, and four people, with their arms out and finger-tips touchin', barely girds round some of them.

"Well my neck was stretched out o' the winda, looking for the first view o' the great house; and all at once we pulled up in front of it.

"A great white-and-black house it is, wi' great black beams across and right up it, and gables lookin' out, as white as a sheet, to the moon, and the shadows o' the trees, two or three up and down in front, you could count the leaves on them, and all the little diamond-shaped winda-panes, glimmering on the great hall winda, and great shutters, in the old fashion, hinged on the wall outside, boulted across all the rest o' the windas in front, for there was but three or four servants, and the old lady in the house, and most o' t' rooms was locked up.

"My heart was in my mouth when I sid the journey was over, and this the great house afoore me, and I sa near my aunt that I never sid till noo, and Dame Crowl, that I was come to wait upon, and was afeard on already.

"My aunt kissed me in the hall, and brought me to her room. She was tall and thin, wi' a pale face and black eyes, and long thin hands wi' black mittins on. She was past fifty, and her word was short; but her word was law. I hev no complaints to make of her; but she was a hard woman, and I think she would hev bin kinder to me if I had bin her sister's child in place of her brother's. But all that's o' no consequence noo.

"The squire—his name was Mr. Chevenix Crowl, he was Dame Crowl's grandson—came down there, by way of seeing that the old lady was well treated, about twice or thrice in the year. I sid him but twice all the time I was at Applewale House.

"I can't say but she was well taken care of, notwithstanding; but that was because my aunt and Meg Wyvern, that was her maid, had a conscience, and did their duty by her.

"Mrs. Wyvern—Meg Wyvern my aunt called her to herself, and Mrs. Wyvern to me—was a fat, jolly lass of fifty, a good height and a good breadth, always good-humoured and walked slow. She had fine wages, but she was a bit stingy, and kept all her fine clothes under lock and key, and wore, mostly, a twilled chocolate cotton, wi' red, and yellow, and green sprigs and balls on it, and it lasted wonderful.

"She never gave me nout, not the vally o' a brass thimble, all the time I was there; but she was good-humoured, and always laughin', and she talked no end o' proas over her tea; and, seeing me sa sackless and dowly, she roused me up wi' her laughin' and stories; and I think I liked her better than my aunt—children is so taken wi' a bit o' fun or a story—though my aunt was very good to me, but a hard woman about some things, and silent always.

"My aunt took me into her bed-chamber, that I might rest myself a bit while she was settin' the tea in her room. But first, she patted me on the shouther, and said I was a tall lass o' my years, and had spired up well, and asked me if I could do plain work and stitchin'; and she looked in my face, and said I was like my father, her brother, that was dead and gone, and she hoped I was a better Christian, and wad na du a' that lids (would not do anything of that sort).

"It was a hard sayin' the first time I set foot in her room, I thought.

"When I went into the next room, the housekeeper's room—very comfortable, yak (oak) all round—there was a fine fire blazin' away, wi' coal, and peat, and wood, all in a low together, and tea on the table, and hot cake, and smokin' meat; and there was Mrs. Wyvern, fat, jolly, and talkin' away, more in an hour than my aunt would in a year.

"While I was still at my tea my aunt went up-stairs to see Madam Crowl.

"'She's agone up to see that old Judith Squailes is awake,' says Mrs. Wyvern. 'Judith sits with Madam Crowl when me and Mrs. Shutters'—that was my aunt's name—'is away. She's a troublesome old lady. Ye'll hev to be sharp wi' her, or she'll be into the fire, or out o' t' winda. She goes on wires, she does, old though she be.'

"'How old, ma'am?' says I.

"'Ninety-three her last birthday, and that's eight months gone,' says she; and she laughed. 'And don't be askin' questions about her before your aunt—mind, I tell ye; just take her as you find her, and that's all.'

"'And what's to be my business about her, please, ma'am?' says I.

"'About the old lady? Well,' says she, 'your aunt, Mrs. Shutters, will tell you that; but I suppose you'll hev to sit in the room with your work, and see she's at no mischief, and let her amuse herself with her things on the table, and get her her food or drink as she calls for it, and keep her out o' mischief, and ring the bell hard if she's troublesome.'

"'Is she deaf, ma'am?'

"'No, nor blind,' says she; 'as sharp as a needle, but she's gone quite aupy, and can't remember nout rightly; and Jack the Giant Killer, or Goody Twoshoes will please her as well as the king's court, or the affairs of the nation.'

"'And what did the little girl go away for, ma'am, that went on Friday last? My aunt wrote to my mother she was to go.'

"'Yes; she's gone.'

"'What for?' says I again.

"'She didn't answer Mrs. Shutters, I do suppose,' says she. 'I don't know. Don't be talkin'; your aunt can't abide a talkin' child.'

"'And please, ma'am, is the old lady well in health?' says I.

"'It ain't no harm to ask that,' says she. 'She's torflin a bit lately, but better this week past, and I dare say she'll last out her hundred years yet. Hish! Here's your aunt coming down the passage.'

"In comes my aunt, and begins talkin' to Mrs. Wyvern, and I, beginnin' to feel more comfortable and at home like, was walkin' about the room lookin' at this thing and at that. There was pretty old china things on the cupboard, and pictures again the wall; and there was a door open in the wainscot, and I sees a queer old leathern jacket, wi' straps and buckles to it, and sleeves as long as the bed-post hangin' up inside.

"'What's that you're at, child?' says my aunt, sharp enough, turning about when I thought she least minded. 'What's that in your hand?'

"'This, ma'am?' says I, turning about with the leathern jacket. 'I don't know what it is, ma'am.'

"Pale as she was, the red came up in her cheeks, and her eyes flashed wi' anger, and I think only she had half a dozen steps to take, between her and me, she'd a gev me a sizzup. But she did gie me a shake by the shouther, and she plucked the thing out o' my hand, and says she, 'While ever you stay here, don't ye meddle wi' nout that don't belong to ye', and she hung it up on the pin that was there, and shut the door wi' a bang and locked it fast.

"Mrs. Wyvern was liftin' up her hands and laughin' all this time, quietly, in her chair, rolling herself a bit in it, as she used when she was kinkin'.

"The tears was in my eyes, and she winked at my aunt, and says she, dryin' her own eyes that was wet wi' the laughin', 'Tut, the child meant no harm—come here to me, child. It's only a pair o' crutches for lame ducks, and ask us no questions mind, and we'll tell ye no lies; and come here and sit down, and drink a mug o' beer before ye go to your bed.'

"My room, mind ye, was upstairs, next to the old lady's, and Mrs. Wyvern's bed was near hers in her room, and I was to be ready at call, if need should be.

"The old lady was in one of her tantrums that night and part of the day before. She used to take fits o' the sulks. Sometimes she would not let them dress her, and at other times she would not let them take her clothes off. She was a great beauty, they said, in her day. But there was no one about Applewale that remembered her in her prime. And she was dreadful fond o' dress, and had thick silks, and stiff satins, and velvets, and laces, and all sorts, enough to set up seven shops at the least. All her dresses was old-fashioned and queer, but worth a fortune.

"Well, I went to my bed. I lay for a while awake; for a' things was new to me; and I think the tea was in my nerves, too, for I wasn't used to it, except now and then on a holiday, or the like. And I heard Mrs. Wyvern talkin', and I listened with my hand to my ear; but I could not hear Mrs. Crowl, and I don't think she said a word.

"There was great care took of her. The people at Applewale knew that when she died they would every one get the sack; and their situations was well paid and easy.

"The doctor came twice a week to see the old lady, and you may be sure they all did as he bid them. One thing was the same every time; they were never to cross or frump her, any way, but to humour and please her in everything.

"So she lay in her clothes all that night, and next day, not a word she said, and I was at my needlework all that day, in my own room, except when I went down to my dinner.

"I would a liked to see the ald lady, and even to hear her speak. But she might as well a' bin in Lunnon a' the time for me.

"When I had my dinner my aunt sent me out for a walk for an hour. I was glad when I came back, the trees was so big, and the place so dark and lonesome, and 'twas a cloudy day, and I cried a deal, thinkin' of home, while I was walkin' alone there. That evening, the candles bein' alight, I was sittin' in my room, and the door was open into Madam Crowl's chamber, where my aunt was. It was, then, for the first time I heard what I suppose was the ald lady talking.

"It was a queer noise like, I couldn't well say which, a bird, or a beast, only it had a bleatin' sound in it, and was very small.

"I pricked my ears to hear all I could. But I could not make out one word she said. And my aunt answered:

"'The evil one can't hurt no one, ma'am, bout the Lord permits.'

"Then the same queer voice from the bed says something more that I couldn't make head nor tail on.

"And my aunt med answer again: 'Let them pull faces, ma'am, and say what they will; if the Lord be for us, who can be against us?'

"I kept listenin' with my ear turned to the door, holdin' my breath, but not another word or sound came in from the room. In about twenty minutes, as I was sittin' by the table, lookin' at the pictures in the old Aesop's Fables, I was aware o' something moving at the door, and lookin' up I sid my aunt's face lookin' in at the door, and her hand raised.

"'Hish!' says she, very soft, and comes over to me on tiptoe, and she says in a whisper: 'Thank God, she's asleep at last, and don't ye make no noise till I come back, for I'm goin' down to take my cup o' tea, and I'll be back i' noo—me and Mrs. Wyvern, and she'll be sleepin' in the room, and you can run down when we come up, and Judith will gie ye yaur supper in my room.'

"And with that she goes.

"I kep' looking at the picture-book, as before, listenin' every noo and then, but there was no sound, not a breath, that I could hear; an' I began whisperin' to the pictures and talkin' to myself to keep my heart up, for I was growin' feared in that big room.

"And at last up I got, and began walkin' about the room, lookin' at this and peepin' at that, to amuse my mind, ye'll understand. And at last what sud I do but peeps into Madam Crowl's bedchamber.

"A grand chamber it was, wi' a great four-poster, wi' flowered silk curtains as tall as the ceilin', and foldin' down on the floor, and drawn close all round. There was a lookin'-glass, the biggest I ever sid before, and the room was a blaze o' light. I counted twenty-two wax candles, all alight. Such was her fancy, and no one dared say her nay.

"I listened at the door, and gaped and wondered all round. When I heard there was not a breath, and did not see so much as a stir in the curtains, I took heart, and walked into the room on tiptoe, and looked round again. Then I takes a keek at myself in the big glass; and at last it came in my head, 'Why couldn't I ha' a keek at the ald lady herself in the bed?

"Ye'd think me a fule if ye knew half how I longed to see Dame Crowl, and I thought to myself if I didn't peep now I might wait many a day before I got so gude a chance again.

"Well, my dear, I came to the side o' the bed, the curtains bein' close, and my heart a'most failed me. But I took courage, and I slips my finger in between the thick curtains, and then my hand. So I waits a bit, but all was still as death. So, softly, softly I draws the curtain, and there, sure enough, I sid before me, stretched out like the painted lady on the tomb-stean in Lexhoe Church, the famous Dame Crowl, of Applewale House. There she was, dressed out. You never sid the like in they days. Satin and silk, and scarlet and green, and gold and pint lace; by Jen! 'twas a sight! A big powdered wig, half as high as herself, was a-top o' her head, and, wow!—was ever such wrinkles?—and her old baggy throat all powdered white, and her cheeks rouged, and mouse-skin eyebrows, that Mrs. Wyvern used to stick on, and there she lay proud and stark, wi' a pair o' clocked silk hose on, and heels to her shoon as tall as nine-pins. Lawk! But her nose was crooked and thin, and half the whites o' her eyes was open. She used to stand, dressed as she was, gigglin' and dribblin' before the lookin'-glass, wi' a fan in her hand and a big nosegay in her bodice. Her wrinkled little hands was stretched down by her sides, and such long nails, all cut into points, I never sid in my days. Could it even a bin the fashion for grit fowk to wear their fingernails so?

"Well, I think ye'd a-bin frightened yourself if ye'd a sid such a sight. I couldn't let go the curtain, nor move an inch, nor take my eyes off her; my very heart stood still. And in an instant she opens her eyes and up she sits, and spins herself round, and down wi' her, wi' a clack on her two tall heels on the floor, facin' me, ogglin' in my face wi' her two great glassy eyes, and a wicked simper wi' her wrinkled lips, and lang fause teeth.

"Well, a corpse is a natural thing; but this was the dreadfullest sight I ever sid. She had her fingers straight out pointin' at me, and her back was crooked, round again wi' age. Says she:

"'Ye little limb! what for did ye say I killed the boy? I'll tickle ye till ye're stiff!'

"If I'd a thought an instant, I'd a turned about and run. But I couldn't take my eyes off her, and I backed from her as soon as I could; and she came clatterin' after like a thing on wires, with her fingers pointing to my throat, and she makin' all the time a sound with her tongue like zizz-zizz-zizz.

"I kept backin' and backin' as quick as I could, and her fingers was only a few inches away from my throat, and I felt I'd lose my wits if she touched me.

"I went back this way, right into the corner, and I gev a yellock, ye'd think saul and body was partin', and that minute my aunt, from the door, calls out wi' a blare, and the ald lady turns round on her, and I turns about, and ran through my room, and down the stairs, as hard as my legs could carry me.

"I cried hearty, I can tell you, when I got down to the housekeeper's room. Mrs. Wyvern laughed a deal when I told her what happened. But she changed her key when she heard the ald lady's words.

"'Say them again,' says she.

"So I told her.

"'Ye little limb! What for did ye say I killed the boy? I'll tickle ye till ye're stiff.'

"'And did ye say she killed a boy?' says she.

"'Not I, ma'am,' says I.

"Judith was always up with me, after that, when the two elder women was away from her. I would a jumped out at winda, rather than stay alone in the same room wi' her.

"It was about a week after, as well as I can remember, Mrs. Wyvern, one day when me and her was alone, told me a thing about Madam Crowl that I did not know before.

"She being young and a great beauty, full seventy year before, had married Squire Crowl, of Applewale. But he was a widower, and had a son about nine years old.

"There never was tale or tidings of this boy after one mornin'. No one could say where he went to. He was allowed too much liberty, and used to be off in the morning, one day, to the keeper's cottage and breakfast wi' him, and away to the warren, and not home, mayhap, till evening; and another time down to the lake, and bathe there, and spend the day fishin' there, or paddlin' about in the boat. Well, no one could say what was gone wi' him; only this, that his hat was found by the lake, under a haathorn that grows thar to this day, and 'twas thought he was drowned bathin'. And the squire's son, by his second marriage, with this Madam Crowl that lived sa dreadful lang, came in far the estates. It was his son, the ald lady's grandson, Squire Chevenix Crowl, that owned the estates at the time I came to Applewale.

"There was a deal o' talk lang before my aunt's time about it; and 'twas said the step-mother knew more than she was like to let out. And she managed her husband, the ald squire, wi' her white-heft and flatteries. And as the boy was never seen more, in course of time the thing died out of fowks' minds.

"I'm goin' to tell ye noo about what I sid wi' my own een.

"I was not there six months, and it was winter time, when the ald lady took her last sickness.

"The doctor was afeard she might a took a fit o' madness, as she did fifteen years befoore, and was buckled up, many a time, in a strait-waistcoat, which was the very leathern jerkin I sid in the closet, off my aunt's room.

"Well, she didn't. She pined, and windered, and went off, torflin', torflin', quiet enough, till a day or two before her flittin', and then she took to rabblin', and sometimes skirlin' in the bed, ye'd think a robber had a knife to her throat, and she used to work out o' the bed, and not being strong enough, then, to walk or stand, she'd fall on the flure, wi' her ald wizened hands stretched before her face, and skirlin' still for mercy.

"Ye may guess I didn't go into the room, and I used to be shiverin' in my bed wi' fear, at her skirlin' and scrafflin' on the flure, and blarin' out words that id make your skin turn blue.

"My aunt, and Mrs. Wyvern, and Judith Squailes, and a woman from Lexhoe, was always about her. At last she took fits, and they wore her out.

"T' sir was there, and prayed for her; but she was past praying with. I suppose it was right, but none could think there was much good in it, and sa at lang last she made her flittin', and a' was over, and old Dame Crowl was shrouded and coffined, and Squire Chevenix was wrote for. But he was away in France, and the delay was sa lang, that t' sir and doctor both agreed it would not du to keep her langer out o' her place, and no one cared but just them two, and my aunt and the rest o' us, from Applewale, to go to the buryin'. So the old lady of Applewale was laid in the vault under Lexhoe Church; and we lived up at the great house till such time as the squire should come to tell his will about us, and pay off such as he chose to discharge.

"I was put into another room, two doors away from what was Dame Crowl's chamber, after her death, and this thing happened the night before Squire Chevenix came to Applewale.

"The room I was in now was a large square chamber, covered wi' yak pannels, but unfurnished except for my bed, which had no curtains to it, and a chair and a table, or so, that looked nothing at all in such a big room. And the big looking-glass, that the old lady used to keek into and admire herself from head to heel, now that there was na mair o' that wark, was put out of the way, and stood against the wall in my room, for there was shiftin' o' many things in her chamber ye may suppose, when she came to be coffined.

"The news had come that day that the squire was to be down next morning at Applewale; and not sorry was I, for I thought I was sure to be sent home again to my mother. And right glad was I, and I was thinkin' of a' at hame, and my sister Janet, and the kitten and the pymag, and Trimmer the tike, and all the rest, and I got sa fidgetty, I couldn't sleep, and the clock struck twelve, and me wide awake, and the room as dark as pick. My back was turned to the door, and my eyes toward the wall opposite.

"Well, it could na be a full quarter past twelve, when I sees a lightin' on the wall befoore me, as if something took fire behind, and the shadas o' the bed, and the chair, and my gown, that was hangin' from the wall, was dancin' up and down on the ceilin' beams and the yak pannels; and I turns my head ower my shouther quick, thinkin' something must a gone a' fire.

"And what sud I see, by Jen! but the likeness o' the ald beldame, bedizened out in her satins and velvets, on her dead body, simperin', wi' her eyes as wide as saucers, and her face like the fiend himself. 'Twas a red light that rose about her in a fuffin low, as if her dress round her feet was blazin'. She was drivin' on right for me, wi' her ald shrivelled hands crooked as if she was goin' to claw me. I could not stir, but she passed me straight by, wi' a blast o' cald air, and I sid her, at the wall, in the alcove as my aunt used to call it, which was a recess where the state bed used to stand in ald times wi' a door open wide, and her hands gropin' in at somethin' was there. I never sid that door befoore. And she turned round to me, like a thing on a pivot, flyrin', and all at once the room was dark, and I standin' at the far side o' the bed; I don't know how I got there, and I found my tongue at last, and if I did na blare a yellock, rennin' down the gallery and almost pulled Mrs. Wyvern's door off t' hooks, and frighted her half out o' wits.

"Ye may guess I did na sleep that night; and wi' the first light, down wi' me to my aunt, as fast as my two legs cud carry me.

"Well my aunt did na frump or flite me, as I thought she would, but she held me by the hand, and looked hard in my face all the time. And she telt me not to be feared; and says she:

"'Hed the appearance a key in its hand?'

"'Yes,' says I, bringin' it to mind, 'a big key in a queer brass handle.'

"'Stop a bit,' says she, lettin' go ma hand, and openin' the cupboard-door. 'Was it like this?' says she, takin' one out in her fingers, and showing it to me, with a dark look in my face.

"'That was it,' says I, quick enough.

"'Are ye sure?' she says, turnin' it round.

"'Sart,' says I, and I felt like I was gain' to faint when I sid it.

"'Well, that will do, child,' says she, saftly thinkin', and she locked it up again.

"'The squire himself will be here today, before twelve o'clock, and ye must tell him all about it,' says she, thinkin', 'and I suppose I'll be leavin' soon, and so the best thing for the present is, that ye should go home this afternoon, and I'll look out another place for you when I can.'

"Fain was I, ye may guess, at that word.

"My aunt packed up my things for me, and the three pounds that was due to me, to bring home, and Squire Crowl himself came down to Applewale that day, a handsome man, about thirty years ald. It was the second time I sid him. But this was the first time he spoke to me.

"My aunt talked wi' him in the housekeeper's room, and I don't know what they said. I was a bit feared on the squire, he bein' a great gentleman down in Lexhoe, and I darn't go near till I was called. And says he, smilin':

"'What's a' this ye a sen, child? it mun be a dream, for ye know there's na sic a thing as a bo or a freet in a' the world. But whatever it was, ma little maid, sit ye down and tell all about it from first to last.'

"Well, so soon as I made an end, he thought a bit, and says he to my aunt:

"'I mind the place well. In old Sir Olivur's time lame Wyndel told me there was a door in that recess, to the left, where the lassie dreamed she saw my grandmother open it. He was past eighty when he told me that, and I but a boy. It's twenty year sen. The plate and jewels used to be kept there, long ago, before the iron closet was made in the arras chamber, and he told me the key had a brass handle, and this ye say was found in the bottom o' the kist where she kept her old fans. Now, would not it be a queer thing if we found some spoons or diamonds forgot there? Ye mun come up wi' us, lassie, and point to the very spot.'

"Loth was I, and my heart in my mouth, and fast I held by my aunt's hand as I stept into that awsome room, and showed them both how she came and passed me by, and the spot where she stood, and where the door seemed to open.

"There was an ald empty press against the wall then, and shoving it aside, sure enough there was the tracing of a door in the wainscot, and a keyhole stopped with wood, and planed across as smooth as the rest, and the joining of the door all stopped wi' putty the colour o' yak, and, but for the hinges that showed a bit when the press was shoved aside, ye would not consayt there was a door there at all.

"'Ha!' says he, wi' a queer smile, 'this looks like it.'

"It took some minutes wi' a small chisel and hammer to pick the bit o' wood out o' the keyhole. The key fitted, sure enough, and, wi' a strang twist and a lang skreak, the boult went back and he pulled the door open.

"There was another door inside, stranger than the first, but the lacks was gone, and it opened easy. Inside was a narrow floor and walls and vault o' brick; we could not see what was in it, for 'twas dark as pick.

"When my aunt had lighted the candle, the squire held it up and stept in.

"My aunt stood on tiptoe tryin' to look over his shouther, and I did na see nout.

"'Ha! ha!' says the squire, steppin' backward. 'What's that? Gi' ma the poker—quick!' says he to my aunt. And as she went to the hearth I peeps beside his arm, and I sid squat down in the far corner a monkey or a flayin' on the chest, or else the maist shrivelled up, wizzened ald wife that ever was sen on yearth.

"'By Jen!' says my aunt, as puttin' the poker in his hand, she keeked by his shouther, and sid the ill-favoured thing, 'hae a care, sir, what ye're doin'. Back wi' ye, and shut to the door!'

"But in place o' that he steps in saftly, wi' the poker pointed like a swoord, and he gies it a poke, and down it a' tumbles together, head and a', in a heap o' bayans and dust, little meyar an' a hatful.

"'Twas the bayans o' a child; a' the rest went to dust at a touch. They said nout for a while, but he turns round the skull, as it lay on the floor.

"Young as I was, I consayted I knew well enough what they was thinkin' on.

"'A dead cat!' says he, pushin' back and blowin' out the can'le, and shuttin' to the door. 'We'll come back, you and me, Mrs. Shutters, and look on the shelves by-and-bye. I've other matters first to speak to ye about; and this little girl's goin' hame, ye say. She has her wages, and I mun mak' her a present,' says he, pattin' my shouther wi' his hand.

"And he did gimma a goud pound and I went aff to Lexhoe about an hour after, and sa hame by the stage-coach, and fain was I to be at hame again; and I never sid Dame Crowl o' Applewale, God be thanked, either in appearance or in dream, at-efter. But when I was grown to be a woman, my aunt spent a day and night wi' me at Littleham, and she telt me there was no doubt it was the poor little boy that was missing sa lang sen, that was shut up to die thar in the dark by that wicked beldame, whar his skirls, or his prayers, or his thumpin' cud na be heard, and his hat was left by the water's edge, whoever did it, to mak' belief he was drowned. The clothes, at the first touch, a' ran into a snuff o' dust in the cell whar the bayans was found. But there was a handful o' jet buttons, and a knife with a green heft, together wi' a couple o' pennies the poor little fella had in his pocket, I suppose, when he was decoyed in thar, and sid his last o' the light. And there was, amang the squire's papers, a copy o' the notice that was prented after he was lost, when the ald squire thought hc might 'a run away, or bin took by gipsies, and it said he had a green-hefted knife wi' him, and that his buttons were o' cut jet. Sa that is a' I hev to say consarnin' ald Dame Crowl, o' Applewale House."

THE DEAD SEXTON

THE DEAD SEXTON

The sunsets were red, the nights were long, and the weather pleasantly frosty; and Christmas, the glorious herald of the New Year, was at hand, when an event—still recounted by winter firesides, with a horror made delightful by the mellowing influence of years—occurred in the beautiful little town of Golden Friars, and signalized, as the scene of its catastrophe, the old inn known throughout a wide region of the Northumbrian counties as the George and Dragon.

Toby Crooke, the sexton, was lying dead in the old coach-house in the inn yard. The body had been discovered, only half an hour before this story begins, under strange circumstances, and in a place where it might have lain the better part of a week undisturbed; and a dreadful suspicion astounded the village of Golden Friars.

A wintry sunset was glaring through a gorge of the western mountains, turning into fire the twigs of the leafless elms, and all the tiny blades of grass on the green by which the quaint little town is surrounded. It is built of light, grey stone, with steep gables and slender chimneys rising with airy lightness from the level sward by the margin of the beautiful lake, and backed by the grand amphitheatre of the fells at the other side, whose snowy peaks show faintly against the sky, tinged with the vaporous red of the western light. As you descend towards the margin of the lake, and see Golden Friars, its taper chimneys and slender gables, its curious old inn and gorgeous sign, and over all the graceful tower and spire of the ancient church, at this hour or by moonlight, in the solemn grandeur and stillness of the natural scenery that surrounds it, it stands before you like a fairy town.

Toby Crooke, the lank sexton, now fifty or upwards, had passed an hour or two with some village cronies, over a solemn pot of purl, in the kitchen of that cosy hostelry, the night before. He generally turned in there at about seven o'clock, and heard the news. This contented him: for he talked little, and looked always surly.

Many things are now raked up and talked over about him.

In early youth, he had been a bit of a scamp. He broke his indentures, and ran away from his master, the tanner of Bryemere; he had got into fifty bad scrapes and out again; and, just as the little world of Golden Friars had come to the conclusion that it would be well for all parties—except, perhaps, himself—and a happy riddance for his afflicted mother, if he were sunk, with a gross of quart pots about his neck, in the bottom of the lake in which the grey gables, the elms, and the towering fells of Golden Friars are mirrored, he suddenly returned, a reformed man at the ripe age of forty.

For twelve years he had disappeared, and no one knew what had become of him. Then, suddenly, as I say, he reappeared at Golden Friars—a very black and silent man, sedate and orderly. His mother was dead and buried; but the "prodigal son" was received good-naturedly. The good vicar, Doctor Jenner, reported to his wife:

"His hard heart has been softened, dear Dolly. I saw him dry his eyes, poor fellow, at the sermon yesterday."

"I don't wonder, Hugh darling. I know the part—'There is joy in Heaven.' I am sure it was—wasn't it? It was quite beautiful. I almost cried myself."

The Vicar laughed gently, and stooped over her chair and kissed her, and patted her cheek fondly.

"You think too well of your old man's sermons," he said. "I preach, you see, Dolly, very much to the *poor*. If *they* understand me, I am pretty sure everyone else must; and I think that my simple style goes more home to both feelings and conscience—"

"You ought to have told me of his crying before. You *are* so eloquent," exclaimed Dolly Jenner. "No one preaches like my man. I have never heard such sermons."

Not many, we may be sure; for the good lady had not heard more than six from any other divine for the last twenty years.

The personages of Golden Friars talked Toby Crooke over on his return. Doctor Lincote said:

"He must have led a hard life; he had *dried in* so, and got a good deal of hard muscle; and he rather fancied he had been soldiering—he stood like a soldier; and the mark over his right eye looked like a gunshot."

People might wonder how he could have survived a gunshot over the eye; but was not Lincote a doctor—and an army doctor to boot—when he was young; and who, in Golden Friars, could dispute with him on points of surgery? And I believe the truth is, that this mark had been really made by a pistol bullet.

Mr. Jarlcot, the attorney, would "go bail" he had picked up some sense in his travels; and honest Turnbull, the host of the George and Dragon, said heartily:

"We must look out something for him to put his hand to. *Now's* the time to make a man of him."

The end of it was that he became, among other things, the sexton of Golden Friars.

He was a punctual sexton. He meddled with no other person's business; but he was a silent man, and by no means popular. He was reserved in company; and he used to walk alone by the shore of the lake, while other fellows played at fives or skittles; and when he visited the kitchen of the George, he had his liquor to himself, and in the midst of the general talk was a saturnine listener. There was something sinister in this man's face; and when things went wrong with him, he could look dangerous enough.

There were whispered stories in Golden Friars about Toby Crooke. Nobody could say how they got there. Nothing is more mysterious than the spread of rumour. It is like a vial poured on the air. It travels, like an epidemic, on the sightless currents of the atmosphere, or by the laws of a telluric influence equally intangible. These stories treated, though darkly, of the long period of his absence from his native village; but they took no well-defined shape, and no one could refer them to any authentic source.

The Vicar's charity was of the kind that thinketh no evil; and in such cases he always insisted on proof. Crooke was, of course, undisturbed in his office.

On the evening before the tragedy came to light—trifles are always remembered after the catastrophe—a boy, returning along the margin of the mere, passed him by seated on a prostrate trunk of a tree, under the "bield" of a rock, counting silver money. His lean body and limbs were bent together, his knees were up to his chin, and his long fingers were telling the coins over hurriedly in the hollow of his other hand. He glanced at the boy, as the old English saying is, like "the devil looking over Lincoln." But a black and sour look from Mr. Crooke, who never had a smile for a child nor a greeting for a wayfarer, was nothing strange.

Toby Crooke lived in the grey stone house, cold and narrow, that stands near the church porch, with the window of its staircase looking out into the churchyard, where so much of his labour, for many a day, had been expended. The greater part of this house was untenanted.

The old woman who was in charge of it slept in a settle-bed, among broken stools, old sacks, rotten chests and other rattle-traps, in the small room at the rear of the house, floored with tiles.

At what time of the night she could not tell, she awoke, and saw a man, with his hat on, in her room. He had a candle in his hand, which he shaded with his coat from her eye; his back was towards her, and he was rummaging in the drawer in which she usually kept her money.

Having got her quarter's pension of two pounds that day, however, she had placed it, folded in a rag, in the corner of her tea caddy, and locked it up in the "eat-malison" or cupboard.

She was frightened when she saw the figure in her room, and she could not tell whether her visitor might not have made his entrance from the contiguous churchyard. So, sitting bolt upright in her bed, her grey hair almost lifting her kerchief off her head, and all over in "a fit o' t' creepins," as she expressed it, she demanded:

"In God's name, what want ye thar?"

"Whar's the peppermint ye used to hev by ye, woman? I'm bad wi' an inward pain."

"It's all gane a month sin'," she answered; and offered to make him a "het" drink if he'd get to his room.

But he said:

"Never mind, I'll try a mouthful o' gin."

And, turning on his heel, he left her.

In the morning the sexton was gone. Not only in his lodging was there no account of him, but, when inquiry began to be extended, nowhere in the village of Golden Friars could he be found.

Still he might have gone off, on business of his own, to some distant village, before the town was stirring; and the sexton had no near kindred to trouble their heads about him. People, therefore, were willing to wait, and take his return ultimately for granted.

At three o'clock the good Vicar, standing at his hall door, looking across the lake towards the noble fells that rise, steep and furrowed, from that beautiful mere, saw two men approaching across the green, in a straight line, from a boat that was moored at the water's edge. They were carrying between them something which, though not very large, seemed ponderous.

"Ye'll ken this, sir," said one of the boatmen as they set down, almost at his feet, a small church bell, such as in old-fashioned chimes yields the treble notes. "This won't be less nor five stean. I ween it's fra' the church steeple yon."

"What! one of our church bells?" ejaculated the Vicar—for a moment lost in horrible amazement. "Oh, no!—*no*, that can't possibly be! Where did you find it?"

He had found the boat, in the morning, moored about fifty yards from her moorings where he had left it the night before, and could not think how that came to pass; and now, as he and his partner were about to take their oars, they discovered this bell in the bottom of the boat, under a bit of canvas, also the sexton's pick and spade—"tom-spey'ad," they termed that peculiar, broad-bladed implement.

"Very extraordinary! We must try whether there is a bell missing from the tower," said the Vicar, getting into a fuss. "Has Crooke come back yet? Does anyone know where he is?"

The sexton had not yet turned up.

"That's odd—that's provoking," said the Vicar. "However, my key will let us in. Place the bell in the hall while I get it; and then we can see what all this means."

To the church, accordingly, they went, the Vicar leading the way, with his own key in his hand. He turned it in the lock, and stood in the shadow of the ground porch, and shut the door.

A sack, half full, lay on the ground, with open mouth, a piece of cord lying beside it. Something clanked within it as one of the men shoved it aside with his clumsy shoe.

The Vicar opened the church door and peeped in. The dusky glow from the western sky, entering through a narrow window, illuminated the shafts and arches, the old oak carvings, and the discoloured monuments, with the melancholy glare of a dying fire.

The Vicar withdrew his head and closed the door. The gloom of the porch was deeper than ever as, stooping, he entered the narrow door that opened at the foot of the winding stair that leads to the first loft; from which a rude ladder-stair of wood, some five and twenty feet in height, mounts through a trap to the ringers' loft.

Up the narrow stairs the Vicar climbed, followed by his attendants, to the first loft. It was very dark: a narrow bow-slit in the thick wall admitted the only light they had to guide them. The ivy leaves, seen from the deep shadow, flashed and flickered redly, and the sparrows twittered among them.

"Will one of you be so good as to go up and count the bells, and see if they are all right?" said the Vicar. "There should be—"

"Agoy! what's that?" exclaimed one of the men, recoiling from the foot of the ladder.

"By Jen!" ejaculated the other, in equal surprise.

"Good gracious!" gasped the Vicar, who, seeing indistinctly a dark mass lying on the floor, had stooped to examine it, and placed his hand upon a cold, dead face.

The men drew the body into the streak of light that traversed the floor.

It was the corpse of Toby Crooke! There was a frightful scar across his forehead.

The alarm was given. Doctor Lincote, and Mr. Jarlcot, and Turnbull, of the George and Dragon, were on the spot immediately; and many curious and horrified spectators of minor importance.

The first thing ascertained was that the man must have been many hours dead. The next was that his skull was fractured, across the forehead, by an awful blow. The next was that his neck was broken.

His hat was found on the floor, where he had probably laid it, with his handkerchief in it.

The mystery now began to clear a little; for a bell—one of the chime hung in the tower—was found where it had rolled to, against the wall, with blood and hair on the rim of it, which corresponded with the grizzly fracture across the front of his head.

The sack that lay in the vestibule was examined, and found to contain all the church plate; a silver salver that had disappeared, about a month before, from Dr. Lincote's store of valuables; the Vicar's gold pencil-case, which he thought he had forgot in the vestry book; silver spoons, and various other contributions, levied from time to time off a dozen different households, the mysterious disappearance of which spoils had, of late years, begun to make the honest little community uncomfortable. Two bells had been taken down from the chime; and now the shrewd part of the assemblage, putting things together, began to comprehend the nefarious plans of the sexton, who lay mangled and dead on the floor of the tower, where only two days ago he had tolled the holy bell to call the good Christians of Golden Friars to worship.

The body was carried into the yard of the George and Dragon and laid in the old coach-house; and the townsfolk came grouping in to have a peep at the corpse, and stood round, looking darkly, and talking as low as if they were in a church.

The Vicar, in gaiters and slightly shovel hat, stood erect, as one in a little circle of notables—the doctor, the attorney, Sir Geoffrey Mardykes, who happened to be in the town, and Turnbull, the host—in the centre of the paved yard, they having made an inspection of the body, at which troops of the village stragglers, to-ing and fro-ing, were gaping and frowning as they whispered their horrible conjectures.

"What d'ye think o' that?" said Tom Scales, the old hostler of the George, looking pale, with a stern, faint smile on his lips, as he and Dick Linklin sauntered out of the coach-house together.

"The deaul will hev his ain noo," answered Dick, in his friend's ear. "T' sexton's got a craigthraw like he gav' the lass over the clints of Scarsdale; ye mind what the ald soger telt us when he hid his face in the kitchen of the George here? By Jen! I'll ne'er forget that story."

"I ween 'twas all true enough," replied the hostler; "and the sizzup he gav' the sleepin' man wi' t' poker across the forehead. See whar the edge o' t' bell took him, and smashed his ain, the self-same lids. By ma sang, I wonder the deaul did na carry awa' his corpse i' the night, as he did wi' Tam Lunder's at Mooltern Mill."

"Hout, man, who ever sid t' deaul inside o' a church?"

"The corpse is ill-faur'd enew to scare Satan himsel', for that matter; though it's true what you say. Ay, ye're reet tul a trippet, thar; for Beelzebub dar'n't show his snout inside the church, not the length o' the black o' my nail."

While this discussion was going on, the gentlefolk who were talking the matter over in the centre of the yard had dispatched a message for the coroner all the way to the town of Hextan.

The last tint of sunset was fading from the sky by this time; so, of course, there was no thought of an inquest earlier than next day.

In the meantime it was horribly clear that the sexton had intended to rob the church of its plate, and had lost his life in the attempt to carry the second bell, as we have seen, down the worn ladder of the tower. He had tumbled backwards and broken his neck upon the floor of the loft; and the heavy bell, in its fall, descended with its edge across his forehead.

Never was a man more completely killed by a double catastrophe, in a moment.

The bells and the contents of the sack, it was surmised, he meant to have conveyed across the lake that night, and with the help of his spade and pick to have buried them in Clousted Forest, and returned, after an absence of but a few hours—as he easily might—before morning, unmissed and unobserved. He would no doubt, having secured his booty, have made such arrangements as would have made it appear that the church had been broken into. He would, of course, have taken all measures to divert suspicion from himself, and have watched a suitable opportunity to repossess himself of the buried treasure and dispose of it in safety.

And now came out, into sharp relief, all the stories that had, one way or other, stolen after him into the town. Old Mrs. Pullen fainted when she saw him, and told Doctor Lincote, after, that she thought he was the highwayman who fired the shot that killed the coachman the night they were robbed on Hounslow Heath. There were the stories also told by the wayfaring old soldier with the wooden leg, and fifty others, up to this more than half disregarded, but which now seized on the popular belief with a startling grasp.

The fleeting light soon expired, and twilight was succeeded by the early night.

The inn yard gradually became quiet; and the dead sexton lay alone, in the dark, on his back, locked up in the old coach-house, the key of which was safe in the pocket of Tom Scales, the trusty old hostler of the George.

It was about eight o'clock, and the hostler, standing alone on the road in the front of the open door of the George and Dragon, had just smoked his pipe out. A bright moon hung in the frosty sky. The fells rose from the opposite edge of the lake like phantom mountains. The air was stirless. Through the boughs and sprays of the leafless elms no sigh or motion, however hushed, was audible. Not a ripple glimmered on the lake, which at one point only reflected the brilliant moon from its dark blue expanse like burnished steel. The road that runs by the inn door, along the margin of the lake, shone dazzlingly white.

White as ghosts, among the dark holly and juniper, stood the tall piers of the Vicar's gate, and their great stone balls, like heads, overlooking the same road, a few hundred yards up the lake, to the left. The early little town of Golden Friars was quiet by this time. Except for the townsfolk who were now collected in the kitchen of the inn itself, no inhabitant was now outside his own threshold.

Tom Scales was thinking of turning in. He was beginning to fell a little queer. He was thinking of the sexton, and could not get the fixed features of the dead man out of his head, when he heard the sharp though distant ring of a horse's hoof upon the frozen road. Tom's instinct apprized him of the approach of a guest to the George and Dragon. His experienced ear told him that the horseman was approaching by the Dardale road, which, after crossing that wide and dismal moss, passes the southern fells by Dunner Cleugh and finally enters the town of Golden Friars by joining the Mardykes road, at the edge of the lake, close to the gate of the Vicar's house.

A clump of tall trees stood at this point; but the moon shone full upon the road and cast their shadow backward.

The hoofs were plainly coming at a gallop, with a hollow rattle. The horseman was a long time in appearing. Tom wondered how he had heard the sound—so sharply frosty as the air was—so very far away.

He was right in his guess. The visitor was coming over the mountainous road from Dardale Moss; and he now saw a horseman, who must have turned the corner of the Vicar's house at the moment when his eye was wearied; for when he saw him for the first time he was advancing, in the hazy moonlight, like the shadow of a cavalier, at a gallop, upon the level strip of road that skirts the margin of the mere, between the George and the Vicar's piers.

The hostler had not long to wonder why the rider pushed his beast at so furious a pace, and how he came to have heard him, as he now calculated, at least three miles away. A very few moments sufficed to bring horse and rider to the inn door.

It was a powerful black horse, something like the great Irish hunter that figured a hundred years ago, and would carry sixteen stone with ease across country. It would have made a grand charger. Not a hair turned. It snorted, it pawed, it arched its neck; then threw back its ears and down its head, and looked ready to lash, and then to rear; and seemed impatient to be off again, and incapable of standing quiet for a moment.

The rider got down

As light as shadow falls.

But he was a tall, sinewy figure. He wore a cape or short mantle, a cocked hat, and a pair of jack-boots, such as held their ground in some primitive corners of England almost to the close of the last century.

"Take him, lad," said he to old Scales. "You need not walk or wisp him—he never sweats or tires. Give him his oats, and let him take his own time to eat them. House!" cried the stranger—in the old-fashioned form of summons which still lingered, at that time, in out-of-the-way places—in a deep and piercing voice.

As Tom Scales led the horse away to the stables it turned its head towards its master with a short, shill neigh.

"About *your* business, old gentleman—we must not go too fast," the stranger cried back again to his horse, with a laugh as harsh and piercing; and he strode into the house.

The hostler led this horse into the inn yard. In passing, it sidled up to the coach-house gate, within which lay the dead sexton—snorted, pawed and lowered its head suddenly, with ear close to the plank, as if listening for a sound from within; then uttered again the same short, piercing neigh.

The hostler was chilled at this mysterious coquetry with the dead. He liked the brute less and less every minute.

In the meantime, its master had proceeded.

"I'll go to the inn kitchen," he said, in his startling bass, to the drawer who met him in the passage.

And on he went, as if he had known the place all his days: not seeming to hurry himself—stepping leisurely, the servant thought—but gliding on at such a rate, nevertheless, that he had passed his guide and was in the kitchen of the George before the drawer had got much more than half-way to it.

A roaring fire of dry wood, peat and coal lighted up this snug but spacious apartment—flashing on pots and pans, and dressers high-piled with pewter plates and dishes; and making the uncertain shadows of the long "hanks" of onions and many a flitch and ham, depending from the ceiling, dance on its glowing surface.

The doctor and the attorney, even Sir Geoffrey Mardykes, did not disdain on this occasion to take chairs and smoke their pipes by the kitchen fire, where they were in the thick of the gossip and discussion excited by the terrible event.

The tall stranger entered uninvited.

He looked like a gaunt, athletic Spaniard of forty, burned half black in the sun, with a bony, flattened nose. A pair of fierce black eyes were just visible under the edge of his hat; and his mouth seemed divided, beneath the moustache, by the deep scar of a hare-lip.

Sir Geoffrey Mardykes and the host of the George, aided by the doctor and the attorney, were discussing and arranging, for the third or fourth time, their theories about the death and the probable plans of Toby Crooke, when the stranger entered.

The new-comer lifted his hat, with a sort of smile, for a moment from his black head.

"What do you call this place, gentlemen?" asked the stranger.

"The town of Golden Friars, sir," answered the doctor politely.

"The George and Dragon, sir: Anthony Turnbull, at your service," answered mine host, with a solemn bow, at the same moment—so that the two voices went together, as if the doctor and the innkeeper were singing a catch.

"The George and the Dragon," repeated the horseman, expanding his long hands over the fire which he had approached. "Saint George, King George, the Dragon, the Devil: it is a very grand idol, that outside your door, sir. You catch all sorts of worshippers—courtiers, fanatics, scamps: all's fish, eh? Everybody welcome, provided he drinks like one. Suppose you brew a bowl or two of punch. I'll stand it. How many are we? *Here*—count, and let us have enough. Gentlemen, I mean to spend the night here, and my horse is in the stable. What holiday, fun, or fair has got so many pleasant faces together? When I last called here—for, now I bethink me, I have seen the place before you all looked sad. It was on a Sunday, that dismalest of holidays; and it would have been positively melancholy only that your sexton—that saint upon earth—Mr. Crooke, was here." He was looking round, over his shoulder, and added: "Ha! don't I see him there?"

Frightened a good deal were some of the company. All gaped in the direction in which, with a nod, he turned his eyes.

"He's *not* thar—he *can't* be thar—we *see* he's not thar," said Turnbull, as dogmatically as old Joe Willet might have delivered himself—for he did not care that the George should earn the reputation of a haunted house. "He's met an accident, sir: he's dead—he's elsewhere—and therefore can't be here."

Upon this the company entertained the stranger with the narrative—which they made easy by a division of labour, two or three generally speaking at a time, and no one being permitted to finish a second sentence without finding himself corrected and supplanted.

"The man's in Heaven, so sure as you're not," said the traveller so soon as the story was ended. "What! he was fiddling with the church bell, was he, and d——d for that—eh? Landlord, get us some drink. A sexton d——d for pulling down a church bell he has been pulling at for ten years!"

"You came, sir, by the Dardale-road, I believe?" said the doctor (village folk are curious). "A dismal moss is Dardale Moss, sir; and a bleak clim' up the fells on t' other side."

"I say 'Yes' to all—from Dardale Moss, as black as pitch and as rotten as the grave, up that zigzag wall you call a road, that looks like chalk in the moonlight, through Dunner Cleugh, as dark as a coal-pit, and down here to the George and the Dragon, where you have a roaring fire, wise men, good punch—here it is—and a corpse in your coach-house. Where the carcase is, there will the eagles be gathered together. Come, landlord, ladle out the nectar. Drink, gentlemen—drink, all. Brew another bowl at the bar. How divinely it stinks of alcohol! I hope you like it, gentlemen: it smells all over of spices, like a mummy. Drink, friends. Ladle, landlord. Drink, all. Serve it out."

The guest fumbled in his pocket, and produced three guineas, which he slipped into Turnbull's fat palm.

"Let punch flow till that's out. I'm an old friend of the house. I call here, back and forward. I know you well, Turnbull, though you don't recognize me."

"You have the advantage of me, sir," said Mr. Turnbull, looking hard on that dark and sinister countenance—which, or the like of which, he could have sworn he had never seen before in his life. But he liked the weight and colour of his guineas, as he dropped them into his pocket. "I hope you will find yourself comfortable while you stay."

"You have given me a bedroom?"

"Yes, sir—the cedar chamber."

"I know it—the very thing. No—no punch for me. By and by, perhaps."

The talk went on, but the stranger had grown silent. He had seated himself on an oak bench by the fire, towards which he extended his feet and hands with seeming enjoyment; his cocked hat being, however, a little over his face.

Gradually the company began to thin. Sir Geoffrey Mardykes was the first to go; then some of the humbler townsfolk. The last bowl of punch was on its last legs. The stranger walked into the passage and said to the drawer:

"Fetch me a lantern. I must see my nag. Light it—hey! That will do. No—you need not come."

The gaunt traveller took it from the man's hand and strode along the passage to the door of the stableyard, which he opened and passed out.

Tom Scales, standing on the pavement, was looking through the stable window at the horses when the stranger plucked his shirtsleeve. With an inward shock the hostler found himself alone in presence of the very person he had been thinking of.

"I say—they tell me you have something to look at in there"—he pointed with his thumb at the old coach-house door. "Let us have a peep."

Tom Scales happened to be at that moment in a state of mind highly favourable to anyone in search of a submissive instrument. He was in great perplexity, and even perturbation. He suffered the stranger to lead him to the coach-house gate.

"You must come in and hold the lantern," said he. "I'll pay you handsomely."

The old hostler applied his key and removed the padlock.

"What are you afraid of? Step in and throw the light on his face," said the stranger grimly. "Throw open the lantern: stand *there*. Stoop over him a little—he won't bite you. Steady, or you may pass the night with him!"

In the meantime the company at the George had dispersed; and, shortly after, Anthony Turnbull—who, like a good landlord, was always last in bed, and first up, in his house—was taking, alone, his last look round the kitchen before making his final visit to the stable-yard, when Tom Scales tottered into the kitchen, looking like death, his hair standing upright; and he sat down on an oak chair, all in a tremble, wiped his forehead with his hand, and, instead of speaking, heaved a great sigh or two.

It was not till after he had swallowed a dram of brandy that he found his voice, and said:

"We've the deaul himsel' in t' house! By Jen! ye'd best send fo t' sir" (the clergyman). "Happen he'll tak him in hand wi' holy writ, and send him elsewhidder deftly. Lord atween us and harm! I'm a sinfu' man. I tell ye, Mr. Turnbull, I dar'n't stop in t' George to-night under the same roof wi' him."

"Ye mean the ra-beyoned, black-feyaced lad, wi' the brocken neb? Why, that's a gentleman wi' a pocket ful o' guineas, man, and a horse worth fifty pounds!"

"That horse is no better nor his rider. The nags that were in the stable wi' him, they all tuk the creepins, and sweated like rain down a thack. I tuk them all out o' that, away from him, into the hack-stable, and I thocht I cud never get them past him. But that's not all. When I was keekin inta t' winda at the nags, he comes behint me and claps his claw on ma shouther, and he gars me gang wi' him, and open the aad coach-house door, and haad the cannle for him, till he pearked into the deed man't feyace; and, as God's my judge, I sid the corpse open its eyes and wark its mouth, like a man smoorin' and strivin' to talk. I cudna move or say a word, though I felt my hair rising on my heed; but at lang-last I gev a yelloch, and say I, 'La! what is that?' And he himsel' looked round on me, like the devil he is; and, wi' a skirl o' a laugh, he strikes the lantern out o' my hand. When I cum to myself we were outside the coach-house door. The moon was shinin' in, ad I cud see the corpse stretched on the table whar we left it; and he kicked the door to wi' a purr o' his foot. 'Lock it,' says he; and so I did. And here's the key for ye—tak it yoursel', sir. He offer'd me money: he said he'd mak me a rich man if I'd sell him the corpse, and help him awa' wi' it."

"Hout, man! What cud he want o' t' corpse? He's not doctor, to do a' that lids. He was takin' a rise out o' ye, lad," said Turnbull.

"Na, na—he wants the corpse. There's summat you a' me can't tell he wants to do wi' 't; and he'd liefer get it wi' sin and thievin', and the damage of my soul. He's one of them freytens a boo or a dobbies off Dardale Moss, that's always astir wi' the like after nightfall; unless—Lord save us!—he be the deaul himsel.'"

"Whar is he noo?" asked the landlord, who was growing uncomfortable.

"He spang'd up the back stair to his room. I wonder you didn't hear him trampin' like a wild horse; and he clapt his door that the house shook again—but

Lord knows whar he is noo. Let us gang awa's up to the Vicar's, and gan *him* come down, and talk wi' him."

"Hoity toity, man—you're too easy scared," said the landlord, pale enough by this time. "'Twould be a fine thing, truly, to send abroad that the house was haunted by the deaul himsel'! Why, 'twould be the ruin o' the George. You're sure ye locked the door on the corpse?"

"Aye, sir—sartain."

"Come wi' me, Tom—we'll gi' a last look round the yard."

So, side by side, with many a jealous look right and left, and over their shoulders, they went in silence. On entering the old-fashioned quadrangle, surrounded by stables and other offices—built in the antique cagework fashion—they stopped for a while under the shadow of the inn gable, and looked round the yard, and listened. All was silent—nothing stirring.

The stable lantern was lighted; and with it in his hand Tony Turnbull, holding Tom Scales by the shoulder, advanced. He hauled Tom after him for a step or two; then stood still and shoved him before him for a step or two more; and thus cautiously—as a pair of skirmishers under fire—they approached the coach-house door.

"There, ye see—all safe," whispered Tom, pointing to the lock, which hung—distinct in the moonlight—in its place. "Cum back, I say!"

"Cum on, say I!" retorted the landlord valorously. "It would never do to allow any tricks to be played with the chap in there"—he pointed to the coachhouse door.

"The coroner here in the morning, and never a corpse to sit on!" He unlocked the padlock with these words, having handed the lantern to Tom. "Here, keck in, Tom," he continued; "ye hev the lantern—and see if all's as ye left it."

"Not me—na, not for the George and a' that's in it!" said Tom, with a shudder, sternly, as he took a step backward.

"What the—what are ye afraid on? Gi' me the lantern—it is all one: *I* will."

And cautiously, little by little, he opened the door; and, holding the lantern over his head in the narrow slit, he peeped in—frowning and pale—with one eye, as if he expected something to fly in his face. He closed the door without speaking, and locked it again.

"As safe as a thief in a mill," he whispered with a nod to his companion. And at that moment a harsh laugh overhead broke the silence startlingly, and set all the poultry in the yard gabbling.

"Thar he be!" said Tom, clutching the landlord's arm—"in the winda—see!"

The window of the cedar-room, up two pair of stairs, was open; and in the shadow a darker outline was visible of a man, with his elbows on the window-stone, looking down upon them.

"Look at his eyes—like two live coals!" gasped Tom.

The landlord could not see all this so sharply, being confused, and not so long-sighted as Tom.

"Time, sir," called Tony Turnbull, turning cold as he thought he saw a pair of eyes shining down redly at him—"time for honest folk to be in their beds, and asleep!"

"As sound as your sexton!" said the jeering voice from above.

"Come out of this," whispered the landlord fiercely to his hostler, plucking him hard by the sleeve.

They got into the house, and shut the door.

"I wish we were shot of him," said the landlord, with something like a groan, as he leaned against the wall of the passage. "I'll sit up, anyhow—and, Tom, you'll sit wi' me. Cum into the gun-room. No one shall steal the dead man out of my yard while I can draw a trigger."

The gun-room in the George is about twelve feet square. It projects into the stable-yard and commands a full view of the old coach-house; and, through a narrow side window, a flanking view of the back door of the inn, through which the yard is reached.

Tony Turnbull took down the blunderbuss—which was the great ordnance of the house—and loaded it with a stiff charge of pistol bullets.

He put on a great-coat which hung there, and was his covering when he went out at night, to shoot wild ducks. Tom made himself comfortable likewise. They then sat down at the window, which was open, looking into the yard, the opposite side of which was white in the brilliant moonlight.

The landlord laid the blunderbuss across his knees, and stared into the yard. His comrade stared also. The door of the gun-room was locked; so they felt tolerably secure.

An hour passed; nothing had occurred. Another. The clock struck one. The shadows had shifted a little; but still the moon shone full on the old coach-house, and the stable where the guest's horse stood.

Turnbull thought he heard a step on the back-stair. Tom was watching the back-door through the side window, with eyes glazing with the intensity of his stare. Anthony Turnbull, holding his breath, listened at the room door. It was a false alarm.

When he came back to the window looking into the yard:

"Hish! Look thar!" said he in a vehement whisper.

From the shadow at the left they saw the figure of the gaunt horseman, in short cloak and jack-boots, emerge. He pushed open the stable door, and led out his powerful black horse. He walked it across the front of the building till he reached the old coach-house door; and there, with its bridle on its neck, he left it standing, while he stalked to the yard gate; and, dealing it a kick with his heel, it sprang back with the rebound, shaking from top to bottom, and stood open. The stranger returned to the side of his horse; and the door which secured the corpse of the dead sexton seemed to swing slowly open of itself as he entered, and returned with the corpse in his arms, and swung it across the shoulders of the horse, and instantly sprang into the saddle.

"Fire!" shouted Tom, and bang went the blunderbuss with a stunning crack. A thousand sparrows' wings winnowed through the air from the thick ivy. The watch-dog yelled a furious bark. There was a strange ring and whistle in the air. The blunderbuss had burst to shivers right down to the very breech. The recoil rolled the inn-keeper upon his back on the floor, and Tom Scales was flung against the side of the recess of the window, which had saved him from a tumble as violent. In this position they heard the searing laugh of the departing horseman, and saw him ride out of the gate with his ghastly burden.

Perhaps some of my readers, like myself, have heard this story told by Roger Turnbull, now host of the George and Dragon, the grandson of the very Tony who then swayed the spigot and keys of that inn, in the identical kitchen of which the fiend treated so many of the neighbours to punch.

What infernal object was subserved by the possession of the dead villain's body, I have not learned. But a very curious story, in which a vampire resuscitation of Crooke the sexton figures, may throw a light upon this part of the tale.

The result of Turnbull's shot at the disappearing fiend certainly justifies old Andrew Moreton's dictum, which is thus expressed in his curious "History of Apparitions": "I warn rash brands who, pretending not to fear the devil, are for using the ordinary violences with him, which affect one man from another—or with an apparition, in which they may be sure to receive some mischief. I knew one fired a gun at an apparition and the gun burst in a hundred pieces in his hand; another struck at an apparition with a sword, and broke his sword in pieces and wounded his hand grievously; and 'tis next to madness for anyone to go that way to work with any spirit, be it angel or be it devil."

Wilkie Collins Collection (complete and unabridged):The Woman in White, The Moonstone, No Name, Armadale
Wilkie Collins
Benediction Classics, 2012
1136 pages
ISBN: 978-1-78139-328-4

Available from www.amazon.com, www.amazon.co.uk

Wilkie Collins (1824-1889) is best known as the innovator of the detective novel. He was a prolific writer, with 30 novels, more than 60 short stories, 14 plays, and more than 100 non-fiction pieces to his name. He was a close friend of Charles Dickens and one of the best known and loved Victorian Fiction writers. After his death, his popularity diminished as Dickens's grew. Now, Collins is once again becoming popular with most of his books in print and film, television and radio adaptations being made. There is much still to be discovered about this great author and this volume contains his four most popular novels.

Henry James - Notable Works, including (complete and unabridged): The American, The Turn of the Screw, The Portrait of a Lady, The Wings of the Dove, Daisy Miller and The Ambassadors
Henry James
Benediction Classics, 2013
1128 pages
ISBN: 978-1-78139-371-0

Available from www.amazon.com, www.amazon.co.uk

Henry James (1843 - 1916) was born in American but eventually settled in England. He is considered to be a key figure of 19th-century literary realism. His writing explores the perceptions of a character, and his works have been compared with impressionist paintings. His novels brought new life and interest into narrative fiction.

This omnibus edition includes his notable works:

The American,
The Turn of the Screw,
The Portrait of a Lady,
The Wings of the Dove,
Daisy Miller,
The Ambassadors

Flaxman Low, Occult Psychologist - Collected Stories
E. and H. Heron
Benediction Classics, 2012
96 pages
ISBN: 978-1-78139-219-5

Available from www.amazon.com, www.amazon.co.uk

E. and H. Heron were the pen names of Hesketh Pritchard and his mother Kate. Their Flaxman Low stories were first published in 1899, and have been reprinted a number of times since. Flaxman Low himself is a psychic detective in the mould of Sherlock Holmes. He investigates psychic mysteries using his immense knowledge of supernatural phenomena and powers of observation. The tales have a dark and macabre mood. Do not read these stories before bed if you don't want to be haunted during the night. The Story of the Spaniards, Hammersmith; The Story of the Moor Road; The Story of Baelbrow; The Story of Yand Manor House; The Story of Sevens Hall; The Story of Saddler's Croft; The Story of Konnor Old House.

The Land of Mist
Sir Arthur Conan Doyle
Benediction Classics, 2011
204 pages
ISBN: 978-1-84902-432-7

Available from www.amazon.com, www.amazon.co.uk

The 'Land of Mist' is the third novel in Arthur Conan Doyle's 'Professor Challenger' series. The first was written in 1912 and is entitled 'The Lost World', describing an expedition to a plateau in South America where dinosaurs still survive. Then in 1913 he wrote 'The Poison Belt', describing a disaster as the earth passes through a cloud of poisonous ether. Finally, in 1926 'The Land of Mist', which is heavily influenced by Doyle's growing belief in Spiritualism after a number of his close relatives died. It is therefore seem as semi-autobiographical, Challenger and Conan Doyle both grieving men and both interested in Spirituality.

Also from Benediction Books ...
Wandering Between Two Worlds: Essays on Faith and Art
Anita Mathias
Benediction Books, 2007
152 pages
ISBN: 0955373700

Available from www.amazon.com, www.amazon.co.uk

In these wide-ranging lyrical essays, Anita Mathias writes, in lush, lovely prose, of her naughty Catholic childhood in Jamshedpur, India; her large, eccentric family in Mangalore, a sea-coast town converted by the Portuguese in the sixteenth century; her rebellion and atheism as a teenager in her Himalayan boarding school, run by German missionary nuns, St. Mary's Convent, Nainital; and her abrupt religious conversion after which she entered Mother Teresa's convent in Calcutta as a novice. Later rich, elegant essays explore the dualities of her life as a writer, mother, and Christian in the United States-- Domesticity and Art, Writing and Prayer, and the experience of being "an alien and stranger" as an immigrant in America, sensing the need for roots.

About the Author

Anita Mathias is the author of *Wandering Between Two Worlds: Essays on Faith and Art*. She has a B.A. and M.A. in English from Somerville College, Oxford University, and an M.A. in Creative Writing from the Ohio State University, USA. Anita won a National Endowment of the Arts fellowship in Creative Nonfiction in 1997. She lives in Oxford, England with her husband, Roy, and her daughters, Zoe and Irene.

Anita's website:
http://www.anitamathias.com, and
Anita's blog Dreaming Beneath the Spires:
http://dreamingbeneaththespires.blogspot.com

The Church That Had Too Much
Anita Mathias
Benediction Books, 2010
52 pages
ISBN: 9781849026567

Available from www.amazon.com, www.amazon.co.uk

The Church That Had Too Much was very well-intentioned. She wanted to love God, she wanted to love people, but she was both hampered by her muchness and the abundance of her possessions, and beset by ambition, power struggles and snobbery. Read about the surprising way The Church That Had Too Much began to resolve her problems in this deceptively simple and enchanting fable.

About the Author

Anita Mathias is the author of *Wandering Between Two Worlds: Essays on Faith and Art*. She has a B.A. and M.A. in English from Somerville College, Oxford University, and an M.A. in Creative Writing from the Ohio State University, USA. Anita won a National Endowment of the Arts fellowship in Creative Non-fiction in 1997. She lives in Oxford, England with her husband, Roy, and her daughters, Zoe and Irene.

Anita's website:
http://www.anitamathias.com, and
Anita's blog Dreaming Beneath the Spires:
http://dreamingbeneaththespires.blogspot.com

www.ingramcontent.com/pod-product-compliance
Lightning Source LLC
Chambersburg PA
CBHW081129300726
48982CB00005B/898

* 9 7 8 1 7 8 1 3 9 4 9 5 3 *